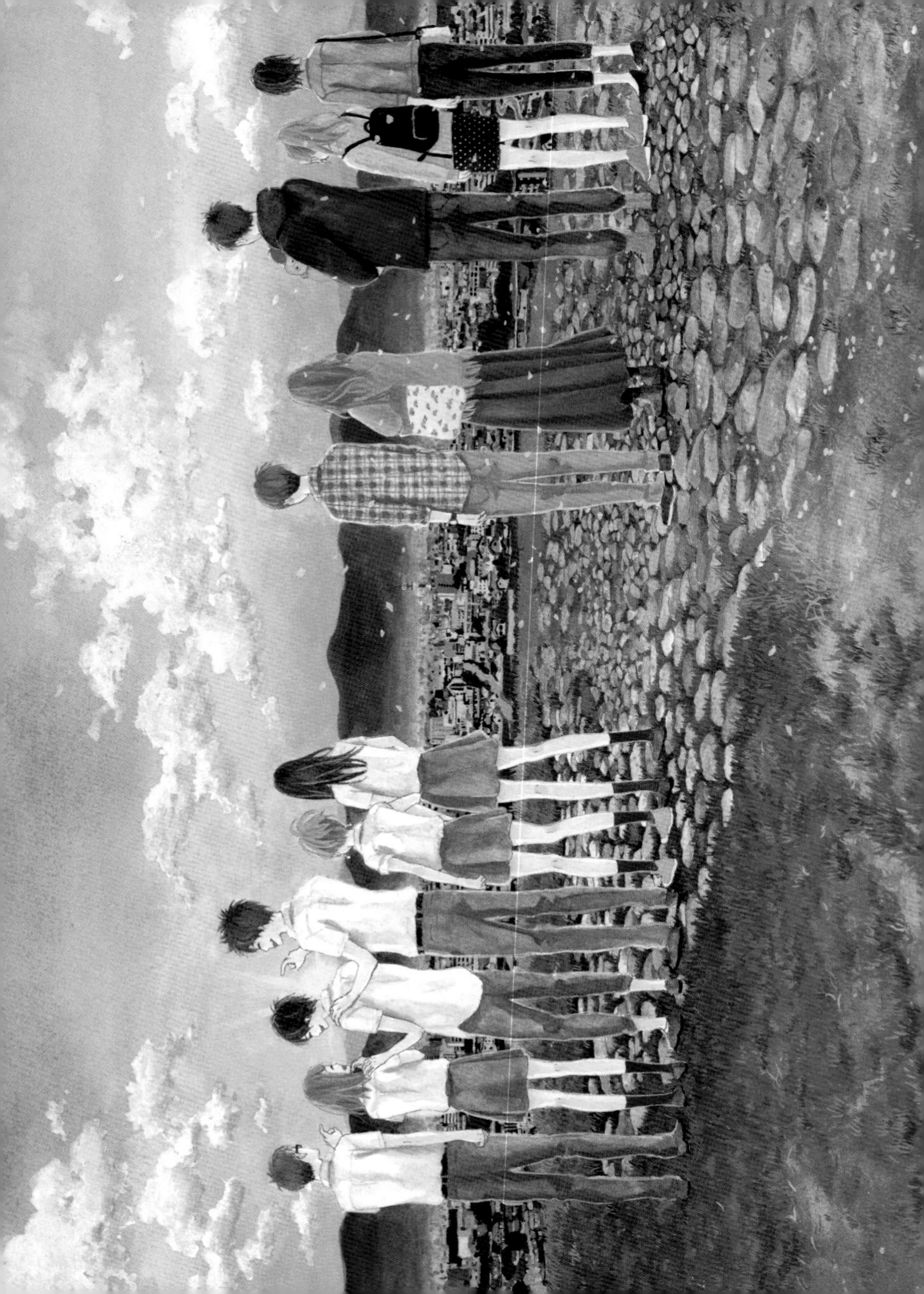

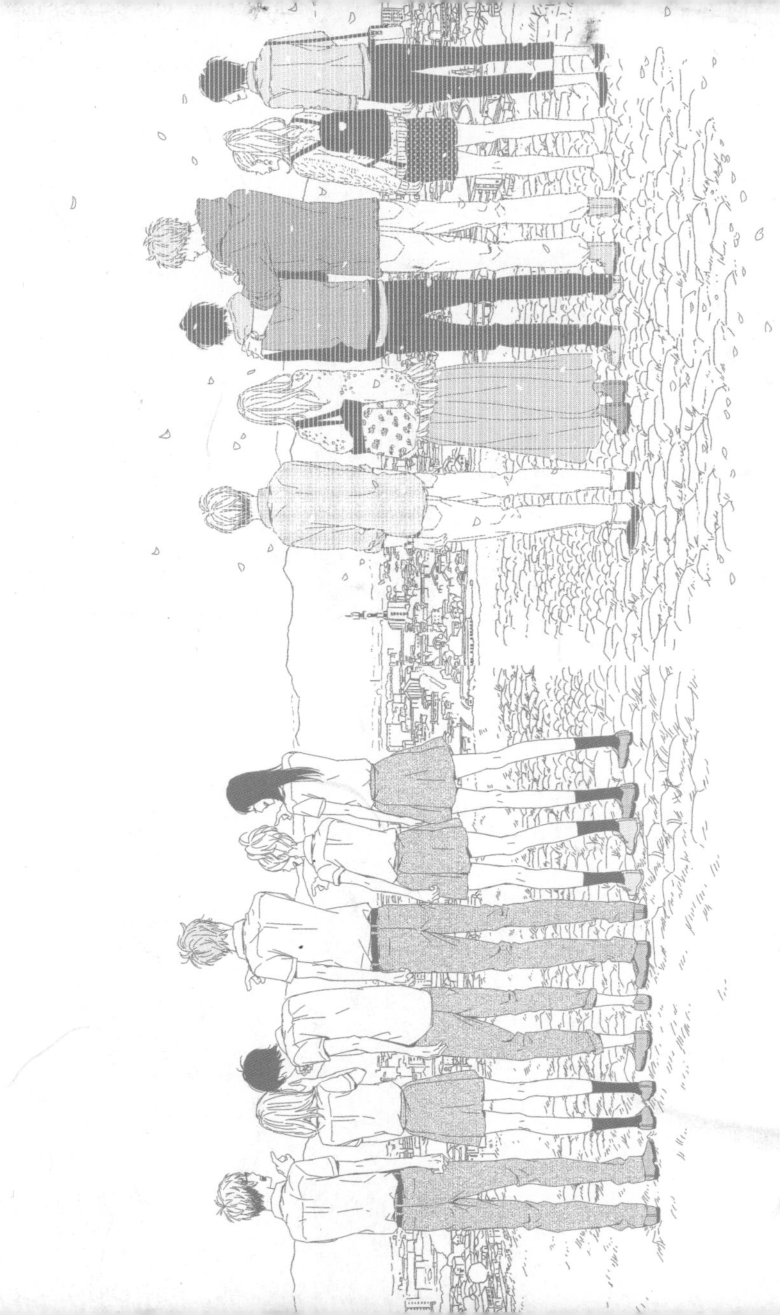

orange

ICHIGO TAKANO presents

4

the fourth
volume

The Story So Far

During the spring of her second year of high school, Naho received a letter from herself ten years in the future. The letter makes predictions about what will happen each day, and also advises her on what to do so that she won't have regrets like her future self. Naho at first thought it was a prank, but as the events written in the letter come true one after another, she starts to think it might be the real deal. When she learns that the letter's main objective is to prevent the death of her classmate Kakeru, Naho works to change herself and the future in order to avoid losing him.

Just when Naho starts to doubt herself, her friends reveal that they too have letters from the future. Armed with their knowledge of the future, the gang is even more determined to save their friend from his fate.

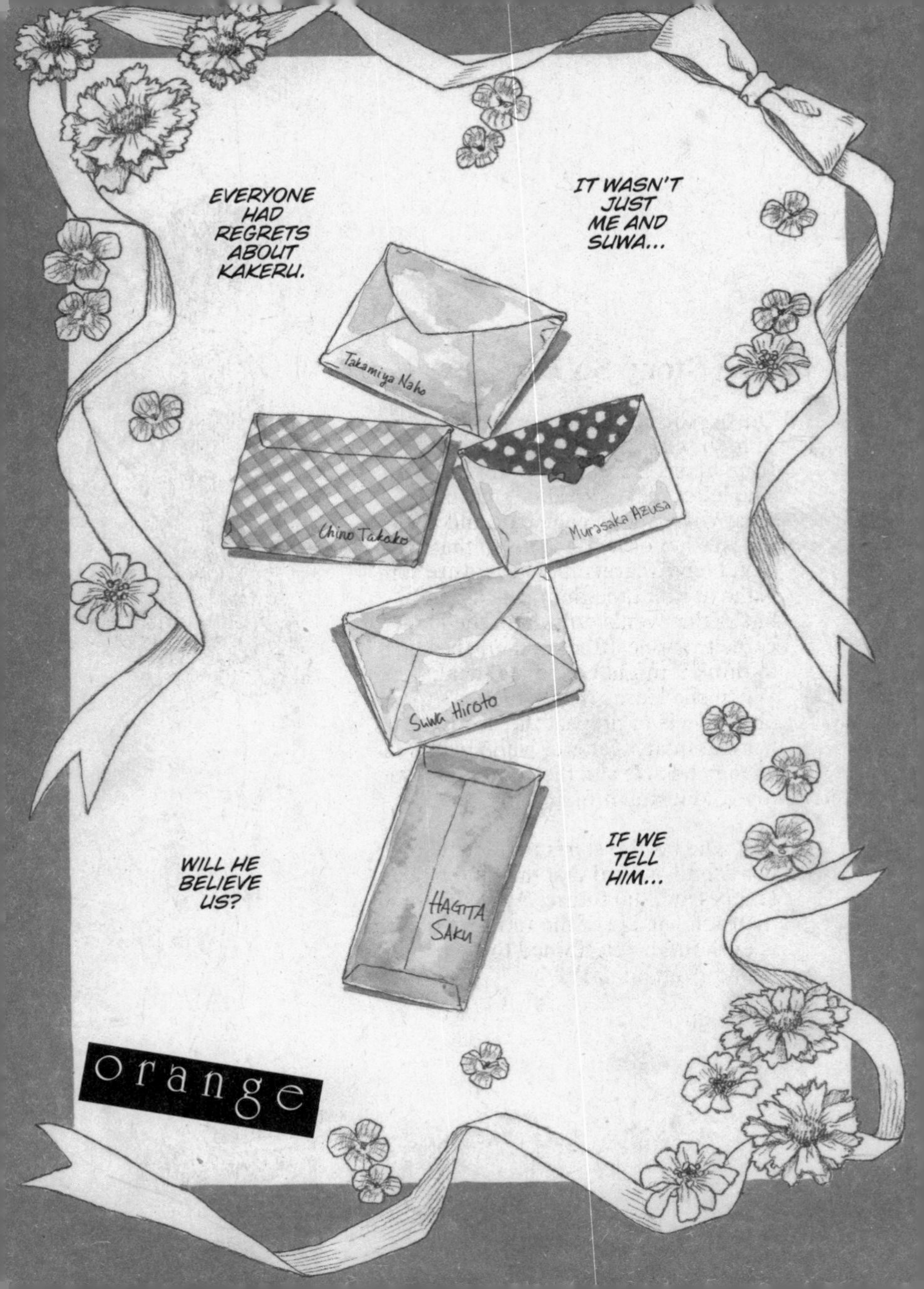
IT WASN'T JUST ME AND SUWA...
EVERYONE HAD REGRETS ABOUT KAKERU.
Takamiya Naho
Murasaka Azusa
Chino Takako
Suwa Hiroto
HAGITA SAKU
IF WE TELL HIM...
WILL HE BELIEVE US?
orange

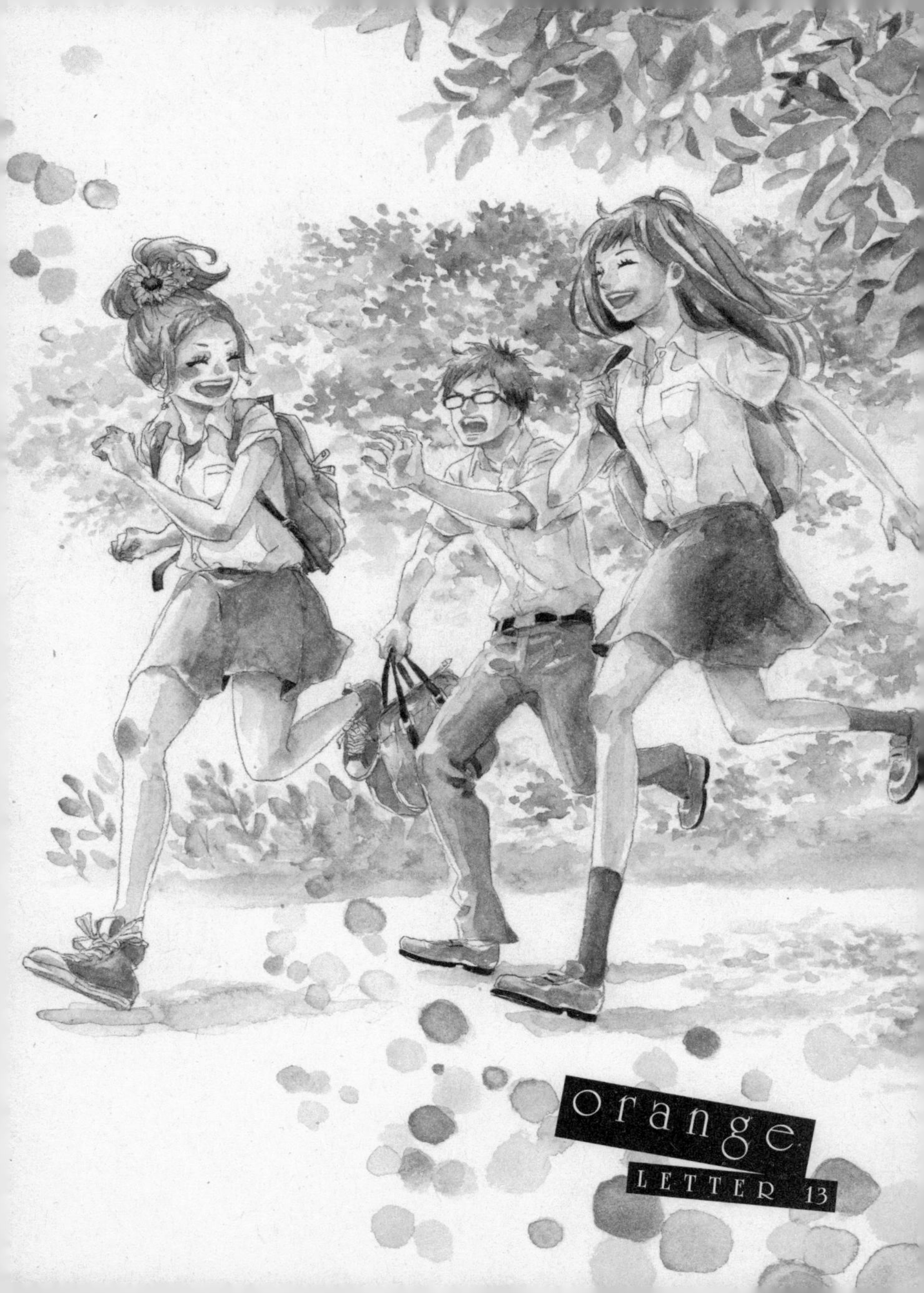

orange
LETTER 13

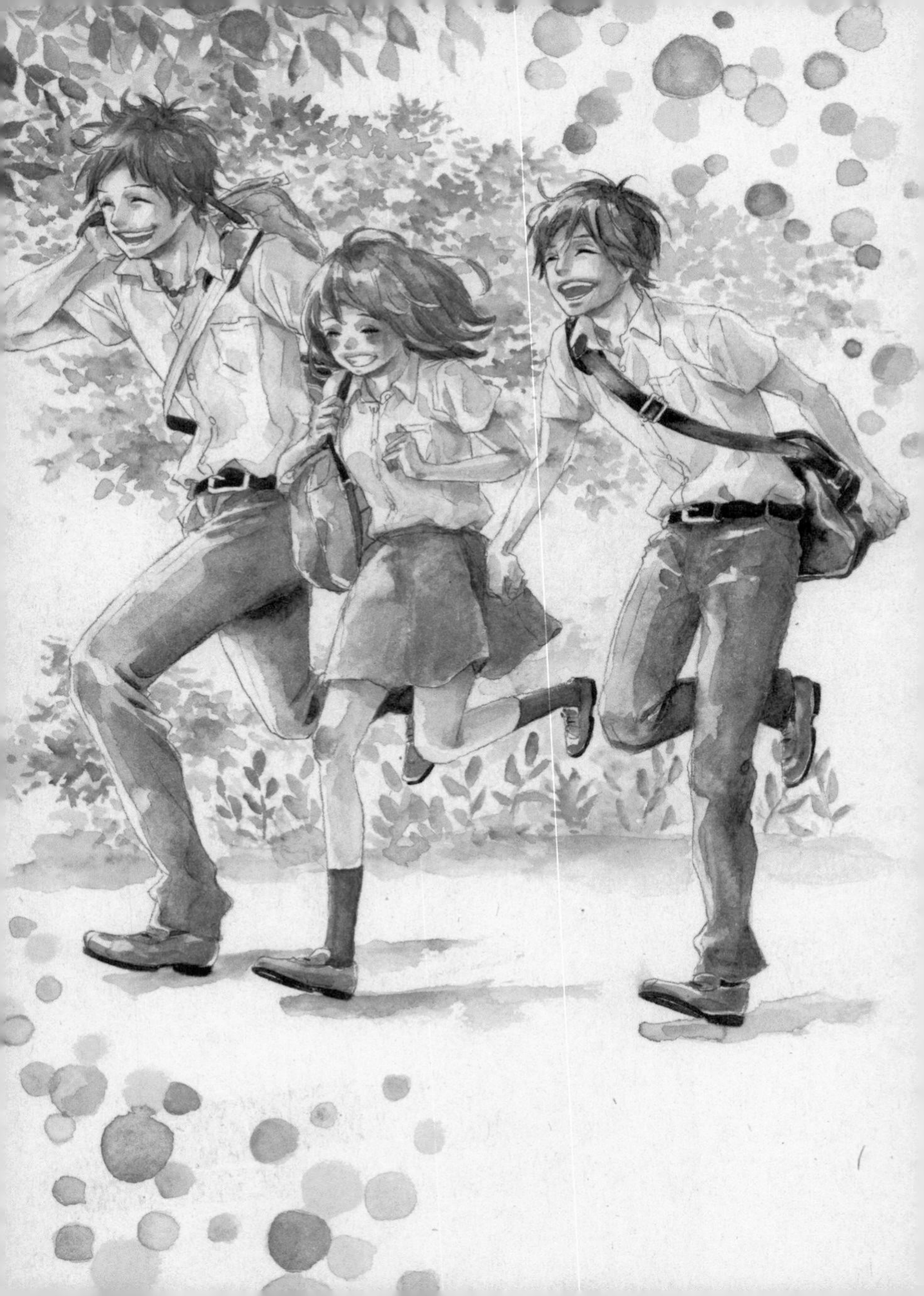

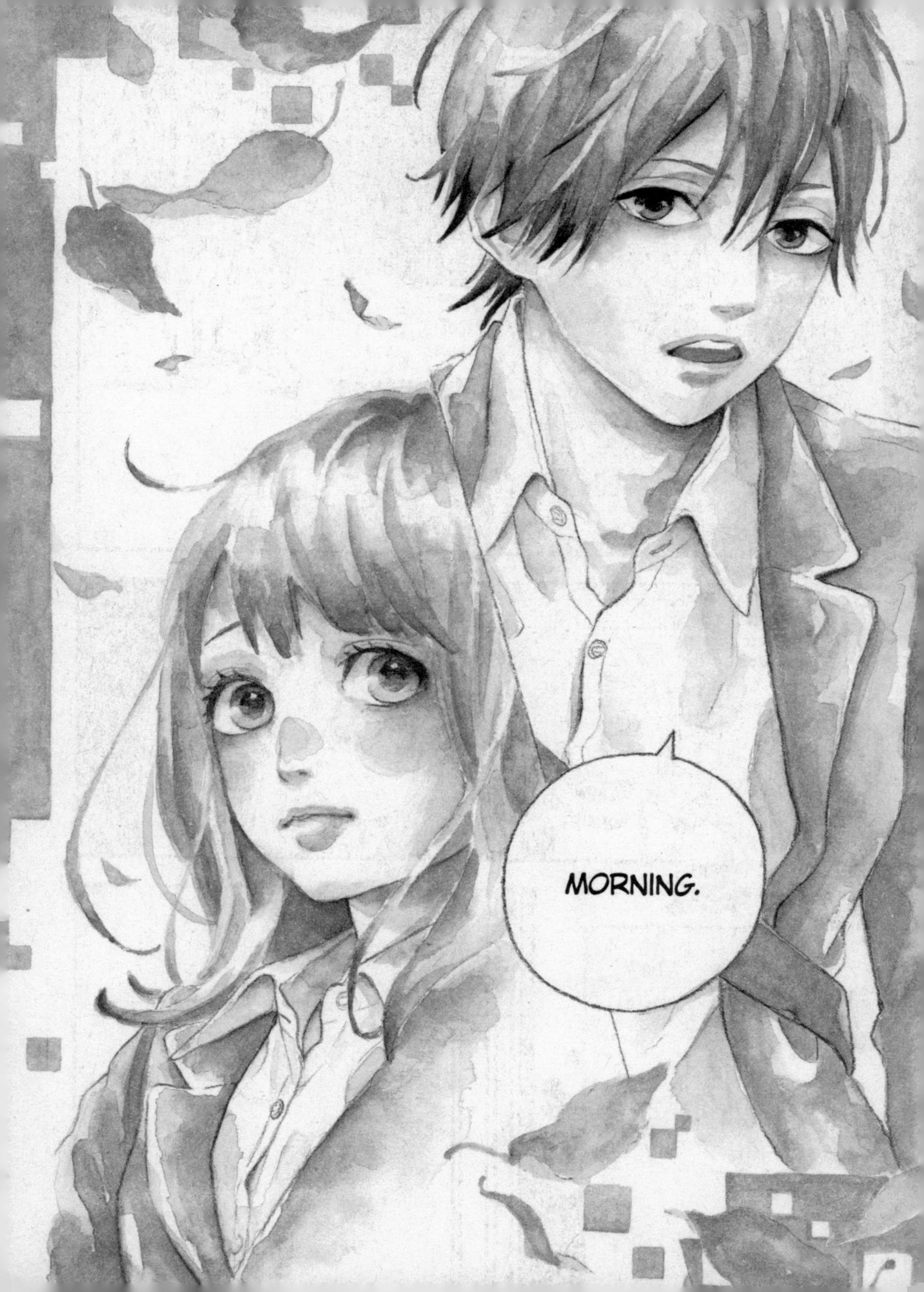
MORNING.

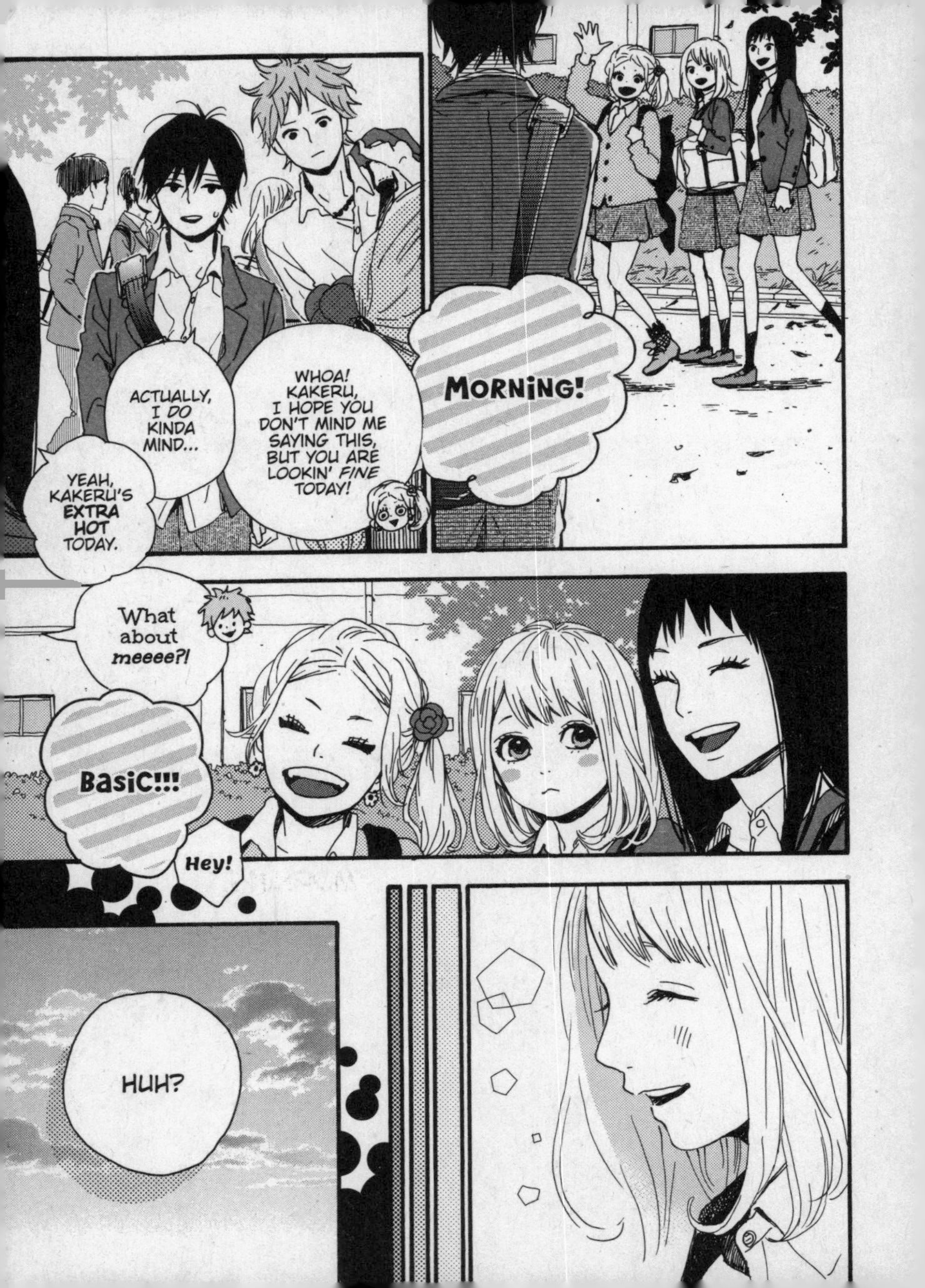
MORNING!
WHOA! KAKERU, I HOPE YOU DON'T MIND ME SAYING THIS, BUT YOU ARE LOOKIN' *FINE* TODAY!
ACTUALLY, I *DO* KINDA MIND...
YEAH, KAKERU'S **EXTRA HOT** TODAY.
What about *meeee?!*
Basic!!!
Hey!
HUH?

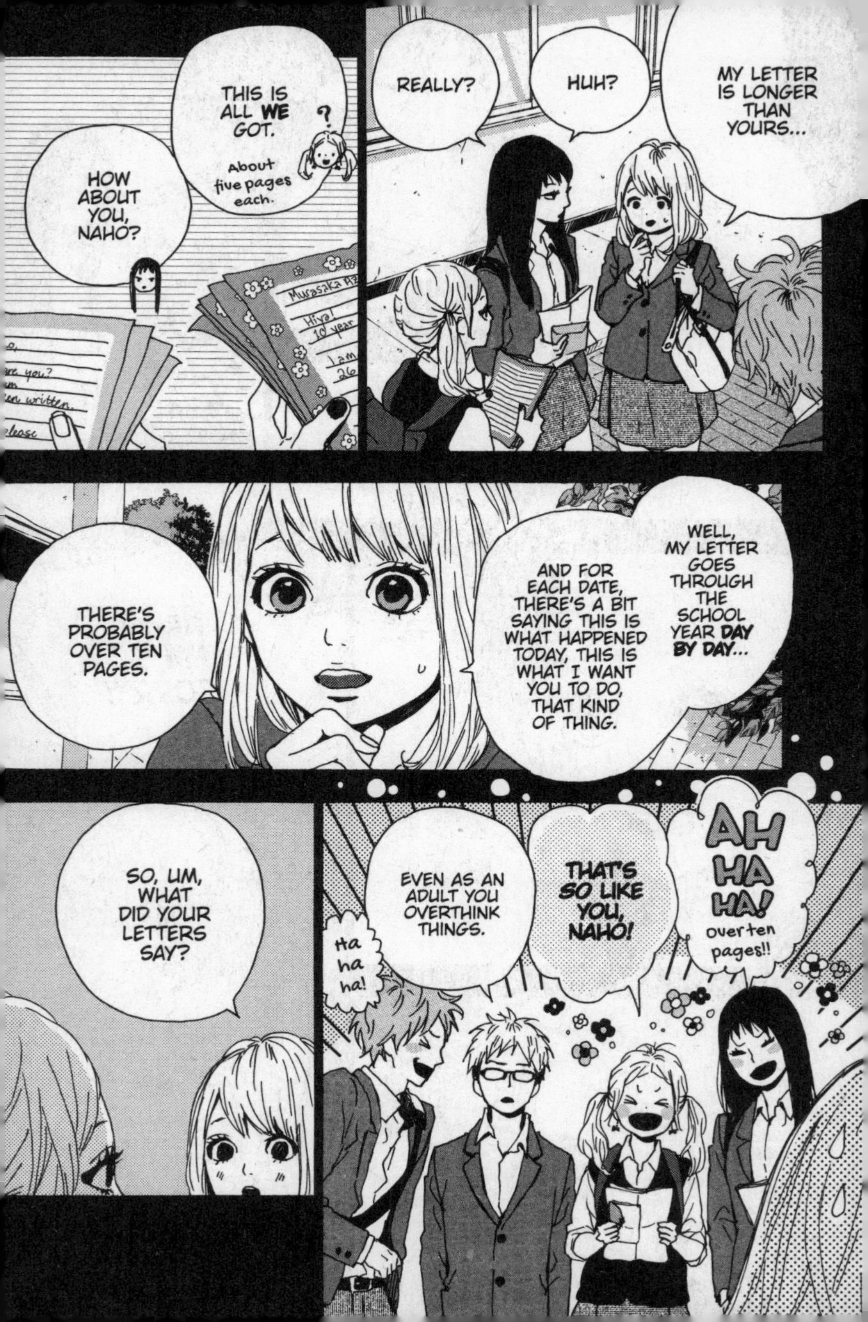

MY LETTER IS LONGER THAN YOURS...
HUH?
REALLY?
THIS IS ALL **WE** GOT.
?
About five pages each.
HOW ABOUT YOU, NAHO?
WELL, MY LETTER GOES THROUGH THE SCHOOL YEAR **DAY BY DAY...**
AND FOR EACH DATE, THERE'S A BIT SAYING THIS IS WHAT HAPPENED TODAY, THIS IS WHAT I WANT YOU TO DO, THAT KIND OF THING.
THERE'S PROBABLY OVER TEN PAGES.
AH HA HA!
over ten pages!!
THAT'S SO LIKE YOU, NAHO!
EVEN AS AN ADULT YOU OVERTHINK THINGS.
Ha ha ha!
SO, UM, WHAT DID YOUR LETTERS SAY?

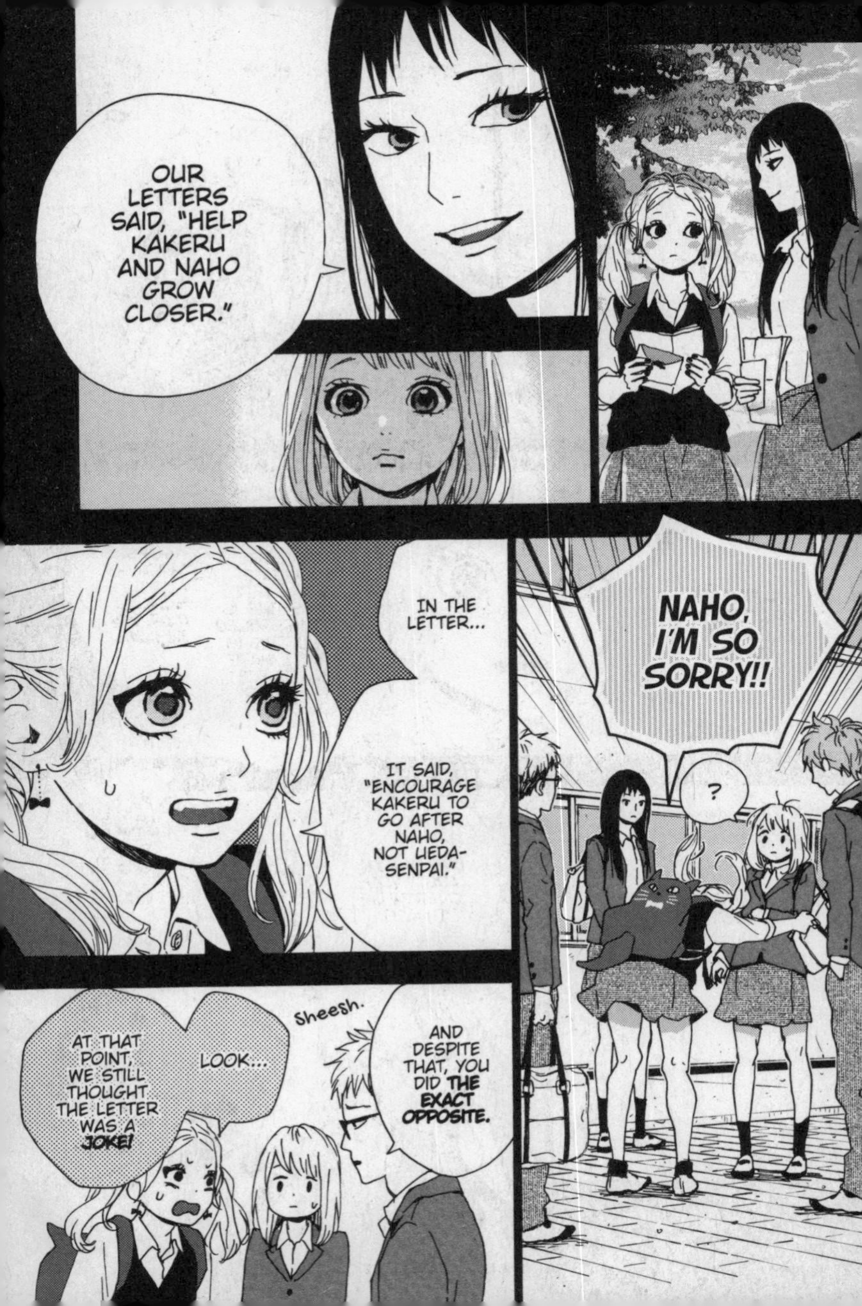
OUR LETTERS SAID, "HELP KAKERU AND NAHO GROW CLOSER."
NAHO, I'M SO SORRY!!
?
IN THE LETTER...
IT SAID, "ENCOURAGE KAKERU TO GO AFTER NAHO, NOT UEDA-SENPAI."
Sheesh.
AND DESPITE THAT, YOU DID THE EXACT OPPOSITE.
LOOK...
AT THAT POINT, WE STILL THOUGHT THE LETTER WAS A JOKE!

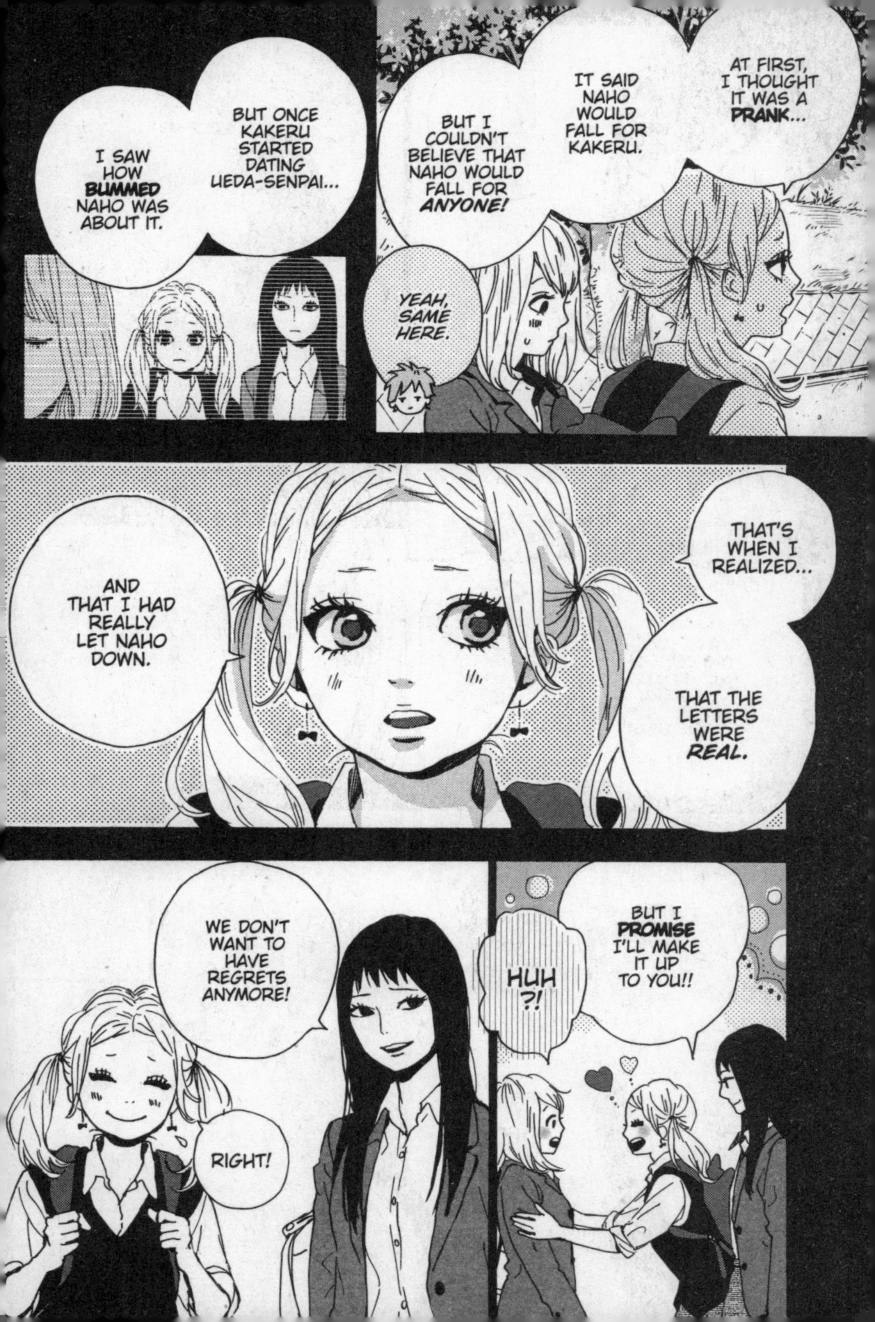
AT FIRST, I THOUGHT IT WAS A PRANK...
IT SAID NAHO WOULD FALL FOR KAKERU.
BUT I COULDN'T BELIEVE THAT NAHO WOULD FALL FOR ANYONE!
YEAH, SAME HERE.
BUT ONCE KAKERU STARTED DATING UEDA-SENPAI...
I SAW HOW BUMMED NAHO WAS ABOUT IT.
THAT'S WHEN I REALIZED...
THAT THE LETTERS WERE REAL.
AND THAT I HAD REALLY LET NAHO DOWN.
BUT I PROMISE I'LL MAKE IT UP TO YOU!!
HUH?!
WE DON'T WANT TO HAVE REGRETS ANYMORE!
RIGHT!

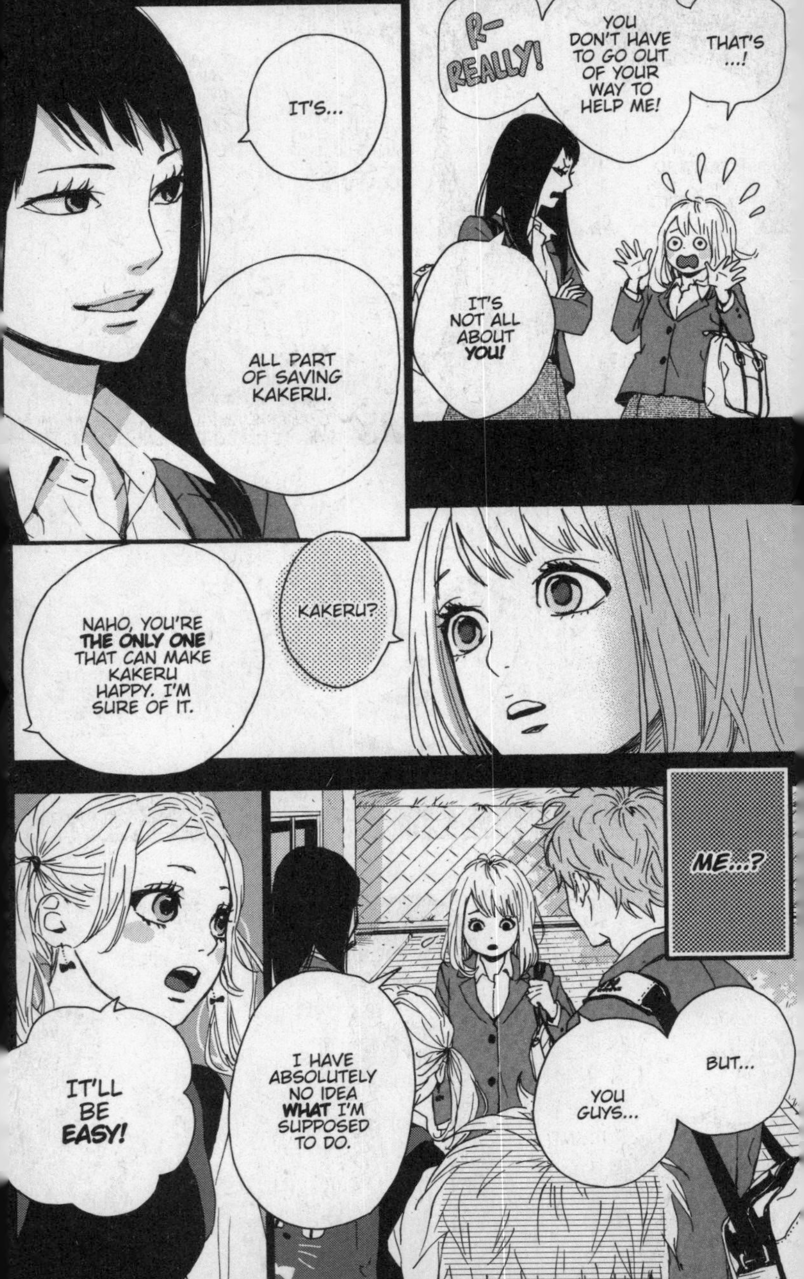
THAT'S ...!
YOU DON'T HAVE TO GO OUT OF YOUR WAY TO HELP ME!
R-REALLY!
IT'S NOT ALL ABOUT YOU!
IT'S...
ALL PART OF SAVING KAKERU.
KAKERU?
NAHO, YOU'RE THE ONLY ONE THAT CAN MAKE KAKERU HAPPY. I'M SURE OF IT.
ME...?
BUT...
YOU GUYS...
I HAVE ABSOLUTELY NO IDEA WHAT I'M SUPPOSED TO DO.
IT'LL BE EASY!

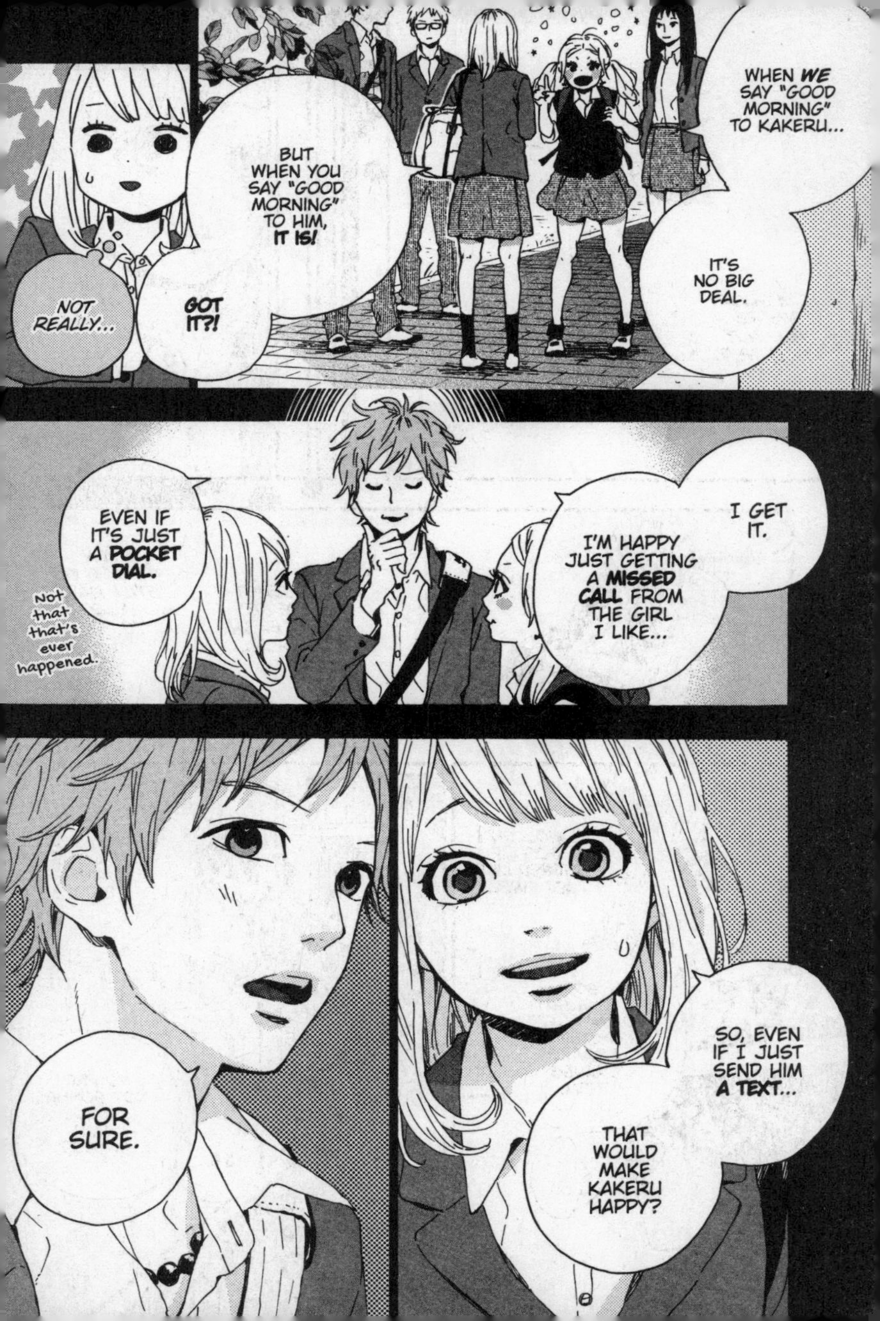
WHEN WE SAY "GOOD MORNING" TO KAKERU...
IT'S NO BIG DEAL.
BUT WHEN YOU SAY "GOOD MORNING" TO HIM, IT IS!
GOT IT?!
NOT REALLY...
I GET IT.
I'M HAPPY JUST GETTING A MISSED CALL FROM THE GIRL I LIKE...
EVEN IF IT'S JUST A POCKET DIAL.
Not that that's ever happened.
SO, EVEN IF I JUST SEND HIM A TEXT...
THAT WOULD MAKE KAKERU HAPPY?
FOR SURE.

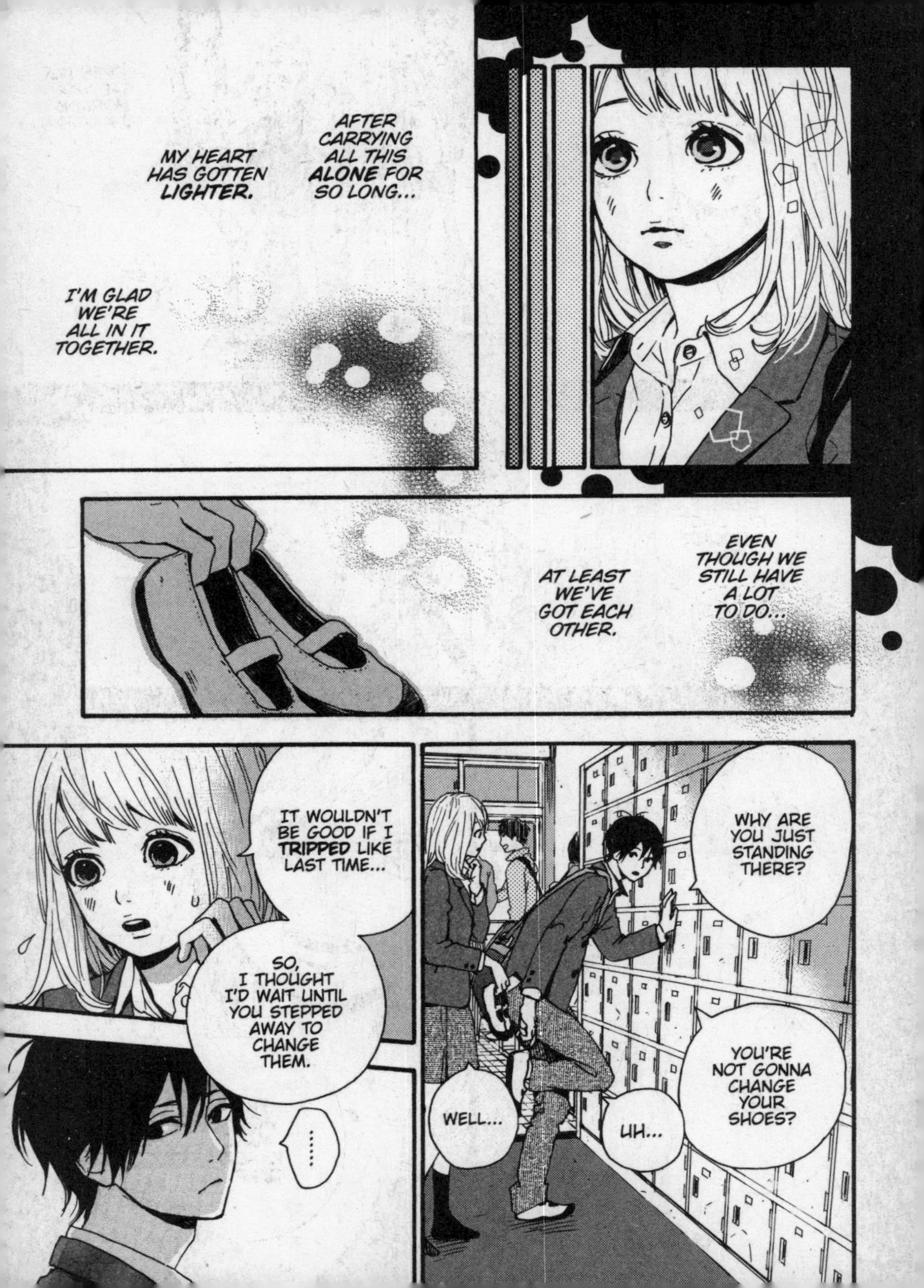
AFTER CARRYING ALL THIS ALONE FOR SO LONG...
MY HEART HAS GOTTEN LIGHTER.
I'M GLAD WE'RE ALL IN IT TOGETHER.
EVEN THOUGH WE STILL HAVE A LOT TO DO...
AT LEAST WE'VE GOT EACH OTHER.
WHY ARE YOU JUST STANDING THERE?
YOU'RE NOT GONNA CHANGE YOUR SHOES?
UH...
WELL...
IT WOULDN'T BE GOOD IF I TRIPPED LIKE LAST TIME...
SO, I THOUGHT I'D WAIT UNTIL YOU STEPPED AWAY TO CHANGE THEM.
......

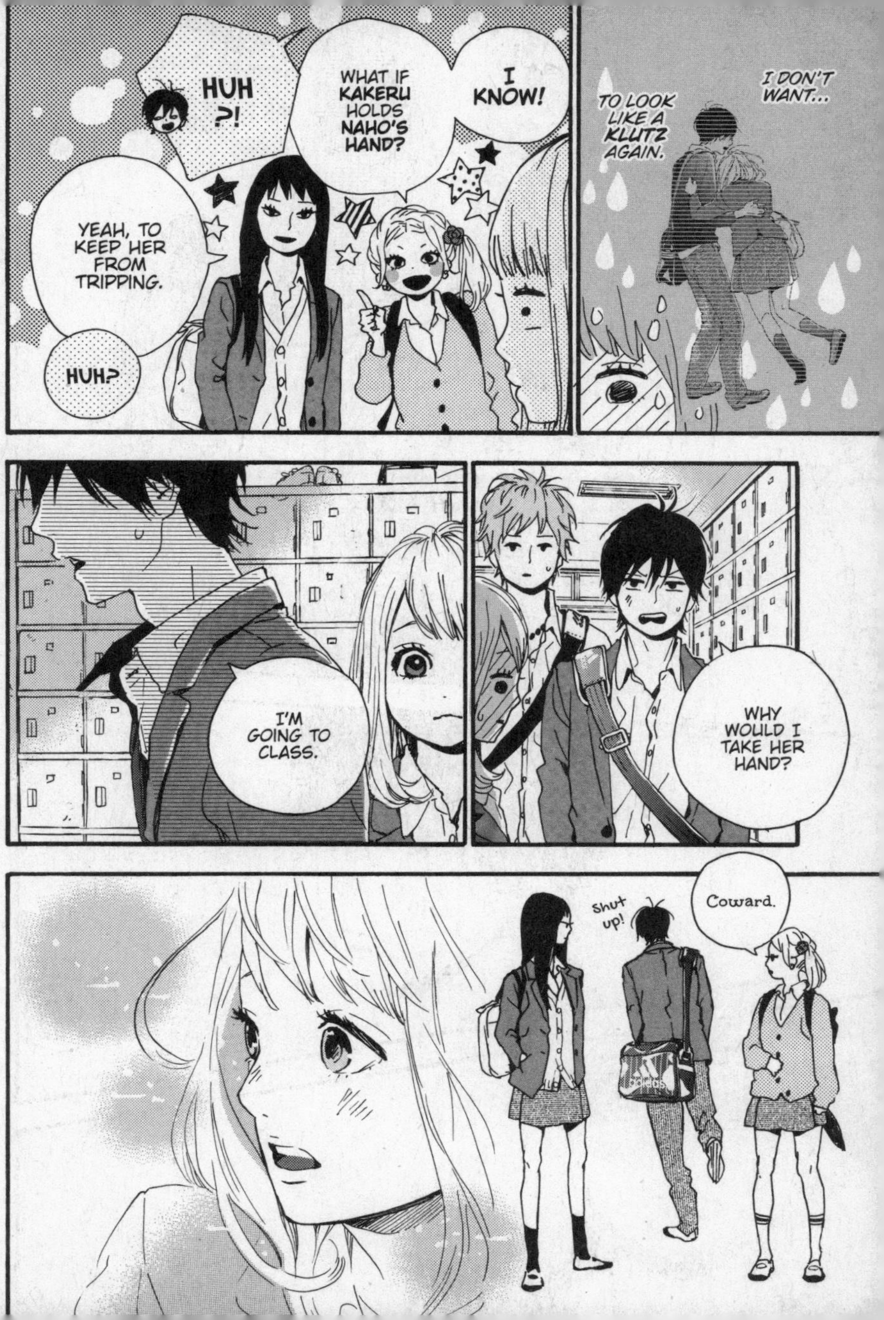
I DON'T WANT...
TO LOOK LIKE A KLUTZ AGAIN.
I KNOW!
WHAT IF KAKERU HOLDS NAHO'S HAND?
HUH ?!
YEAH, TO KEEP HER FROM TRIPPING.
HUH?
WHY WOULD I TAKE HER HAND?
I'M GOING TO CLASS.
Coward.
Shut up!

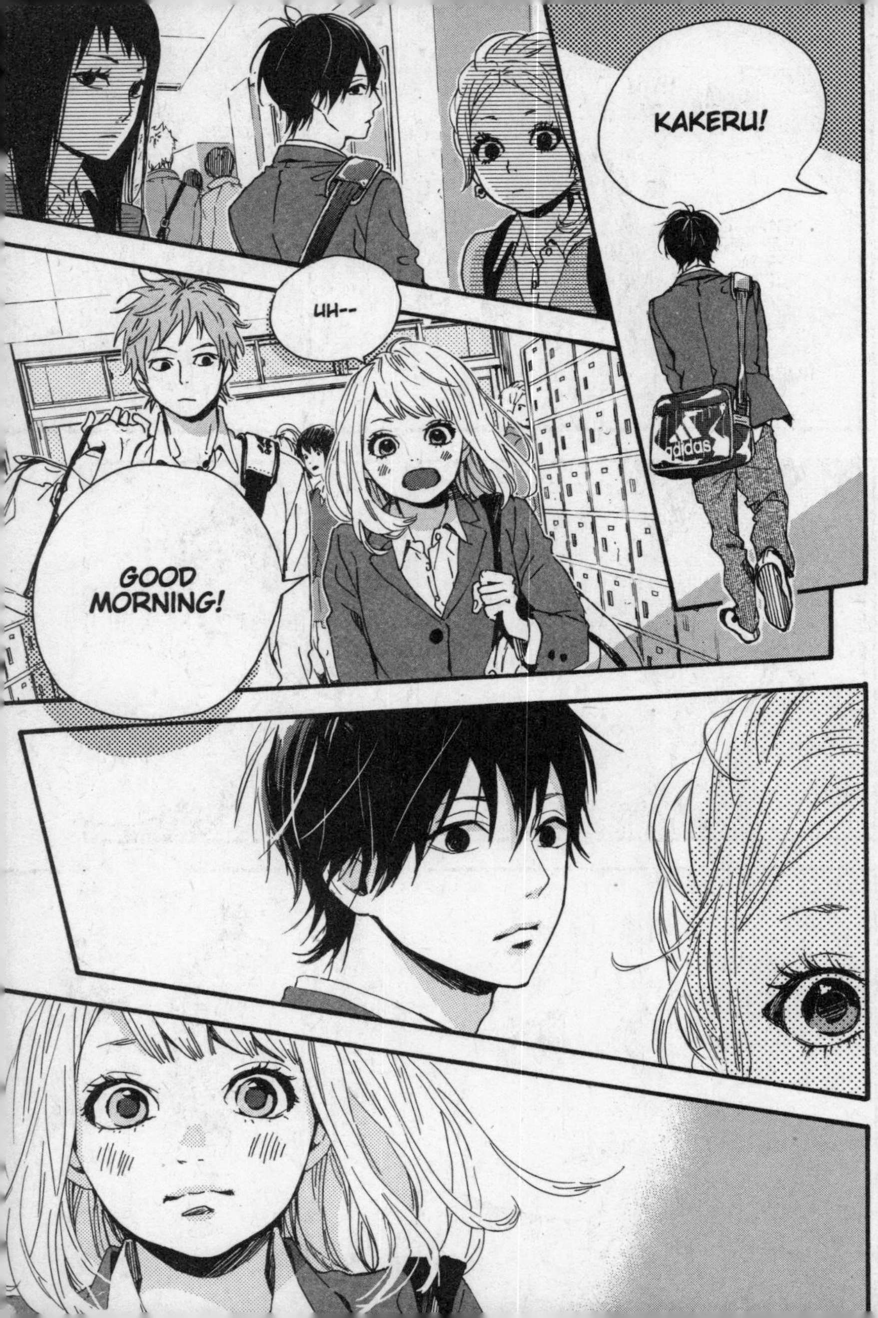
KAKERU!
adidas
UH--
GOOD MORNING!

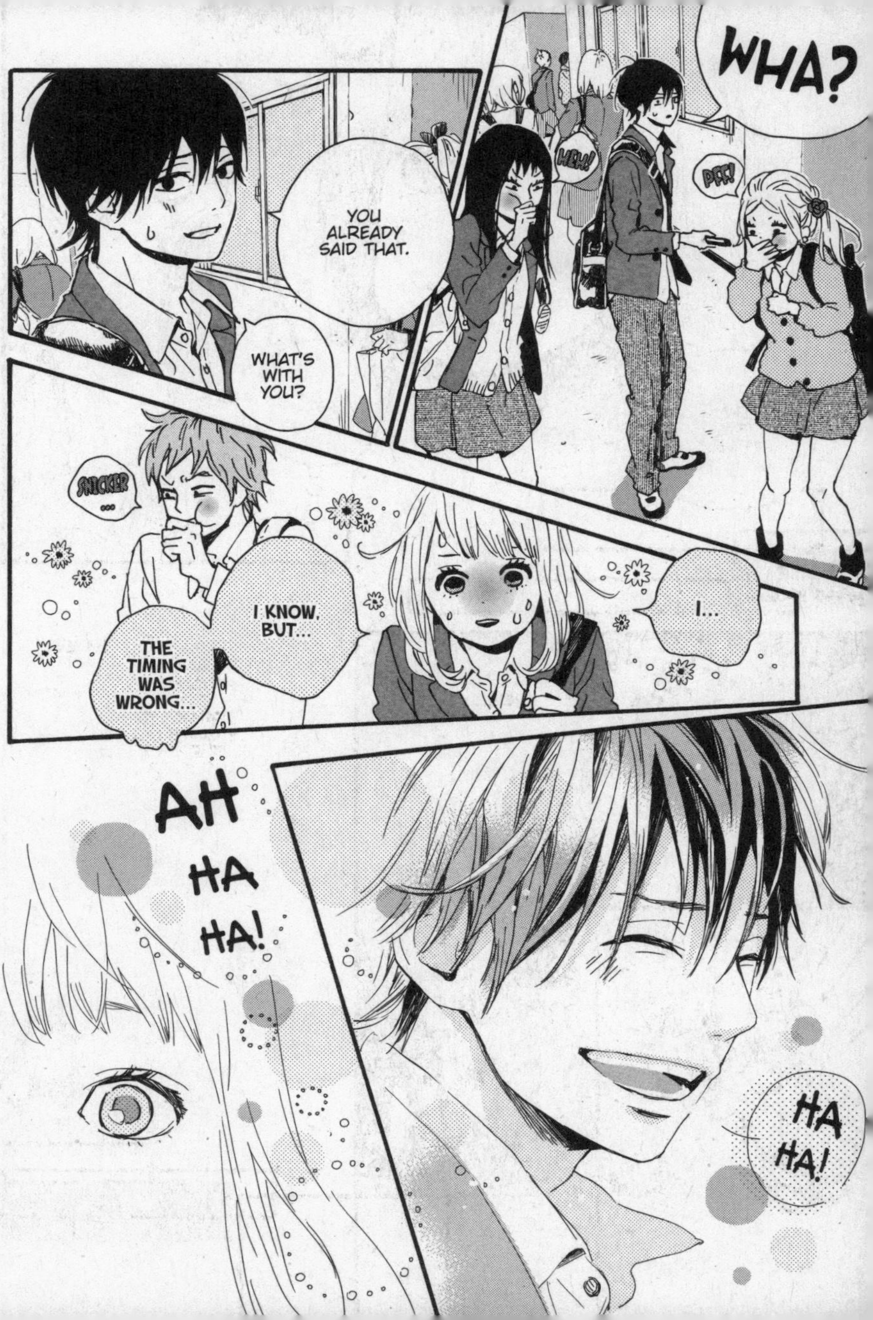

WHA?
HEH!
PFF!
YOU ALREADY SAID THAT.
WHAT'S WITH YOU?
I...
I KNOW, BUT...
THE TIMING WAS WRONG...
SNICKER...
HA HA!
AH HA HA!

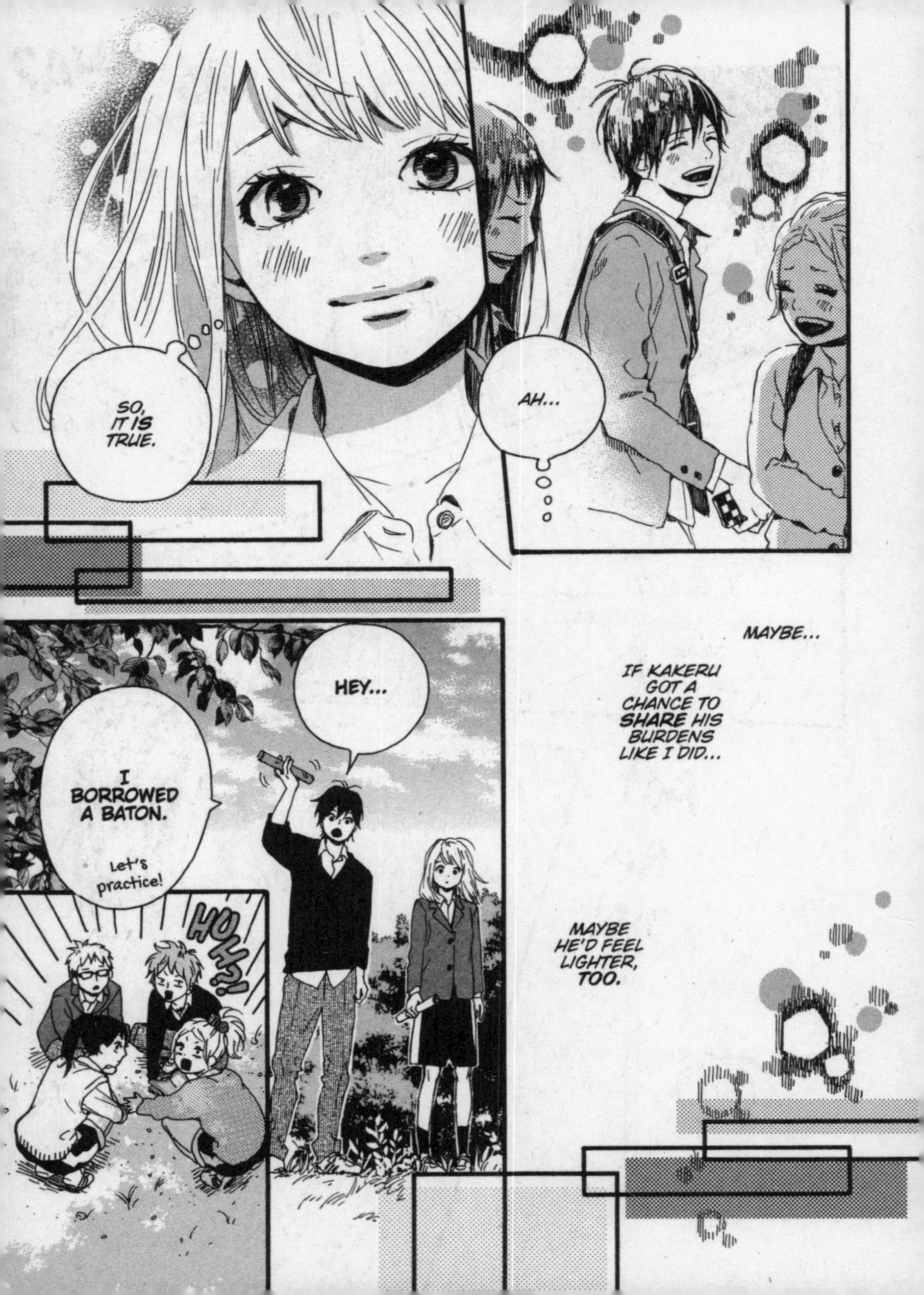
AH...
SO, IT IS TRUE.
MAYBE...
IF KAKERU GOT A CHANCE TO SHARE HIS BURDENS LIKE I DID...
MAYBE HE'D FEEL LIGHTER, TOO.
HEY...
I BORROWED A BATON.
Let's practice!
HUH?!

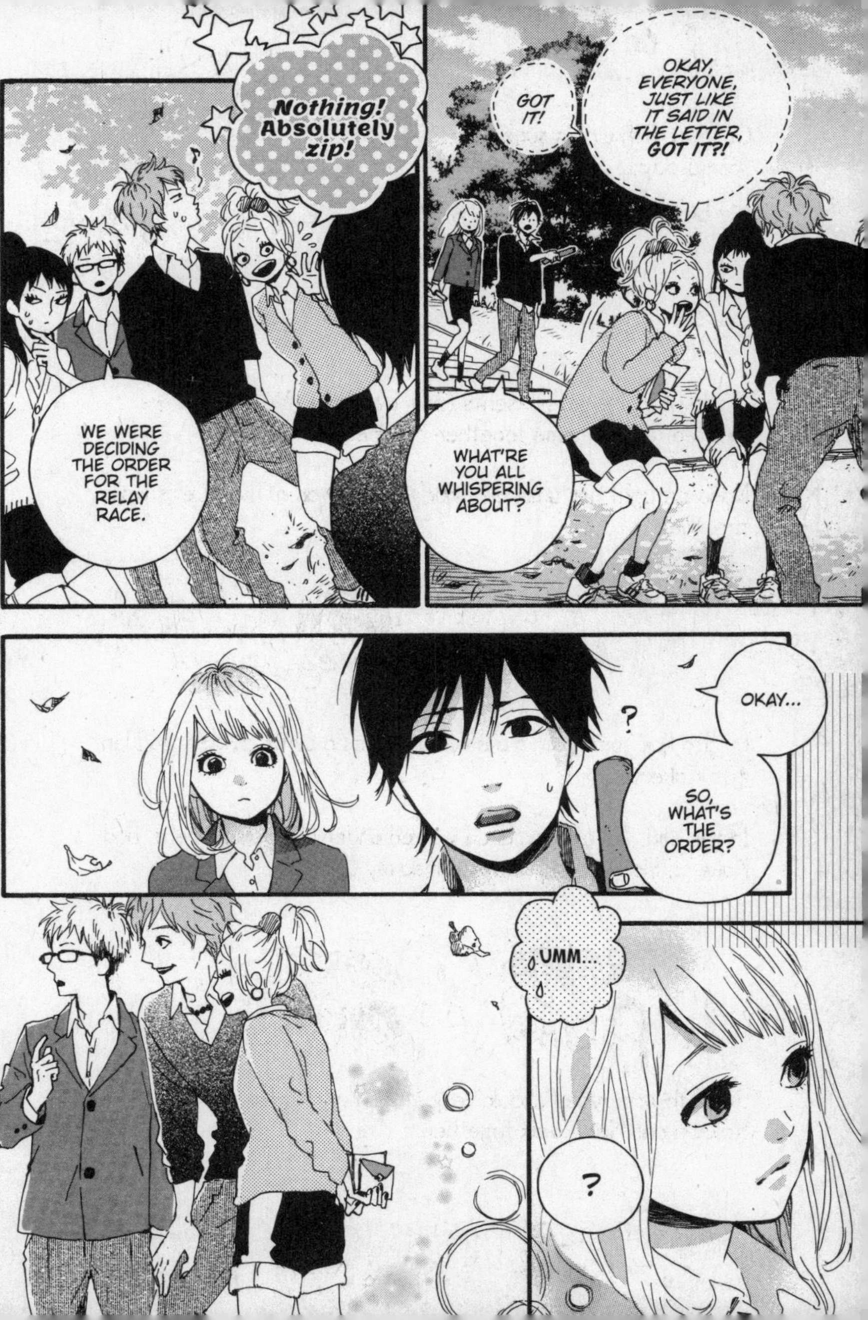
OKAY, EVERYONE, JUST LIKE IT SAID IN THE LETTER, GOT IT?!
GOT IT!
WHAT'RE YOU ALL WHISPERING ABOUT?
Nothing! Absolutely zip!
WE WERE DECIDING THE ORDER FOR THE RELAY RACE.
OKAY...
SO, WHAT'S THE ORDER?
?
UMM...
?

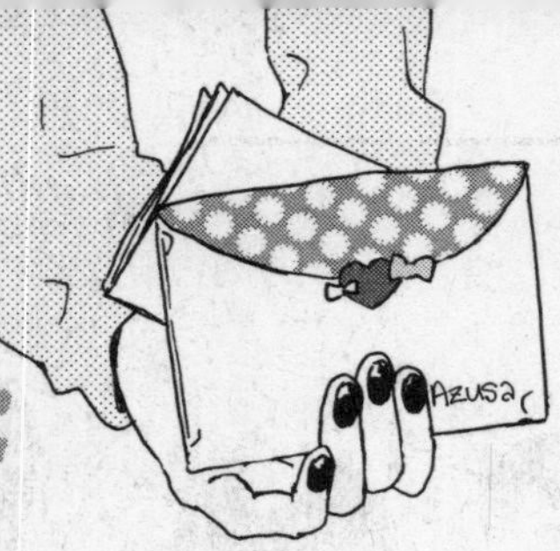
Azusa

October 5th was a super special day...

My birthday!

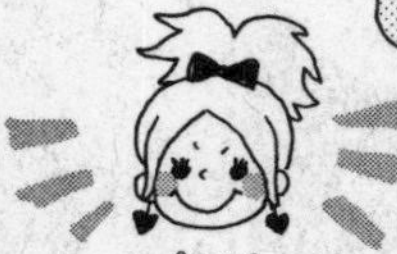

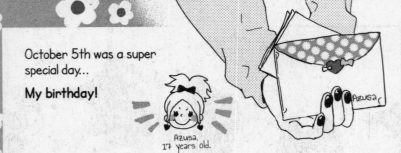

Azusa, 17 years old.

After school, I got presents from everyone. But just as we started to walk home together, it rained!

Naho brought her umbrella, and Kakeru was all like, "Let's walk together."

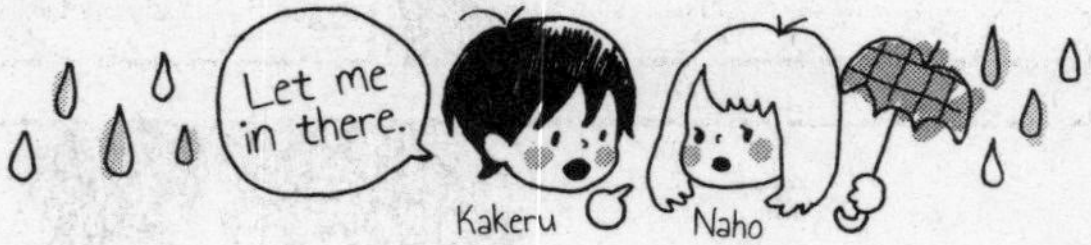
Let me in there.
Kakeru
Naho

Hagita had just given me an umbrella as a birthday gift, so I lent it to Kakeru.

In the end, Taka-chan and I walked under Naho's umbrella, and Kakeru, Hagita, and Suwa shared my umbrella.

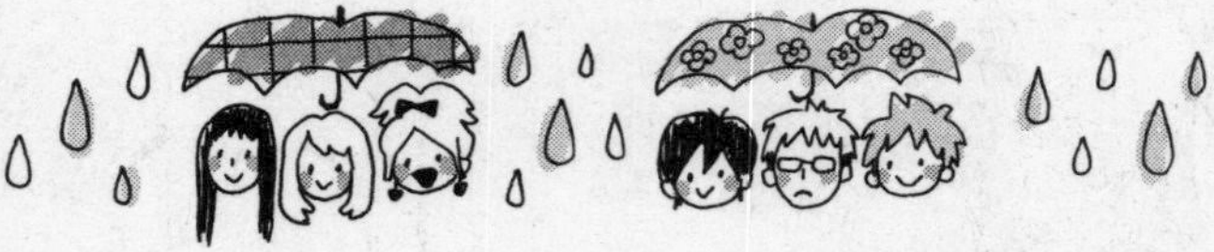

But I think maybe I should've just kept my big mouth shut and let Kakeru and Naho walk together.

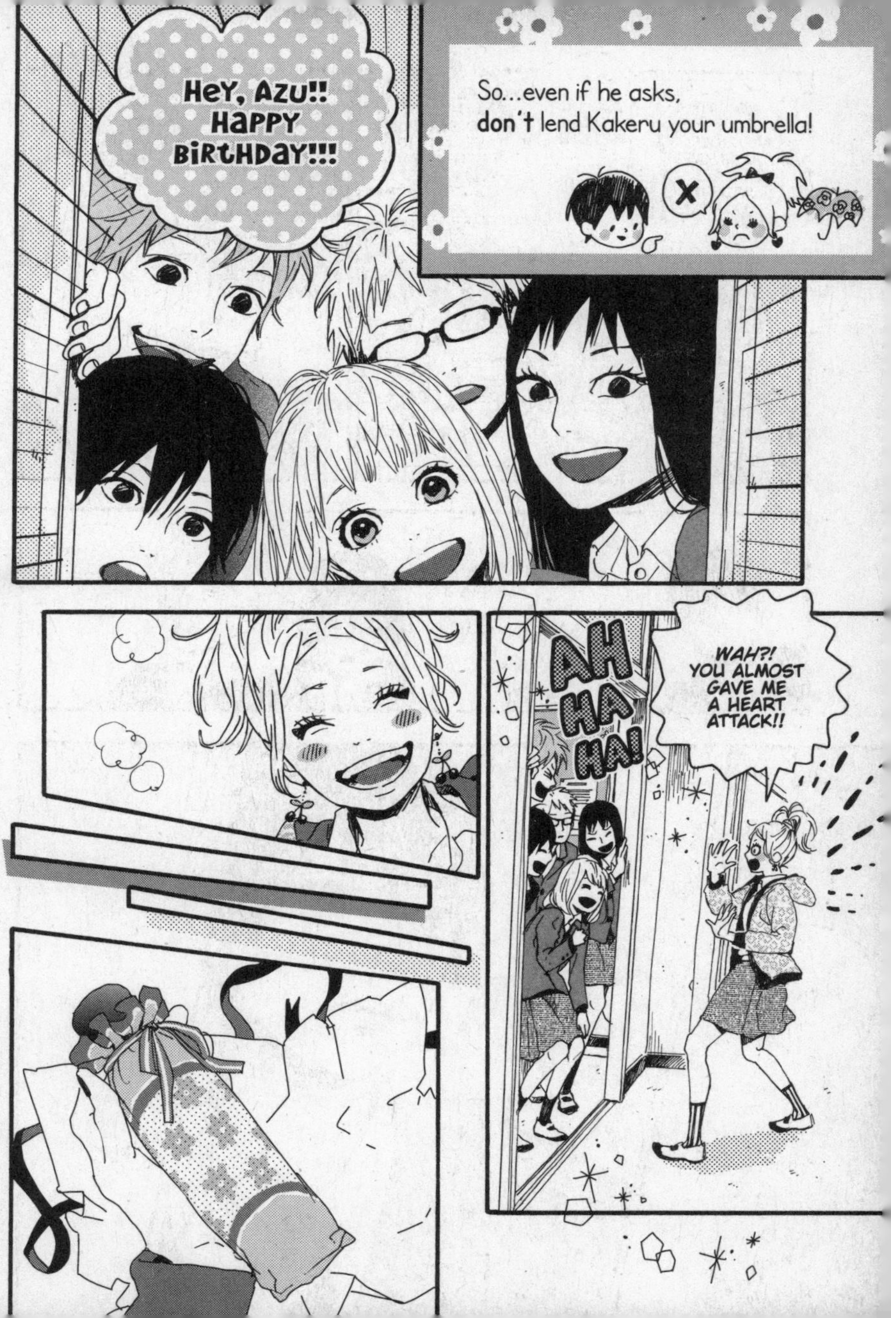
So…even if he asks,
don't lend Kakeru your umbrella!
HEY, AZU!! HAPPY BIRTHDAY!!!
WAH?! YOU ALMOST GAVE ME A HEART ATTACK!!
AH HA HA HA!

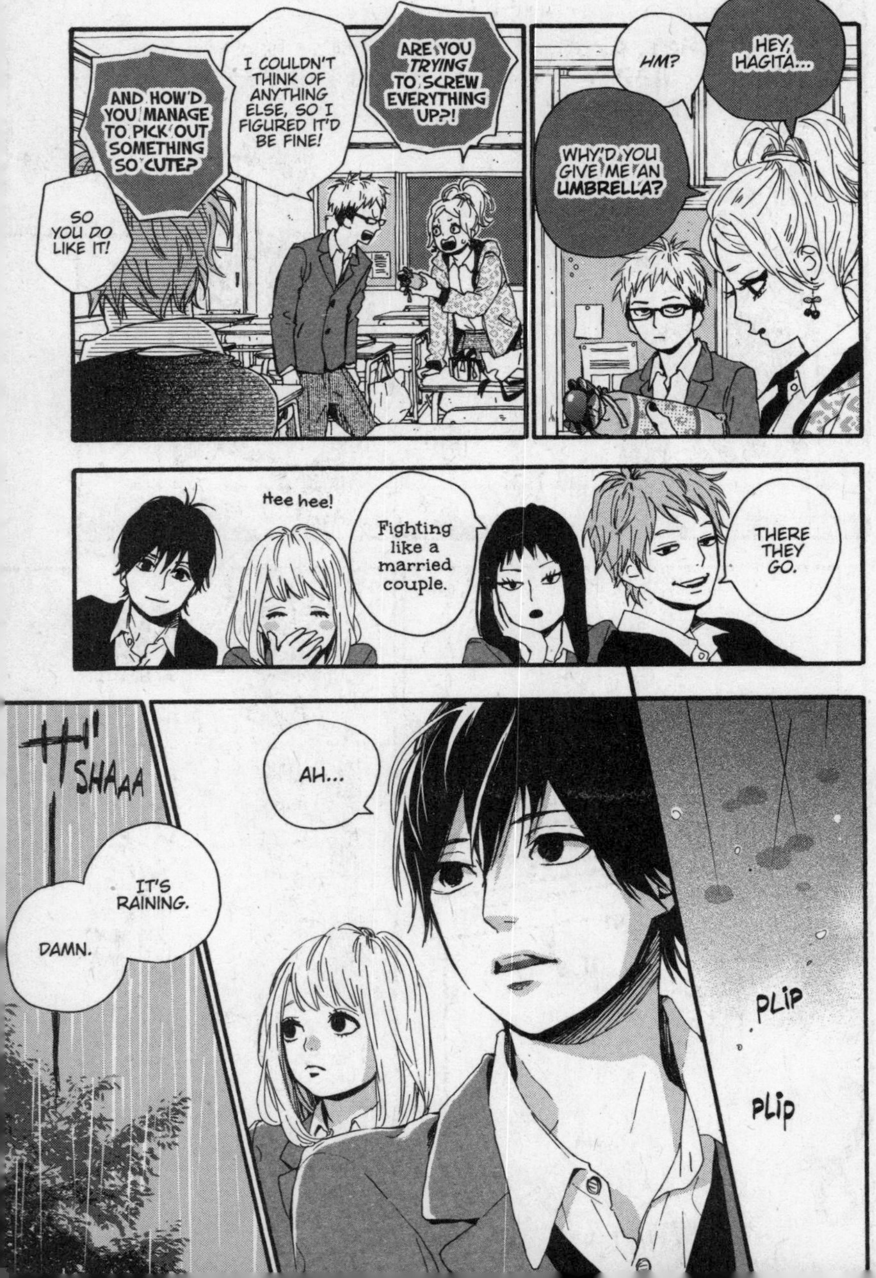
HEY, HAGITA...
HM?
WHY'D YOU GIVE ME AN UMBRELLA?
ARE YOU TRYING TO SCREW EVERYTHING UP?!
I COULDN'T THINK OF ANYTHING ELSE, SO I FIGURED IT'D BE FINE!
AND HOW'D YOU MANAGE TO PICK OUT SOMETHING SO CUTE?
SO YOU DO LIKE IT!
THERE THEY GO.
Fighting like a married couple.
Hee hee!
AH...
PLIP
PLIP
SHAAA
IT'S RAINING.
DAMN.

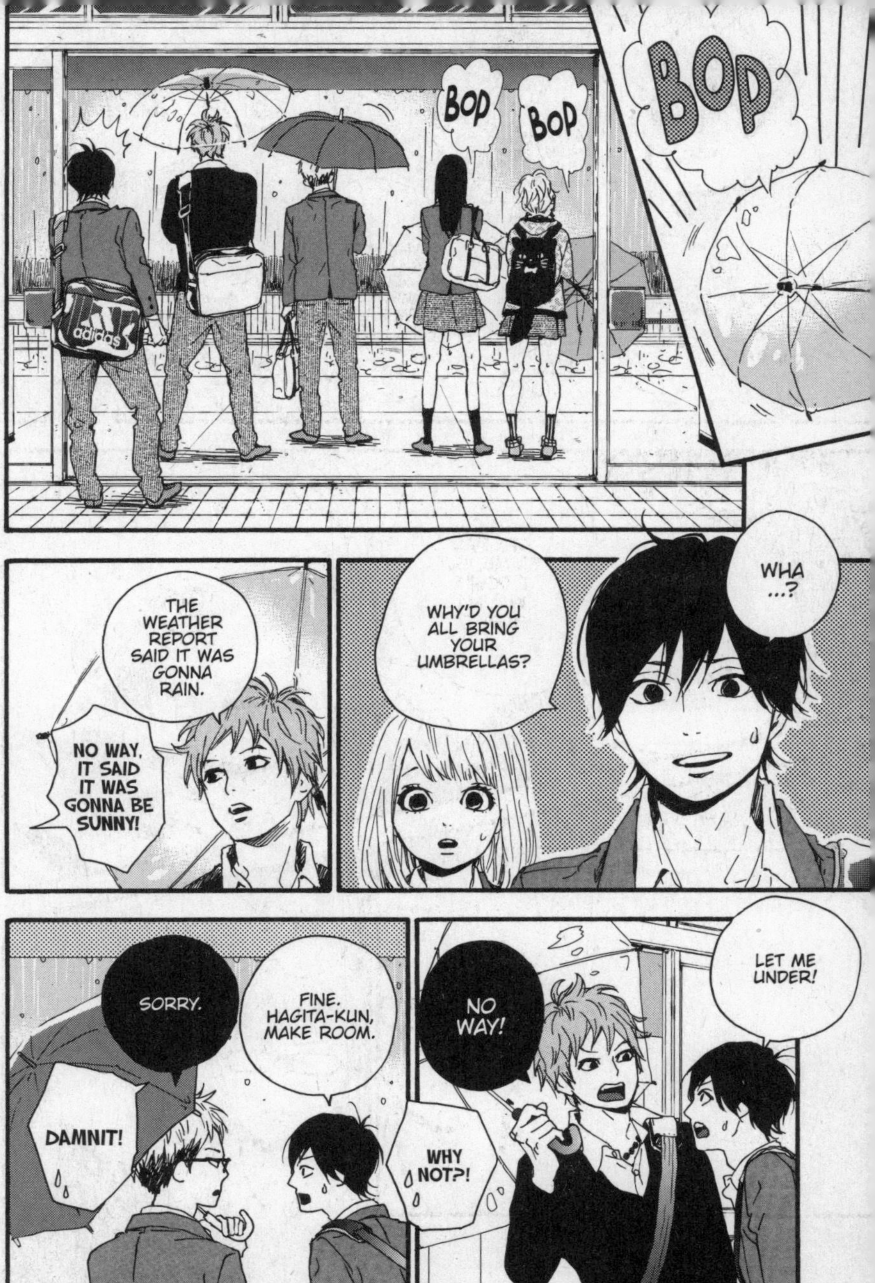
BOP
BOP
BOP
WHA ...?
WHY'D YOU ALL BRING YOUR UMBRELLAS?
THE WEATHER REPORT SAID IT WAS GONNA RAIN.
NO WAY, IT SAID IT WAS GONNA BE SUNNY!
LET ME UNDER!
NO WAY!
WHY NOT?!
FINE. HAGITA-KUN, MAKE ROOM.
SORRY.
DAMNIT!

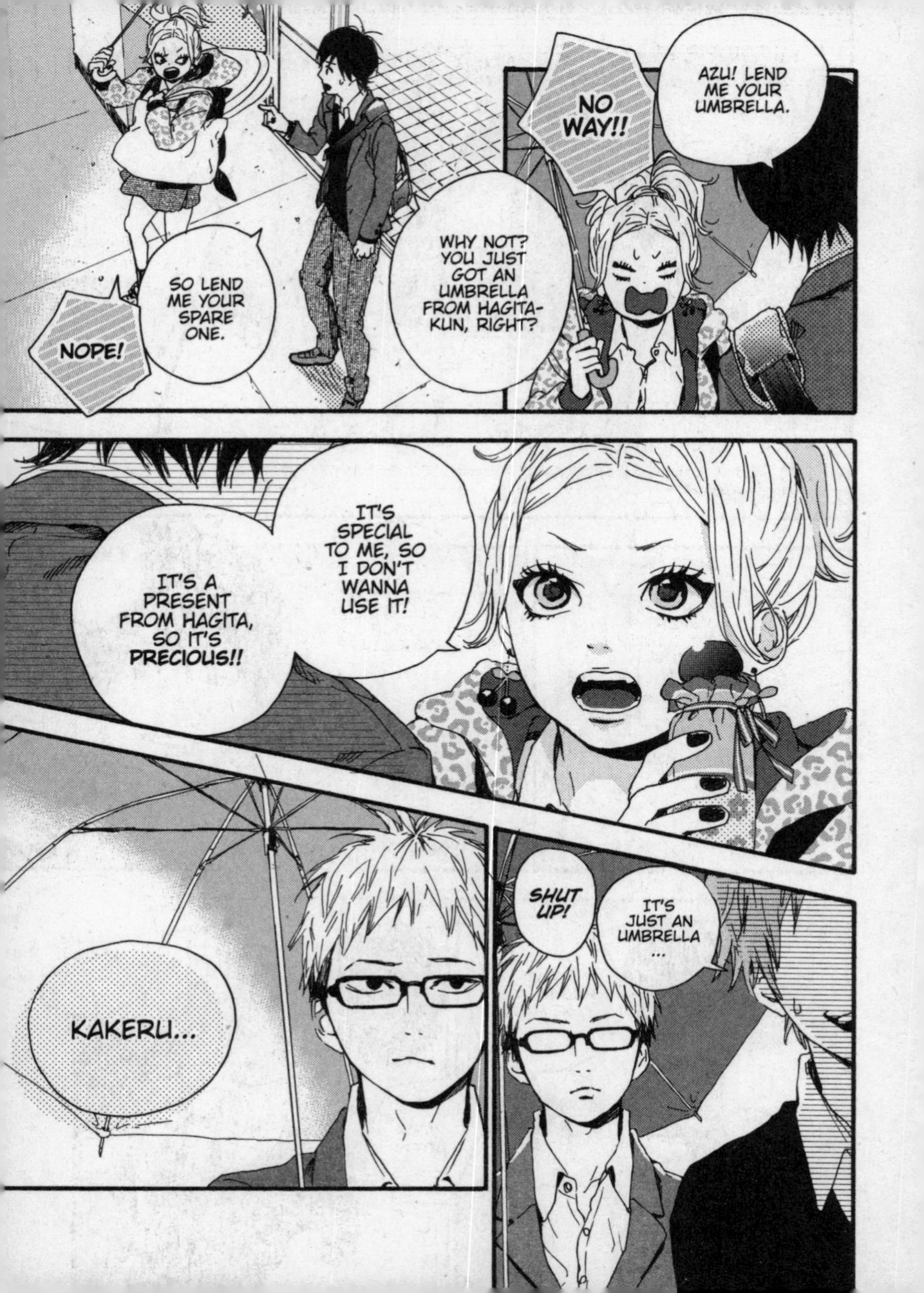
AZU! LEND ME YOUR UMBRELLA.
NO WAY!!
WHY NOT? YOU JUST GOT AN UMBRELLA FROM HAGITA-KUN, RIGHT?
SO LEND ME YOUR SPARE ONE.
NOPE!
IT'S SPECIAL TO ME, SO I DON'T WANNA USE IT!
IT'S A PRESENT FROM HAGITA, SO IT'S PRECIOUS!!
IT'S JUST AN UMBRELLA ...
SHUT UP!
KAKERU...

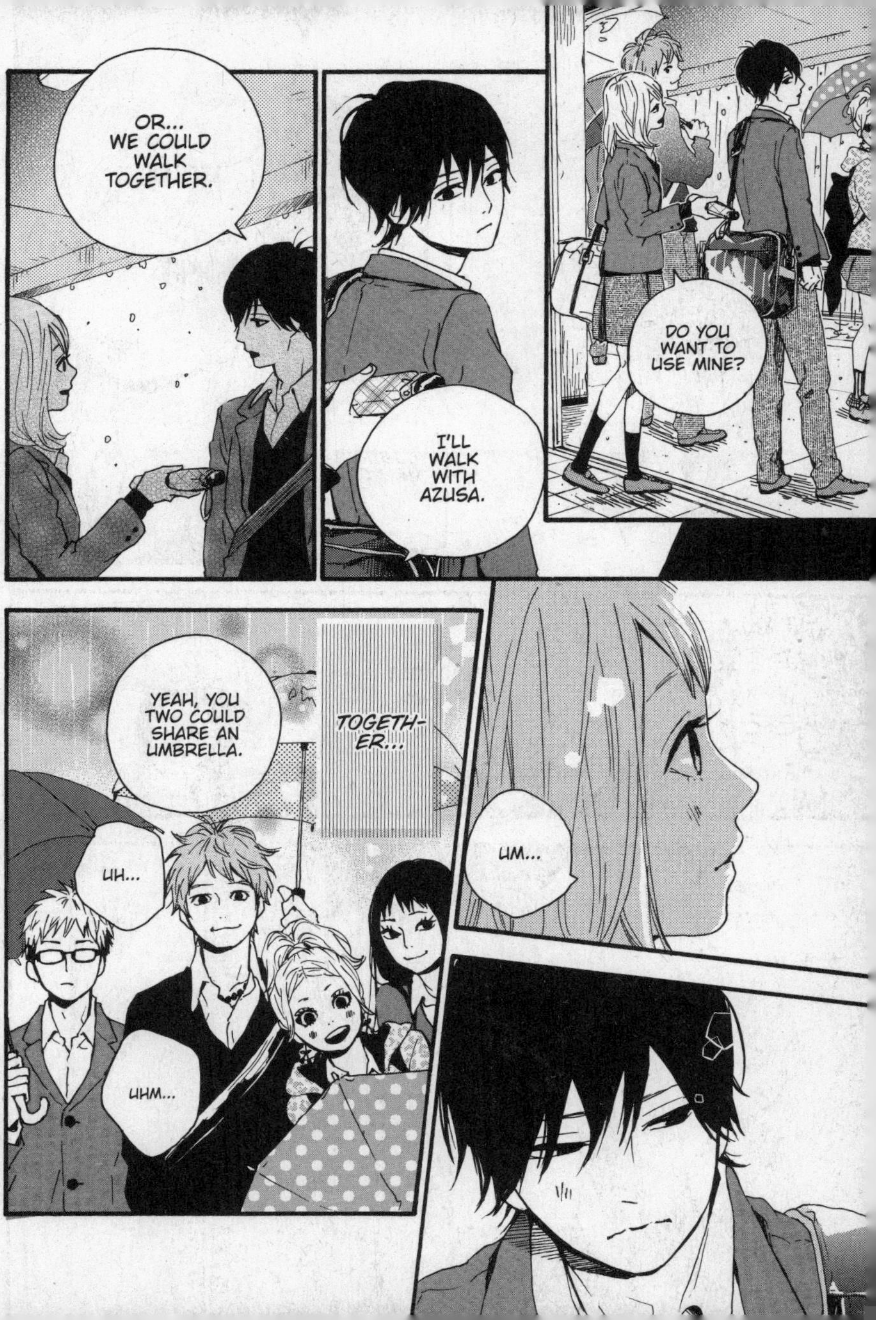
DO YOU WANT TO USE MINE?
I'LL WALK WITH AZUSA.
OR... WE COULD WALK TOGETHER.
UM...
YEAH, YOU TWO COULD SHARE AN UMBRELLA.
TOGETH-ER...
UH...
UHM...

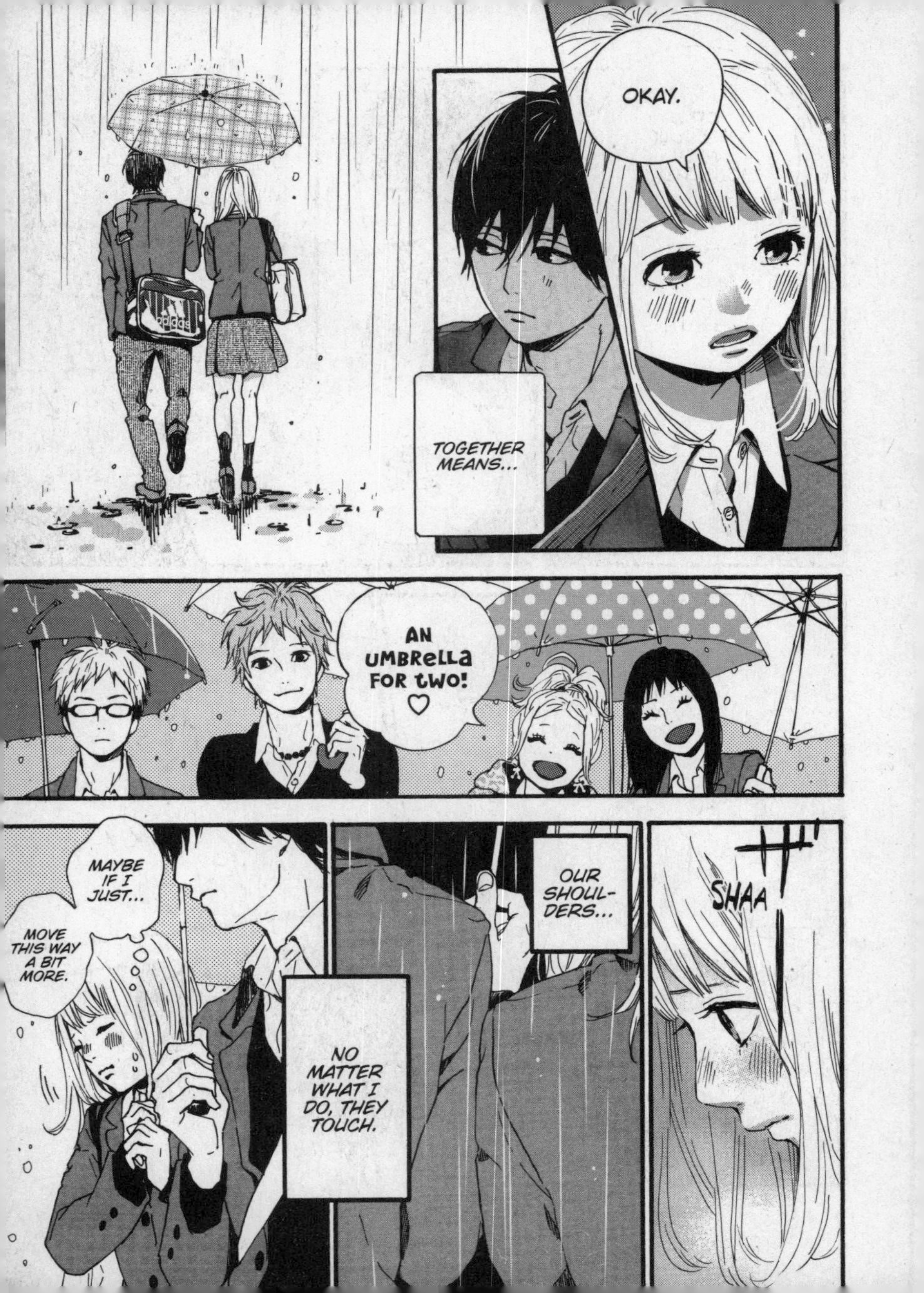
OKAY.
TOGETHER MEANS...
AN UMBRELLA FOR TWO! ♡
SHAA
OUR SHOULDERS...
NO MATTER WHAT I DO, THEY TOUCH.
MAYBE IF I JUST...
MOVE THIS WAY A BIT MORE.

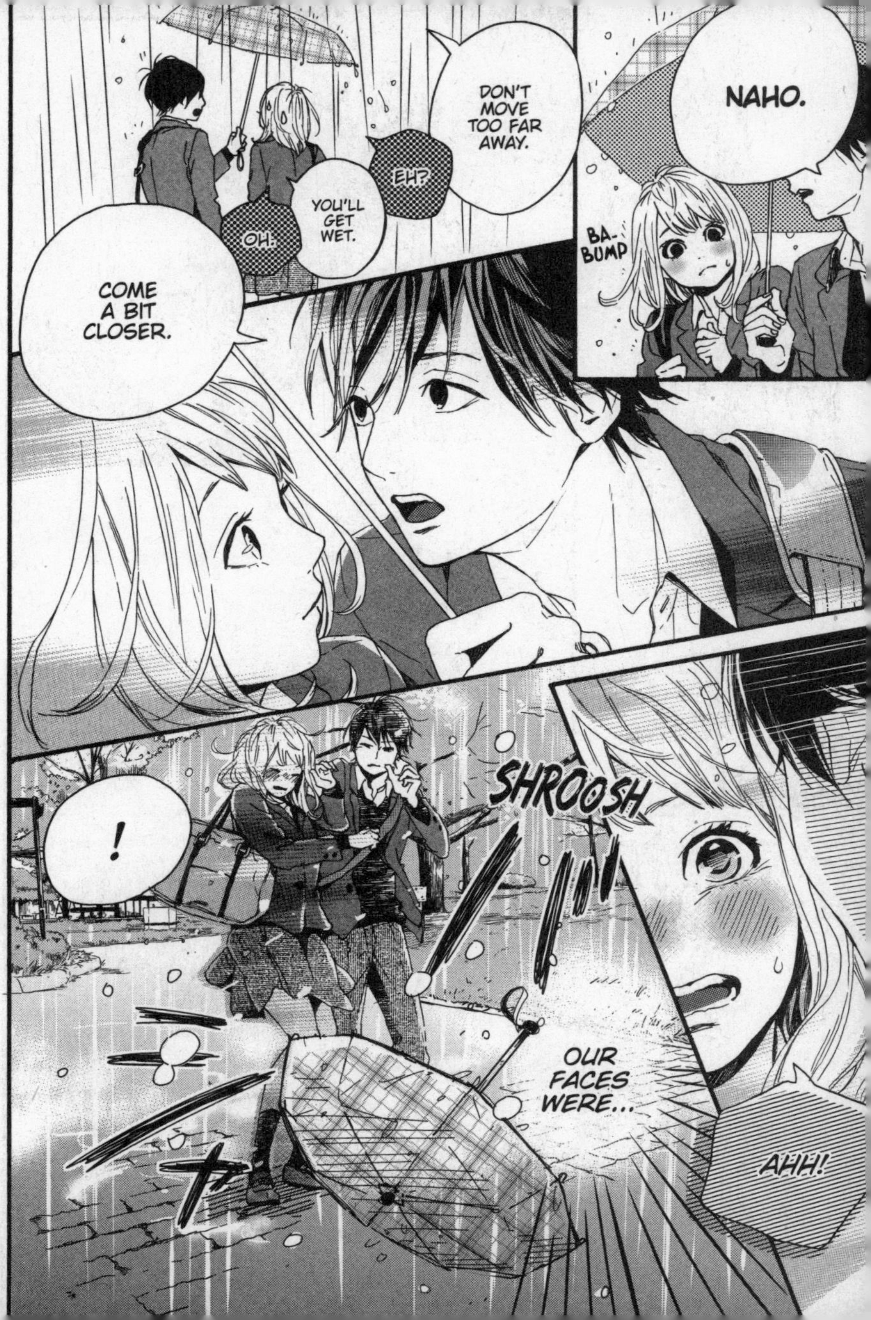
NAHO.
BA-BUMP
DON'T MOVE TOO FAR AWAY.
EH?
YOU'LL GET WET.
OH.
COME A BIT CLOSER.
SHROOSH
OUR FACES WERE...
AHH!
!

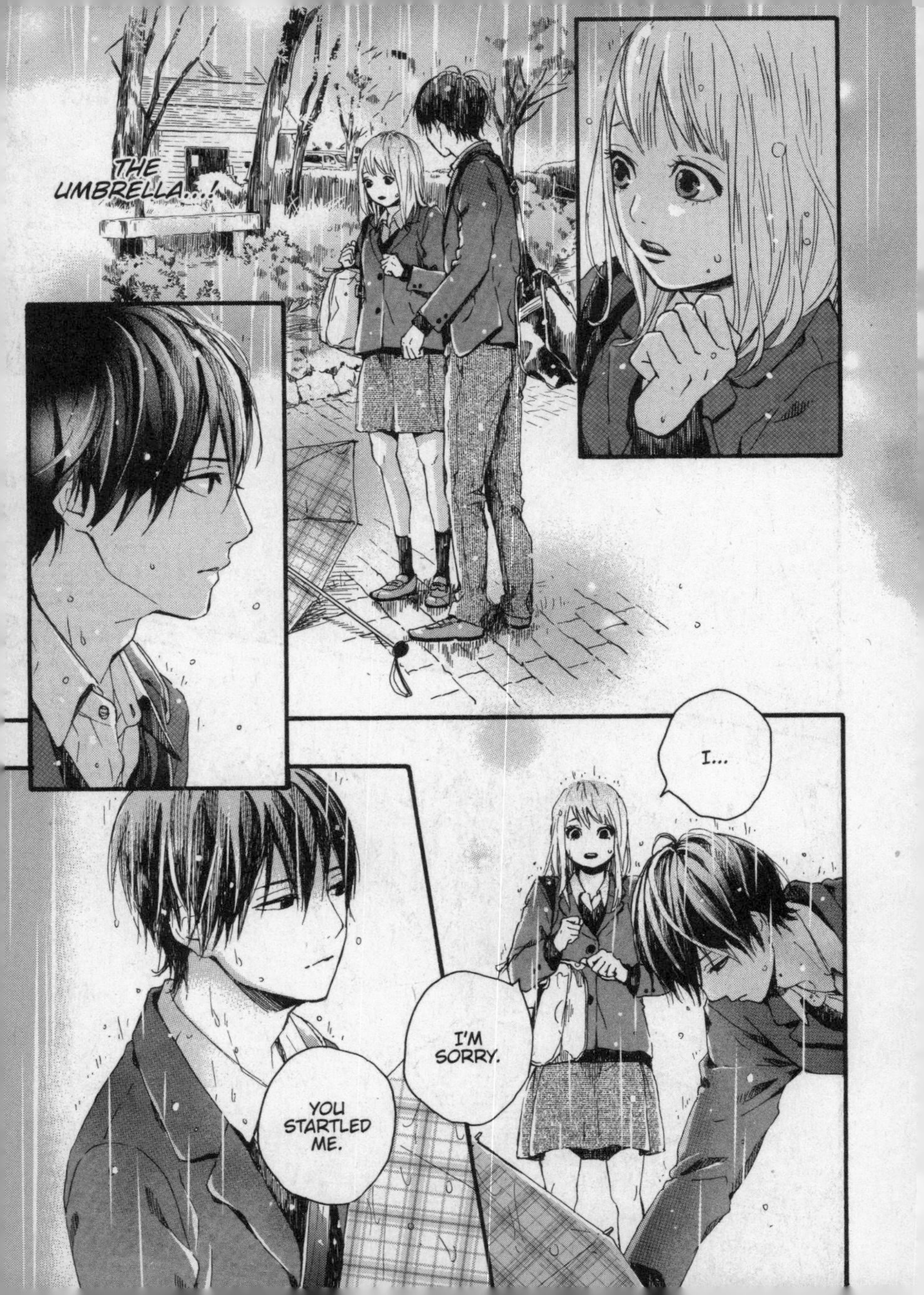
THE UMBRELLA...!
I...
I'M SORRY.
YOU STARTLED ME.

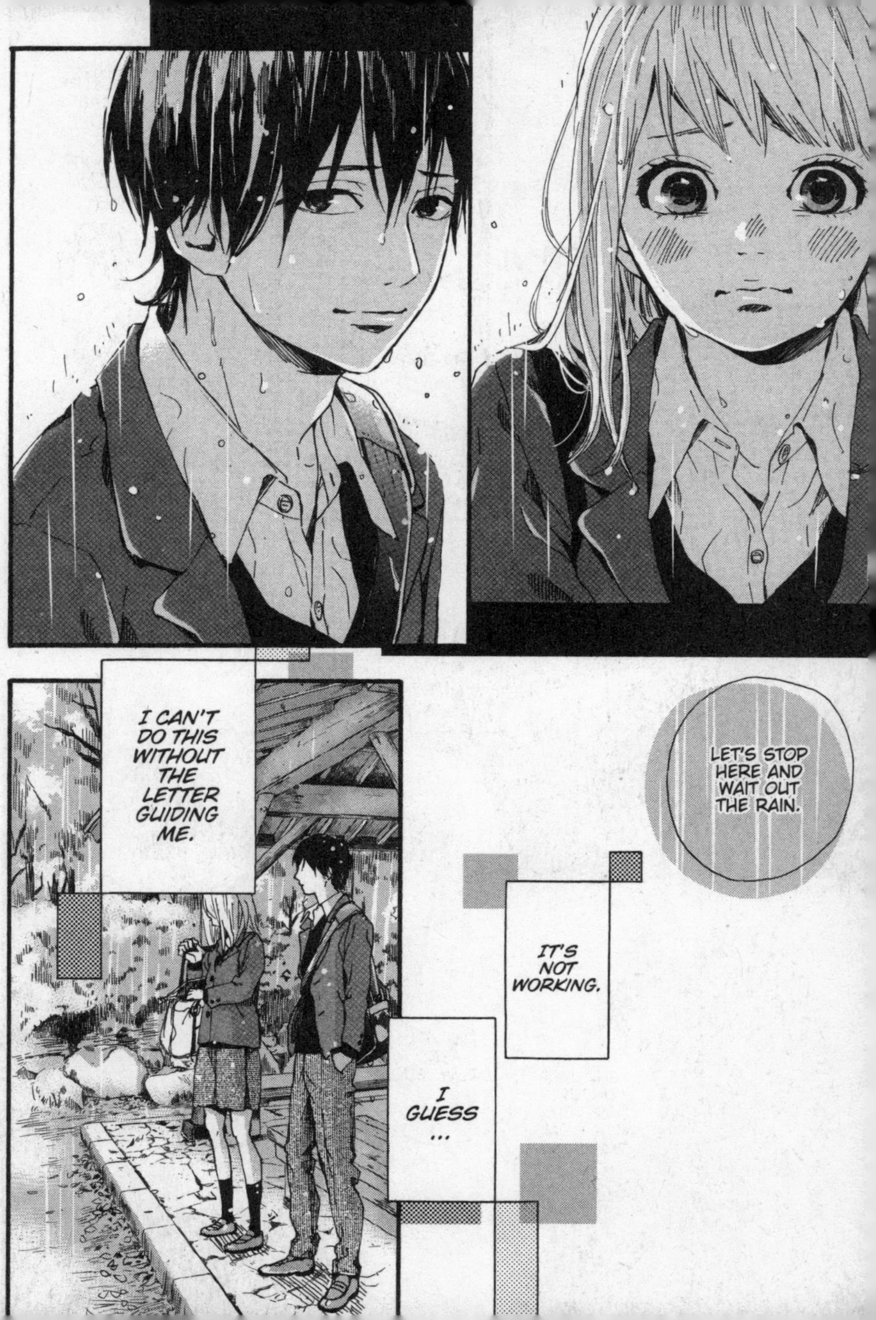
LET'S STOP HERE AND WAIT OUT THE RAIN.
IT'S NOT WORKING.
I GUESS ...
I CAN'T DO THIS WITHOUT THE LETTER GUIDING ME.

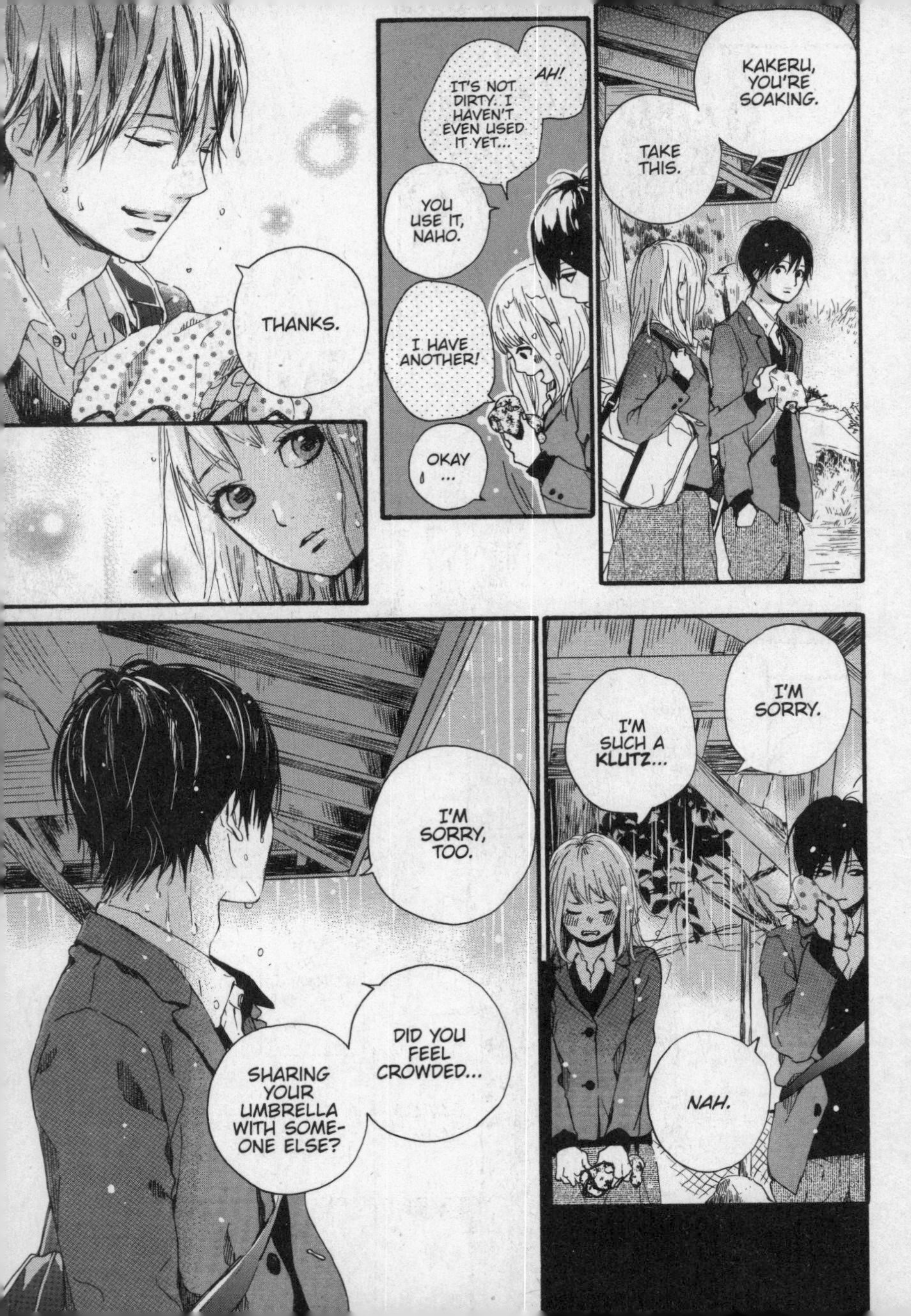
KAKERU, YOU'RE SOAKING.
TAKE THIS.
AH!
IT'S NOT DIRTY. I HAVEN'T EVEN USED IT YET...
YOU USE IT, NAHO.
I HAVE ANOTHER!
OKAY ...
THANKS.
I'M SORRY.
I'M SUCH A KLUTZ...
NAH.
I'M SORRY, TOO.
DID YOU FEEL CROWDED...
SHARING YOUR UMBRELLA WITH SOME-ONE ELSE?

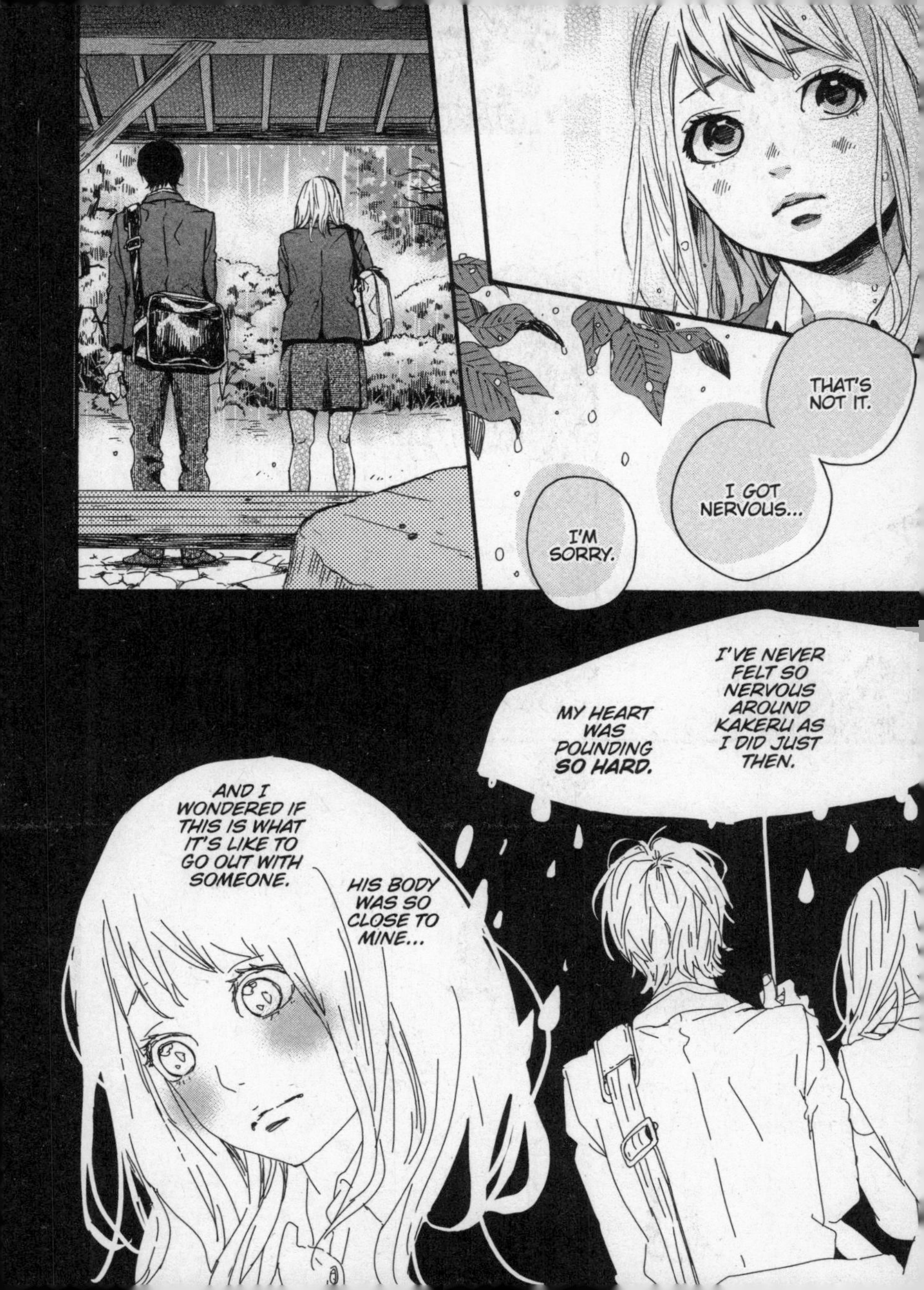
THAT'S NOT IT.
I GOT NERVOUS...
I'M SORRY.
I'VE NEVER FELT SO NERVOUS AROUND KAKERU AS I DID JUST THEN.
MY HEART WAS POUNDING SO HARD.
HIS BODY WAS SO CLOSE TO MINE...
AND I WONDERED IF THIS IS WHAT IT'S LIKE TO GO OUT WITH SOMEONE.

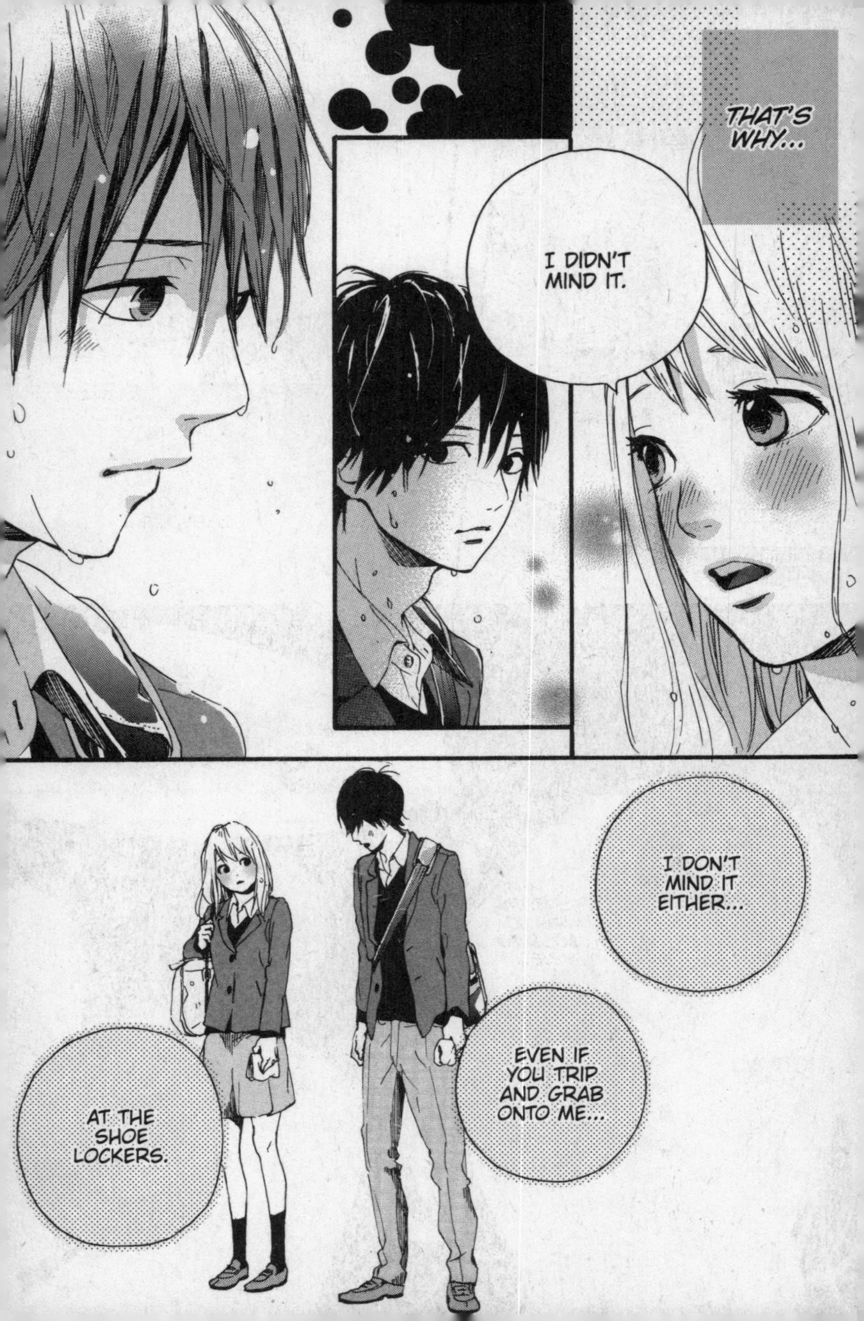
THAT'S WHY...
I DIDN'T MIND IT.
I DON'T MIND IT EITHER...
EVEN IF YOU TRIP AND GRAB ONTO ME...
AT THE SHOE LOCKERS.

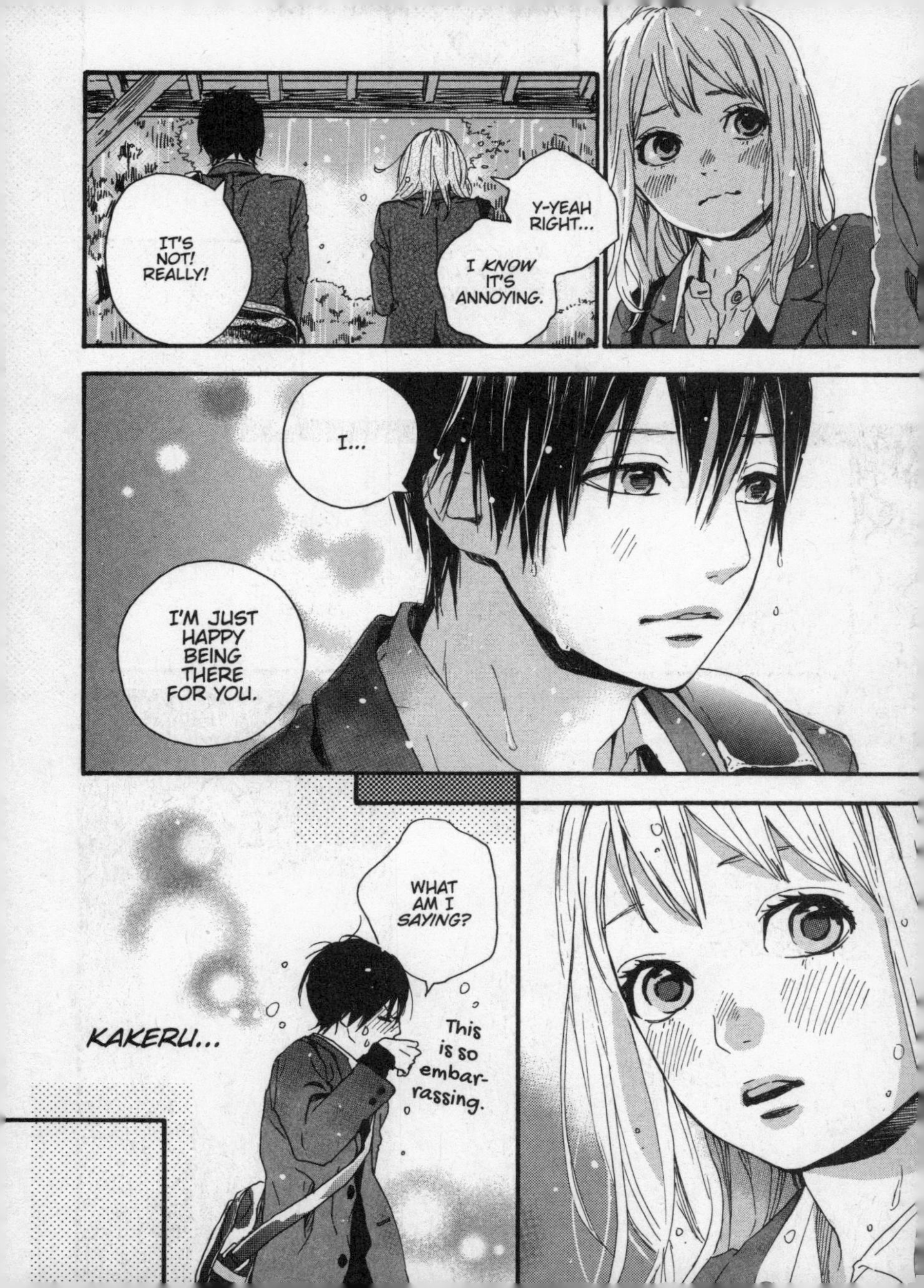
Y-YEAH RIGHT...
I *KNOW* IT'S ANNOYING.
IT'S NOT! REALLY!
I...
I'M JUST HAPPY BEING THERE FOR YOU.
WHAT AM I SAYING?
This is so embarrassing.
KAKERU...

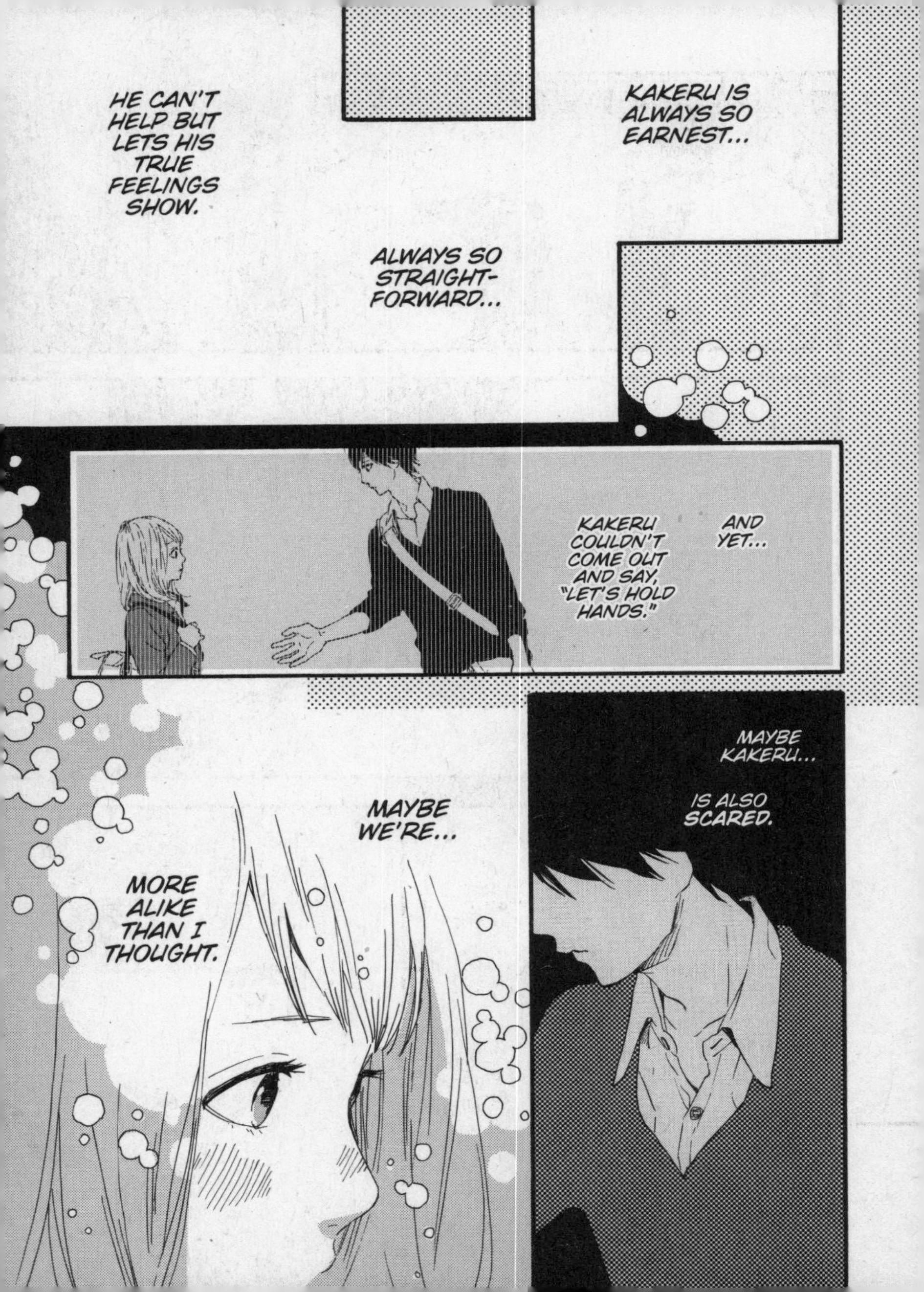
KAKERU IS ALWAYS SO EARNEST...
HE CAN'T HELP BUT LETS HIS TRUE FEELINGS SHOW.
ALWAYS SO STRAIGHT-FORWARD...
AND YET...
KAKERU COULDN'T COME OUT AND SAY, "LET'S HOLD HANDS."
MAYBE KAKERU...
IS ALSO SCARED.
MAYBE WE'RE...
MORE ALIKE THAN I THOUGHT.

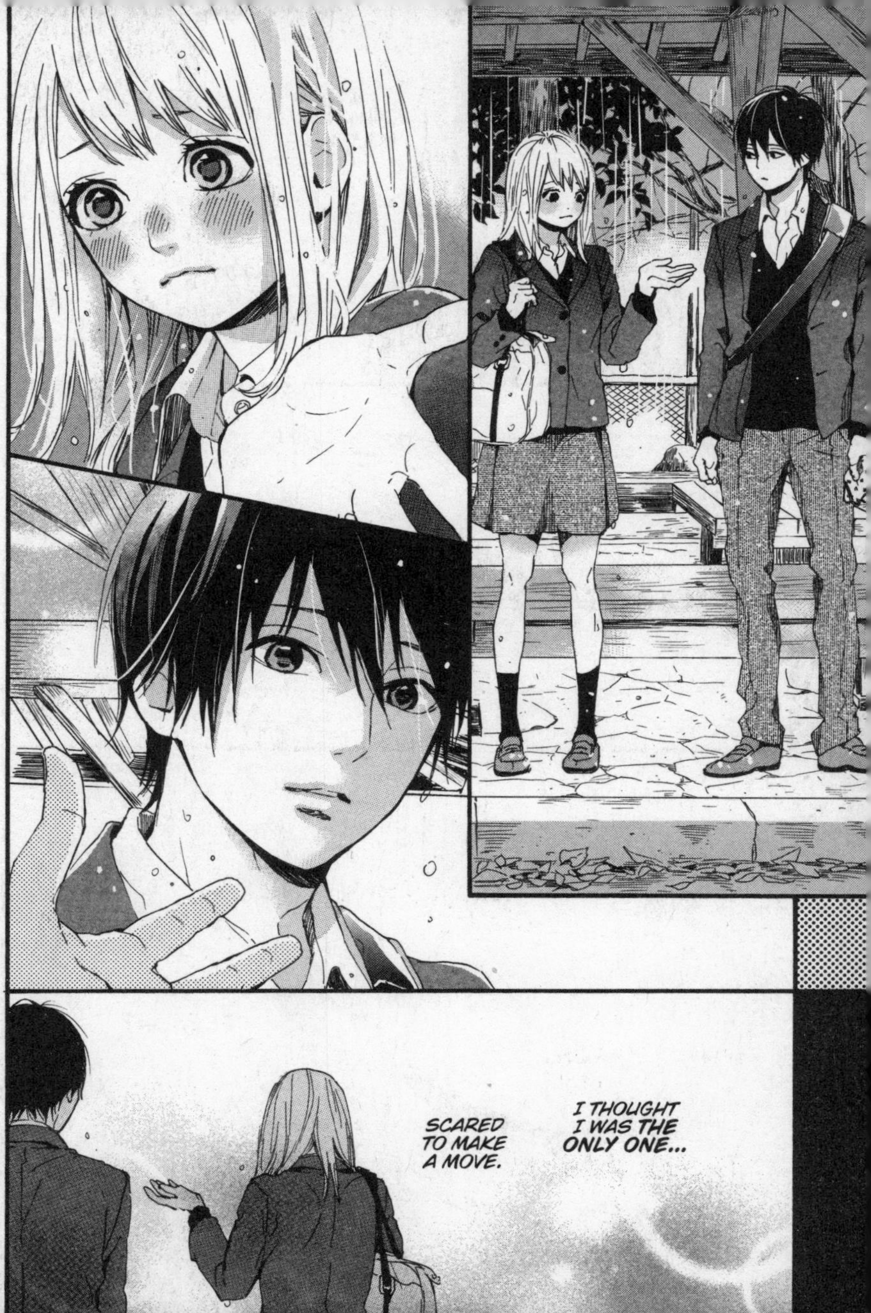
I THOUGHT
I WAS THE
ONLY ONE...
SCARED
TO MAKE
A MOVE.

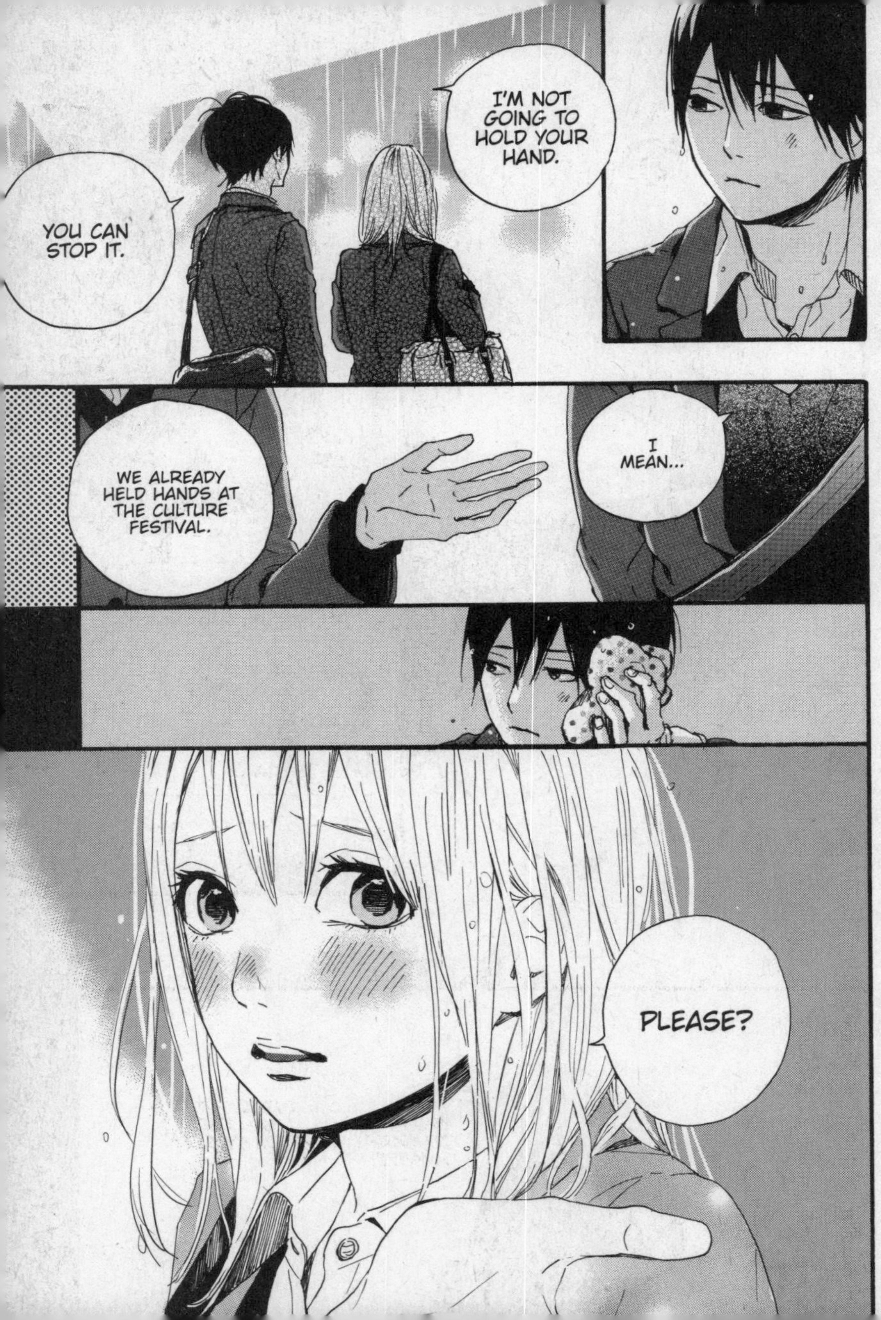
I'M NOT GOING TO HOLD YOUR HAND.
YOU CAN STOP IT.
I MEAN...
WE ALREADY HELD HANDS AT THE CULTURE FESTIVAL.
PLEASE?

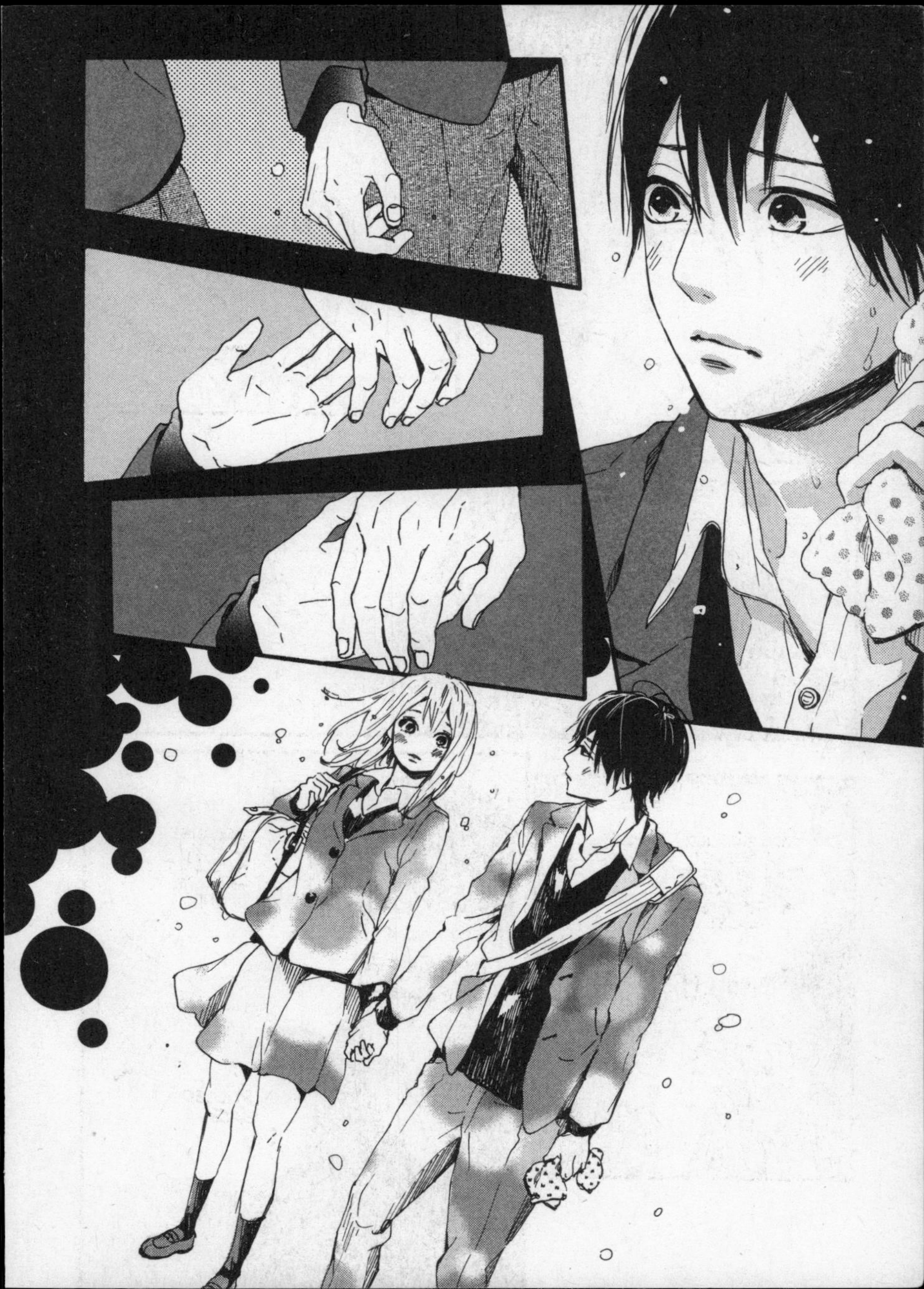

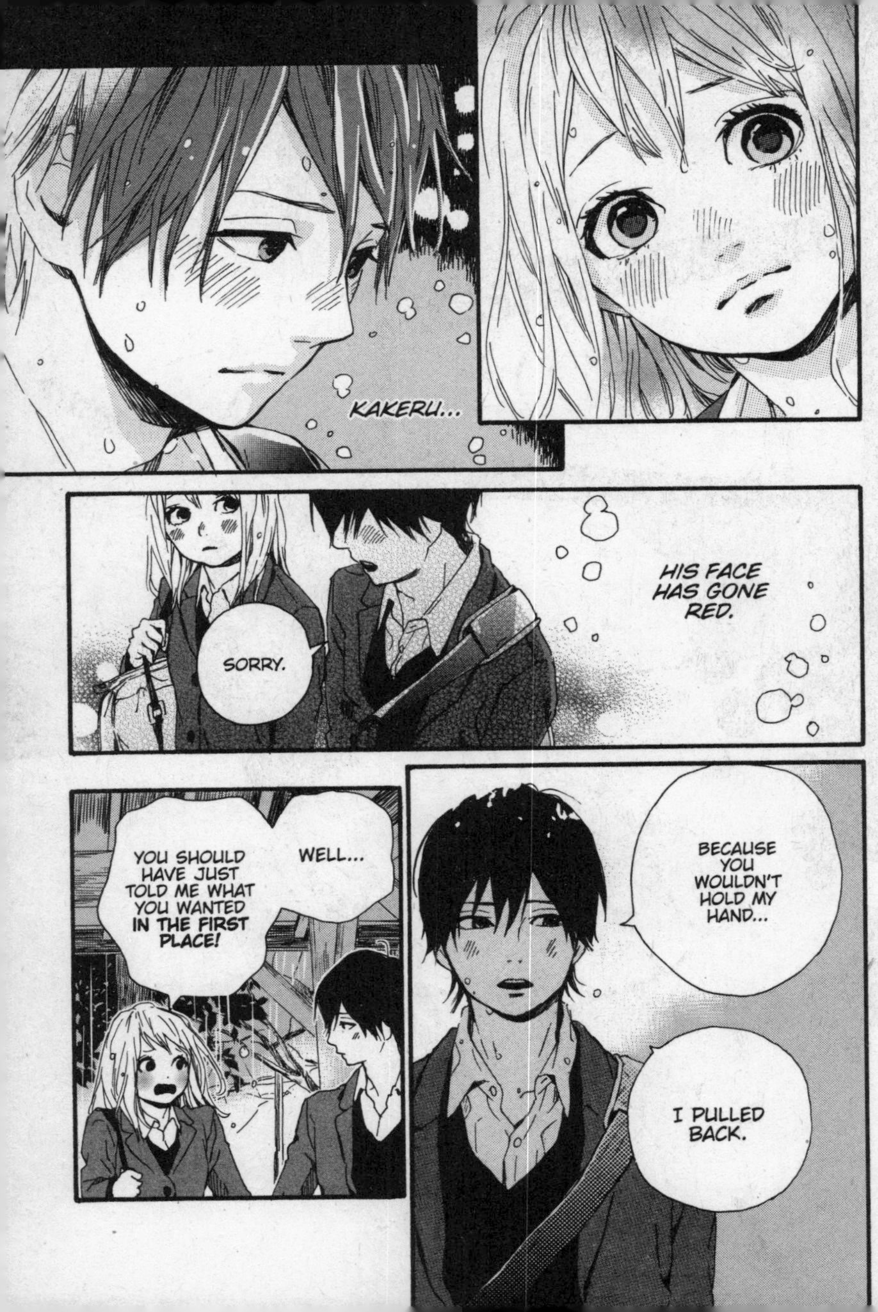
KAKERU...
HIS FACE HAS GONE RED.
SORRY.
BECAUSE YOU WOULDN'T HOLD MY HAND...
I PULLED BACK.
WELL...
YOU SHOULD HAVE JUST TOLD ME WHAT YOU WANTED IN THE FIRST PLACE!

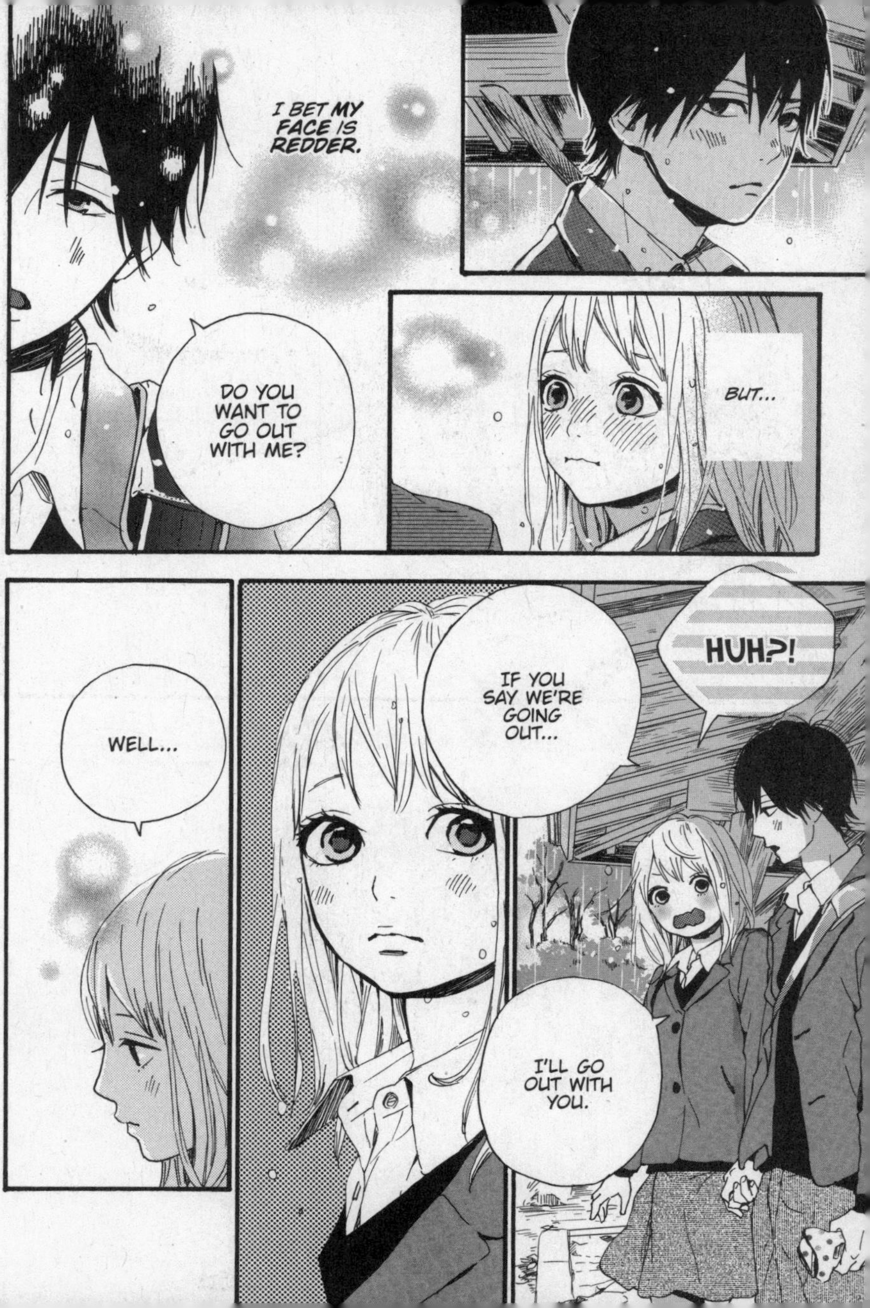
BUT...
I BET MY FACE IS REDDER.
DO YOU WANT TO GO OUT WITH ME?
HUH?!
IF YOU SAY WE'RE GOING OUT...
I'LL GO OUT WITH YOU.
WELL...

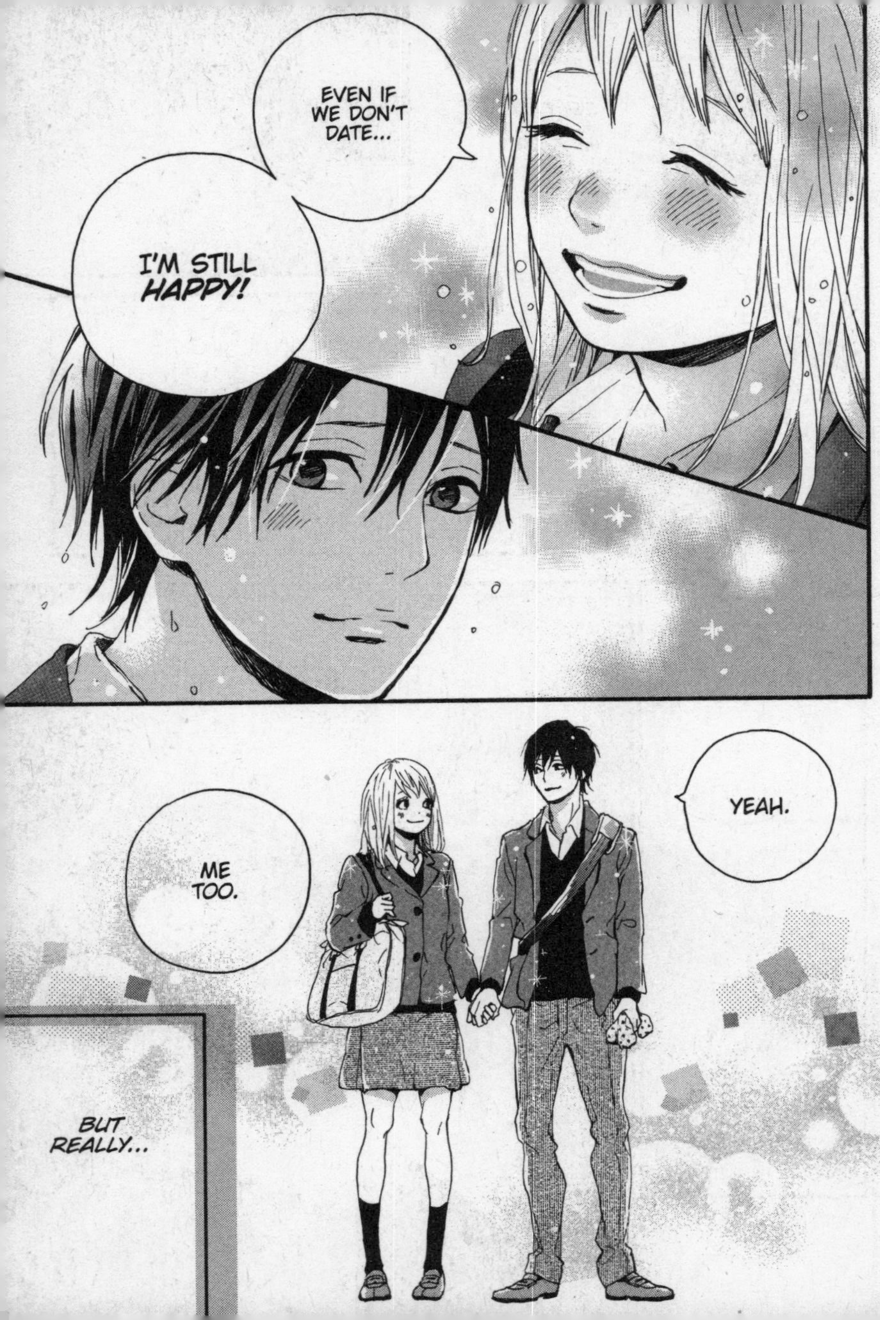
EVEN IF WE DON'T DATE...
I'M STILL *HAPPY!*
YEAH.
ME TOO.
BUT REALLY...

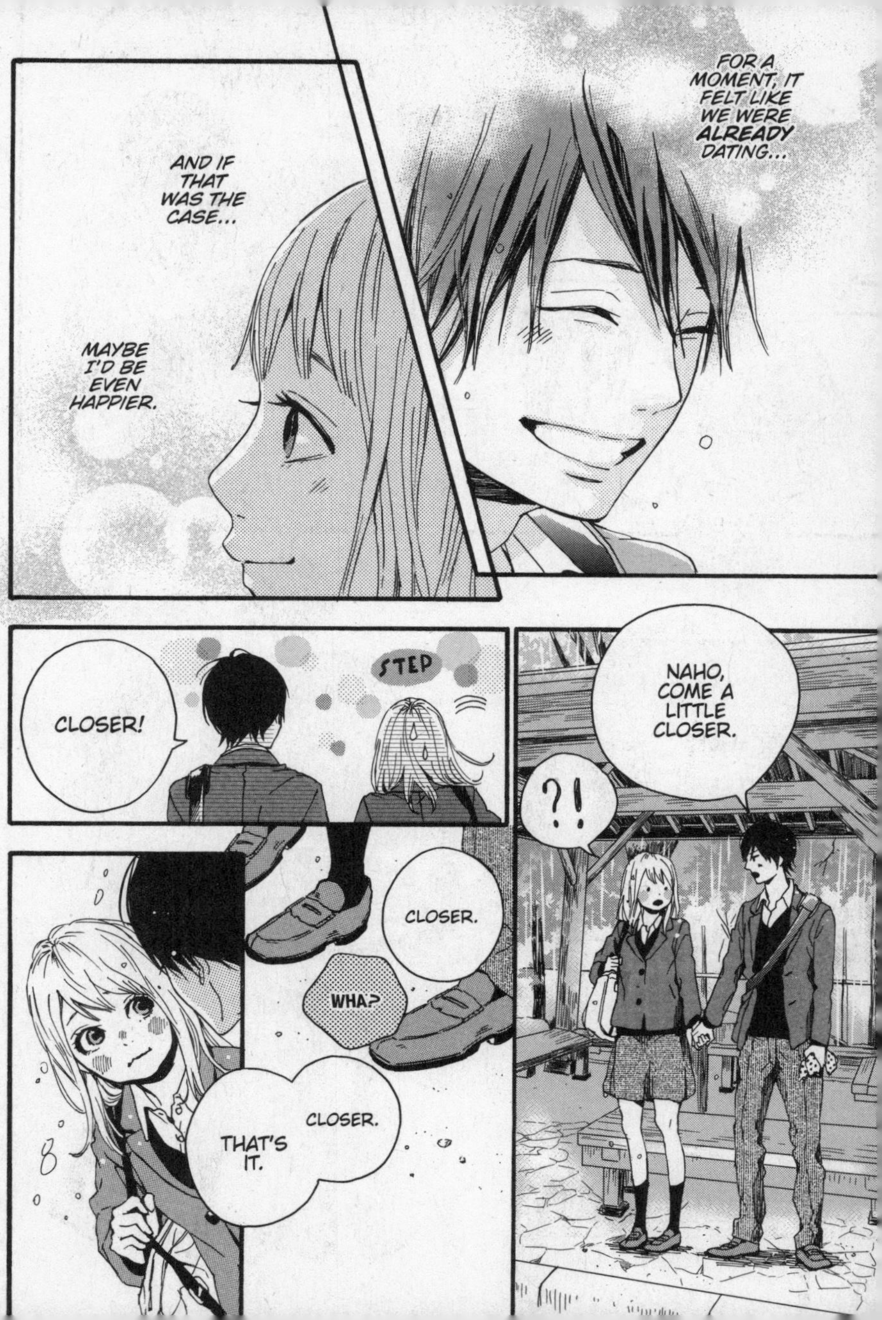
FOR A MOMENT, IT FELT LIKE WE WERE **ALREADY** DATING...
AND IF THAT WAS THE CASE...
MAYBE I'D BE EVEN HAPPIER.
NAHO, COME A LITTLE CLOSER.
?!
STEP
CLOSER!
CLOSER.
WHA?
CLOSER.
THAT'S IT.

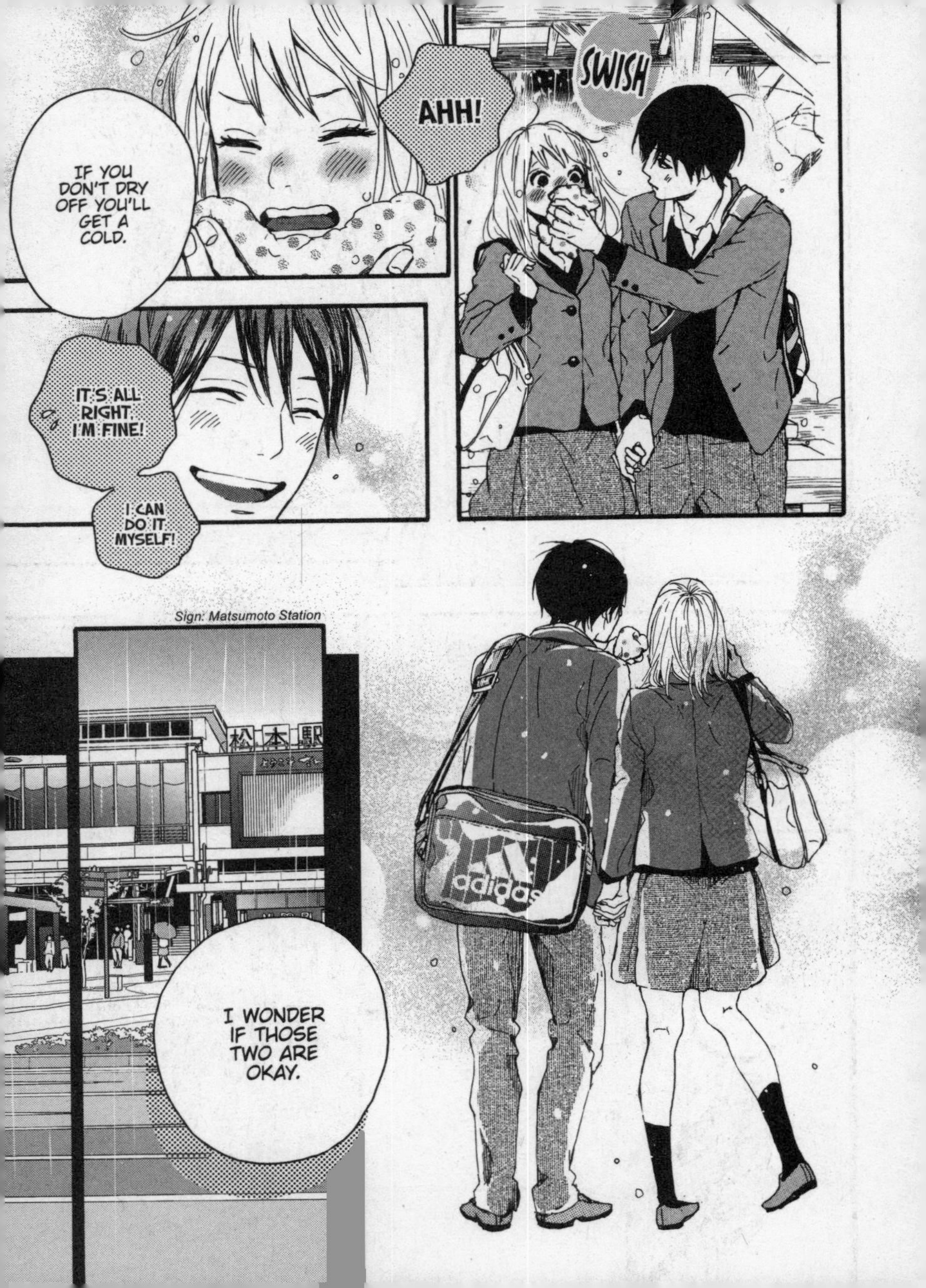
SWISH
AHH!
IF YOU DON'T DRY OFF YOU'LL GET A COLD.
IT'S ALL RIGHT, I'M FINE!
I CAN DO IT MYSELF!
Sign: Matsumoto Station
松本駅
I WONDER IF THOSE TWO ARE OKAY.

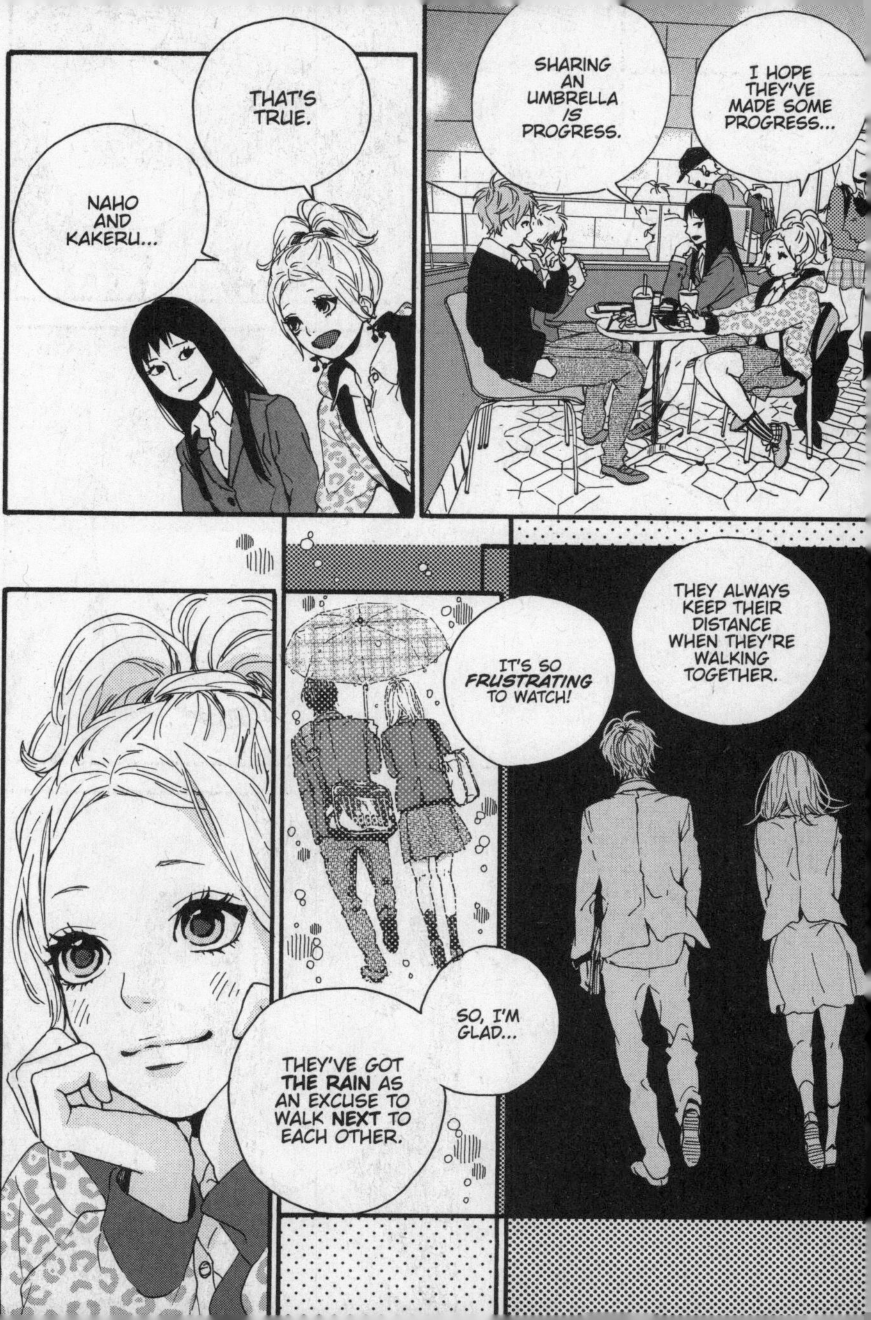
I HOPE THEY'VE MADE SOME PROGRESS...
SHARING AN UMBRELLA *IS* PROGRESS.
THAT'S TRUE.
NAHO AND KAKERU...
THEY ALWAYS KEEP THEIR DISTANCE WHEN THEY'RE WALKING TOGETHER.
IT'S SO ***FRUSTRATING*** TO WATCH!
SO, I'M GLAD...
THEY'VE GOT **THE RAIN** AS AN EXCUSE TO WALK **NEXT** TO EACH OTHER.

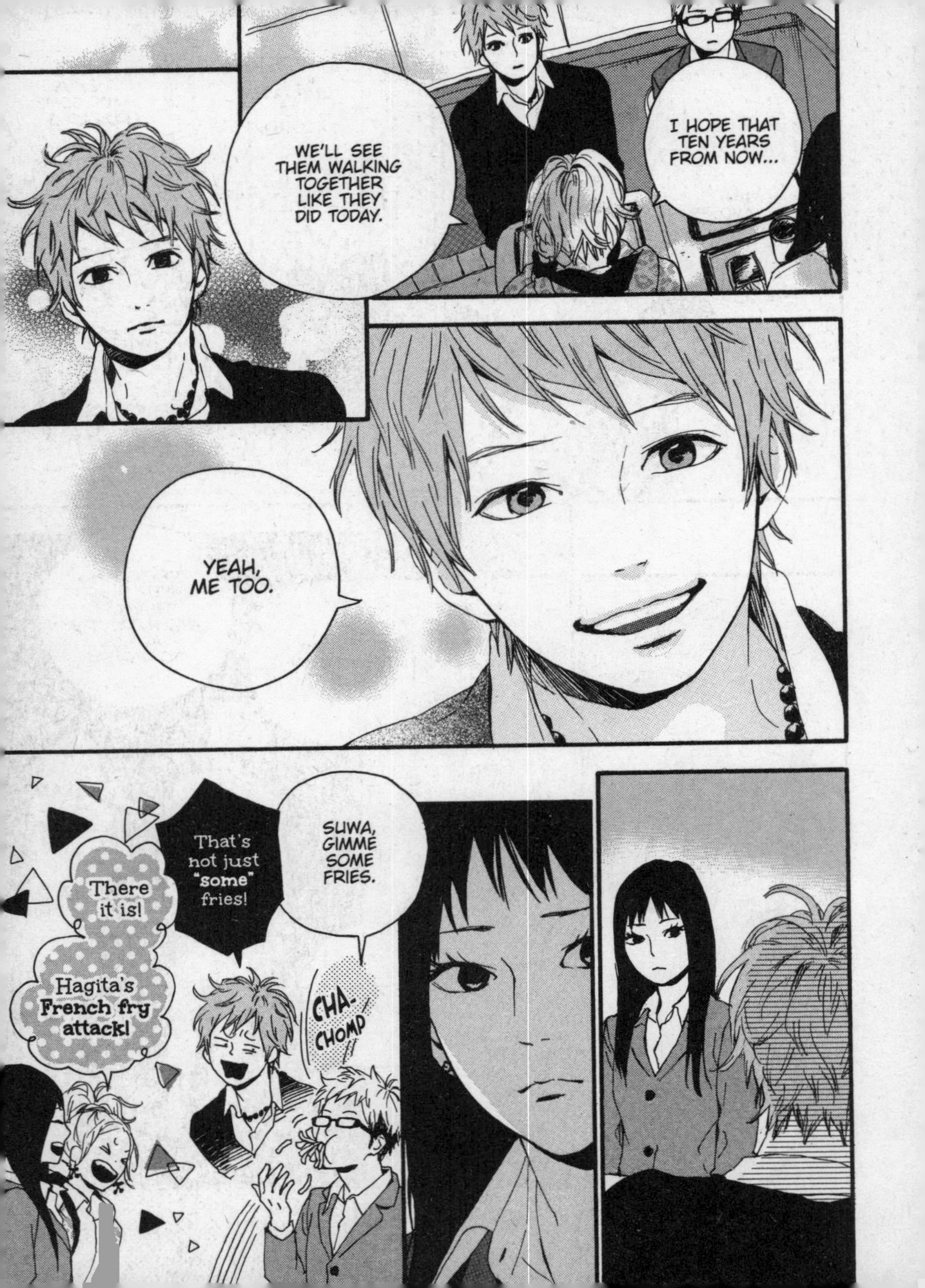
I HOPE THAT TEN YEARS FROM NOW...
WE'LL SEE THEM WALKING TOGETHER LIKE THEY DID TODAY.
YEAH, ME TOO.
SUWA, GIMME SOME FRIES.
That's not just "some" fries!
There it is!
Hagita's French fry attack!
CHA-CHOMP

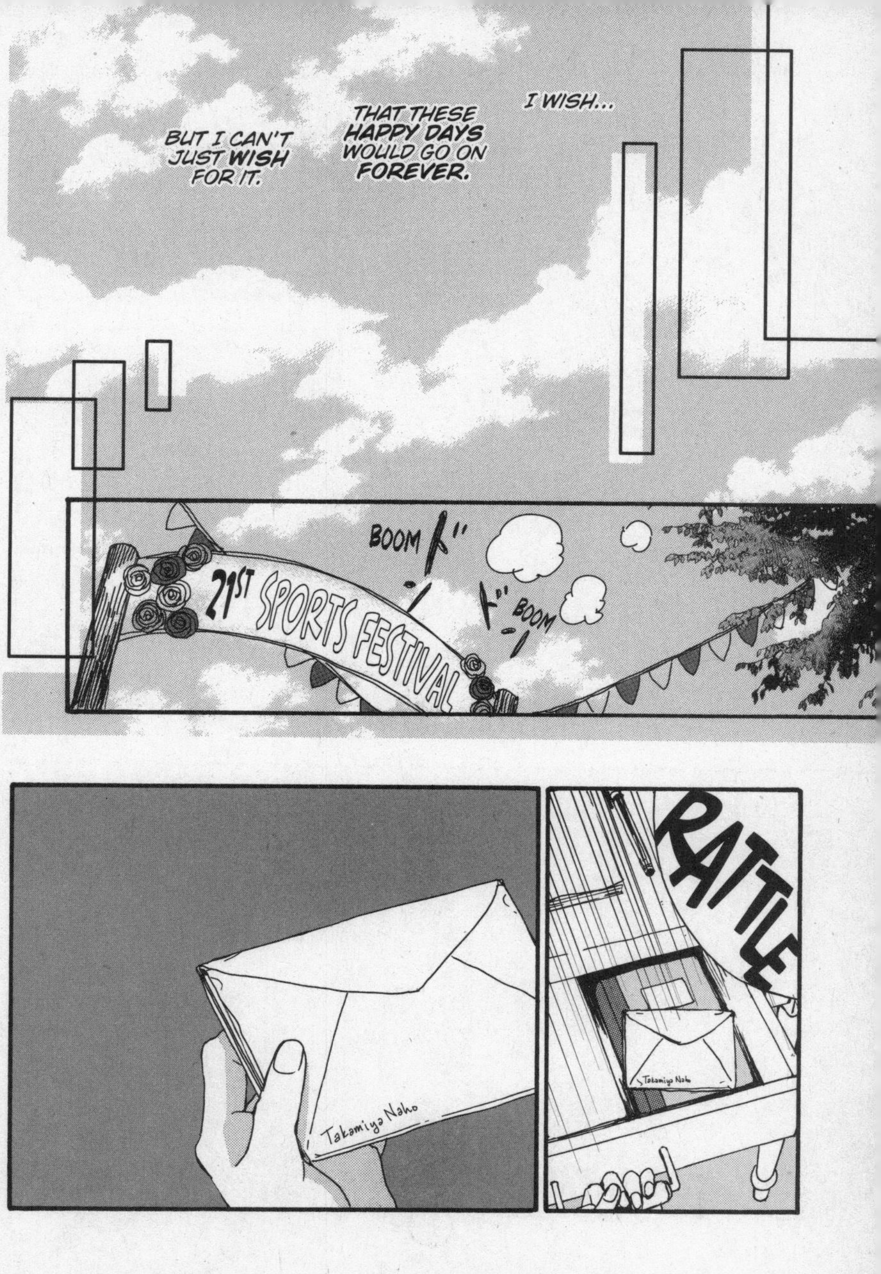
I WISH...
THAT THESE HAPPY DAYS WOULD GO ON FOREVER.
BUT I CAN'T JUST WISH FOR IT.
21ST SPORTS FESTIVAL
BOOM
BOOM
RATTLE
Takamiya Naho
Takamiya Naho

orange

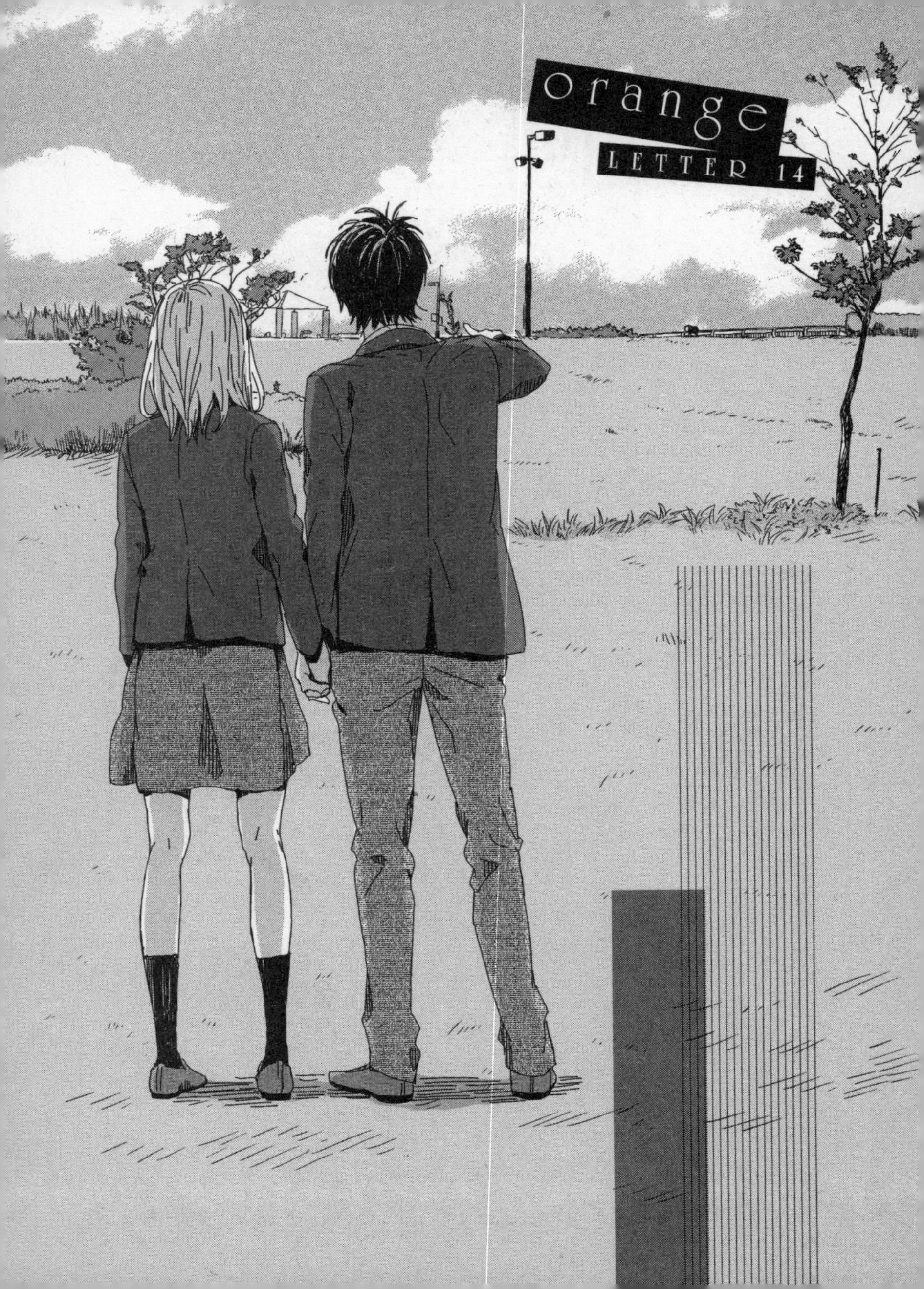
orange
LETTER 14

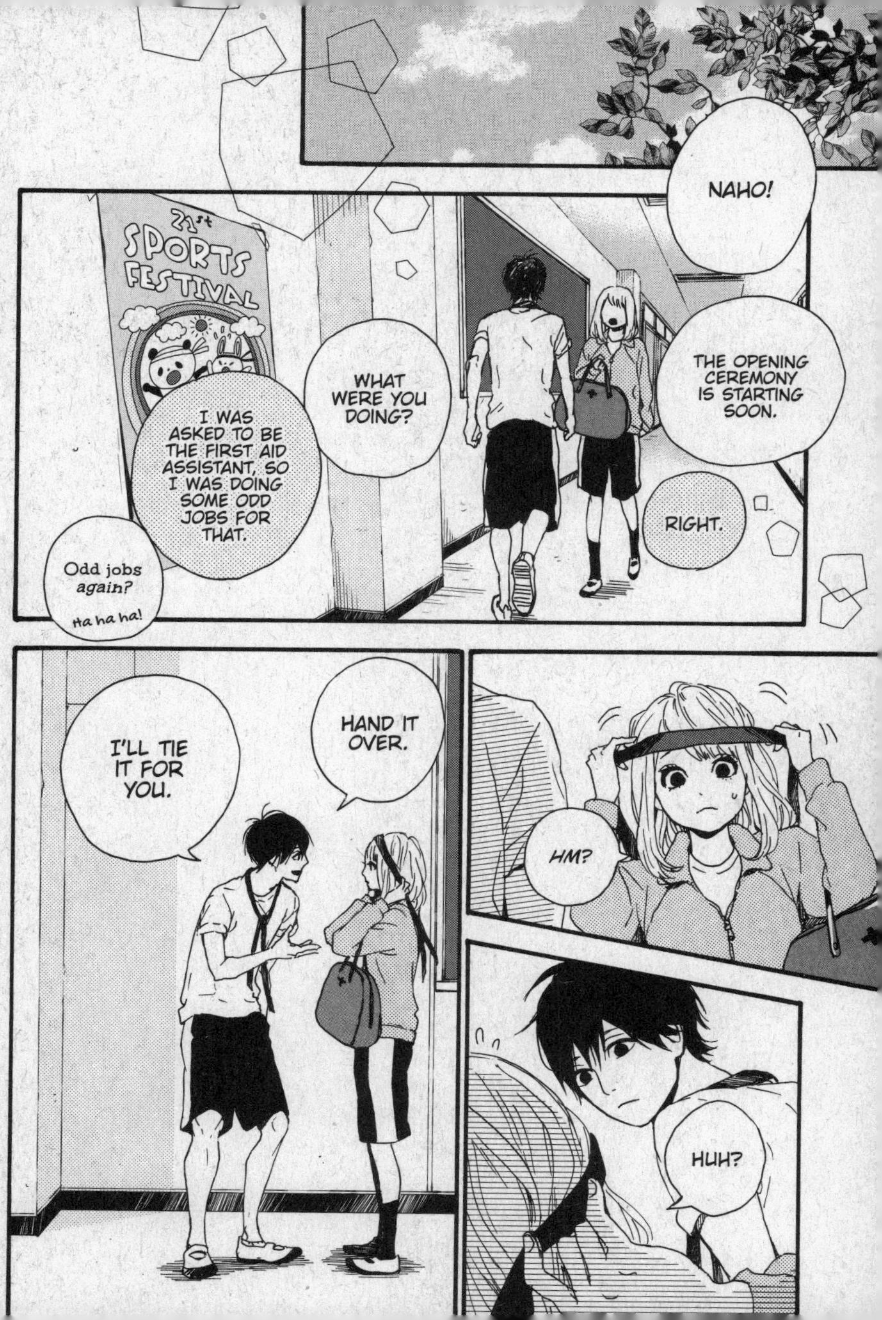
NAHO!
THE OPENING CEREMONY IS STARTING SOON.
RIGHT.
WHAT WERE YOU DOING?
I WAS ASKED TO BE THE FIRST AID ASSISTANT, SO I WAS DOING SOME ODD JOBS FOR THAT.
Odd jobs again?
Ha ha ha!
21st SPORTS FESTIVAL
HM?
HUH?
HAND IT OVER.
I'LL TIE IT FOR YOU.

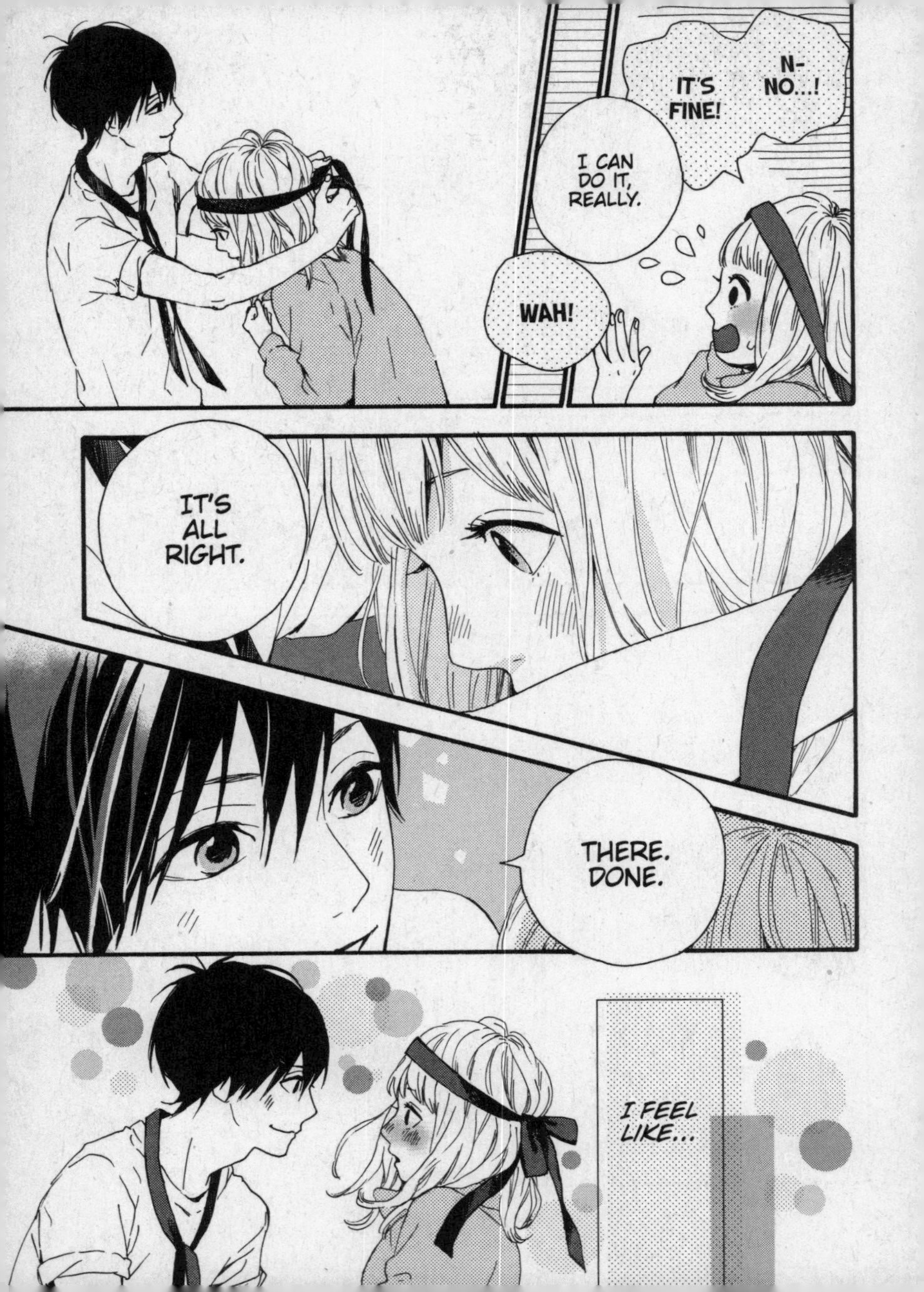
N-NO...!
IT'S FINE!
I CAN DO IT, REALLY.
WAH!
IT'S ALL RIGHT.
THERE. DONE.
I FEEL LIKE...

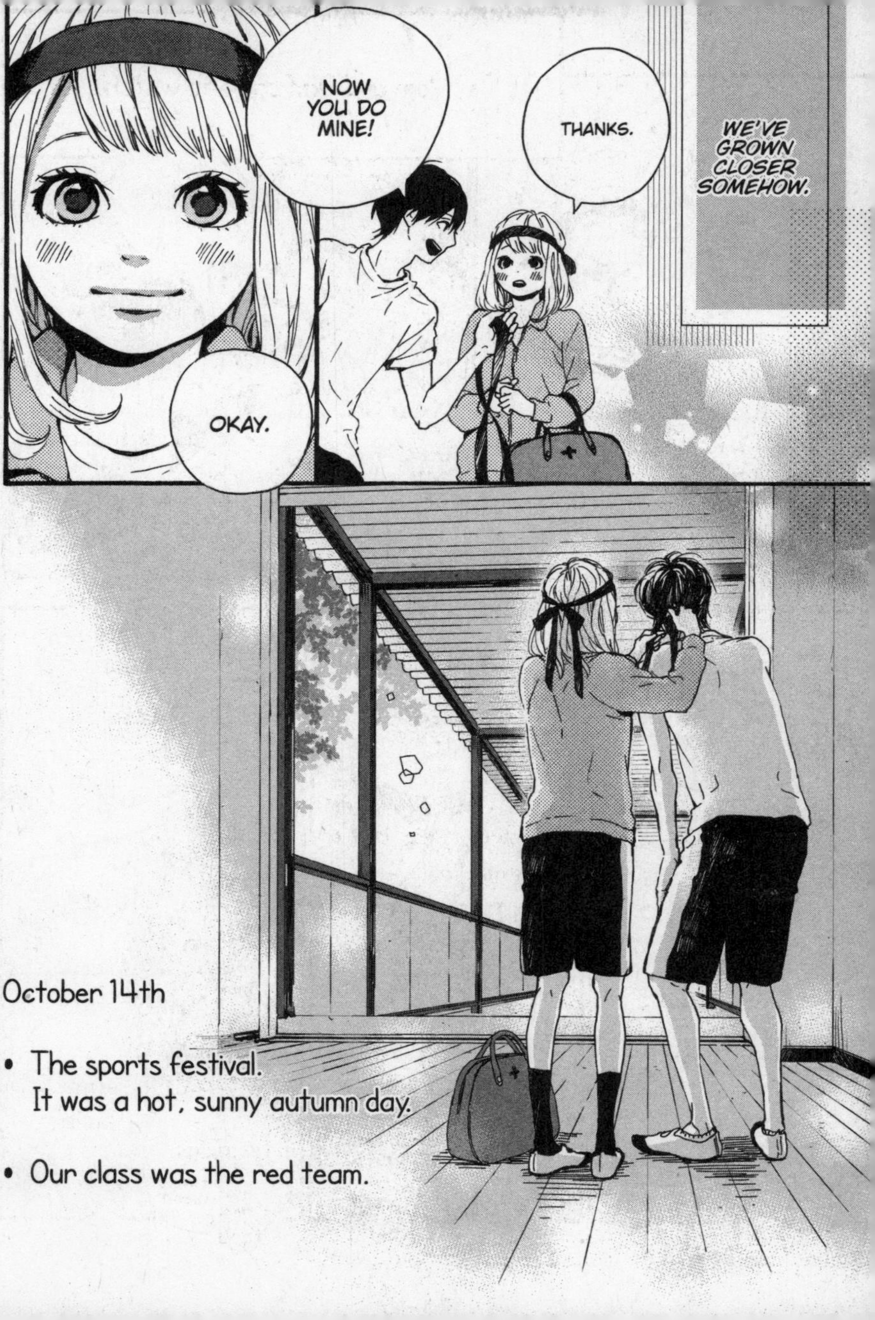
WE'VE GROWN CLOSER SOMEHOW.
THANKS.
NOW YOU DO MINE!
OKAY.
October 14th
• The sports festival. It was a hot, sunny autumn day.
• Our class was the red team.

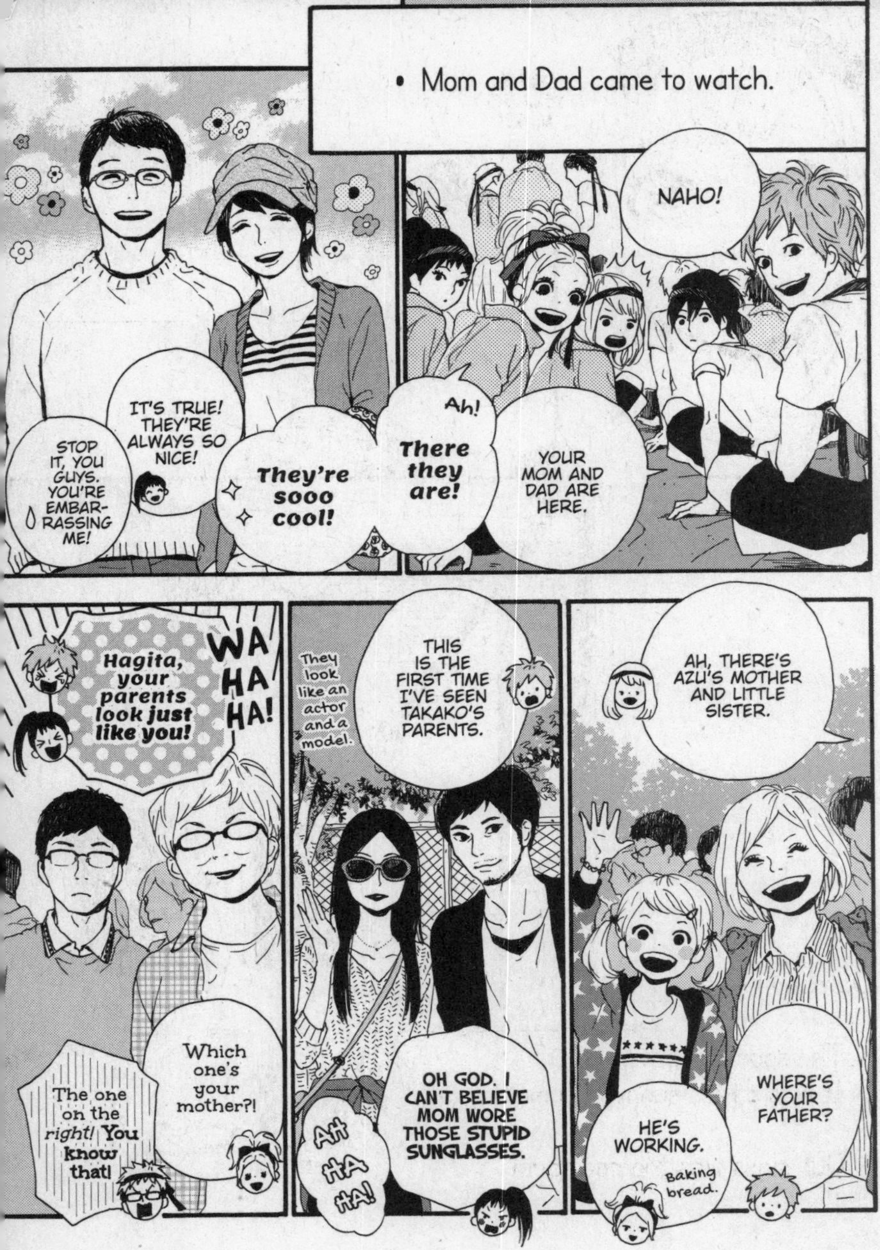
• Mom and Dad came to watch.
NAHO!
YOUR MOM AND DAD ARE HERE.
Ah! There they are!
They're sooo cool!
IT'S TRUE! THEY'RE ALWAYS SO NICE!
STOP IT, YOU GUYS. YOU'RE EMBARRASSING ME!
AH, THERE'S AZU'S MOTHER AND LITTLE SISTER.
WHERE'S YOUR FATHER?
HE'S WORKING.
Baking bread.
THIS IS THE FIRST TIME I'VE SEEN TAKAKO'S PARENTS.
They look like an actor and a model.
OH GOD. I CAN'T BELIEVE MOM WORE THOSE STUPID SUNGLASSES.
AH HA HA!
Hagita, your parents look just like you!
WA HA HA!
Which one's your mother?!
The one on the right! You know that!

• Everyone's parents came to see them run the race except for Kakeru's.

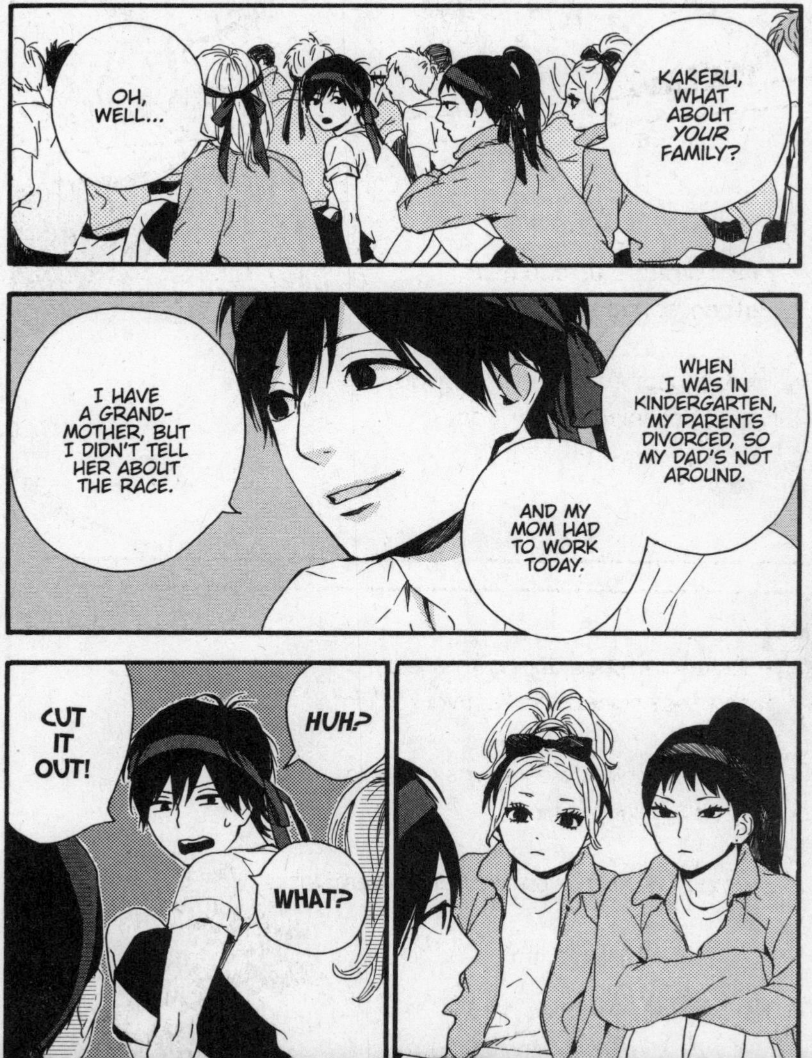
KAKERU, WHAT ABOUT *YOUR* FAMILY?
OH, WELL...
WHEN I WAS IN KINDERGARTEN, MY PARENTS DIVORCED, SO MY DAD'S NOT AROUND.
AND MY MOM HAD TO WORK TODAY.
I HAVE A GRAND-MOTHER, BUT I DIDN'T TELL HER ABOUT THE RACE.
HUH?
CUT IT OUT!
WHAT?

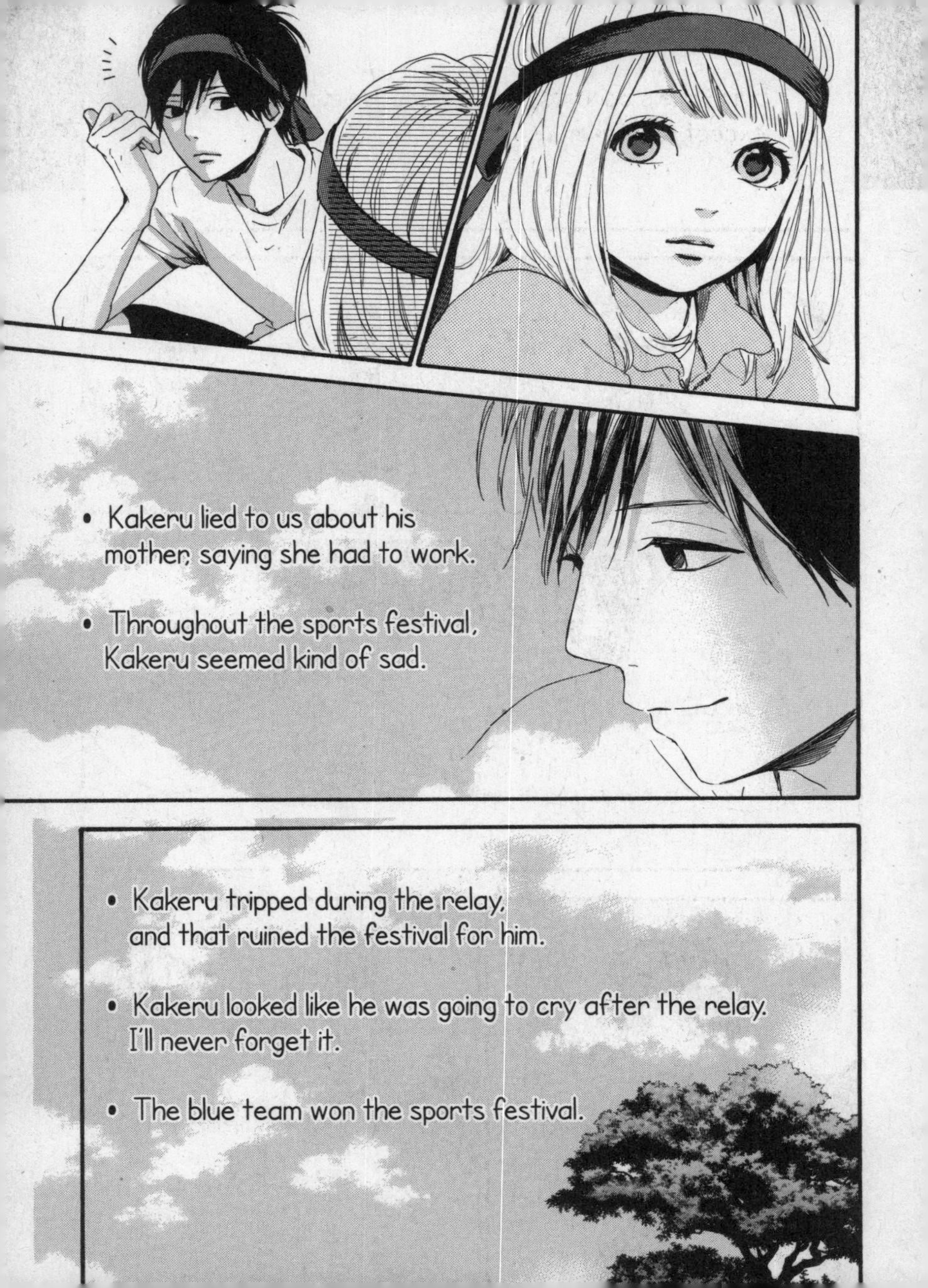

• Kakeru lied to us about his mother, saying she had to work.
• Throughout the sports festival, Kakeru seemed kind of sad.
• Kakeru tripped during the relay, and that ruined the festival for him.
• Kakeru looked like he was going to cry after the relay. I'll never forget it.
• The blue team won the sports festival.

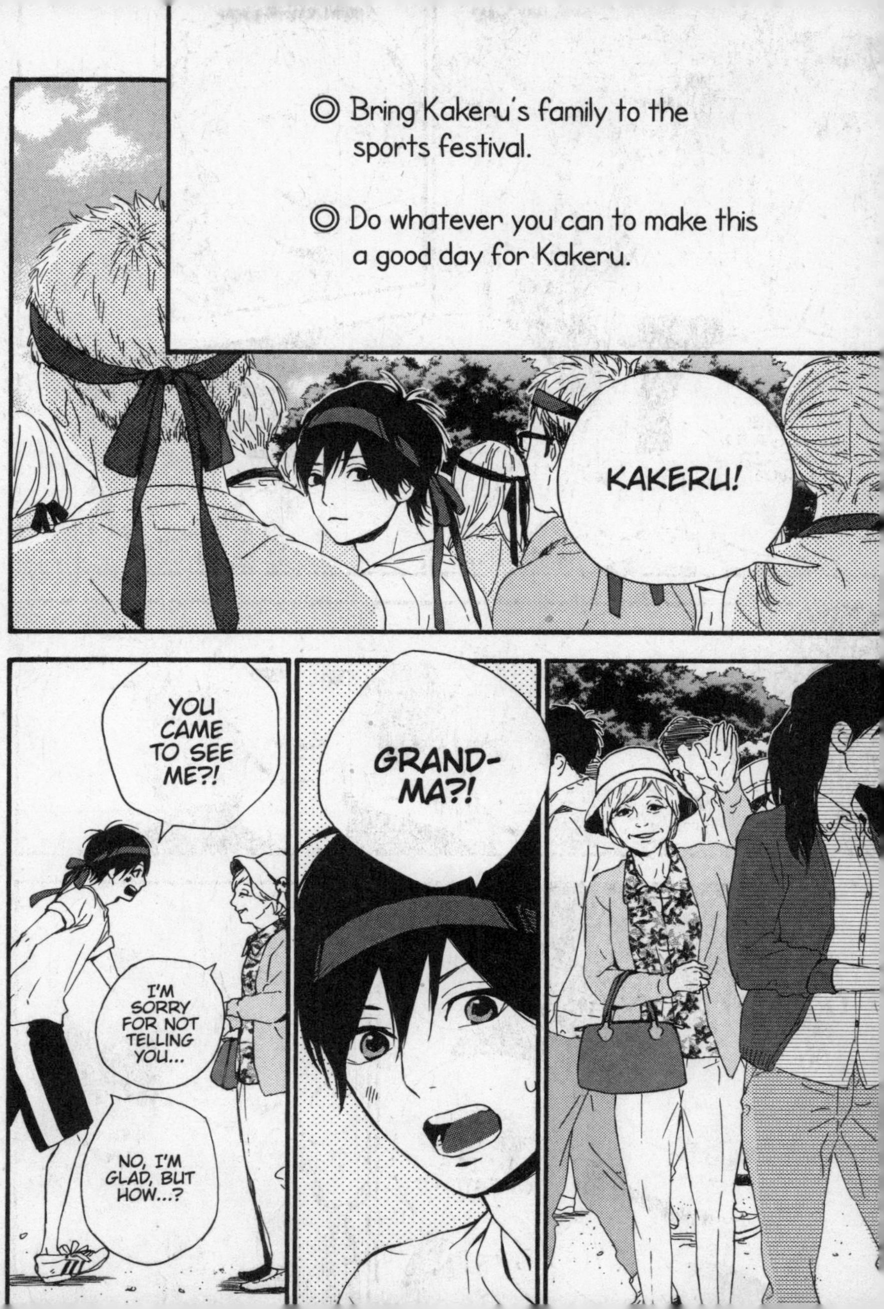
◎ Bring Kakeru's family to the sports festival.
◎ Do whatever you can to make this a good day for Kakeru.
KAKERU!
GRAND-MA?!
YOU CAME TO SEE ME?!
I'M SORRY FOR NOT TELLING YOU...
NO, I'M GLAD, BUT HOW...?

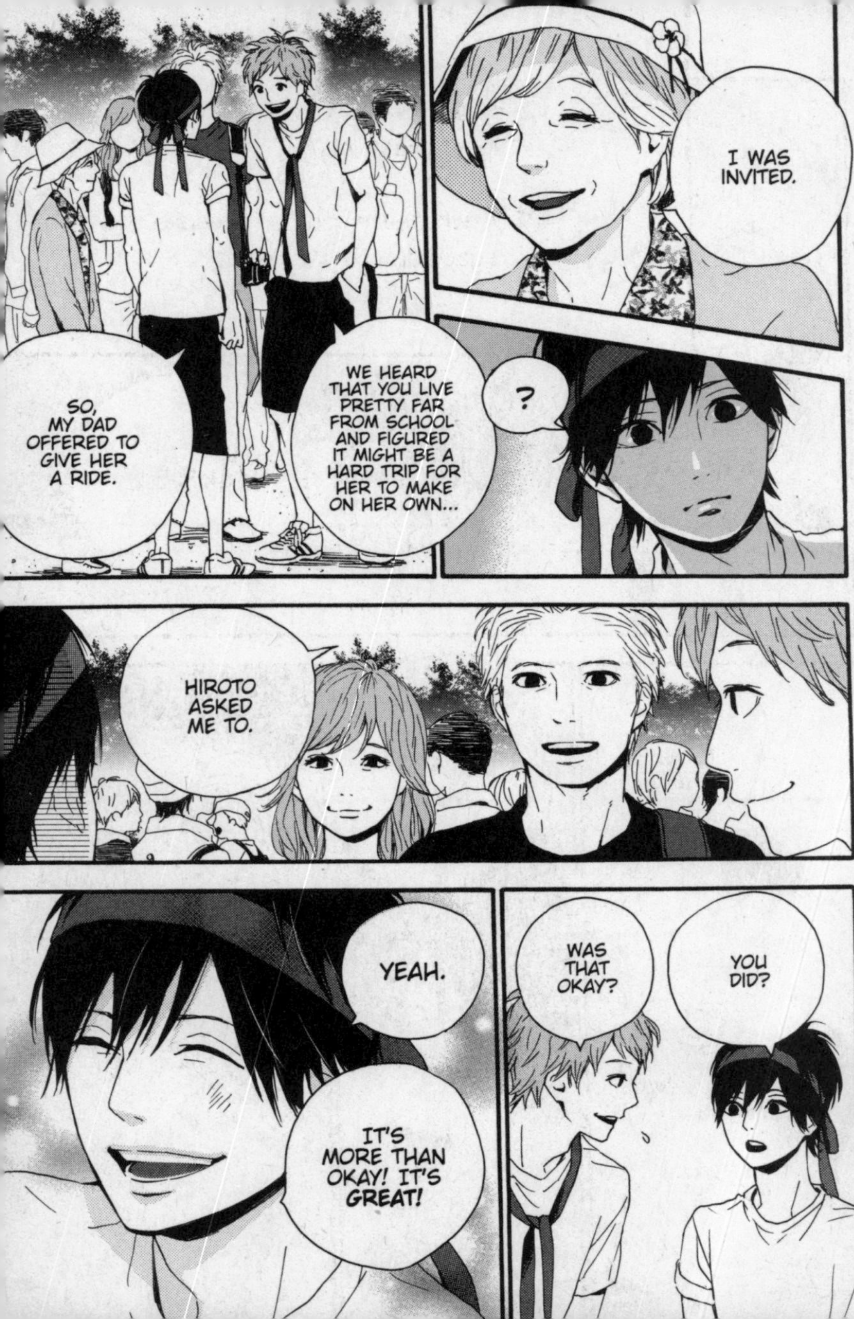
I WAS INVITED.
?
WE HEARD THAT YOU LIVE PRETTY FAR FROM SCHOOL AND FIGURED IT MIGHT BE A HARD TRIP FOR HER TO MAKE ON HER OWN...
SO, MY DAD OFFERED TO GIVE HER A RIDE.
HIROTO ASKED ME TO.
YOU DID?
WAS THAT OKAY?
YEAH.
IT'S MORE THAN OKAY! IT'S GREAT!

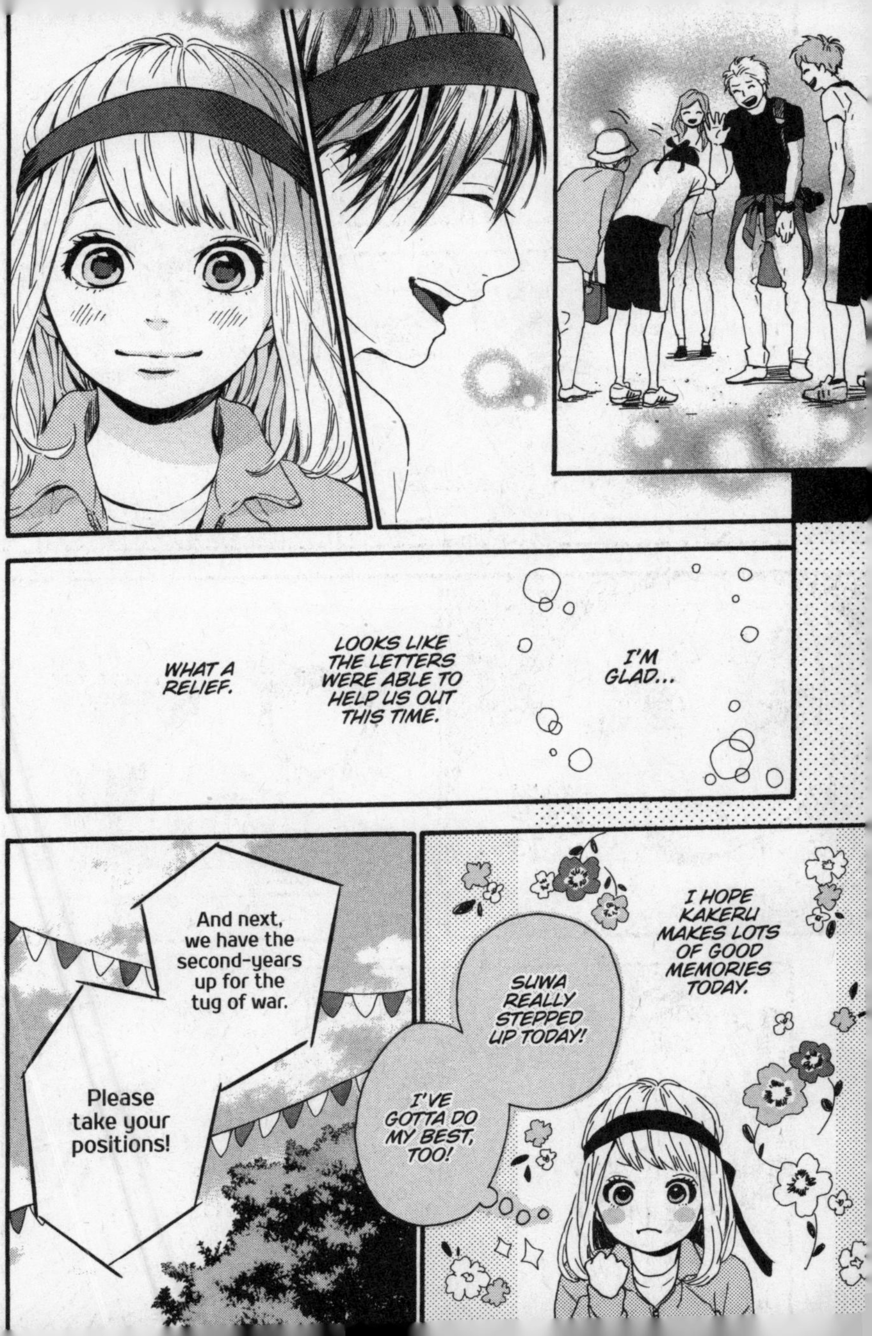
I'M GLAD...
LOOKS LIKE THE LETTERS WERE ABLE TO HELP US OUT THIS TIME.
WHAT A RELIEF.
I HOPE KAKERU MAKES LOTS OF GOOD MEMORIES TODAY.
SUWA REALLY STEPPED UP TODAY!
I'VE GOTTA DO MY BEST, TOO!
And next, we have the second-years up for the tug of war.
Please take your positions!

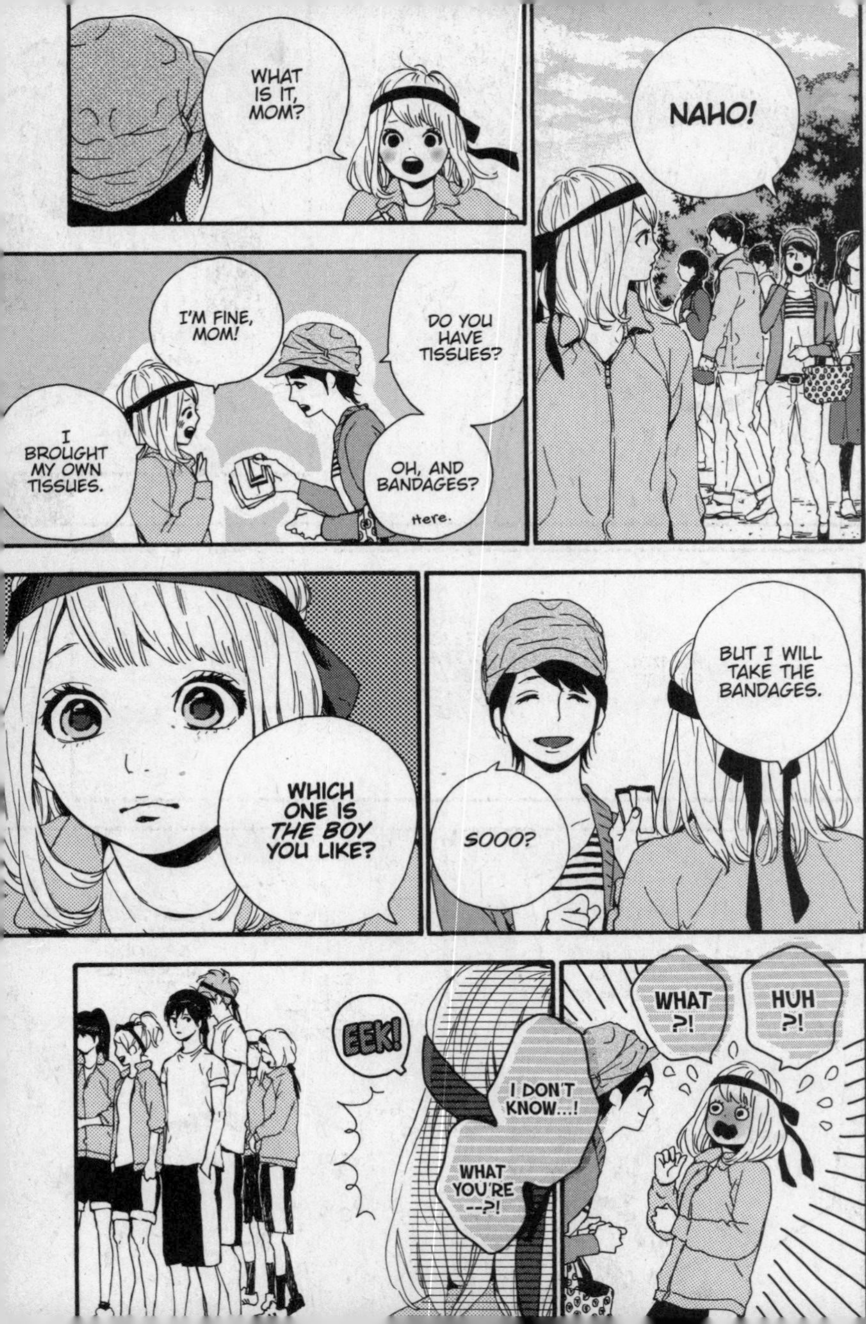
NAHO!
WHAT IS IT, MOM?
DO YOU HAVE TISSUES?
OH, AND BANDAGES?
Here.
I'M FINE, MOM!
I BROUGHT MY OWN TISSUES.
BUT I WILL TAKE THE BANDAGES.
SOOO?
WHICH ONE IS *THE BOY* YOU LIKE?
HUH ?!
WHAT ?!
I DON'T KNOW...!
WHAT YOU'RE --?!
EEK!

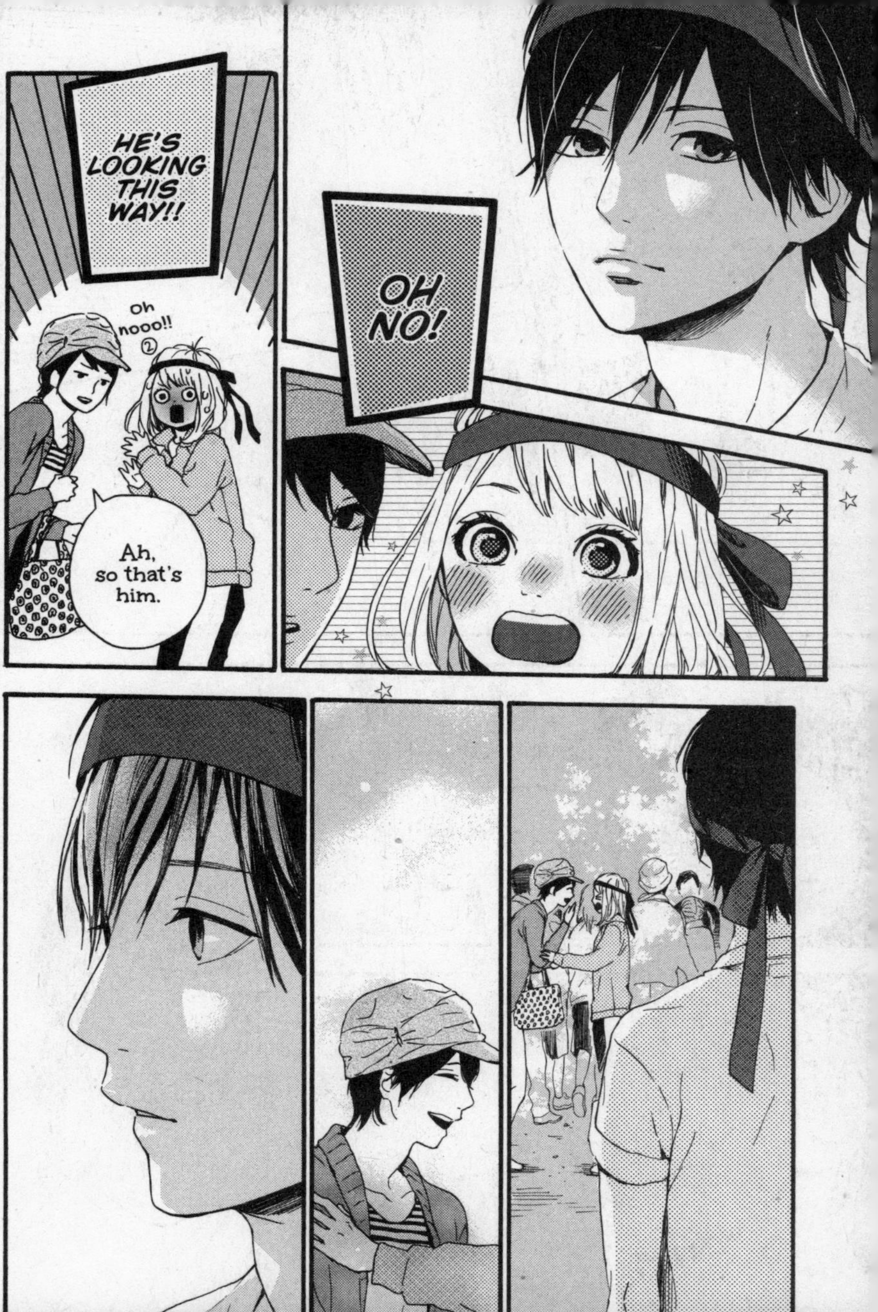
OH NO!
HE'S LOOKING THIS WAY!!
Oh nooo!!
Ah, so that's him.

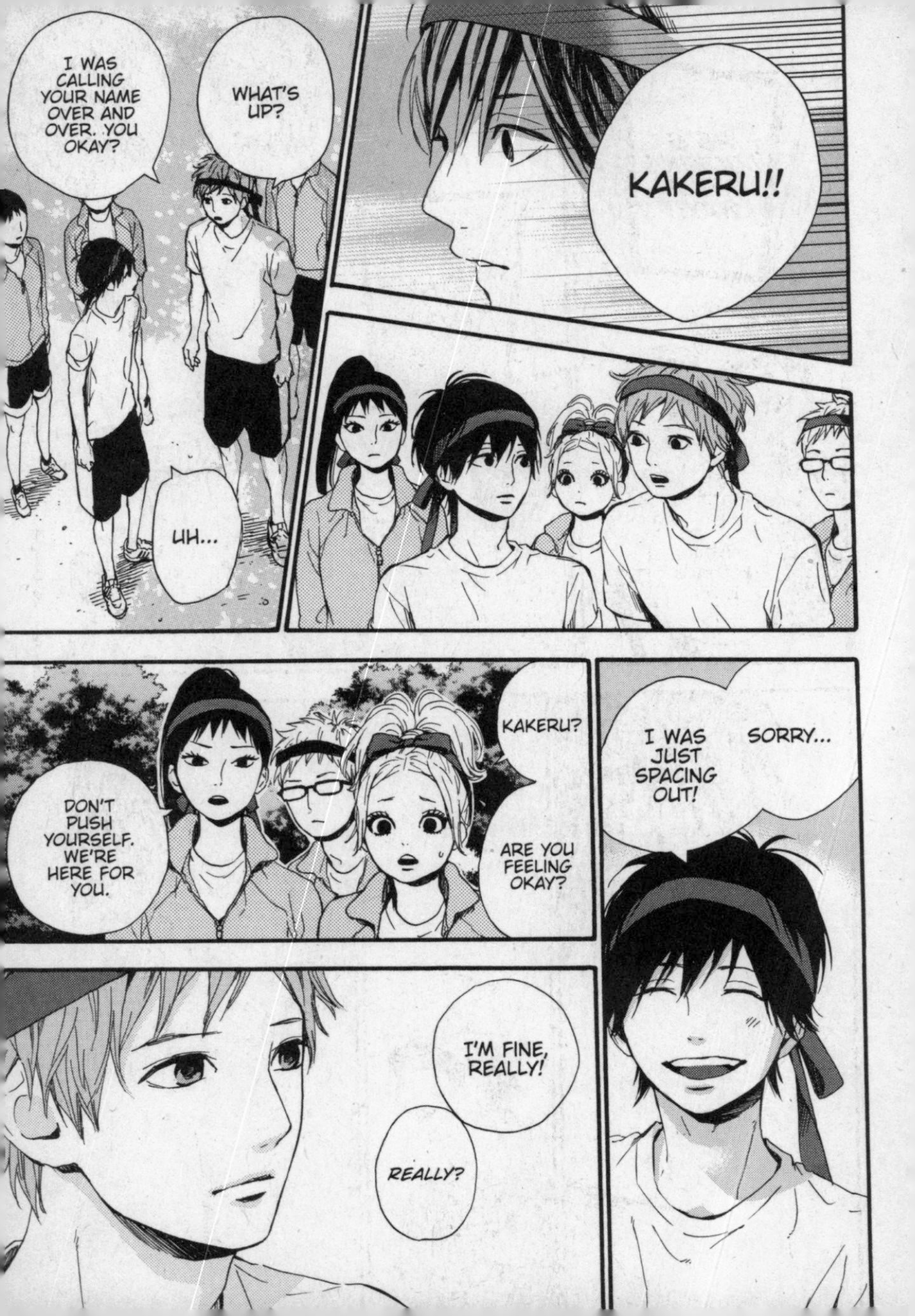
KAKERU!!
WHAT'S UP?
I WAS CALLING YOUR NAME OVER AND OVER. YOU OKAY?
UH...
SORRY...
I WAS JUST SPACING OUT!
KAKERU?
ARE YOU FEELING OKAY?
DON'T PUSH YOURSELF. WE'RE HERE FOR YOU.
I'M FINE, REALLY!
REALLY?

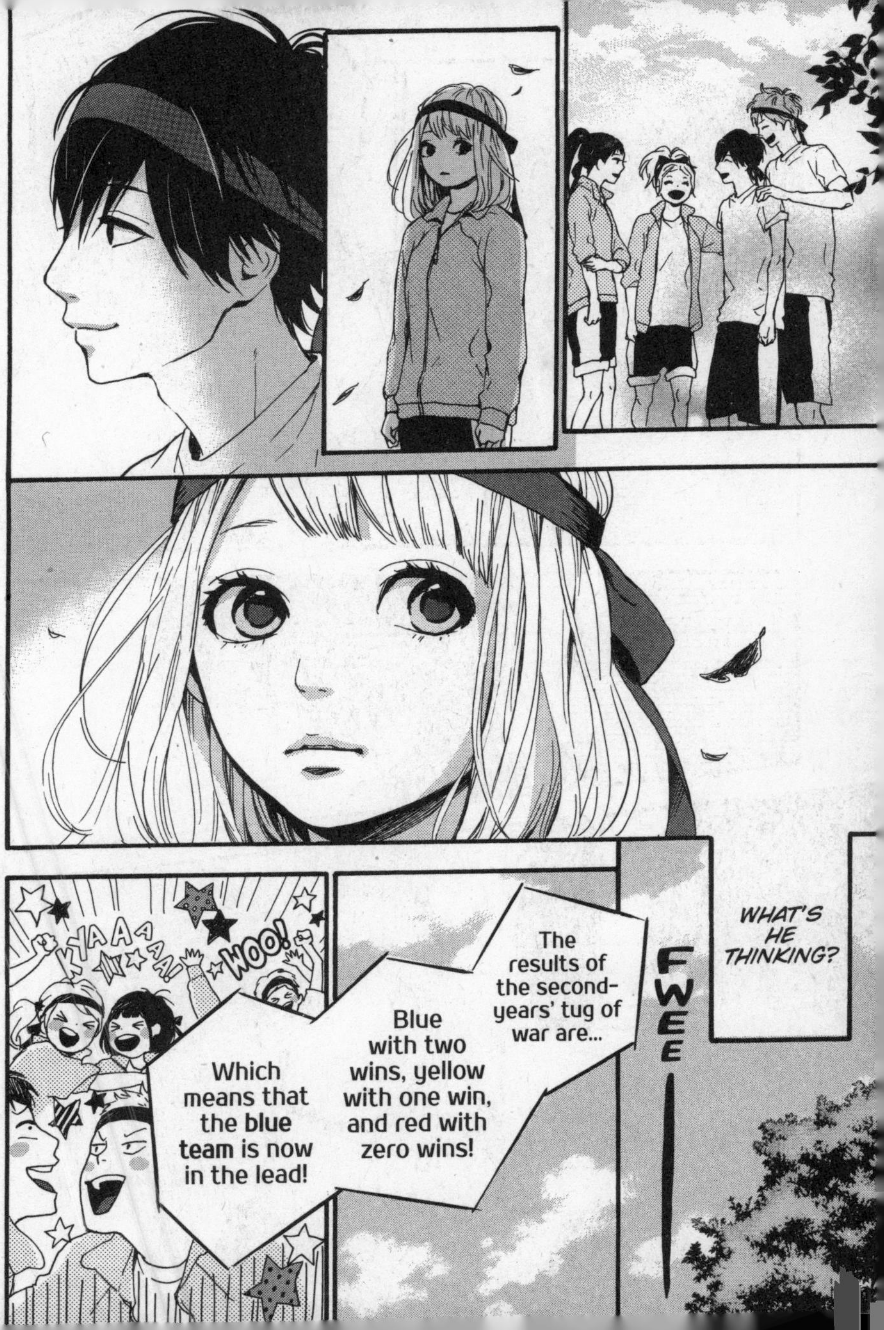
WHAT'S HE THINKING?
FWEE—
The results of the second-years' tug of war are...
Blue with two wins, yellow with one win, and red with zero wins!
Which means that the blue team is now in the lead!
KYAAAAAA!
WOO!

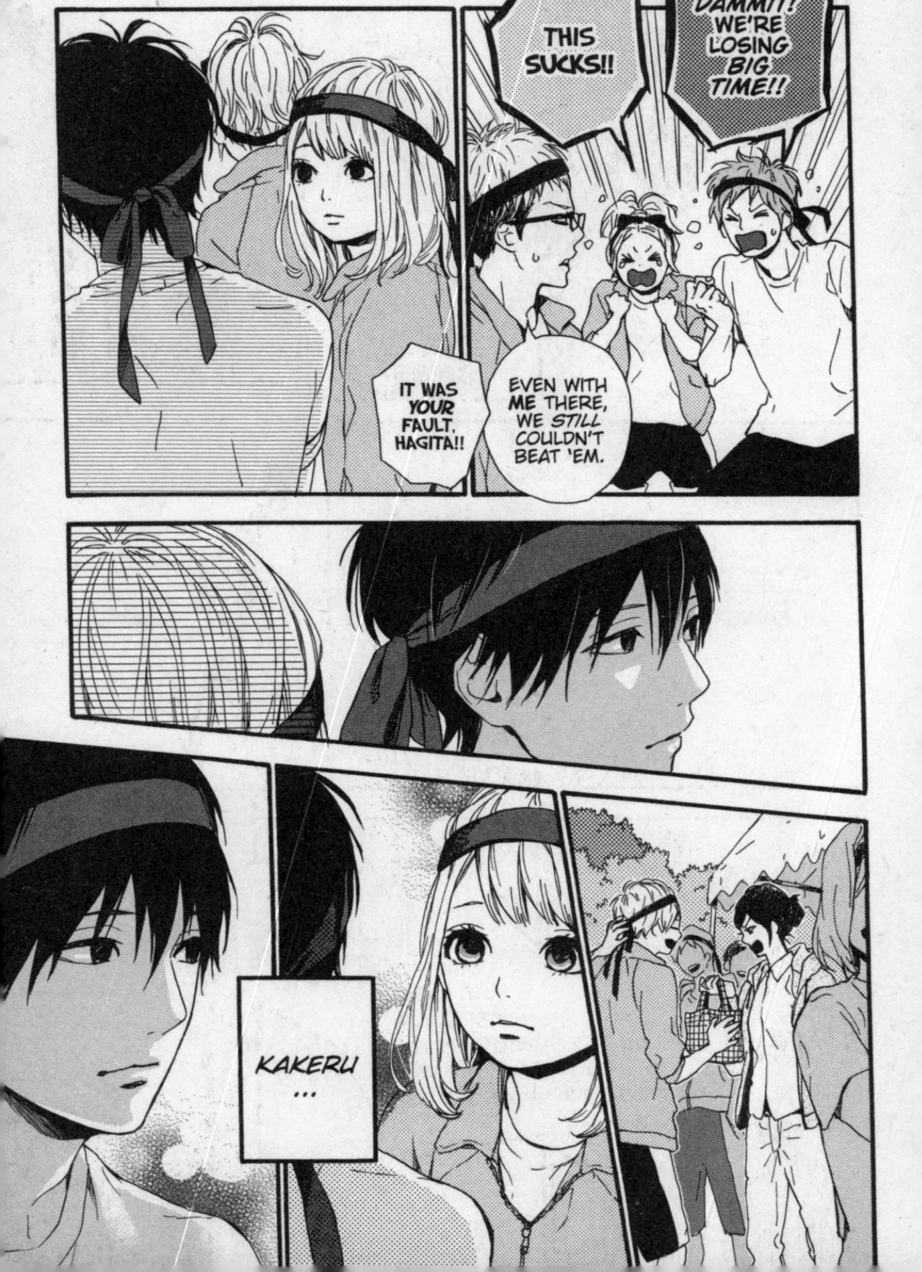
DAMMIT! WE'RE LOSING BIG TIME!!
THIS SUCKS!!
EVEN WITH ME THERE, WE STILL COULDN'T BEAT 'EM.
IT WAS YOUR FAULT, HAGITA!!
KAKERU ...

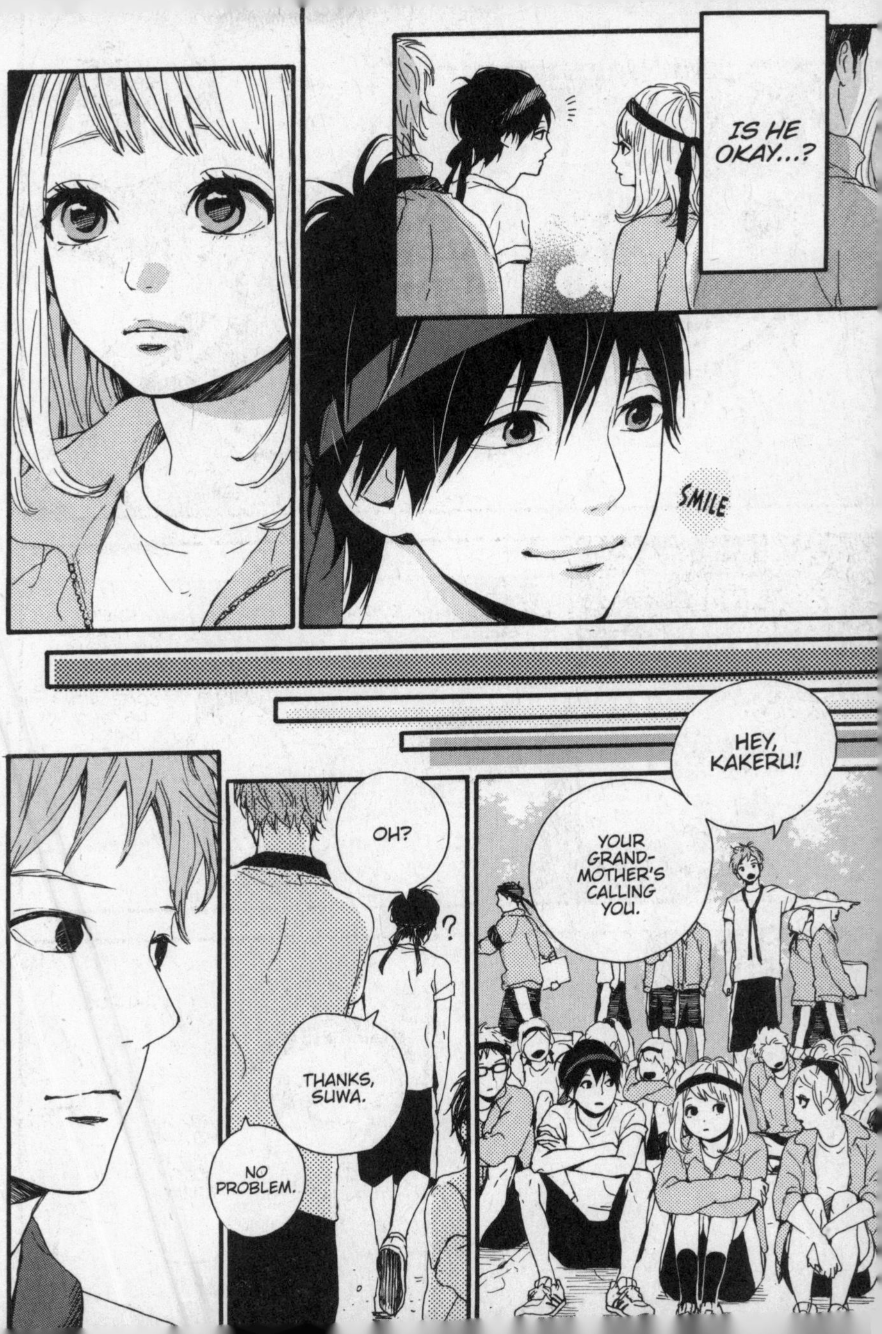
IS HE OKAY...?
SMILE
HEY, KAKERU!
YOUR GRAND-MOTHER'S CALLING YOU.
OH?
?
THANKS, SUWA.
NO PROBLEM.

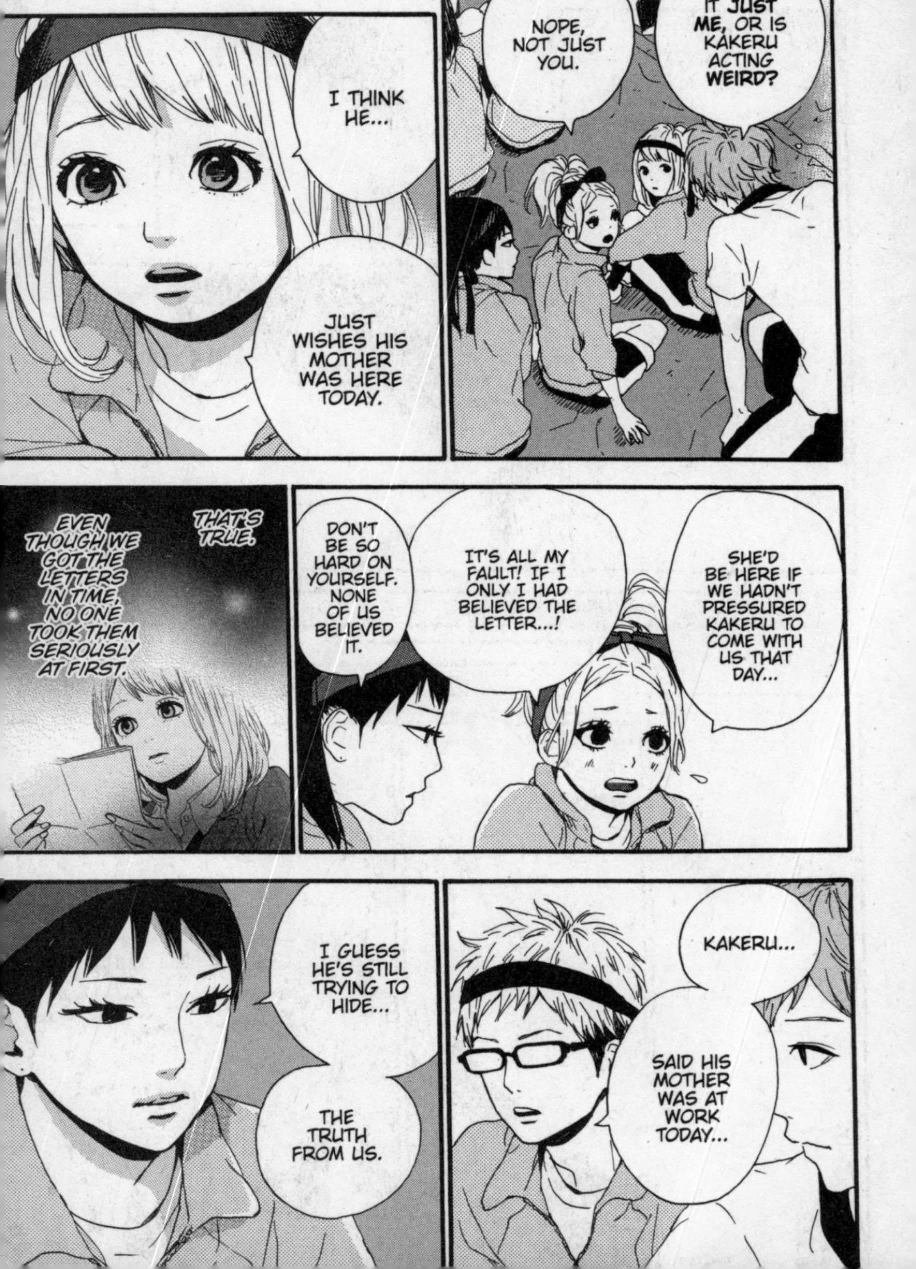
IS IT JUST ME, OR IS KAKERU ACTING WEIRD?
NOPE, NOT JUST YOU.
I THINK HE...
JUST WISHES HIS MOTHER WAS HERE TODAY.
SHE'D BE HERE IF WE HADN'T PRESSURED KAKERU TO COME WITH US THAT DAY...
IT'S ALL MY FAULT! IF I ONLY I HAD BELIEVED THE LETTER...!
DON'T BE SO HARD ON YOURSELF. NONE OF US BELIEVED IT.
THAT'S TRUE.
EVEN THOUGH WE GOT THE LETTERS IN TIME, NO ONE TOOK THEM SERIOUSLY AT FIRST.
KAKERU...
SAID HIS MOTHER WAS AT WORK TODAY...
I GUESS HE'S STILL TRYING TO HIDE...
THE TRUTH FROM US.

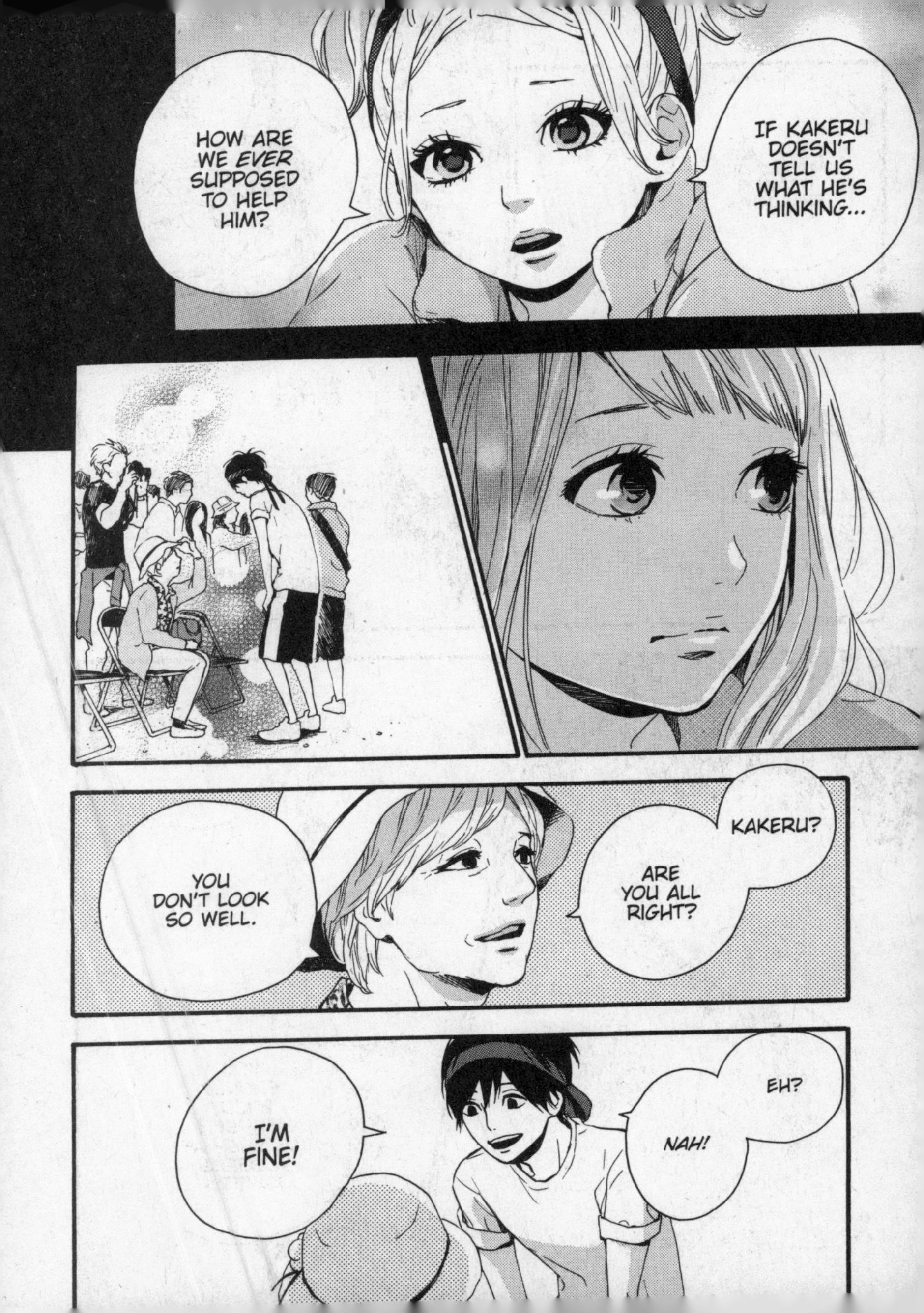
IF KAKERU DOESN'T TELL US WHAT HE'S THINKING...
HOW ARE WE *EVER* SUPPOSED TO HELP HIM?
KAKERU?
ARE YOU ALL RIGHT?
YOU DON'T LOOK SO WELL.
EH?
NAH!
I'M FINE!

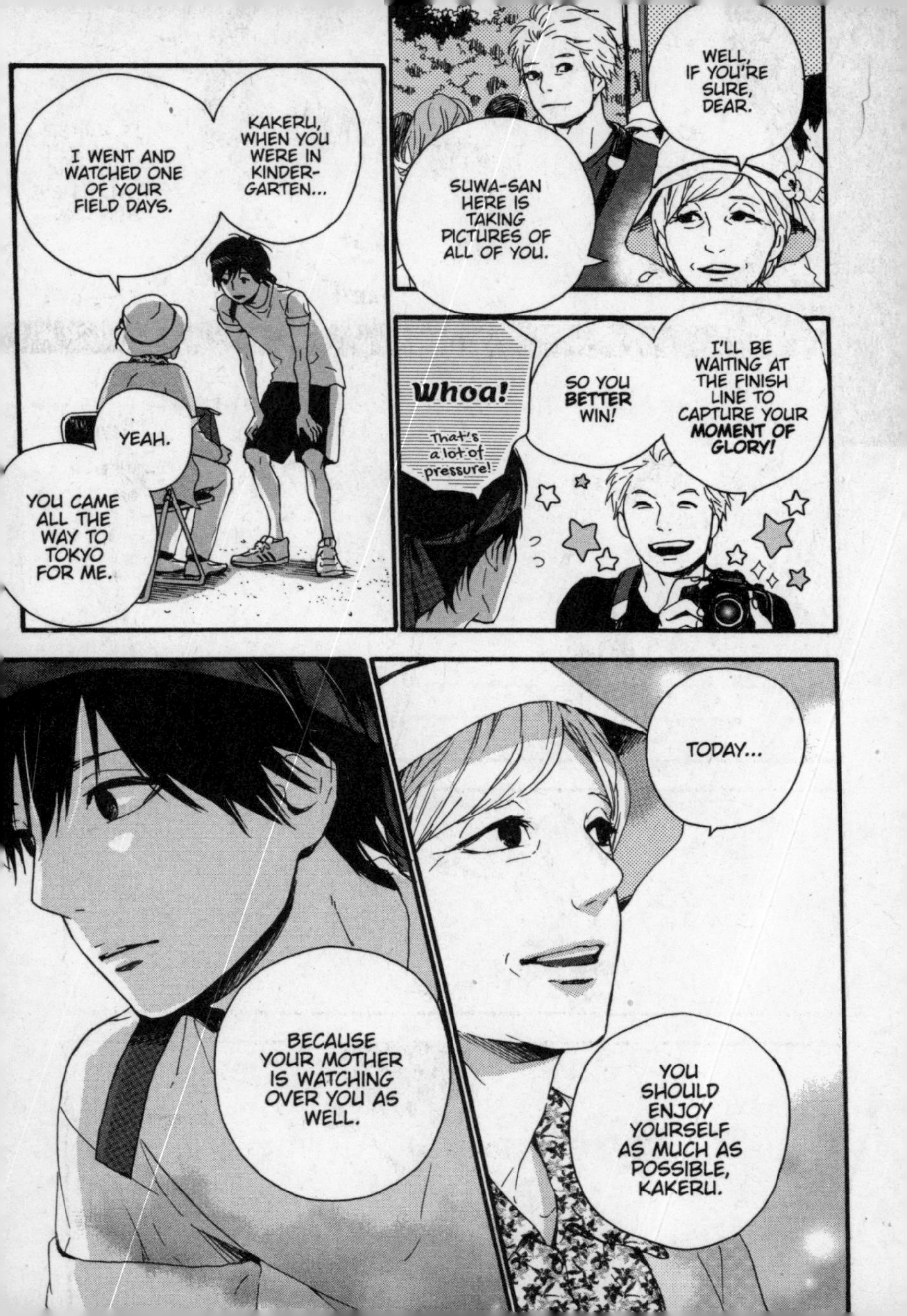
WELL, IF YOU'RE SURE, DEAR.
SUWA-SAN HERE IS TAKING PICTURES OF ALL OF YOU.
I'LL BE WAITING AT THE FINISH LINE TO CAPTURE YOUR MOMENT OF GLORY!
SO YOU BETTER WIN!
Whoa!
That's a lot of pressure!
KAKERU, WHEN YOU WERE IN KINDERGARTEN...
I WENT AND WATCHED ONE OF YOUR FIELD DAYS.
YEAH.
YOU CAME ALL THE WAY TO TOKYO FOR ME.
TODAY...
YOU SHOULD ENJOY YOURSELF AS MUCH AS POSSIBLE, KAKERU.
BECAUSE YOUR MOTHER IS WATCHING OVER YOU AS WELL.

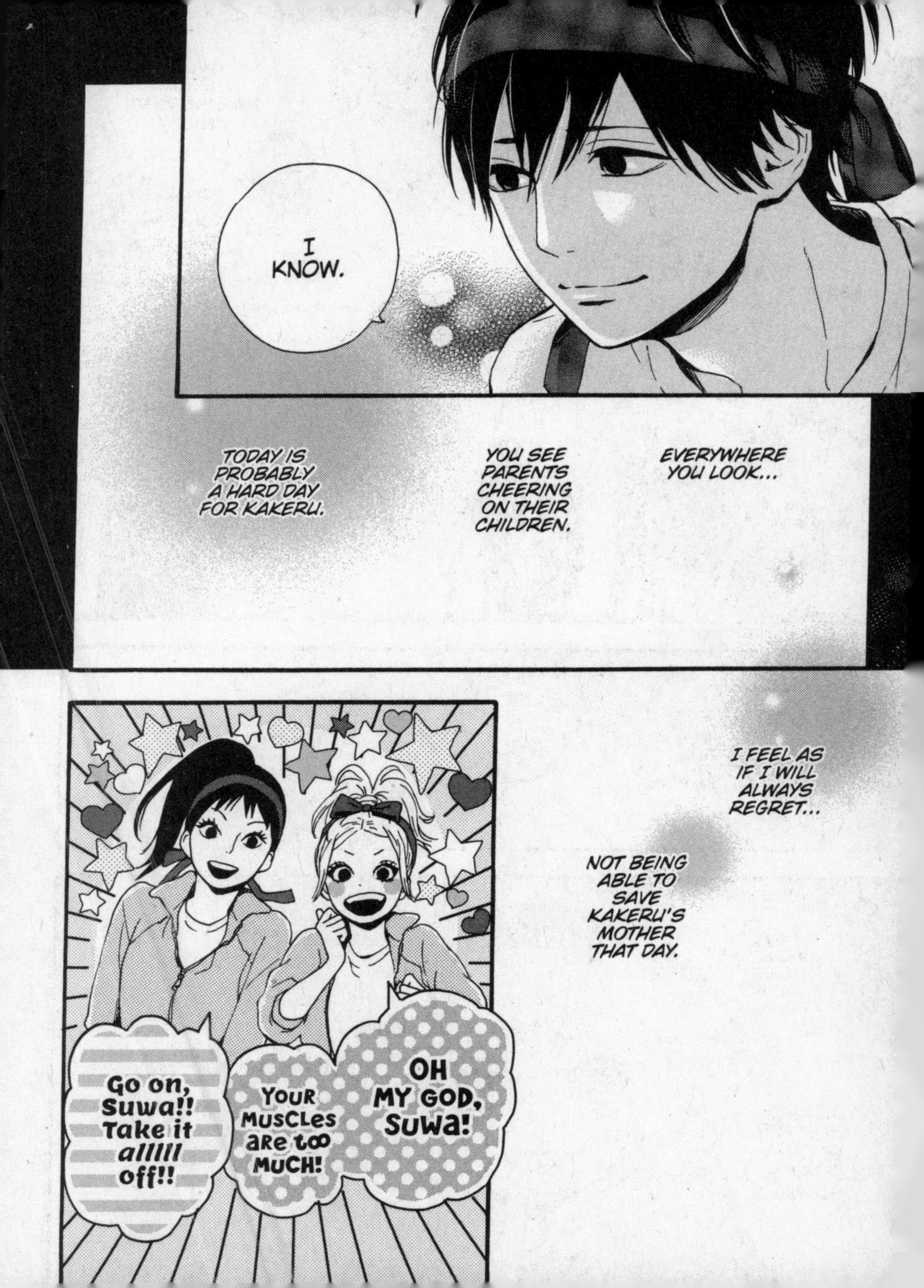
I KNOW.
EVERYWHERE YOU LOOK...
YOU SEE PARENTS CHEERING ON THEIR CHILDREN.
TODAY IS PROBABLY A HARD DAY FOR KAKERU.
I FEEL AS IF I WILL ALWAYS REGRET...
NOT BEING ABLE TO SAVE KAKERU'S MOTHER THAT DAY.
OH MY GOD, SUWA!
YOUR MUSCLES are too MUCH!
Go on, Suwa!! Take it allllll off!!

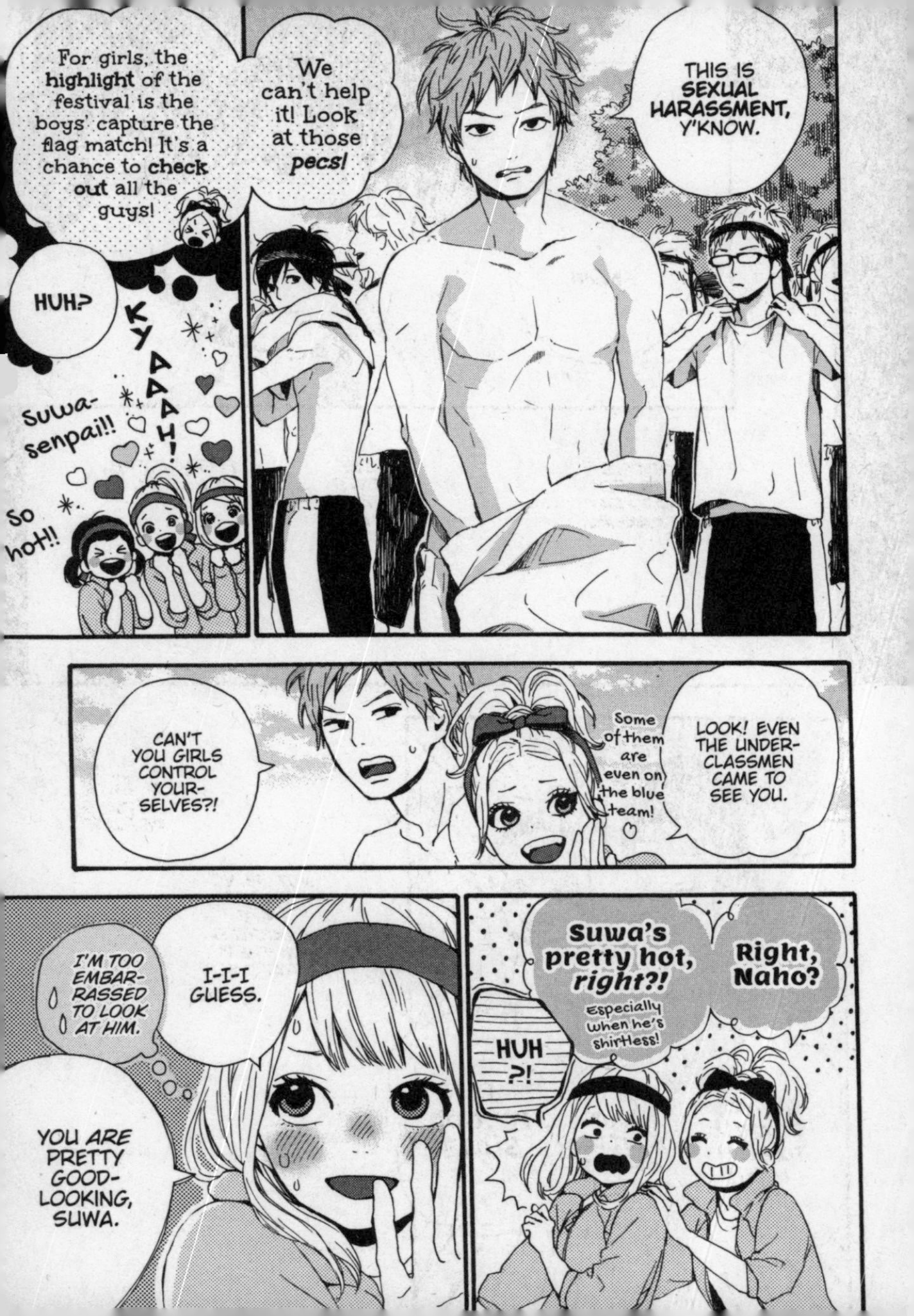
THIS IS SEXUAL HARASSMENT, Y'KNOW.
We can't help it! Look at those *pecs!*
For girls, the **highlight** of the festival is the boys' capture the flag match! It's a chance to **check out** all the guys!
HUH?
KYAAAH!
Suwa-senpai!!
So hot!!
LOOK! EVEN THE UNDER-CLASSMEN CAME TO SEE YOU.
Some of them are even on the blue team!
CAN'T YOU GIRLS CONTROL YOUR-SELVES?!
Right, Naho?
Suwa's pretty hot, *right?!*
Especially when he's shirtless!
HUH ?!
I-I-I GUESS.
I'M TOO EMBAR-RASSED TO LOOK AT HIM.
YOU ARE PRETTY GOOD-LOOKING, SUWA.

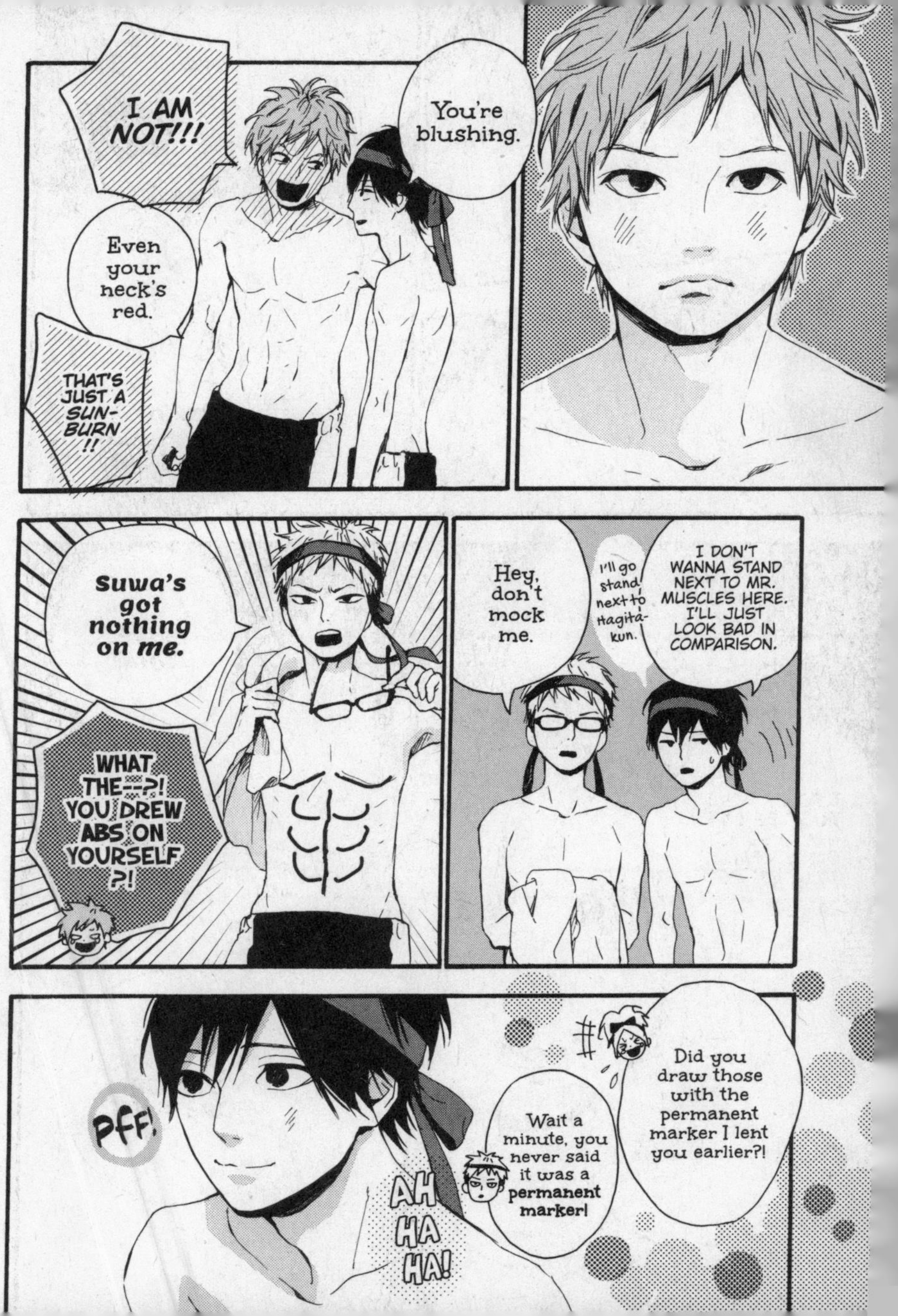
You're blushing.
I AM NOT!!!
Even your neck's red.
THAT'S JUST A SUNBURN!!
I DON'T WANNA STAND NEXT TO MR. MUSCLES HERE. I'LL JUST LOOK BAD IN COMPARISON.
I'll go stand next to Hagita-kun.
Hey, don't mock me.
Suwa's got nothing on me.
WHAT THE--?! YOU DREW ABS ON YOURSELF?!
Did you draw those with the permanent marker I lent you earlier?!
Wait a minute, you never said it was a permanent marker!
AH HA HA!
PFF!

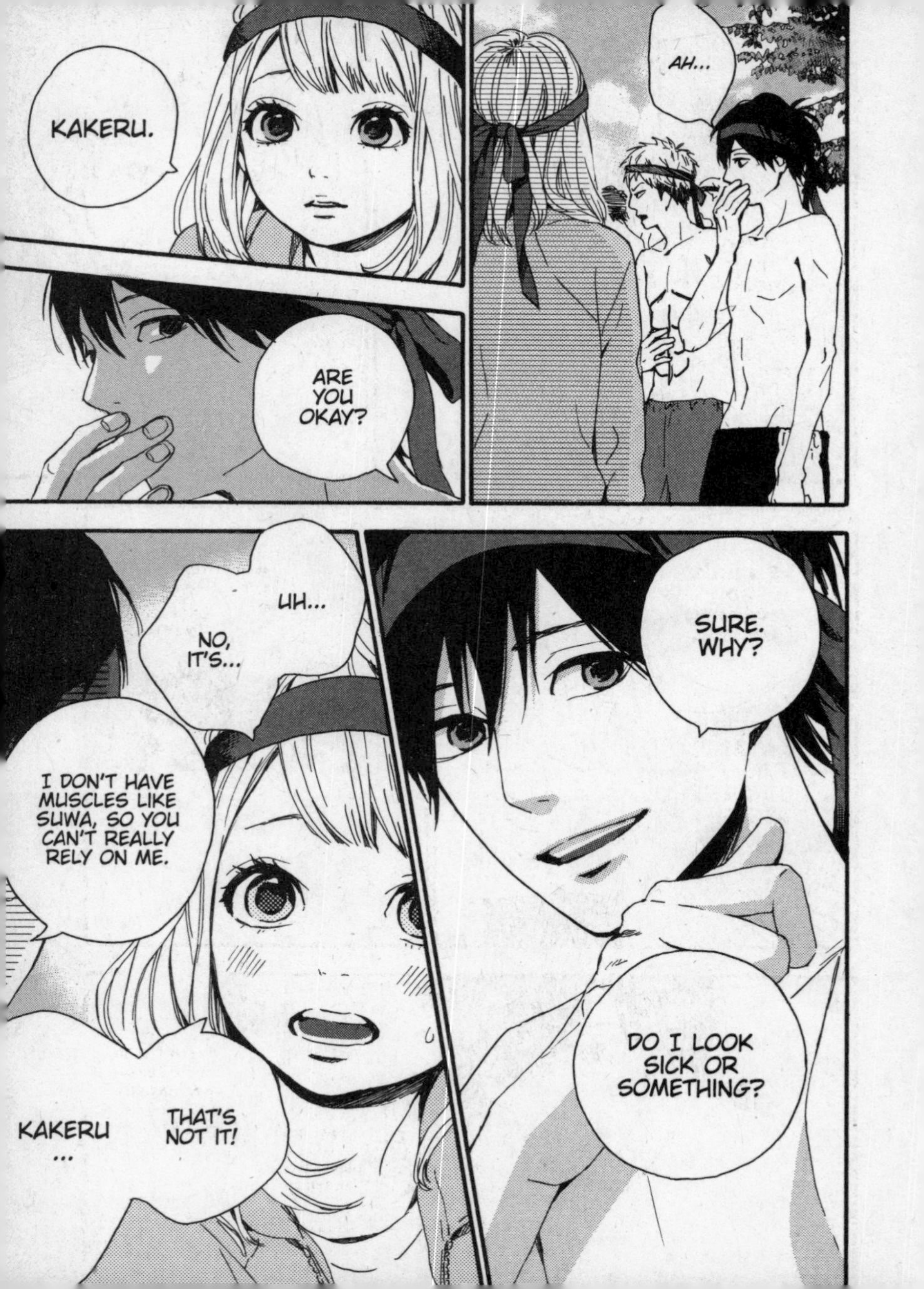
AH...
KAKERU.
ARE YOU OKAY?
SURE. WHY?
DO I LOOK SICK OR SOMETHING?
UH...
NO, IT'S...
I DON'T HAVE MUSCLES LIKE SUWA, SO YOU CAN'T REALLY RELY ON ME.
THAT'S NOT IT!
KAKERU ...

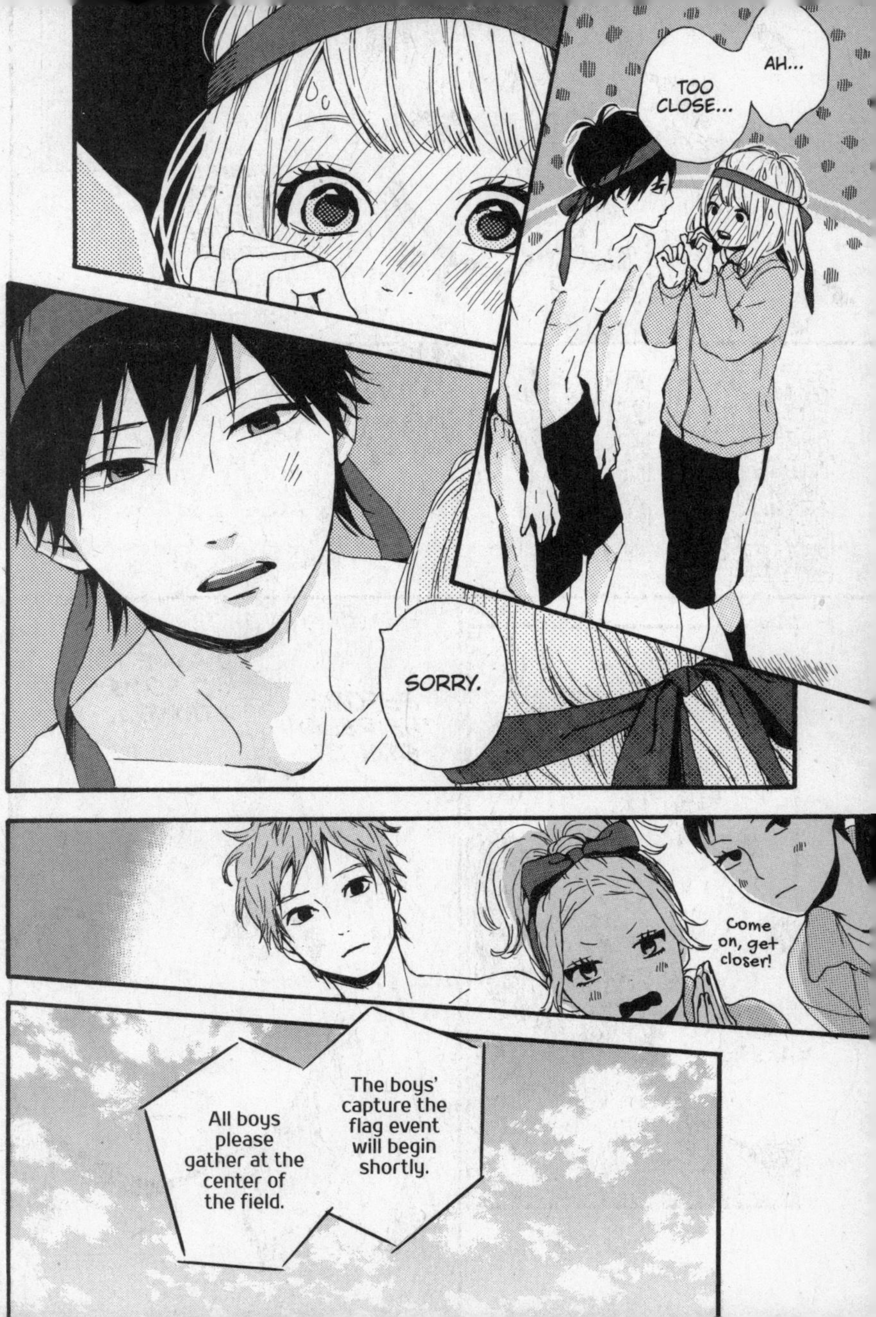
AH...
TOO CLOSE...
SORRY.
Come on, get closer!
The boys' capture the flag event will begin shortly.
All boys please gather at the center of the field.

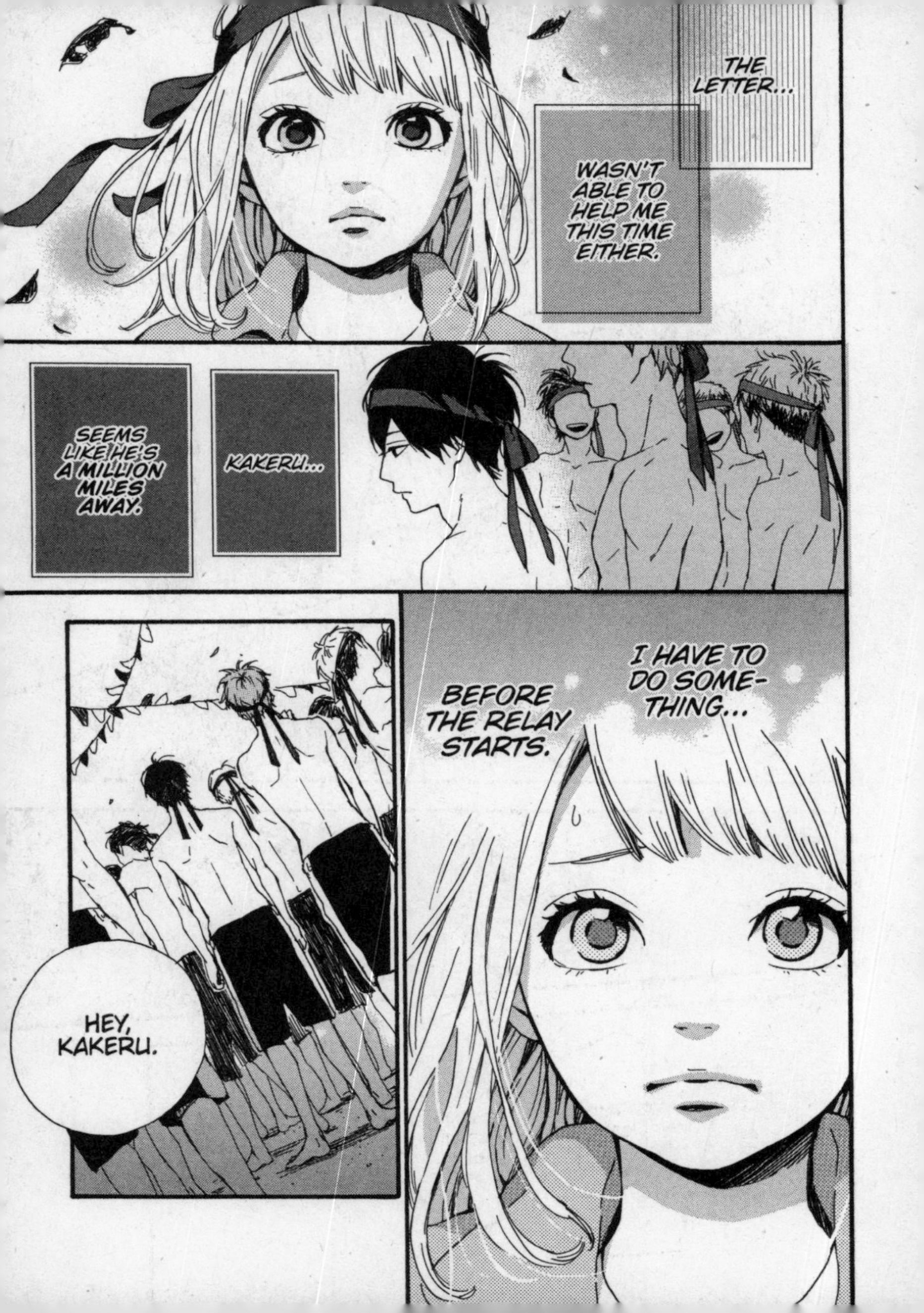
THE LETTER...
WASN'T ABLE TO HELP ME THIS TIME EITHER.
KAKERU...
SEEMS LIKE HE'S A MILLION MILES AWAY.
I HAVE TO DO SOME-THING...
BEFORE THE RELAY STARTS.
HEY, KAKERU.

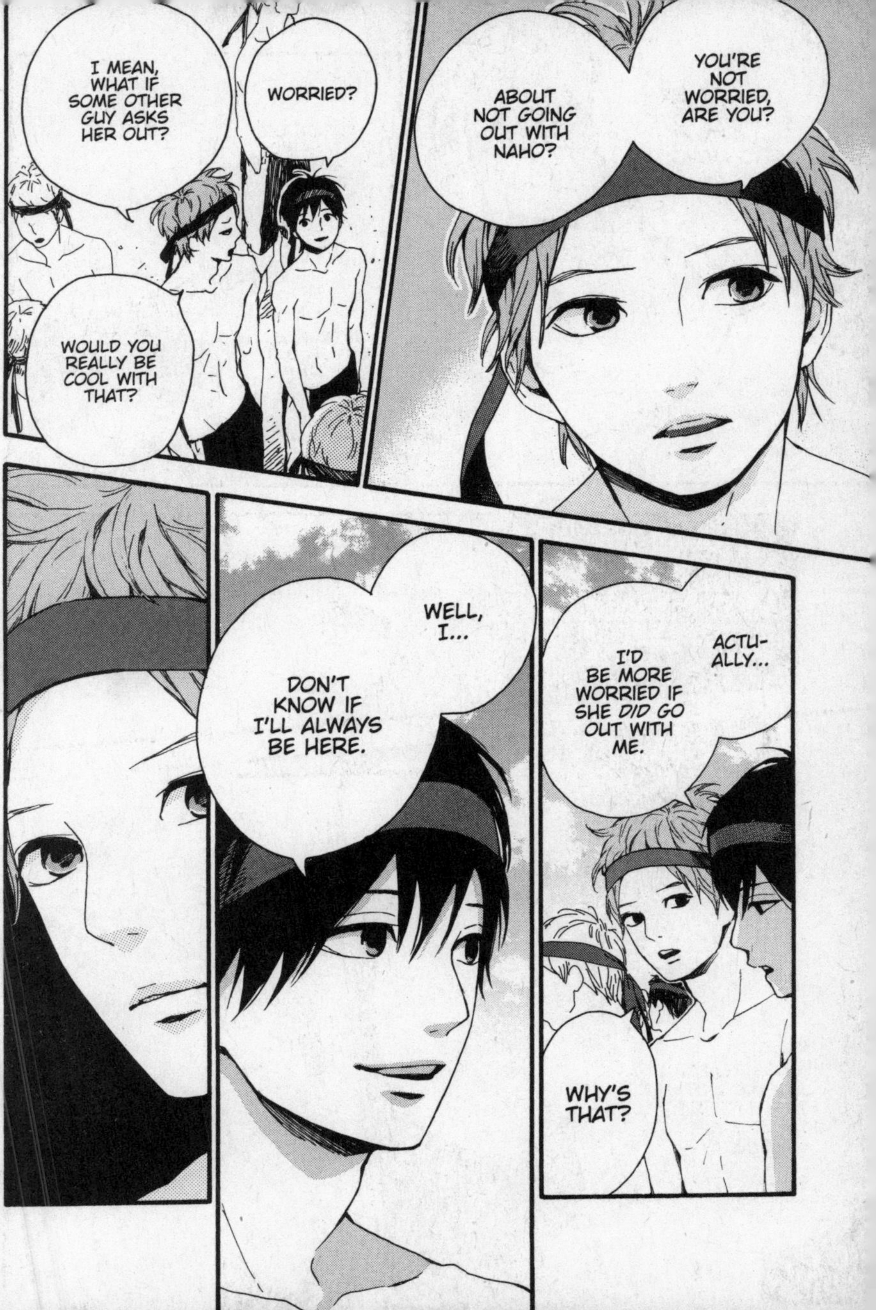
YOU'RE NOT WORRIED, ARE YOU?
ABOUT NOT GOING OUT WITH NAHO?
WORRIED?
I MEAN, WHAT IF SOME OTHER GUY ASKS HER OUT?
WOULD YOU REALLY BE COOL WITH THAT?
ACTU-ALLY...
I'D BE MORE WORRIED IF SHE *DID* GO OUT WITH ME.
WHY'S THAT?
WELL, I...
DON'T KNOW IF I'LL ALWAYS BE HERE.

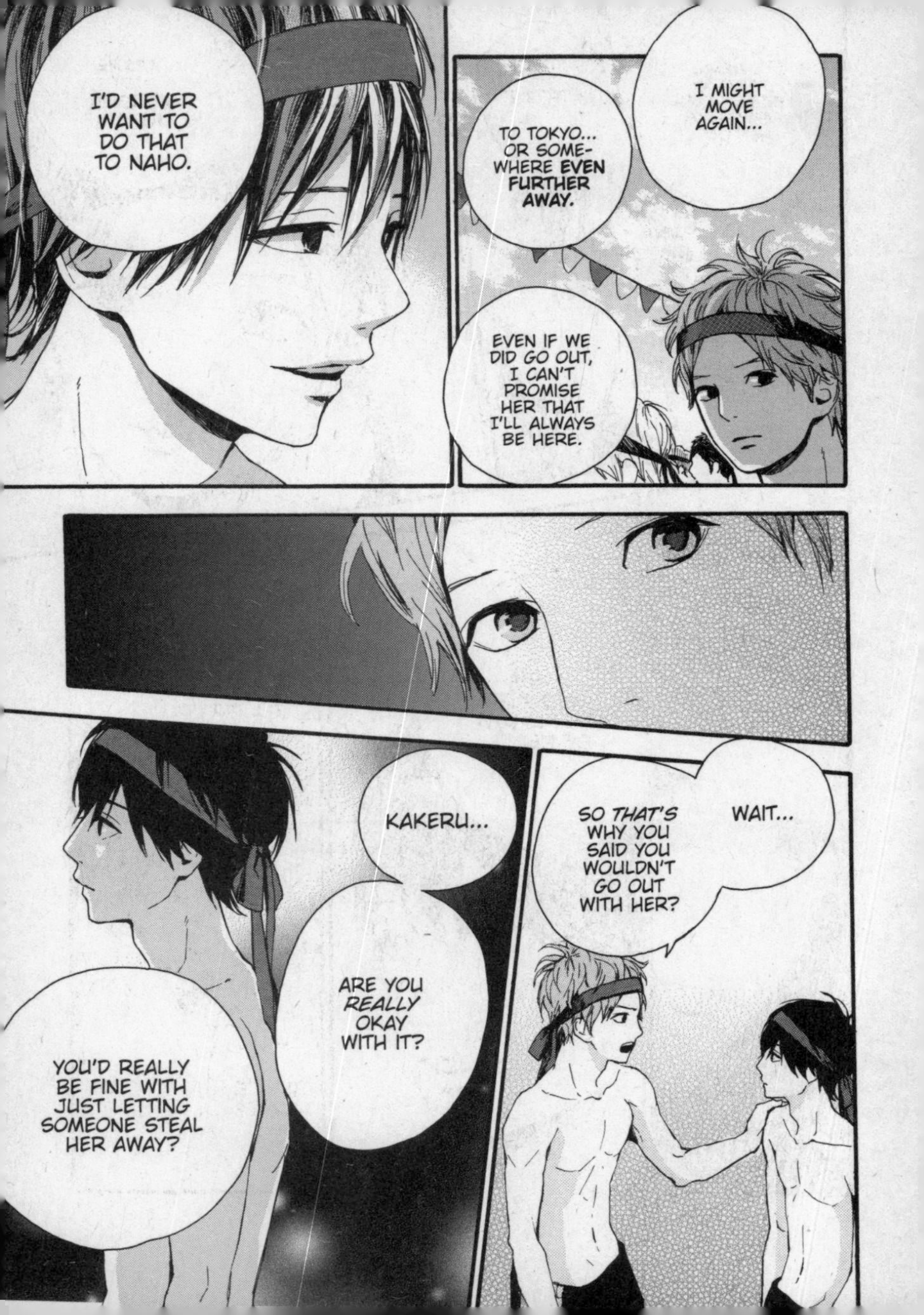
I MIGHT MOVE AGAIN...
TO TOKYO... OR SOME-WHERE **EVEN FURTHER AWAY.**
EVEN IF WE DID GO OUT, I CAN'T PROMISE HER THAT I'LL ALWAYS BE HERE.
I'D NEVER WANT TO DO THAT TO NAHO.
WAIT...
SO *THAT'S* WHY YOU SAID YOU WOULDN'T GO OUT WITH HER?
KAKERU...
ARE YOU *REALLY* OKAY WITH IT?
YOU'D REALLY BE FINE WITH JUST LETTING SOMEONE STEAL HER AWAY?

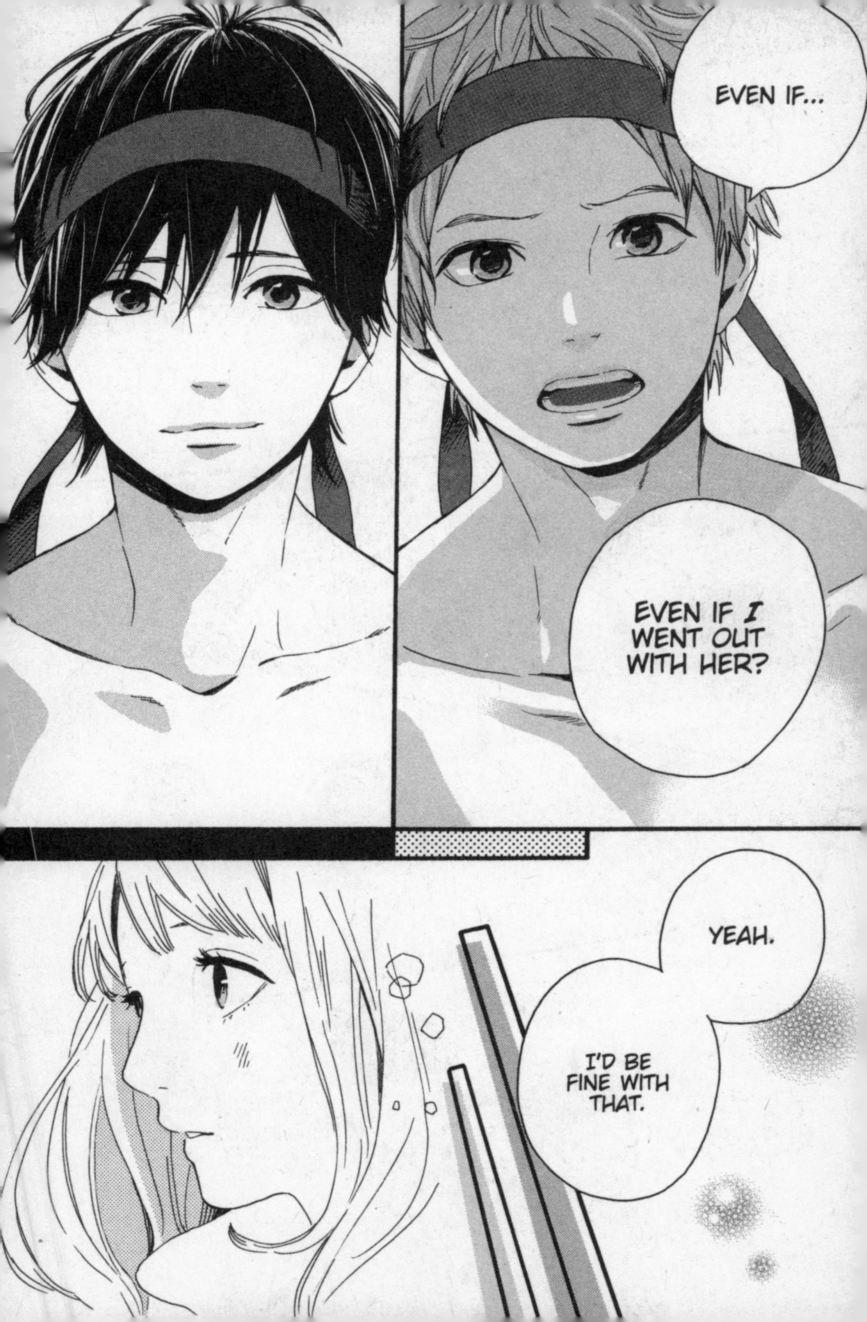
EVEN IF...
EVEN IF *I* WENT OUT WITH HER?
YEAH.
I'D BE FINE WITH THAT.

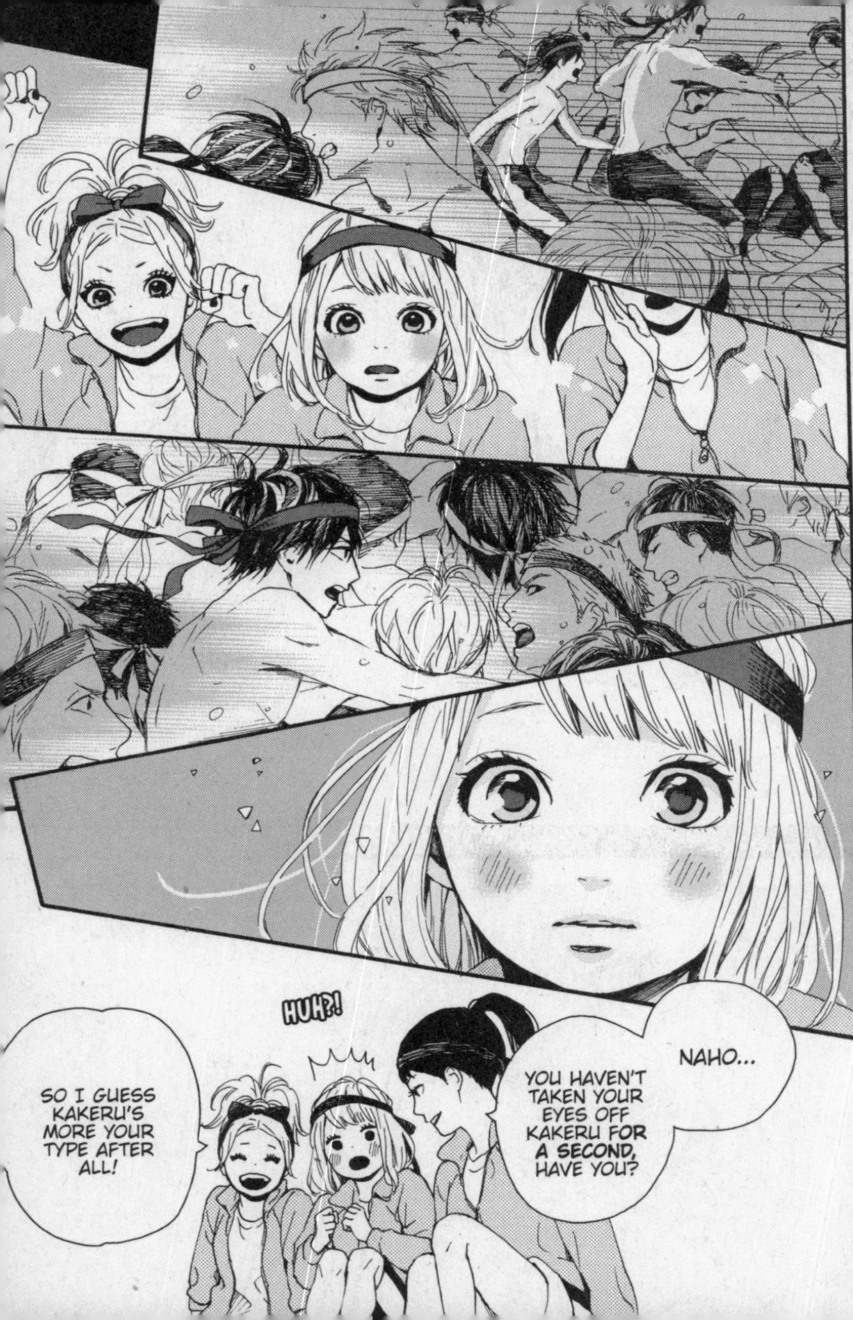
NAHO...
YOU HAVEN'T TAKEN YOUR EYES OFF KAKERU FOR A SECOND, HAVE YOU?
HUH?!
SO I GUESS KAKERU'S MORE YOUR TYPE AFTER ALL!

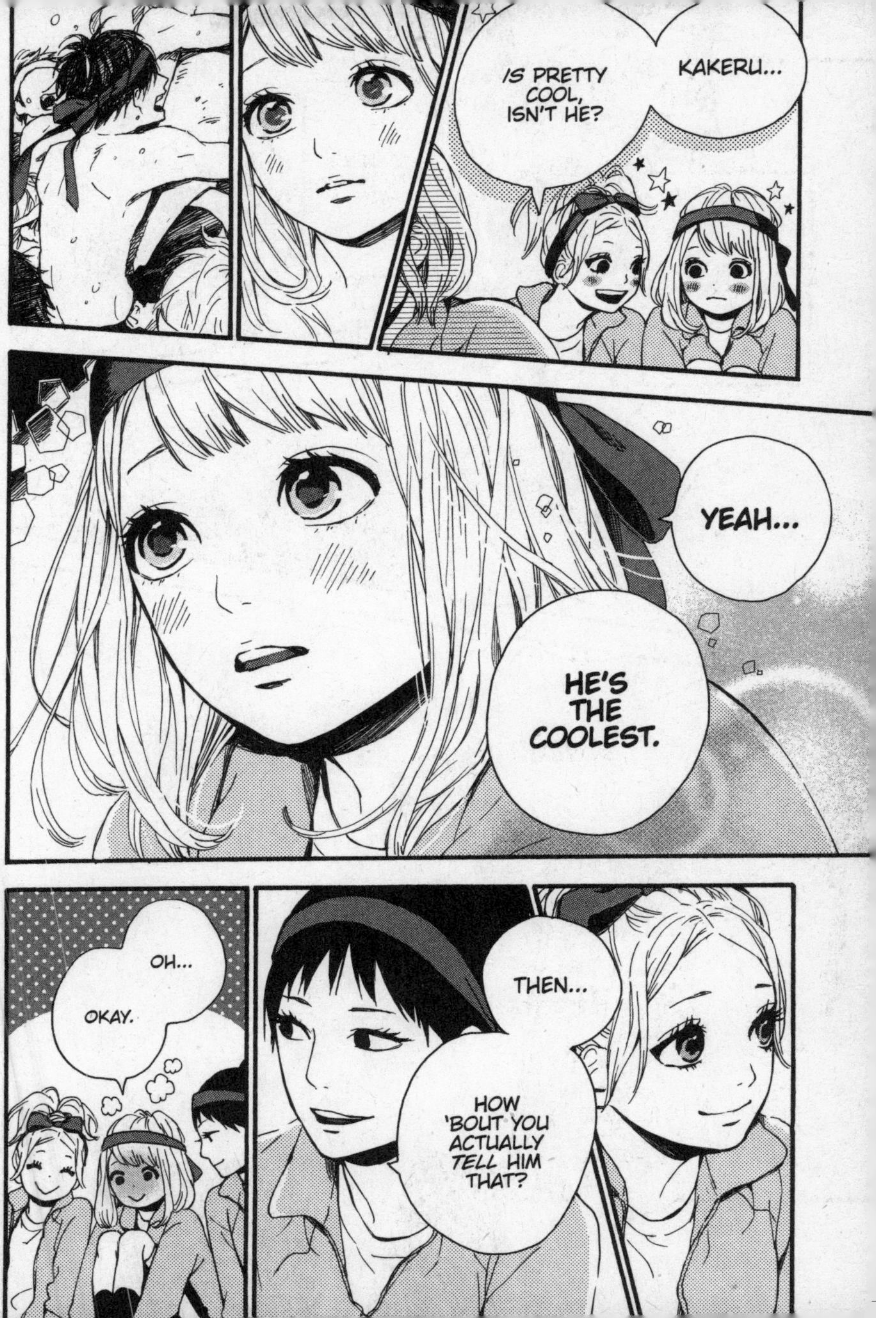
KAKERU... IS PRETTY COOL, ISN'T HE?
YEAH...
HE'S THE COOLEST.
THEN...
HOW 'BOUT YOU ACTUALLY *TELL* HIM THAT?
OH... OKAY.

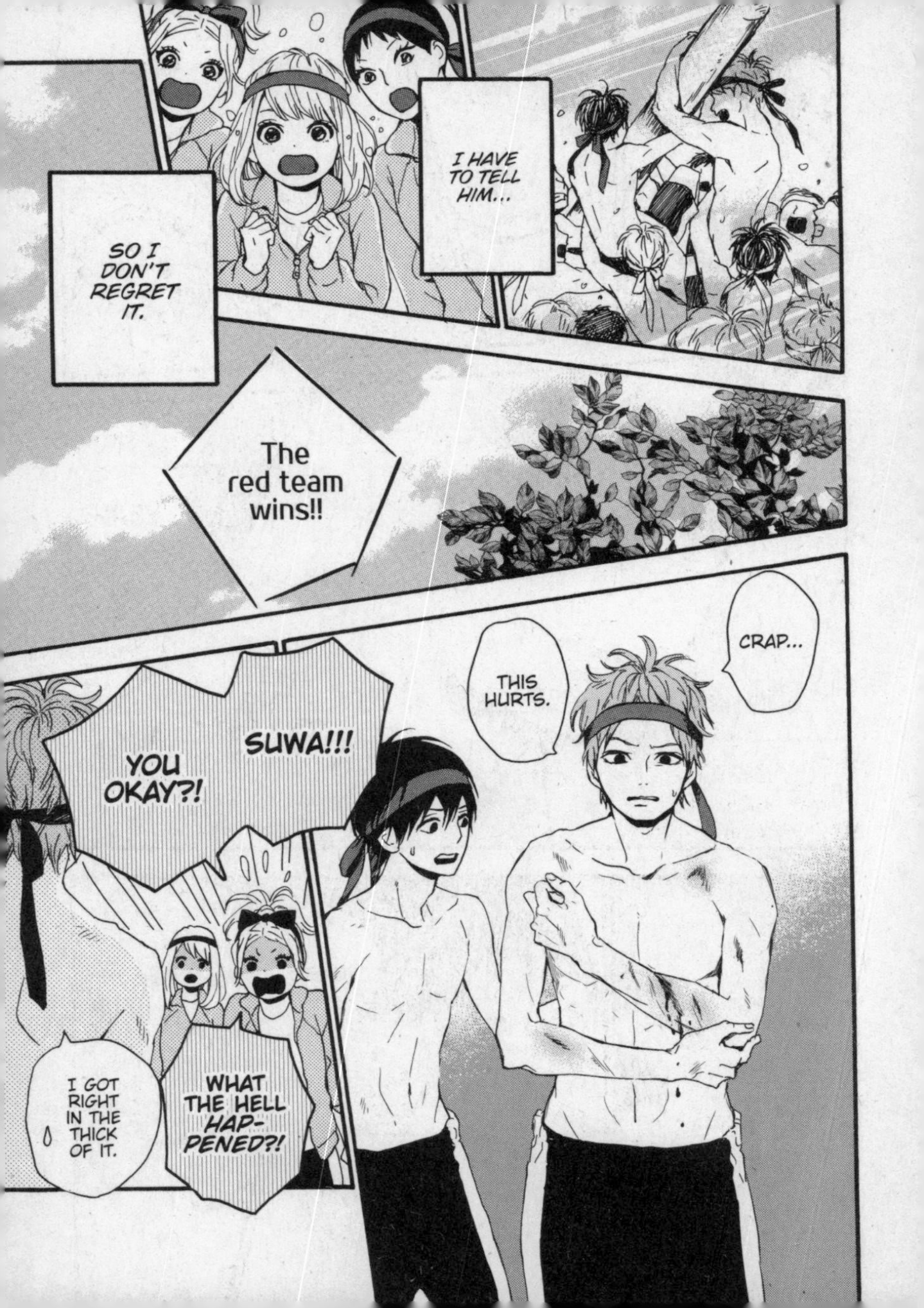
I HAVE TO TELL HIM...
SO I DON'T REGRET IT.
The red team wins!!
CRAP...
THIS HURTS.
SUWA!!!
YOU OKAY?!
WHAT THE HELL HAP-PENED?!
I GOT RIGHT IN THE THICK OF IT.

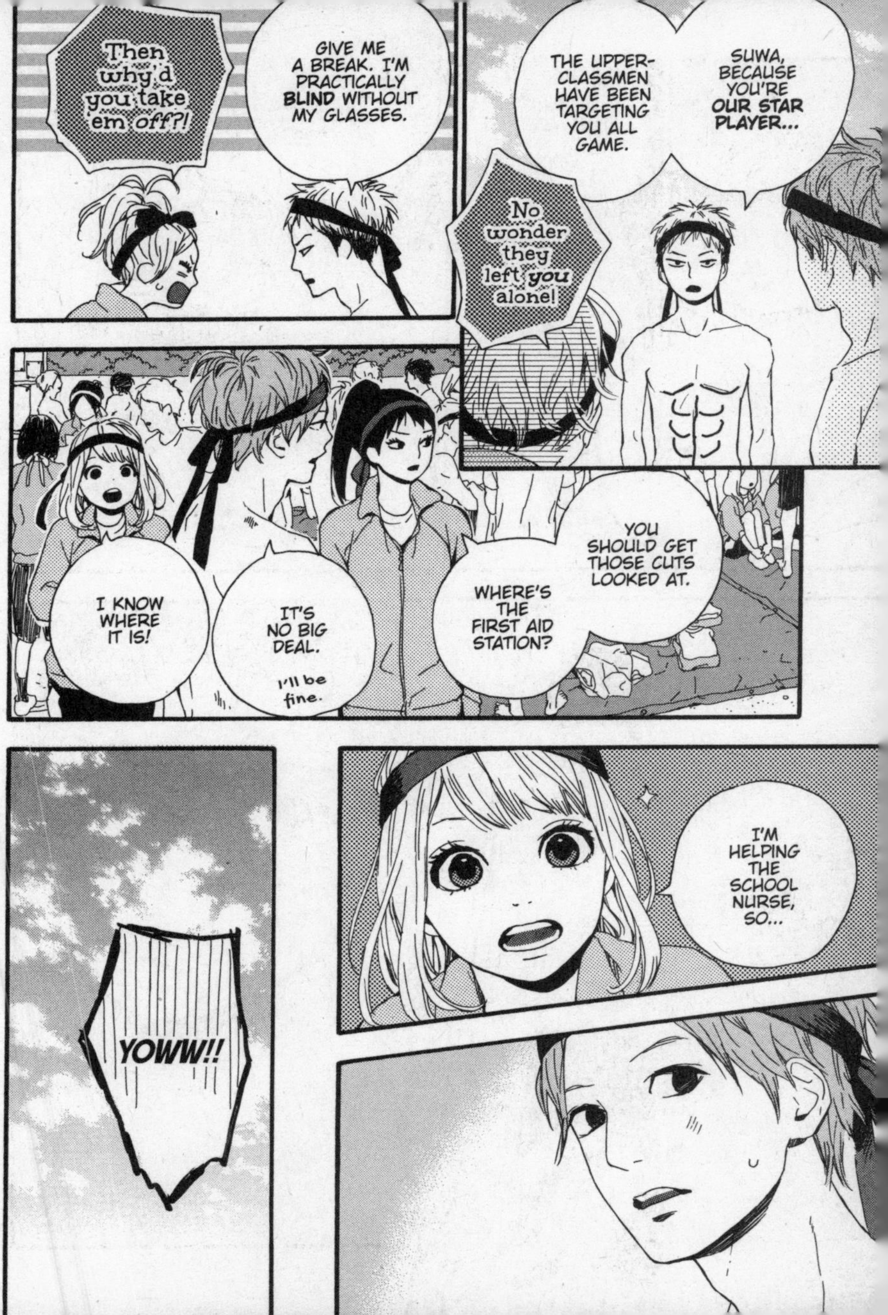
SUWA, BECAUSE YOU'RE OUR STAR PLAYER...
THE UPPER-CLASSMEN HAVE BEEN TARGETING YOU ALL GAME.
No wonder they left you alone!
GIVE ME A BREAK. I'M PRACTICALLY BLIND WITHOUT MY GLASSES.
Then why'd you take em off?!
YOU SHOULD GET THOSE CUTS LOOKED AT.
WHERE'S THE FIRST AID STATION?
IT'S NO BIG DEAL.
I'll be fine.
I KNOW WHERE IT IS!
I'M HELPING THE SCHOOL NURSE, SO...
YOWW!!

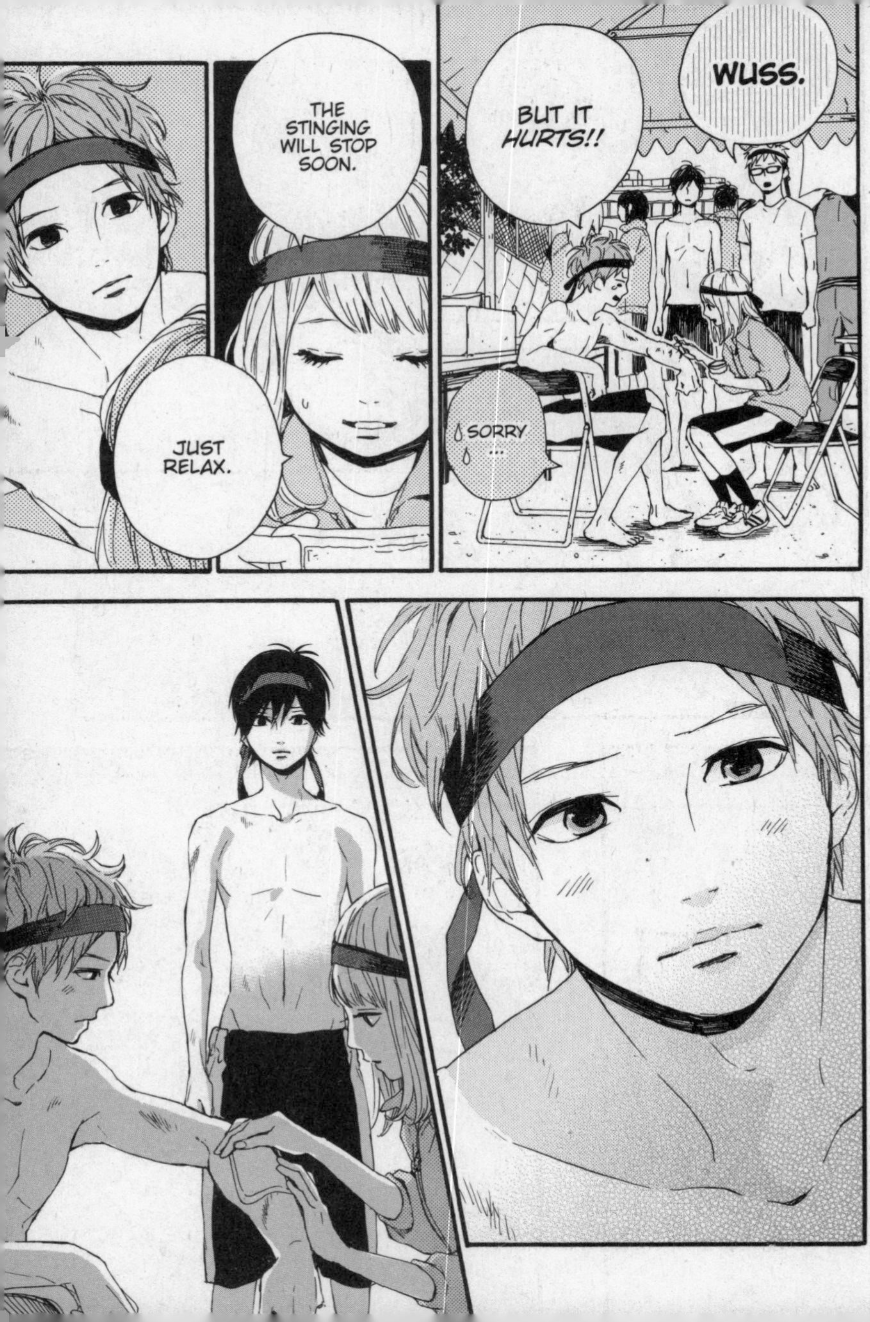
WUSS.
BUT IT HURTS!!
SORRY ...
THE STINGING WILL STOP SOON.
JUST RELAX.

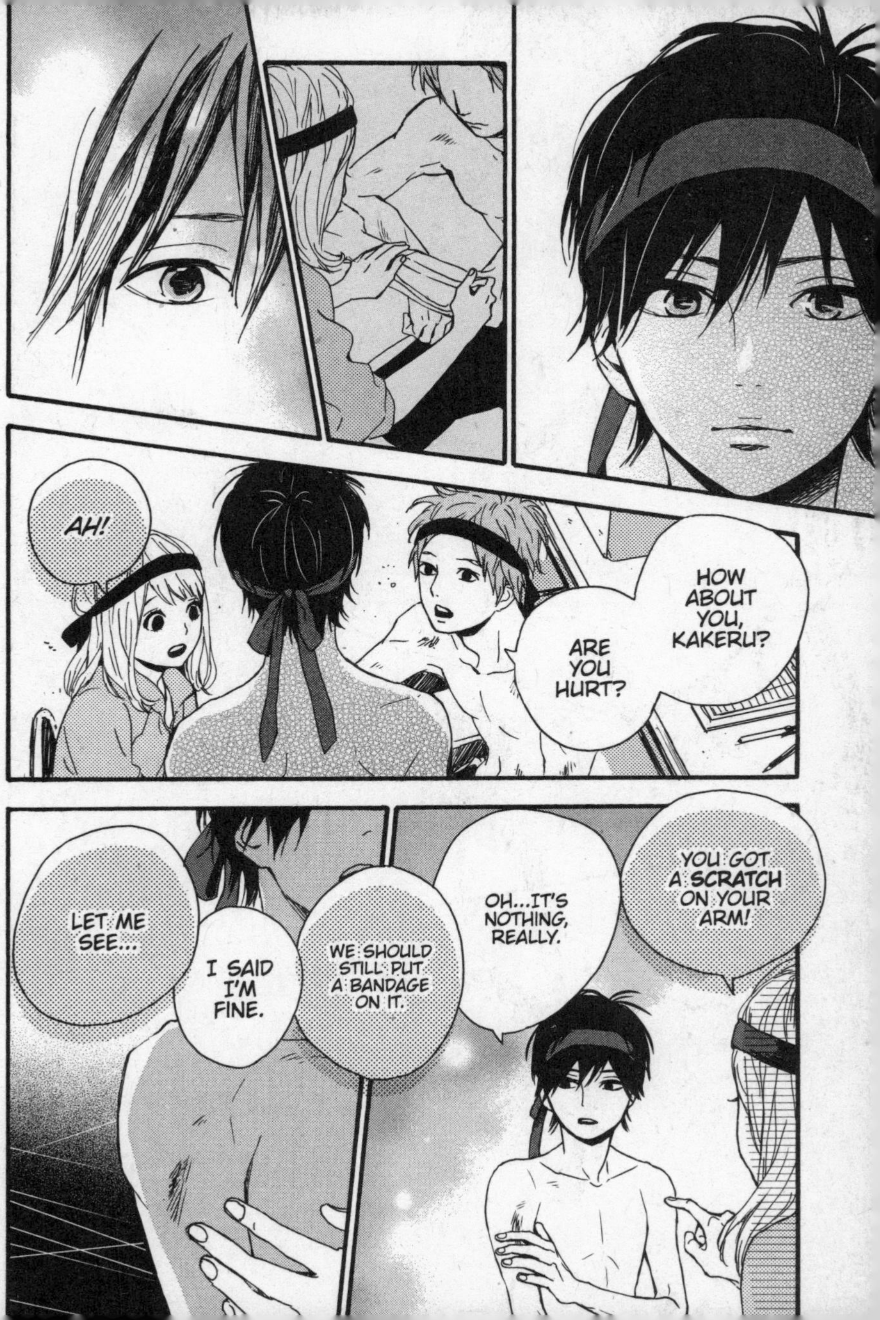
HOW ABOUT YOU, KAKERU?
ARE YOU HURT?
AH!
YOU GOT A SCRATCH ON YOUR ARM!
OH...IT'S NOTHING, REALLY.
WE SHOULD STILL PUT A BANDAGE ON IT.
I SAID I'M FINE.
LET ME SEE...

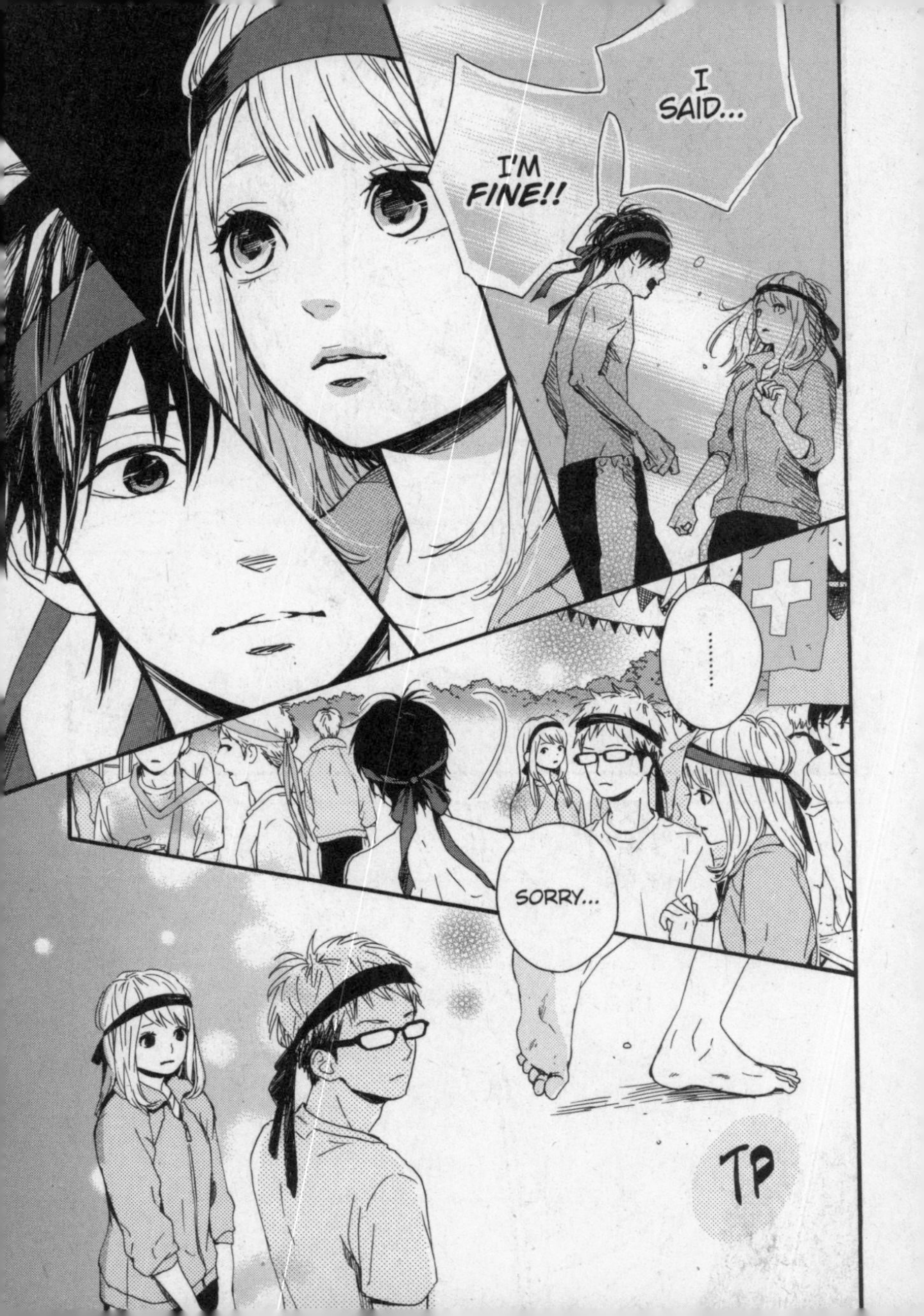
I SAID...
I'M FINE!!
......
SORRY...
TP

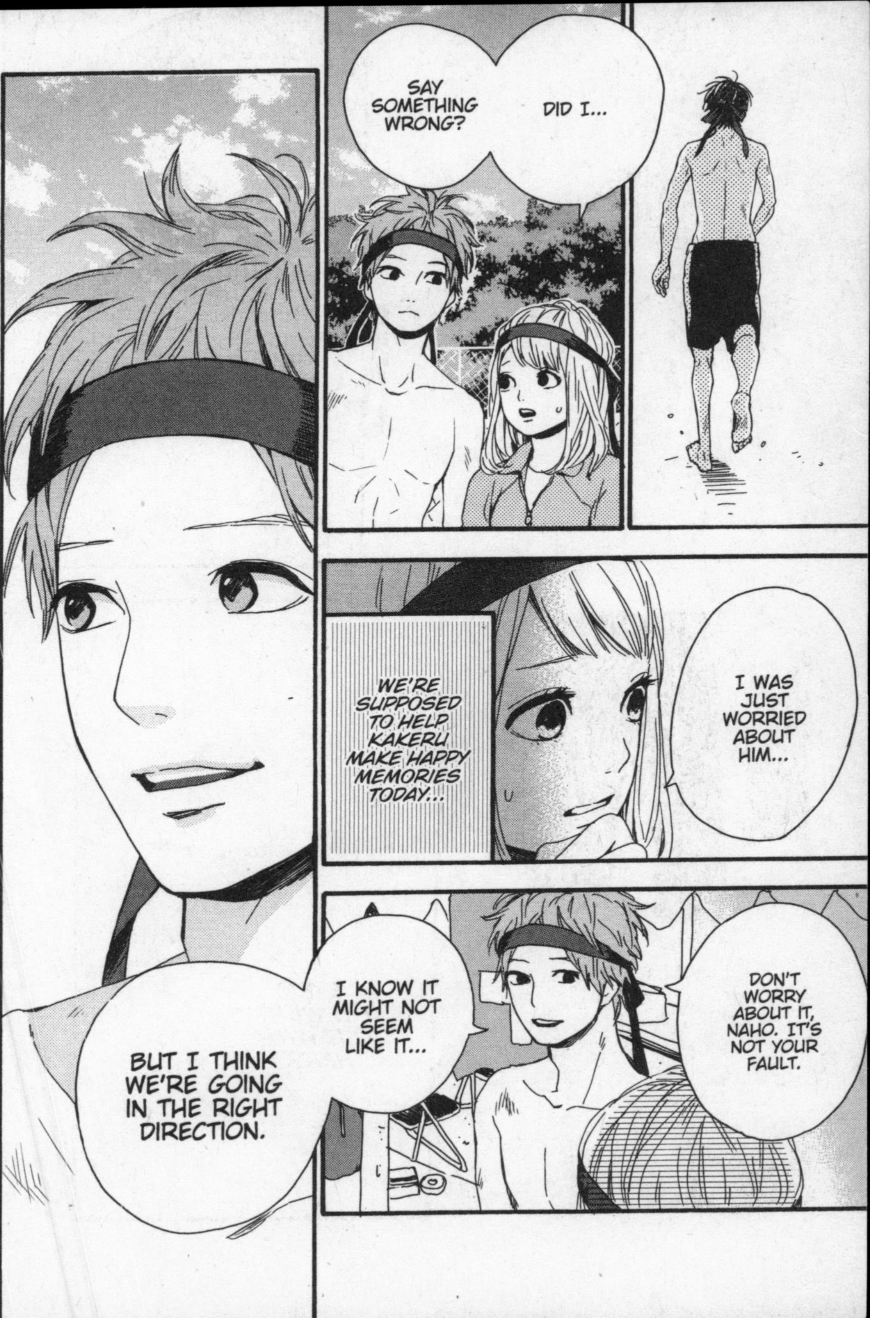
DID I...
SAY SOMETHING WRONG?
I WAS JUST WORRIED ABOUT HIM...
WE'RE SUPPOSED TO HELP KAKERU MAKE HAPPY MEMORIES TODAY...
DON'T WORRY ABOUT IT, NAHO. IT'S NOT YOUR FAULT.
I KNOW IT MIGHT NOT SEEM LIKE IT...
BUT I THINK WE'RE GOING IN THE RIGHT DIRECTION.

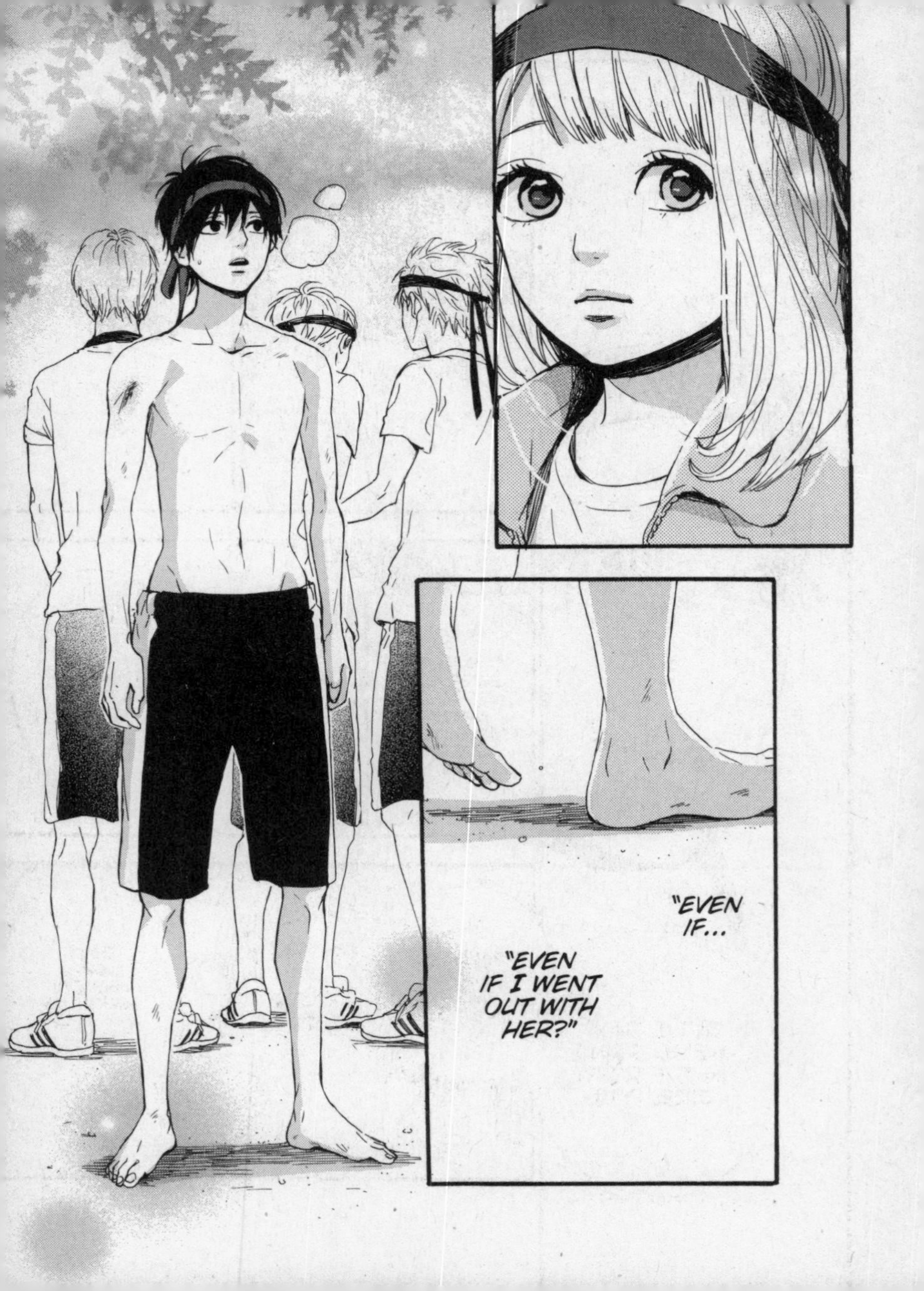
"EVEN IF...
"EVEN IF I WENT OUT WITH HER?"

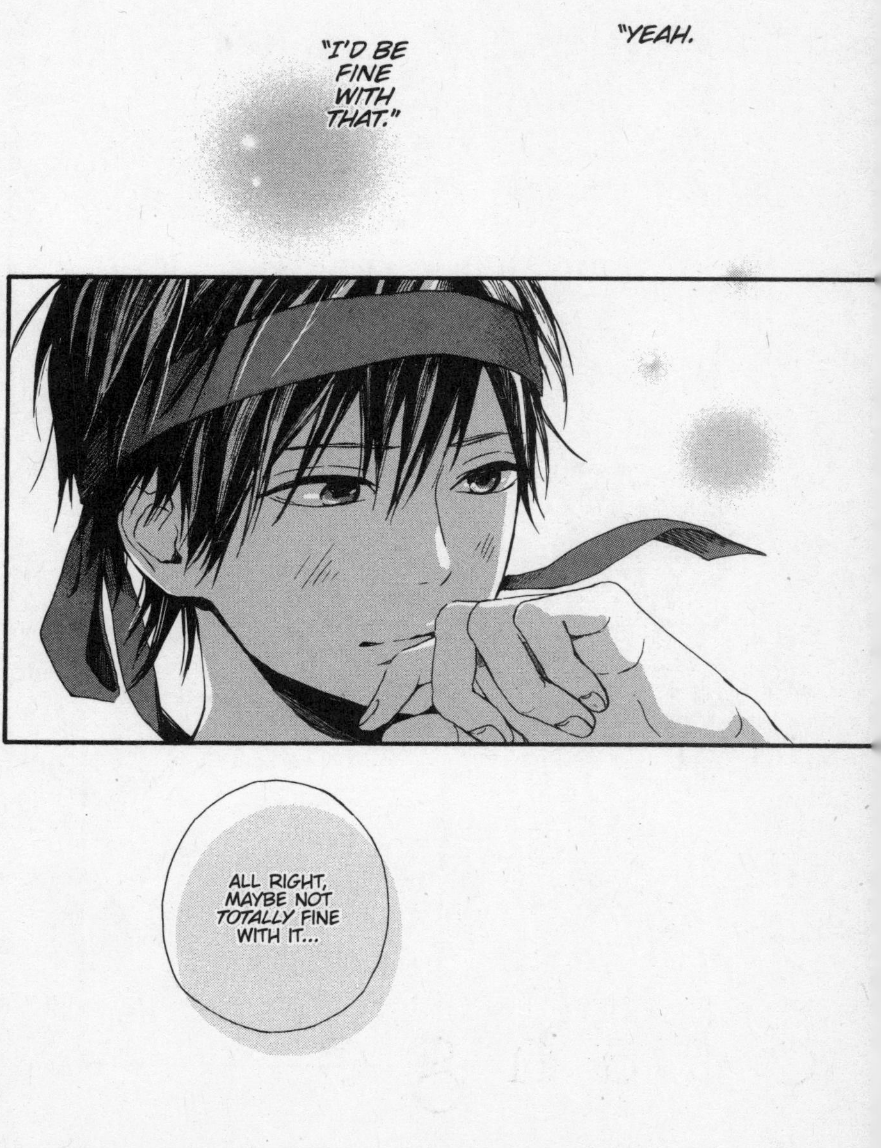
"YEAH.
"I'D BE FINE WITH THAT."
ALL RIGHT, MAYBE NOT *TOTALLY* FINE WITH IT...

orange

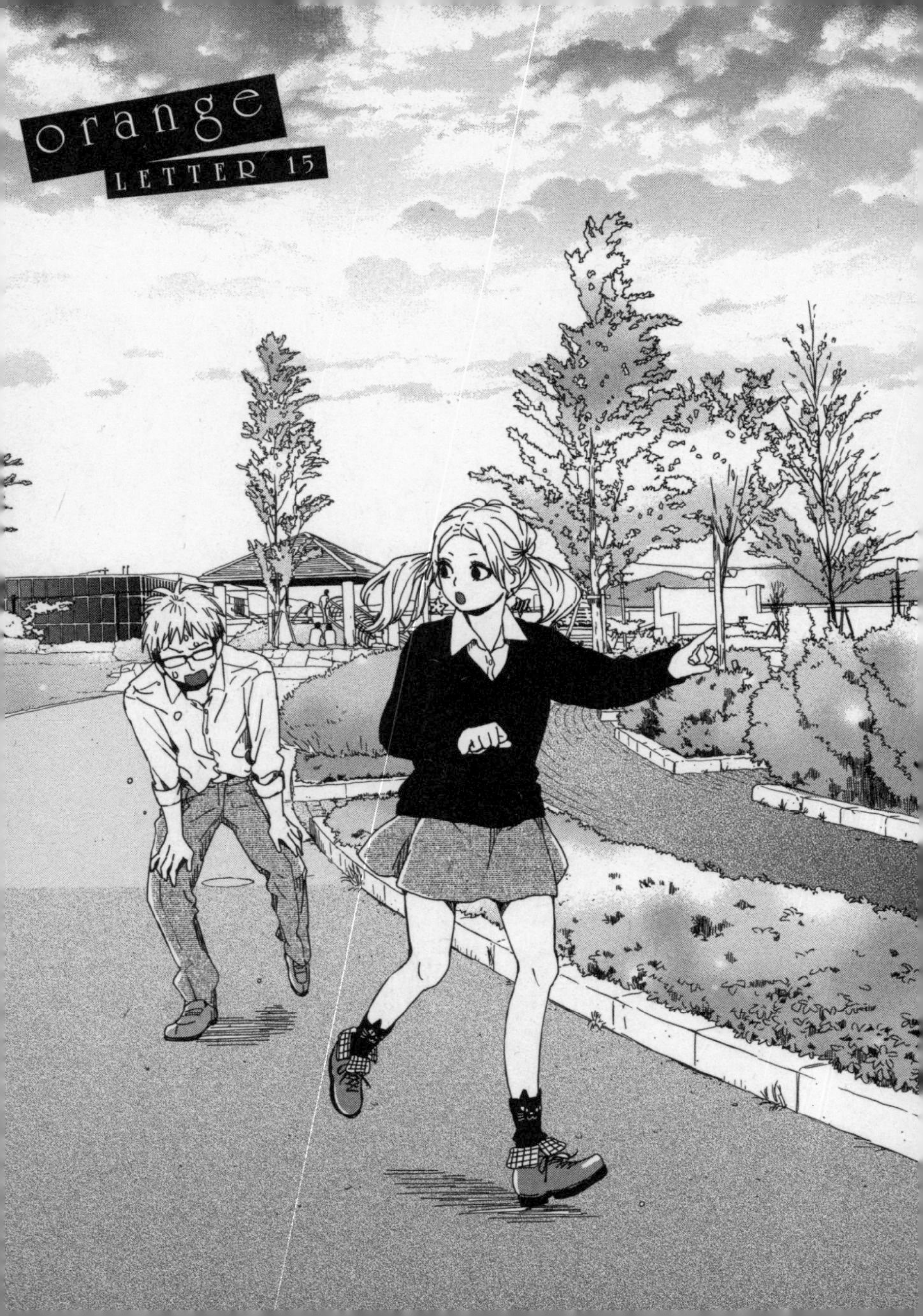
orange
LETTER 15

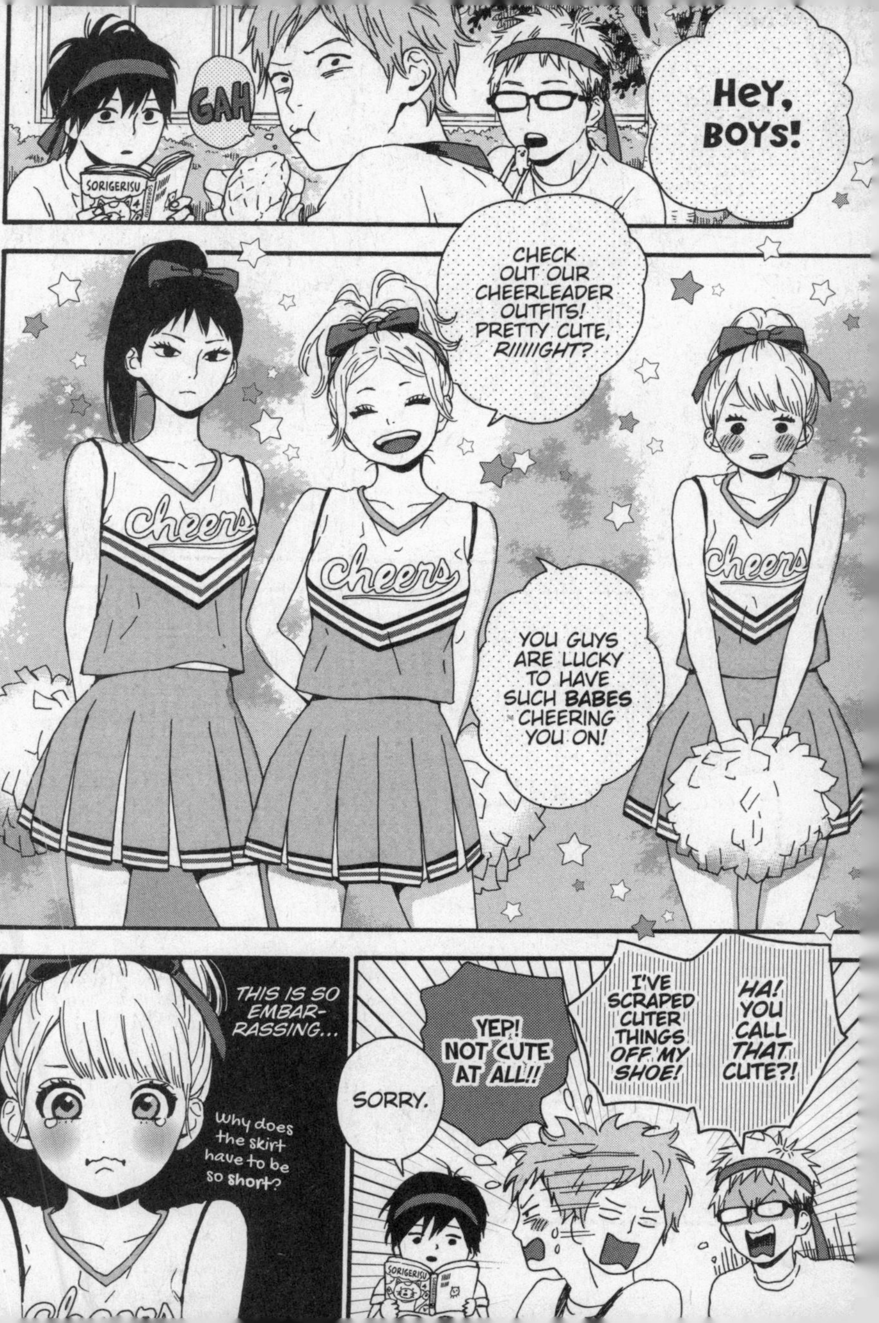
HEY, BOYS!
GAH
SORIGERISU
CHECK OUT OUR CHEERLEADER OUTFITS! PRETTY CUTE, RIIIIIGHT?
cheers
YOU GUYS ARE LUCKY TO HAVE SUCH BABES CHEERING YOU ON!
HA! YOU CALL THAT CUTE?!
I'VE SCRAPED CUTER THINGS OFF MY SHOE!
YEP! NOT CUTE AT ALL!!
SORRY.
SORIGERISU
THIS IS SO EMBAR-RASSING...
Why does the skirt have to be so short?

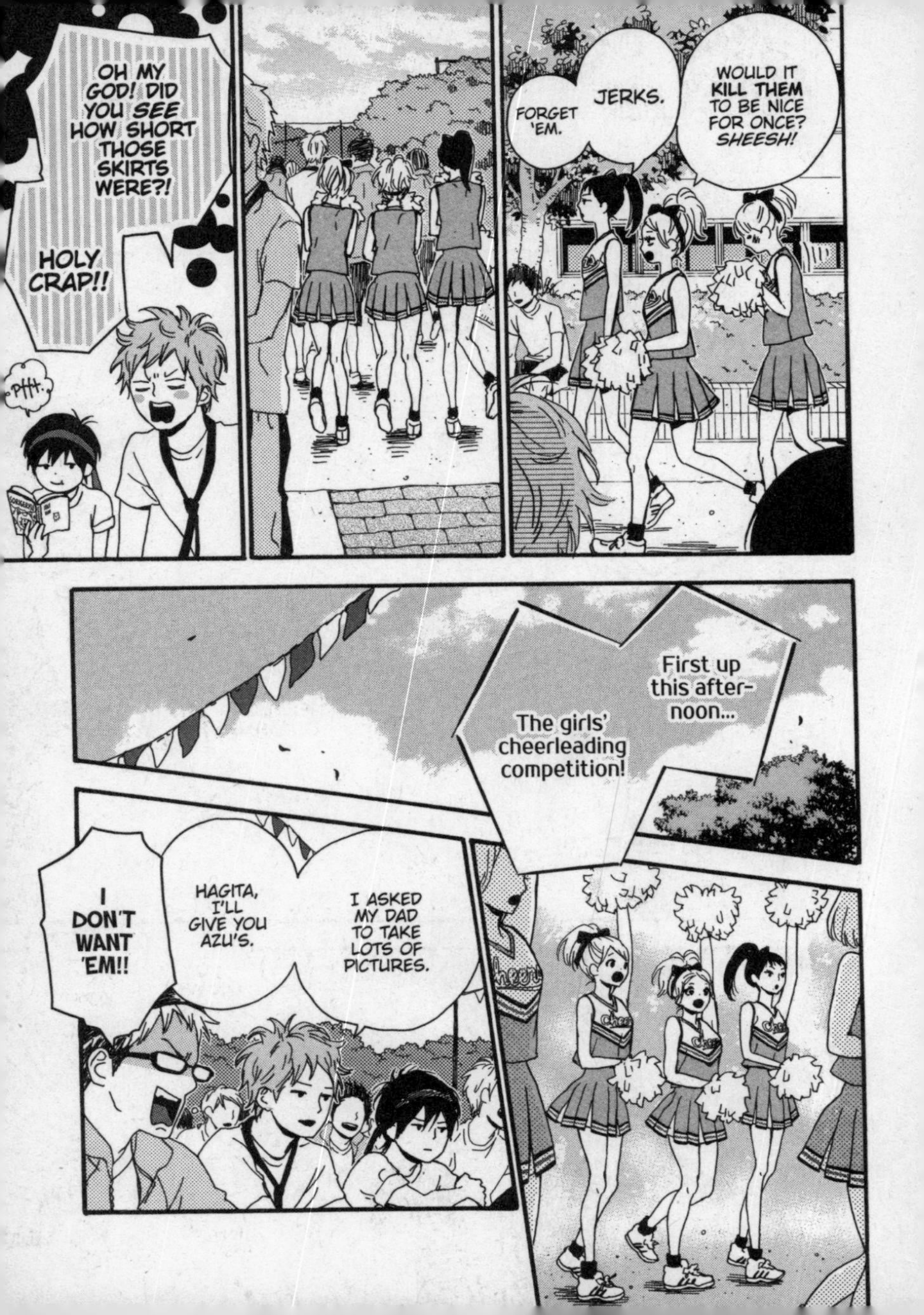
WOULD IT KILL THEM TO BE NICE FOR ONCE? SHEESH!
JERKS.
FORGET 'EM.
OH MY GOD! DID YOU SEE HOW SHORT THOSE SKIRTS WERE?!
HOLY CRAP!!
First up this after-noon...
The girls' cheerleading competition!
I ASKED MY DAD TO TAKE LOTS OF PICTURES.
HAGITA, I'LL GIVE YOU AZU'S.
I DON'T WANT 'EM!!

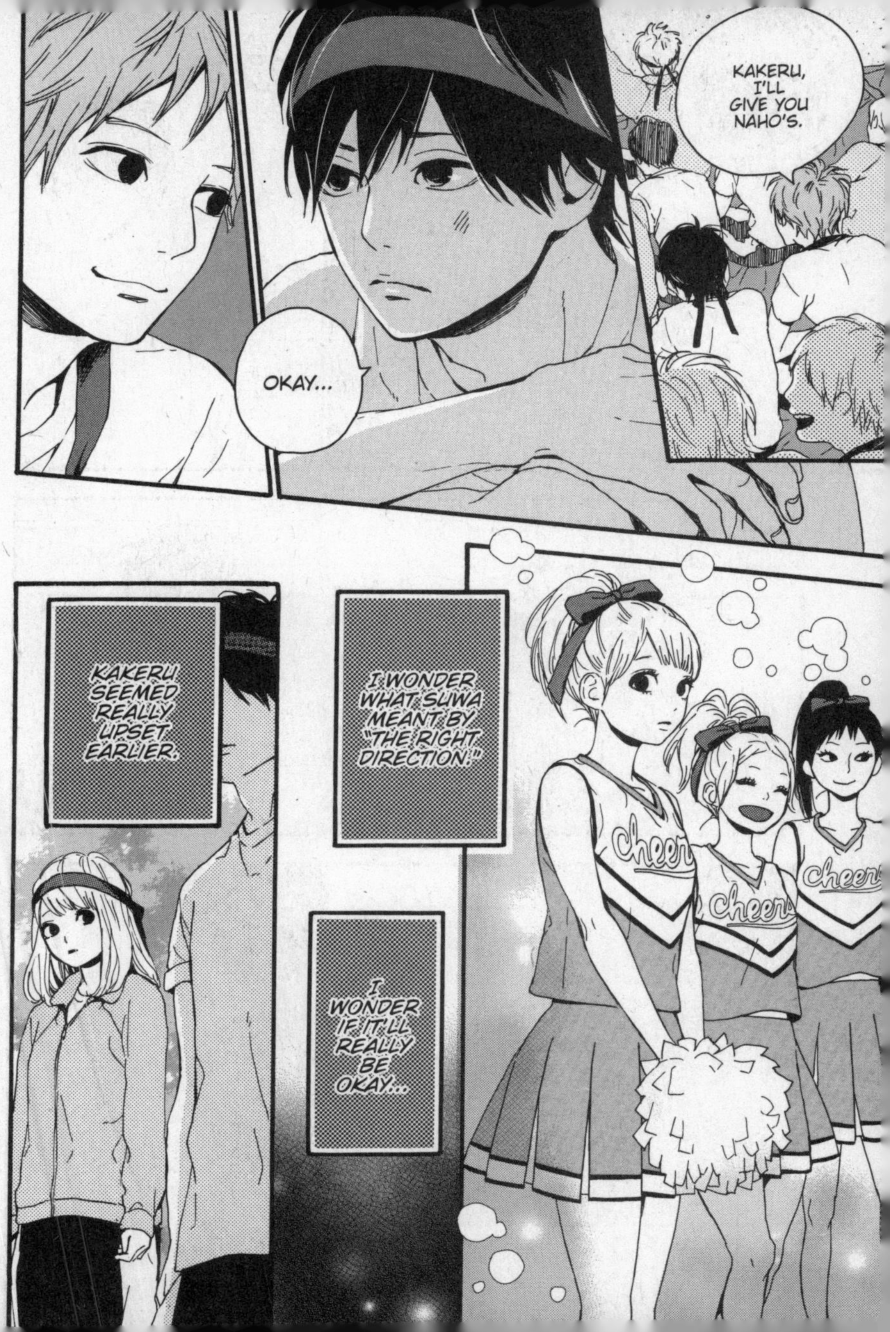
KAKERU, I'LL GIVE YOU NAHO'S.
OKAY...
cheers
I WONDER WHAT SUWA MEANT BY "THE RIGHT DIRECTION."
I WONDER IF IT'LL REALLY BE OKAY...
KAKERU SEEMED REALLY UPSET EARLIER.

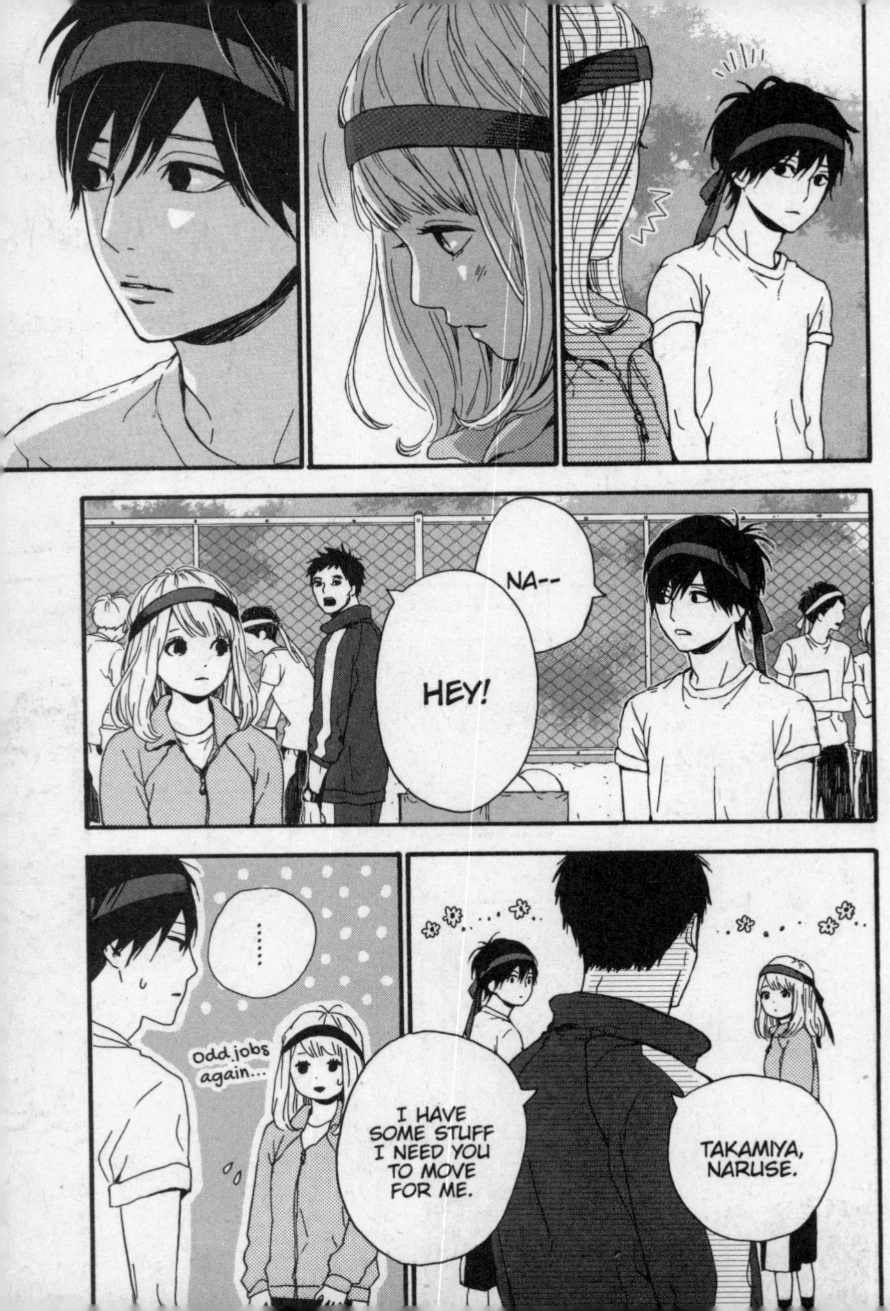
NA--
HEY!
TAKAMIYA, NARUSE.
I HAVE SOME STUFF I NEED YOU TO MOVE FOR ME.
......
Odd jobs again...

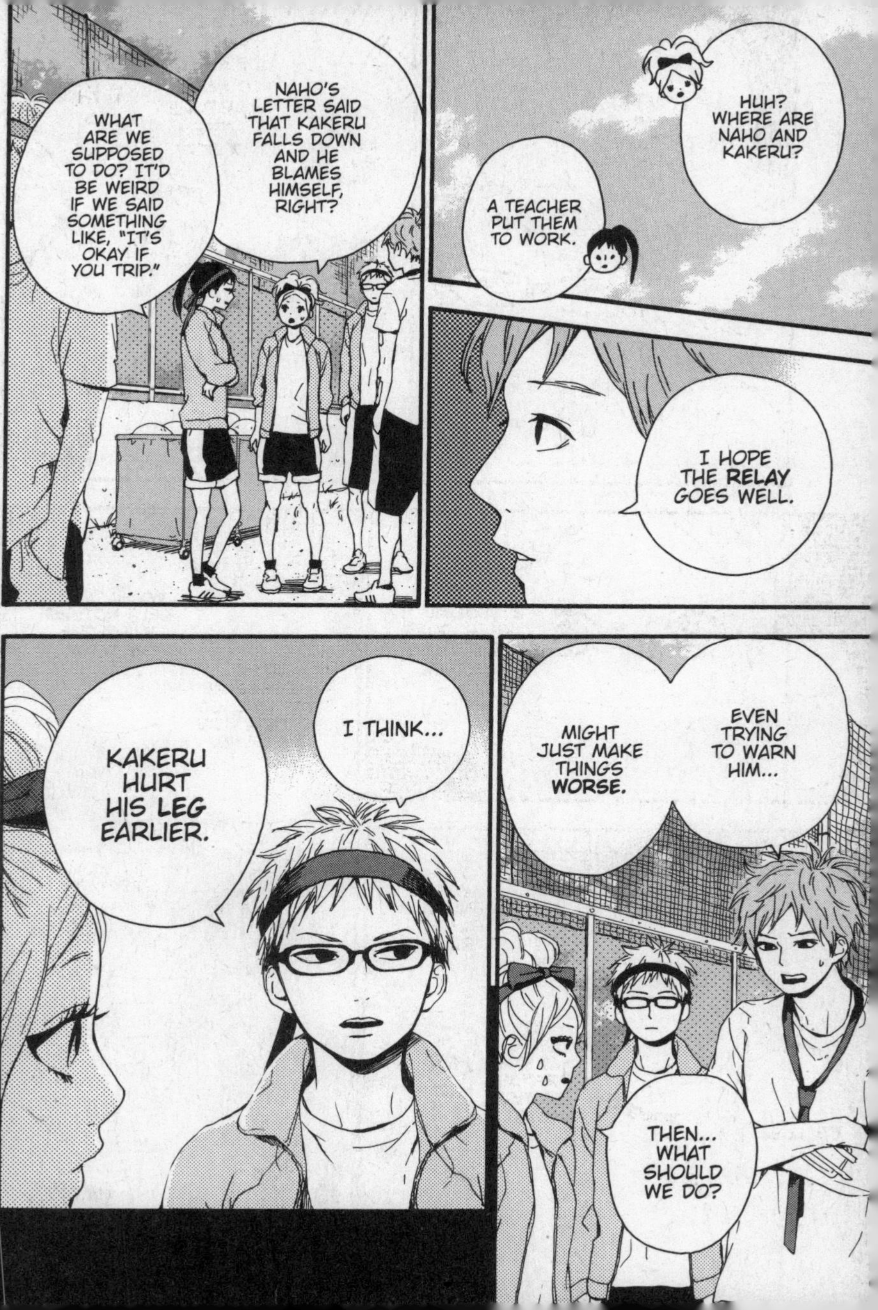
HUH? WHERE ARE NAHO AND KAKERU?
A TEACHER PUT THEM TO WORK.
I HOPE THE RELAY GOES WELL.
NAHO'S LETTER SAID THAT KAKERU FALLS DOWN AND HE BLAMES HIMSELF, RIGHT?
WHAT ARE WE SUPPOSED TO DO? IT'D BE WEIRD IF WE SAID SOMETHING LIKE, "IT'S OKAY IF YOU TRIP."
EVEN TRYING TO WARN HIM...
MIGHT JUST MAKE THINGS WORSE.
THEN... WHAT SHOULD WE DO?
I THINK...
KAKERU HURT HIS LEG EARLIER.

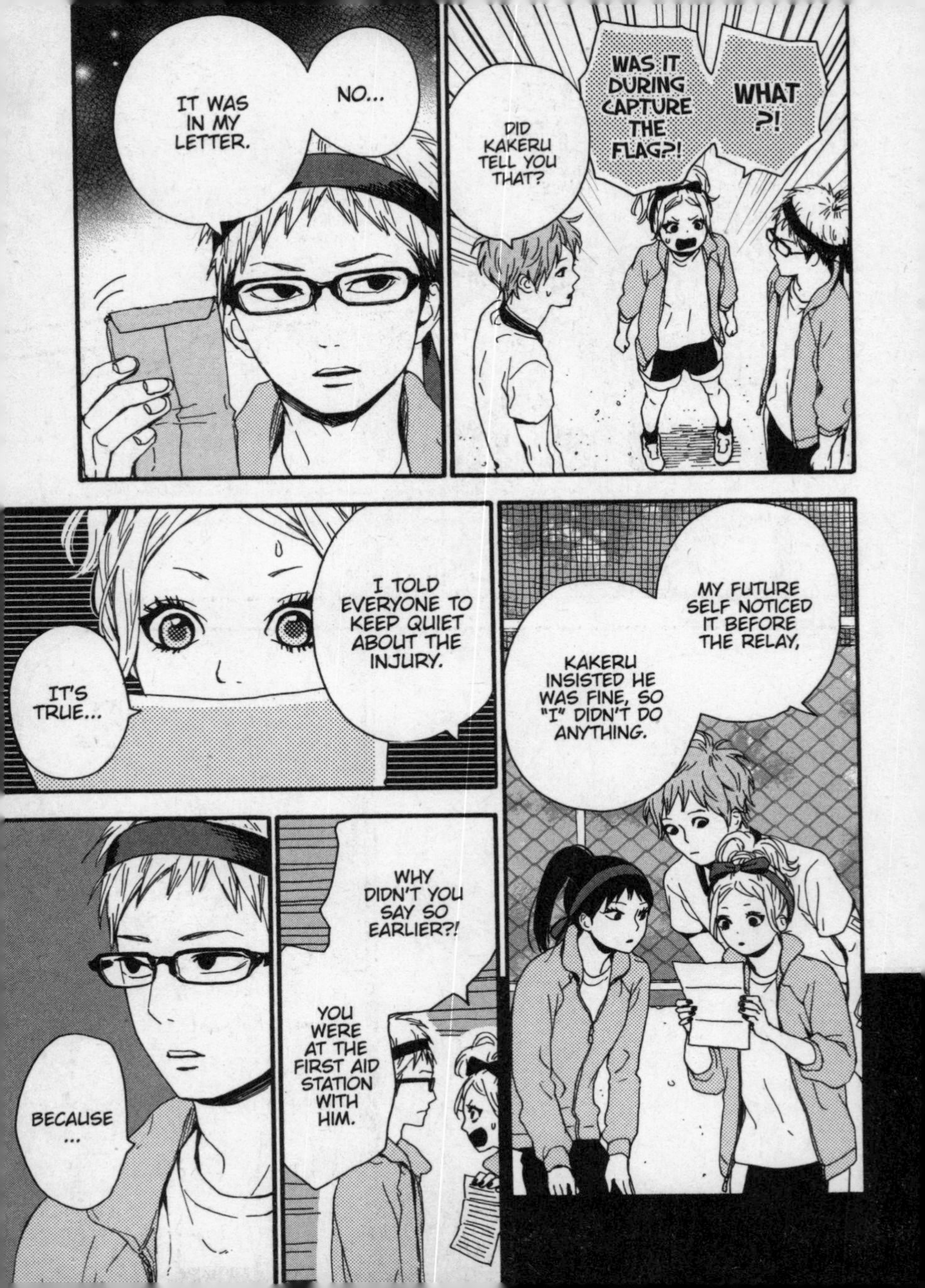
WHAT ?!
WAS IT DURING CAPTURE THE FLAG?!
DID KAKERU TELL YOU THAT?
NO...
IT WAS IN MY LETTER.
MY FUTURE SELF NOTICED IT BEFORE THE RELAY,
KAKERU INSISTED HE WAS FINE, SO "I" DIDN'T DO ANYTHING.
I TOLD EVERYONE TO KEEP QUIET ABOUT THE INJURY.
IT'S TRUE...
WHY DIDN'T YOU SAY SO EARLIER?!
YOU WERE AT THE FIRST AID STATION WITH HIM.
BECAUSE ...

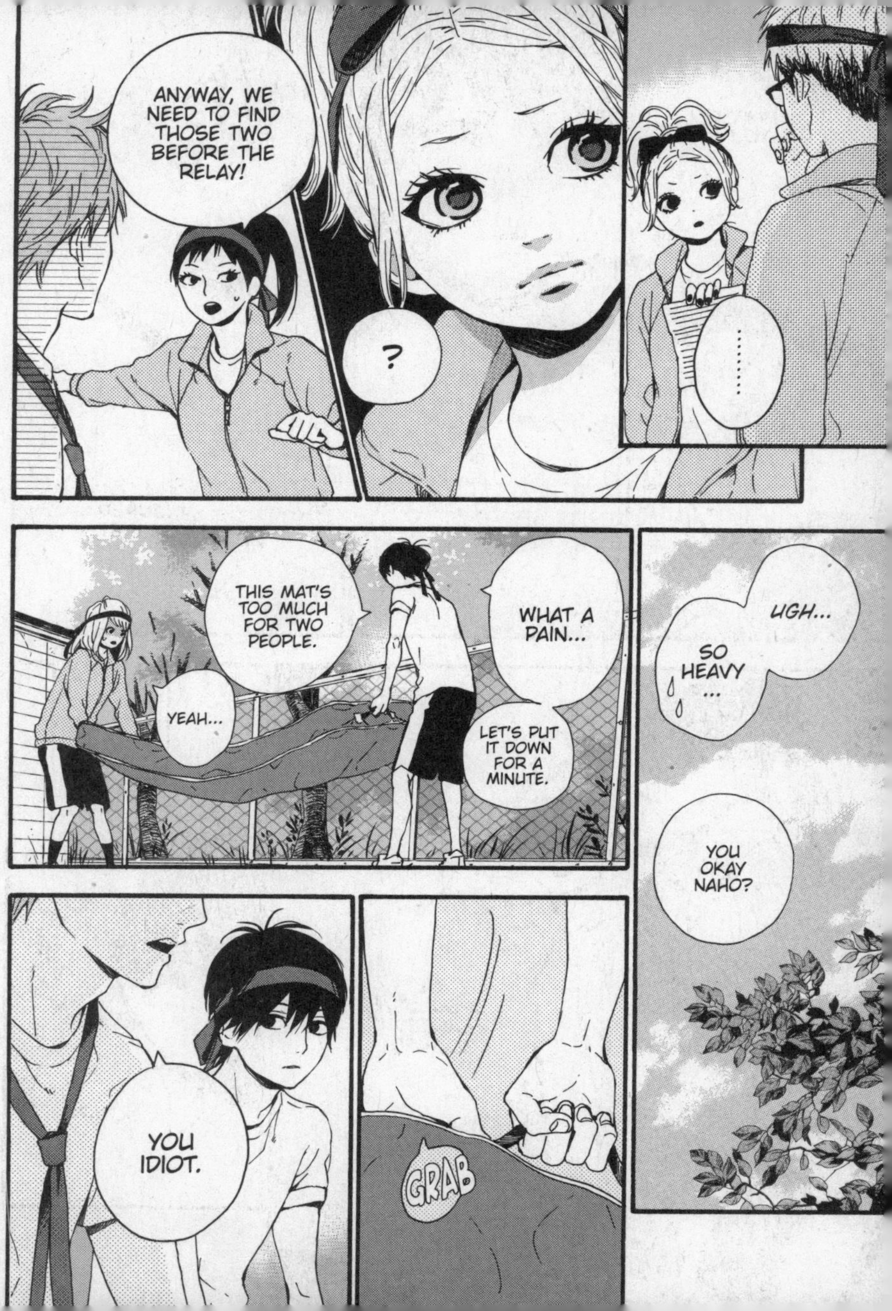
......
?
ANYWAY, WE NEED TO FIND THOSE TWO BEFORE THE RELAY!
UGH...
SO HEAVY...
YOU OKAY NAHO?
WHAT A PAIN...
THIS MAT'S TOO MUCH FOR TWO PEOPLE.
LET'S PUT IT DOWN FOR A MINUTE.
YEAH...
GRAB
YOU IDIOT.

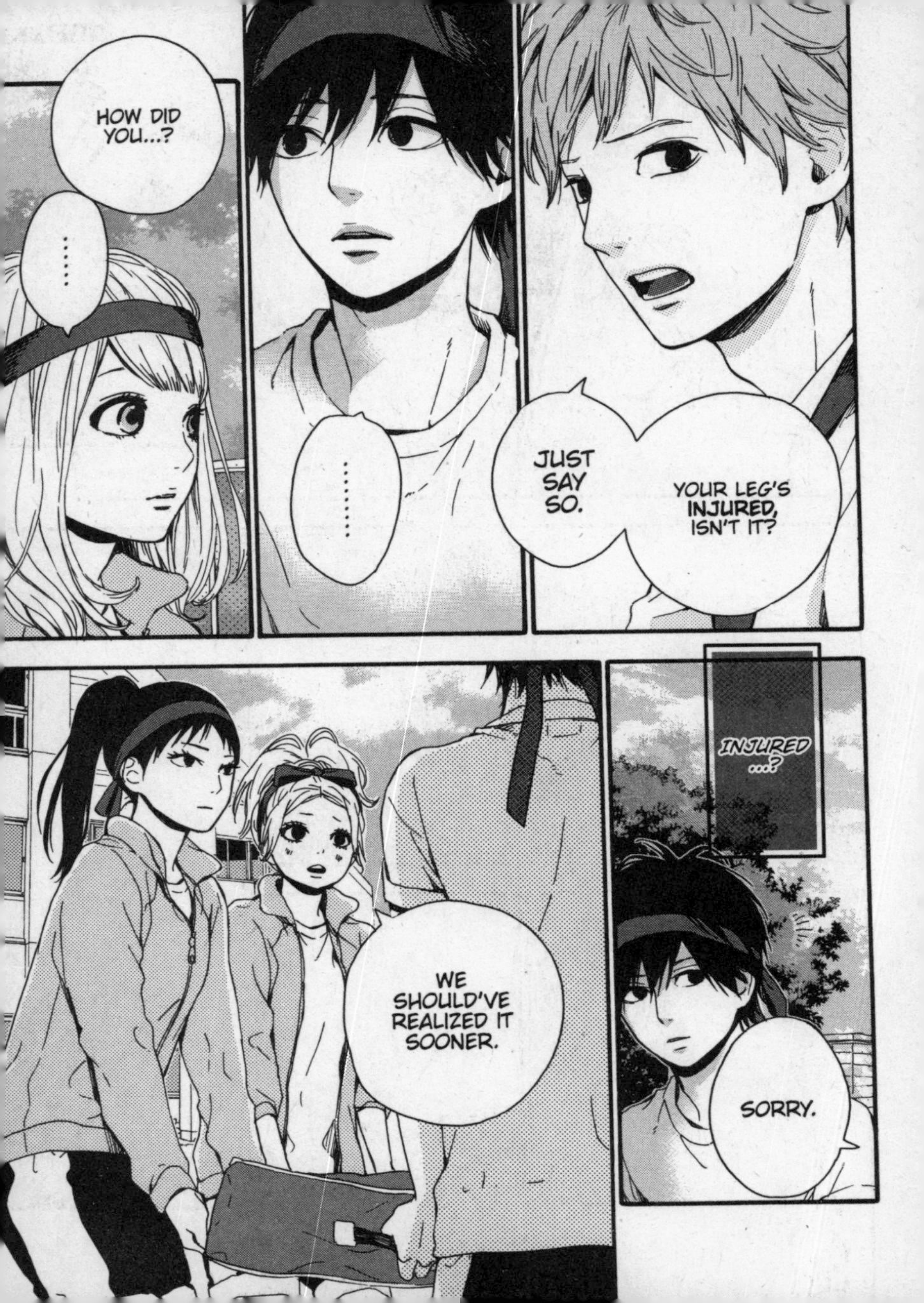
YOUR LEG'S INJURED, ISN'T IT?
JUST SAY SO.
......
HOW DID YOU...?
......
INJURED ...?
SORRY.
WE SHOULD'VE REALIZED IT SOONER.

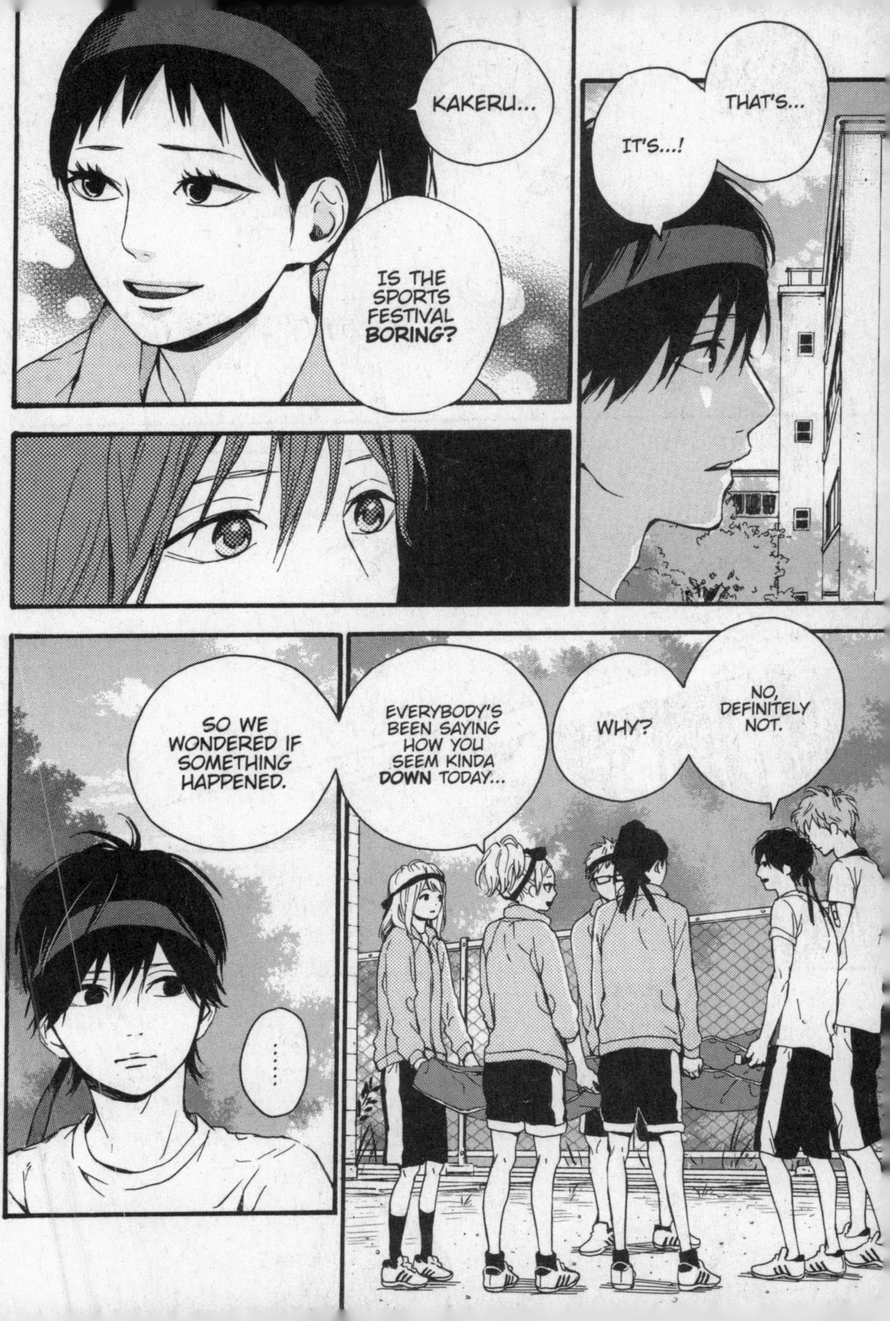
THAT'S...
IT'S...!
KAKERU...
IS THE SPORTS FESTIVAL BORING?
NO, DEFINITELY NOT.
WHY?
EVERYBODY'S BEEN SAYING HOW YOU SEEM KINDA DOWN TODAY...
SO WE WONDERED IF SOMETHING HAPPENED.
......

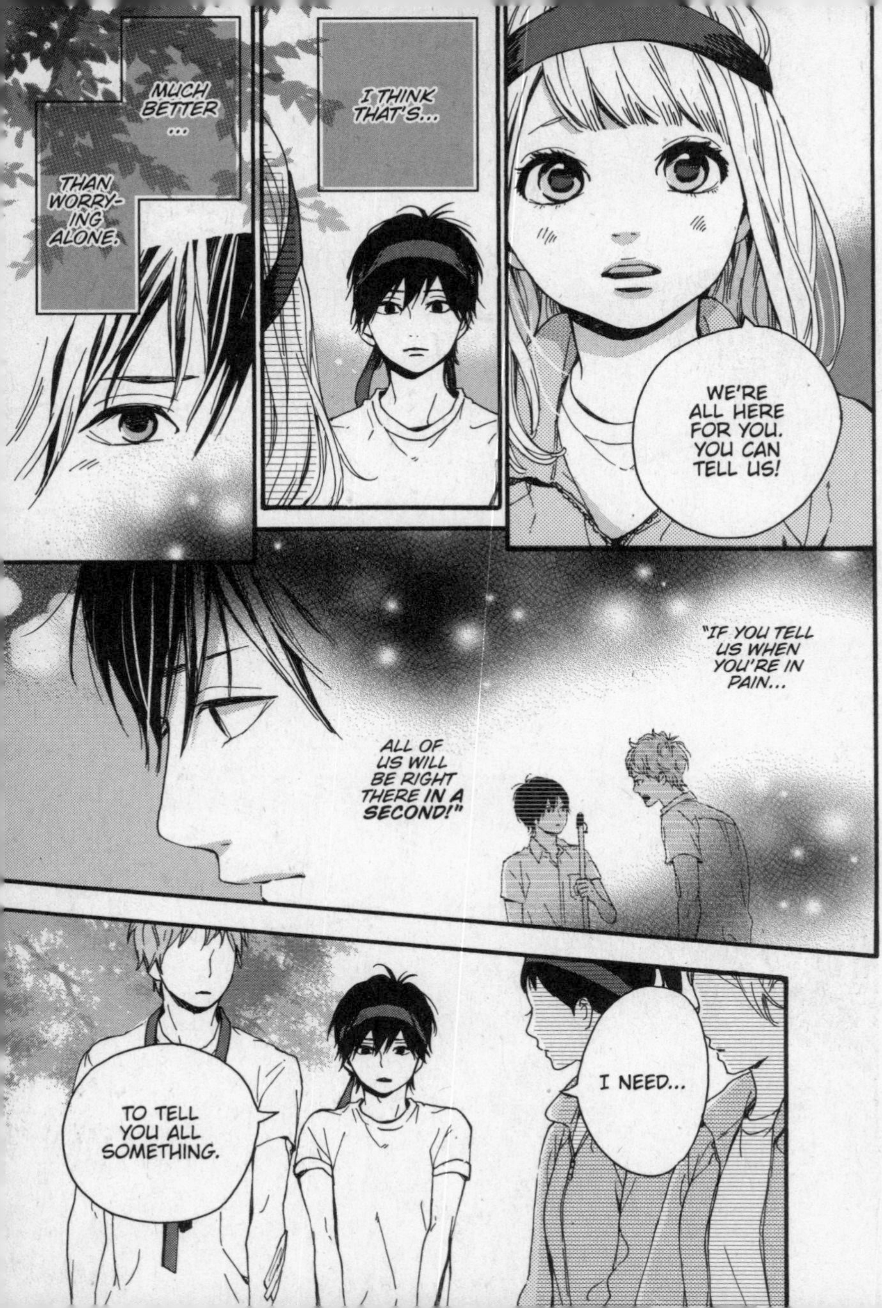
WE'RE ALL HERE FOR YOU. YOU CAN TELL US!
I THINK THAT'S...
MUCH BETTER ...
THAN WORRYING ALONE.
"IF YOU TELL US WHEN YOU'RE IN PAIN...
ALL OF US WILL BE RIGHT THERE IN A SECOND!"
I NEED...
TO TELL YOU ALL SOMETHING.

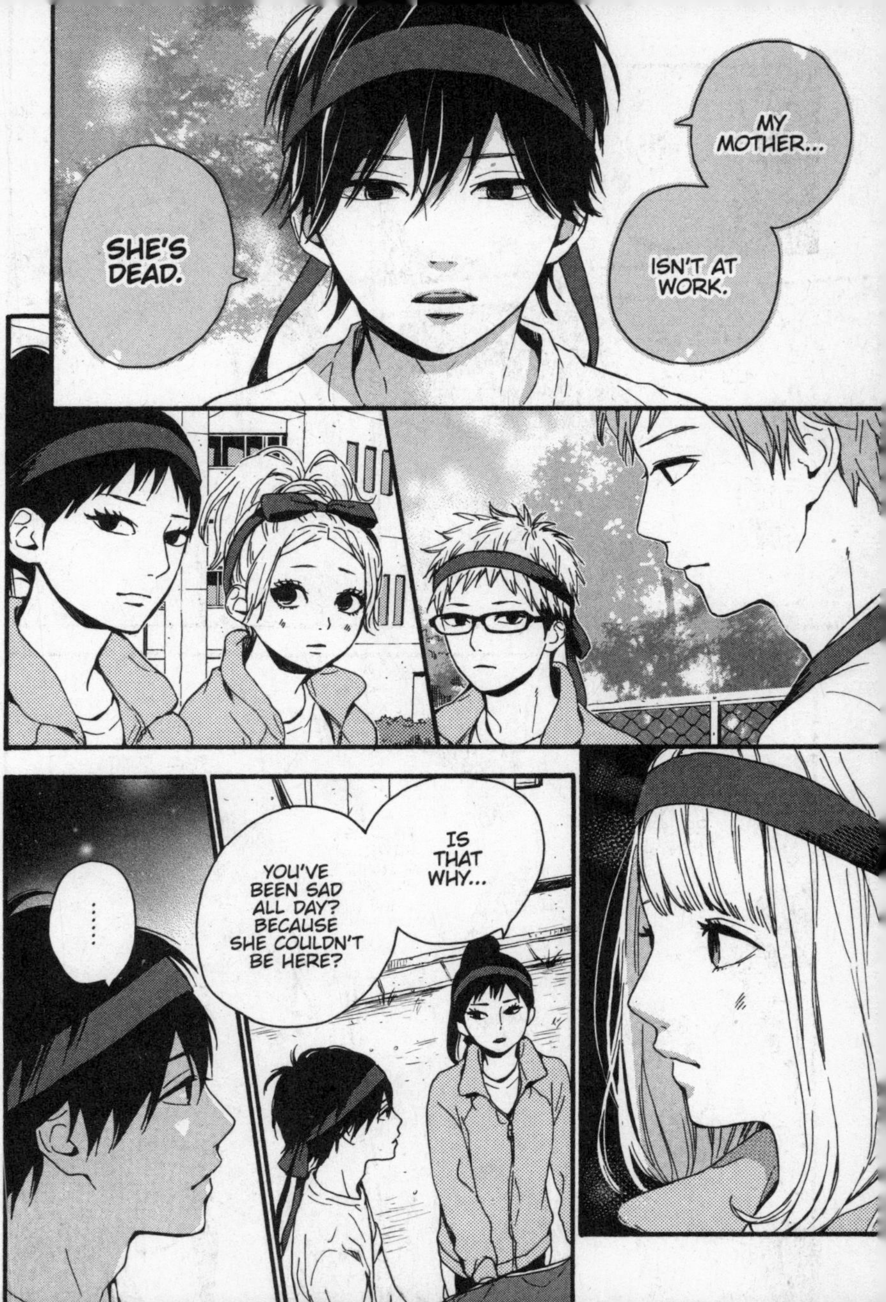
MY MOTHER...
ISN'T AT WORK.
SHE'S DEAD.
IS THAT WHY...
YOU'VE BEEN SAD ALL DAY? BECAUSE SHE COULDN'T BE HERE?
......

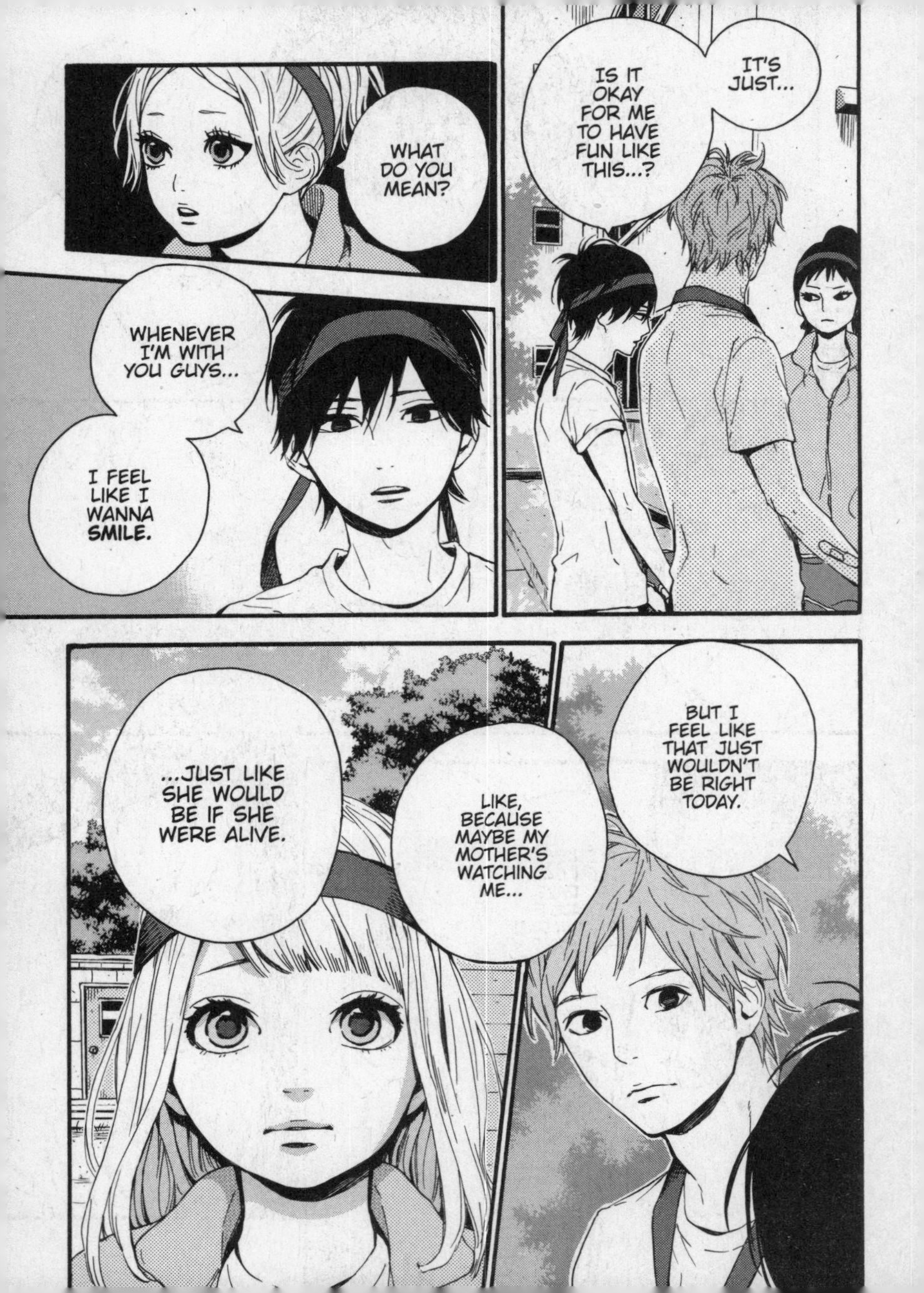
IT'S JUST...
IS IT OKAY FOR ME TO HAVE FUN LIKE THIS...?
WHAT DO YOU MEAN?
WHENEVER I'M WITH YOU GUYS...
I FEEL LIKE I WANNA SMILE.
BUT I FEEL LIKE THAT JUST WOULDN'T BE RIGHT TODAY.
LIKE, BECAUSE MAYBE MY MOTHER'S WATCHING ME...
...JUST LIKE SHE WOULD BE IF SHE WERE ALIVE.

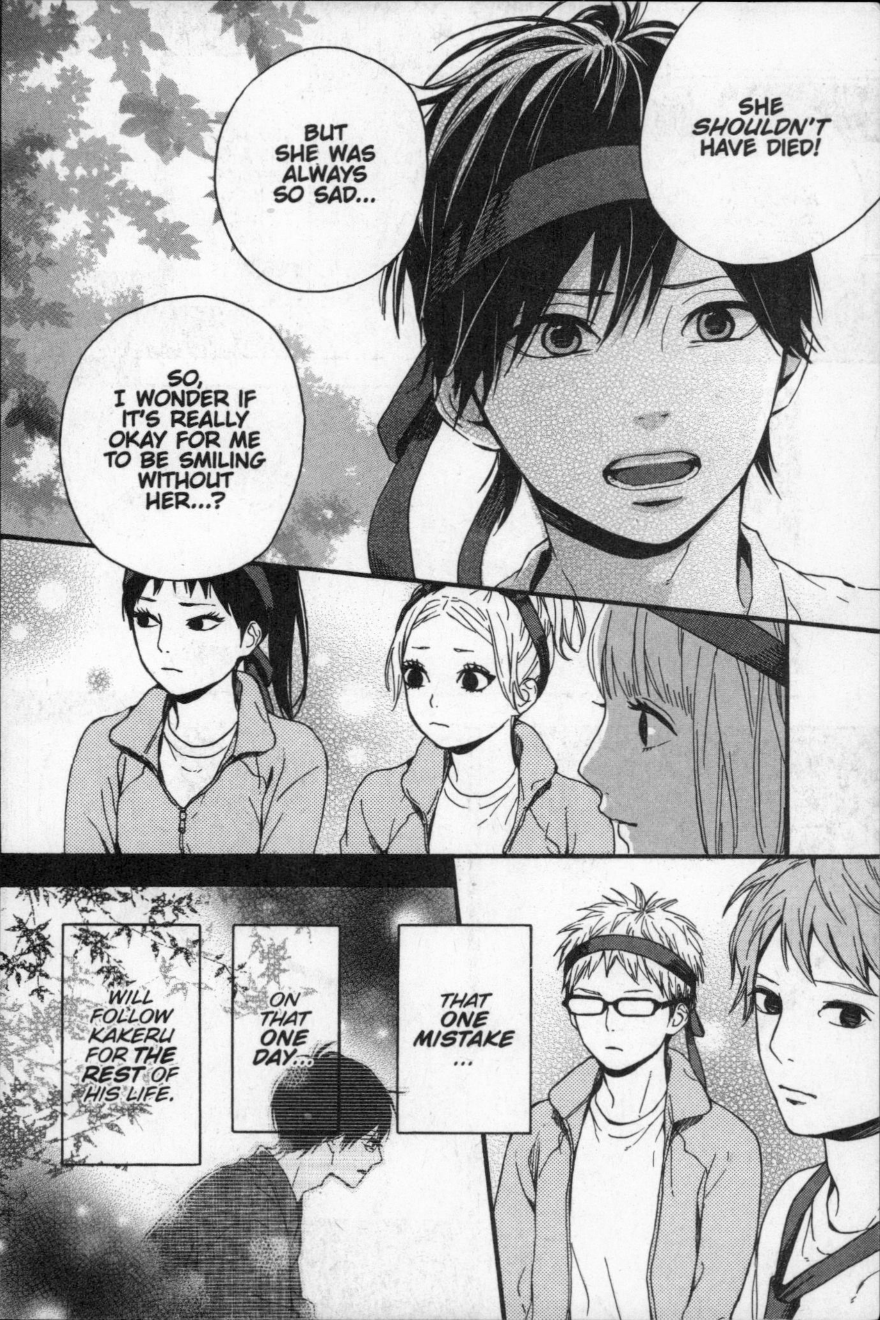
SHE SHOULDN'T HAVE DIED!
BUT SHE WAS ALWAYS SO SAD...
SO, I WONDER IF IT'S REALLY OKAY FOR ME TO BE SMILING WITHOUT HER...?
THAT ONE MISTAKE ...
ON THAT ONE DAY...
WILL FOLLOW KAKERU FOR THE REST OF HIS LIFE.

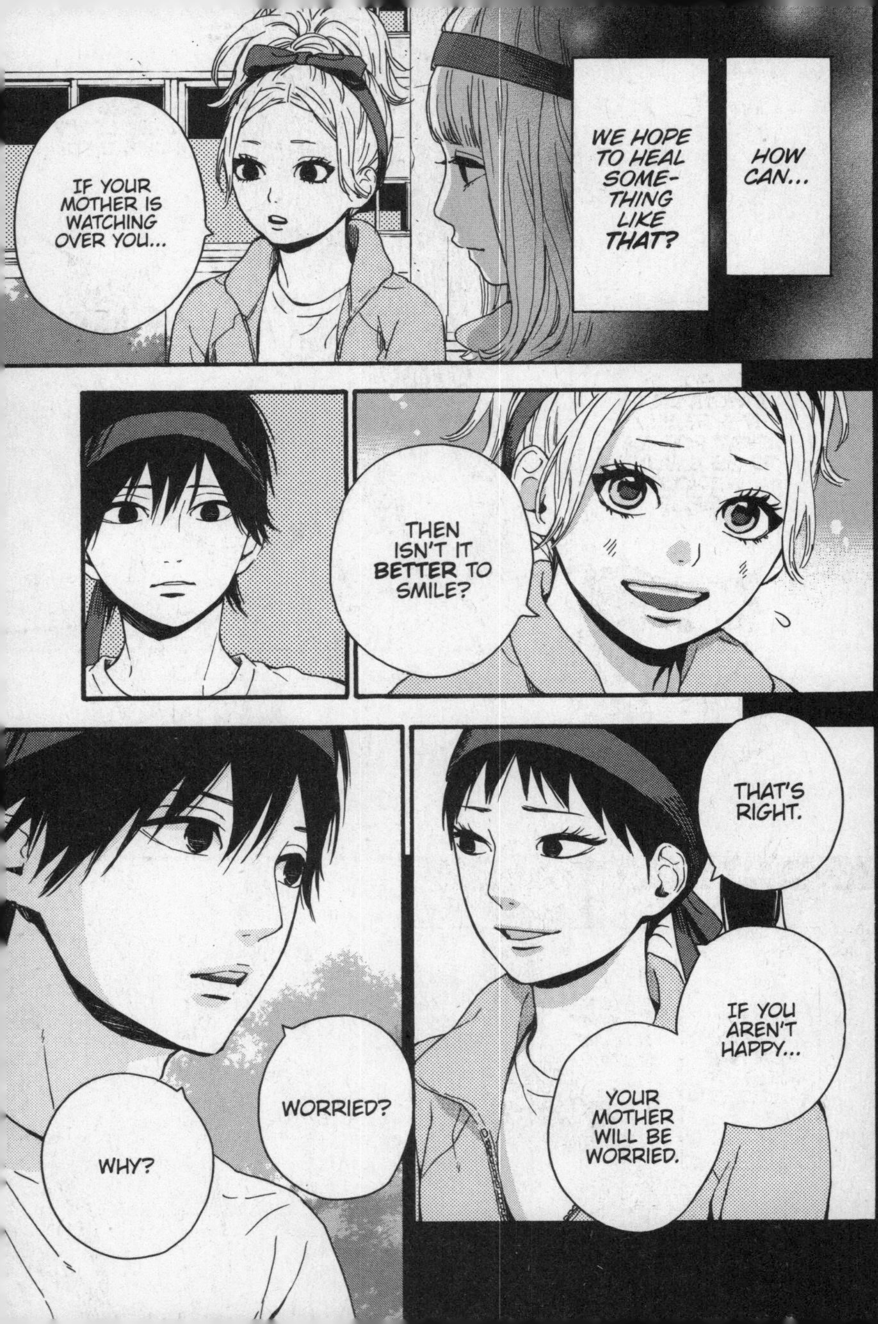
HOW CAN...
WE HOPE TO HEAL SOME-THING LIKE THAT?
IF YOUR MOTHER IS WATCHING OVER YOU...
THEN ISN'T IT BETTER TO SMILE?
THAT'S RIGHT.
IF YOU AREN'T HAPPY...
YOUR MOTHER WILL BE WORRIED.
WORRIED?
WHY?

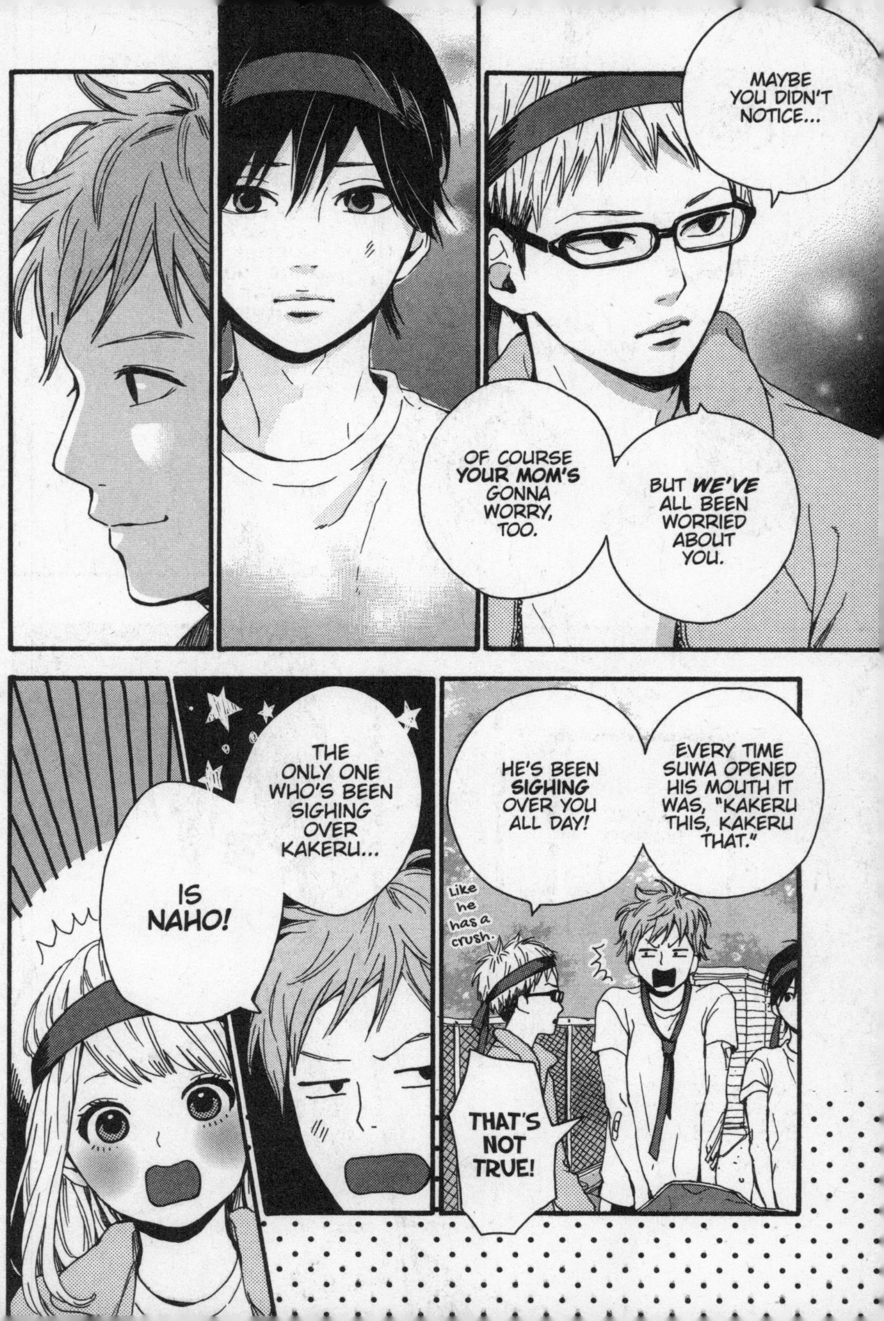
MAYBE YOU DIDN'T NOTICE...
BUT WE'VE ALL BEEN WORRIED ABOUT YOU.
OF COURSE YOUR MOM'S GONNA WORRY, TOO.
EVERY TIME SUWA OPENED HIS MOUTH IT WAS, "KAKERU THIS, KAKERU THAT."
HE'S BEEN SIGHING OVER YOU ALL DAY!
Like he has a crush.
THAT'S NOT TRUE!
THE ONLY ONE WHO'S BEEN SIGHING OVER KAKERU...
IS NAHO!

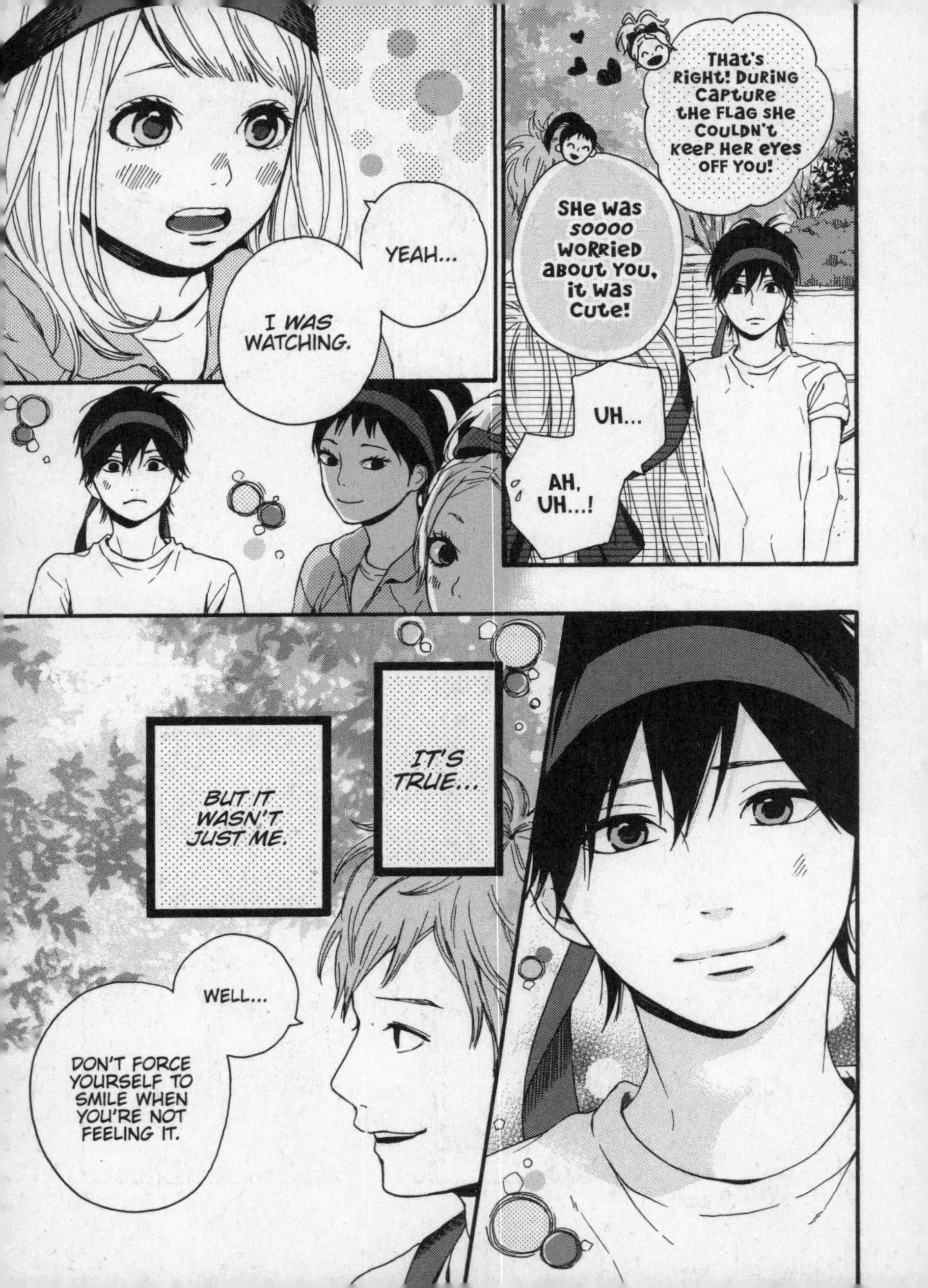
THAT'S RIGHT! DURING CAPTURE THE FLAG SHE COULDN'T KEEP HER EYES OFF YOU!
SHE WAS SOOOO WORRIED ABOUT YOU, IT WAS CUTE!
UH...
AH, UH...!
YEAH...
I WAS WATCHING.
IT'S TRUE...
BUT IT WASN'T JUST ME.
WELL...
DON'T FORCE YOURSELF TO SMILE WHEN YOU'RE NOT FEELING IT.

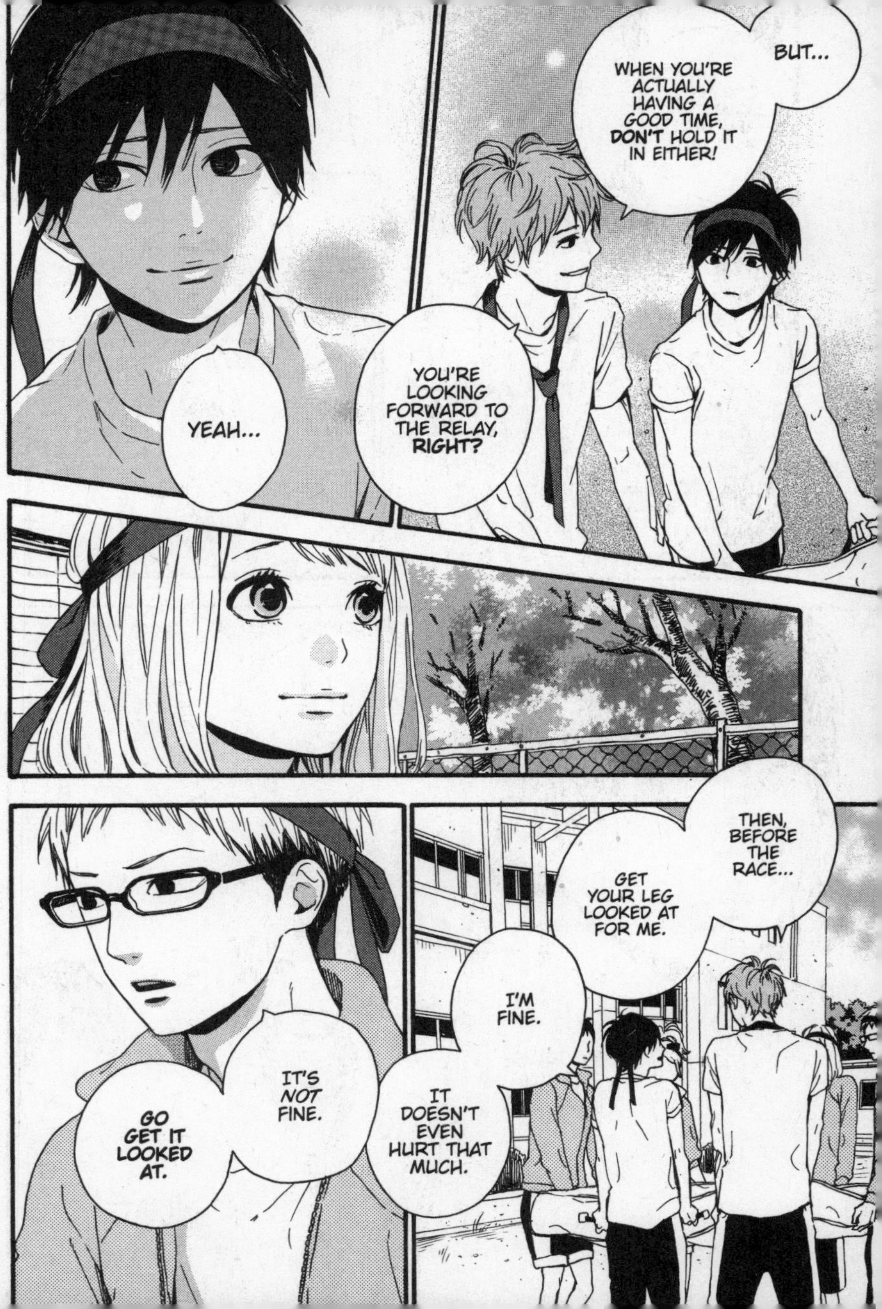
BUT...
WHEN YOU'RE ACTUALLY HAVING A GOOD TIME, DON'T HOLD IT IN EITHER!
YOU'RE LOOKING FORWARD TO THE RELAY, RIGHT?
YEAH...
THEN, BEFORE THE RACE...
GET YOUR LEG LOOKED AT FOR ME.
I'M FINE.
IT DOESN'T EVEN HURT THAT MUCH.
IT'S *NOT* FINE.
GO GET IT LOOKED AT.

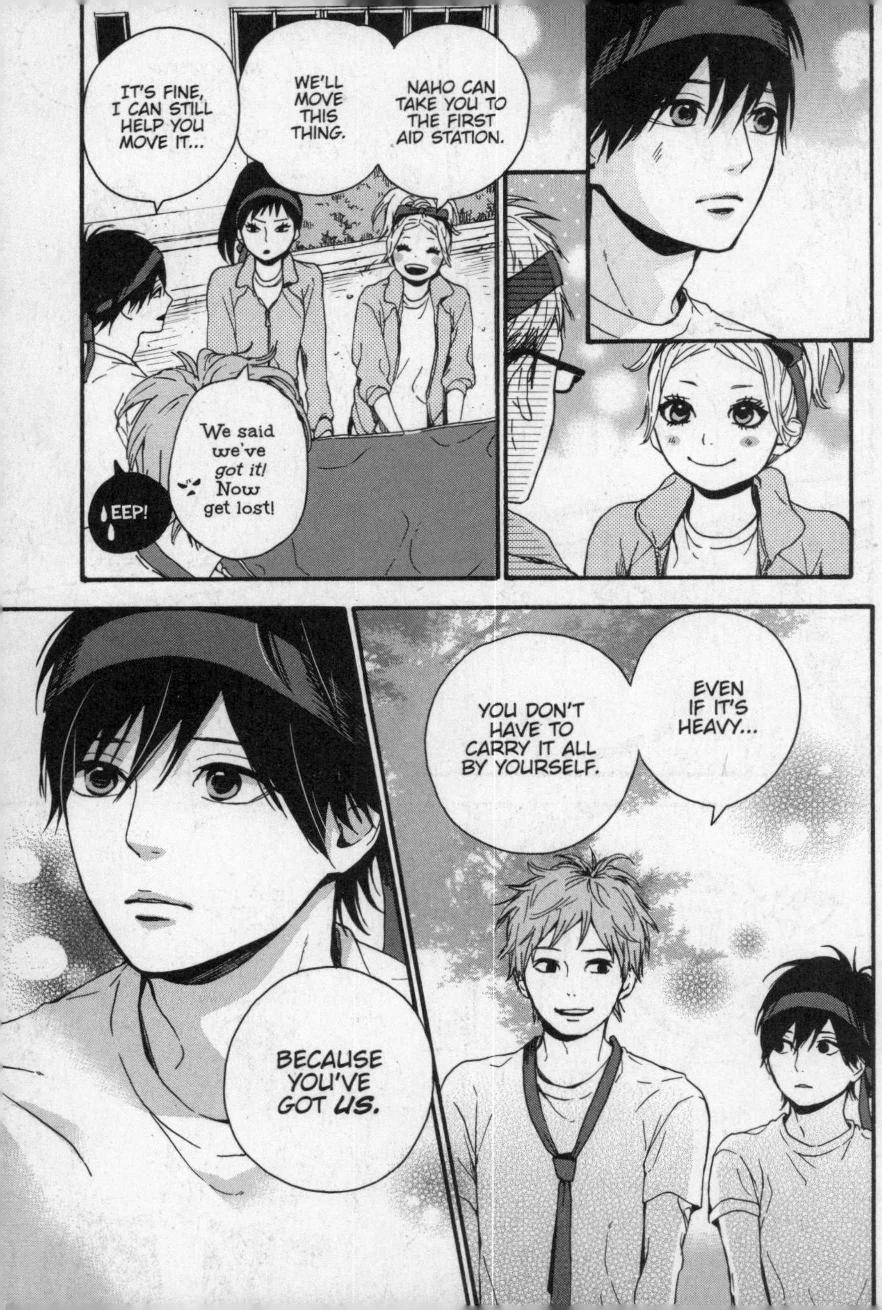
NAHO CAN TAKE YOU TO THE FIRST AID STATION.
WE'LL MOVE THIS THING.
IT'S FINE, I CAN STILL HELP YOU MOVE IT...
We said we've *got it!* Now get lost!
EEP!
EVEN IF IT'S HEAVY...
YOU DON'T HAVE TO CARRY IT ALL BY YOURSELF.
BECAUSE YOU'VE GOT ***US.***

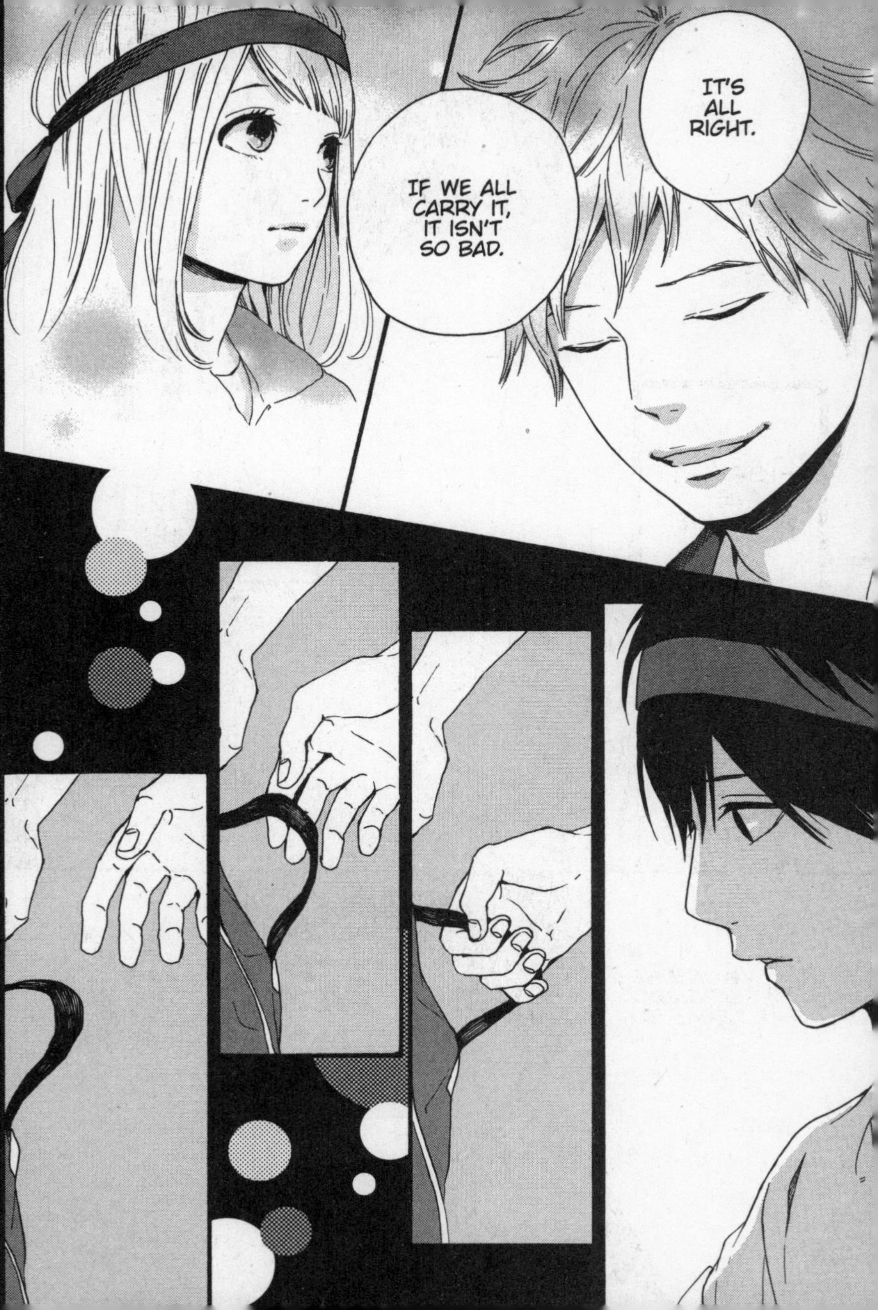
IT'S ALL RIGHT.
IF WE ALL CARRY IT, IT ISN'T SO BAD.

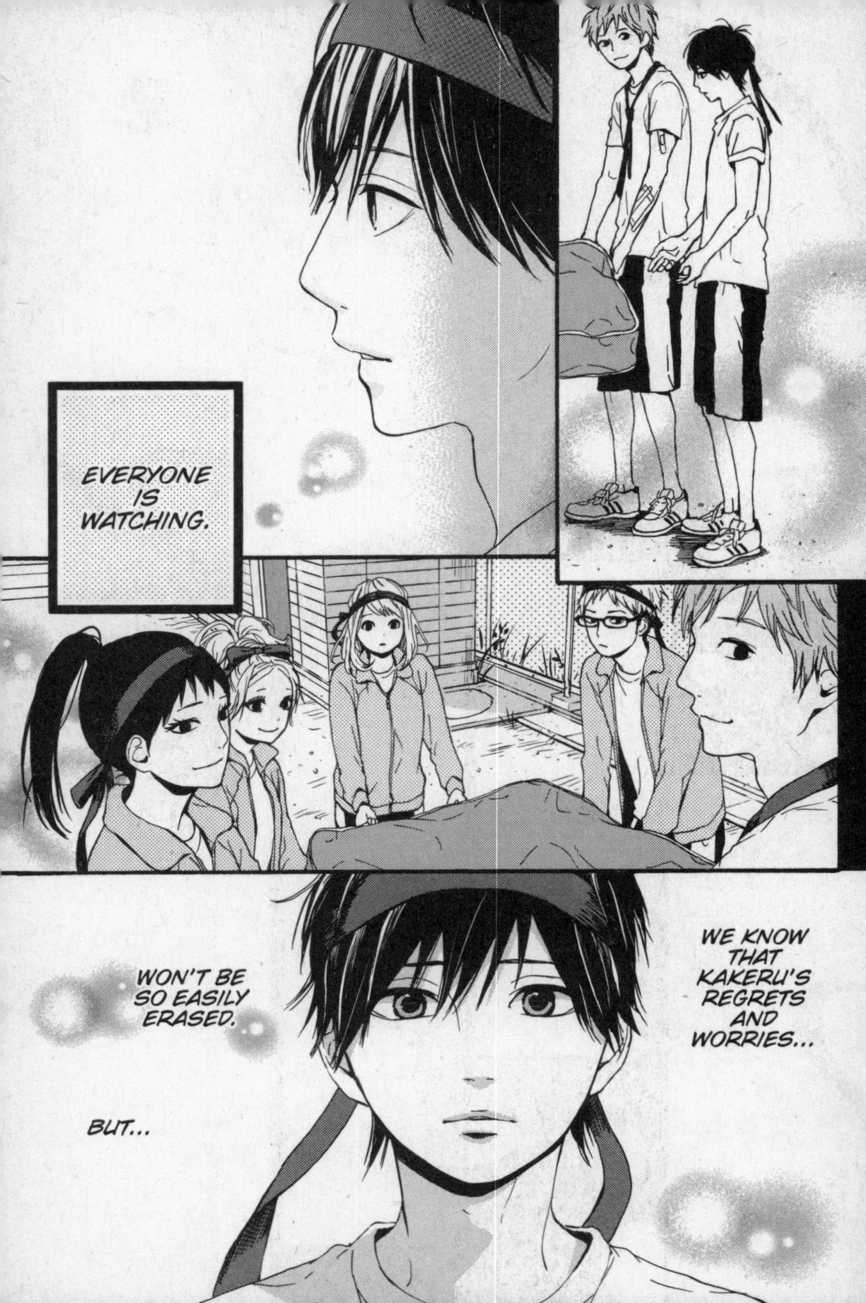
EVERYONE IS WATCHING.
WE KNOW THAT KAKERU'S REGRETS AND WORRIES...
WON'T BE SO EASILY ERASED.
BUT...

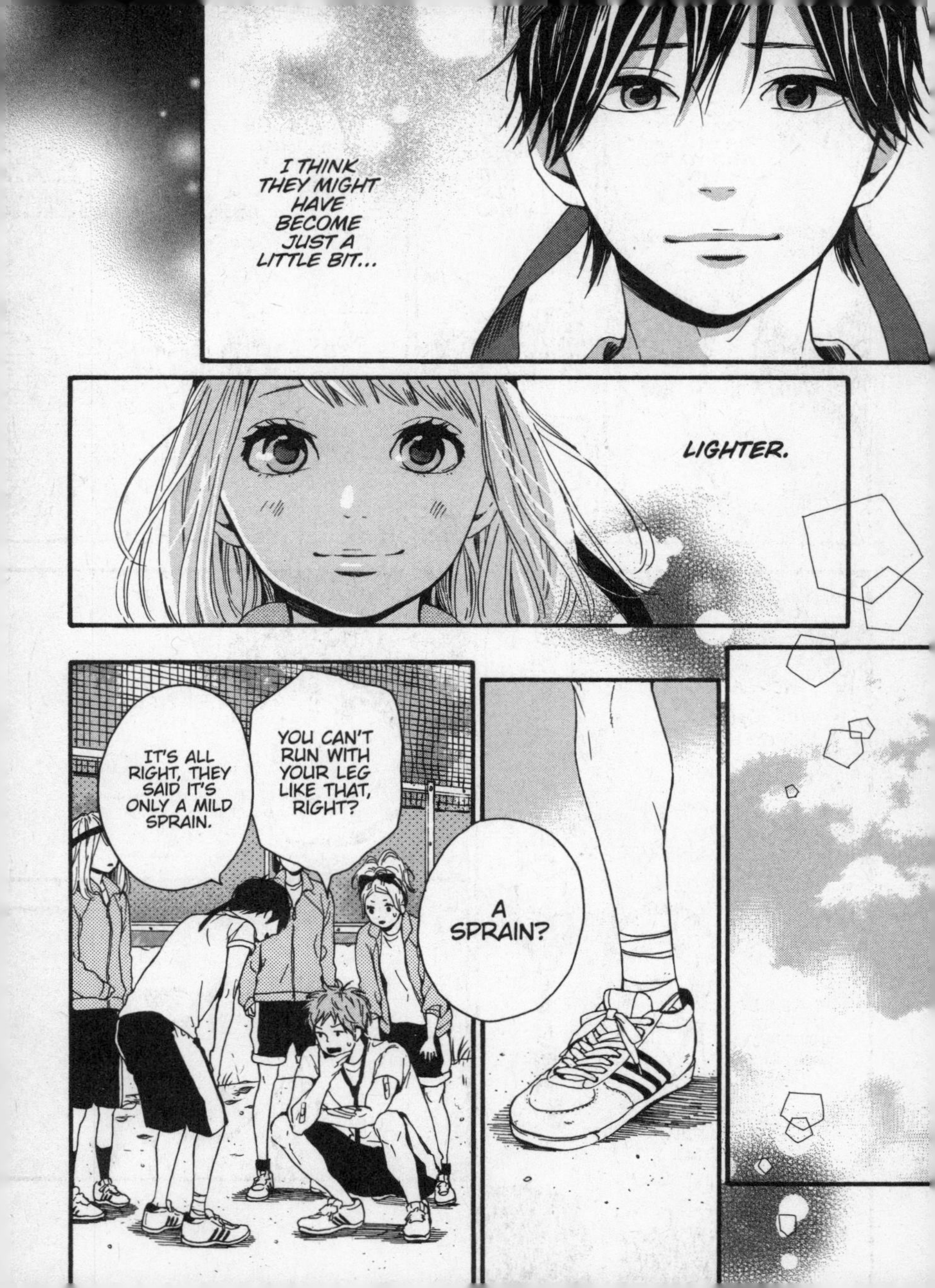
I THINK THEY MIGHT HAVE BECOME JUST A LITTLE BIT...
LIGHTER.
A SPRAIN?
YOU CAN'T RUN WITH YOUR LEG LIKE THAT, RIGHT?
IT'S ALL RIGHT, THEY SAID IT'S ONLY A MILD SPRAIN.

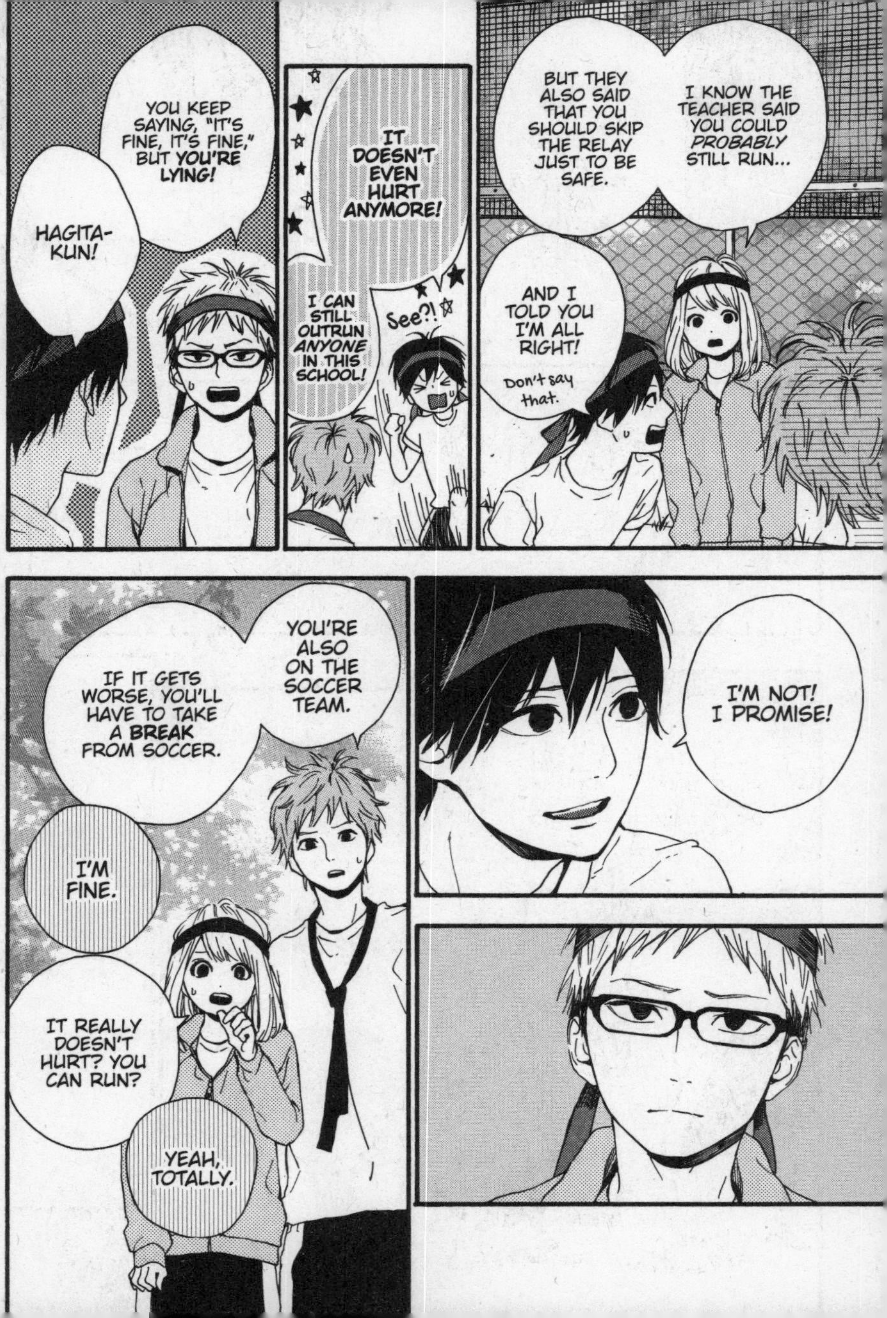
I KNOW THE TEACHER SAID YOU COULD *PROBABLY* STILL RUN...
BUT THEY ALSO SAID THAT YOU SHOULD SKIP THE RELAY JUST TO BE SAFE.
AND I TOLD YOU I'M ALL RIGHT!
Don't say that.
IT DOESN'T EVEN HURT ANYMORE!
See?!
I CAN STILL OUTRUN *ANYONE* IN THIS SCHOOL!
YOU KEEP SAYING, "IT'S FINE, IT'S FINE," BUT **YOU'RE** LYING!
HAGITA-KUN!
I'M NOT! I PROMISE!
YOU'RE ALSO ON THE SOCCER TEAM.
IF IT GETS WORSE, YOU'LL HAVE TO TAKE A **BREAK** FROM SOCCER.
I'M FINE.
IT REALLY DOESN'T HURT? YOU CAN RUN?
YEAH, TOTALLY.

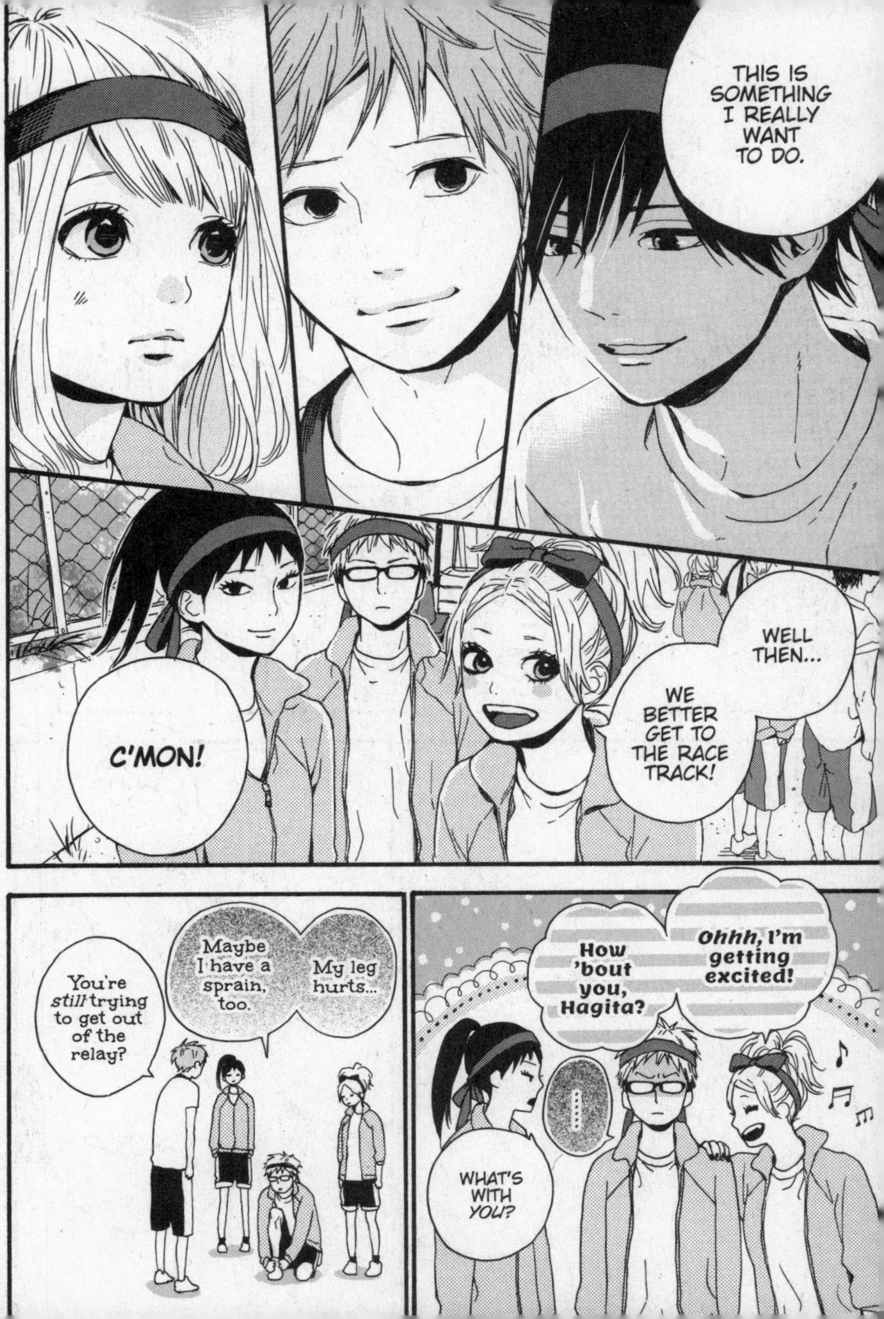
THIS IS SOMETHING I REALLY WANT TO DO.
WELL THEN...
WE BETTER GET TO THE RACE TRACK!
C'MON!
Ohhh, I'm getting excited!
How 'bout you, Hagita?
WHAT'S WITH YOU?
My leg hurts...
Maybe I have a sprain, too.
You're still trying to get out of the relay?

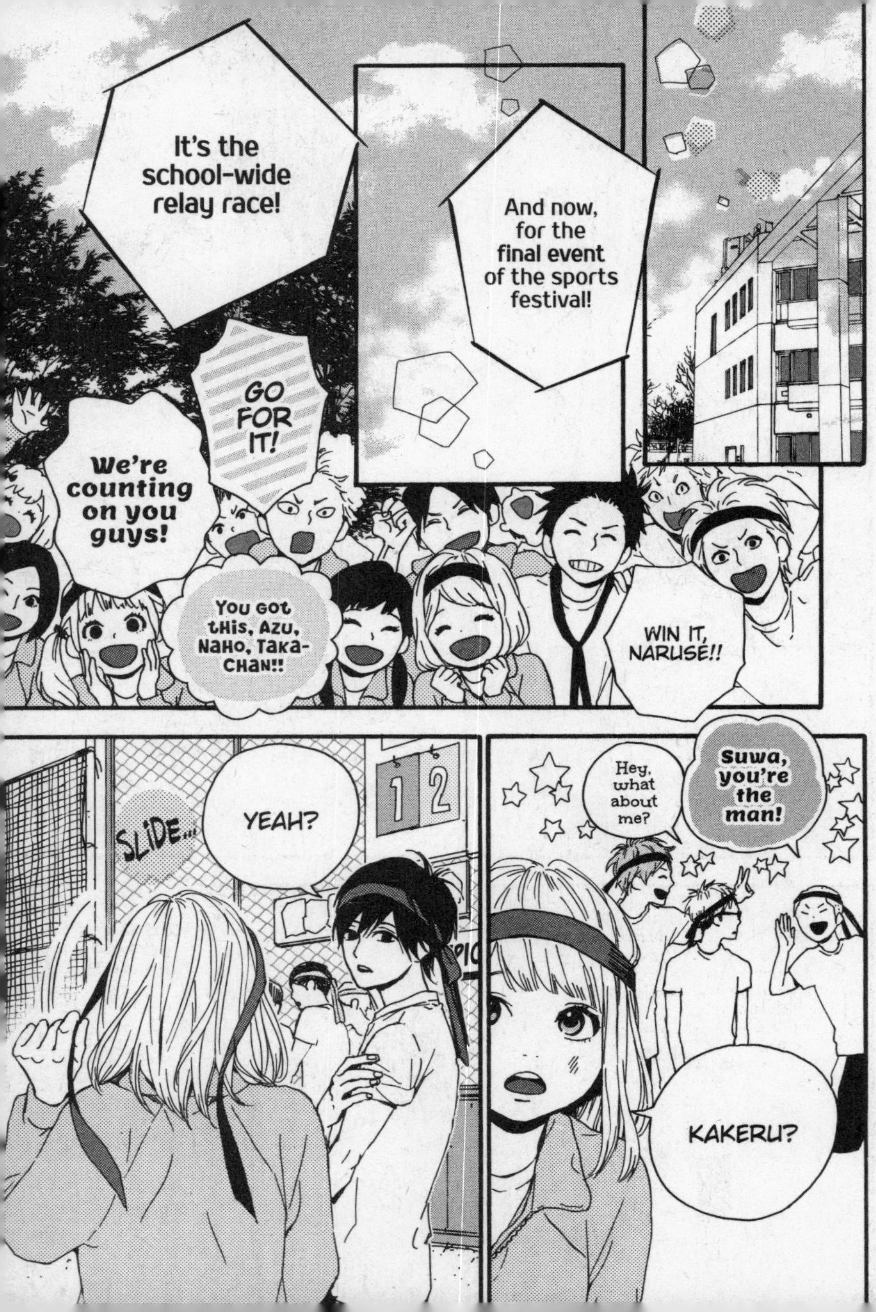
And now, for the final event of the sports festival!
It's the school-wide relay race!
WIN IT, NARUSE!!
GO FOR IT!
We're counting on you guys!
You got this, Azu, Naho, Taka-chan!!
Suwa, you're the man!
Hey, what about me?
KAKERU?
YEAH?
SLIDE...

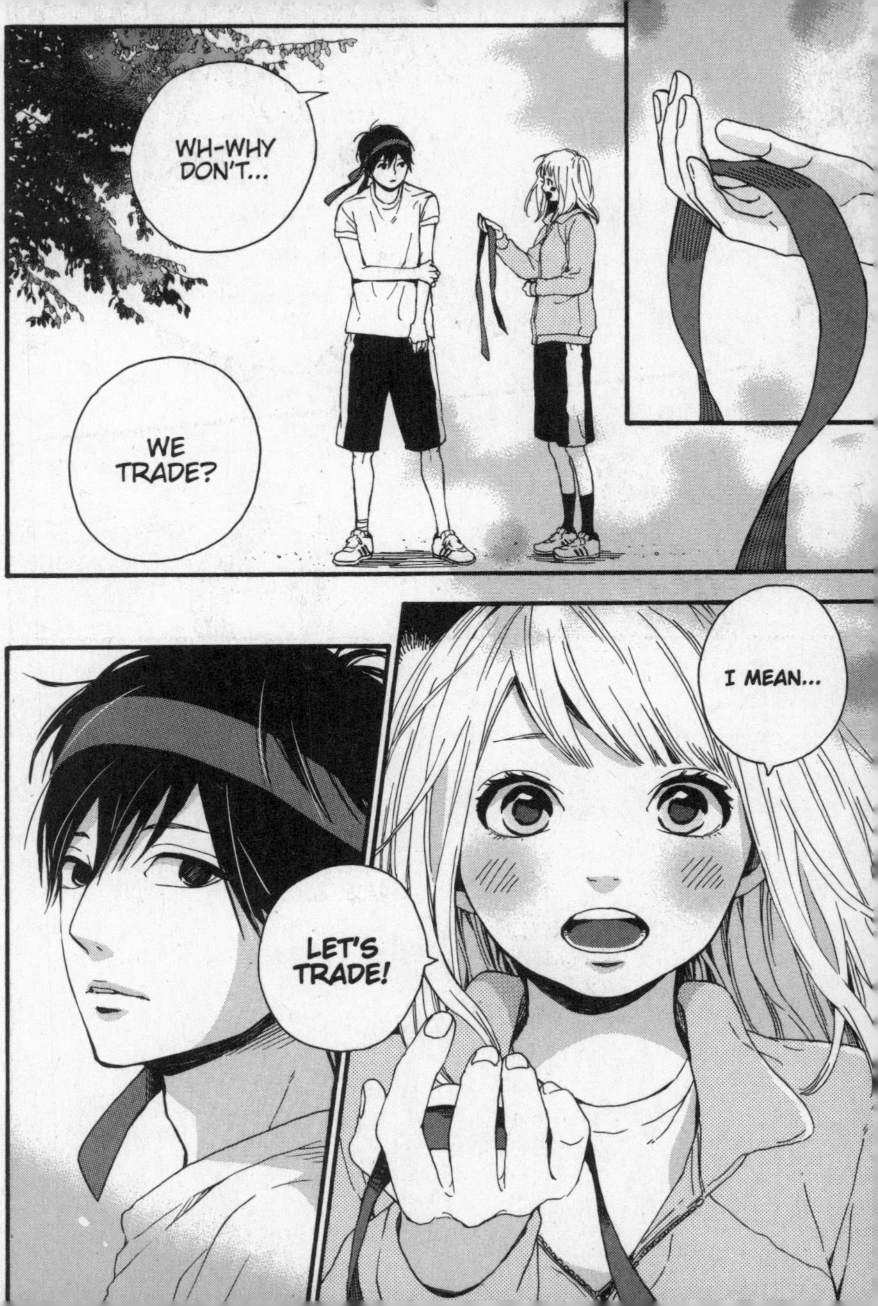
WH-WHY DON'T...
WE TRADE?
I MEAN...
LET'S TRADE!

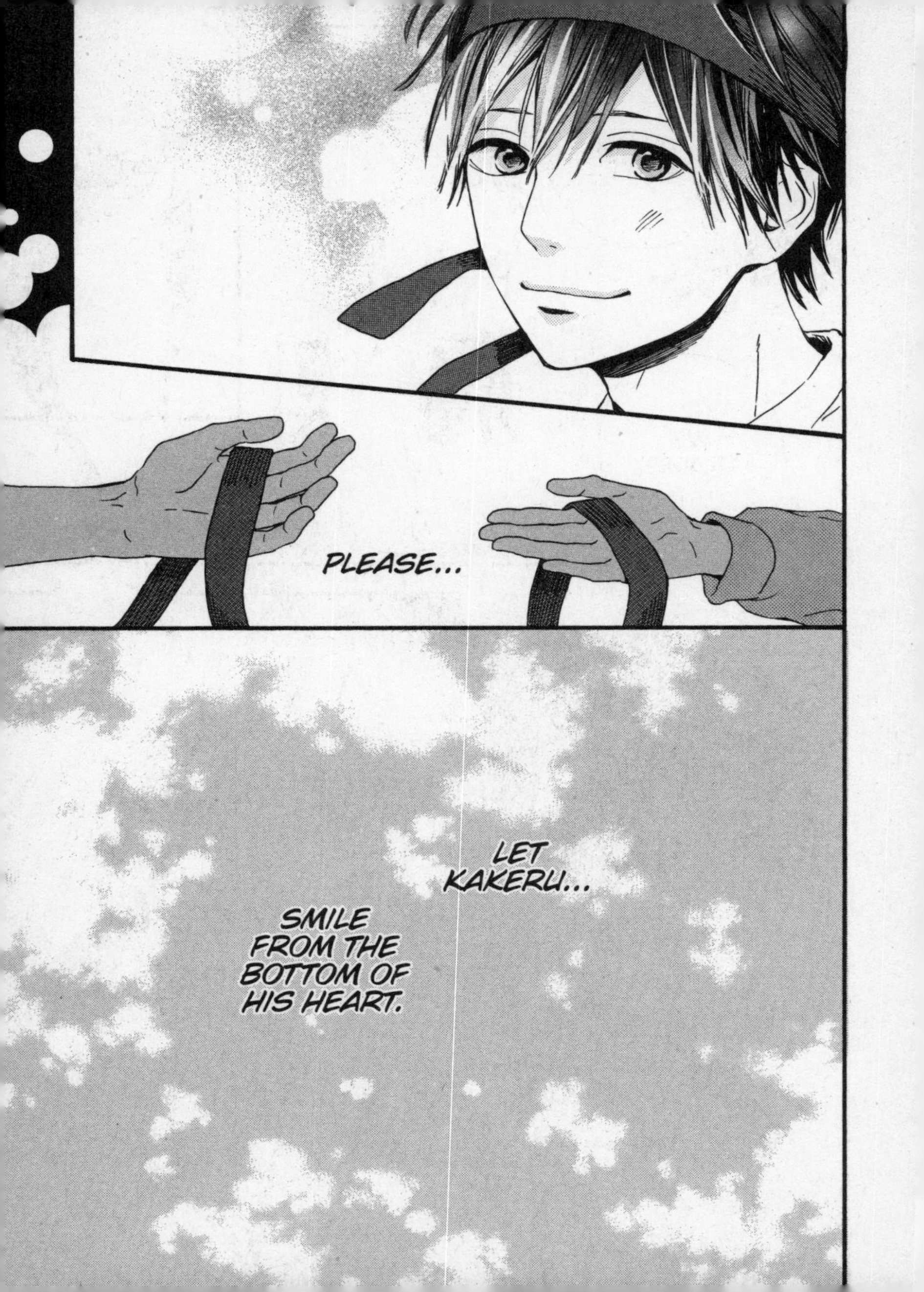
PLEASE...
LET KAKERU...
SMILE FROM THE BOTTOM OF HIS HEART.

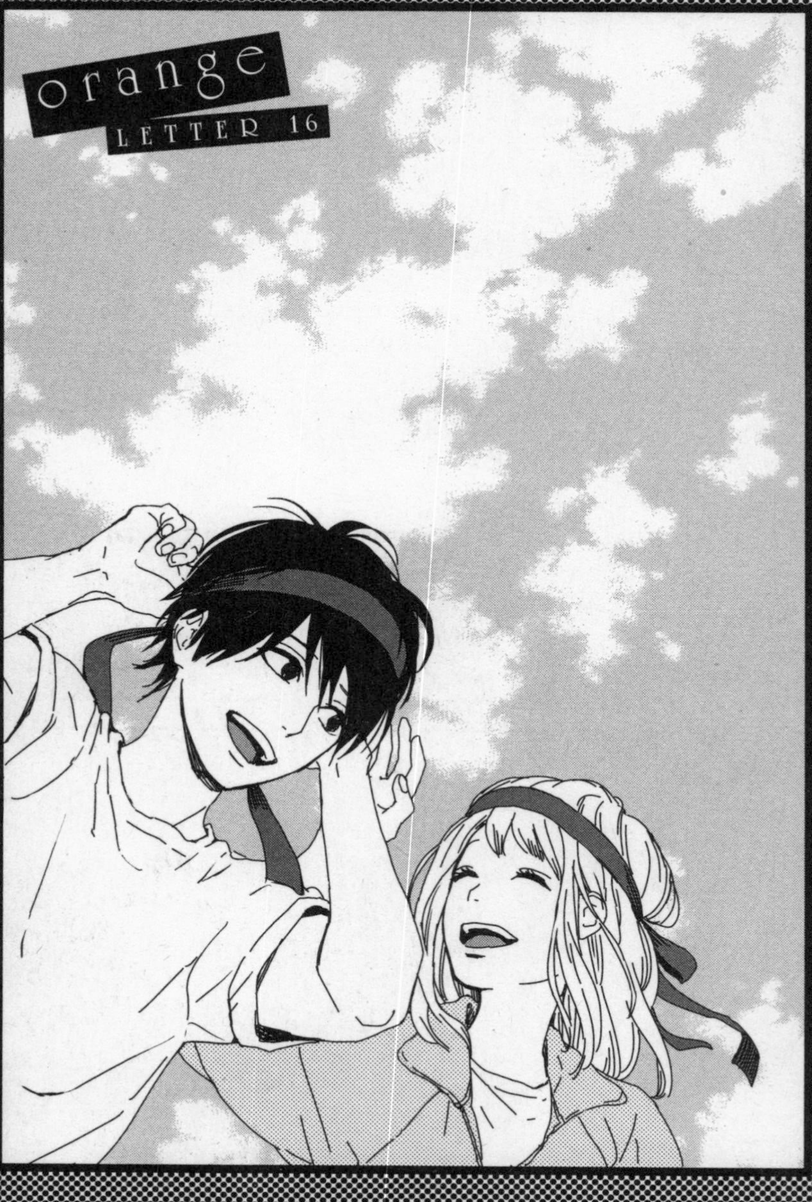
orange
LETTER 16

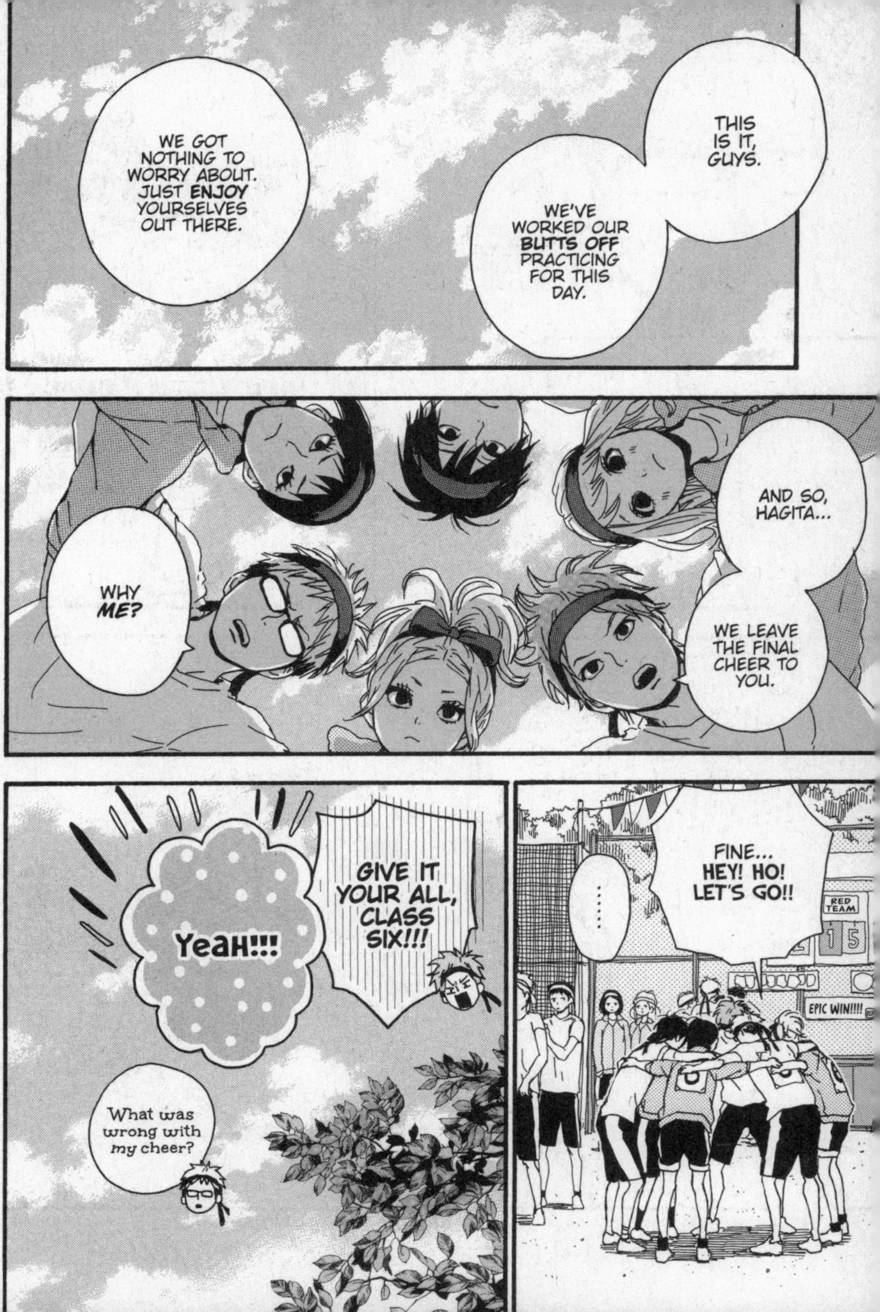
THIS IS IT, GUYS.
WE'VE WORKED OUR BUTTS OFF PRACTICING FOR THIS DAY.
WE GOT NOTHING TO WORRY ABOUT. JUST ENJOY YOURSELVES OUT THERE.
AND SO, HAGITA...
WE LEAVE THE FINAL CHEER TO YOU.
WHY ME?
FINE... HEY! HO! LET'S GO!!
......
RED TEAM
15
EPIC WIN!!!!
GIVE IT YOUR ALL, CLASS SIX!!!
Yeah!!!
What was wrong with my cheer?

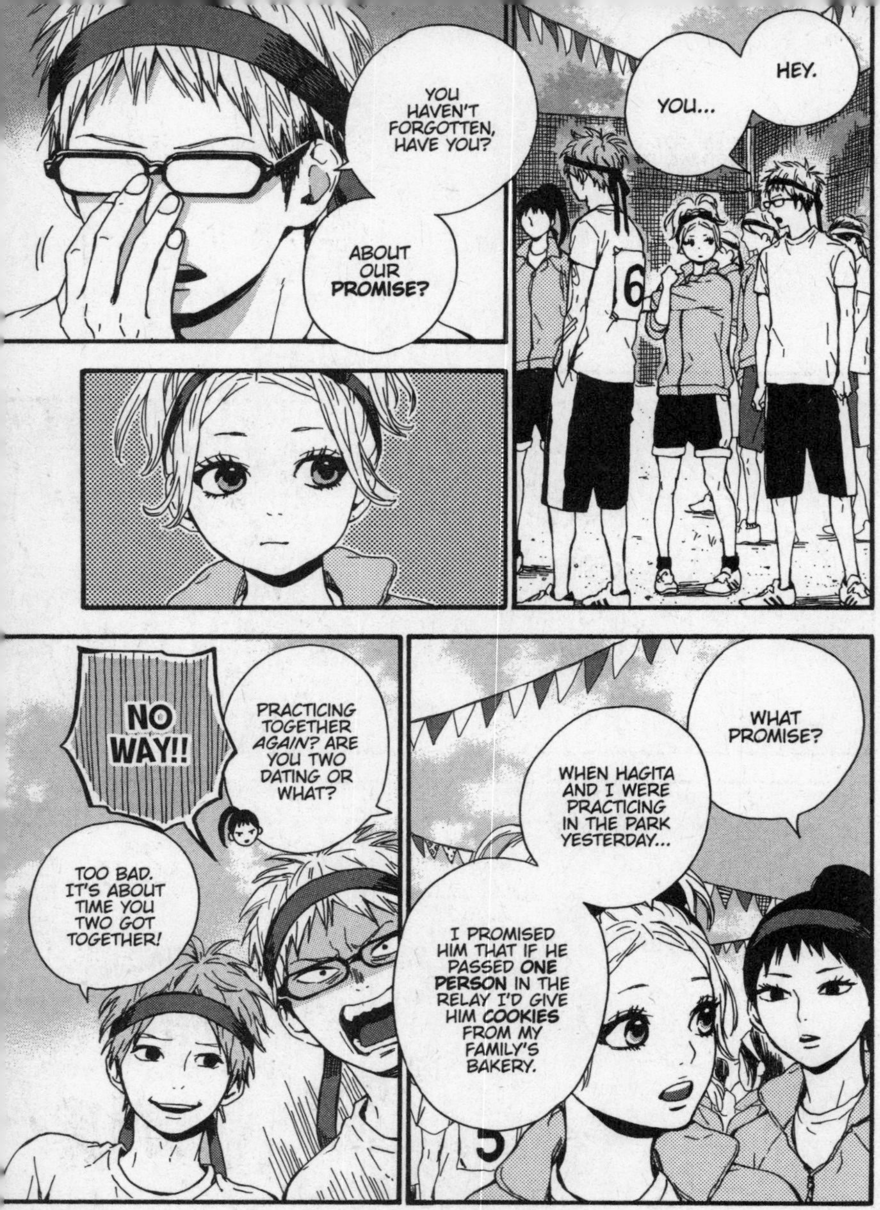
HEY.
YOU...
YOU HAVEN'T FORGOTTEN, HAVE YOU?
ABOUT OUR **PROMISE?**
WHAT PROMISE?
WHEN HAGITA AND I WERE PRACTICING IN THE PARK YESTERDAY...
I PROMISED HIM THAT IF HE PASSED **ONE PERSON** IN THE RELAY I'D GIVE HIM **COOKIES** FROM MY FAMILY'S BAKERY.
PRACTICING TOGETHER *AGAIN?* ARE YOU TWO DATING OR WHAT?
NO WAY!!
TOO BAD. IT'S ABOUT TIME YOU TWO GOT TOGETHER!

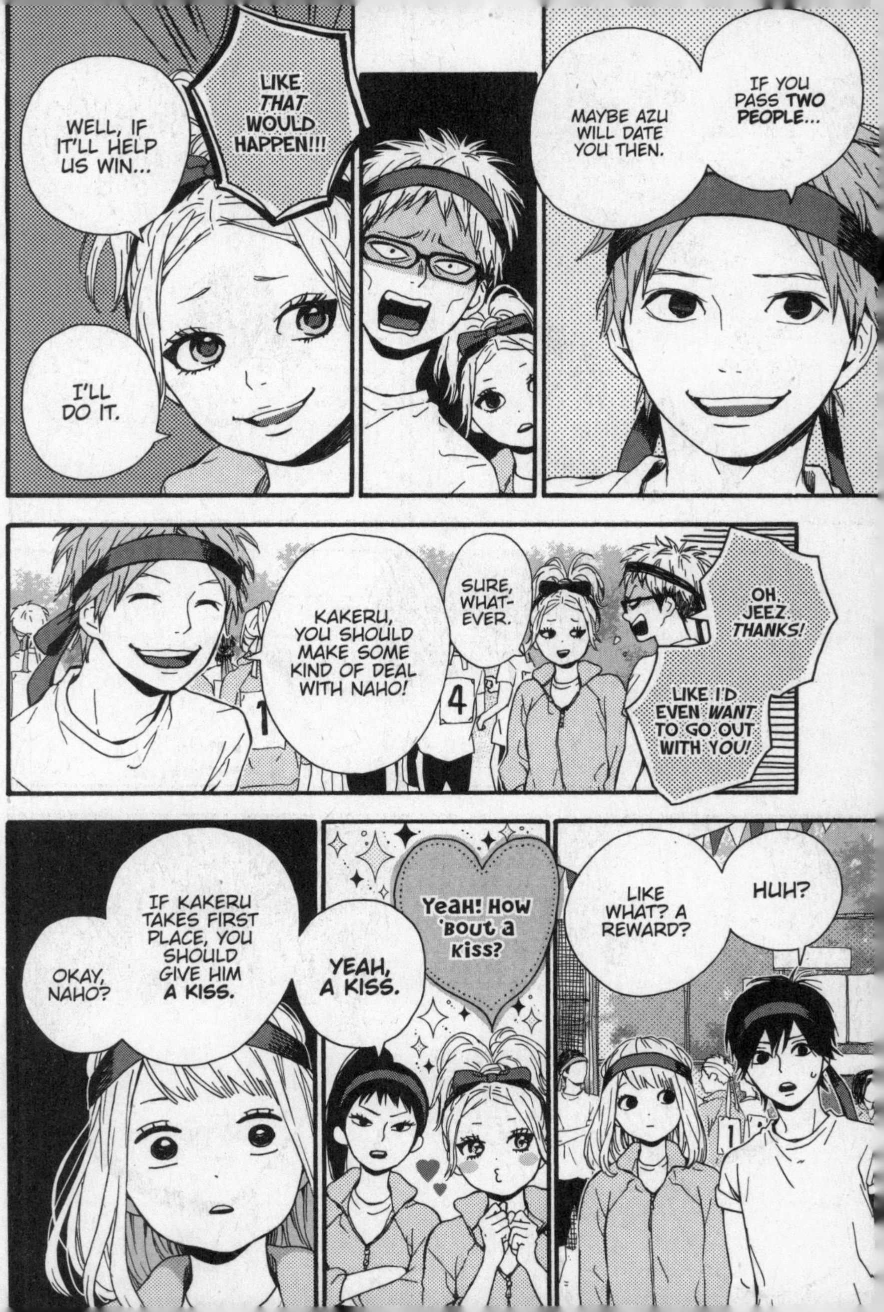
IF YOU PASS TWO PEOPLE...
MAYBE AZU WILL DATE YOU THEN.
LIKE THAT WOULD HAPPEN!!!
WELL, IF IT'LL HELP US WIN...
I'LL DO IT.
SURE, WHATEVER.
OH, JEEZ. THANKS!
LIKE I'D EVEN WANT TO GO OUT WITH YOU!
KAKERU, YOU SHOULD MAKE SOME KIND OF DEAL WITH NAHO!
HUH?
LIKE WHAT? A REWARD?
Yeah! How 'bout a kiss?
YEAH, A KISS.
IF KAKERU TAKES FIRST PLACE, YOU SHOULD GIVE HIM A KISS.
OKAY, NAHO?

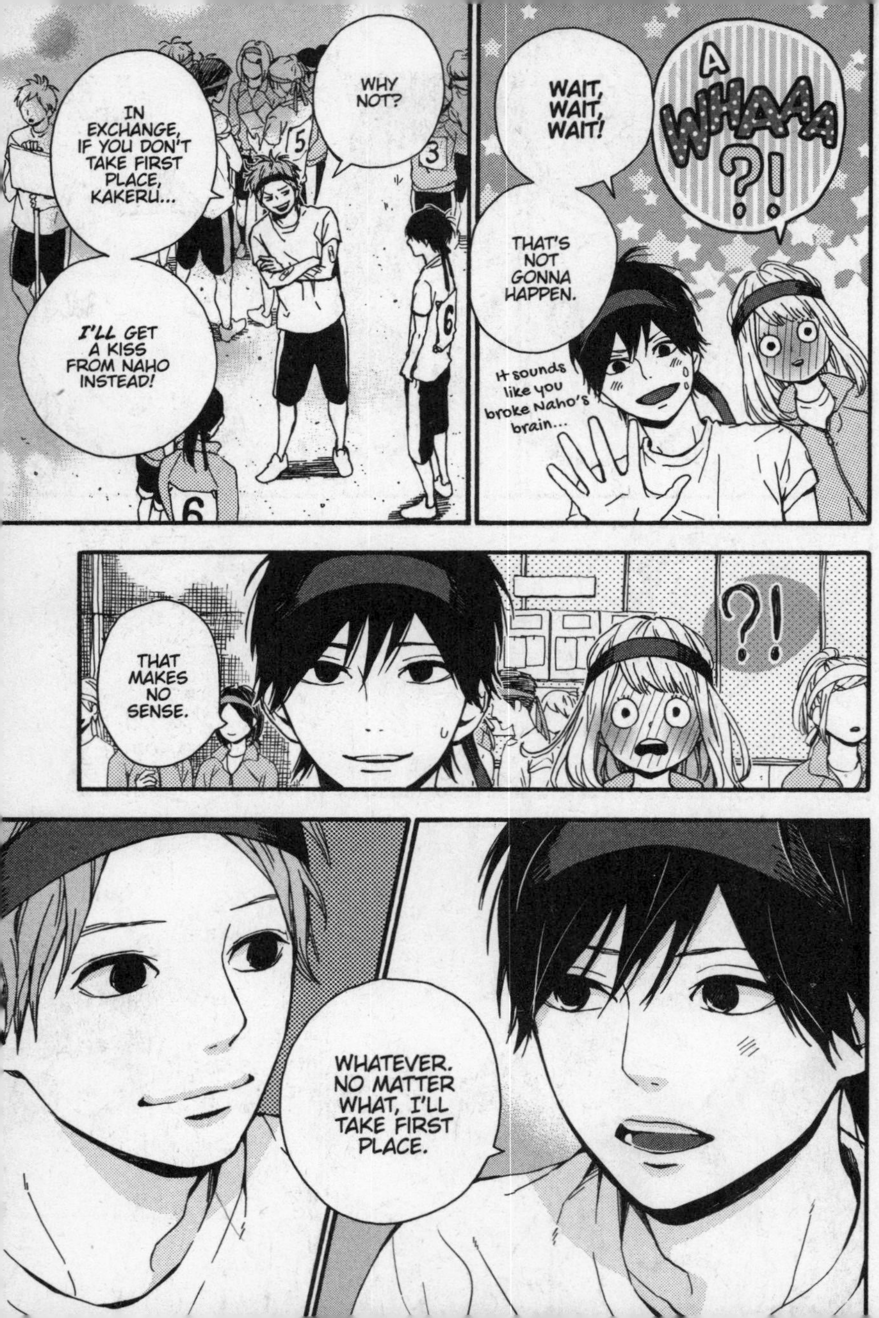
A WHAAA ?!
WAIT, WAIT, WAIT!
THAT'S NOT GONNA HAPPEN.
It sounds like you broke Naho's brain...
WHY NOT?
IN EXCHANGE, IF YOU DON'T TAKE FIRST PLACE, KAKERU...
I'LL GET A KISS FROM NAHO INSTEAD!
5
3
6
6
?!
THAT MAKES NO SENSE.
WHATEVER. NO MATTER WHAT, I'LL TAKE FIRST PLACE.

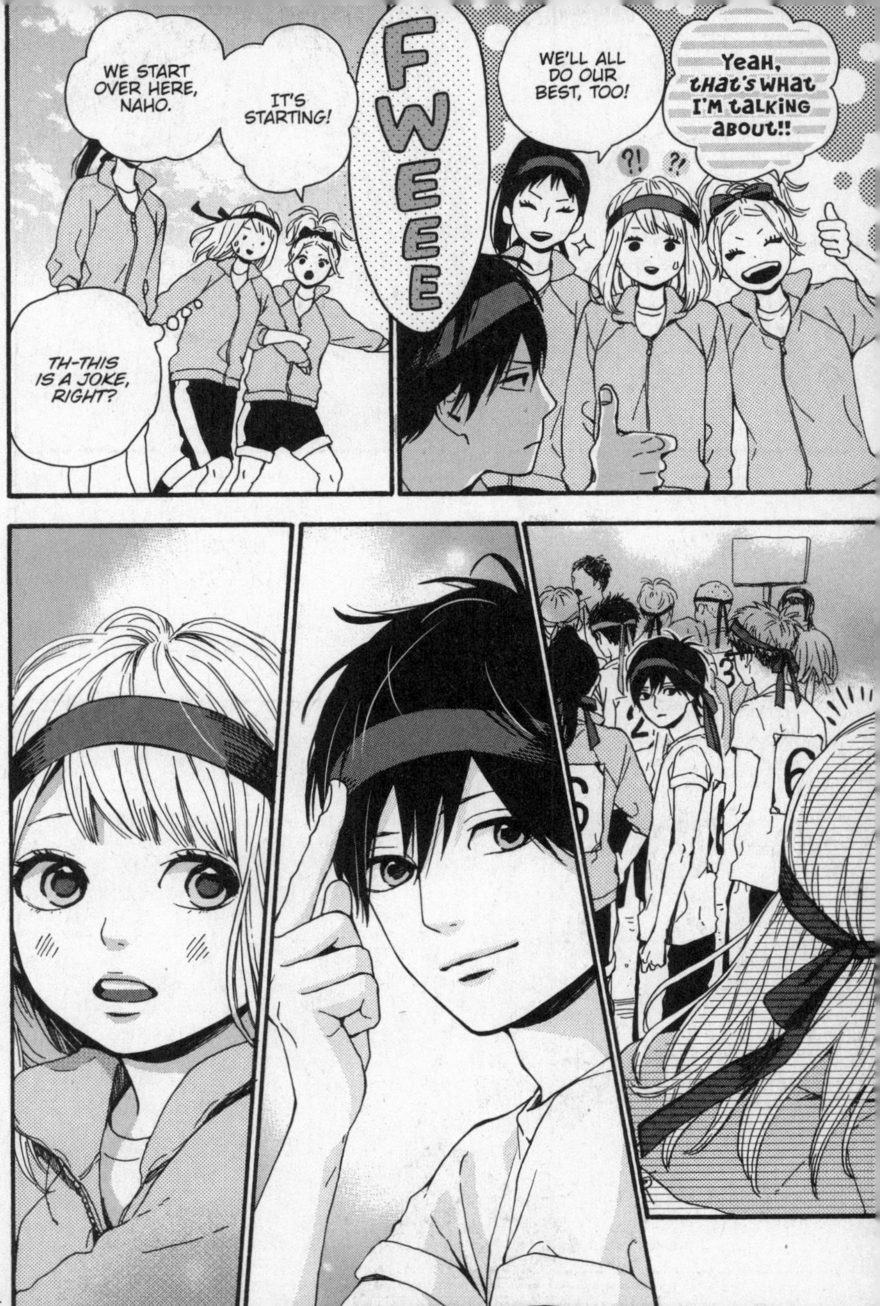
Yeah, that's what I'm talking about!!
?!
?!
WE'LL ALL DO OUR BEST, TOO!
FWEEE
IT'S STARTING!
WE START OVER HERE, NAHO.
TH-THIS IS A JOKE, RIGHT?

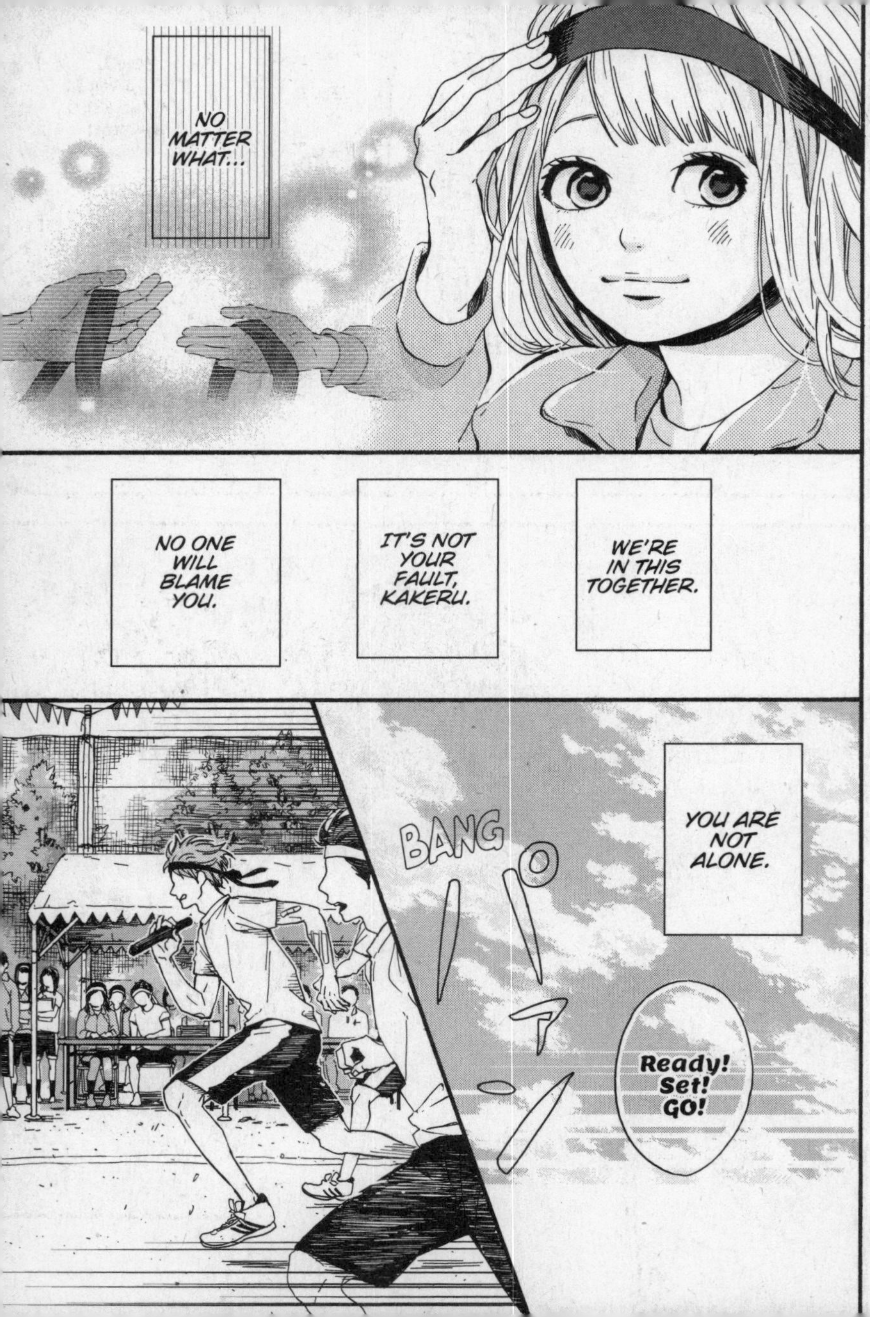
NO MATTER WHAT...
WE'RE IN THIS TOGETHER.
IT'S NOT YOUR FAULT, KAKERU.
NO ONE WILL BLAME YOU.
YOU ARE NOT ALONE.
Ready! Set! GO!
BANG

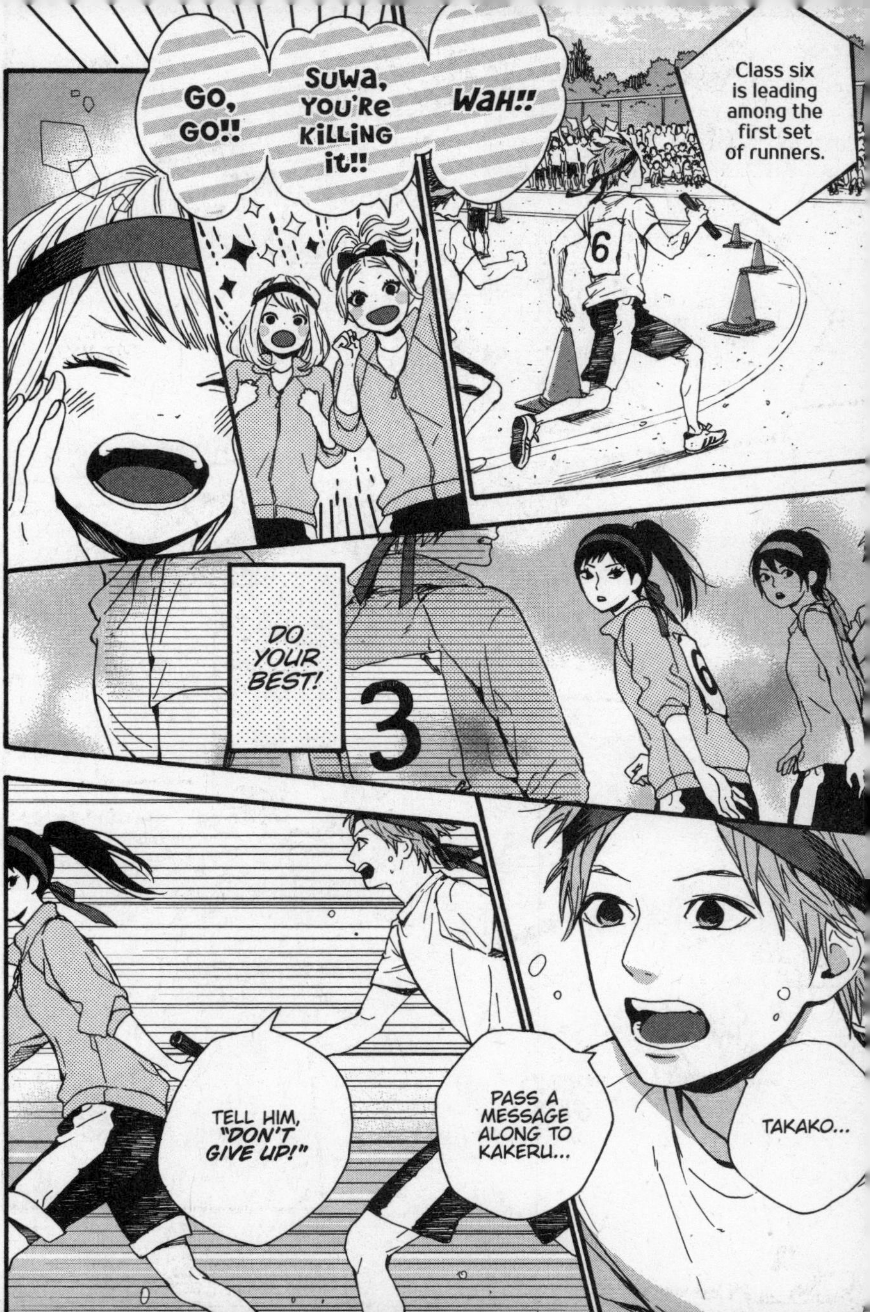
Class six is leading among the first set of runners.
GO, GO!!
SUWA, YOU'RE KILLING IT!!
WAH!!
DO YOUR BEST!
TAKAKO...
PASS A MESSAGE ALONG TO KAKERU...
TELL HIM, "DON'T GIVE UP!"

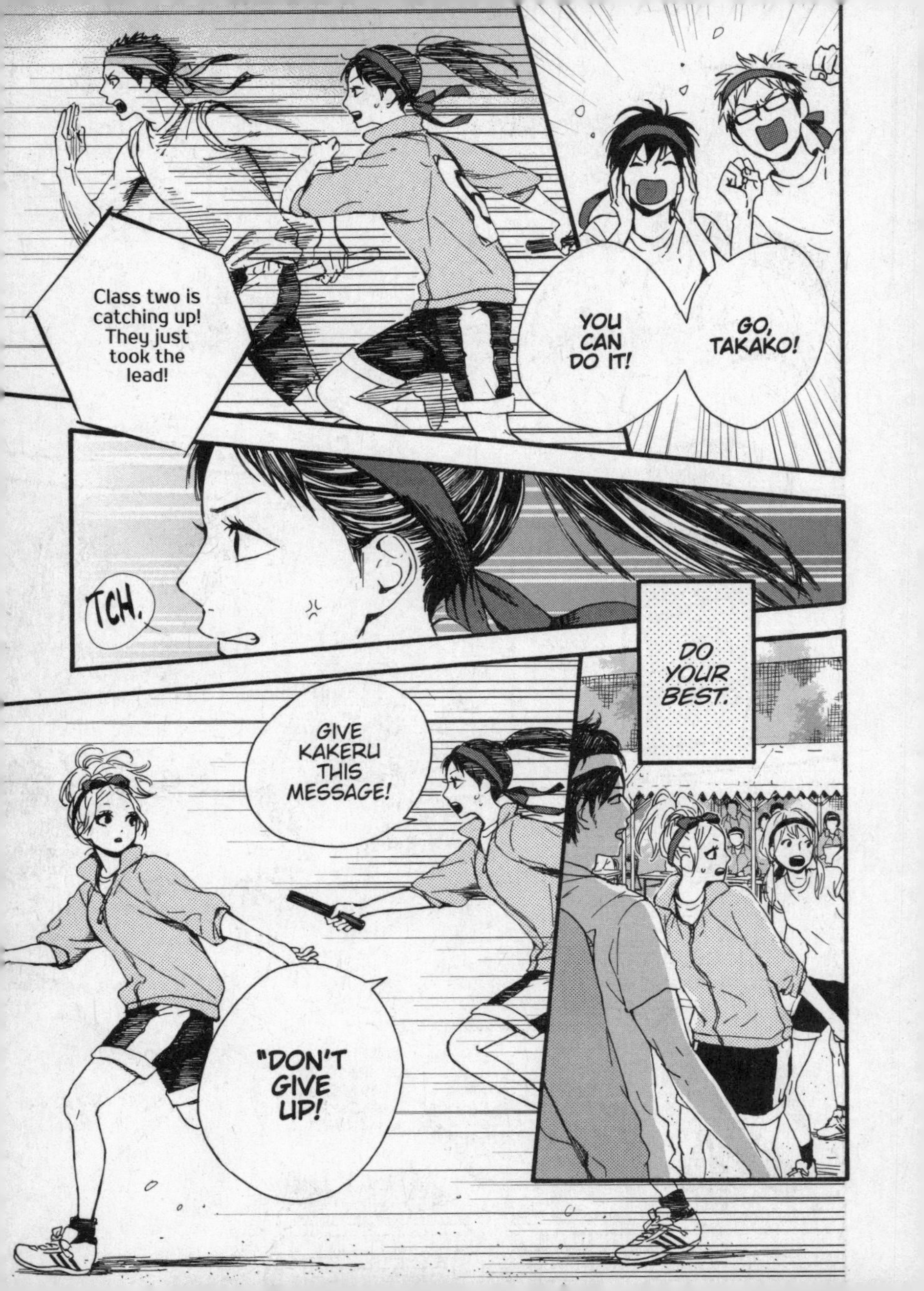
GO, TAKAKO!
YOU CAN DO IT!
Class two is catching up! They just took the lead!
TCH.
DO YOUR BEST.
GIVE KAKERU THIS MESSAGE!
"DON'T GIVE UP!

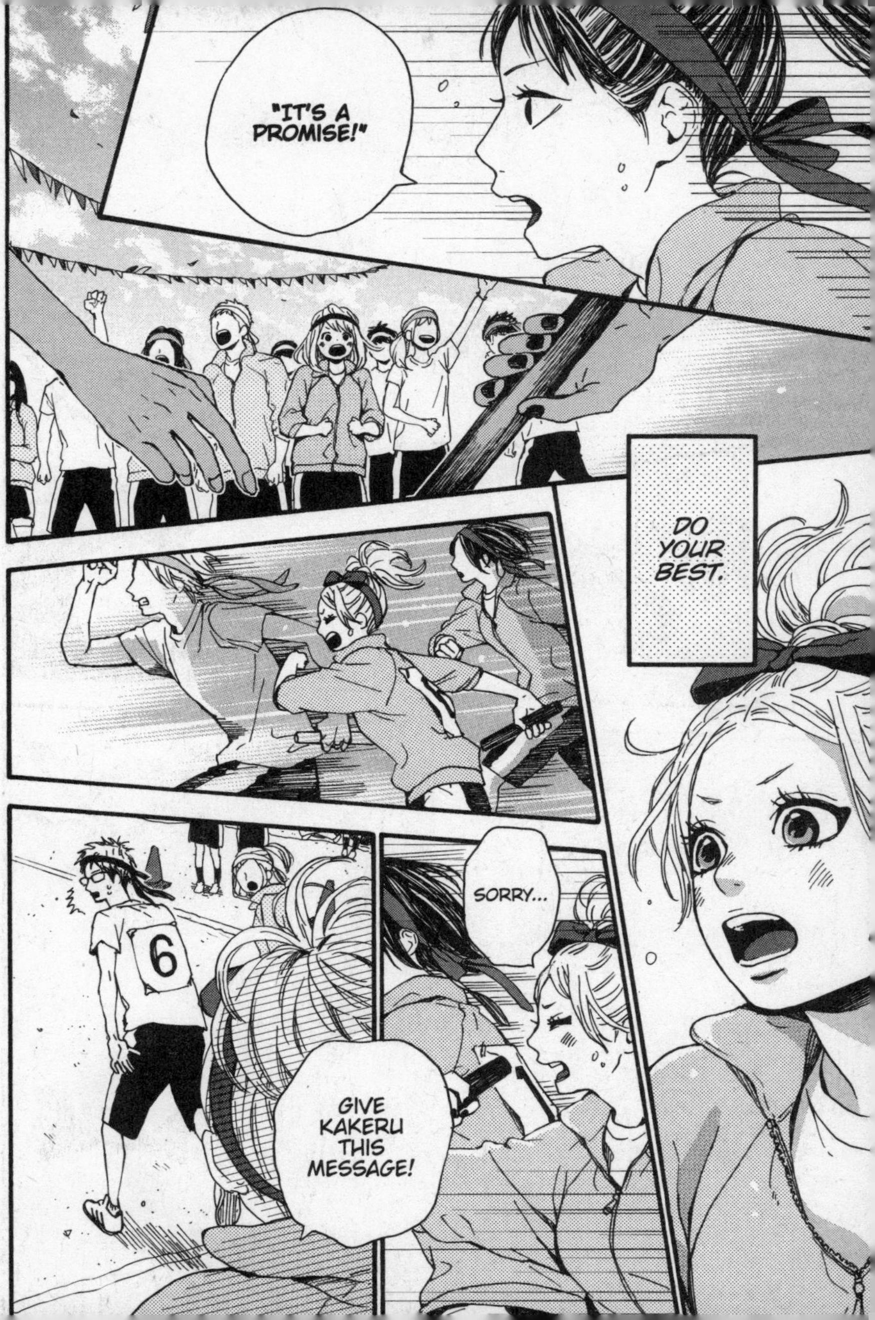
"IT'S A PROMISE!"
DO YOUR BEST.
SORRY...
GIVE KAKERU THIS MESSAGE!

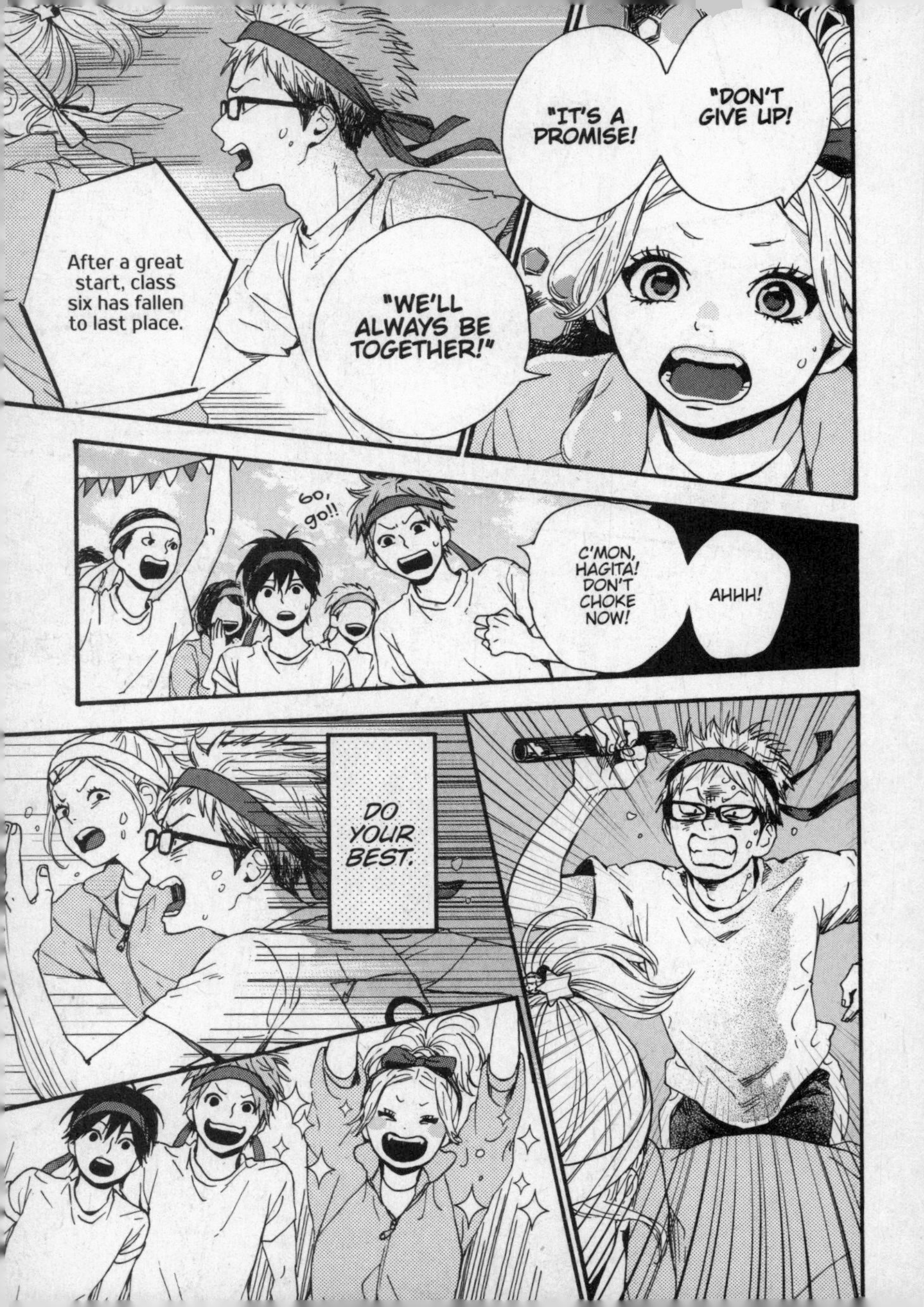
"DON'T GIVE UP!
"IT'S A PROMISE!
"WE'LL ALWAYS BE TOGETHER!"
After a great start, class six has fallen to last place.
AHHH!
C'MON, HAGITA! DON'T CHOKE NOW!
Go, go!!
DO YOUR BEST.

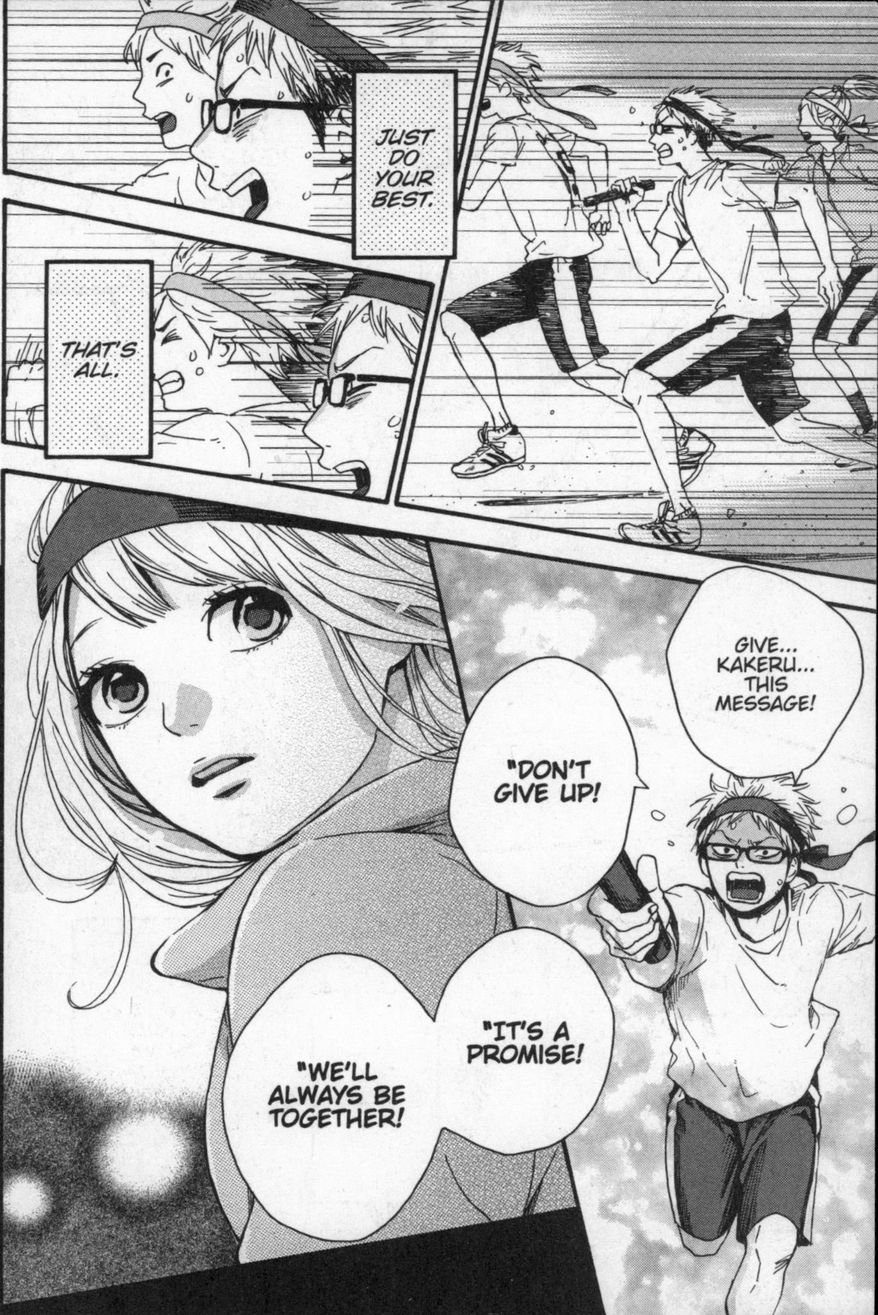
JUST DO YOUR BEST.
THAT'S ALL.
GIVE... KAKERU... THIS MESSAGE!
"DON'T GIVE UP!
"IT'S A PROMISE!
"WE'LL ALWAYS BE TOGETHER!

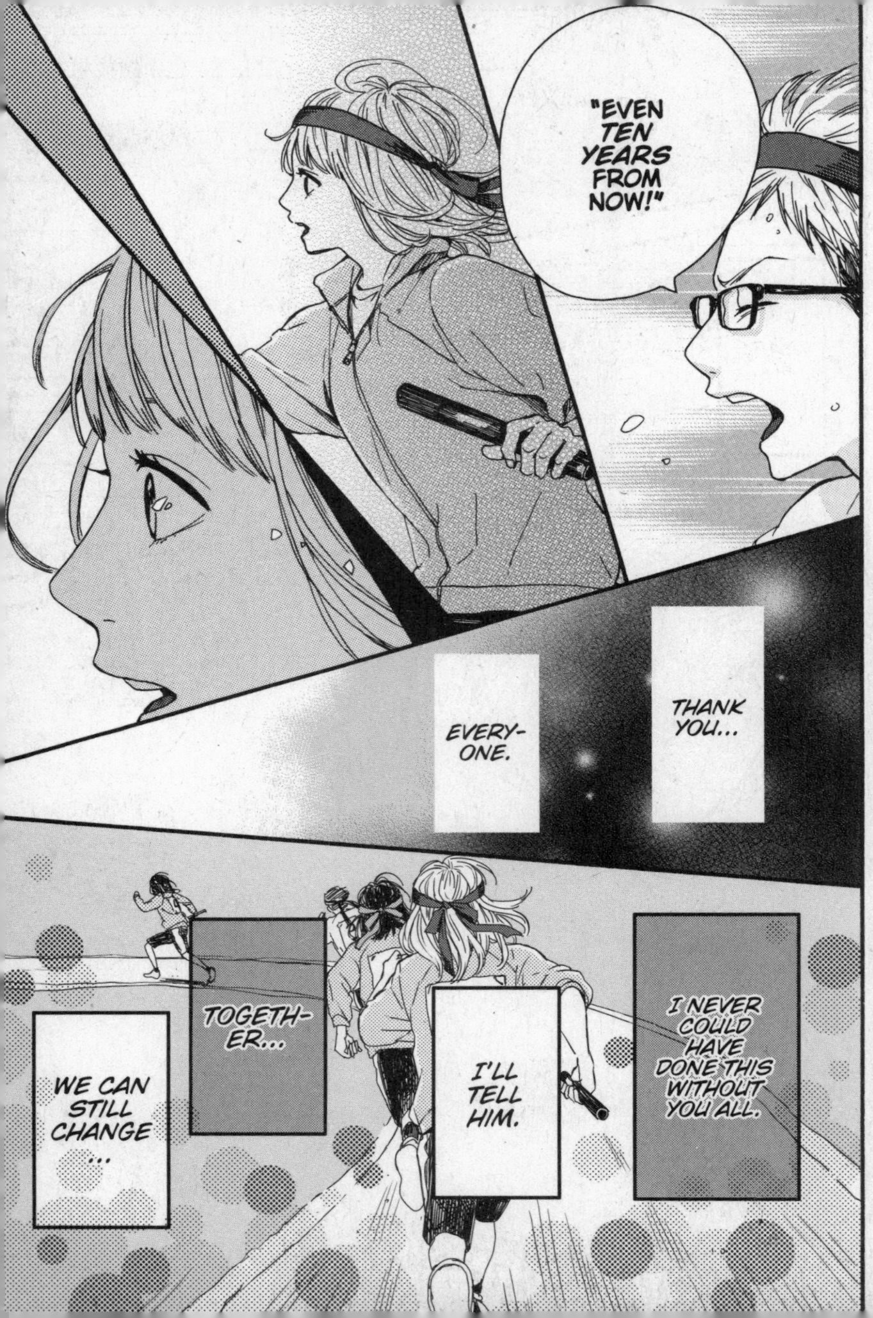
"EVEN TEN YEARS FROM NOW!"
THANK YOU...
EVERY-ONE.
I NEVER COULD HAVE DONE THIS WITHOUT YOU ALL.
I'LL TELL HIM.
TOGETH-ER...
WE CAN STILL CHANGE ...

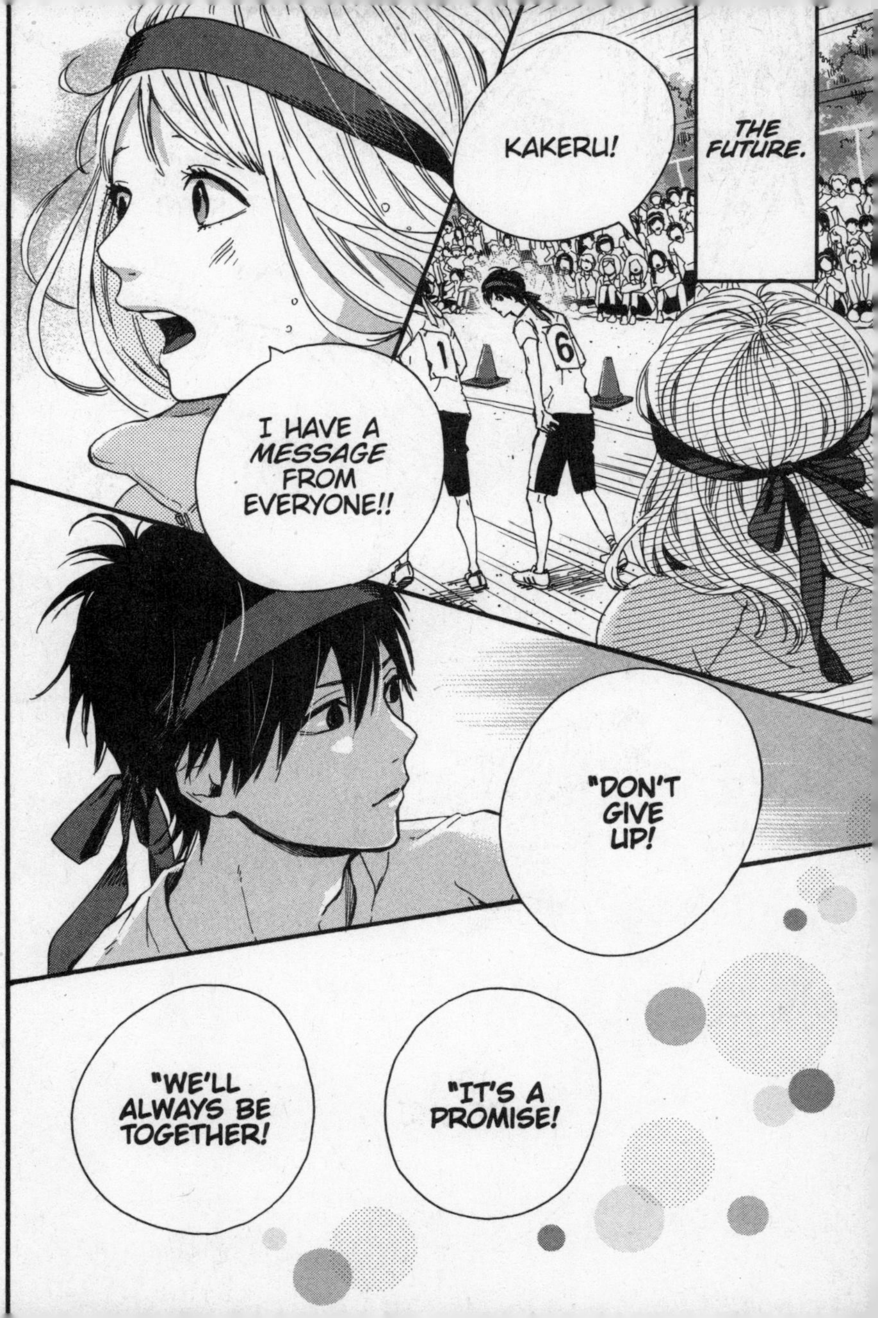
THE FUTURE.
KAKERU!
I HAVE A MESSAGE FROM EVERYONE!!
"DON'T GIVE UP!
"IT'S A PROMISE!
"WE'LL ALWAYS BE TOGETHER!

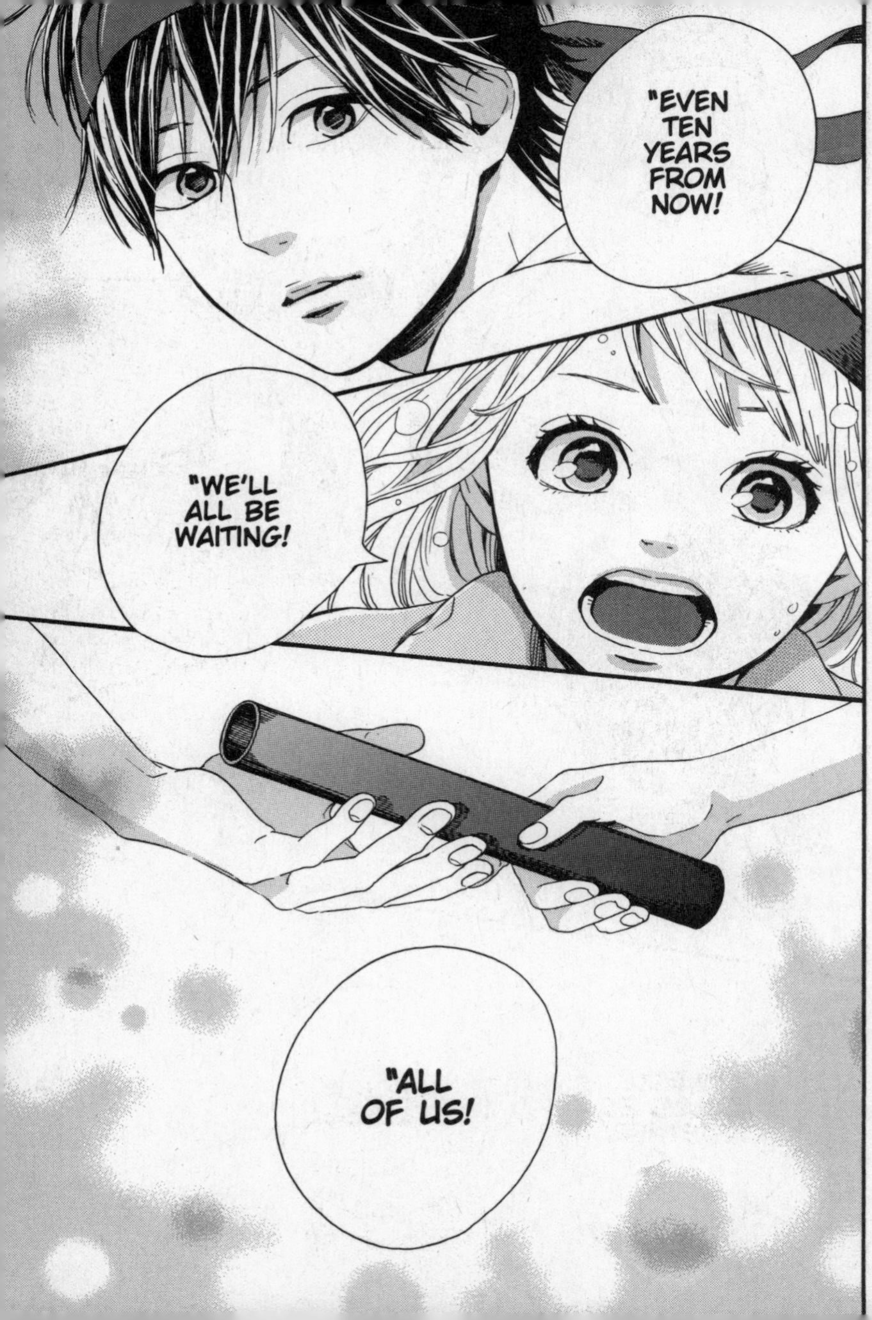
"EVEN TEN YEARS FROM NOW!
"WE'LL ALL BE WAITING!
"ALL OF US!

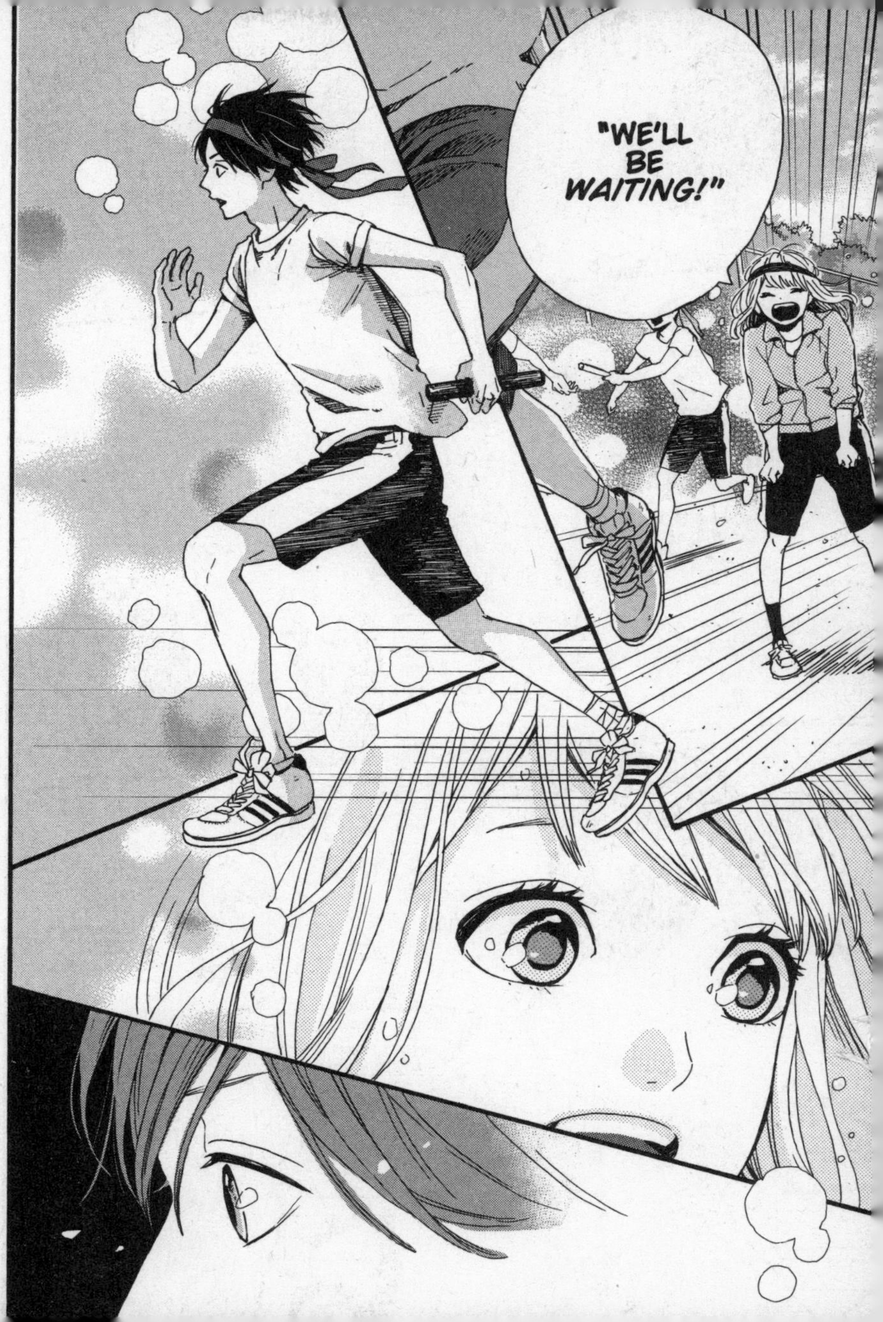
"WE'LL BE WAITING!"

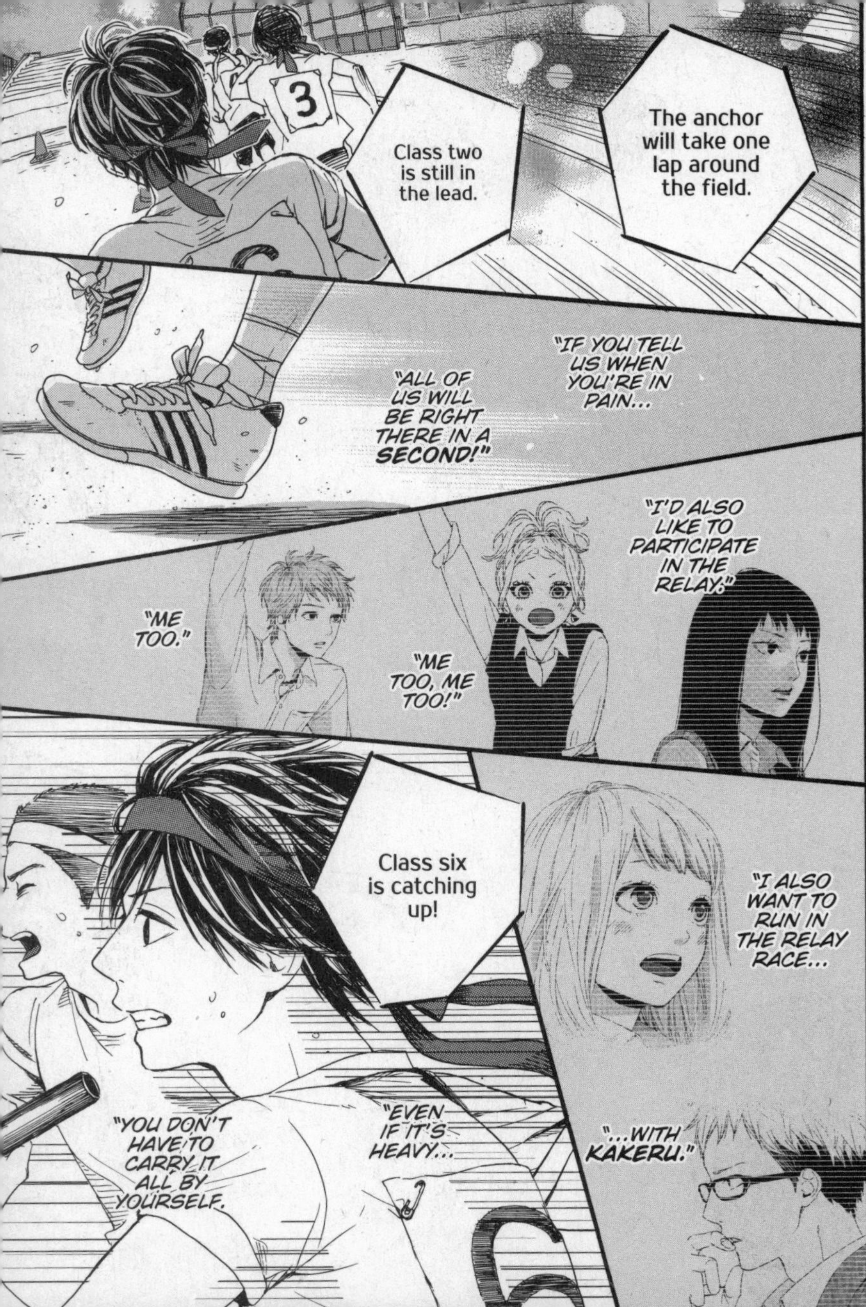
The anchor will take one lap around the field.
Class two is still in the lead.
"IF YOU TELL US WHEN YOU'RE IN PAIN...
"ALL OF US WILL BE RIGHT THERE IN A SECOND!"
"I'D ALSO LIKE TO PARTICIPATE IN THE RELAY."
"ME TOO, ME TOO!"
"ME TOO."
"I ALSO WANT TO RUN IN THE RELAY RACE...
"...WITH KAKERU."
Class six is catching up!
"EVEN IF IT'S HEAVY...
"YOU DON'T HAVE TO CARRY IT ALL BY YOURSELF.

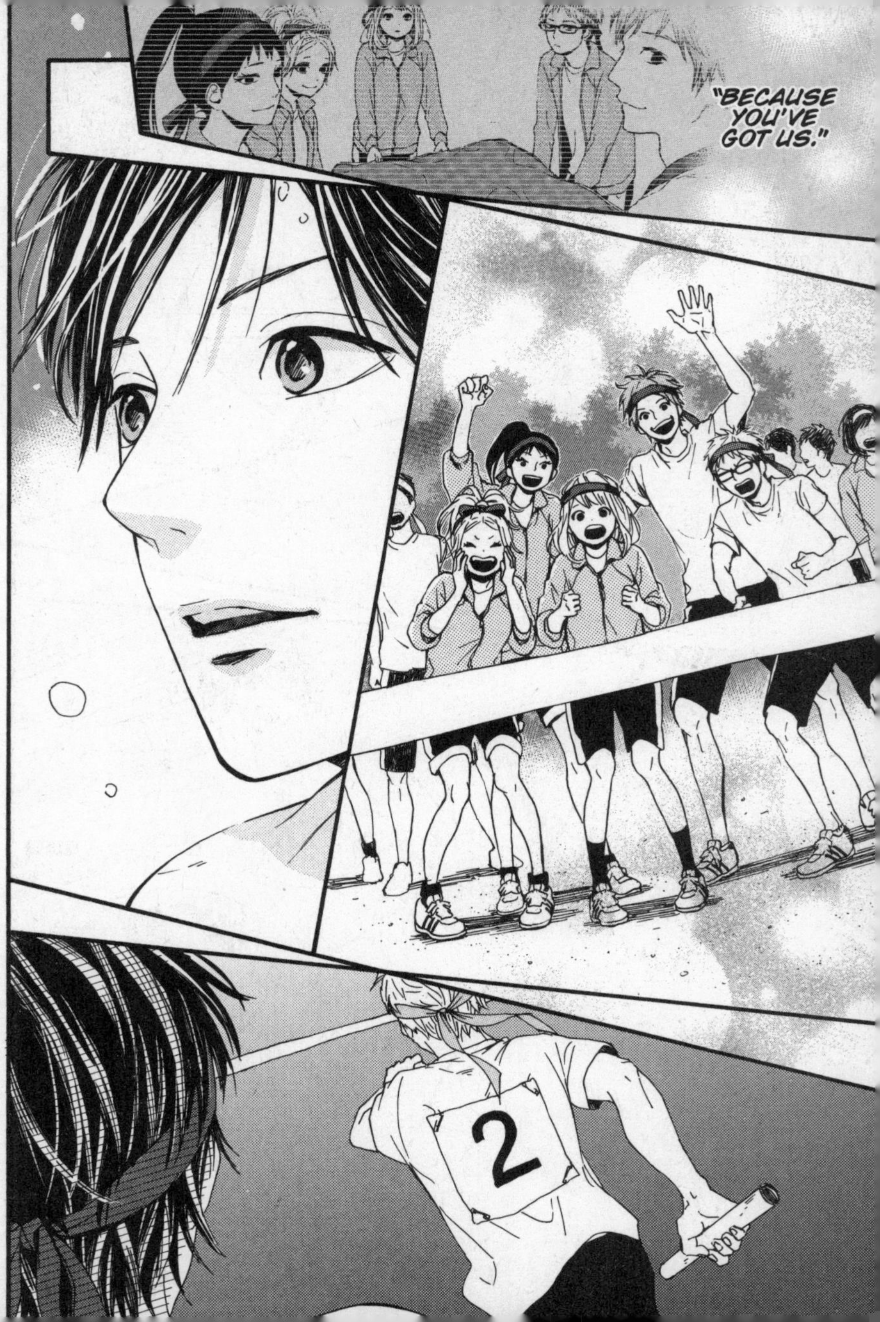
"BECAUSE YOU'VE GOT US."
2

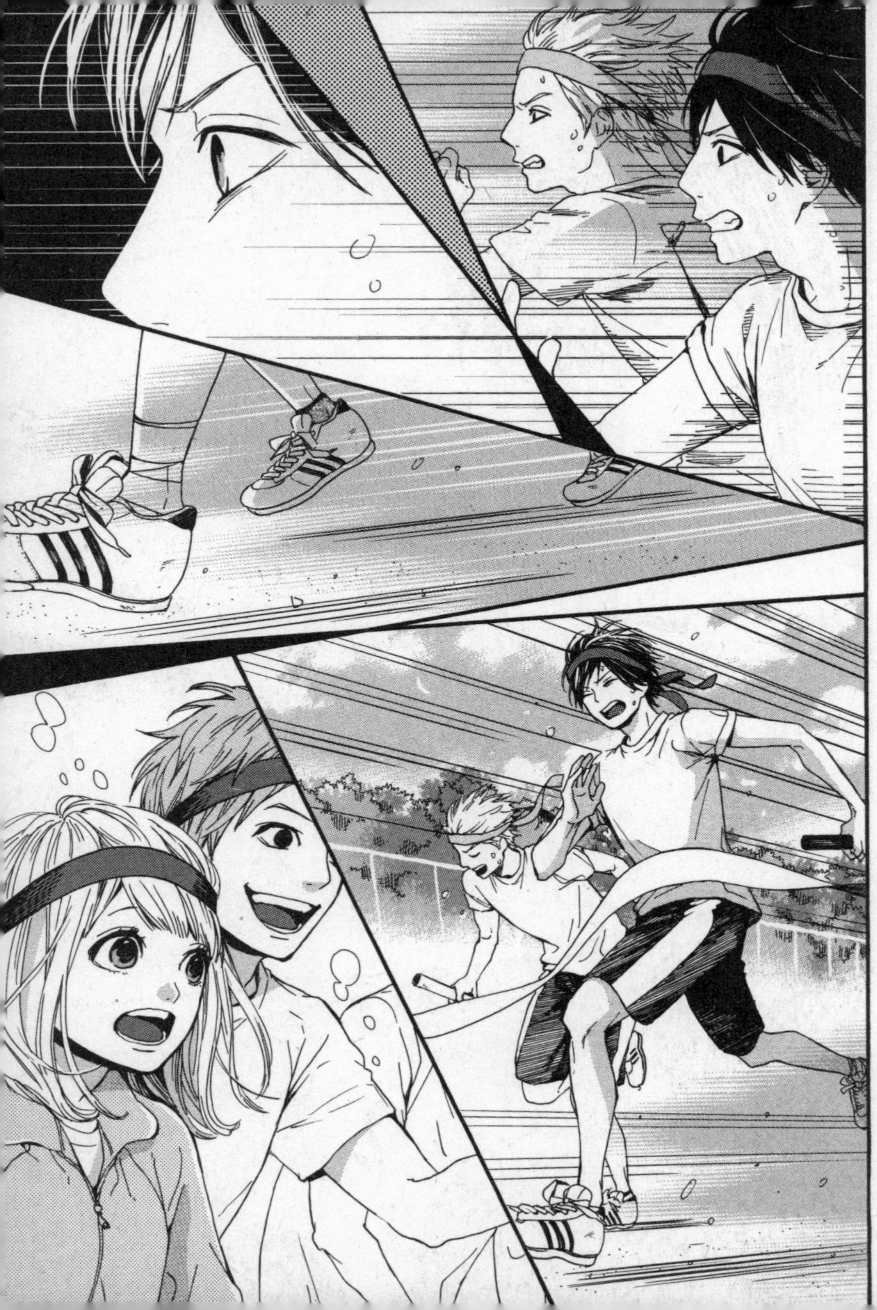

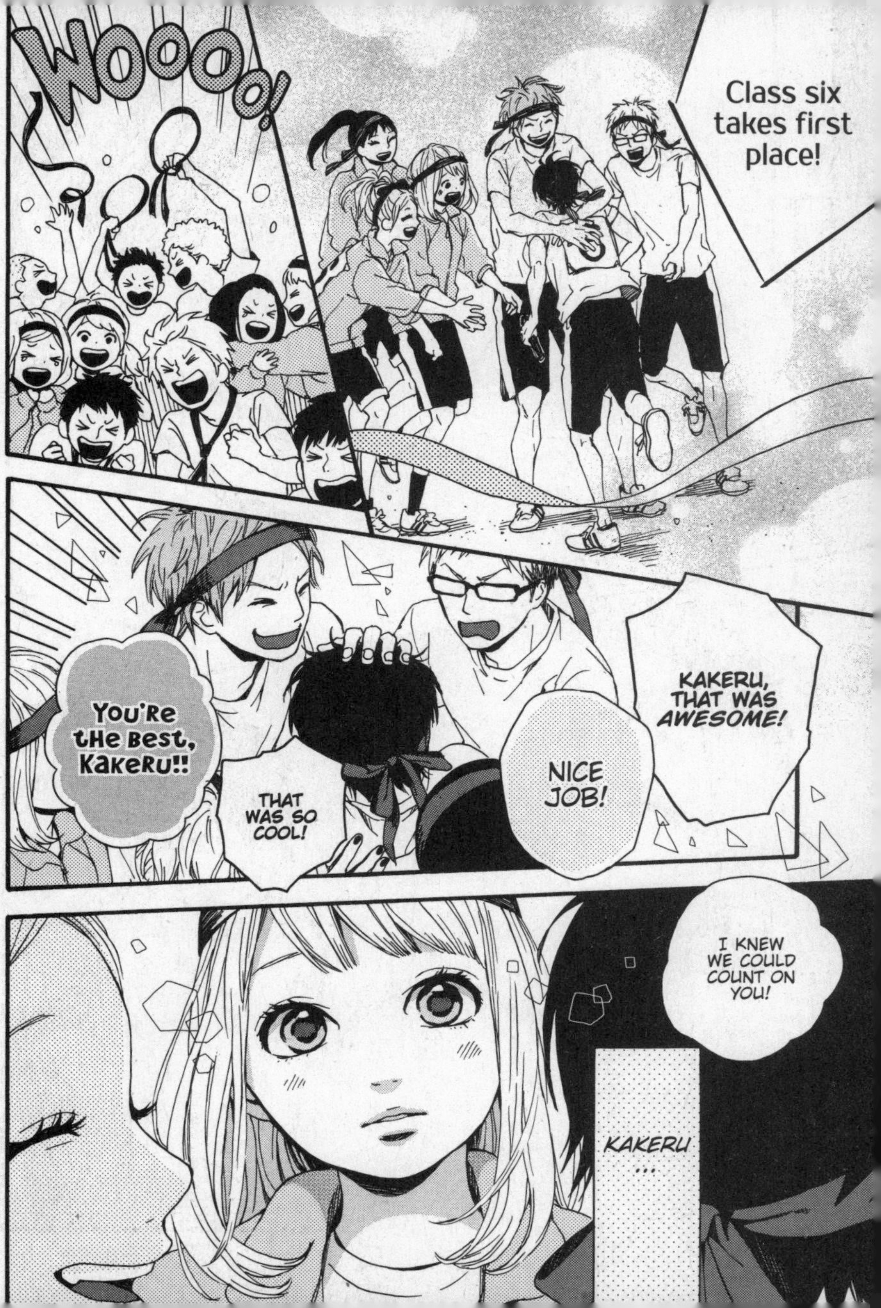
Class six takes first place!
WOOOO!
KAKERU, THAT WAS AWESOME!
NICE JOB!
THAT WAS SO COOL!
You're the best, Kakeru!!
I KNEW WE COULD COUNT ON YOU!
KAKERU ...

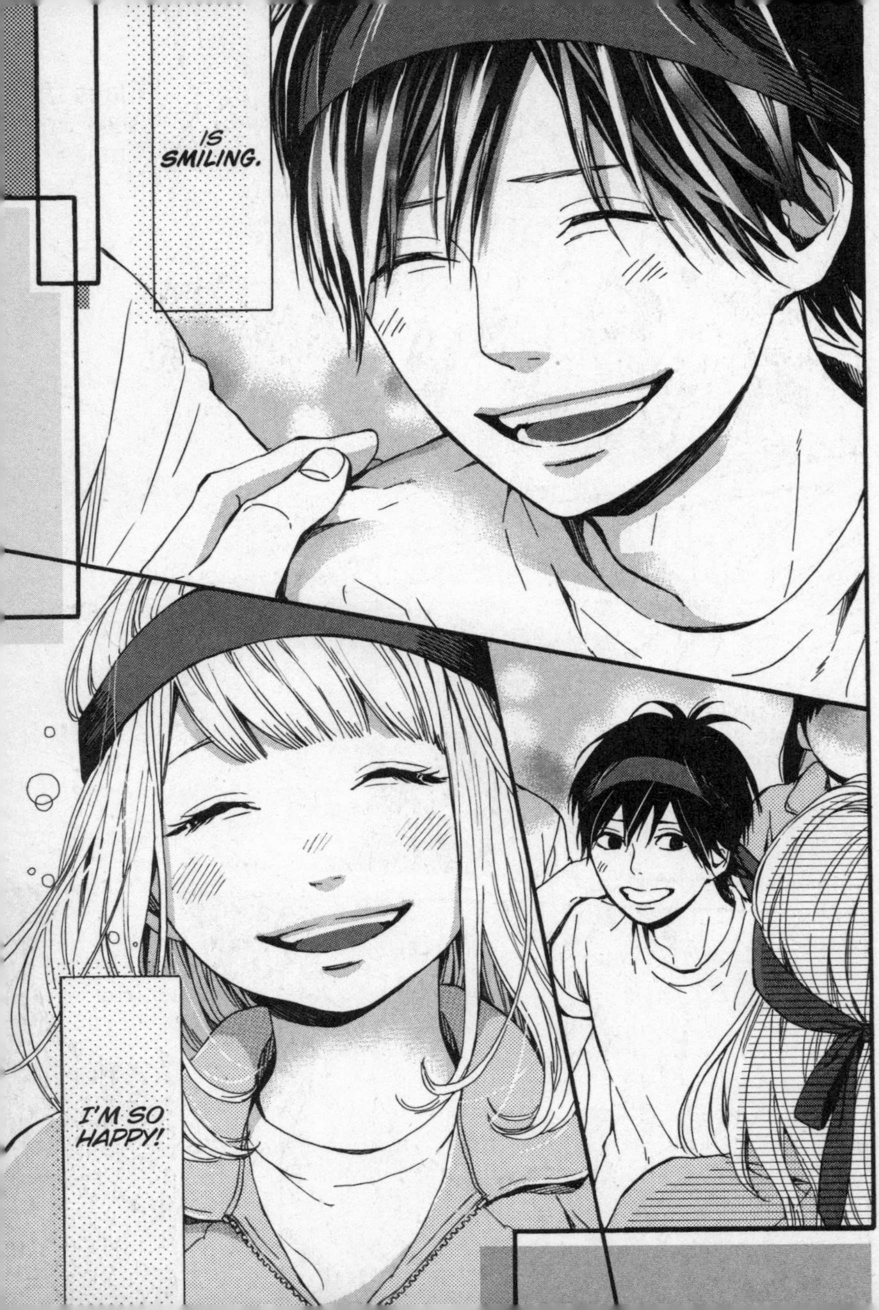
IS SMILING.
I'M SO HAPPY!

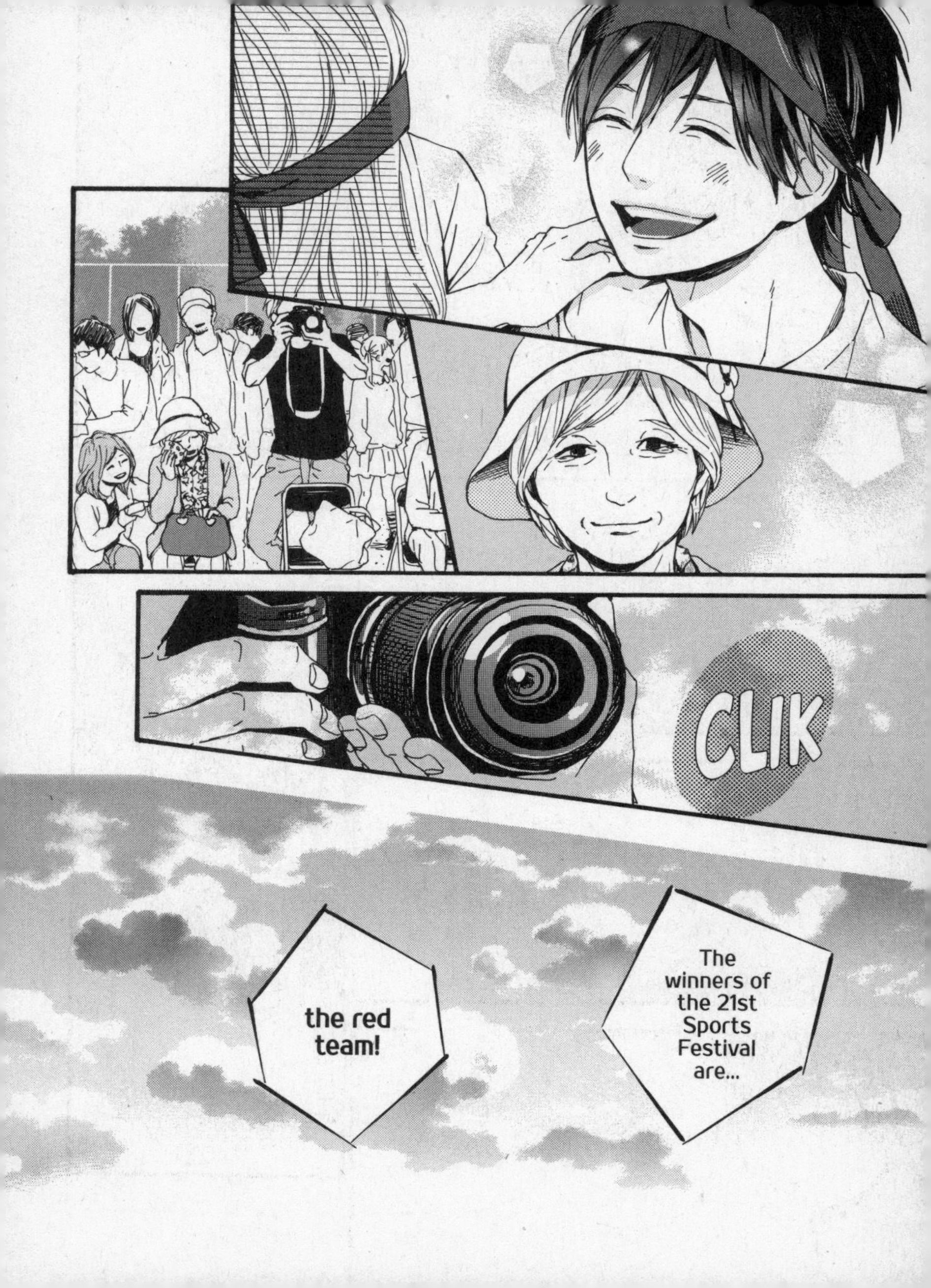
CLIK
The winners of the 21st Sports Festival are...
the red team!

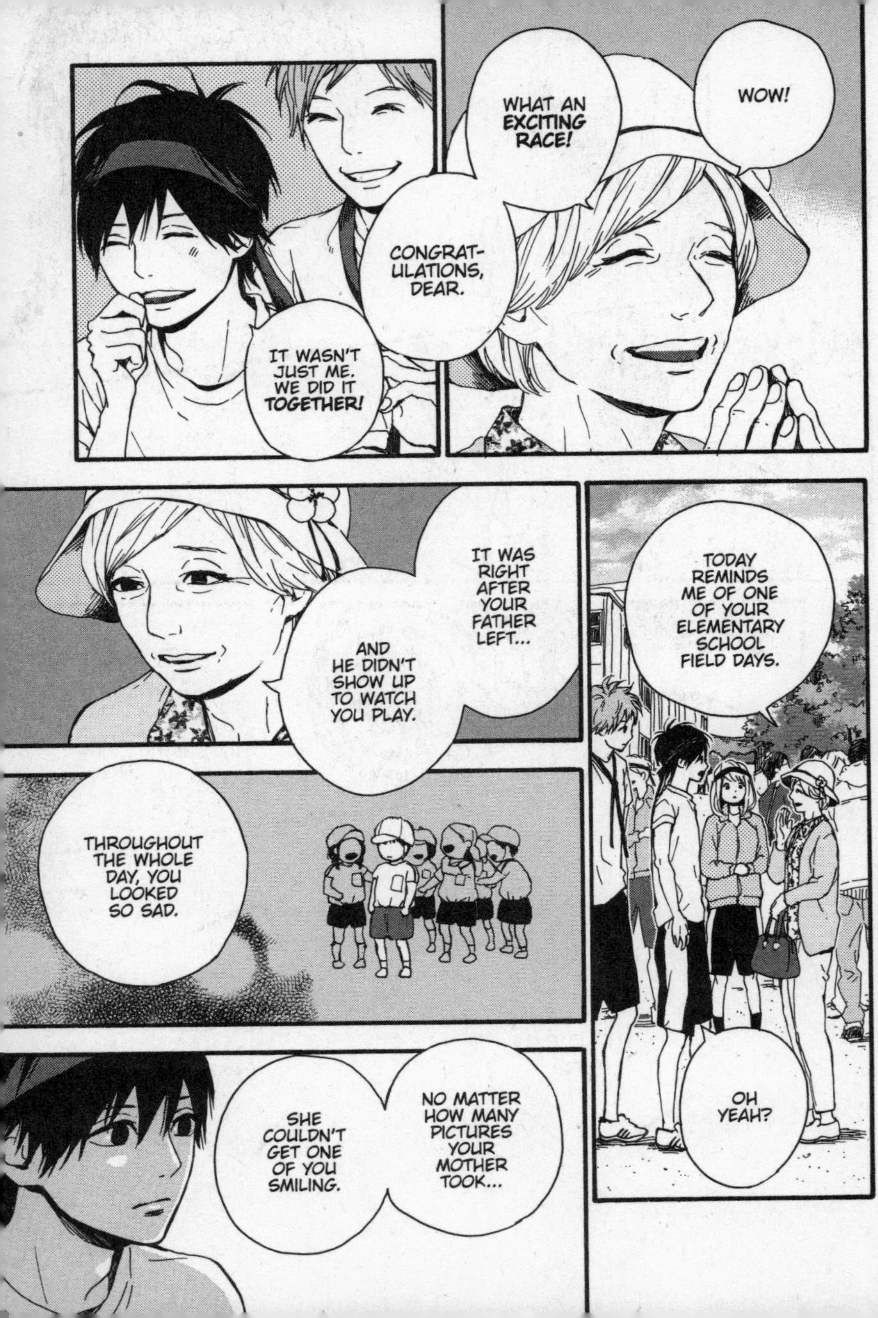
WOW!
WHAT AN EXCITING RACE!
CONGRATULATIONS, DEAR.
IT WASN'T JUST ME. WE DID IT TOGETHER!
TODAY REMINDS ME OF ONE OF YOUR ELEMENTARY SCHOOL FIELD DAYS.
OH YEAH?
IT WAS RIGHT AFTER YOUR FATHER LEFT...
AND HE DIDN'T SHOW UP TO WATCH YOU PLAY.
THROUGHOUT THE WHOLE DAY, YOU LOOKED SO SAD.
NO MATTER HOW MANY PICTURES YOUR MOTHER TOOK...
SHE COULDN'T GET ONE OF YOU SMILING.

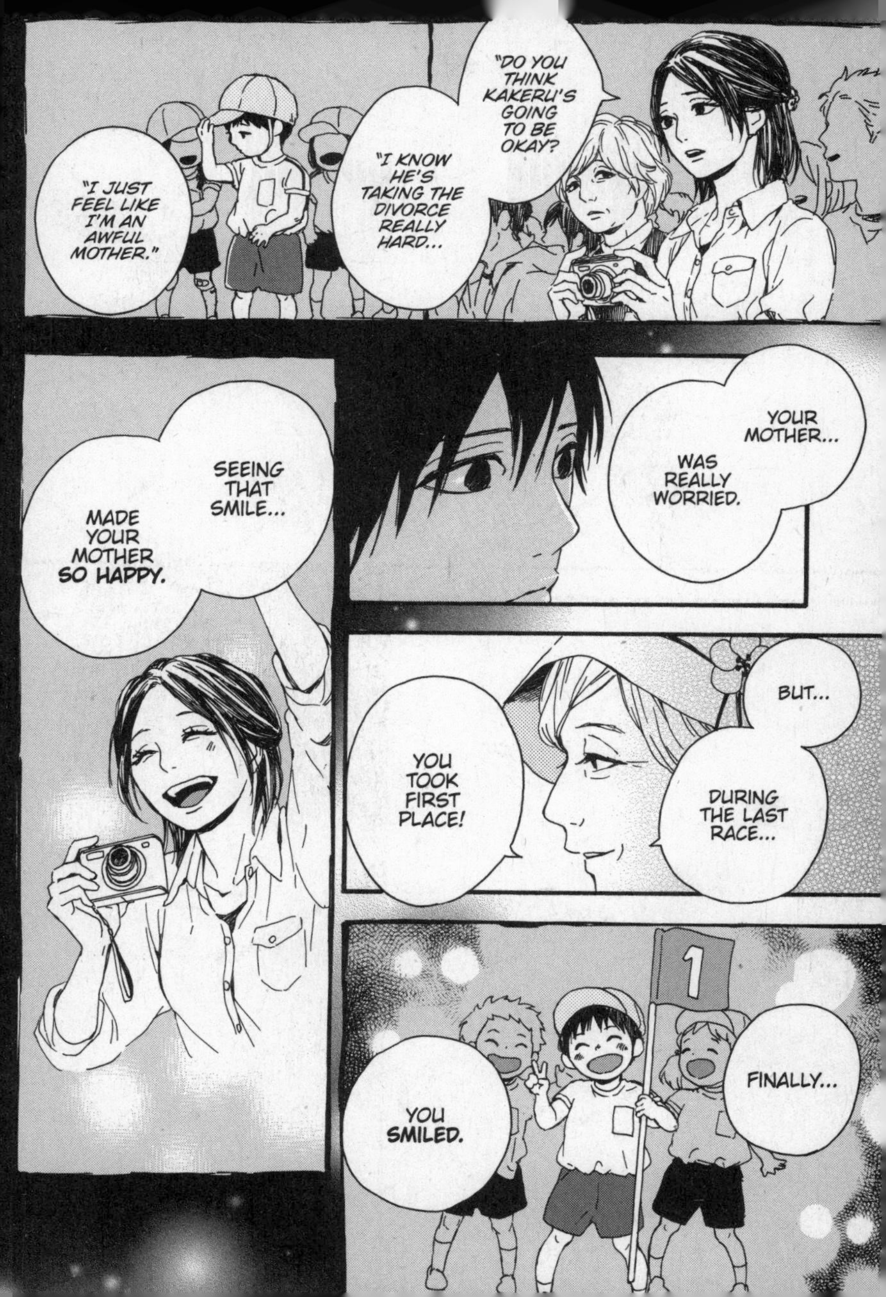
"DO YOU THINK KAKERU'S GOING TO BE OKAY?
"I KNOW HE'S TAKING THE DIVORCE REALLY HARD...
"I JUST FEEL LIKE I'M AN AWFUL MOTHER."
YOUR MOTHER...
WAS REALLY WORRIED.
BUT...
DURING THE LAST RACE...
YOU TOOK FIRST PLACE!
FINALLY...
YOU SMILED.
SEEING THAT SMILE...
MADE YOUR MOTHER SO HAPPY.

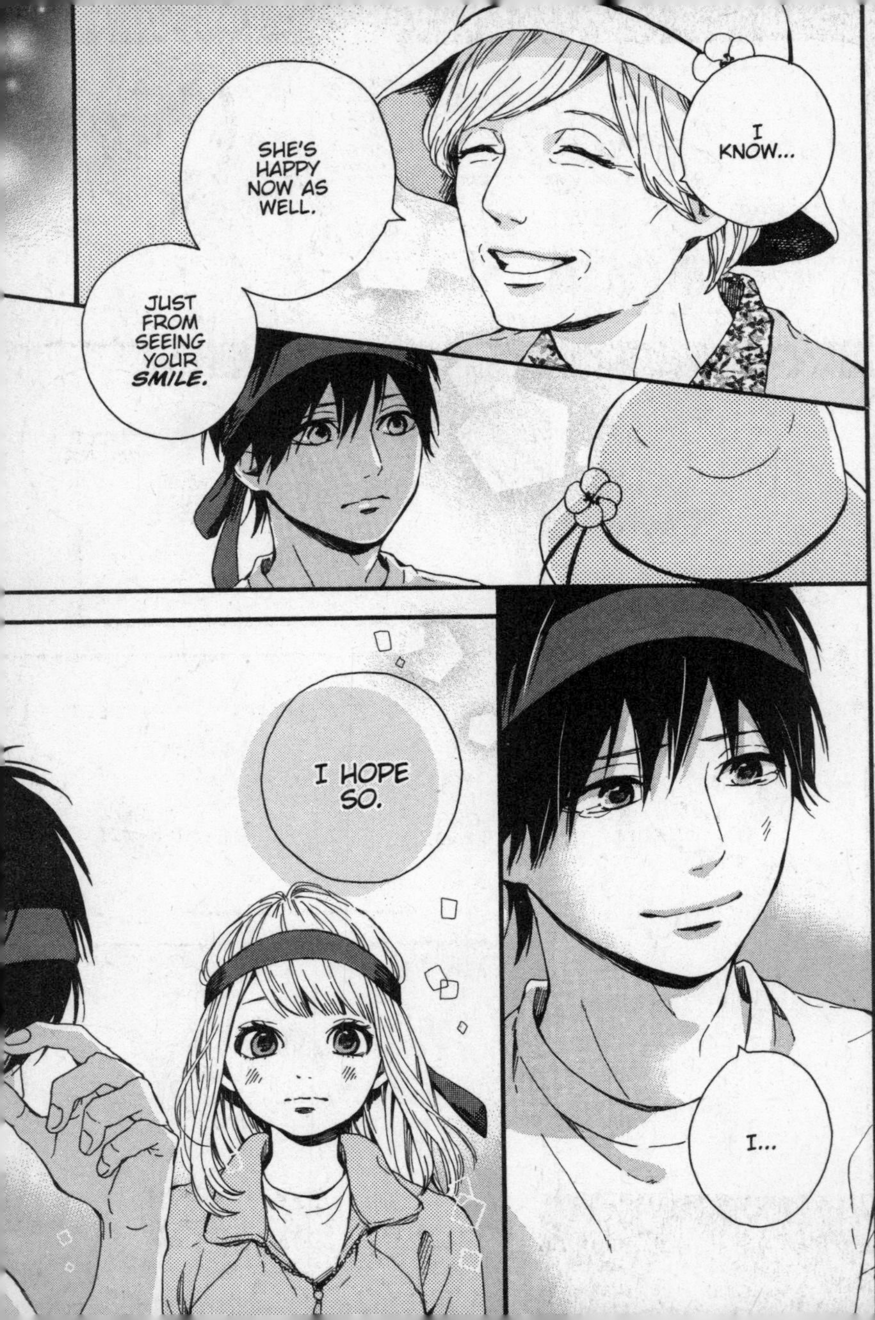
I KNOW...
SHE'S HAPPY NOW AS WELL.
JUST FROM SEEING YOUR *SMILE.*
I...
I HOPE SO.

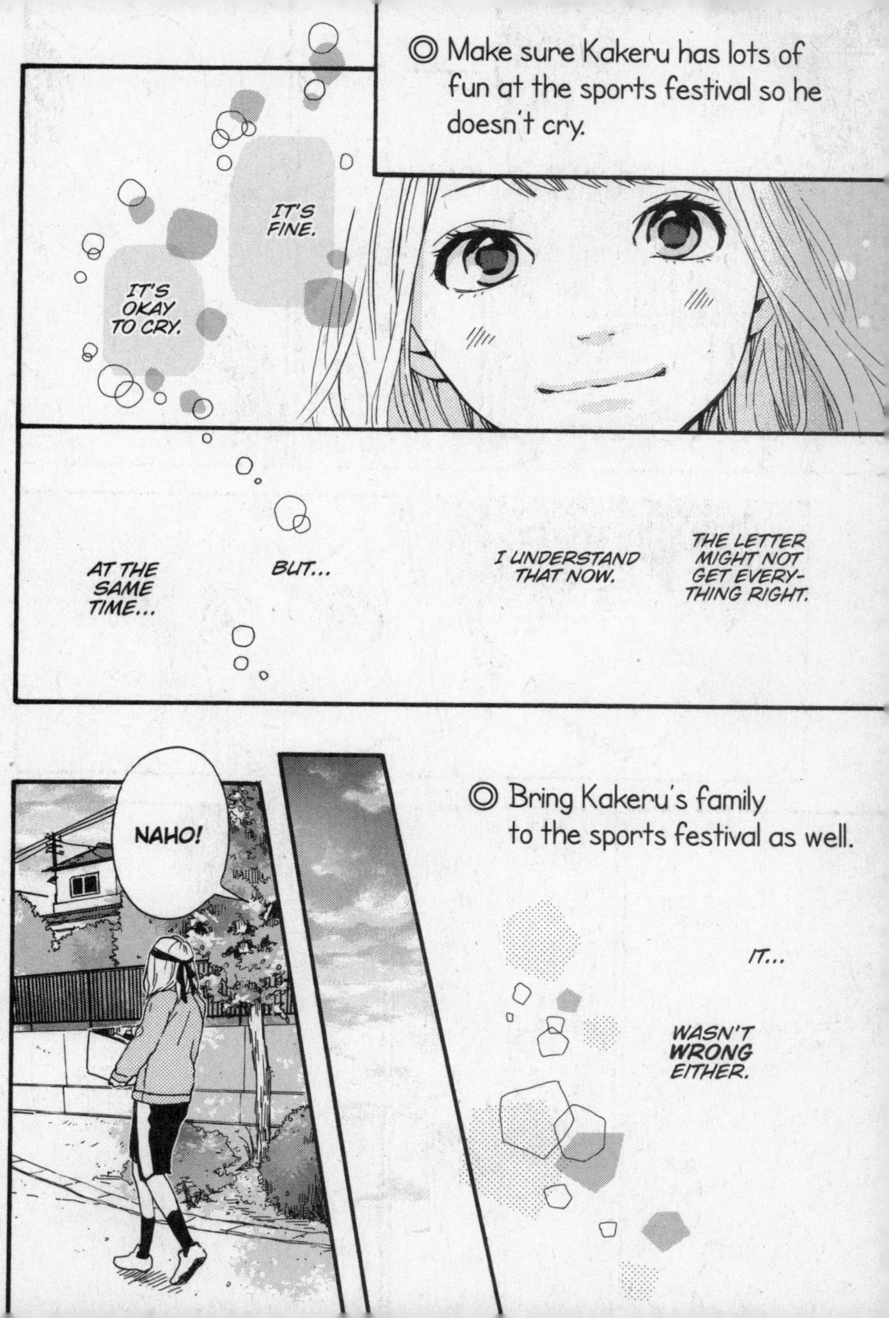
Make sure Kakeru has lots of fun at the sports festival so he doesn't cry.
IT'S FINE.
IT'S OKAY TO CRY.
THE LETTER MIGHT NOT GET EVERYTHING RIGHT.
I UNDERSTAND THAT NOW.
BUT...
AT THE SAME TIME...
Bring Kakeru's family to the sports festival as well.
IT...
WASN'T WRONG EITHER.
NAHO!

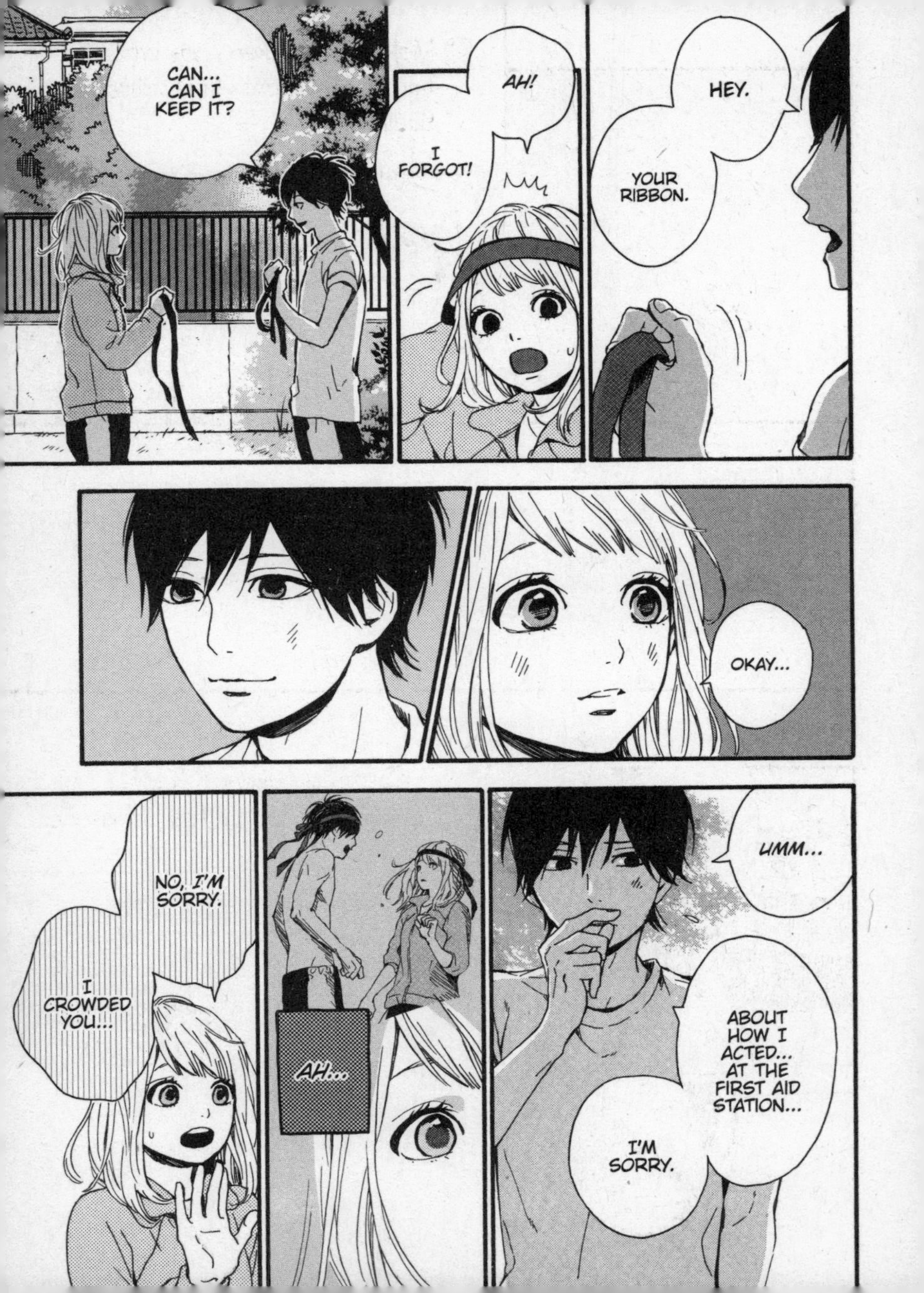
HEY.
YOUR RIBBON.
AH!
I FORGOT!
CAN... CAN I KEEP IT?
OKAY...
UMM...
ABOUT HOW I ACTED... AT THE FIRST AID STATION...
I'M SORRY.
AH...
NO, *I'M* SORRY.
I CROWDED YOU...

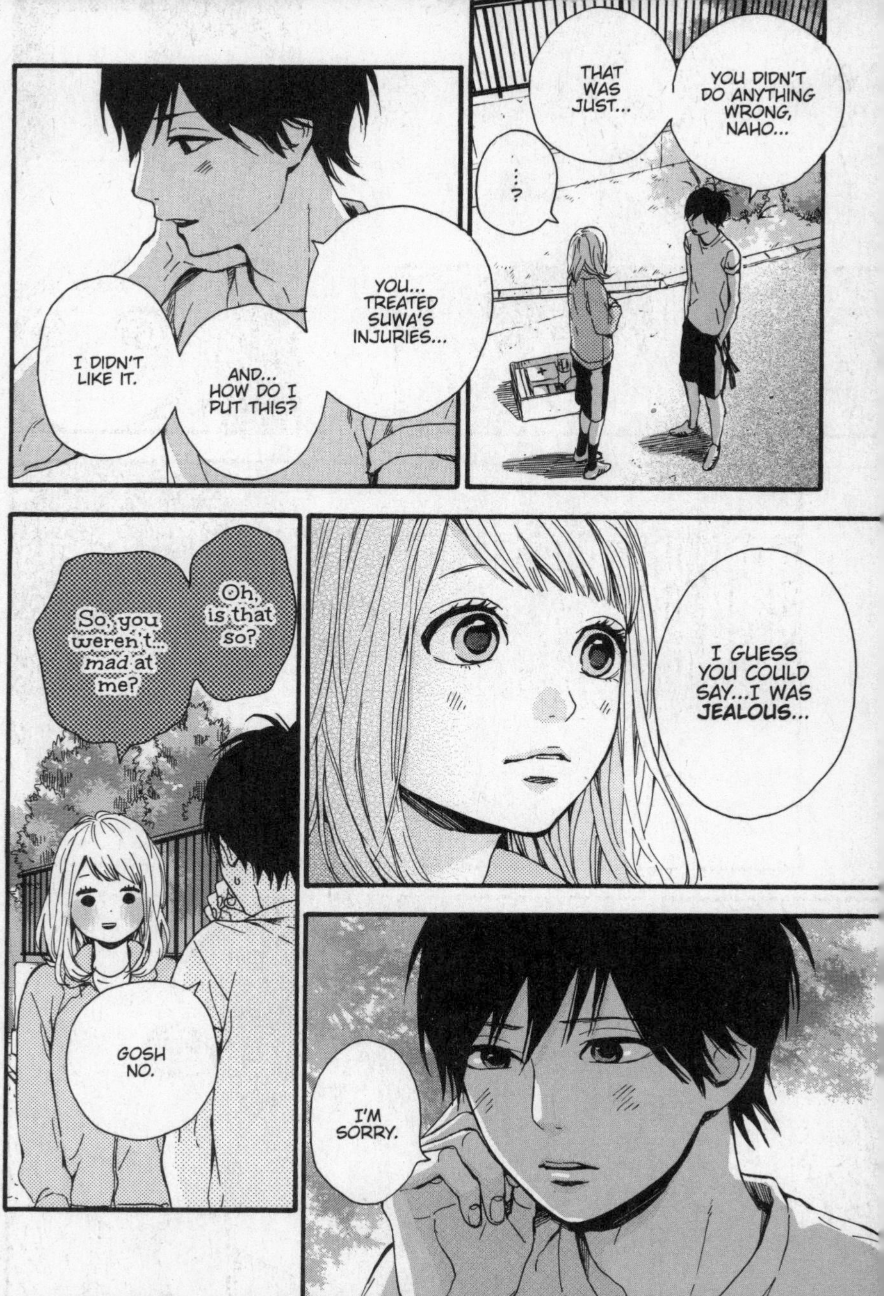
YOU DIDN'T DO ANYTHING WRONG, NAHO...
THAT WAS JUST...
...?
YOU... TREATED SUWA'S INJURIES...
AND... HOW DO I PUT THIS?
I DIDN'T LIKE IT.
I GUESS YOU COULD SAY...I WAS JEALOUS...
I'M SORRY.
Oh, is that so?
So, you weren't... mad at me?
GOSH NO.

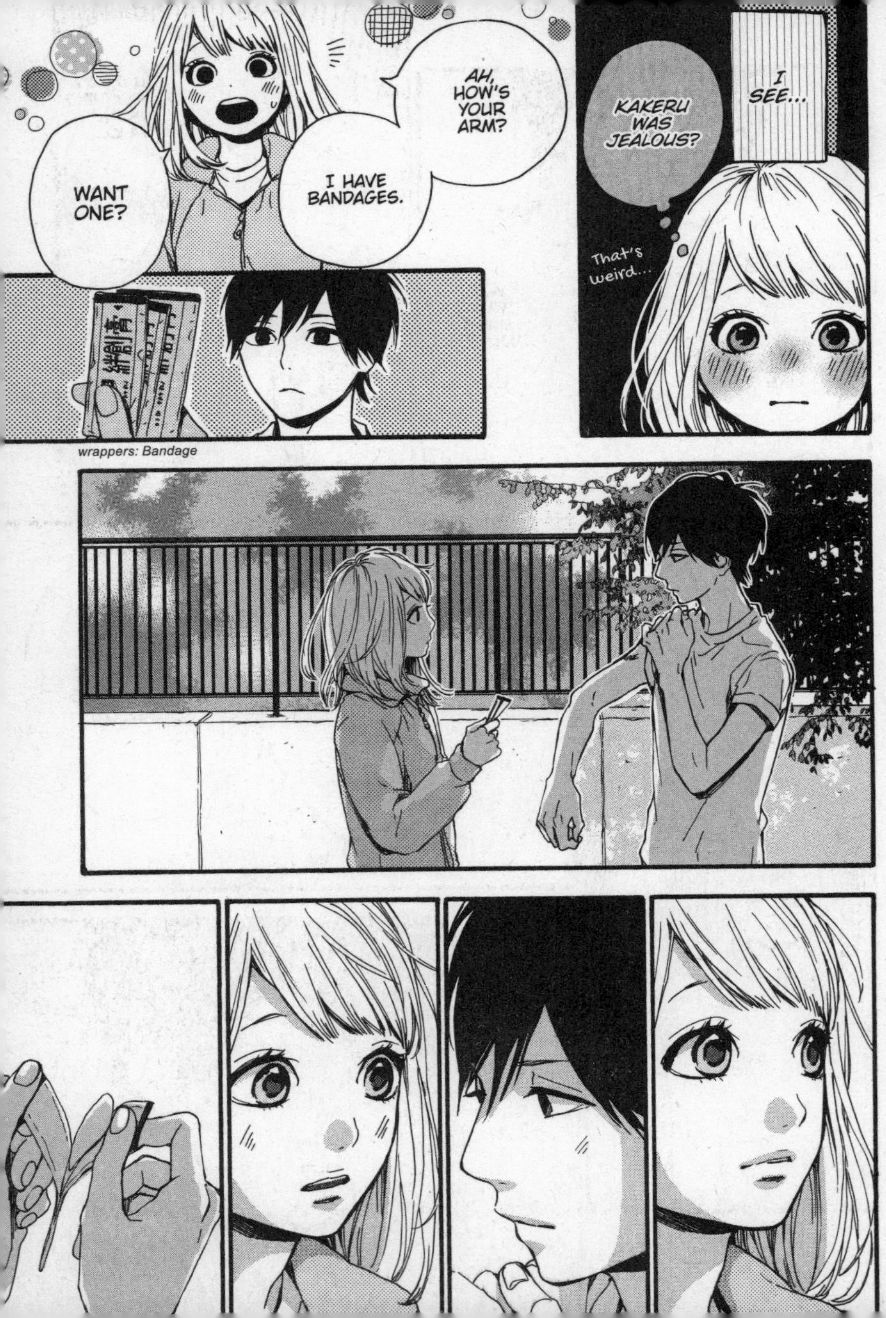
I SEE...
KAKERU WAS JEALOUS?
That's weird...
AH, HOW'S YOUR ARM?
I HAVE BANDAGES.
WANT ONE?
wrappers: Bandage

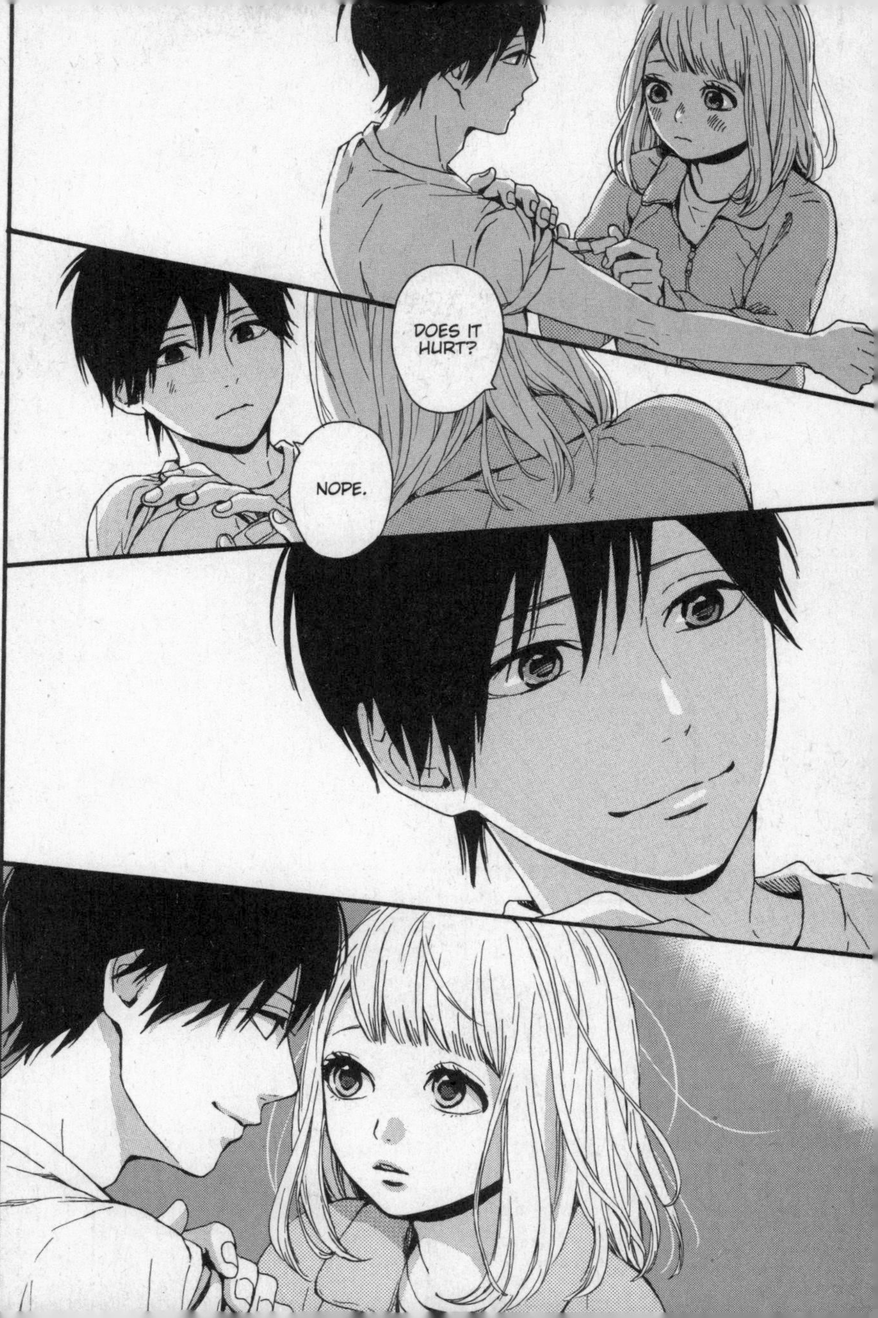
DOES IT HURT?
NOPE.

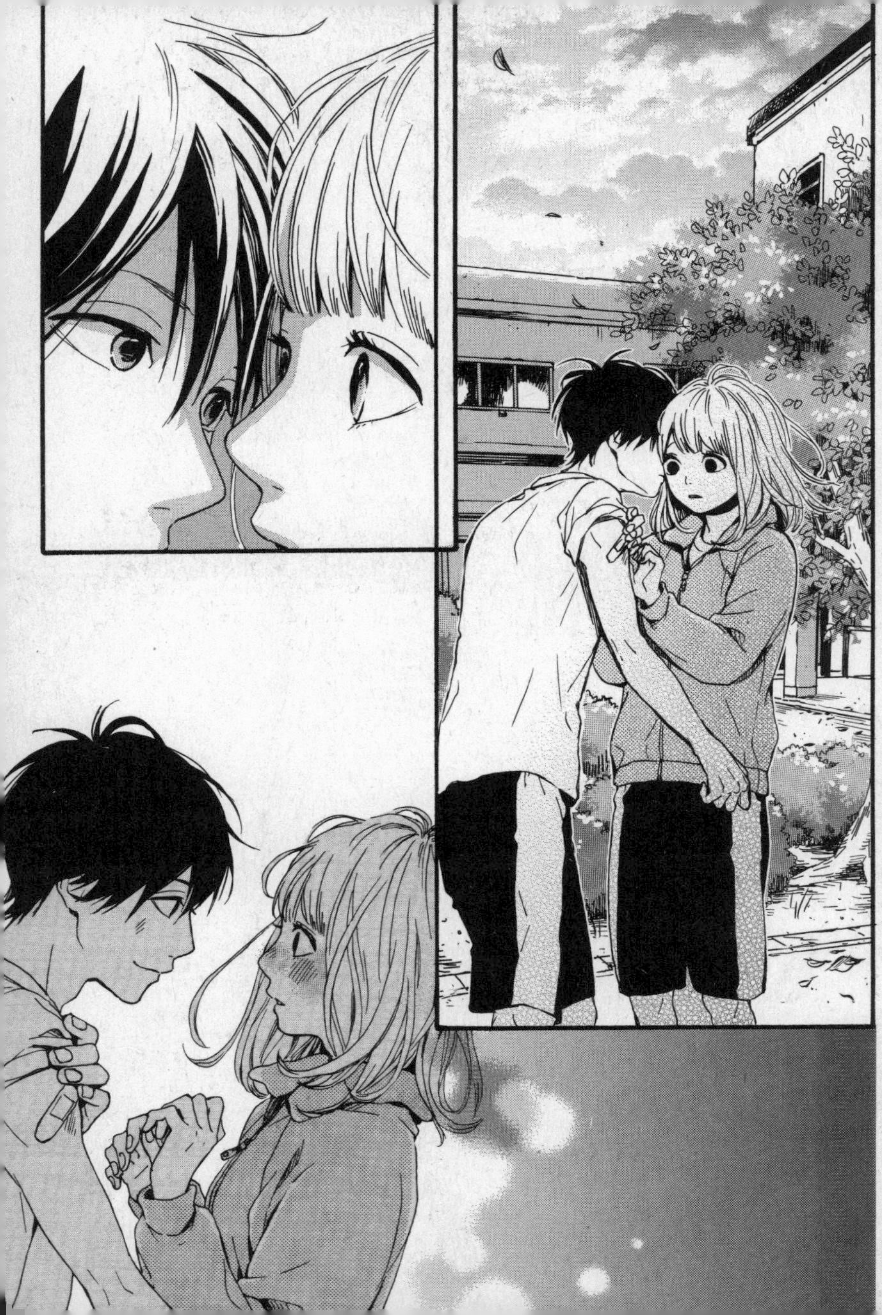

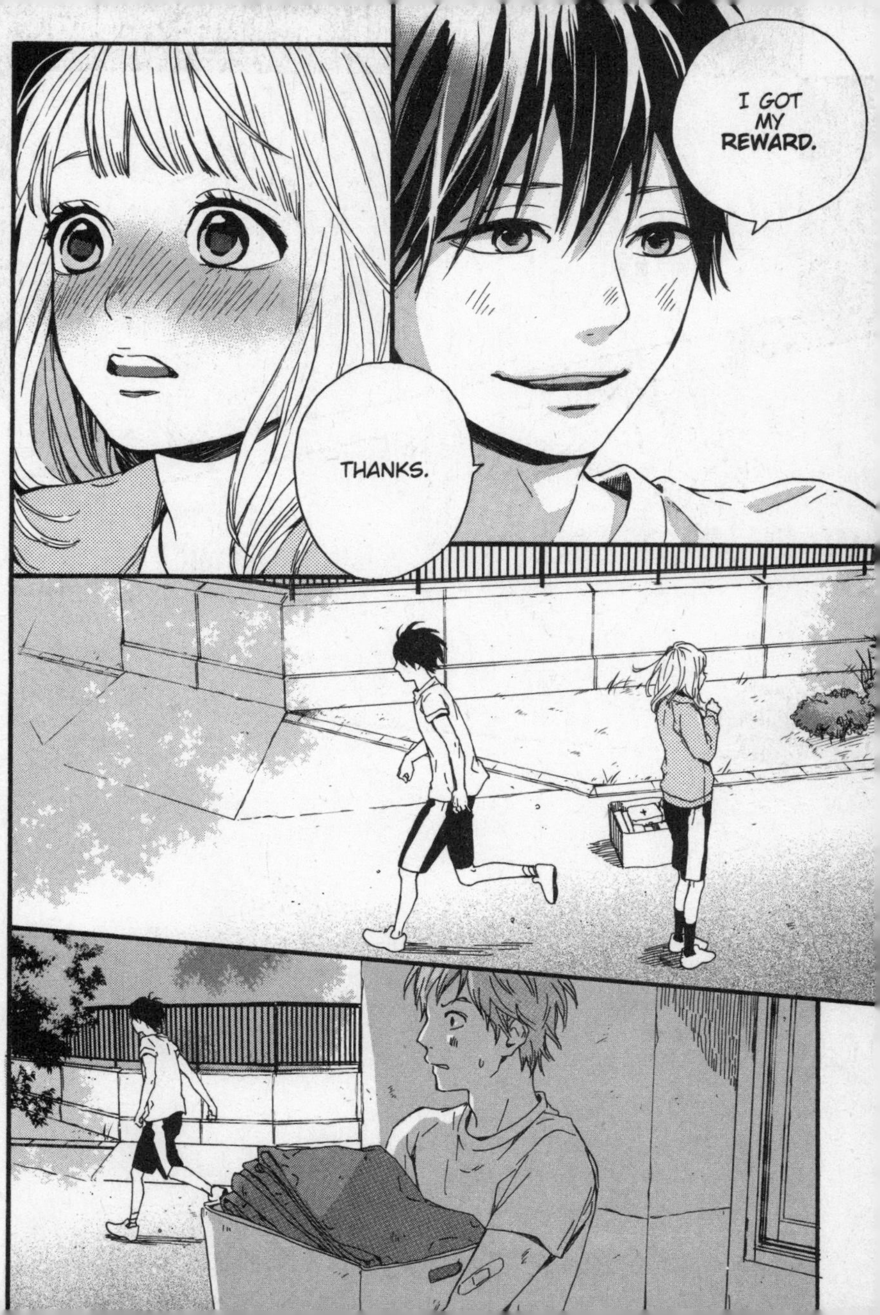
I GOT MY REWARD.
THANKS.

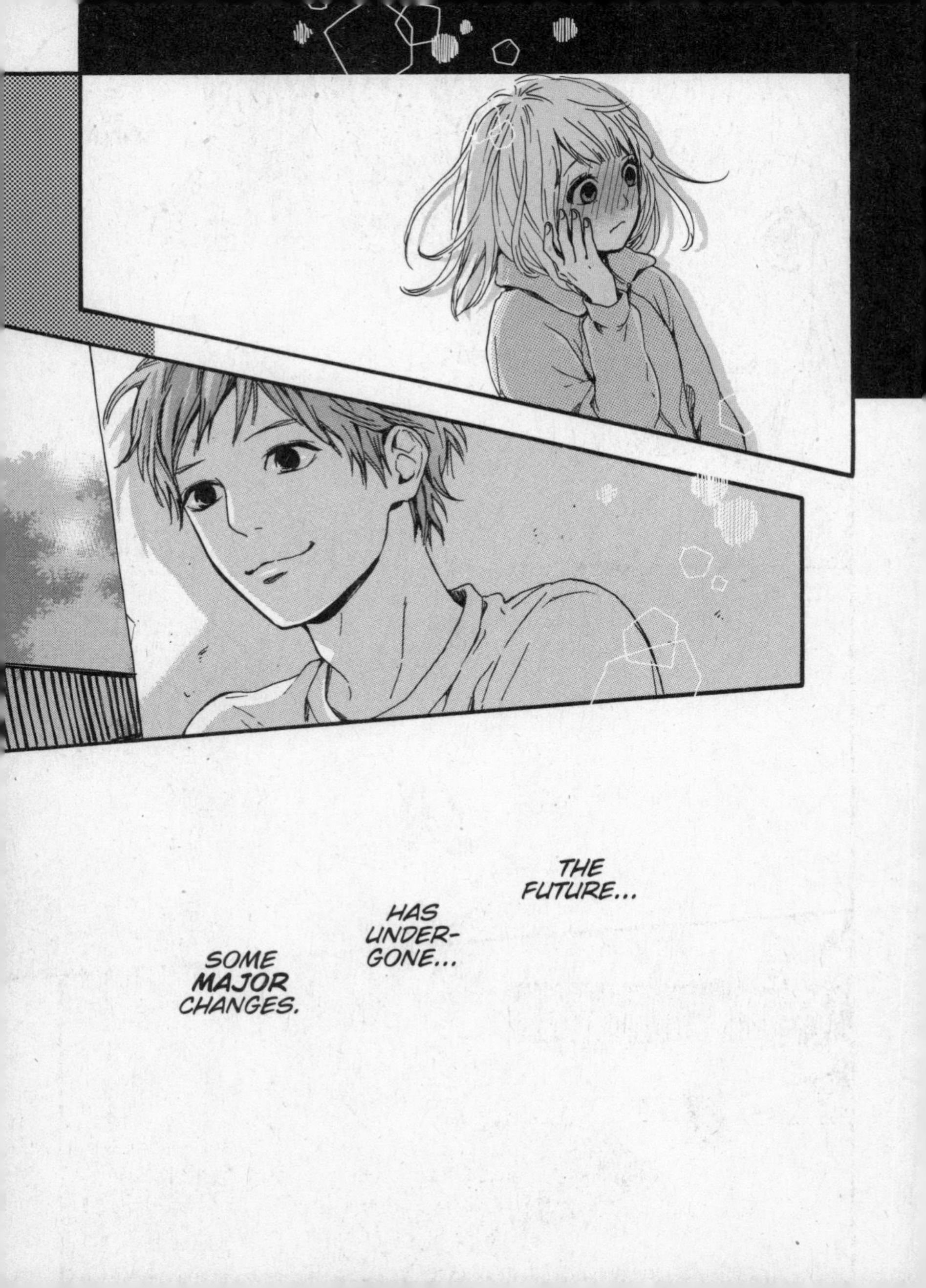
THE FUTURE...
HAS UNDER-GONE...
SOME MAJOR CHANGES.

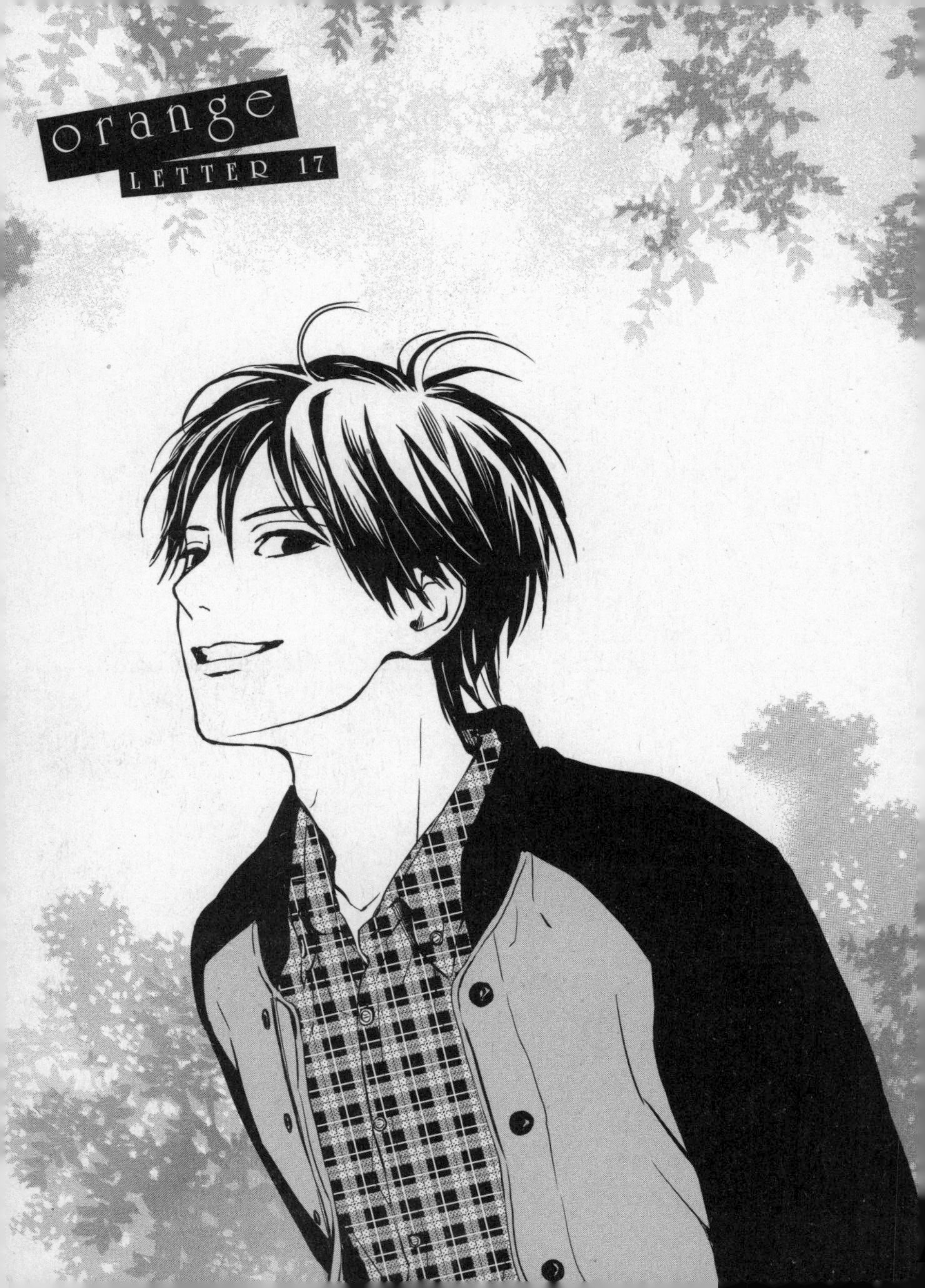
orange
LETTER 17

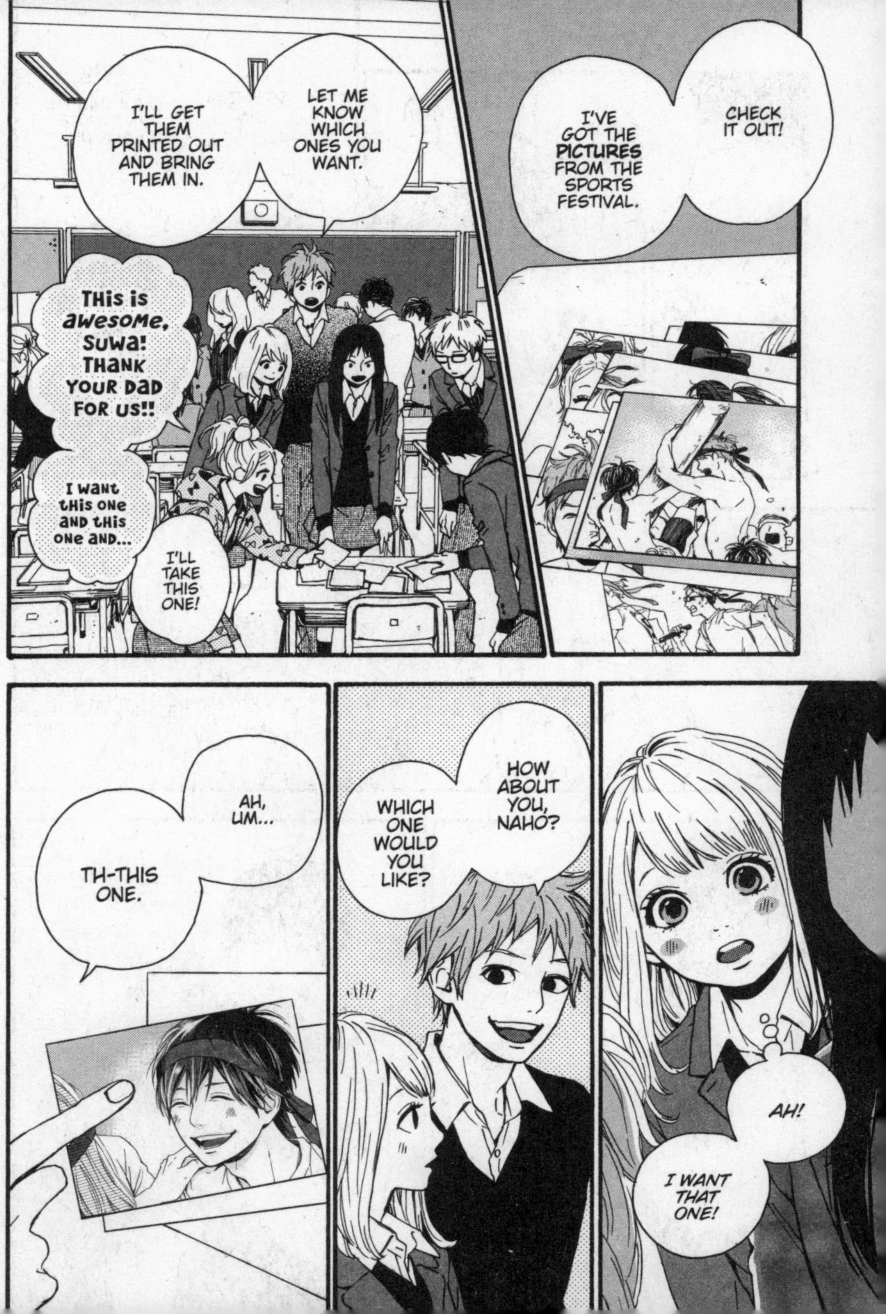
CHECK IT OUT!
I'VE GOT THE **PICTURES** FROM THE SPORTS FESTIVAL.
LET ME KNOW WHICH ONES YOU WANT.
I'LL GET THEM PRINTED OUT AND BRING THEM IN.
THIS is *awesome*, SUWA! THANK YOUR DAD FOR US!!
I want this one and this one and...
I'LL TAKE THIS ONE!
AH!
I WANT THAT ONE!
HOW ABOUT YOU, NAHO?
WHICH ONE WOULD YOU LIKE?
AH, UM...
TH-THIS ONE.

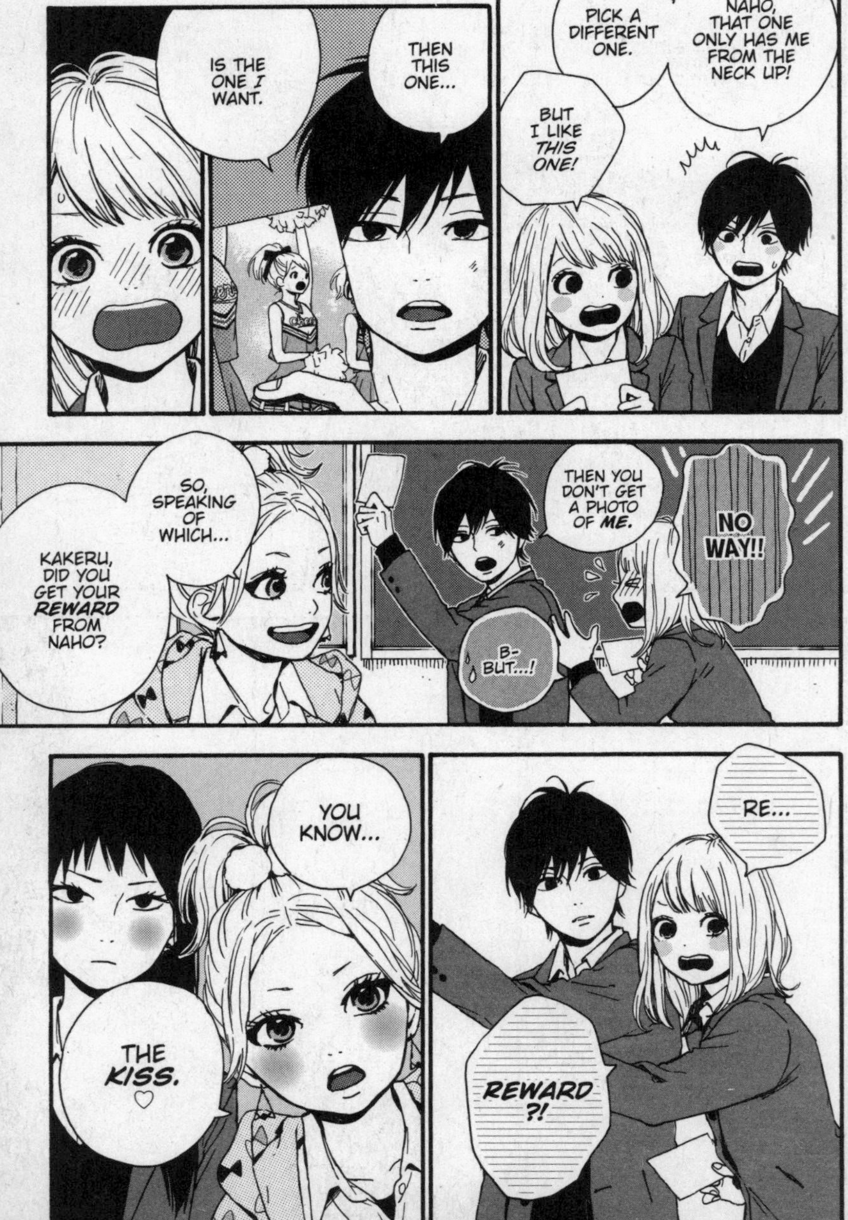
NAHO, THAT ONE ONLY HAS ME FROM THE NECK UP!
PICK A DIFFERENT ONE.
BUT I LIKE *THIS ONE!*
THEN THIS ONE...
IS THE ONE *I* WANT.
NO WAY!!
THEN YOU DON'T GET A PHOTO OF **ME.**
B-BUT...!
SO, SPEAKING OF WHICH...
KAKERU, DID YOU GET YOUR ***REWARD*** FROM NAHO?
RE...
REWARD ?!
YOU KNOW...
THE ***KISS.*** ♡

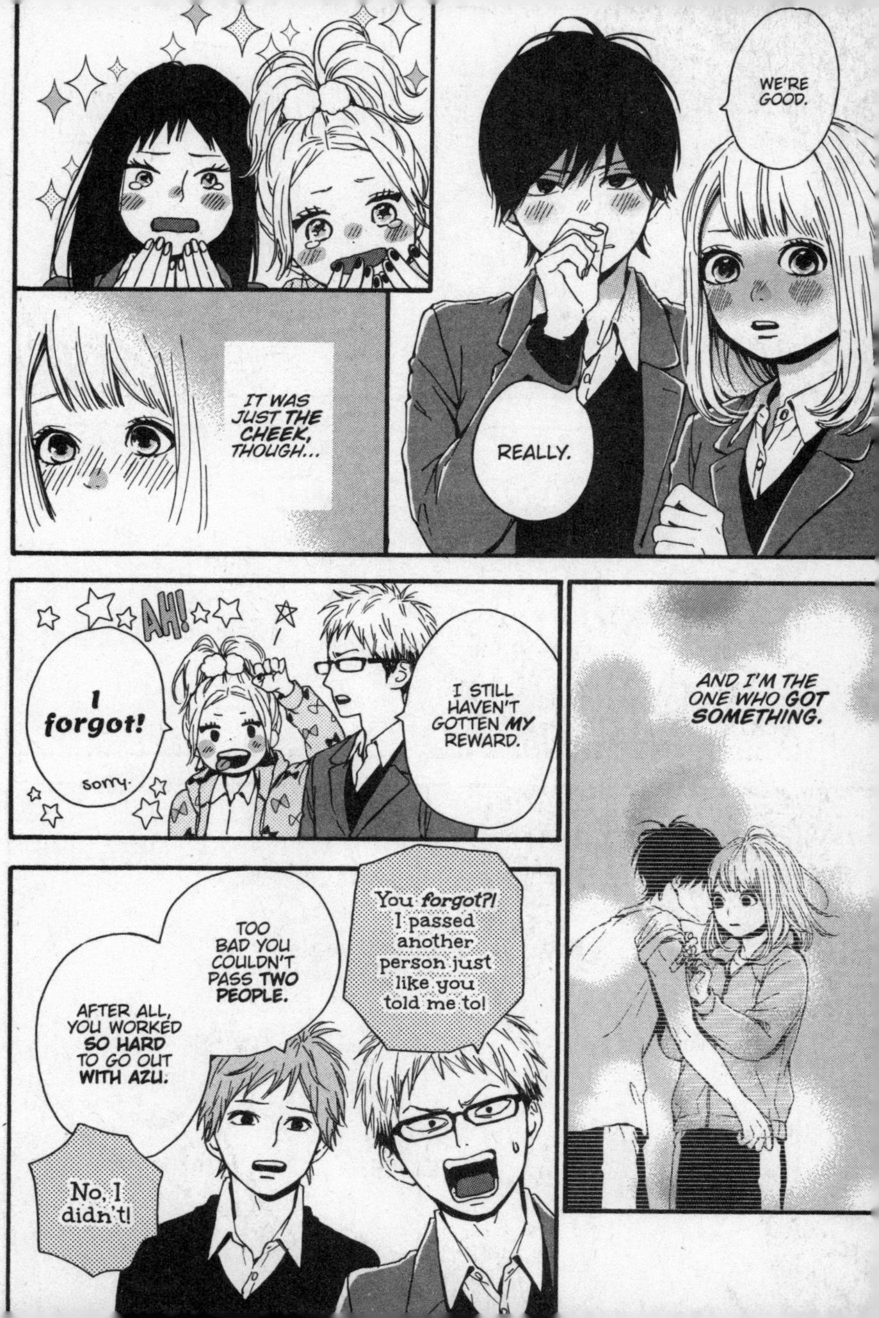
WE'RE GOOD.
REALLY.
IT WAS JUST THE CHEEK, THOUGH...
AND I'M THE ONE WHO GOT SOMETHING.
I STILL HAVEN'T GOTTEN MY REWARD.
AH!
I forgot!
sorry.
You forgot?! I passed another person just like you told me to!
TOO BAD YOU COULDN'T PASS TWO PEOPLE.
AFTER ALL, YOU WORKED SO HARD TO GO OUT WITH AZU.
No, I didn't!

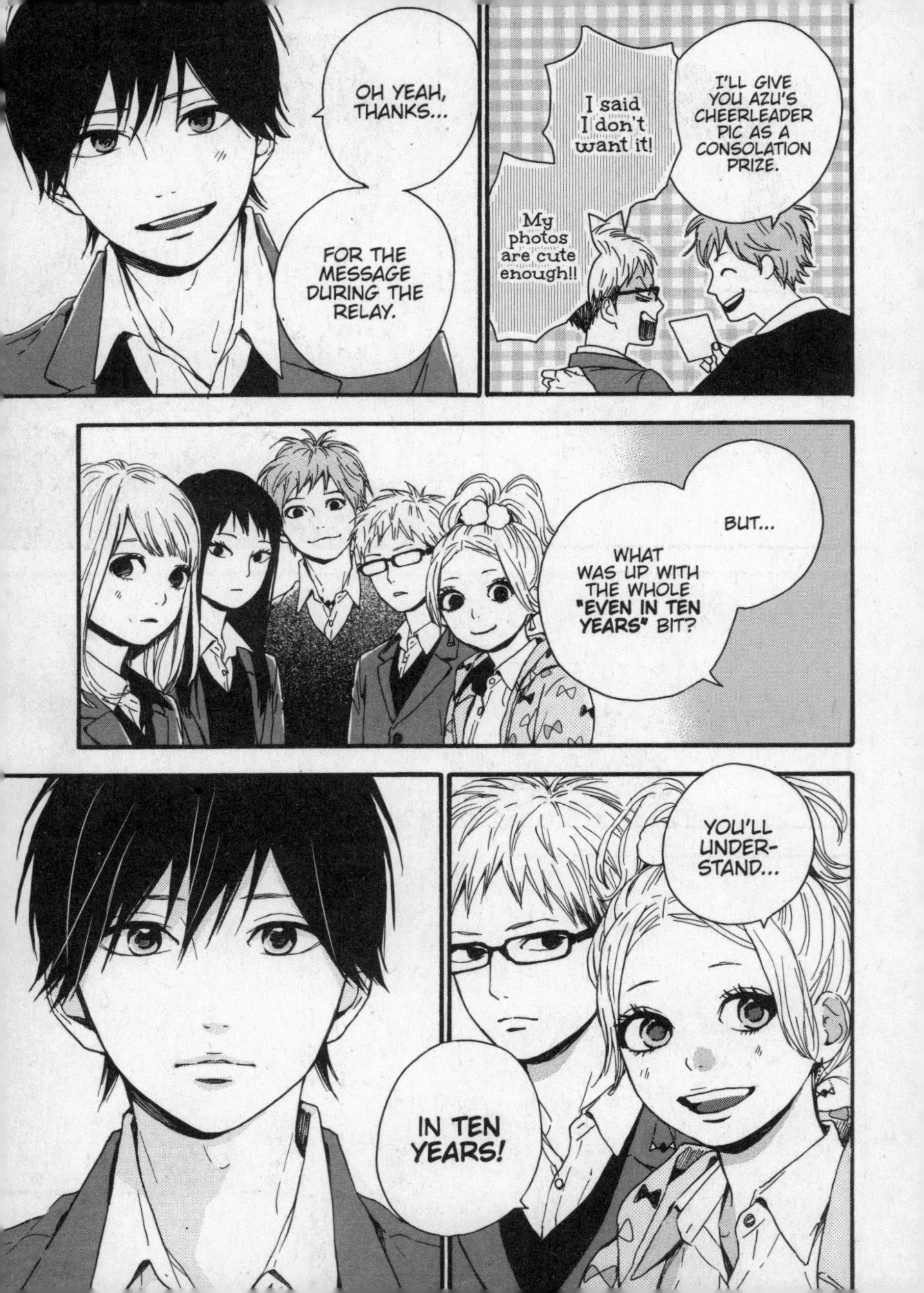
I'LL GIVE YOU AZU'S CHEERLEADER PIC AS A CONSOLATION PRIZE.
I said I don't want it!
My photos are cute enough!!
OH YEAH, THANKS...
FOR THE MESSAGE DURING THE RELAY.
BUT...
WHAT WAS UP WITH THE WHOLE "EVEN IN TEN YEARS" BIT?
YOU'LL UNDER-STAND...
IN TEN YEARS!

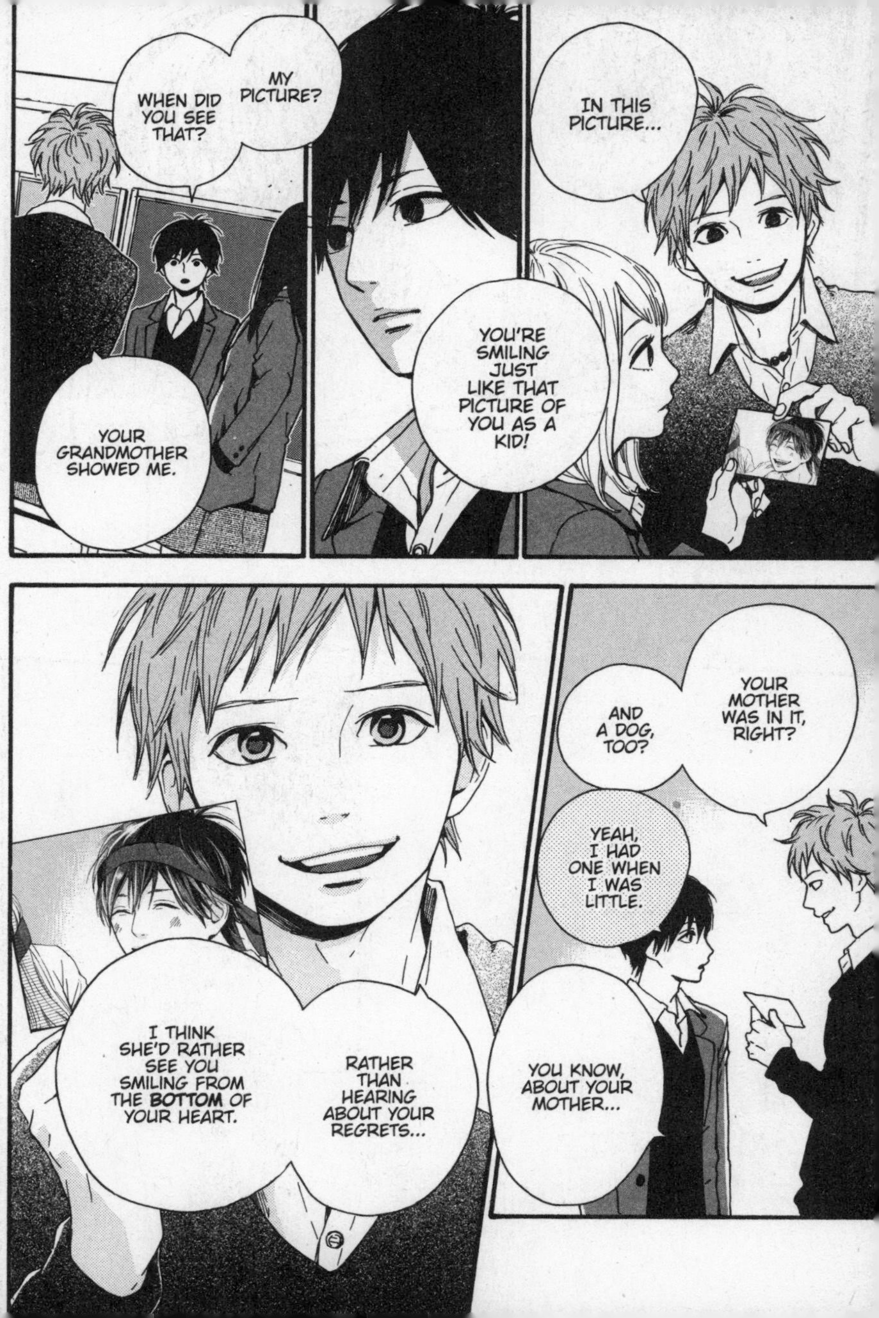
IN THIS PICTURE...
YOU'RE SMILING JUST LIKE THAT PICTURE OF YOU AS A KID!
MY PICTURE?
WHEN DID YOU SEE THAT?
YOUR GRANDMOTHER SHOWED ME.
YOUR MOTHER WAS IN IT, RIGHT?
AND A DOG, TOO?
YEAH, I HAD ONE WHEN I WAS LITTLE.
YOU KNOW, ABOUT YOUR MOTHER...
RATHER THAN HEARING ABOUT YOUR REGRETS...
I THINK SHE'D RATHER SEE YOU SMILING FROM THE **BOTTOM** OF YOUR HEART.

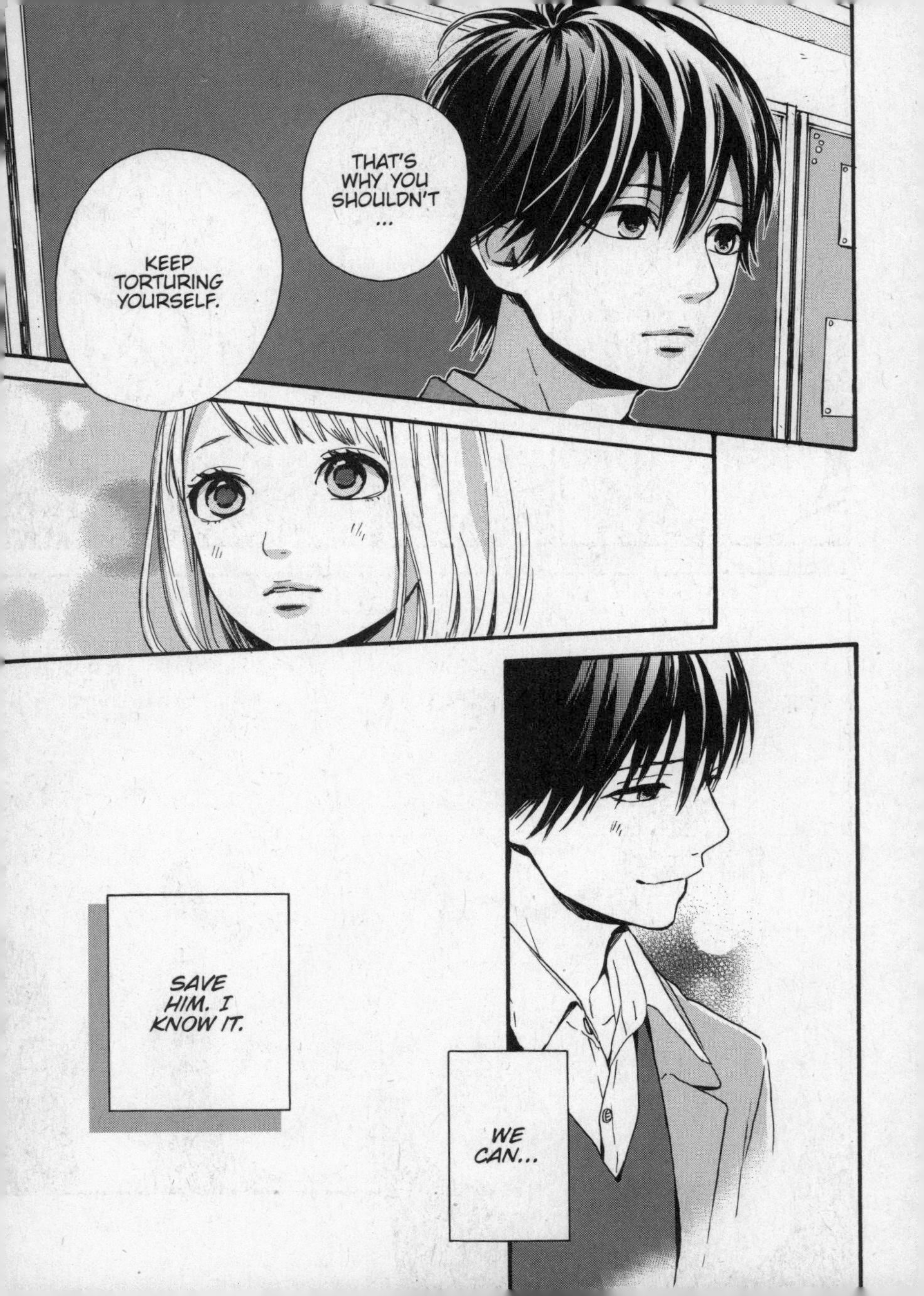
THAT'S WHY YOU SHOULDN'T ...
KEEP TORTURING YOURSELF.
WE CAN...
SAVE HIM. I KNOW IT.

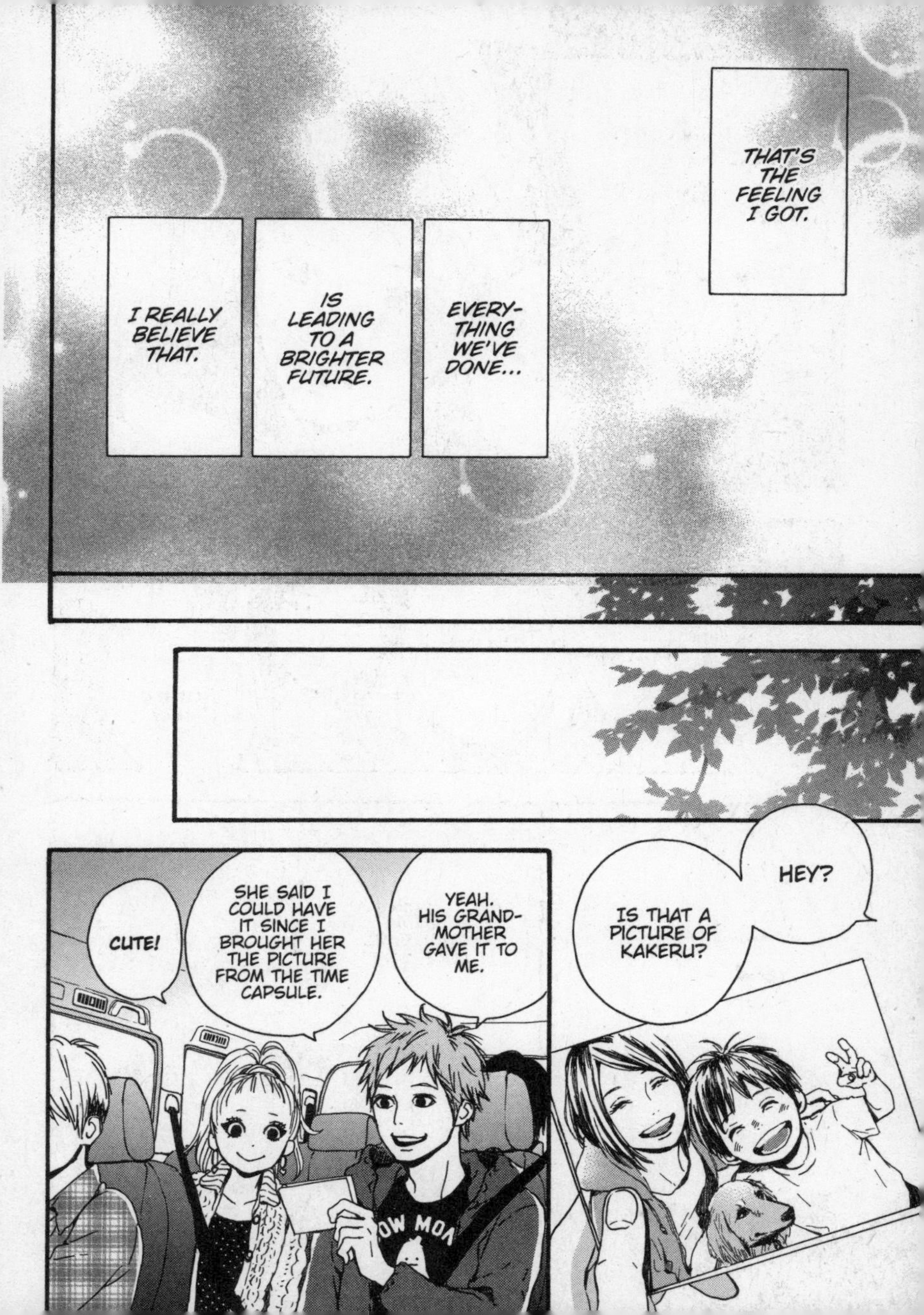
THAT'S THE FEELING I GOT.
EVERY-THING WE'VE DONE...
IS LEADING TO A BRIGHTER FUTURE.
I REALLY BELIEVE THAT.
HEY?
IS THAT A PICTURE OF KAKERU?
YEAH. HIS GRAND-MOTHER GAVE IT TO ME.
SHE SAID I COULD HAVE IT SINCE I BROUGHT HER THE PICTURE FROM THE TIME CAPSULE.
CUTE!
OW MOA

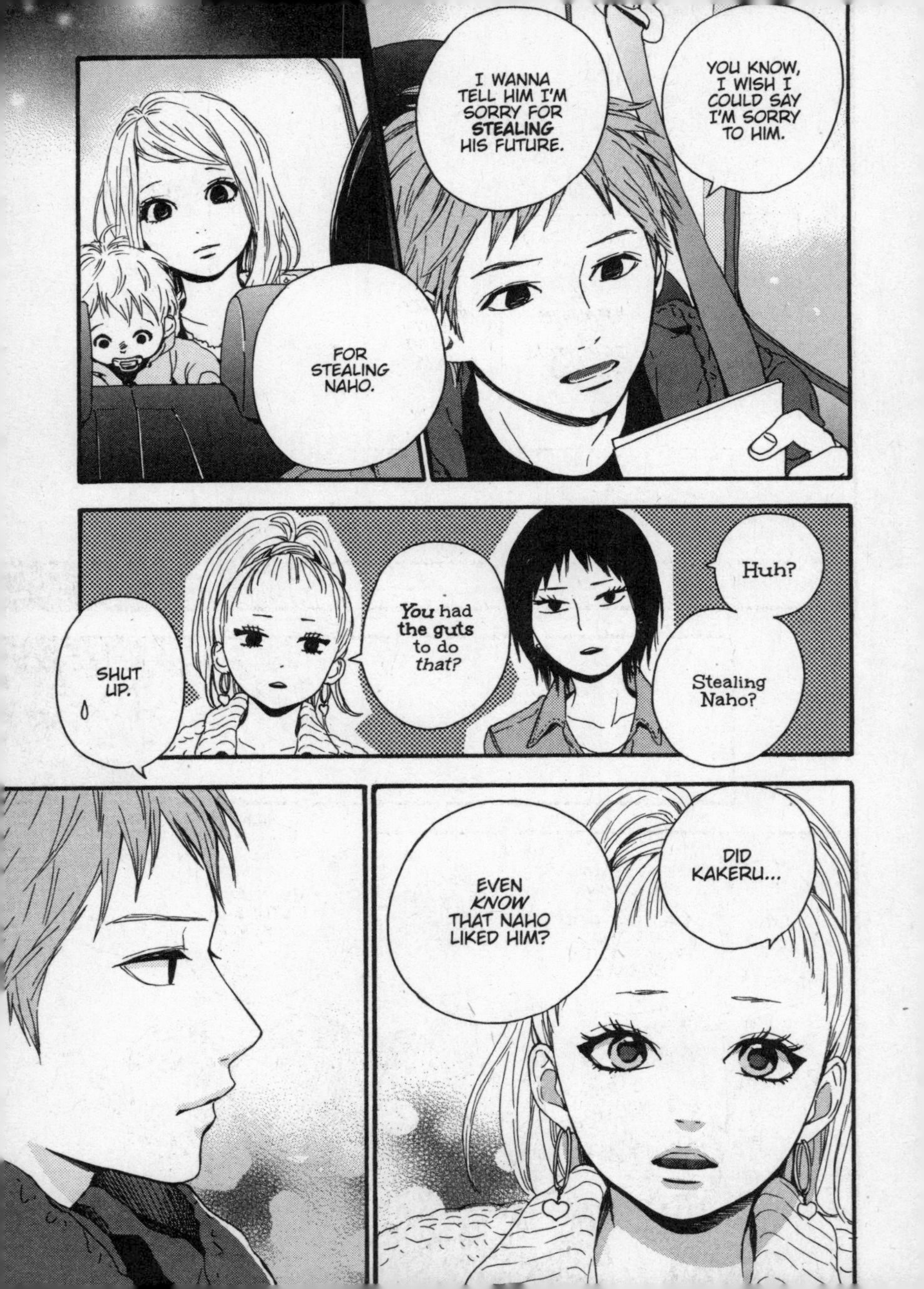
YOU KNOW, I WISH I COULD SAY I'M SORRY TO HIM.
I WANNA TELL HIM I'M SORRY FOR **STEALING** HIS FUTURE.
FOR STEALING NAHO.
Huh?
Stealing Naho?
You had the guts to do *that?*
SHUT UP.
DID KAKERU...
EVEN *KNOW* THAT NAHO LIKED HIM?

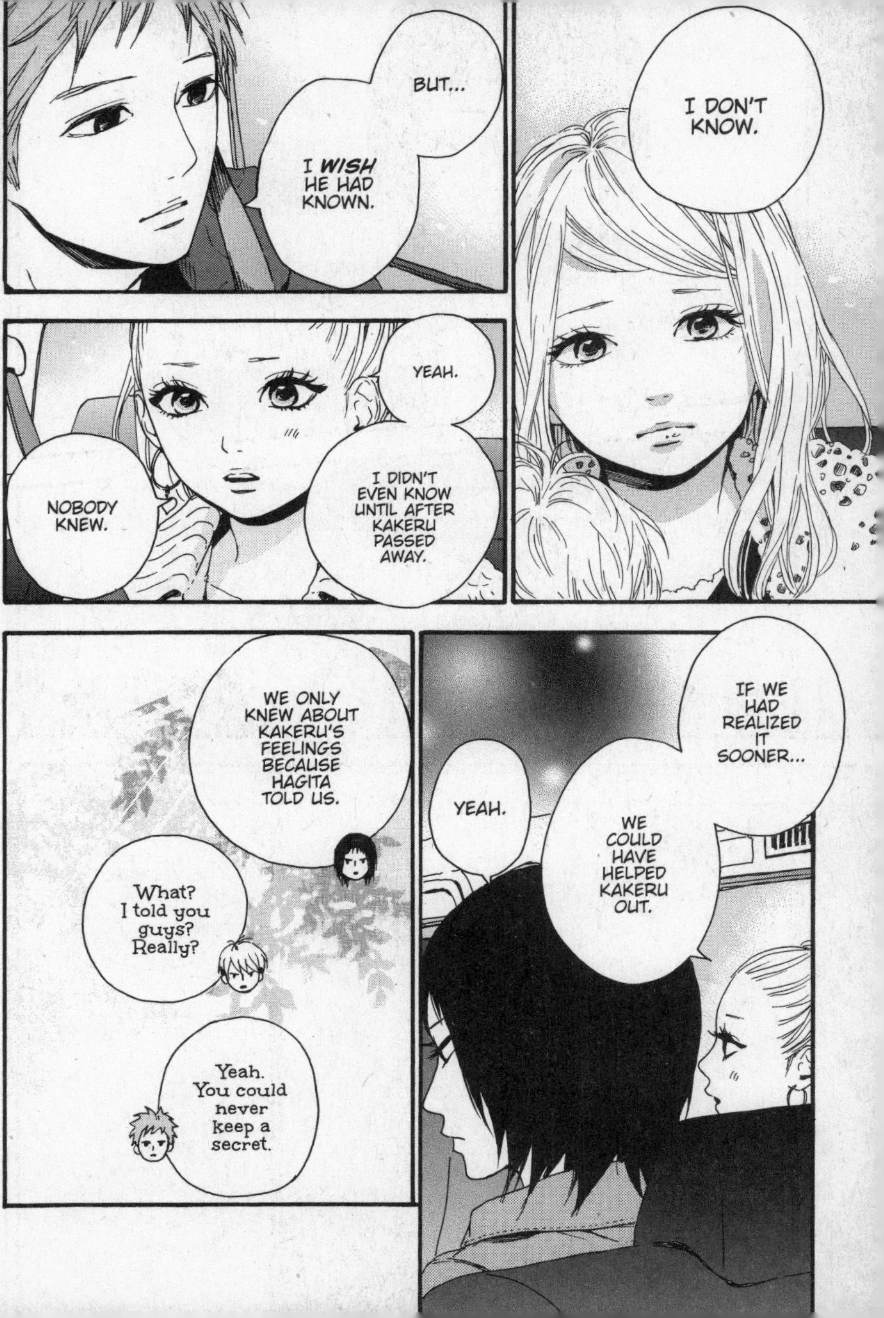
I DON'T KNOW.
BUT...
I *WISH* HE HAD KNOWN.
YEAH.
I DIDN'T EVEN KNOW UNTIL AFTER KAKERU PASSED AWAY.
NOBODY KNEW.
IF WE HAD REALIZED IT SOONER...
WE COULD HAVE HELPED KAKERU OUT.
YEAH.
WE ONLY KNEW ABOUT KAKERU'S FEELINGS BECAUSE HAGITA TOLD US.
What? I told you guys? Really?
Yeah. You could never keep a secret.

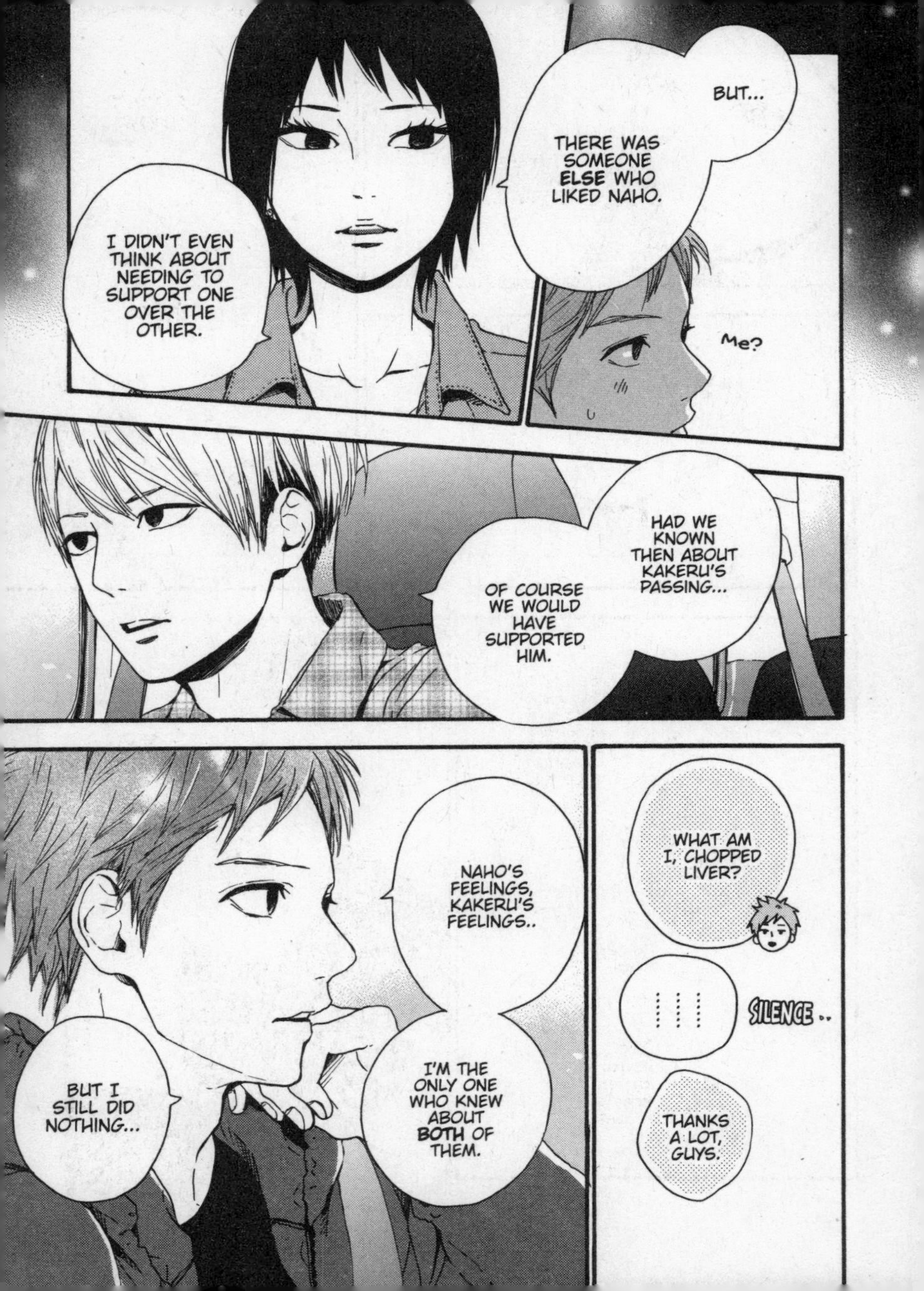
BUT...
THERE WAS SOMEONE ELSE WHO LIKED NAHO.
Me?
I DIDN'T EVEN THINK ABOUT NEEDING TO SUPPORT ONE OVER THE OTHER.
HAD WE KNOWN THEN ABOUT KAKERU'S PASSING...
OF COURSE WE WOULD HAVE SUPPORTED HIM.
WHAT AM I, CHOPPED LIVER?
......
SILENCE..
THANKS A LOT, GUYS.
NAHO'S FEELINGS, KAKERU'S FEELINGS..
I'M THE ONLY ONE WHO KNEW ABOUT BOTH OF THEM.
BUT I STILL DID NOTHING...

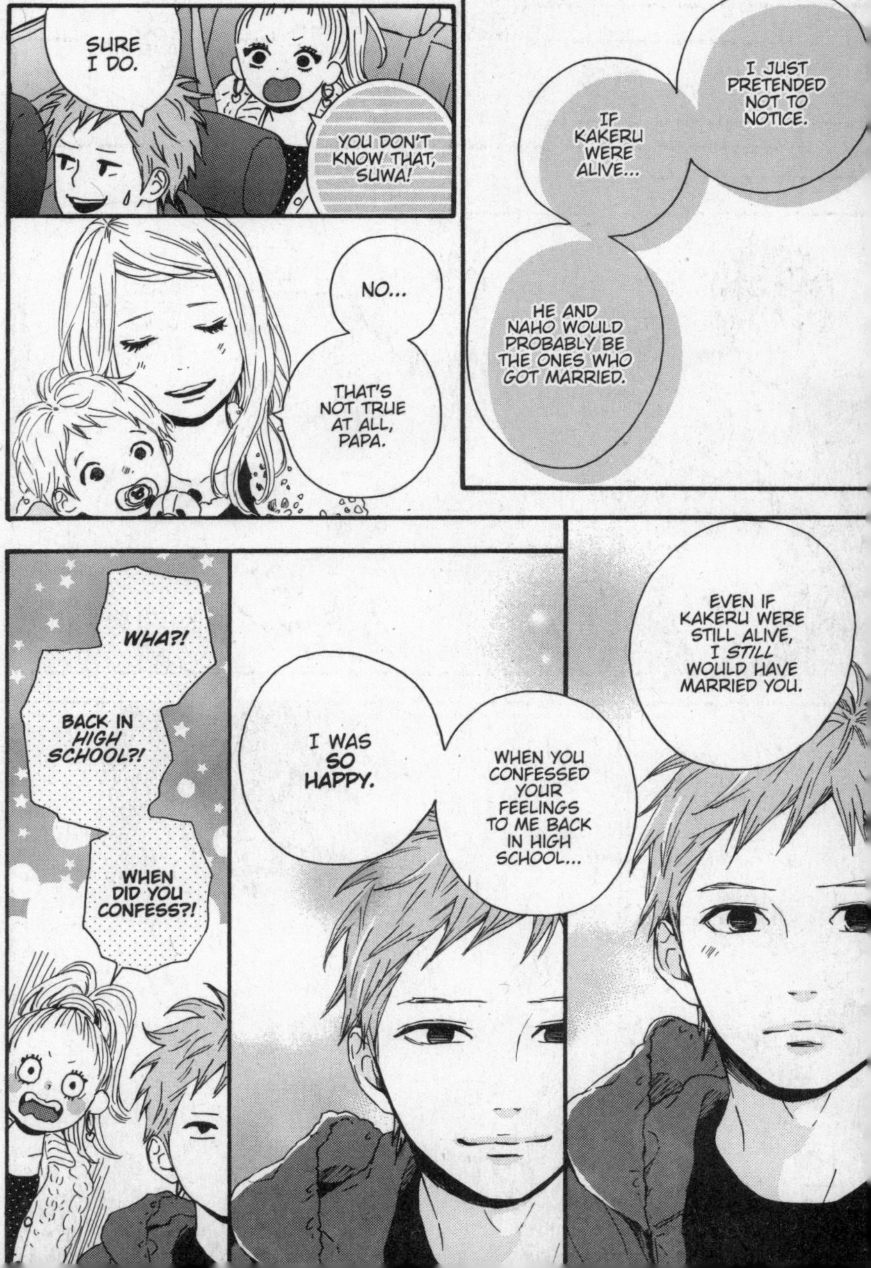
I JUST PRETENDED NOT TO NOTICE.
IF KAKERU WERE ALIVE...
HE AND NAHO WOULD PROBABLY BE THE ONES WHO GOT MARRIED.
SURE I DO.
YOU DON'T KNOW THAT, SUWA!
NO...
THAT'S NOT TRUE AT ALL, PAPA.
EVEN IF KAKERU WERE STILL ALIVE, I *STILL* WOULD HAVE MARRIED YOU.
WHEN YOU CONFESSED YOUR FEELINGS TO ME BACK IN HIGH SCHOOL...
I WAS **SO HAPPY.**
WHA?!
BACK IN *HIGH SCHOOL?!*
WHEN DID YOU CONFESS?!

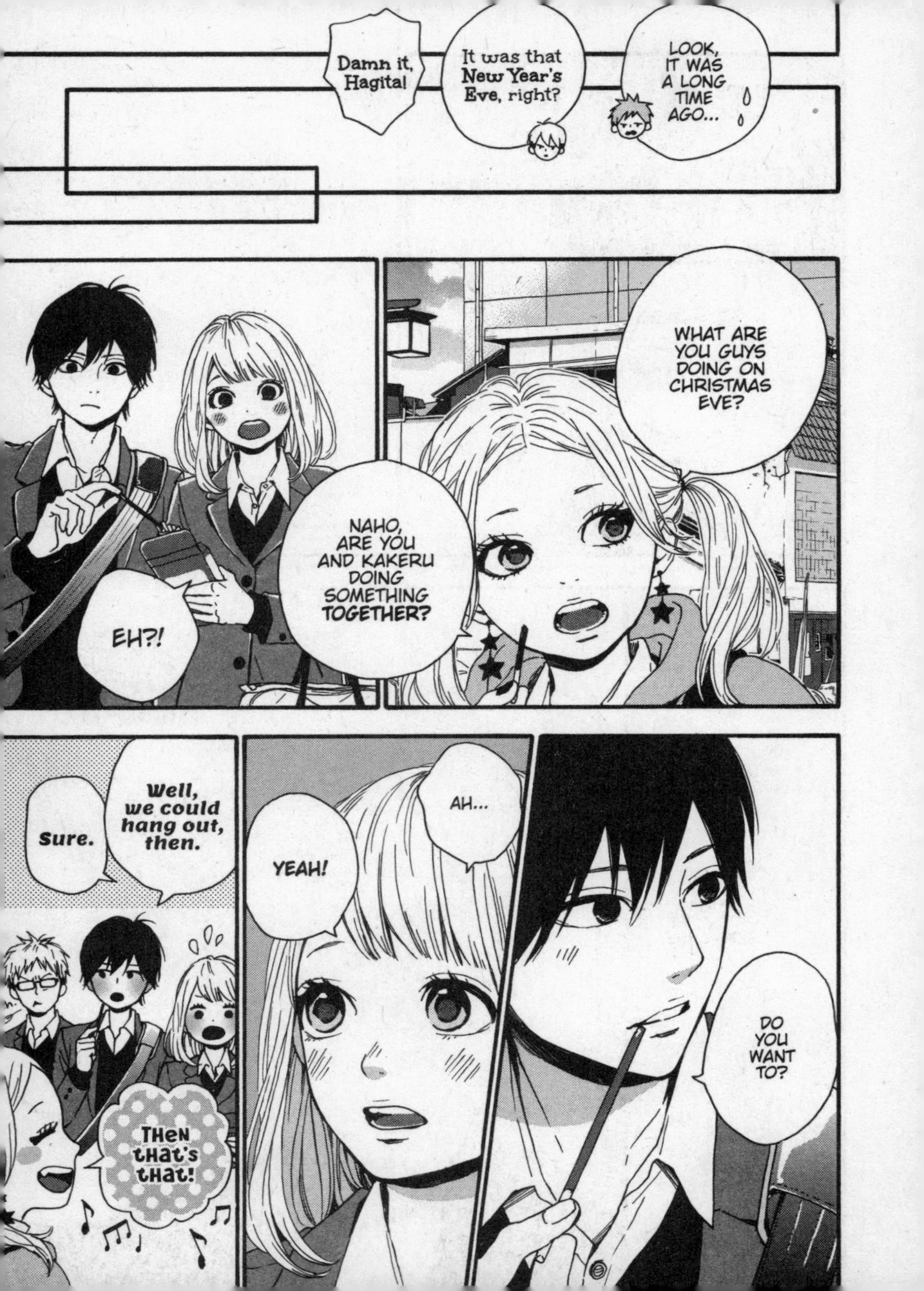
LOOK, IT WAS A LONG TIME AGO...
It was that New Year's Eve, right?
Damn it, Hagita!
WHAT ARE YOU GUYS DOING ON CHRISTMAS EVE?
NAHO, ARE YOU AND KAKERU DOING SOMETHING TOGETHER?
EH?!
DO YOU WANT TO?
AH...
YEAH!
Well, we could hang out, then.
Sure.
THEN that's that!

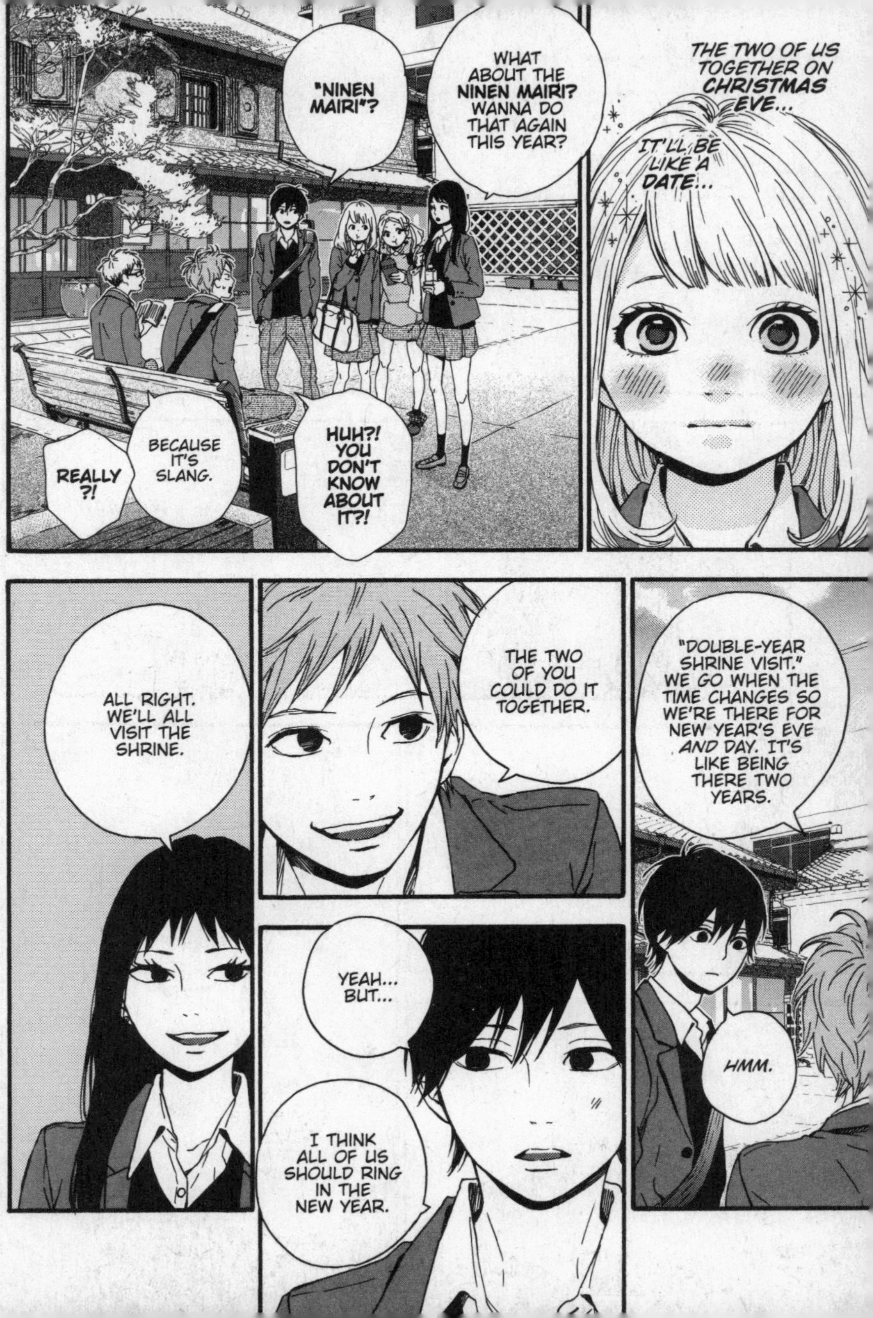
THE TWO OF US TOGETHER ON CHRISTMAS EVE...
IT'LL BE LIKE A DATE...
WHAT ABOUT THE NINEN MAIRI? WANNA DO THAT AGAIN THIS YEAR?
"NINEN MAIRI"?
HUH?! YOU DON'T KNOW ABOUT IT?!
BECAUSE IT'S SLANG.
REALLY ?!
"DOUBLE-YEAR SHRINE VISIT." WE GO WHEN THE TIME CHANGES SO WE'RE THERE FOR NEW YEAR'S EVE AND DAY. IT'S LIKE BEING THERE TWO YEARS.
HMM.
THE TWO OF YOU COULD DO IT TOGETHER.
YEAH... BUT...
I THINK ALL OF US SHOULD RING IN THE NEW YEAR.
ALL RIGHT. WE'LL ALL VISIT THE SHRINE.

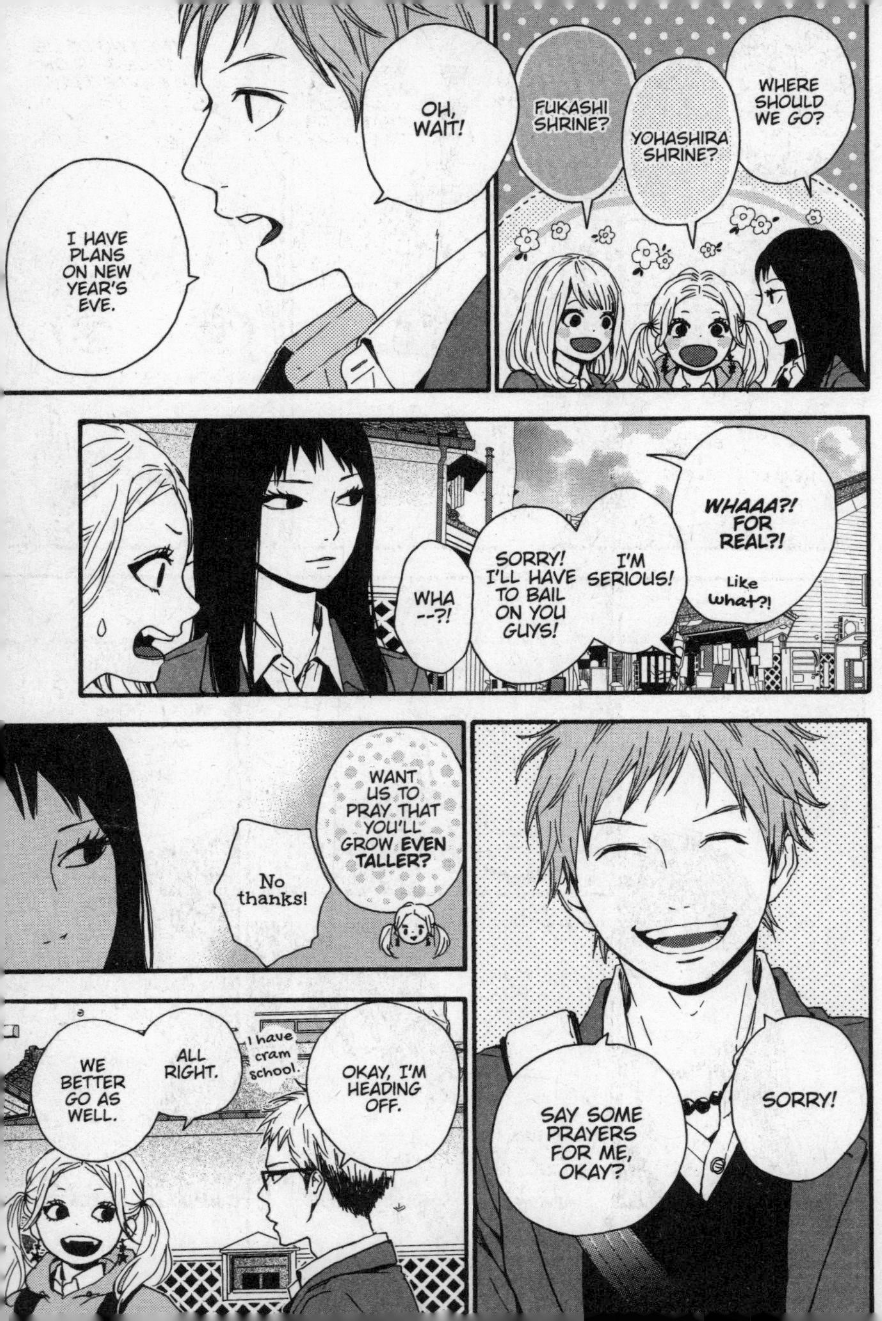
WHERE SHOULD WE GO?
YOHASHIRA SHRINE?
FUKASHI SHRINE?
OH, WAIT!
I HAVE PLANS ON NEW YEAR'S EVE.
WHAAA?! FOR REAL?!
Like what?!
I'M SERIOUS!
SORRY! I'LL HAVE TO BAIL ON YOU GUYS!
WHA --?!
SORRY!
SAY SOME PRAYERS FOR ME, OKAY?
WANT US TO PRAY THAT YOU'LL GROW EVEN TALLER?
No thanks!
OKAY, I'M HEADING OFF.
I have cram school.
ALL RIGHT.
WE BETTER GO AS WELL.

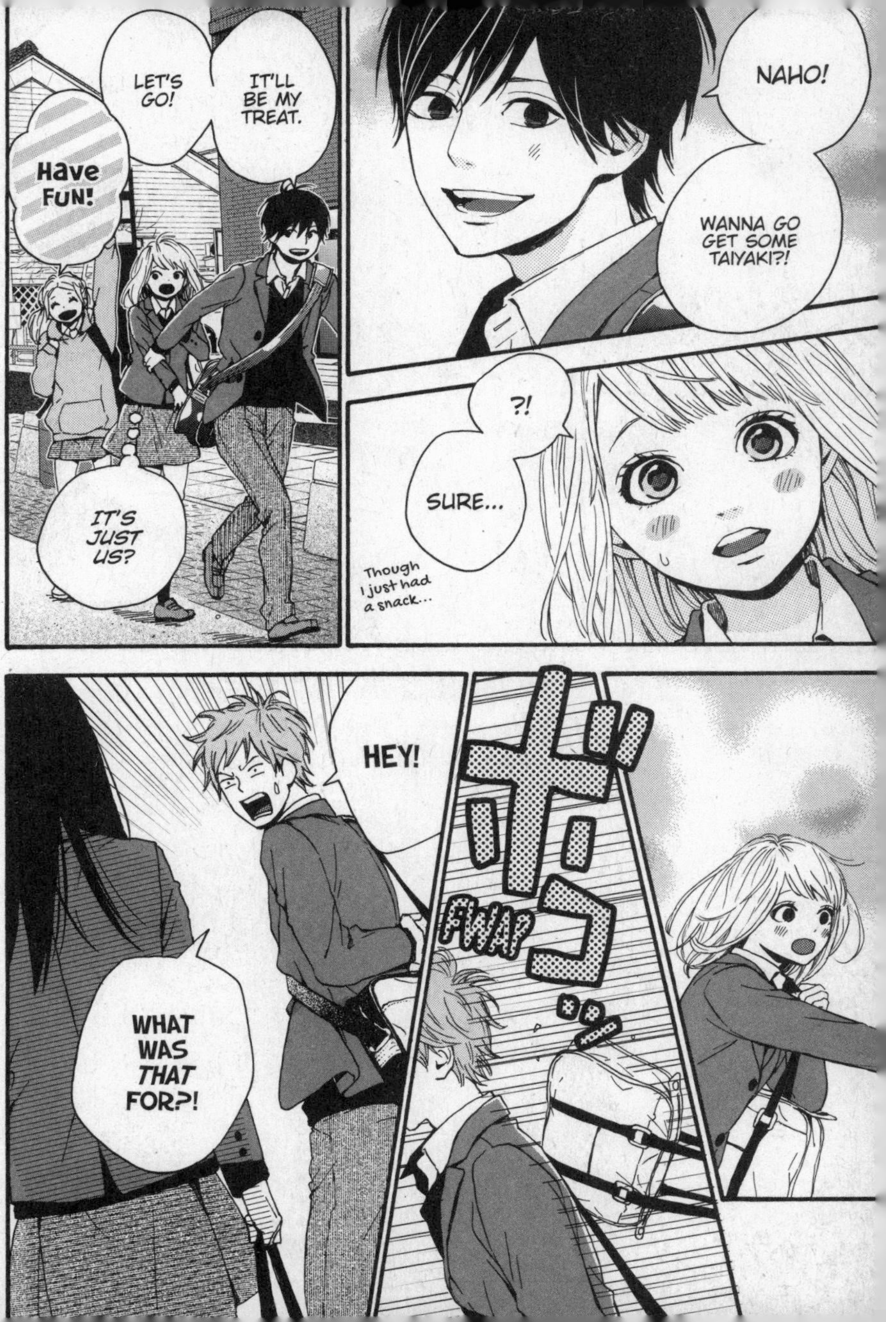
NAHO!
WANNA GO GET SOME TAIYAKI?!
?!
SURE...
Though I just had a snack...
IT'LL BE MY TREAT.
LET'S GO!
Have FUN!
IT'S JUST US?
ボコッ
FWAP
HEY!
WHAT WAS THAT FOR?!

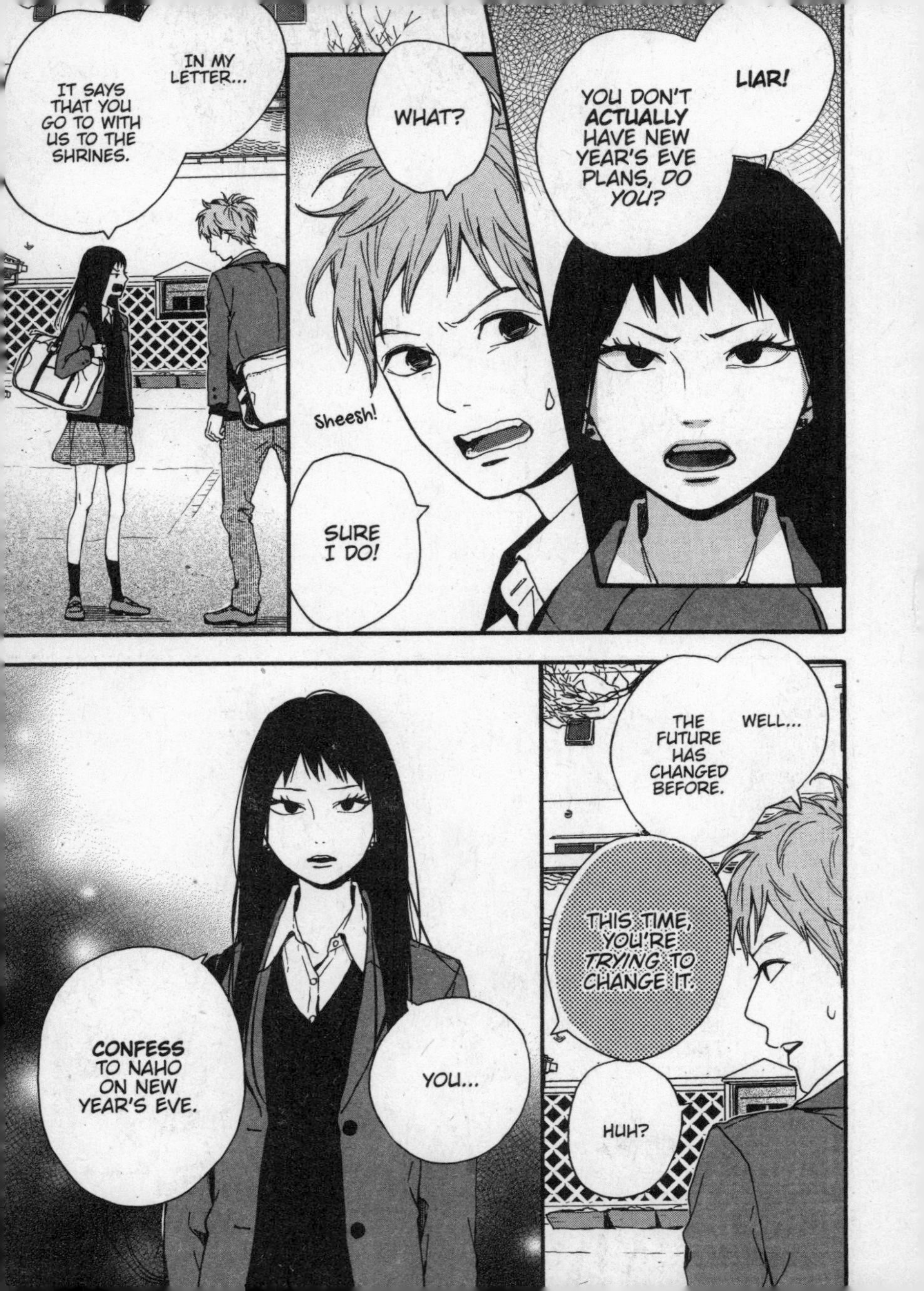
LIAR!
YOU DON'T ACTUALLY HAVE NEW YEAR'S EVE PLANS, DO YOU?
WHAT?
Sheesh!
SURE I DO!
IN MY LETTER...
IT SAYS THAT YOU GO TO WITH US TO THE SHRINES.
WELL...
THE FUTURE HAS CHANGED BEFORE.
THIS TIME, YOU'RE TRYING TO CHANGE IT.
HUH?
YOU...
CONFESS TO NAHO ON NEW YEAR'S EVE.

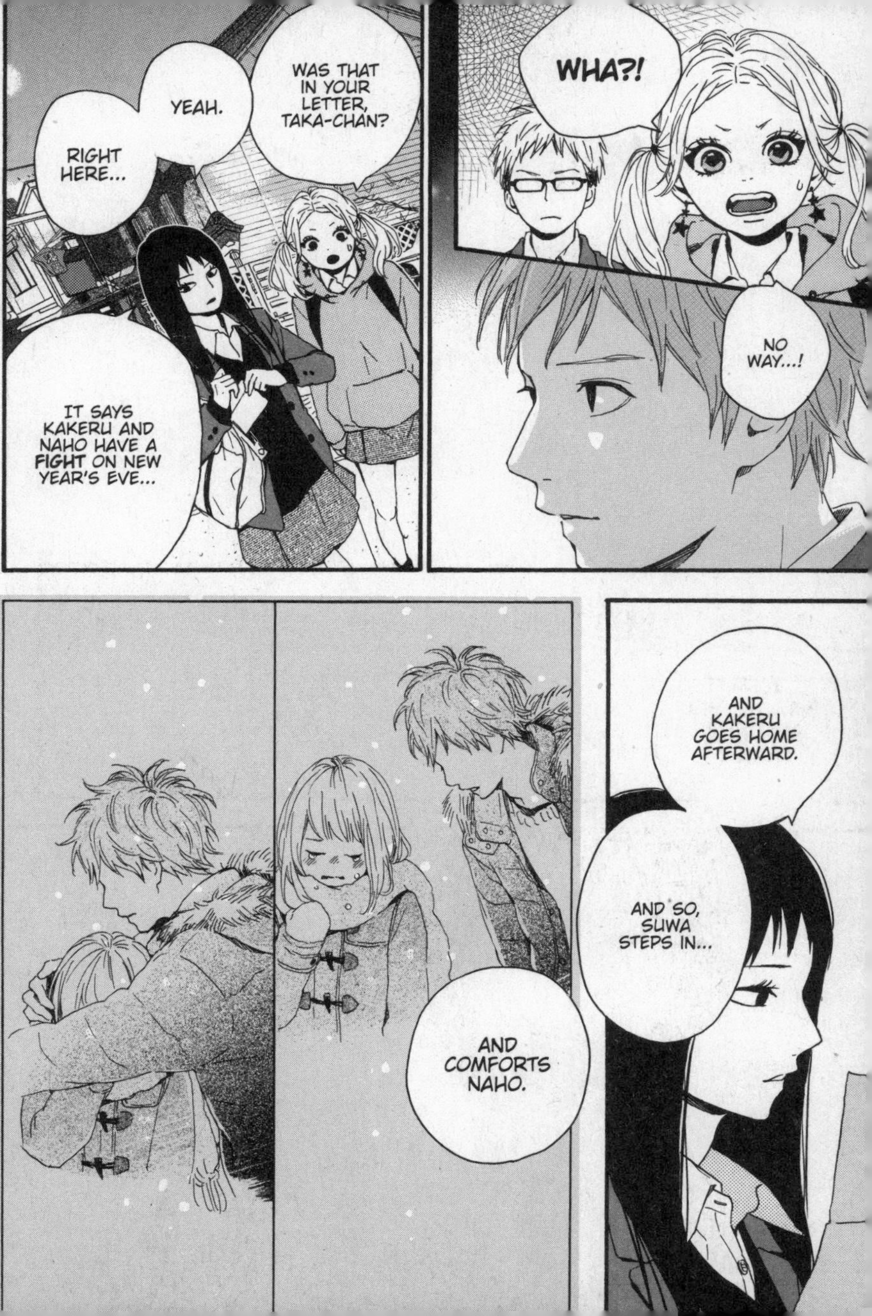
WHA?!
NO WAY...!
WAS THAT IN YOUR LETTER, TAKA-CHAN?
YEAH.
RIGHT HERE...
IT SAYS KAKERU AND NAHO HAVE A **FIGHT** ON NEW YEAR'S EVE...
AND KAKERU GOES HOME AFTERWARD.
AND SO, SUWA STEPS IN...
AND COMFORTS NAHO.

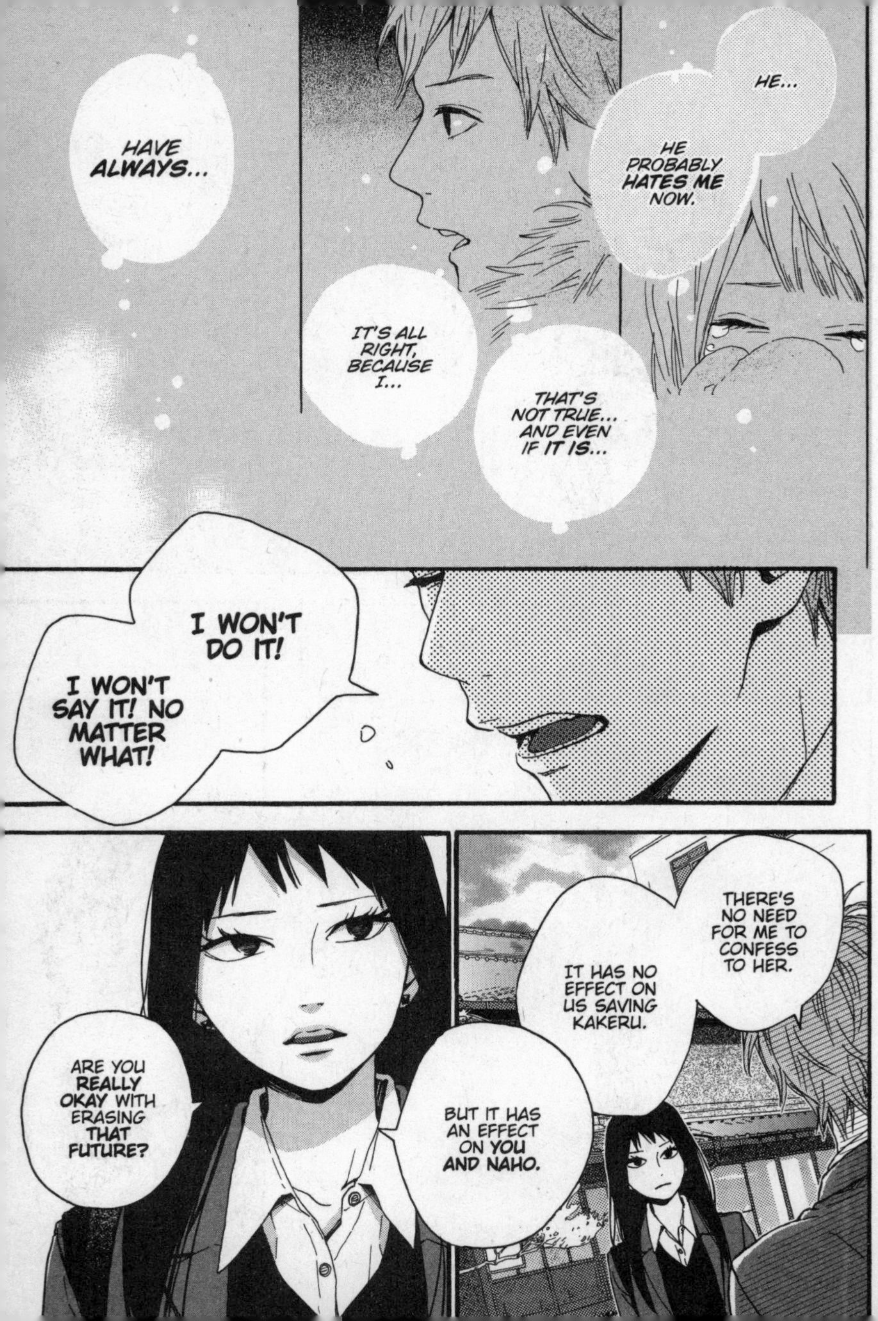
HE...
HE PROBABLY HATES ME NOW.
THAT'S NOT TRUE... AND EVEN IF IT IS...
IT'S ALL RIGHT, BECAUSE I...
HAVE ALWAYS...
I WON'T DO IT!
I WON'T SAY IT! NO MATTER WHAT!
THERE'S NO NEED FOR ME TO CONFESS TO HER.
IT HAS NO EFFECT ON US SAVING KAKERU.
BUT IT HAS AN EFFECT ON YOU AND NAHO.
ARE YOU REALLY OKAY WITH ERASING THAT FUTURE?

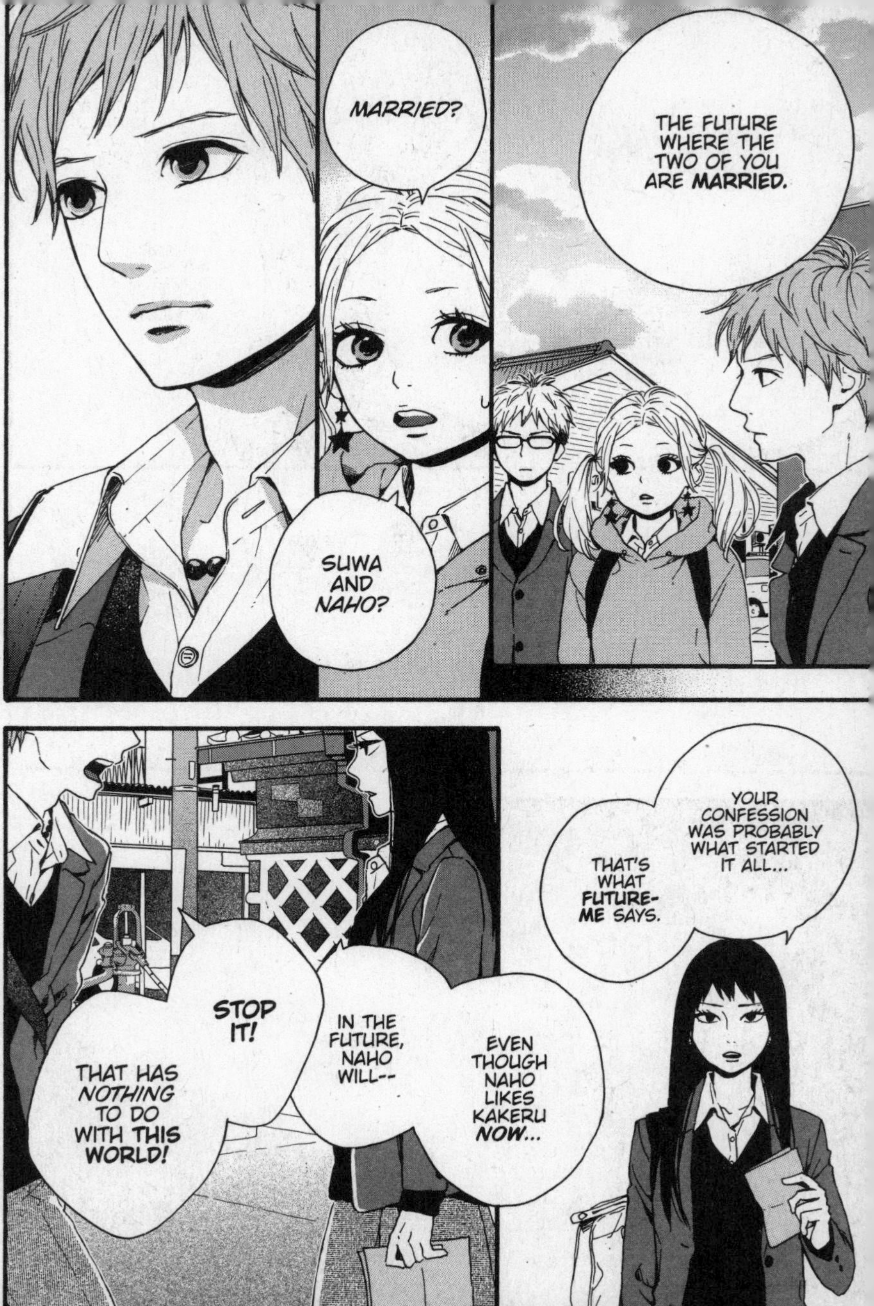
THE FUTURE WHERE THE TWO OF YOU ARE MARRIED.
MARRIED?
SUWA AND NAHO?
YOUR CONFESSION WAS PROBABLY WHAT STARTED IT ALL...
THAT'S WHAT FUTURE-ME SAYS.
EVEN THOUGH NAHO LIKES KAKERU NOW...
IN THE FUTURE, NAHO WILL--
STOP IT!
THAT HAS NOTHING TO DO WITH THIS WORLD!

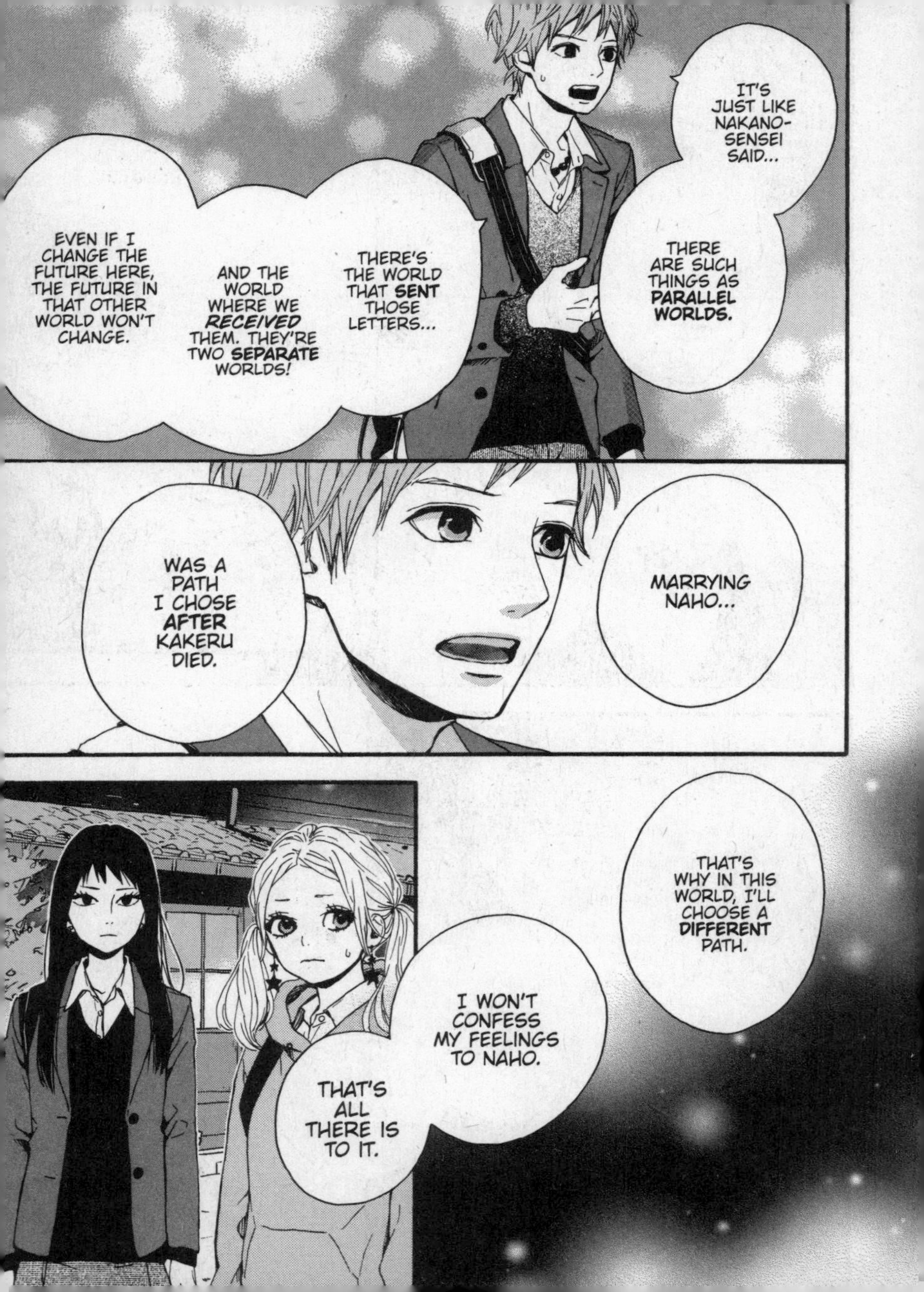
IT'S JUST LIKE NAKANO-SENSEI SAID...
THERE ARE SUCH THINGS AS **PARALLEL WORLDS.**
THERE'S THE WORLD THAT **SENT** THOSE LETTERS...
AND THE WORLD WHERE WE ***RECEIVED*** THEM. THEY'RE TWO **SEPARATE** WORLDS!
EVEN IF I CHANGE THE FUTURE HERE, THE FUTURE IN THAT OTHER WORLD WON'T CHANGE.
MARRYING NAHO...
WAS A PATH I CHOSE **AFTER** KAKERU DIED.
THAT'S WHY IN THIS WORLD, I'LL CHOOSE A **DIFFERENT** PATH.
I WON'T CONFESS MY FEELINGS TO NAHO.
THAT'S ALL THERE IS TO IT.

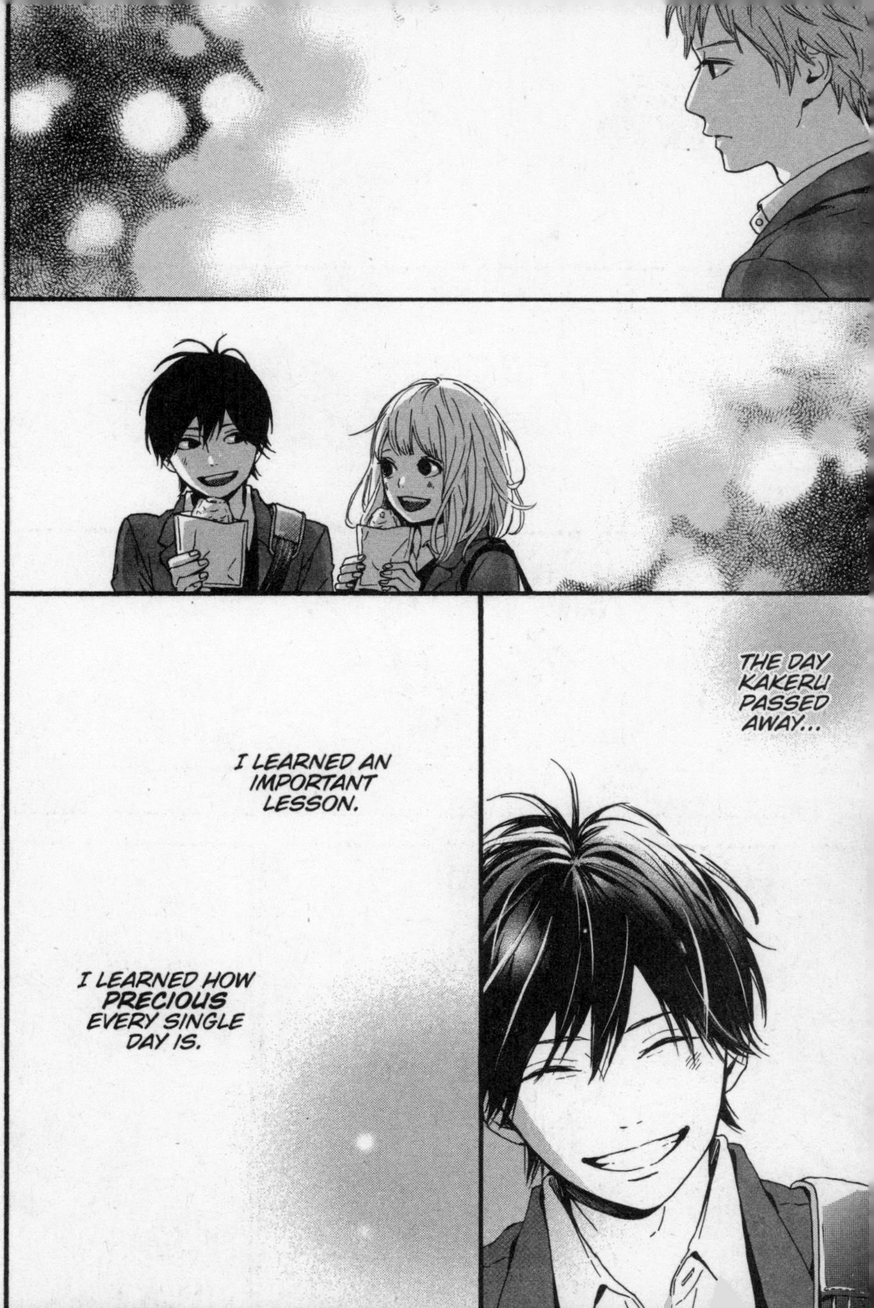
THE DAY KAKERU PASSED AWAY...
I LEARNED AN IMPORTANT LESSON.
I LEARNED HOW PRECIOUS EVERY SINGLE DAY IS.

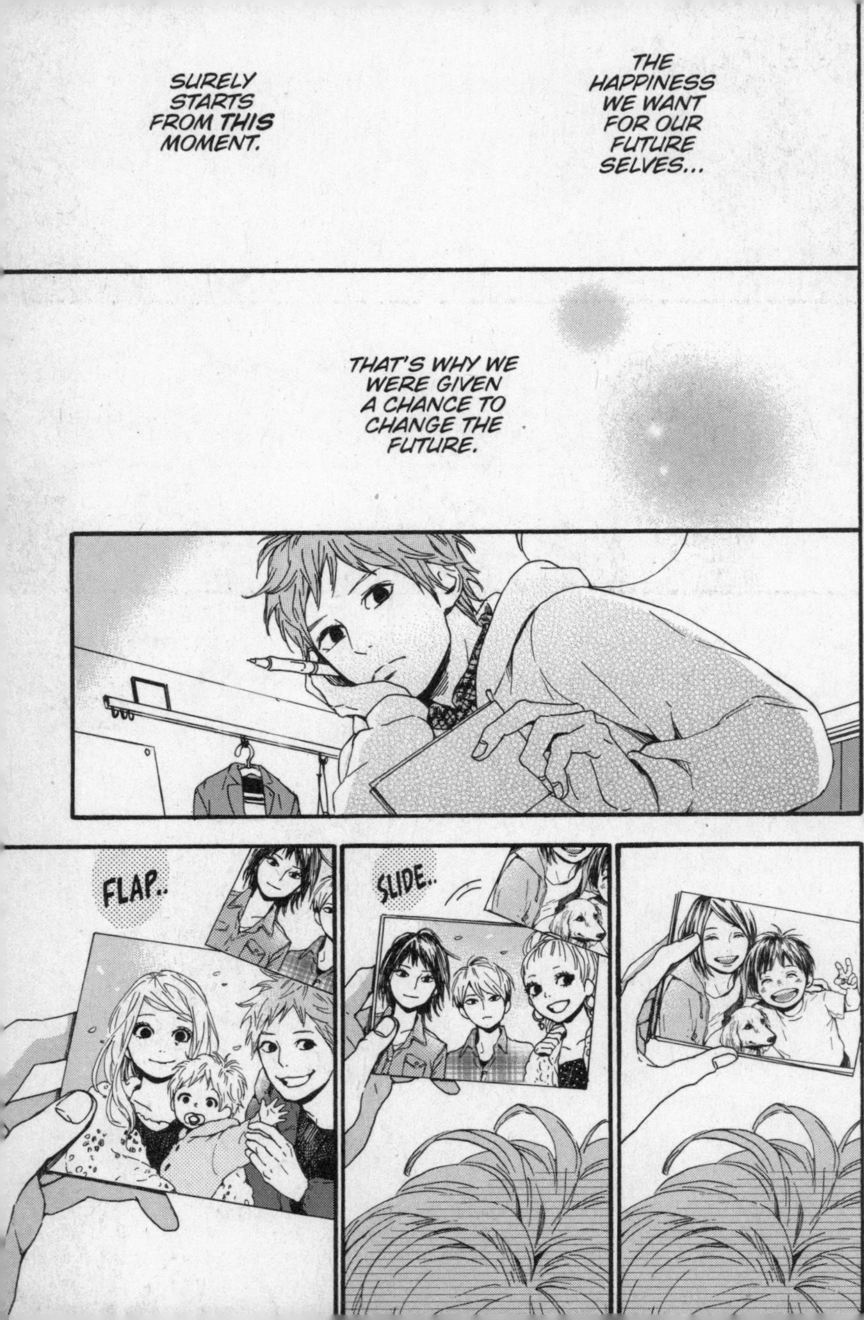
THE HAPPINESS WE WANT FOR OUR FUTURE SELVES...
SURELY STARTS FROM THIS MOMENT.
THAT'S WHY WE WERE GIVEN A CHANCE TO CHANGE THE FUTURE.
SLIDE..
FLAP..

December 31

- Everyone does the Double-Year Shrine Visit.
- Later on, I have an argument with Kakeru.
- After this, the distance between Kakeru and me grows. We don't talk as much as before.

- Kakeru passed away without me ever really apologizing to him.

orange

orange

ICHIGO TAKANO presents

5

the fifth
volume

orange

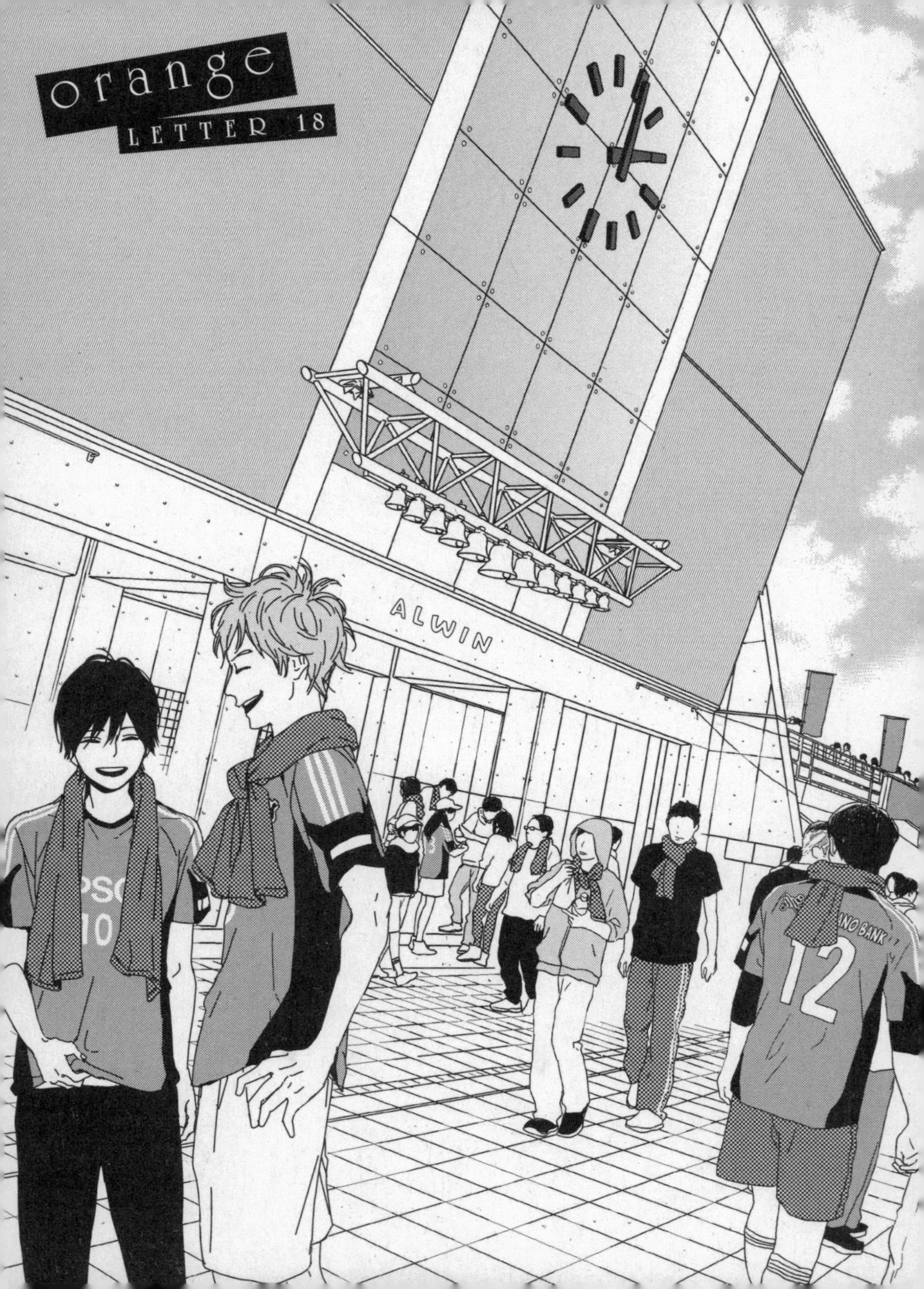
orange
LETTER 18
ALWIN
12

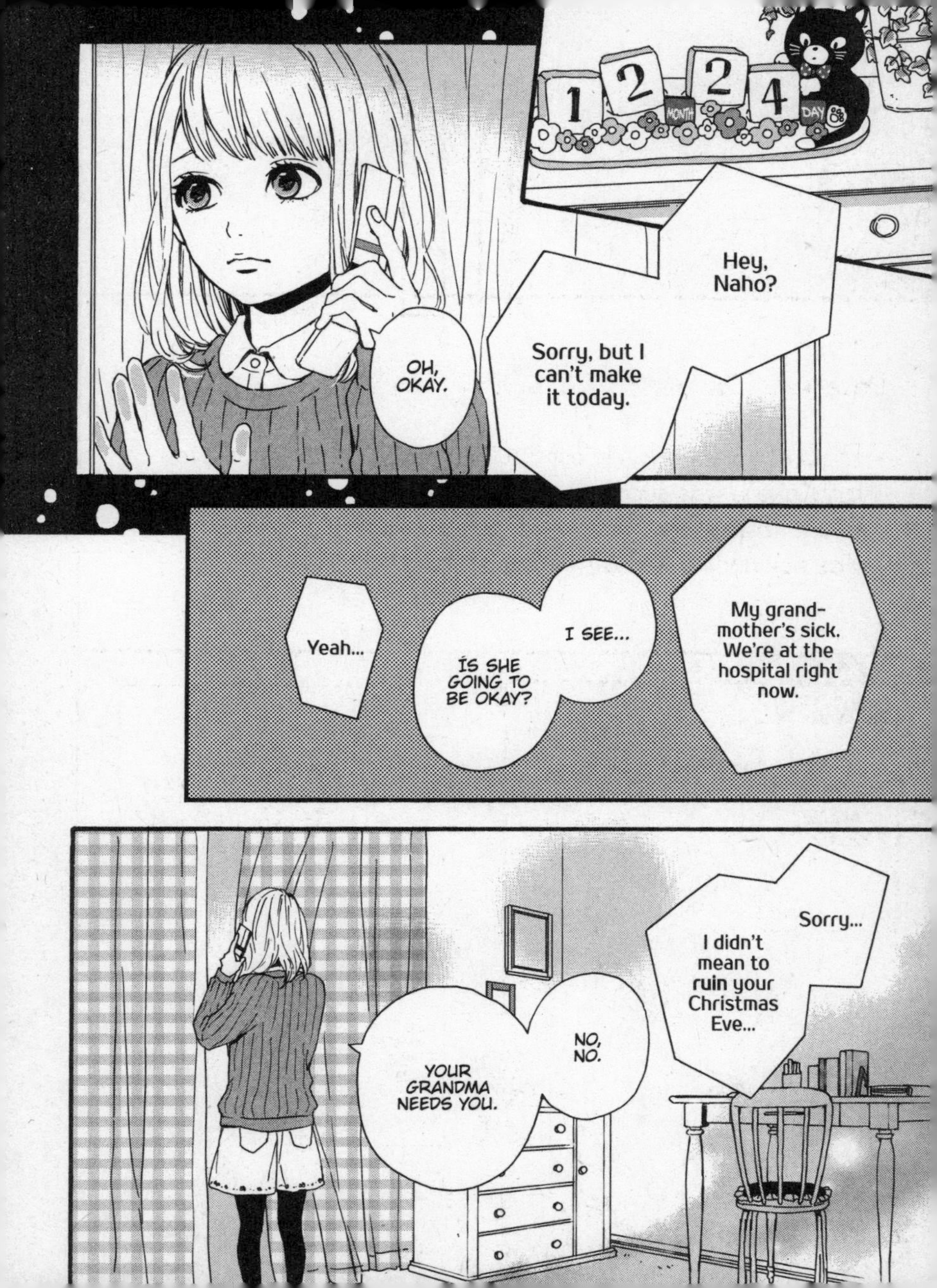
12 MONTH 24 DAY
Hey, Naho?
Sorry, but I can't make it today.
OH, OKAY.
My grand-mother's sick. We're at the hospital right now.
I SEE...
IS SHE GOING TO BE OKAY?
Yeah...
Sorry...
I didn't mean to ruin your Christmas Eve...
NO, NO.
YOUR GRANDMA NEEDS YOU.

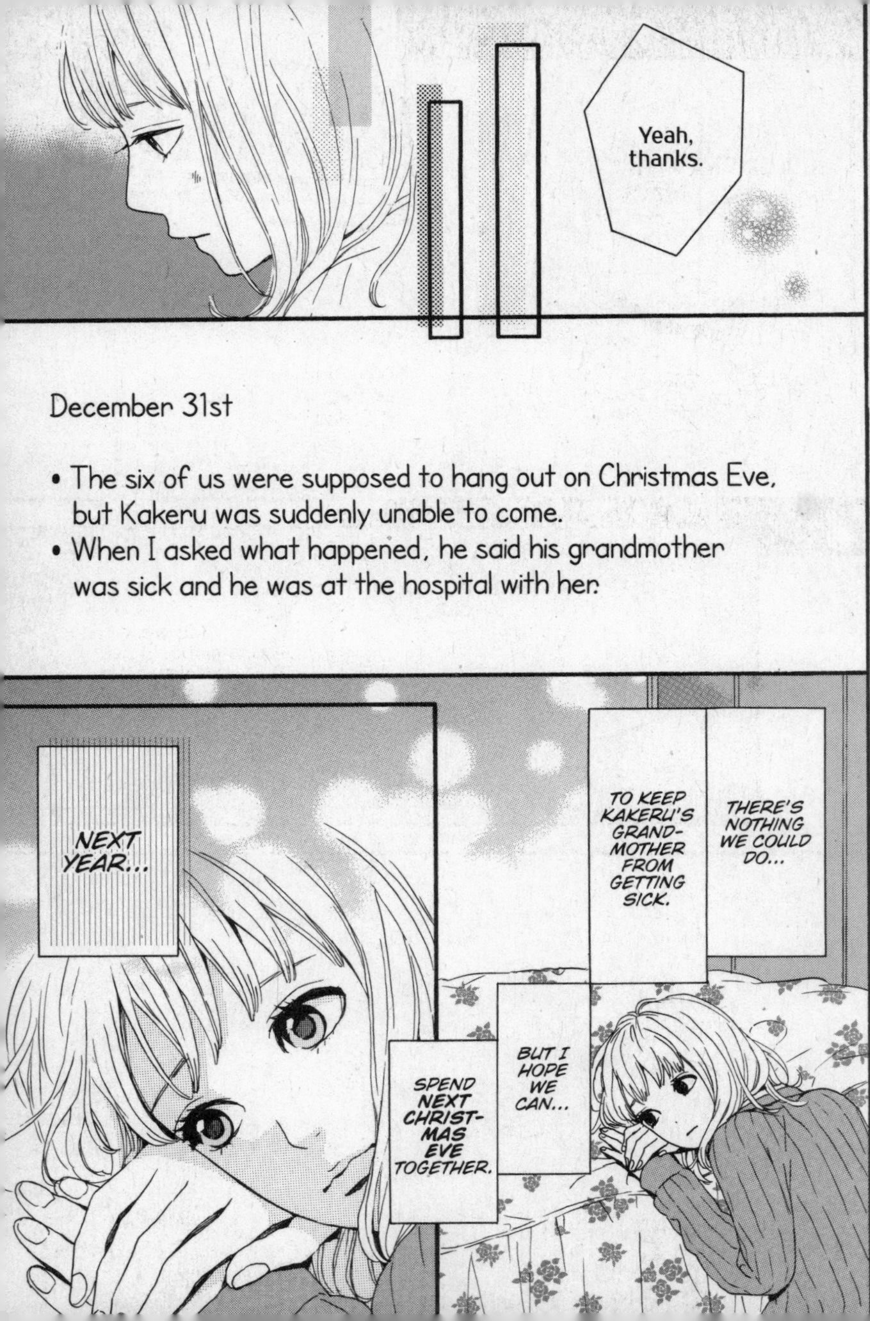
Yeah, thanks.
December 31st
• The six of us were supposed to hang out on Christmas Eve, but Kakeru was suddenly unable to come.
• When I asked what happened, he said his grandmother was sick and he was at the hospital with her.
THERE'S NOTHING WE COULD DO...
TO KEEP KAKERU'S GRAND-MOTHER FROM GETTING SICK.
NEXT YEAR...
BUT I HOPE WE CAN...
SPEND NEXT CHRIST-MAS EVE TOGETHER.

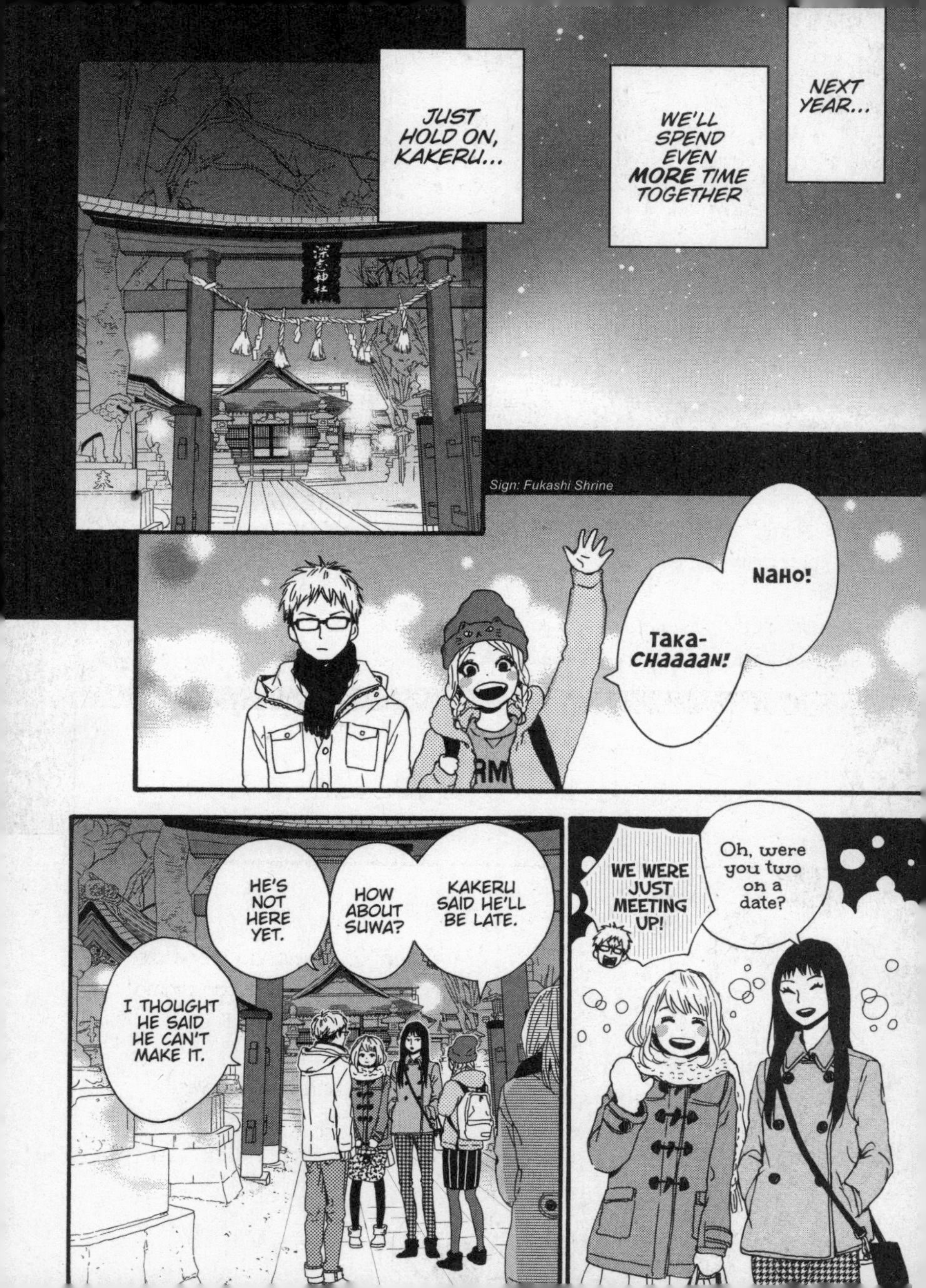
NEXT YEAR...
WE'LL SPEND EVEN MORE TIME TOGETHER
JUST HOLD ON, KAKERU...
Sign: Fukashi Shrine
NAHO!
TAKA-CHAAAAN!
Oh, were you two on a date?
WE WERE JUST MEETING UP!
KAKERU SAID HE'LL BE LATE.
HOW ABOUT SUWA?
HE'S NOT HERE YET.
I THOUGHT HE SAID HE CAN'T MAKE IT.

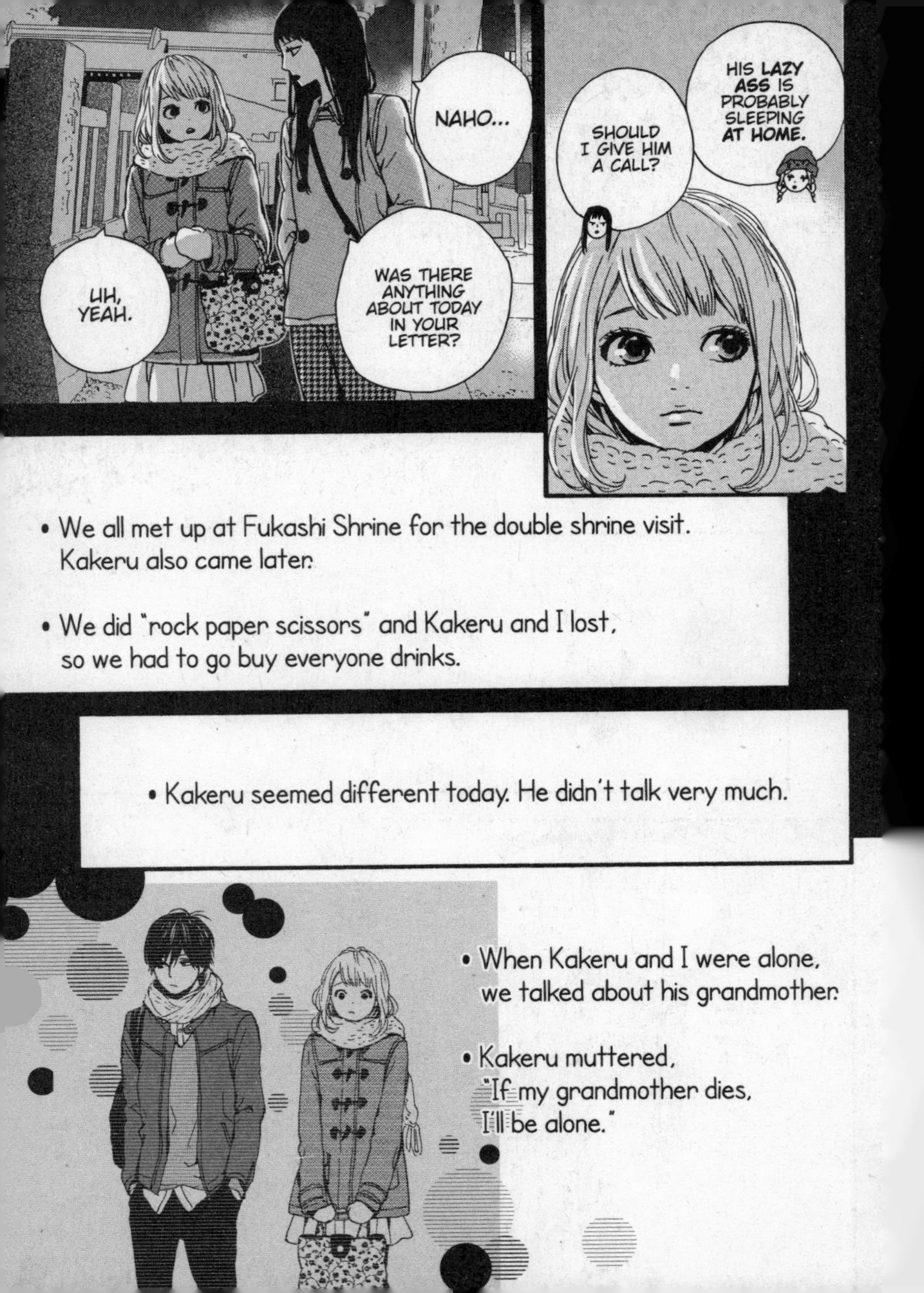

HIS LAZY ASS IS PROBABLY SLEEPING AT HOME.
SHOULD I GIVE HIM A CALL?
NAHO...
WAS THERE ANYTHING ABOUT TODAY IN YOUR LETTER?
UH, YEAH.
• We all met up at Fukashi Shrine for the double shrine visit. Kakeru also came later.
• We did "rock paper scissors" and Kakeru and I lost, so we had to go buy everyone drinks.
• Kakeru seemed different today. He didn't talk very much.
• When Kakeru and I were alone, we talked about his grandmother.
• Kakeru muttered, "If my grandmother dies, I'll be alone."

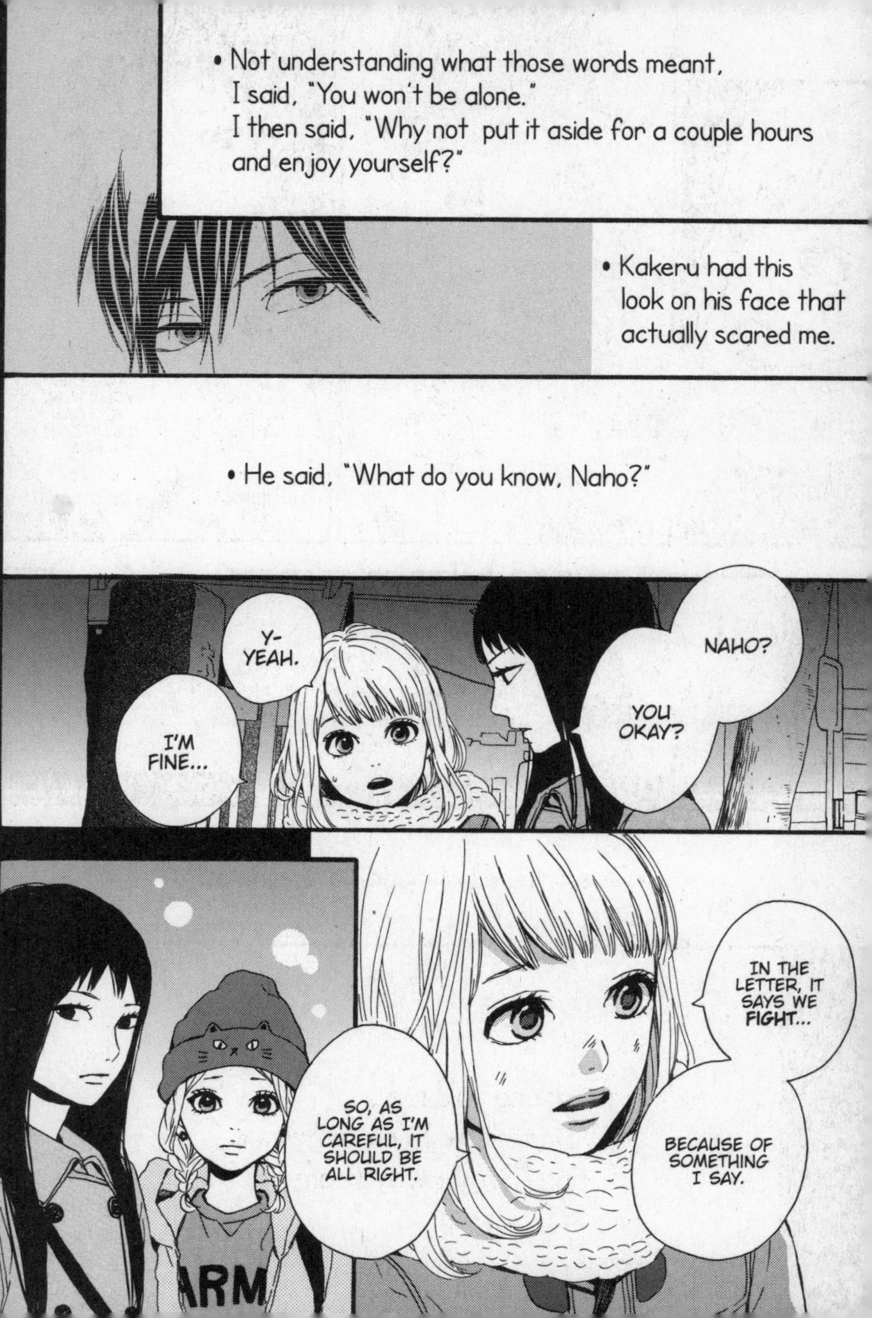
• Not understanding what those words meant, I said, "You won't be alone." I then said, "Why not put it aside for a couple hours and enjoy yourself?"
• Kakeru had this look on his face that actually scared me.
• He said, "What do you know, Naho?"
NAHO?
YOU OKAY?
Y-YEAH.
I'M FINE...
IN THE LETTER, IT SAYS WE FIGHT...
BECAUSE OF SOMETHING I SAY.
SO, AS LONG AS I'M CAREFUL, IT SHOULD BE ALL RIGHT.
ARM

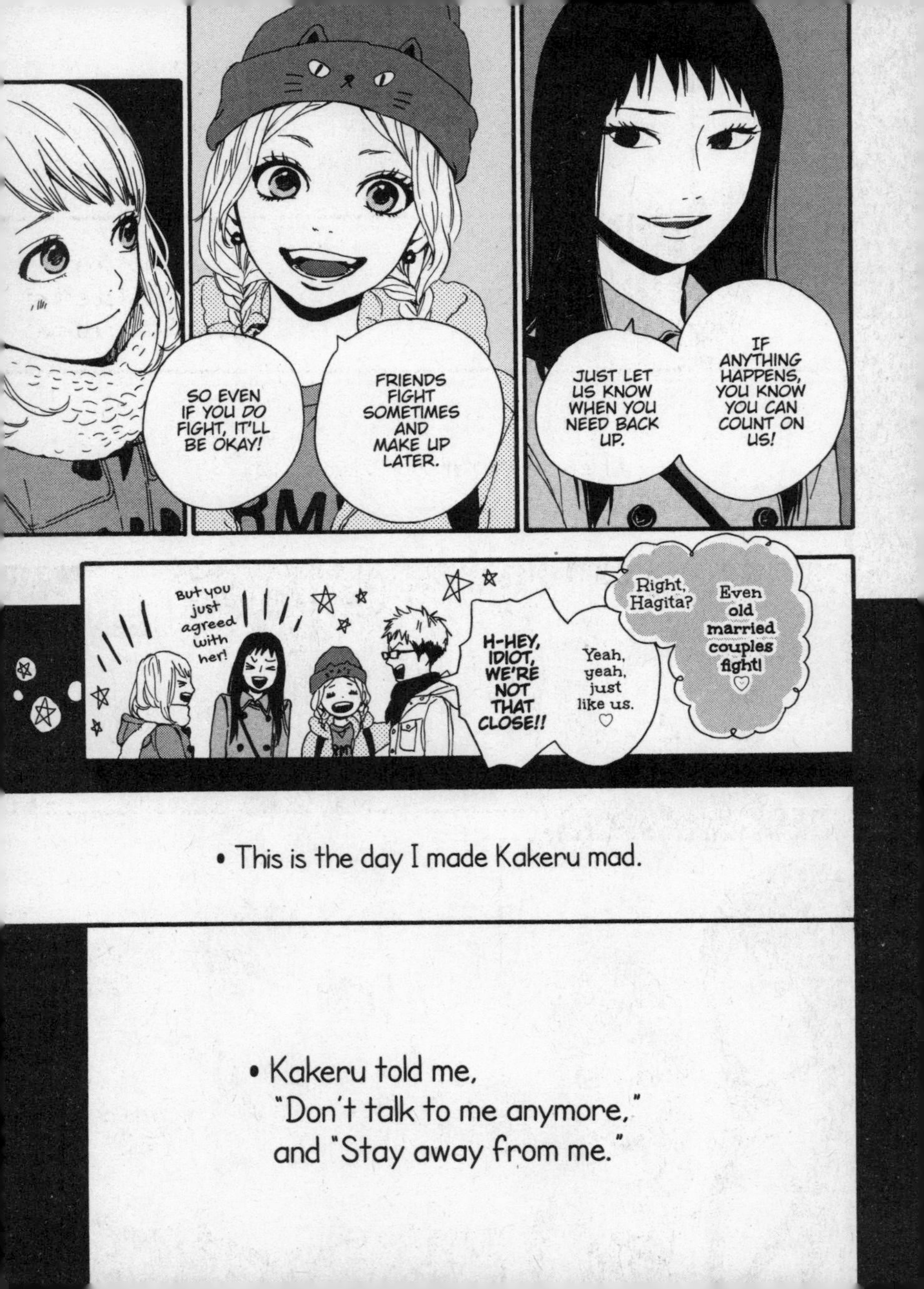
IF ANYTHING HAPPENS, YOU KNOW YOU CAN COUNT ON US!
JUST LET US KNOW WHEN YOU NEED BACK UP.
FRIENDS FIGHT SOMETIMES AND MAKE UP LATER.
SO EVEN IF YOU DO FIGHT, IT'LL BE OKAY!
Even old married couples fight! ♡
Right, Hagita?
Yeah, yeah, just like us. ♡
H-HEY, IDIOT, WE'RE NOT THAT CLOSE!!
But you just agreed with her!
• This is the day I made Kakeru mad.
• Kakeru told me, "Don't talk to me anymore," and "Stay away from me."

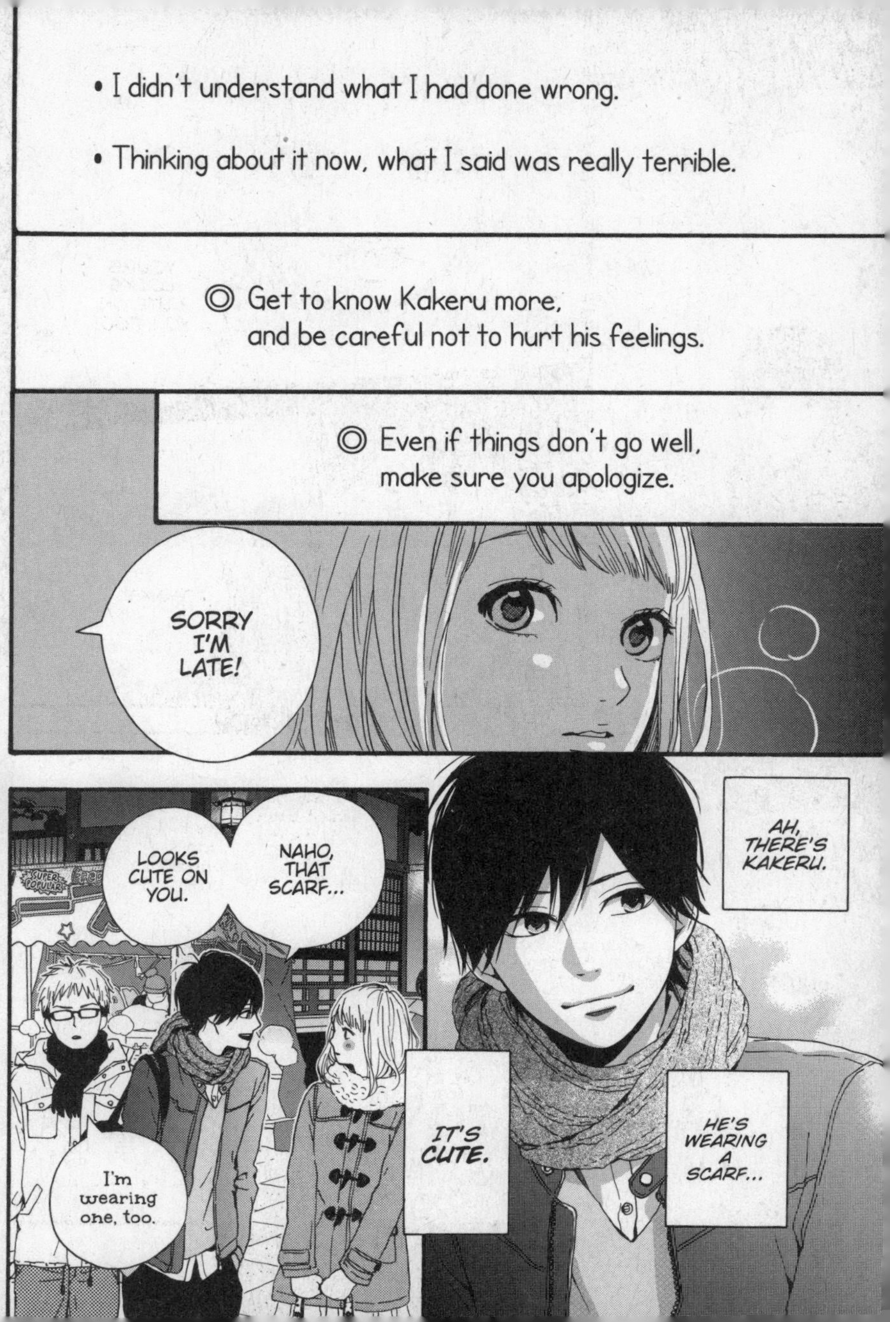
• I didn't understand what I had done wrong.
• Thinking about it now, what I said was really terrible.
◎ Get to know Kakeru more, and be careful not to hurt his feelings.
◎ Even if things don't go well, make sure you apologize.
SORRY I'M LATE!
AH, THERE'S KAKERU.
HE'S WEARING A SCARF...
IT'S CUTE.
NAHO, THAT SCARF...
LOOKS CUTE ON YOU.
SUPER POPULAR
I'm wearing one, too.

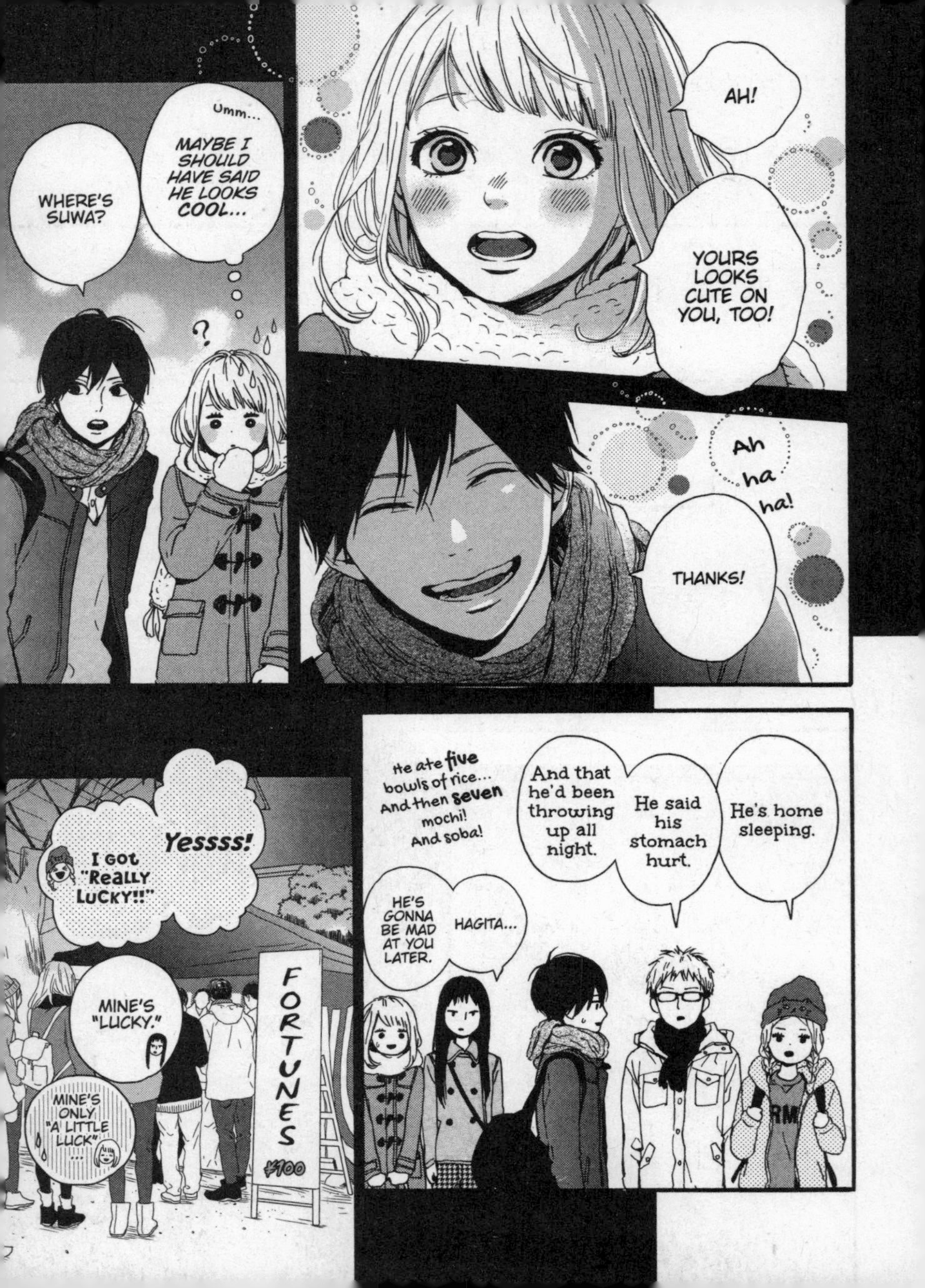
AH!
YOURS LOOKS CUTE ON YOU, TOO!
Ah ha ha!
THANKS!
Umm... MAYBE I SHOULD HAVE SAID HE LOOKS COOL...
WHERE'S SUWA?
He's home sleeping.
He said his stomach hurt.
And that he'd been throwing up all night.
He ate five bowls of rice... And then seven mochi! And soba!
HAGITA...
HE'S GONNA BE MAD AT YOU LATER.
Yessss!
I got "Really Lucky!!"
MINE'S "LUCKY."
FORTUNES ¥100
MINE'S ONLY "A LITTLE LUCK"...

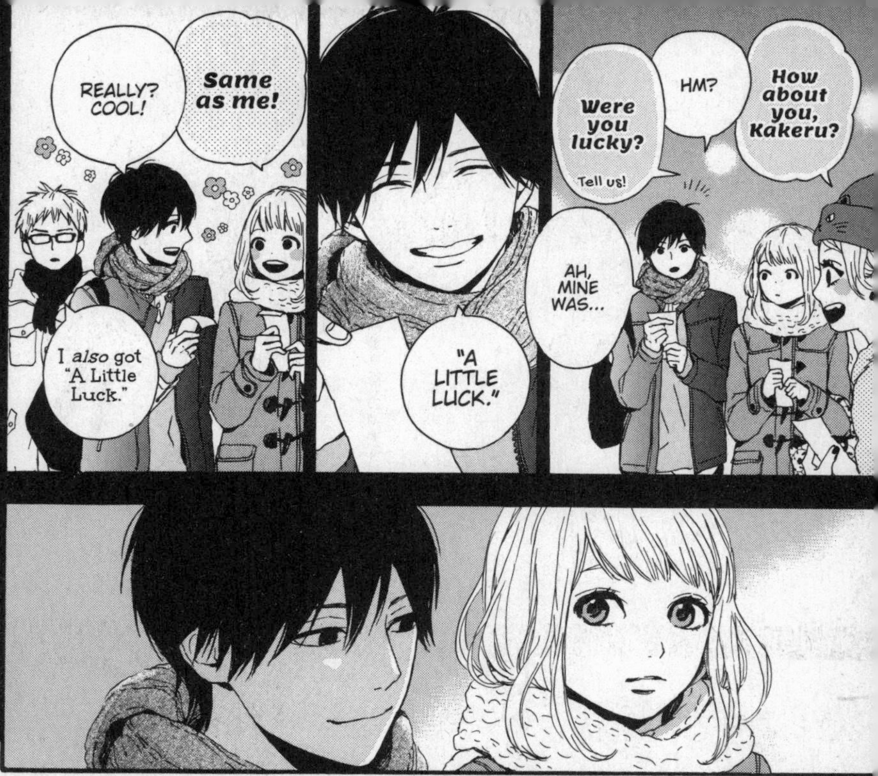
How about you, Kakeru?
HM?
Were you lucky?
Tell us!
AH, MINE WAS...
"A LITTLE LUCK."
Same as me!
REALLY? COOL!
I *also* got "A Little Luck."

Signs: Best Wishes for the New Year, Fukashi Shrine / Lantern: Blessings and Longevity, Fukashi Shrine

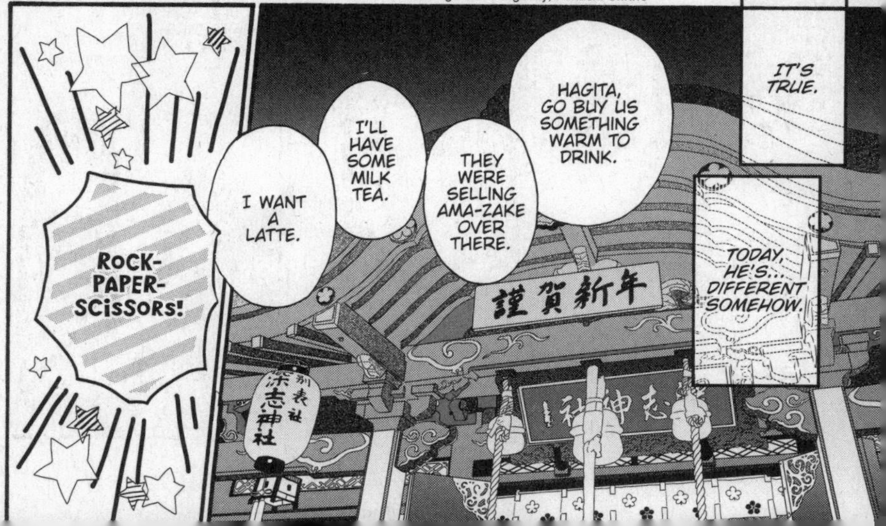
IT'S TRUE.
TODAY, HE'S... DIFFERENT SOMEHOW.
HAGITA, GO BUY US SOMETHING WARM TO DRINK.
THEY WERE SELLING AMA-ZAKE OVER THERE.
I'LL HAVE SOME MILK TEA.
I WANT A LATTE.
謹賀新年
ROCK-PAPER-SCISSORS!

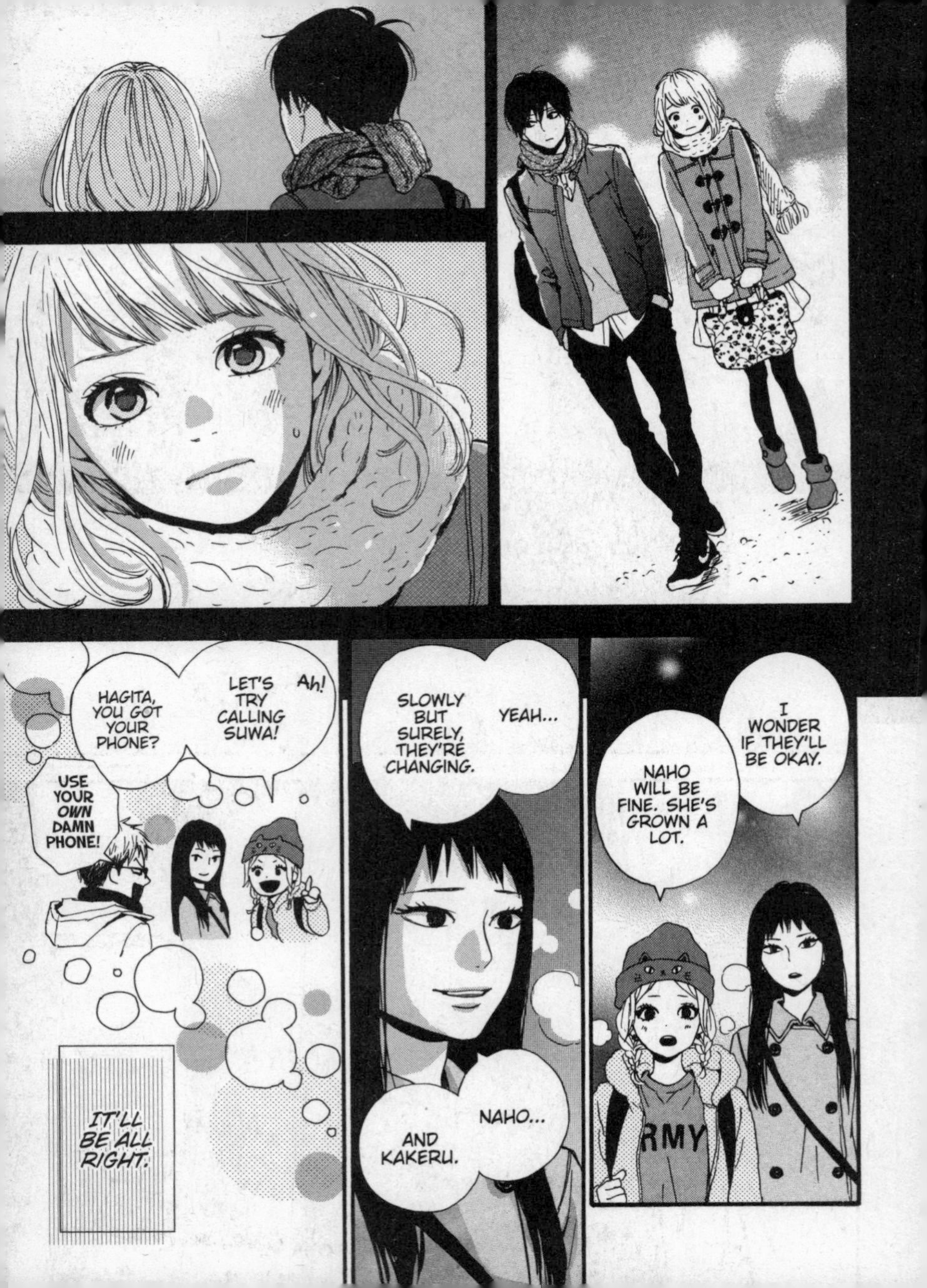
I WONDER IF THEY'LL BE OKAY.
NAHO WILL BE FINE. SHE'S GROWN A LOT.
YEAH...
SLOWLY BUT SURELY, THEY'RE CHANGING.
NAHO...
AND KAKERU.
Ah!
LET'S TRY CALLING SUWA!
HAGITA, YOU GOT YOUR PHONE?
USE YOUR *OWN* DAMN PHONE!
IT'LL BE ALL RIGHT.

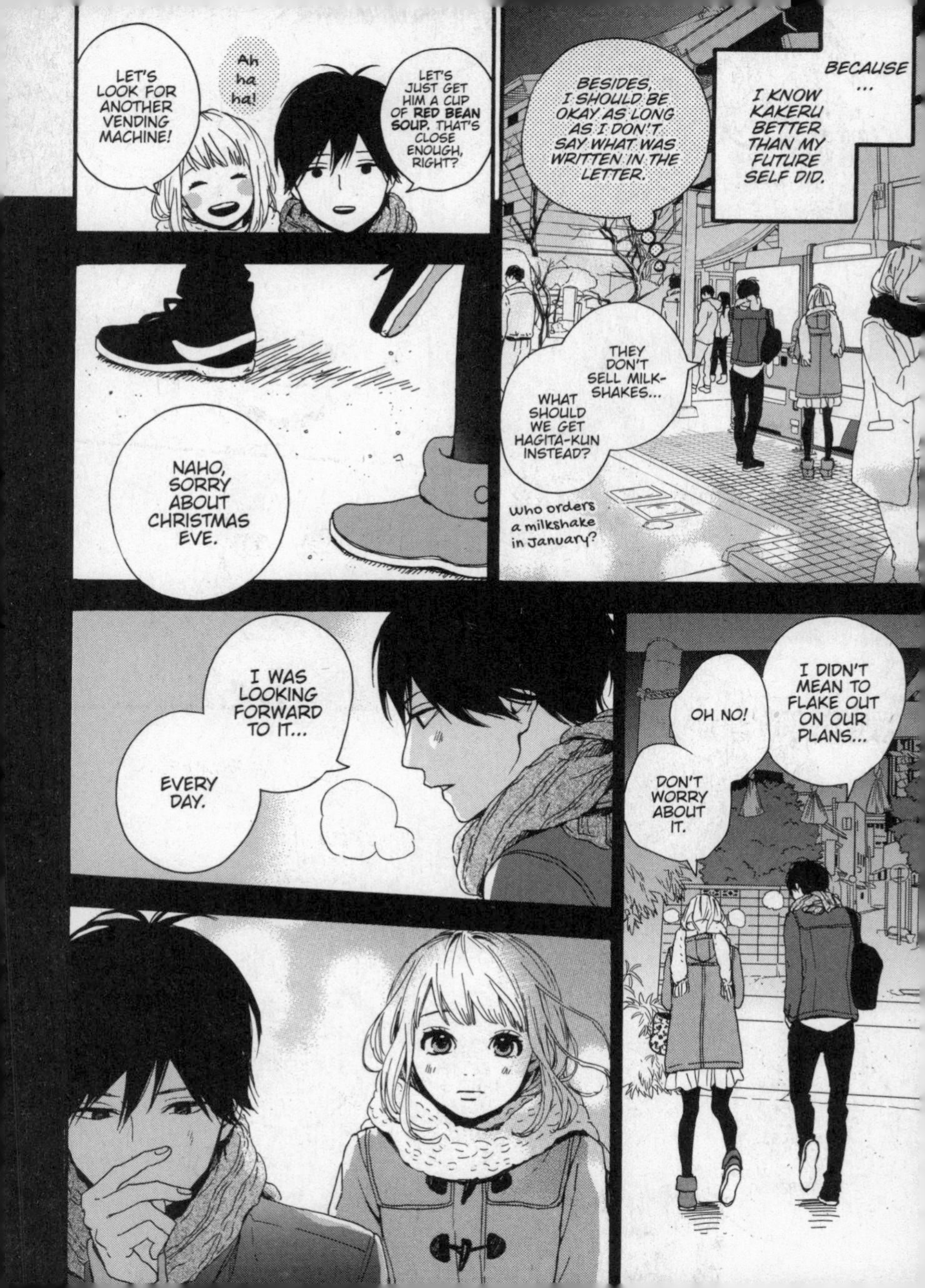
BECAUSE ... I KNOW KAKERU BETTER THAN MY FUTURE SELF DID.
BESIDES, I SHOULD BE OKAY AS LONG AS I DON'T SAY WHAT WAS WRITTEN IN THE LETTER.
THEY DON'T SELL MILK-SHAKES...
WHAT SHOULD WE GET HAGITA-KUN INSTEAD?
Who orders a milkshake in January?
LET'S JUST GET HIM A CUP OF RED BEAN SOUP. THAT'S CLOSE ENOUGH, RIGHT?
Ah ha ha!
LET'S LOOK FOR ANOTHER VENDING MACHINE!
NAHO, SORRY ABOUT CHRISTMAS EVE.
I DIDN'T MEAN TO FLAKE OUT ON OUR PLANS...
OH NO!
DON'T WORRY ABOUT IT.
I WAS LOOKING FORWARD TO IT...
EVERY DAY.

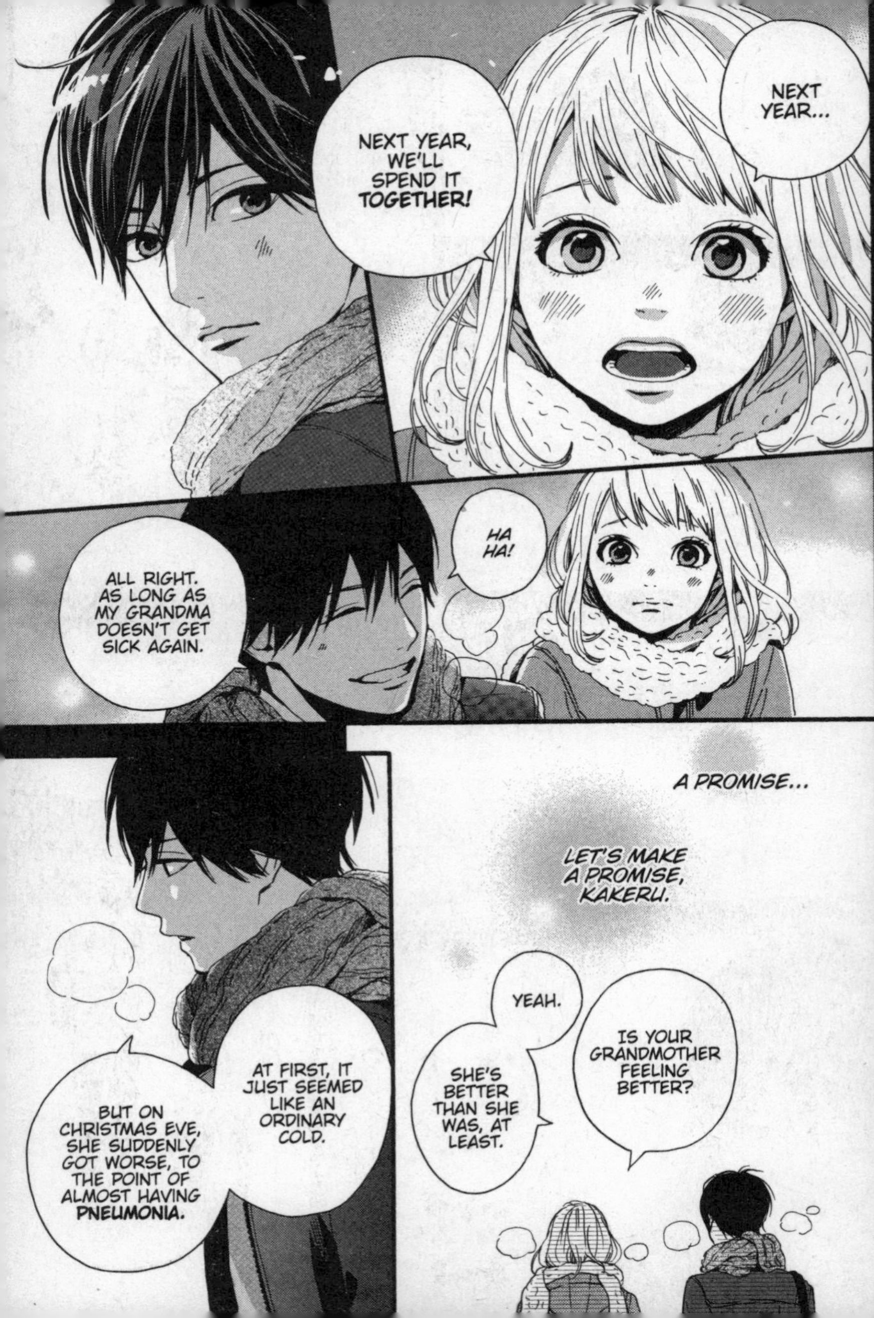
NEXT YEAR...
NEXT YEAR, WE'LL SPEND IT TOGETHER!
HA HA!
ALL RIGHT. AS LONG AS MY GRANDMA DOESN'T GET SICK AGAIN.
A PROMISE...
LET'S MAKE A PROMISE, KAKERU.
IS YOUR GRANDMOTHER FEELING BETTER?
YEAH.
SHE'S BETTER THAN SHE WAS, AT LEAST.
AT FIRST, IT JUST SEEMED LIKE AN ORDINARY COLD.
BUT ON CHRISTMAS EVE, SHE SUDDENLY GOT WORSE, TO THE POINT OF ALMOST HAVING PNEUMONIA.

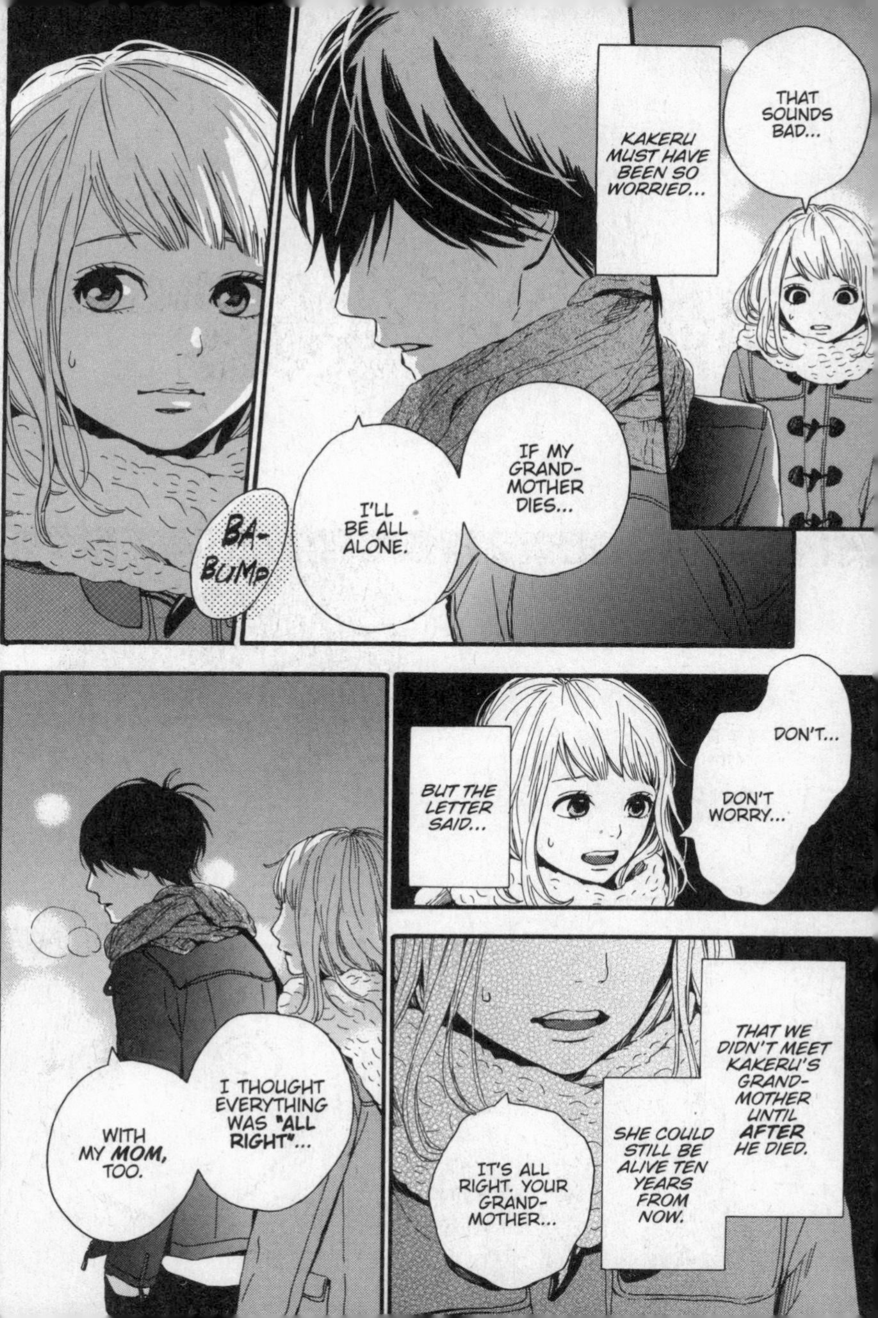

THAT SOUNDS BAD...
KAKERU MUST HAVE BEEN SO WORRIED...
IF MY GRAND-MOTHER DIES...
I'LL BE ALL ALONE.
BA-BUMP
DON'T...
DON'T WORRY...
BUT THE LETTER SAID...
THAT WE DIDN'T MEET KAKERU'S GRAND-MOTHER UNTIL **AFTER** HE DIED.
SHE COULD STILL BE ALIVE TEN YEARS FROM NOW.
IT'S ALL RIGHT. YOUR GRAND-MOTHER...
I THOUGHT EVERYTHING WAS **"ALL RIGHT"**...
WITH MY **MOM,** TOO.

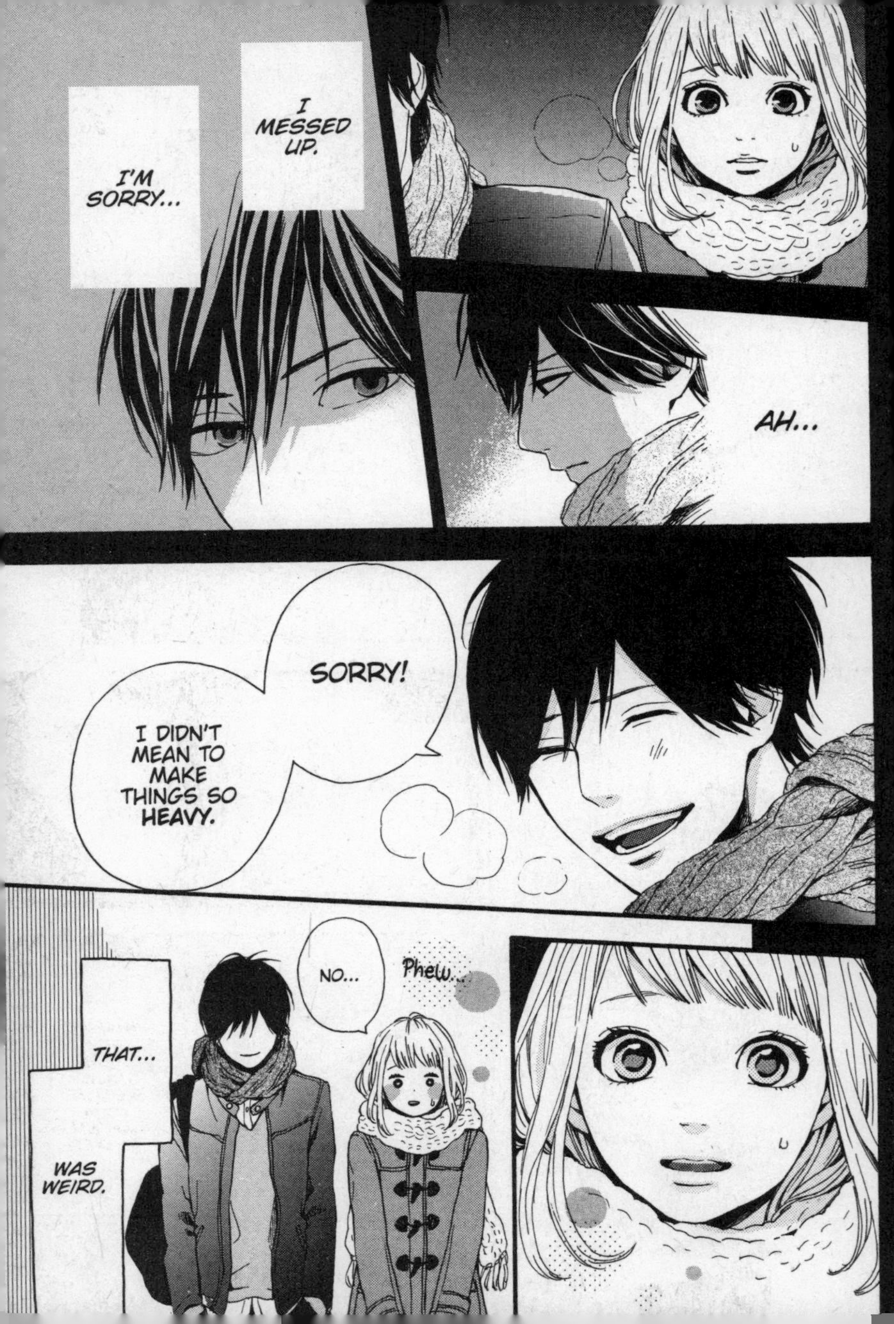
AH...
I MESSED UP.
I'M SORRY...
SORRY!
I DIDN'T MEAN TO MAKE THINGS SO HEAVY.
Phew...
NO...
THAT...
WAS WEIRD.

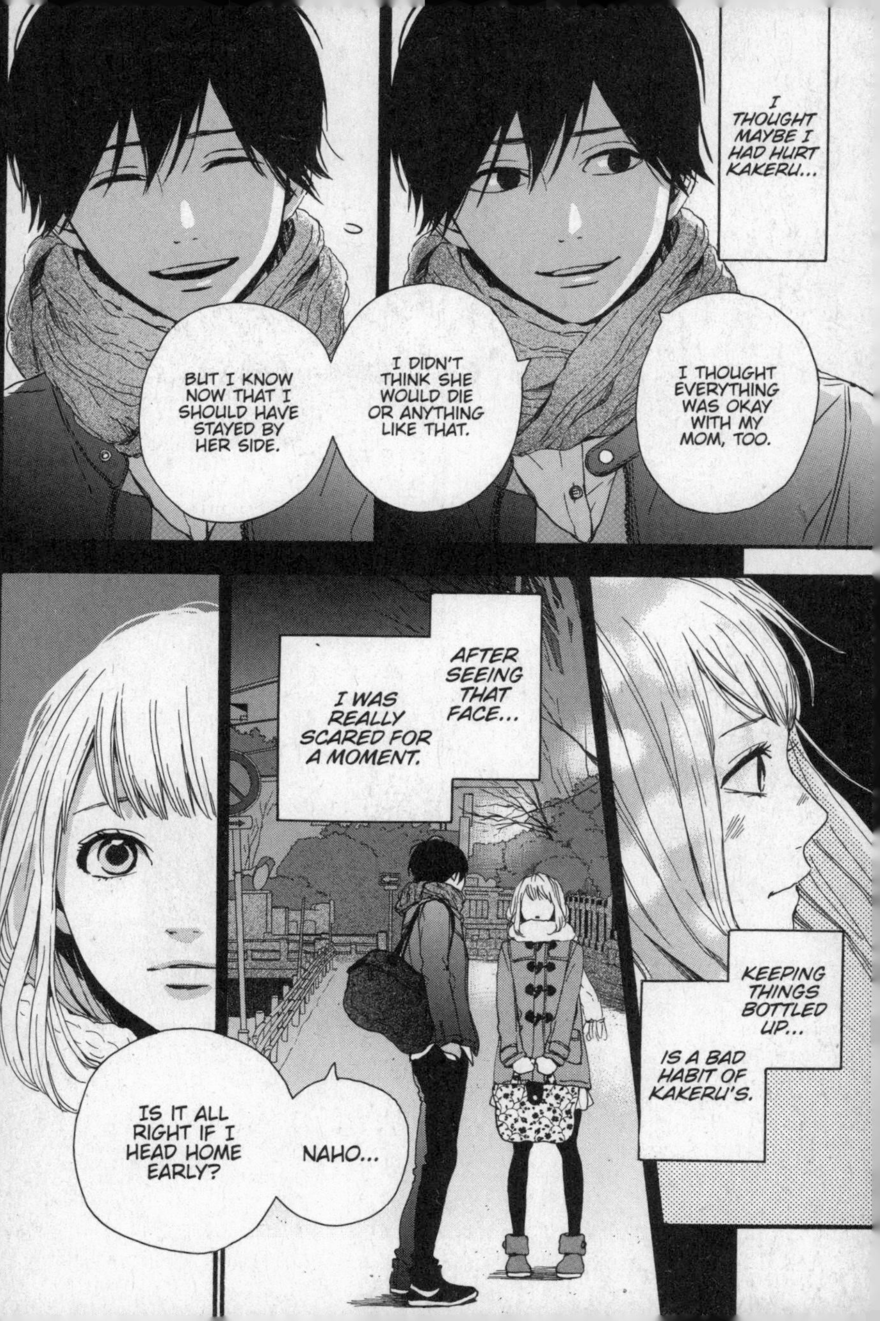
I THOUGHT MAYBE I HAD HURT KAKERU...
I THOUGHT EVERYTHING WAS OKAY WITH MY MOM, TOO.
I DIDN'T THINK SHE WOULD DIE OR ANYTHING LIKE THAT.
BUT I KNOW NOW THAT I SHOULD HAVE STAYED BY HER SIDE.
KEEPING THINGS BOTTLED UP...
IS A BAD HABIT OF KAKERU'S.
AFTER SEEING THAT FACE...
I WAS REALLY SCARED FOR A MOMENT.
NAHO...
IS IT ALL RIGHT IF I HEAD HOME EARLY?

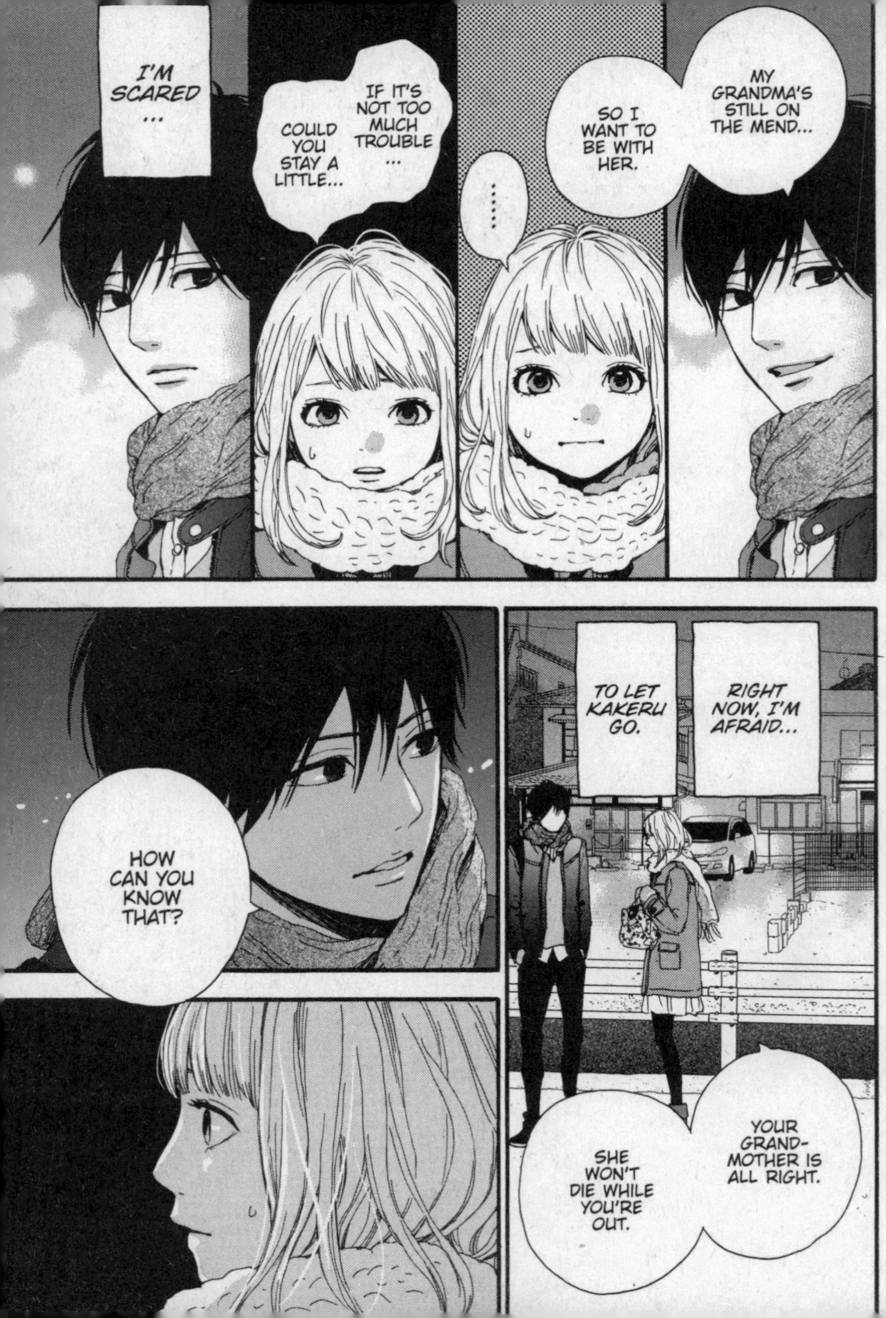
MY GRANDMA'S STILL ON THE MEND...
SO I WANT TO BE WITH HER.
......
IF IT'S NOT TOO MUCH TROUBLE ...
COULD YOU STAY A LITTLE...
I'M SCARED ...
RIGHT NOW, I'M AFRAID...
TO LET KAKERU GO.
YOUR GRAND-MOTHER IS ALL RIGHT.
SHE WON'T DIE WHILE YOU'RE OUT.
HOW CAN YOU KNOW THAT?

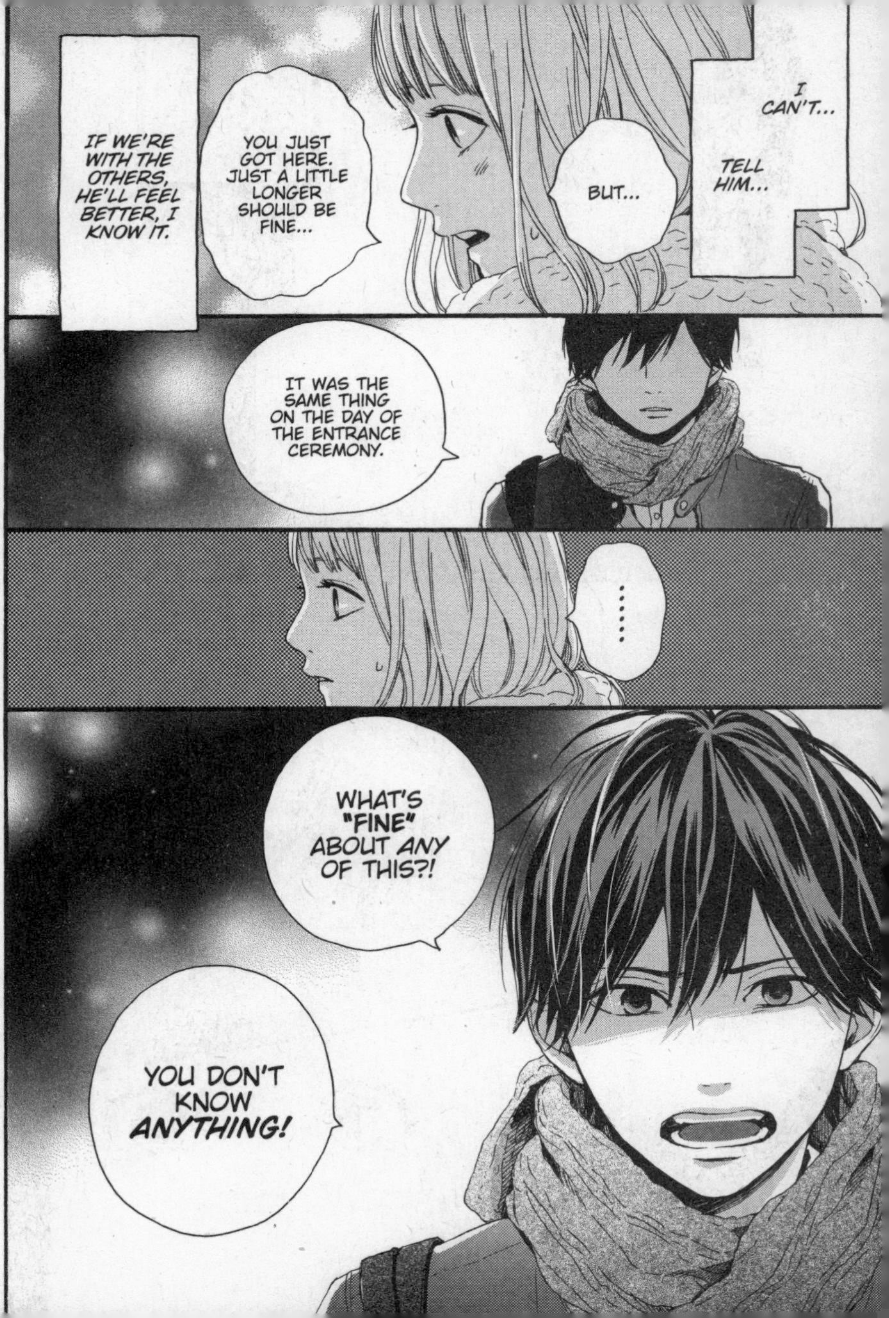
I CAN'T...
TELL HIM...
BUT...
YOU JUST GOT HERE. JUST A LITTLE LONGER SHOULD BE FINE...
IF WE'RE WITH THE OTHERS, HE'LL FEEL BETTER, I KNOW IT.
IT WAS THE SAME THING ON THE DAY OF THE ENTRANCE CEREMONY.
......
WHAT'S "FINE" ABOUT ANY OF THIS?!
YOU DON'T KNOW ANYTHING!

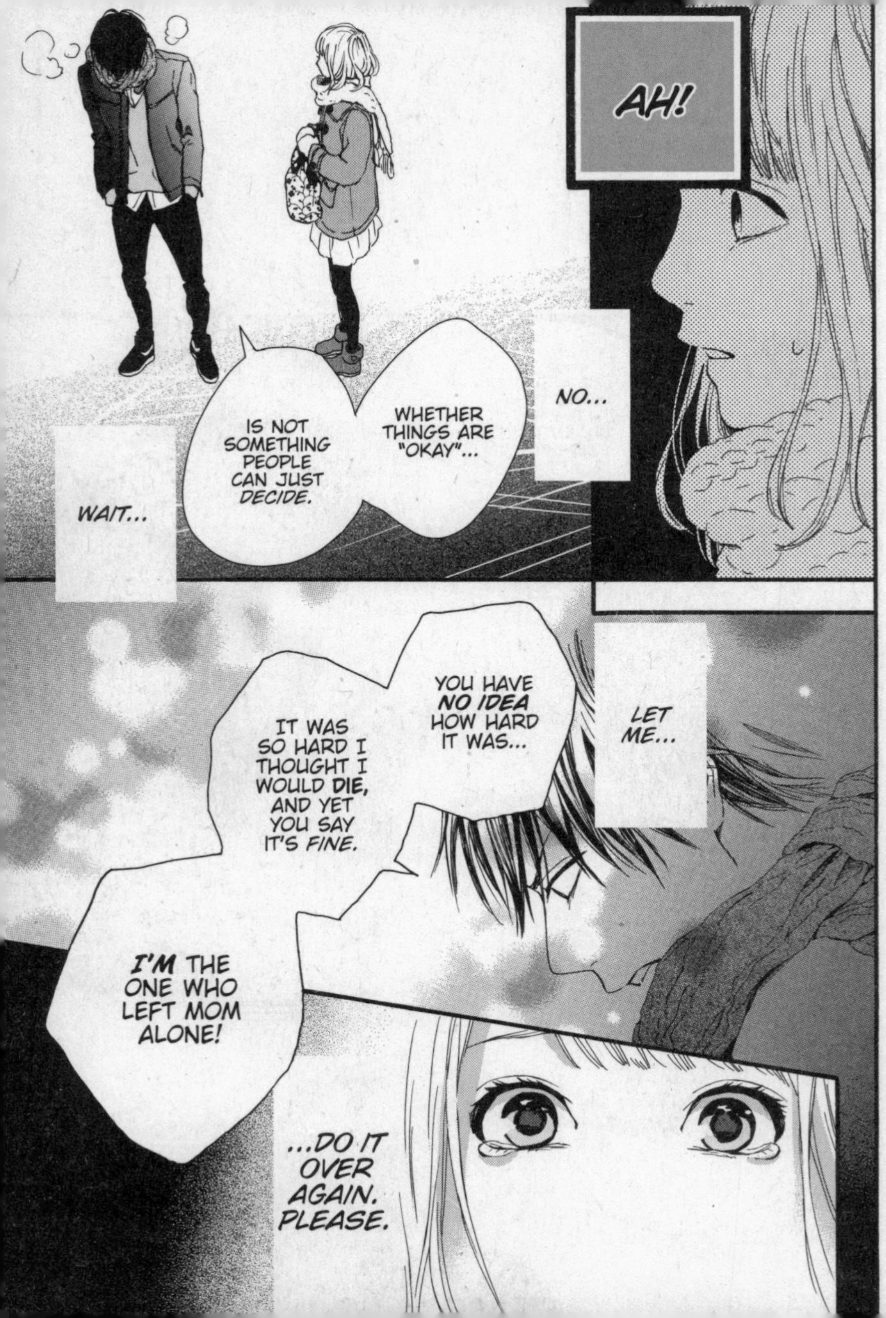
AH!
NO...
WHETHER THINGS ARE "OKAY"...
IS NOT SOMETHING PEOPLE CAN JUST DECIDE.
WAIT...
LET ME...
YOU HAVE NO IDEA HOW HARD IT WAS...
IT WAS SO HARD I THOUGHT I WOULD DIE, AND YET YOU SAY IT'S FINE.
I'M THE ONE WHO LEFT MOM ALONE!
...DO IT OVER AGAIN. PLEASE.

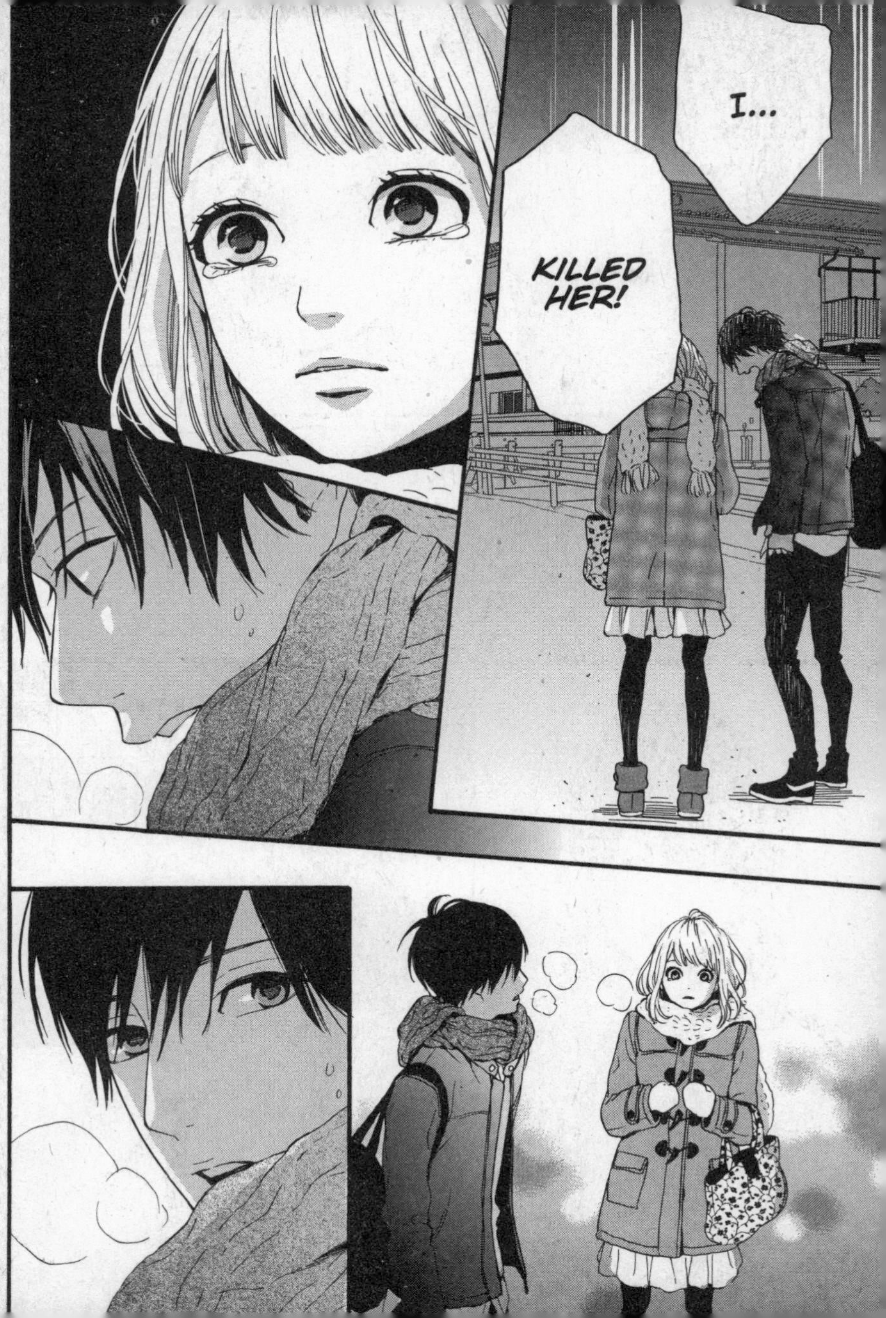
I...
KILLED HER!

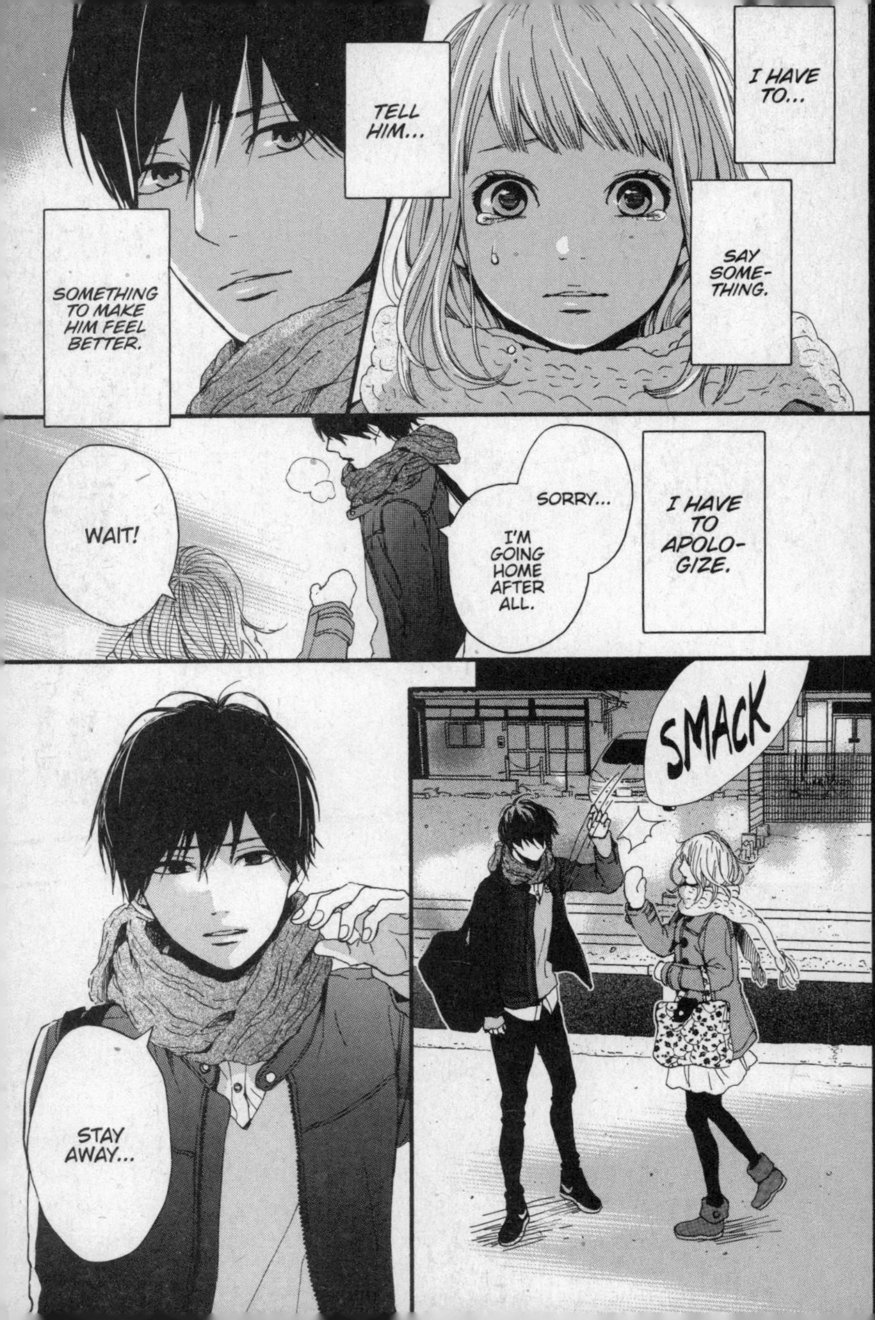
I HAVE TO...
SAY SOME-THING.
TELL HIM...
SOMETHING TO MAKE HIM FEEL BETTER.
I HAVE TO APOLO-GIZE.
SORRY...
I'M GOING HOME AFTER ALL.
WAIT!
SMACK
STAY AWAY...

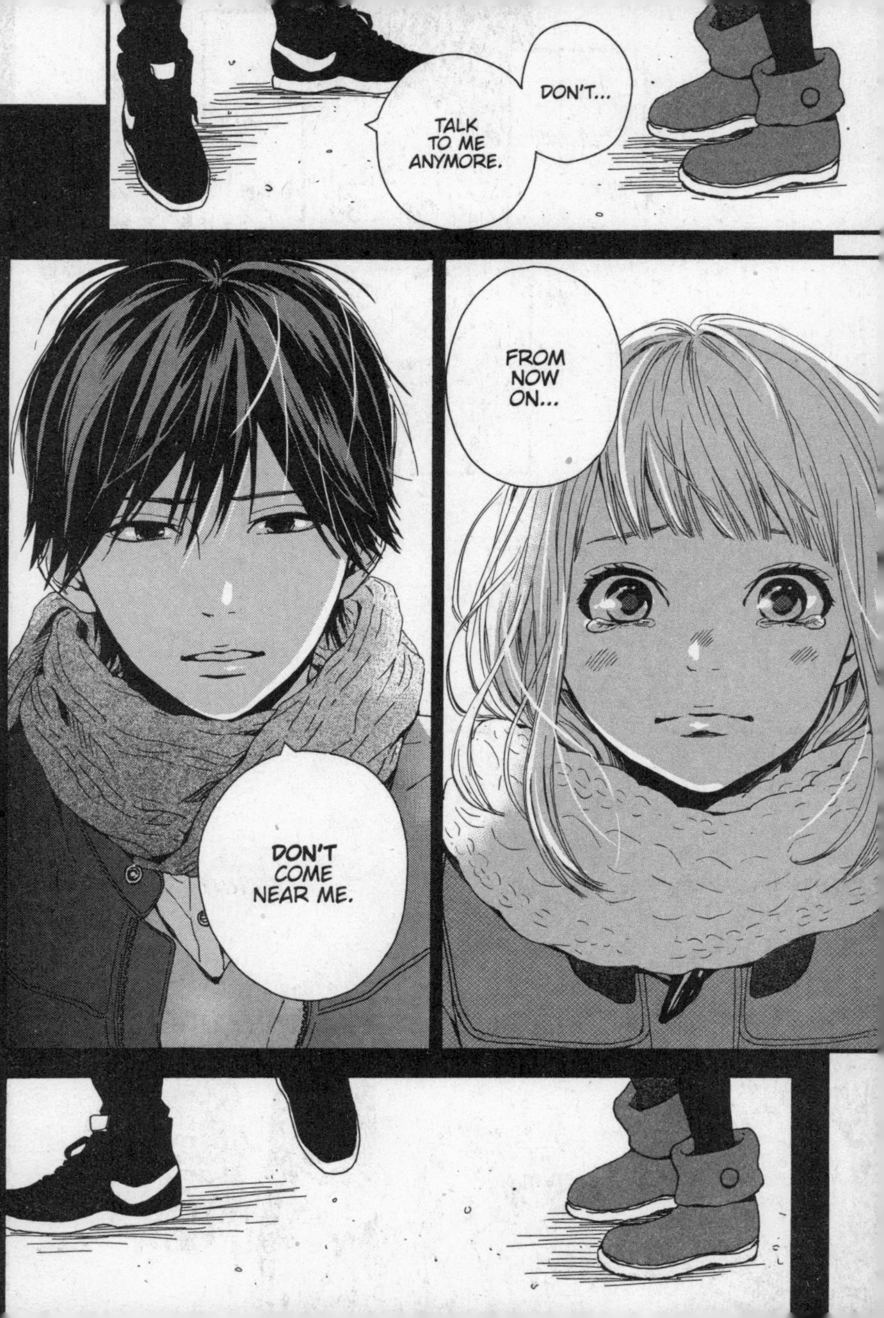
DON'T...
TALK TO ME ANYMORE.
FROM NOW ON...
DON'T COME NEAR ME.

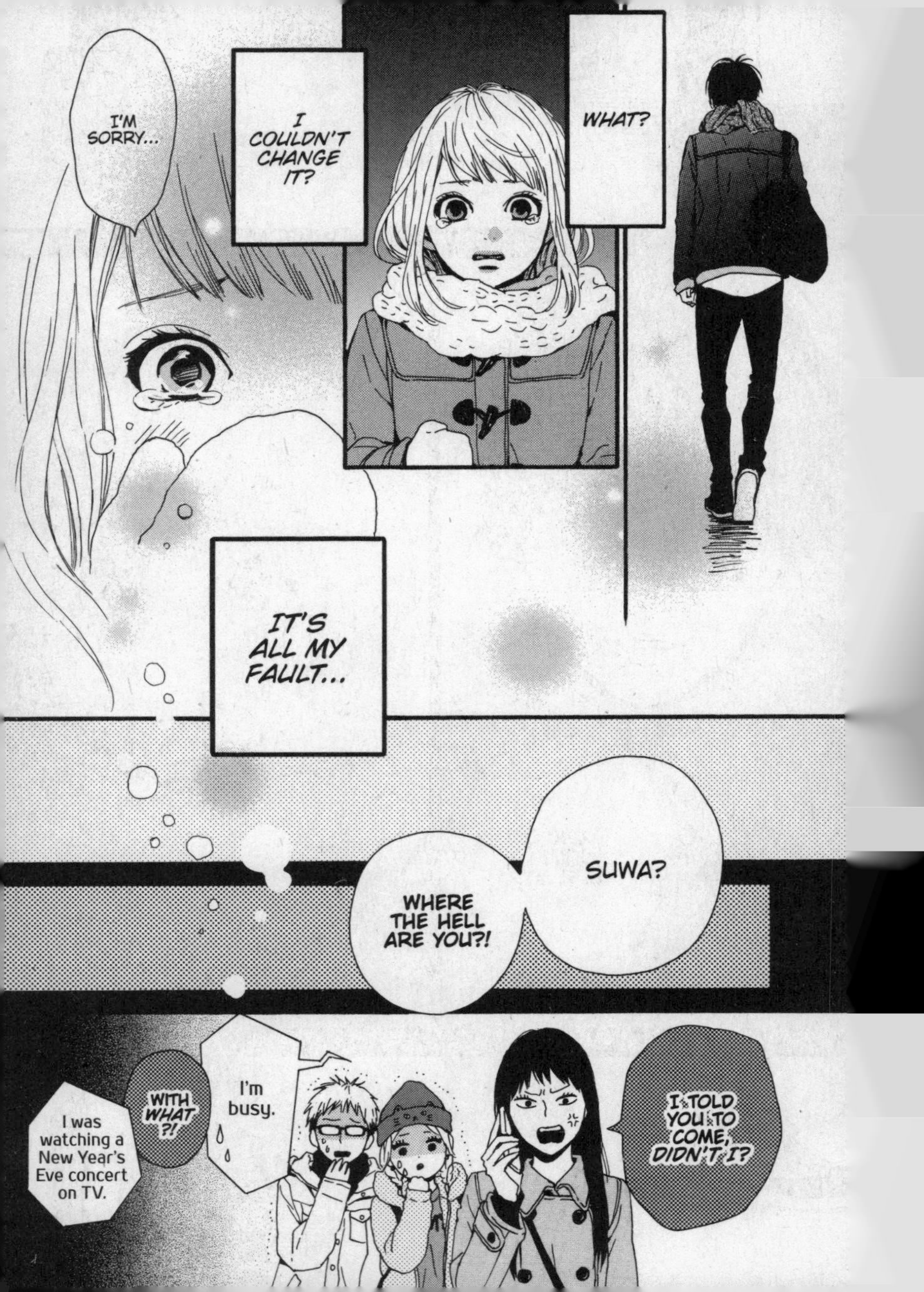
WHAT?
I COULDN'T CHANGE IT?
I'M SORRY...
IT'S ALL MY FAULT...
SUWA?
WHERE THE HELL ARE YOU?!
I TOLD YOU TO COME, DIDN'T I?
I'm busy.
WITH WHAT?!
I was watching a New Year's Eve concert on TV.

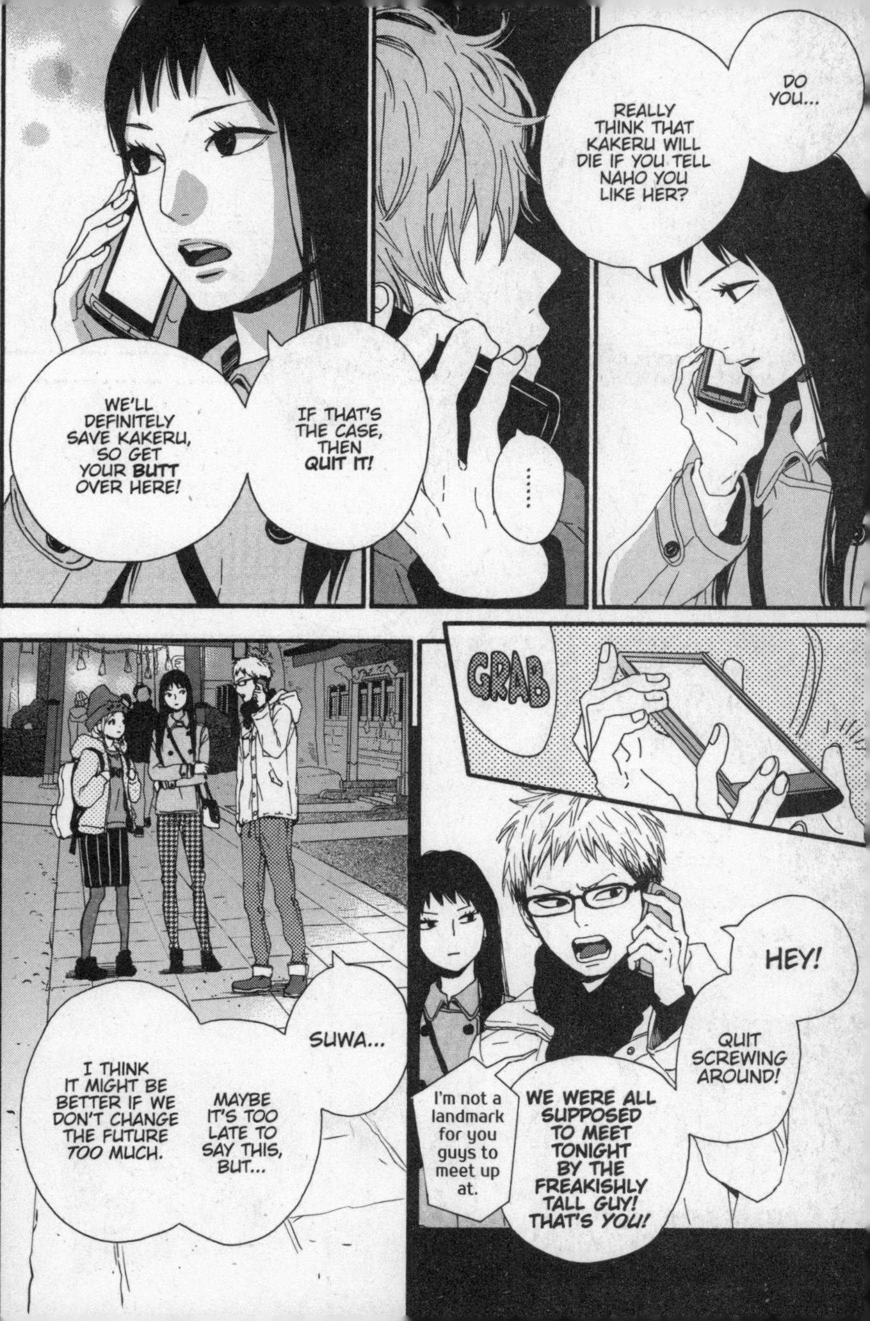
DO YOU...
REALLY THINK THAT KAKERU WILL DIE IF YOU TELL NAHO YOU LIKE HER?
......
IF THAT'S THE CASE, THEN **QUIT IT!**
WE'LL DEFINITELY SAVE KAKERU, SO GET YOUR **BUTT** OVER HERE!
GRAB
HEY!
QUIT SCREWING AROUND!
WE WERE ALL SUPPOSED TO MEET TONIGHT BY THE FREAKISHLY TALL GUY! THAT'S *YOU!*
I'm not a landmark for you guys to meet up at.
SUWA...
MAYBE IT'S TOO LATE TO SAY THIS, BUT...
I THINK IT MIGHT BE BETTER IF WE DON'T CHANGE THE FUTURE *TOO* MUCH.

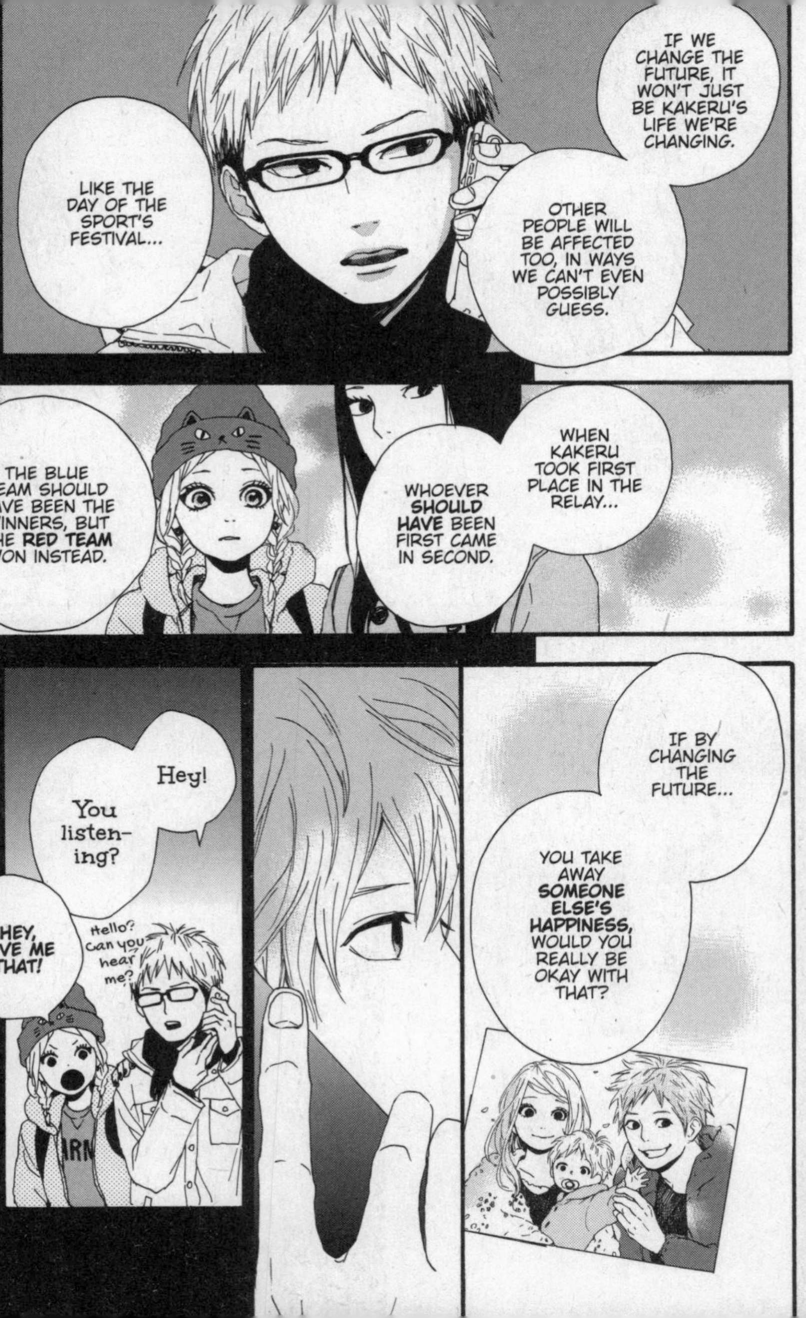
IF WE CHANGE THE FUTURE, IT WON'T JUST BE KAKERU'S LIFE WE'RE CHANGING.
OTHER PEOPLE WILL BE AFFECTED TOO, IN WAYS WE CAN'T EVEN POSSIBLY GUESS.
LIKE THE DAY OF THE SPORT'S FESTIVAL...
WHEN KAKERU TOOK FIRST PLACE IN THE RELAY...
WHOEVER **SHOULD HAVE** BEEN FIRST CAME IN SECOND.
THE BLUE TEAM SHOULD HAVE BEEN THE WINNERS, BUT THE **RED TEAM** WON INSTEAD.
IF BY CHANGING THE FUTURE...
YOU TAKE AWAY **SOMEONE ELSE'S HAPPINESS,** WOULD YOU REALLY BE OKAY WITH THAT?
Hey! You listening?
Hello? Can you hear me?
HEY, GIVE ME THAT!

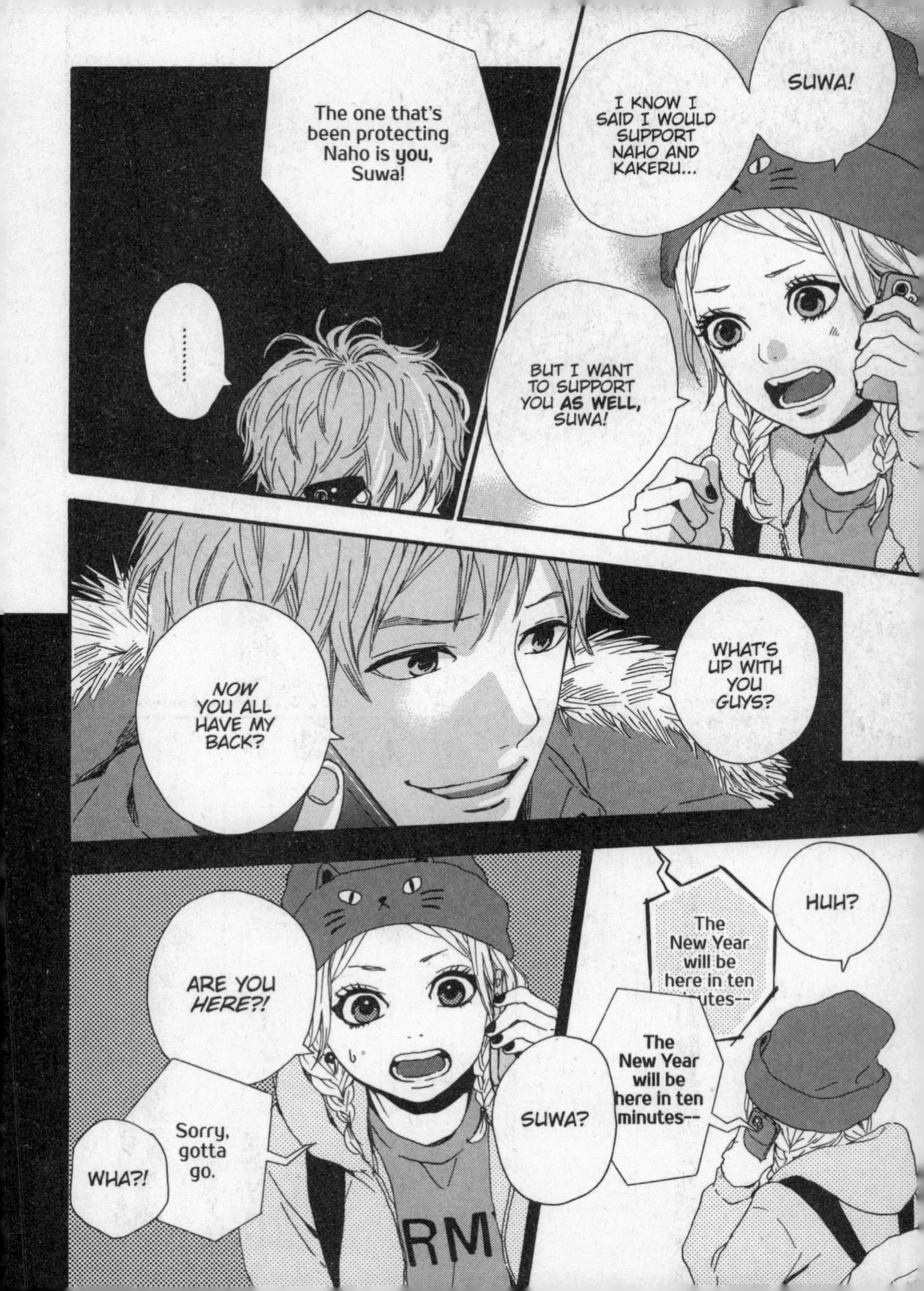
SUWA!
I KNOW I SAID I WOULD SUPPORT NAHO AND KAKERU...
BUT I WANT TO SUPPORT YOU AS WELL, SUWA!
The one that's been protecting Naho is you, Suwa!
......
WHAT'S UP WITH YOU GUYS?
NOW YOU ALL HAVE MY BACK?
HUH?
The New Year will be here in ten
utes--
The New Year will be here in ten minutes--
SUWA?
ARE YOU HERE?!
Sorry, gotta go.
WHA?!

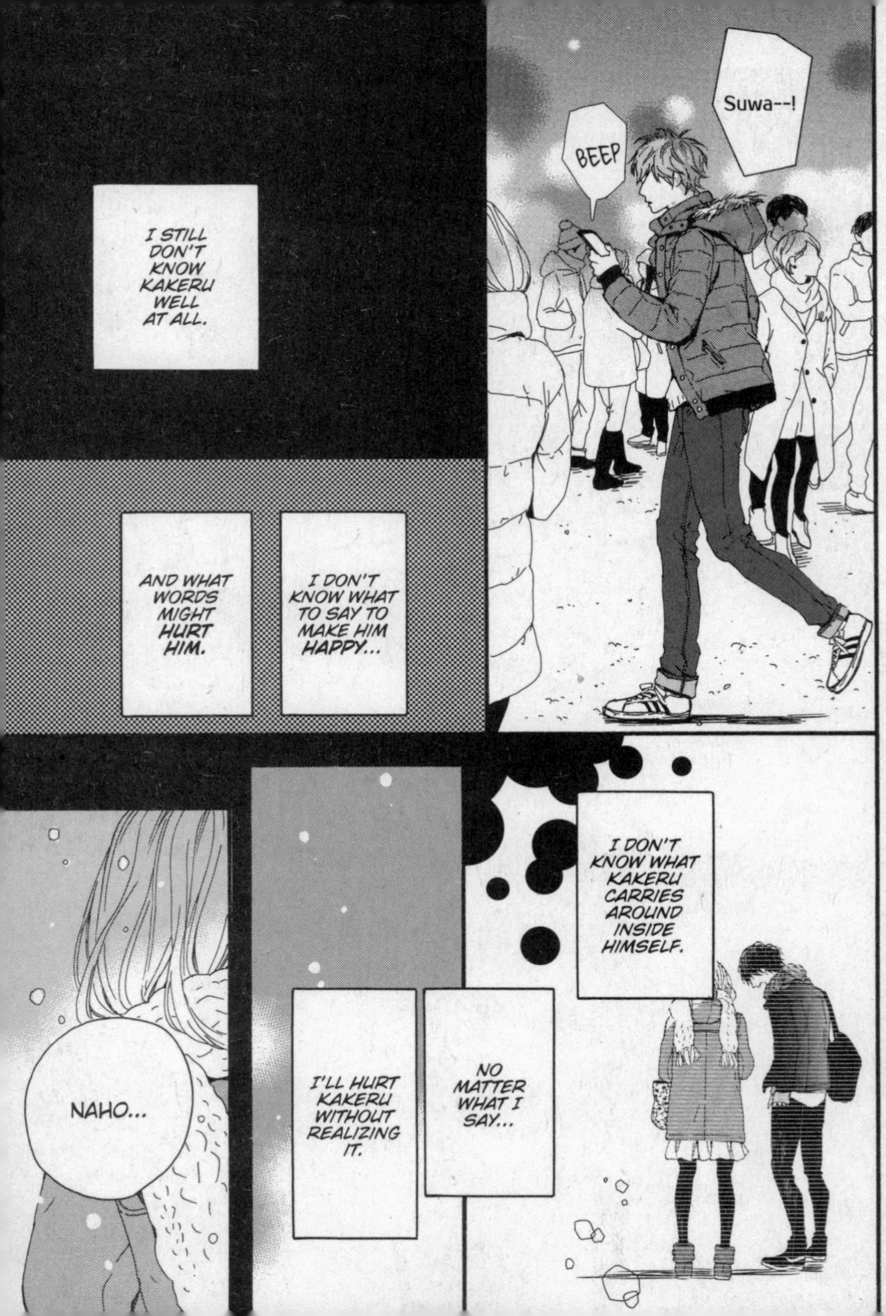
Suwa--!
BEEP
I STILL DON'T KNOW KAKERU WELL AT ALL.
I DON'T KNOW WHAT TO SAY TO MAKE HIM HAPPY...
AND WHAT WORDS MIGHT HURT HIM.
I DON'T KNOW WHAT KAKERU CARRIES AROUND INSIDE HIMSELF.
NO MATTER WHAT I SAY...
I'LL HURT KAKERU WITHOUT REALIZING IT.
NAHO...

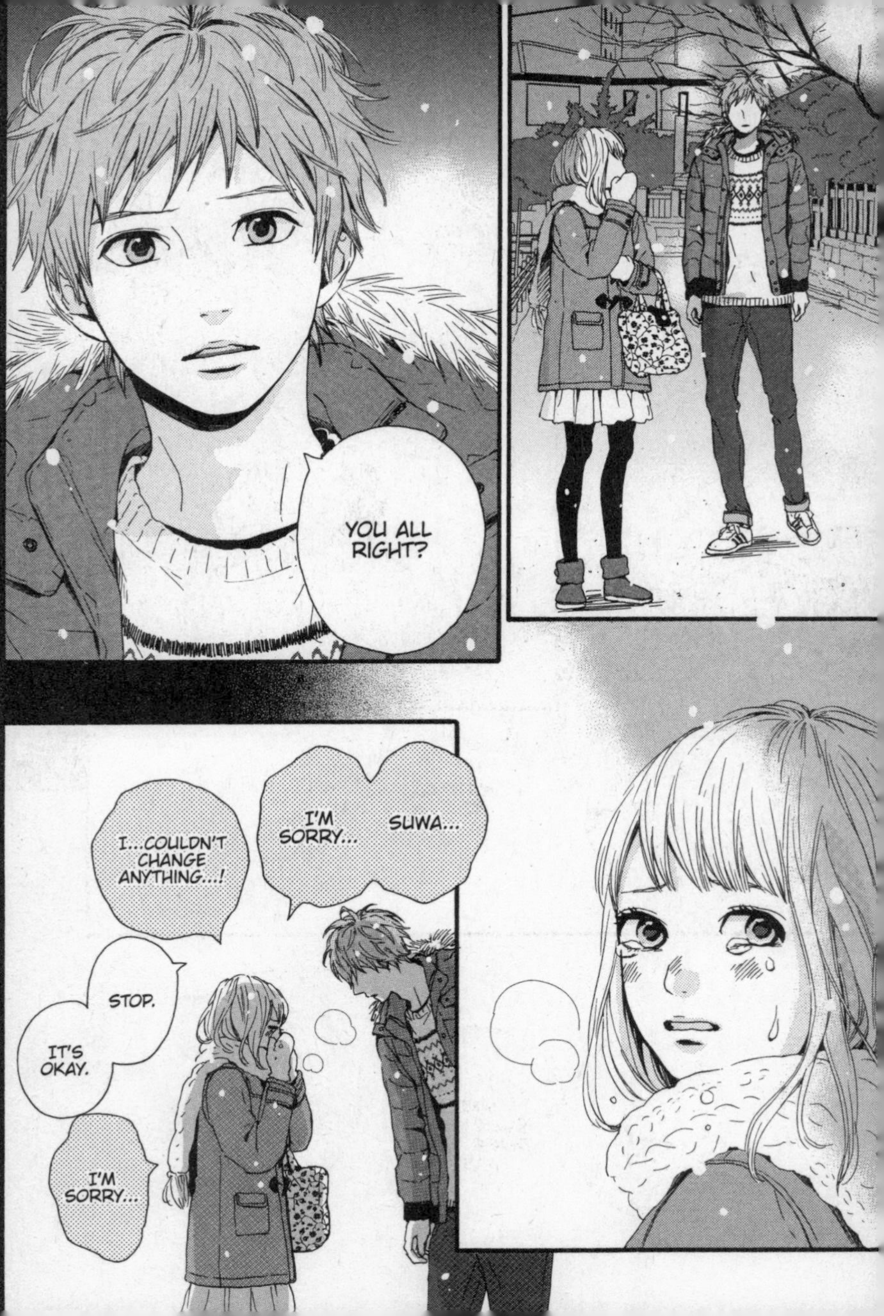
YOU ALL RIGHT?
I'M SORRY... SUWA...
I...COULDN'T CHANGE ANYTHING...!
STOP.
IT'S OKAY.
I'M SORRY...

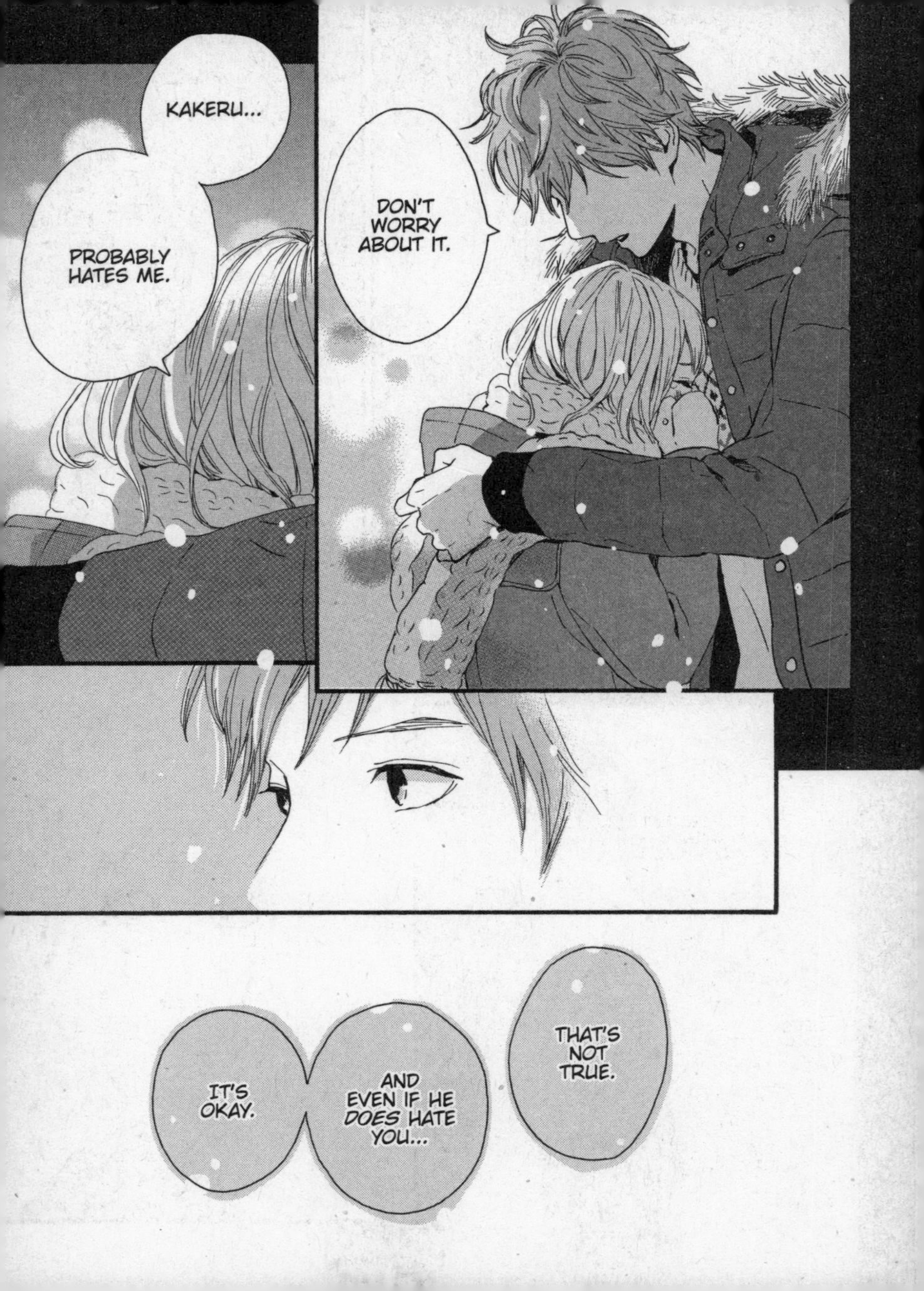
DON'T WORRY ABOUT IT.
KAKERU...
PROBABLY HATES ME.
THAT'S NOT TRUE.
AND EVEN IF HE DOES HATE YOU...
IT'S OKAY.

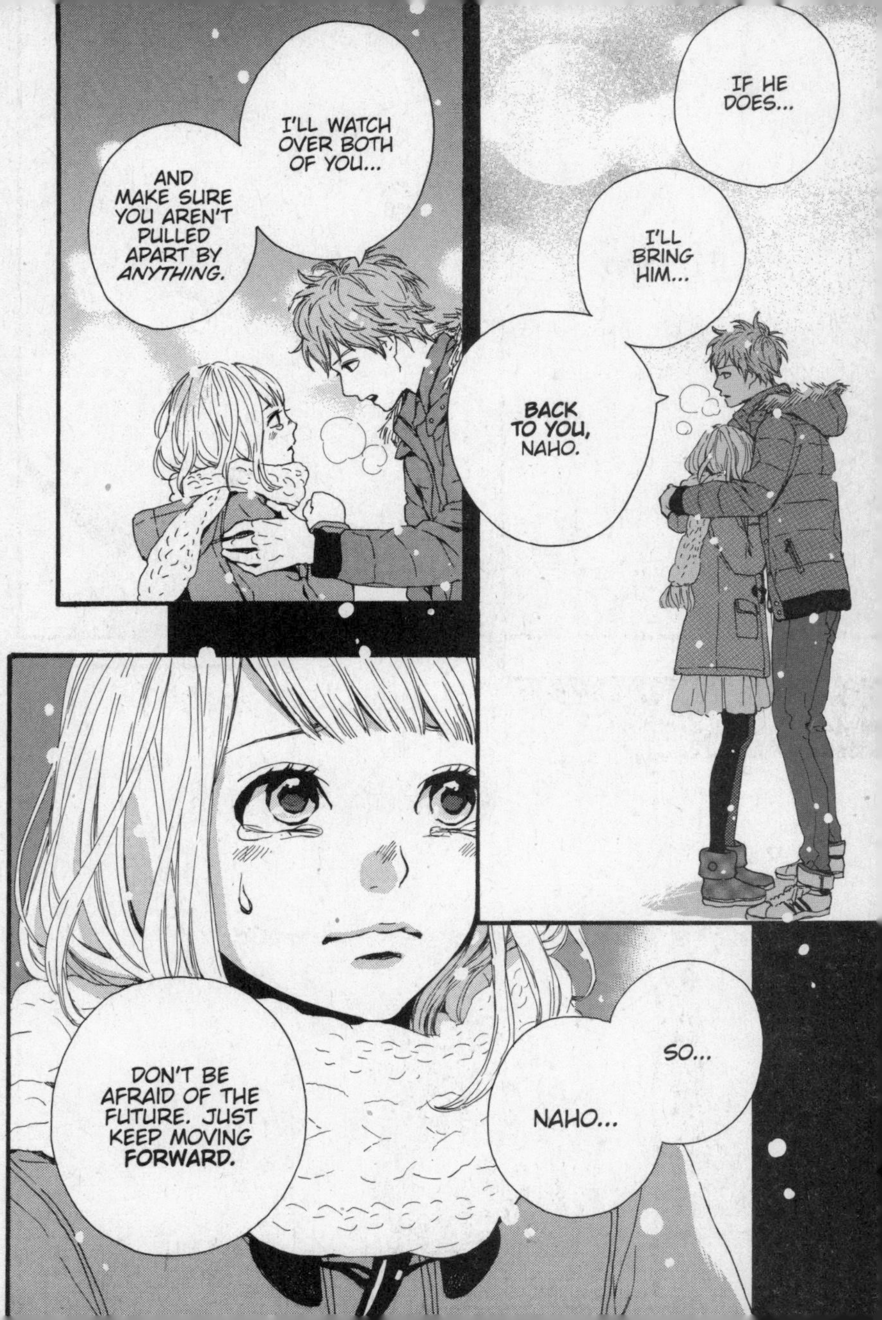
IF HE DOES...
I'LL BRING HIM...
BACK TO YOU, NAHO.
I'LL WATCH OVER BOTH OF YOU...
AND MAKE SURE YOU AREN'T PULLED APART BY *ANYTHING.*
SO...
NAHO...
DON'T BE AFRAID OF THE FUTURE. JUST KEEP MOVING **FORWARD.**

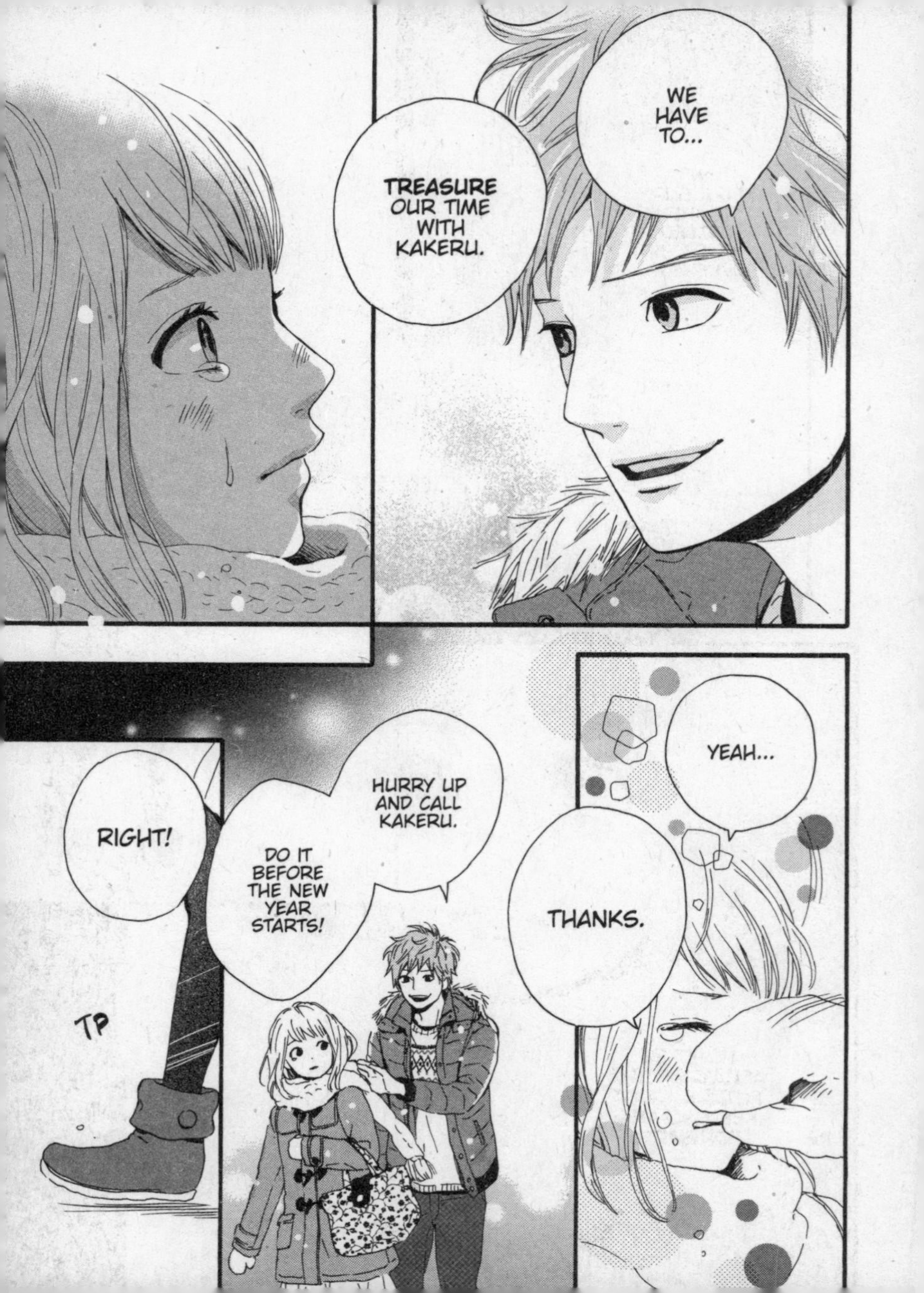
WE HAVE TO...
TREASURE OUR TIME WITH KAKERU.
YEAH...
THANKS.
HURRY UP AND CALL KAKERU.
DO IT BEFORE THE NEW YEAR STARTS!
RIGHT!
TP

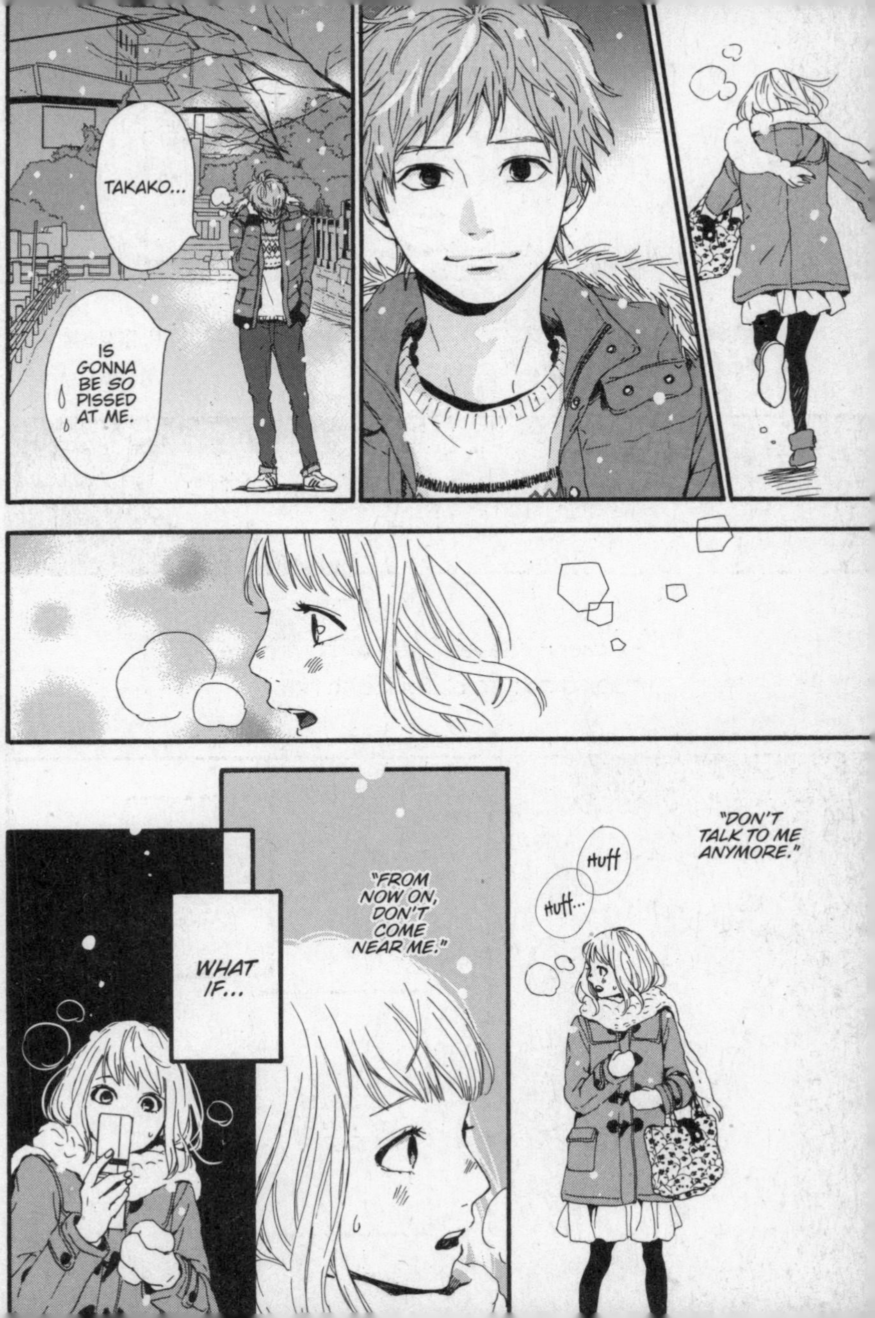
TAKAKO...
IS GONNA BE SO PISSED AT ME.
"DON'T TALK TO ME ANYMORE."
Huff
Huff...
"FROM NOW ON, DON'T COME NEAR ME."
WHAT IF...

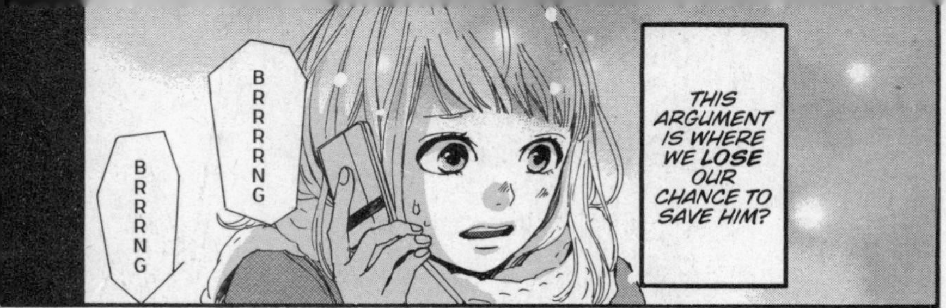
THIS ARGUMENT IS WHERE WE LOSE OUR CHANCE TO SAVE HIM?
BRRRRRNG
BRRRRNG

• After this day, the distance between Kakeru and me grows. We don't talk as much as before.

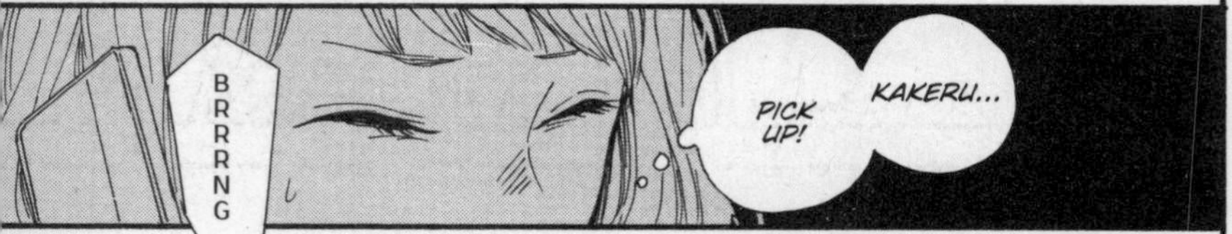
KAKERU...
PICK UP!
BRRRRNG

• Kakeru passed away without me ever being able to apologize to him.

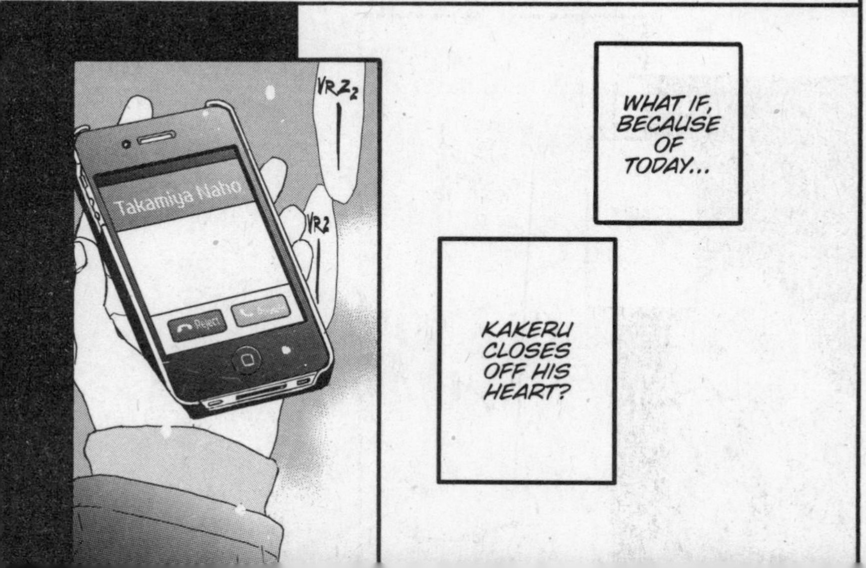
WHAT IF, BECAUSE OF TODAY...
KAKERU CLOSES OFF HIS HEART?
VRZZ
VRZ
Takamiya Naho
Reject

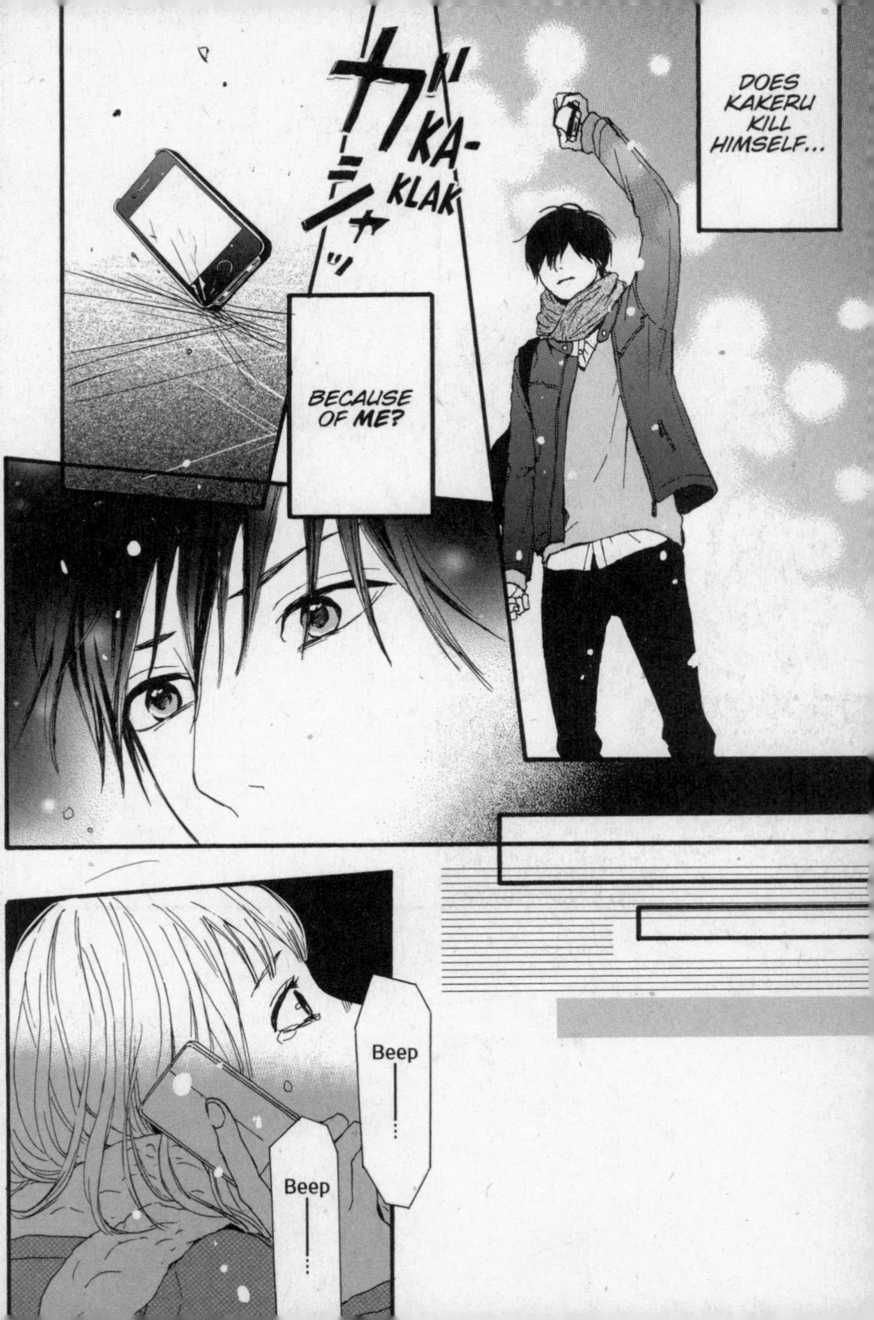
DOES KAKERU KILL HIMSELF...
KA-KLAK
BECAUSE OF ME?
Beep——......
Beep——......

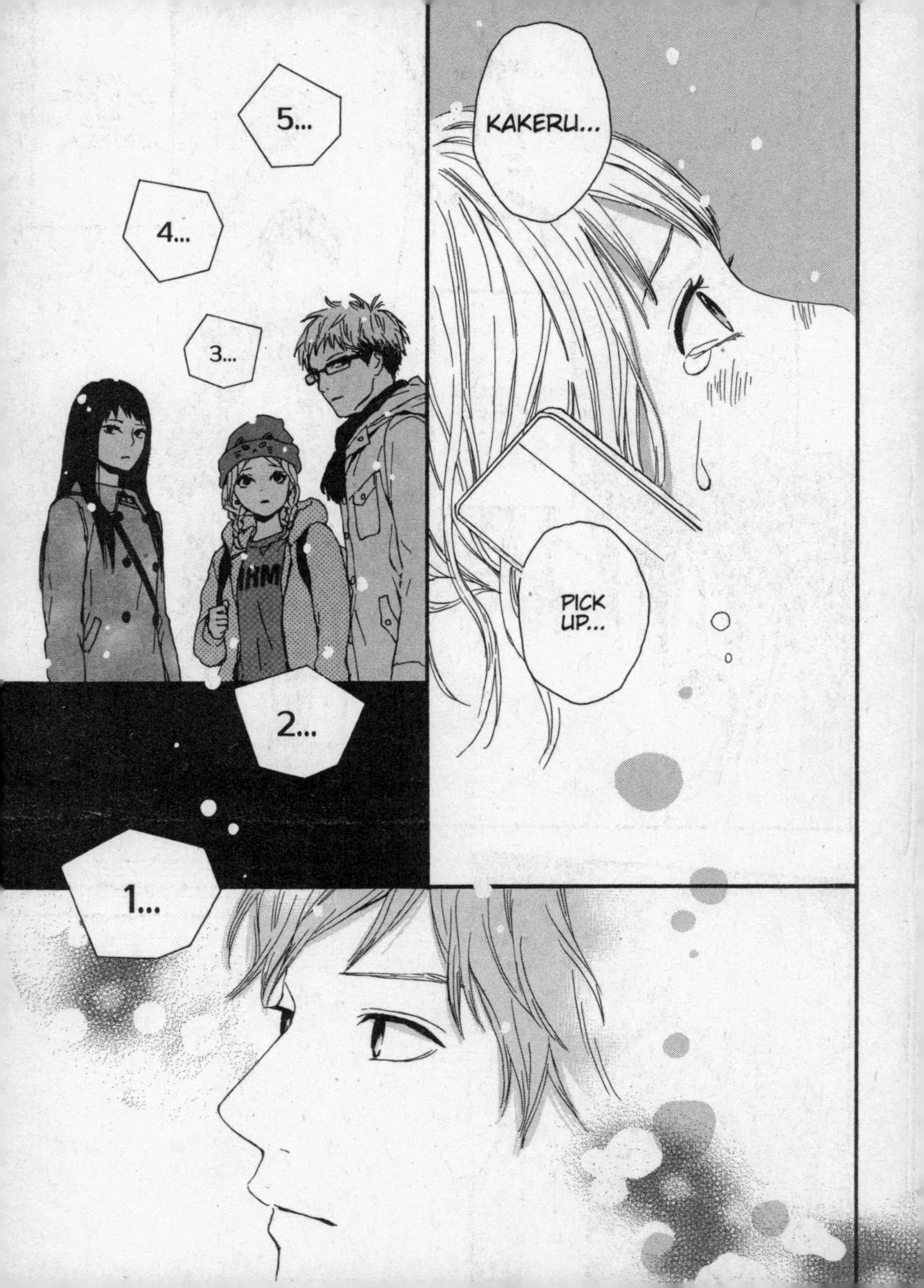
KAKERU...
PICK UP...
5...
4...
3...
2...
1...

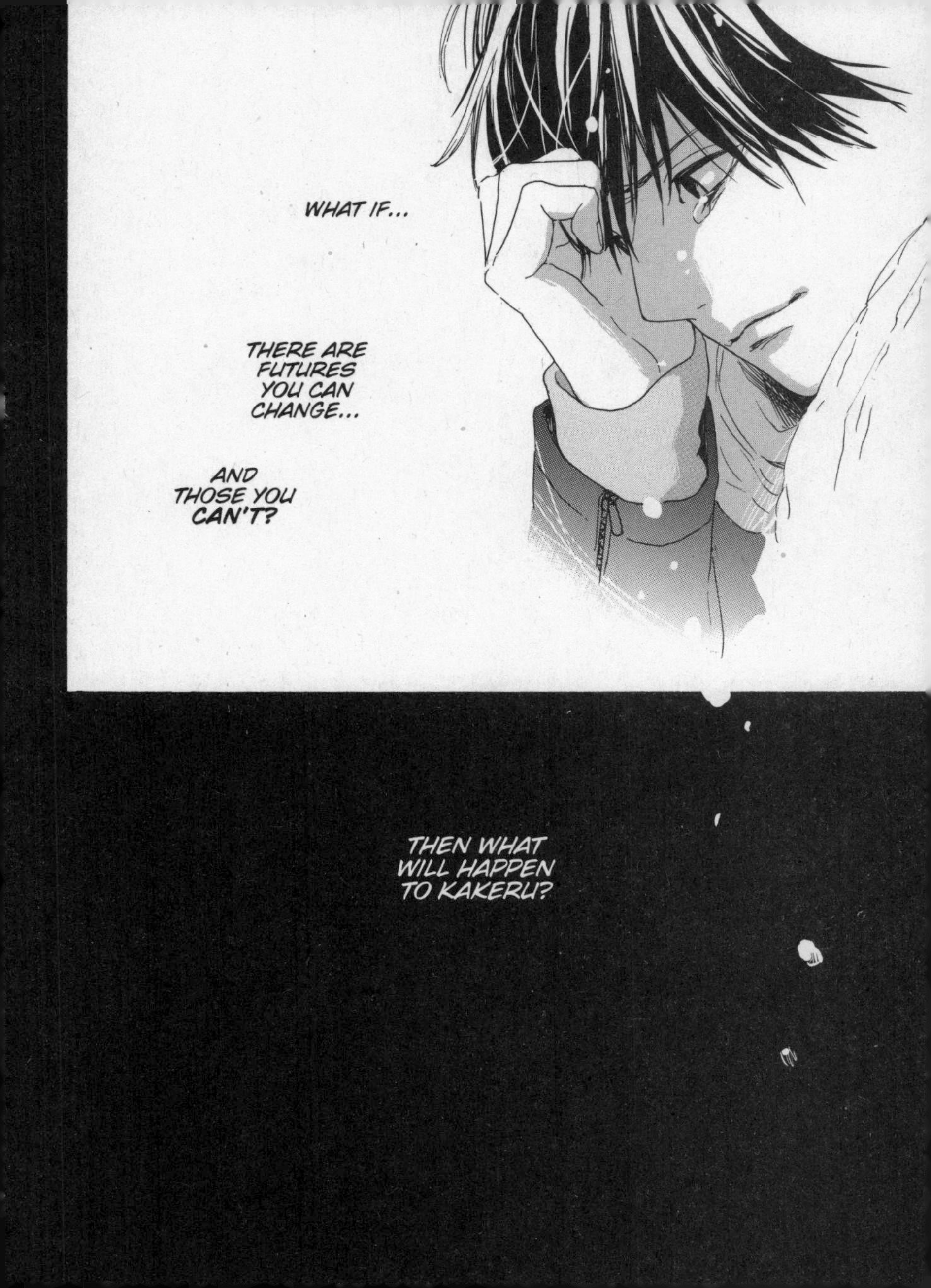
WHAT IF...
THERE ARE FUTURES YOU CAN CHANGE...
AND THOSE YOU CAN'T?
THEN WHAT WILL HAPPEN TO KAKERU?

orange

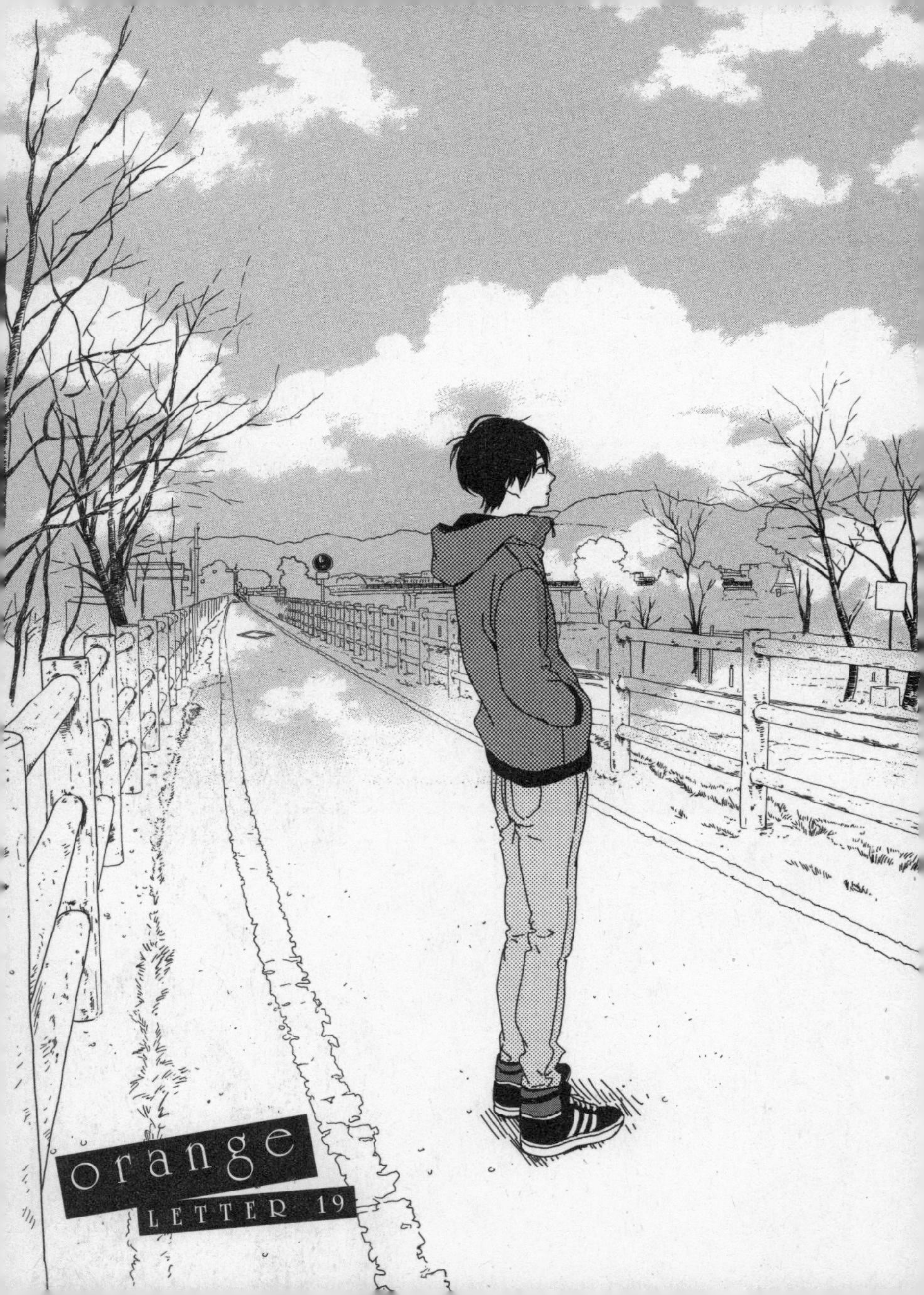
orange
LETTER 19

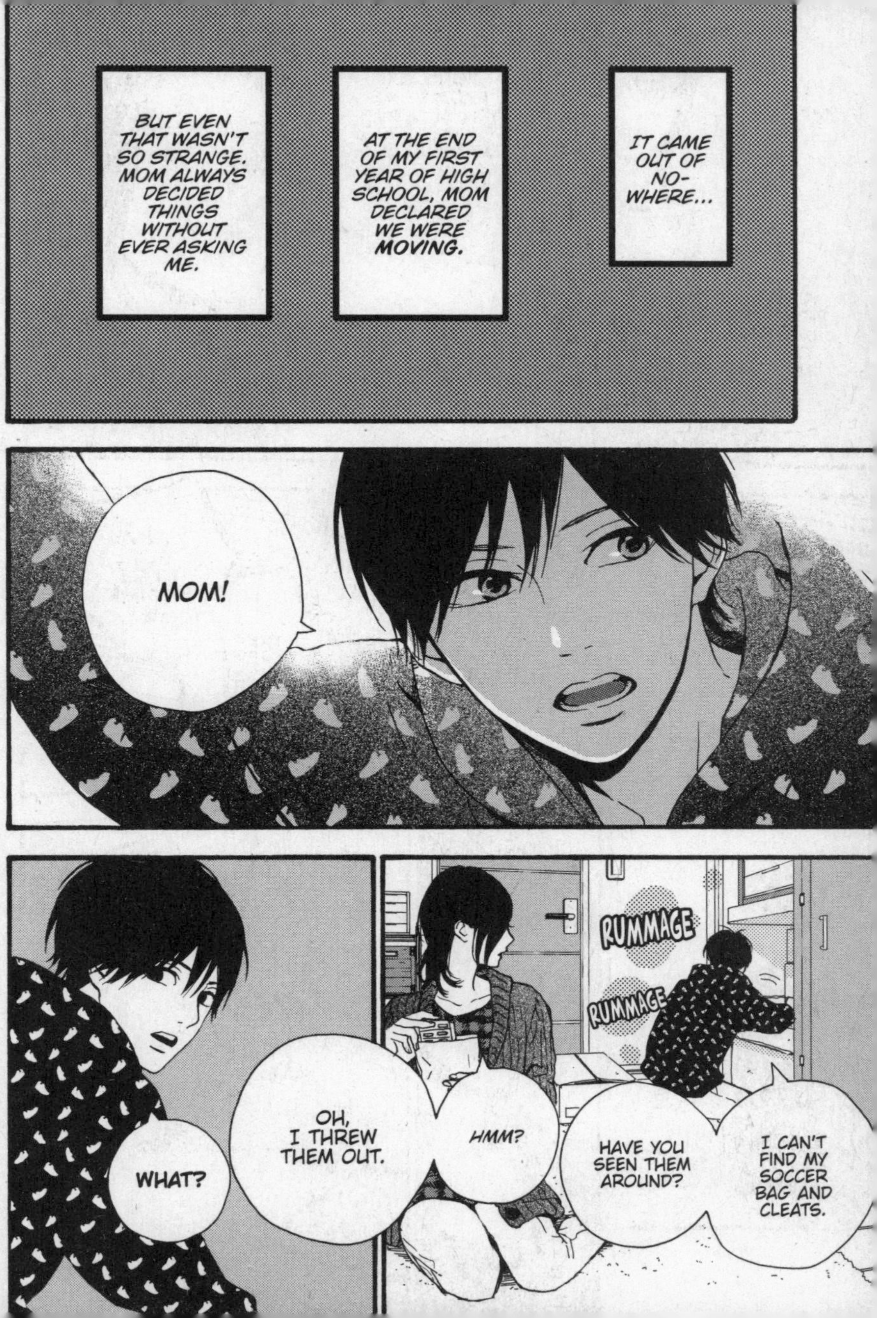
IT CAME OUT OF NO-WHERE...
AT THE END OF MY FIRST YEAR OF HIGH SCHOOL, MOM DECLARED WE WERE MOVING.
BUT EVEN THAT WASN'T SO STRANGE. MOM ALWAYS DECIDED THINGS WITHOUT EVER ASKING ME.
MOM!
RUMMAGE
RUMMAGE
I CAN'T FIND MY SOCCER BAG AND CLEATS.
HAVE YOU SEEN THEM AROUND?
HMM?
OH, I THREW THEM OUT.
WHAT?

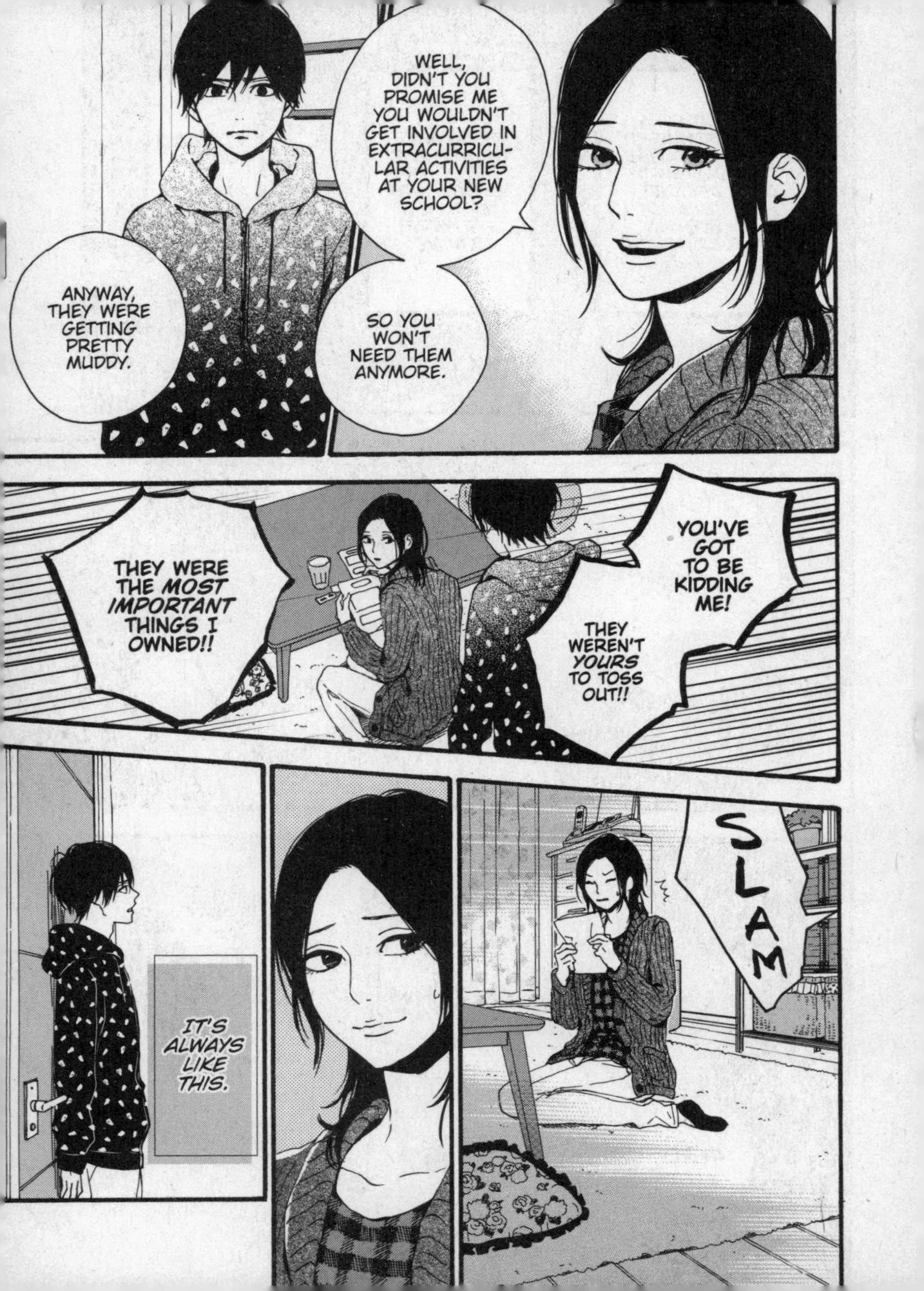
WELL, DIDN'T YOU PROMISE ME YOU WOULDN'T GET INVOLVED IN EXTRACURRICULAR ACTIVITIES AT YOUR NEW SCHOOL?
SO YOU WON'T NEED THEM ANYMORE.
ANYWAY, THEY WERE GETTING PRETTY MUDDY.
YOU'VE GOT TO BE KIDDING ME!
THEY WEREN'T *YOURS* TO TOSS OUT!!
THEY WERE THE *MOST IMPORTANT* THINGS I OWNED!!
SLAM
IT'S ALWAYS LIKE THIS.

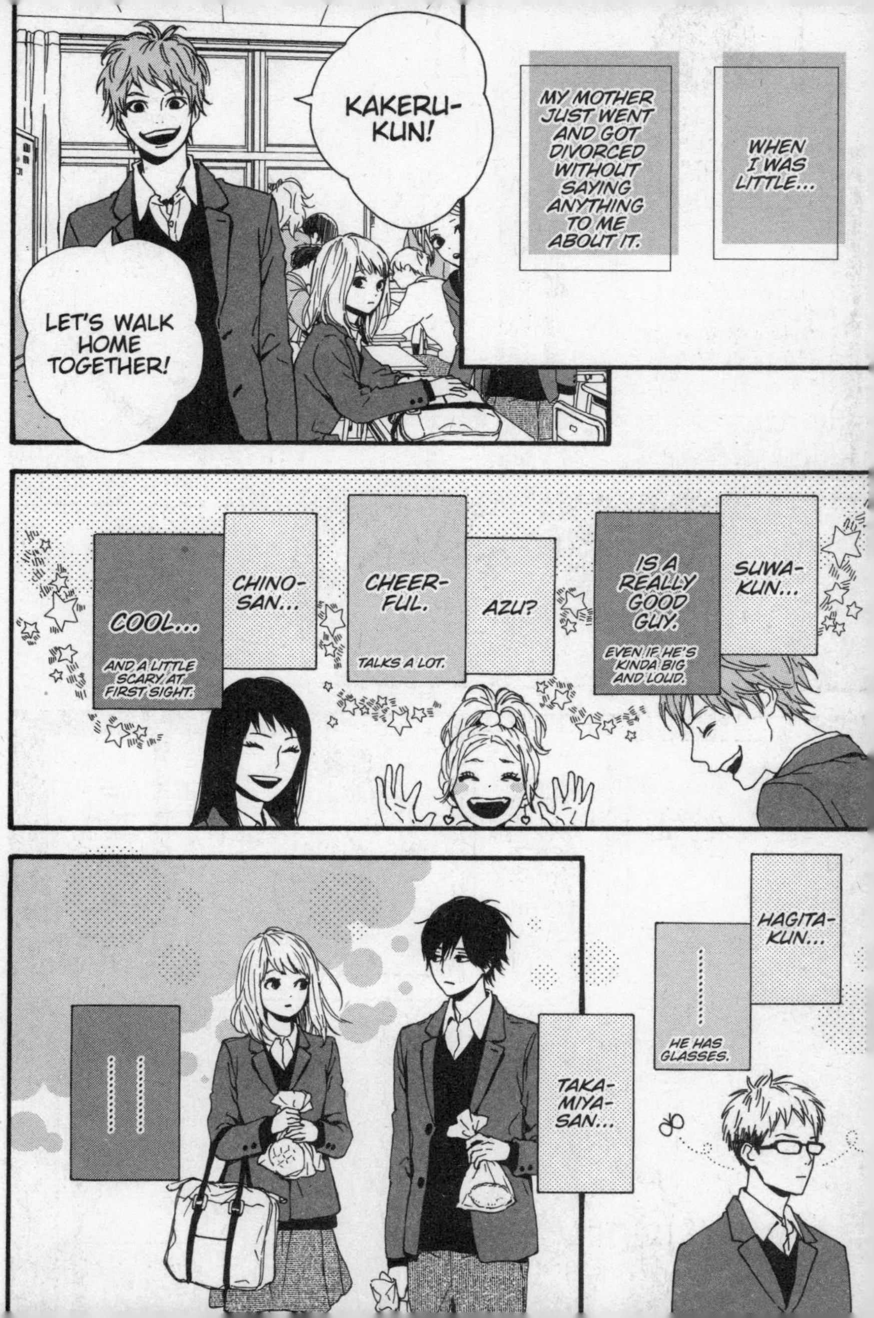
WHEN I WAS LITTLE...
MY MOTHER JUST WENT AND GOT DIVORCED WITHOUT SAYING ANYTHING TO ME ABOUT IT.
KAKERU-KUN!
LET'S WALK HOME TOGETHER!
SUWA-KUN...
IS A REALLY GOOD GUY.
EVEN IF HE'S KINDA BIG AND LOUD.
AZU?
CHEER-FUL.
TALKS A LOT.
CHINO-SAN...
COOL...
AND A LITTLE SCARY AT FIRST SIGHT.
HAGITA-KUN...
......
HE HAS GLASSES.
TAKA-MIYA-SAN...
......
......

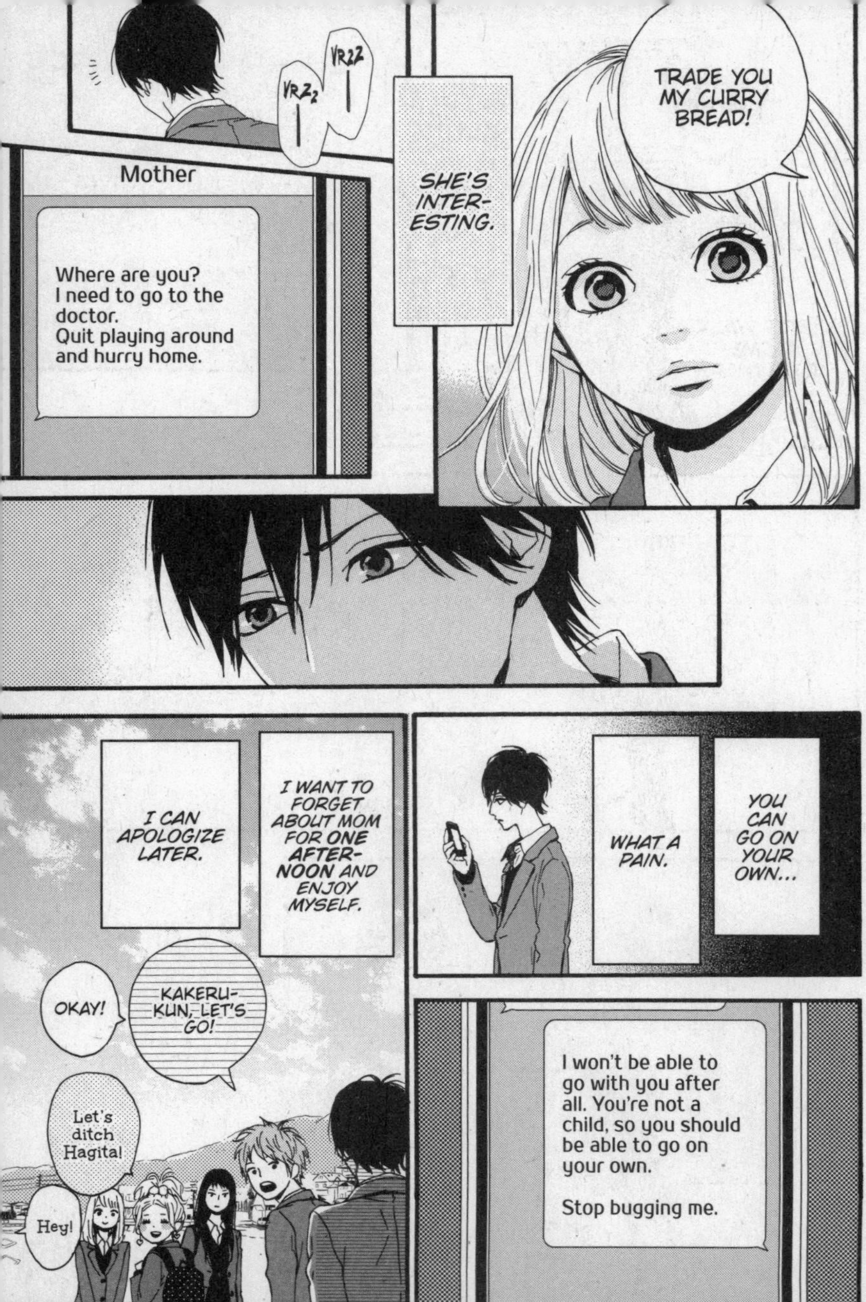
TRADE YOU MY CURRY BREAD!
SHE'S INTER-ESTING.
VRZZ
VRZZ
Mother
Where are you? I need to go to the doctor. Quit playing around and hurry home.
YOU CAN GO ON YOUR OWN...
WHAT A PAIN.
I WANT TO FORGET ABOUT MOM FOR ONE AFTER-NOON AND ENJOY MYSELF.
I CAN APOLOGIZE LATER.
I won't be able to go with you after all. You're not a child, so you should be able to go on your own.
Stop bugging me.
KAKERU-KUN, LET'S GO!
OKAY!
Let's ditch Hagita!
Hey!

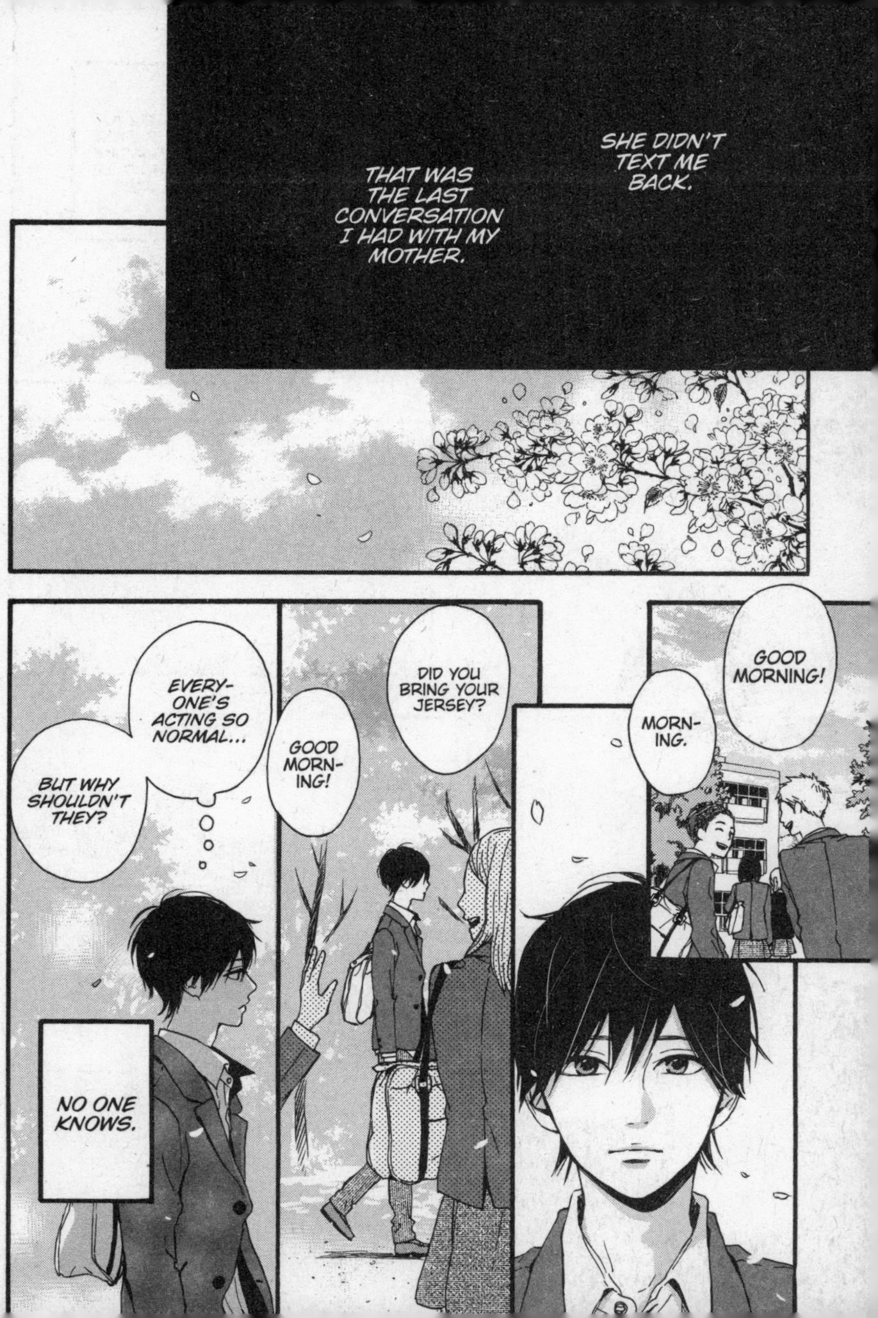
SHE DIDN'T TEXT ME BACK.
THAT WAS THE LAST CONVERSATION I HAD WITH MY MOTHER.
GOOD MORNING!
MORN-ING.
DID YOU BRING YOUR JERSEY?
GOOD MORN-ING!
EVERY-ONE'S ACTING SO NORMAL...
BUT WHY SHOULDN'T THEY?
NO ONE KNOWS.

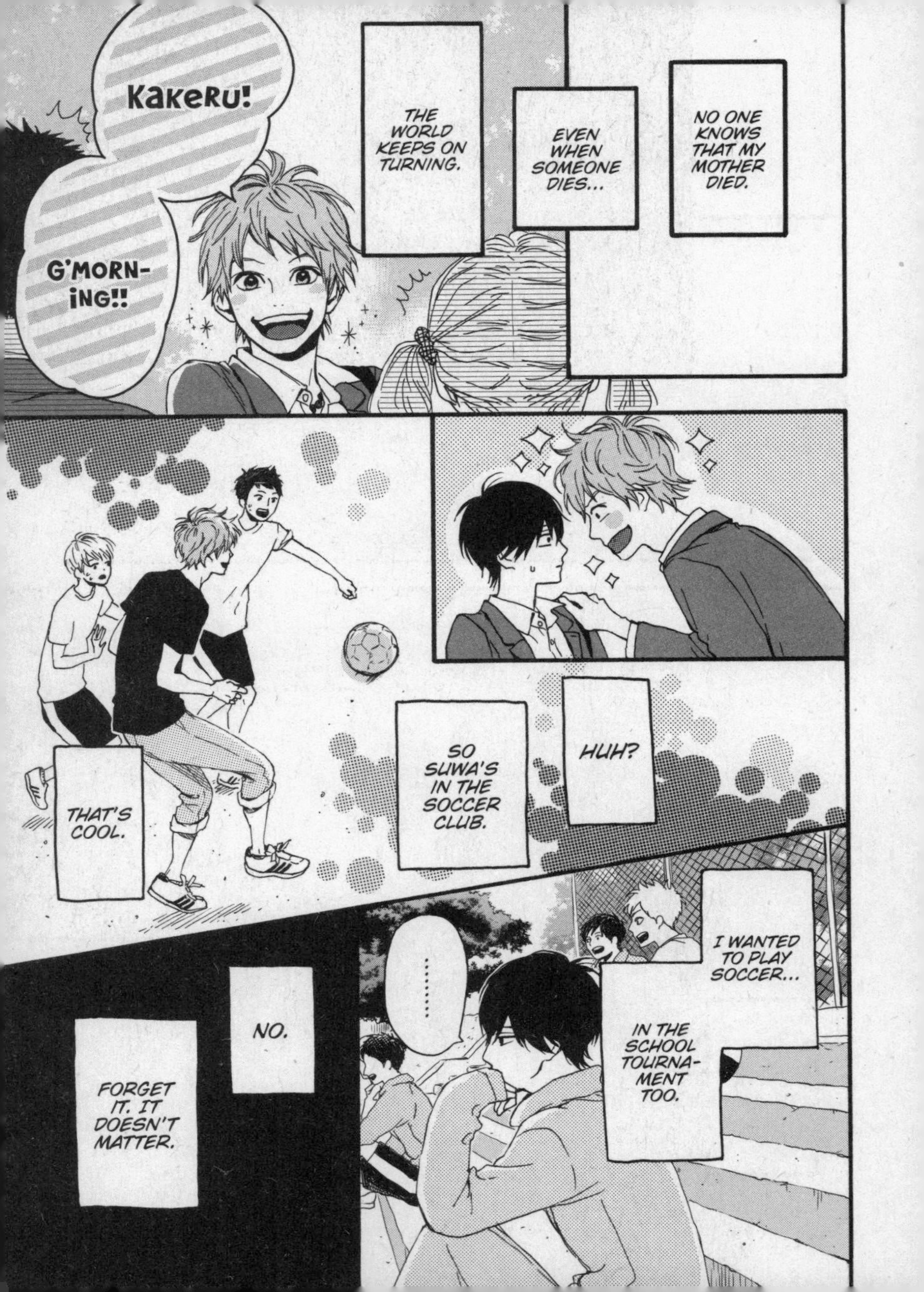
NO ONE KNOWS THAT MY MOTHER DIED.
EVEN WHEN SOMEONE DIES...
THE WORLD KEEPS ON TURNING.
KAKERU!
G'MORN-ING!!
HUH?
SO SUWA'S IN THE SOCCER CLUB.
THAT'S COOL.
I WANTED TO PLAY SOCCER...
IN THE SCHOOL TOURNA-MENT TOO.
......
NO.
FORGET IT. IT DOESN'T MATTER.

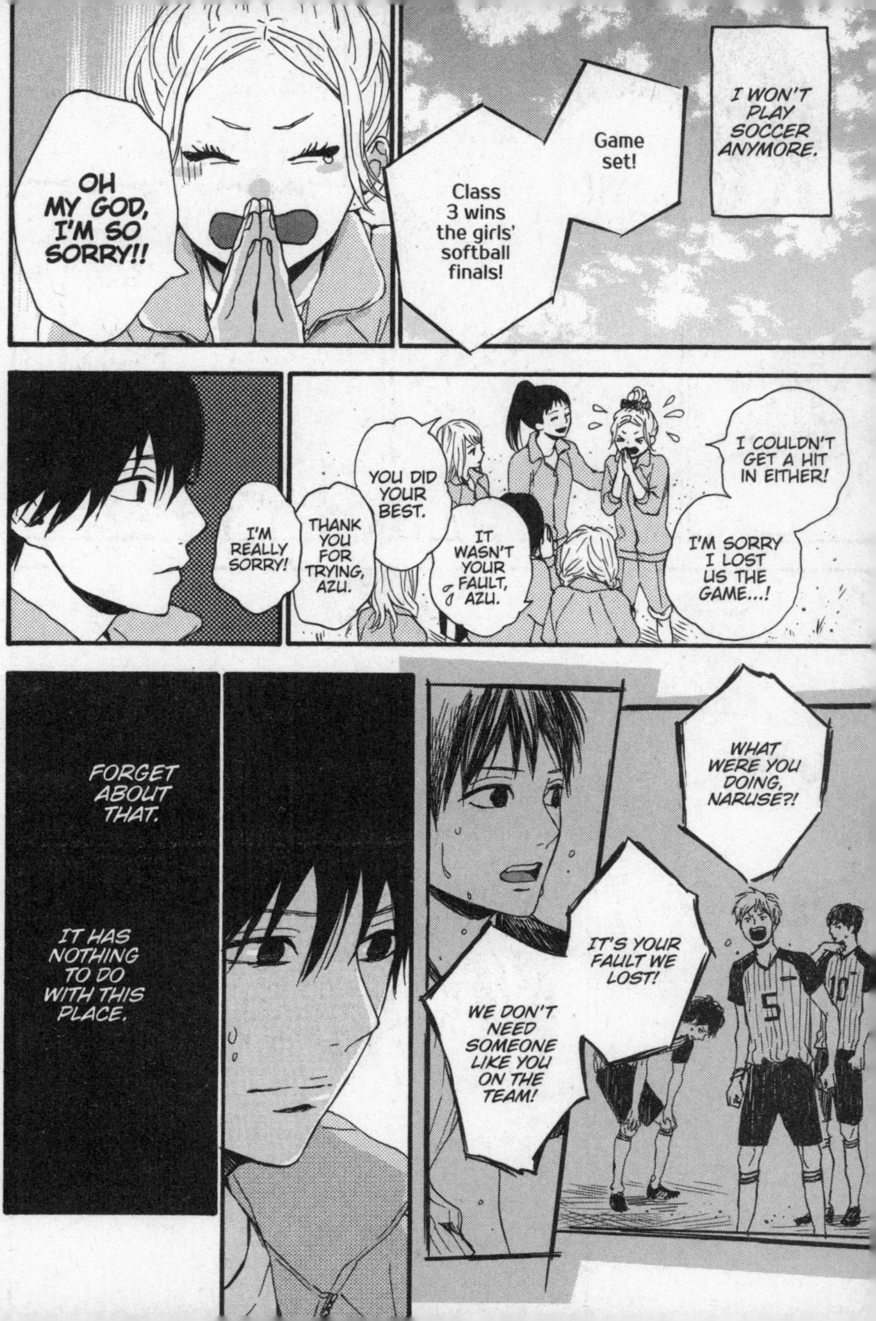
I WON'T PLAY SOCCER ANYMORE.
Game set!
Class 3 wins the girls' softball finals!
OH MY GOD, I'M SO SORRY!!
I COULDN'T GET A HIT IN EITHER!
I'M SORRY I LOST US THE GAME...!
YOU DID YOUR BEST.
IT WASN'T YOUR FAULT, AZU.
THANK YOU FOR TRYING, AZU.
I'M REALLY SORRY!
WHAT WERE YOU DOING, NARUSE?!
IT'S YOUR FAULT WE LOST!
WE DON'T NEED SOMEONE LIKE YOU ON THE TEAM!
FORGET ABOUT THAT.
IT HAS NOTHING TO DO WITH THIS PLACE.

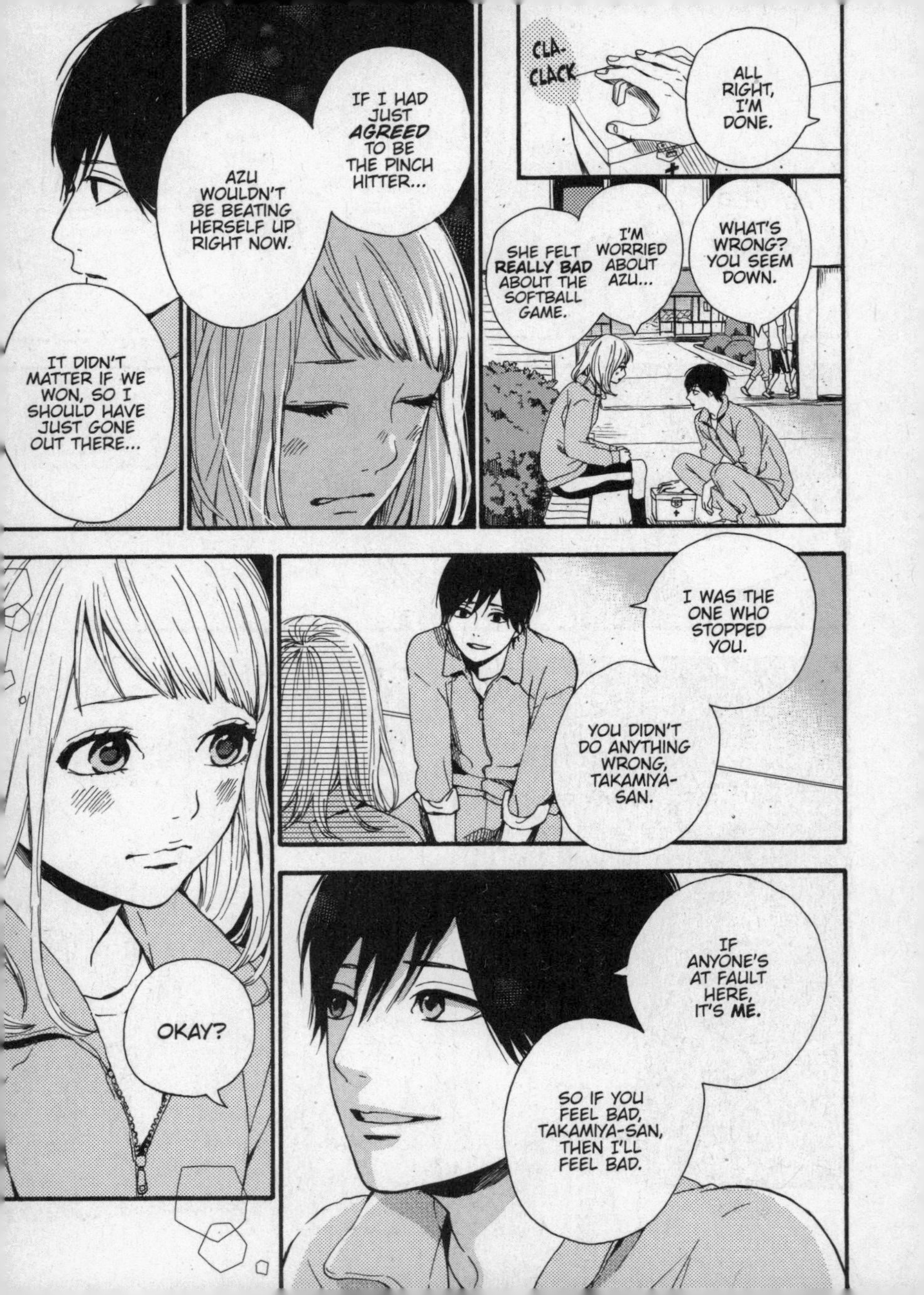
CLA-CLACK
ALL RIGHT, I'M DONE.
WHAT'S WRONG? YOU SEEM DOWN.
I'M WORRIED ABOUT AZU...
SHE FELT REALLY BAD ABOUT THE SOFTBALL GAME.
IF I HAD JUST AGREED TO BE THE PINCH HITTER...
AZU WOULDN'T BE BEATING HERSELF UP RIGHT NOW.
IT DIDN'T MATTER IF WE WON, SO I SHOULD HAVE JUST GONE OUT THERE...
I WAS THE ONE WHO STOPPED YOU.
YOU DIDN'T DO ANYTHING WRONG, TAKAMIYA-SAN.
IF ANYONE'S AT FAULT HERE, IT'S ME.
SO IF YOU FEEL BAD, TAKAMIYA-SAN, THEN I'LL FEEL BAD.
OKAY?

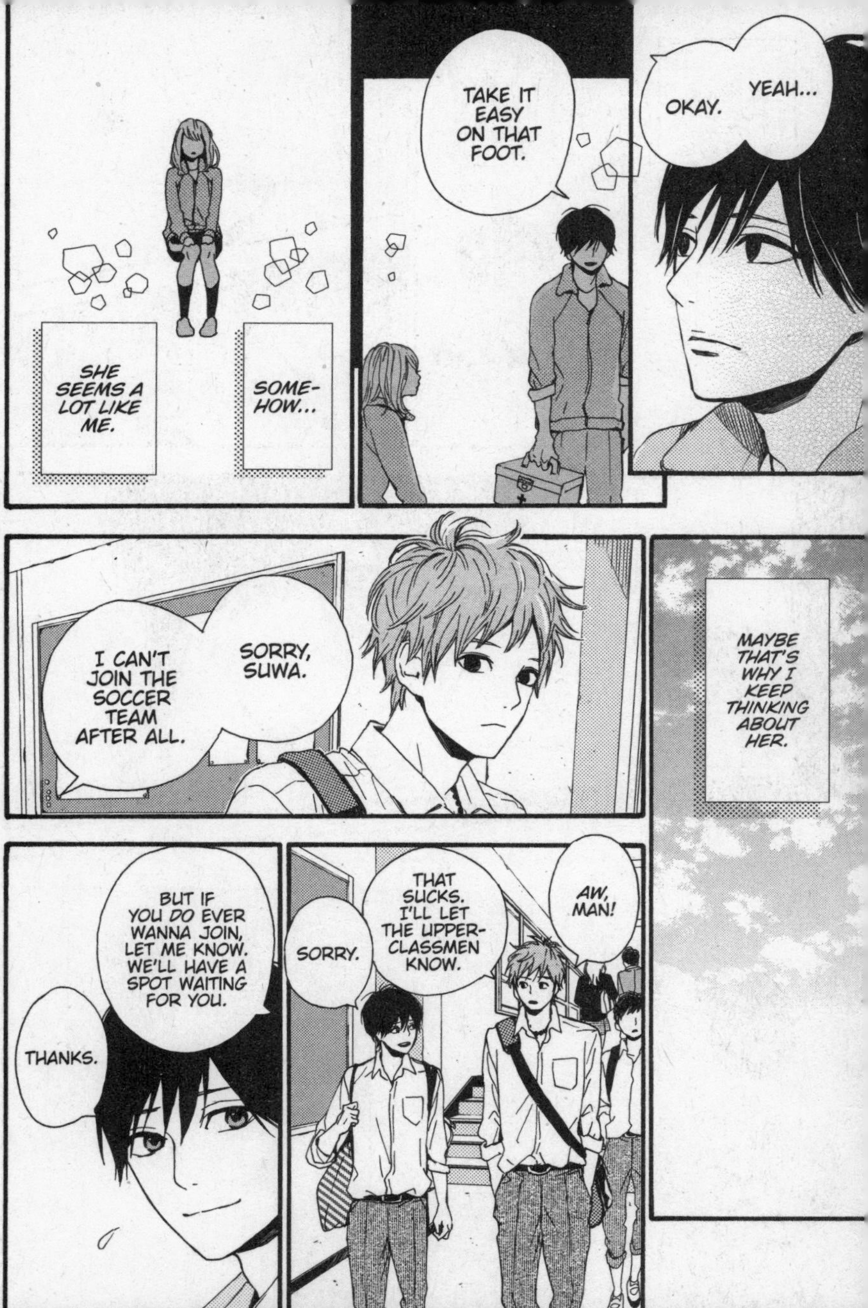
YEAH... OKAY.
TAKE IT EASY ON THAT FOOT.
SOME-HOW...
SHE SEEMS A LOT LIKE ME.
MAYBE THAT'S WHY I KEEP THINKING ABOUT HER.
SORRY, SUWA.
I CAN'T JOIN THE SOCCER TEAM AFTER ALL.
AW, MAN!
THAT SUCKS. I'LL LET THE UPPER-CLASSMEN KNOW.
SORRY.
BUT IF YOU DO EVER WANNA JOIN, LET ME KNOW. WE'LL HAVE A SPOT WAITING FOR YOU.
THANKS.

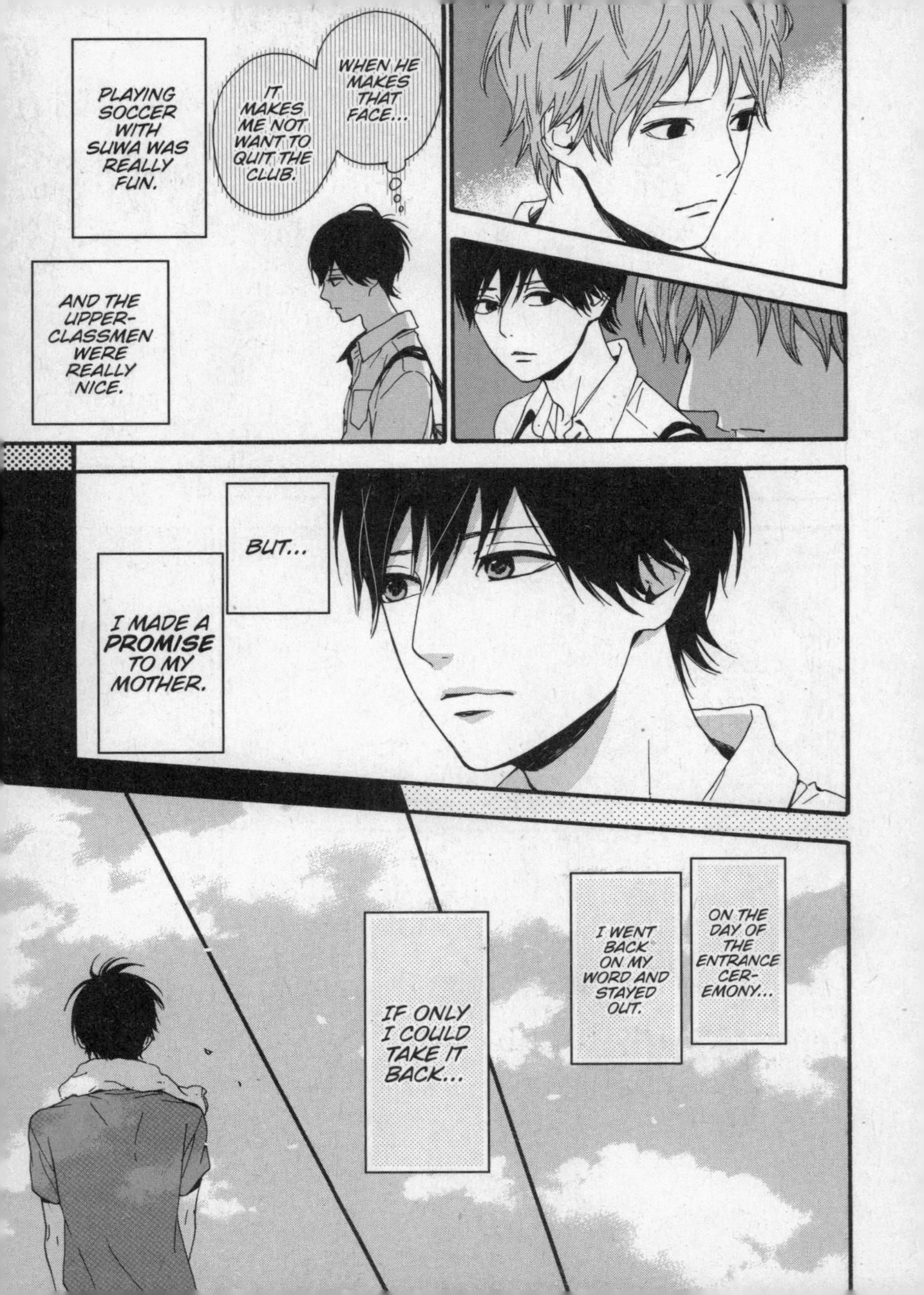
WHEN HE MAKES THAT FACE...
IT MAKES ME NOT WANT TO QUIT THE CLUB.
PLAYING SOCCER WITH SUWA WAS REALLY FUN.
AND THE UPPER-CLASSMEN WERE REALLY NICE.
BUT...
I MADE A **PROMISE** TO MY MOTHER.
ON THE DAY OF THE ENTRANCE CER-EMONY...
I WENT BACK ON MY WORD AND STAYED OUT.
IF ONLY I COULD TAKE IT BACK...

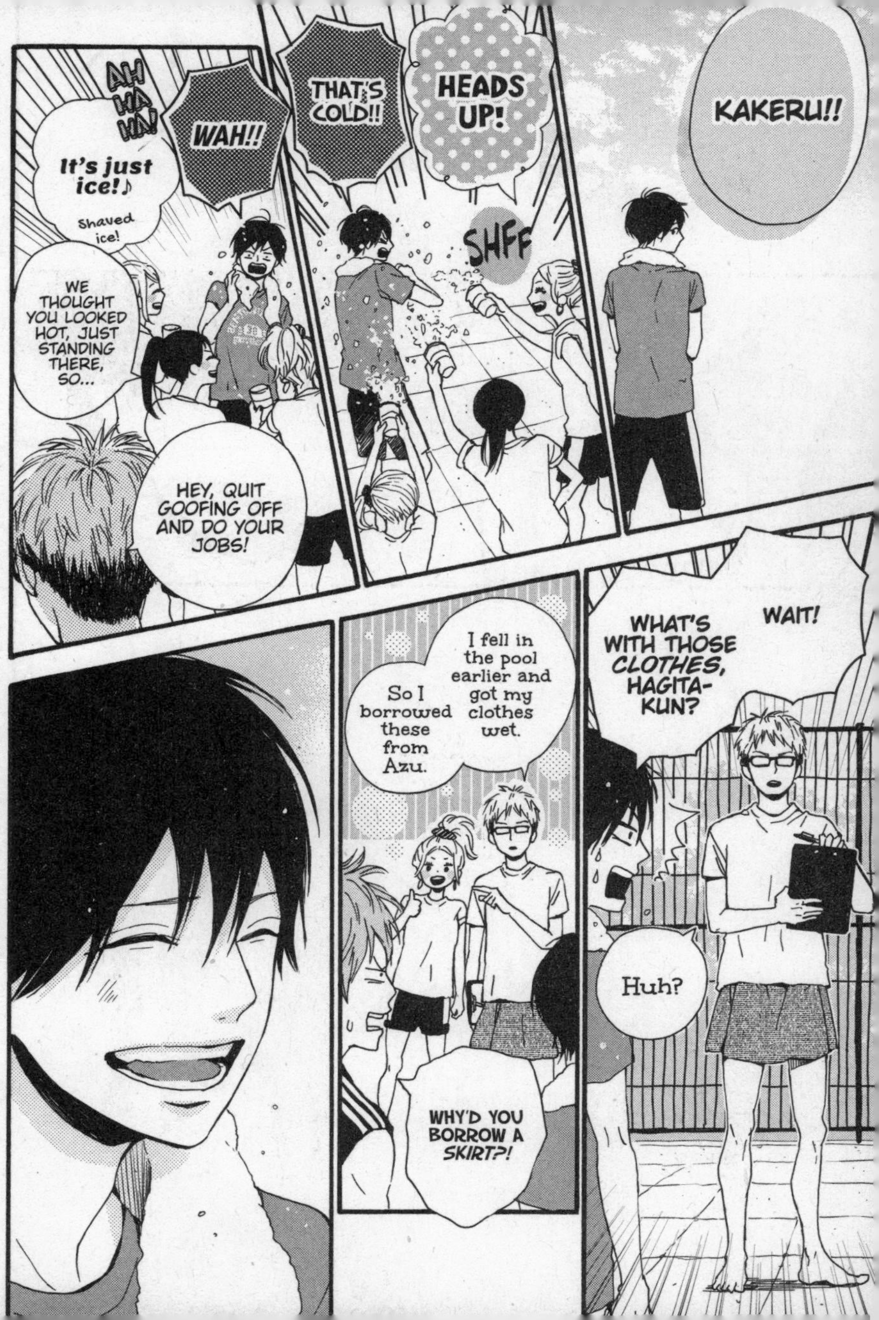
KAKERU!!
HEADS UP!
THAT'S COLD!!
SHFF
WAH!!
AH HA HA!
It's just ice!♪
Shaved ice!
WE THOUGHT YOU LOOKED HOT, JUST STANDING THERE, SO...
HEY, QUIT GOOFING OFF AND DO YOUR JOBS!
WAIT!
WHAT'S WITH THOSE CLOTHES, HAGITA-KUN?
Huh?
I fell in the pool earlier and got my clothes wet.
So I borrowed these from Azu.
WHY'D YOU BORROW A SKIRT?!

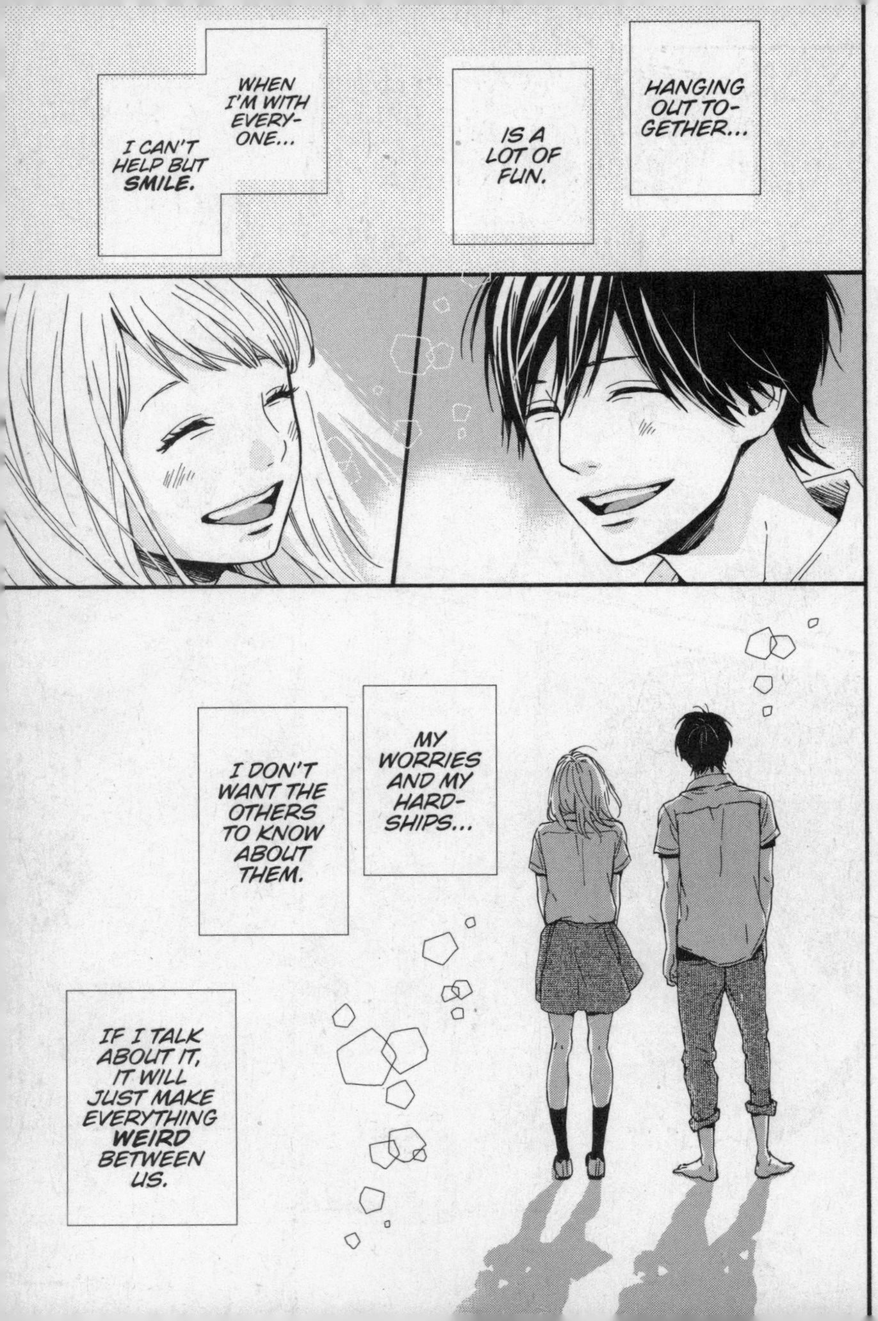
HANGING OUT TO-GETHER...
IS A LOT OF FUN.
WHEN I'M WITH EVERY-ONE...
I CAN'T HELP BUT SMILE.
MY WORRIES AND MY HARD-SHIPS...
I DON'T WANT THE OTHERS TO KNOW ABOUT THEM.
IF I TALK ABOUT IT, IT WILL JUST MAKE EVERYTHING WEIRD BETWEEN US.

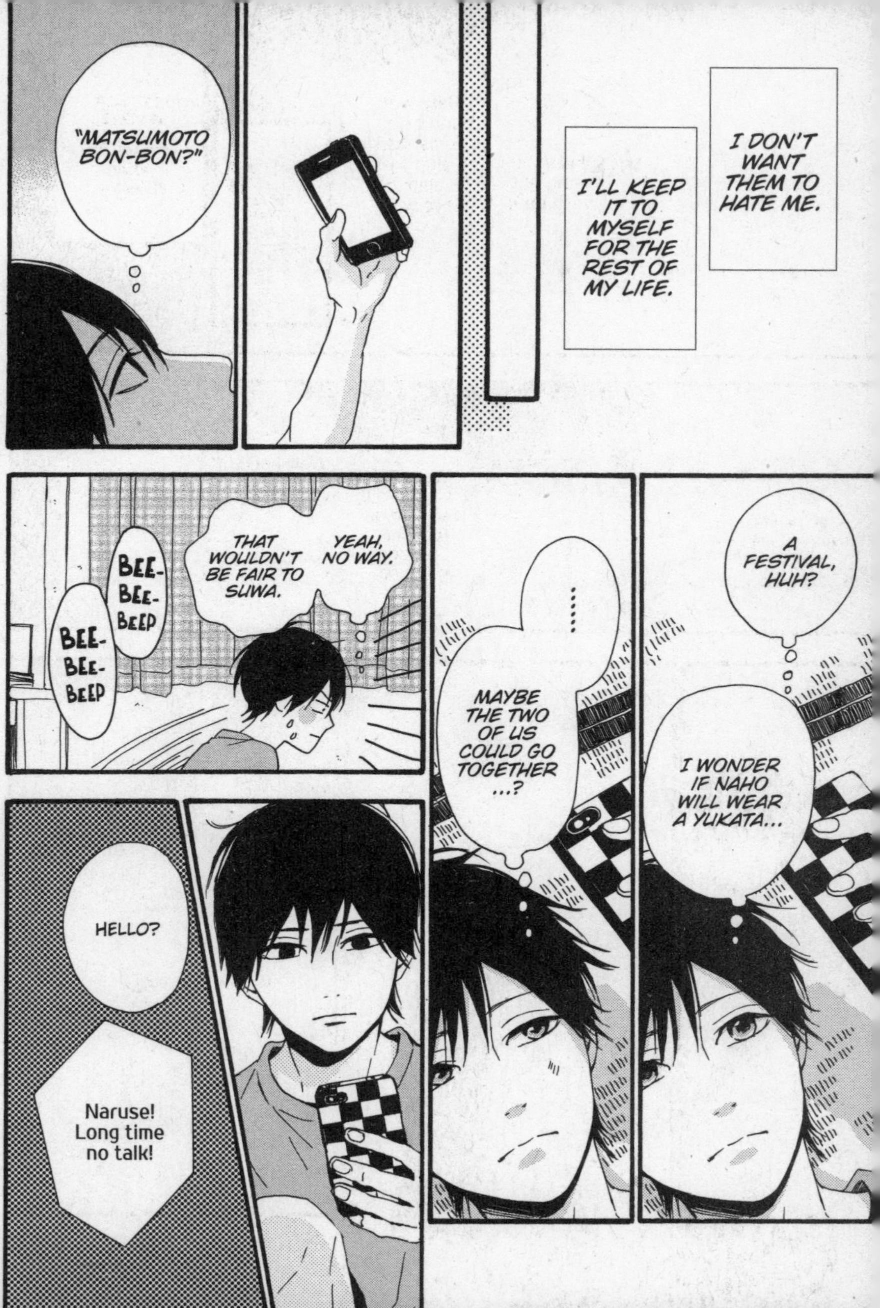
I DON'T WANT THEM TO HATE ME.
I'LL KEEP IT TO MYSELF FOR THE REST OF MY LIFE.
"MATSUMOTO BON-BON?"
A FESTIVAL, HUH?
I WONDER IF NAHO WILL WEAR A YUKATA...
......
MAYBE THE TWO OF US COULD GO TOGETHER ...?
YEAH, NO WAY.
THAT WOULDN'T BE FAIR TO SUWA.
BEE-BEE-BEEP
BEE-BEE-BEEP
HELLO?
Naruse! Long time no talk!

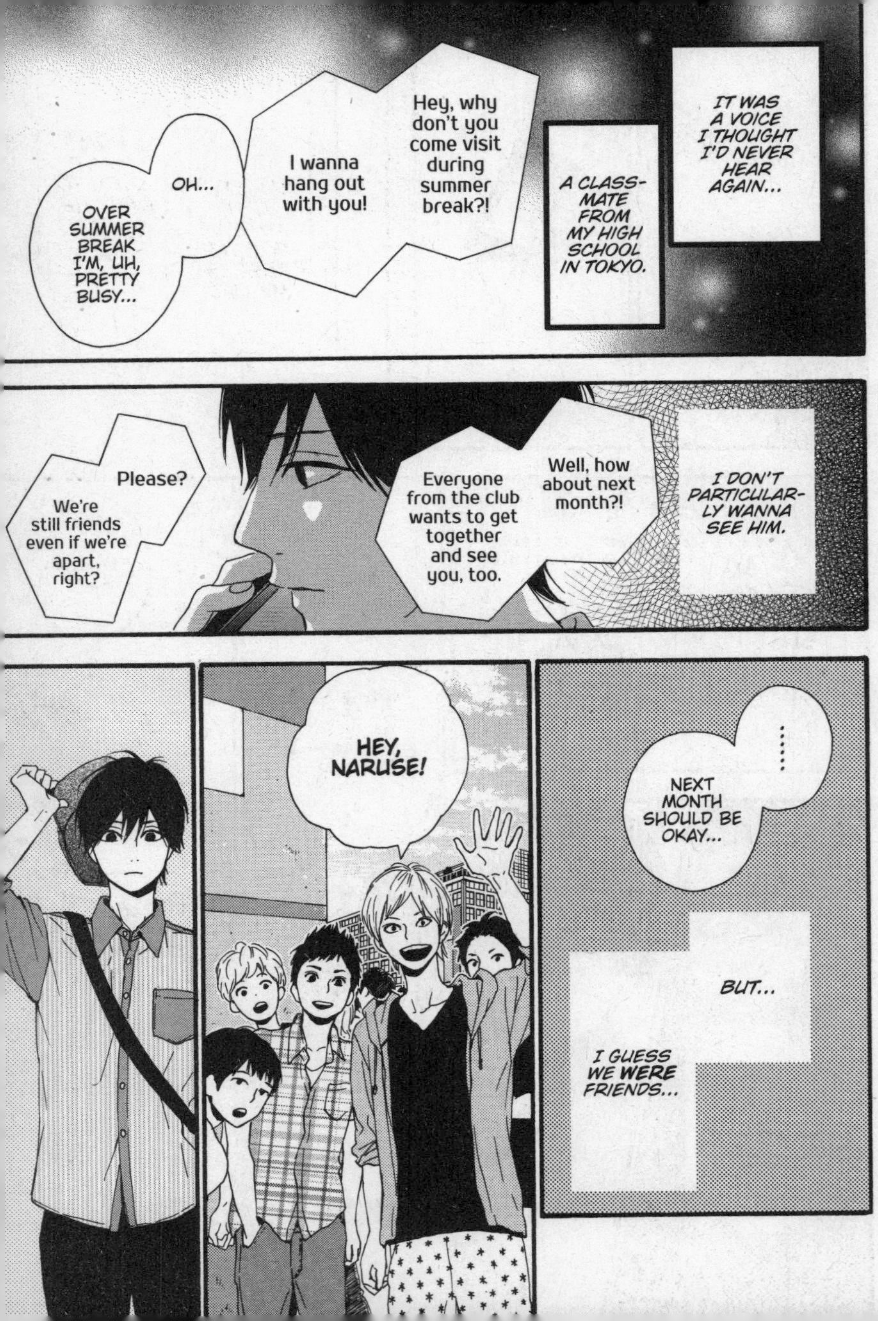
IT WAS A VOICE I THOUGHT I'D NEVER HEAR AGAIN...
A CLASS-MATE FROM MY HIGH SCHOOL IN TOKYO.
Hey, why don't you come visit during summer break?!
I wanna hang out with you!
OH...
OVER SUMMER BREAK I'M, UH, PRETTY BUSY...
I DON'T PARTICULAR-LY WANNA SEE HIM.
Well, how about next month?!
Everyone from the club wants to get together and see you, too.
Please?
We're still friends even if we're apart, right?
......
NEXT MONTH SHOULD BE OKAY...
BUT...
I GUESS WE WERE FRIENDS...
HEY, NARUSE!

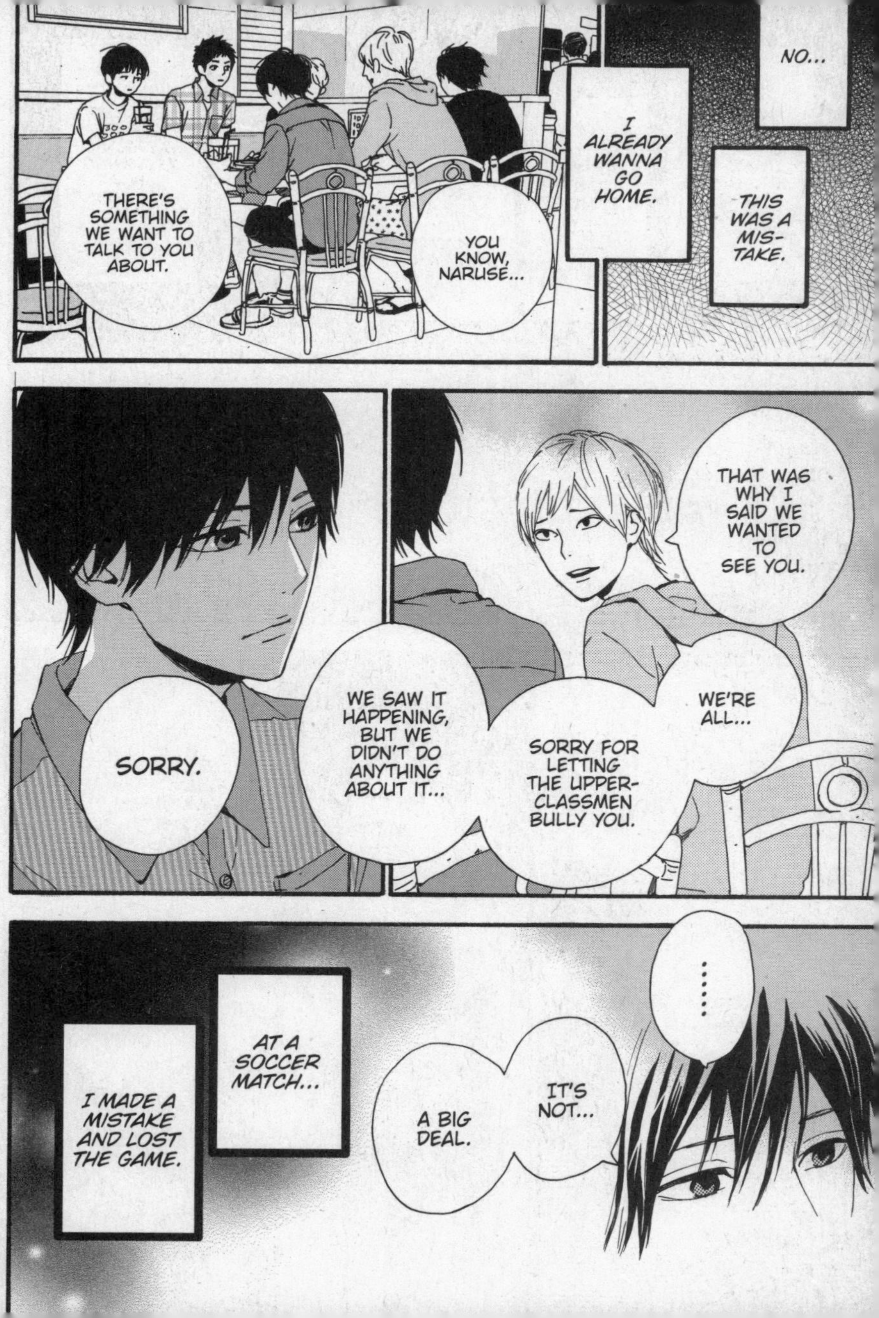
NO...
I ALREADY WANNA GO HOME.
THIS WAS A MIS-TAKE.
YOU KNOW, NARUSE...
THERE'S SOMETHING WE WANT TO TALK TO YOU ABOUT.
THAT WAS WHY I SAID WE WANTED TO SEE YOU.
WE'RE ALL...
SORRY FOR LETTING THE UPPER-CLASSMEN BULLY YOU.
WE SAW IT HAPPENING, BUT WE DIDN'T DO ANYTHING ABOUT IT...
SORRY.
......
IT'S NOT...
A BIG DEAL.
AT A SOCCER MATCH...
I MADE A MISTAKE AND LOST THE GAME.

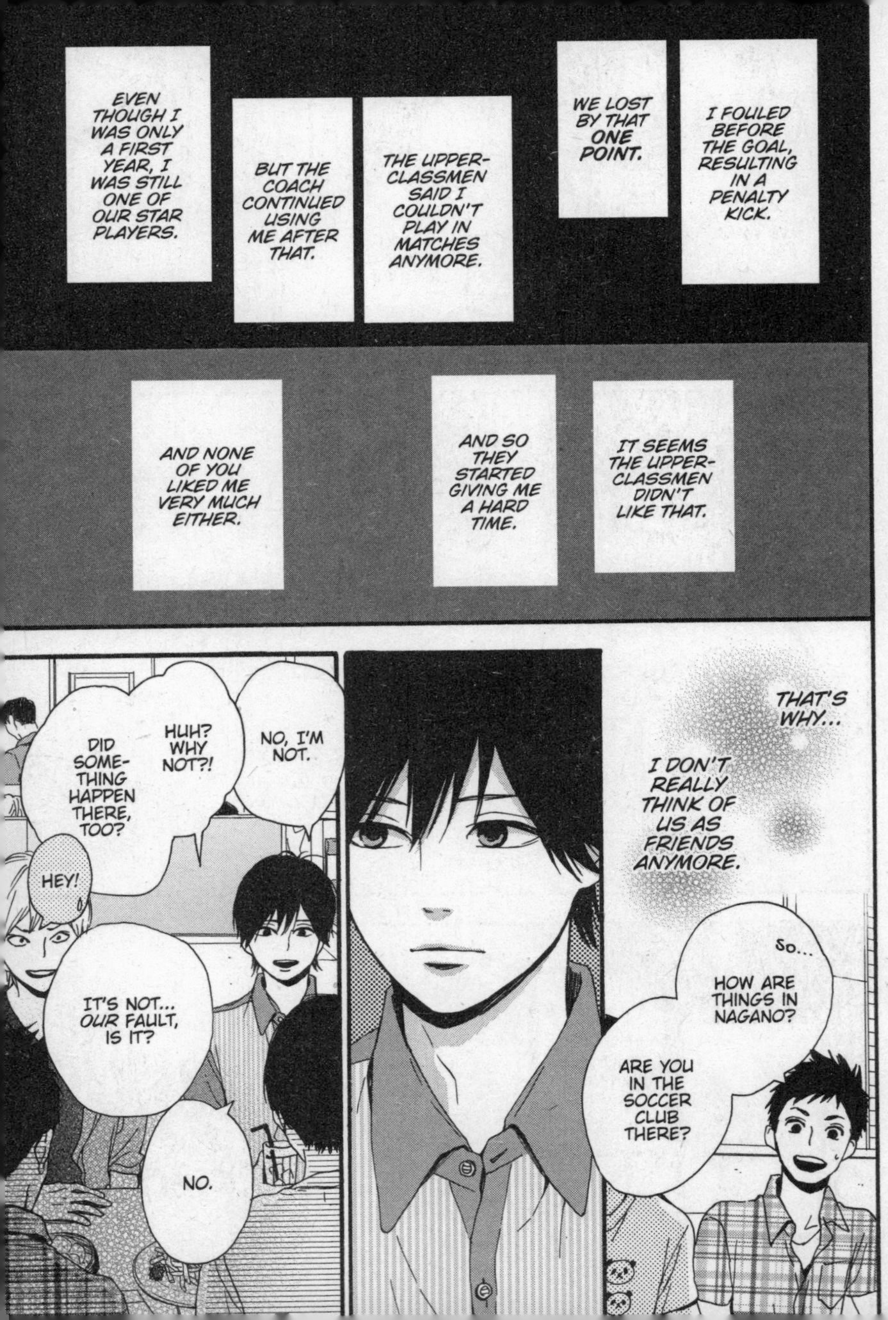
I FOULED BEFORE THE GOAL, RESULTING IN A PENALTY KICK.
WE LOST BY THAT ONE POINT.
THE UPPER-CLASSMEN SAID I COULDN'T PLAY IN MATCHES ANYMORE.
BUT THE COACH CONTINUED USING ME AFTER THAT.
EVEN THOUGH I WAS ONLY A FIRST YEAR, I WAS STILL ONE OF OUR STAR PLAYERS.
IT SEEMS THE UPPER-CLASSMEN DIDN'T LIKE THAT.
AND SO THEY STARTED GIVING ME A HARD TIME.
AND NONE OF YOU LIKED ME VERY MUCH EITHER.
THAT'S WHY...
I DON'T REALLY THINK OF US AS FRIENDS ANYMORE.
SO...
HOW ARE THINGS IN NAGANO?
ARE YOU IN THE SOCCER CLUB THERE?
NO, I'M NOT.
HUH? WHY NOT?!
DID SOMETHING HAPPEN THERE, TOO?
HEY!
IT'S NOT... OUR FAULT, IS IT?
NO.

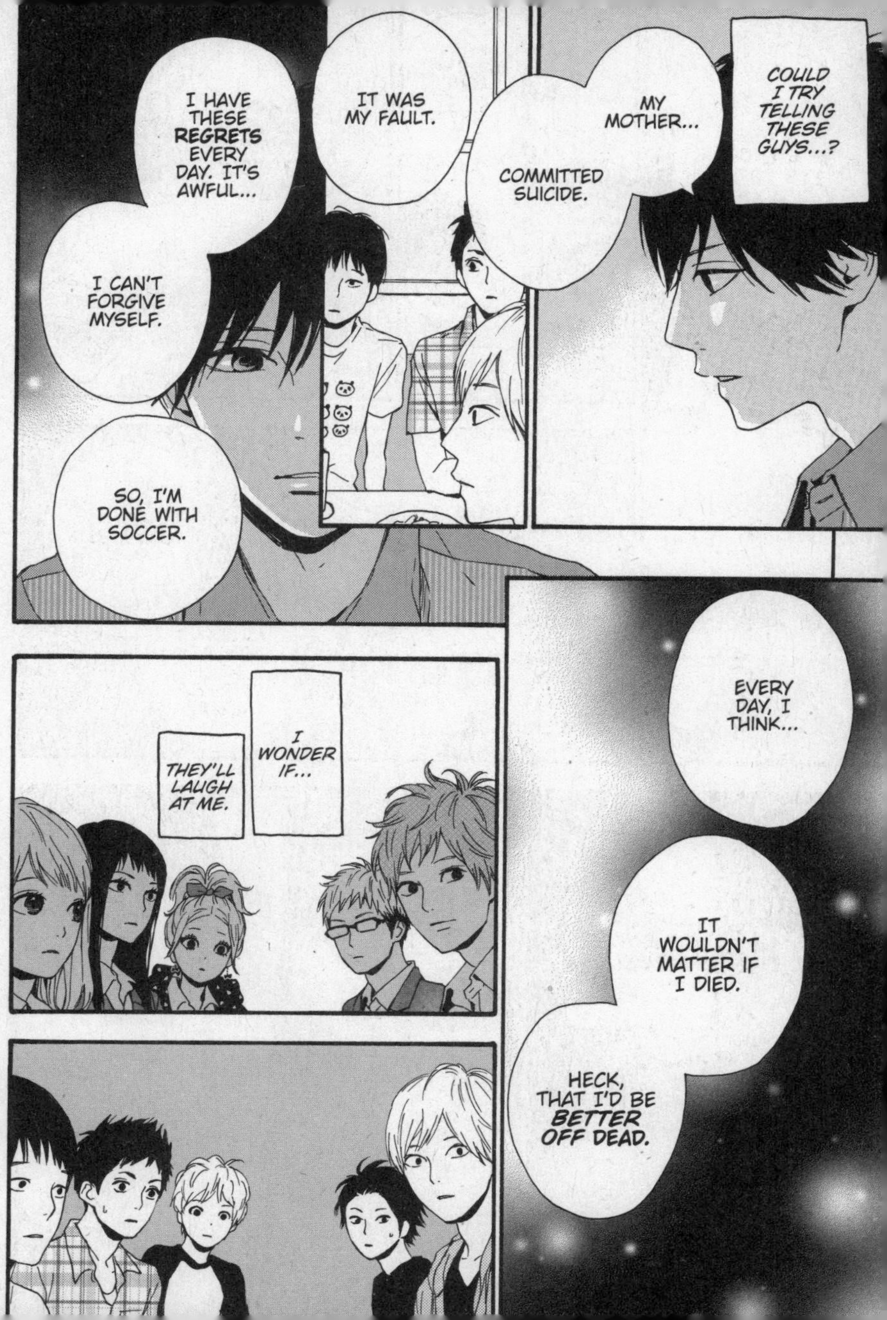
COULD I TRY TELLING THESE GUYS...?
MY MOTHER...
COMMITTED SUICIDE.
IT WAS MY FAULT.
I HAVE THESE REGRETS EVERY DAY. IT'S AWFUL...
I CAN'T FORGIVE MYSELF.
SO, I'M DONE WITH SOCCER.
EVERY DAY, I THINK...
IT WOULDN'T MATTER IF I DIED.
HECK, THAT I'D BE BETTER OFF DEAD.
I WONDER IF...
THEY'LL LAUGH AT ME.

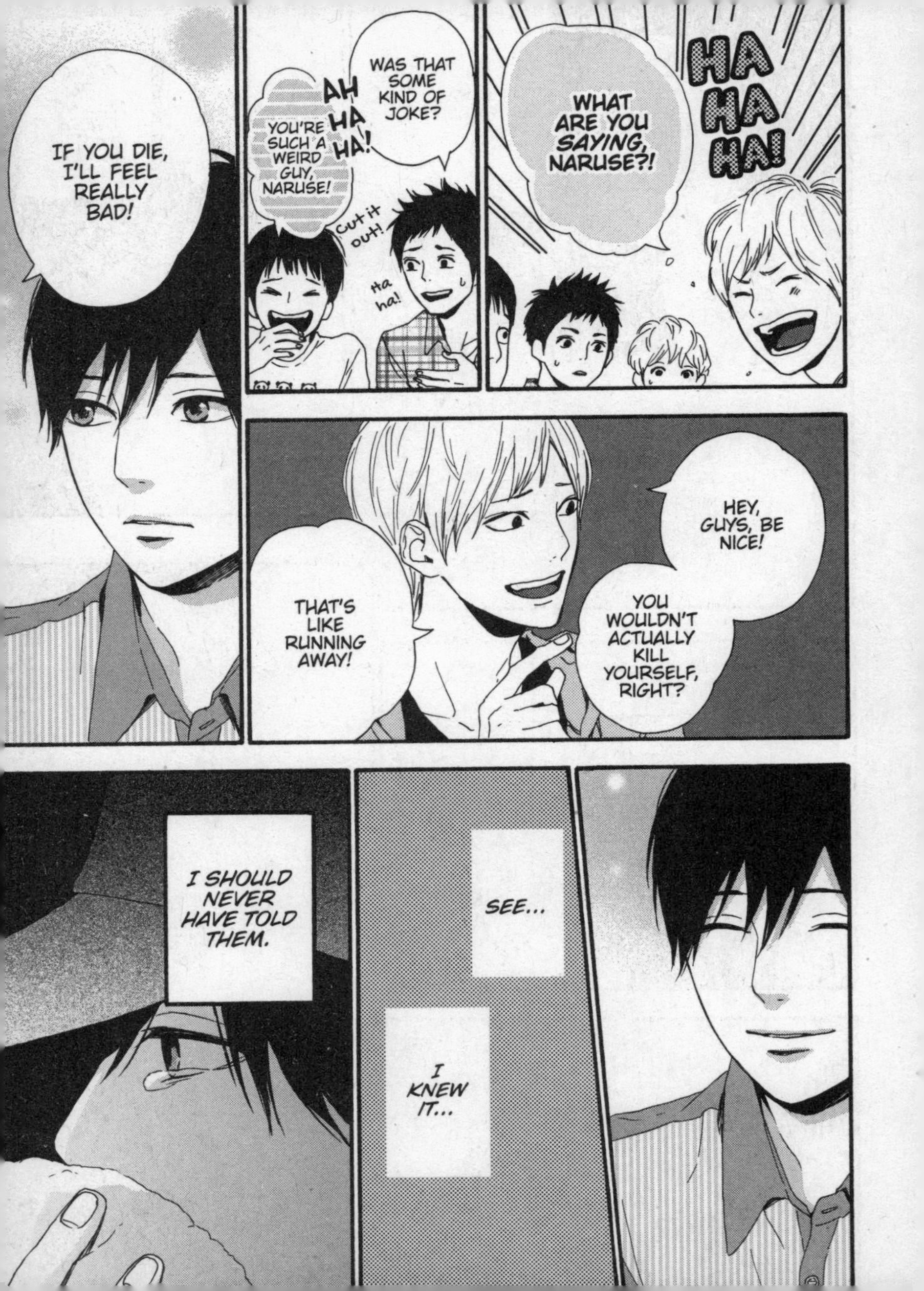
HA HA HA!
WHAT ARE YOU SAYING, NARUSE?!
WAS THAT SOME KIND OF JOKE?
AH HA HA!
YOU'RE SUCH A WEIRD GUY, NARUSE!
Cut it out!
Ha ha!
HEY, GUYS, BE NICE!
YOU WOULDN'T ACTUALLY KILL YOURSELF, RIGHT?
THAT'S LIKE RUNNING AWAY!
IF YOU DIE, I'LL FEEL REALLY BAD!
SEE...
I KNEW IT...
I SHOULD NEVER HAVE TOLD THEM.

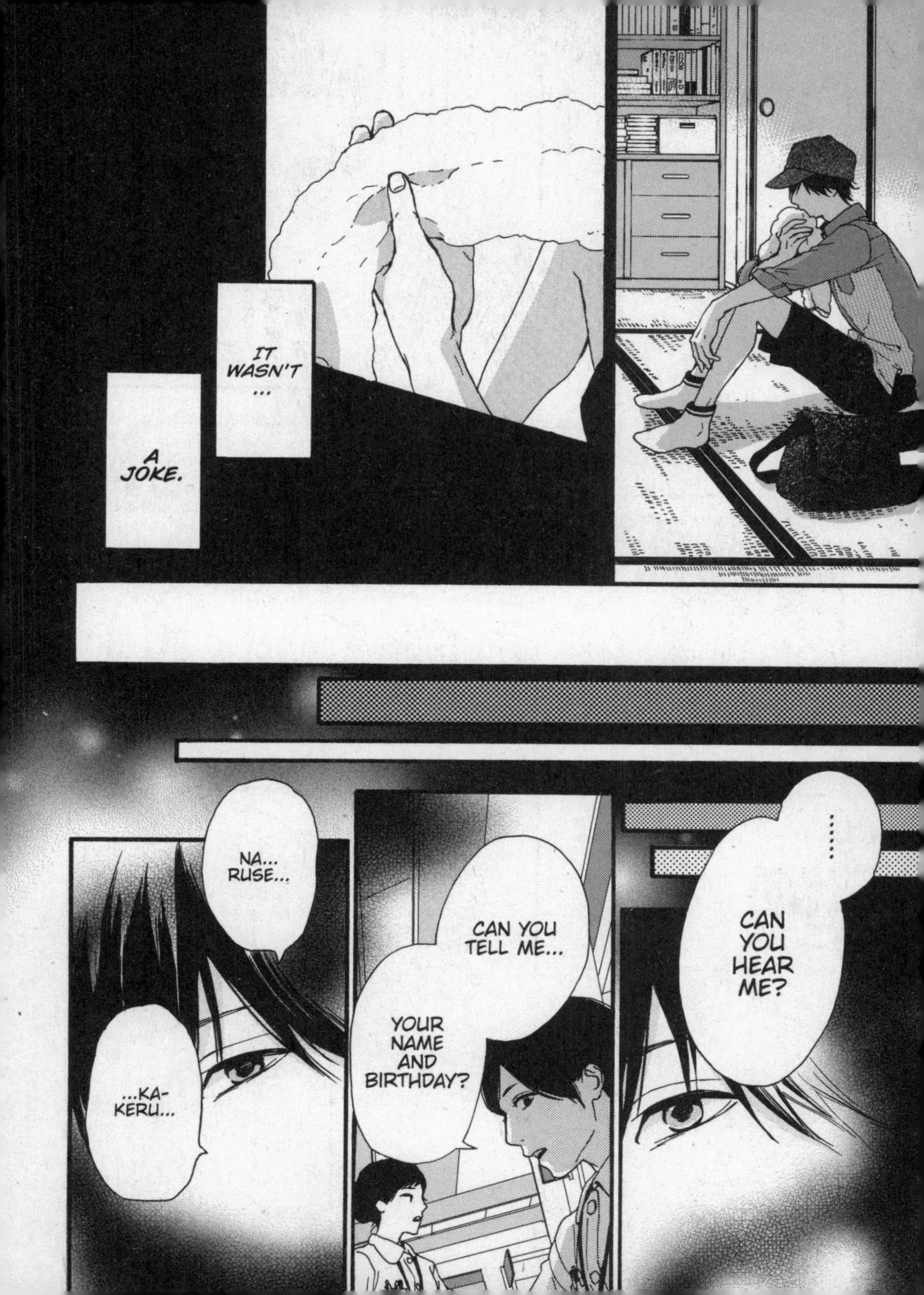
IT WASN'T ...
A JOKE.
.....
CAN YOU HEAR ME?
CAN YOU TELL ME...
YOUR NAME AND BIRTHDAY?
NA... RUSE...
...KA-KERU...

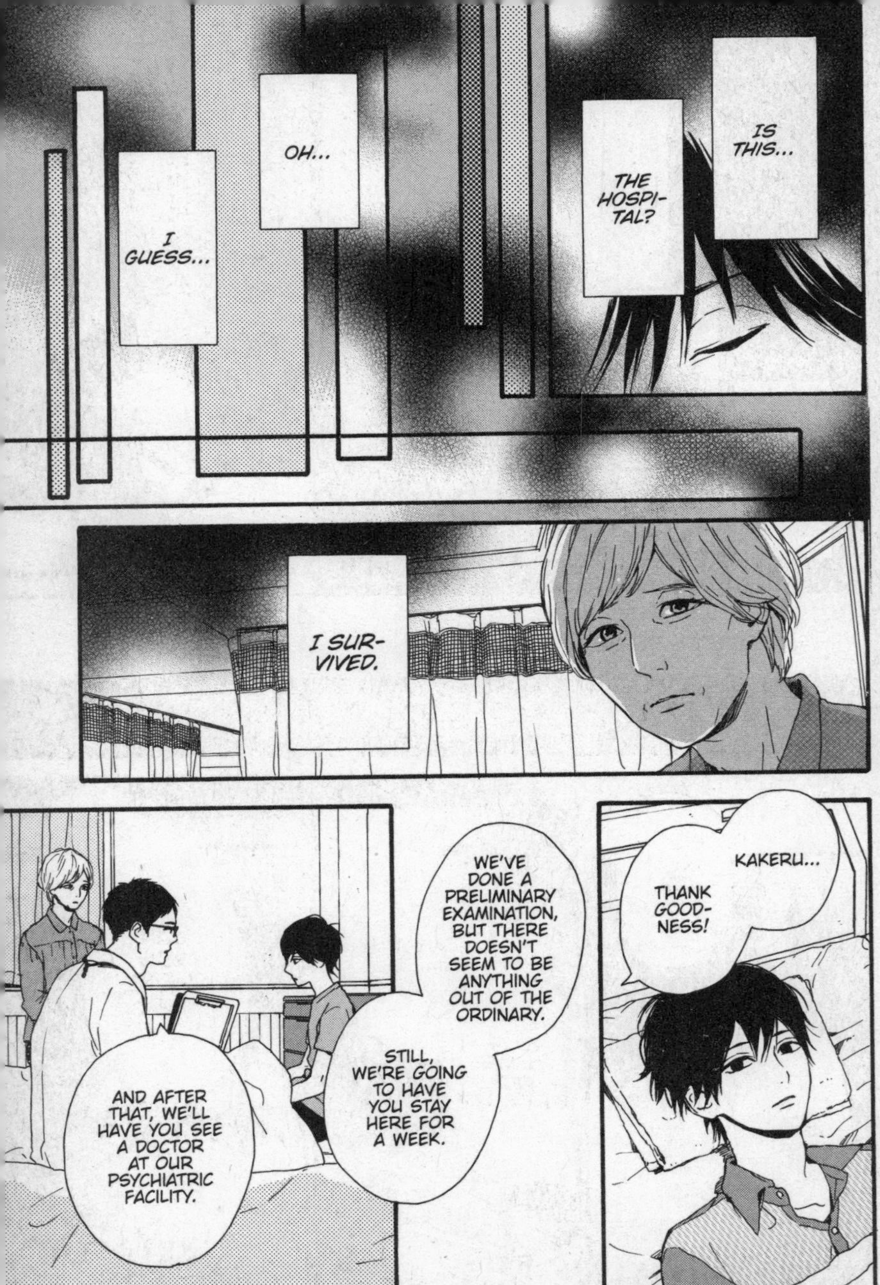
IS THIS...
THE HOSPITAL?
OH...
I GUESS...
I SURVIVED.
KAKERU... THANK GOODNESS!
WE'VE DONE A PRELIMINARY EXAMINATION, BUT THERE DOESN'T SEEM TO BE ANYTHING OUT OF THE ORDINARY.
STILL, WE'RE GOING TO HAVE YOU STAY HERE FOR A WEEK.
AND AFTER THAT, WE'LL HAVE YOU SEE A DOCTOR AT OUR PSYCHIATRIC FACILITY.

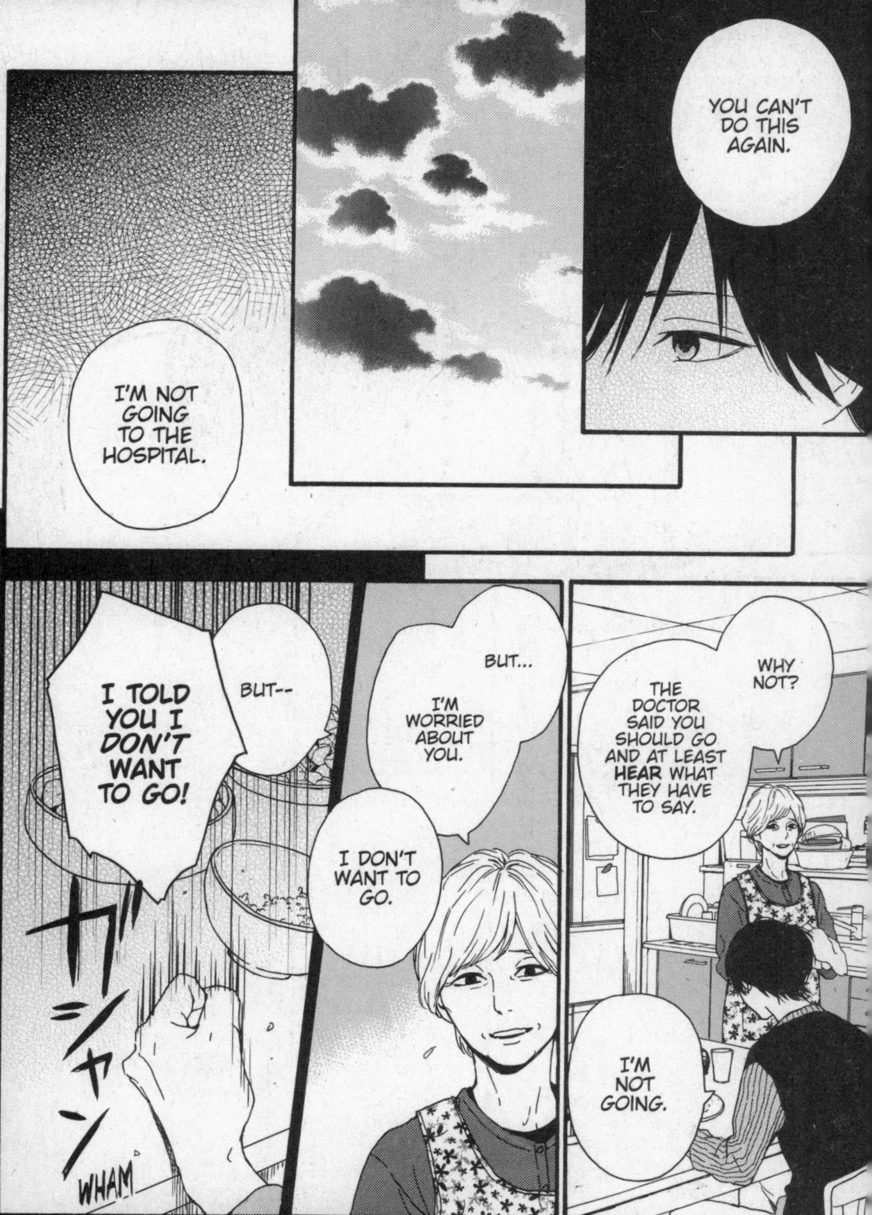
YOU CAN'T DO THIS AGAIN.
I'M NOT GOING TO THE HOSPITAL.
WHY NOT?
THE DOCTOR SAID YOU SHOULD GO AND AT LEAST **HEAR** WHAT THEY HAVE TO SAY.
I'M NOT GOING.
BUT...
I'M WORRIED ABOUT YOU.
I DON'T WANT TO GO.
BUT--
I TOLD YOU I *DON'T* WANT TO GO!
ガシャン
WHAM

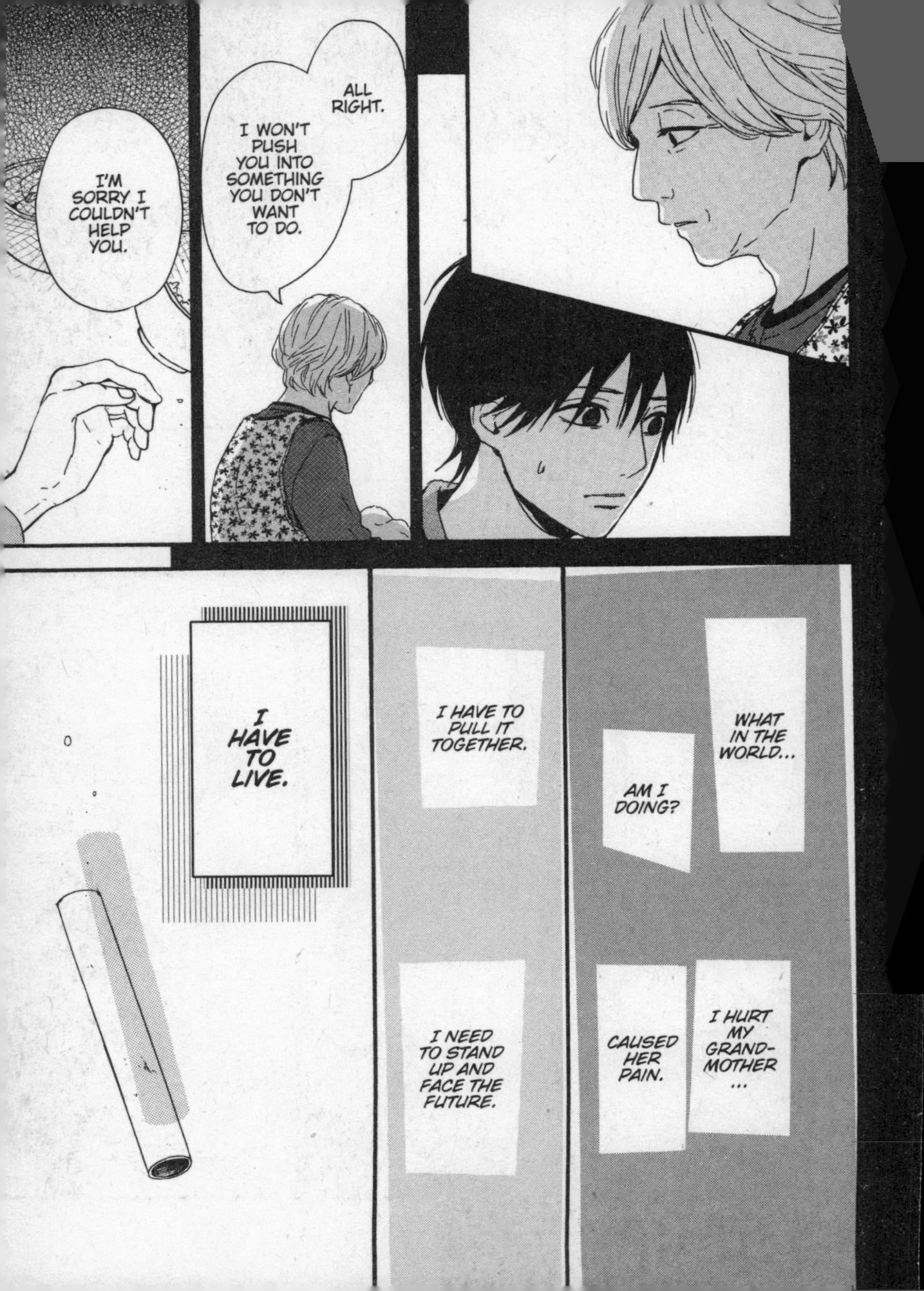
ALL RIGHT.
I WON'T PUSH YOU INTO SOMETHING YOU DON'T WANT TO DO.
I'M SORRY I COULDN'T HELP YOU.
WHAT IN THE WORLD...
AM I DOING?
I HURT MY GRANDMOTHER...
CAUSED HER PAIN.
I HAVE TO PULL IT TOGETHER.
I NEED TO STAND UP AND FACE THE FUTURE.
I HAVE TO LIVE.

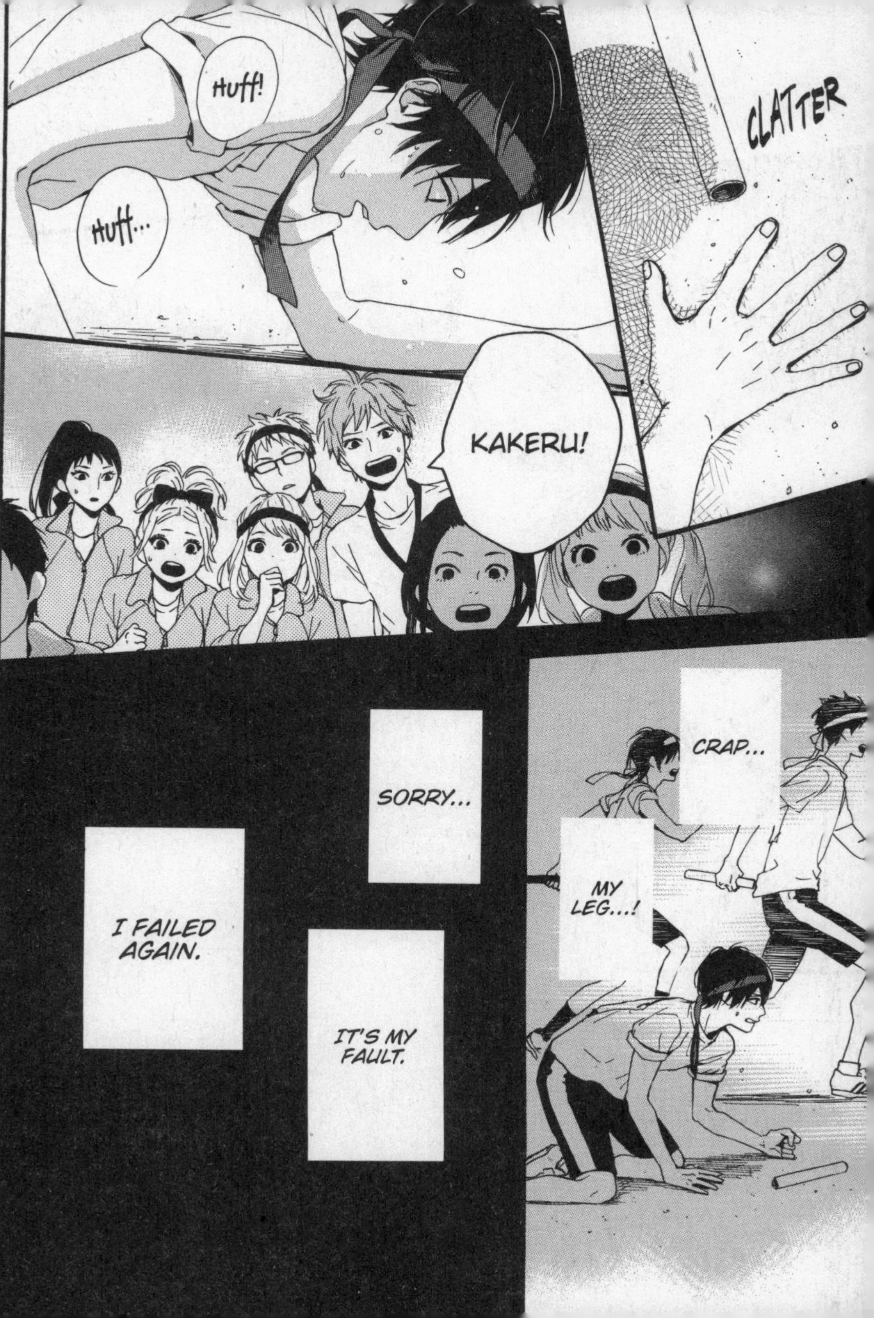
CLATTER
Huff!
Huff...
KAKERU!
CRAP...
MY LEG...!
SORRY...
I FAILED AGAIN.
IT'S MY FAULT.

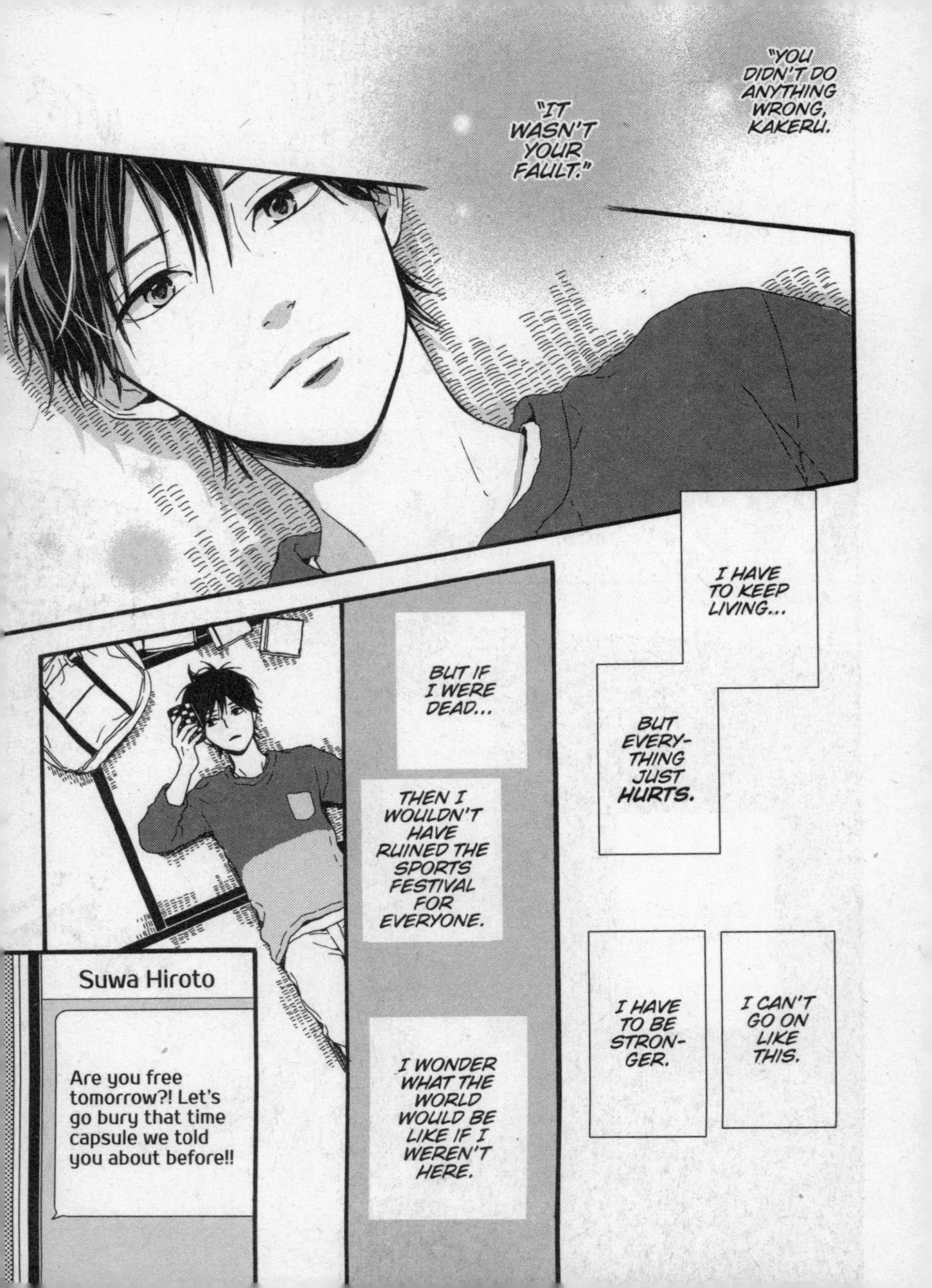
"YOU DIDN'T DO ANYTHING WRONG, KAKERU.
"IT WASN'T YOUR FAULT."
I HAVE TO KEEP LIVING...
BUT EVERY-THING JUST HURTS.
I CAN'T GO ON LIKE THIS.
I HAVE TO BE STRON-GER.
BUT IF I WERE DEAD...
THEN I WOULDN'T HAVE RUINED THE SPORTS FESTIVAL FOR EVERYONE.
I WONDER WHAT THE WORLD WOULD BE LIKE IF I WEREN'T HERE.
Suwa Hiroto
Are you free tomorrow?! Let's go bury that time capsule we told you about before!!

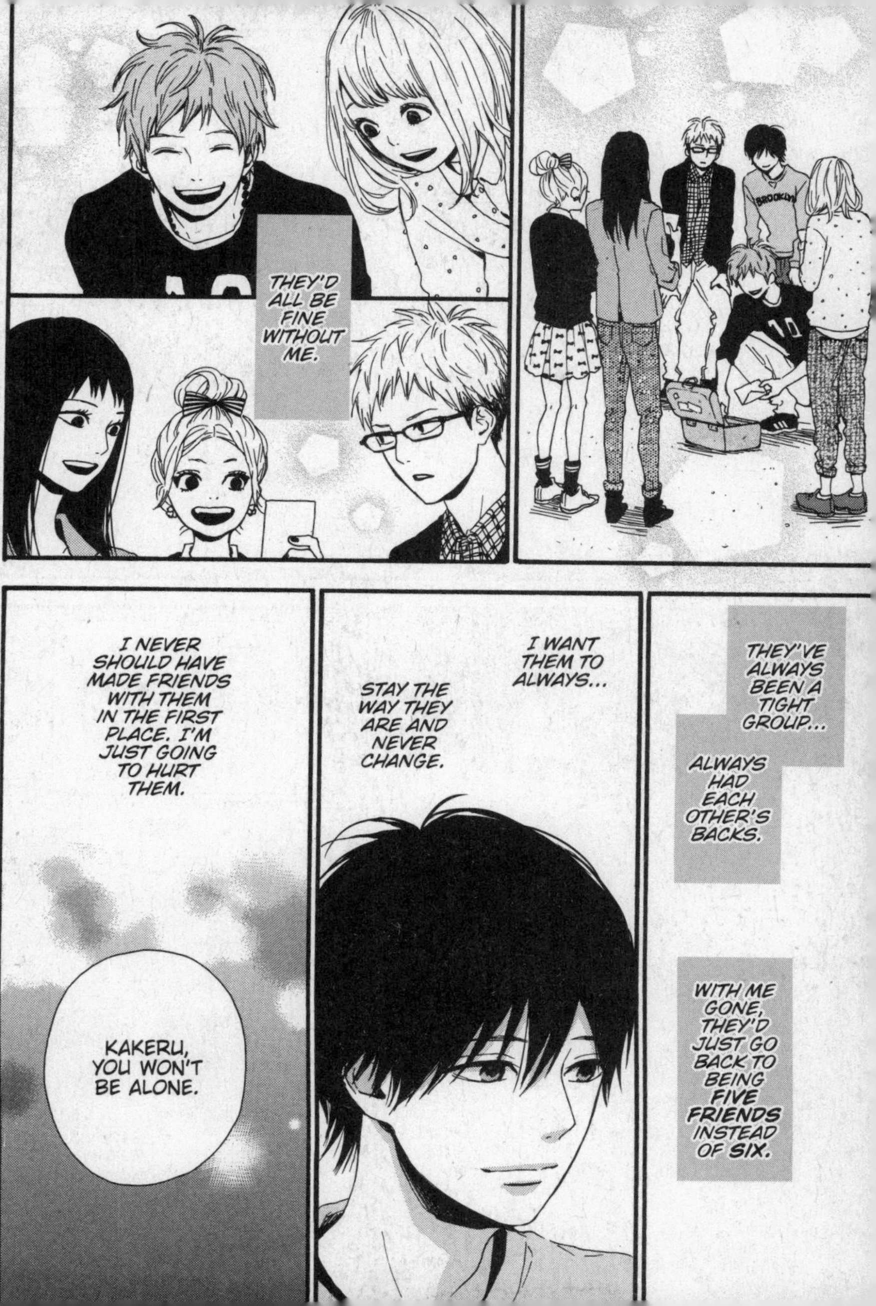
THEY'D ALL BE FINE WITHOUT ME.
THEY'VE ALWAYS BEEN A TIGHT GROUP...
ALWAYS HAD EACH OTHER'S BACKS.
WITH ME GONE, THEY'D JUST GO BACK TO BEING **FIVE FRIENDS** INSTEAD OF **SIX**.
I WANT THEM TO ALWAYS...
STAY THE WAY THEY ARE AND NEVER CHANGE.
I NEVER SHOULD HAVE MADE FRIENDS WITH THEM IN THE FIRST PLACE. I'M JUST GOING TO HURT THEM.
KAKERU, YOU WON'T BE ALONE.

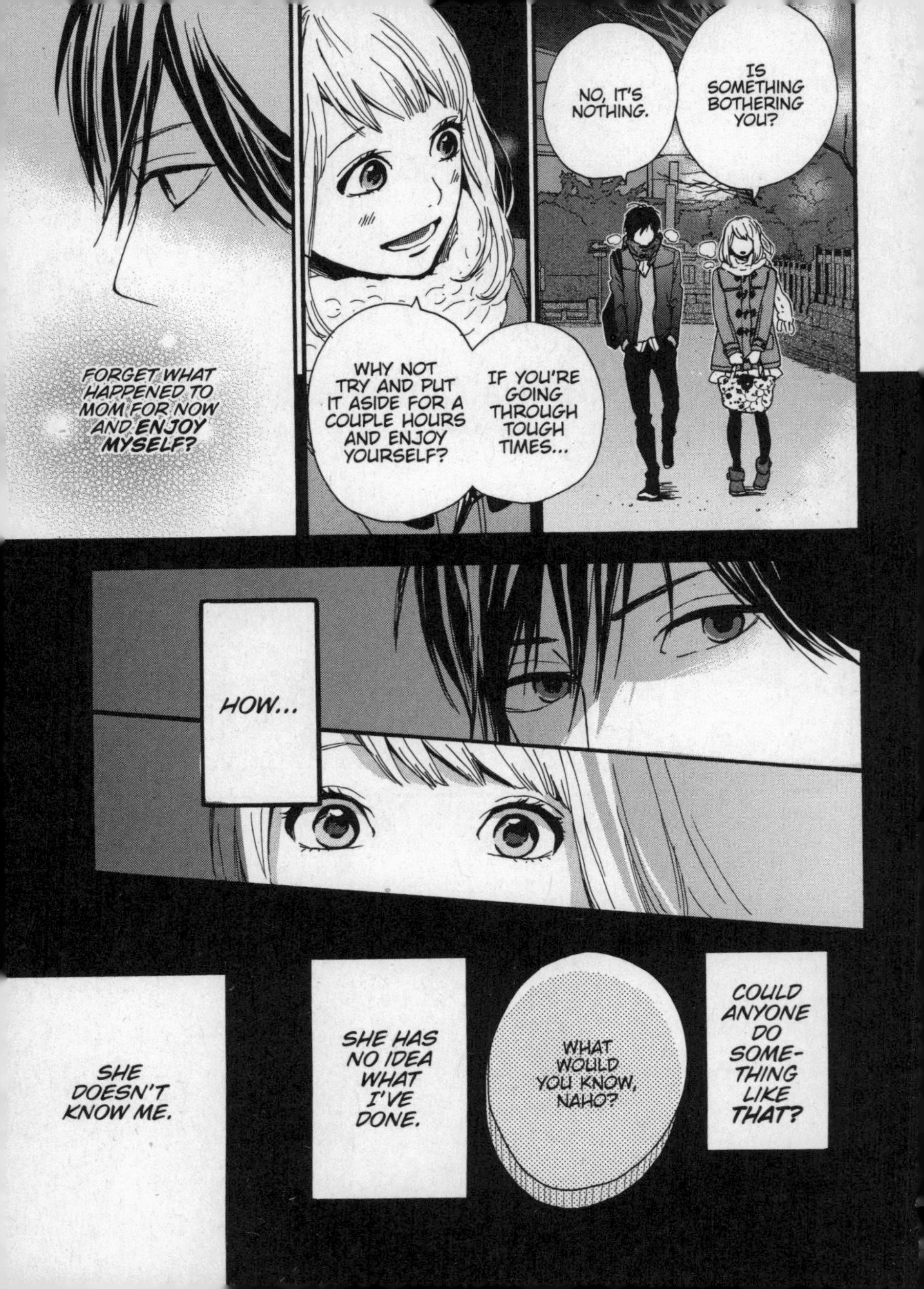
IS SOMETHING BOTHERING YOU?
NO, IT'S NOTHING.
IF YOU'RE GOING THROUGH TOUGH TIMES...
WHY NOT TRY AND PUT IT ASIDE FOR A COUPLE HOURS AND ENJOY YOURSELF?
FORGET WHAT HAPPENED TO MOM FOR NOW AND ENJOY MYSELF?
HOW...
COULD ANYONE DO SOME-THING LIKE THAT?
WHAT WOULD YOU KNOW, NAHO?
SHE HAS NO IDEA WHAT I'VE DONE.
SHE DOESN'T KNOW ME.

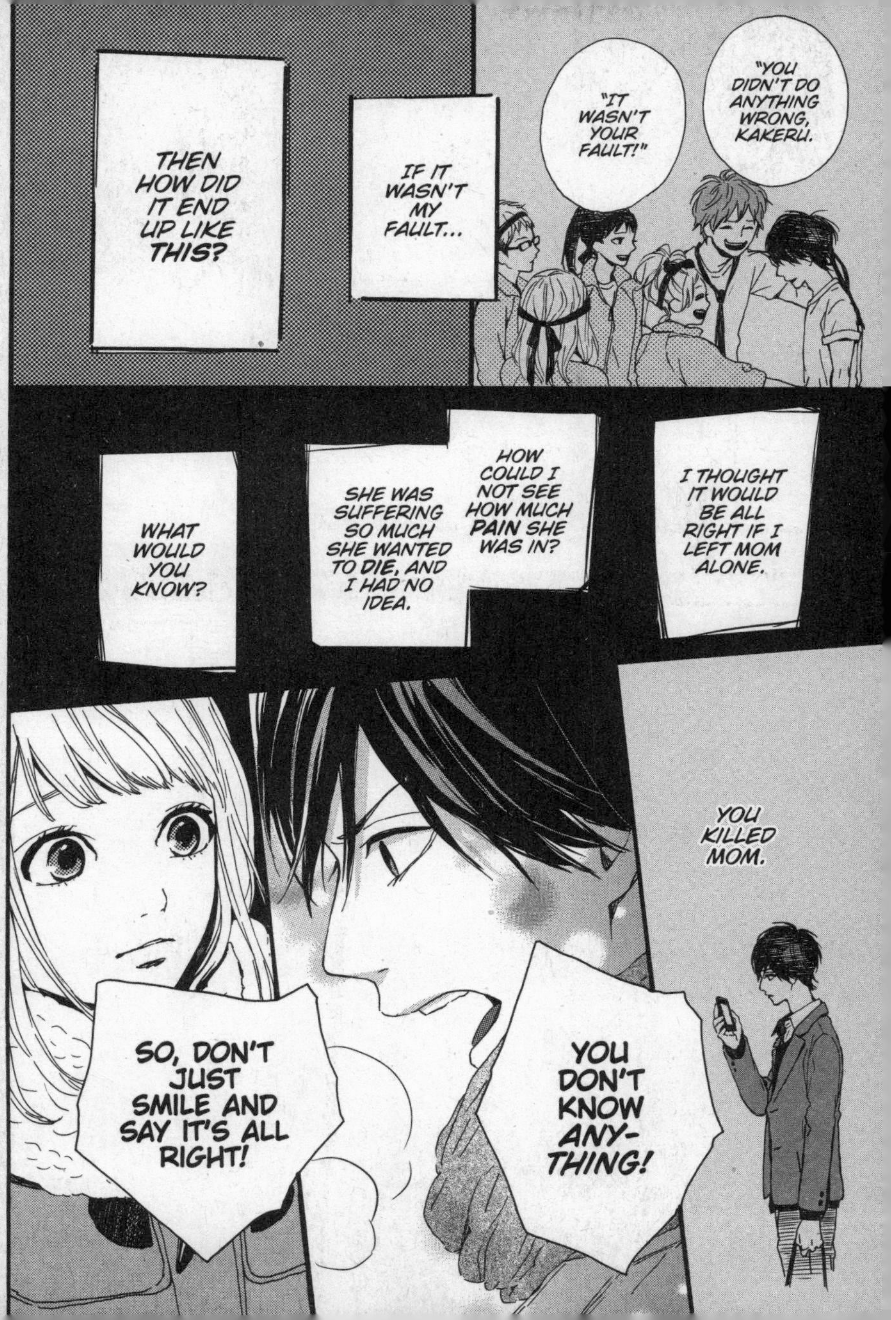
"YOU DIDN'T DO ANYTHING WRONG, KAKERU.
"IT WASN'T YOUR FAULT!"
IF IT WASN'T MY FAULT...
THEN HOW DID IT END UP LIKE THIS?
I THOUGHT IT WOULD BE ALL RIGHT IF I LEFT MOM ALONE.
HOW COULD I NOT SEE HOW MUCH PAIN SHE WAS IN?
SHE WAS SUFFERING SO MUCH SHE WANTED TO DIE, AND I HAD NO IDEA.
WHAT WOULD YOU KNOW?
YOU KILLED MOM.
YOU DON'T KNOW ANY-THING!
SO, DON'T JUST SMILE AND SAY IT'S ALL RIGHT!

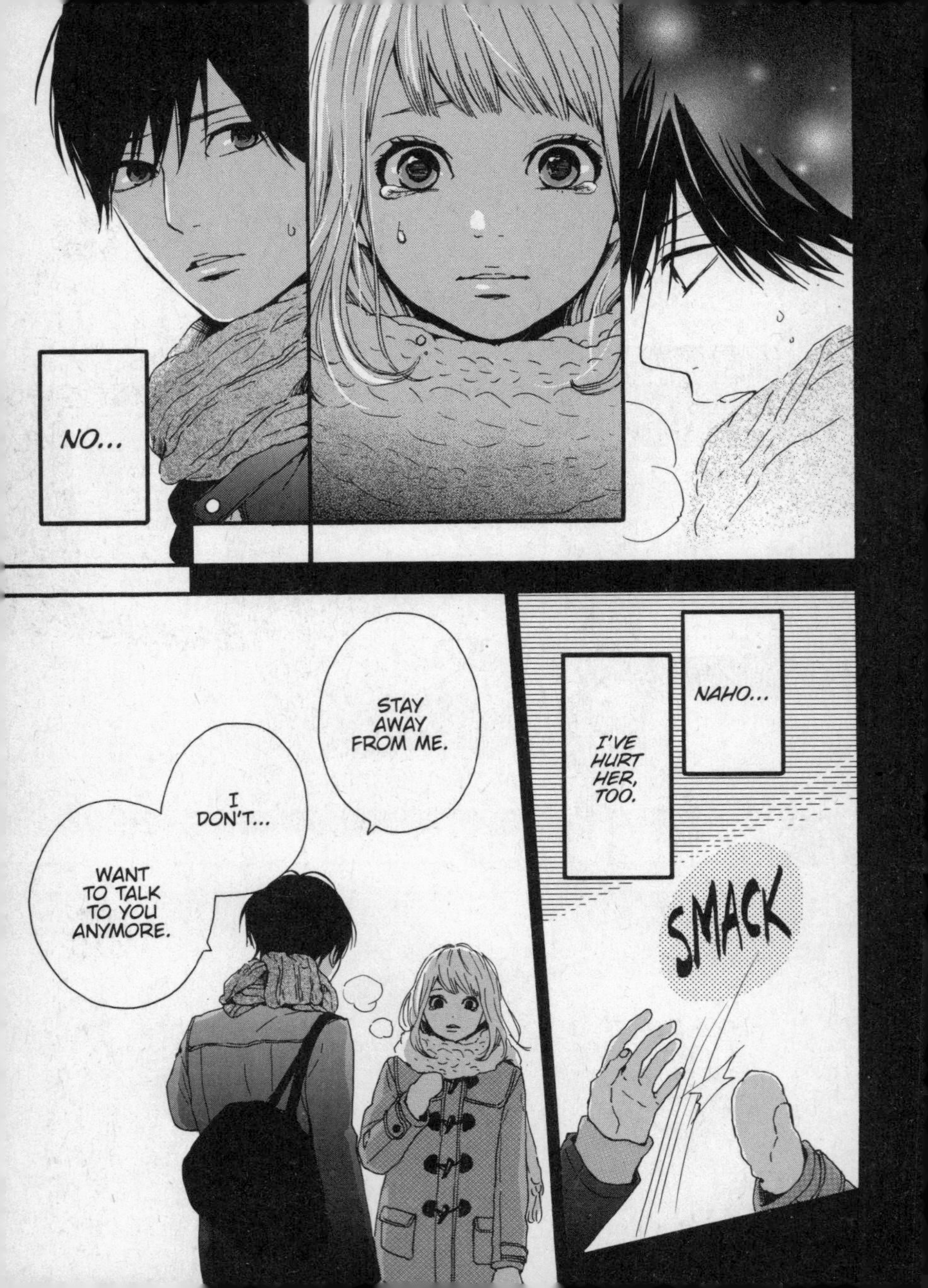
NO...
NAHO...
I'VE HURT HER, TOO.
SMACK
STAY AWAY FROM ME.
I DON'T...
WANT TO TALK TO YOU ANYMORE.

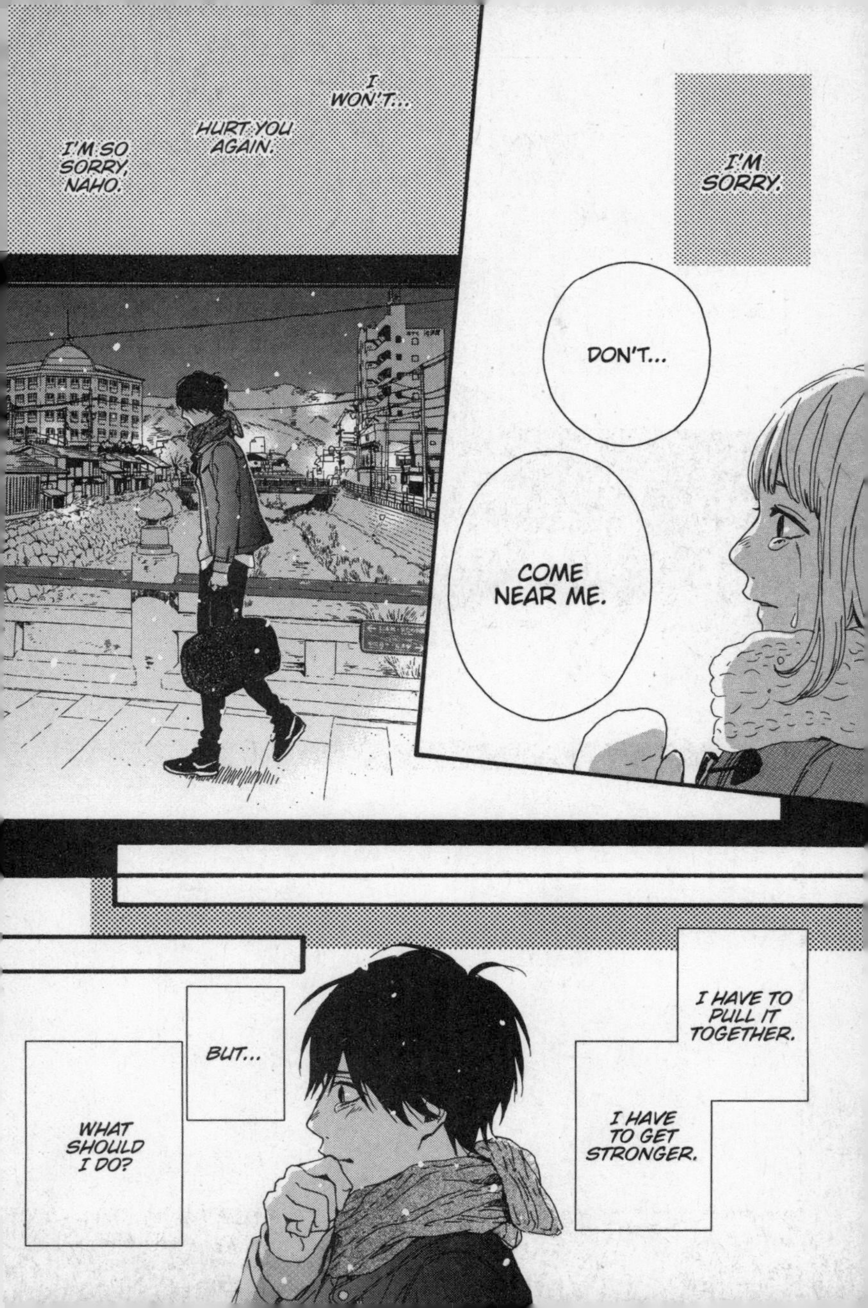
I'M SORRY.
DON'T...
COME NEAR ME.
I WON'T...
HURT YOU AGAIN.
I'M SO SORRY, NAHO.
I HAVE TO PULL IT TOGETHER.
I HAVE TO GET STRONGER.
BUT...
WHAT SHOULD I DO?

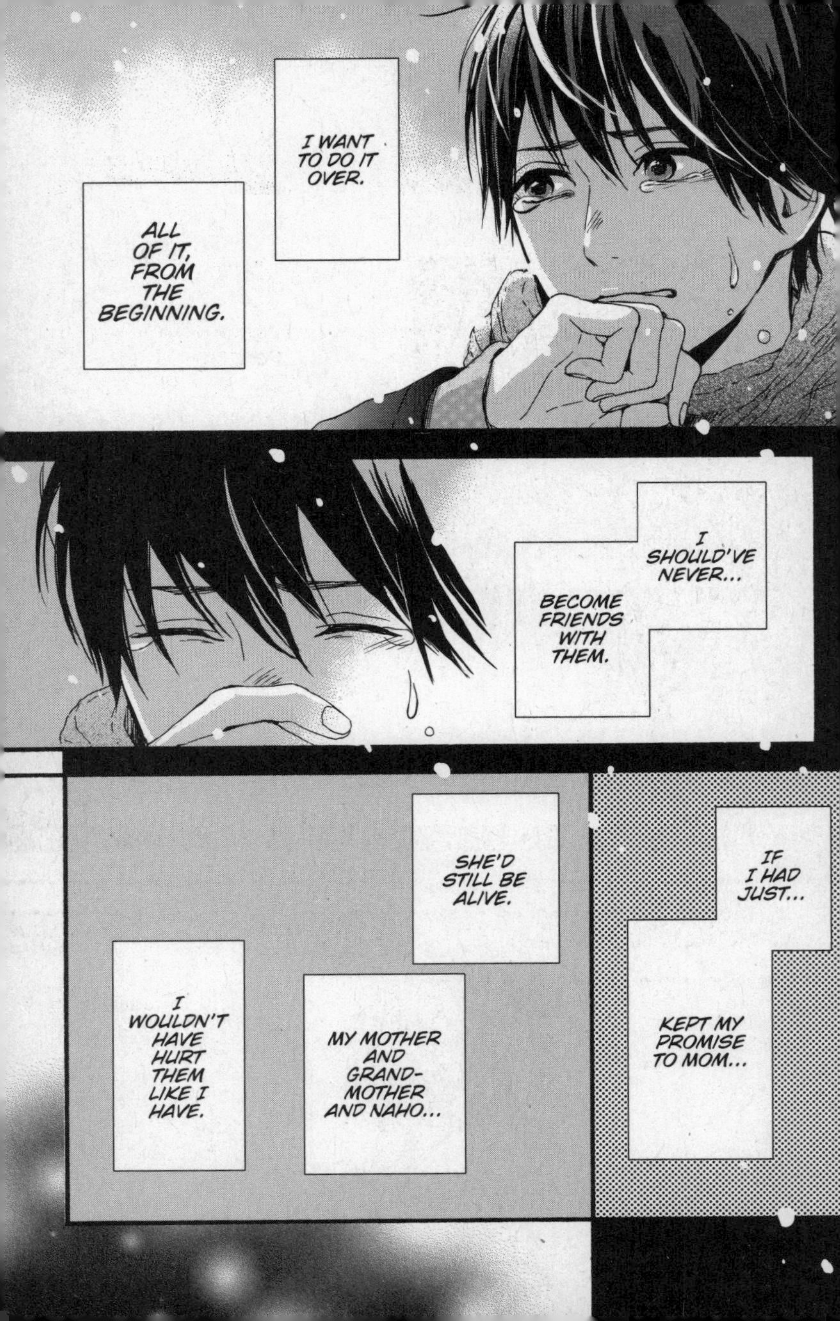
I WANT TO DO IT OVER.
ALL OF IT, FROM THE BEGINNING.
I SHOULD'VE NEVER...
BECOME FRIENDS WITH THEM.
IF I HAD JUST...
KEPT MY PROMISE TO MOM...
SHE'D STILL BE ALIVE.
MY MOTHER AND GRAND-MOTHER AND NAHO...
I WOULDN'T HAVE HURT THEM LIKE I HAVE.

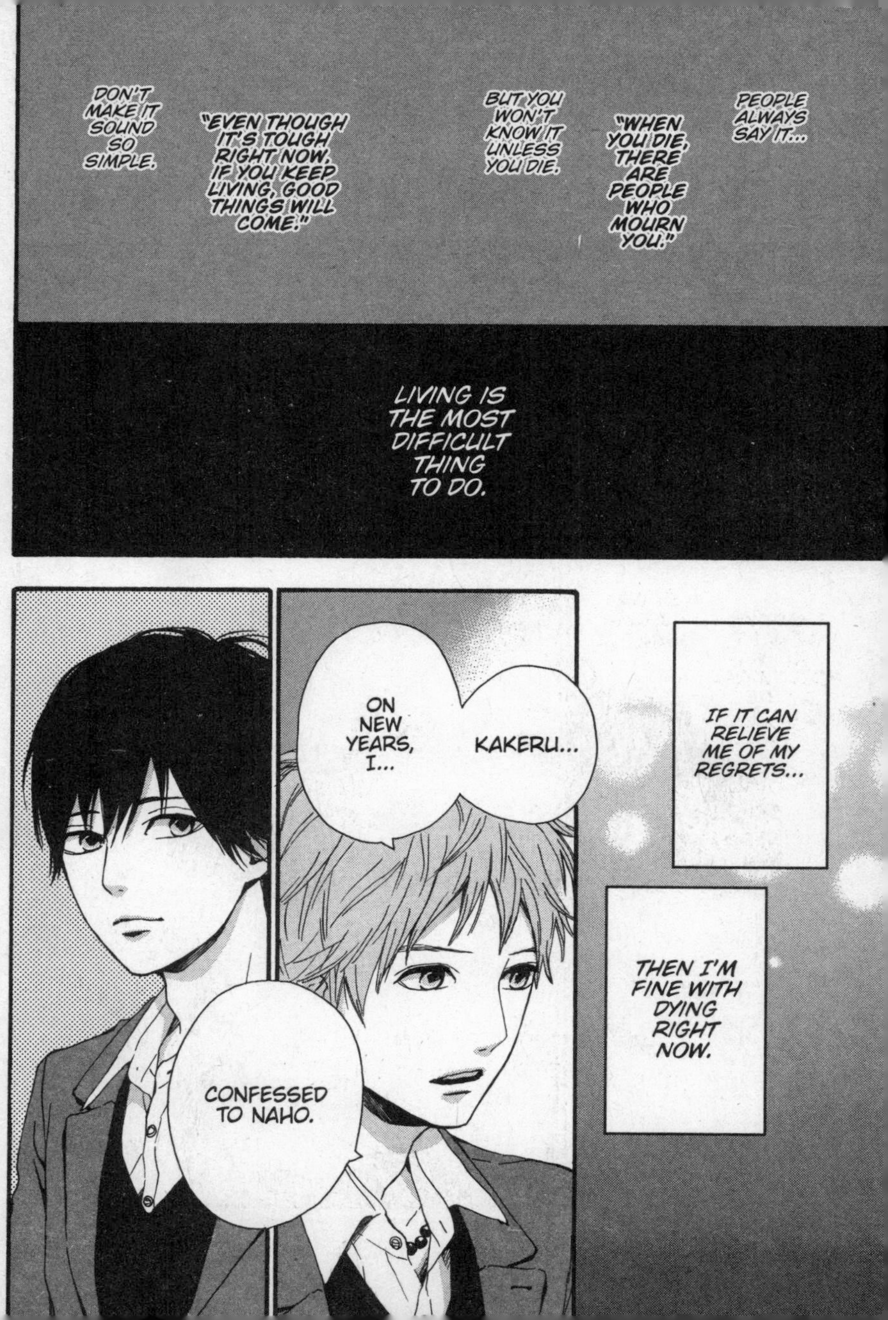
PEOPLE ALWAYS SAY IT...
"WHEN YOU DIE, THERE ARE PEOPLE WHO MOURN YOU."
BUT YOU WON'T KNOW IT UNLESS YOU DIE.
"EVEN THOUGH IT'S TOUGH RIGHT NOW, IF YOU KEEP LIVING, GOOD THINGS WILL COME."
DON'T MAKE IT SOUND SO SIMPLE.
LIVING IS THE MOST DIFFICULT THING TO DO.
IF IT CAN RELIEVE ME OF MY REGRETS...
THEN I'M FINE WITH DYING RIGHT NOW.
KAKERU...
ON NEW YEARS, I...
CONFESSED TO NAHO.

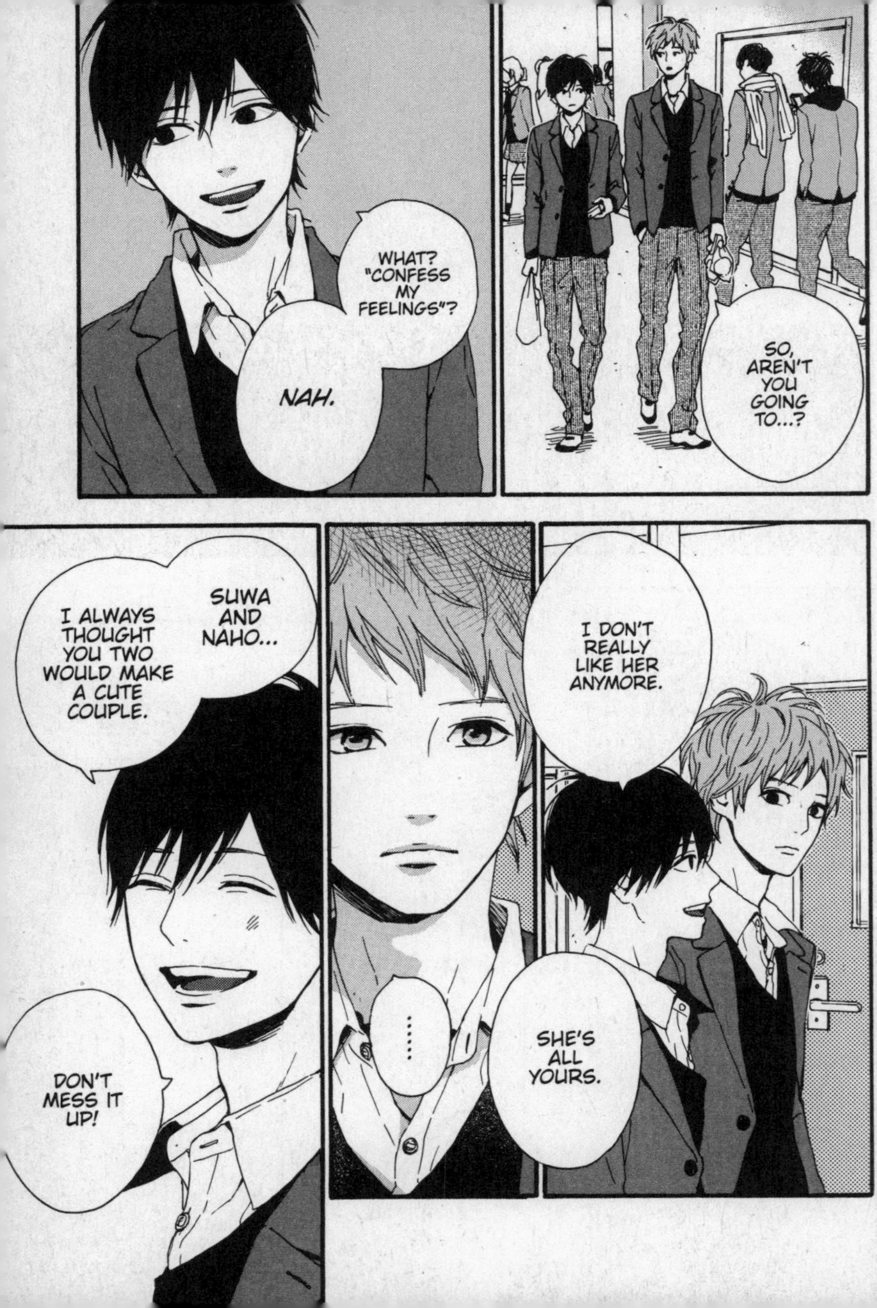
SO, AREN'T YOU GOING TO...?
WHAT? "CONFESS MY FEELINGS"?
NAH.
I DON'T REALLY LIKE HER ANYMORE.
SHE'S ALL YOURS.
......
SUWA AND NAHO...
I ALWAYS THOUGHT YOU TWO WOULD MAKE A CUTE COUPLE.
DON'T MESS IT UP!

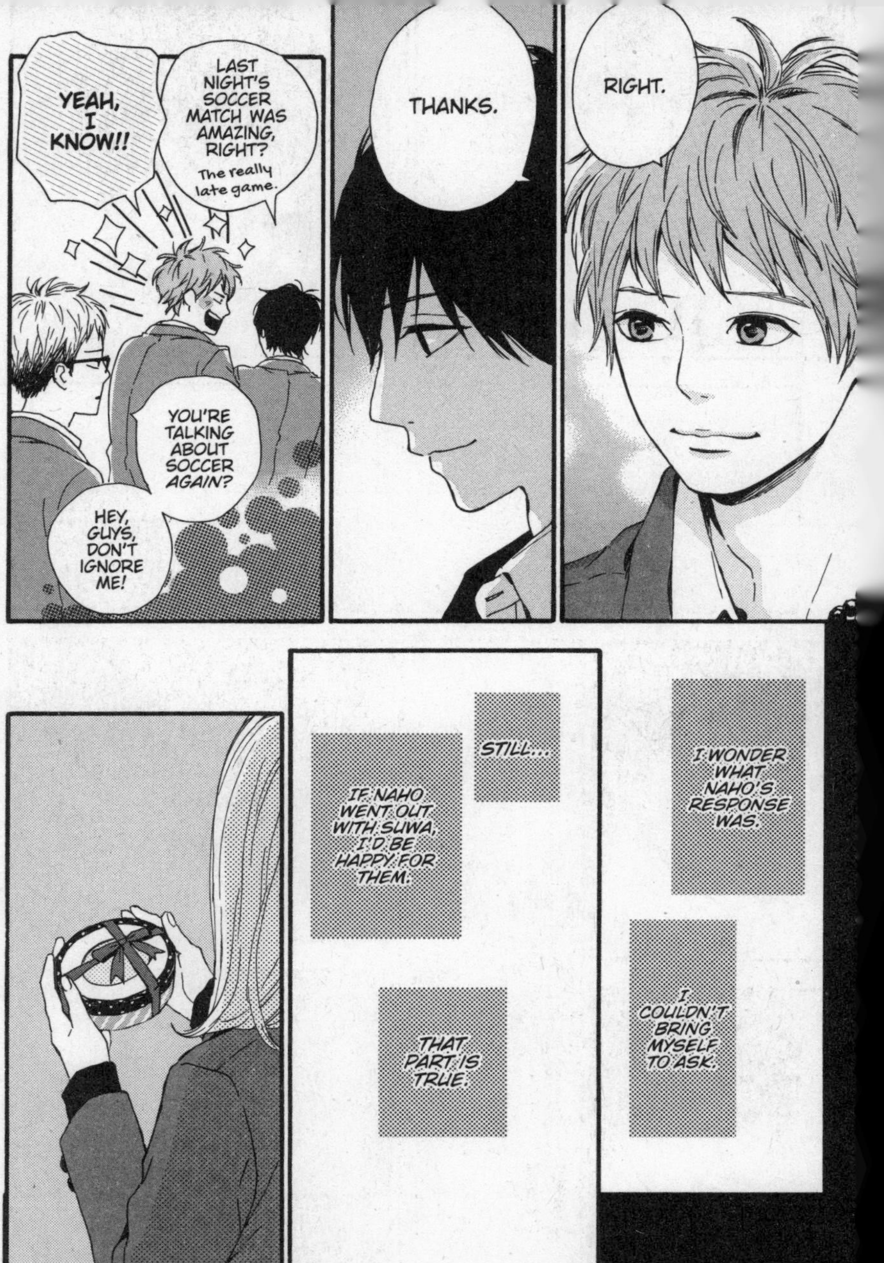
RIGHT.
THANKS.
LAST NIGHT'S SOCCER MATCH WAS AMAZING, RIGHT? The really late game.
YEAH, I KNOW!!
YOU'RE TALKING ABOUT SOCCER AGAIN?
HEY, GUYS, DON'T IGNORE ME!
I WONDER WHAT NAHO'S RESPONSE WAS.
I COULDN'T BRING MYSELF TO ASK.
STILL...
IF NAHO WENT OUT WITH SUWA, I'D BE HAPPY FOR THEM.
THAT PART IS TRUE.

ARE THOSE VALENTINE'S DAY CHOCOLATES?

WAH!

YOU GONNA GIVE THEM TO SOMEONE?

YEAH...

TO THE GUY YOU LIKE?

OH.

YEAH...

HUNH.

I WONDER IF IT IS?

IT'S GOTTA BE.

IS IT SUWA?

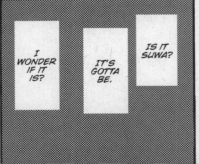

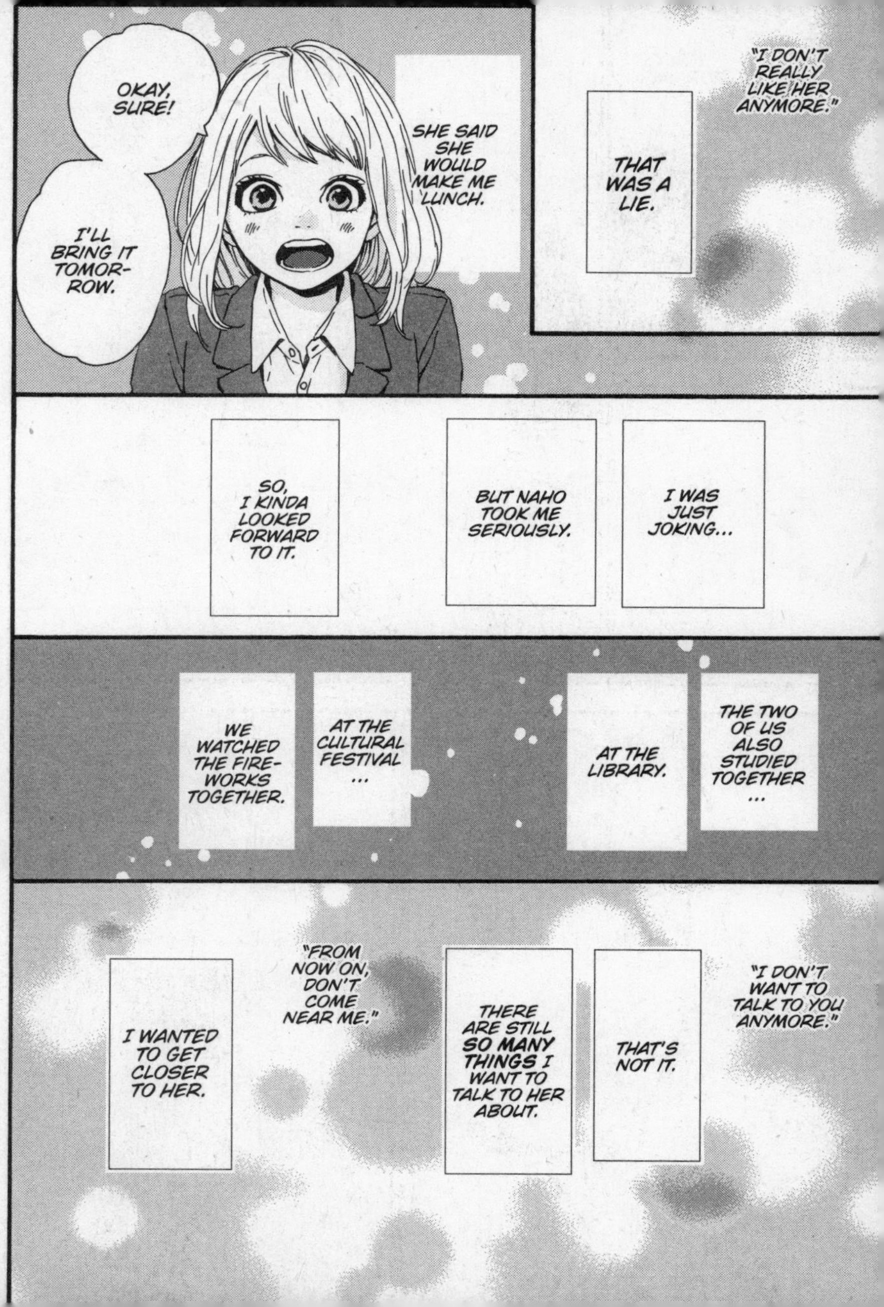
"I DON'T REALLY LIKE HER ANYMORE."
THAT WAS A LIE.
SHE SAID SHE WOULD MAKE ME LUNCH.
OKAY, SURE!
I'LL BRING IT TOMOR-ROW.
I WAS JUST JOKING...
BUT NAHO TOOK ME SERIOUSLY.
SO, I KINDA LOOKED FORWARD TO IT.
THE TWO OF US ALSO STUDIED TOGETHER ...
AT THE LIBRARY.
AT THE CULTURAL FESTIVAL ...
WE WATCHED THE FIRE-WORKS TOGETHER.
"I DON'T WANT TO TALK TO YOU ANYMORE."
THAT'S NOT IT.
THERE ARE STILL **SO MANY THINGS** I WANT TO TALK TO HER ABOUT.
"FROM NOW ON, DON'T COME NEAR ME."
I WANTED TO GET CLOSER TO HER.

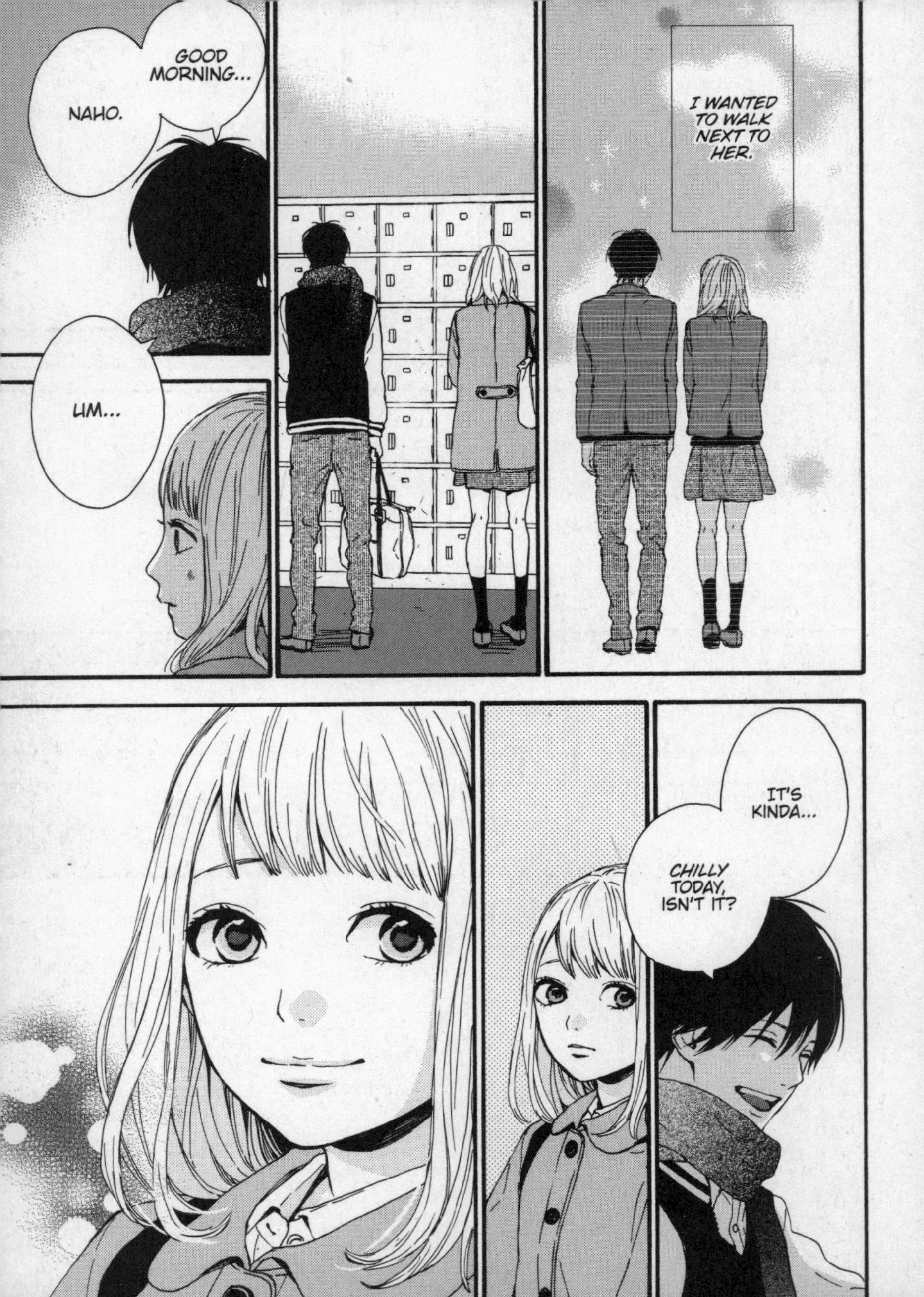
I WANTED TO WALK NEXT TO HER.
GOOD MORNING...
NAHO.
UM...
IT'S KINDA...
CHILLY TODAY, ISN'T IT?

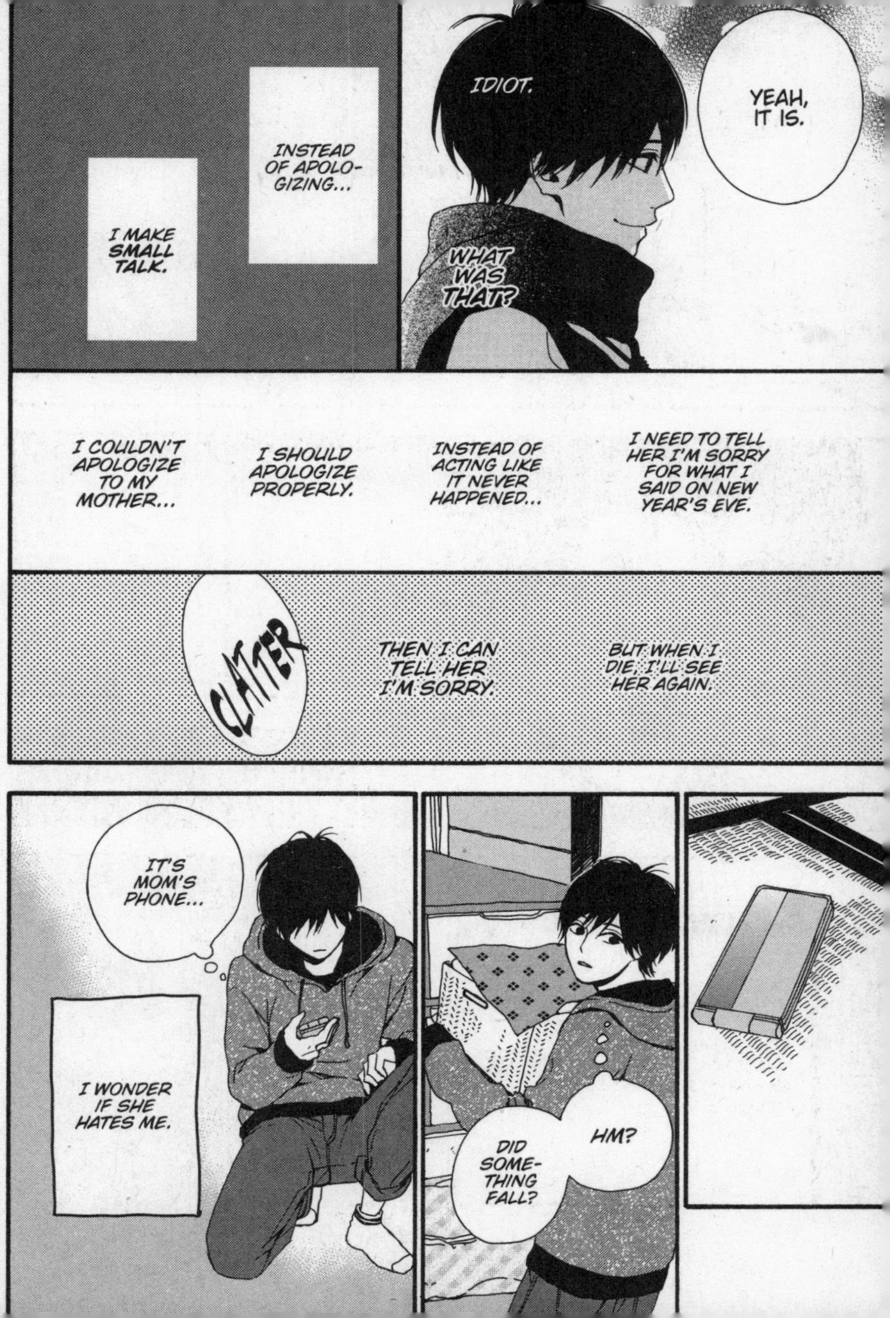
YEAH, IT IS.
IDIOT.
WHAT WAS THAT?
INSTEAD OF APOLO-GIZING...
I MAKE SMALL TALK.
I NEED TO TELL HER I'M SORRY FOR WHAT I SAID ON NEW YEAR'S EVE.
INSTEAD OF ACTING LIKE IT NEVER HAPPENED...
I SHOULD APOLOGIZE PROPERLY.
I COULDN'T APOLOGIZE TO MY MOTHER...
BUT WHEN I DIE, I'LL SEE HER AGAIN.
THEN I CAN TELL HER I'M SORRY.
CLATTER
HM?
DID SOME-THING FALL?
IT'S MOM'S PHONE...
I WONDER IF SHE HATES ME.

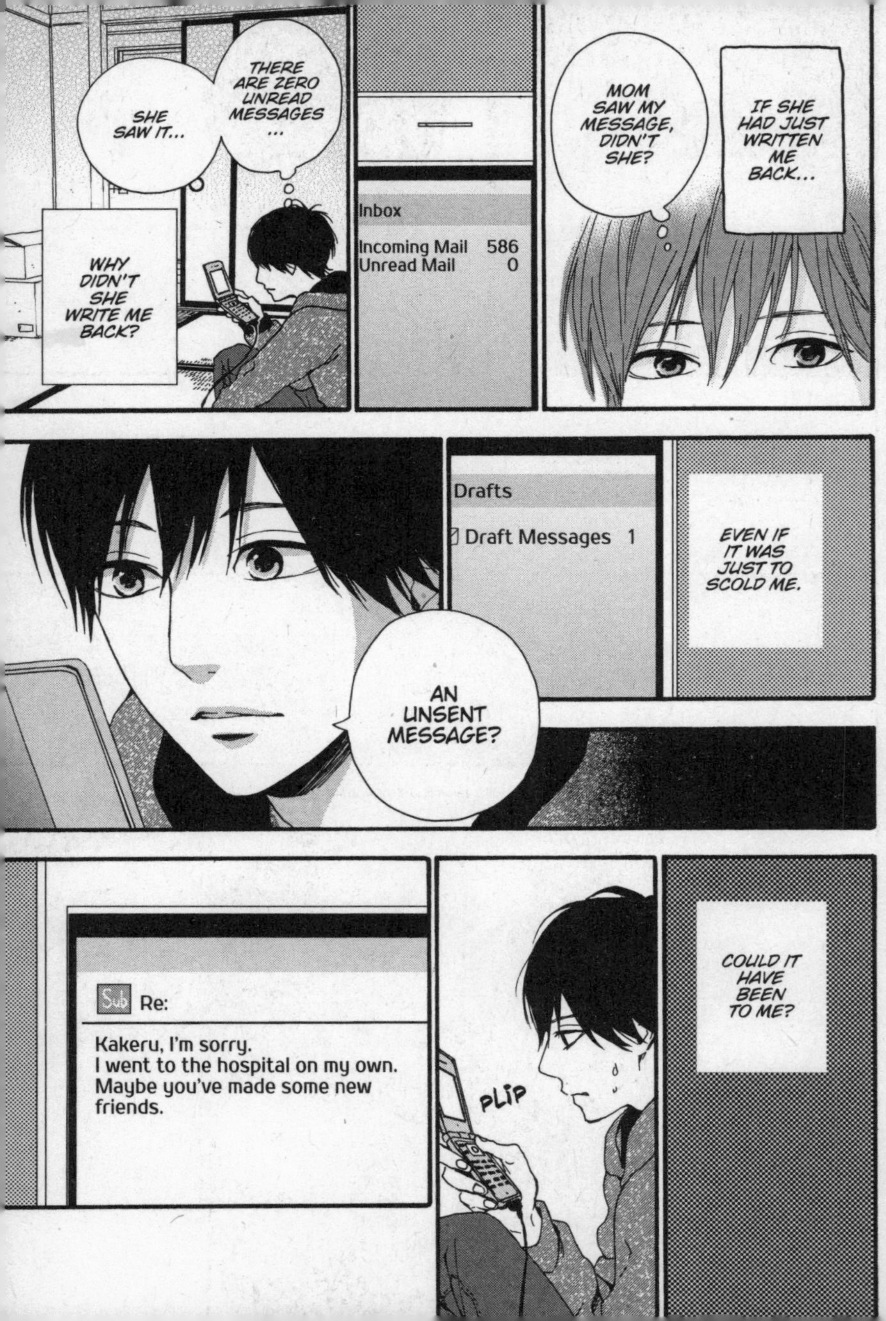
IF SHE HAD JUST WRITTEN ME BACK...
MOM SAW MY MESSAGE, DIDN'T SHE?
Inbox
Incoming Mail 586
Unread Mail 0
THERE ARE ZERO UNREAD MESSAGES ...
SHE SAW IT...
WHY DIDN'T SHE WRITE ME BACK?
EVEN IF IT WAS JUST TO SCOLD ME.
Drafts
Draft Messages 1
AN UNSENT MESSAGE?
COULD IT HAVE BEEN TO ME?
PLIP
Sub Re:
Kakeru, I'm sorry.
I went to the hospital on my own.
Maybe you've made some new friends.

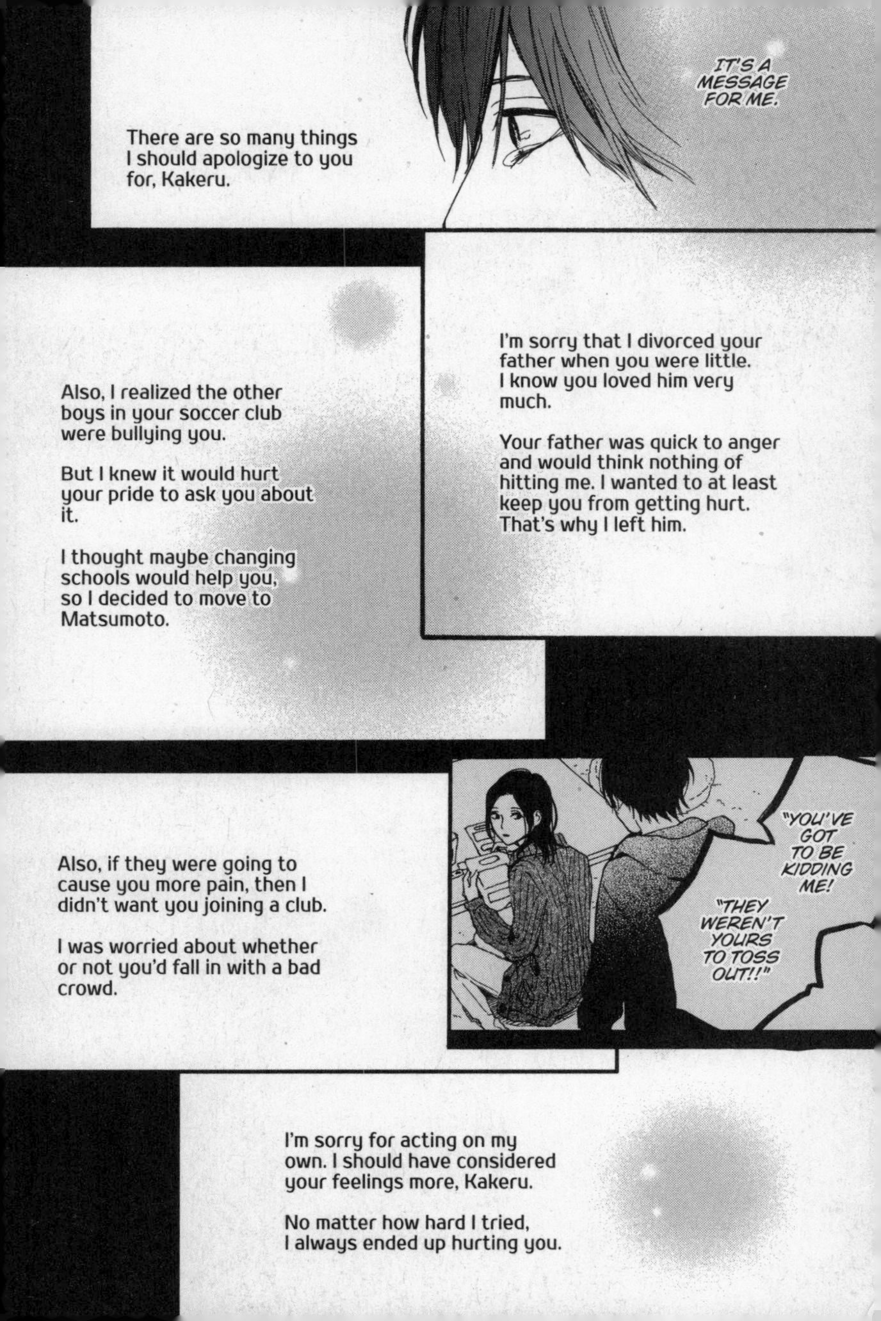
IT'S A MESSAGE FOR ME.
There are so many things I should apologize to you for, Kakeru.
I'm sorry that I divorced your father when you were little. I know you loved him very much.
Your father was quick to anger and would think nothing of hitting me. I wanted to at least keep you from getting hurt. That's why I left him.
Also, I realized the other boys in your soccer club were bullying you.
But I knew it would hurt your pride to ask you about it.
I thought maybe changing schools would help you, so I decided to move to Matsumoto.
"YOU'VE GOT TO BE KIDDING ME!
"THEY WEREN'T YOURS TO TOSS OUT!!"
Also, if they were going to cause you more pain, then I didn't want you joining a club.
I was worried about whether or not you'd fall in with a bad crowd.
I'm sorry for acting on my own. I should have considered your feelings more, Kakeru.
No matter how hard I tried, I always ended up hurting you.

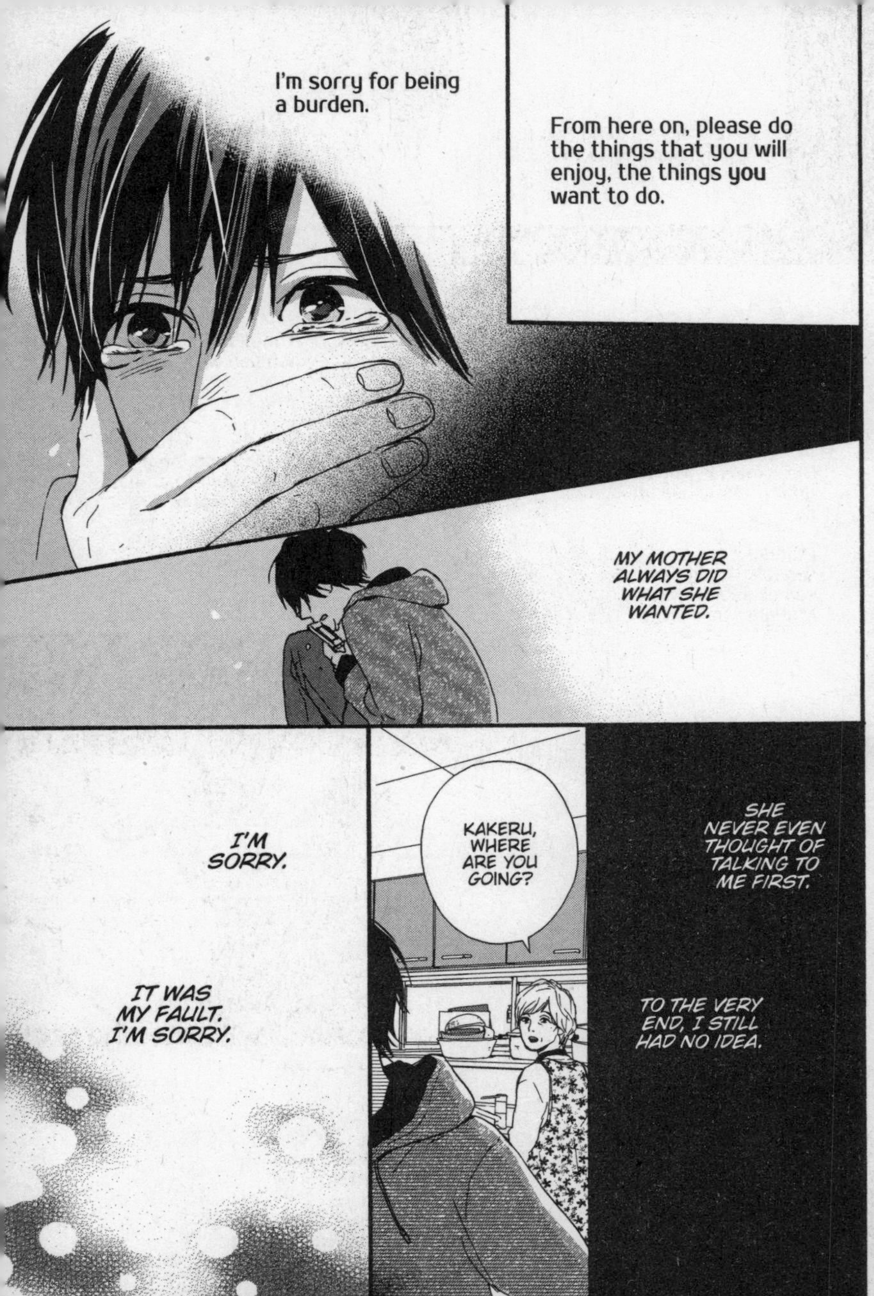
From here on, please do the things that you will enjoy, the things you want to do.
I'm sorry for being a burden.
MY MOTHER ALWAYS DID WHAT SHE WANTED.
SHE NEVER EVEN THOUGHT OF TALKING TO ME FIRST.
TO THE VERY END, I STILL HAD NO IDEA.
KAKERU, WHERE ARE YOU GOING?
I'M SORRY.
IT WAS MY FAULT. I'M SORRY.

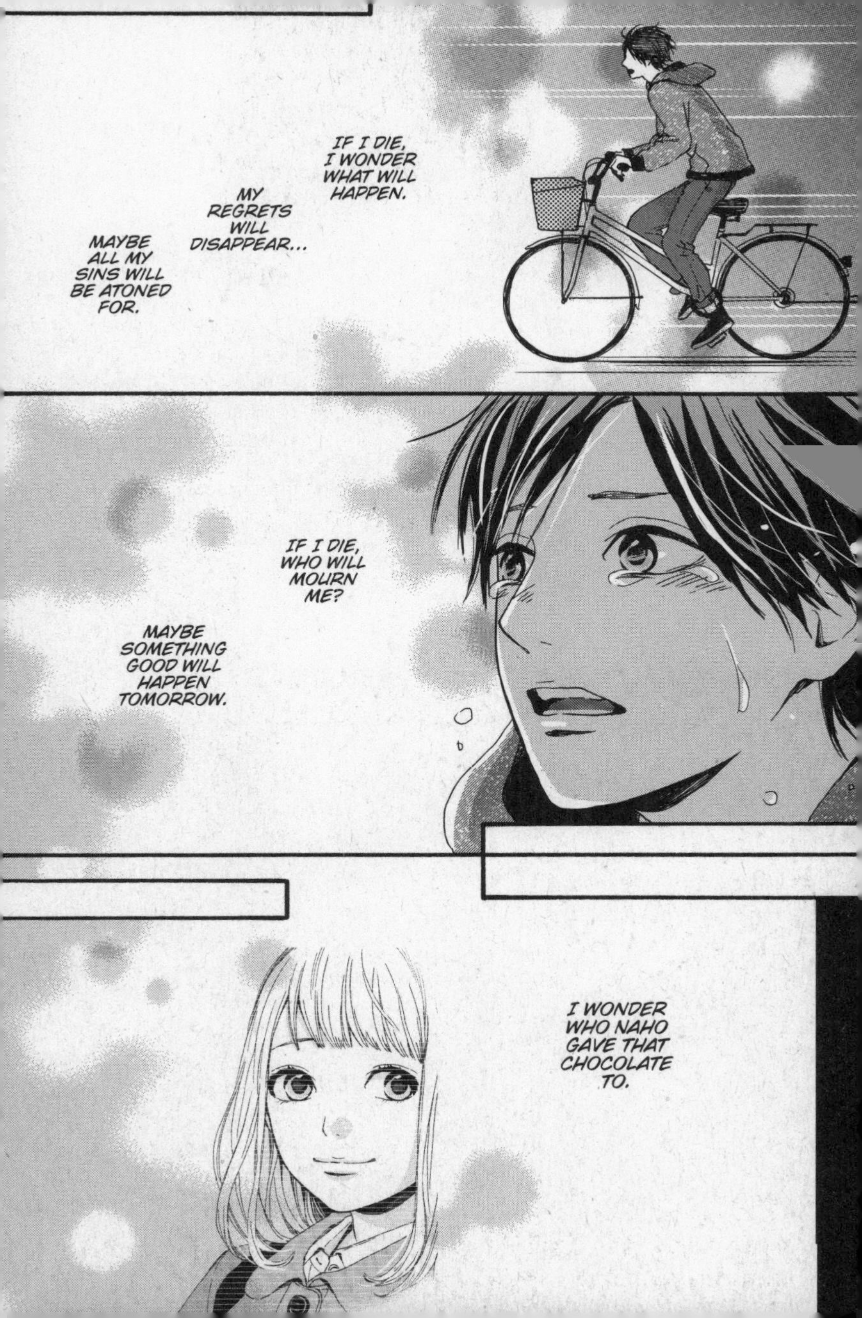
IF I DIE, I WONDER WHAT WILL HAPPEN.
MY REGRETS WILL DISAPPEAR...
MAYBE ALL MY SINS WILL BE ATONED FOR.
IF I DIE, WHO WILL MOURN ME?
MAYBE SOMETHING GOOD WILL HAPPEN TOMORROW.
I WONDER WHO NAHO GAVE THAT CHOCOLATE TO.

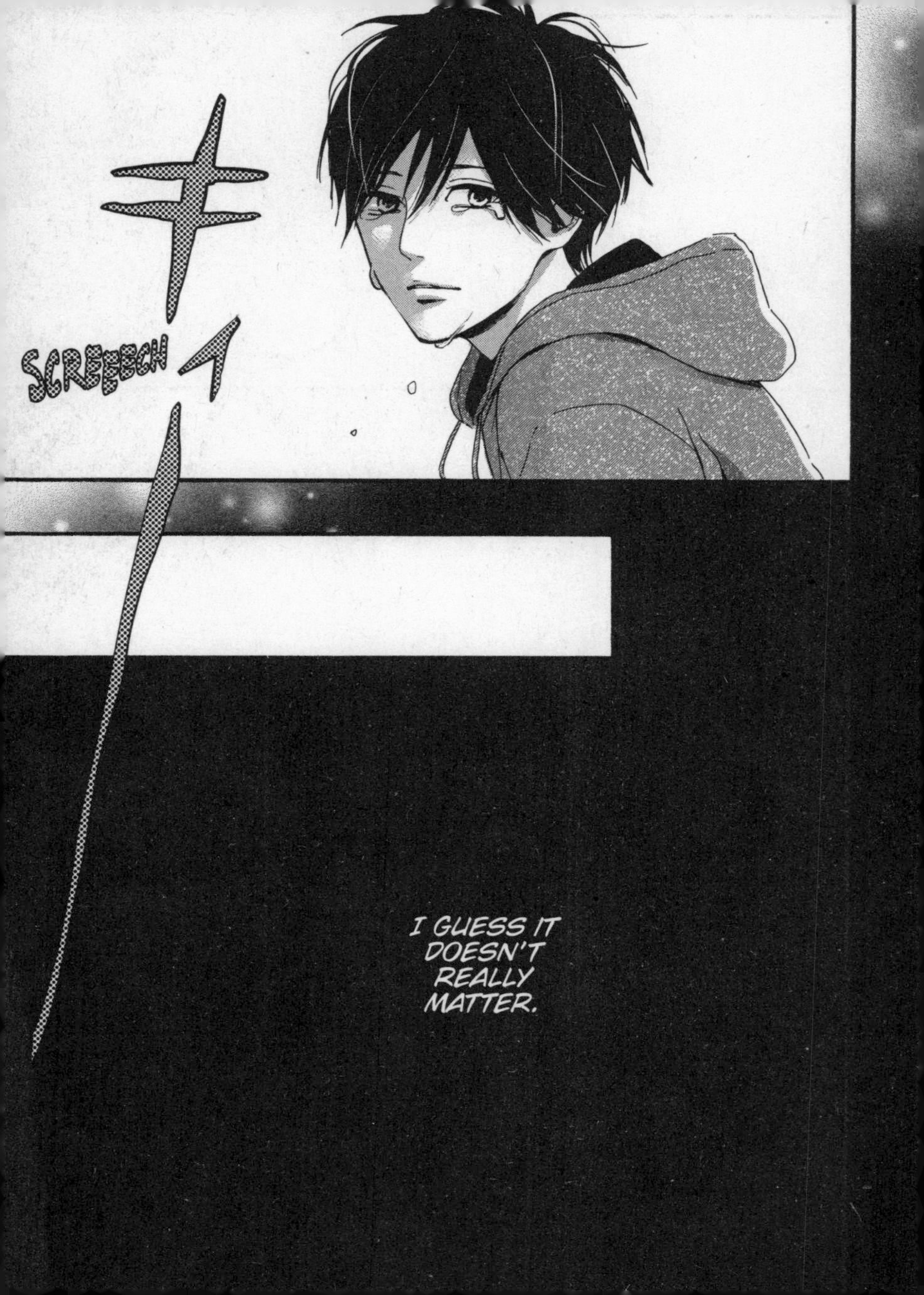
キイ
SCREEECH
I GUESS IT DOESN'T REALLY MATTER.

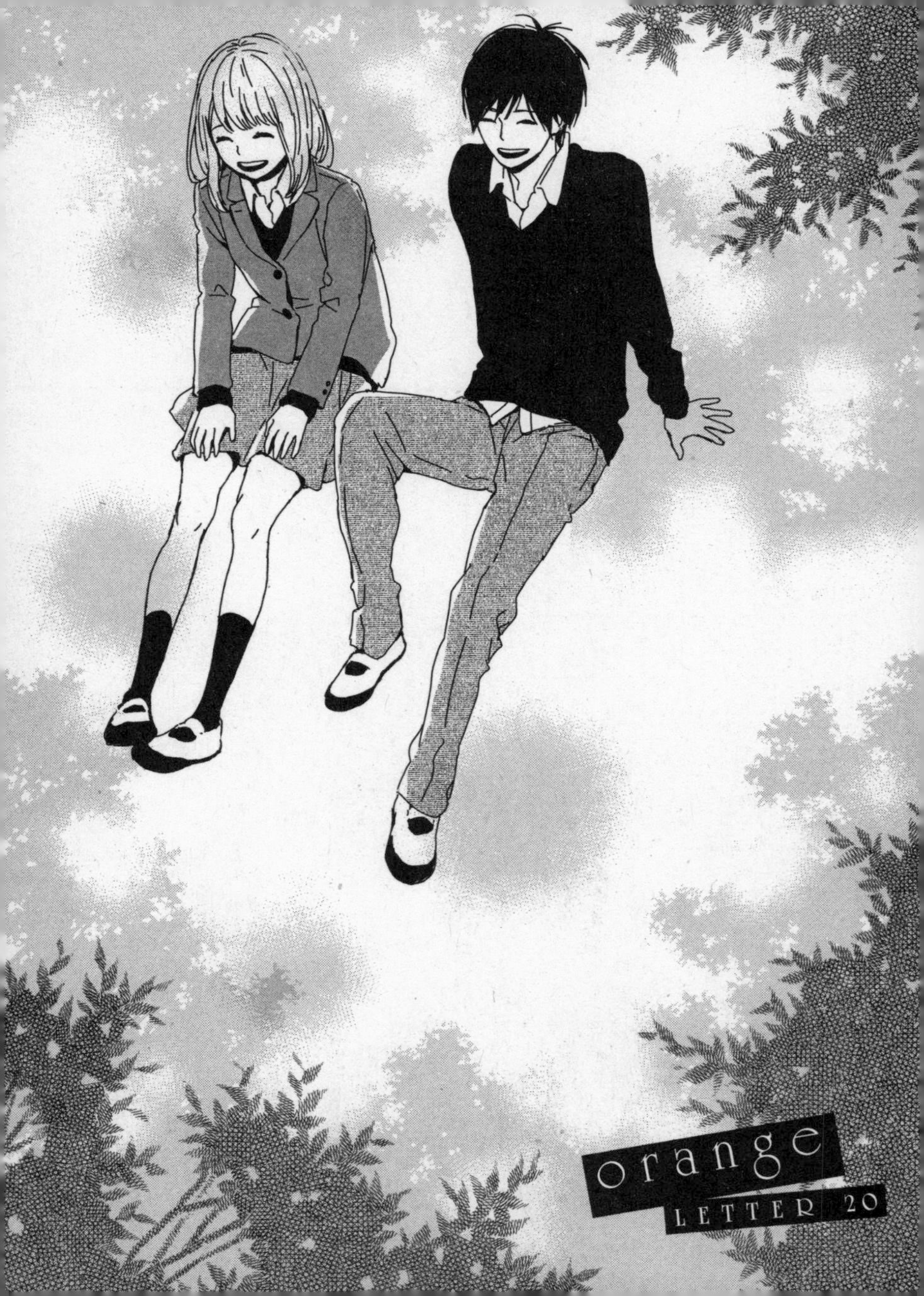
orange
LETTER 20

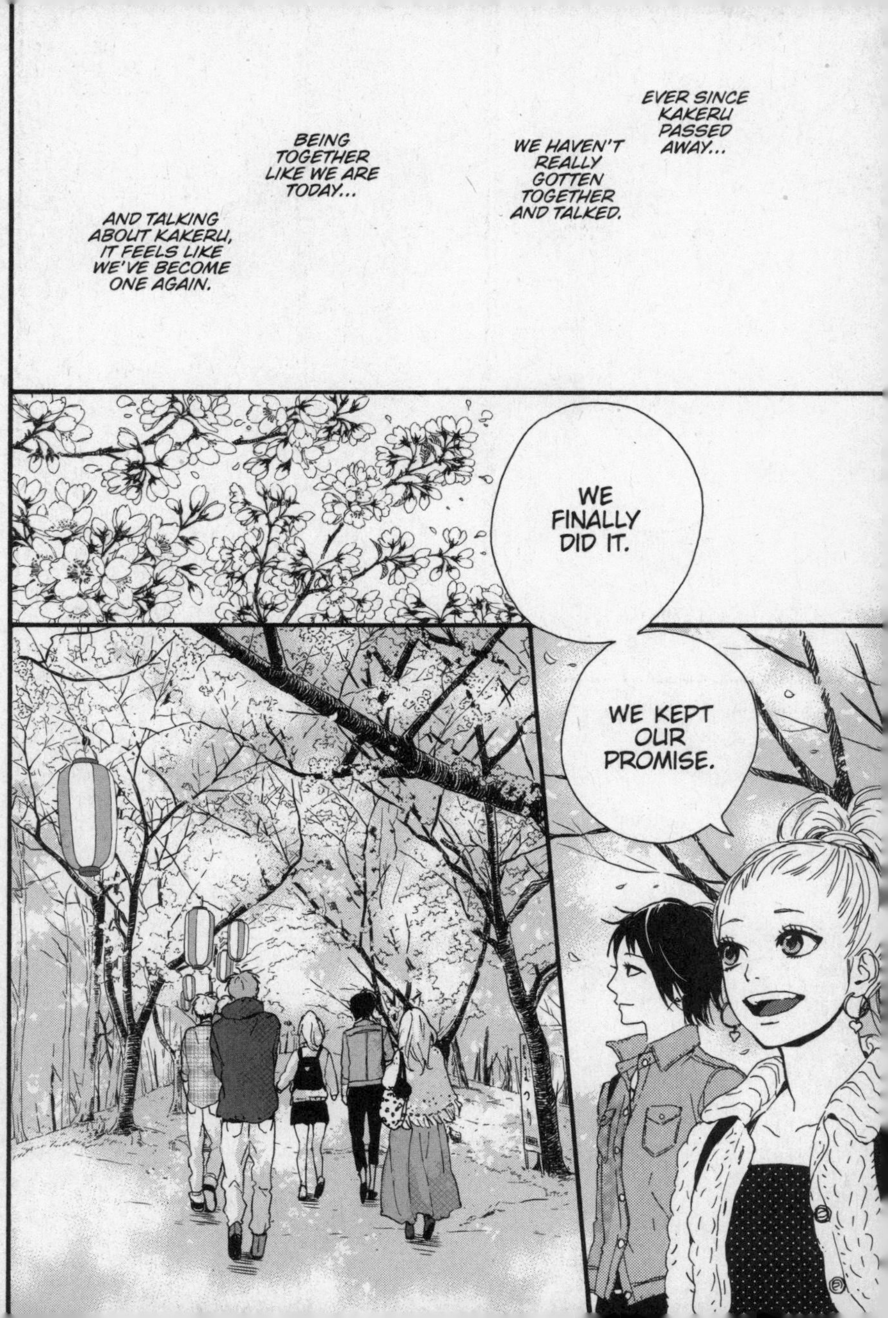
EVER SINCE KAKERU PASSED AWAY...
WE HAVEN'T REALLY GOTTEN TOGETHER AND TALKED.
BEING TOGETHER LIKE WE ARE TODAY...
AND TALKING ABOUT KAKERU, IT FEELS LIKE WE'VE BECOME ONE AGAIN.
WE FINALLY DID IT.
WE KEPT OUR PROMISE.

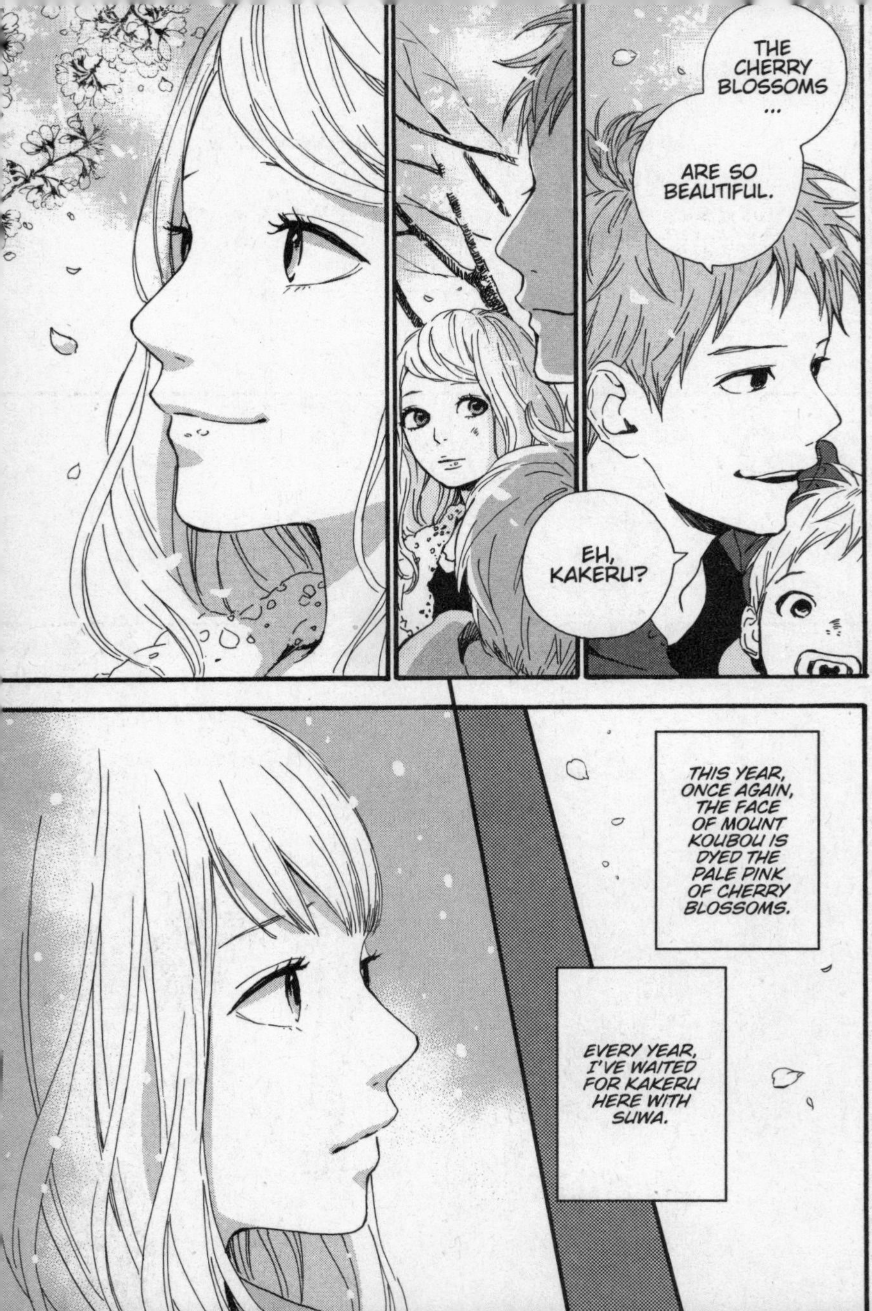
THE CHERRY BLOSSOMS ...
ARE SO BEAUTIFUL.
EH, KAKERU?
THIS YEAR, ONCE AGAIN, THE FACE OF MOUNT KOUBOU IS DYED THE PALE PINK OF CHERRY BLOSSOMS.
EVERY YEAR, I'VE WAITED FOR KAKERU HERE WITH SUWA.

January 7th

- I started winter break having fought with Kakeru on New Year's Eve.
- In the morning when I saw Kakeru, I felt awkward.

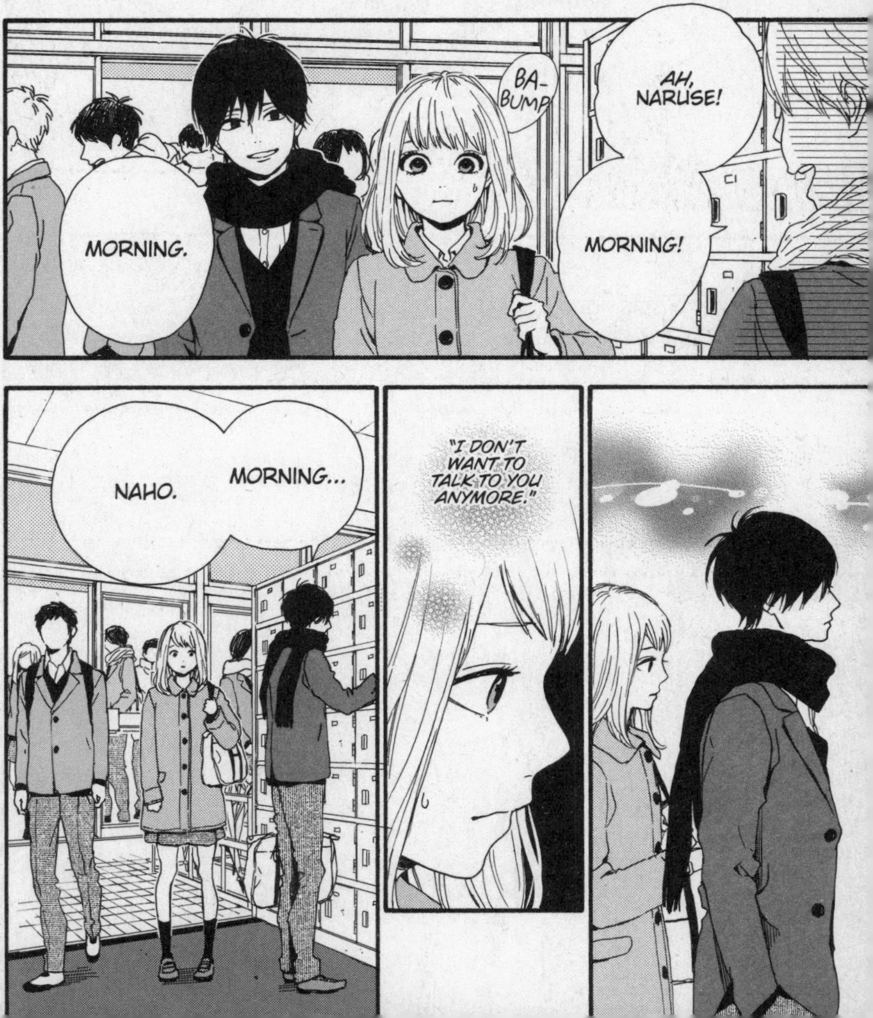
AH, NARUSE!
BA-BUMP
MORNING!
MORNING.
"I DON'T WANT TO TALK TO YOU ANYMORE."
MORNING...
NAHO.

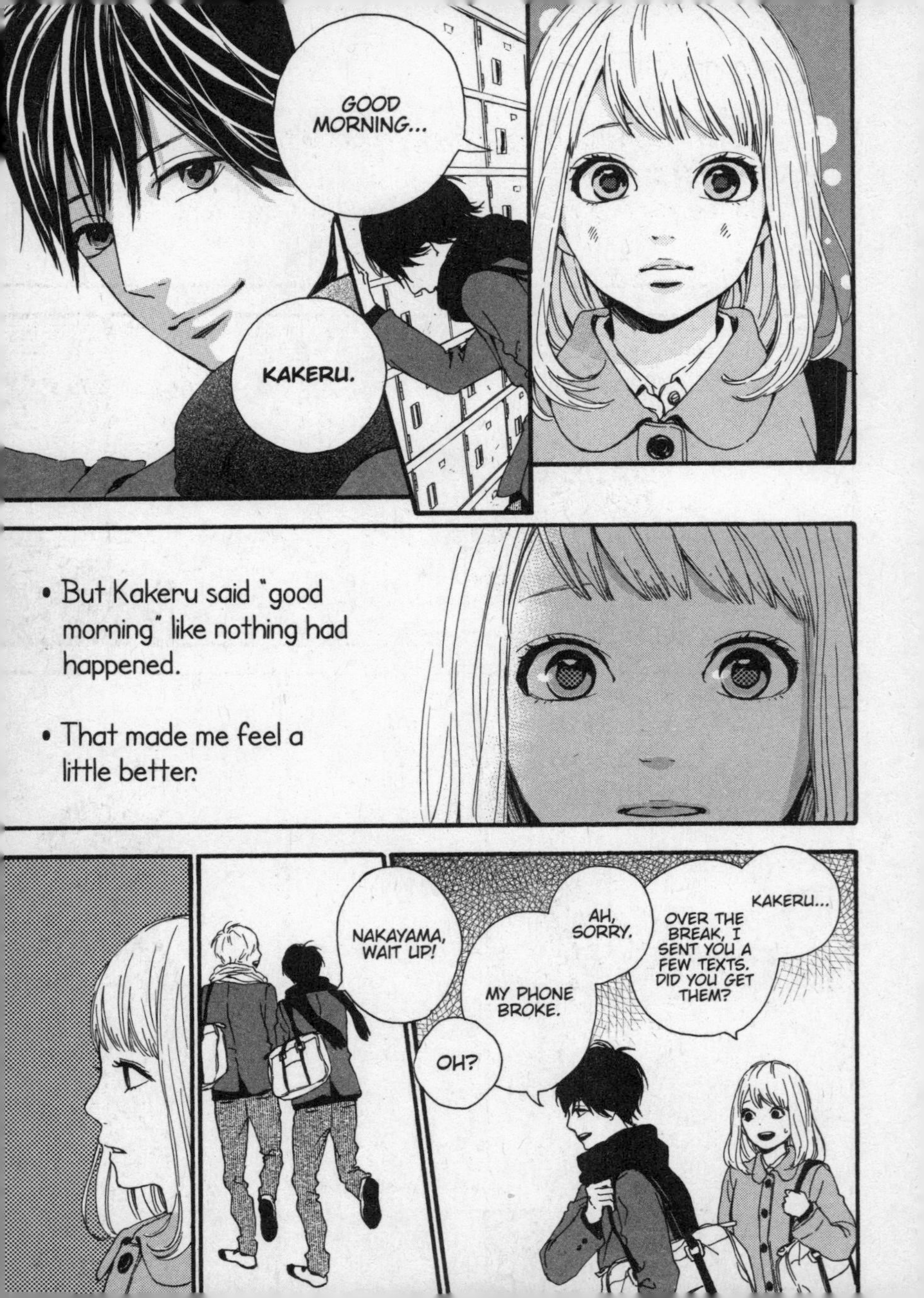
GOOD MORNING...
KAKERU.
• But Kakeru said "good morning" like nothing had happened.
• That made me feel a little better.
KAKERU...
OVER THE BREAK, I SENT YOU A FEW TEXTS. DID YOU GET THEM?
AH, SORRY.
MY PHONE BROKE.
OH?
NAKAYAMA, WAIT UP!

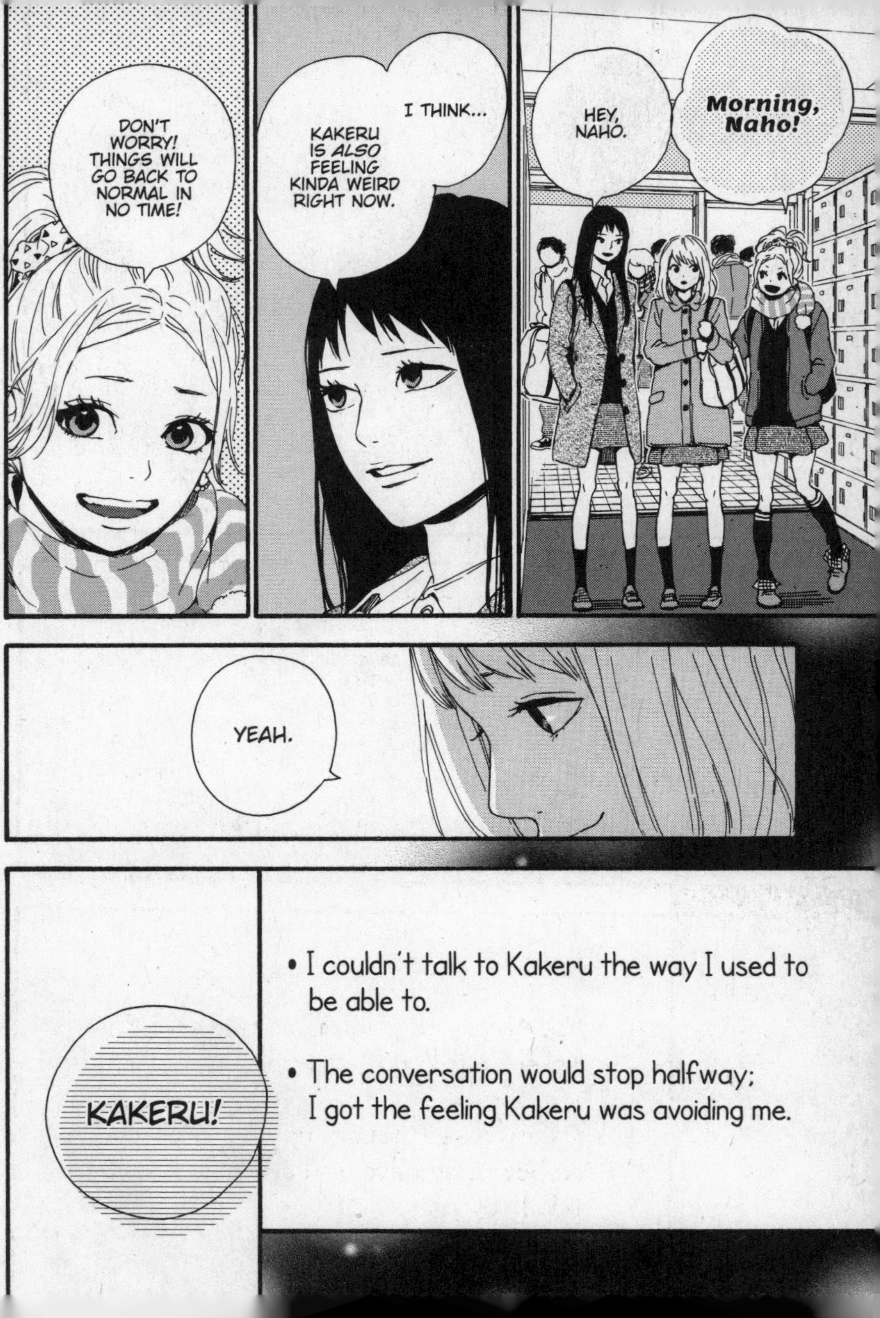
Morning, Naho!
HEY, NAHO.
I THINK...
KAKERU IS *ALSO* FEELING KINDA WEIRD RIGHT NOW.
DON'T WORRY! THINGS WILL GO BACK TO NORMAL IN NO TIME!
YEAH.
• I couldn't talk to Kakeru the way I used to be able to.
• The conversation would stop halfway; I got the feeling Kakeru was avoiding me.
KAKERU!

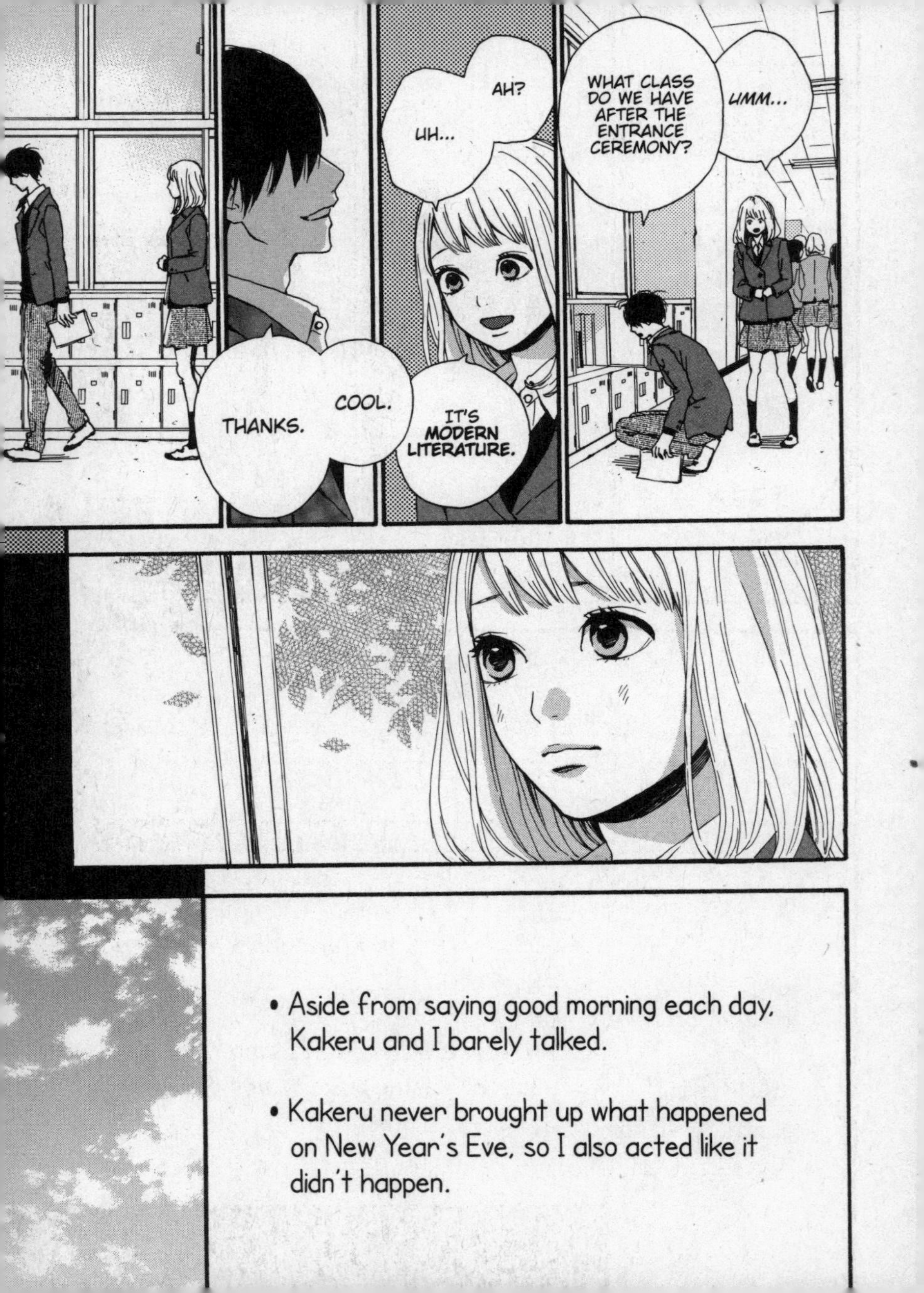
UMM...
WHAT CLASS DO WE HAVE AFTER THE ENTRANCE CEREMONY?
AH?
UH...
IT'S MODERN LITERATURE.
COOL.
THANKS.
• Aside from saying good morning each day, Kakeru and I barely talked.
• Kakeru never brought up what happened on New Year's Eve, so I also acted like it didn't happen.

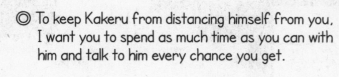

◎ To keep Kakeru from distancing himself from you, I want you to spend as much time as you can with him and talk to him every chance you get.

KAKERU!

GOOD MORNING!

I WANT TO APOLOGIZE TO YOU!!

UM...

MORNING.

UM...

HEY, SUWA--

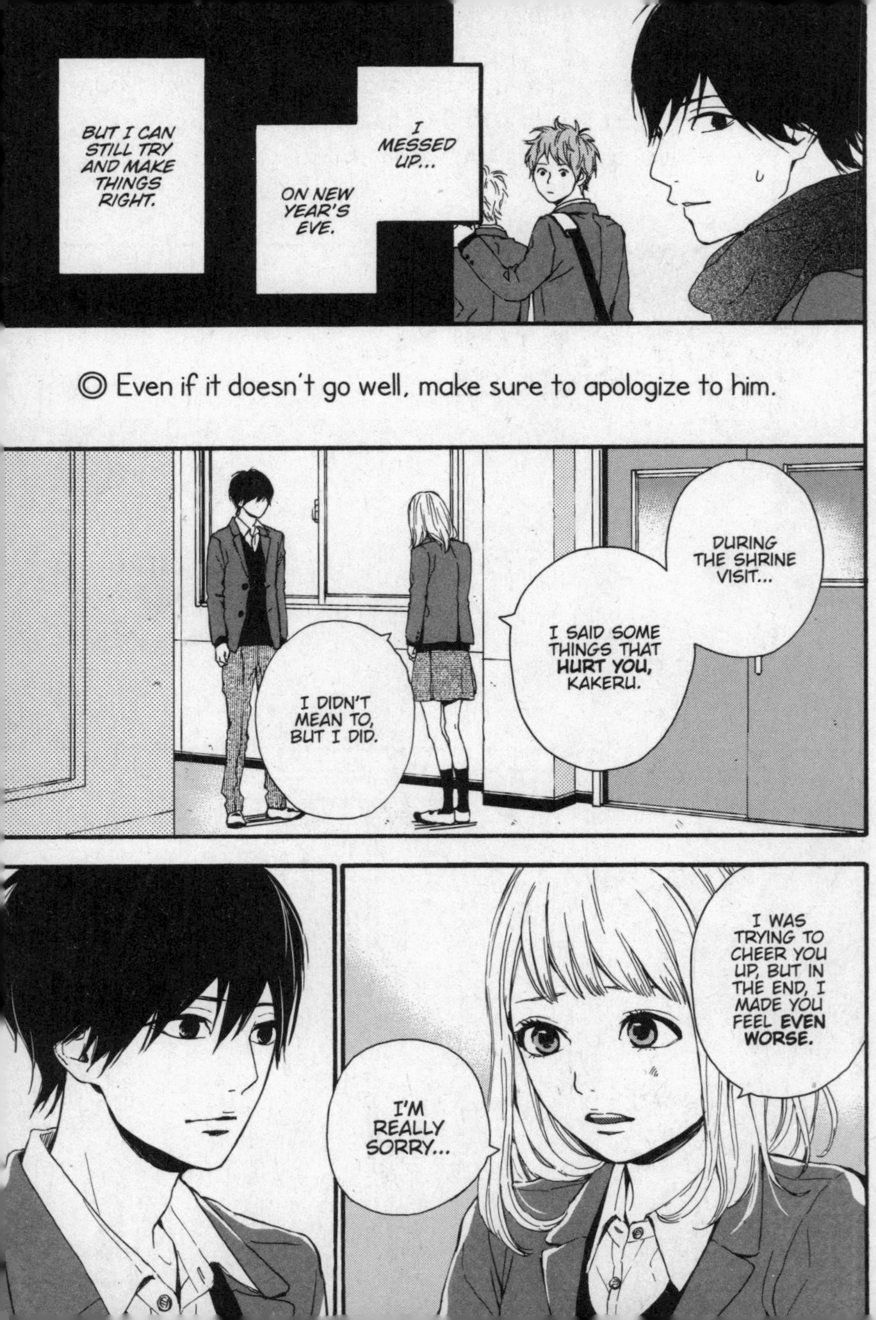
I MESSED UP...
ON NEW YEAR'S EVE.
BUT I CAN STILL TRY AND MAKE THINGS RIGHT.
◎ Even if it doesn't go well, make sure to apologize to him.
DURING THE SHRINE VISIT...
I SAID SOME THINGS THAT HURT YOU, KAKERU.
I DIDN'T MEAN TO, BUT I DID.
I WAS TRYING TO CHEER YOU UP, BUT IN THE END, I MADE YOU FEEL EVEN WORSE.
I'M REALLY SORRY...

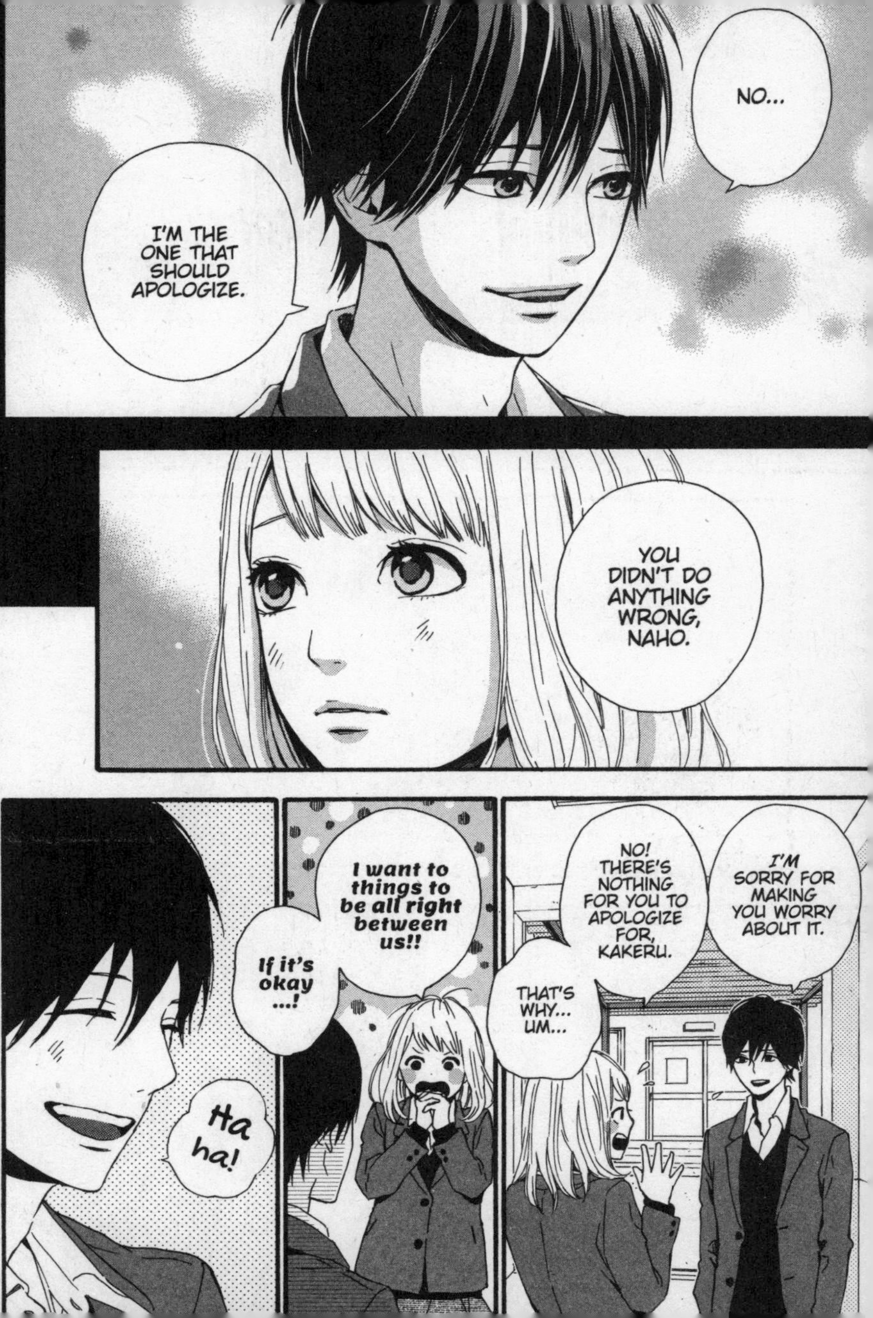
NO...
I'M THE ONE THAT SHOULD APOLOGIZE.
YOU DIDN'T DO ANYTHING WRONG, NAHO.
I'M SORRY FOR MAKING YOU WORRY ABOUT IT.
NO! THERE'S NOTHING FOR YOU TO APOLOGIZE FOR, KAKERU.
THAT'S WHY... UM...
I want to things to be all right between us!!
If it's okay ...!
Ha ha!

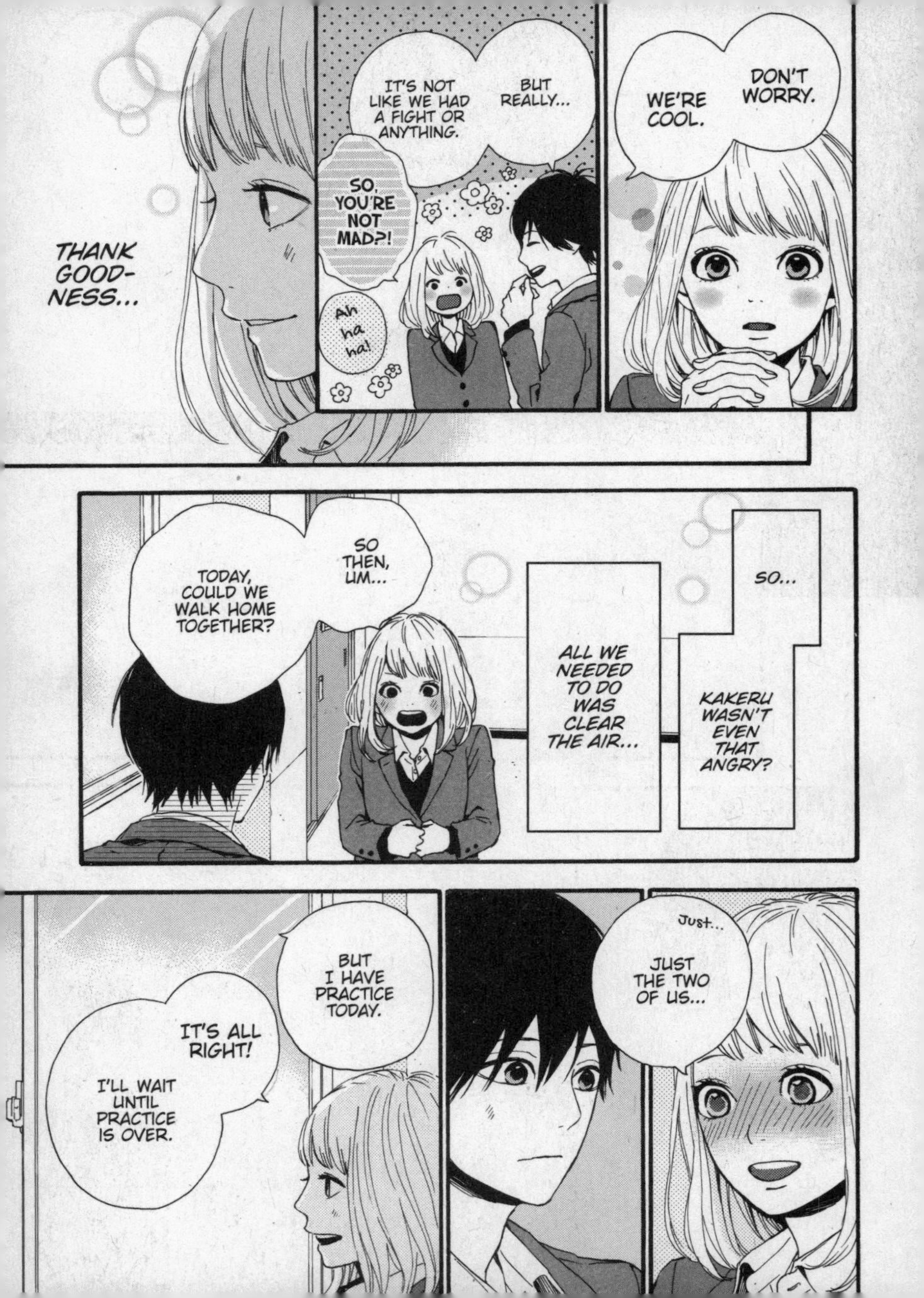
DON'T WORRY.
WE'RE COOL.
BUT REALLY...
IT'S NOT LIKE WE HAD A FIGHT OR ANYTHING.
SO, YOU'RE NOT MAD?!
Ah ha ha!
THANK GOOD-NESS...
SO...
KAKERU WASN'T EVEN THAT ANGRY?
ALL WE NEEDED TO DO WAS CLEAR THE AIR...
SO THEN, UM...
TODAY, COULD WE WALK HOME TOGETHER?
Just...
JUST THE TWO OF US...
BUT I HAVE PRACTICE TODAY.
IT'S ALL RIGHT!
I'LL WAIT UNTIL PRACTICE IS OVER.

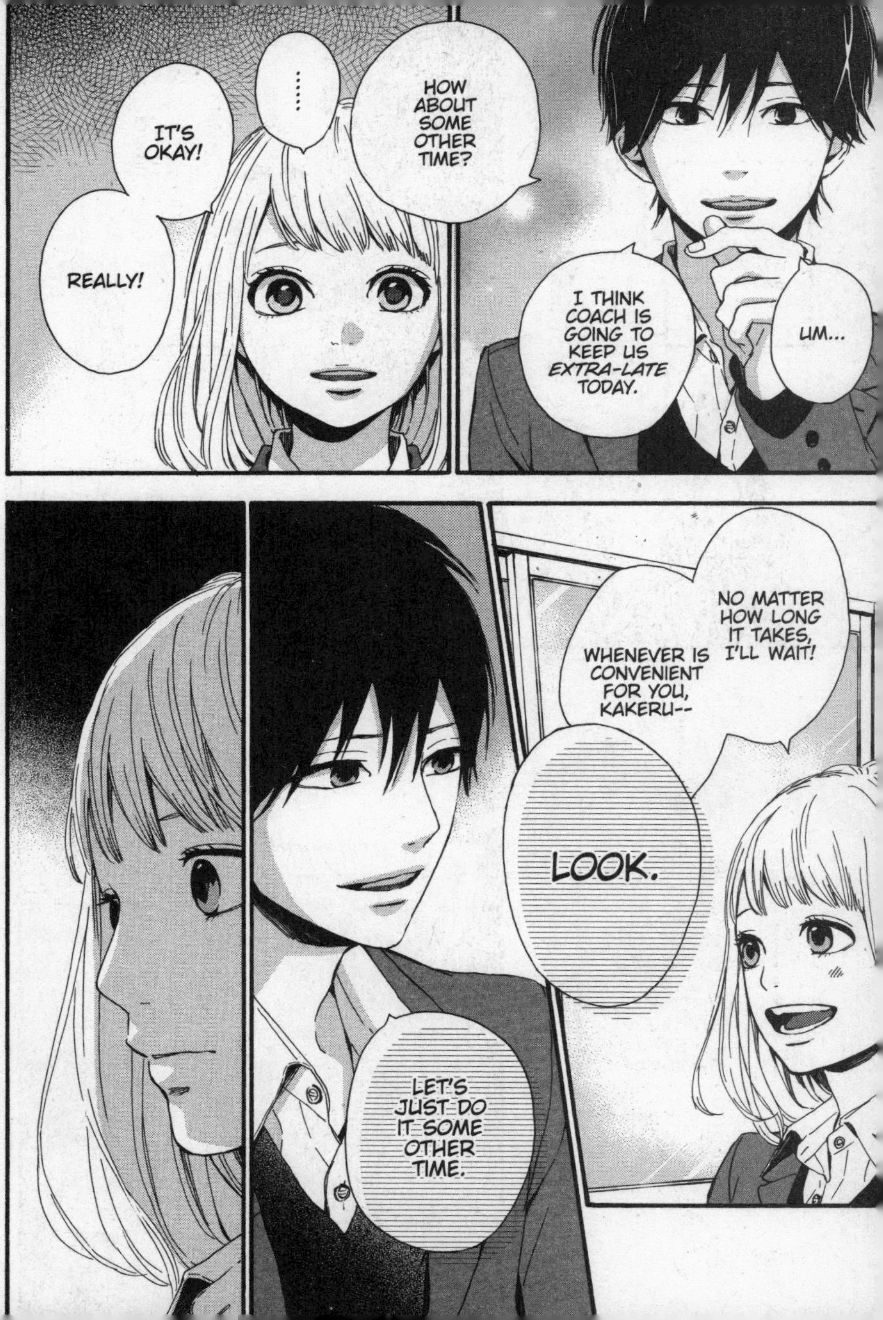
UM...
I THINK COACH IS GOING TO KEEP US EXTRA-LATE TODAY.
HOW ABOUT SOME OTHER TIME?
......
IT'S OKAY!
REALLY!
NO MATTER HOW LONG IT TAKES, I'LL WAIT!
WHENEVER IS CONVENIENT FOR YOU, KAKERU--
LOOK.
LET'S JUST DO IT SOME OTHER TIME.

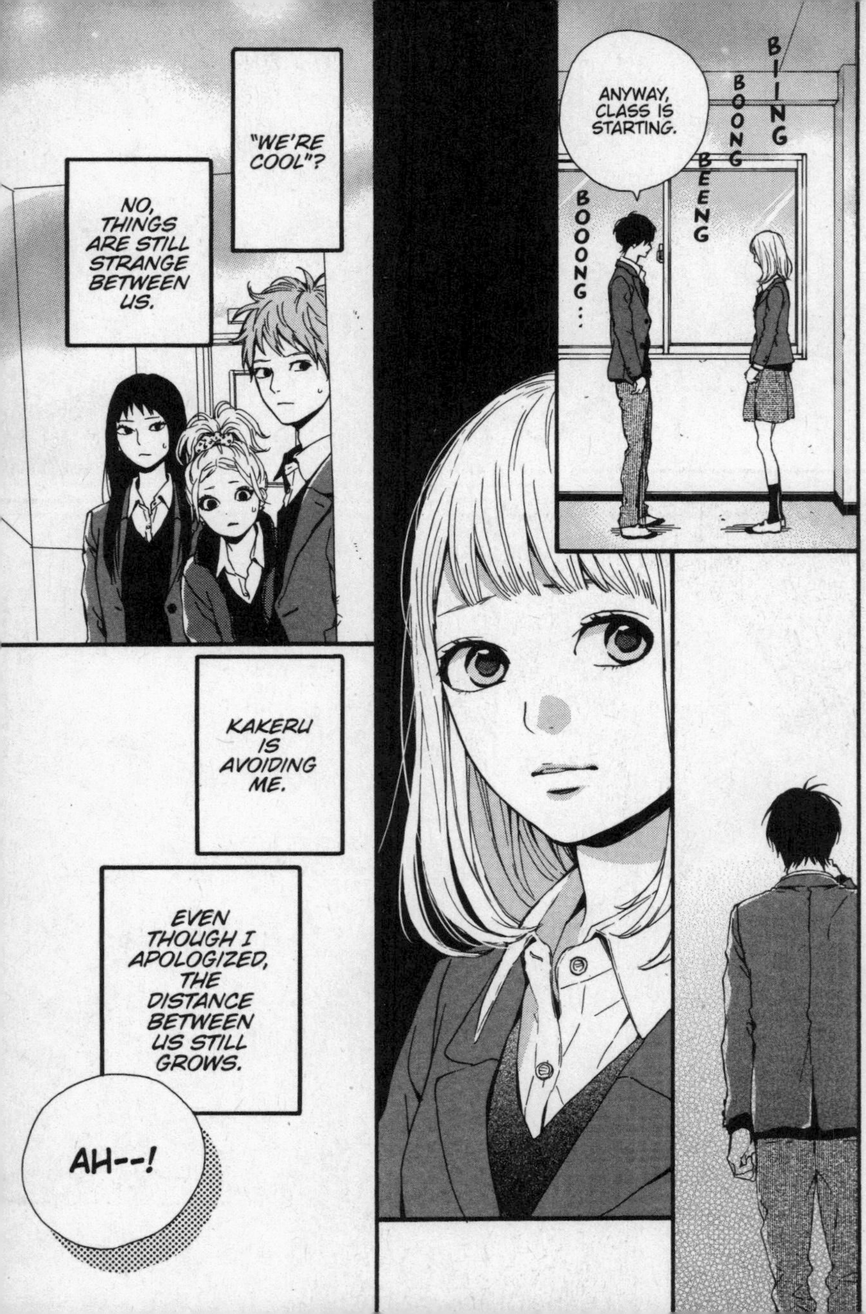
ANYWAY, CLASS IS STARTING.
BING
BOONG
BEENG
BOOONG...
"WE'RE COOL"?
NO, THINGS ARE STILL STRANGE BETWEEN US.
KAKERU IS AVOIDING ME.
EVEN THOUGH I APOLOGIZED, THE DISTANCE BETWEEN US STILL GROWS.
AH--!

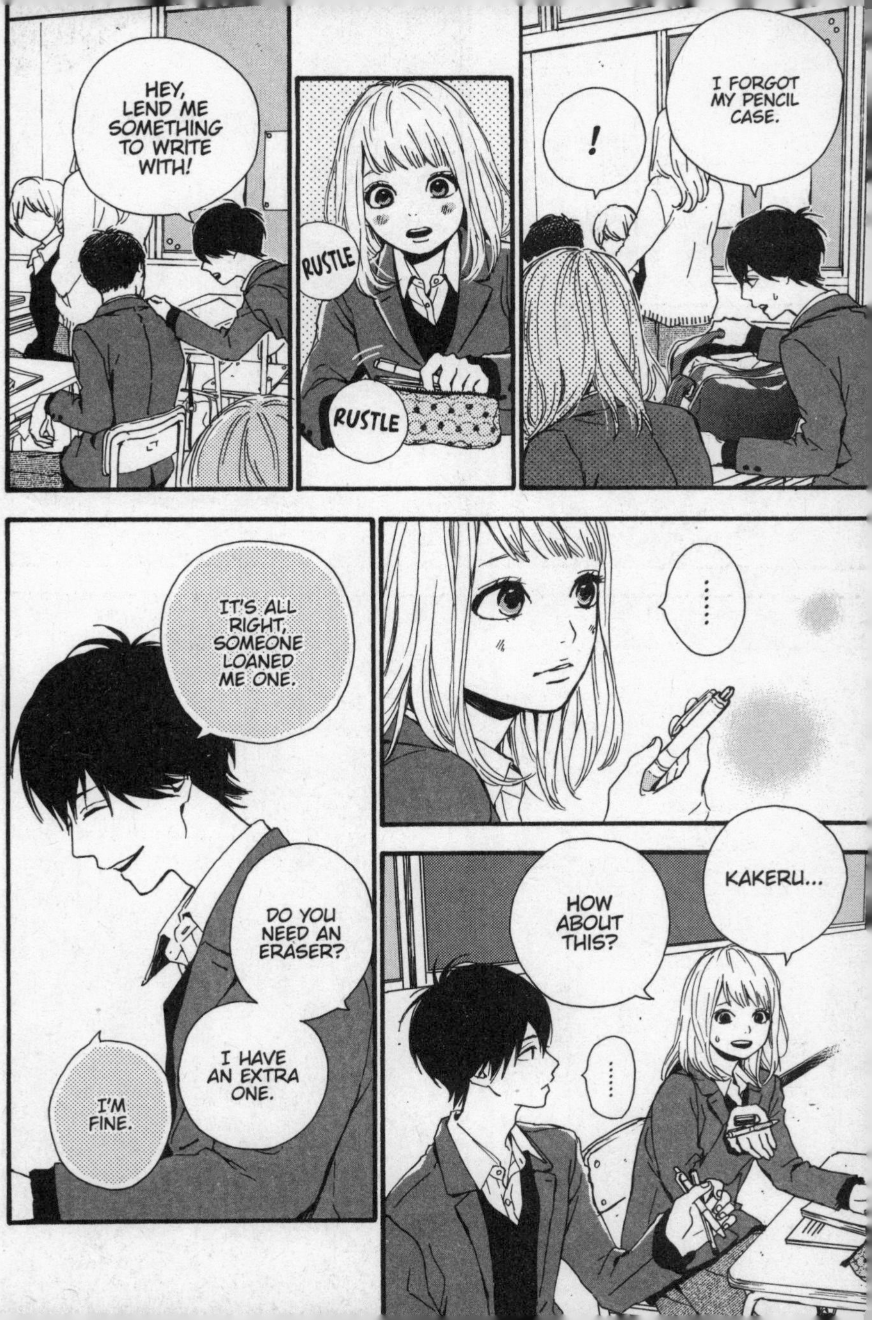
I FORGOT MY PENCIL CASE.
!
RUSTLE
RUSTLE
HEY, LEND ME SOMETHING TO WRITE WITH!
......
KAKERU...
HOW ABOUT THIS?
......
IT'S ALL RIGHT, SOMEONE LOANED ME ONE.
DO YOU NEED AN ERASER?
I HAVE AN EXTRA ONE.
I'M FINE.

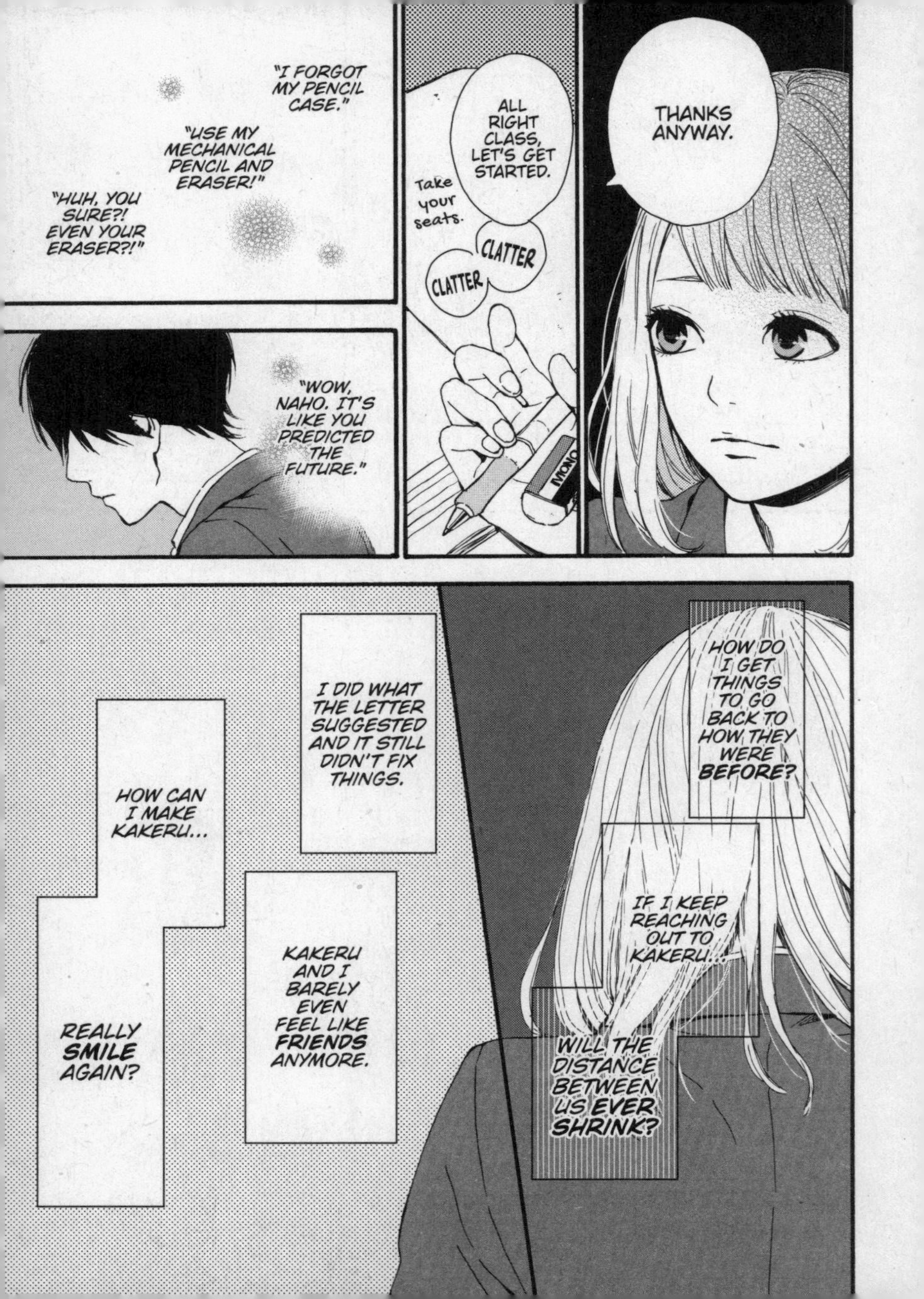
THANKS ANYWAY.
ALL RIGHT CLASS, LET'S GET STARTED.
Take your seats.
CLATTER
CLATTER
"I FORGOT MY PENCIL CASE."
"USE MY MECHANICAL PENCIL AND ERASER!"
"HUH, YOU SURE?! EVEN YOUR ERASER?!"
"WOW, NAHO. IT'S LIKE YOU PREDICTED THE FUTURE."
HOW DO I GET THINGS TO GO BACK TO HOW THEY WERE **BEFORE**?
IF I KEEP REACHING OUT TO KAKERU...
WILL THE DISTANCE BETWEEN US **EVER** SHRINK?
I DID WHAT THE LETTER SUGGESTED AND IT STILL DIDN'T FIX THINGS.
KAKERU AND I BARELY EVEN FEEL LIKE **FRIENDS** ANYMORE.
HOW CAN I MAKE KAKERU...
REALLY **SMILE** AGAIN?

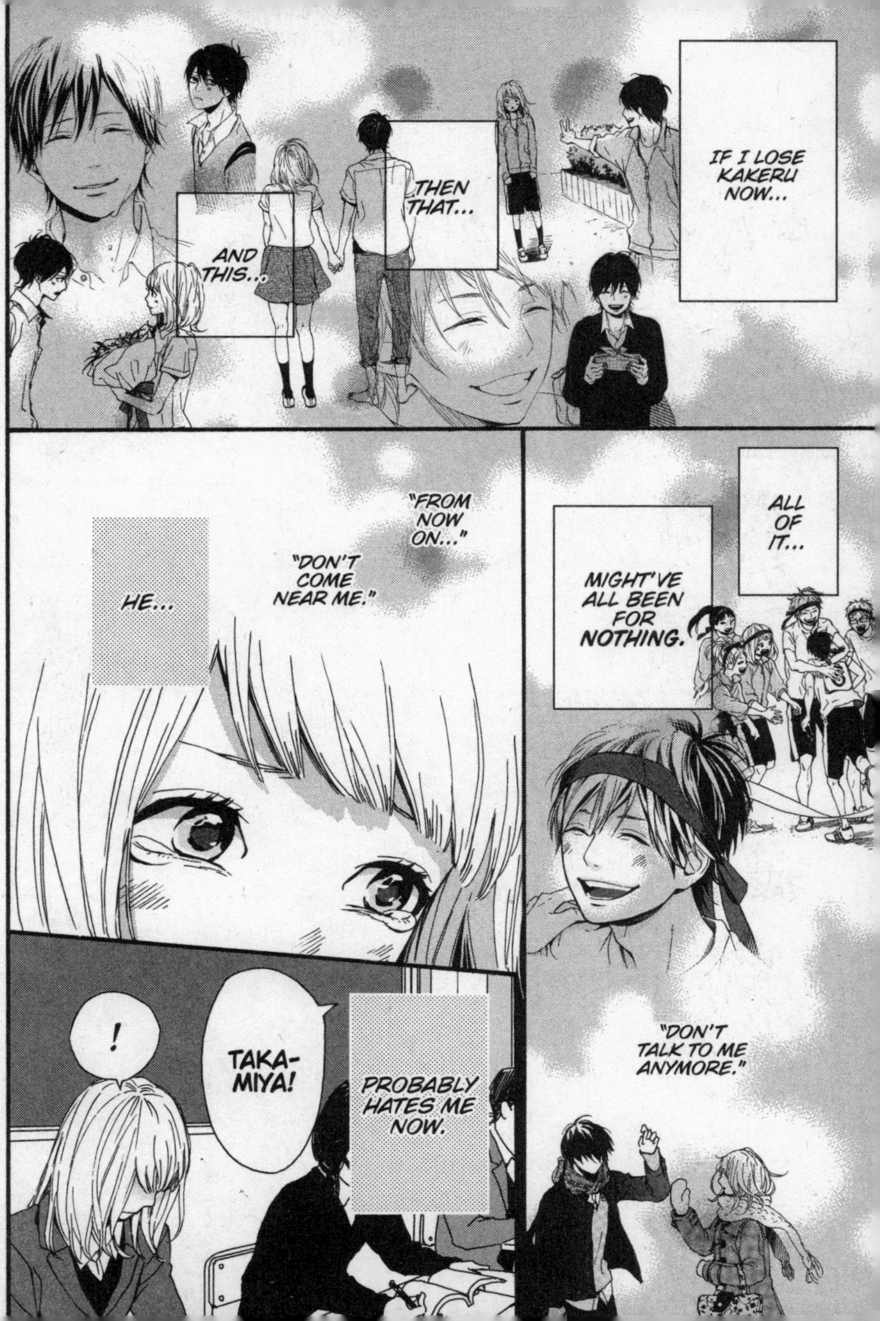
IF I LOSE KAKERU NOW...
THEN THAT...
AND THIS...
ALL OF IT...
MIGHT'VE ALL BEEN FOR NOTHING.
"DON'T TALK TO ME ANYMORE."
"FROM NOW ON..."
"DON'T COME NEAR ME."
HE...
PROBABLY HATES ME NOW.
TAKA-MIYA!
!

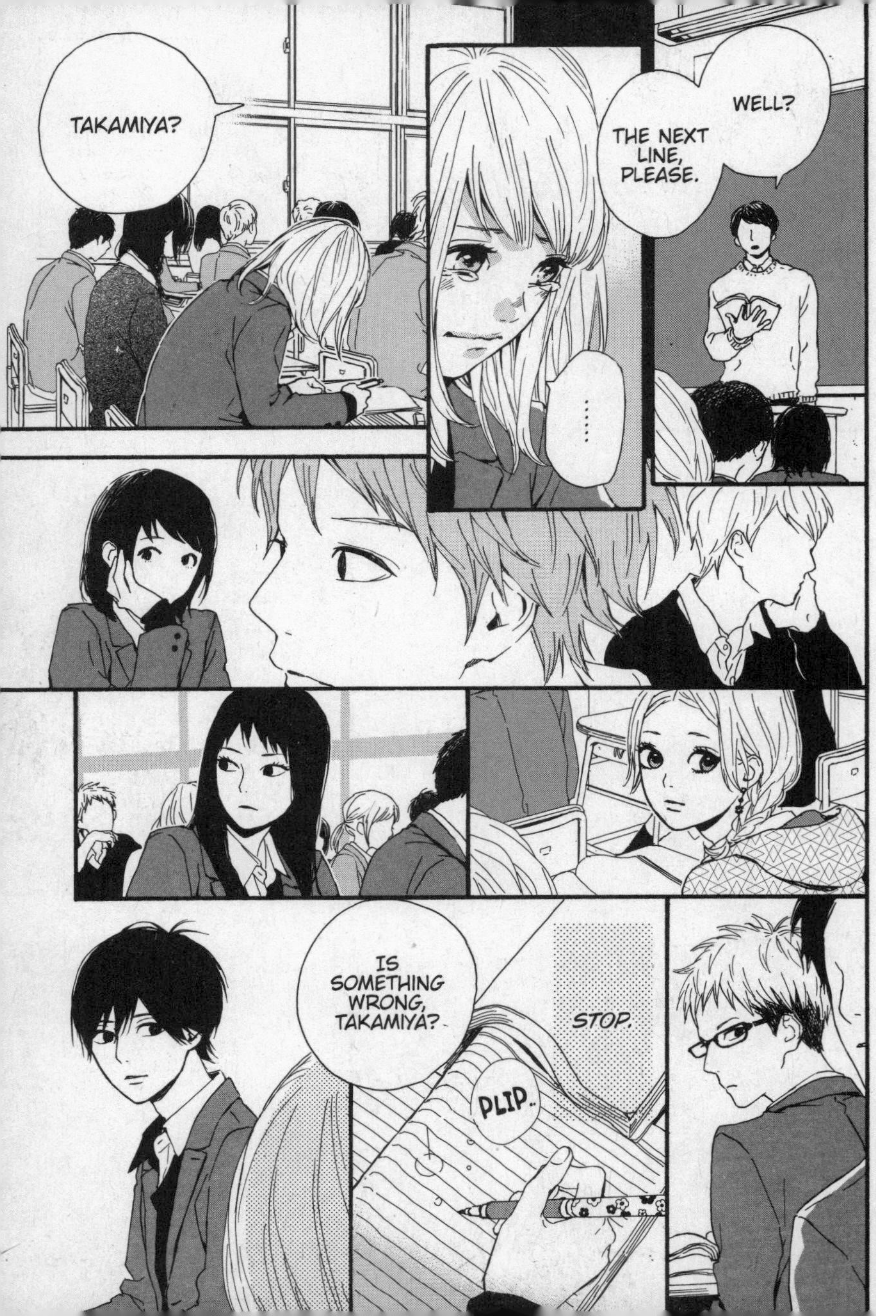
WELL?
THE NEXT LINE, PLEASE.
......
TAKAMIYA?
IS SOMETHING WRONG, TAKAMIYA?
STOP.
PLIP..

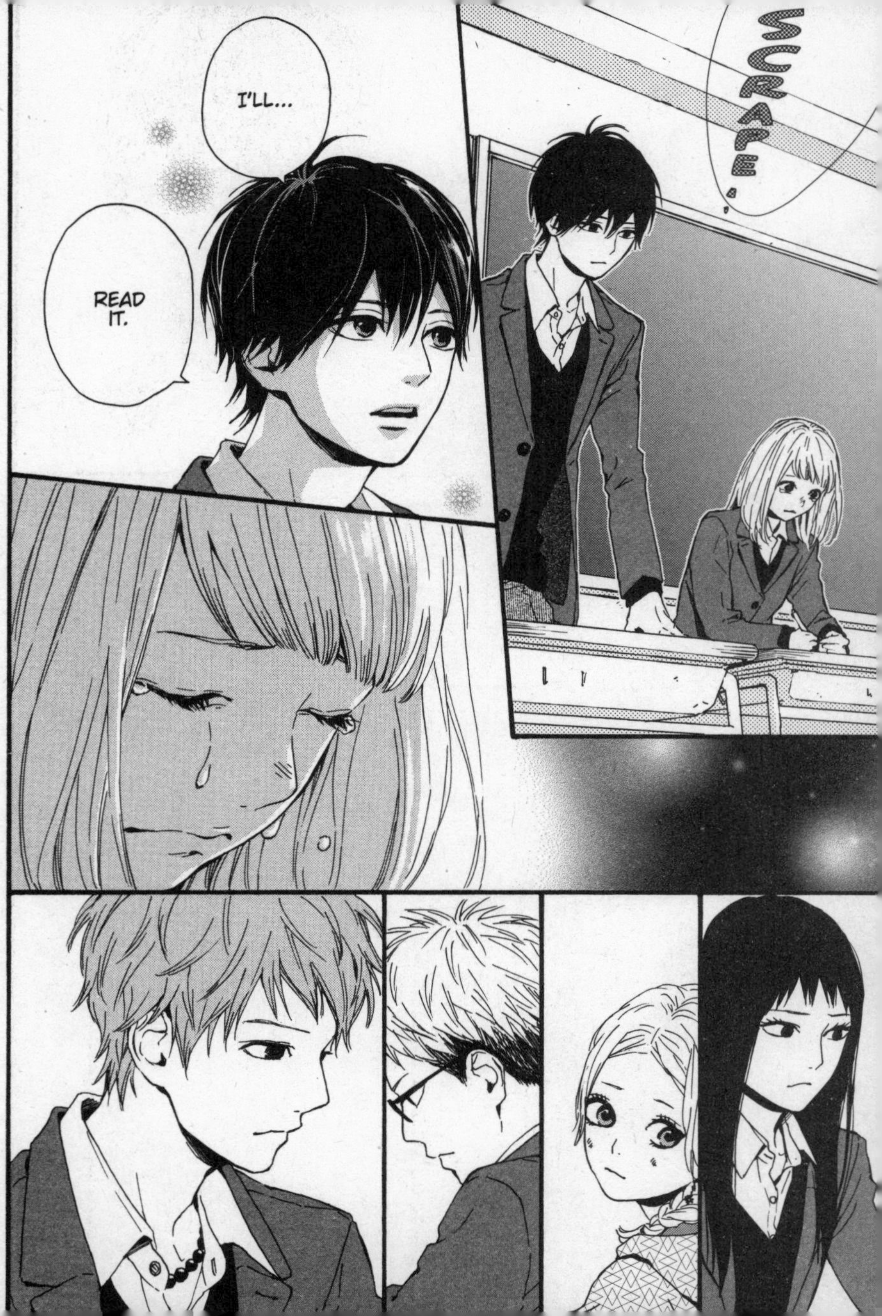
SCRAPE
I'LL...
READ IT.

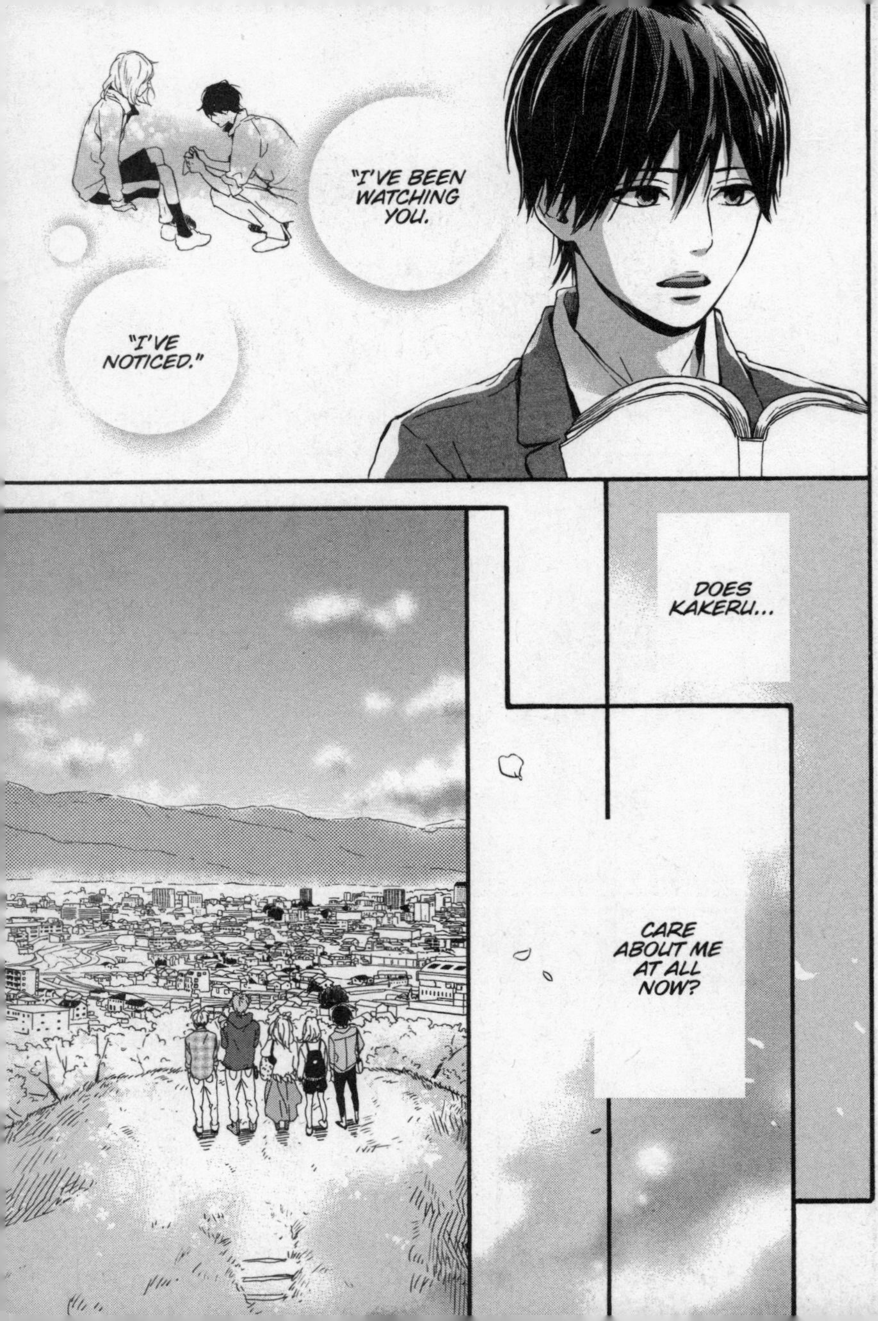
"I'VE BEEN WATCHING YOU.
"I'VE NOTICED."
DOES KAKERU...
CARE ABOUT ME AT ALL NOW?

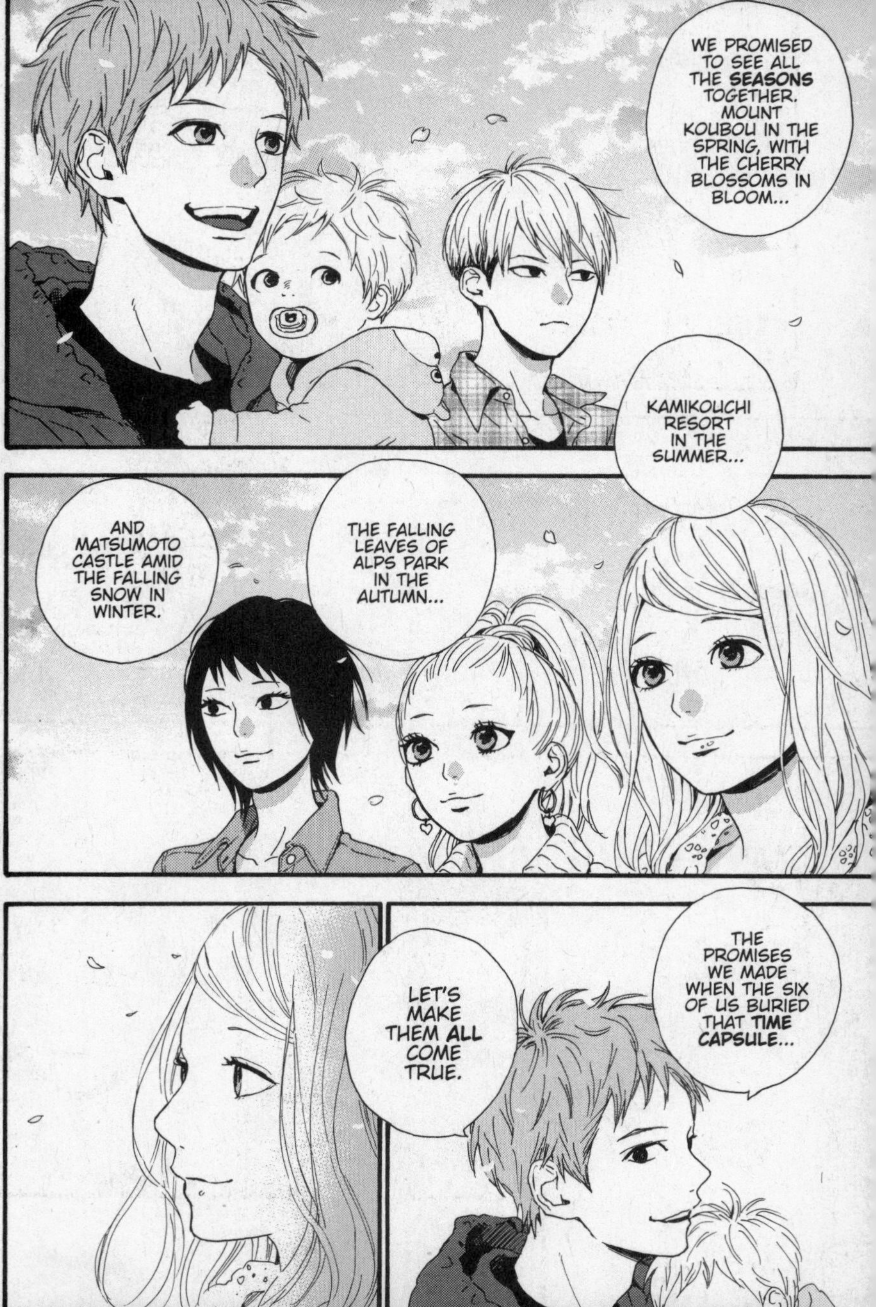
WE PROMISED TO SEE ALL THE **SEASONS** TOGETHER. MOUNT KOUBOU IN THE SPRING, WITH THE CHERRY BLOSSOMS IN BLOOM...
KAMIKOUCHI RESORT IN THE SUMMER...
THE FALLING LEAVES OF ALPS PARK IN THE AUTUMN...
AND MATSUMOTO CASTLE AMID THE FALLING SNOW IN WINTER.
THE PROMISES WE MADE WHEN THE SIX OF US BURIED THAT **TIME CAPSULE**...
LET'S MAKE THEM **ALL** COME TRUE.

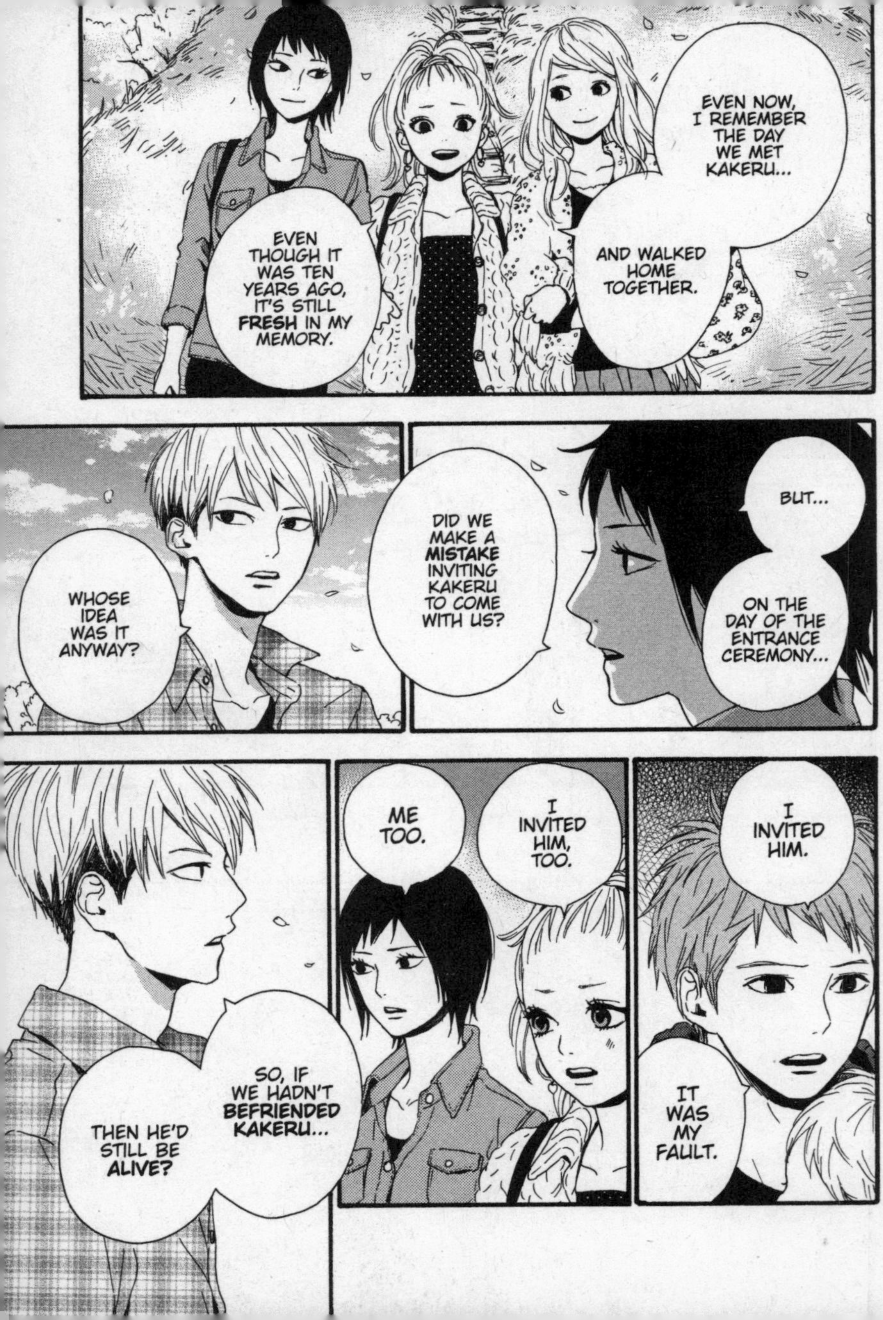
EVEN NOW, I REMEMBER THE DAY WE MET KAKERU...
AND WALKED HOME TOGETHER.
EVEN THOUGH IT WAS TEN YEARS AGO, IT'S STILL FRESH IN MY MEMORY.
BUT...
ON THE DAY OF THE ENTRANCE CEREMONY...
DID WE MAKE A MISTAKE INVITING KAKERU TO COME WITH US?
WHOSE IDEA WAS IT ANYWAY?
I INVITED HIM.
IT WAS MY FAULT.
I INVITED HIM, TOO.
ME TOO.
SO, IF WE HADN'T BEFRIENDED KAKERU...
THEN HE'D STILL BE ALIVE?

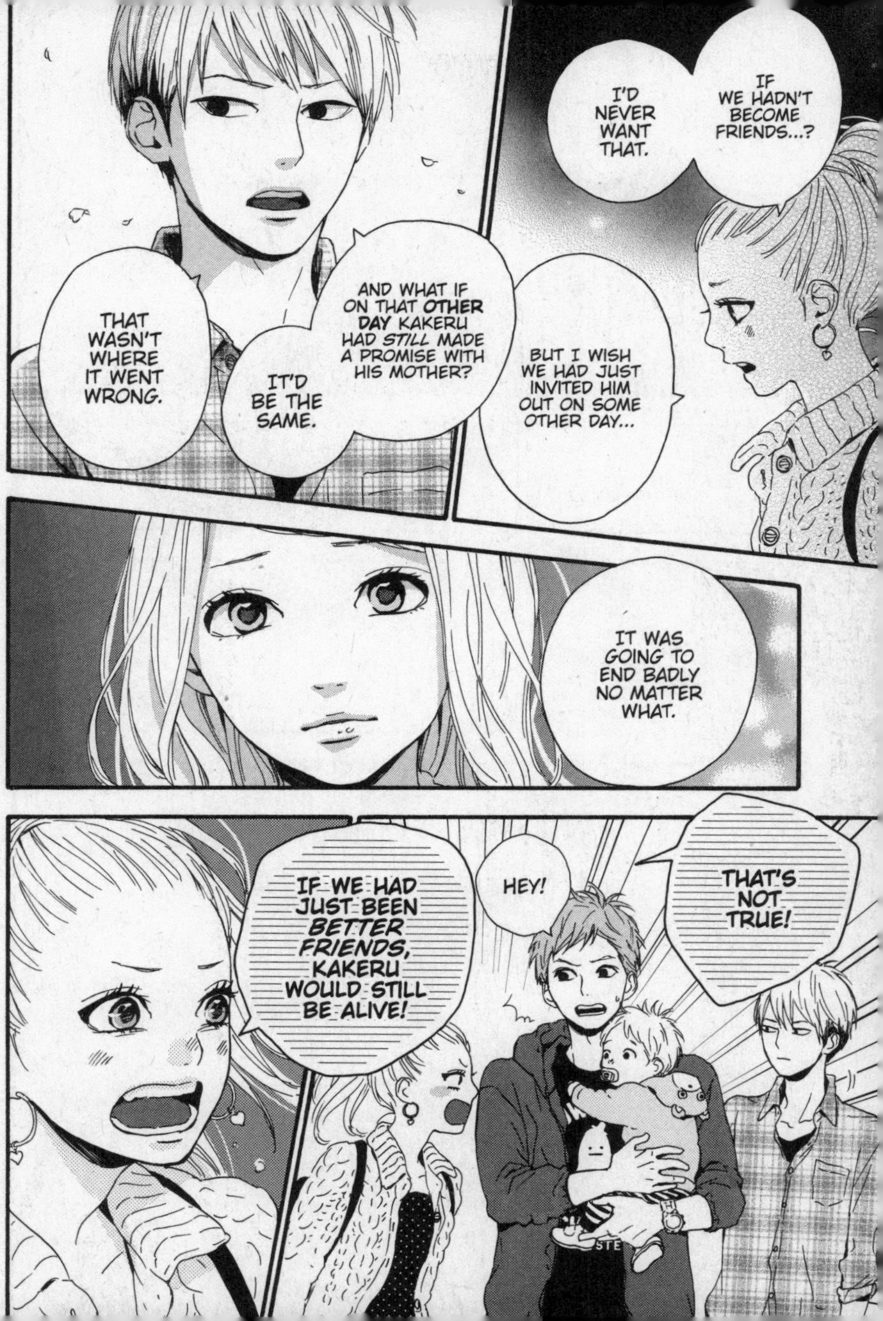
IF WE HADN'T BECOME FRIENDS...?
I'D NEVER WANT THAT.
BUT I WISH WE HAD JUST INVITED HIM OUT ON SOME OTHER DAY...
AND WHAT IF ON THAT **OTHER DAY** KAKERU HAD *STILL* MADE A PROMISE WITH HIS MOTHER?
IT'D BE THE SAME.
THAT WASN'T WHERE IT WENT WRONG.
IT WAS GOING TO END BADLY NO MATTER WHAT.
THAT'S NOT TRUE!
HEY!
IF WE HAD JUST BEEN *BETTER FRIENDS,* KAKERU WOULD STILL BE ALIVE!

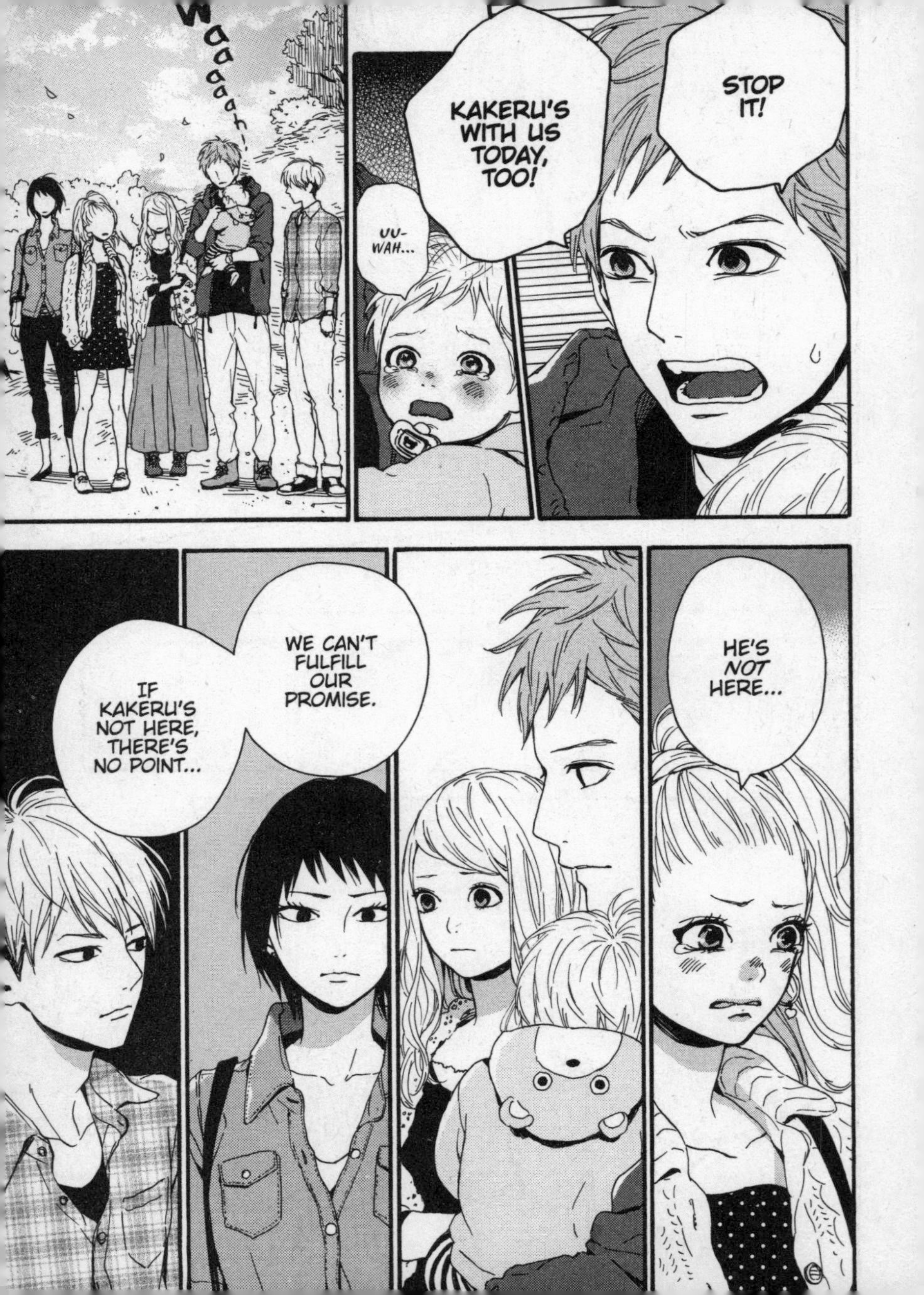
STOP IT!
KAKERU'S WITH US TODAY, TOO!
UU-WAH...
Waaaaah!
HE'S *NOT* HERE...
WE CAN'T FULFILL OUR PROMISE.
IF KAKERU'S NOT HERE, THERE'S NO POINT...

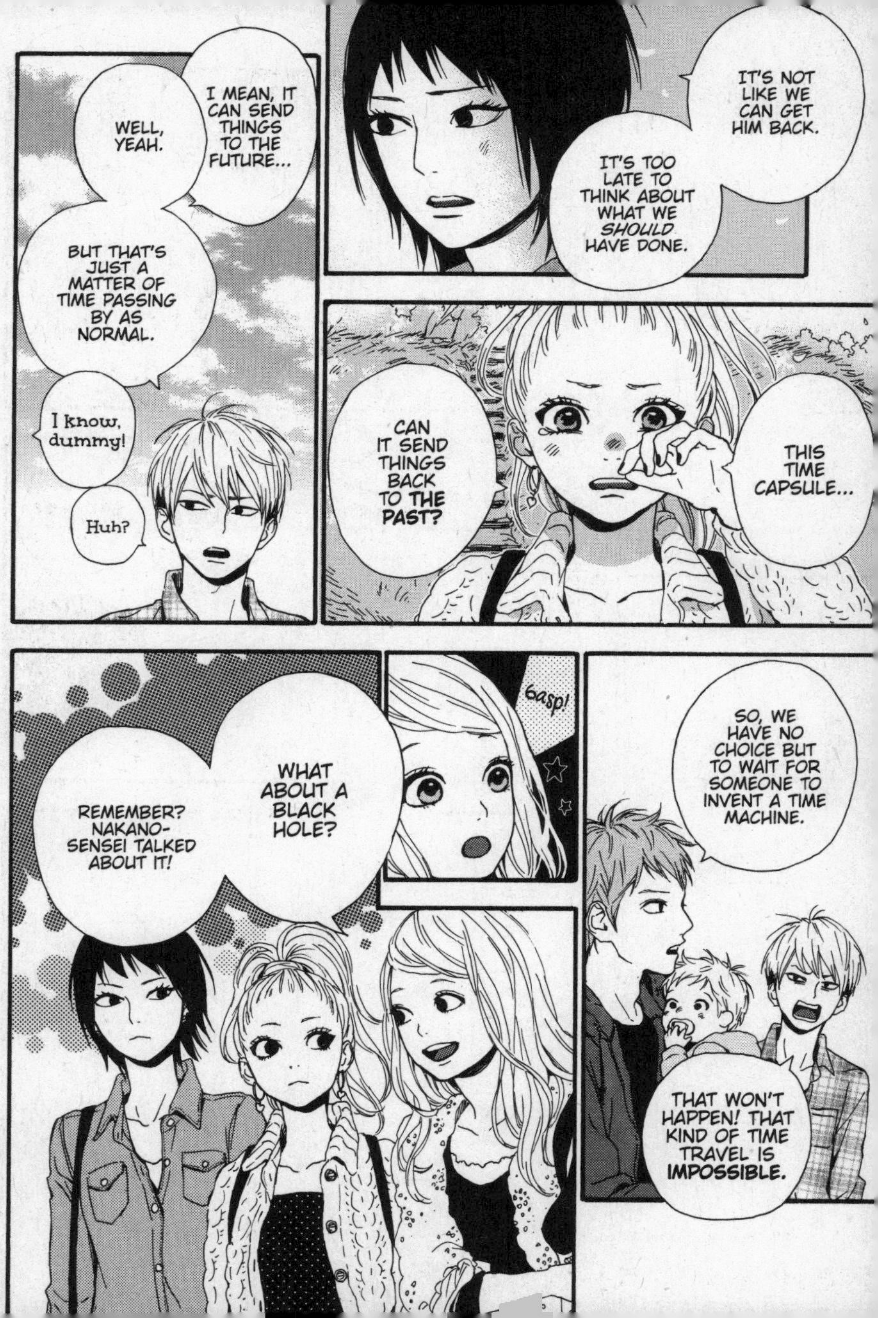
IT'S NOT LIKE WE CAN GET HIM BACK.
IT'S TOO LATE TO THINK ABOUT WHAT WE *SHOULD* HAVE DONE.
THIS TIME CAPSULE...
CAN IT SEND THINGS BACK TO THE PAST?
WELL, YEAH.
I MEAN, IT CAN SEND THINGS TO THE FUTURE...
BUT THAT'S JUST A MATTER OF TIME PASSING BY AS NORMAL.
I know, dummy!
Huh?
SO, WE HAVE NO CHOICE BUT TO WAIT FOR SOMEONE TO INVENT A TIME MACHINE.
THAT WON'T HAPPEN! THAT KIND OF TIME TRAVEL IS **IMPOSSIBLE.**
Gasp!
WHAT ABOUT A BLACK HOLE?
REMEMBER? NAKANO-SENSEI TALKED ABOUT IT!

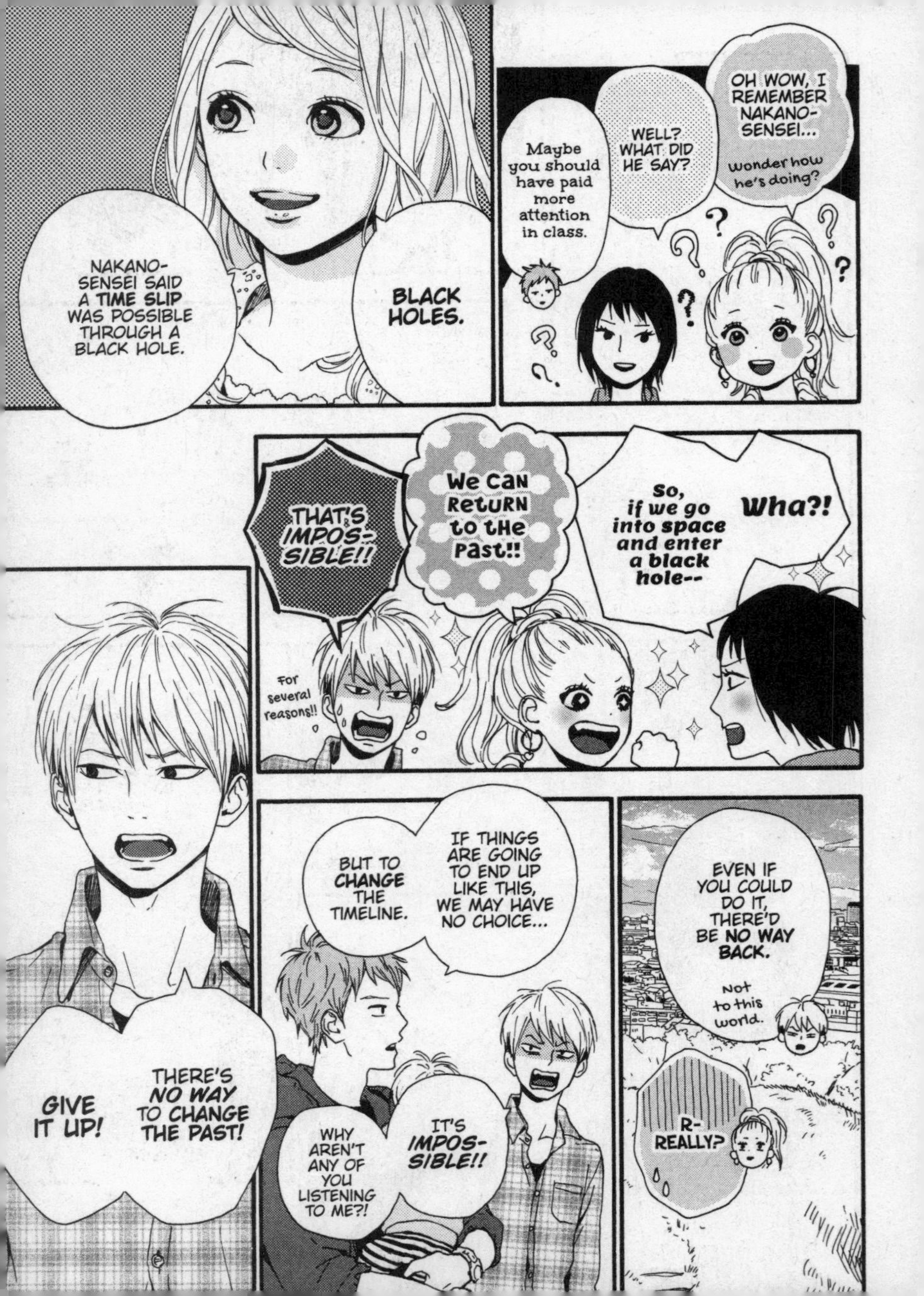
OH WOW, I REMEMBER NAKANO-SENSEI...
wonder how he's doing?
WELL? WHAT DID HE SAY?
Maybe you should have paid more attention in class.
BLACK HOLES.
NAKANO-SENSEI SAID A TIME SLIP WAS POSSIBLE THROUGH A BLACK HOLE.
Wha?!
So, if we go into space and enter a black hole--
We can return to the past!!
THAT'S IMPOSSIBLE!!
For several reasons!!
EVEN IF YOU COULD DO IT, THERE'D BE NO WAY BACK.
Not to this world.
R-REALLY?
IF THINGS ARE GOING TO END UP LIKE THIS, WE MAY HAVE NO CHOICE...
BUT TO CHANGE THE TIMELINE.
IT'S IMPOSSIBLE!!
WHY AREN'T ANY OF YOU LISTENING TO ME?!
THERE'S NO WAY TO CHANGE THE PAST!
GIVE IT UP!

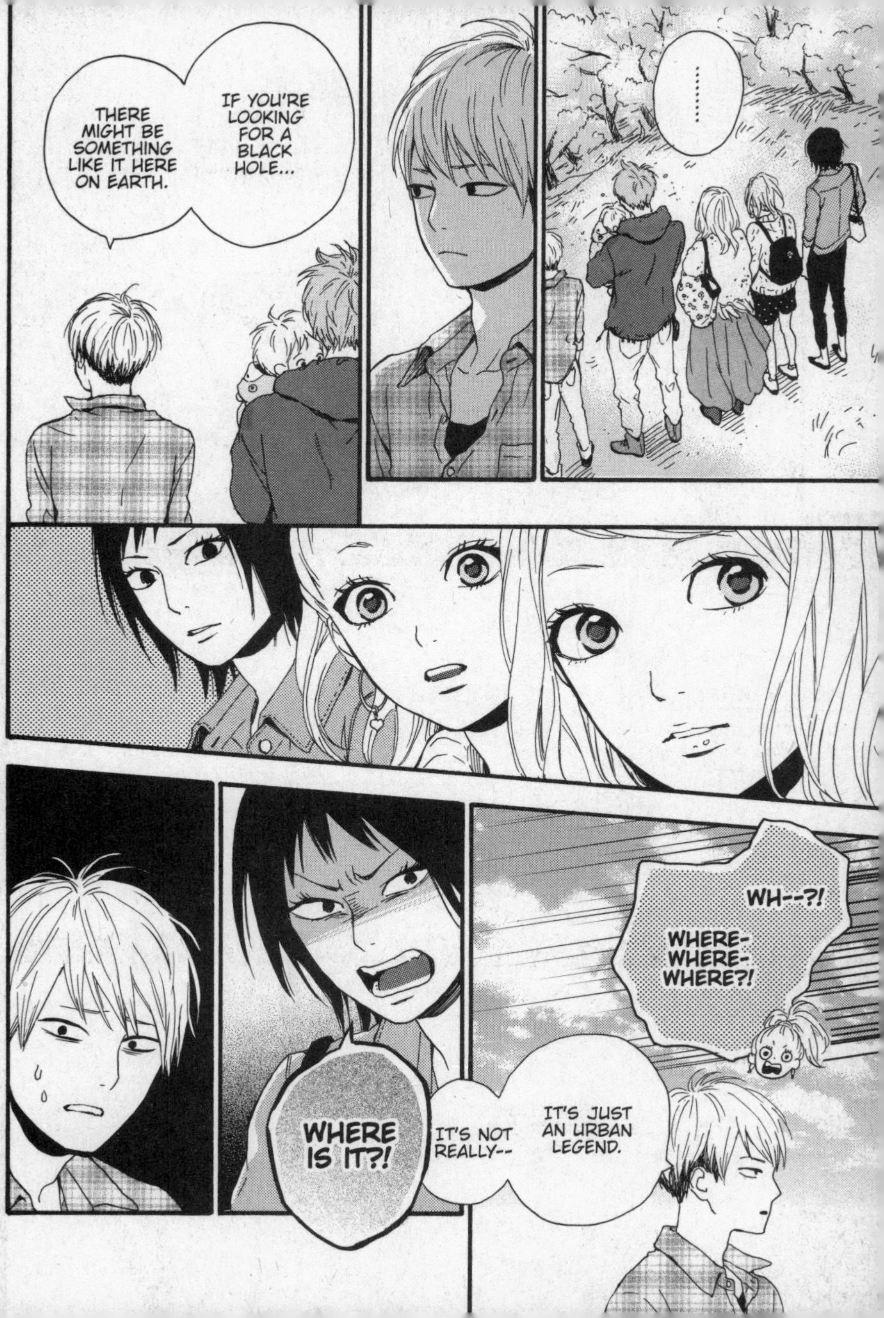
......
IF YOU'RE LOOKING FOR A BLACK HOLE...
THERE MIGHT BE SOMETHING LIKE IT HERE ON EARTH.
WH--?!
WHERE-WHERE-WHERE?!
WHERE IS IT?!
IT'S NOT REALLY--
IT'S JUST AN URBAN LEGEND.

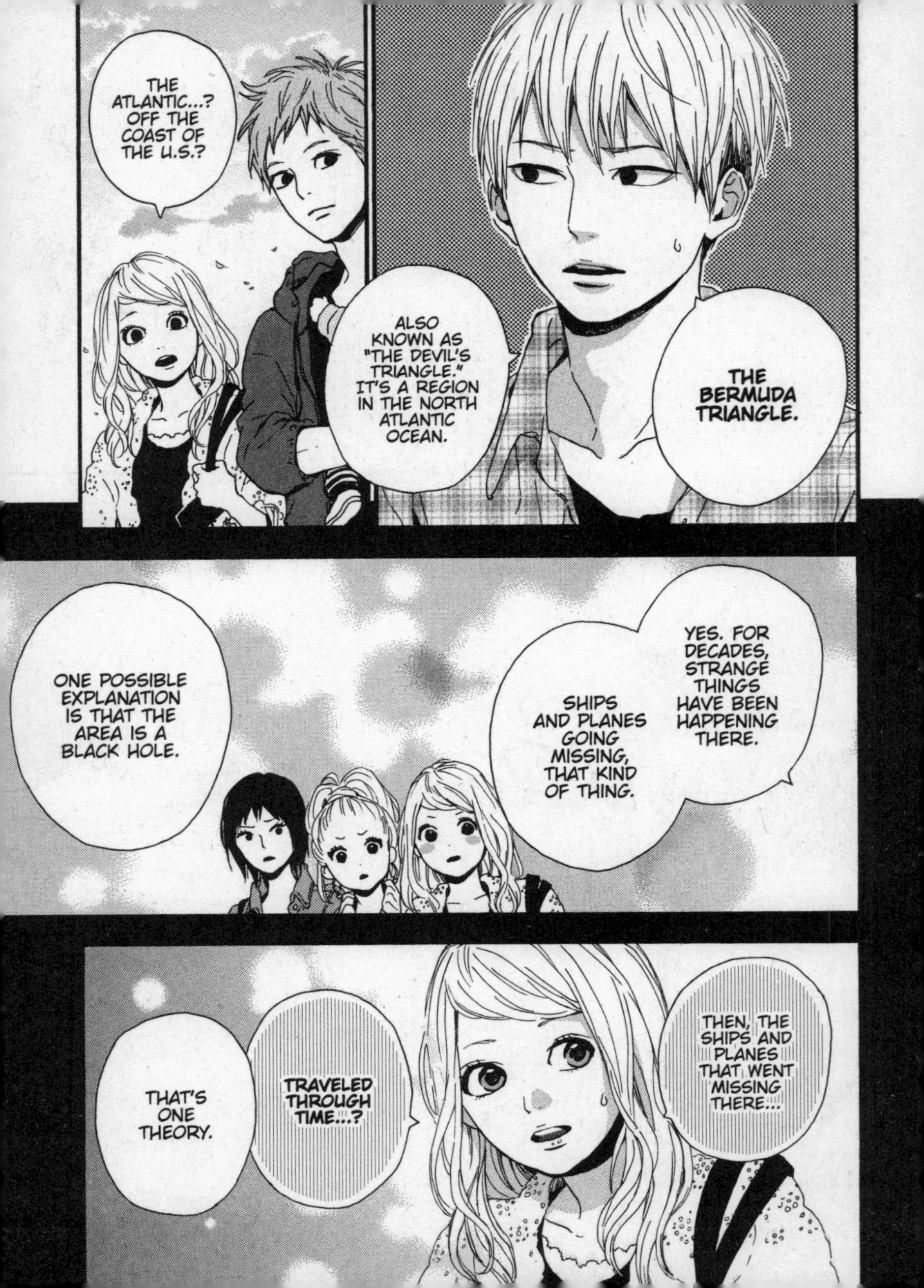
THE BERMUDA TRIANGLE.
ALSO KNOWN AS "THE DEVIL'S TRIANGLE." IT'S A REGION IN THE NORTH ATLANTIC OCEAN.
THE ATLANTIC...? OFF THE COAST OF THE U.S.?
YES. FOR DECADES, STRANGE THINGS HAVE BEEN HAPPENING THERE.
SHIPS AND PLANES GOING MISSING, THAT KIND OF THING.
ONE POSSIBLE EXPLANATION IS THAT THE AREA IS A BLACK HOLE.
THEN, THE SHIPS AND PLANES THAT WENT MISSING THERE...
TRAVELED THROUGH TIME...?
THAT'S ONE THEORY.

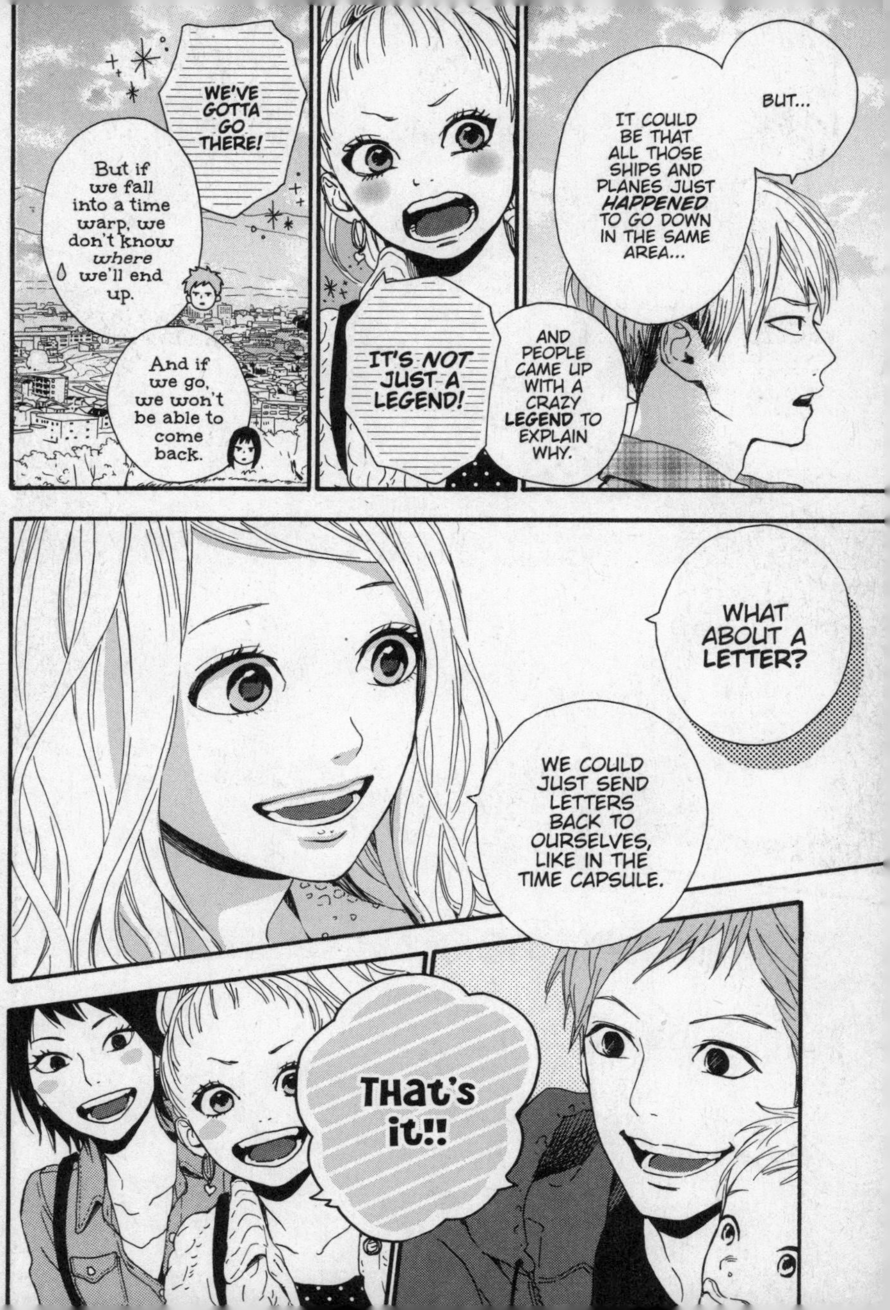
BUT...
IT COULD BE THAT ALL THOSE SHIPS AND PLANES JUST HAPPENED TO GO DOWN IN THE SAME AREA...
AND PEOPLE CAME UP WITH A CRAZY LEGEND TO EXPLAIN WHY.
IT'S NOT JUST A LEGEND!
WE'VE GOTTA GO THERE!
But if we fall into a time warp, we don't know where we'll end up.
And if we go, we won't be able to come back.
WHAT ABOUT A LETTER?
WE COULD JUST SEND LETTERS BACK TO OURSELVES, LIKE IN THE TIME CAPSULE.
That's it!!

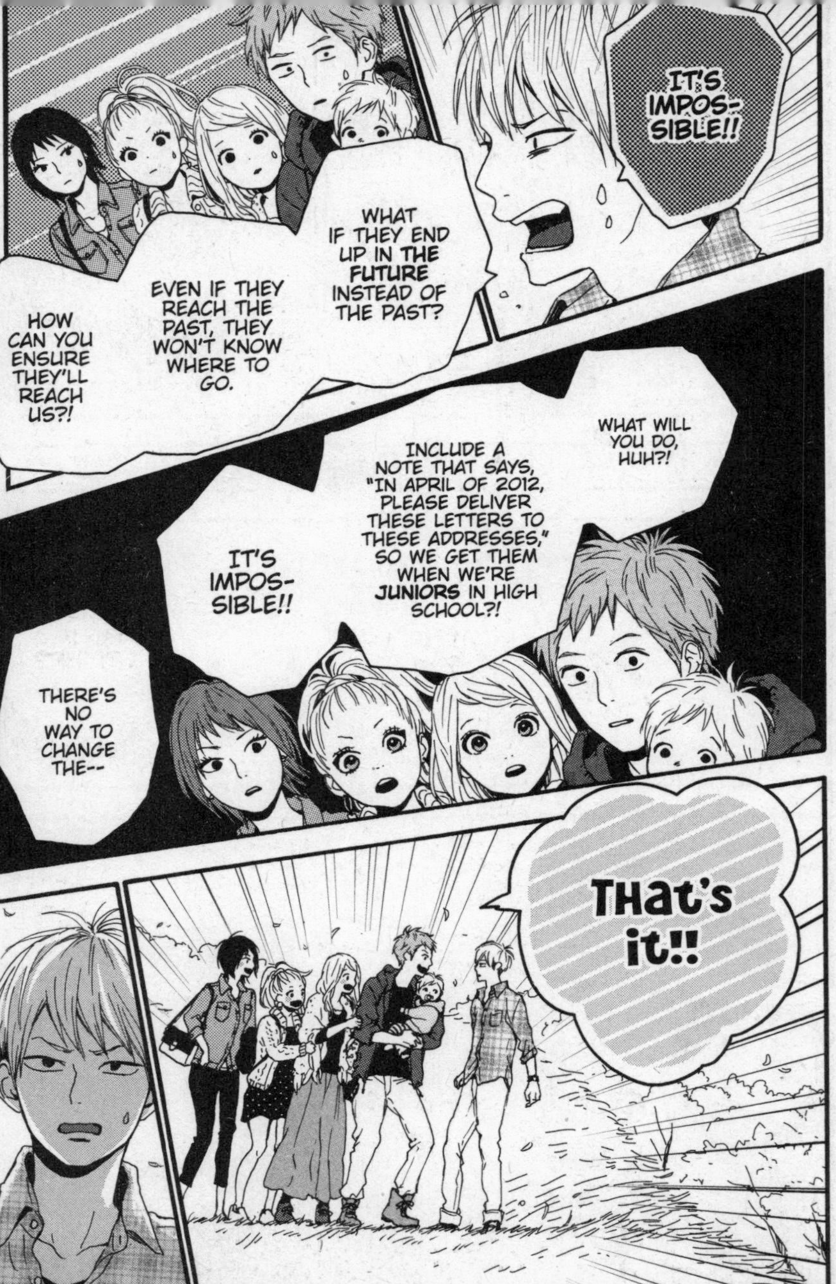
IT'S IMPOSSIBLE!!
WHAT IF THEY END UP IN THE FUTURE INSTEAD OF THE PAST?
EVEN IF THEY REACH THE PAST, THEY WON'T KNOW WHERE TO GO.
HOW CAN YOU ENSURE THEY'LL REACH US?!
WHAT WILL YOU DO, HUH?!
INCLUDE A NOTE THAT SAYS, "IN APRIL OF 2012, PLEASE DELIVER THESE LETTERS TO THESE ADDRESSES," SO WE GET THEM WHEN WE'RE JUNIORS IN HIGH SCHOOL?!
IT'S IMPOSSIBLE!!
THERE'S NO WAY TO CHANGE THE--
THAT's it!!

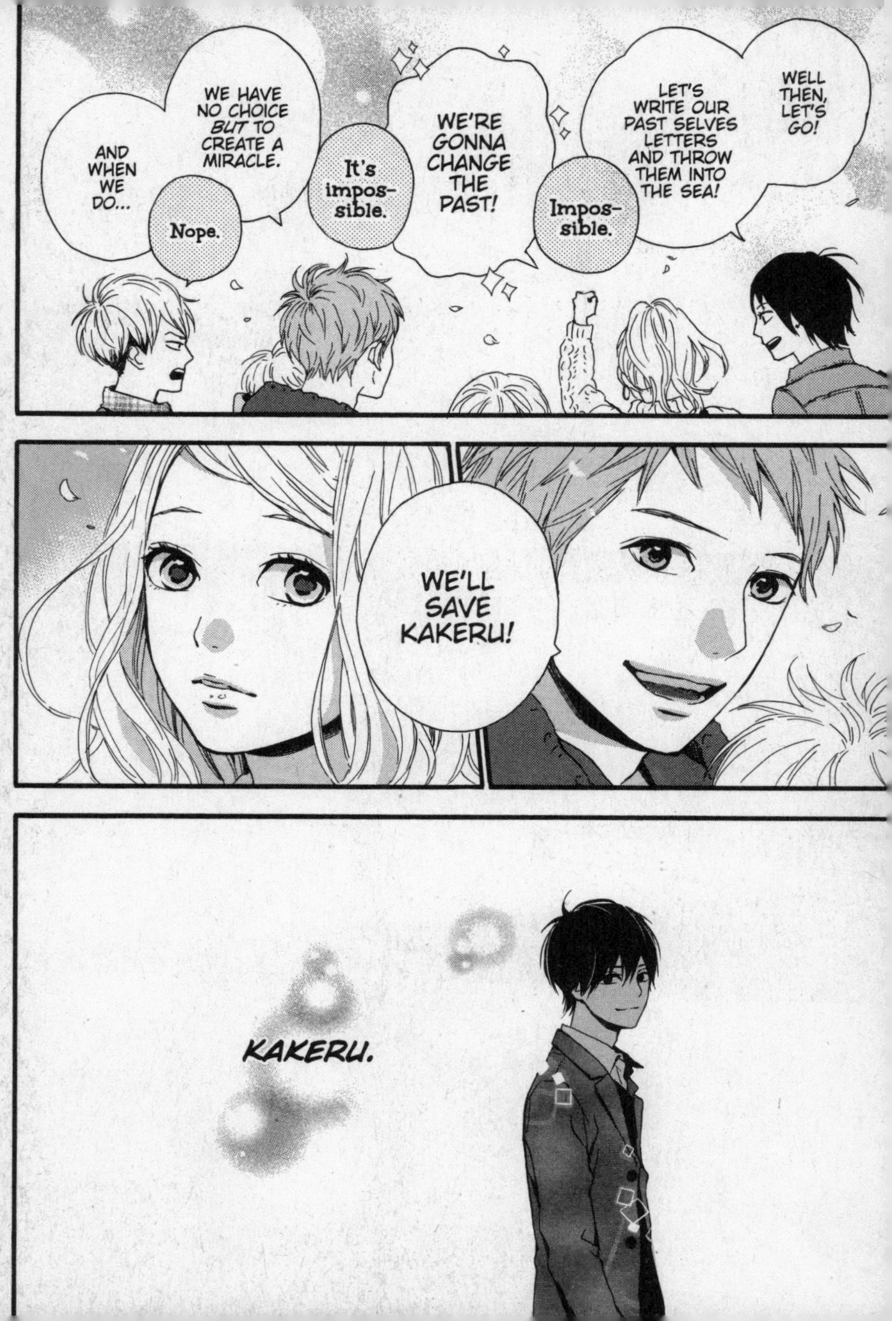
WELL THEN, LET'S GO!
LET'S WRITE OUR PAST SELVES LETTERS AND THROW THEM INTO THE SEA!
Impos-sible.
WE'RE GONNA CHANGE THE PAST!
It's impos-sible.
WE HAVE NO CHOICE *BUT* TO CREATE A MIRACLE.
Nope.
AND WHEN WE DO...
WE'LL SAVE KAKERU!
KAKERU.

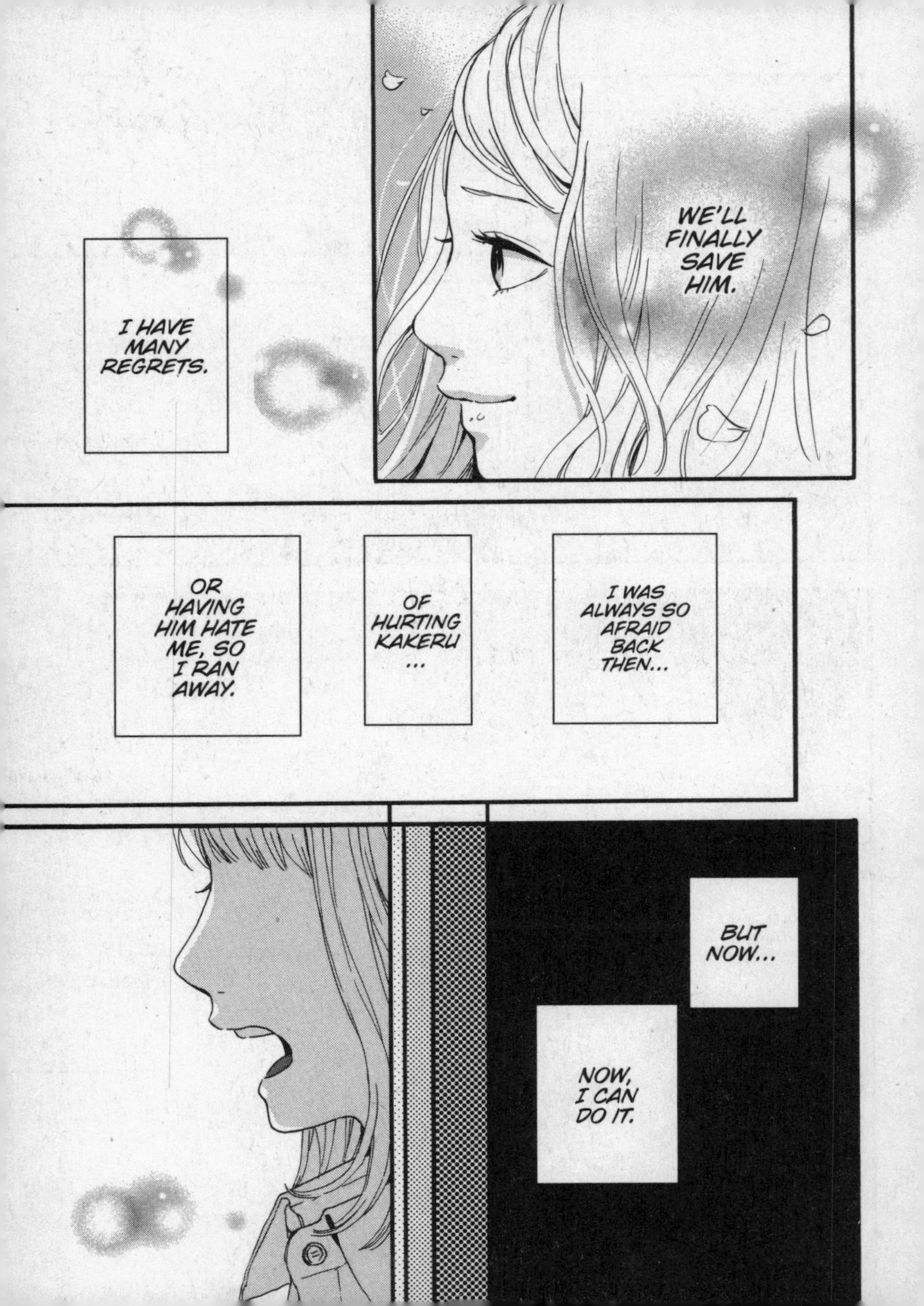
WE'LL FINALLY SAVE HIM.
I HAVE MANY REGRETS.
I WAS ALWAYS SO AFRAID BACK THEN...
OF HURTING KAKERU...
OR HAVING HIM HATE ME, SO I RAN AWAY.
BUT NOW...
NOW, I CAN DO IT.

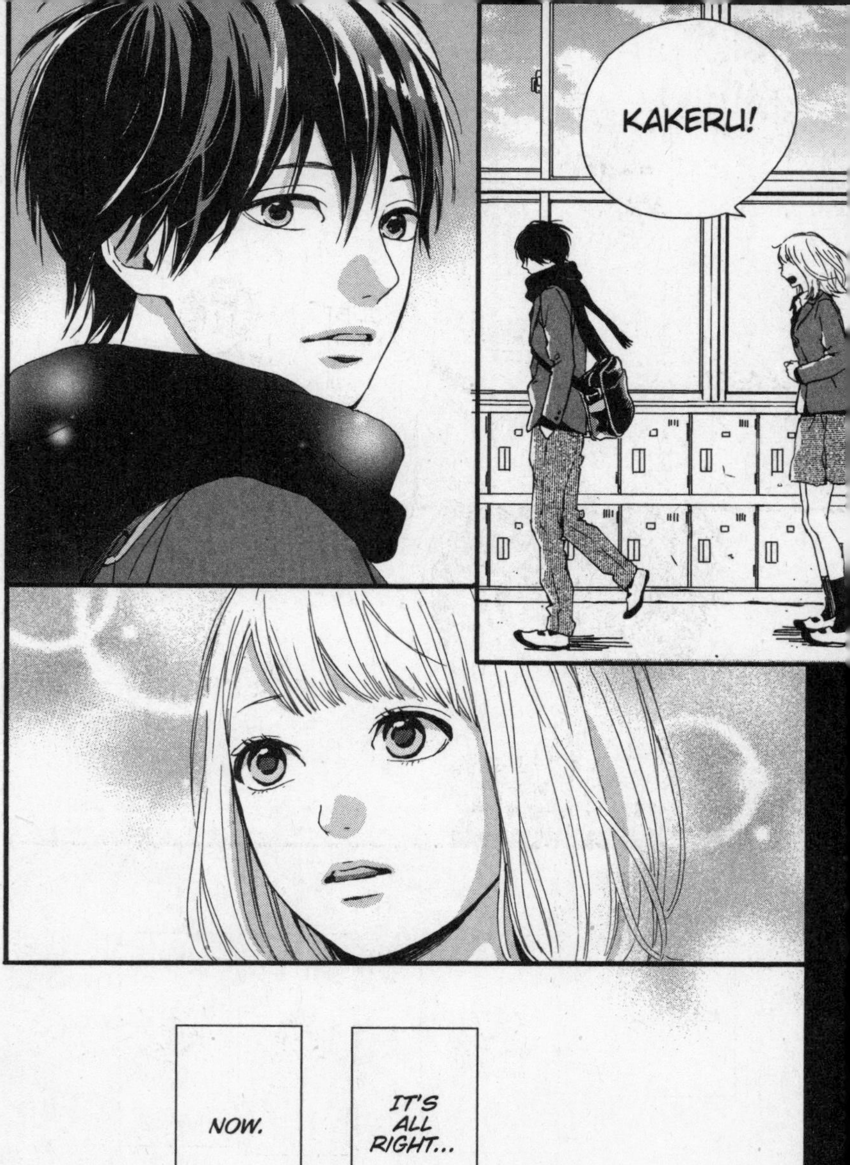
KAKERU!
IT'S ALL RIGHT...
NOW.

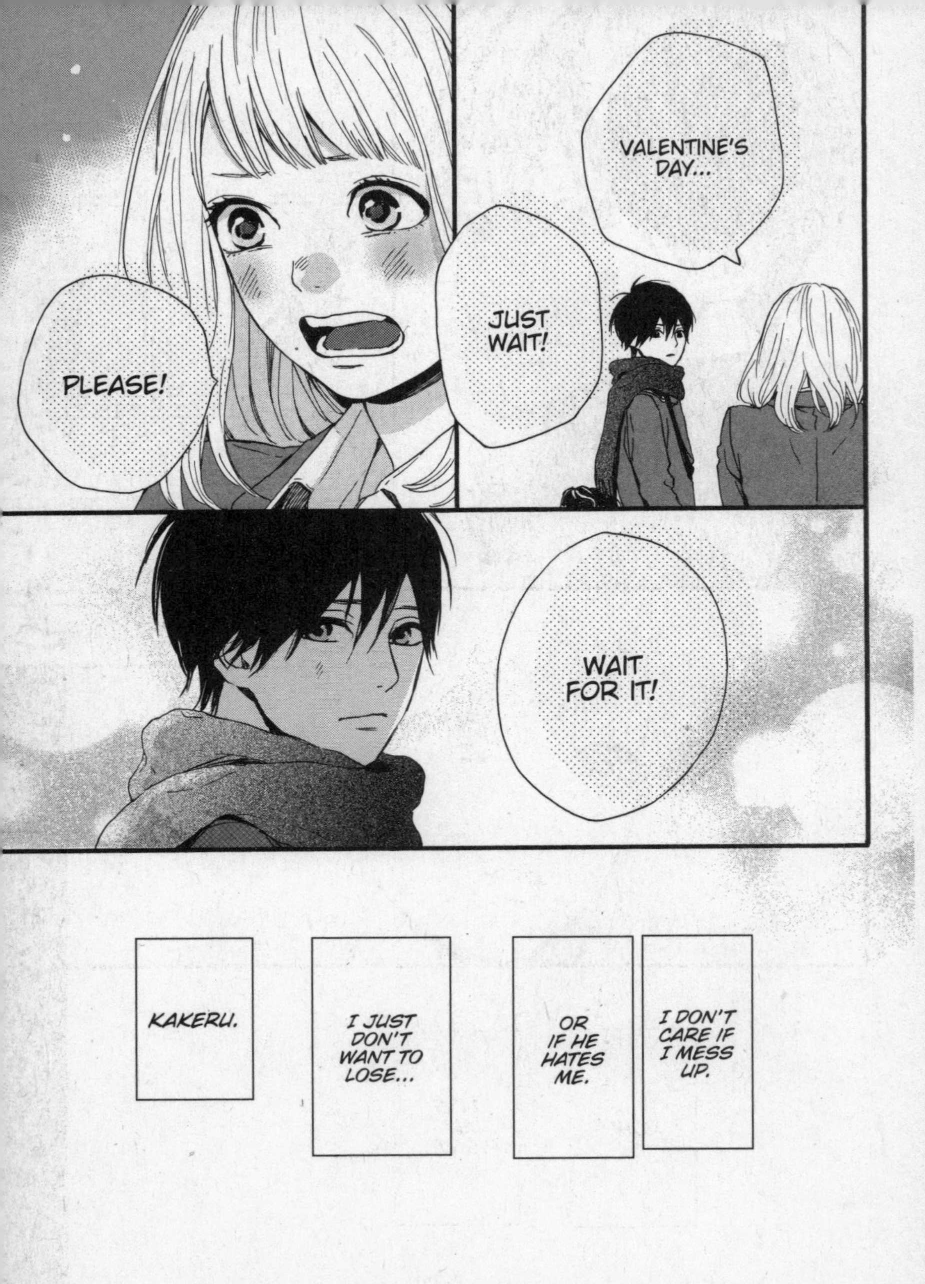
VALENTINE'S DAY...
JUST WAIT!
PLEASE!
WAIT FOR IT!
I DON'T CARE IF I MESS UP.
OR IF HE HATES ME.
I JUST DON'T WANT TO LOSE...
KAKERU.

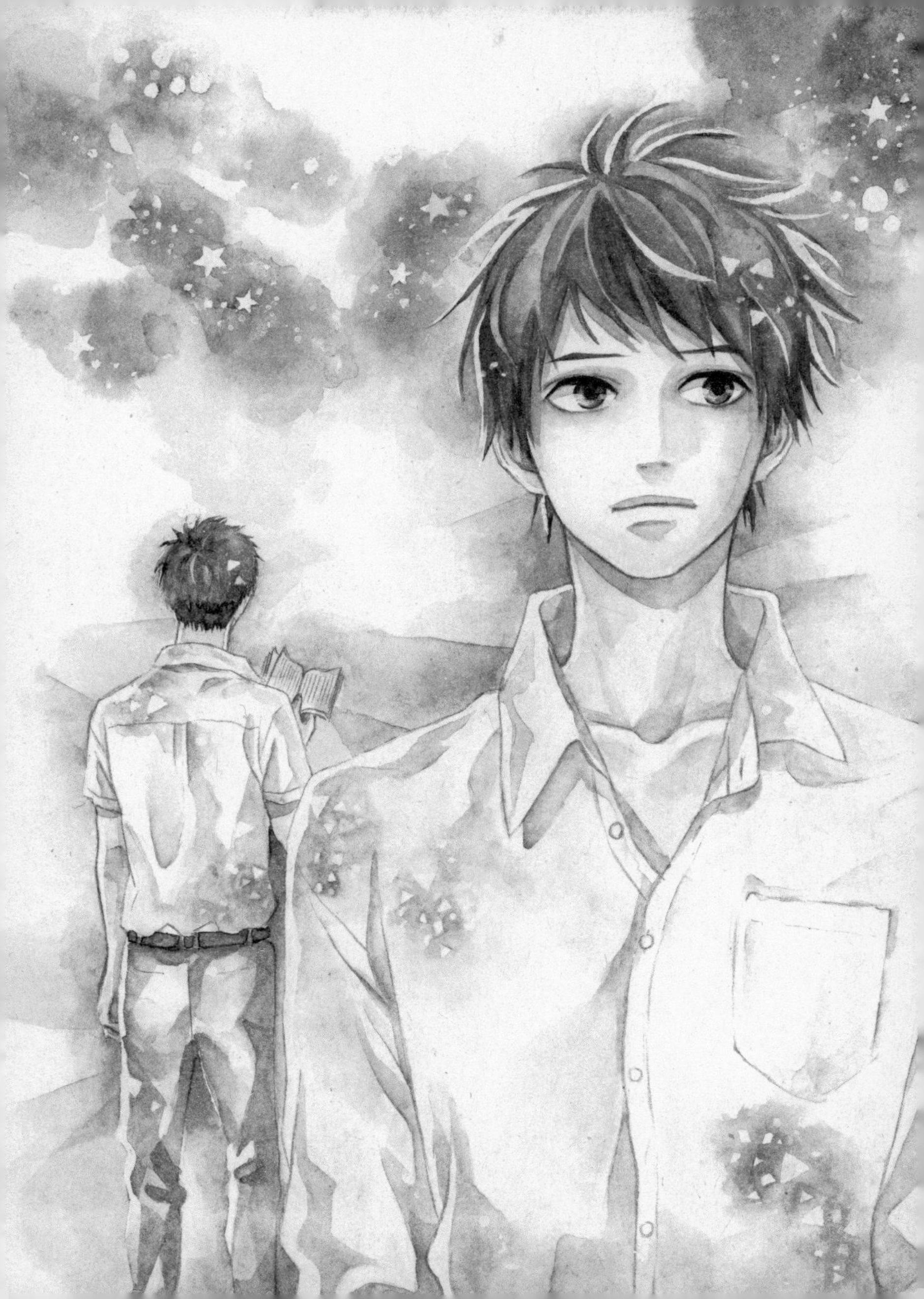

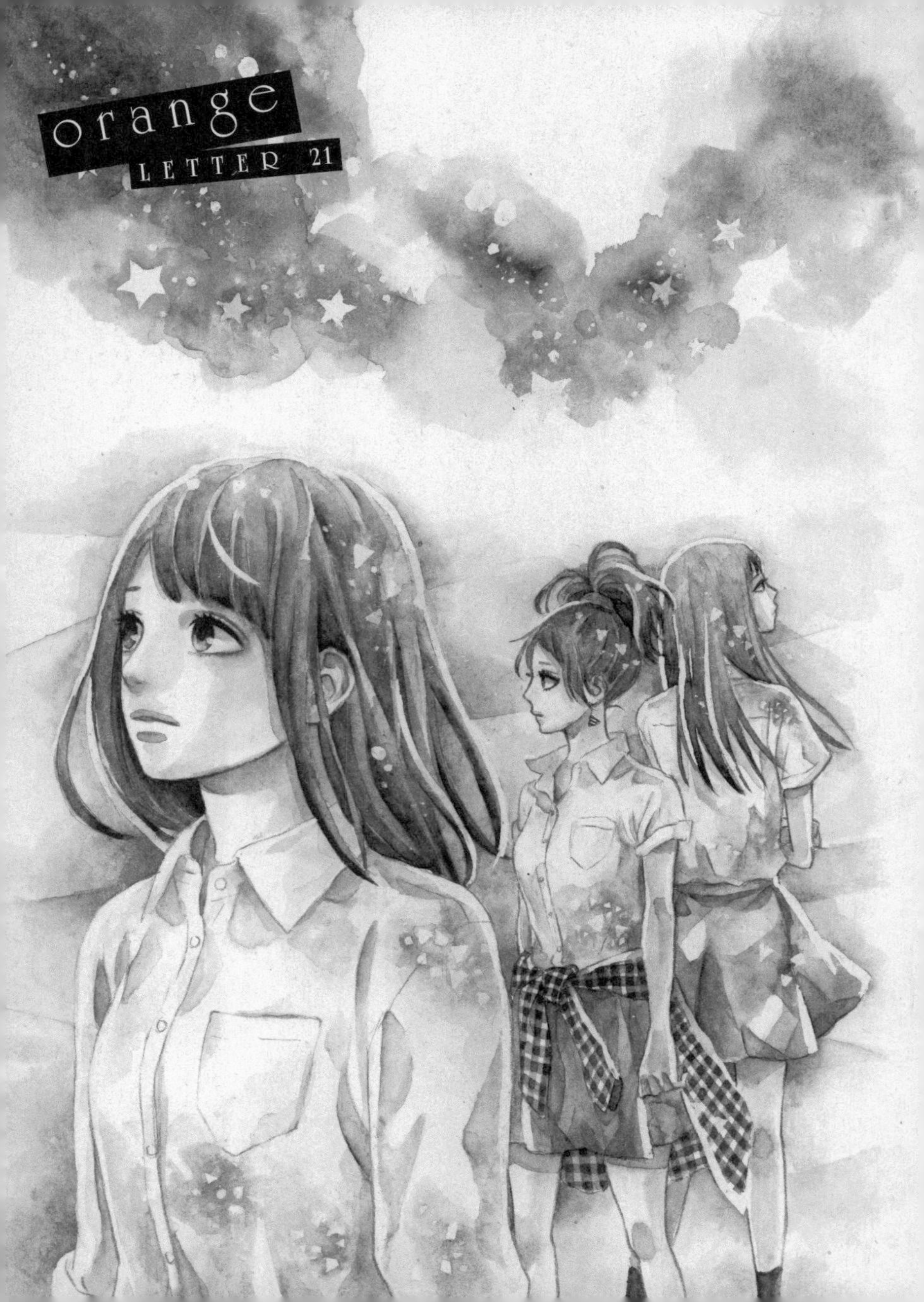
orange
LETTER 21

orange

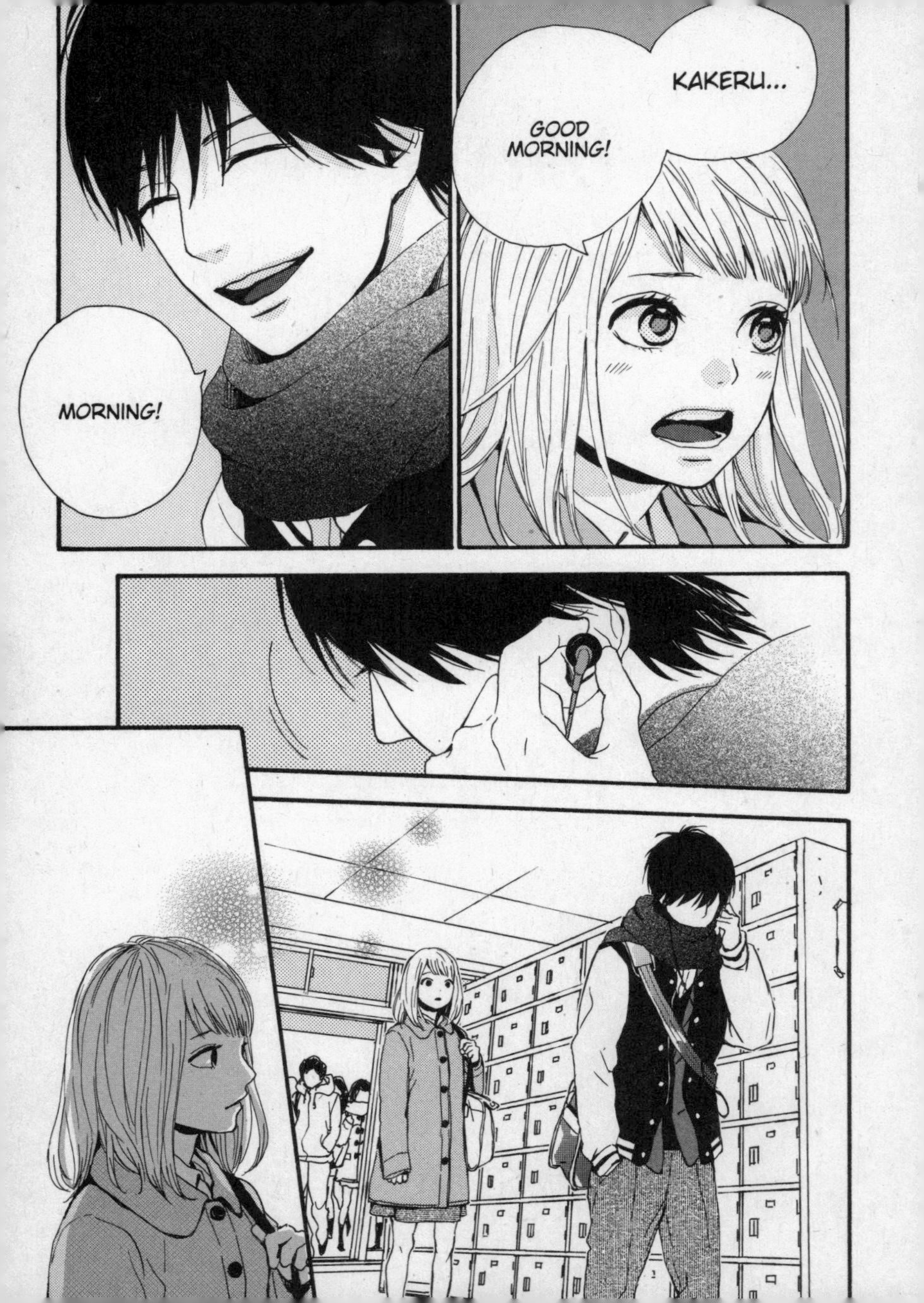
KAKERU...
GOOD MORNING!
MORNING!

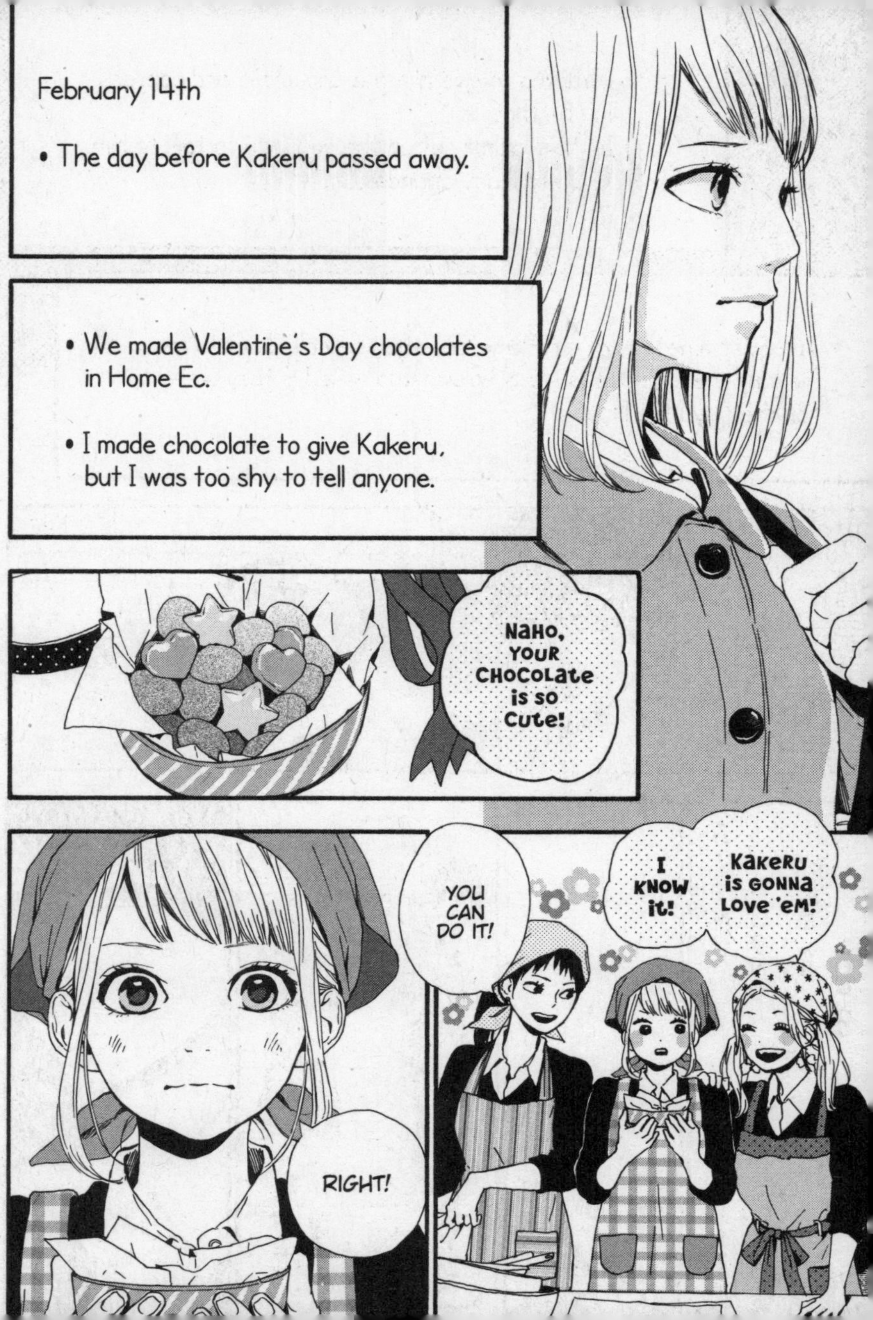
February 14th
• The day before Kakeru passed away.
• We made Valentine's Day chocolates in Home Ec.
• I made chocolate to give Kakeru, but I was too shy to tell anyone.
Naho, your chocolate is so cute!
Kakeru is gonna love 'em!
I know it!
You can do it!
Right!

- I wanted to give him the chocolate and confess my feelings.
- But I couldn't get up the courage to talk to him. I had so many chances...

- The first time was after Home Ec, when he called out to me. He saw the chocolates I was holding and asked if they were for the guy I liked.

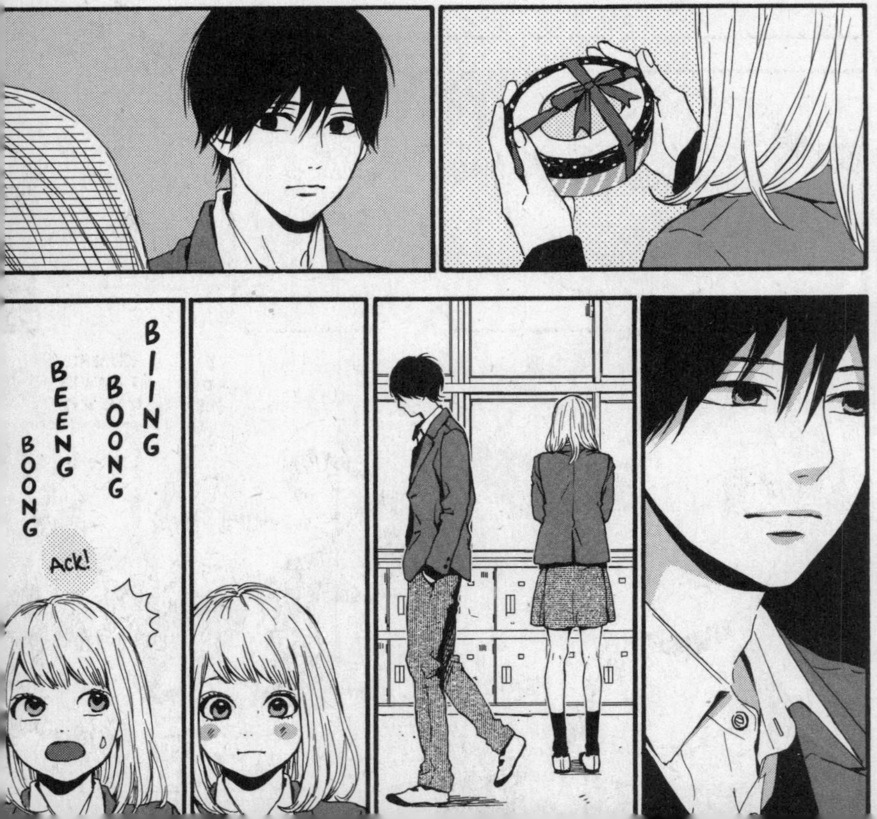
BIING
BOONG
BEENG
BOONG
Ack!

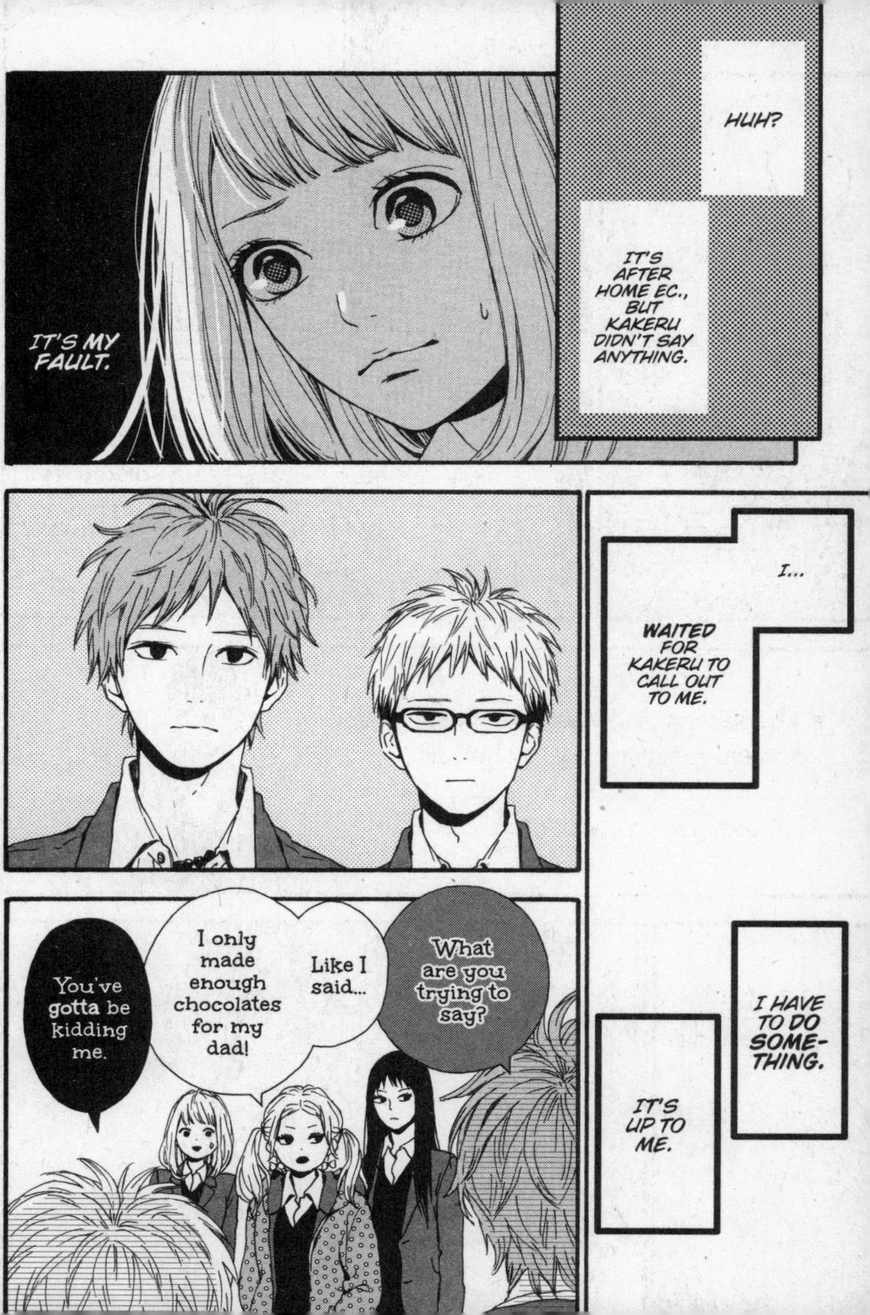
HUH?
IT'S AFTER HOME EC., BUT KAKERU DIDN'T SAY ANYTHING.
IT'S MY FAULT.
I...
WAITED FOR KAKERU TO CALL OUT TO ME.
I HAVE TO DO SOME-THING.
IT'S UP TO ME.
What are you trying to say?
Like I said...
I only made enough chocolates for my dad!
You've gotta be kidding me.

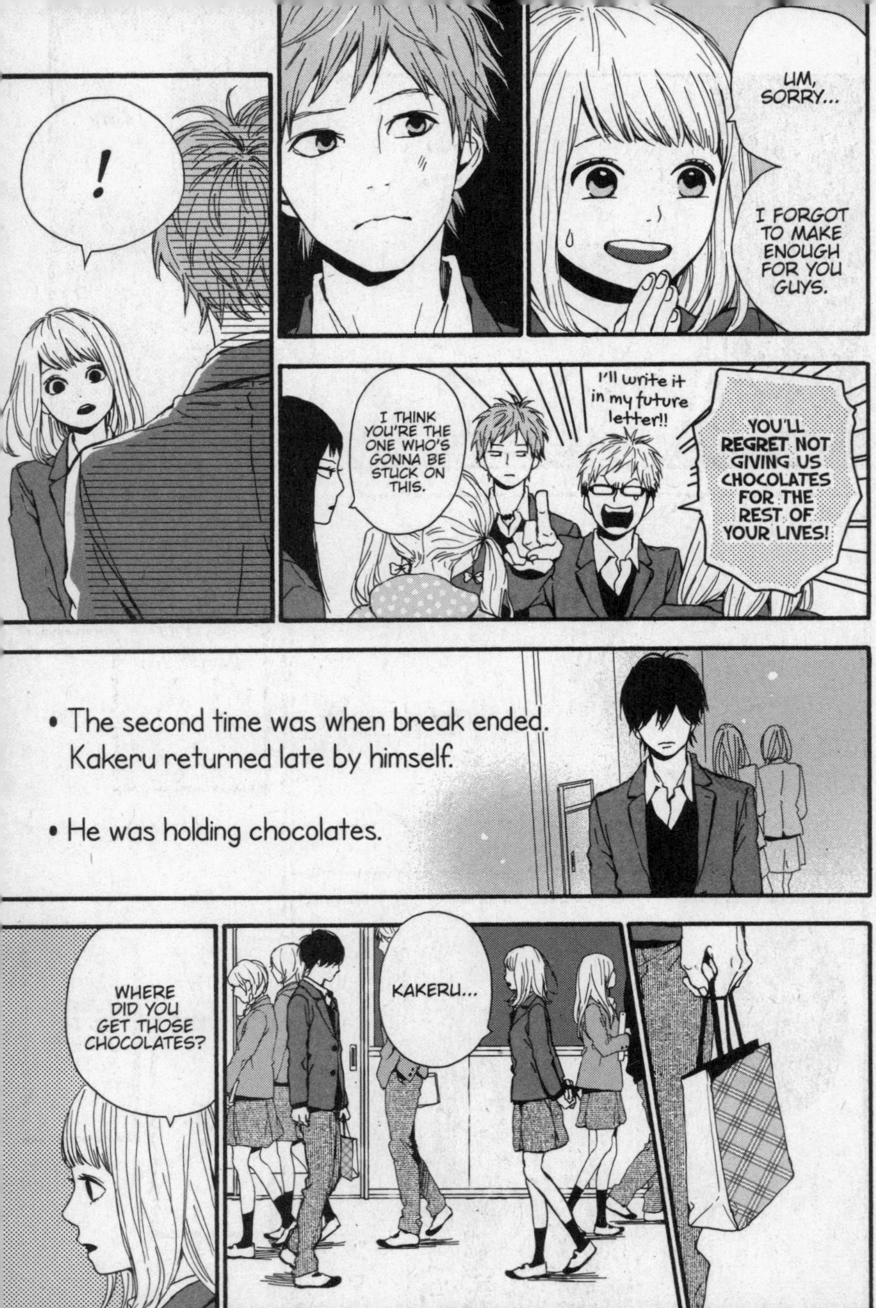
UM, SORRY...
I FORGOT TO MAKE ENOUGH FOR YOU GUYS.
YOU'LL REGRET NOT GIVING US CHOCOLATES FOR THE REST OF YOUR LIVES!
I'll write it in my future letter!!
I THINK YOU'RE THE ONE WHO'S GONNA BE STUCK ON THIS.
!
• The second time was when break ended. Kakeru returned late by himself.
• He was holding chocolates.
KAKERU...
WHERE DID YOU GET THOSE CHOCOLATES?

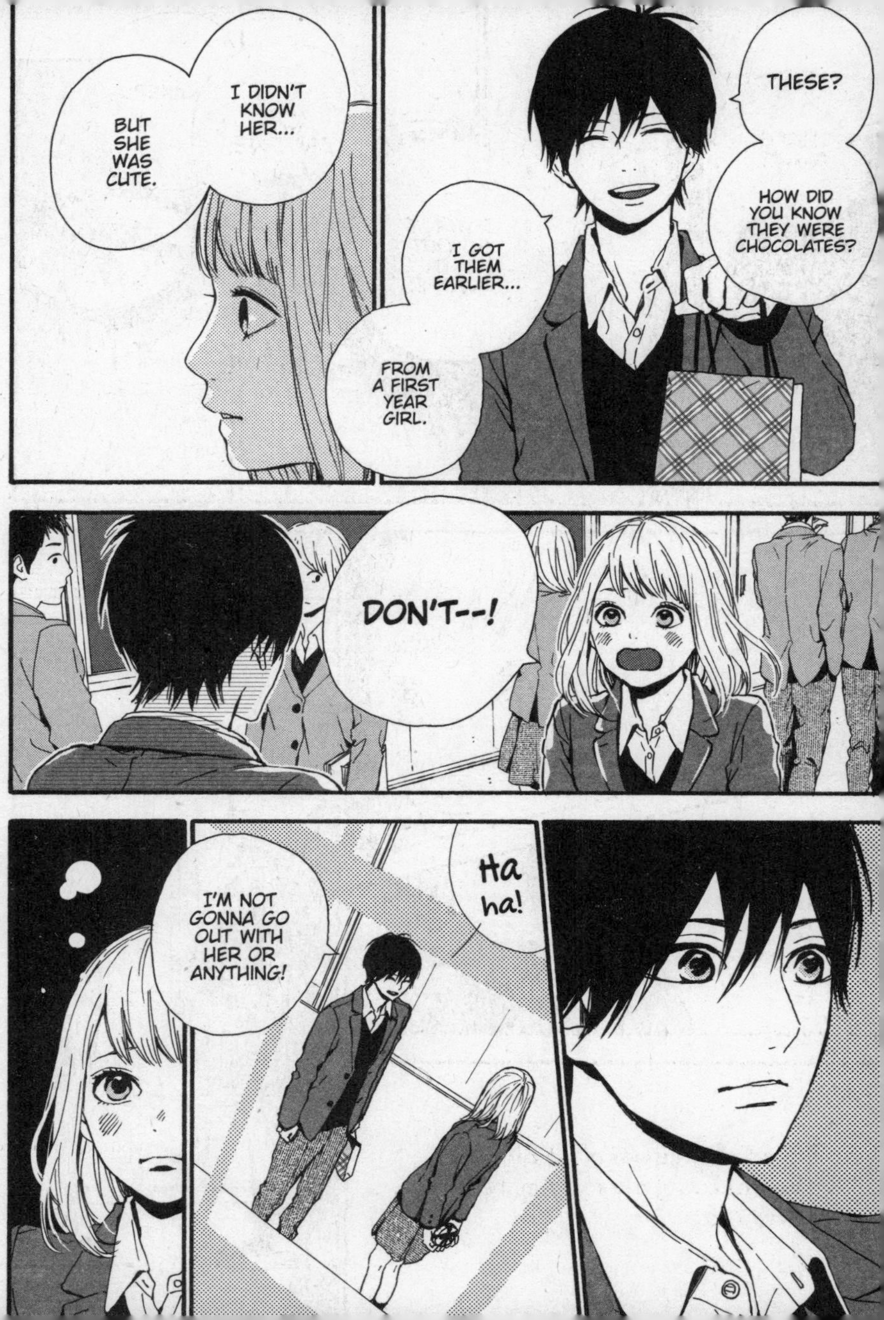
THESE?
HOW DID YOU KNOW THEY WERE CHOCOLATES?
I GOT THEM EARLIER...
FROM A FIRST YEAR GIRL.
I DIDN'T KNOW HER...
BUT SHE WAS CUTE.
DON'T--!
Ha ha!
I'M NOT GONNA GO OUT WITH HER OR ANYTHING!

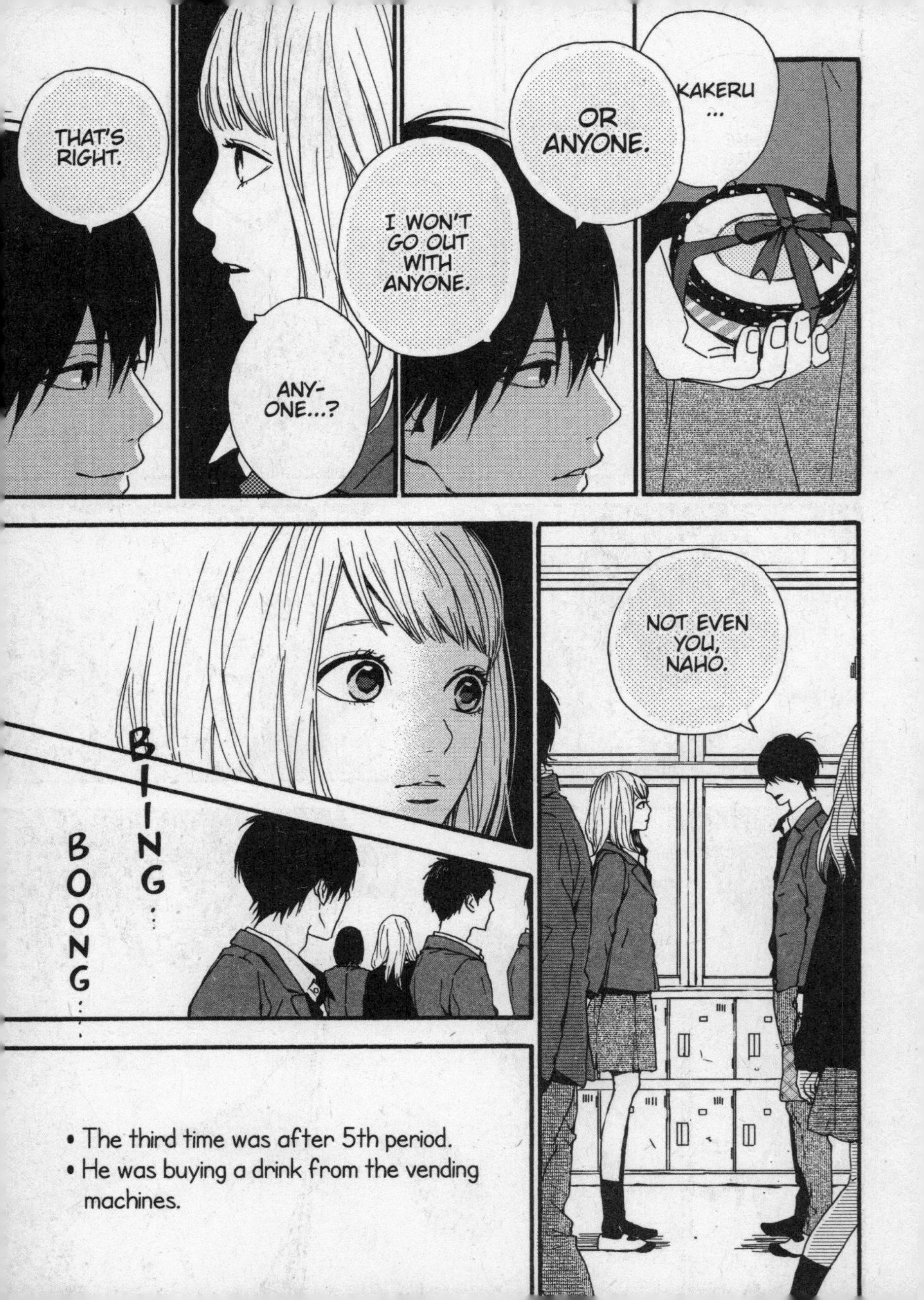
KAKERU ...
OR ANYONE.
I WON'T GO OUT WITH ANYONE.
ANY-ONE...?
THAT'S RIGHT.
NOT EVEN YOU, NAHO.
BING... BOONG...
• The third time was after 5th period.
• He was buying a drink from the vending machines.

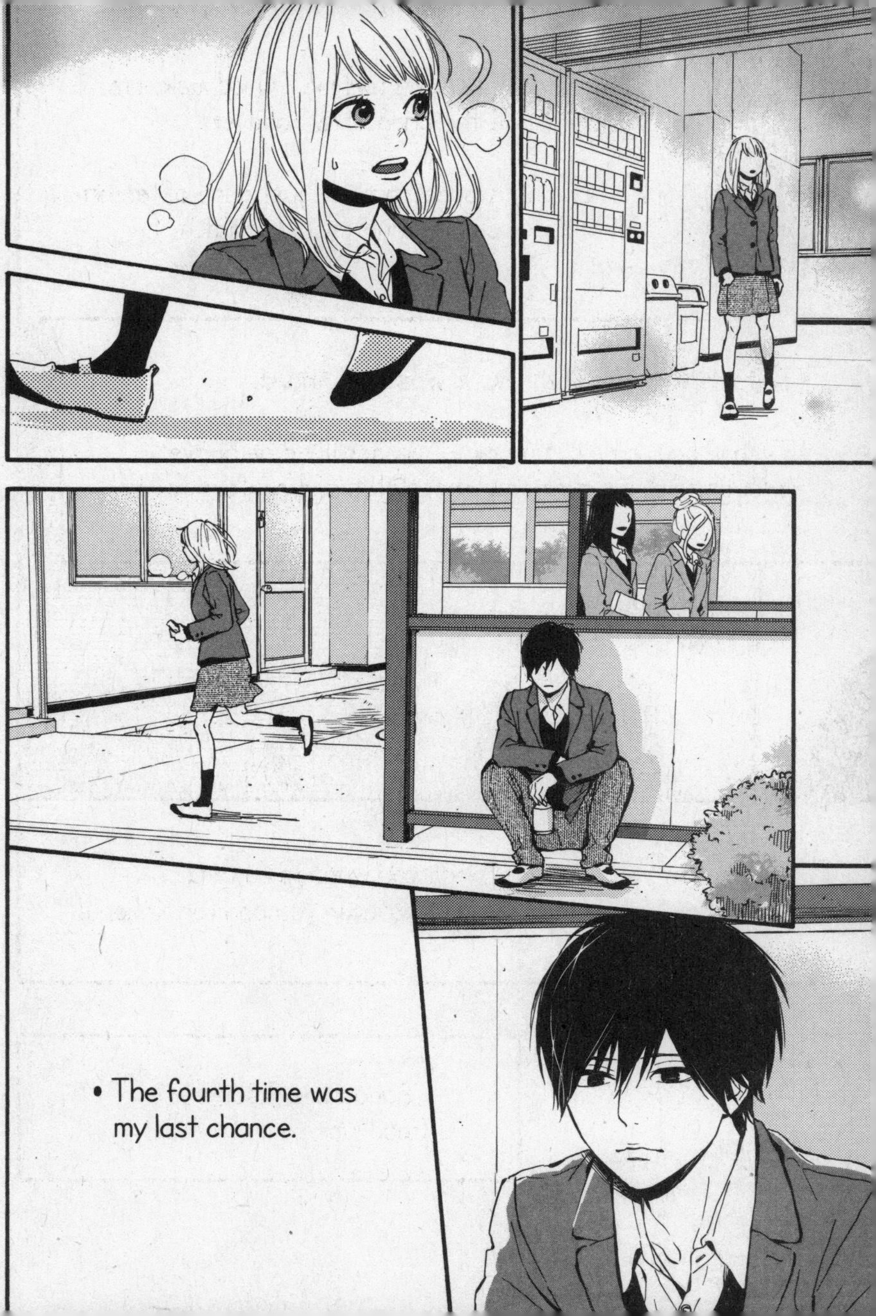
The fourth time was my last chance.

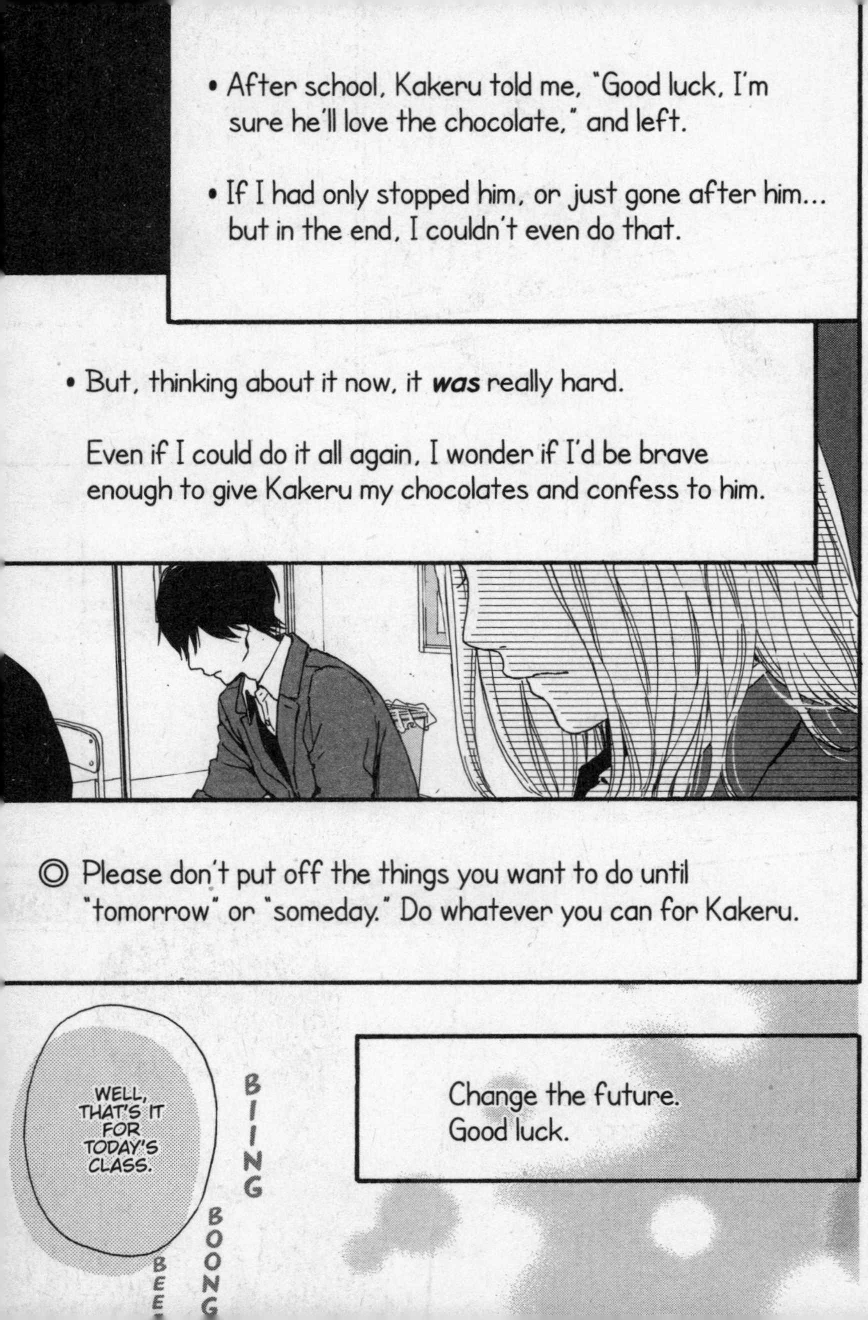

• After school, Kakeru told me, "Good luck, I'm sure he'll love the chocolate," and left.
• If I had only stopped him, or just gone after him... but in the end, I couldn't even do that.
• But, thinking about it now, it *was* really hard.
Even if I could do it all again, I wonder if I'd be brave enough to give Kakeru my chocolates and confess to him.
◎ Please don't put off the things you want to do until "tomorrow" or "someday." Do whatever you can for Kakeru.
Change the future.
Good luck.
BIING
WELL, THAT'S IT FOR TODAY'S CLASS.
BOONG
BEE

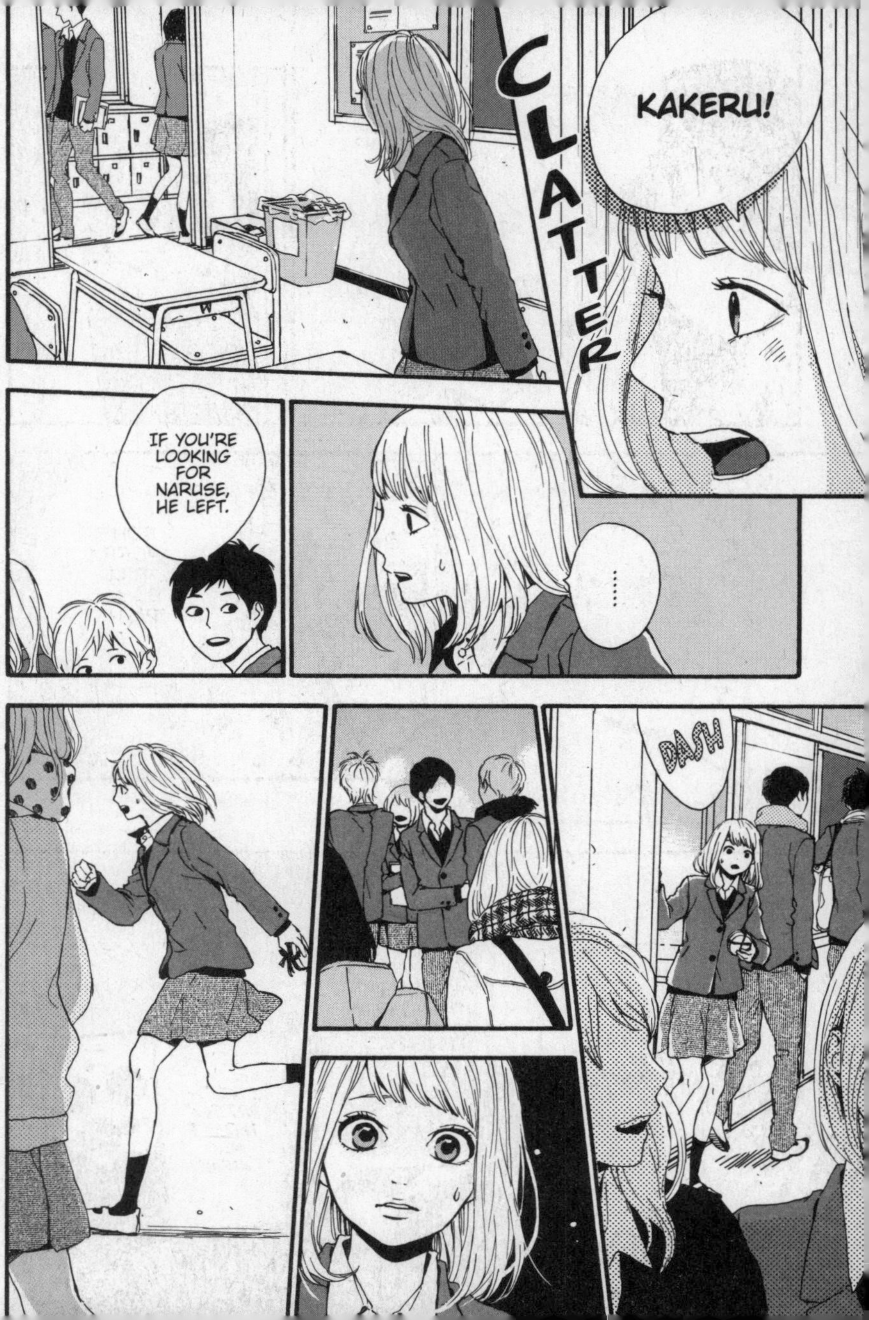
CLATTER
KAKERU!
……
IF YOU'RE LOOKING FOR NARUSE, HE LEFT.
DASH

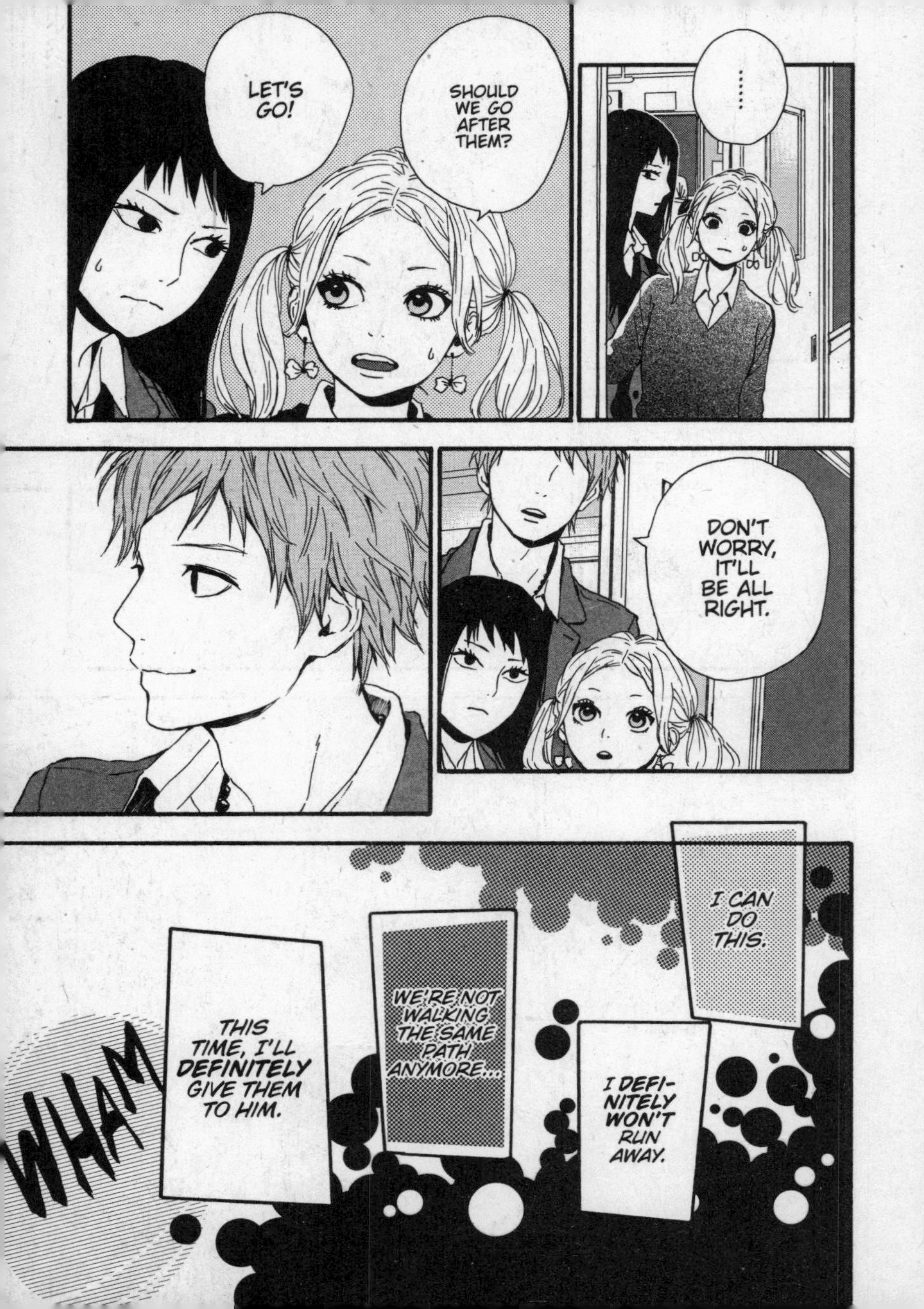
......
SHOULD WE GO AFTER THEM?
LET'S GO!
DON'T WORRY, IT'LL BE ALL RIGHT.
I CAN DO THIS.
I DEFINITELY WON'T RUN AWAY.
WE'RE NOT WALKING THE SAME PATH ANYMORE...
THIS TIME, I'LL DEFINITELY GIVE THEM TO HIM.
WHAM

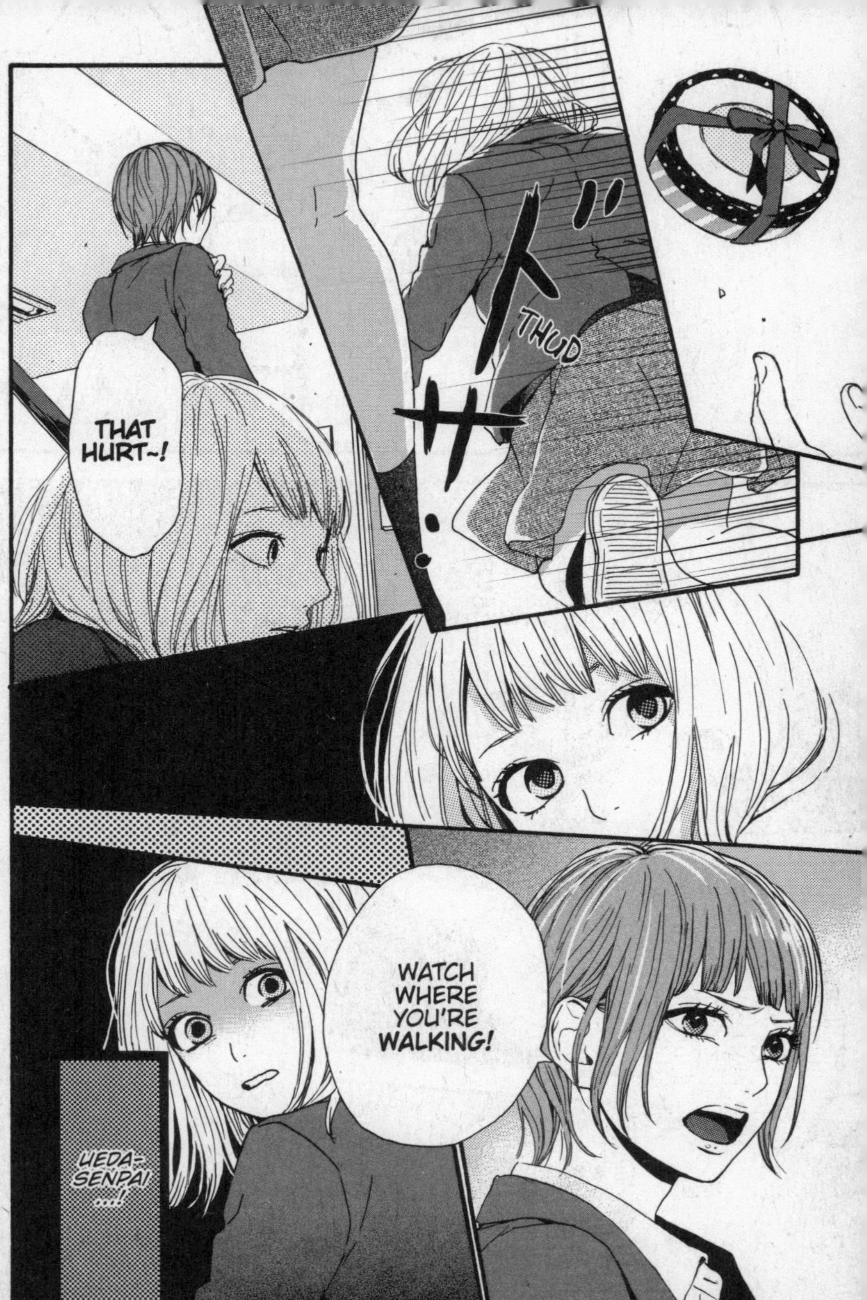
THUD
THAT HURT~!
WATCH WHERE YOU'RE WALKING!
UEDA-SENPAI...!

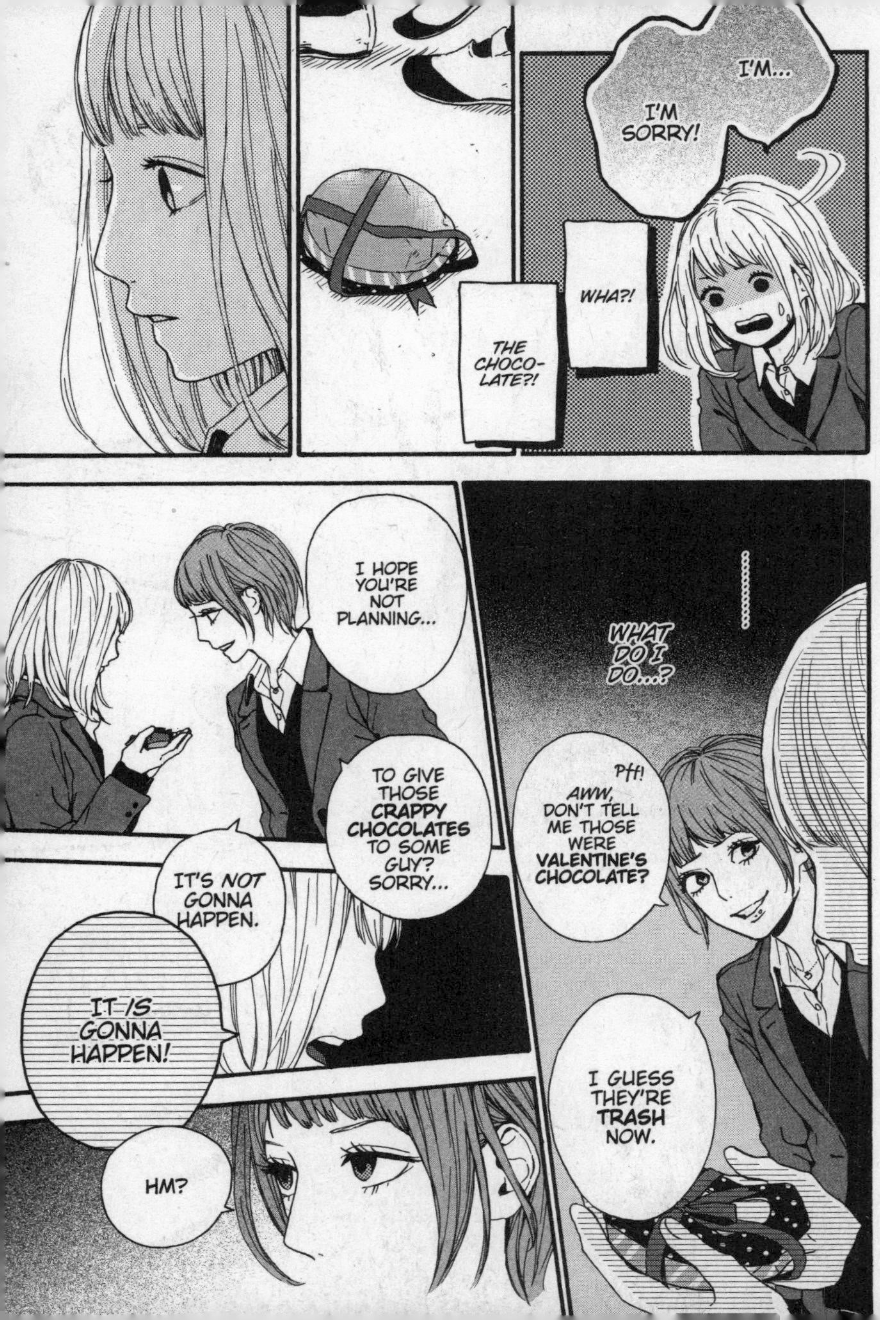
I'M...
I'M SORRY!
WHA?!
THE CHOCO-LATE?!
......
WHAT DO I DO...?
Pff!
AWW, DON'T TELL ME THOSE WERE VALENTINE'S CHOCOLATE?
I GUESS THEY'RE TRASH NOW.
I HOPE YOU'RE NOT PLANNING...
TO GIVE THOSE CRAPPY CHOCOLATES TO SOME GUY? SORRY...
IT'S NOT GONNA HAPPEN.
IT IS GONNA HAPPEN!
HM?

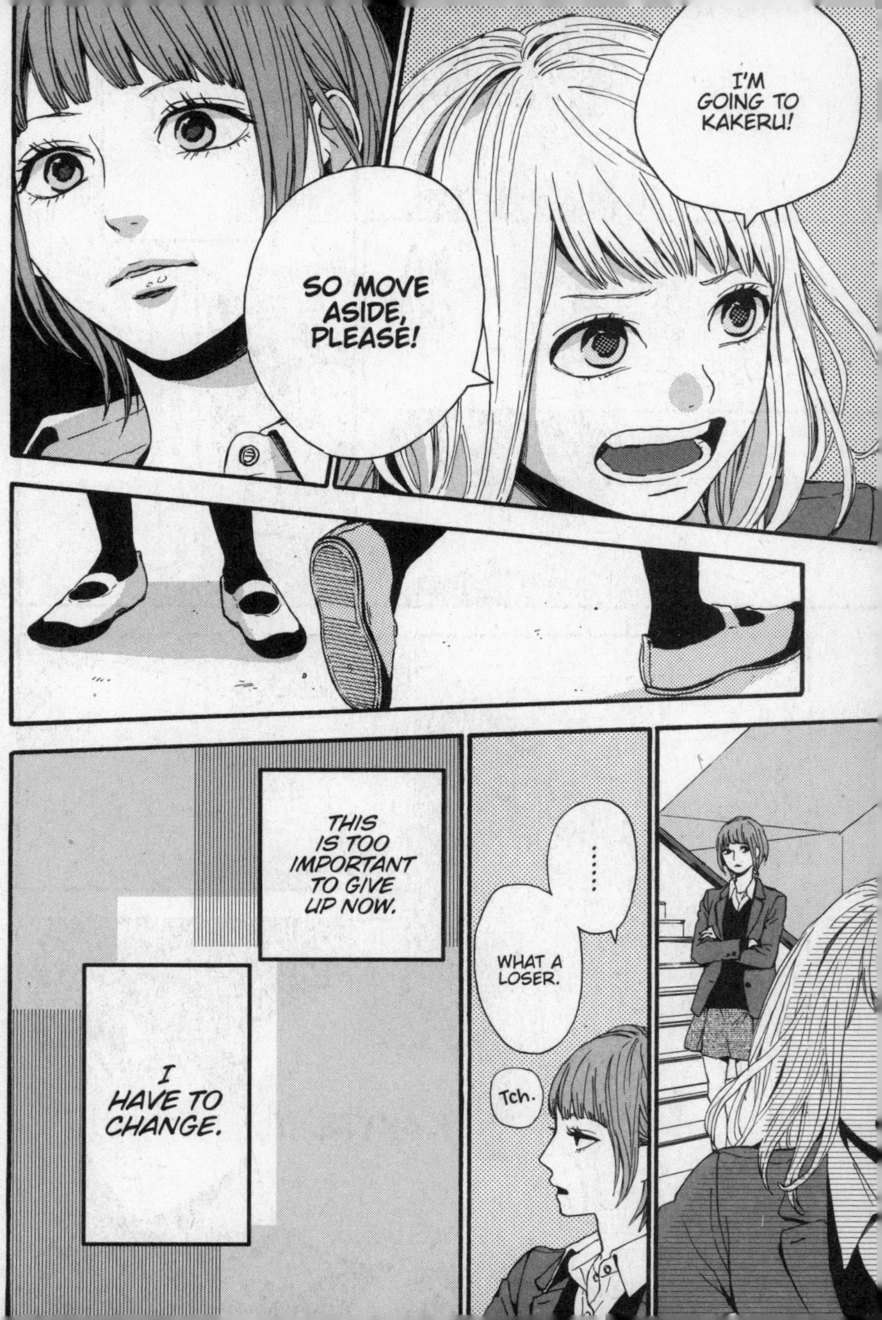
I'M GOING TO KAKERU!
SO MOVE ASIDE, PLEASE!
......
WHAT A LOSER.
Tch.
THIS IS TOO IMPORTANT TO GIVE UP NOW.
I HAVE TO CHANGE.

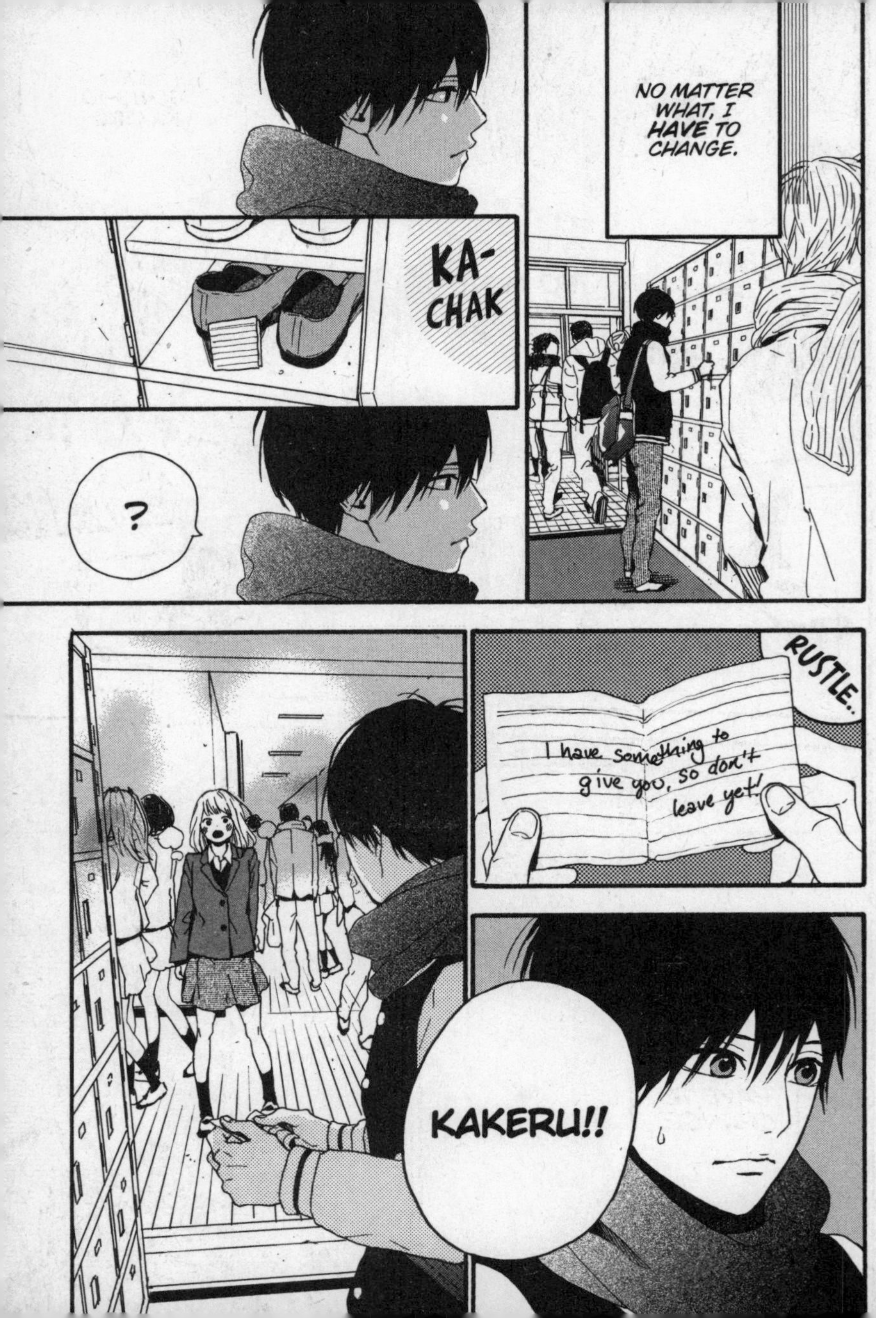
NO MATTER WHAT, I HAVE TO CHANGE.
KA-CHAK
?
RUSTLE...
I have something to give you, so don't leave yet!
KAKERU!!

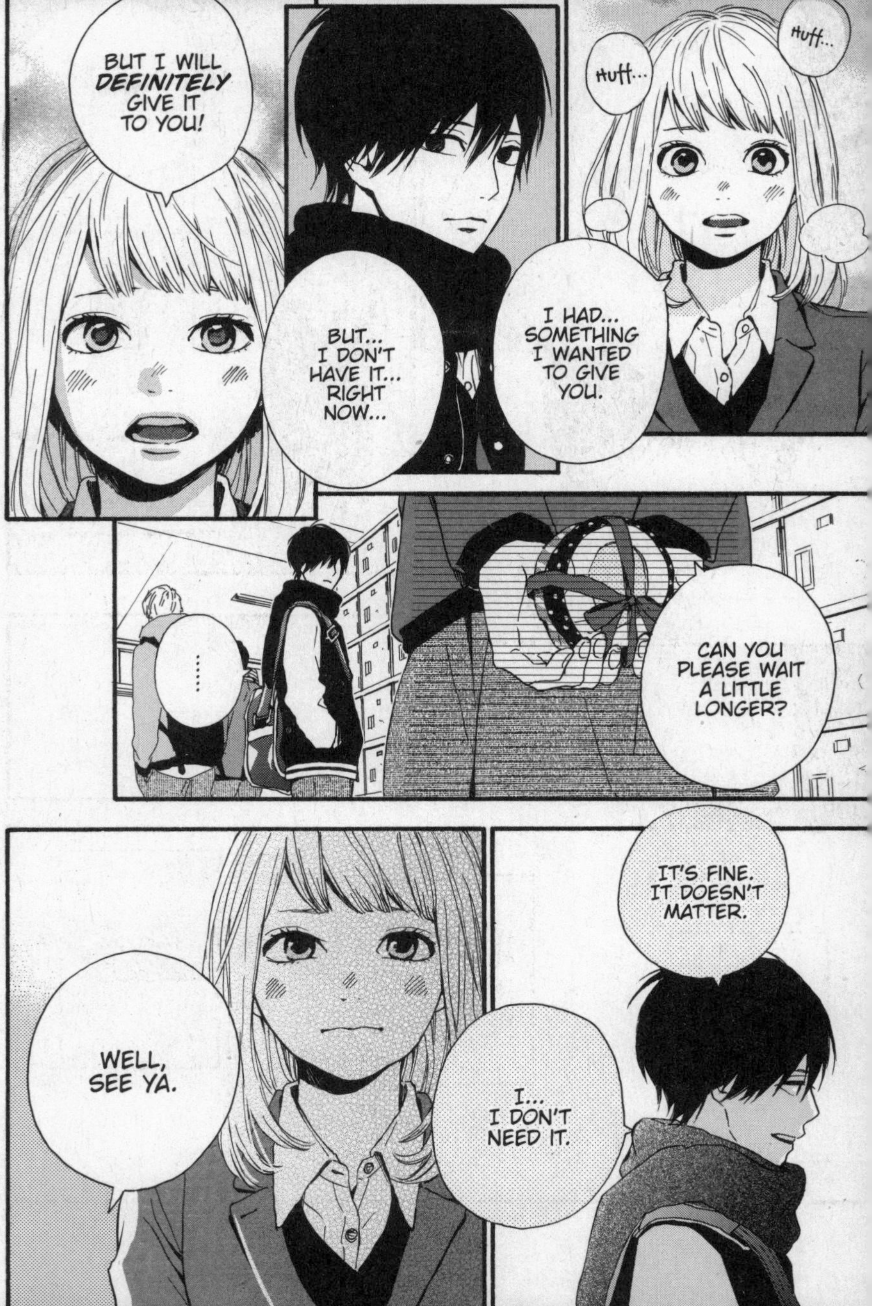
Huff...
Huff...
I HAD... SOMETHING I WANTED TO GIVE YOU.
BUT... I DON'T HAVE IT... RIGHT NOW...
BUT I WILL DEFINITELY GIVE IT TO YOU!
CAN YOU PLEASE WAIT A LITTLE LONGER?
......
IT'S FINE. IT DOESN'T MATTER.
I... I DON'T NEED IT.
WELL, SEE YA.

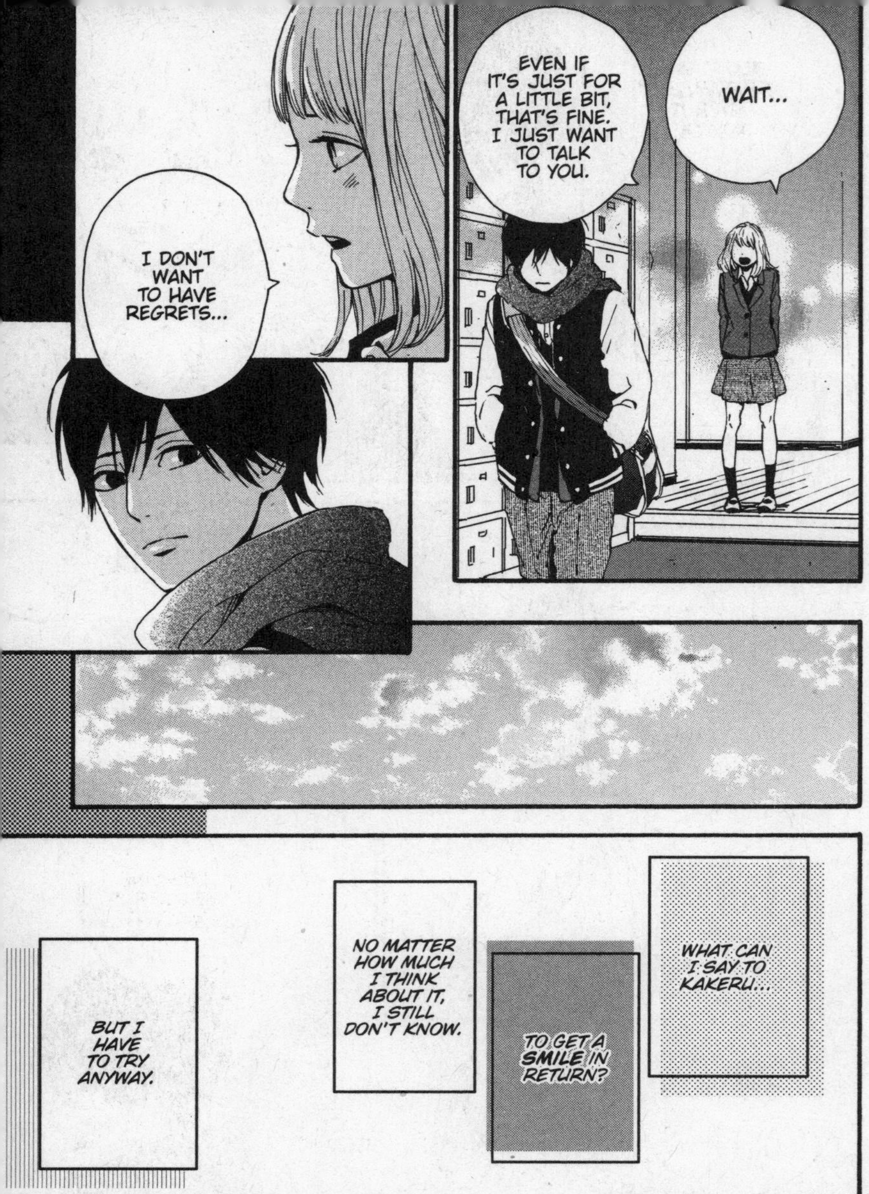
WAIT...
EVEN IF IT'S JUST FOR A LITTLE BIT, THAT'S FINE. I JUST WANT TO TALK TO YOU.
I DON'T WANT TO HAVE REGRETS...
WHAT CAN I SAY TO KAKERU...
TO GET A SMILE IN RETURN?
NO MATTER HOW MUCH I THINK ABOUT IT, I STILL DON'T KNOW.
BUT I HAVE TO TRY ANYWAY.

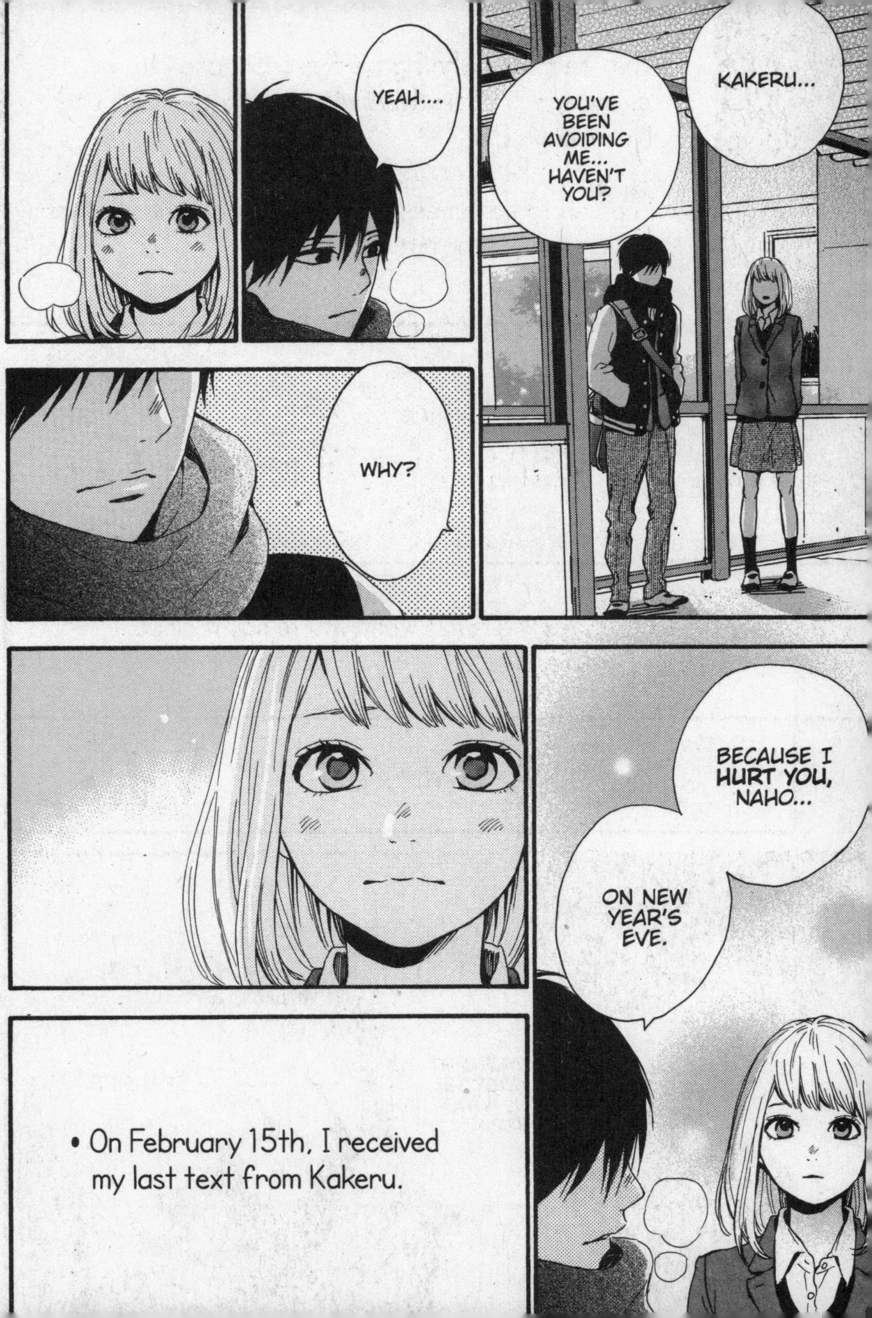
KAKERU...
YOU'VE BEEN AVOIDING ME... HAVEN'T YOU?
YEAH....
WHY?
BECAUSE I HURT YOU, NAHO...
ON NEW YEAR'S EVE.
• On February 15th, I received my last text from Kakeru.

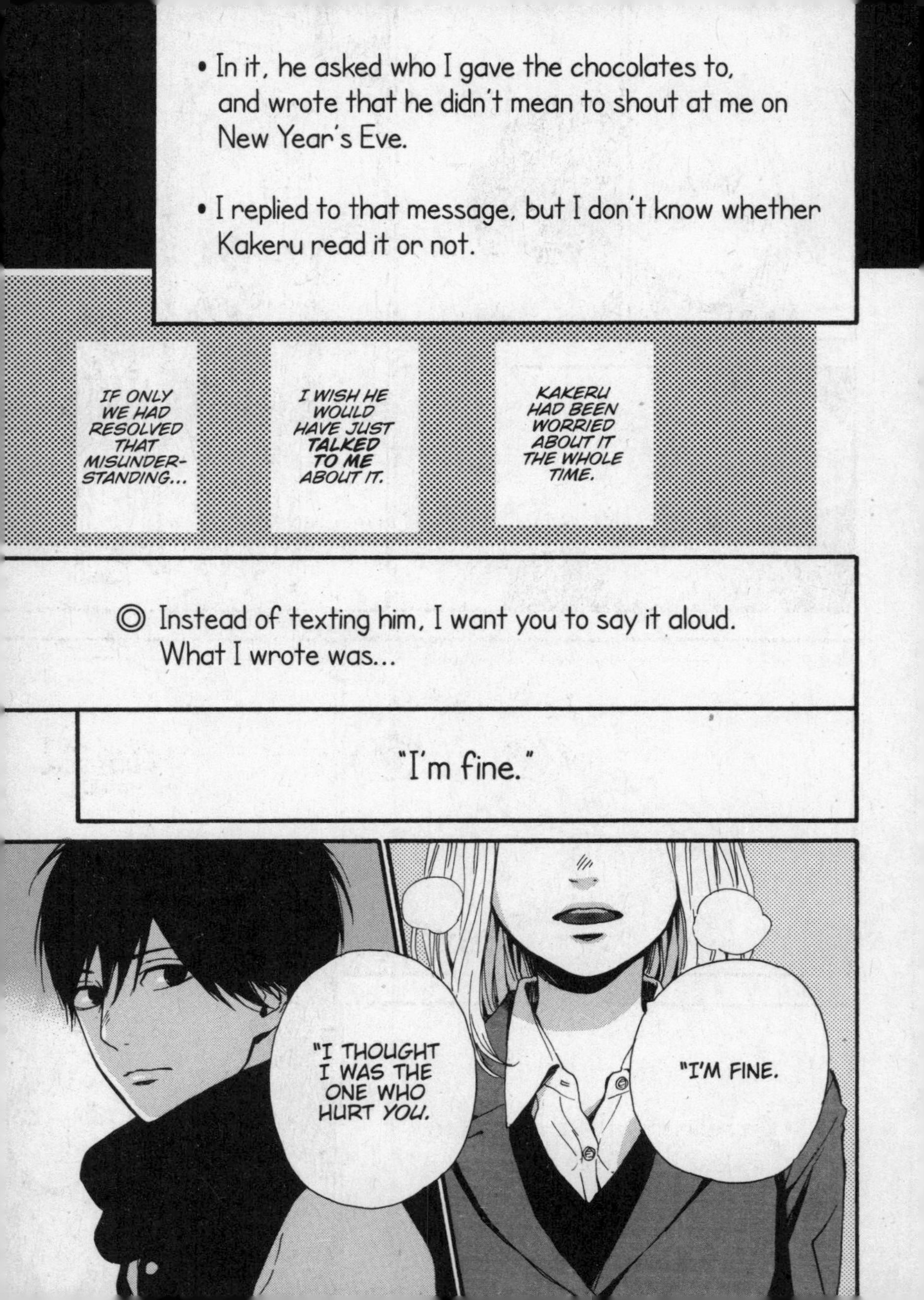
• In it, he asked who I gave the chocolates to, and wrote that he didn't mean to shout at me on New Year's Eve.
• I replied to that message, but I don't know whether Kakeru read it or not.
KAKERU HAD BEEN WORRIED ABOUT IT THE WHOLE TIME.
I WISH HE WOULD HAVE JUST TALKED TO ME ABOUT IT.
IF ONLY WE HAD RESOLVED THAT MISUNDERSTANDING...
◎ Instead of texting him, I want you to say it aloud. What I wrote was...
"I'm fine."
"I'M FINE.
"I THOUGHT I WAS THE ONE WHO HURT *YOU*.

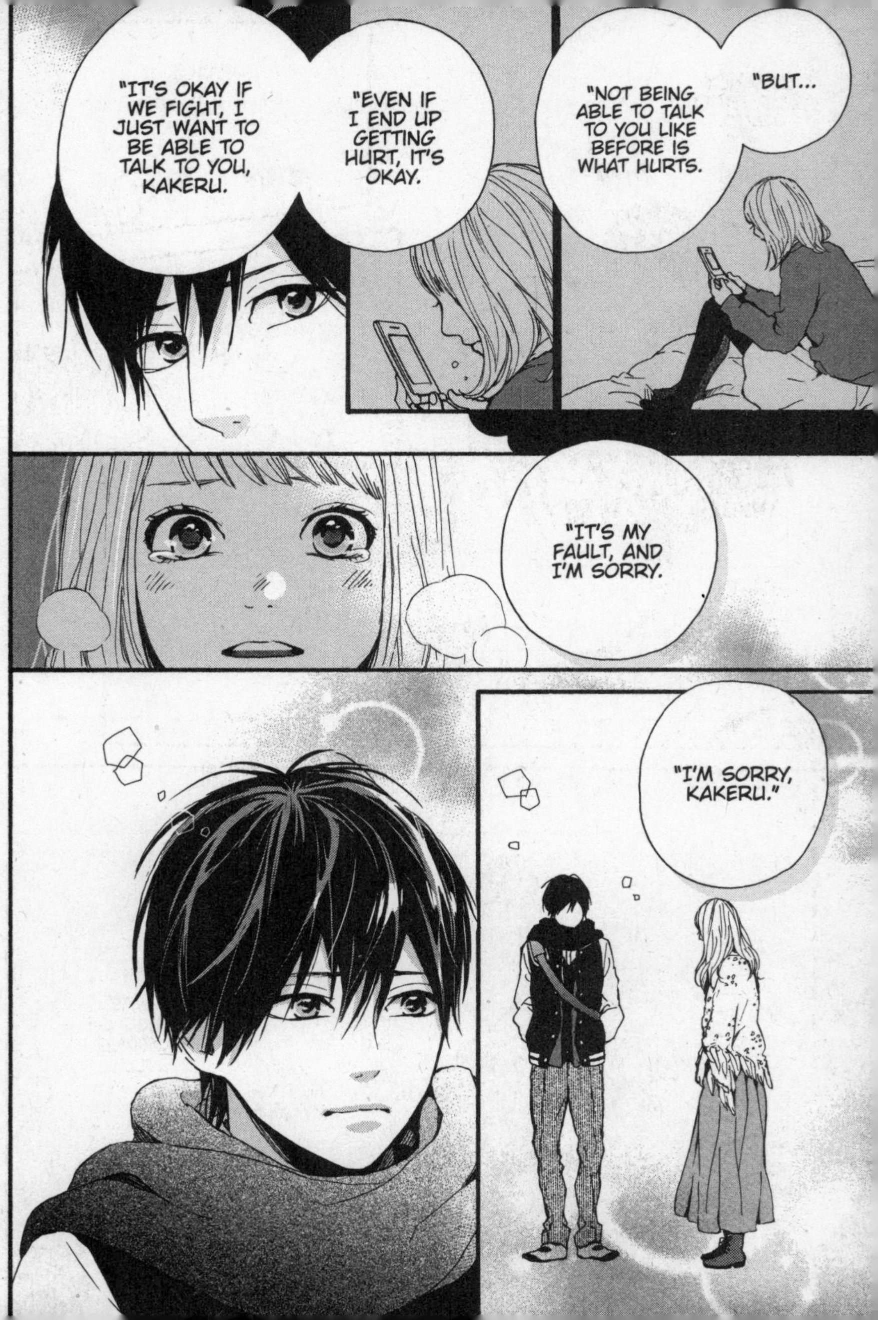

"BUT...
"NOT BEING ABLE TO TALK TO YOU LIKE BEFORE IS WHAT HURTS.
"EVEN IF I END UP GETTING HURT, IT'S OKAY.
"IT'S OKAY IF WE FIGHT, I JUST WANT TO BE ABLE TO TALK TO YOU, KAKERU.
"IT'S MY FAULT, AND I'M SORRY.
"I'M SORRY, KAKERU."

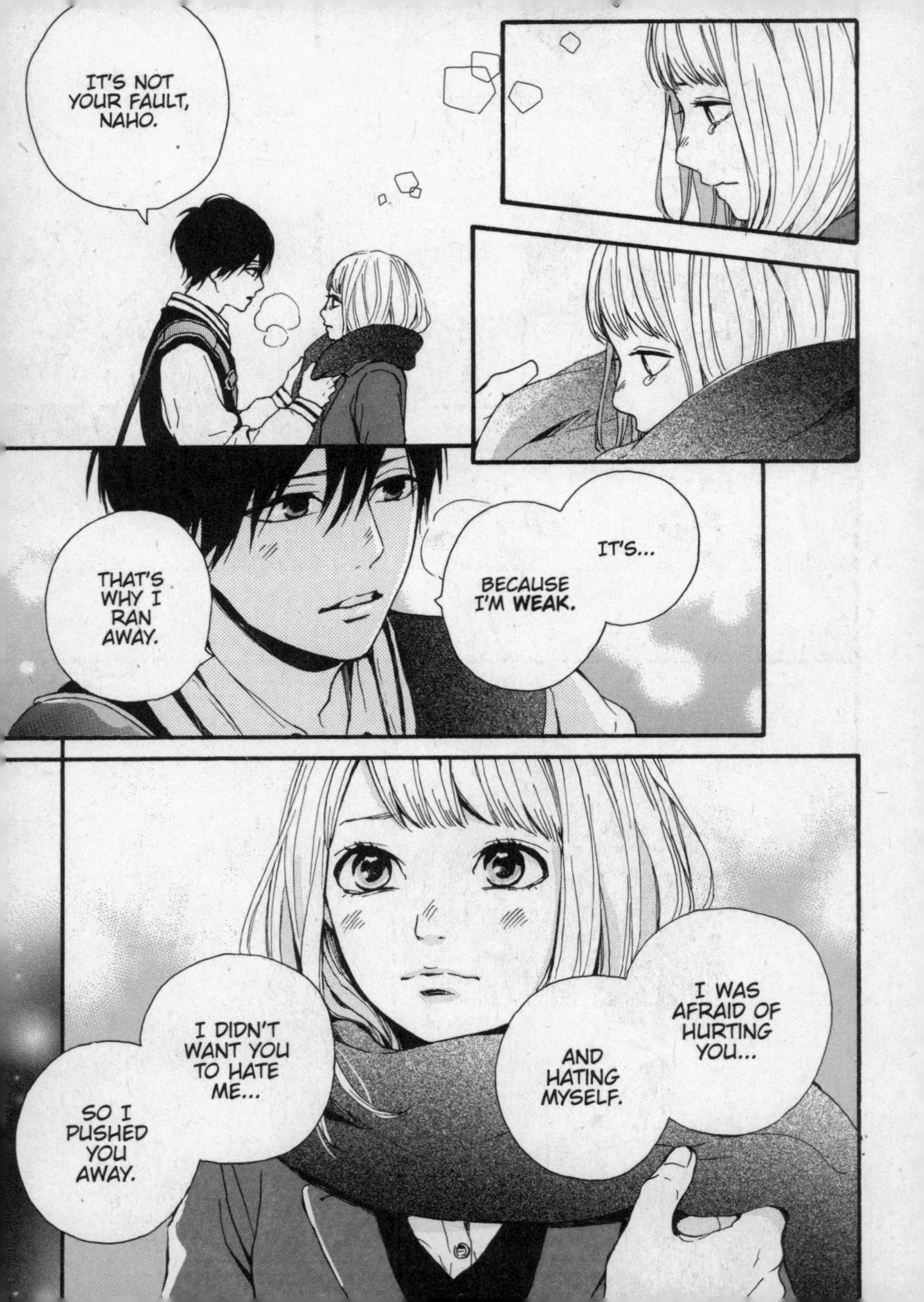
IT'S NOT YOUR FAULT, NAHO.
IT'S... BECAUSE I'M **WEAK.**
THAT'S WHY I RAN AWAY.
I WAS AFRAID OF HURTING YOU...
AND HATING MYSELF.
I DIDN'T WANT YOU TO HATE ME...
SO I PUSHED YOU AWAY.

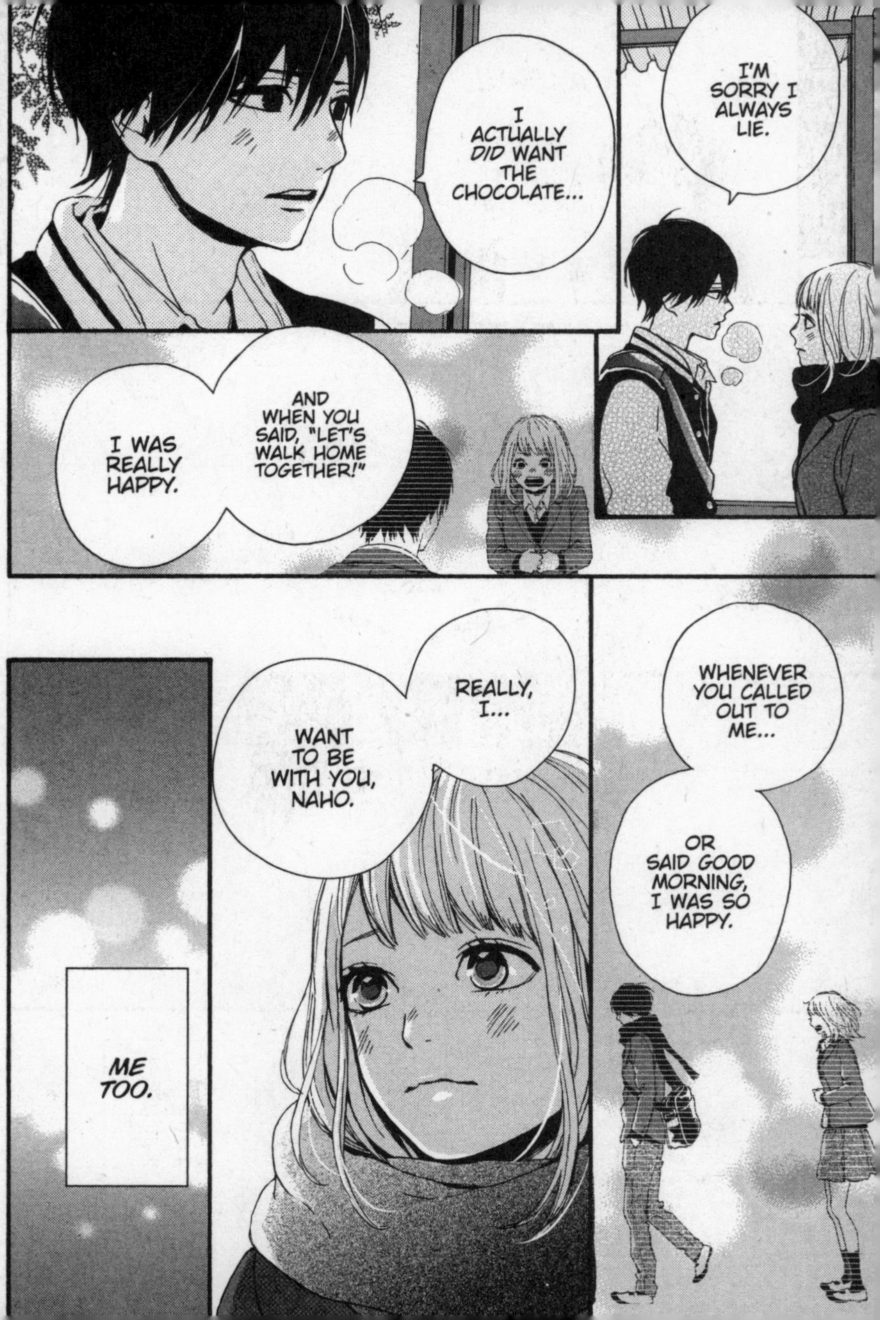
I'M SORRY I ALWAYS LIE.
I ACTUALLY *DID* WANT THE CHOCOLATE...
AND WHEN YOU SAID, "LET'S WALK HOME TOGETHER!"
I WAS REALLY HAPPY.
WHENEVER YOU CALLED OUT TO ME...
OR SAID GOOD MORNING, I WAS SO HAPPY.
REALLY, I...
WANT TO BE WITH YOU, NAHO.
ME TOO.

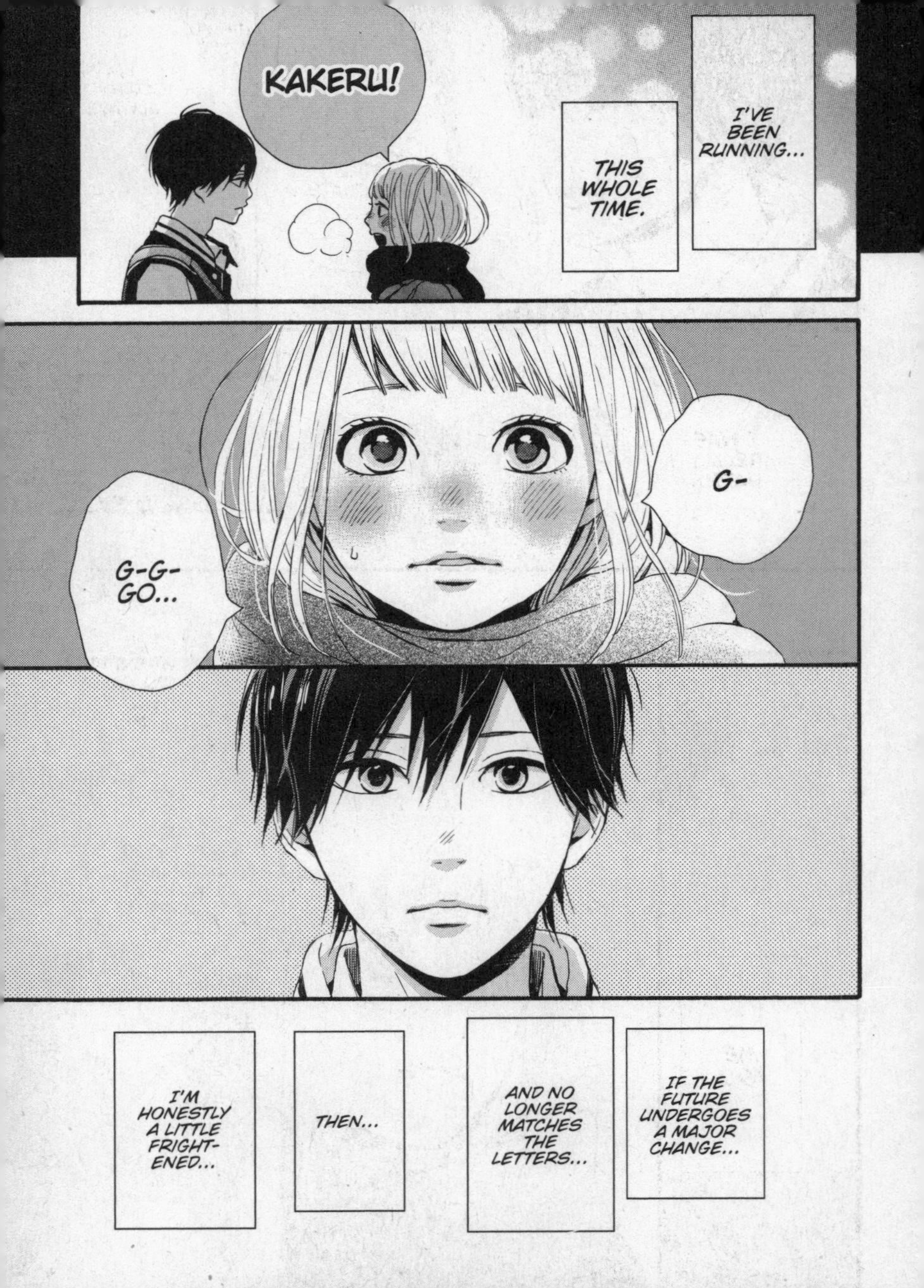
I'VE BEEN RUNNING...
THIS WHOLE TIME.
KAKERU!
G-
G-G-GO...
IF THE FUTURE UNDERGOES A MAJOR CHANGE...
AND NO LONGER MATCHES THE LETTERS...
THEN...
I'M HONESTLY A LITTLE FRIGHT-ENED...

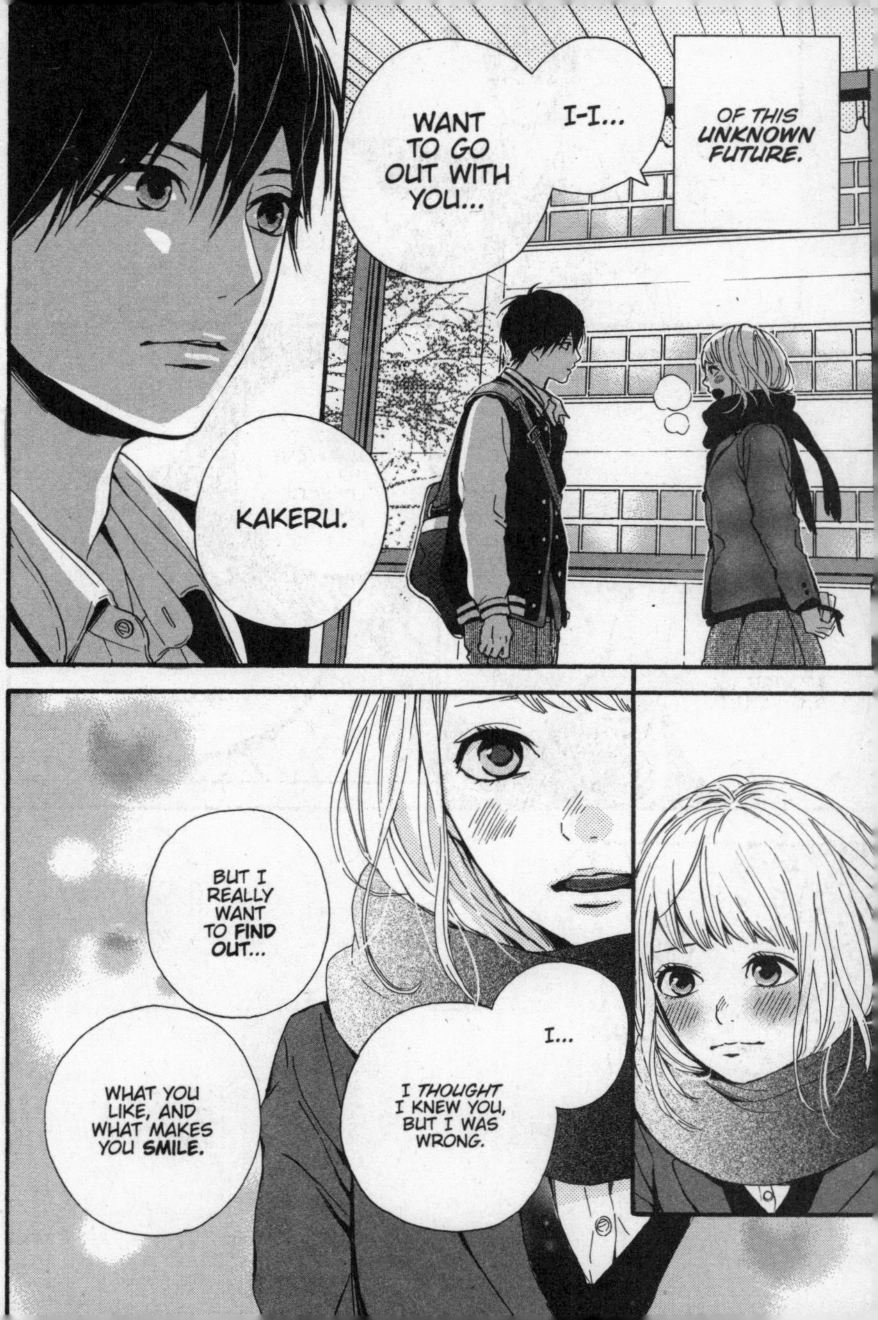
OF THIS UNKNOWN FUTURE.
I-I...
WANT TO GO OUT WITH YOU...
KAKERU.
I...
I *THOUGHT* I KNEW YOU, BUT I WAS WRONG.
BUT I REALLY WANT TO **FIND** OUT...
WHAT YOU LIKE, AND WHAT MAKES YOU **SMILE**.

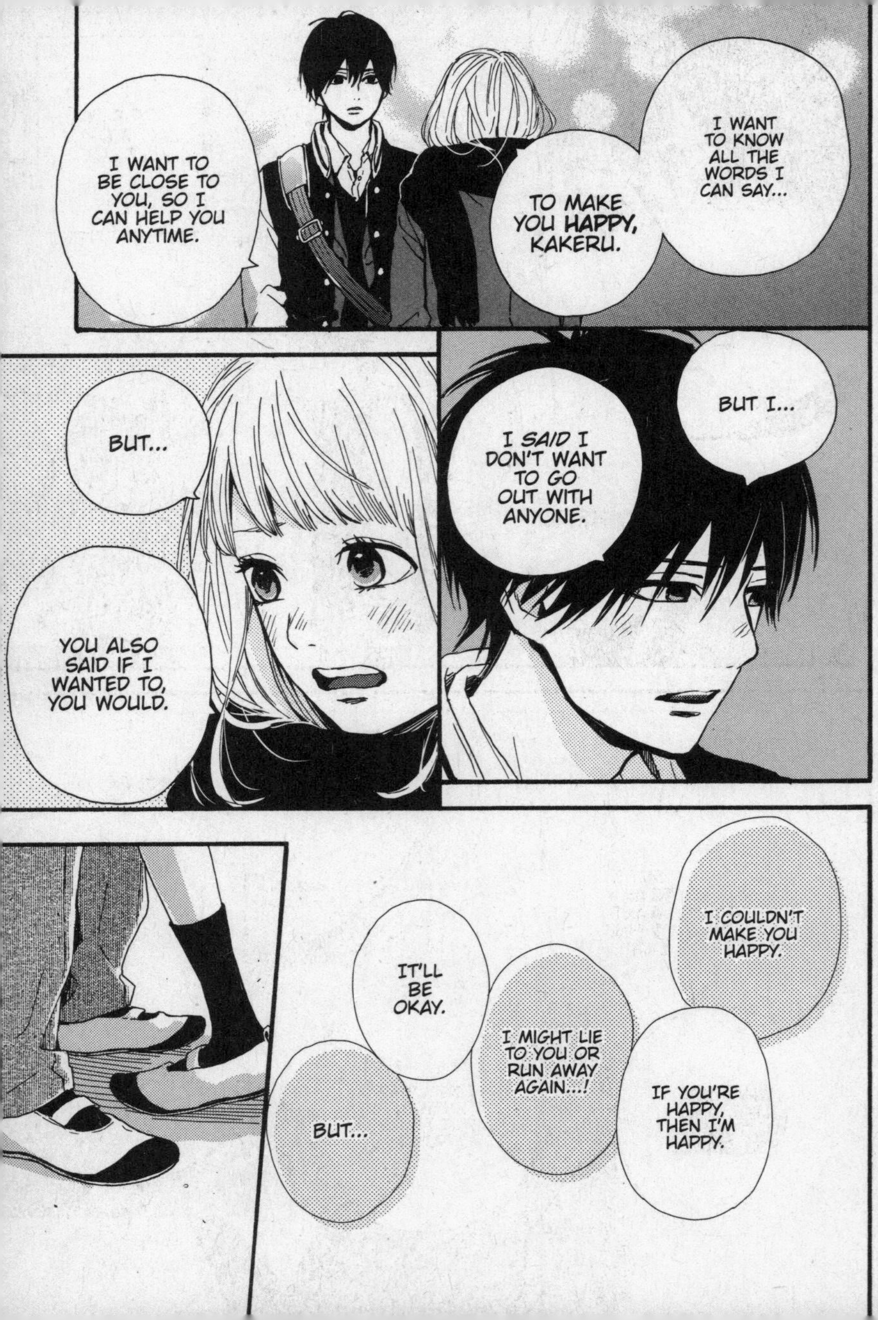
I WANT TO KNOW ALL THE WORDS I CAN SAY...
TO MAKE YOU **HAPPY**, KAKERU.
I WANT TO BE CLOSE TO YOU, SO I CAN HELP YOU ANYTIME.
BUT I...
I *SAID* I DON'T WANT TO GO OUT WITH ANYONE.
BUT...
YOU ALSO SAID IF I WANTED TO, YOU WOULD.
I COULDN'T MAKE YOU HAPPY.
IF YOU'RE HAPPY, THEN I'M HAPPY.
I MIGHT LIE TO YOU OR RUN AWAY AGAIN...!
IT'LL BE OKAY.
BUT...

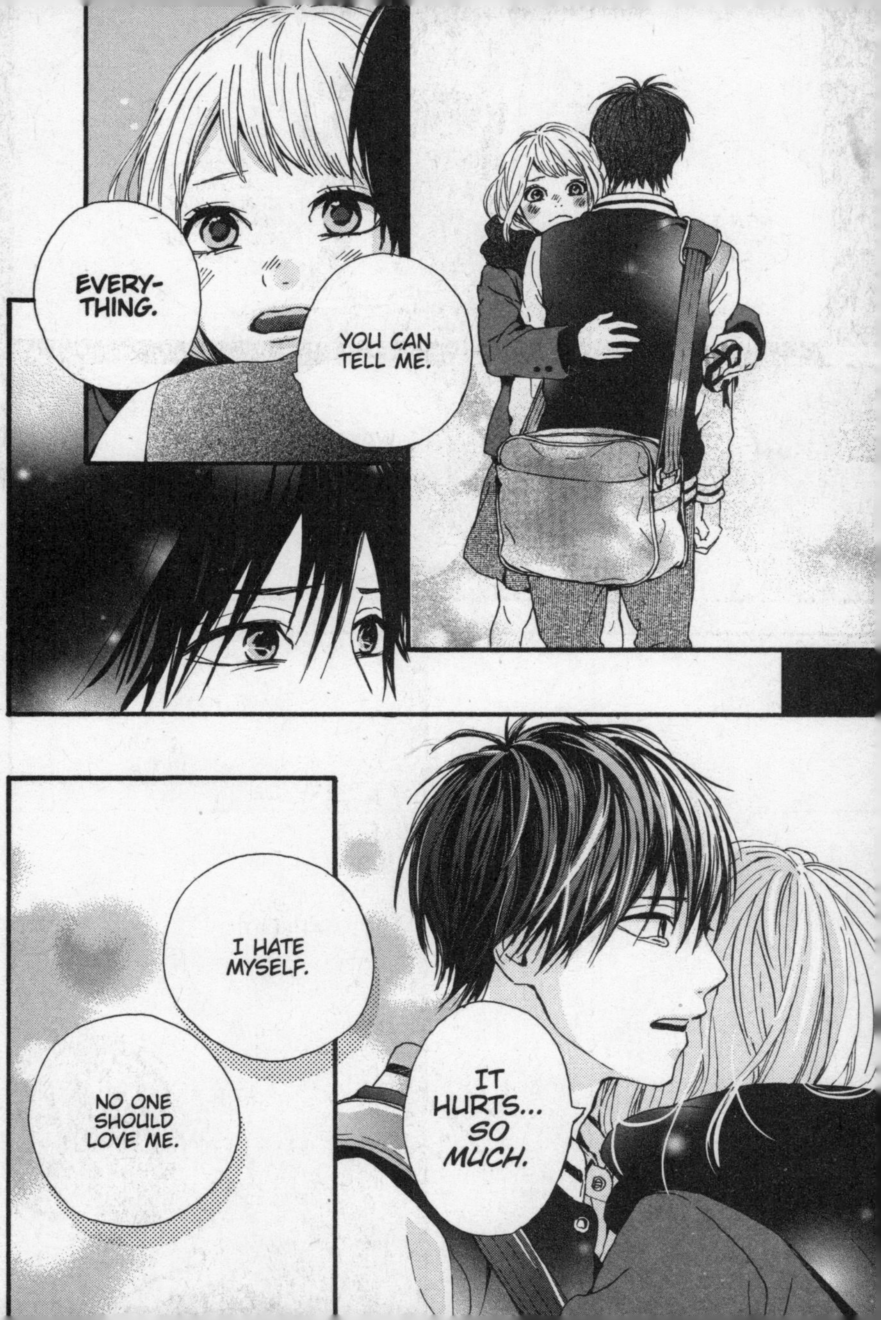
YOU CAN TELL ME.
EVERYTHING.
IT HURTS... SO MUCH.
I HATE MYSELF.
NO ONE SHOULD LOVE ME.

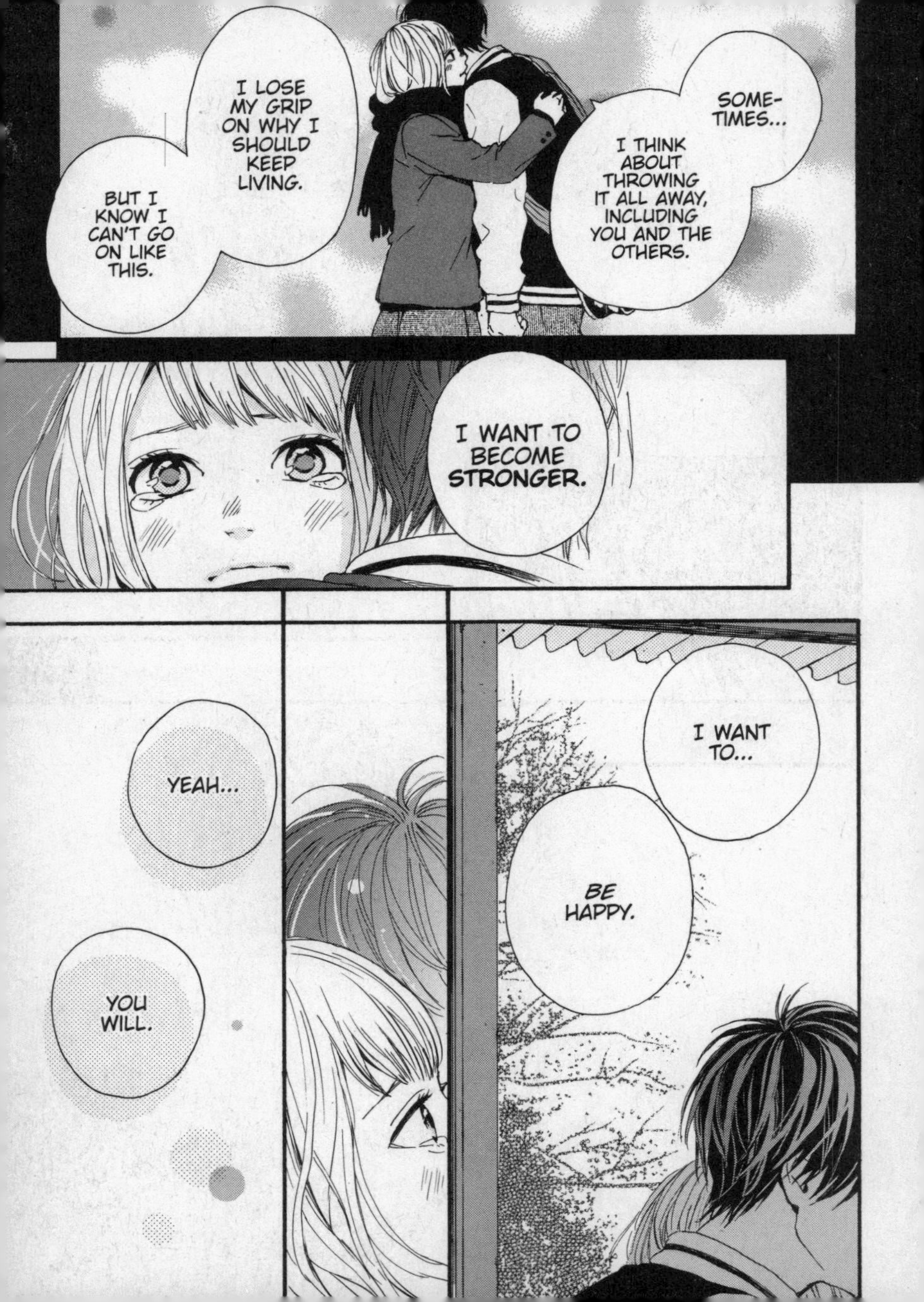
SOME-TIMES...
I THINK ABOUT THROWING IT ALL AWAY, INCLUDING YOU AND THE OTHERS.
I LOSE MY GRIP ON WHY I SHOULD KEEP LIVING.
BUT I KNOW I CAN'T GO ON LIKE THIS.
I WANT TO BECOME STRONGER.
I WANT TO...
BE HAPPY.
YEAH...
YOU WILL.

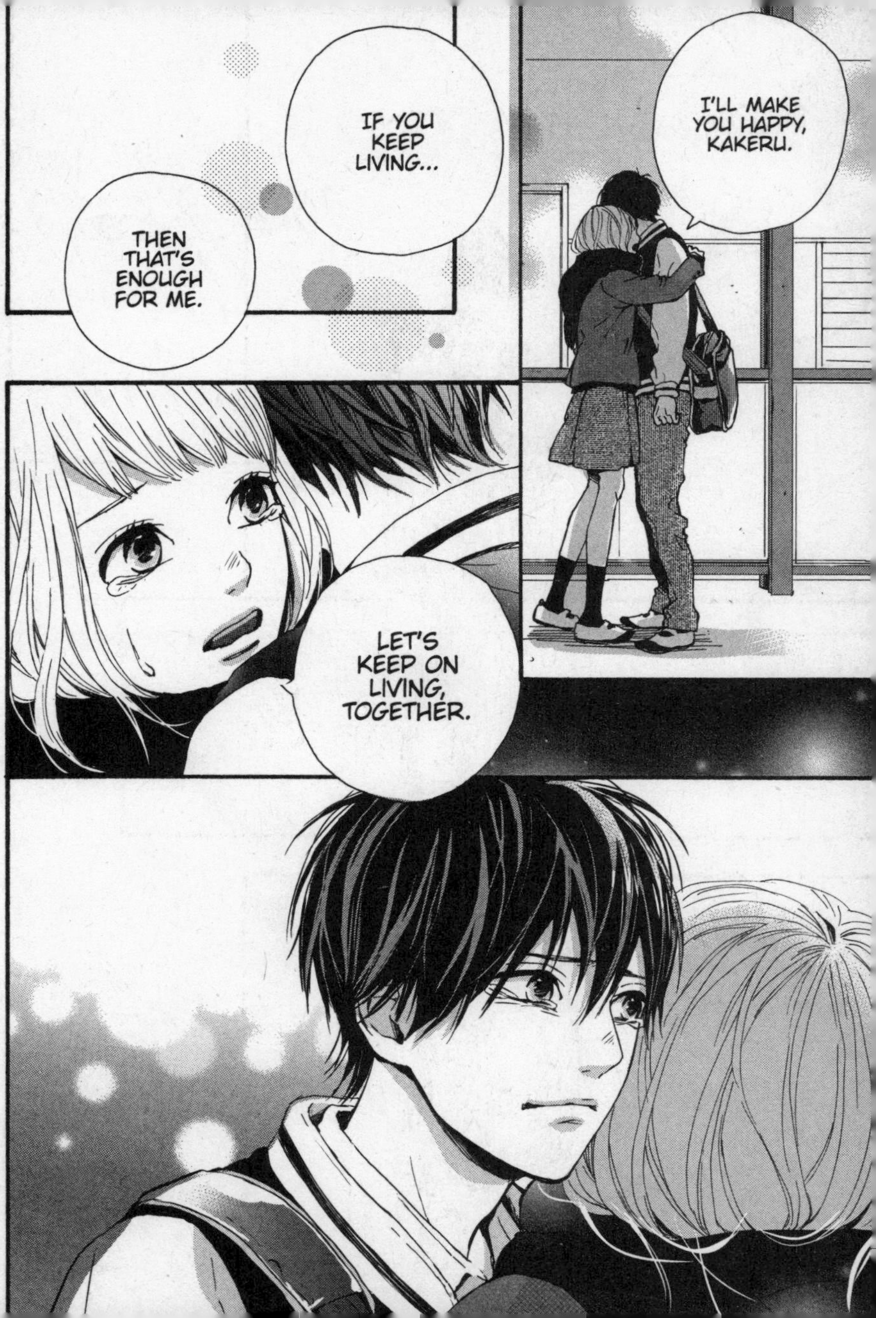
I'LL MAKE YOU HAPPY, KAKERU.
IF YOU KEEP LIVING...
THEN THAT'S ENOUGH FOR ME.
LET'S KEEP ON LIVING, TOGETHER.

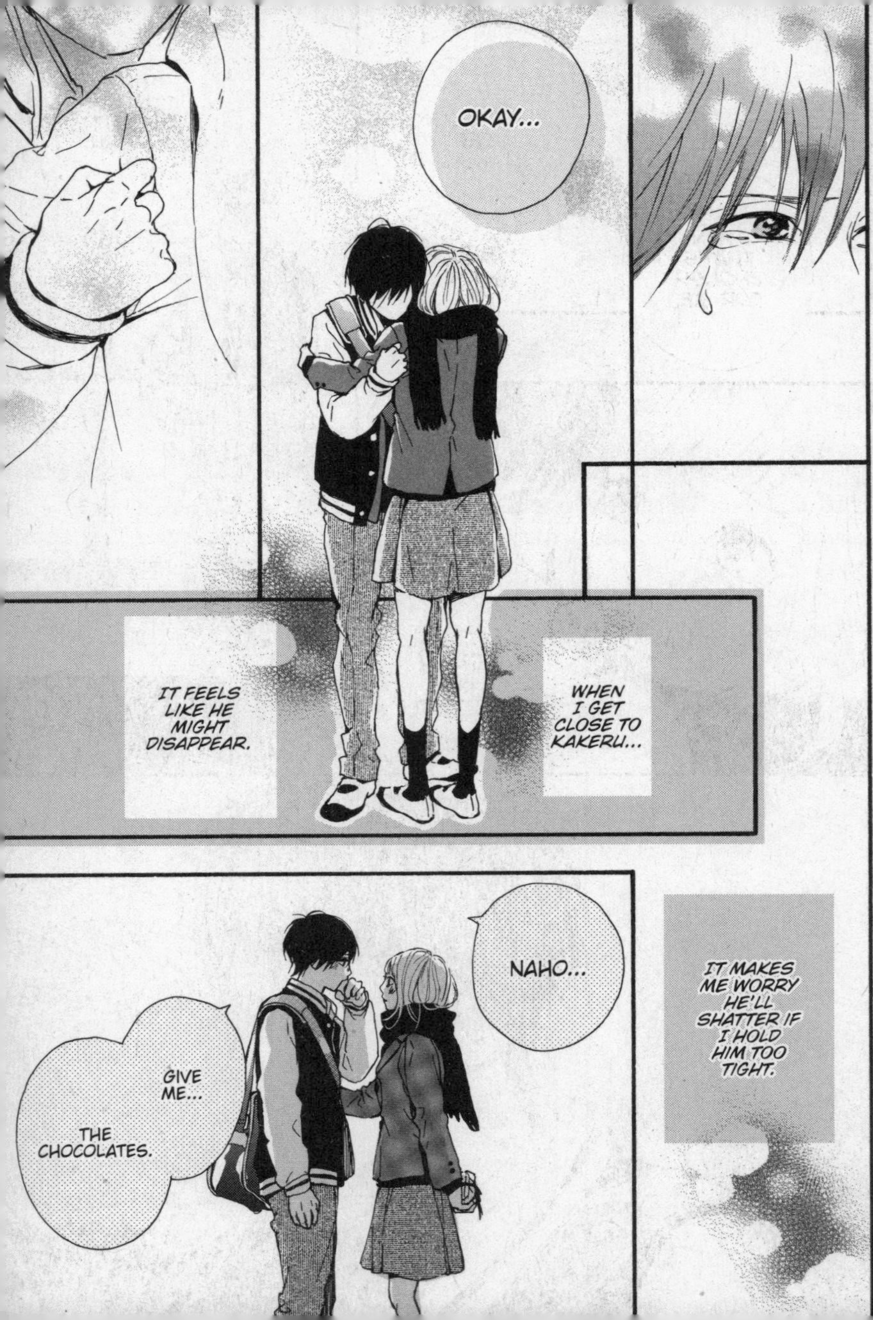
OKAY...
WHEN I GET CLOSE TO KAKERU...
IT FEELS LIKE HE MIGHT DISAPPEAR.
IT MAKES ME WORRY HE'LL SHATTER IF I HOLD HIM TOO TIGHT.
NAHO...
GIVE ME...
THE CHOCOLATES.

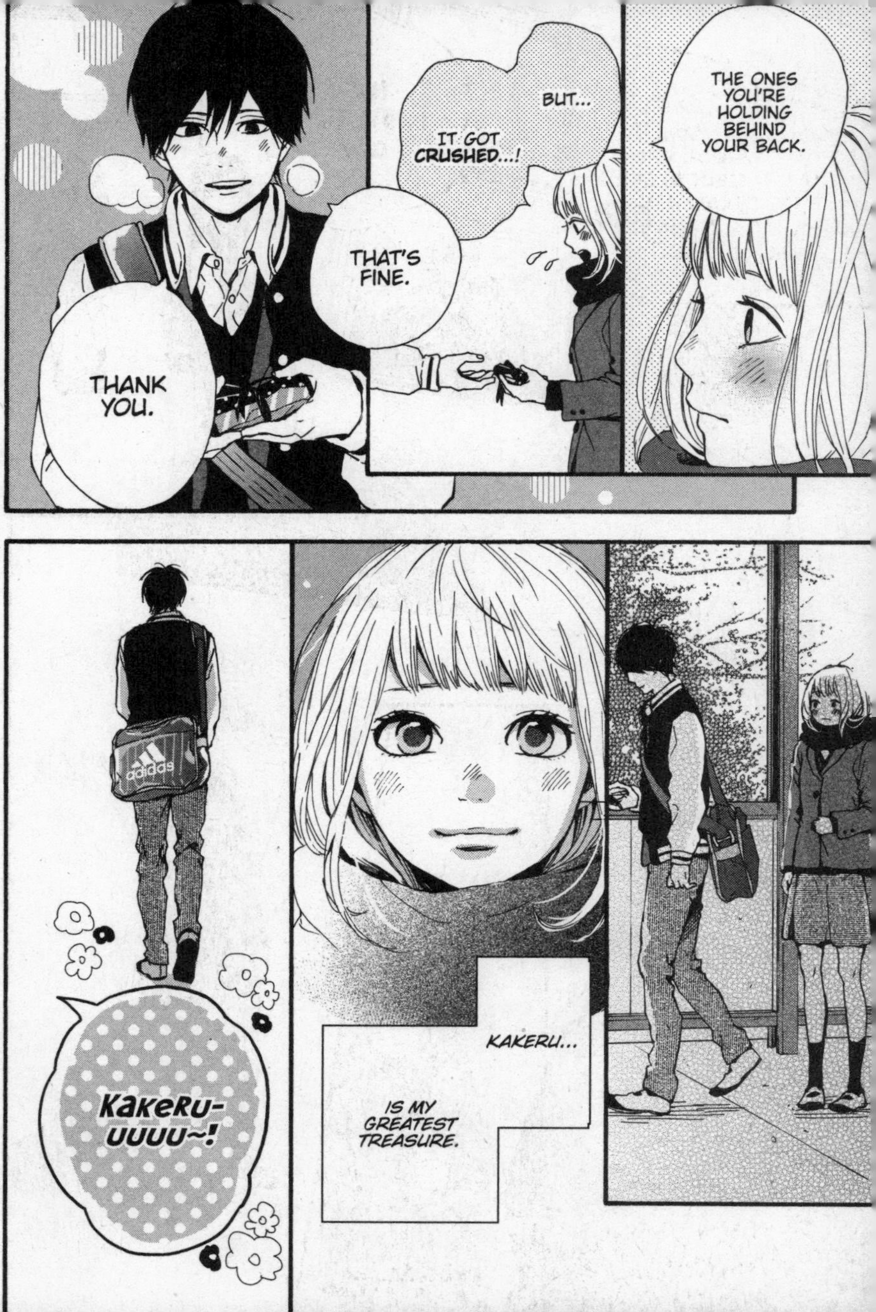
THE ONES YOU'RE HOLDING BEHIND YOUR BACK.
BUT...
IT GOT CRUSHED...!
THAT'S FINE.
THANK YOU.
KAKERU...
IS MY GREATEST TREASURE.
KaKeRu-uuuu~!

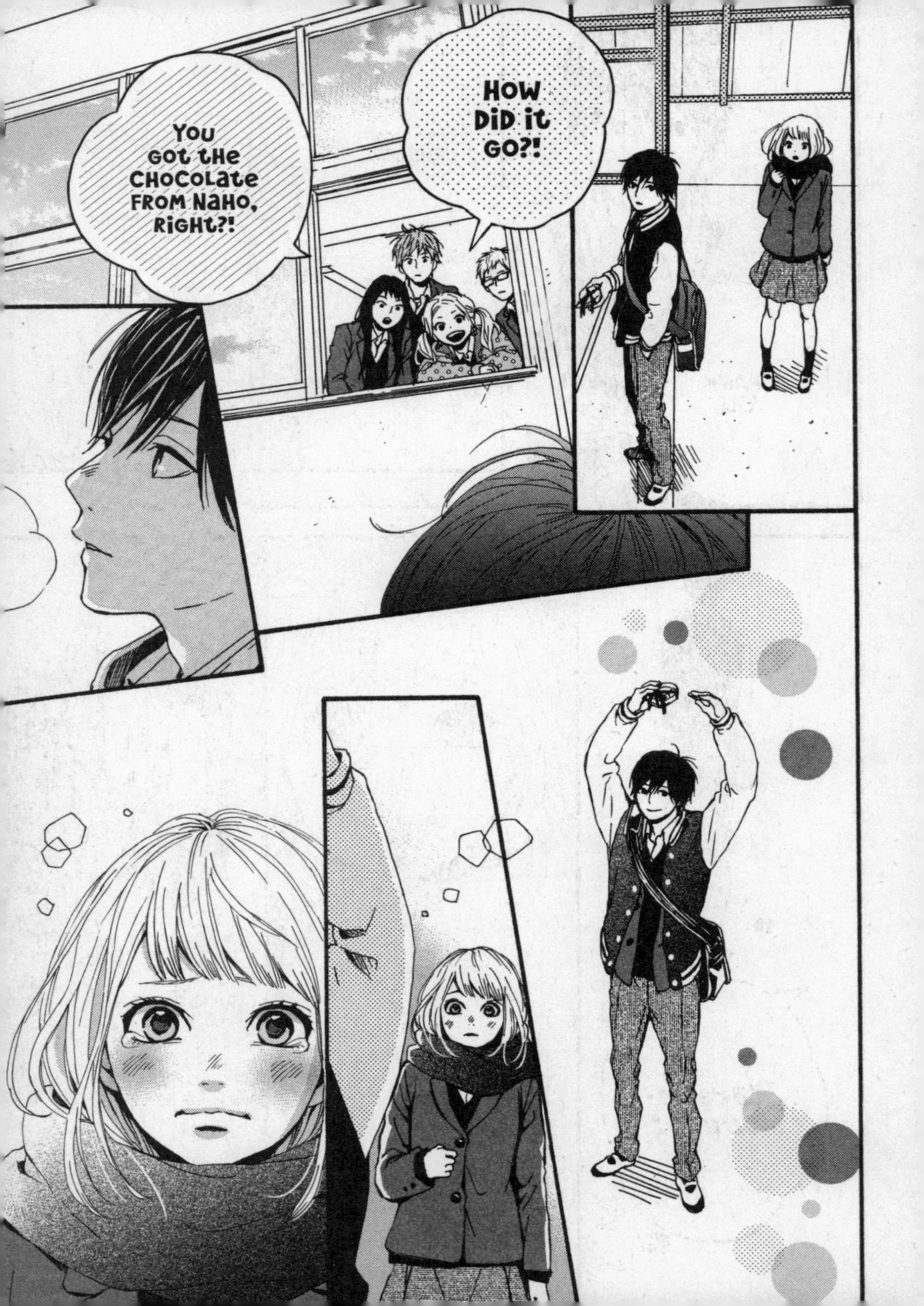
HOW DID IT GO?!
YOU GOT THE CHOCOLATE FROM NAHO, RIGHT?!

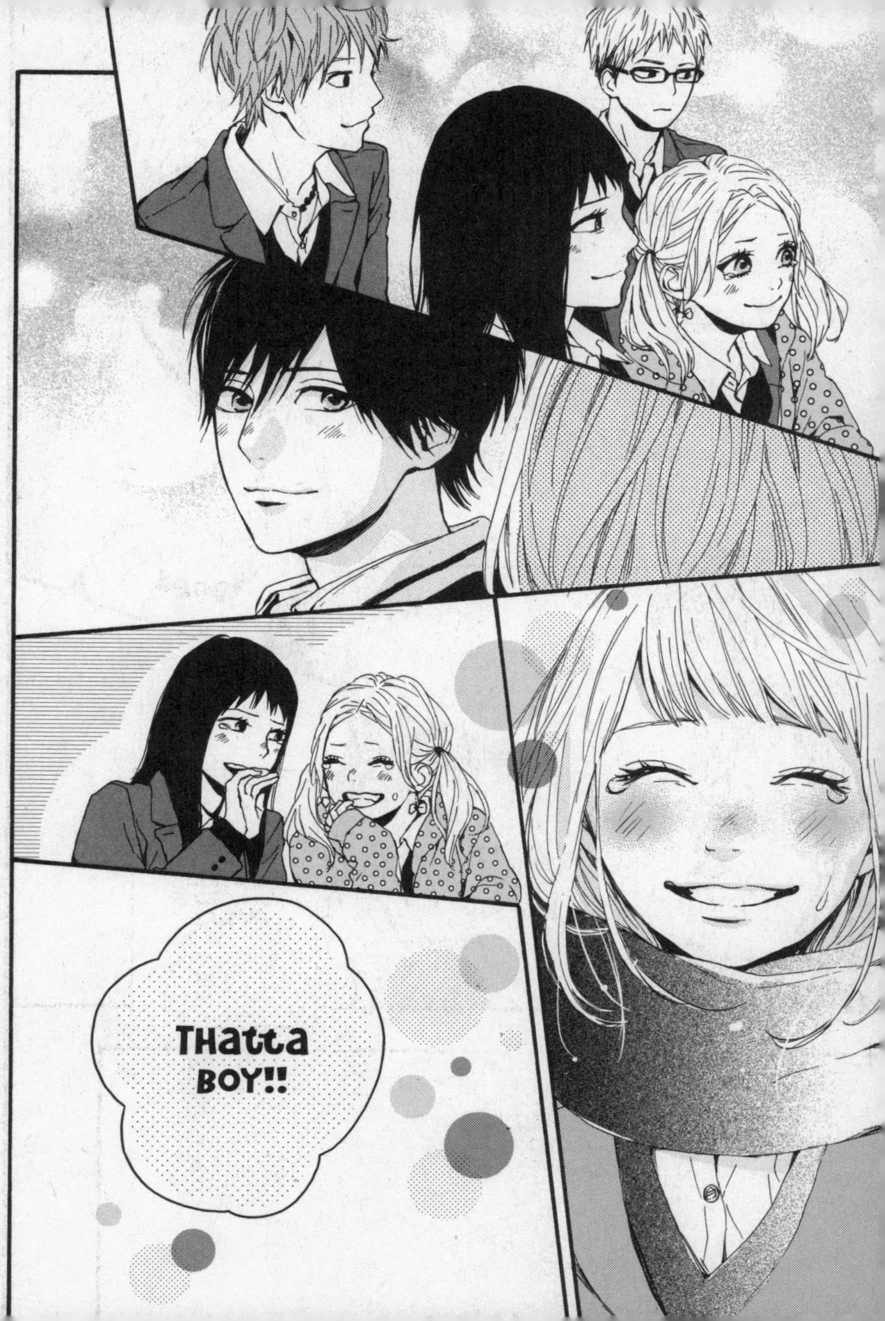
THATTA BOY!!

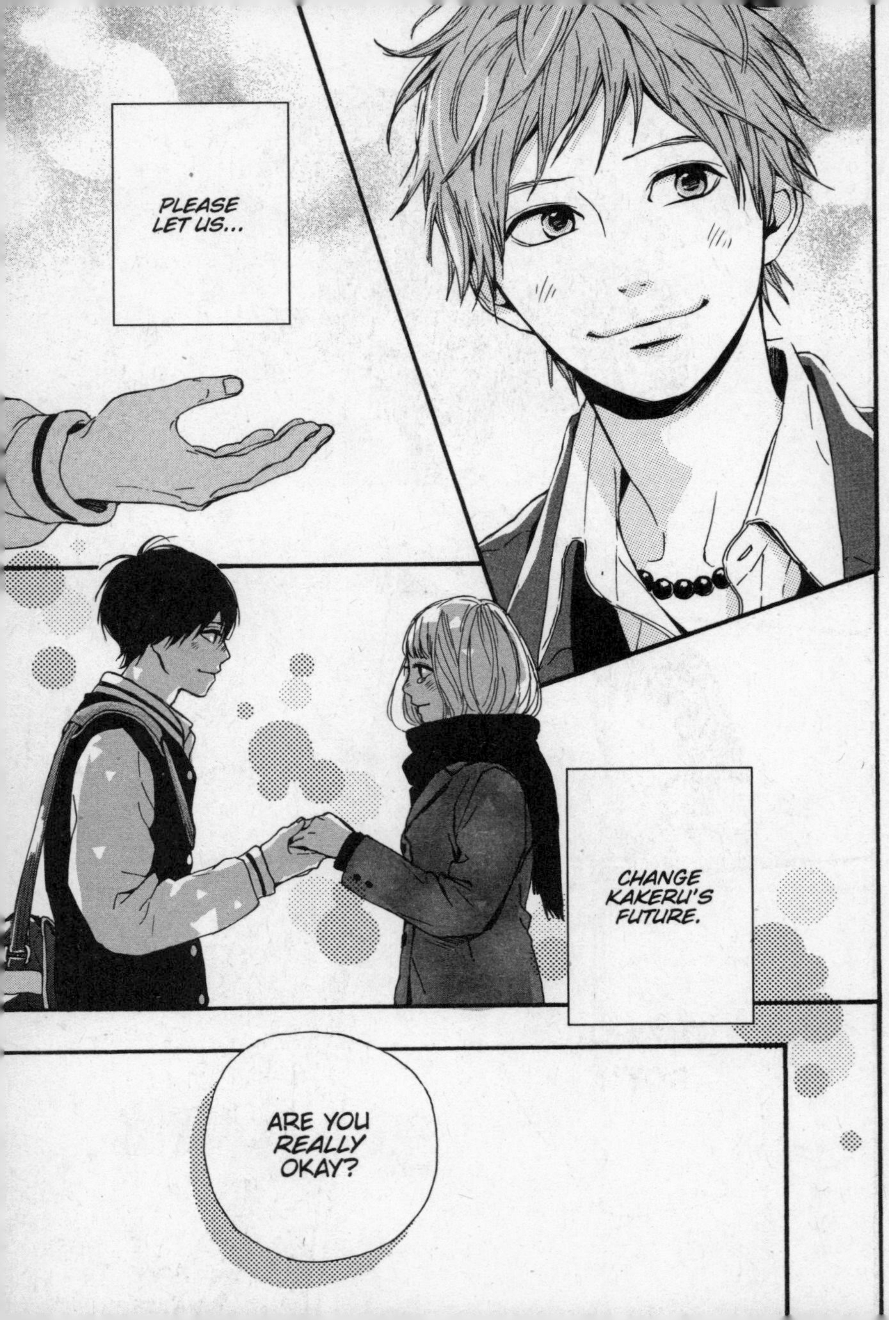
PLEASE LET US...
CHANGE KAKERU'S FUTURE.
ARE YOU REALLY OKAY?

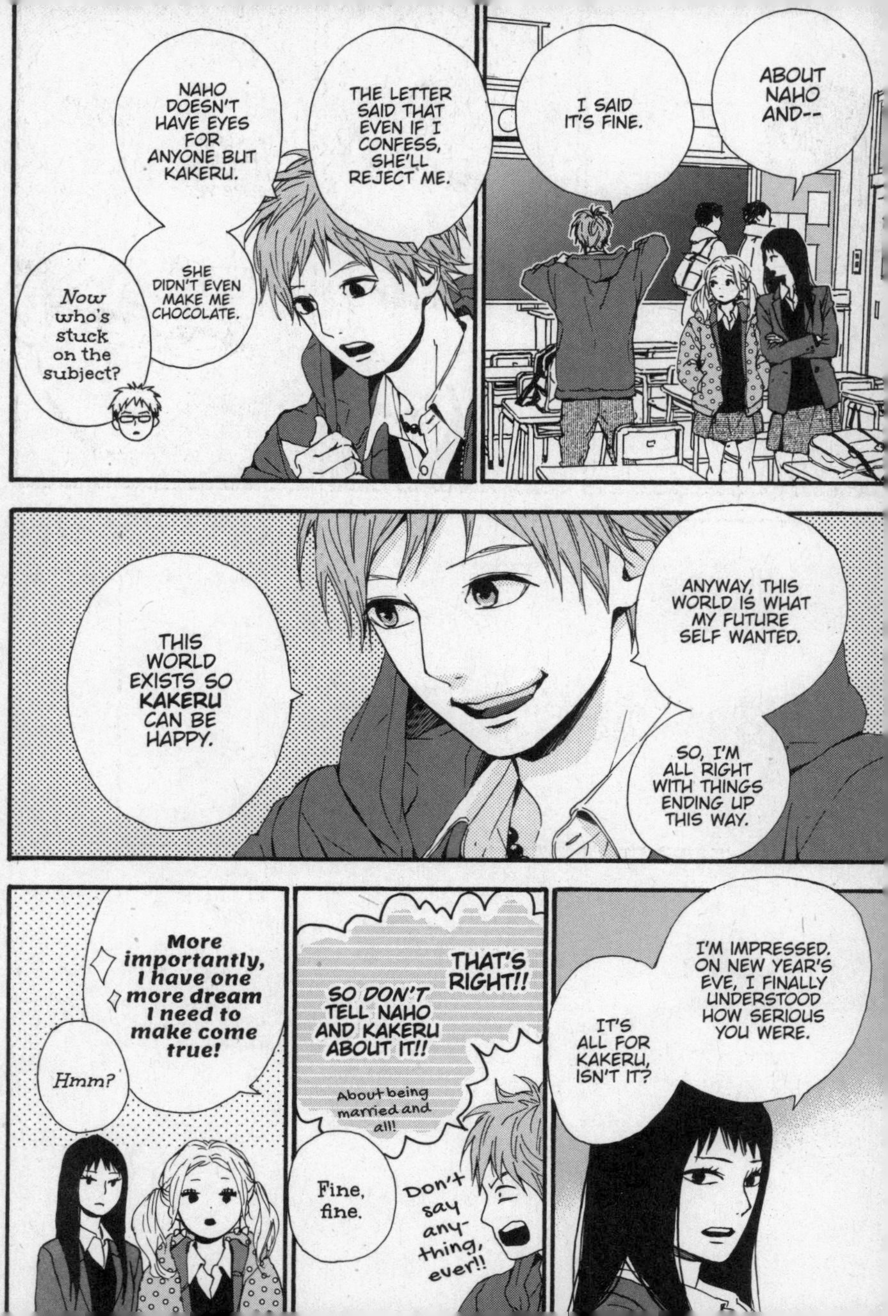
ABOUT NAHO AND--
I SAID IT'S FINE.
THE LETTER SAID THAT EVEN IF I CONFESS, SHE'LL REJECT ME.
NAHO DOESN'T HAVE EYES FOR ANYONE BUT KAKERU.
SHE DIDN'T EVEN MAKE ME CHOCOLATE.
Now who's stuck on the subject?
ANYWAY, THIS WORLD IS WHAT MY FUTURE SELF WANTED.
SO, I'M ALL RIGHT WITH THINGS ENDING UP THIS WAY.
THIS WORLD EXISTS SO KAKERU CAN BE HAPPY.
I'M IMPRESSED. ON NEW YEAR'S EVE, I FINALLY UNDERSTOOD HOW SERIOUS YOU WERE.
IT'S ALL FOR KAKERU, ISN'T IT?
THAT'S RIGHT!!
SO DON'T TELL NAHO AND KAKERU ABOUT IT!!
About being married and all!
Don't say any-thing, ever!!
Fine, fine.
More importantly, I have one more dream I need to make come true!
Hmm?

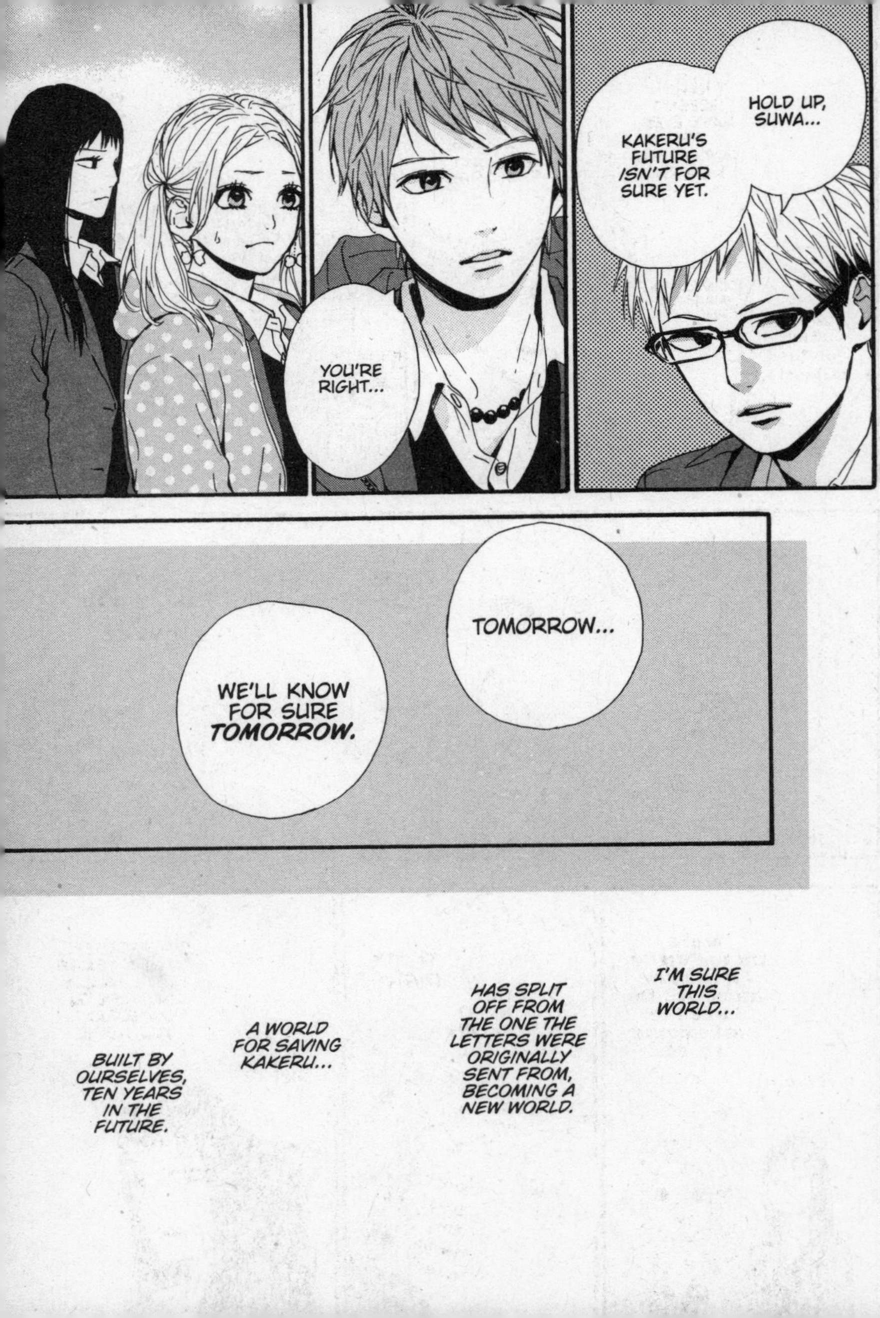
HOLD UP, SUWA...
KAKERU'S FUTURE *ISN'T* FOR SURE YET.
YOU'RE RIGHT...
TOMORROW...
WE'LL KNOW FOR SURE ***TOMORROW.***
I'M SURE THIS WORLD...
HAS SPLIT OFF FROM THE ONE THE LETTERS WERE ORIGINALLY SENT FROM, BECOMING A NEW WORLD.
A WORLD FOR SAVING KAKERU...
BUILT BY OURSELVES, TEN YEARS IN THE FUTURE.

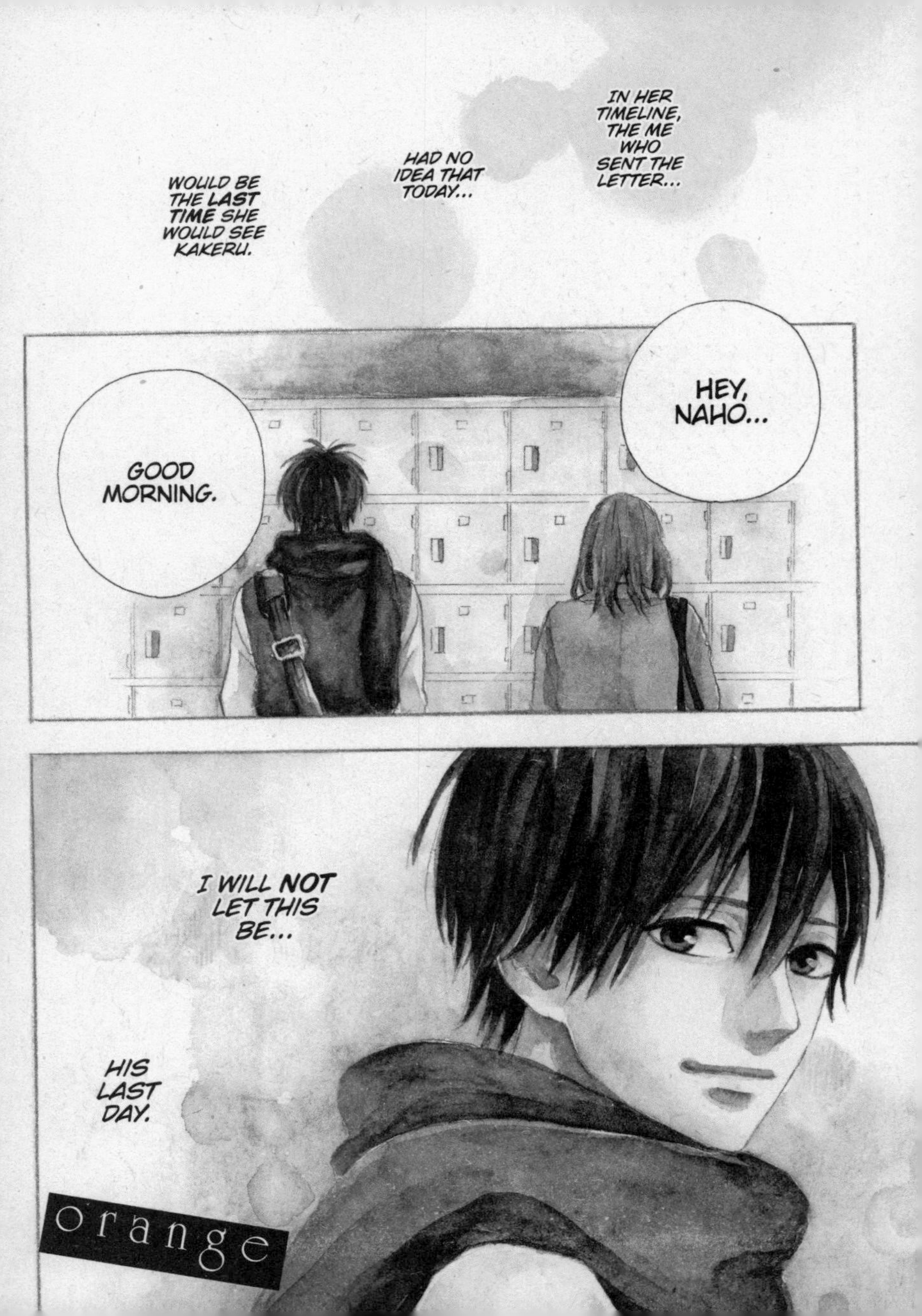
IN HER TIMELINE, THE ME WHO SENT THE LETTER...
HAD NO IDEA THAT TODAY...
WOULD BE THE **LAST TIME** SHE WOULD SEE KAKERU.
HEY, NAHO...
GOOD MORNING.
I WILL **NOT** LET THIS BE...
HIS LAST DAY.
orange

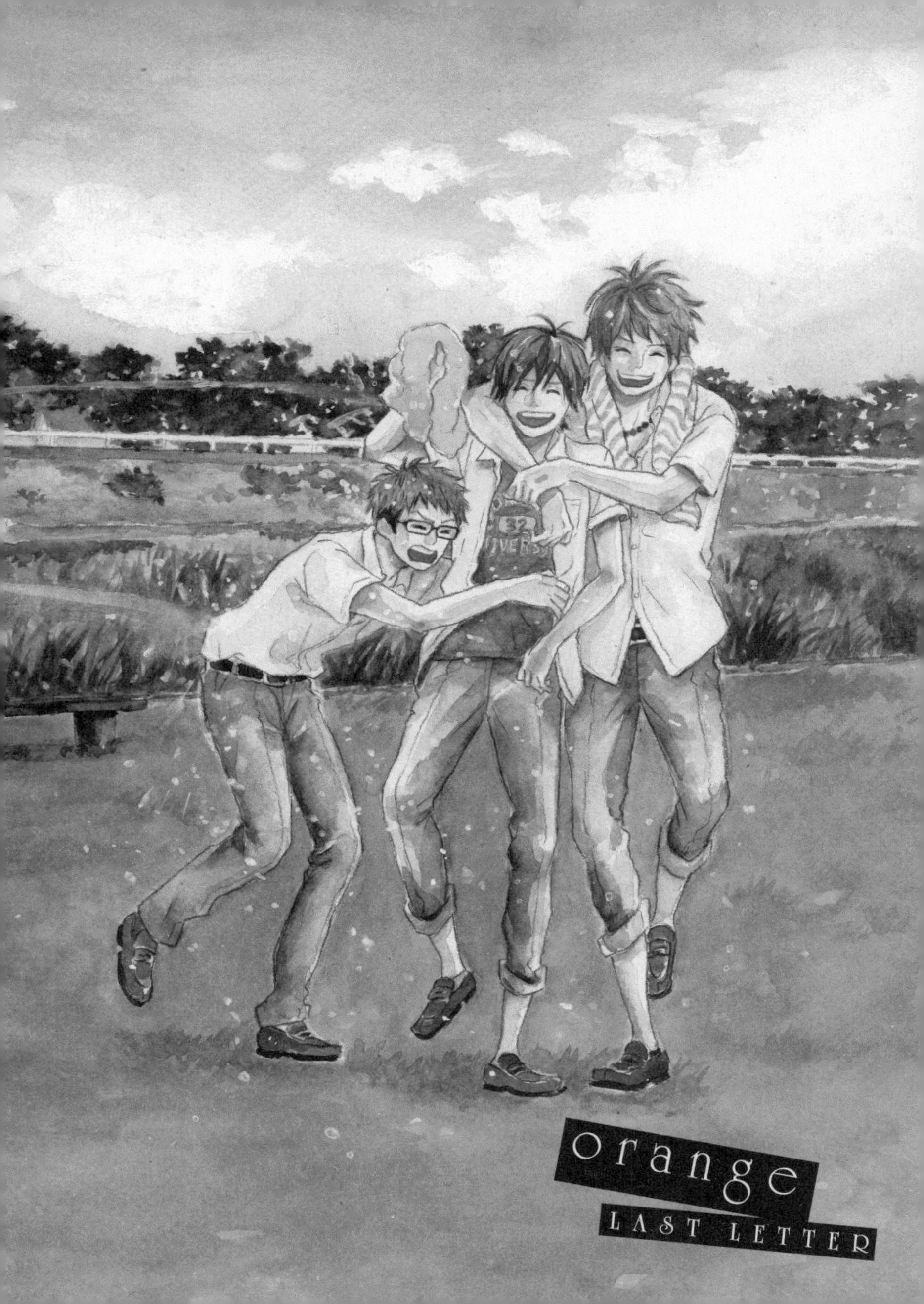
orange
LAST LETTER

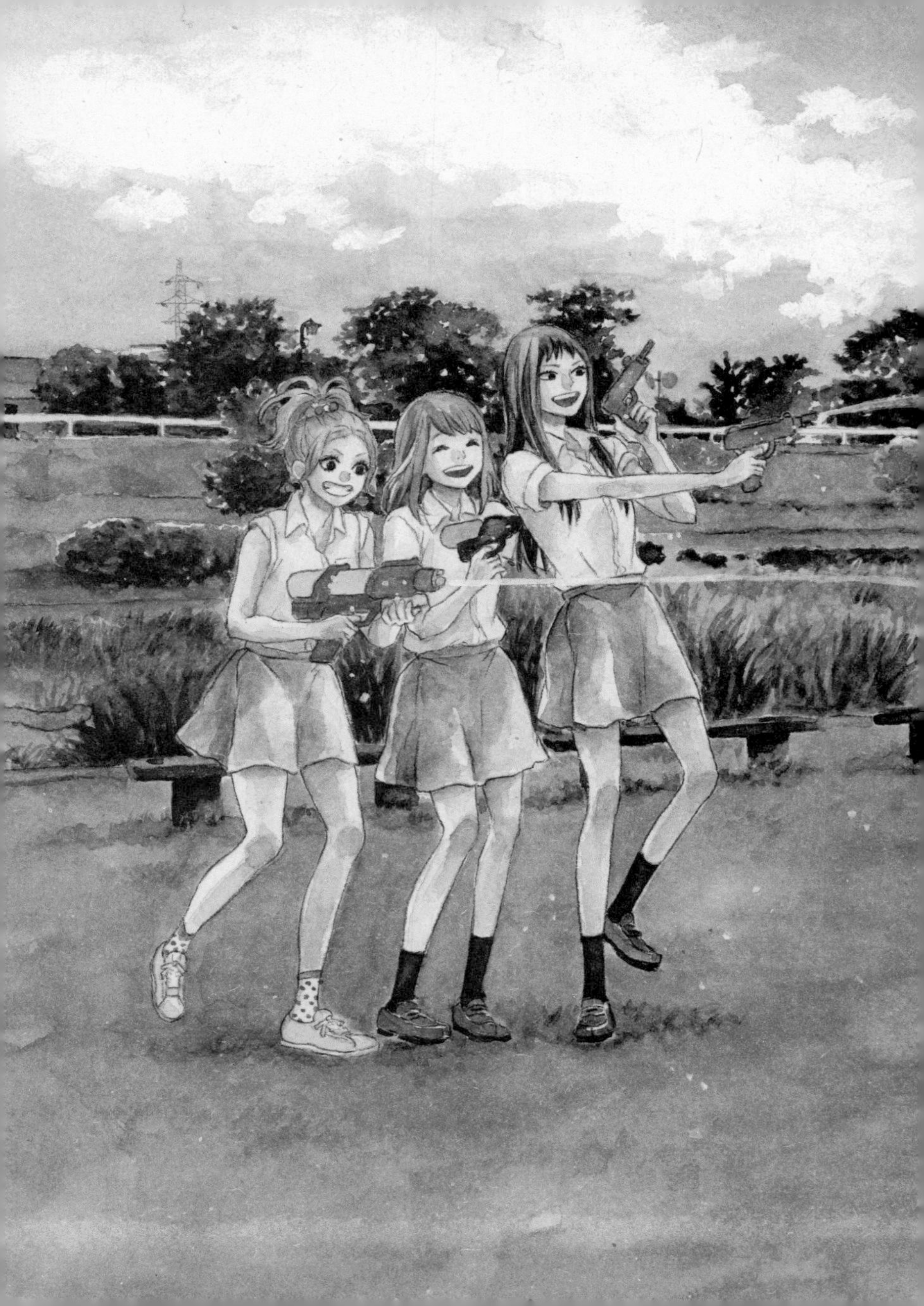

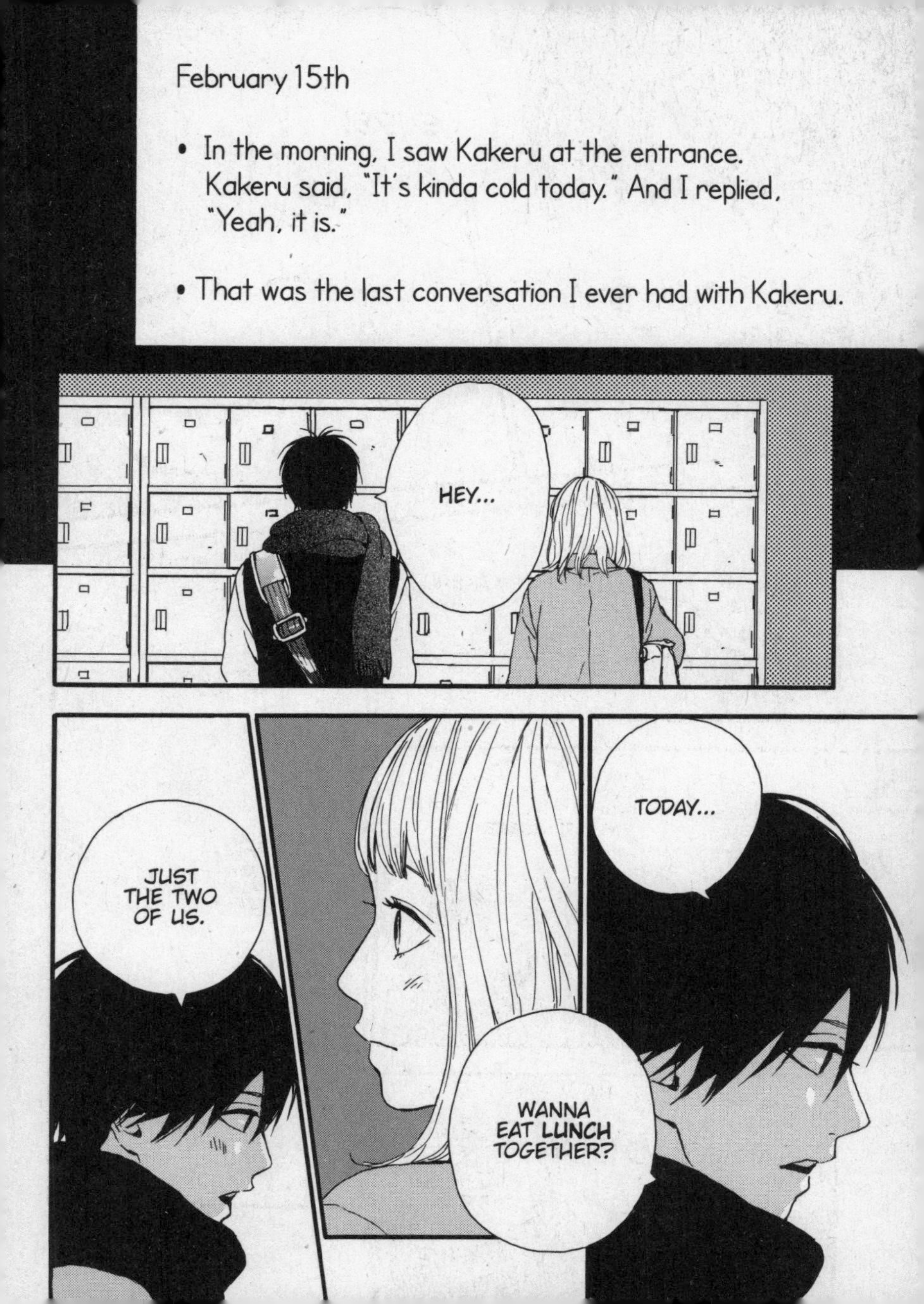
February 15th
• In the morning, I saw Kakeru at the entrance. Kakeru said, "It's kinda cold today." And I replied, "Yeah, it is."
• That was the last conversation I ever had with Kakeru.
HEY...
TODAY...
WANNA EAT LUNCH TOGETHER?
JUST THE TWO OF US.

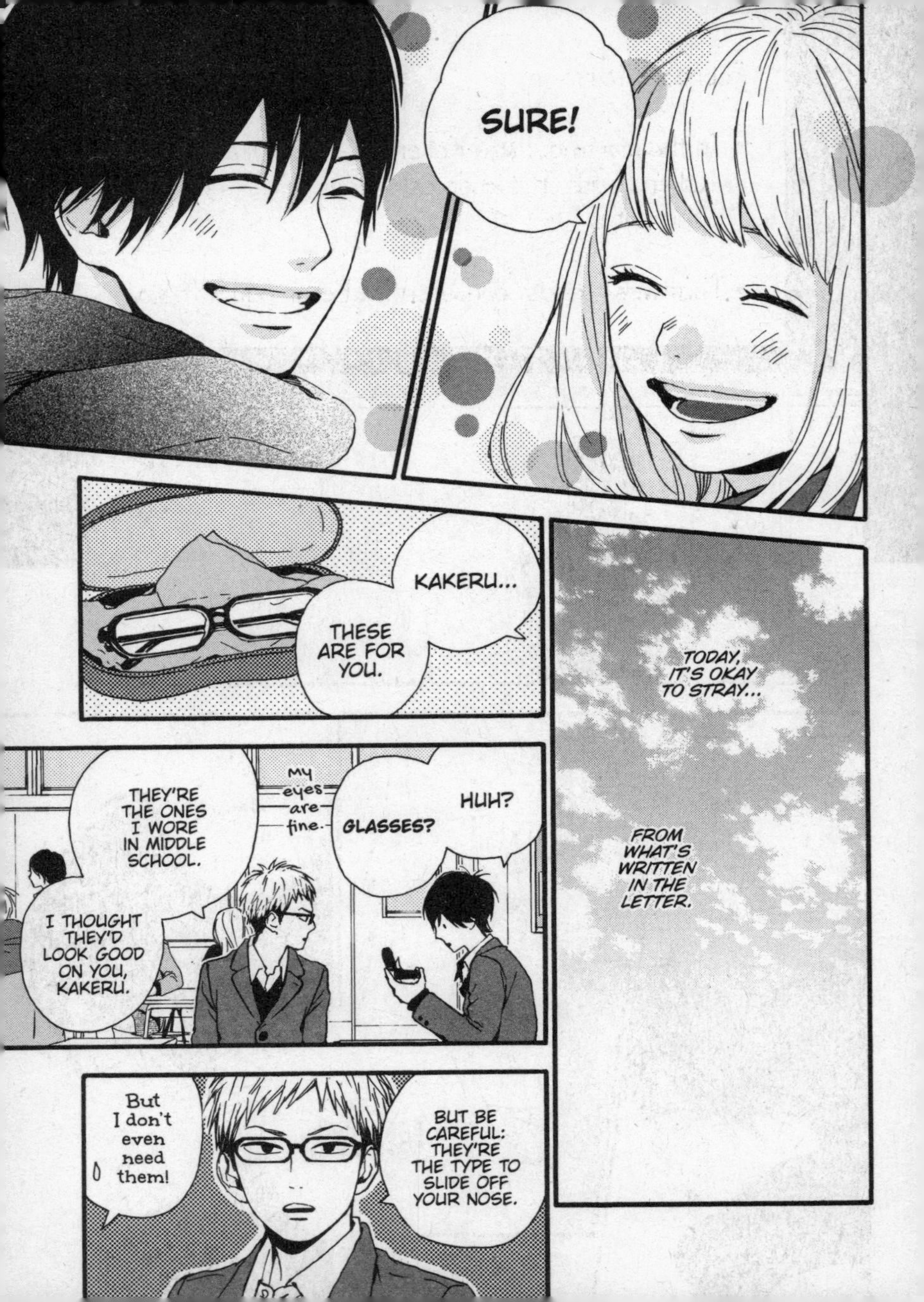
SURE!
TODAY, IT'S OKAY TO STRAY...
FROM WHAT'S WRITTEN IN THE LETTER.
KAKERU...
THESE ARE FOR YOU.
HUH?
GLASSES?
My eyes are fine.
THEY'RE THE ONES I WORE IN MIDDLE SCHOOL.
I THOUGHT THEY'D LOOK GOOD ON YOU, KAKERU.
BUT BE CAREFUL: THEY'RE THE TYPE TO SLIDE OFF YOUR NOSE.
But I don't even need them!

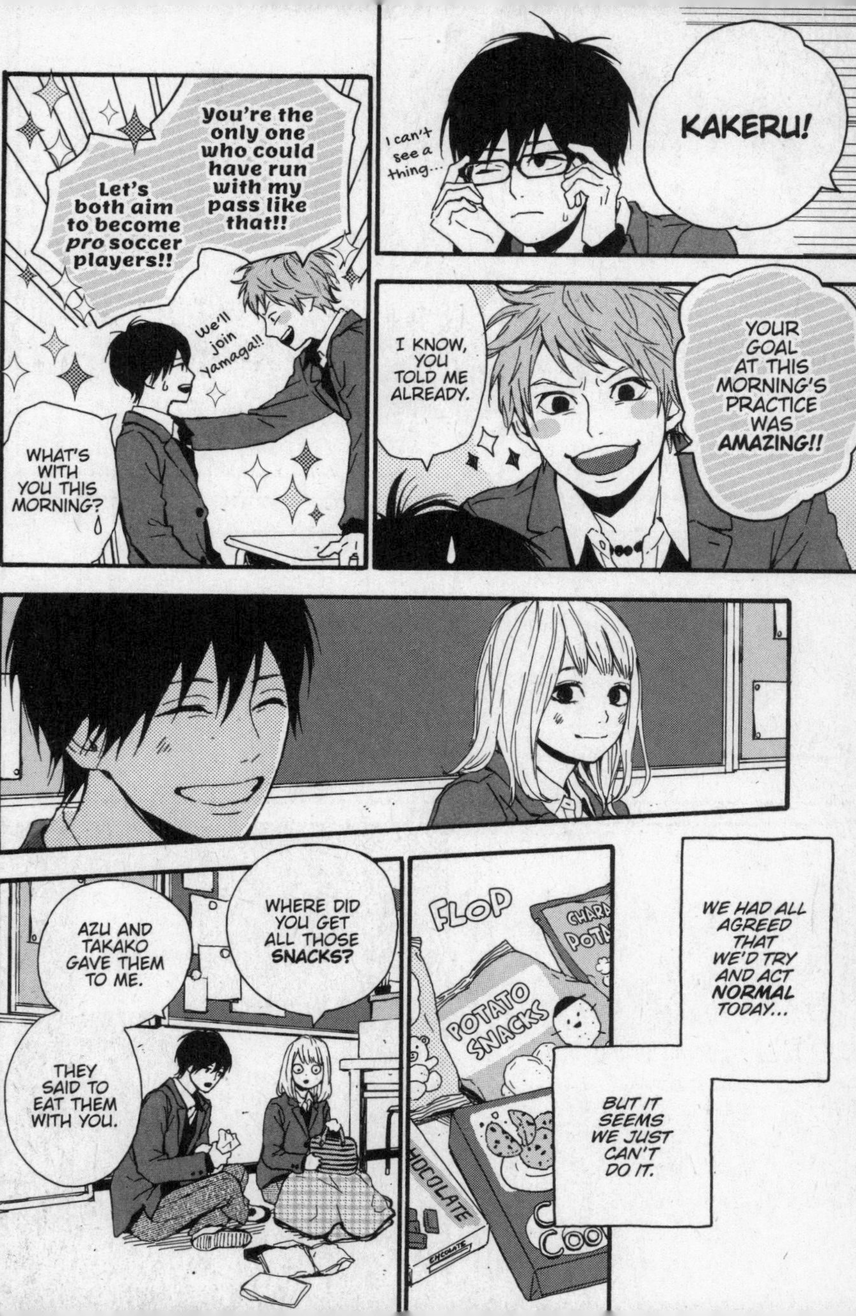
KAKERU!
I can't see a thing...
YOUR GOAL AT THIS MORNING'S PRACTICE WAS AMAZING!!
I KNOW, YOU TOLD ME ALREADY.
You're the only one who could have run with my pass like that!!
Let's both aim to become pro soccer players!!
We'll join Yamaga!!
WHAT'S WITH YOU THIS MORNING?
WE HAD ALL AGREED THAT WE'D TRY AND ACT NORMAL TODAY...
BUT IT SEEMS WE JUST CAN'T DO IT.
FLOP
POTATO SNACKS
CHOCOLATE
WHERE DID YOU GET ALL THOSE SNACKS?
AZU AND TAKAKO GAVE THEM TO ME.
THEY SAID TO EAT THEM WITH YOU.

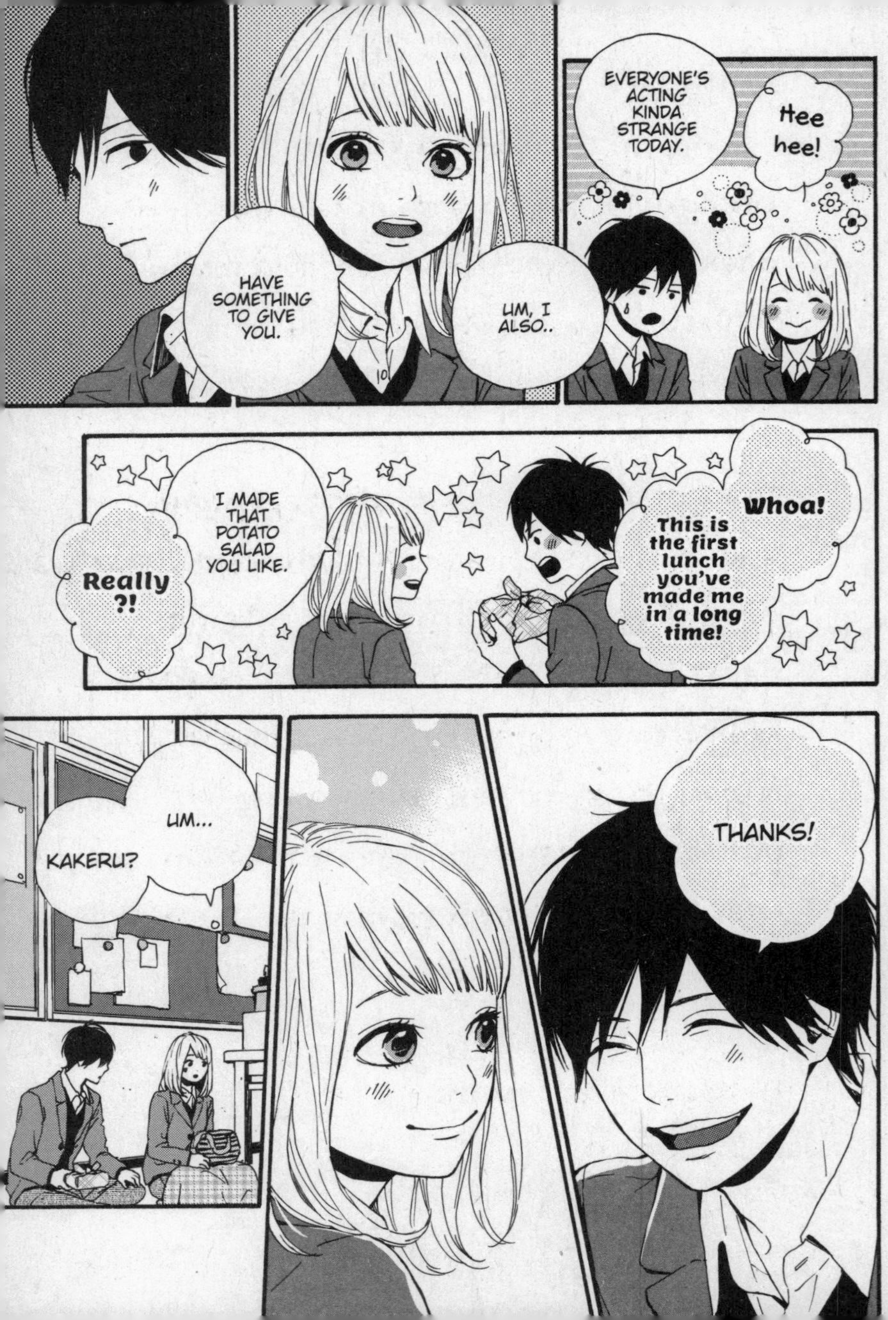
EVERYONE'S ACTING KINDA STRANGE TODAY.
Hee hee!
UM, I ALSO..
HAVE SOMETHING TO GIVE YOU.
Whoa!
This is the first lunch you've made me in a long time!
I MADE THAT POTATO SALAD YOU LIKE.
Really?!
THANKS!
UM...
KAKERU?

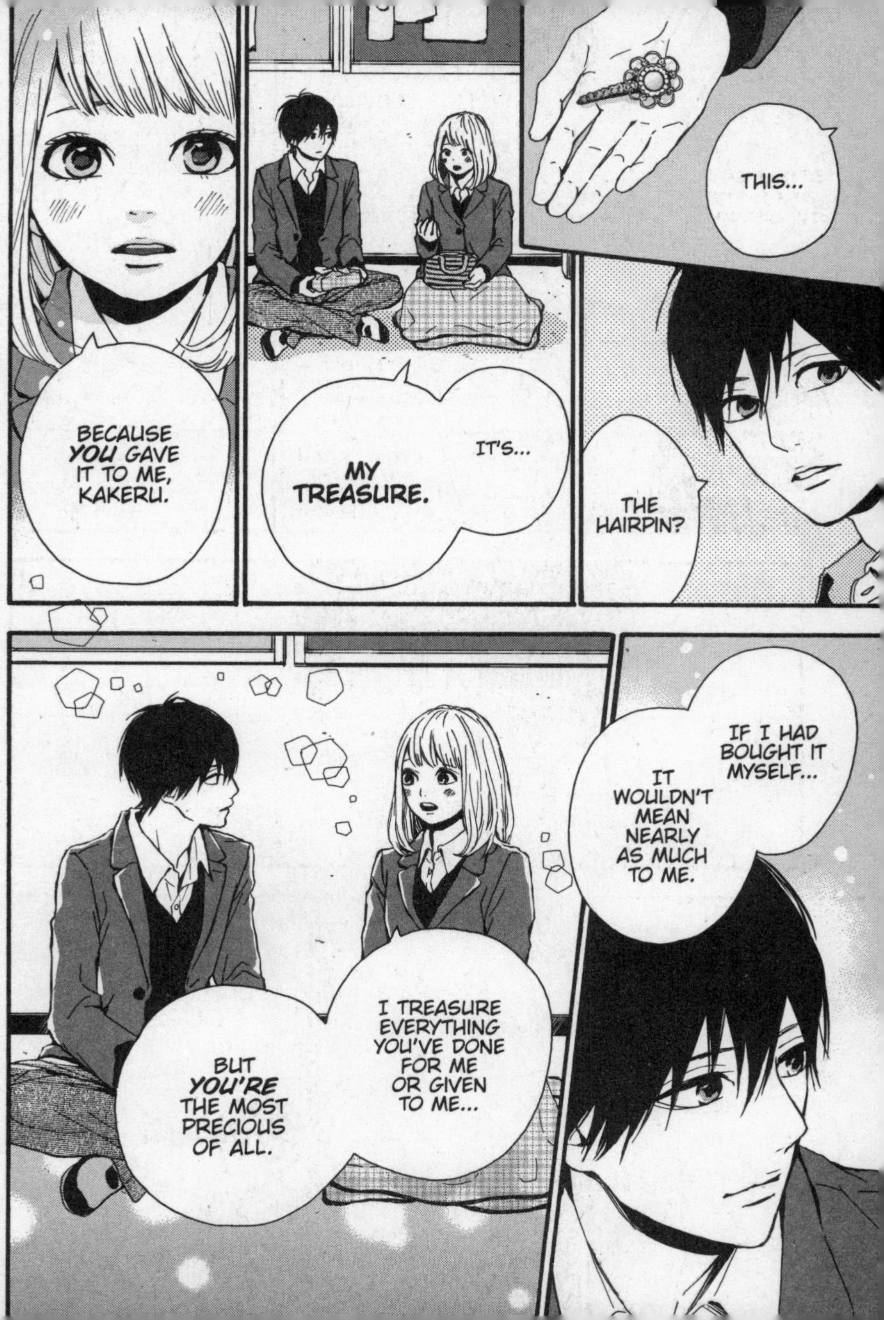
THIS...
THE HAIRPIN?
IT'S...
MY TREASURE.
BECAUSE YOU GAVE IT TO ME, KAKERU.
IF I HAD BOUGHT IT MYSELF...
IT WOULDN'T MEAN NEARLY AS MUCH TO ME.
I TREASURE EVERYTHING YOU'VE DONE FOR ME OR GIVEN TO ME...
BUT YOU'RE THE MOST PRECIOUS OF ALL.

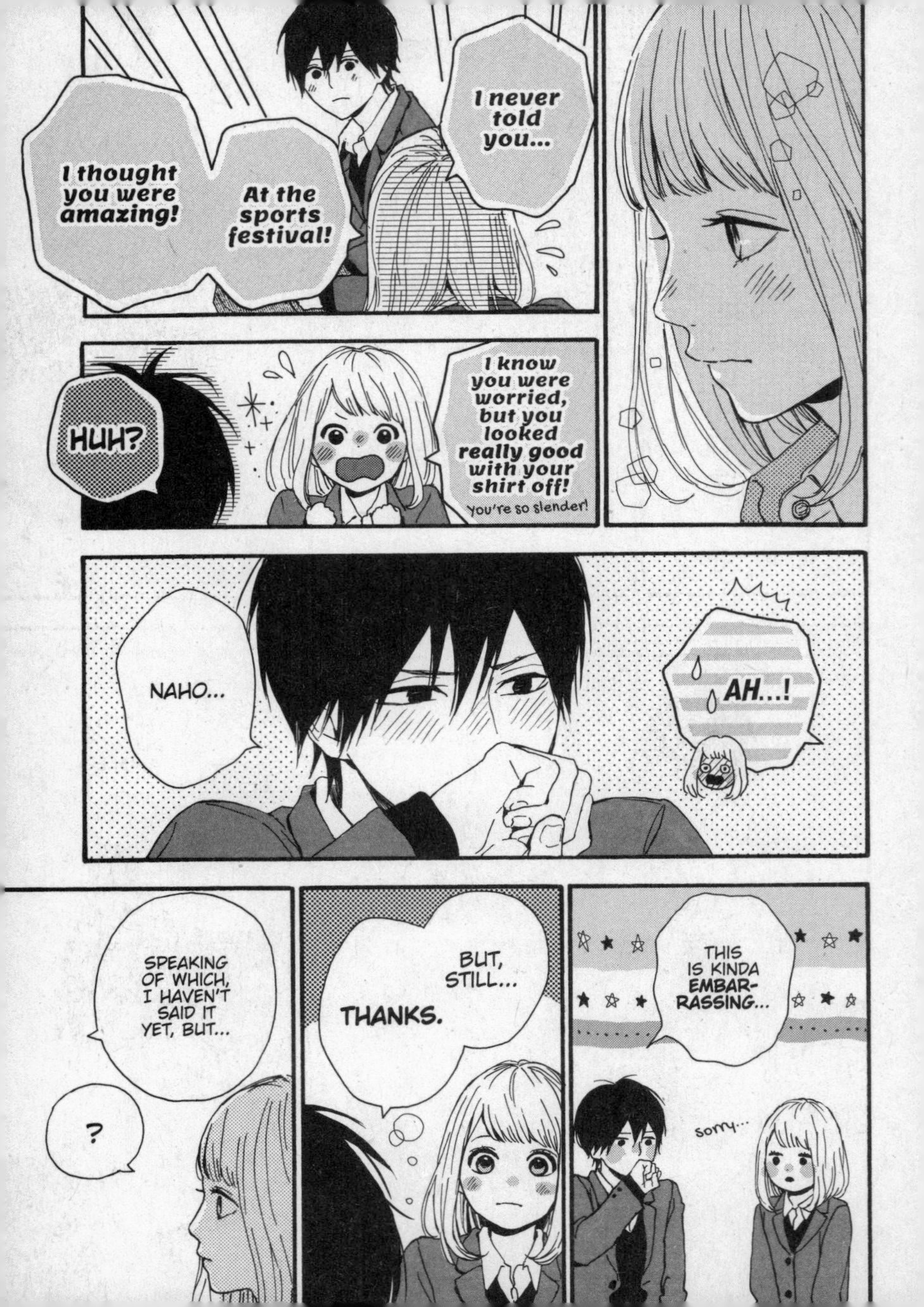
I never told you...
At the sports festival!
I thought you were amazing!
I know you were worried, but you looked really good with your shirt off!
You're so slender!
HUH?
AH...!
NAHO...
THIS IS KINDA EMBARRASSING...
sorry...
BUT, STILL...
THANKS.
SPEAKING OF WHICH, I HAVEN'T SAID IT YET, BUT...
?

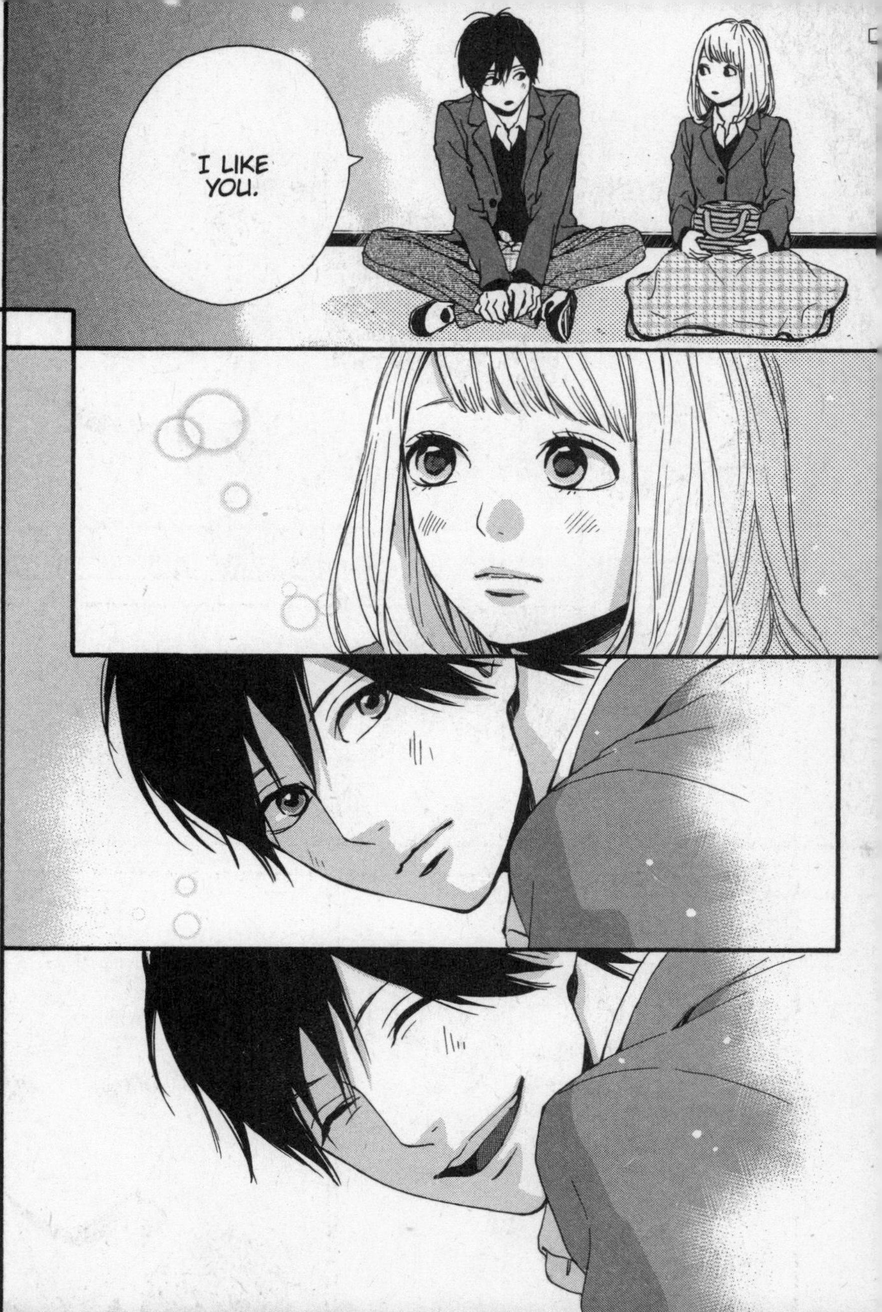
I LIKE YOU.

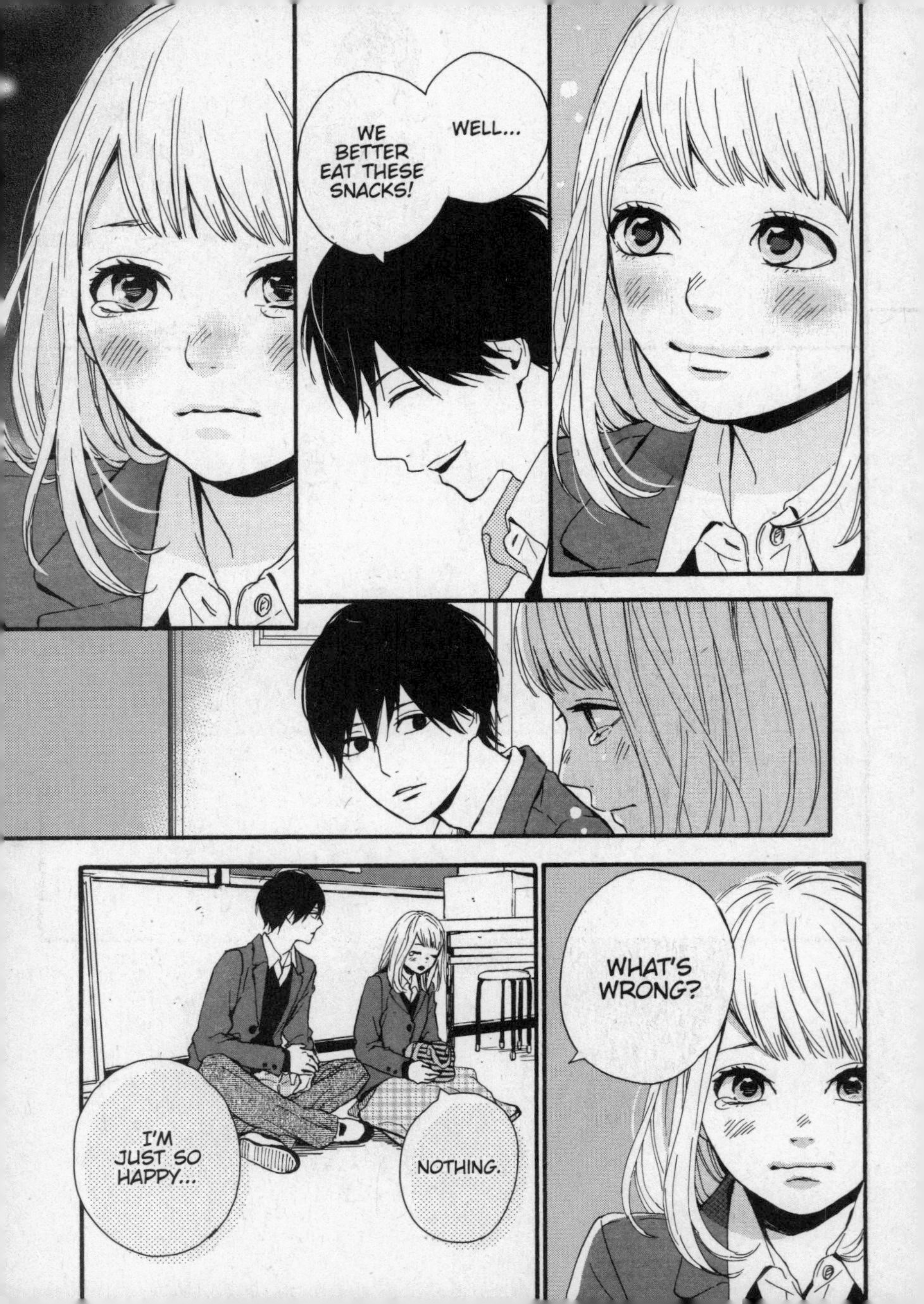
WELL...
WE BETTER EAT THESE SNACKS!
WHAT'S WRONG?
NOTHING.
I'M JUST SO HAPPY...

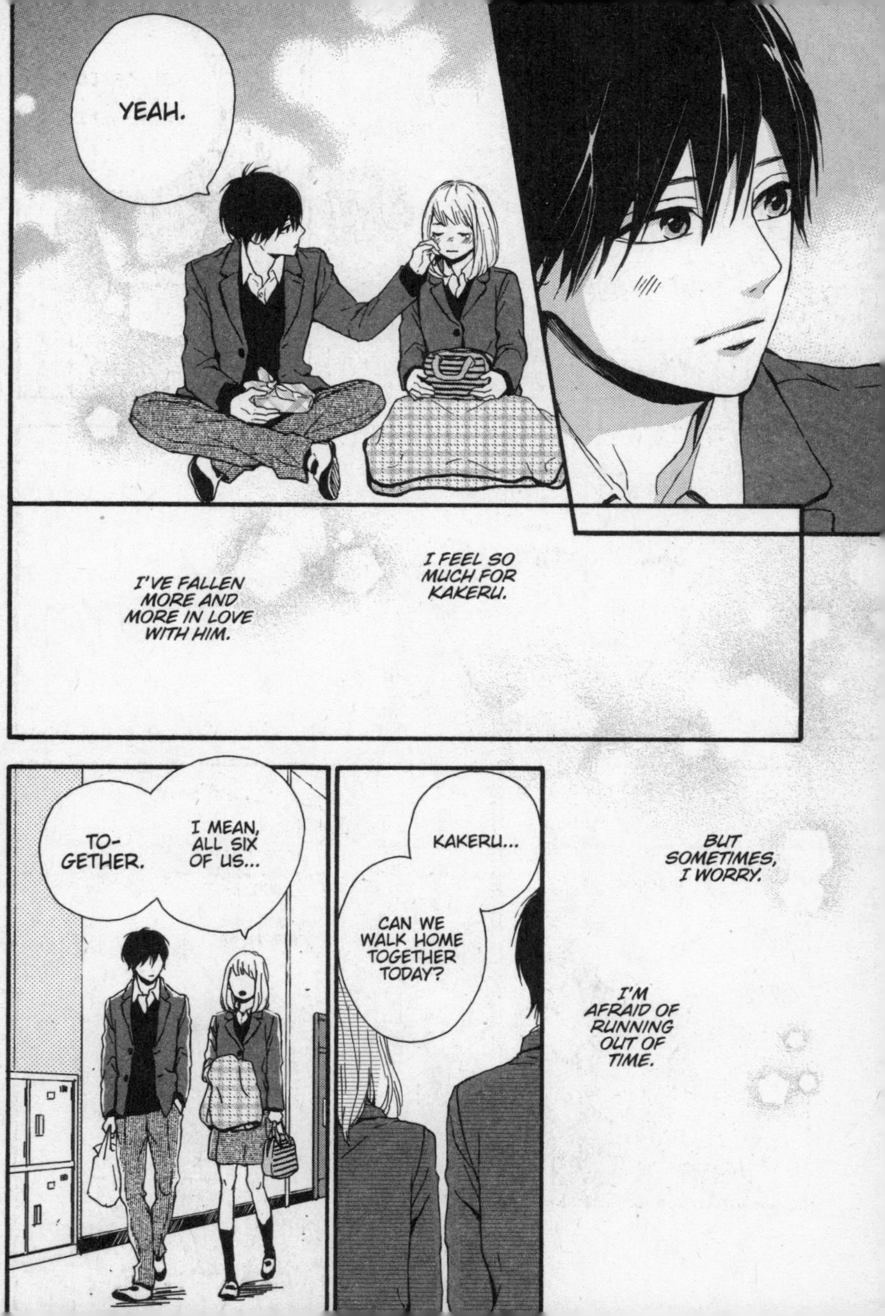
YEAH.
I FEEL SO MUCH FOR KAKERU.
I'VE FALLEN MORE AND MORE IN LOVE WITH HIM.
BUT SOMETIMES, I WORRY.
I'M AFRAID OF RUNNING OUT OF TIME.
KAKERU...
CAN WE WALK HOME TOGETHER TODAY?
I MEAN, ALL SIX OF US...
TO-GETHER.

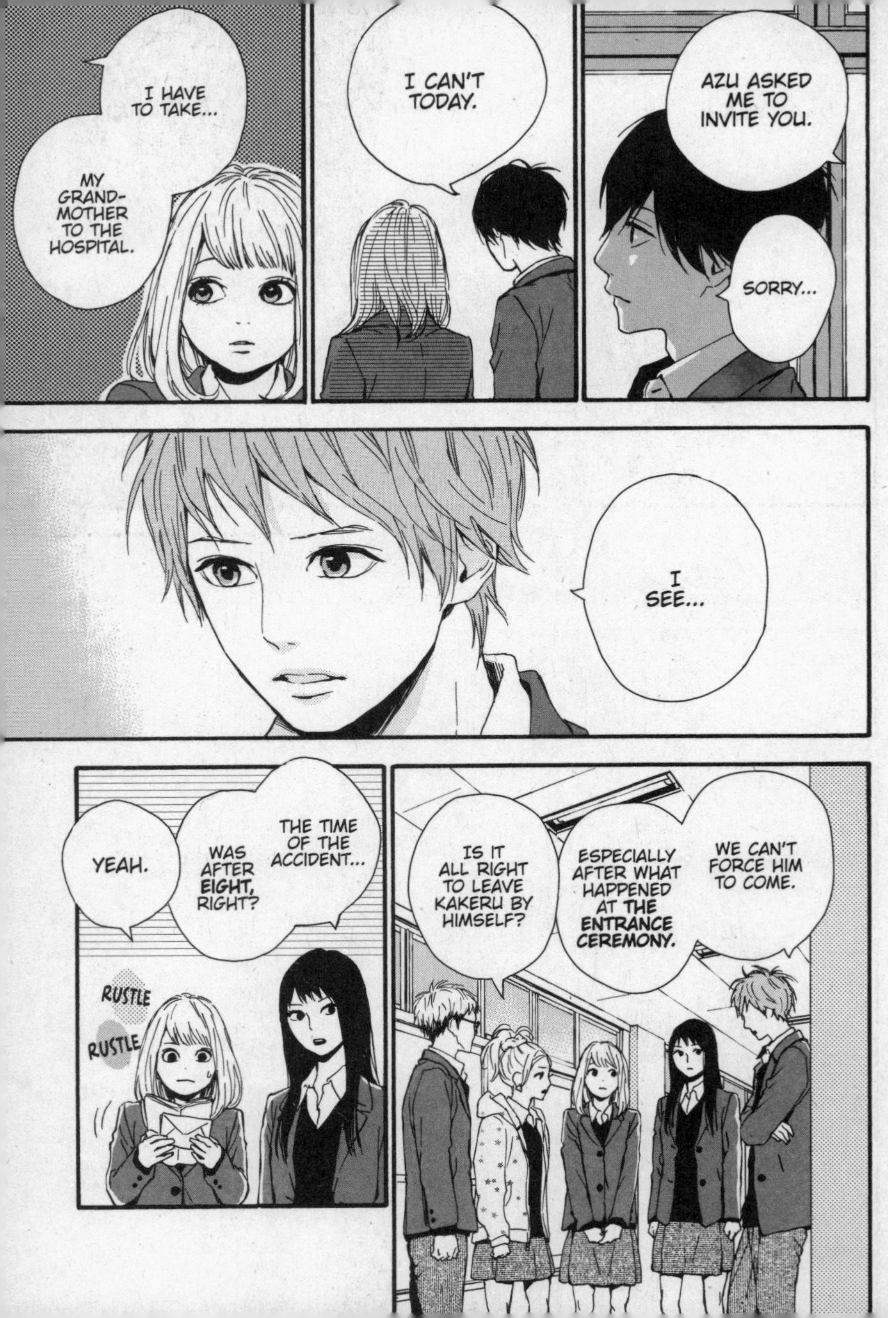
AZU ASKED ME TO INVITE YOU.
SORRY...
I CAN'T TODAY.
I HAVE TO TAKE...
MY GRAND-MOTHER TO THE HOSPITAL.
I SEE...
WE CAN'T FORCE HIM TO COME.
ESPECIALLY AFTER WHAT HAPPENED AT THE ENTRANCE CEREMONY.
IS IT ALL RIGHT TO LEAVE KAKERU BY HIMSELF?
THE TIME OF THE ACCIDENT...
WAS AFTER EIGHT, RIGHT?
YEAH.
RUSTLE
RUSTLE

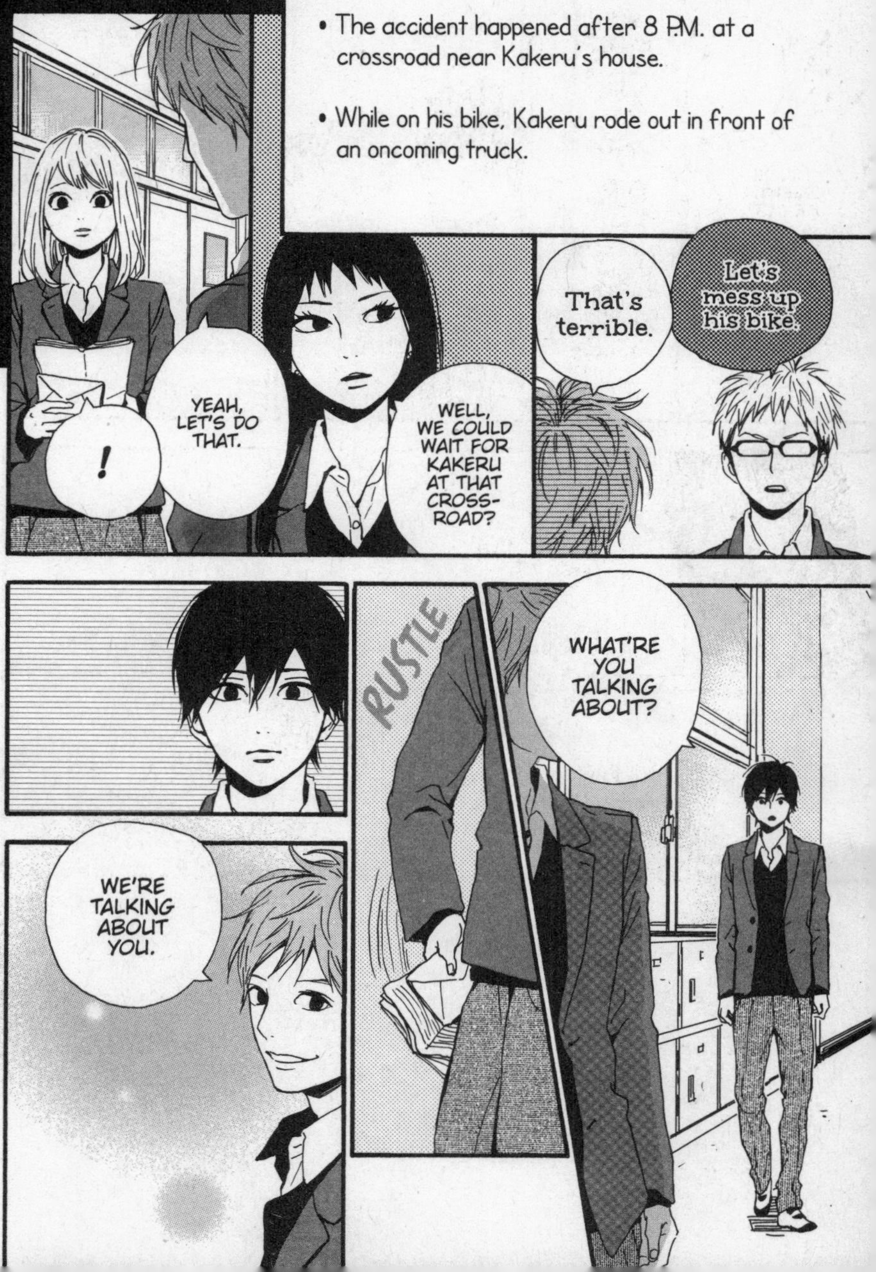
• The accident happened after 8 P.M. at a crossroad near Kakeru's house.
• While on his bike, Kakeru rode out in front of an oncoming truck.
Let's mess up his bike.
That's terrible.
WELL, WE COULD WAIT FOR KAKERU AT THAT CROSS-ROAD?
YEAH, LET'S DO THAT.
!
WHAT'RE YOU TALKING ABOUT?
RUSTLE
WE'RE TALKING ABOUT YOU.

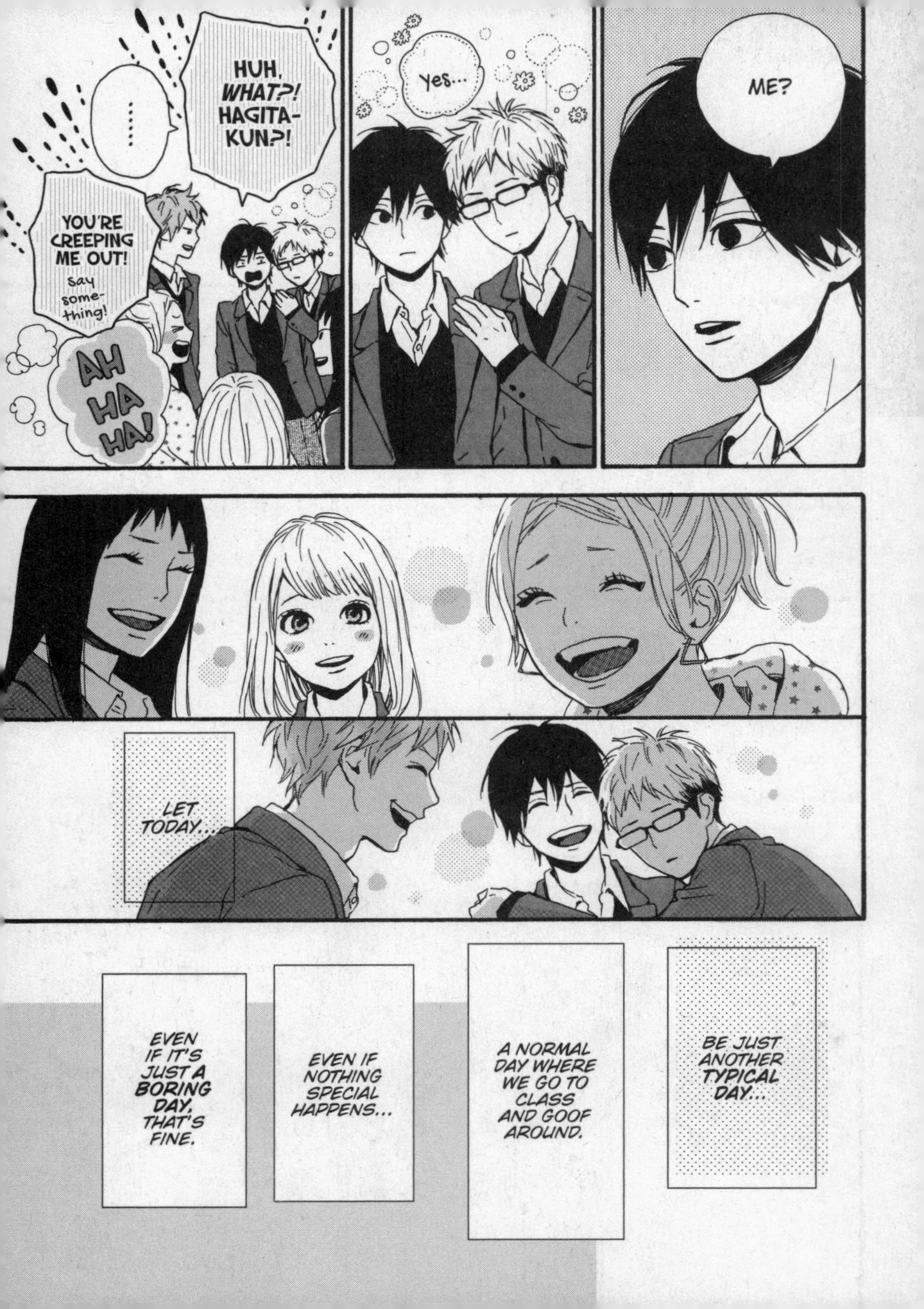
ME?
Yes...
HUH, WHAT?! HAGITA-KUN?!
......
YOU'RE CREEPING ME OUT!
say something!
AH HA HA HA!
LET TODAY...
BE JUST ANOTHER TYPICAL DAY...
A NORMAL DAY WHERE WE GO TO CLASS AND GOOF AROUND.
EVEN IF NOTHING SPECIAL HAPPENS...
EVEN IF IT'S JUST A BORING DAY, THAT'S FINE.

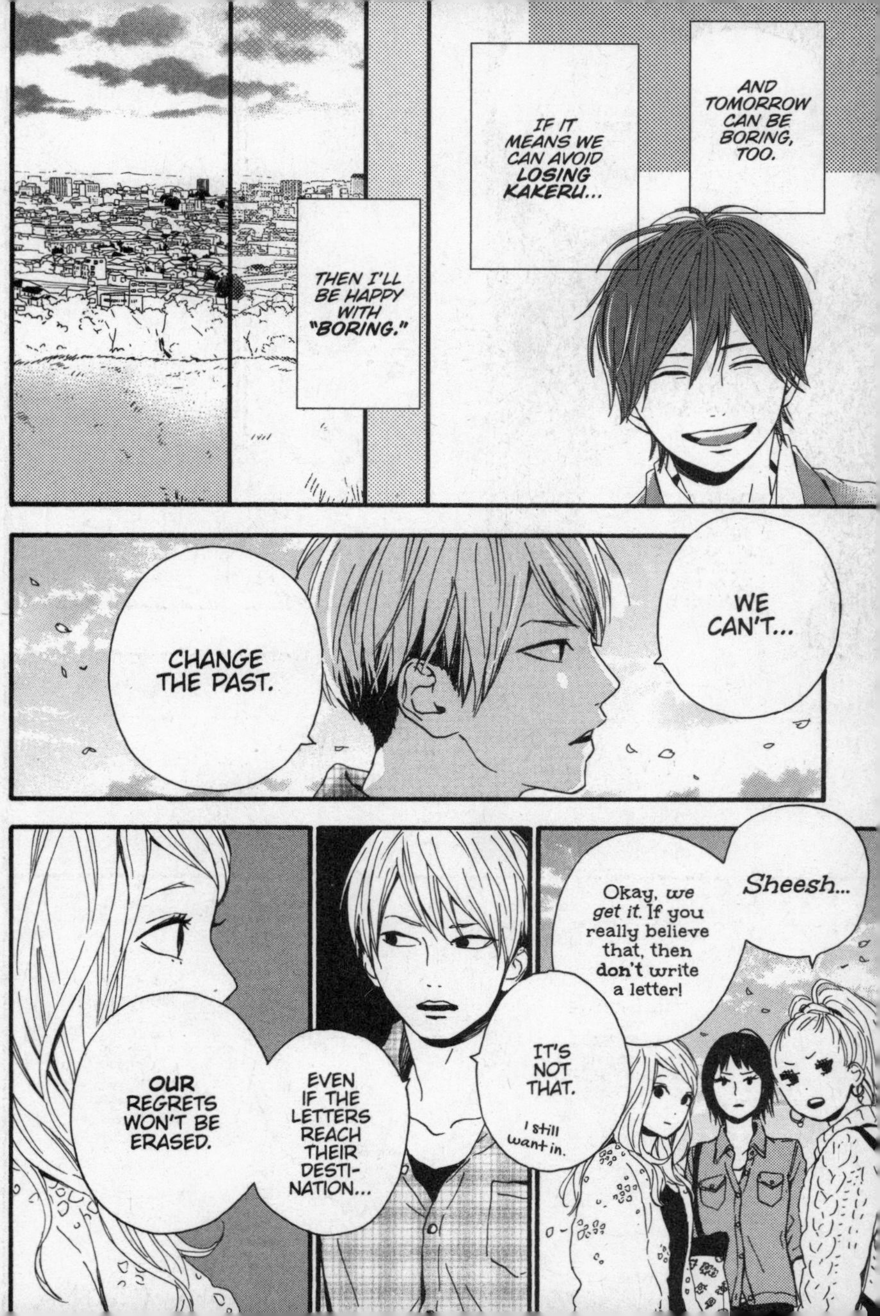
AND TOMORROW CAN BE BORING, TOO.
IF IT MEANS WE CAN AVOID LOSING KAKERU...
THEN I'LL BE HAPPY WITH "BORING."
WE CAN'T...
CHANGE THE PAST.
Sheesh...
Okay, we get it. If you really believe that, then don't write a letter!
IT'S NOT THAT.
I still want in.
EVEN IF THE LETTERS REACH THEIR DESTINATION...
OUR REGRETS WON'T BE ERASED.

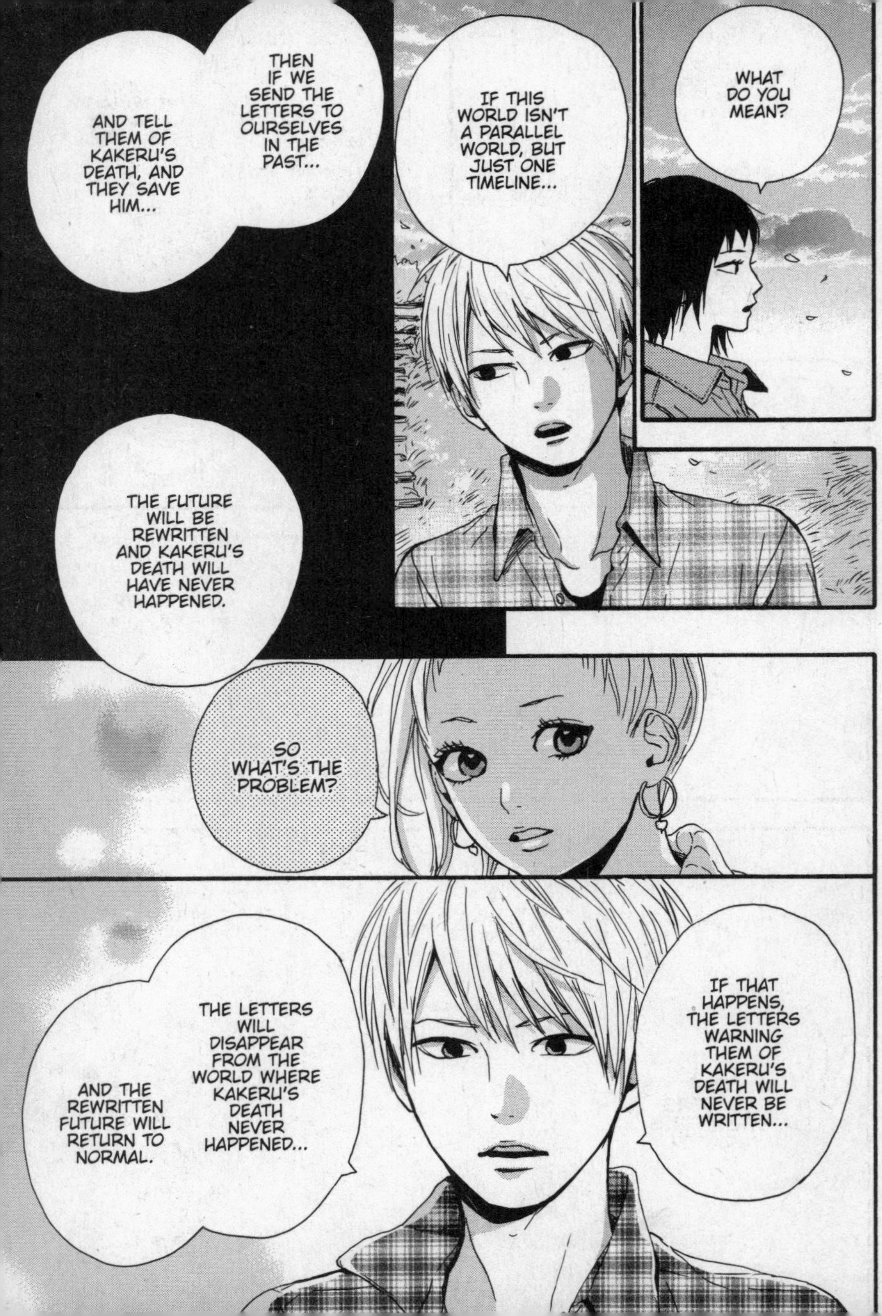
WHAT DO YOU MEAN?
IF THIS WORLD ISN'T A PARALLEL WORLD, BUT JUST ONE TIMELINE...
THEN IF WE SEND THE LETTERS TO OURSELVES IN THE PAST...
AND TELL THEM OF KAKERU'S DEATH, AND THEY SAVE HIM...
THE FUTURE WILL BE REWRITTEN AND KAKERU'S DEATH WILL HAVE NEVER HAPPENED.
SO WHAT'S THE PROBLEM?
IF THAT HAPPENS, THE LETTERS WARNING THEM OF KAKERU'S DEATH WILL NEVER BE WRITTEN...
THE LETTERS WILL DISAPPEAR FROM THE WORLD WHERE KAKERU'S DEATH NEVER HAPPENED...
AND THE REWRITTEN FUTURE WILL RETURN TO NORMAL.

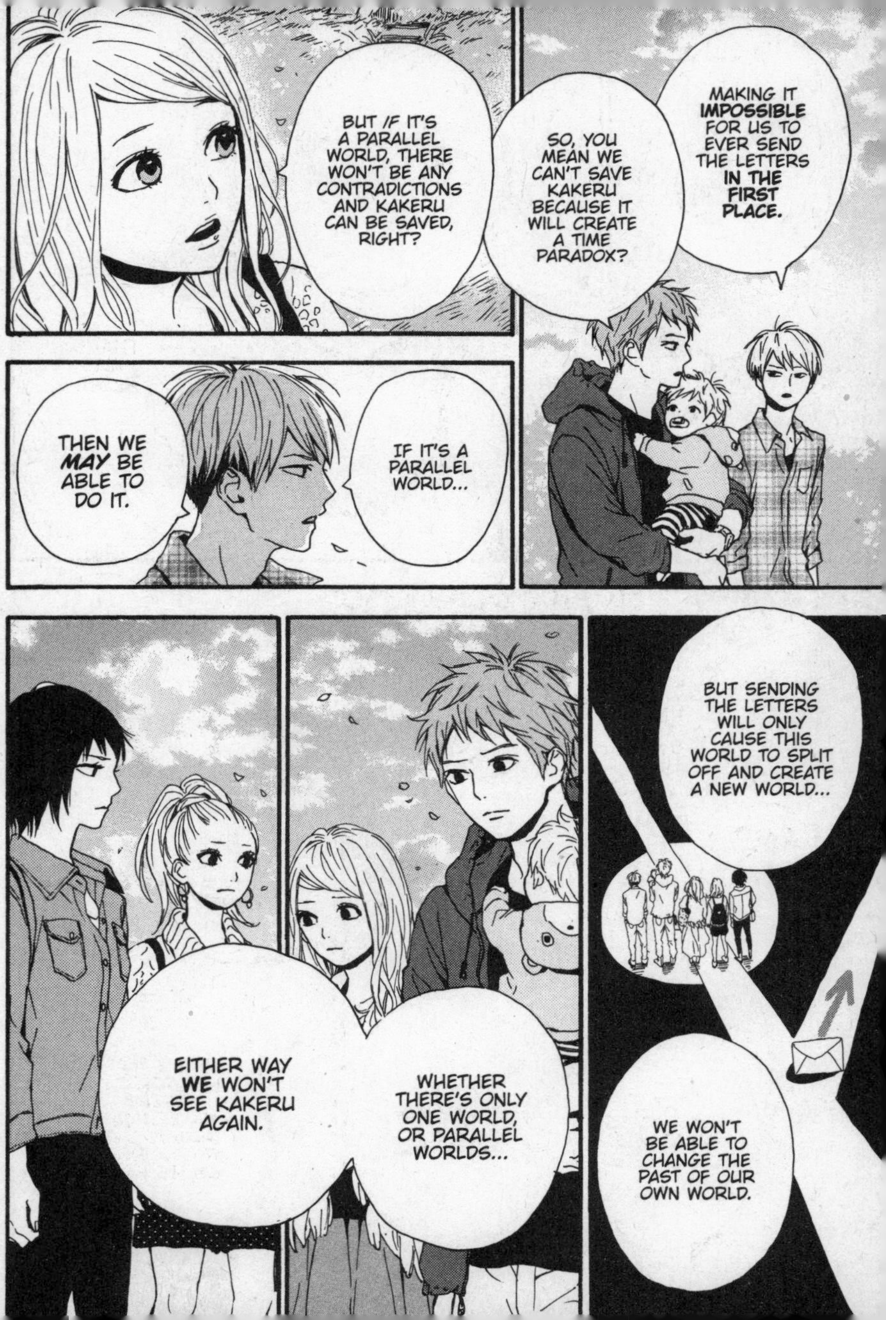
MAKING IT **IMPOSSIBLE** FOR US TO EVER SEND THE LETTERS **IN THE FIRST PLACE.**
SO, YOU MEAN WE CAN'T SAVE KAKERU BECAUSE IT WILL CREATE A TIME PARADOX?
BUT *IF* IT'S A PARALLEL WORLD, THERE WON'T BE ANY CONTRADICTIONS AND KAKERU CAN BE SAVED, RIGHT?
IF IT'S A PARALLEL WORLD...
THEN WE ***MAY*** BE ABLE TO DO IT.
BUT SENDING THE LETTERS WILL ONLY CAUSE THIS WORLD TO SPLIT OFF AND CREATE A NEW WORLD...
WE WON'T BE ABLE TO CHANGE THE PAST OF OUR OWN WORLD.
WHETHER THERE'S ONLY ONE WORLD, OR PARALLEL WORLDS...
EITHER WAY **WE** WON'T SEE KAKERU AGAIN.

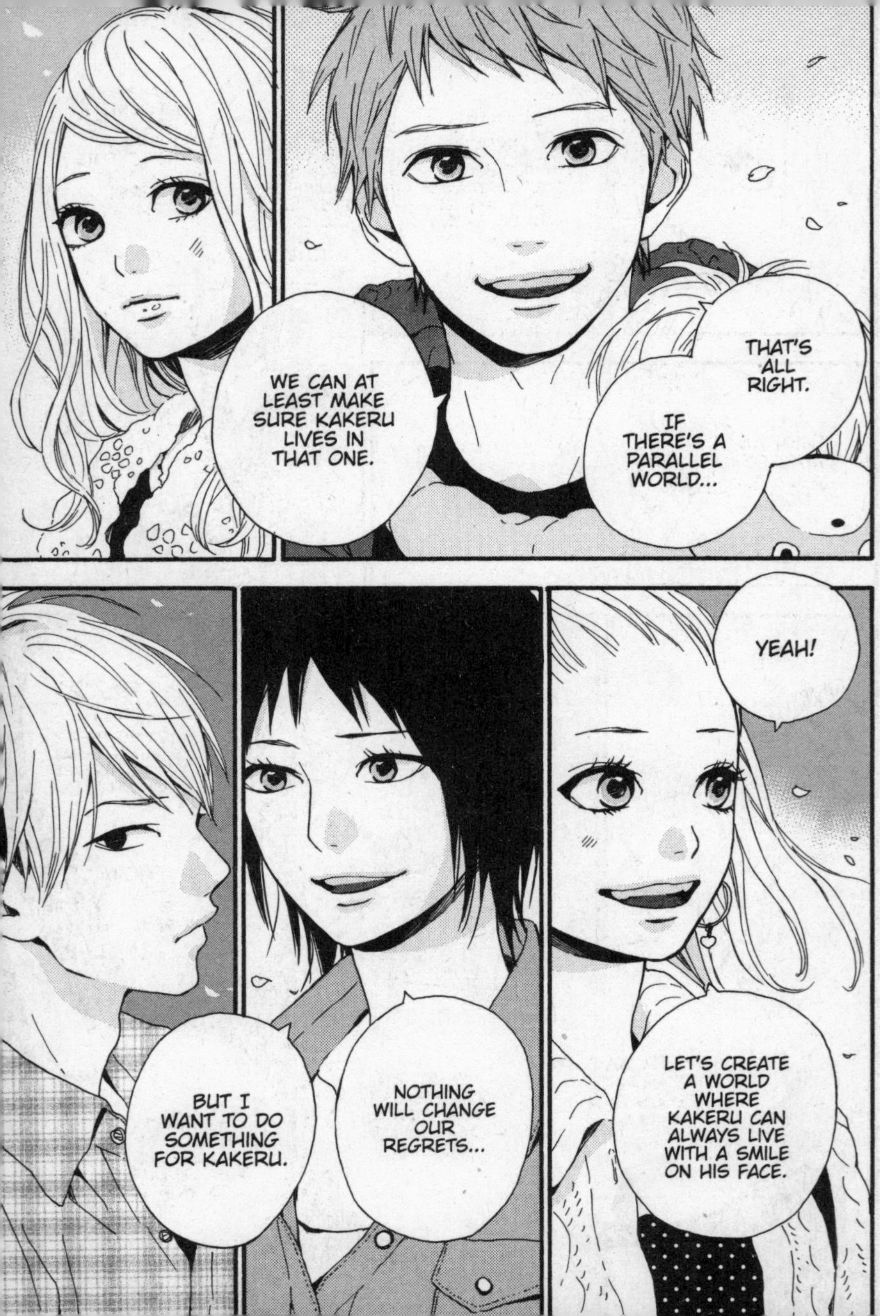
THAT'S ALL RIGHT.
IF THERE'S A PARALLEL WORLD...
WE CAN AT LEAST MAKE SURE KAKERU LIVES IN THAT ONE.
YEAH!
LET'S CREATE A WORLD WHERE KAKERU CAN ALWAYS LIVE WITH A SMILE ON HIS FACE.
NOTHING WILL CHANGE OUR REGRETS...
BUT I WANT TO DO SOMETHING FOR KAKERU.

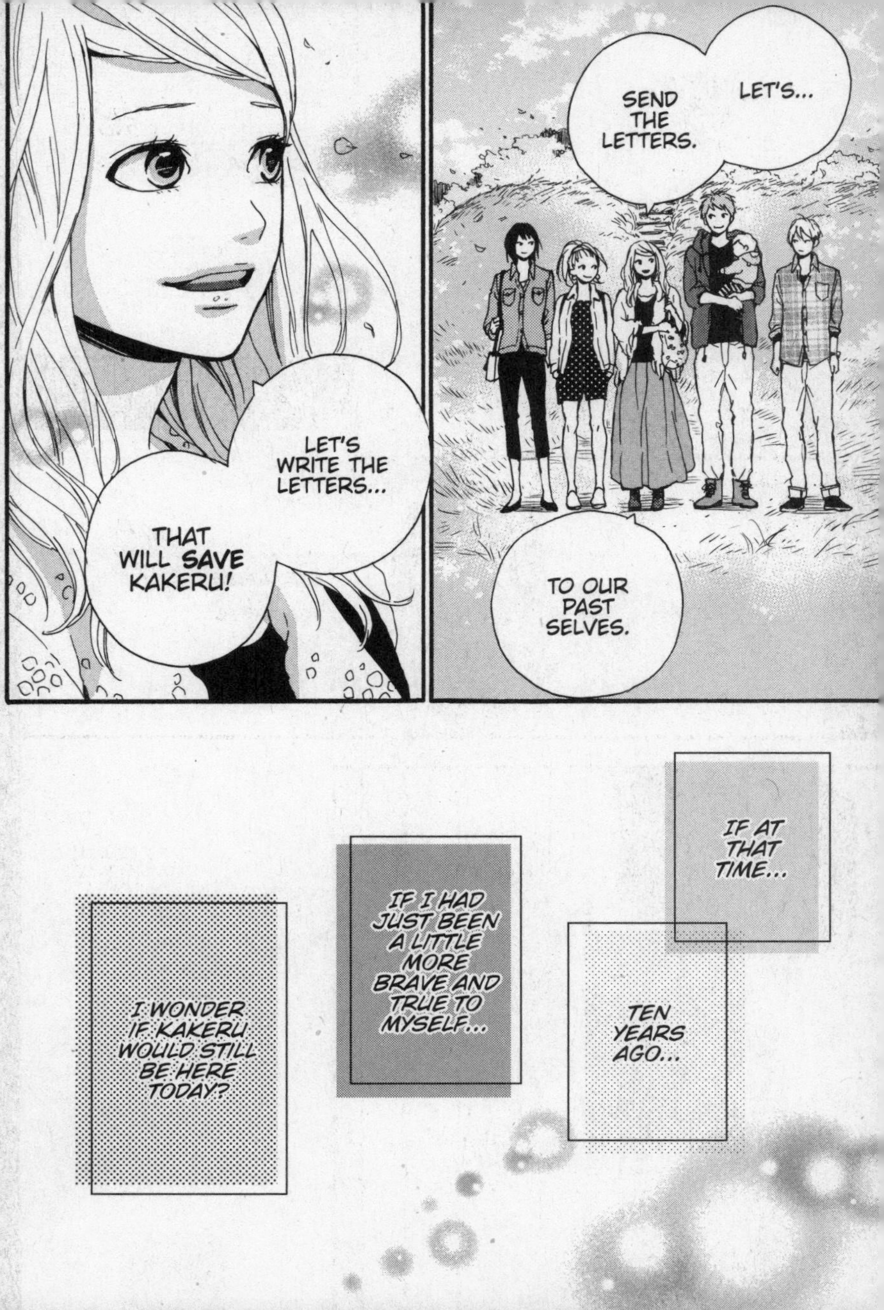
LET'S...
SEND THE LETTERS.
TO OUR PAST SELVES.
LET'S WRITE THE LETTERS...
THAT WILL SAVE KAKERU!
IF AT THAT TIME...
TEN YEARS AGO...
IF I HAD JUST BEEN A LITTLE MORE BRAVE AND TRUE TO MYSELF...
I WONDER IF KAKERU WOULD STILL BE HERE TODAY?

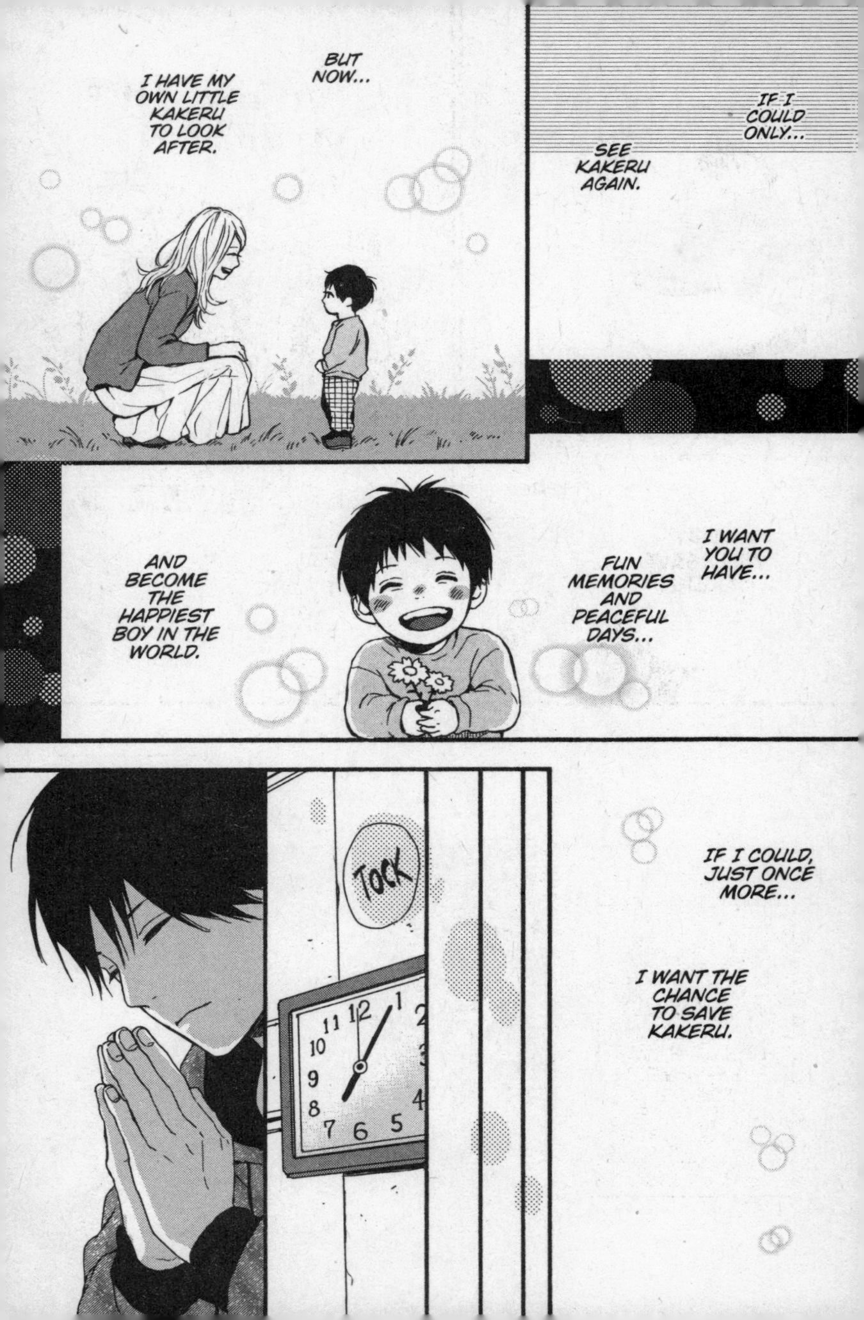
IF I COULD ONLY...
SEE KAKERU AGAIN.
BUT NOW...
I HAVE MY OWN LITTLE KAKERU TO LOOK AFTER.
I WANT YOU TO HAVE...
FUN MEMORIES AND PEACEFUL DAYS...
AND BECOME THE HAPPIEST BOY IN THE WORLD.
IF I COULD, JUST ONCE MORE...
I WANT THE CHANCE TO SAVE KAKERU.
TOCK

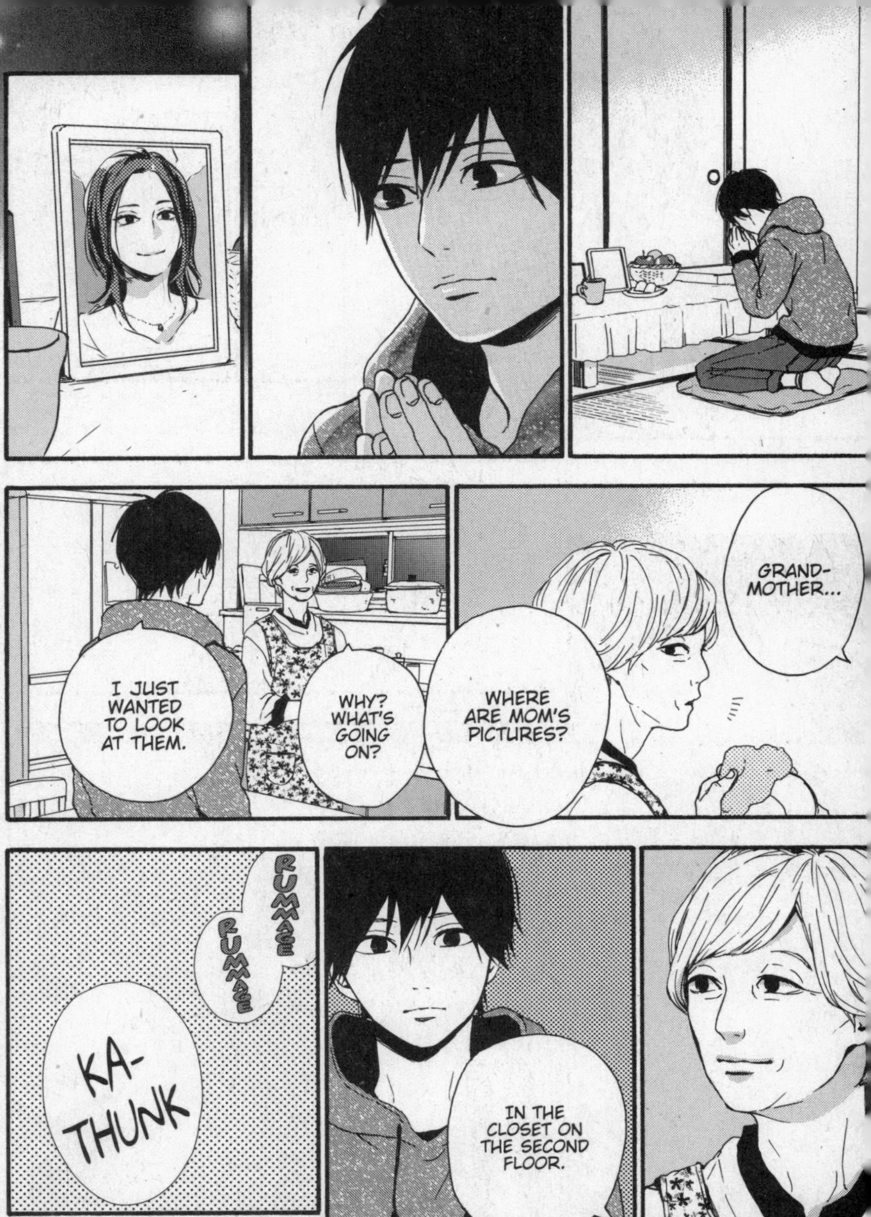
GRAND-MOTHER...
WHERE ARE MOM'S PICTURES?
WHY? WHAT'S GOING ON?
I JUST WANTED TO LOOK AT THEM.
IN THE CLOSET ON THE SECOND FLOOR.
RUMMAGE
RUMMAGE
KA-THUNK

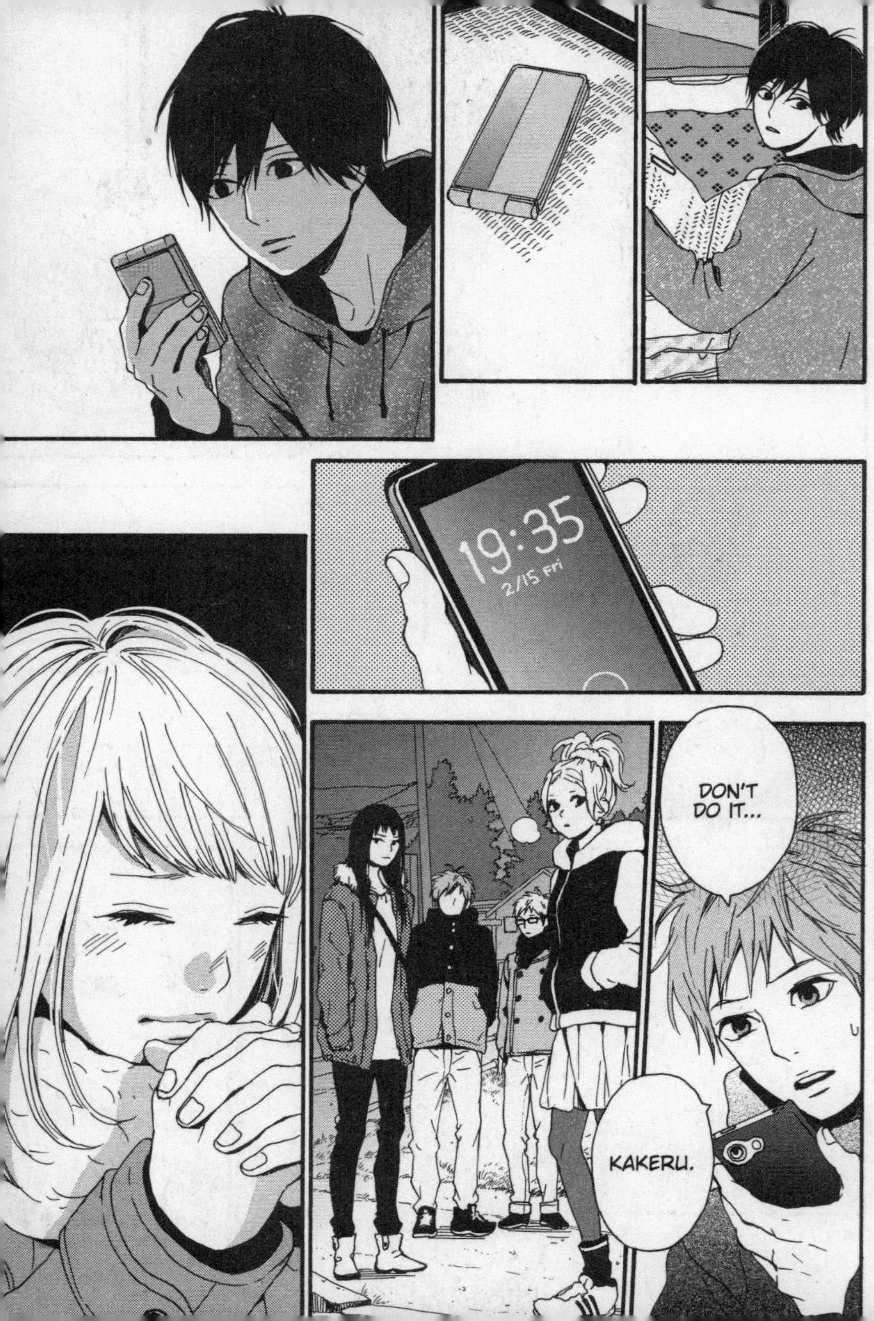

19:35
2/15 Fri
DON'T DO IT...
KAKERU.

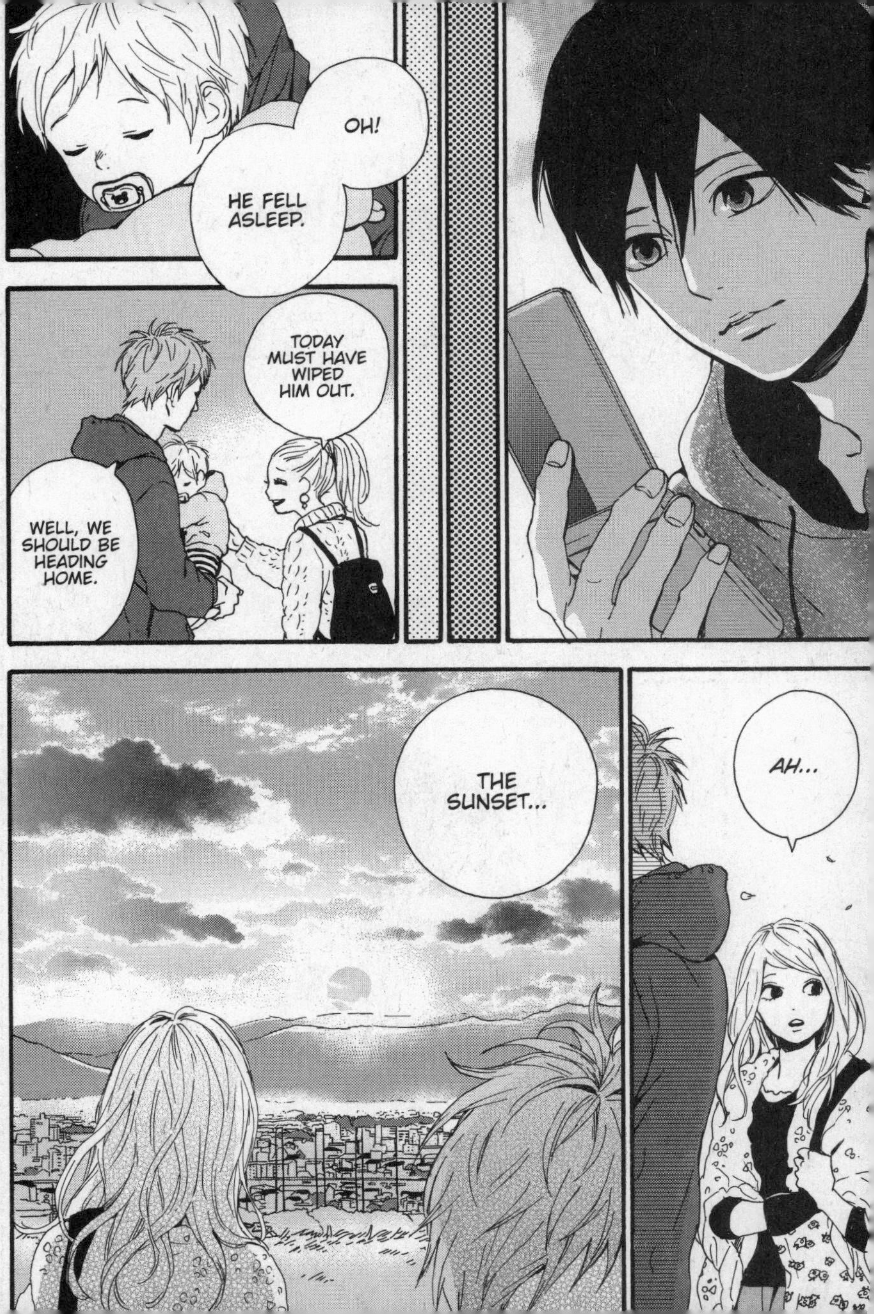
OH!
HE FELL ASLEEP.
TODAY MUST HAVE WIPED HIM OUT.
WELL, WE SHOULD BE HEADING HOME.
AH...
THE SUNSET...

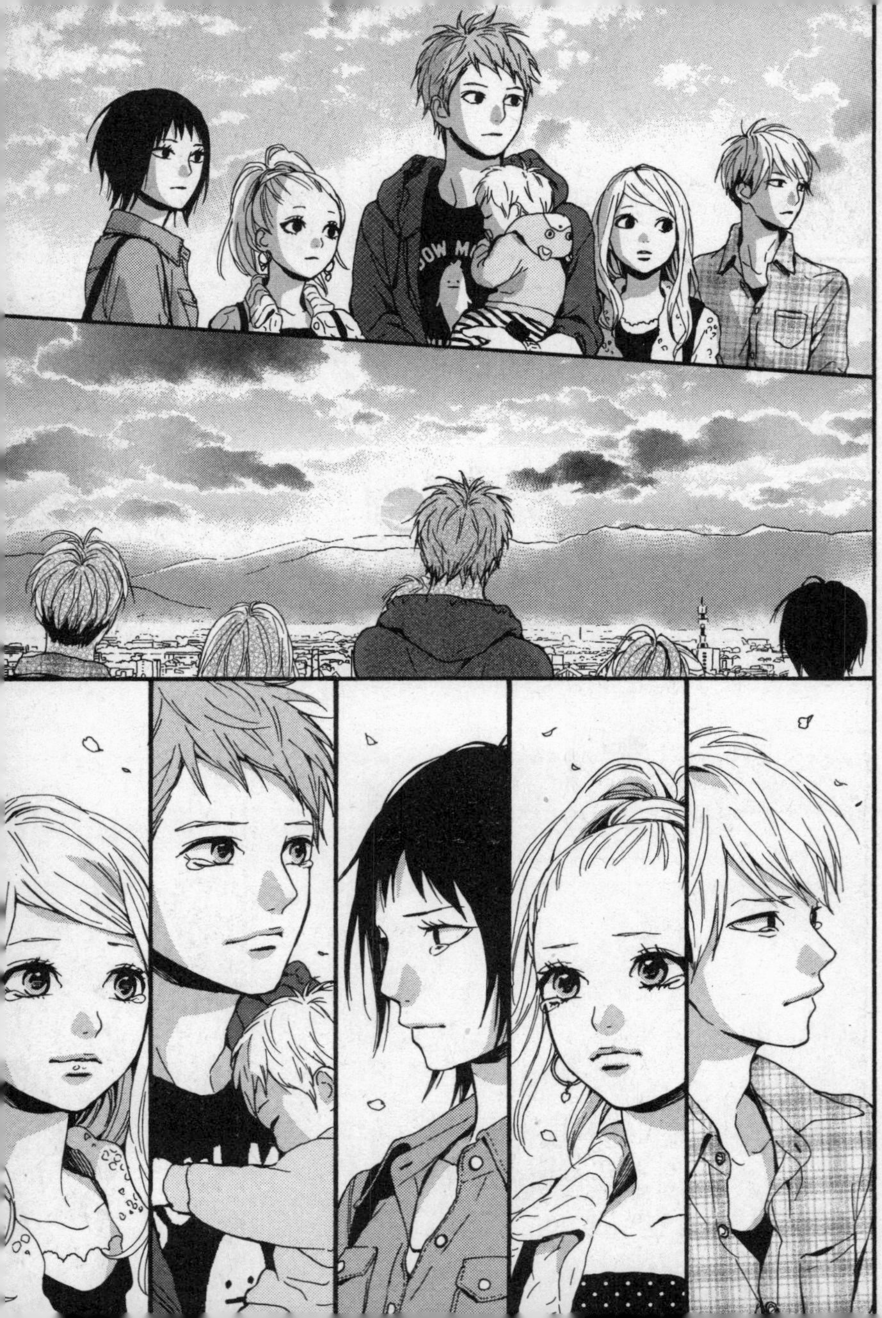

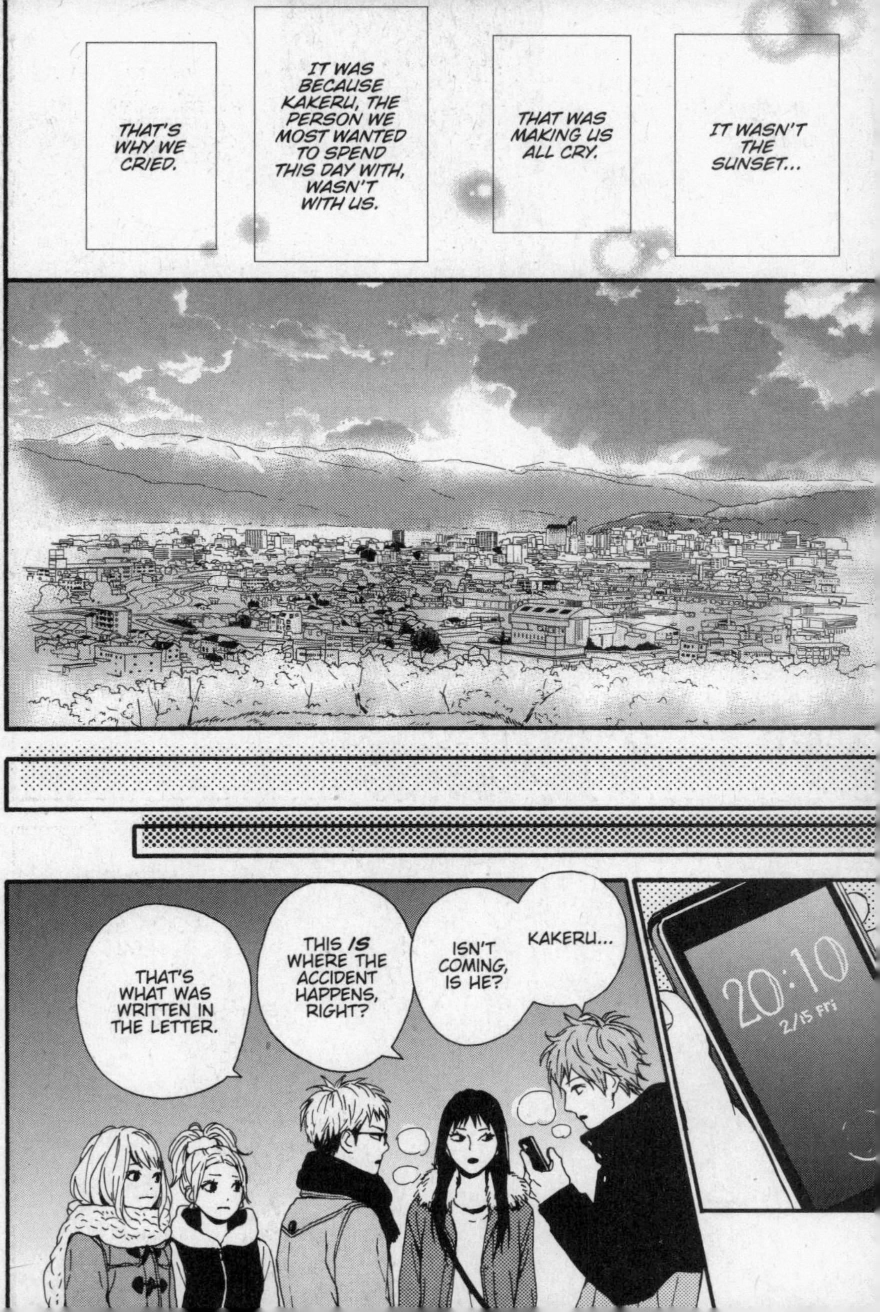
IT WASN'T THE SUNSET...
THAT WAS MAKING US ALL CRY.
IT WAS BECAUSE KAKERU, THE PERSON WE MOST WANTED TO SPEND THIS DAY WITH, WASN'T WITH US.
THAT'S WHY WE CRIED.
20:10
2/15 Fri
KAKERU...
ISN'T COMING, IS HE?
THIS *IS* WHERE THE ACCIDENT HAPPENS, RIGHT?
THAT'S WHAT WAS WRITTEN IN THE LETTER.

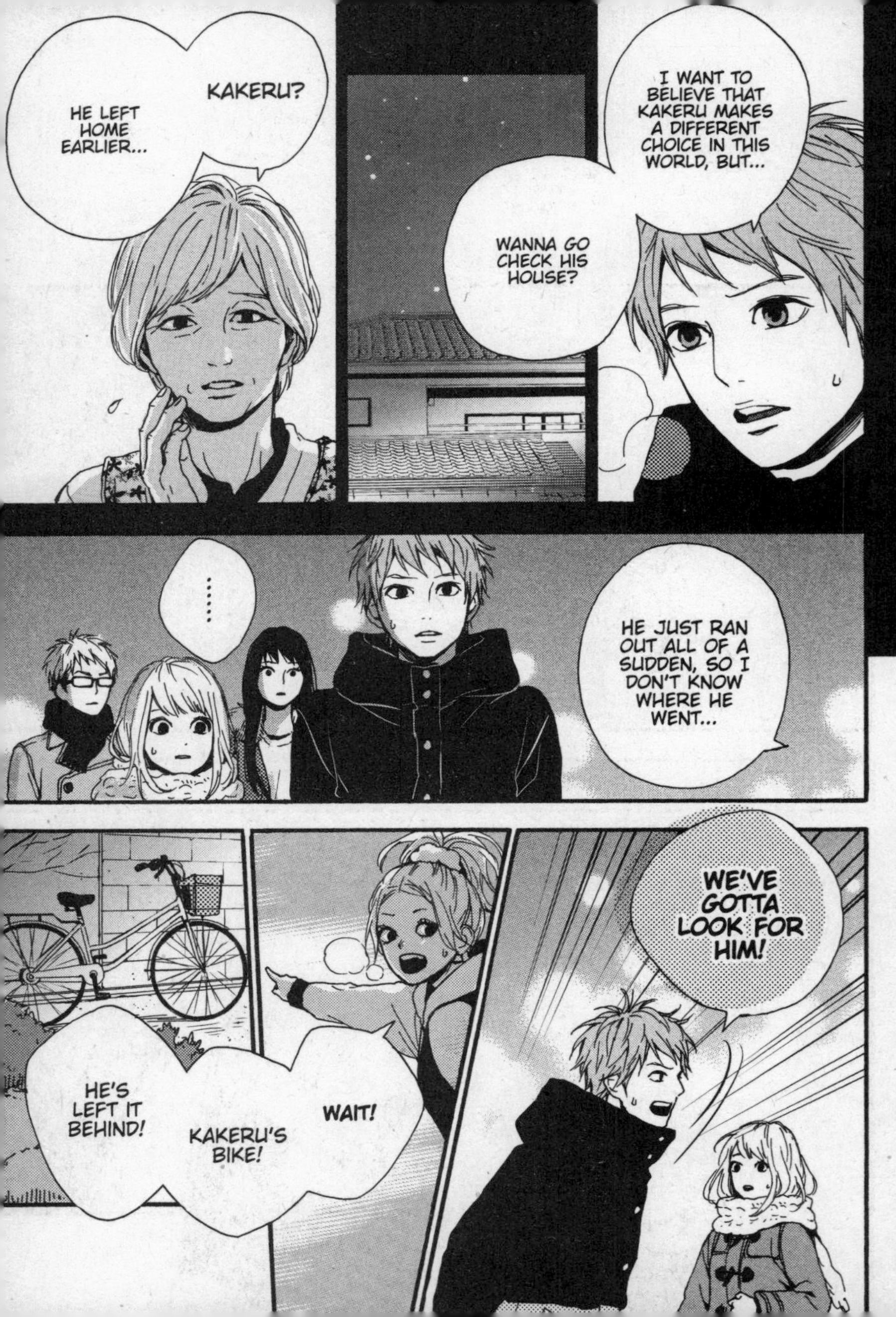
I WANT TO BELIEVE THAT KAKERU MAKES A DIFFERENT CHOICE IN THIS WORLD, BUT...
WANNA GO CHECK HIS HOUSE?
KAKERU?
HE LEFT HOME EARLIER...
HE JUST RAN OUT ALL OF A SUDDEN, SO I DON'T KNOW WHERE HE WENT...
......
WE'VE GOTTA LOOK FOR HIM!
WAIT!
KAKERU'S BIKE!
HE'S LEFT IT BEHIND!

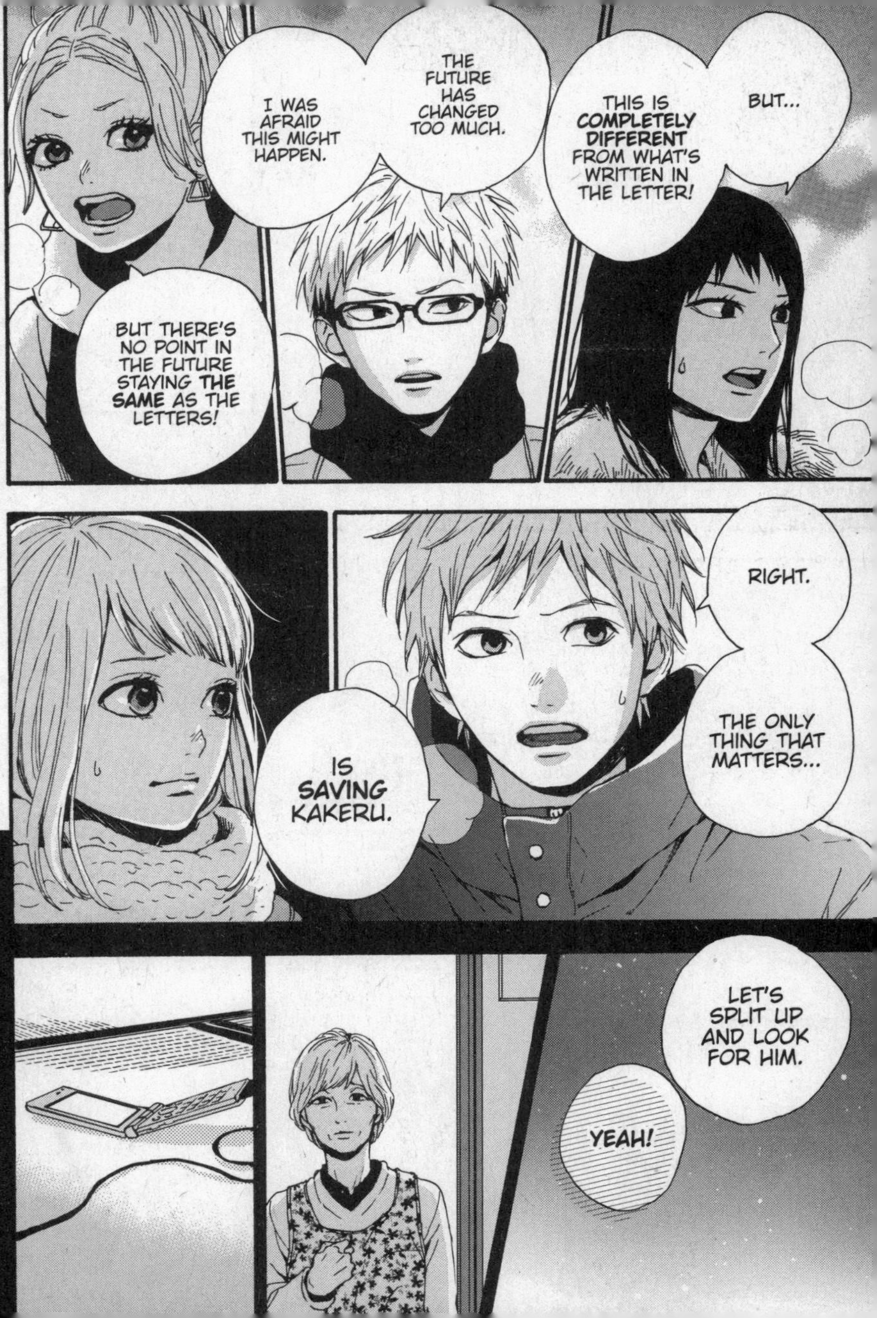
BUT...
THIS IS COMPLETELY DIFFERENT FROM WHAT'S WRITTEN IN THE LETTER!
THE FUTURE HAS CHANGED TOO MUCH.
I WAS AFRAID THIS MIGHT HAPPEN.
BUT THERE'S NO POINT IN THE FUTURE STAYING THE SAME AS THE LETTERS!
RIGHT.
THE ONLY THING THAT MATTERS...
IS SAVING KAKERU.
LET'S SPLIT UP AND LOOK FOR HIM.
YEAH!

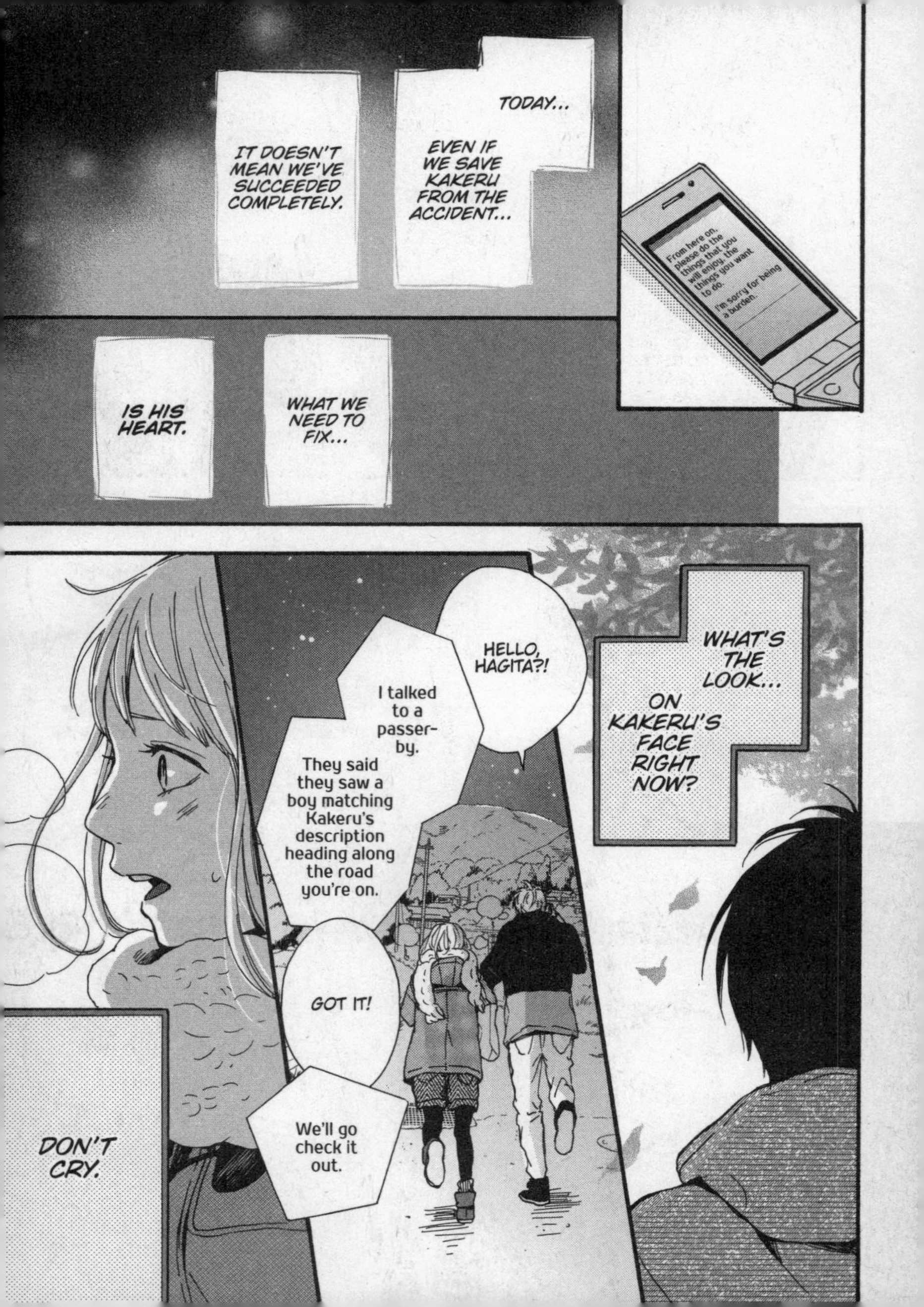

From here on, please do the things that you will enjoy, the things you want to do.
I'm sorry for being a burden.
TODAY...
EVEN IF WE SAVE KAKERU FROM THE ACCIDENT...
IT DOESN'T MEAN WE'VE SUCCEEDED COMPLETELY.
WHAT WE NEED TO FIX...
IS HIS HEART.
WHAT'S THE LOOK...
ON KAKERU'S FACE RIGHT NOW?
HELLO, HAGITA?!
I talked to a passer-by.
They said they saw a boy matching Kakeru's description heading along the road you're on.
GOT IT!
We'll go check it out.
DON'T CRY.

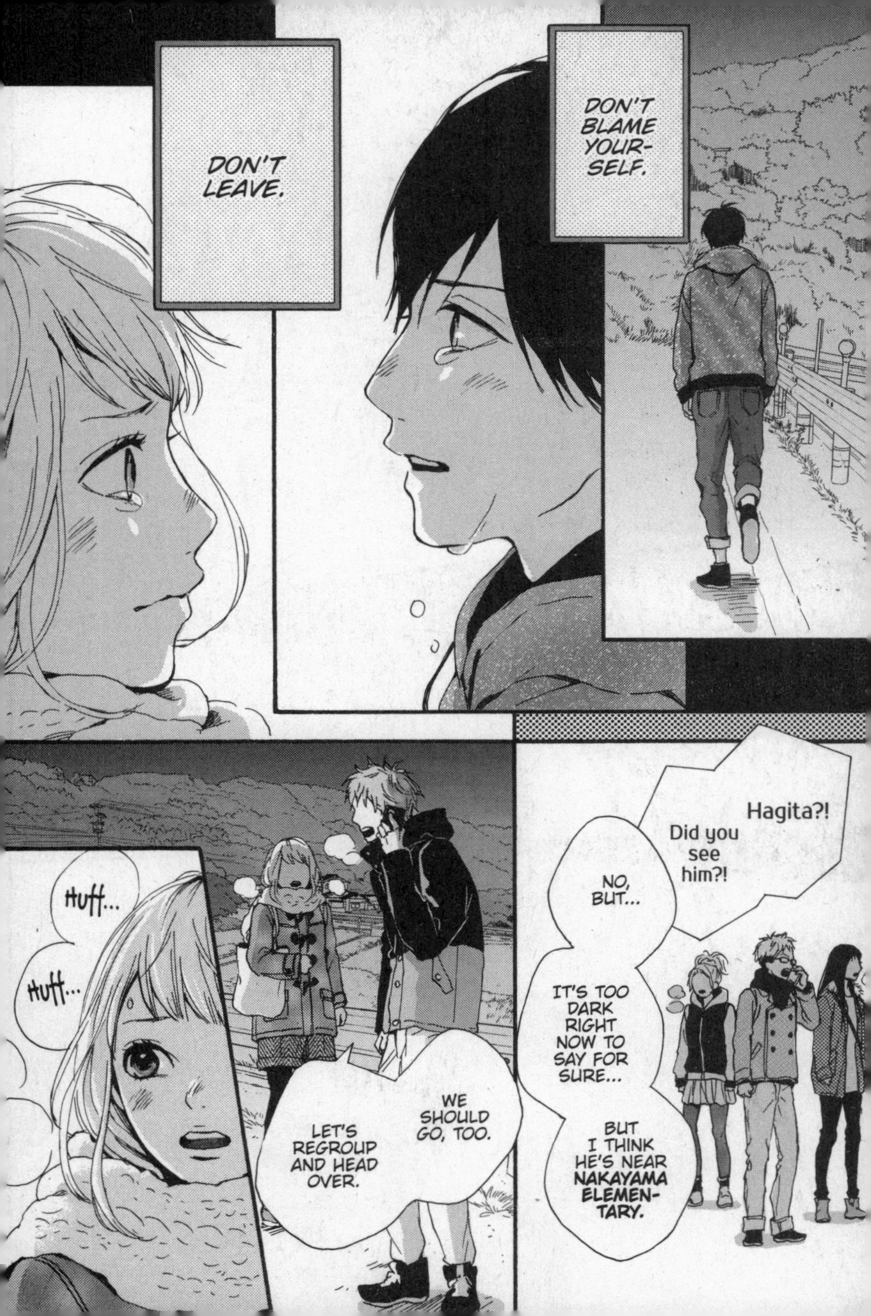
DON'T BLAME YOURSELF.
DON'T LEAVE.
Hagita?! Did you see him?!
NO, BUT...
IT'S TOO DARK RIGHT NOW TO SAY FOR SURE...
BUT I THINK HE'S NEAR **NAKAYAMA ELEMENTARY.**
Huff...
Huff...
WE SHOULD GO, TOO.
LET'S REGROUP AND HEAD OVER.

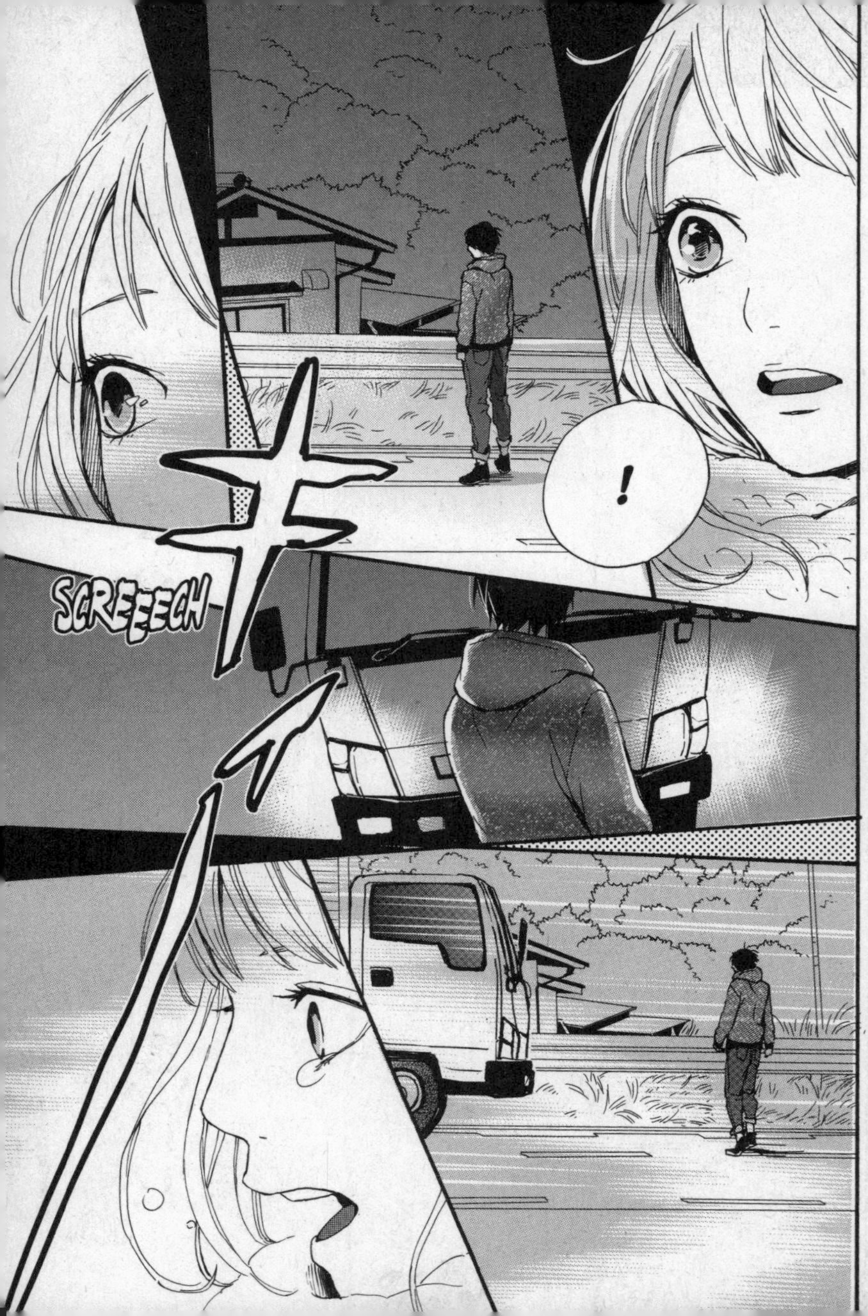
!
SCREEEECH

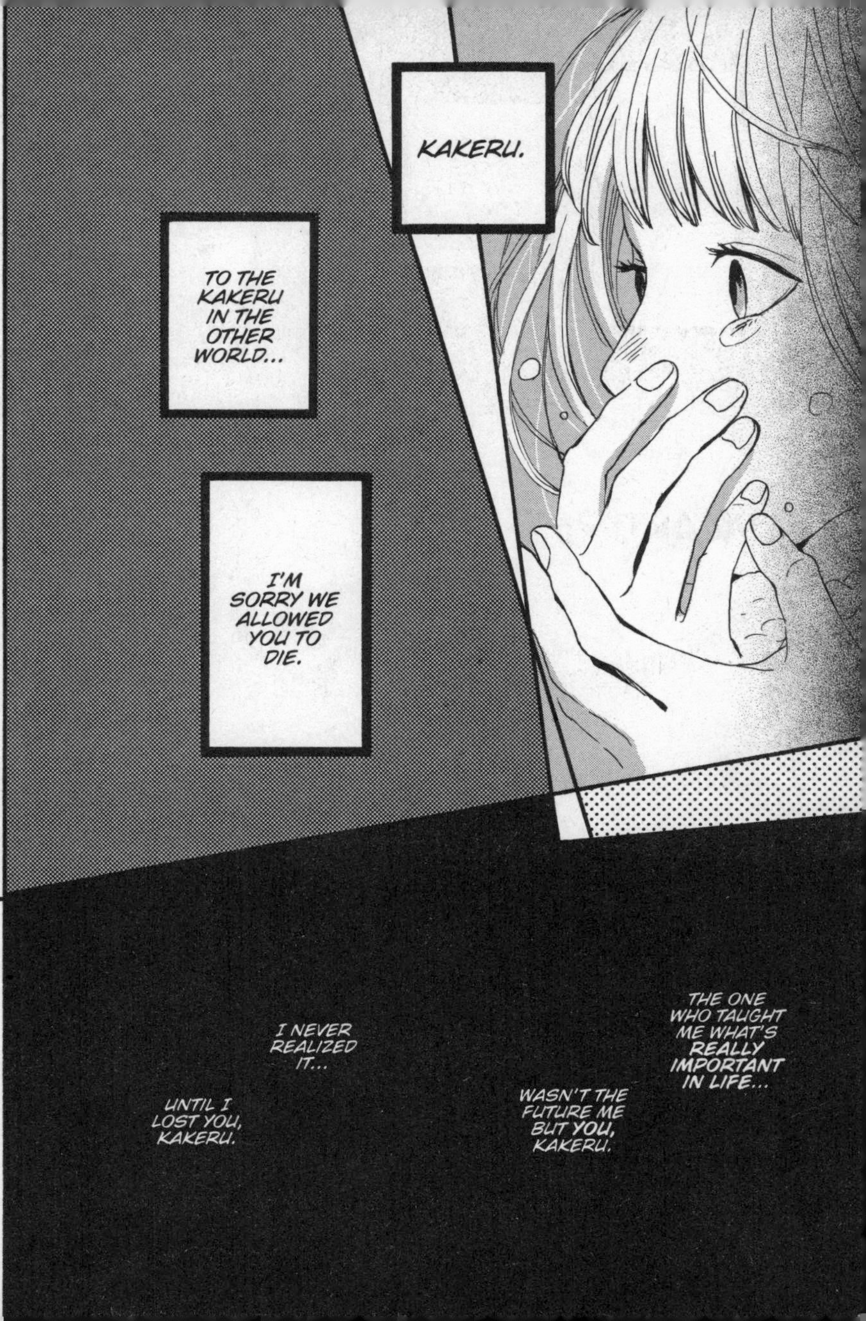
KAKERU.
TO THE KAKERU IN THE OTHER WORLD...
I'M SORRY WE ALLOWED YOU TO DIE.
THE ONE WHO TAUGHT ME WHAT'S REALLY IMPORTANT IN LIFE...
WASN'T THE FUTURE ME BUT YOU, KAKERU.
I NEVER REALIZED IT...
UNTIL I LOST YOU, KAKERU.

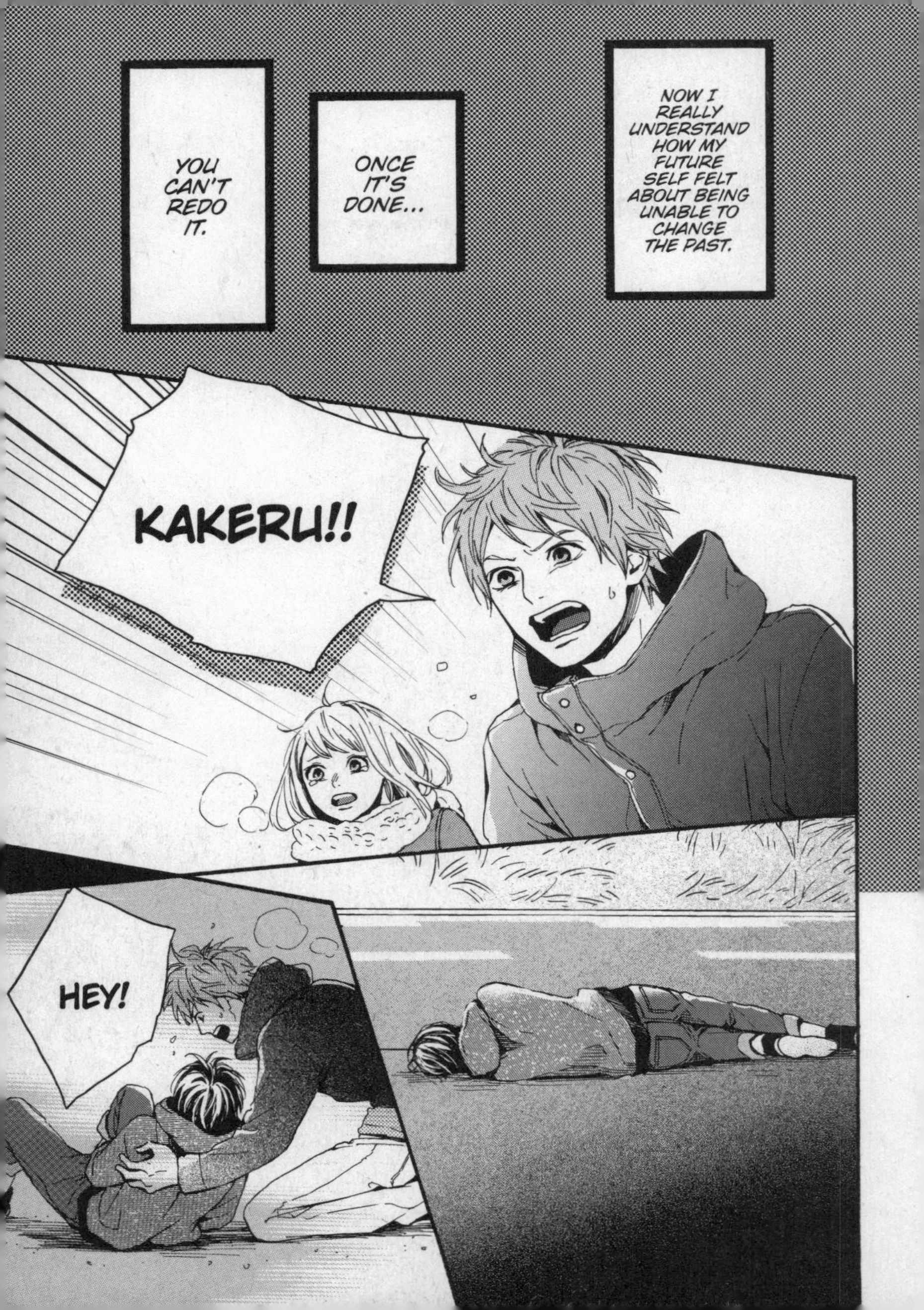
NOW I REALLY UNDERSTAND HOW MY FUTURE SELF FELT ABOUT BEING UNABLE TO CHANGE THE PAST.
ONCE IT'S DONE...
YOU CAN'T REDO IT.
KAKERU!!
HEY!

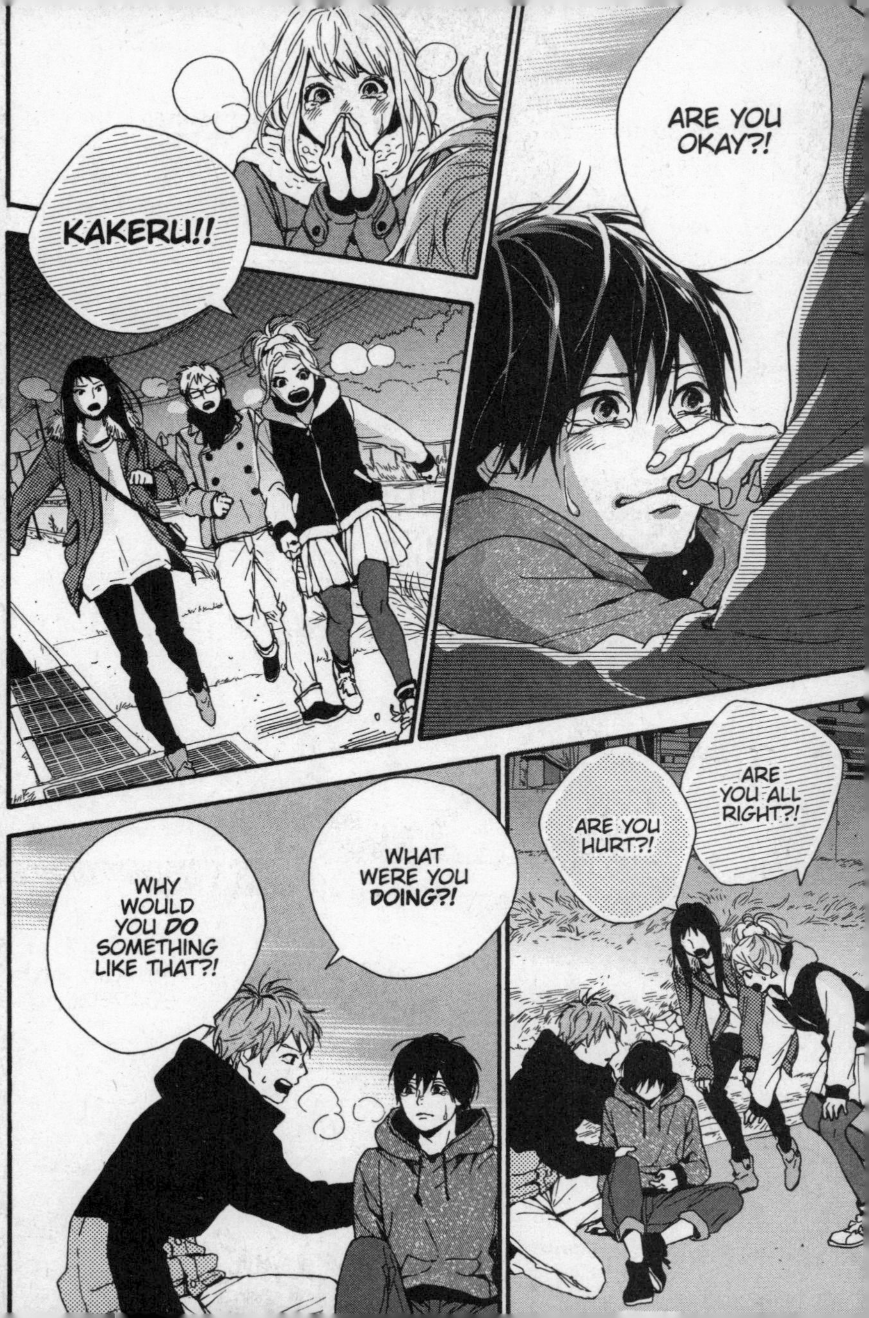
ARE YOU OKAY?!
KAKERU!!
ARE YOU ALL RIGHT?!
ARE YOU HURT?!
WHAT WERE YOU DOING?!
WHY WOULD YOU DO SOMETHING LIKE THAT?!

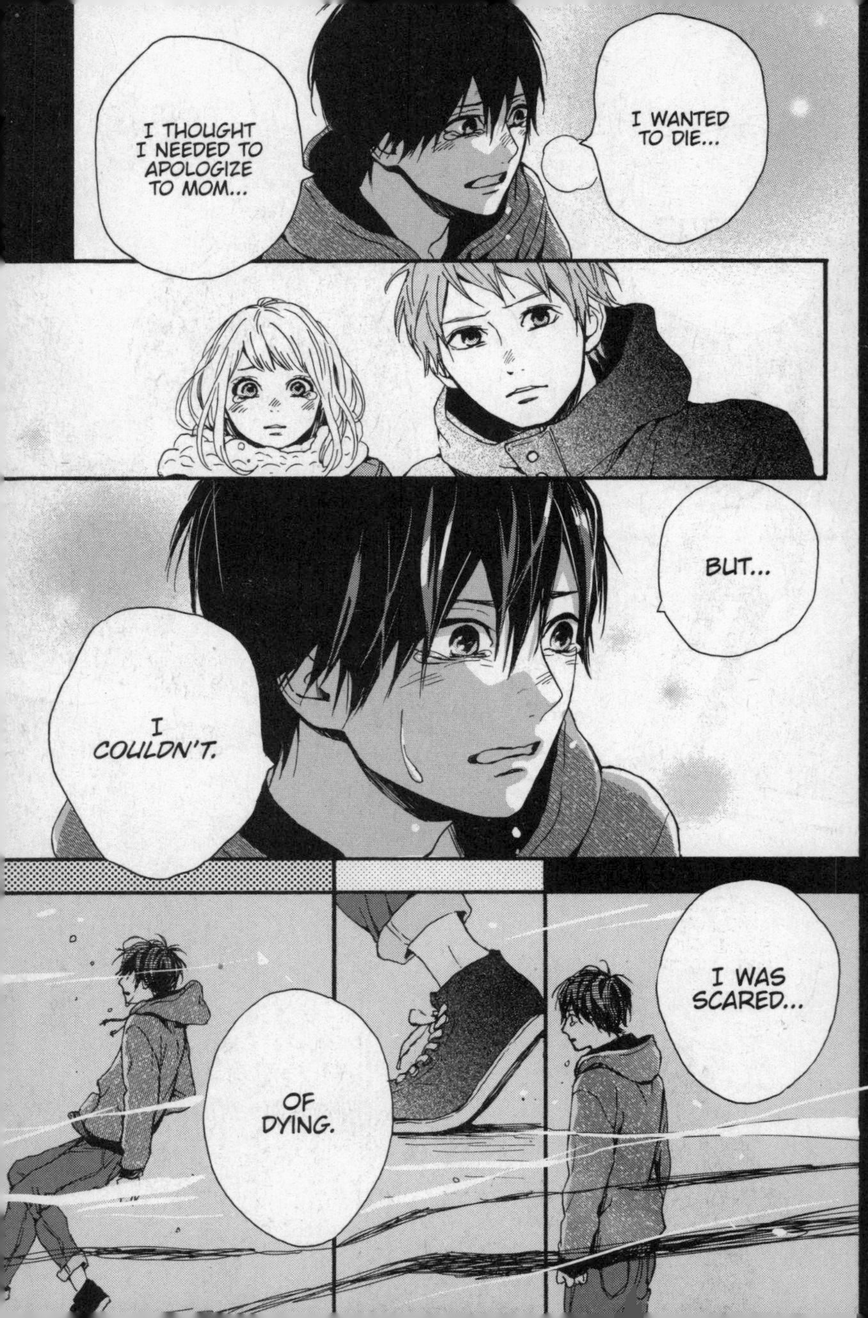
I WANTED TO DIE...
I THOUGHT I NEEDED TO APOLOGIZE TO MOM...
BUT...
I COULDN'T.
I WAS SCARED...
OF DYING.

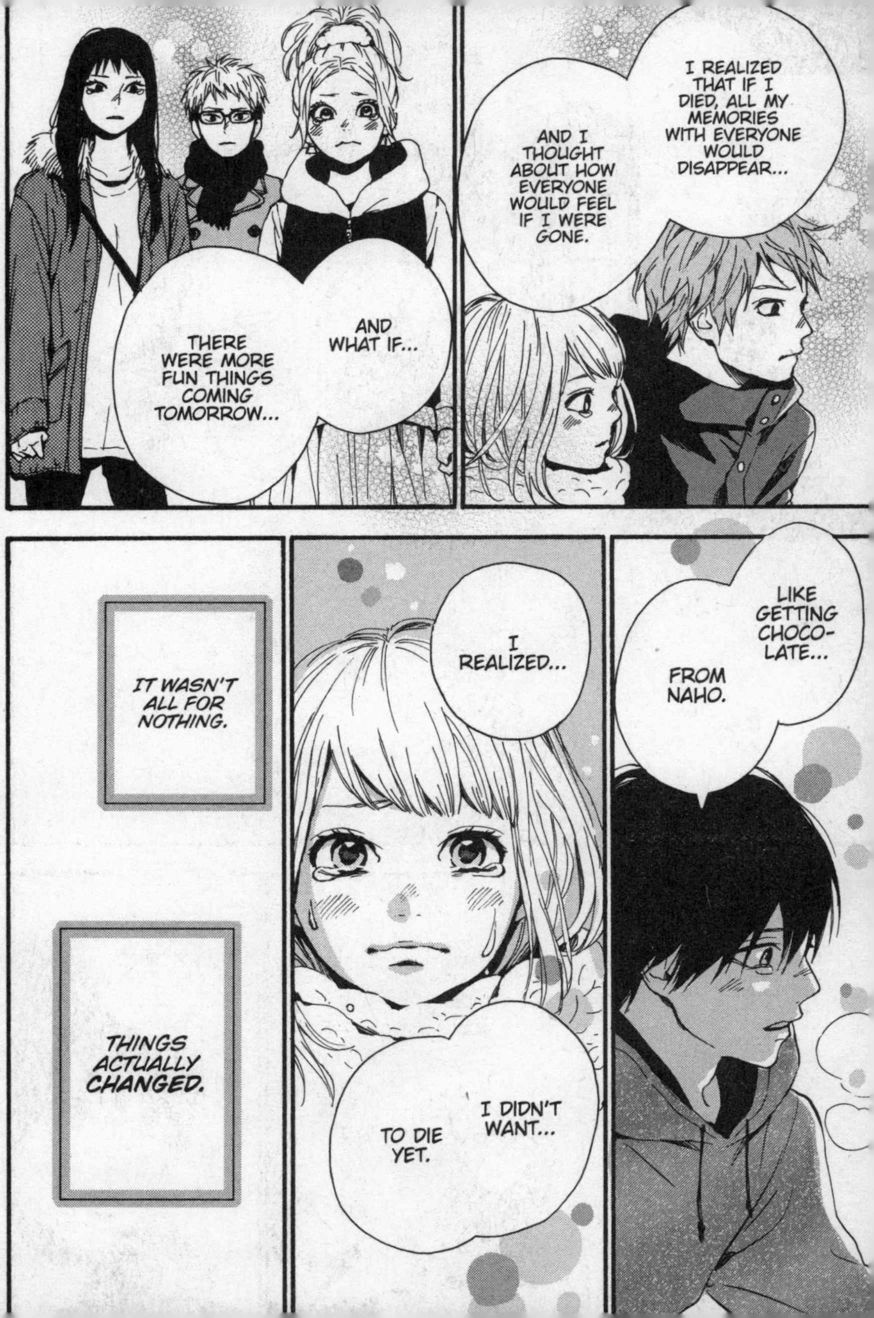
I REALIZED THAT IF I DIED, ALL MY MEMORIES WITH EVERYONE WOULD DISAPPEAR...
AND I THOUGHT ABOUT HOW EVERYONE WOULD FEEL IF I WERE GONE.
AND WHAT IF...
THERE WERE MORE FUN THINGS COMING TOMORROW...
LIKE GETTING CHOCO-LATE...
FROM NAHO.
I REALIZED...
I DIDN'T WANT...
TO DIE YET.
IT WASN'T ALL FOR NOTHING.
THINGS ACTUALLY CHANGED.

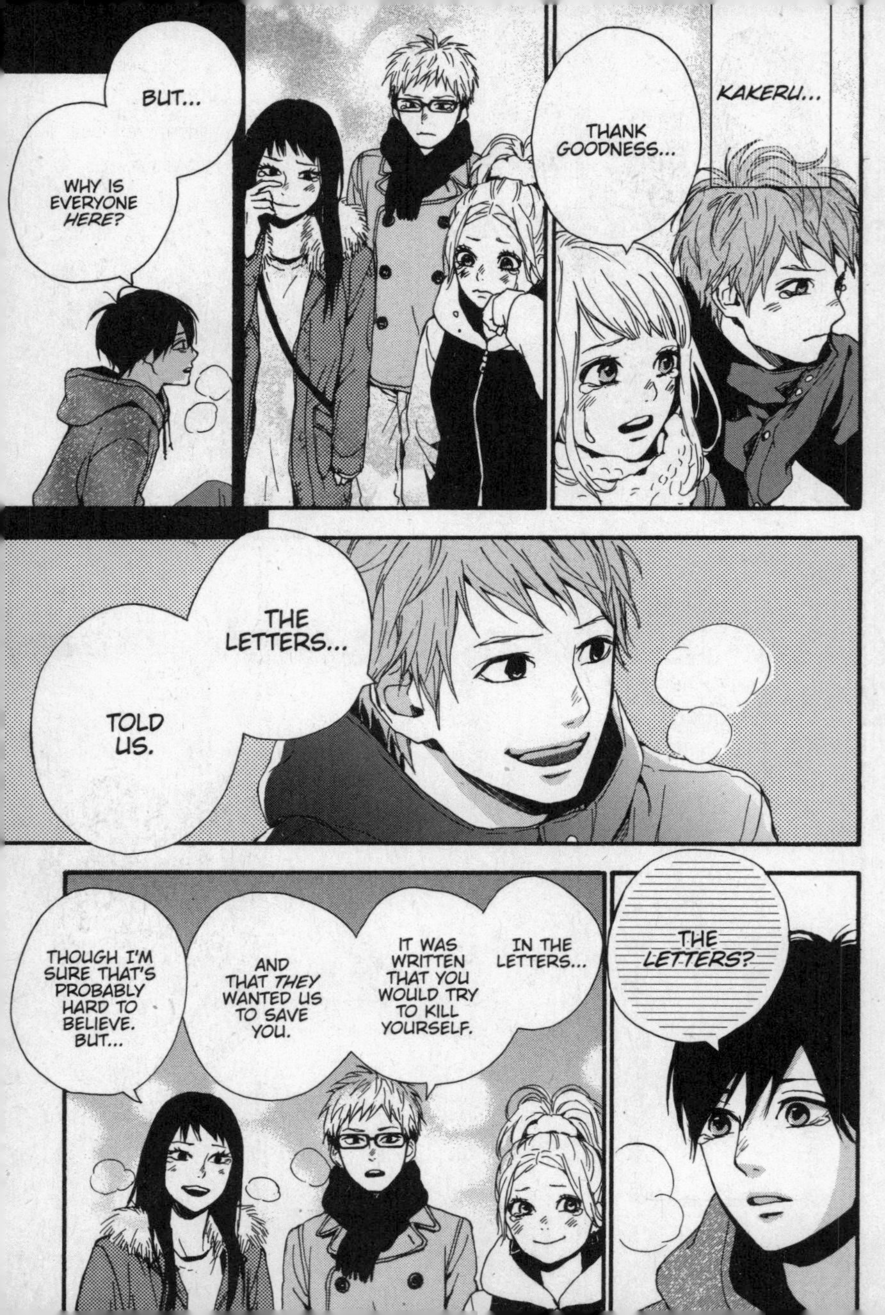
KAKERU...
THANK GOODNESS...
BUT...
WHY IS EVERYONE *HERE*?
THE LETTERS...
TOLD US.
THE *LETTERS*?
IN THE LETTERS...
IT WAS WRITTEN THAT YOU WOULD TRY TO KILL YOURSELF.
AND THAT *THEY* WANTED US TO SAVE YOU.
THOUGH I'M SURE THAT'S PROBABLY HARD TO BELIEVE. BUT...

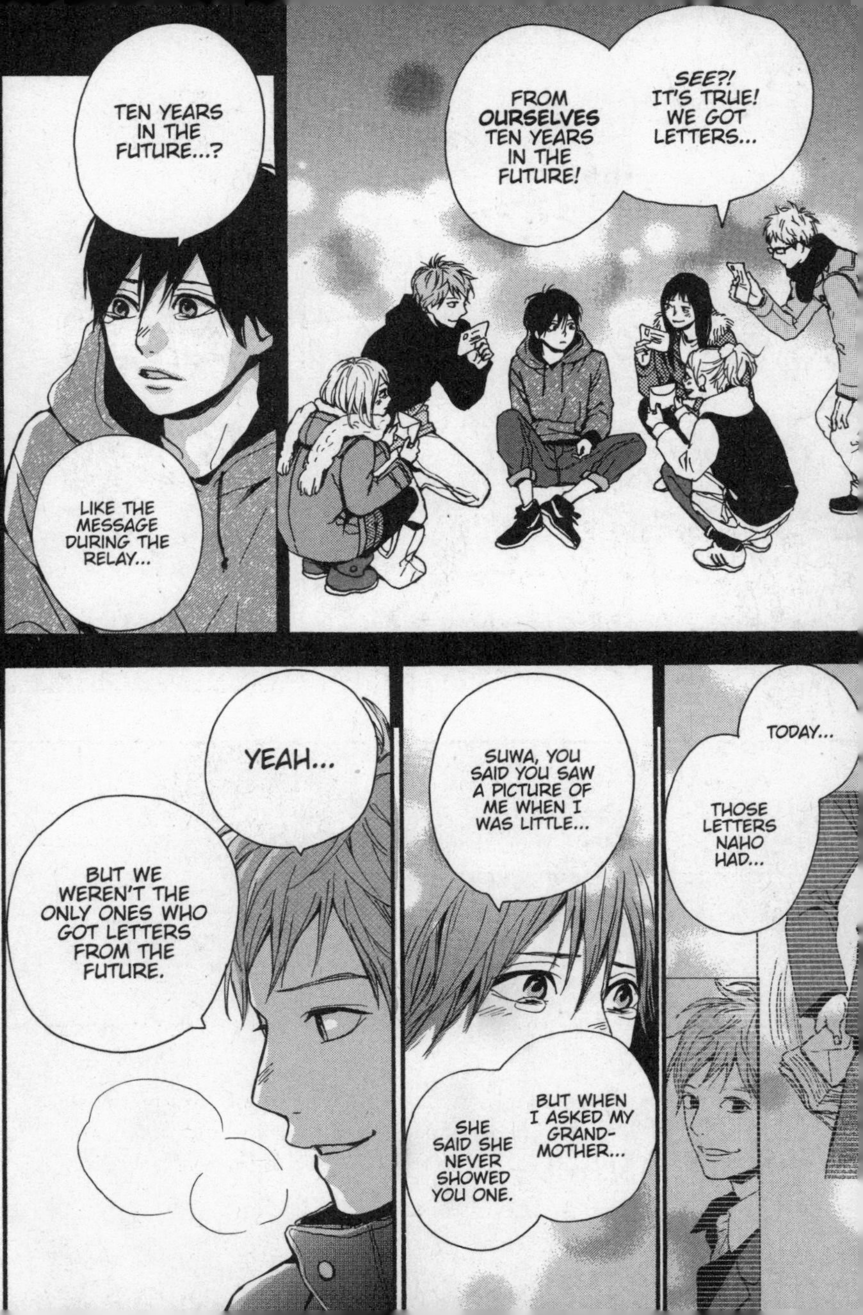
SEE?! IT'S TRUE! WE GOT LETTERS...
FROM OURSELVES TEN YEARS IN THE FUTURE!
TEN YEARS IN THE FUTURE...?
LIKE THE MESSAGE DURING THE RELAY...
TODAY...
THOSE LETTERS NAHO HAD...
SUWA, YOU SAID YOU SAW A PICTURE OF ME WHEN I WAS LITTLE...
BUT WHEN I ASKED MY GRANDMOTHER...
SHE SAID SHE NEVER SHOWED YOU ONE.
YEAH...
BUT WE WEREN'T THE ONLY ONES WHO GOT LETTERS FROM THE FUTURE.

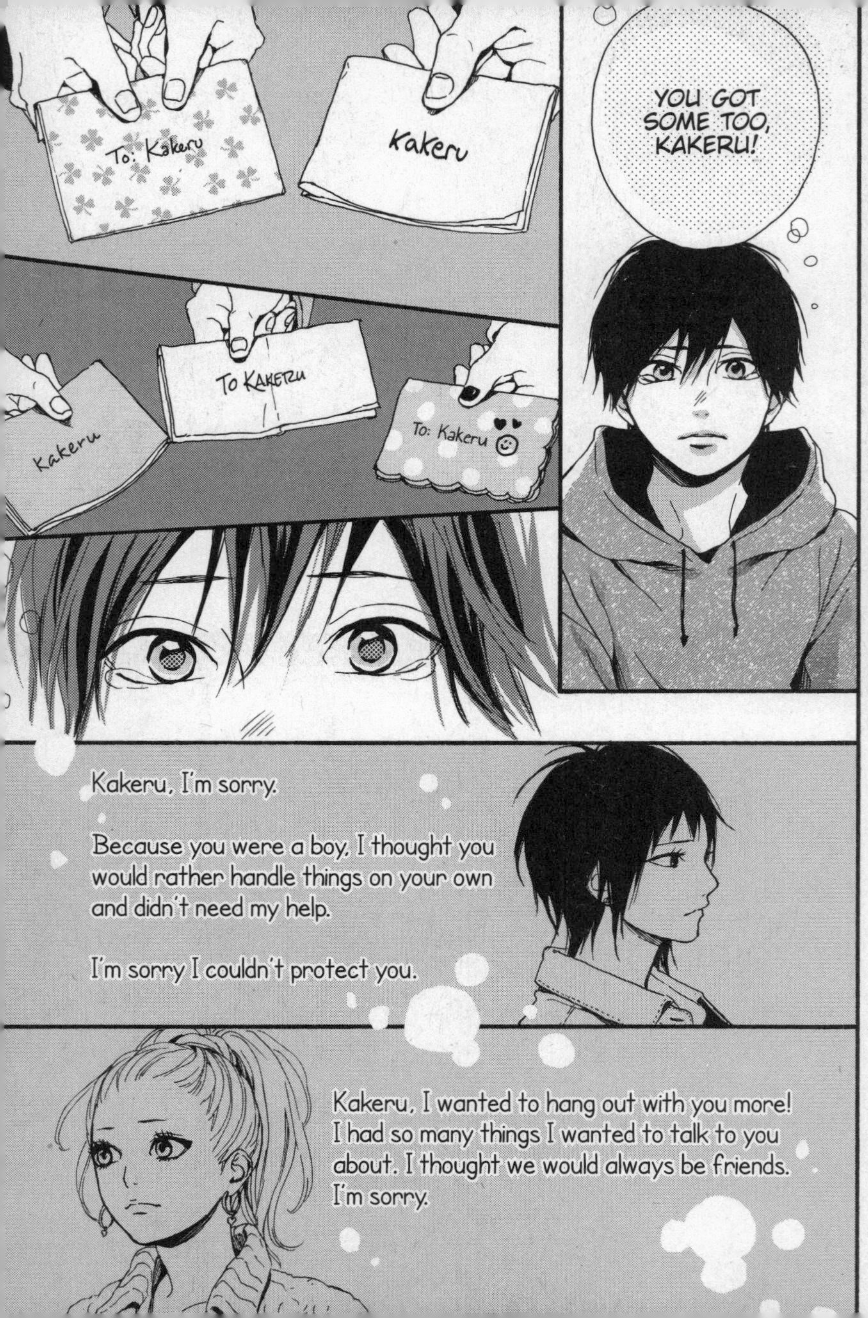
YOU GOT SOME TOO, KAKERU!
Kakeru
To: Kakeru
To: Kakeru
TO KAKERU
Kakeru
Kakeru, I'm sorry.
Because you were a boy, I thought you would rather handle things on your own and didn't need my help.
I'm sorry I couldn't protect you.
Kakeru, I wanted to hang out with you more! I had so many things I wanted to talk to you about. I thought we would always be friends. I'm sorry.

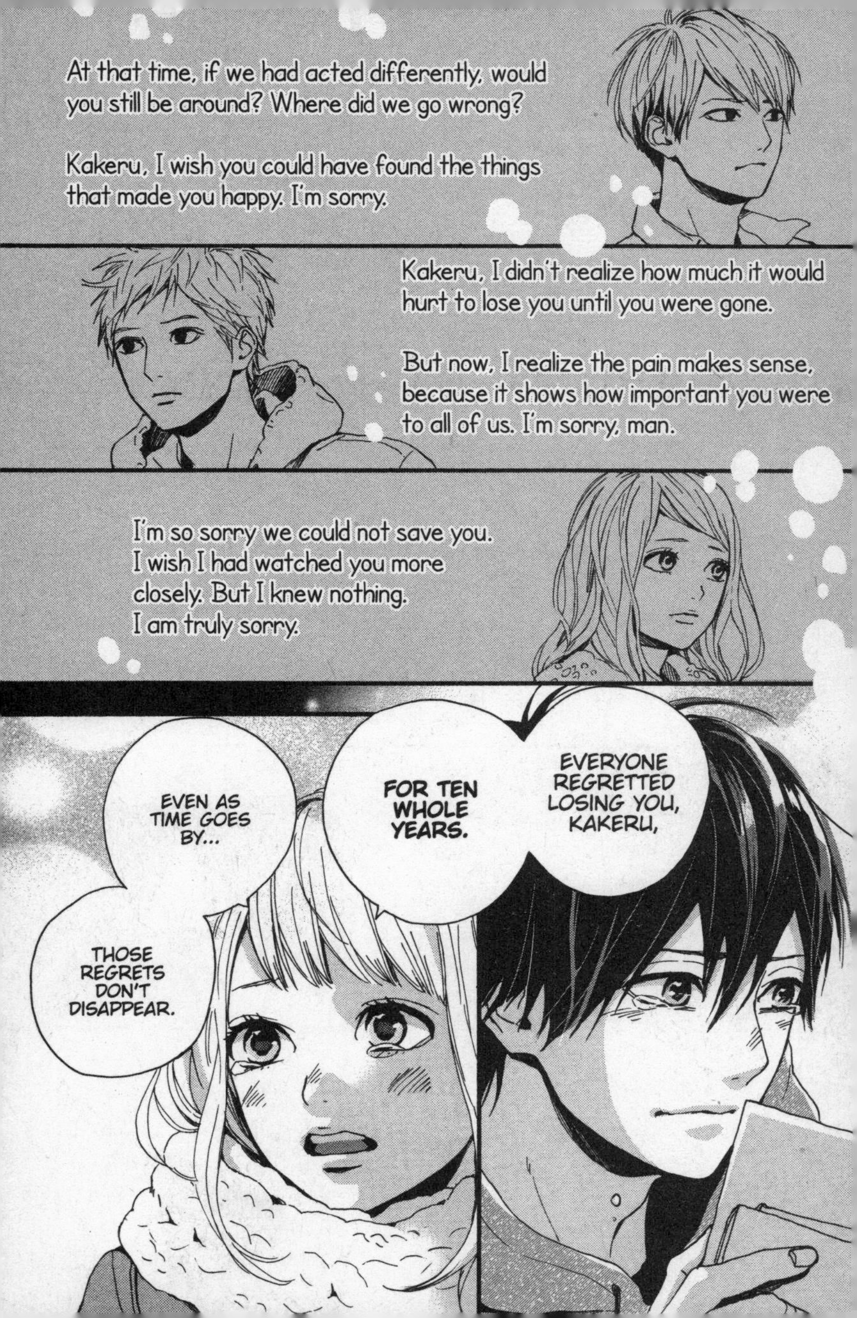
At that time, if we had acted differently, would you still be around? Where did we go wrong?
Kakeru, I wish you could have found the things that made you happy. I'm sorry.
Kakeru, I didn't realize how much it would hurt to lose you until you were gone.
But now, I realize the pain makes sense, because it shows how important you were to all of us. I'm sorry, man.
I'm so sorry we could not save you. I wish I had watched you more closely. But I knew nothing. I am truly sorry.
EVERYONE REGRETTED LOSING YOU, KAKERU,
FOR TEN WHOLE YEARS.
EVEN AS TIME GOES BY...
THOSE REGRETS DON'T DISAPPEAR.

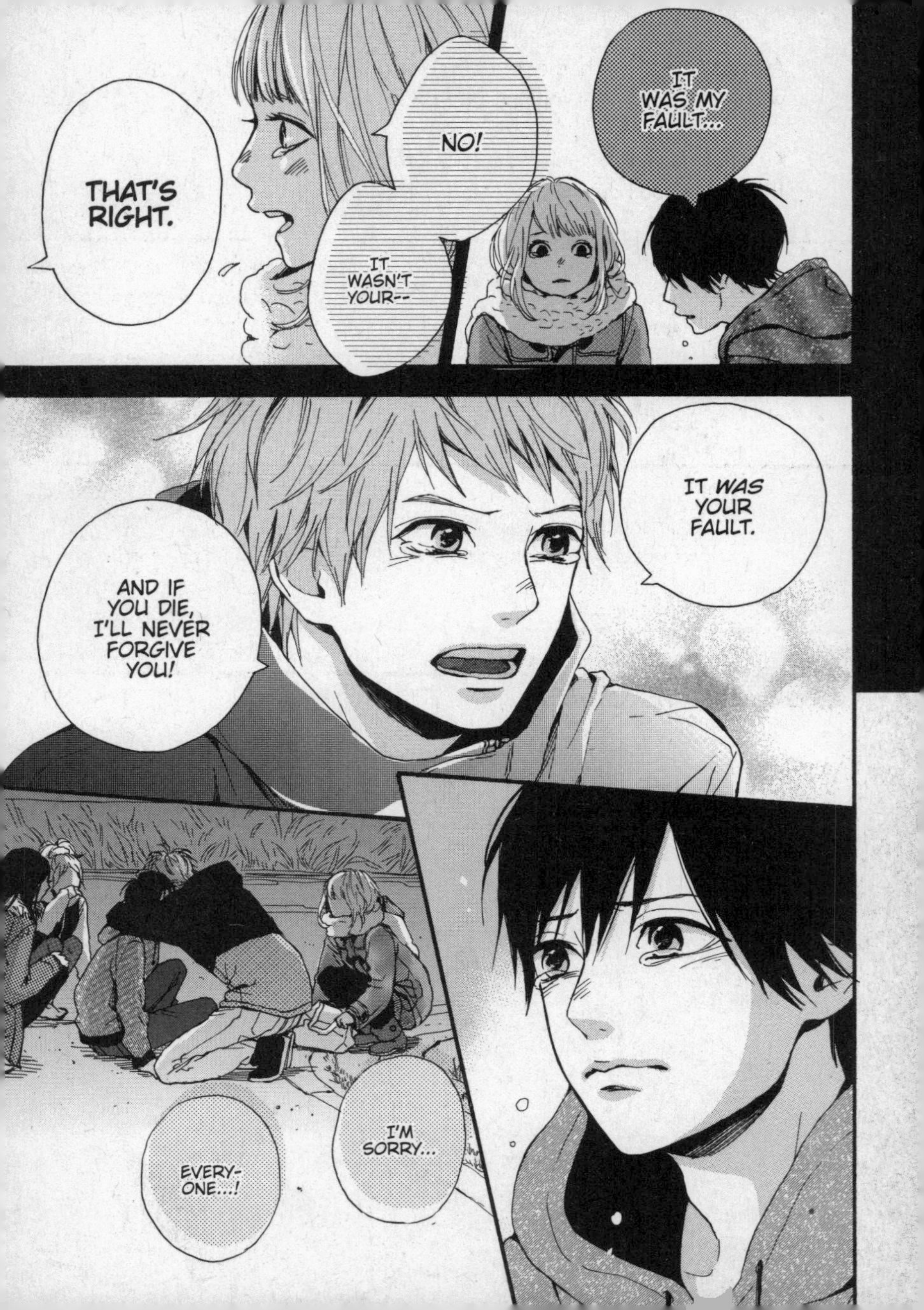
IT WAS MY FAULT...
NO!
IT WASN'T YOUR--
THAT'S RIGHT.
IT *WAS* YOUR FAULT.
AND IF YOU DIE, I'LL NEVER FORGIVE YOU!
I'M SORRY...
EVERY-ONE...!

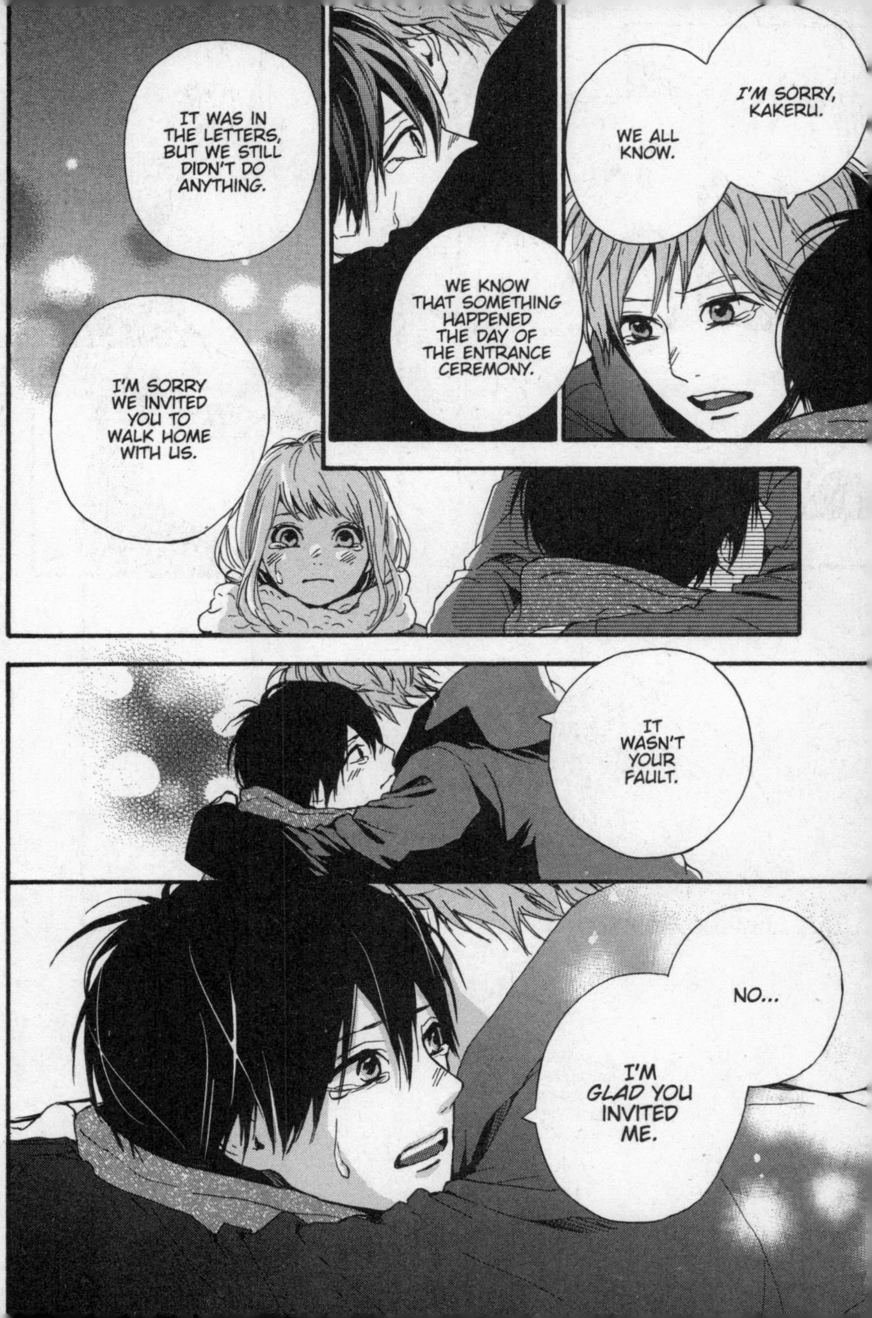
I'M SORRY, KAKERU.
WE ALL KNOW.
WE KNOW THAT SOMETHING HAPPENED THE DAY OF THE ENTRANCE CEREMONY.
IT WAS IN THE LETTERS, BUT WE STILL DIDN'T DO ANYTHING.
I'M SORRY WE INVITED YOU TO WALK HOME WITH US.
IT WASN'T YOUR FAULT.
NO...
I'M GLAD YOU INVITED ME.

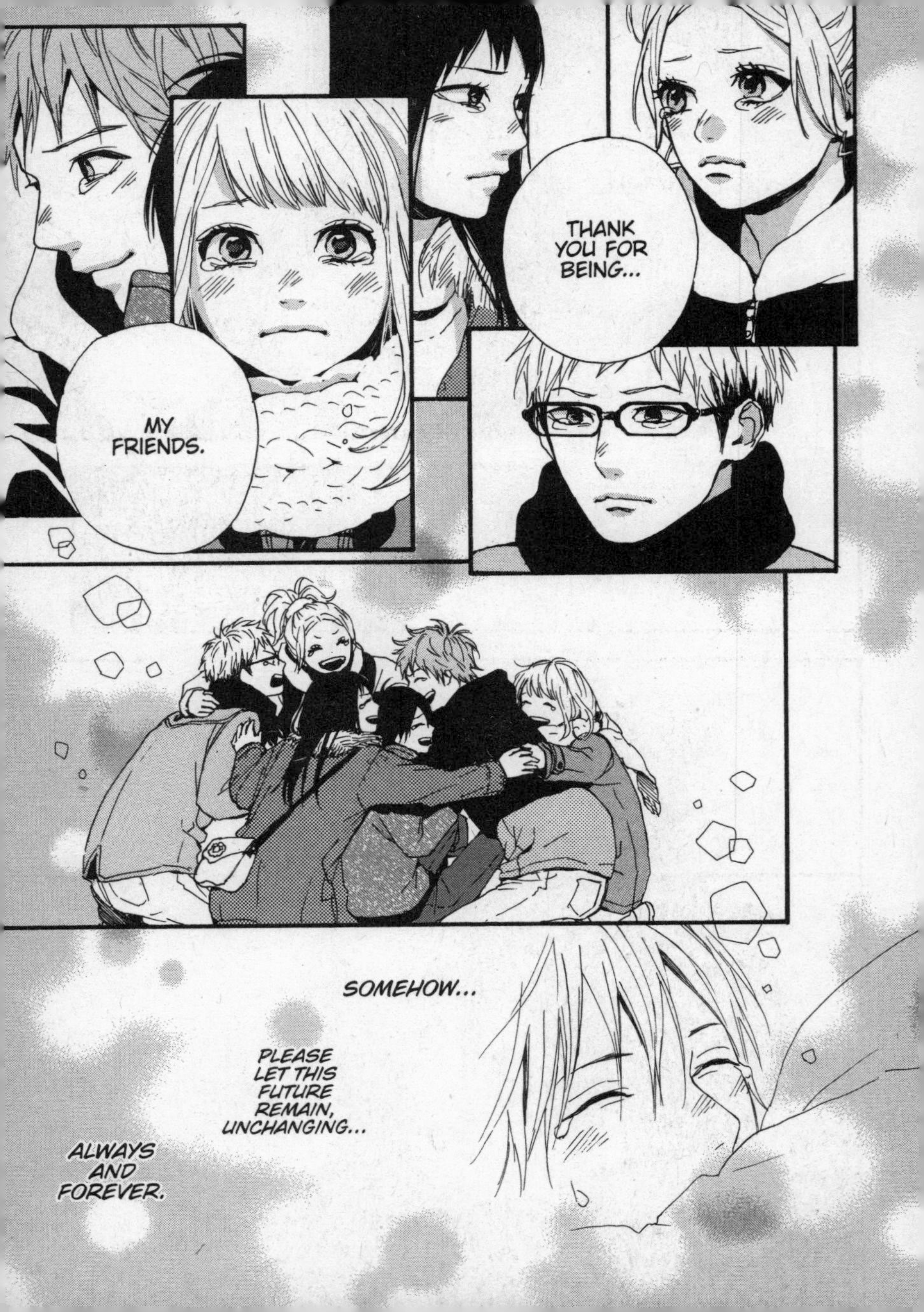
THANK YOU FOR BEING...
MY FRIENDS.
SOMEHOW...
PLEASE LET THIS FUTURE REMAIN, UNCHANGING...
ALWAYS AND FOREVER.

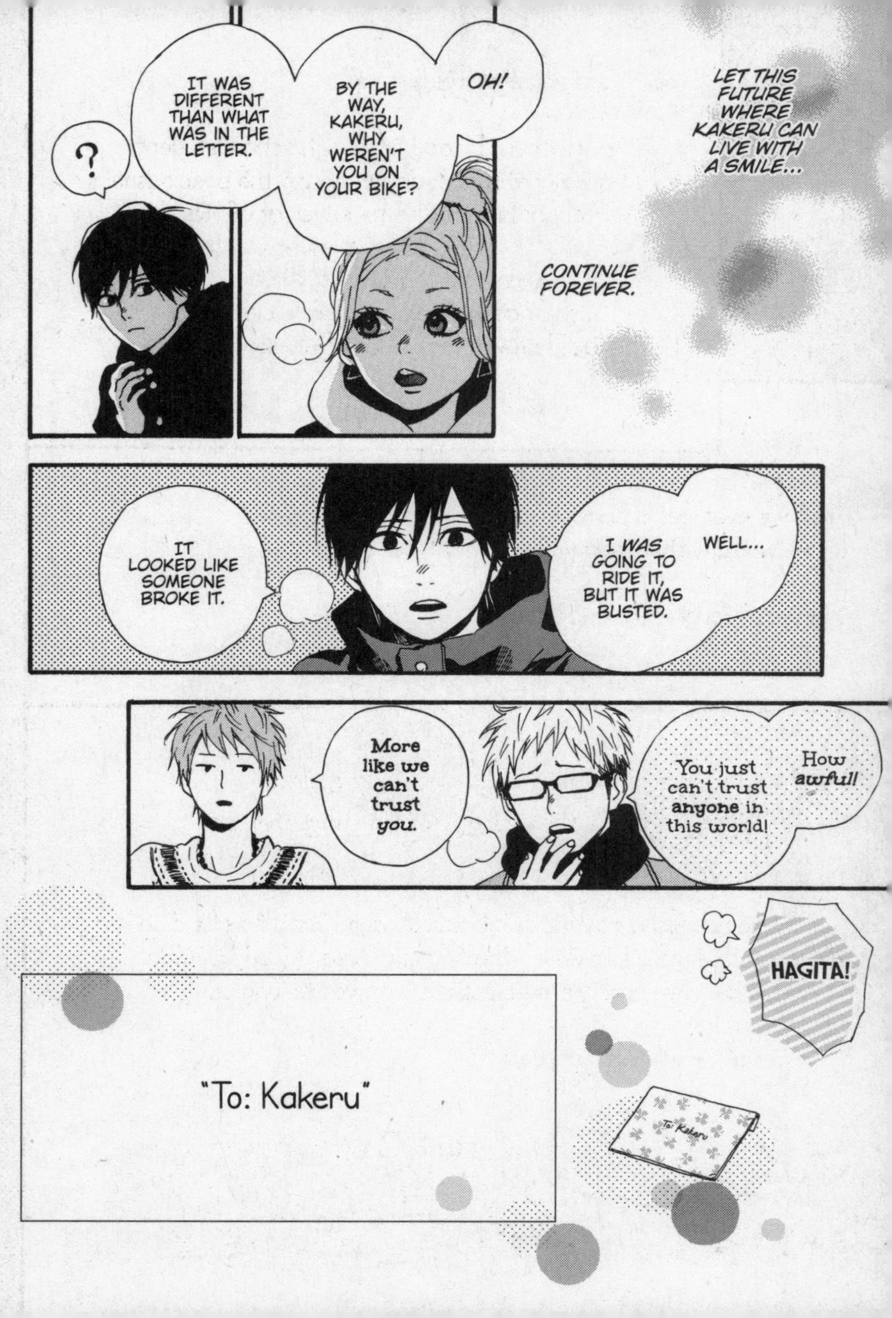
LET THIS FUTURE WHERE KAKERU CAN LIVE WITH A SMILE...
CONTINUE FOREVER.
OH!
BY THE WAY, KAKERU, WHY WEREN'T YOU ON YOUR BIKE?
IT WAS DIFFERENT THAN WHAT WAS IN THE LETTER.
?
WELL...
I WAS GOING TO RIDE IT, BUT IT WAS BUSTED.
IT LOOKED LIKE SOMEONE BROKE IT.
How awful!
You just can't trust anyone in this world!
More like we can't trust you.
HAGITA!
"To: Kakeru"
To: Kakeru

Can you ever forgive us?

Back then, I was just a high school student,
still a child who could not grasp the preciousness
of each day nor the true weight of life.

I'm so sorry we could not save you.
I wish I had watched you more closely.
But I knew nothing, I am truly sorry.

If we ever get a chance to do it over again,
we would watch over you with all of our might.

Please forgive us, and live on.

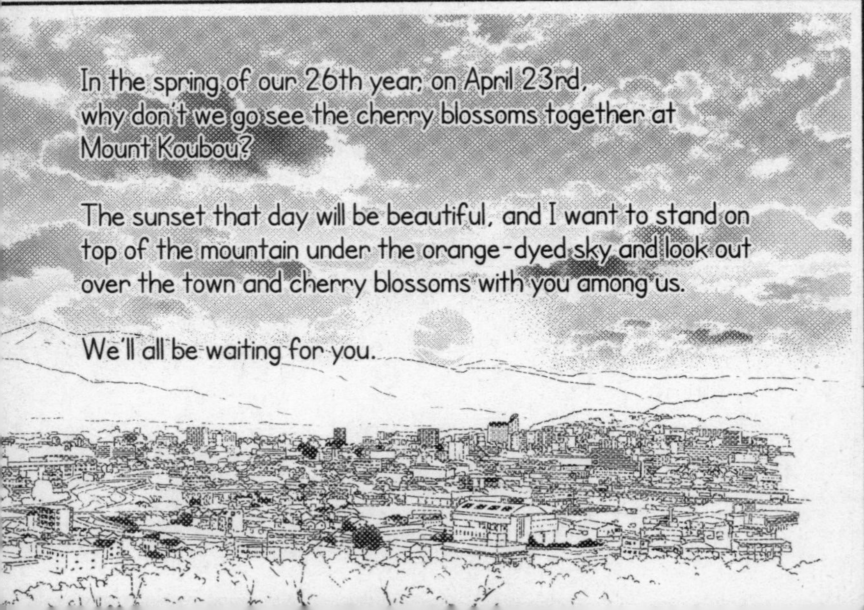
In the spring of our 26th year, on April 23rd, why don't we go see the cherry blossoms together at Mount Koubou?
The sunset that day will be beautiful, and I want to stand on top of the mountain under the orange-dyed sky and look out over the town and cherry blossoms with you among us.
We'll all be waiting for you.

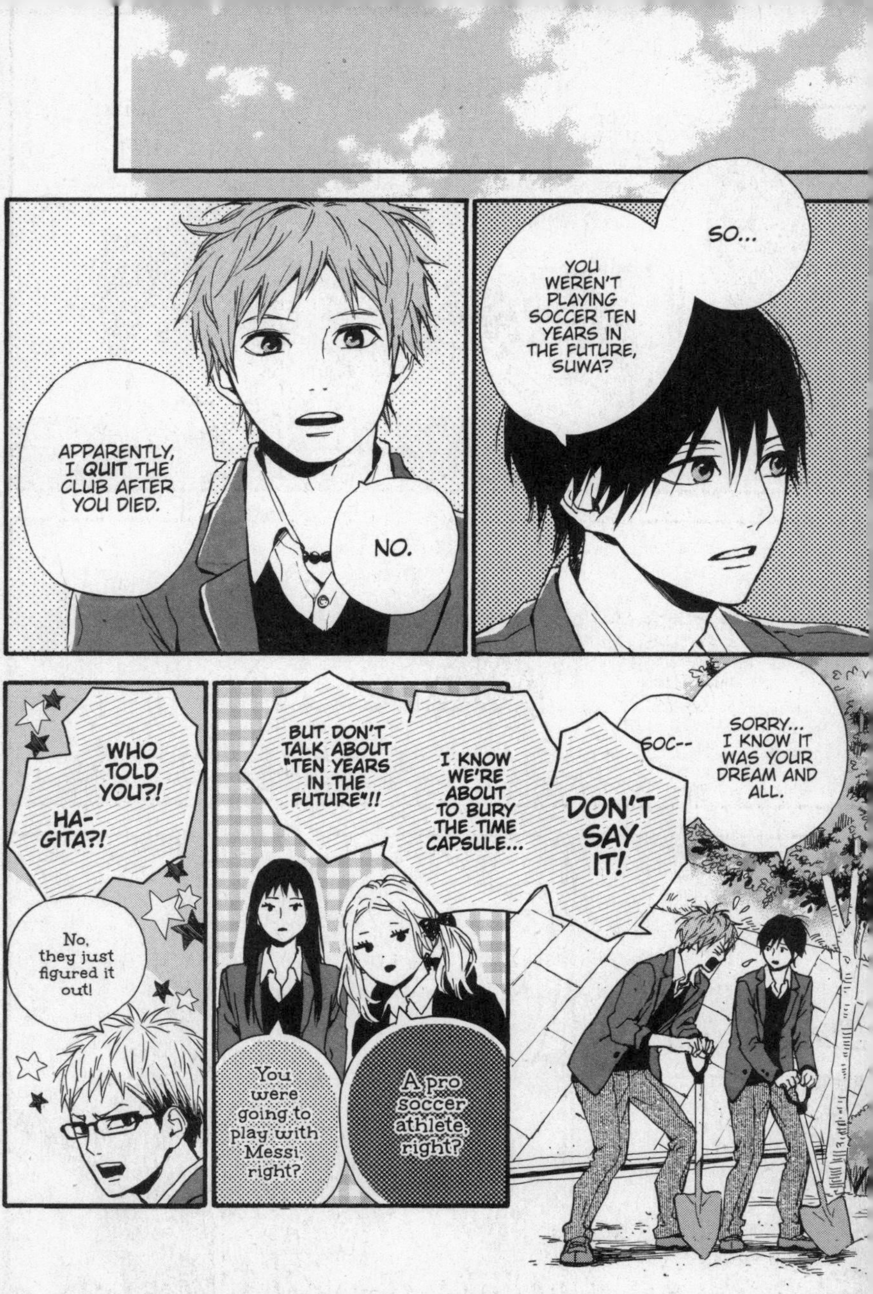
SO...
YOU WEREN'T PLAYING SOCCER TEN YEARS IN THE FUTURE, SUWA?
NO.
APPARENTLY, I QUIT THE CLUB AFTER YOU DIED.
SORRY... I KNOW IT WAS YOUR DREAM AND ALL.
SOC--
DON'T SAY IT!
I KNOW WE'RE ABOUT TO BURY THE TIME CAPSULE...
BUT DON'T TALK ABOUT "TEN YEARS IN THE FUTURE"!!
A pro soccer athlete, right?
You were going to play with Messi, right?
WHO TOLD YOU?!
HA-GITA?!
No, they just figured it out!

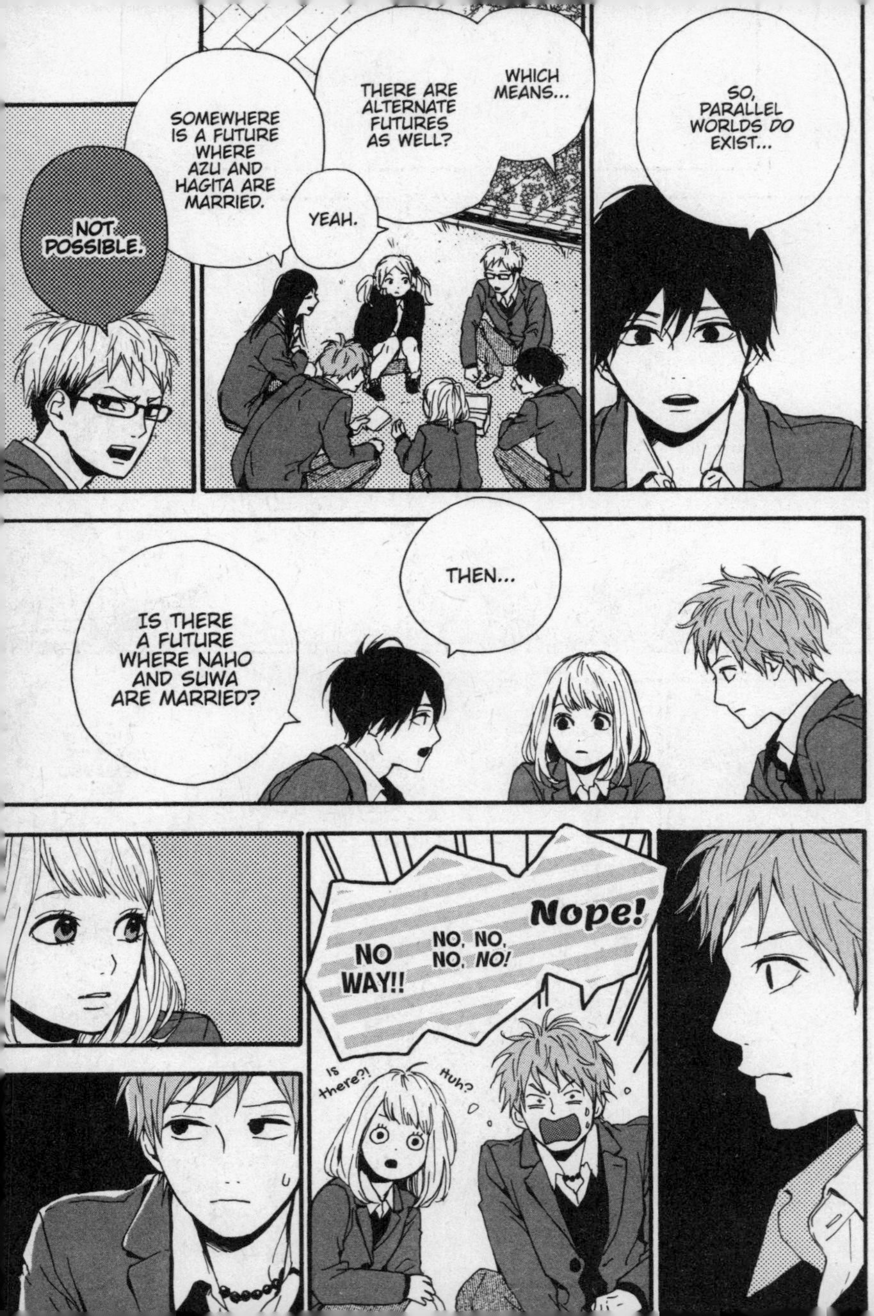
SO, PARALLEL WORLDS DO EXIST...
WHICH MEANS...
THERE ARE ALTERNATE FUTURES AS WELL?
YEAH.
SOMEWHERE IS A FUTURE WHERE AZU AND HAGITA ARE MARRIED.
NOT POSSIBLE.
THEN...
IS THERE A FUTURE WHERE NAHO AND SUWA ARE MARRIED?
Nope!
NO, NO, NO, *NO!*
NO WAY!!
Huh?
Is there?!

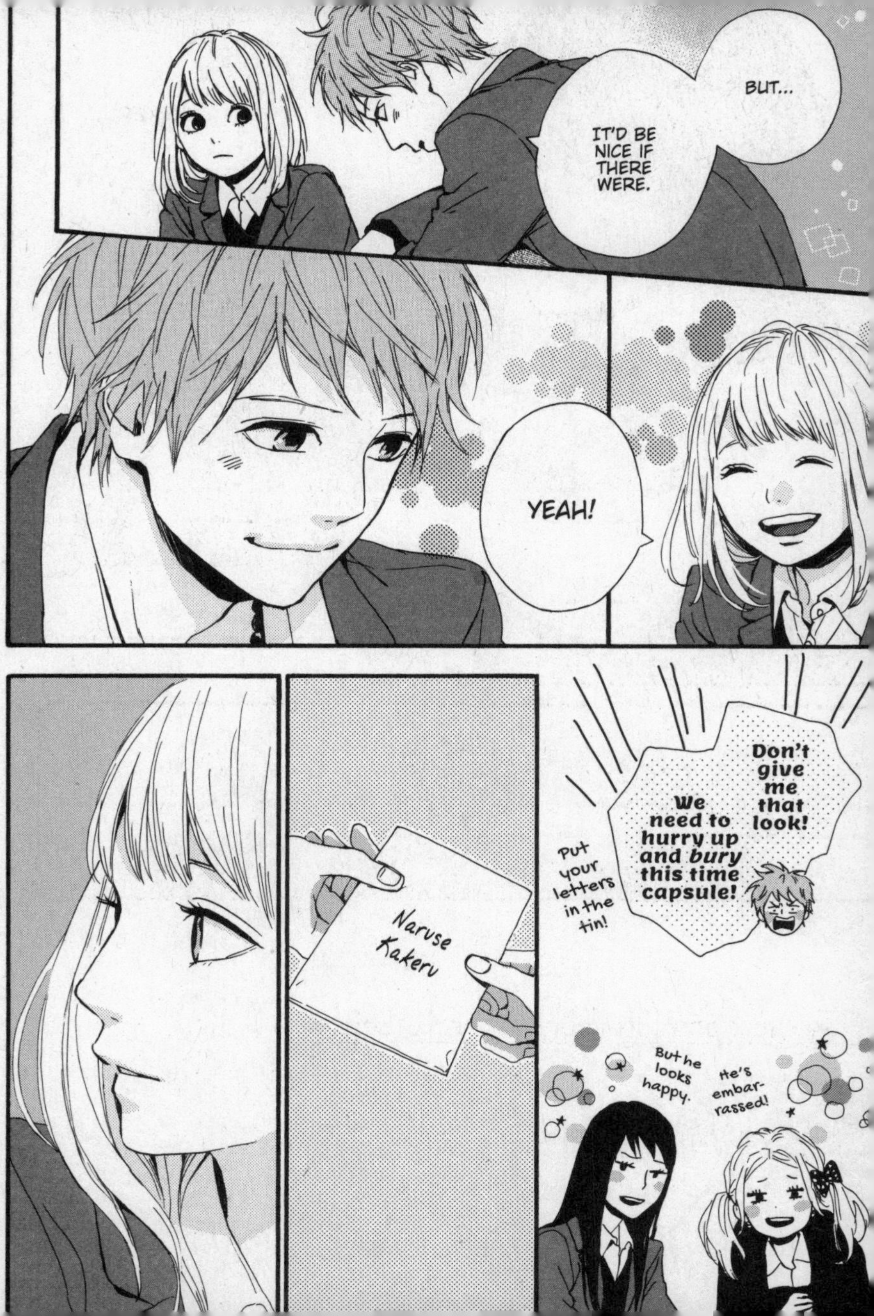
BUT...
IT'D BE NICE IF THERE WERE.
YEAH!
Don't give me that look!
We need to hurry up and *bury* this time capsule!
Put your letters in the tin!
He's embarrassed!
But he looks happy.
Naruse Kakeru

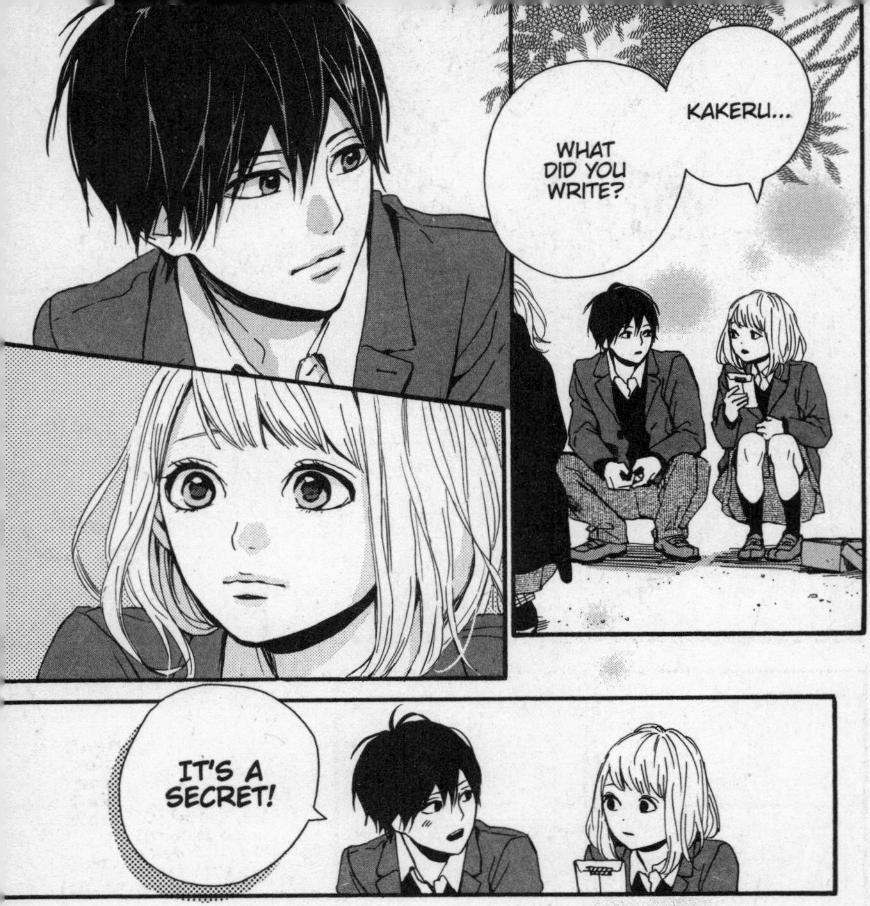
KAKERU...
WHAT DID YOU WRITE?
IT'S A SECRET!

To everyone ten years in the future...

Are you all doing well?

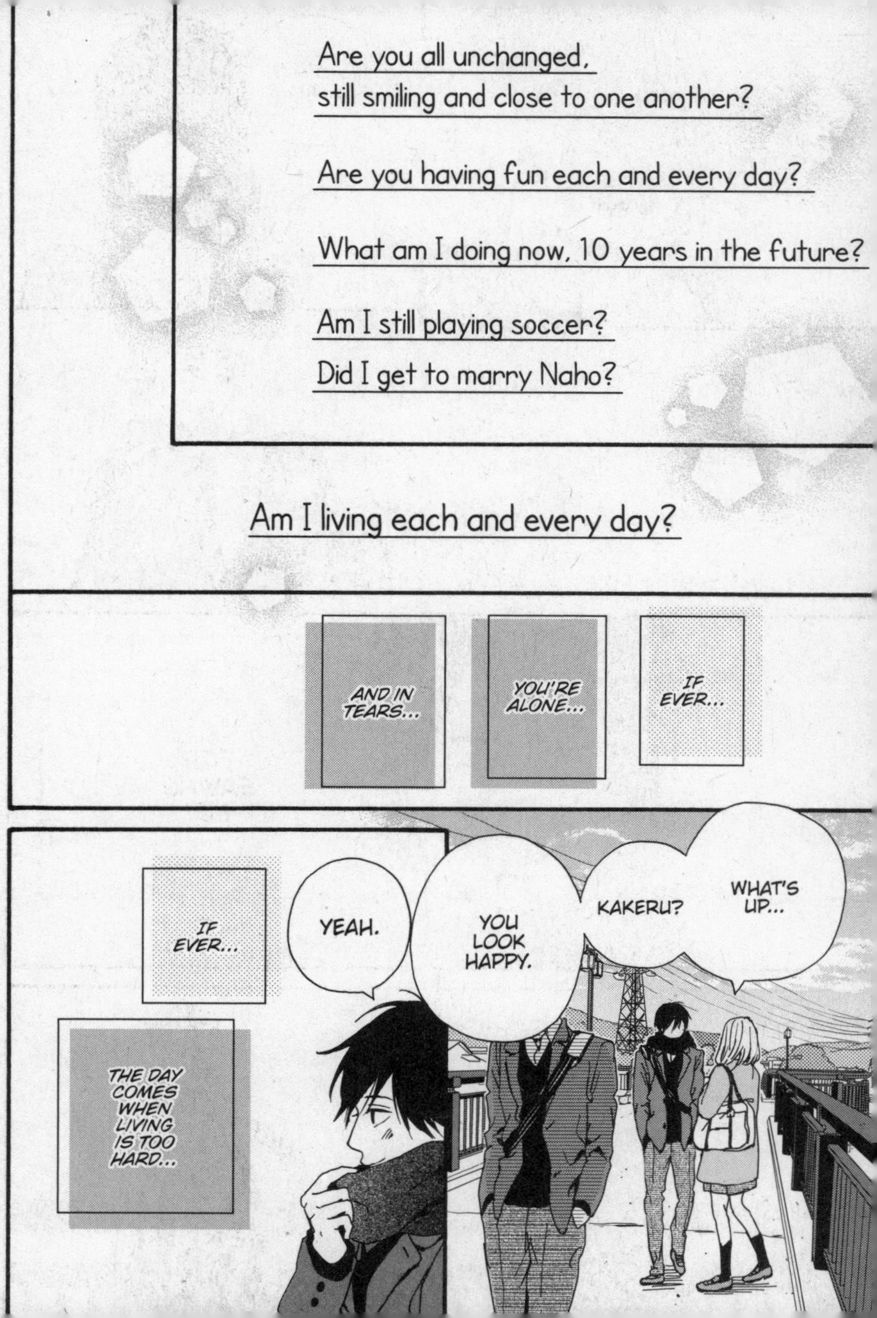
Are you all unchanged,
still smiling and close to one another?
Are you having fun each and every day?
What am I doing now, 10 years in the future?
Am I still playing soccer?
Did I get to marry Naho?
Am I living each and every day?
IF EVER...
YOU'RE ALONE...
AND IN TEARS...
WHAT'S UP...
KAKERU?
YOU LOOK HAPPY.
YEAH.
IF EVER...
THE DAY COMES WHEN LIVING IS TOO HARD...

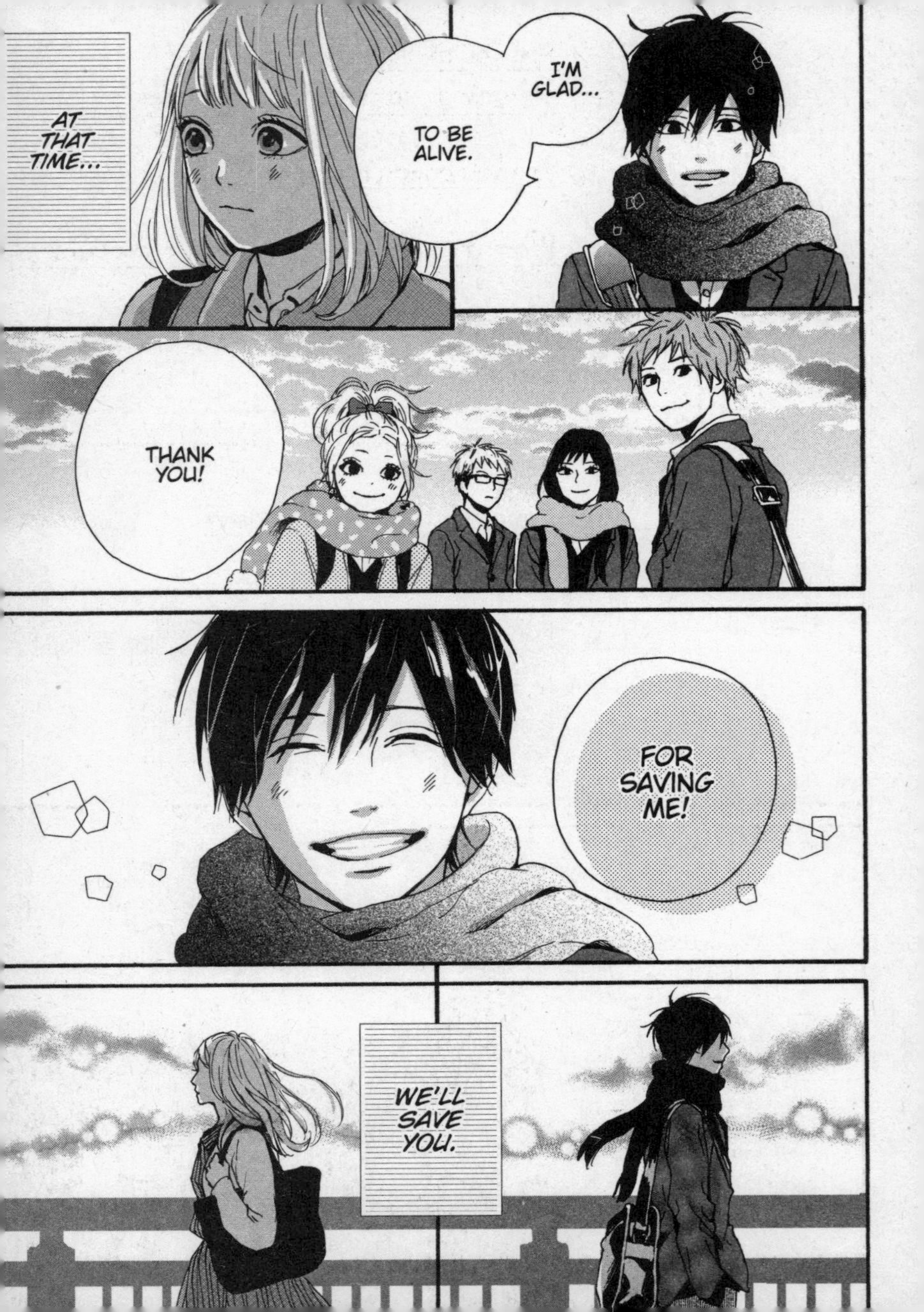
I'M GLAD...
TO BE ALIVE.
AT THAT TIME...
THANK YOU!
FOR SAVING ME!
WE'LL SAVE YOU.

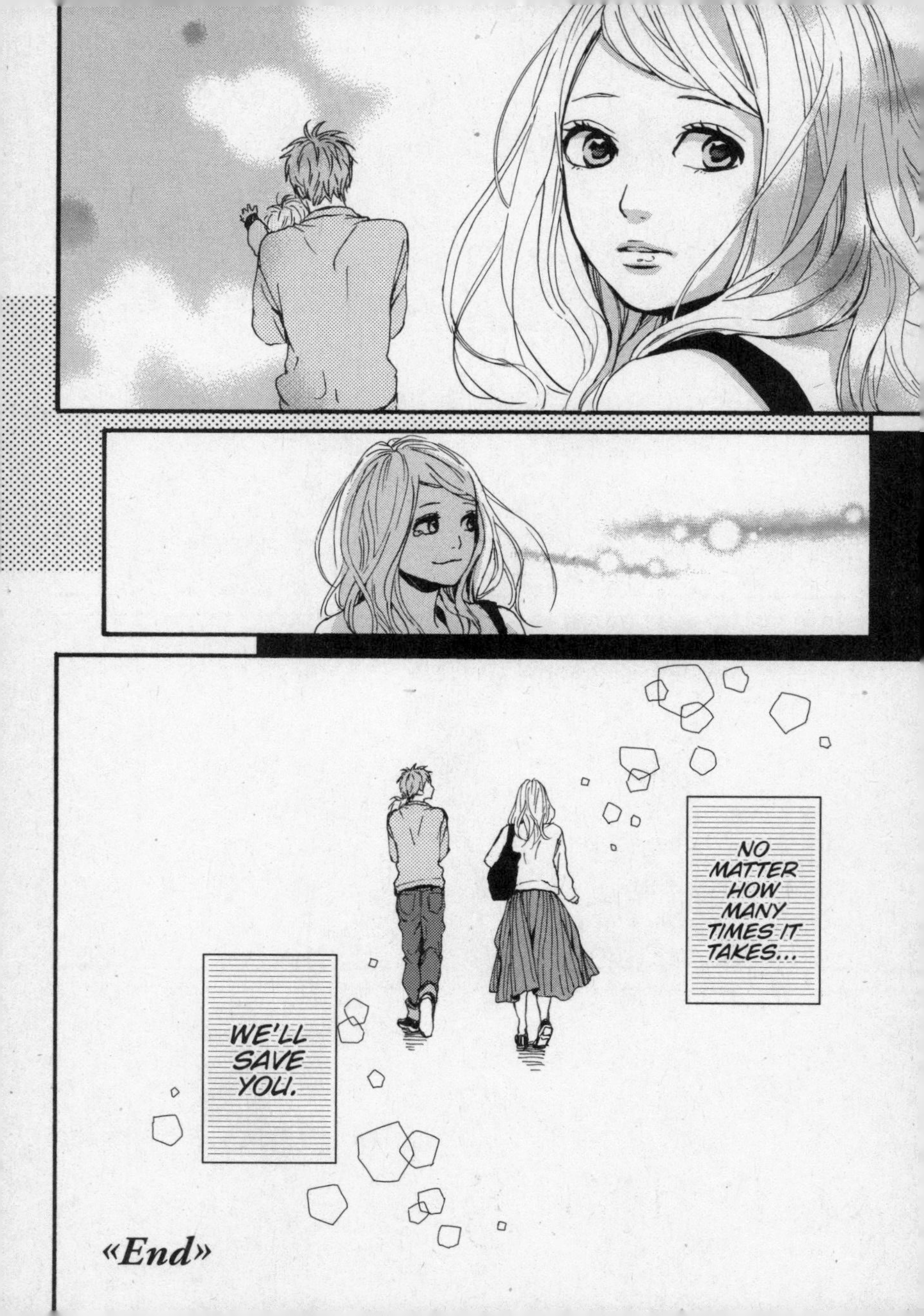
NO MATTER HOW MANY TIMES IT TAKES...
WE'LL SAVE YOU.
«End»

orange

Hello, I'm Takano.

orange has finally finished. To everyone who read until the end, thank you so very, very much. I was able to draw everything I wanted to in this story.

To all of you who read orange, I hope your future is a happy one, that you are still going on without regrets ten years from now. If you have someone like Kakeru in your life, please find a way to save them. Every life is precious. Please treasure each and every day, the present, the moment, and yourself.

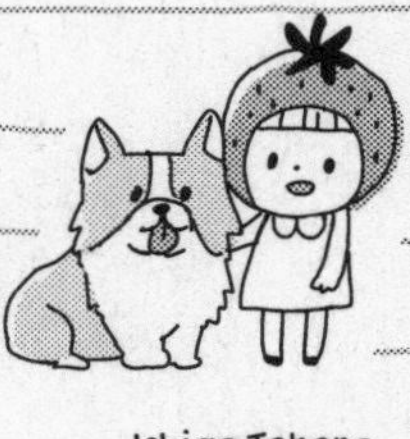

Thank you very much.

Ichigo Takano

2015.11. 高野苺

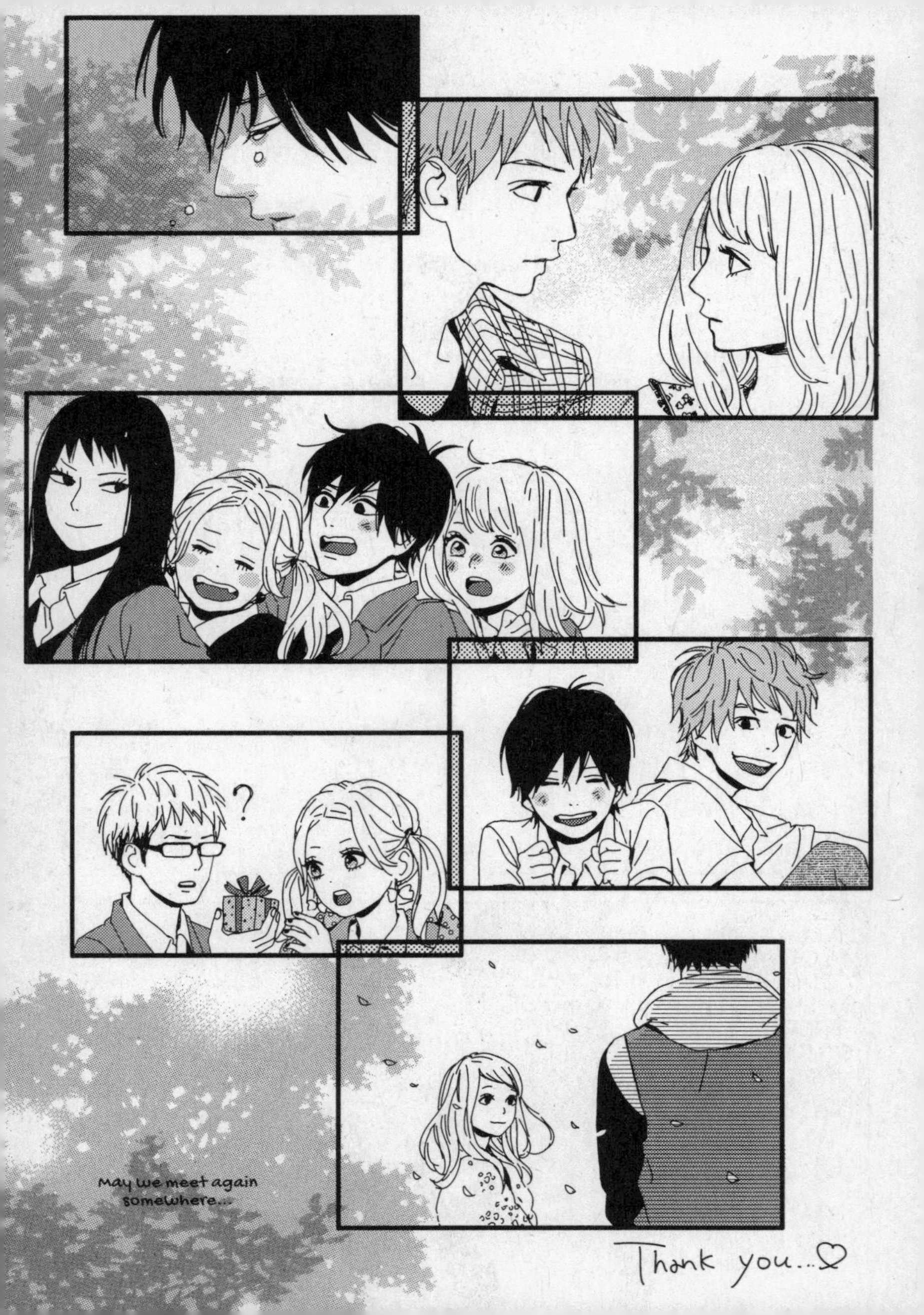
?
May we meet again somewhere...
Thank you...♡

About HARUIRO ÄSTRONAUT☆

With this story, at first, I just wanted to draw **a super cute girl**. But then, if *that* was the case, I decided I would draw **a super hot guy** to go with her! I wanted to use all my favorite shoujo romance tropes! The protagonist has a twin sister. The key to telling them apart is the bangs. Also, Mami has the polka dots, and Chiki has stripes. Drawing a super hot guy is hard...this is my best attempt.

Please enjoy!

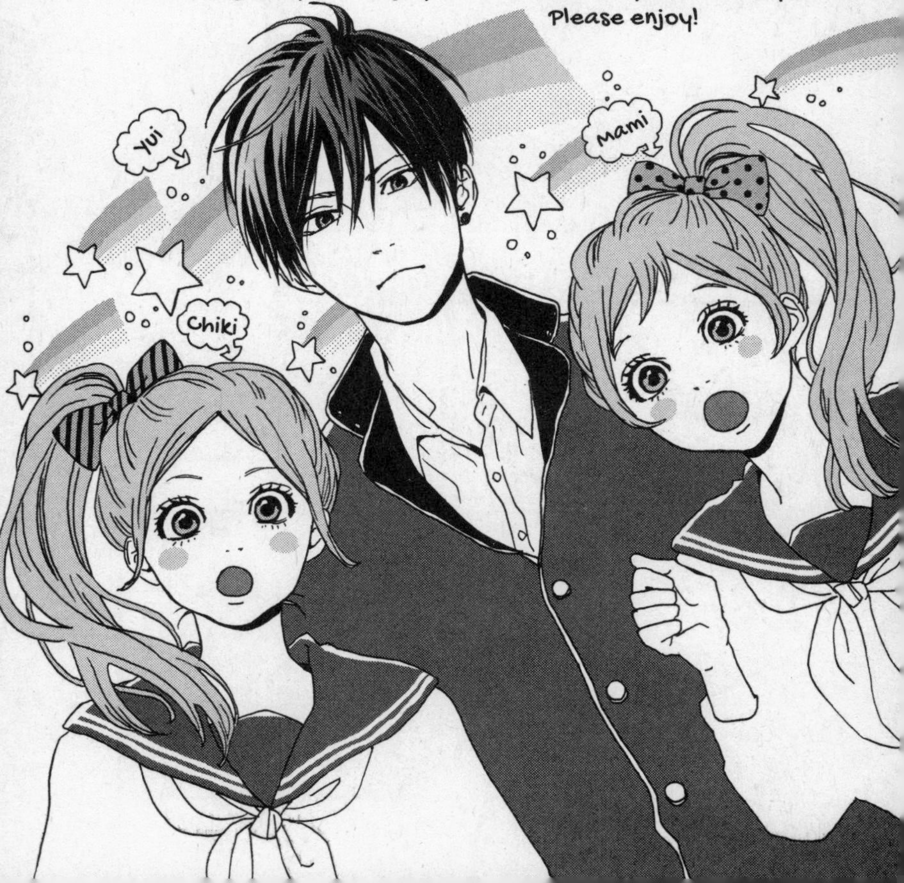
Mami
Yui
Chiki

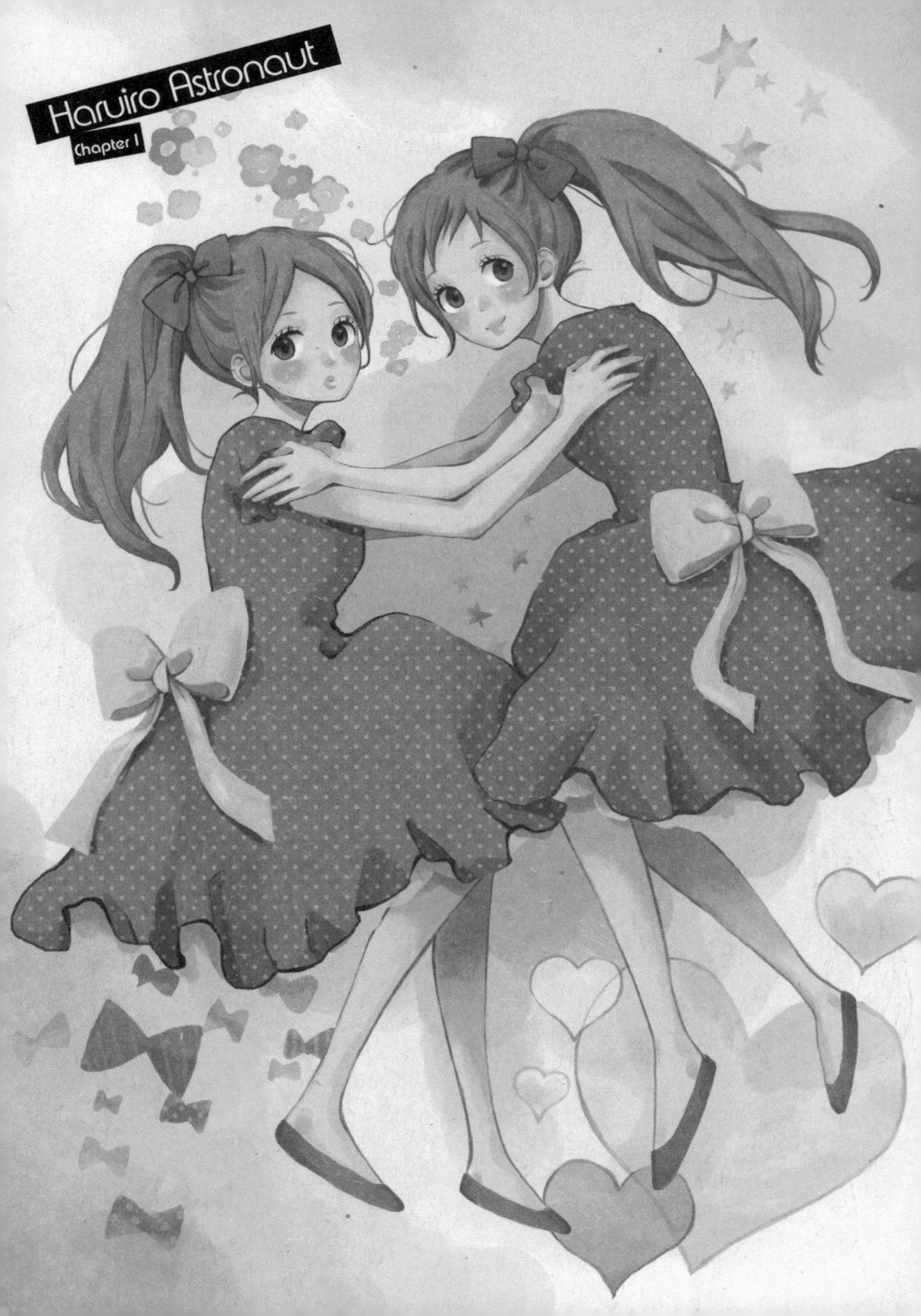
Haruiro Astronaut
Chapter 1

Haruiro
Astronaut

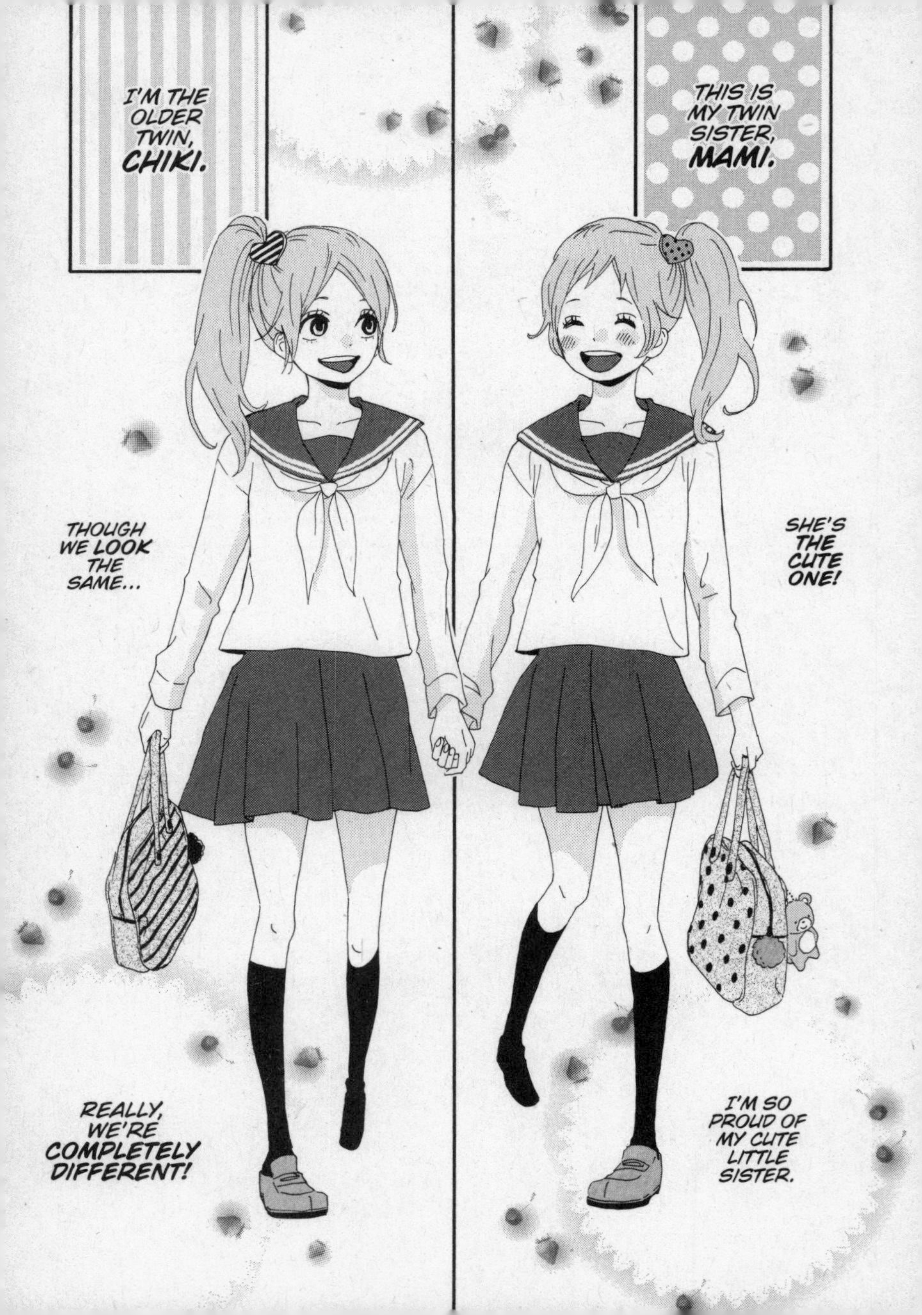
THIS IS MY TWIN SISTER, MAMI.
SHE'S THE CUTE ONE!
I'M SO PROUD OF MY CUTE LITTLE SISTER.
I'M THE OLDER TWIN, CHIKI.
THOUGH WE LOOK THE SAME...
REALLY, WE'RE COMPLETELY DIFFERENT!

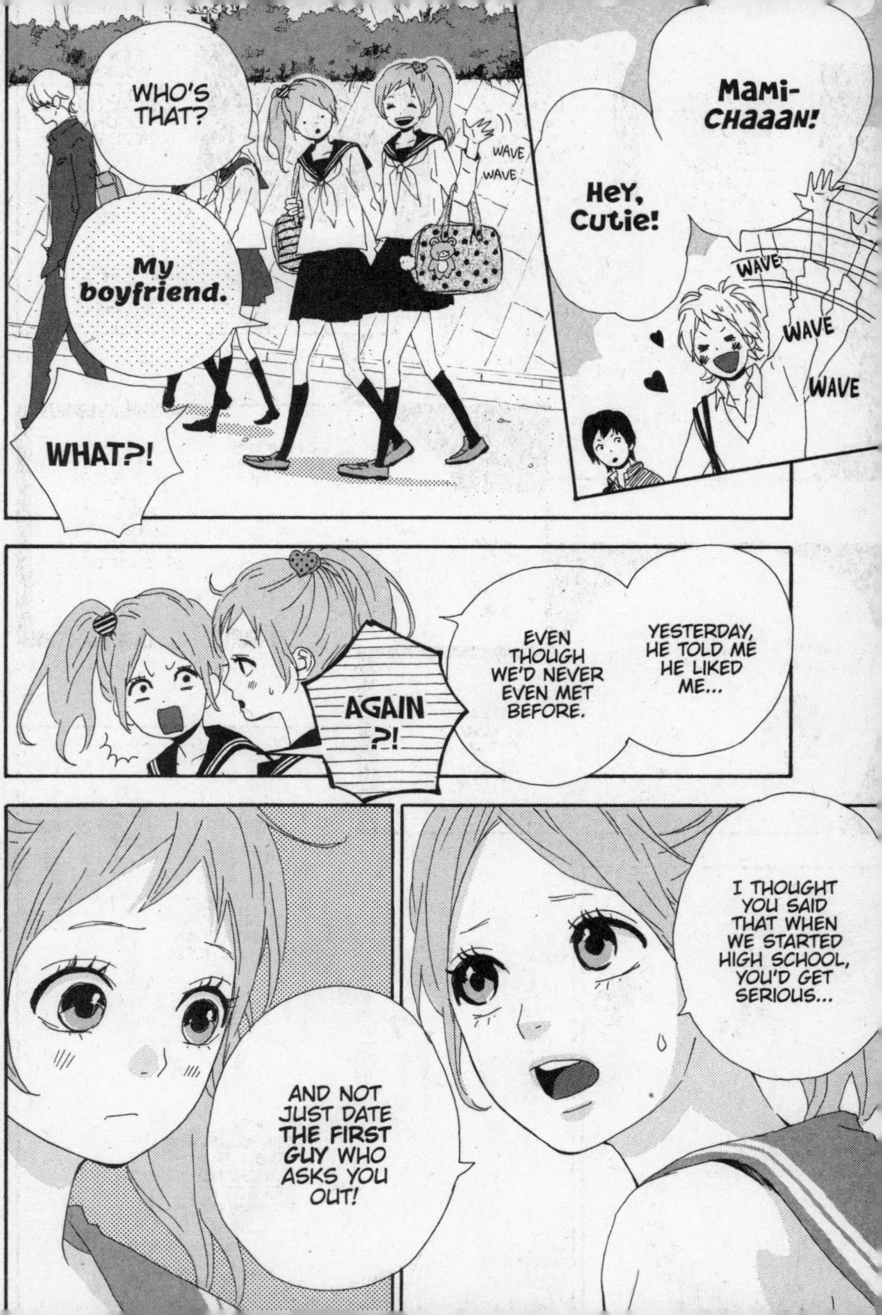
Mami-chaaan!
Hey, Cutie!
WAVE
WAVE
WAVE
WAVE
WAVE
WHO'S THAT?
My boyfriend.
WHAT?!
YESTERDAY, HE TOLD ME HE LIKED ME...
EVEN THOUGH WE'D NEVER EVEN MET BEFORE.
AGAIN?!
I THOUGHT YOU SAID THAT WHEN WE STARTED HIGH SCHOOL, YOU'D GET SERIOUS...
AND NOT JUST DATE THE FIRST GUY WHO ASKS YOU OUT!

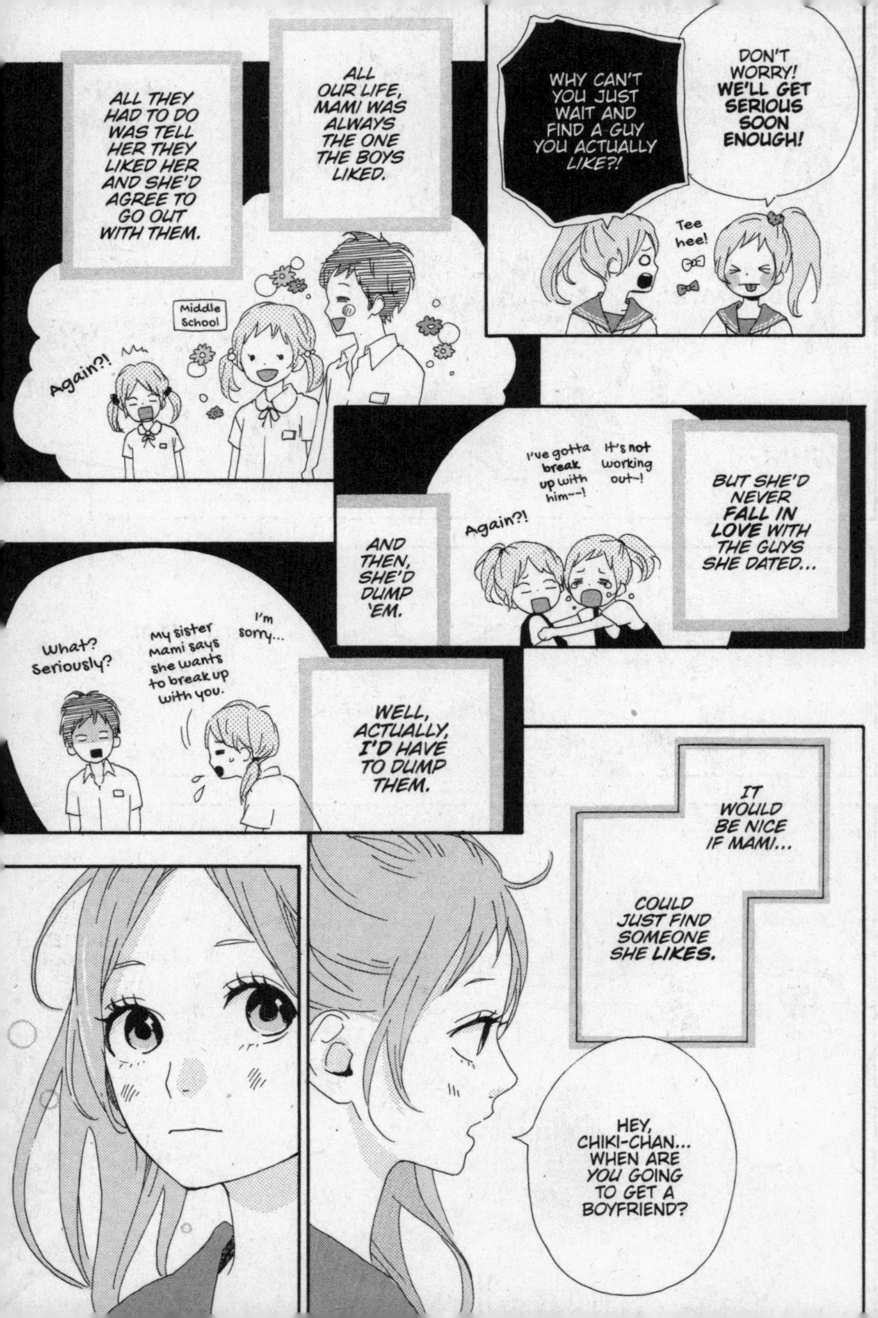
DON'T WORRY! WE'LL GET SERIOUS SOON ENOUGH!
WHY CAN'T YOU JUST WAIT AND FIND A GUY YOU ACTUALLY LIKE?!
Tee hee!
ALL OUR LIFE, MAMI WAS ALWAYS THE ONE THE BOYS LIKED.
ALL THEY HAD TO DO WAS TELL HER THEY LIKED HER AND SHE'D AGREE TO GO OUT WITH THEM.
Middle School
Again?!
BUT SHE'D NEVER FALL IN LOVE WITH THE GUYS SHE DATED...
It's not working out~!
I've gotta break up with him~~!
Again?!
AND THEN, SHE'D DUMP 'EM.
WELL, ACTUALLY, I'D HAVE TO DUMP THEM.
I'm sorry...
My sister Mami says she wants to break up with you.
What? Seriously?
IT WOULD BE NICE IF MAMI...
COULD JUST FIND SOMEONE SHE LIKES.
HEY, CHIKI-CHAN... WHEN ARE YOU GOING TO GET A BOYFRIEND?

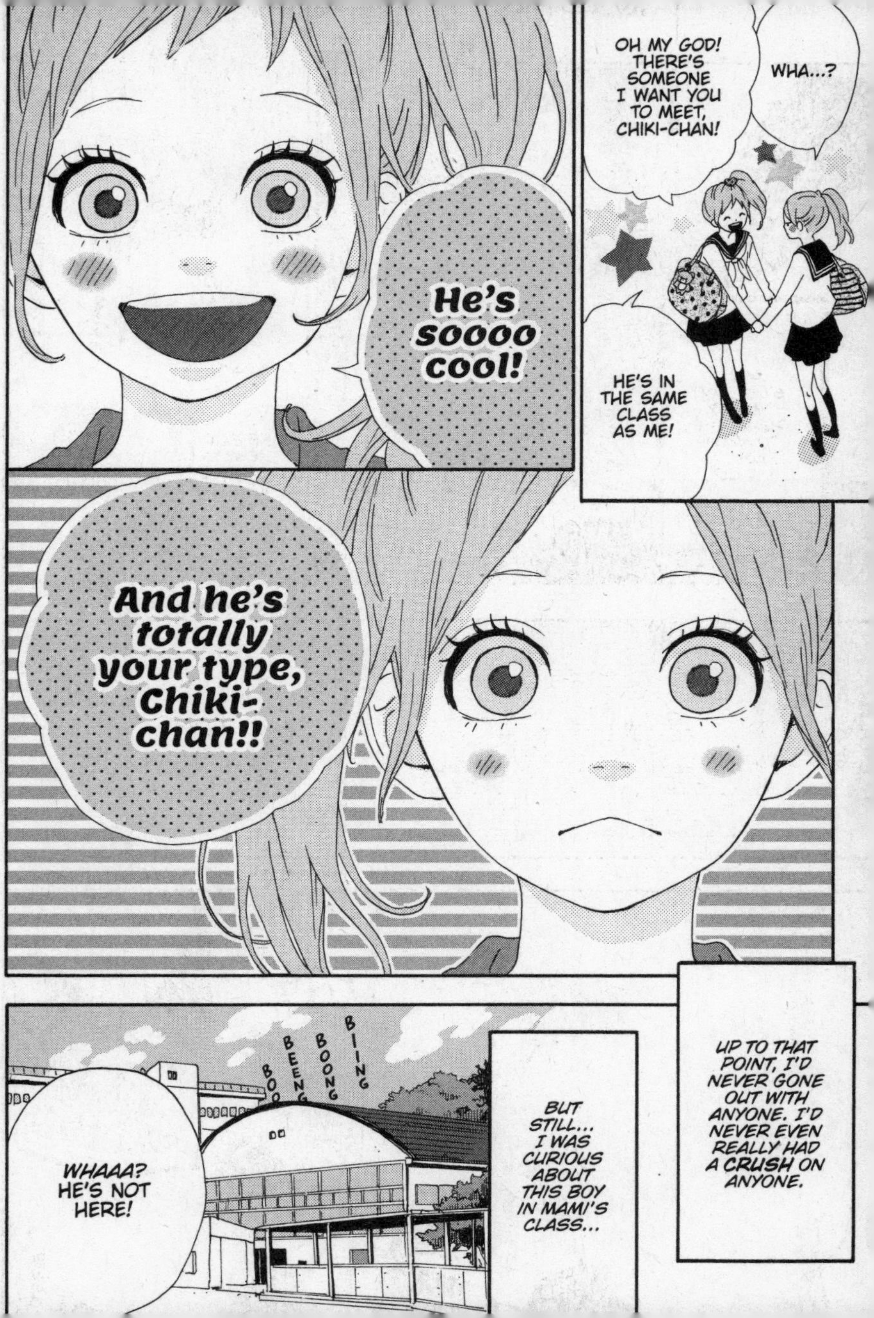
OH MY GOD! THERE'S SOMEONE I WANT YOU TO MEET, CHIKI-CHAN!
WHA...?
HE'S IN THE SAME CLASS AS ME!
He's soooo cool!
And he's totally your type, Chiki-chan!!
UP TO THAT POINT, I'D NEVER GONE OUT WITH ANYONE. I'D NEVER EVEN REALLY HAD A **CRUSH** ON ANYONE.
BUT STILL... I WAS CURIOUS ABOUT THIS BOY IN MAMI'S CLASS...
BIING
BOONG
BEENG
BOO
WHAAA? HE'S NOT HERE!

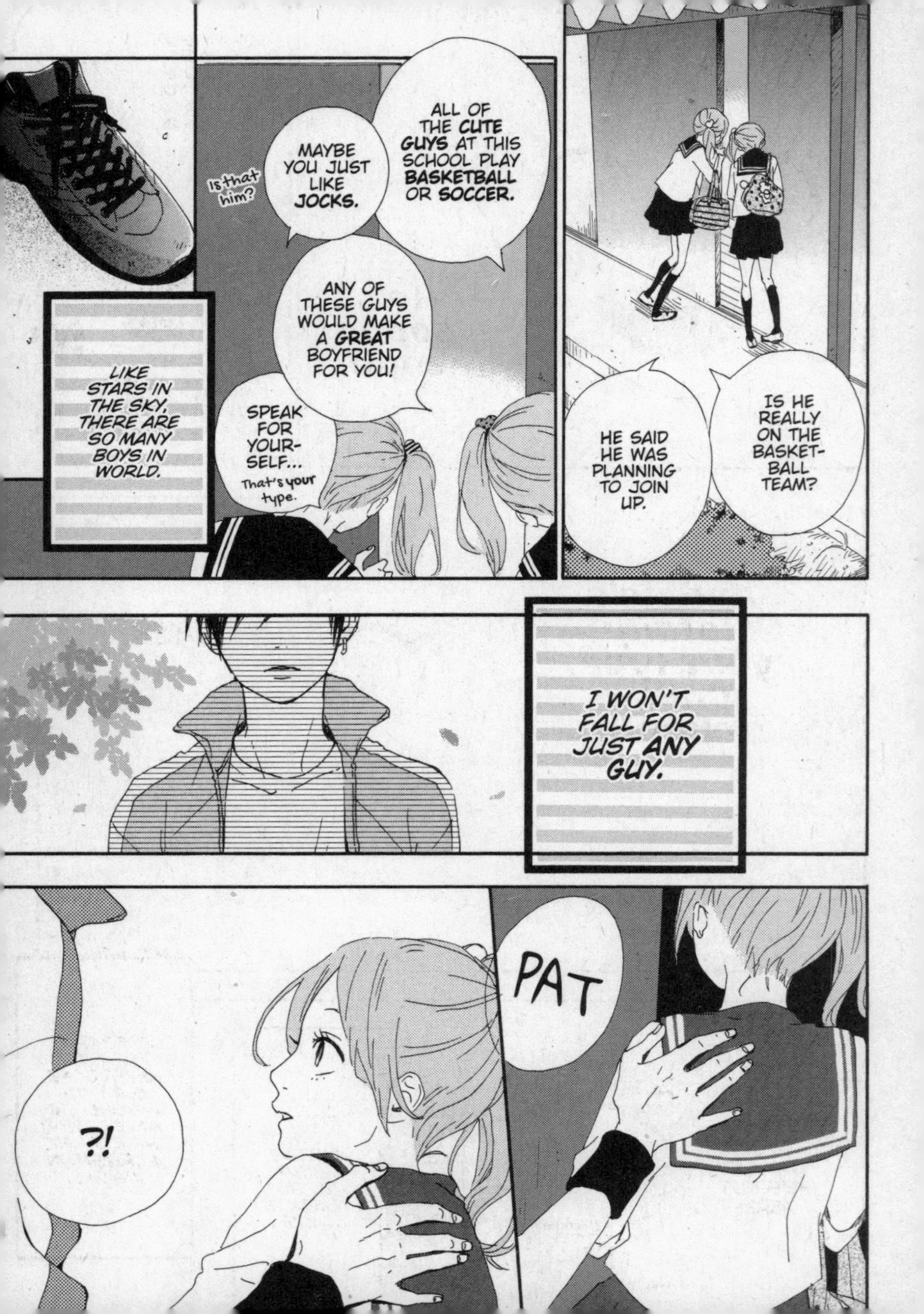
IS HE REALLY ON THE BASKETBALL TEAM?
HE SAID HE WAS PLANNING TO JOIN UP.
ALL OF THE CUTE GUYS AT THIS SCHOOL PLAY BASKETBALL OR SOCCER.
MAYBE YOU JUST LIKE JOCKS.
Is that him?
ANY OF THESE GUYS WOULD MAKE A GREAT BOYFRIEND FOR YOU!
SPEAK FOR YOURSELF...
That's your type.
LIKE STARS IN THE SKY, THERE ARE SO MANY BOYS IN WORLD.
I WON'T FALL FOR JUST ANY GUY.
PAT
?!

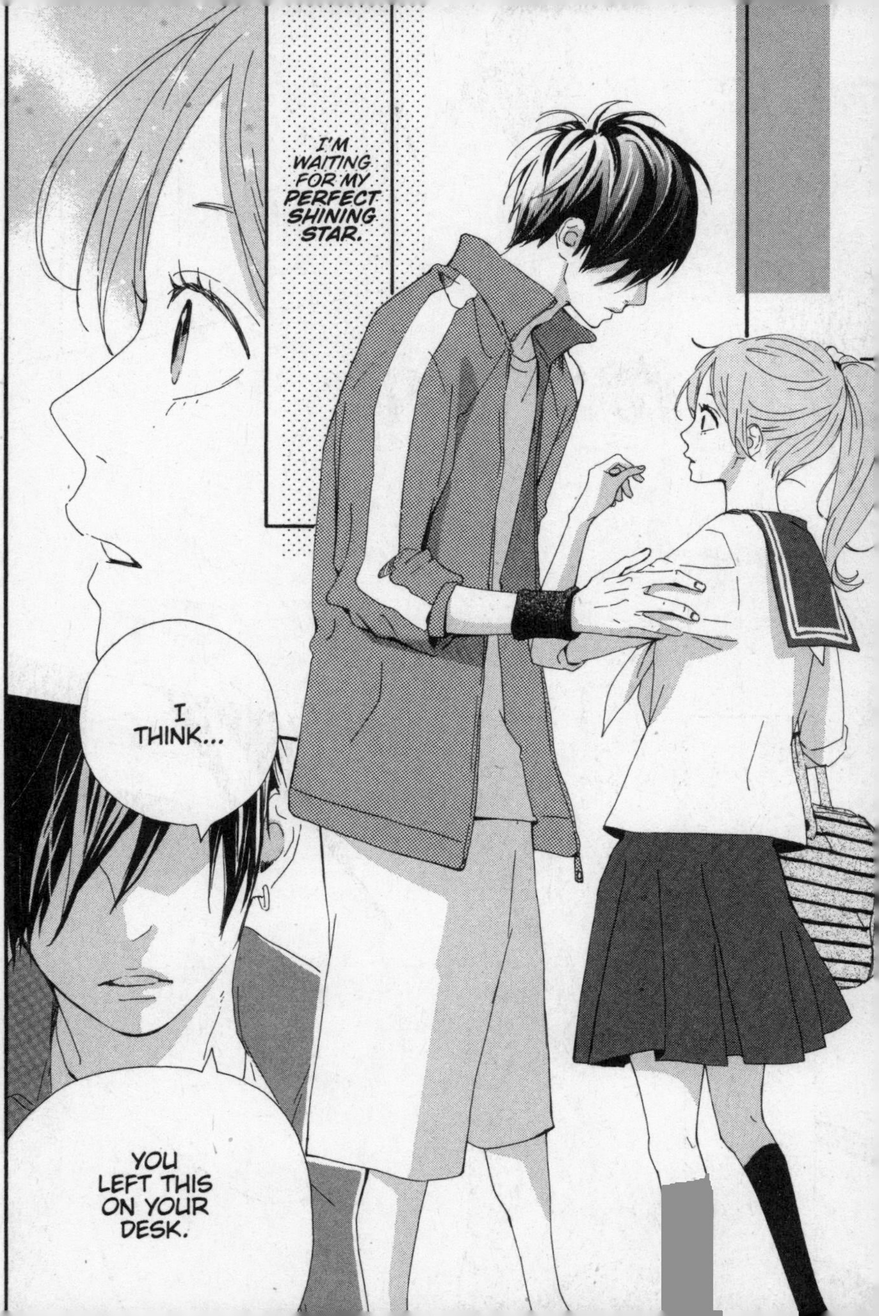
I'M WAITING FOR MY PERFECT SHINING STAR.
I THINK...
YOU LEFT THIS ON YOUR DESK.

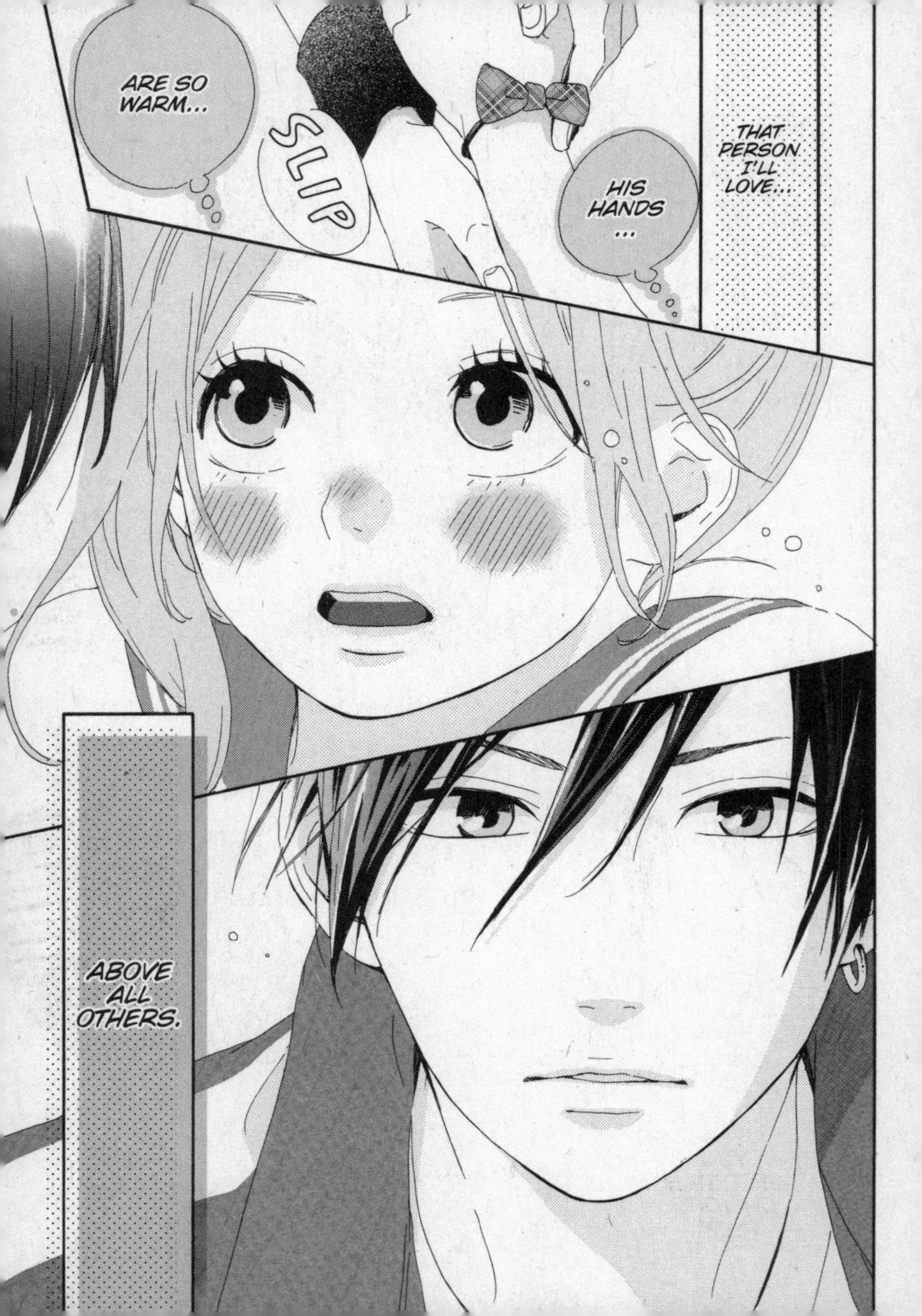
THAT PERSON I'LL LOVE...
HIS HANDS ...
SLIP
ARE SO WARM...
ABOVE ALL OTHERS.

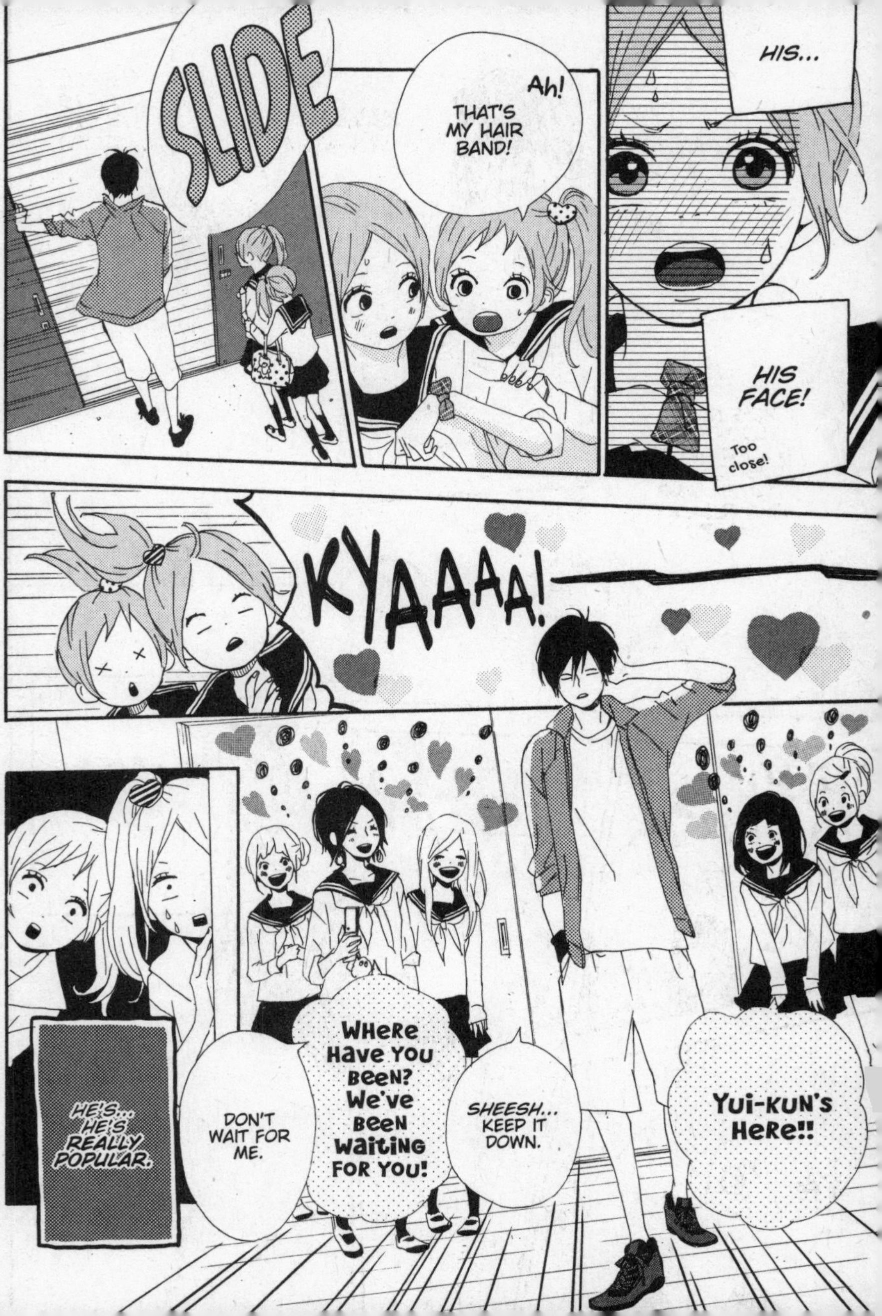
HIS...
HIS FACE!
Too close!
Ah!
THAT'S MY HAIR BAND!
SLIDE
KYAAAA!
Yui-KUN's Here!!
SHEESH... KEEP IT DOWN.
Where Have You Been? We've Been Waiting For You!
DON'T WAIT FOR ME.
HE'S... HE'S REALLY POPULAR.

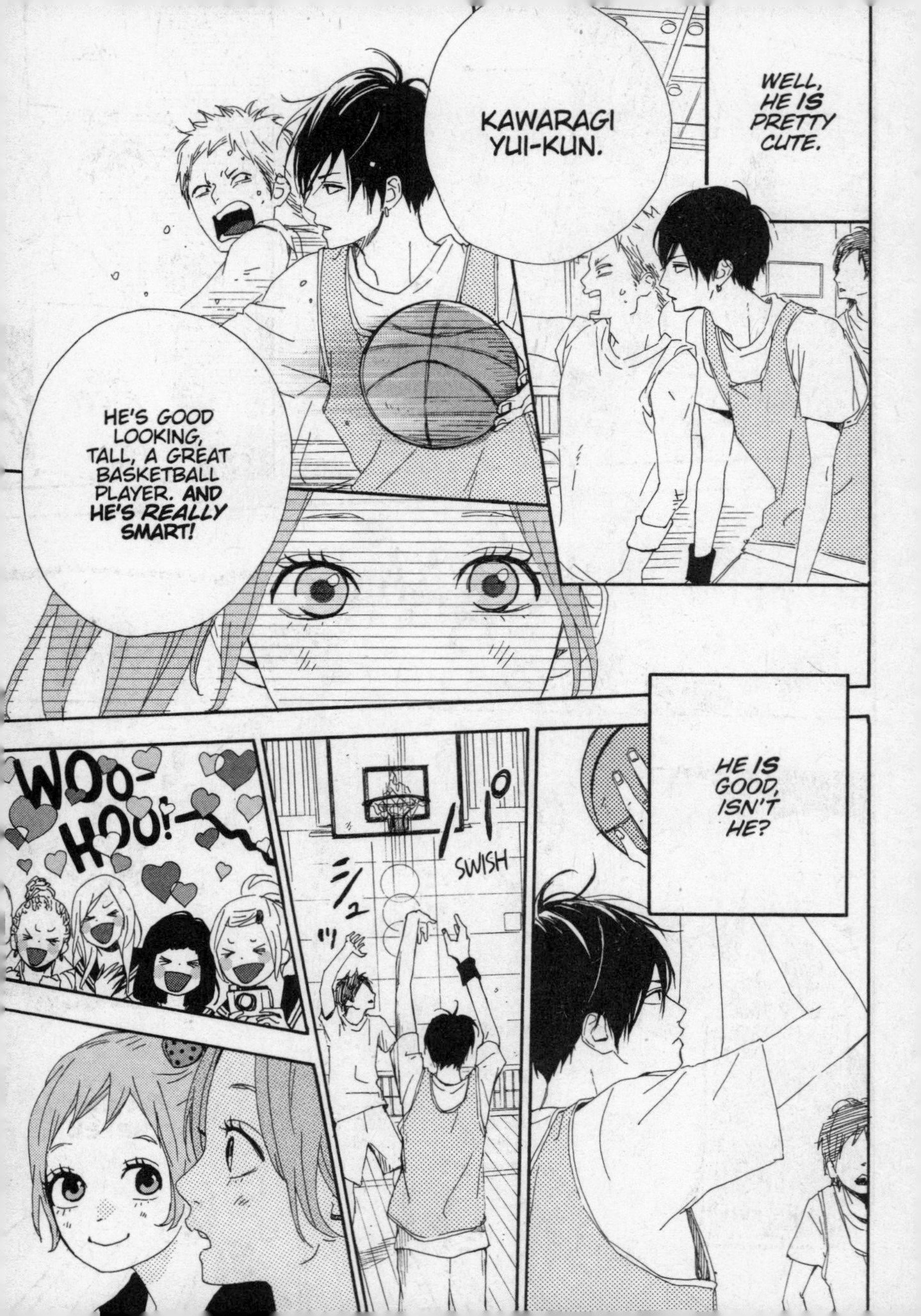
WELL, HE IS PRETTY CUTE.
KAWARAGI YUI-KUN.
HE'S GOOD LOOKING, TALL, A GREAT BASKETBALL PLAYER. AND HE'S *REALLY* SMART!
HE IS GOOD, ISN'T HE?
SWISH
WOO-HOO!

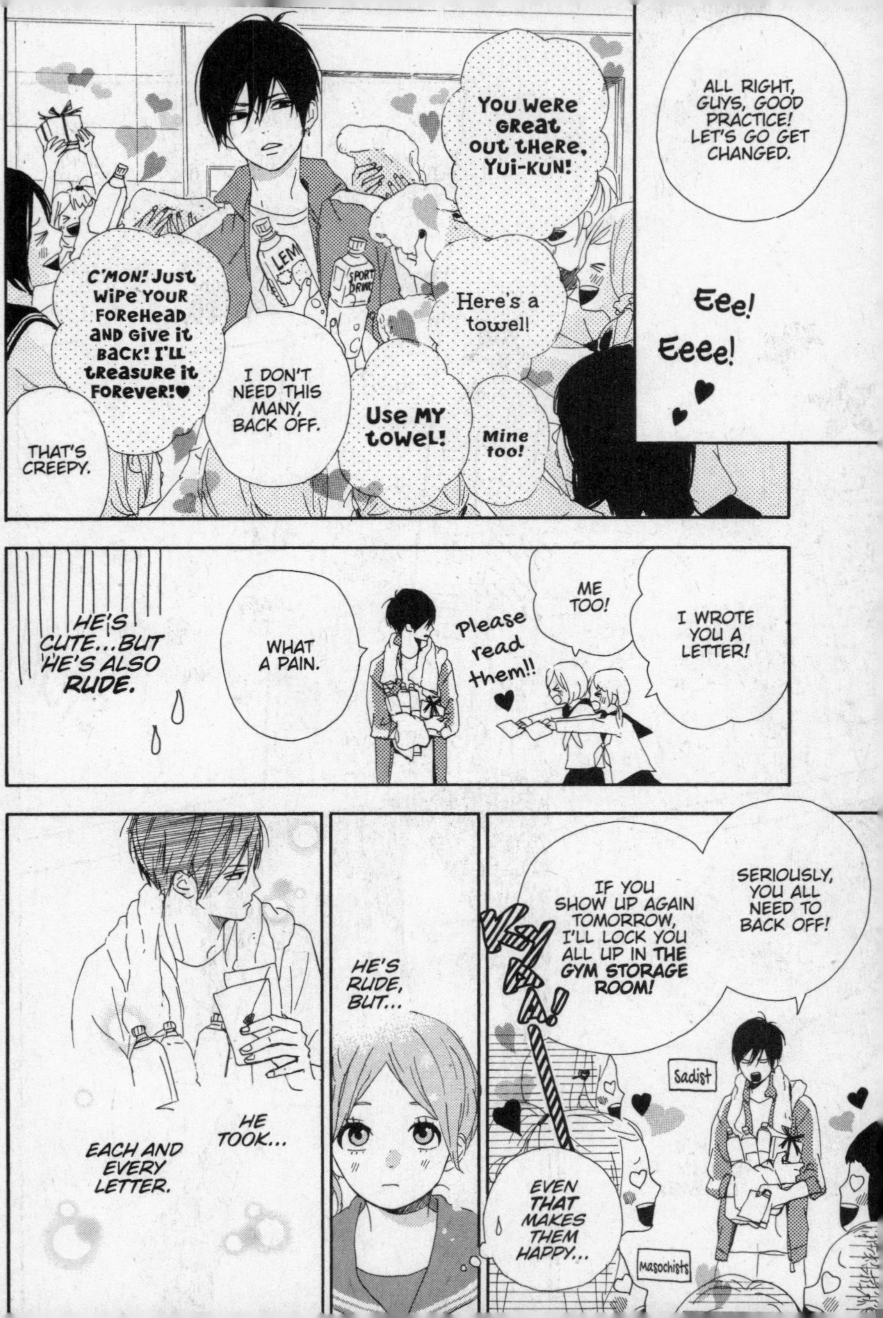
ALL RIGHT, GUYS, GOOD PRACTICE! LET'S GO GET CHANGED.
Eee!
Eeee!
You were great out there, Yui-kun!
Here's a towel!
C'MON! Just wipe your forehead and give it back! I'll treasure it forever!♥
I DON'T NEED THIS MANY, BACK OFF.
Use MY towel!
Mine too!
THAT'S CREEPY.
I WROTE YOU A LETTER!
ME TOO!
Please read them!!
WHAT A PAIN.
HE'S CUTE...BUT HE'S ALSO RUDE.
SERIOUSLY, YOU ALL NEED TO BACK OFF!
IF YOU SHOW UP AGAIN TOMORROW, I'LL LOCK YOU ALL UP IN THE GYM STORAGE ROOM!
Sadist
EVEN THAT MAKES THEM HAPPY...
Masochists
HE'S RUDE, BUT...
HE TOOK...
EACH AND EVERY LETTER.

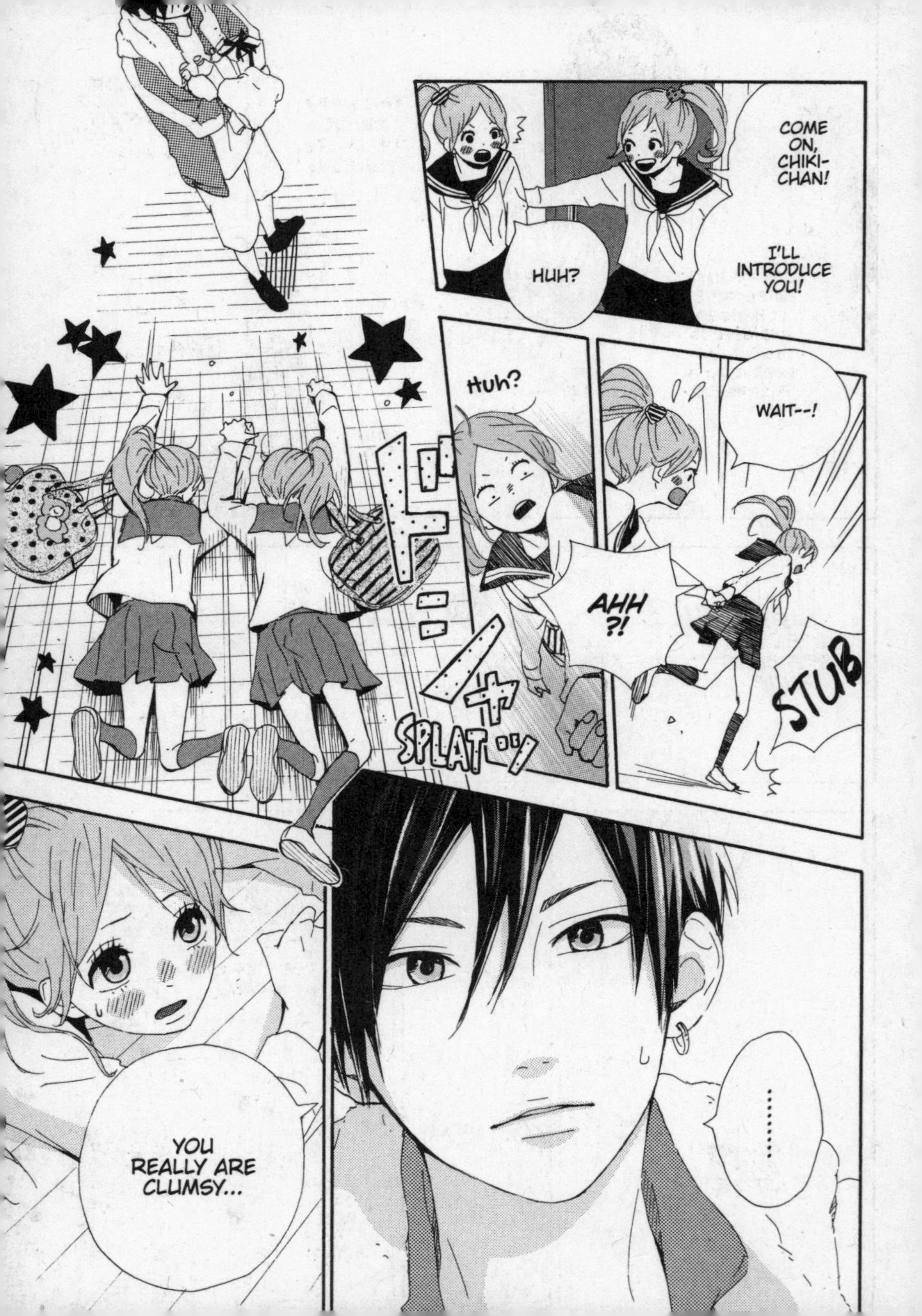
COME ON, CHIKI-CHAN!
I'LL INTRODUCE YOU!
HUH?
WAIT--!
AHH ?!
STUB
Huh?
SPLAT
......
YOU REALLY ARE CLUMSY...

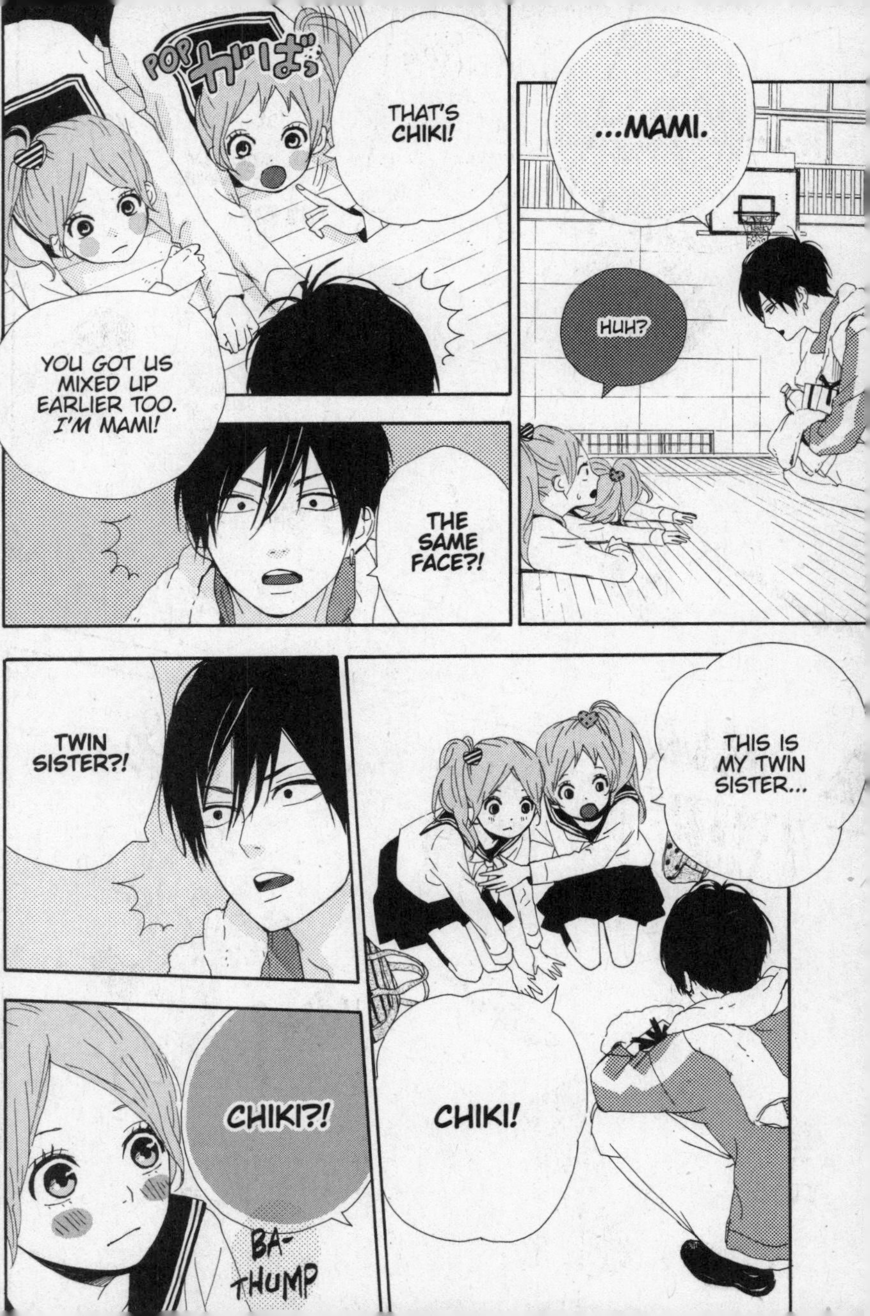
...MAMI.
HUH?
POP がばっ
THAT'S CHIKI!
YOU GOT US MIXED UP EARLIER TOO. I'M MAMI!
THE SAME FACE?!
THIS IS MY TWIN SISTER...
TWIN SISTER?!
CHIKI!
CHIKI?!
BA-THUMP

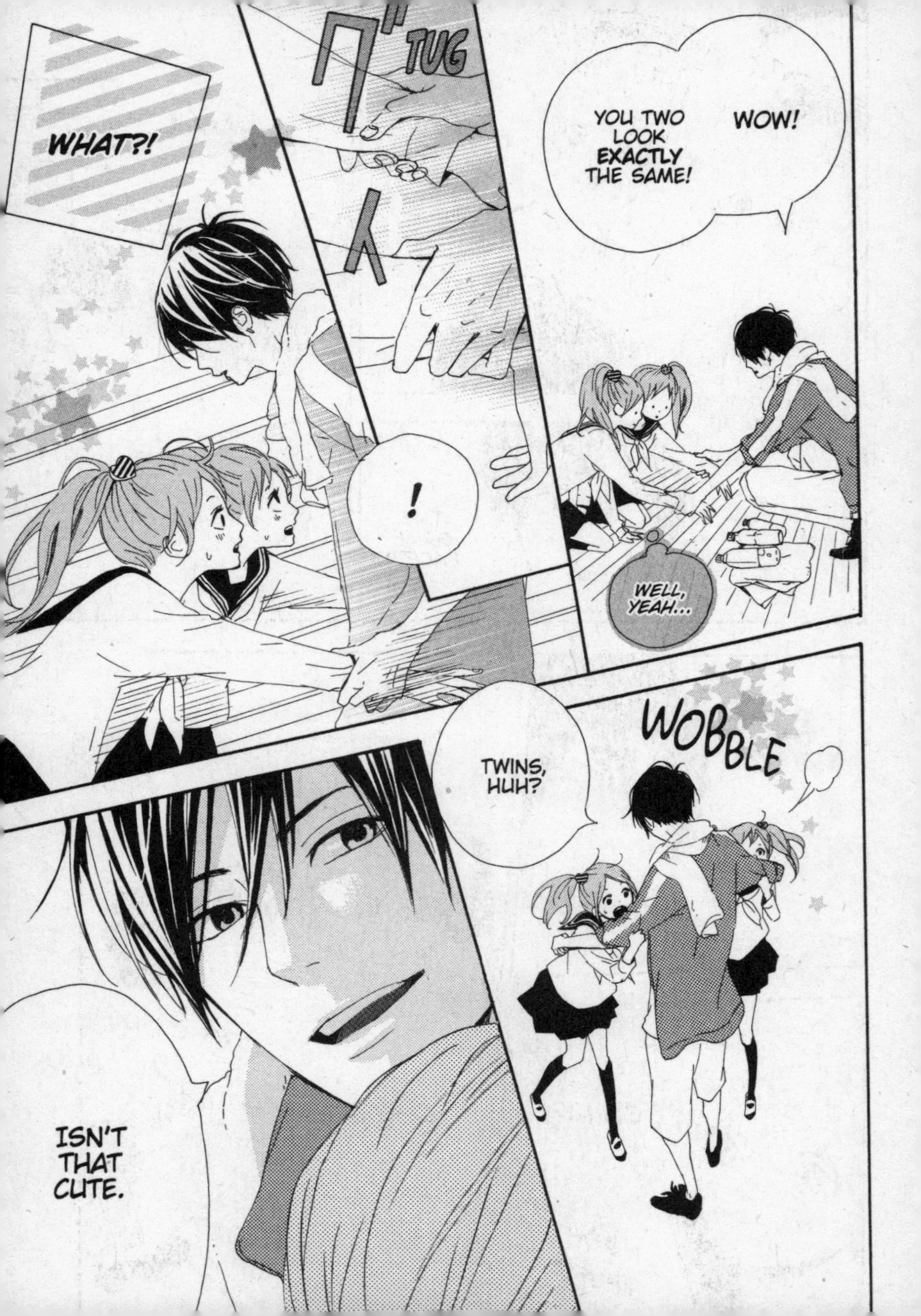
WOW!
YOU TWO LOOK EXACTLY THE SAME!
WELL, YEAH...
TUG
!
WHAT?!
WOBBLE
TWINS, HUH?
ISN'T THAT CUTE.

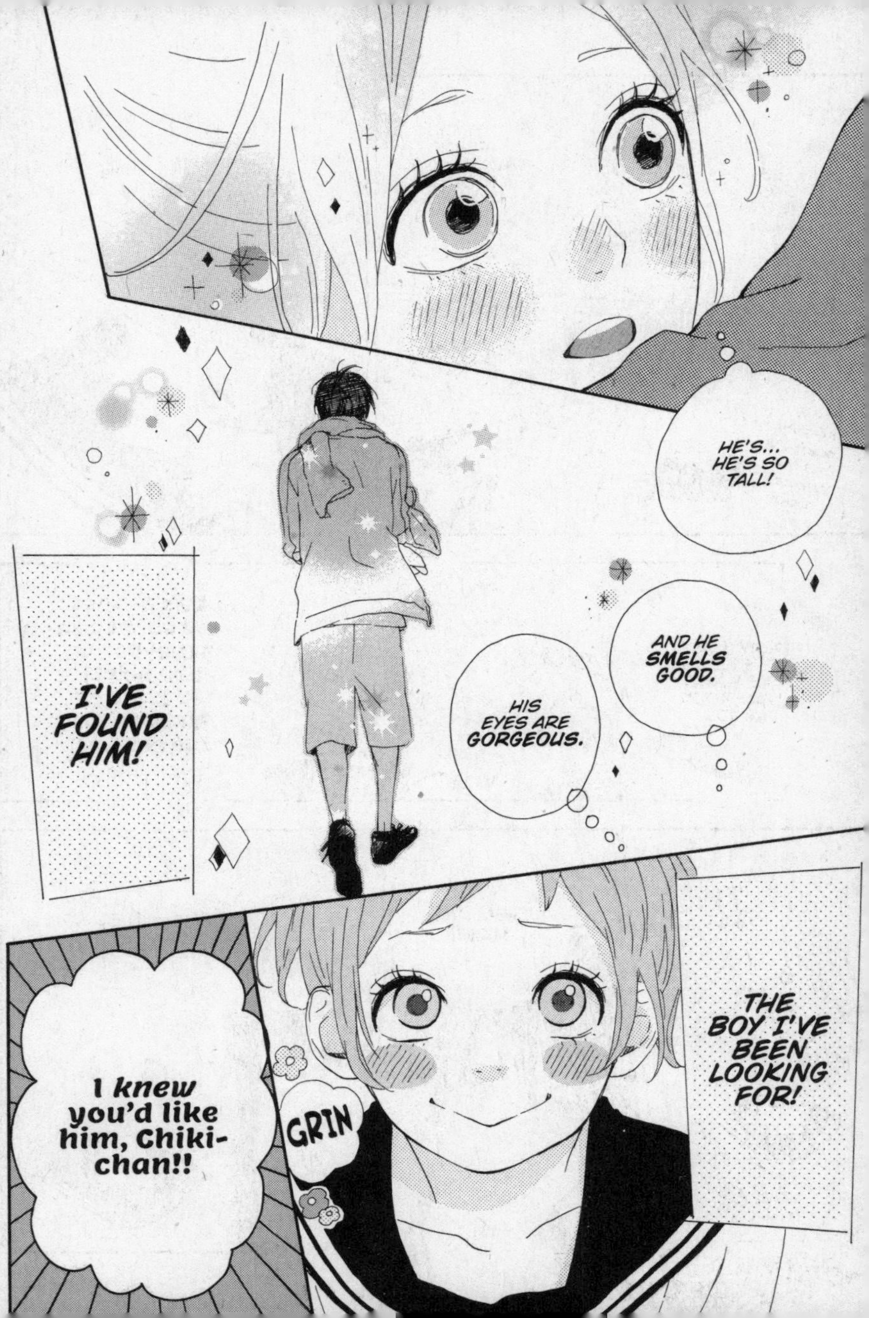
HE'S... HE'S SO TALL!
AND HE SMELLS GOOD.
HIS EYES ARE GORGEOUS.
I'VE FOUND HIM!
THE BOY I'VE BEEN LOOKING FOR!
GRIN
I knew you'd like him, Chiki-chan!!

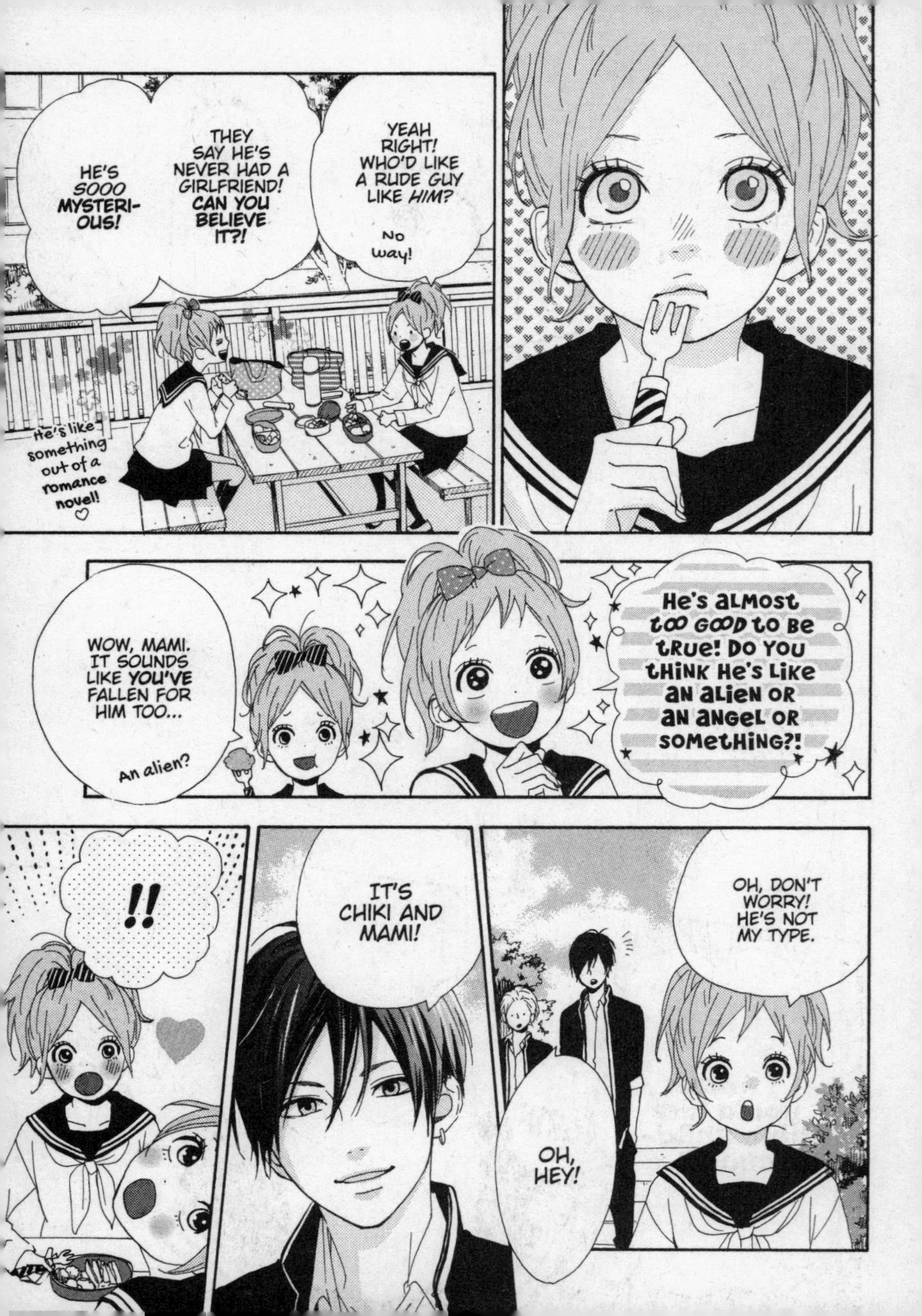
YEAH RIGHT! WHO'D LIKE A RUDE GUY LIKE HIM?
No way!
THEY SAY HE'S NEVER HAD A GIRLFRIEND! CAN YOU BELIEVE IT?!
HE'S SOOO MYSTERIOUS!
He's like something out of a romance novel! ♡
He's almost too good to be true! Do you think he's like an alien or an angel or something?!
WOW, MAMI. IT SOUNDS LIKE YOU'VE FALLEN FOR HIM TOO...
An alien?
OH, DON'T WORRY! HE'S NOT MY TYPE.
OH, HEY!
IT'S CHIKI AND MAMI!
!!

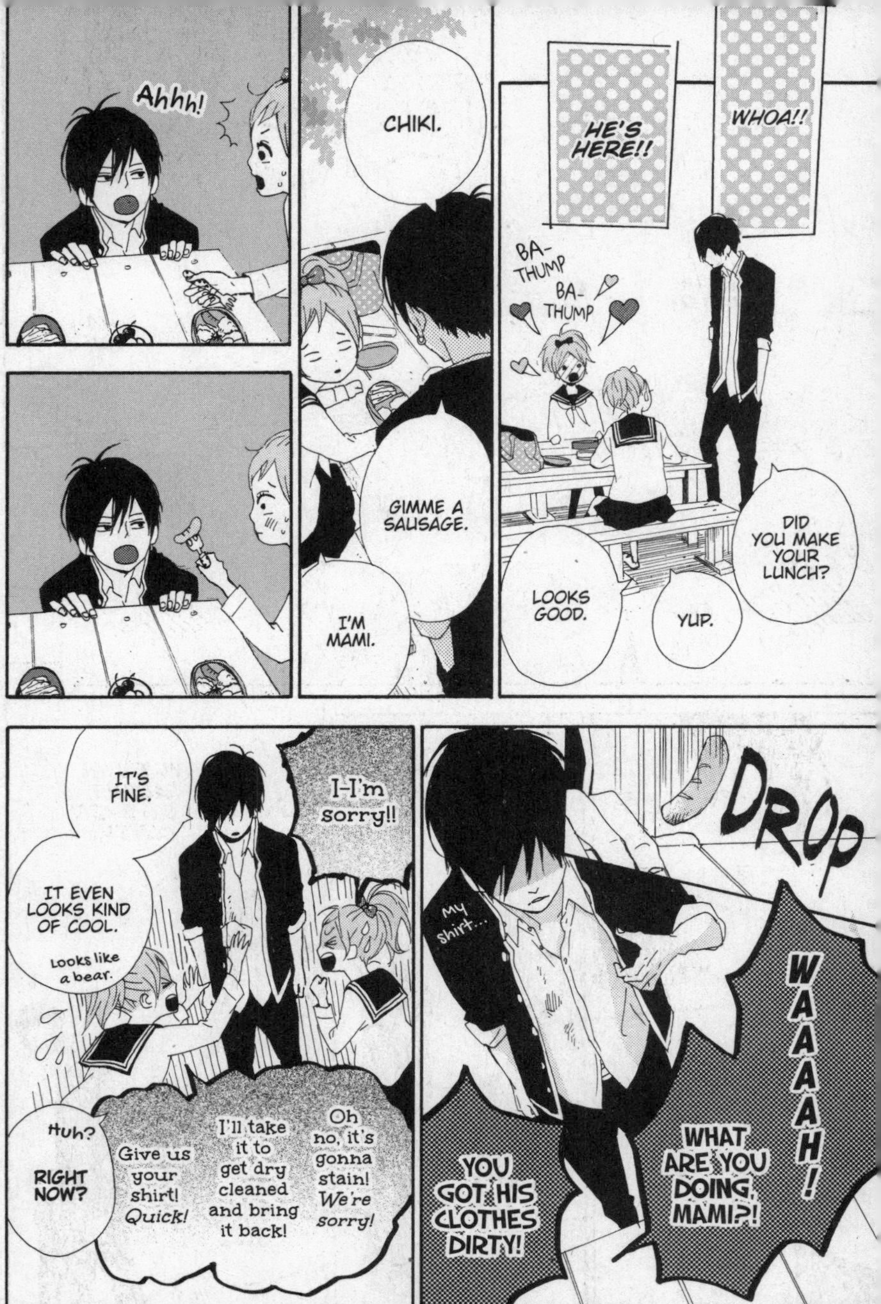
WHOA!!
HE'S HERE!!
BA-THUMP BA-THUMP
DID YOU MAKE YOUR LUNCH?
YUP.
LOOKS GOOD.
CHIKI.
GIMME A SAUSAGE.
I'M MAMI.
Ahhh!
DROP
WAAAAAH!
WHAT ARE YOU DOING, MAMI?!
YOU GOT HIS CLOTHES DIRTY!
My shirt...
I-I'm sorry!!
IT'S FINE.
IT EVEN LOOKS KIND OF COOL.
Looks like a bear.
Oh no, it's gonna stain! We're sorry!
I'll take it to get dry cleaned and bring it back!
Give us your shirt! Quick!
Huh?
RIGHT NOW?

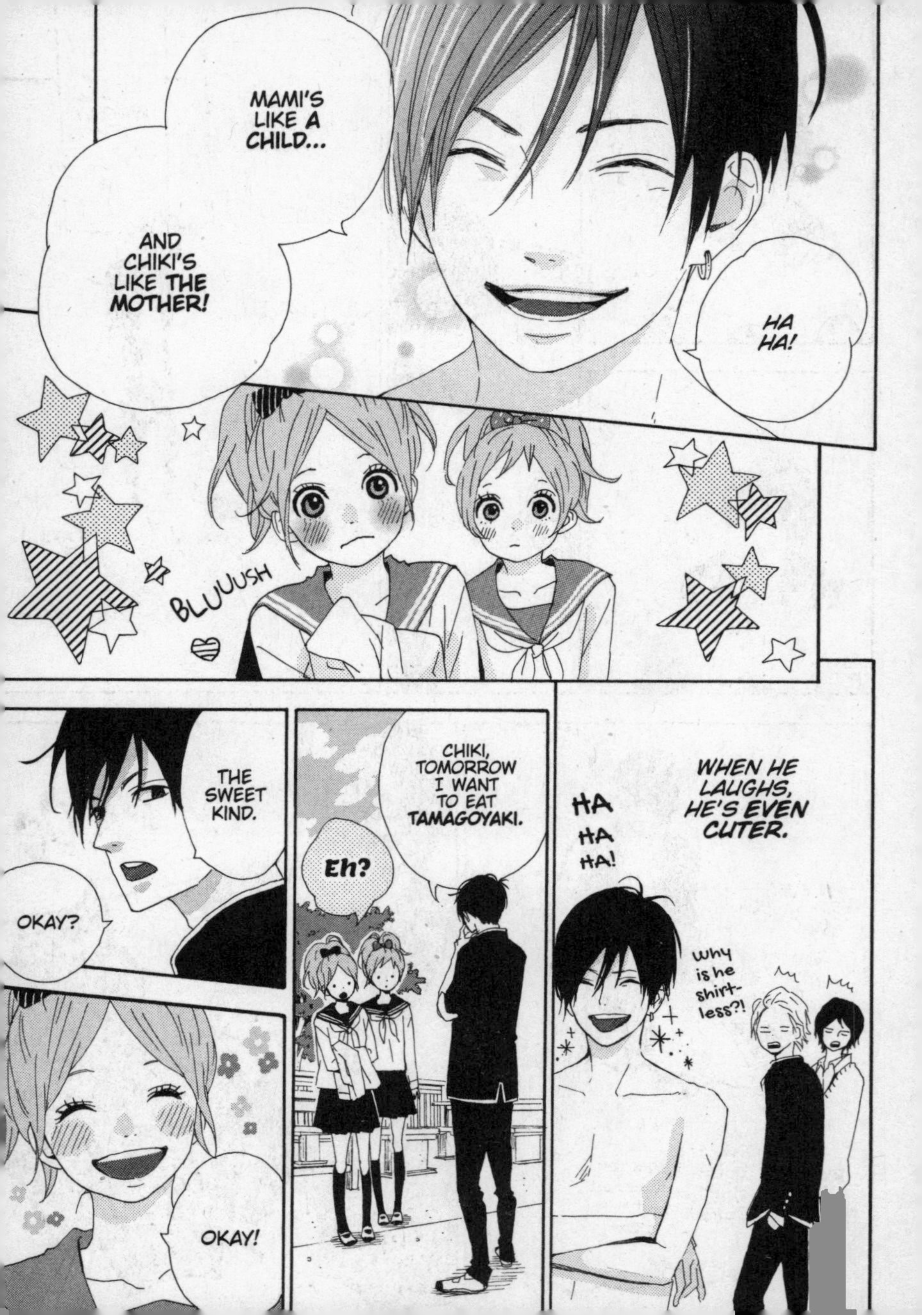

MAMI'S LIKE A CHILD...
AND CHIKI'S LIKE THE MOTHER!
HA HA!
BLUUUSH
WHEN HE LAUGHS, HE'S EVEN CUTER.
HA HA HA!
Why is he shirt-less?!
CHIKI, TOMORROW I WANT TO EAT TAMAGOYAKI.
Eh?
THE SWEET KIND.
OKAY?
OKAY!

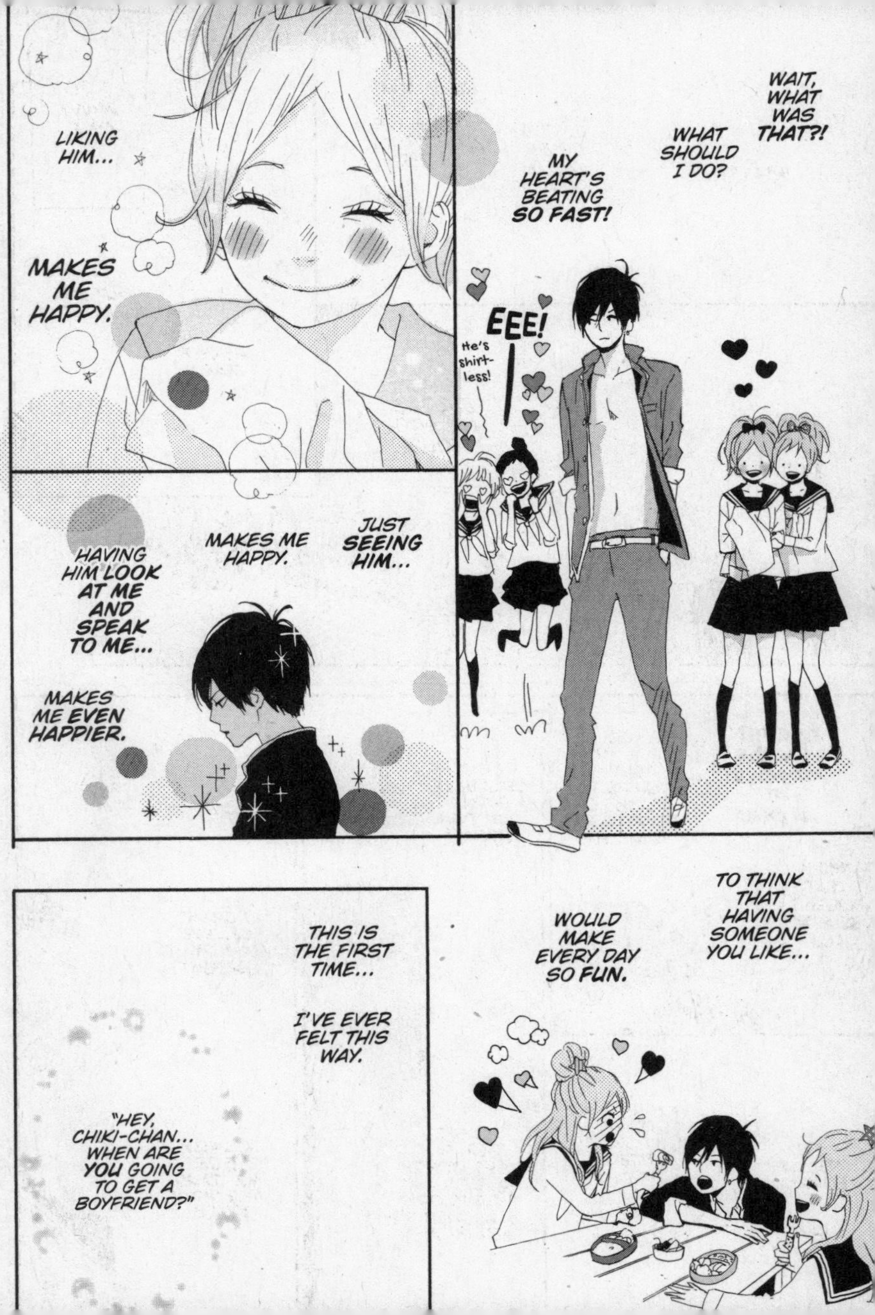
WAIT, WHAT WAS THAT?!
WHAT SHOULD I DO?
MY HEART'S BEATING SO FAST!
EEE!
He's shirtless!
LIKING HIM...
MAKES ME HAPPY.
JUST SEEING HIM...
MAKES ME HAPPY.
HAVING HIM LOOK AT ME AND SPEAK TO ME...
MAKES ME EVEN HAPPIER.
TO THINK THAT HAVING SOMEONE YOU LIKE...
WOULD MAKE EVERY DAY SO FUN.
THIS IS THE FIRST TIME...
I'VE EVER FELT THIS WAY.
"HEY, CHIKI-CHAN... WHEN ARE YOU GOING TO GET A BOYFRIEND?"

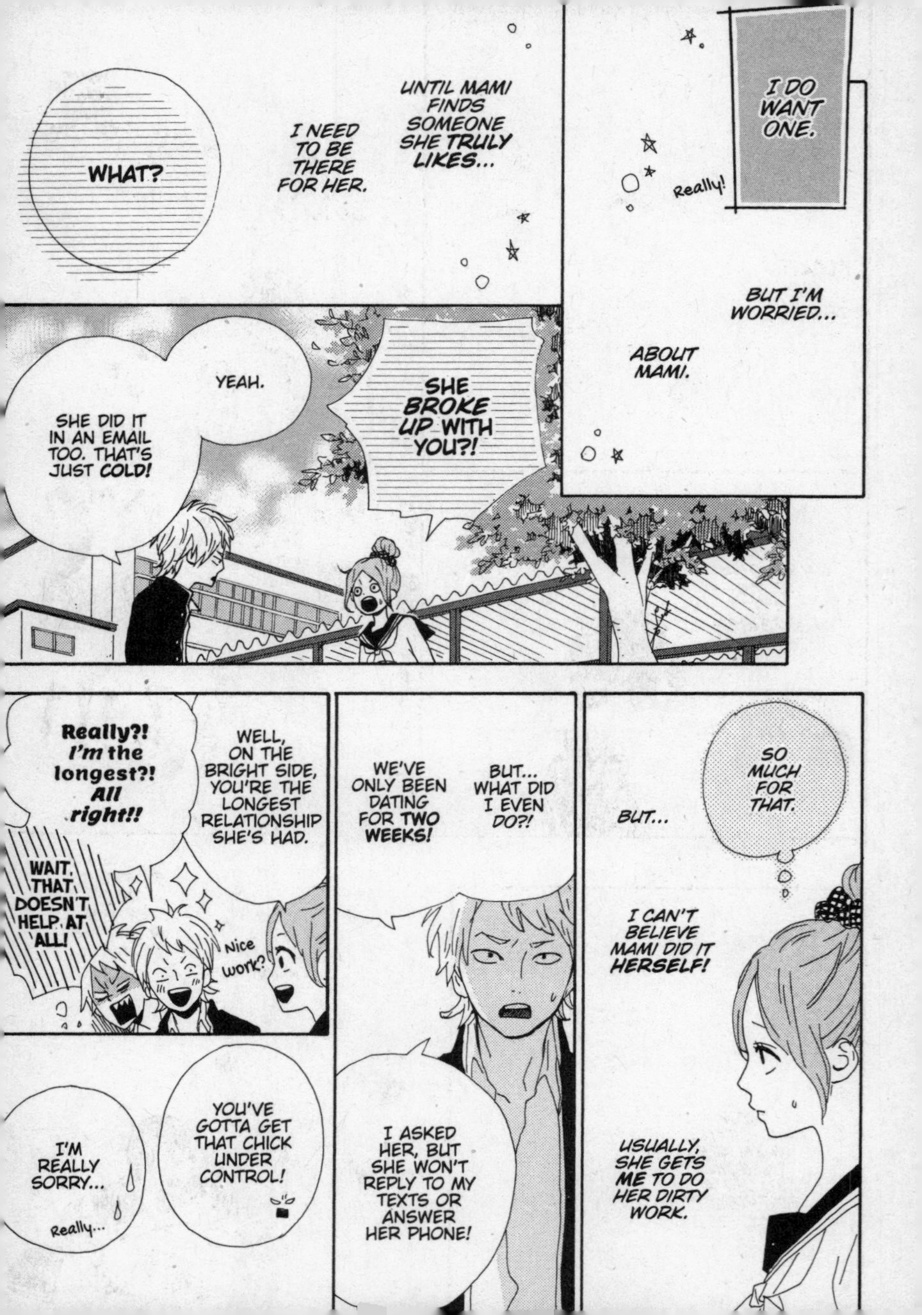
I DO WANT ONE.
Really!
BUT I'M WORRIED...
ABOUT MAMI.
UNTIL MAMI FINDS SOMEONE SHE TRULY LIKES...
I NEED TO BE THERE FOR HER.
WHAT?
SHE BROKE UP WITH YOU?!
YEAH.
SHE DID IT IN AN EMAIL TOO. THAT'S JUST COLD!
SO MUCH FOR THAT.
BUT...
I CAN'T BELIEVE MAMI DID IT HERSELF!
USUALLY, SHE GETS ME TO DO HER DIRTY WORK.
BUT... WHAT DID I EVEN DO?!
WE'VE ONLY BEEN DATING FOR TWO WEEKS!
I ASKED HER, BUT SHE WON'T REPLY TO MY TEXTS OR ANSWER HER PHONE!
WELL, ON THE BRIGHT SIDE, YOU'RE THE LONGEST RELATIONSHIP SHE'S HAD.
Really?! I'm the longest?! All right!!
Nice work?
WAIT, THAT DOESN'T HELP AT ALL!
YOU'VE GOTTA GET THAT CHICK UNDER CONTROL!
I'M REALLY SORRY...
Really...

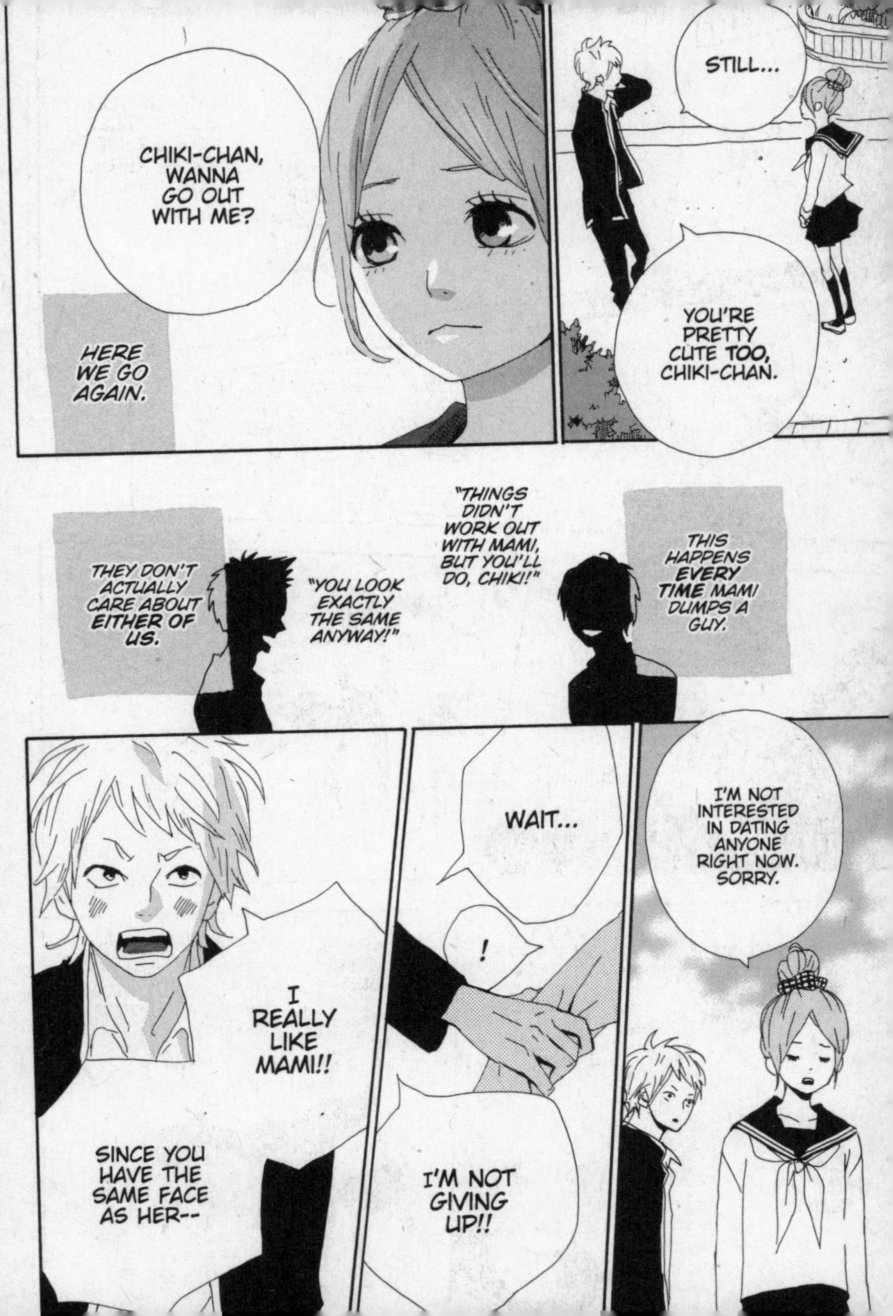
STILL...
YOU'RE PRETTY CUTE TOO, CHIKI-CHAN.
CHIKI-CHAN, WANNA GO OUT WITH ME?
HERE WE GO AGAIN.
THIS HAPPENS EVERY TIME MAMI DUMPS A GUY.
"THINGS DIDN'T WORK OUT WITH MAMI, BUT YOU'LL DO, CHIKI!"
"YOU LOOK EXACTLY THE SAME ANYWAY!"
THEY DON'T ACTUALLY CARE ABOUT EITHER OF US.
I'M NOT INTERESTED IN DATING ANYONE RIGHT NOW. SORRY.
WAIT...
!
I'M NOT GIVING UP!!
I REALLY LIKE MAMI!!
SINCE YOU HAVE THE SAME FACE AS HER--

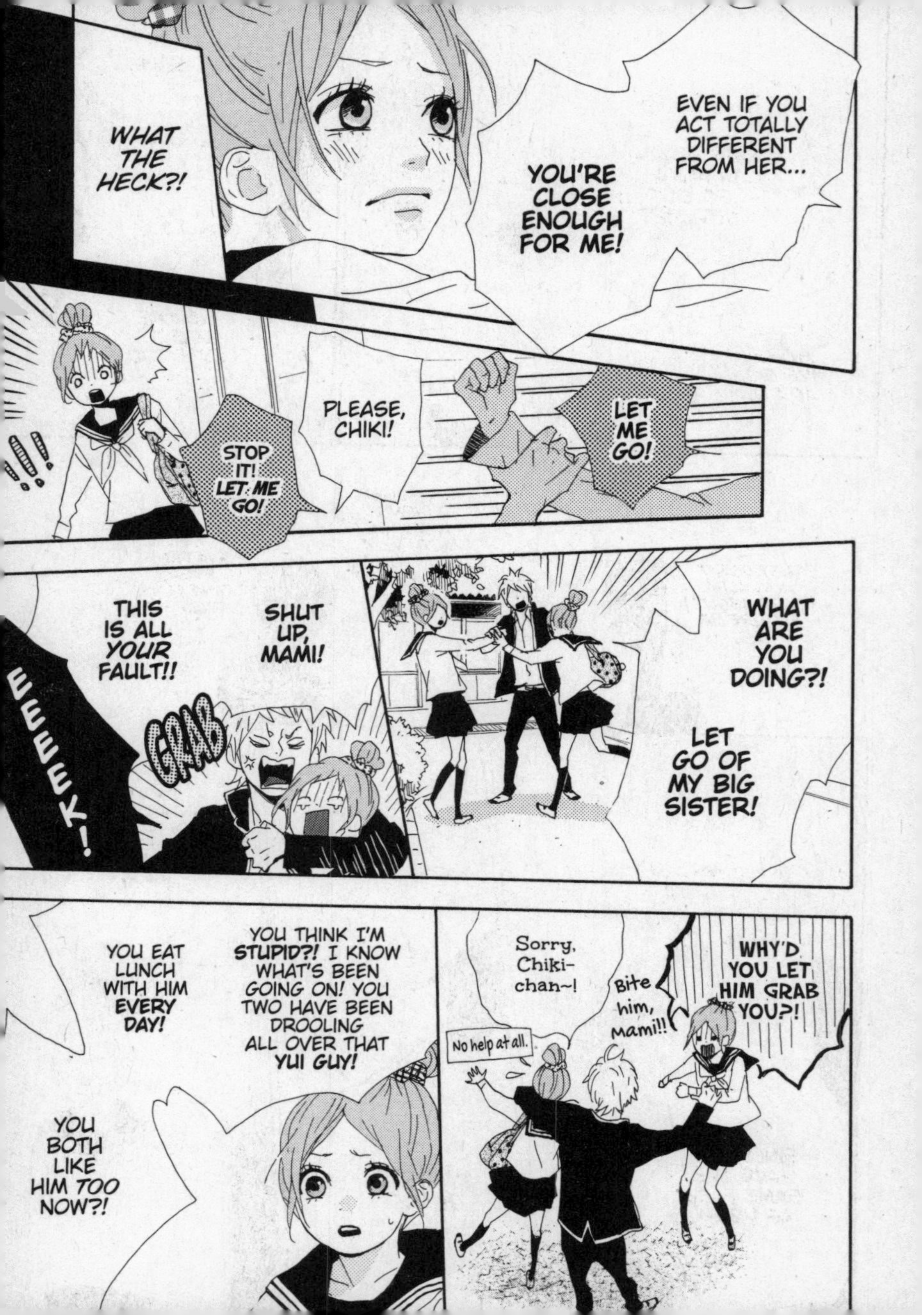
EVEN IF YOU ACT TOTALLY DIFFERENT FROM HER...
YOU'RE CLOSE ENOUGH FOR ME!
WHAT THE HECK?!
LET ME GO!
PLEASE, CHIKI!
STOP IT! LET ME GO!
!!!
WHAT ARE YOU DOING?!
LET GO OF MY BIG SISTER!
SHUT UP, MAMI!
THIS IS ALL YOUR FAULT!!
GRAB
EEEEK!
WHY'D YOU LET HIM GRAB YOU?!
Bite him, Mami!!
Sorry, Chiki-chan~!
No help at all.
YOU THINK I'M STUPID?! I KNOW WHAT'S BEEN GOING ON! YOU TWO HAVE BEEN DROOLING ALL OVER THAT YUI GUY!
YOU EAT LUNCH WITH HIM EVERY DAY!
YOU BOTH LIKE HIM TOO NOW?!

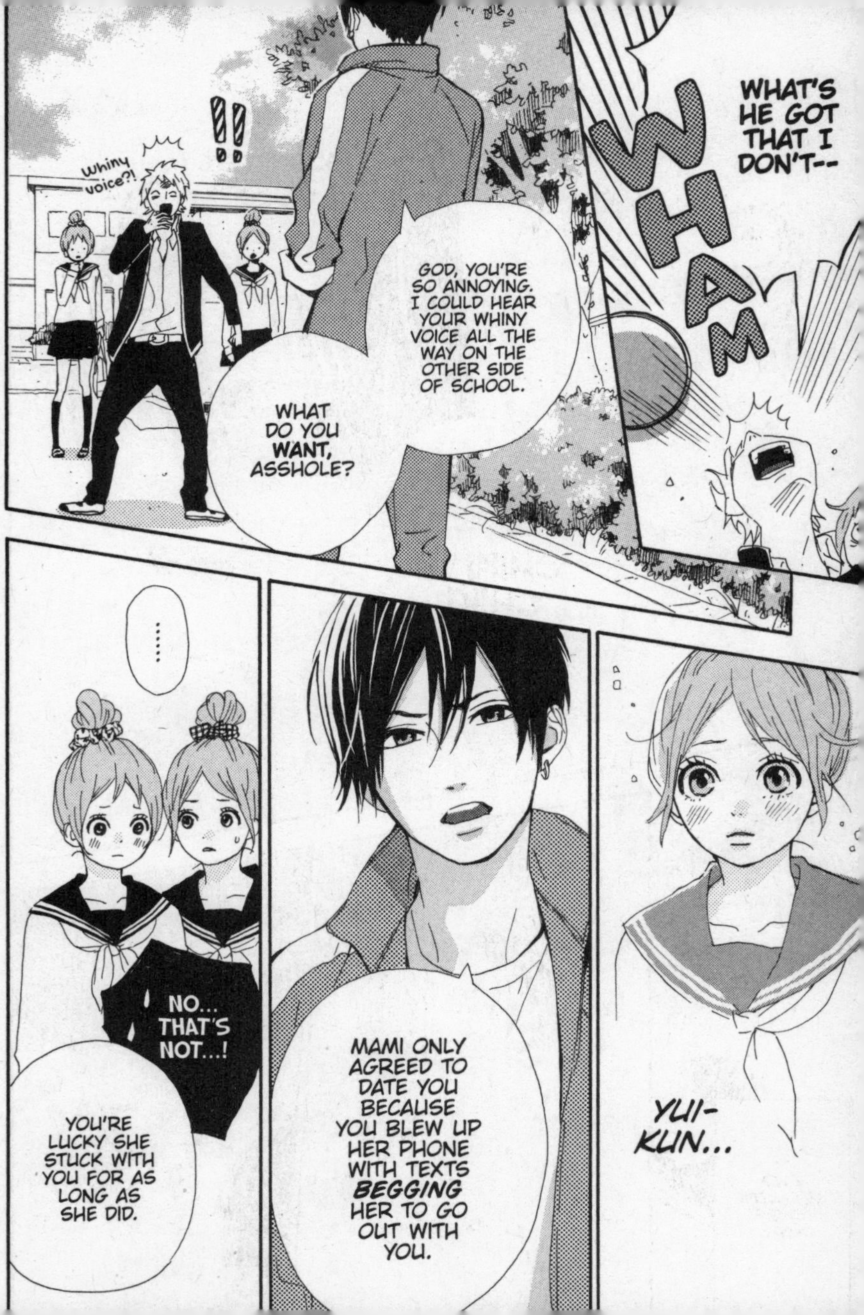
WHAM
WHAT'S HE GOT THAT I DON'T--
!!
Whiny voice?!
GOD, YOU'RE SO ANNOYING. I COULD HEAR YOUR WHINY VOICE ALL THE WAY ON THE OTHER SIDE OF SCHOOL.
WHAT DO YOU WANT, ASSHOLE?
YUI-KUN...
MAMI ONLY AGREED TO DATE YOU BECAUSE YOU BLEW UP HER PHONE WITH TEXTS BEGGING HER TO GO OUT WITH YOU.
......
NO... THAT'S NOT...!
YOU'RE LUCKY SHE STUCK WITH YOU FOR AS LONG AS SHE DID.

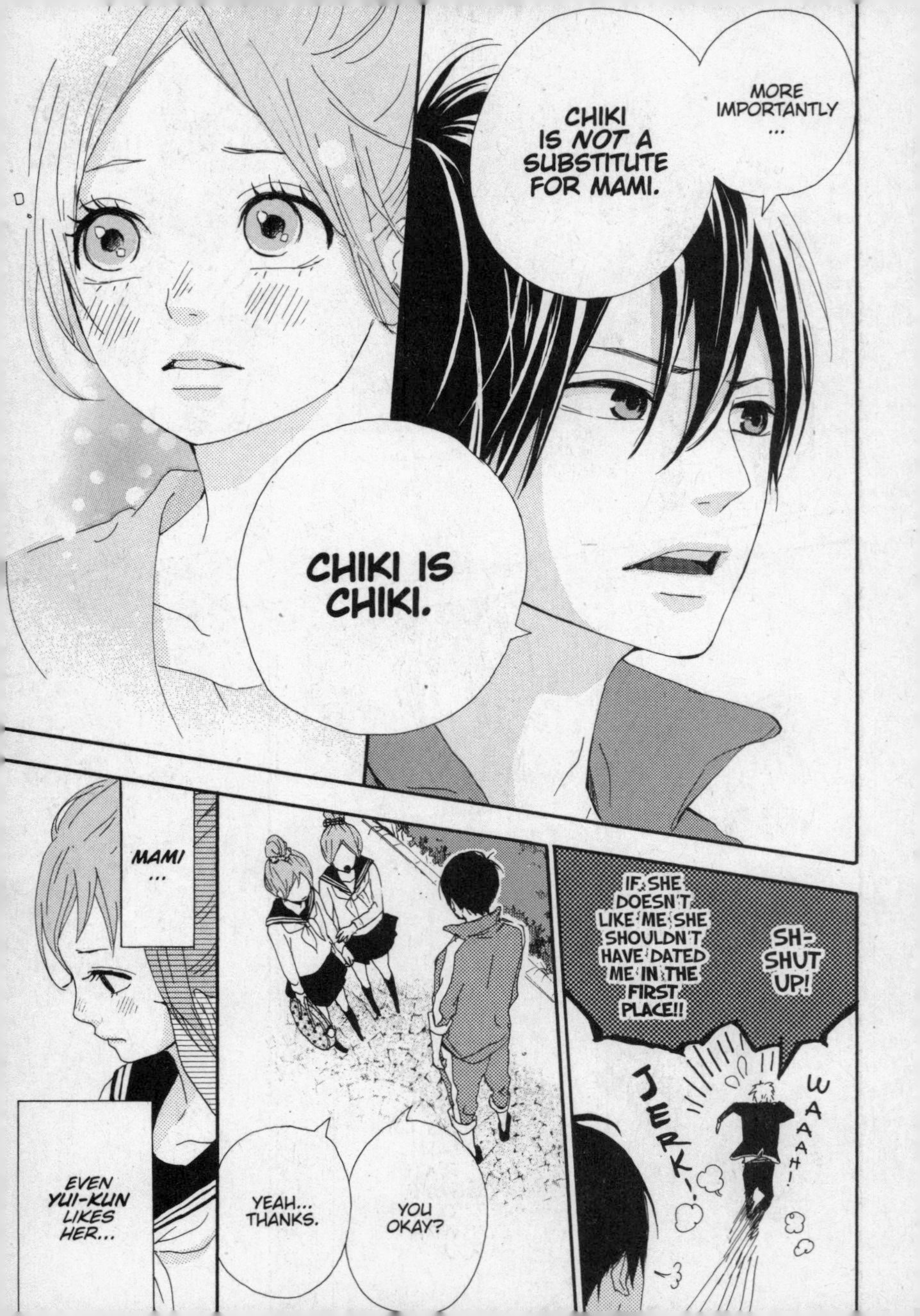
MORE IMPORTANTLY ...
CHIKI IS *NOT* A SUBSTITUTE FOR MAMI.
CHIKI IS CHIKI.
IF SHE DOESN'T LIKE ME SHE SHOULDN'T HAVE DATED ME IN THE FIRST PLACE!!
SH- SHUT UP!
JERK!
WAAAH!
YOU OKAY?
YEAH... THANKS.
MAMI ...
EVEN YUI-KUN LIKES HER...

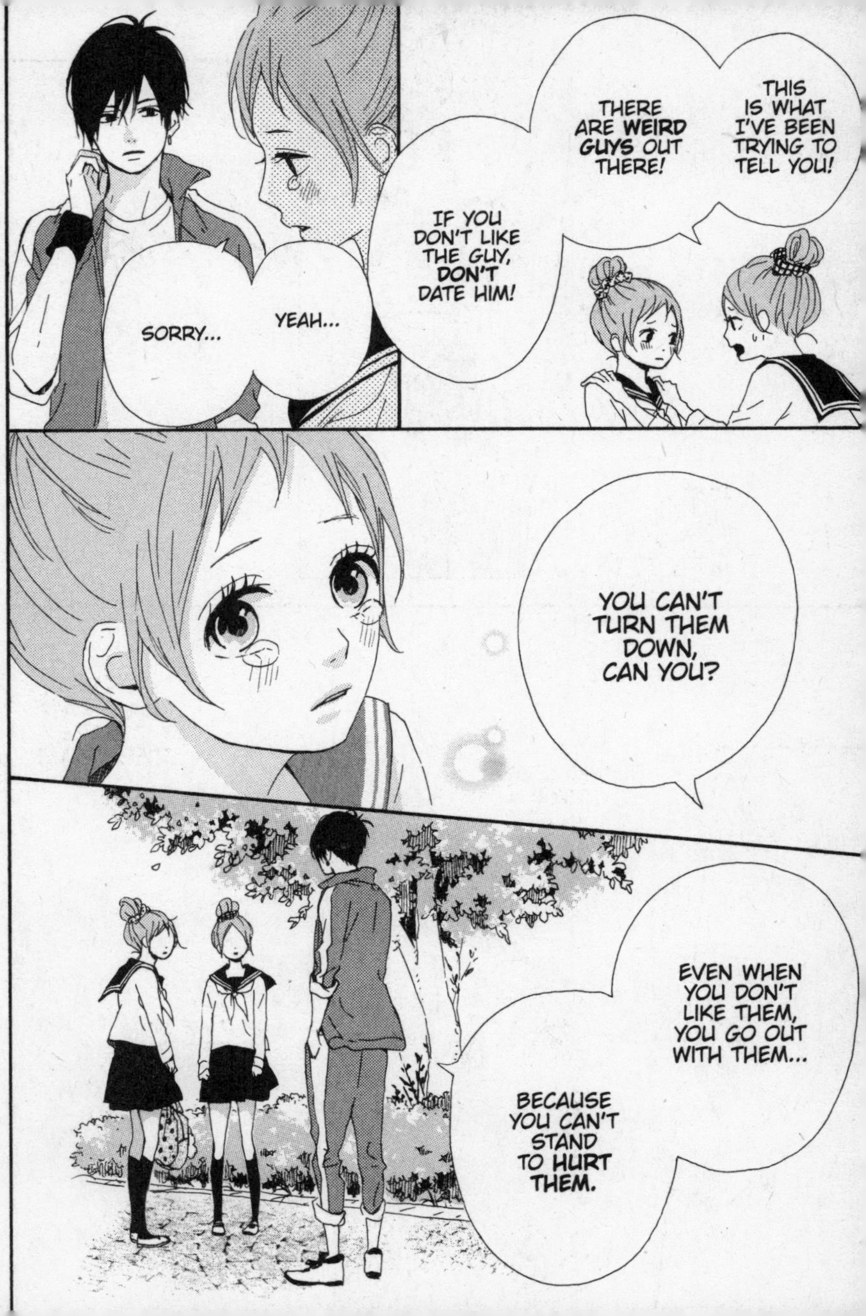
THIS IS WHAT I'VE BEEN TRYING TO TELL YOU!
THERE ARE WEIRD GUYS OUT THERE!
IF YOU DON'T LIKE THE GUY, DON'T DATE HIM!
YEAH...
SORRY...
YOU CAN'T TURN THEM DOWN, CAN YOU?
EVEN WHEN YOU DON'T LIKE THEM, YOU GO OUT WITH THEM...
BECAUSE YOU CAN'T STAND TO HURT THEM.

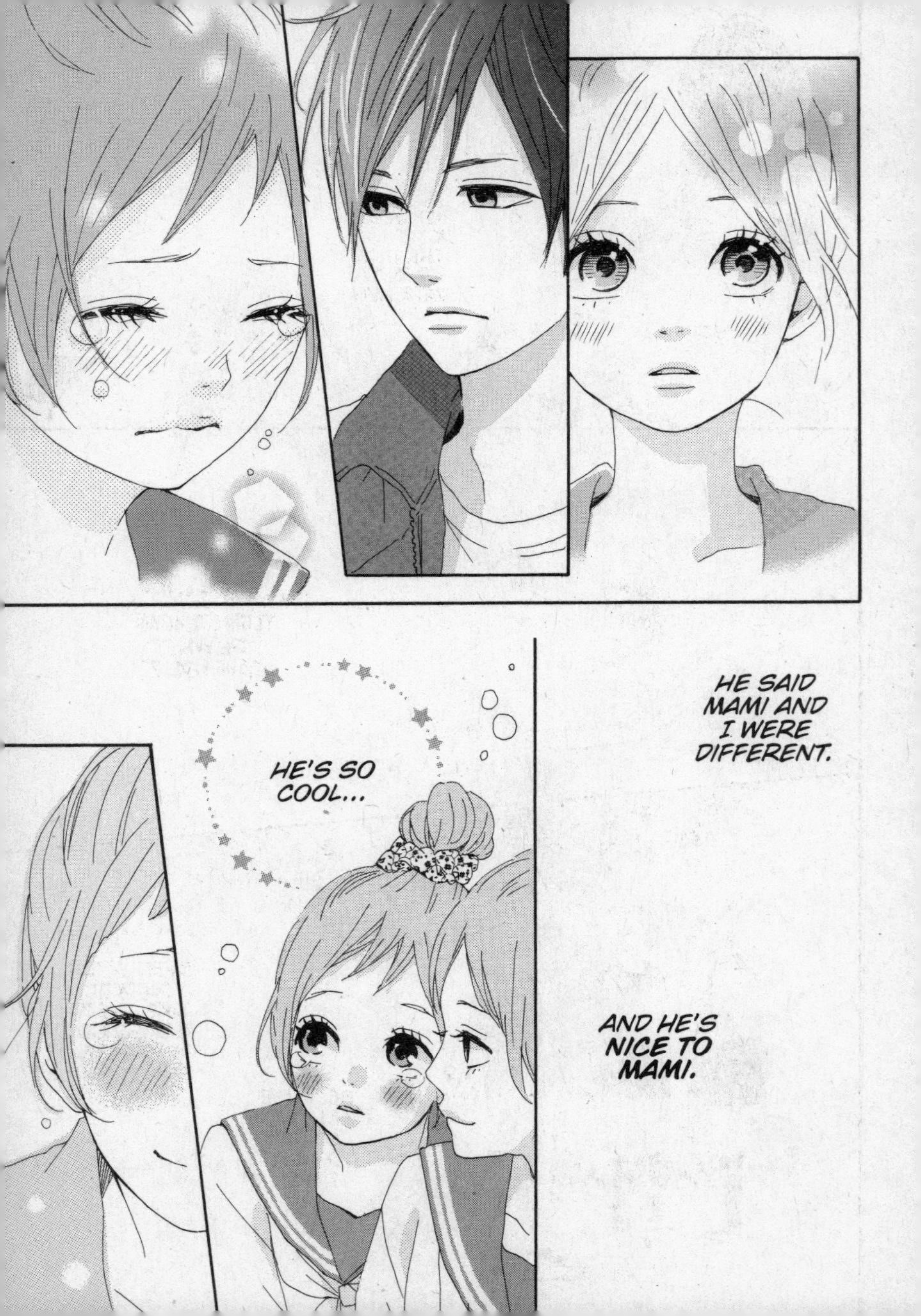
HE SAID MAMI AND I WERE DIFFERENT.
AND HE'S NICE TO MAMI.
HE'S SO COOL...

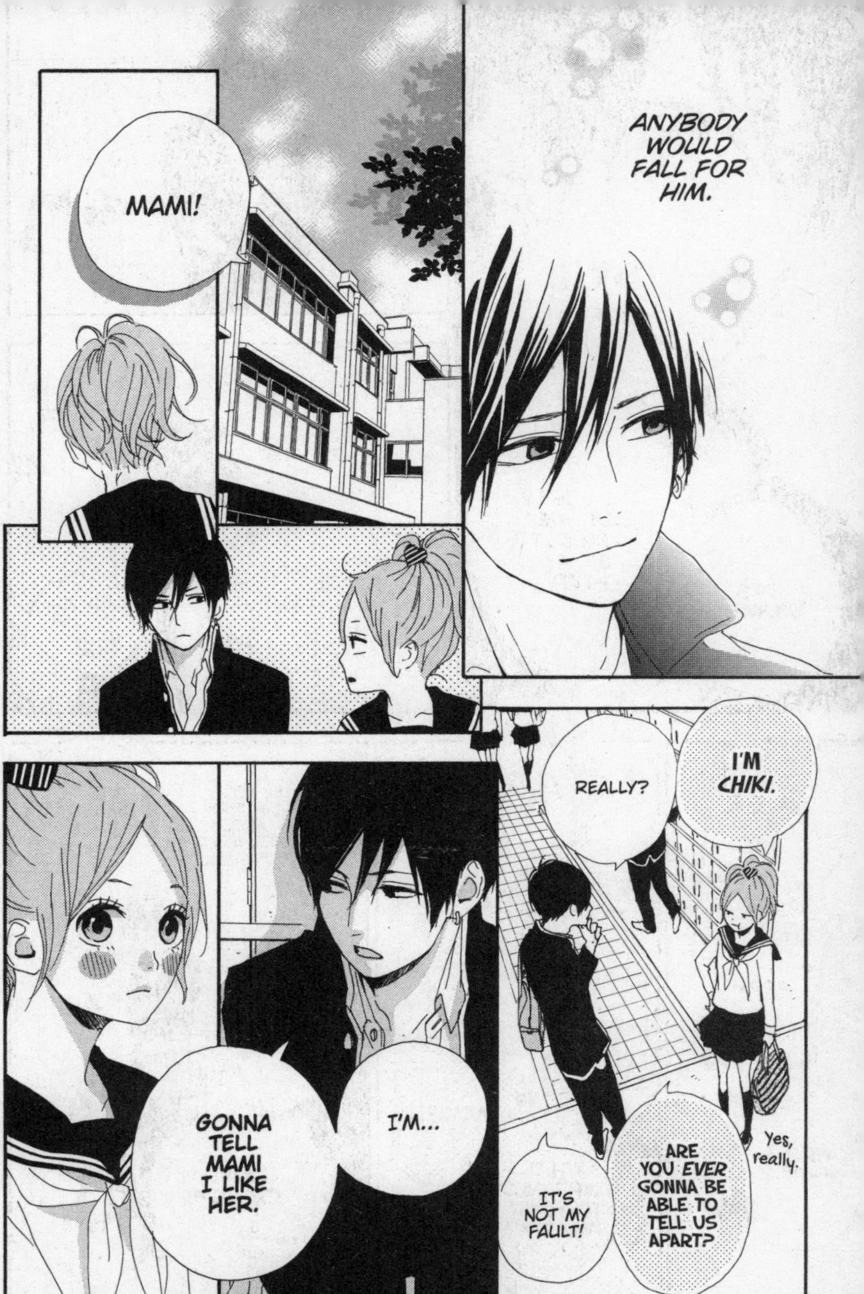
ANYBODY WOULD FALL FOR HIM.
MAMI!
I'M CHIKI.
REALLY?
Yes, really.
ARE YOU EVER GONNA BE ABLE TO TELL US APART?
IT'S NOT MY FAULT!
I'M...
GONNA TELL MAMI I LIKE HER.

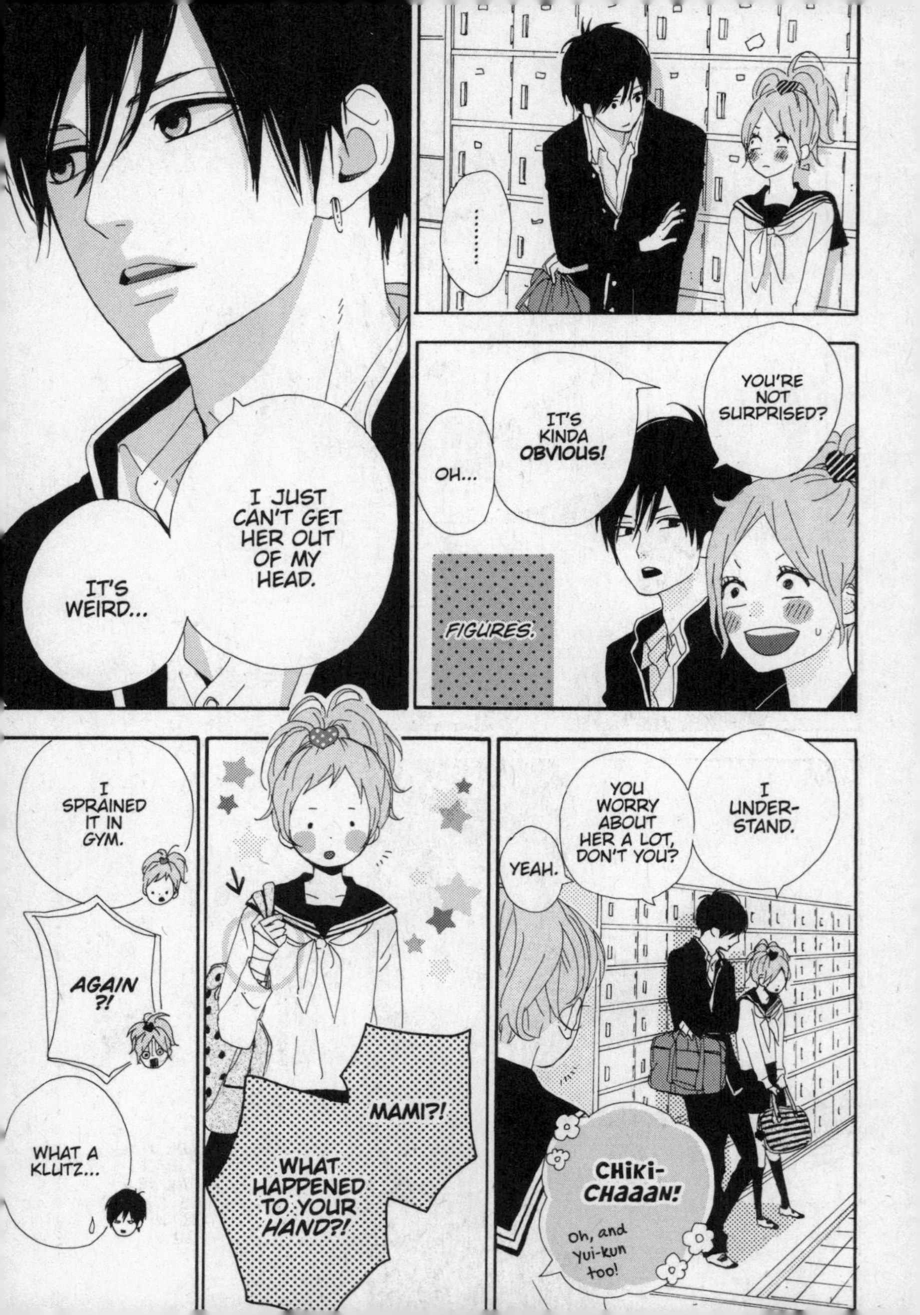
......
YOU'RE NOT SURPRISED?
IT'S KINDA OBVIOUS!
OH...
FIGURES.
I JUST CAN'T GET HER OUT OF MY HEAD.
IT'S WEIRD...
I UNDERSTAND.
YOU WORRY ABOUT HER A LOT, DON'T YOU?
YEAH.
CHIKI-CHAAAN!
Oh, and Yui-kun too!
MAMI?!
WHAT HAPPENED TO YOUR HAND?!
I SPRAINED IT IN GYM.
AGAIN?!
WHAT A KLUTZ...

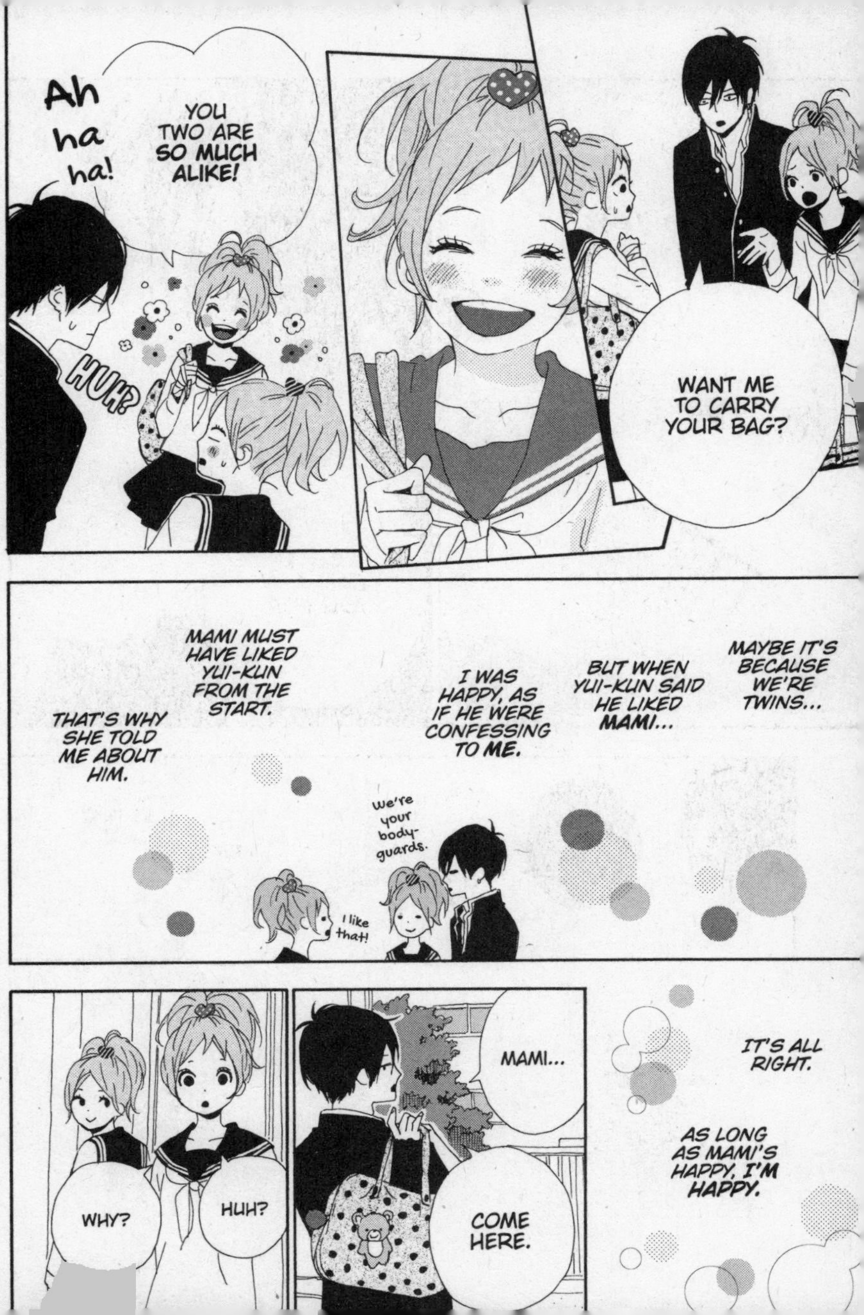
WANT ME TO CARRY YOUR BAG?
Ah ha ha!
YOU TWO ARE SO MUCH ALIKE!
HUH?
MAYBE IT'S BECAUSE WE'RE TWINS...
BUT WHEN YUI-KUN SAID HE LIKED MAMI...
I WAS HAPPY, AS IF HE WERE CONFESSING TO ME.
MAMI MUST HAVE LIKED YUI-KUN FROM THE START.
THAT'S WHY SHE TOLD ME ABOUT HIM.
We're your body-guards.
I like that!
IT'S ALL RIGHT.
AS LONG AS MAMI'S HAPPY, I'M HAPPY.
MAMI...
COME HERE.
HUH?
WHY?

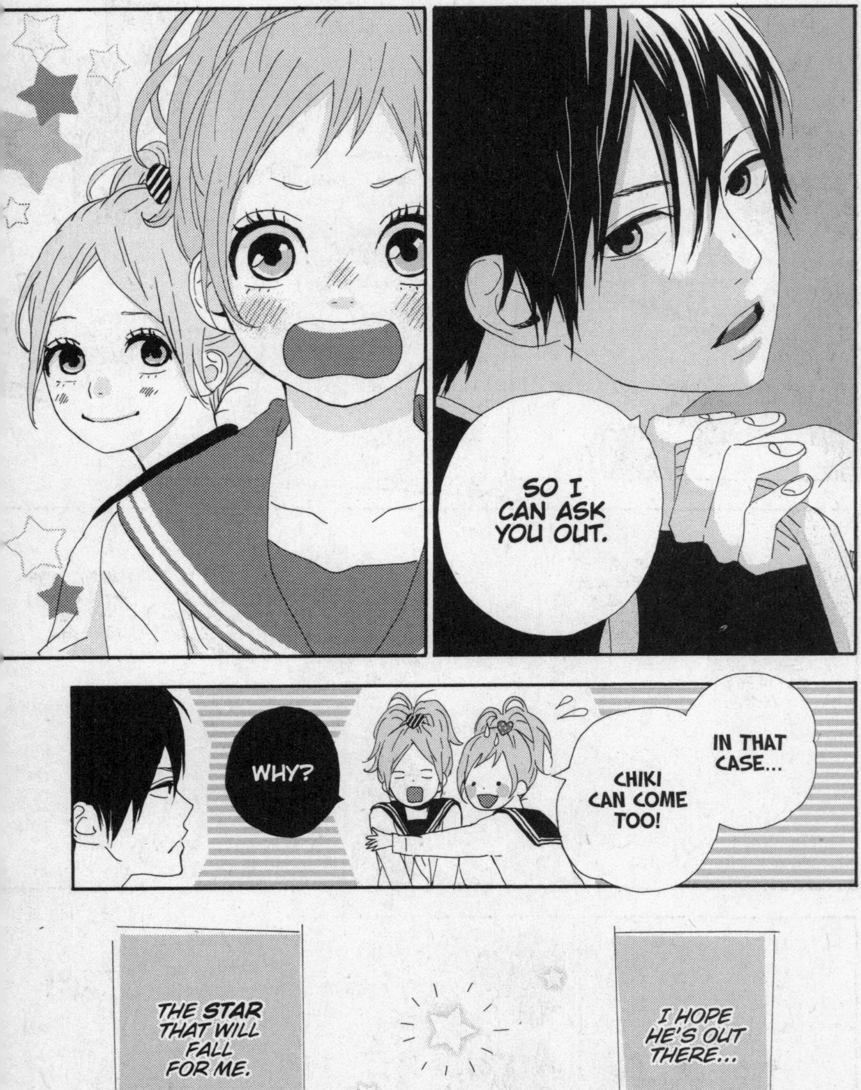
SO I CAN ASK YOU OUT.
IN THAT CASE... CHIKI CAN COME TOO!
WHY?
I HOPE HE'S OUT THERE...
THE STAR THAT WILL FALL FOR ME.

About HARUIRO ASTRONAUT ☆ 2

This is the second chapter! New characters show up, but I was able to create one I really like. It's this guy here, Tatsuaki. Once this character appeared, I couldn't stop drawing him. It quickly became a very silly series. Because of how goofy it is, it's a nice change of pace from *Orange*. Try reading it while taking a break.

At any rate, I plan to draw more.

Please enjoy it!

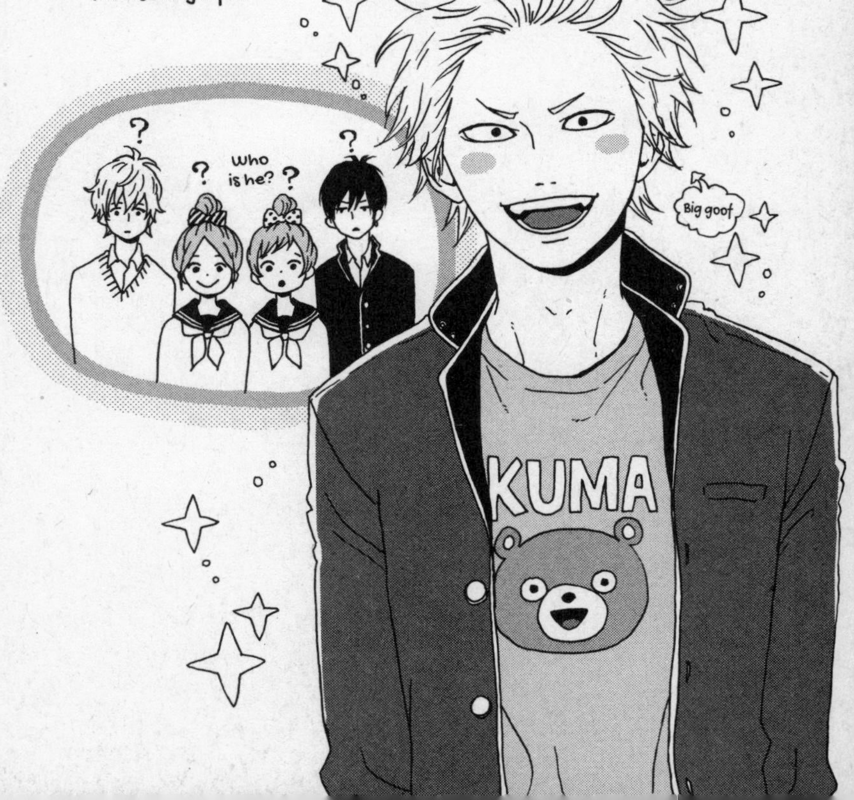

Who is he?
Big goof
KUMA

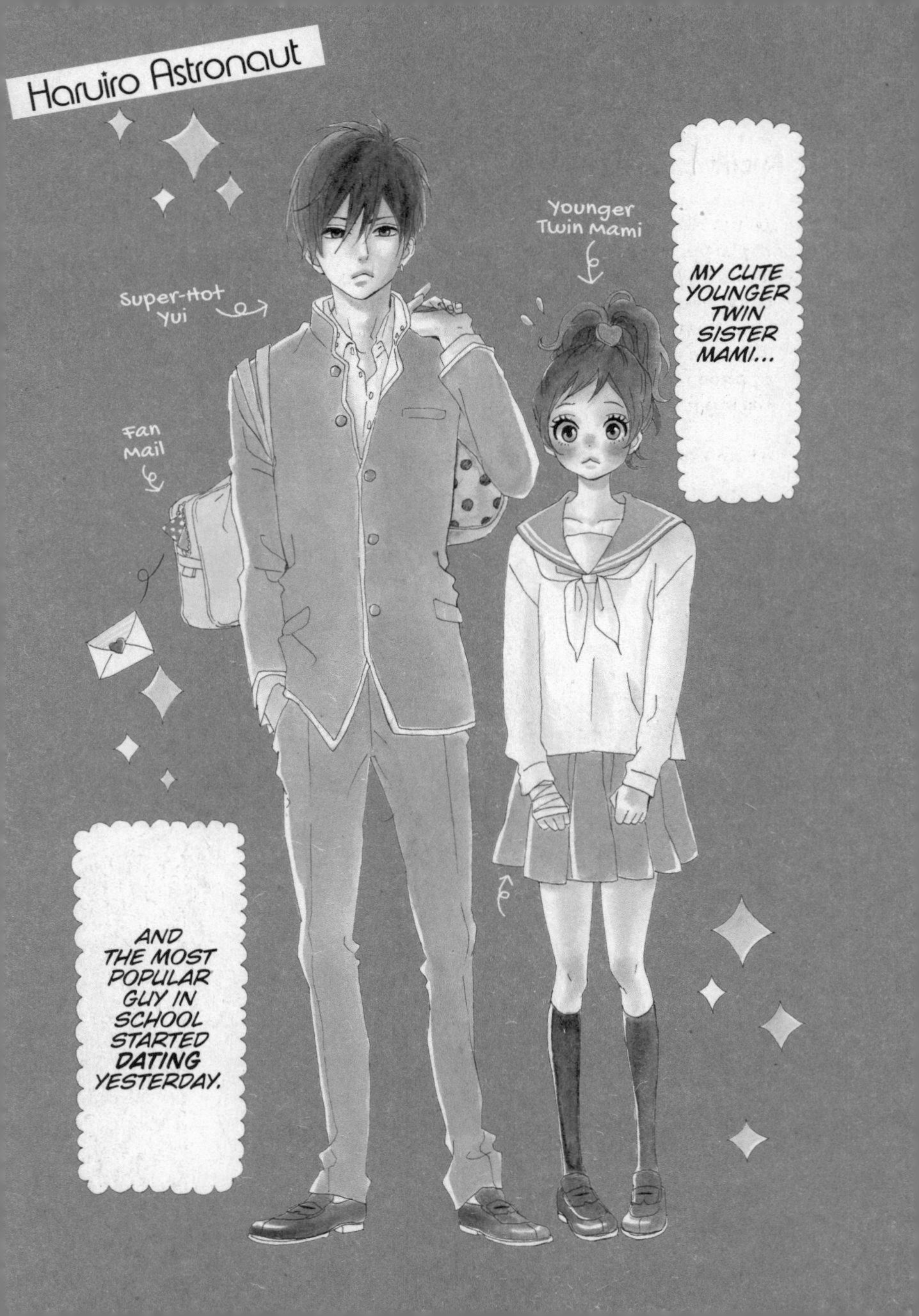
Haruiro Astronaut
MY CUTE YOUNGER TWIN SISTER MAMI...
Younger Twin Mami
Super-Hot Yui
Fan Mail
AND THE MOST POPULAR GUY IN SCHOOL STARTED DATING YESTERDAY.

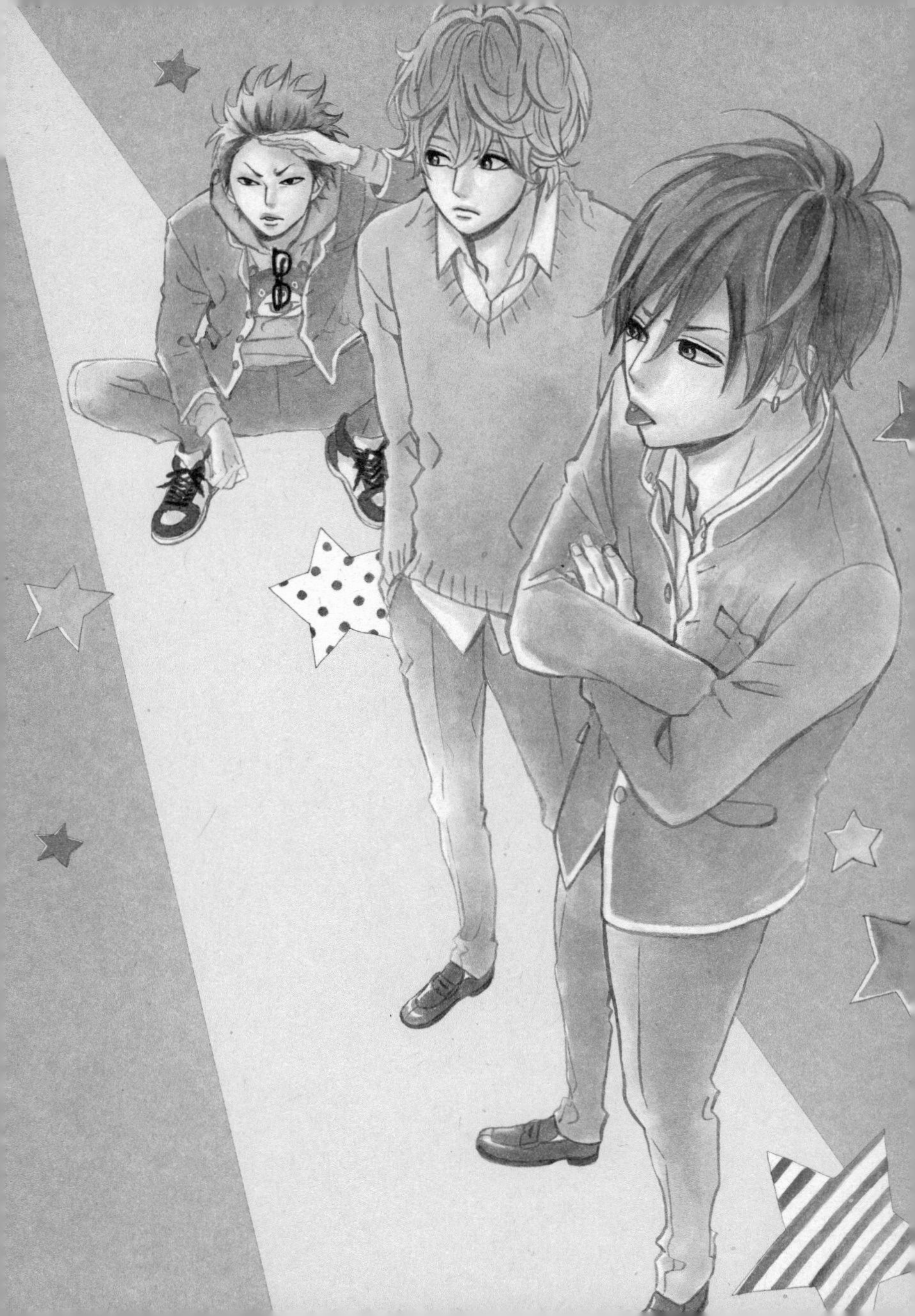

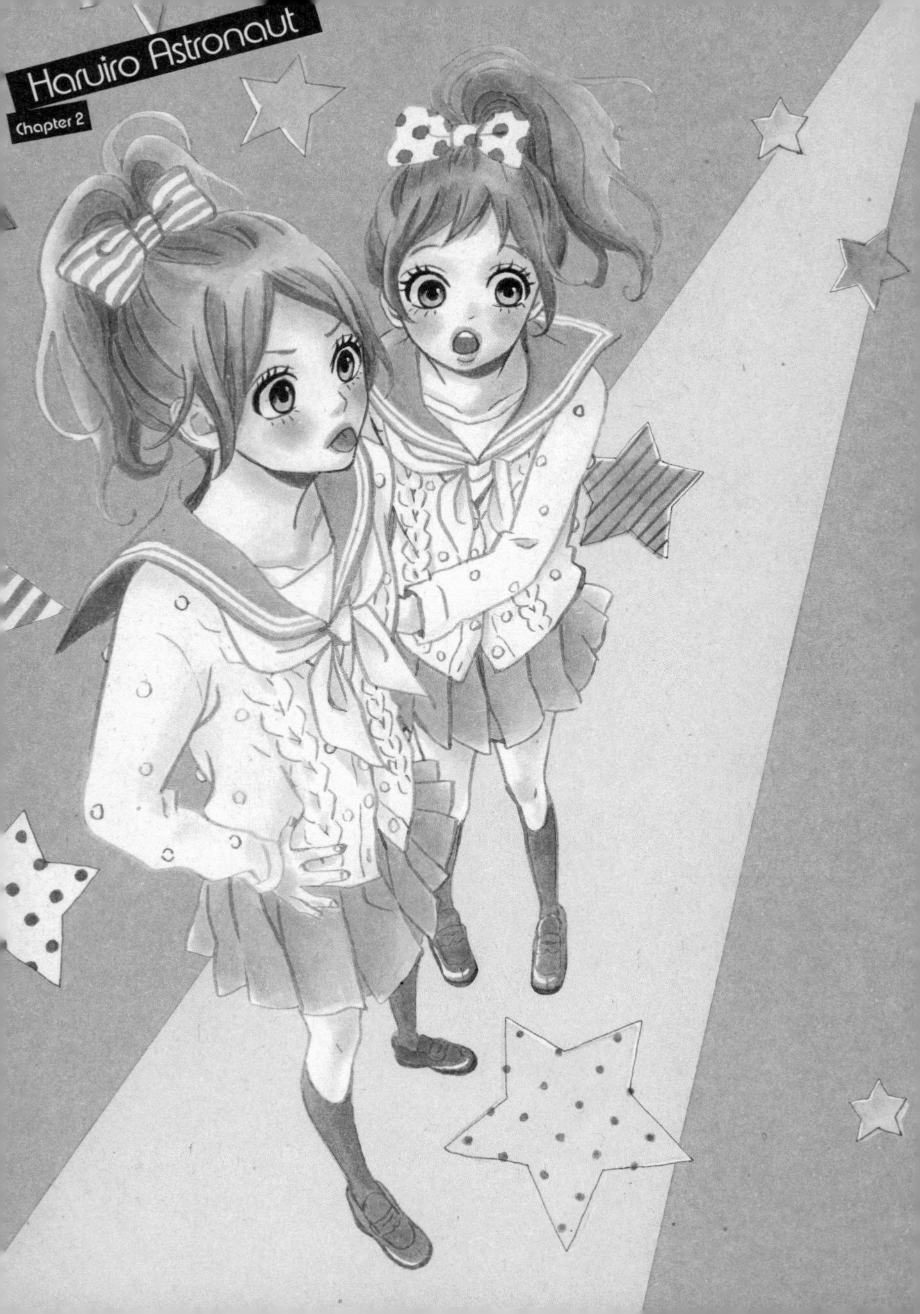
Haruiro Astronaut
Chapter 2

Haruiro Astronaut

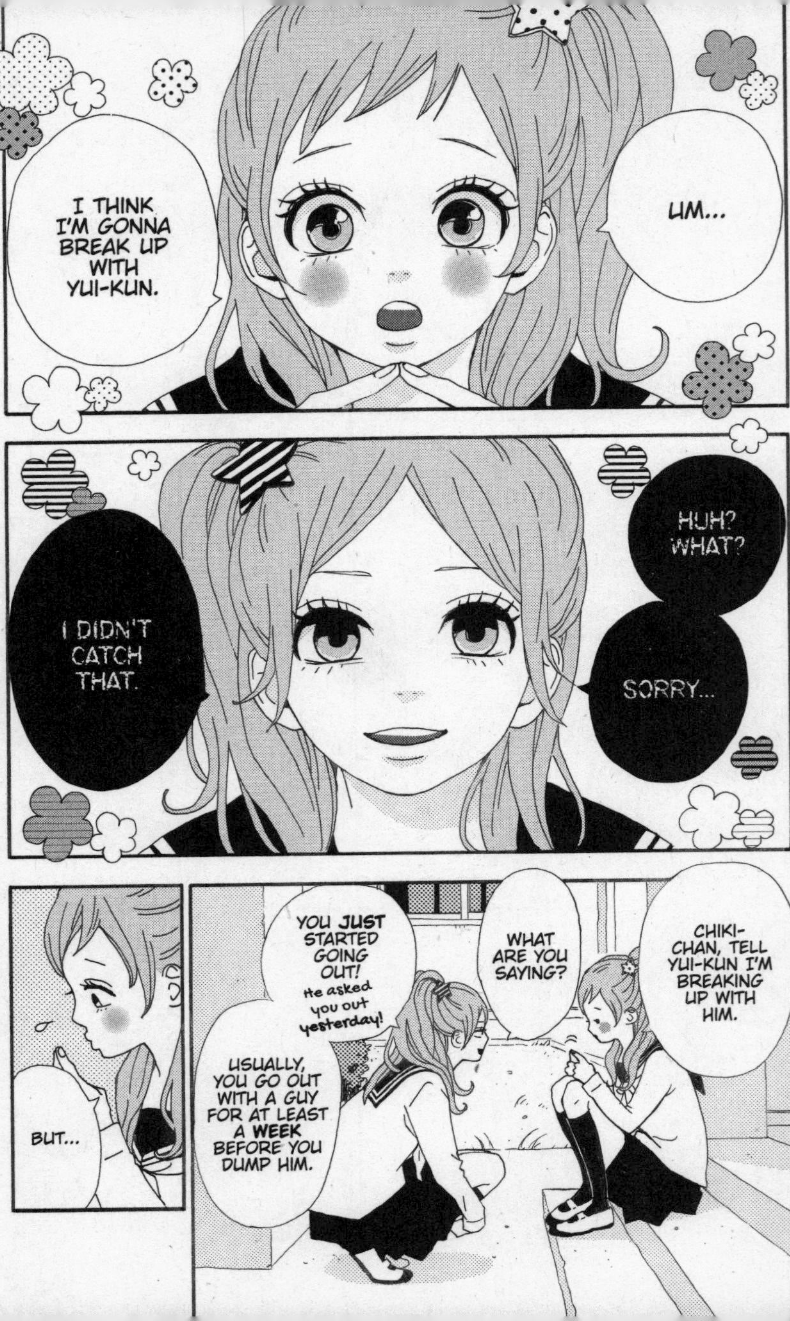
UM...
I THINK I'M GONNA BREAK UP WITH YUI-KUN.
HUH? WHAT?
SORRY...
I DIDN'T CATCH THAT.
CHIKI-CHAN, TELL YUI-KUN I'M BREAKING UP WITH HIM.
WHAT ARE YOU SAYING?
YOU JUST STARTED GOING OUT! He asked you out yesterday!
USUALLY, YOU GO OUT WITH A GUY FOR AT LEAST A WEEK BEFORE YOU DUMP HIM.
BUT...

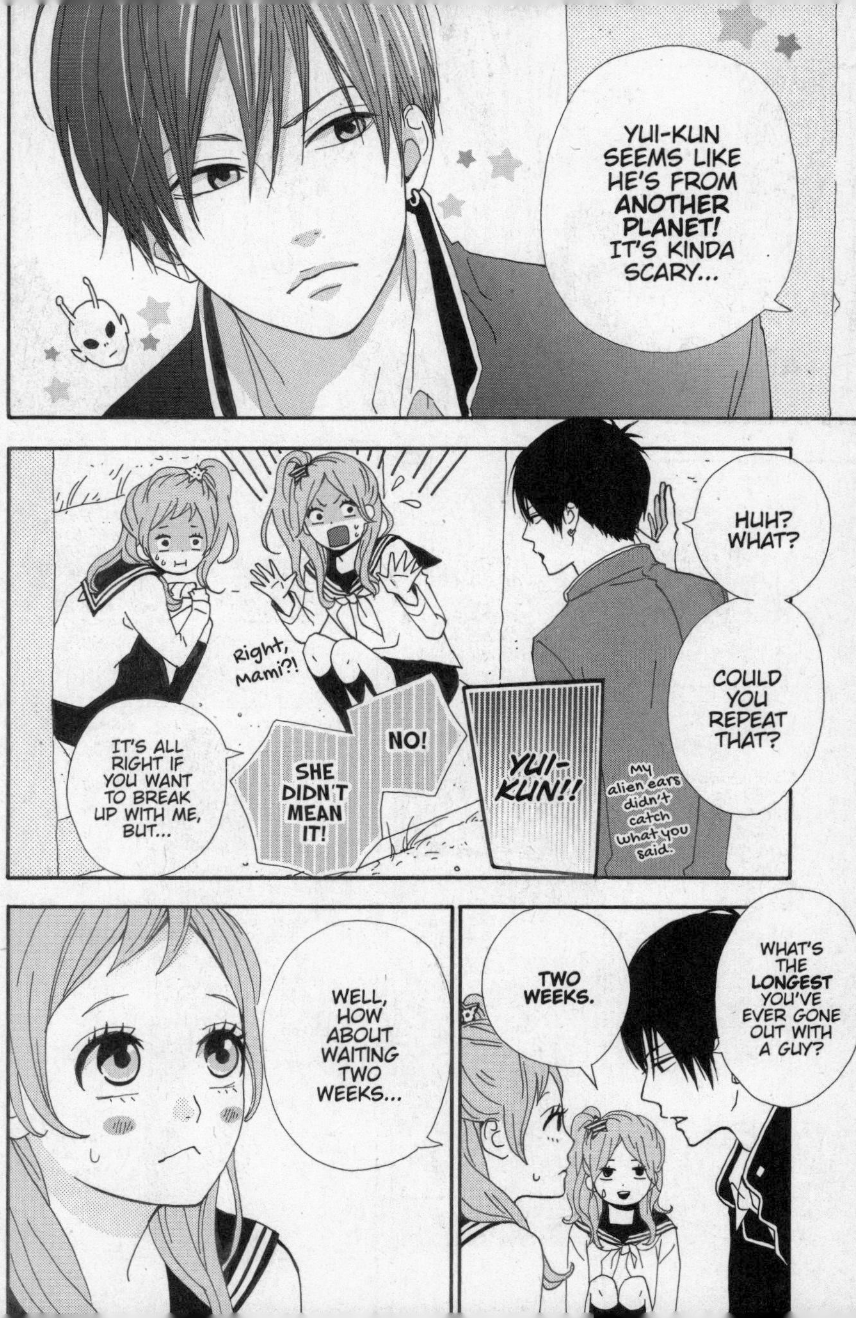
YUI-KUN SEEMS LIKE HE'S FROM ANOTHER PLANET! IT'S KINDA SCARY...
HUH? WHAT?
COULD YOU REPEAT THAT?
My alien ears didn't catch what you said.
YUI-KUN!!
NO!
SHE DIDN'T MEAN IT!
Right, Mami?!
IT'S ALL RIGHT IF YOU WANT TO BREAK UP WITH ME, BUT...
WHAT'S THE LONGEST YOU'VE EVER GONE OUT WITH A GUY?
TWO WEEKS.
WELL, HOW ABOUT WAITING TWO WEEKS...

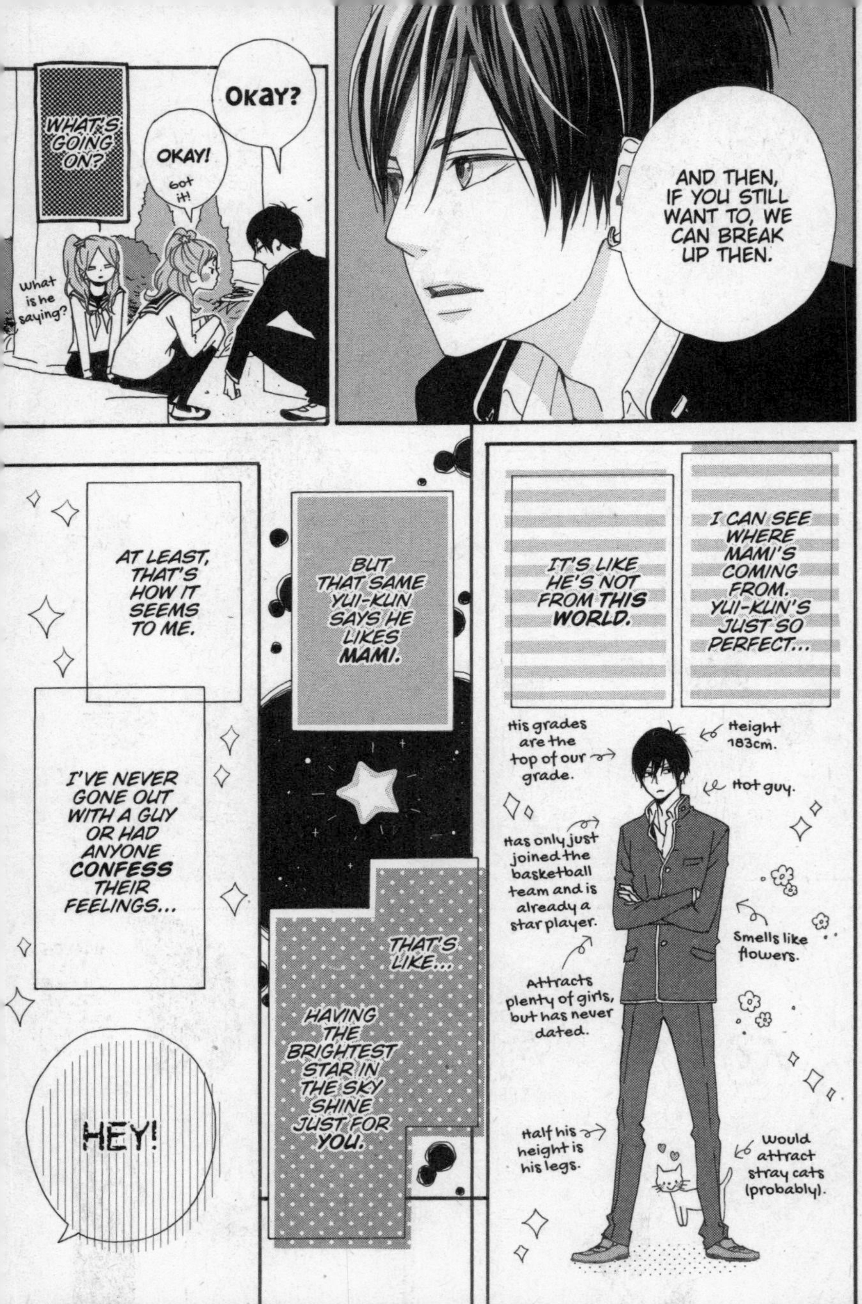
AND THEN, IF YOU STILL WANT TO, WE CAN BREAK UP THEN.
OKAY?
OKAY!
Got it!
WHAT'S GOING ON?
What is he saying?
I CAN SEE WHERE MAMI'S COMING FROM. YUI-KUN'S JUST SO PERFECT...
IT'S LIKE HE'S NOT FROM THIS WORLD.
Height 183cm.
His grades are the top of our grade.
Hot guy.
Has only just joined the basketball team and is already a star player.
Smells like flowers.
Attracts plenty of girls, but has never dated.
Would attract stray cats (probably).
Half his height is his legs.
BUT THAT SAME YUI-KUN SAYS HE LIKES MAMI.
THAT'S LIKE...
HAVING THE BRIGHTEST STAR IN THE SKY SHINE JUST FOR YOU.
AT LEAST, THAT'S HOW IT SEEMS TO ME.
I'VE NEVER GONE OUT WITH A GUY OR HAD ANYONE CONFESS THEIR FEELINGS...
HEY!

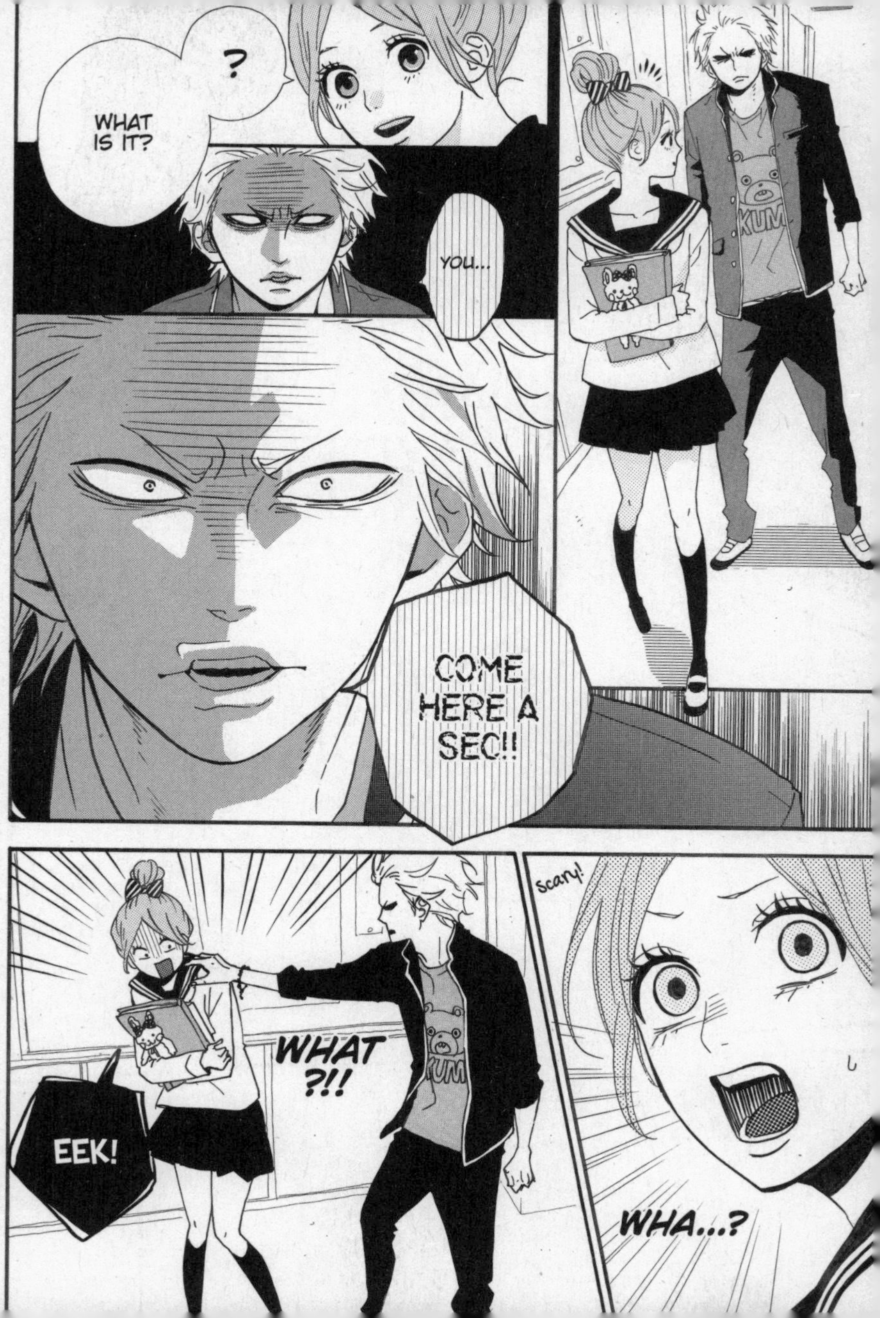
KUM
?
WHAT IS IT?
YOU...
COME HERE A SEC!!
Scary!
WHA...?
WHAT ?!!
KUM
EEK!

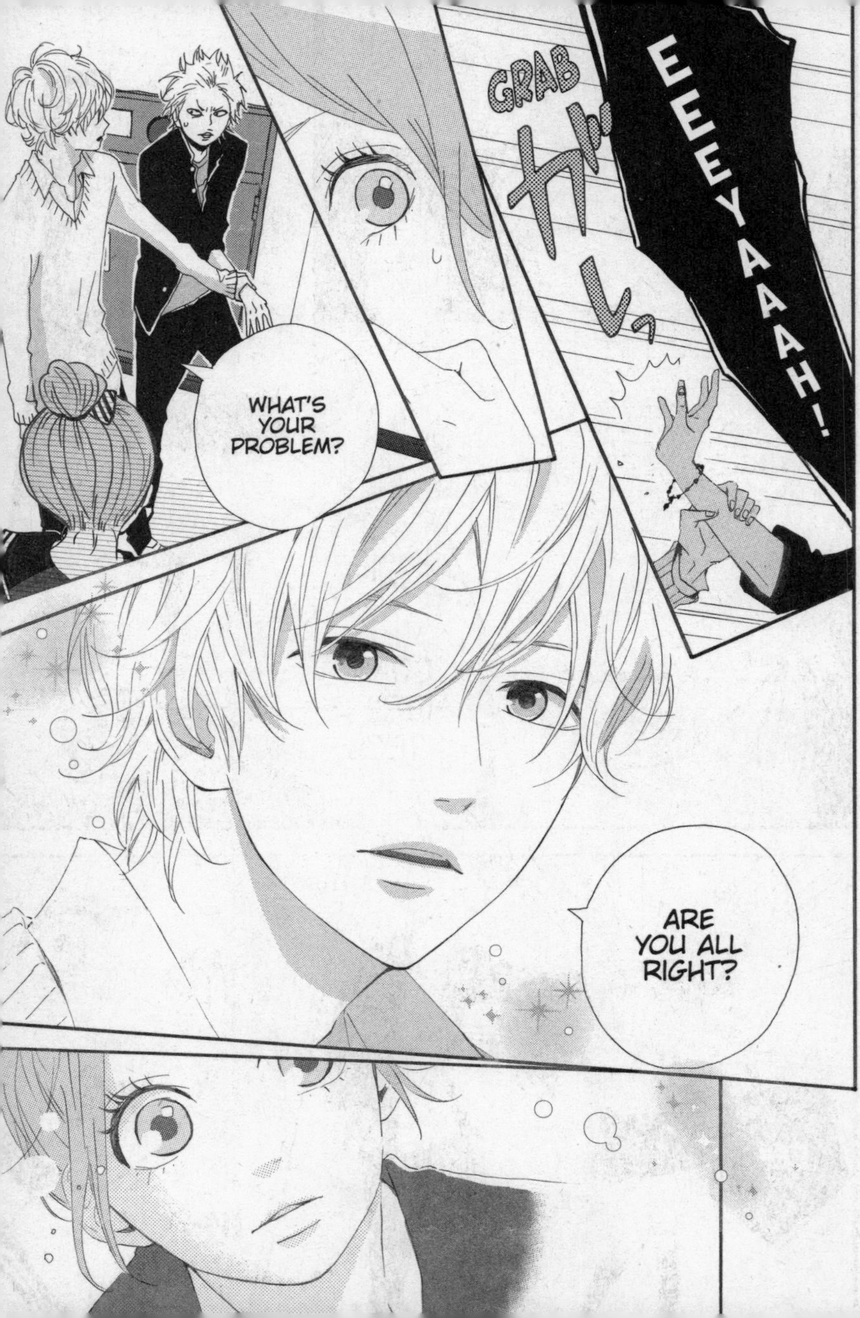
EEEEYAAAAH!
GRAB
WHAT'S YOUR PROBLEM?
ARE YOU ALL RIGHT?

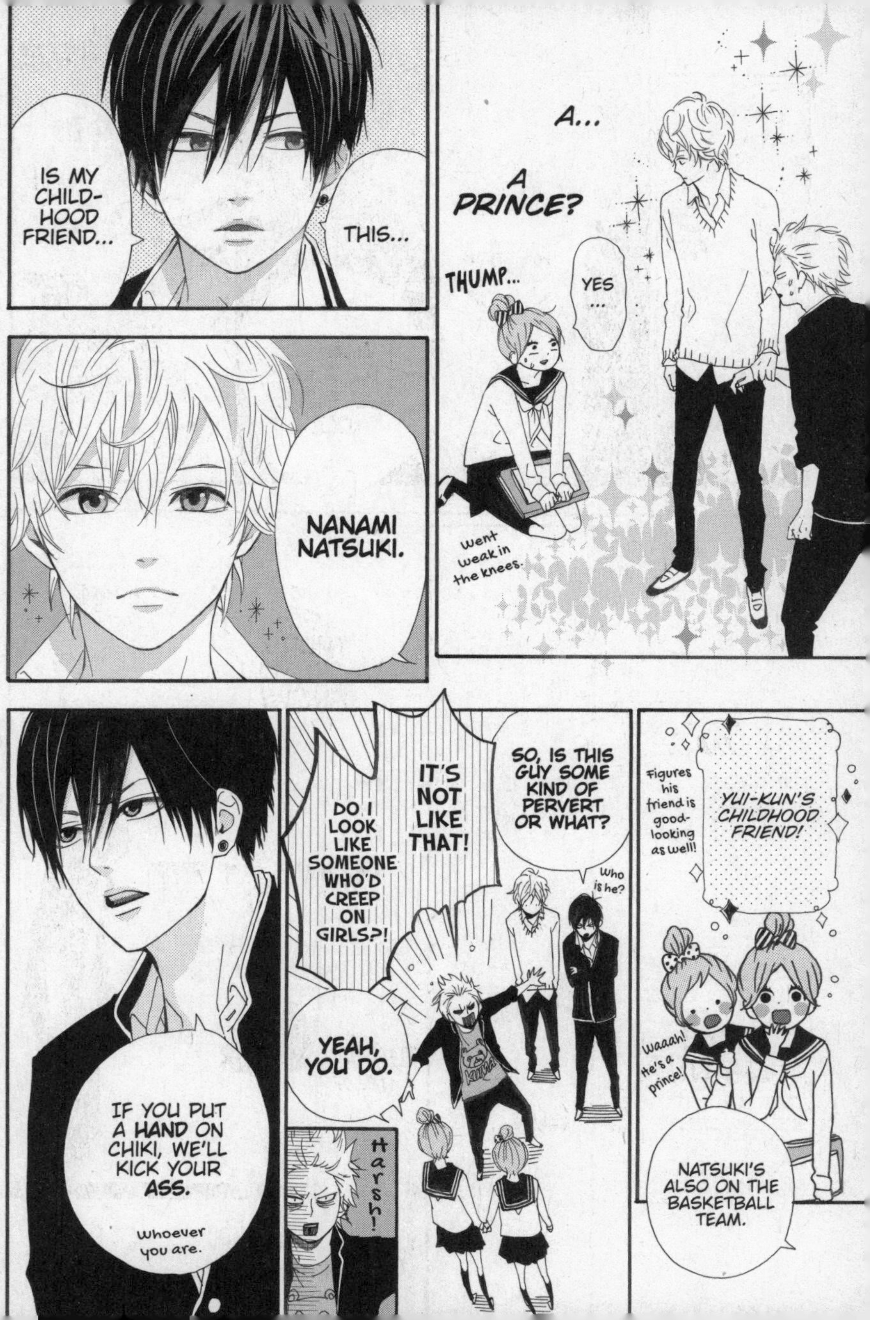
A...
A PRINCE?
YES ...
THUMP...
Went weak in the knees.
THIS...
IS MY CHILDHOOD FRIEND...
NANAMI NATSUKI.
YUI-KUN'S CHILDHOOD FRIEND!
Figures his friend is good-looking as well!
Waaah! He's a prince!
NATSUKI'S ALSO ON THE BASKETBALL TEAM.
SO, IS THIS GUY SOME KIND OF PERVERT OR WHAT?
Who is he?
IT'S NOT LIKE THAT!
DO I LOOK LIKE SOMEONE WHO'D CREEP ON GIRLS?!
YEAH, YOU DO.
Harsh!
IF YOU PUT A HAND ON CHIKI, WE'LL KICK YOUR ASS.
Whoever you are.

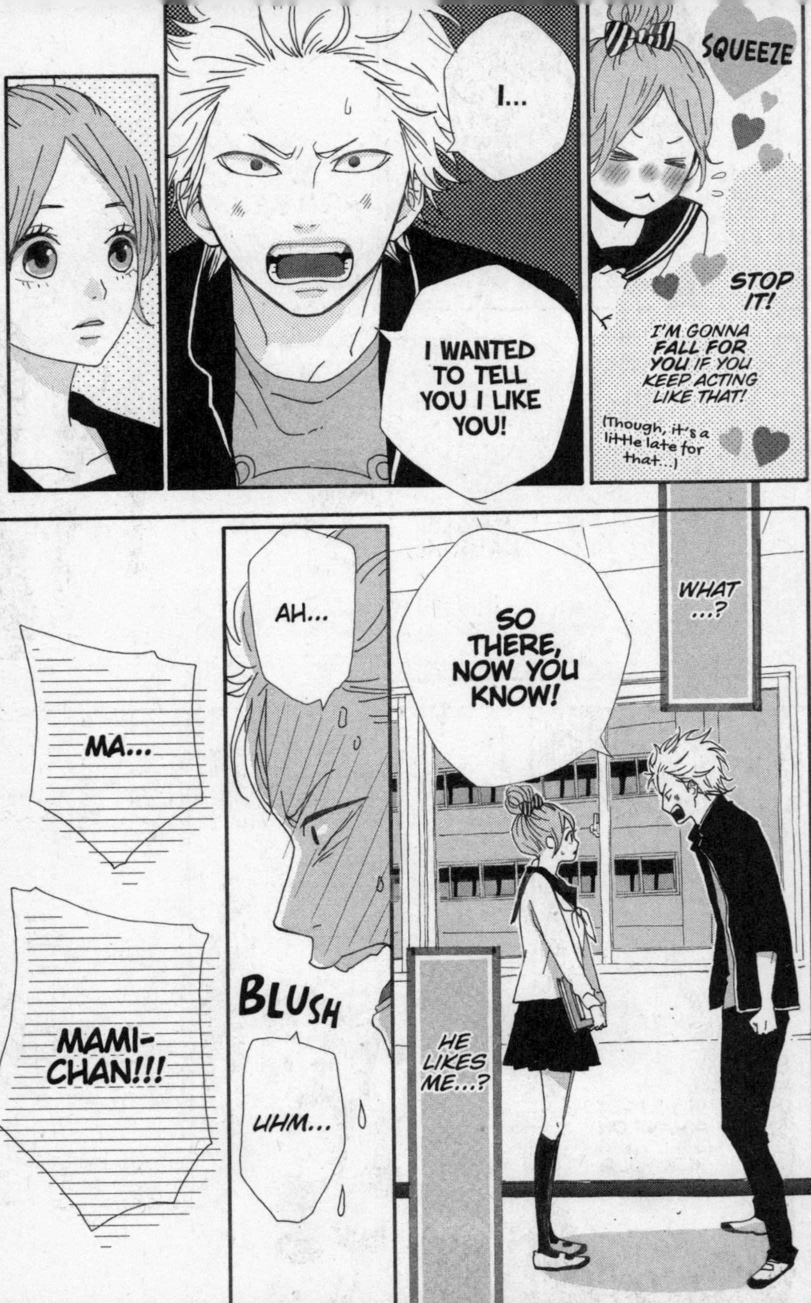
SQUEEZE
STOP IT!
I'M GONNA FALL FOR YOU IF YOU KEEP ACTING LIKE THAT!
(Though, it's a little late for that...)
I...
I WANTED TO TELL YOU I LIKE YOU!
WHAT ...?
SO THERE, NOW YOU KNOW!
HE LIKES ME...?
AH...
BLUSH
UHM...
MA...
MAMI-CHAN!!!

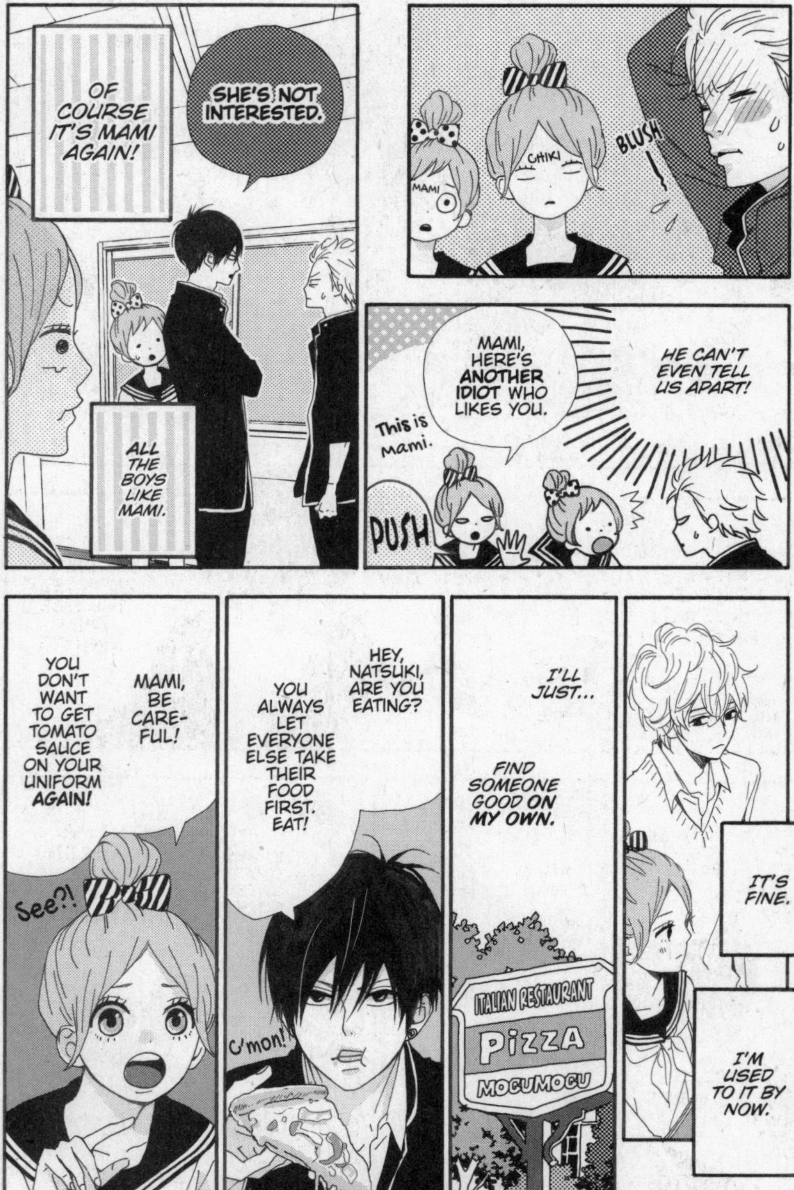
MAMI
CHIKI
BLUSH
HE CAN'T EVEN TELL US APART!
MAMI, HERE'S ANOTHER IDIOT WHO LIKES YOU.
This is Mami.
PUSH
SHE'S NOT INTERESTED.
OF COURSE IT'S MAMI AGAIN!
ALL THE BOYS LIKE MAMI.
IT'S FINE.
I'M USED TO IT BY NOW.
I'LL JUST...
FIND SOMEONE GOOD ON MY OWN.
ITALIAN RESTAURANT
PiZZA
MOCUMOCU
HEY, NATSUKI, ARE YOU EATING?
YOU ALWAYS LET EVERYONE ELSE TAKE THEIR FOOD FIRST. EAT!
C'mon!
MAMI, BE CAREFUL!
YOU DON'T WANT TO GET TOMATO SAUCE ON YOUR UNIFORM AGAIN!
See?!

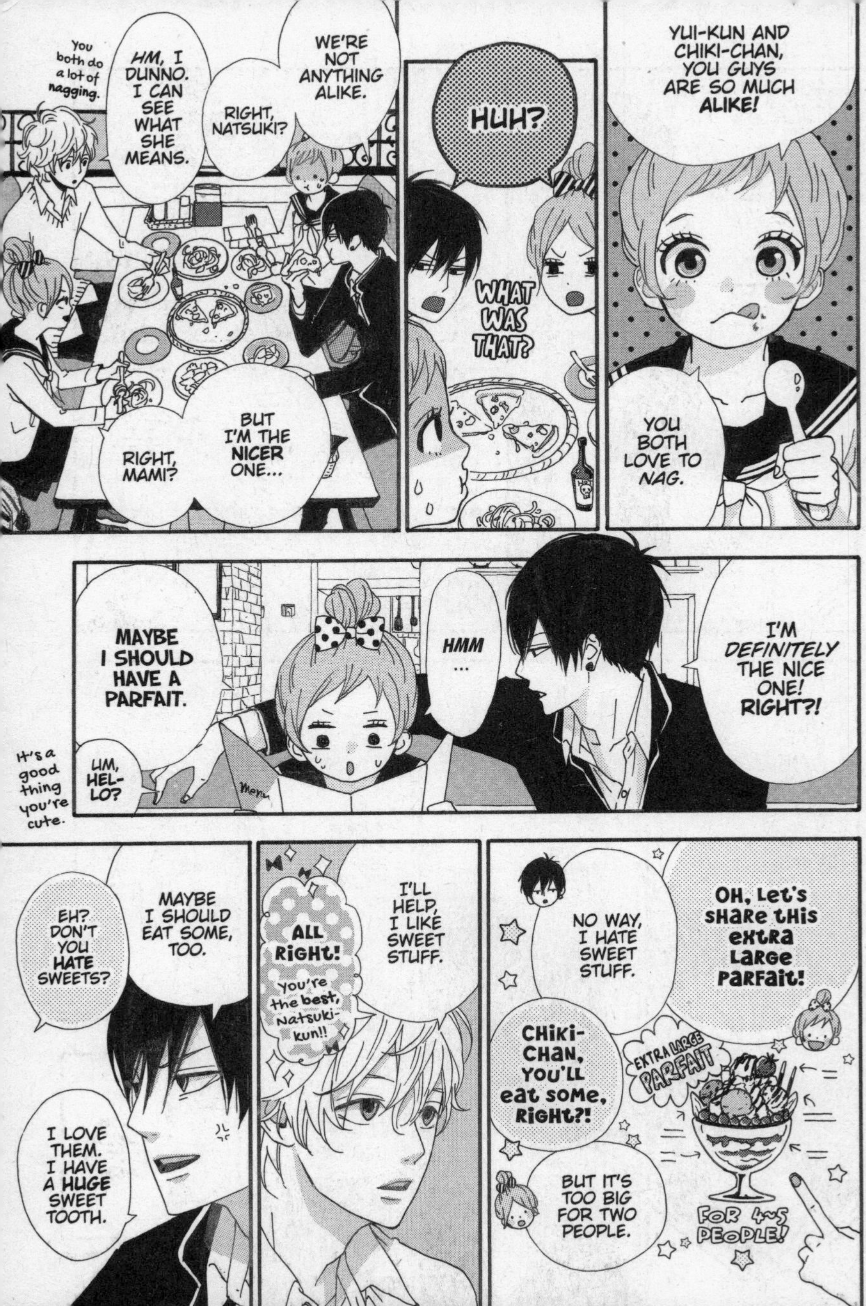
YUI-KUN AND CHIKI-CHAN, YOU GUYS ARE SO MUCH ALIKE!
YOU BOTH LOVE TO NAG.
HUH?
WHAT WAS THAT?
WE'RE NOT ANYTHING ALIKE.
RIGHT, NATSUKI?
HM, I DUNNO. I CAN SEE WHAT SHE MEANS.
You both do a lot of nagging.
BUT I'M THE NICER ONE...
RIGHT, MAMI?
I'M DEFINITELY THE NICE ONE! RIGHT?!
HMM ...
MAYBE I SHOULD HAVE A PARFAIT.
Menu
UM, HELLO?
It's a good thing you're cute.
OH, Let's share this extra large parfait!
NO WAY, I HATE SWEET STUFF.
CHIKI-CHAN, YOU'LL eat some, RIGHT?!
EXTRA LARGE PARFAIT
BUT IT'S TOO BIG FOR TWO PEOPLE.
FOR 4~5 PEOPLE!
I'LL HELP, I LIKE SWEET STUFF.
ALL RIGHT!
You're the best, Natsuki-kun!!
MAYBE I SHOULD EAT SOME, TOO.
EH? DON'T YOU HATE SWEETS?
I LOVE THEM. I HAVE A HUGE SWEET TOOTH.

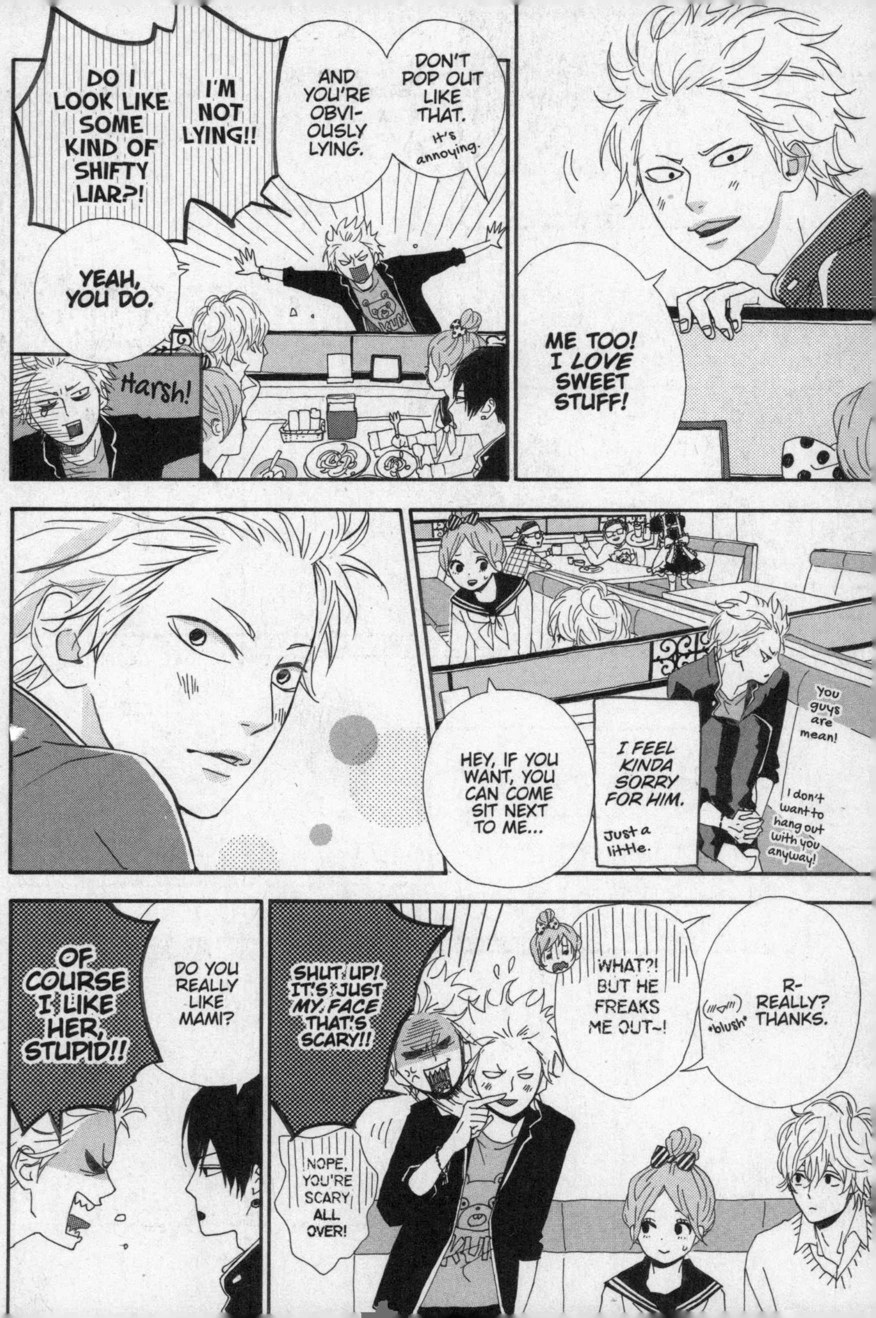
ME TOO! I LOVE SWEET STUFF!
DON'T POP OUT LIKE THAT.
It's annoying.
AND YOU'RE OBVI-OUSLY LYING.
I'M NOT LYING!!
DO I LOOK LIKE SOME KIND OF SHIFTY LIAR?!
YEAH, YOU DO.
Harsh!
You guys are mean!
I don't want to hang out with you anyway!
I FEEL KINDA SORRY FOR HIM.
Just a little.
HEY, IF YOU WANT, YOU CAN COME SIT NEXT TO ME...
R-REALLY? THANKS.
blush
WHAT?! BUT HE FREAKS ME OUT~!
SHUT UP! IT'S JUST MY FACE THAT'S SCARY!!
NOPE, YOU'RE SCARY ALL OVER!
DO YOU REALLY LIKE MAMI?
OF COURSE I LIKE HER, STUPID!!

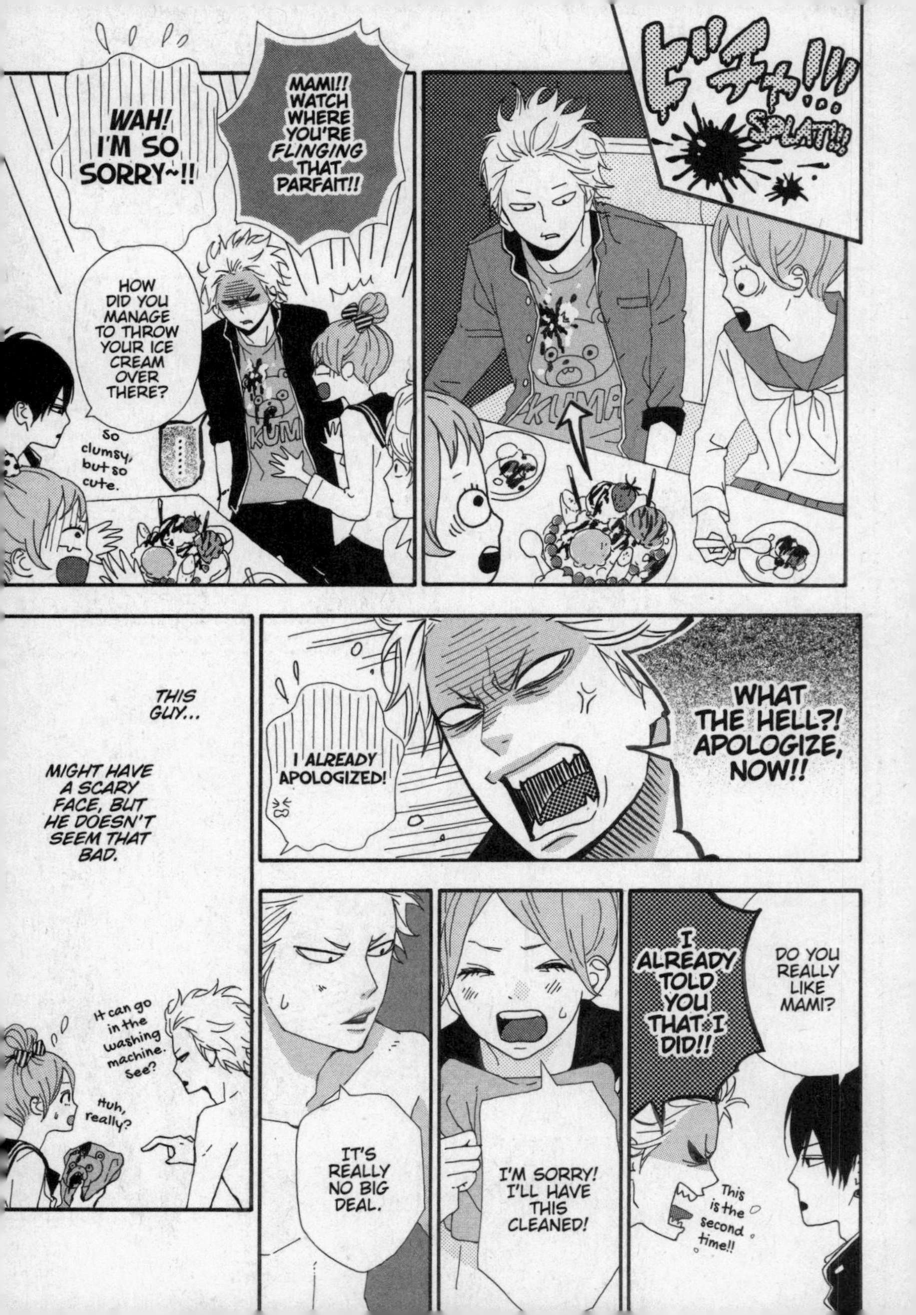
ビチャ!!!
SPLAT!!!
MAMI!! WATCH WHERE YOU'RE FLINGING THAT PARFAIT!!
WAH! I'M SO SORRY~!!
HOW DID YOU MANAGE TO THROW YOUR ICE CREAM OVER THERE?
So clumsy, but so cute.
WHAT THE HELL?! APOLOGIZE, NOW!!
I ALREADY APOLOGIZED!
THIS GUY...
MIGHT HAVE A SCARY FACE, BUT HE DOESN'T SEEM THAT BAD.
DO YOU REALLY LIKE MAMI?
I ALREADY TOLD YOU THAT I DID!!
This is the second time!!
I'M SORRY! I'LL HAVE THIS CLEANED!
IT'S REALLY NO BIG DEAL.
It can go in the washing machine. See?
Huh, really?

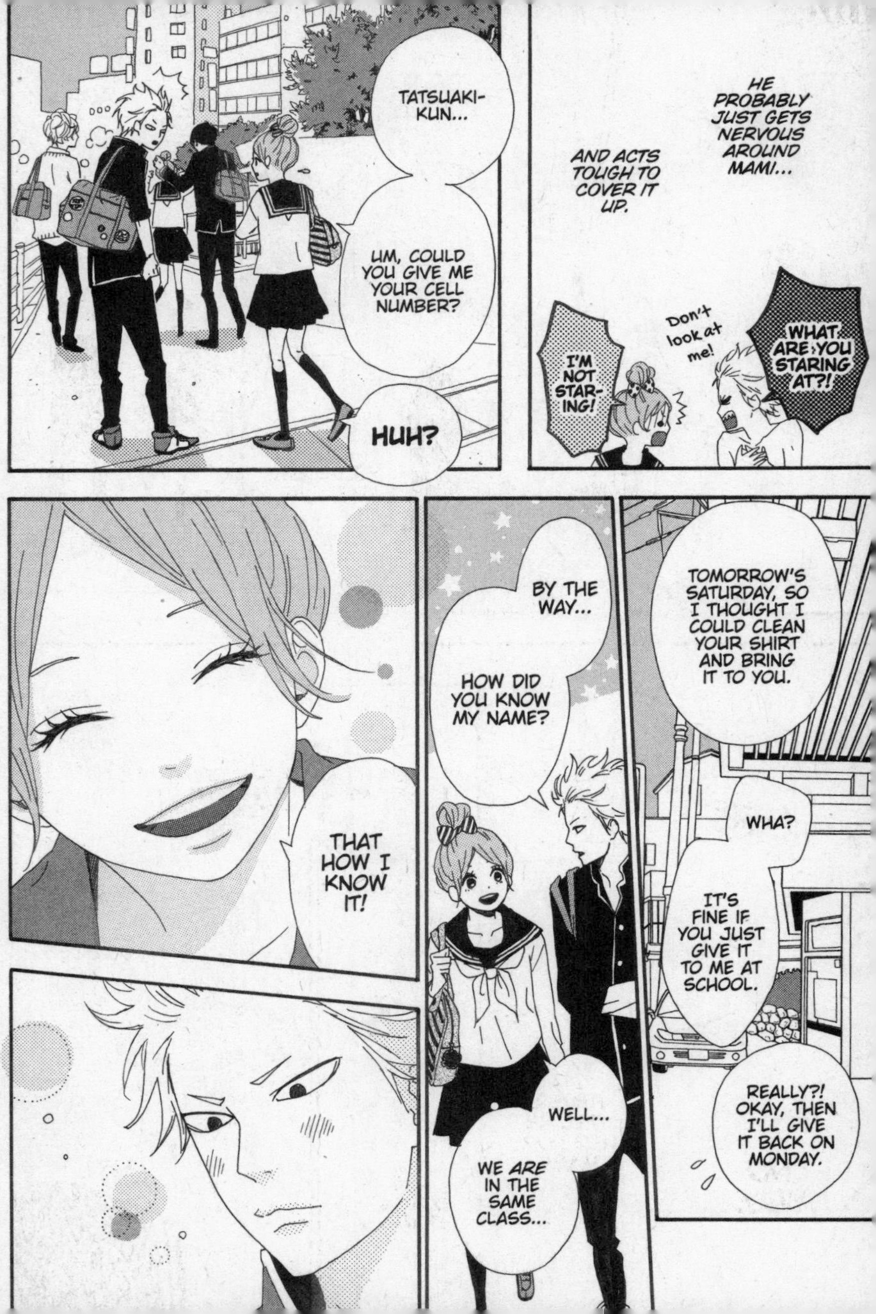
HE PROBABLY JUST GETS NERVOUS AROUND MAMI...
AND ACTS TOUGH TO COVER IT UP.
WHAT ARE YOU STARING AT?!
Don't look at me!
I'M NOT STAR-ING!
TATSUAKI-KUN...
UM, COULD YOU GIVE ME YOUR CELL NUMBER?
HUH?
TOMORROW'S SATURDAY, SO I THOUGHT I COULD CLEAN YOUR SHIRT AND BRING IT TO YOU.
WHA?
IT'S FINE IF YOU JUST GIVE IT TO ME AT SCHOOL.
REALLY?! OKAY, THEN I'LL GIVE IT BACK ON MONDAY.
BY THE WAY...
HOW DID YOU KNOW MY NAME?
WELL...
WE ARE IN THE SAME CLASS...
THAT HOW I KNOW IT!

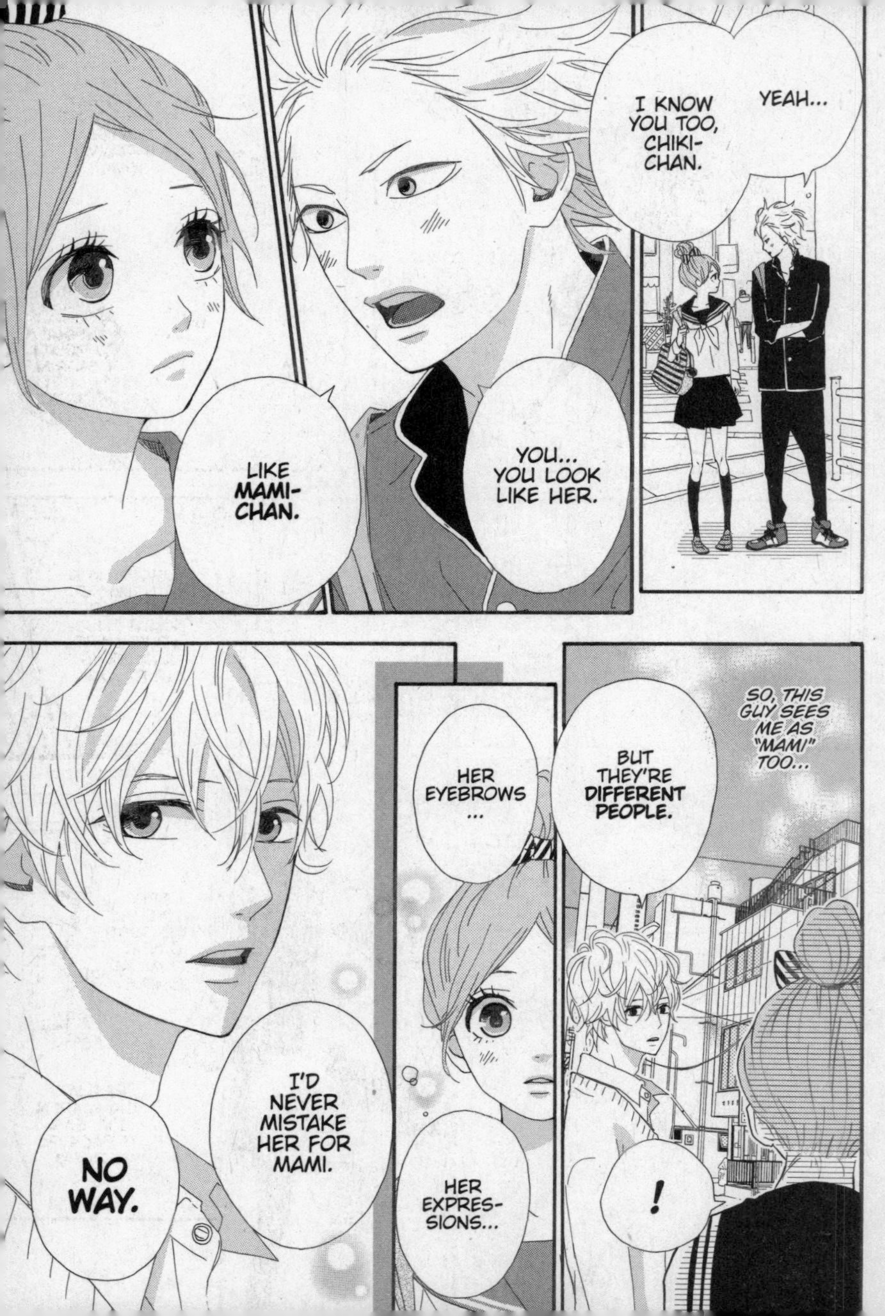
YEAH...
I KNOW YOU TOO, CHIKI-CHAN.
YOU... YOU LOOK LIKE HER.
LIKE MAMI-CHAN.
SO, THIS GUY SEES ME AS "MAMI" TOO...
BUT THEY'RE DIFFERENT PEOPLE.
!
HER EYEBROWS...
HER EXPRESSIONS...
I'D NEVER MISTAKE HER FOR MAMI.
NO WAY.

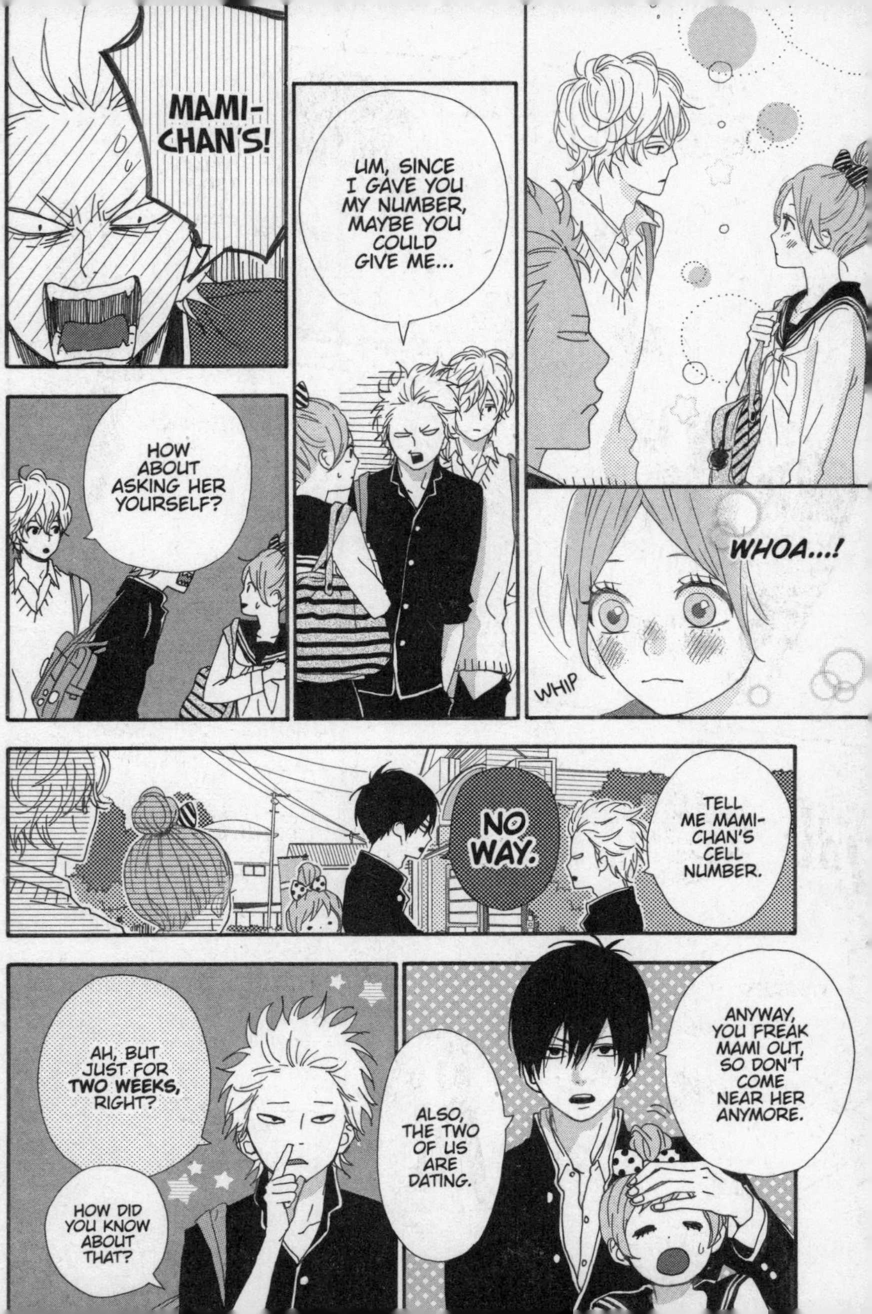
WHOA...!
WHIP
UM, SINCE I GAVE YOU MY NUMBER, MAYBE YOU COULD GIVE ME...
MAMI-CHAN'S!
HOW ABOUT ASKING HER YOURSELF?
TELL ME MAMI-CHAN'S CELL NUMBER.
NO WAY.
ANYWAY, YOU FREAK MAMI OUT, SO DON'T COME NEAR HER ANYMORE.
ALSO, THE TWO OF US ARE DATING.
AH, BUT JUST FOR TWO WEEKS, RIGHT?
HOW DID YOU KNOW ABOUT THAT?

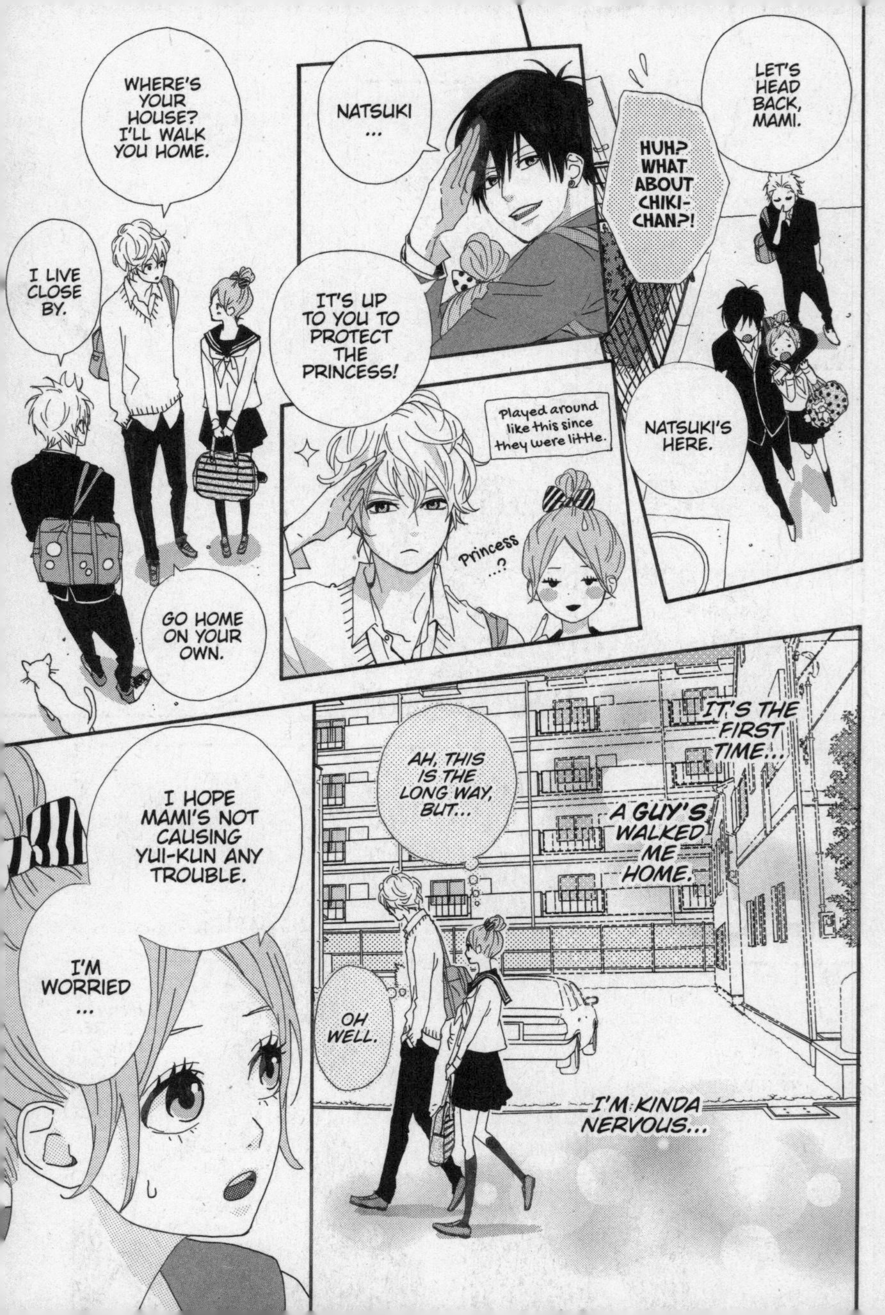
LET'S HEAD BACK, MAMI.
HUH? WHAT ABOUT CHIKI-CHAN?!
NATSUKI'S HERE.
NATSUKI ...
IT'S UP TO YOU TO PROTECT THE PRINCESS!
Played around like this since they were little.
Princess ...?
WHERE'S YOUR HOUSE? I'LL WALK YOU HOME.
I LIVE CLOSE BY.
GO HOME ON YOUR OWN.
IT'S THE FIRST TIME...
A GUY'S WALKED ME HOME.
AH, THIS IS THE LONG WAY, BUT...
OH WELL.
I'M KINDA NERVOUS...
I HOPE MAMI'S NOT CAUSING YUI-KUN ANY TROUBLE.
I'M WORRIED ...

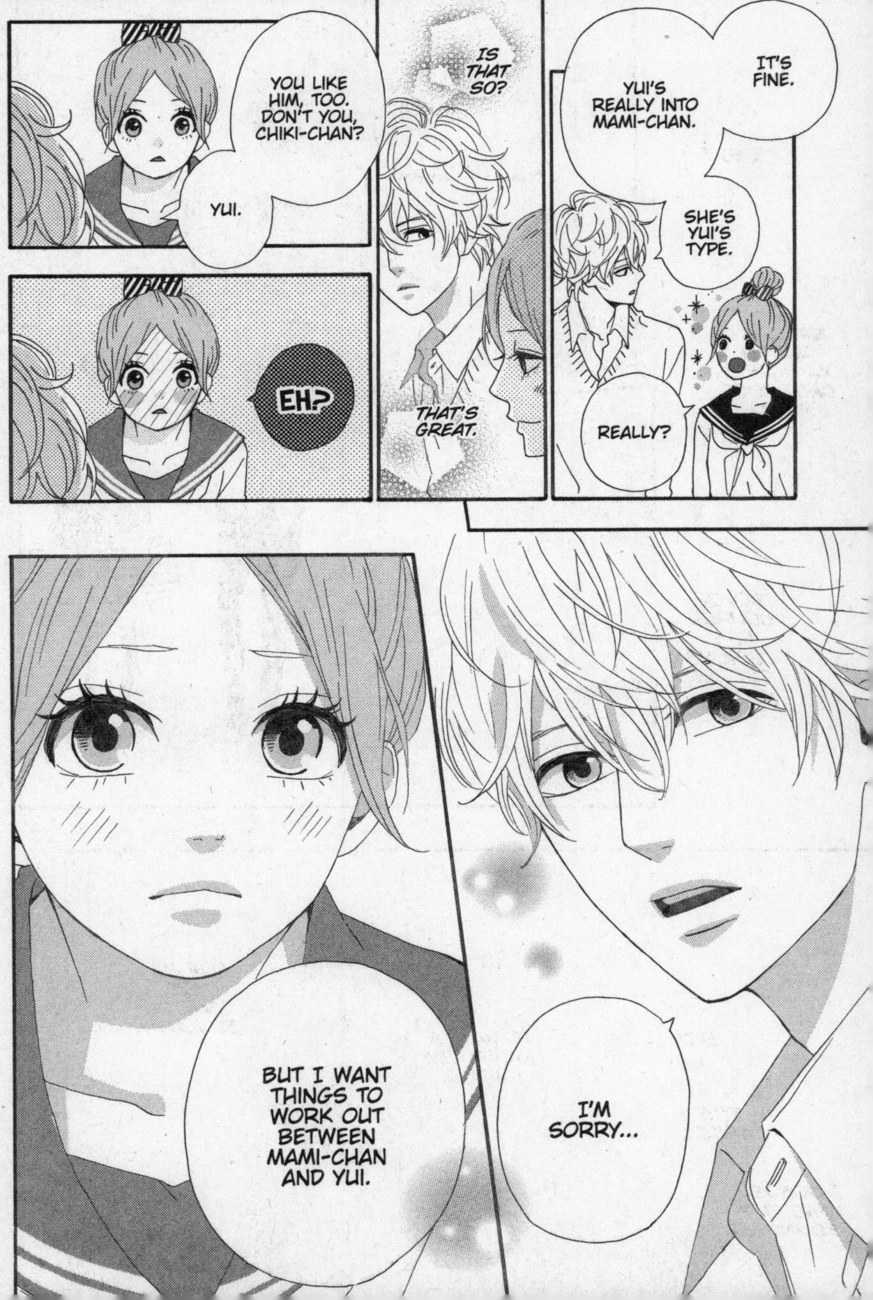
IT'S FINE.
YUI'S REALLY INTO MAMI-CHAN.
SHE'S YUI'S TYPE.
REALLY?
IS THAT SO?
THAT'S GREAT.
YOU LIKE HIM, TOO. DON'T YOU, CHIKI-CHAN?
YUI.
EH?
I'M SORRY...
BUT I WANT THINGS TO WORK OUT BETWEEN MAMI-CHAN AND YUI.

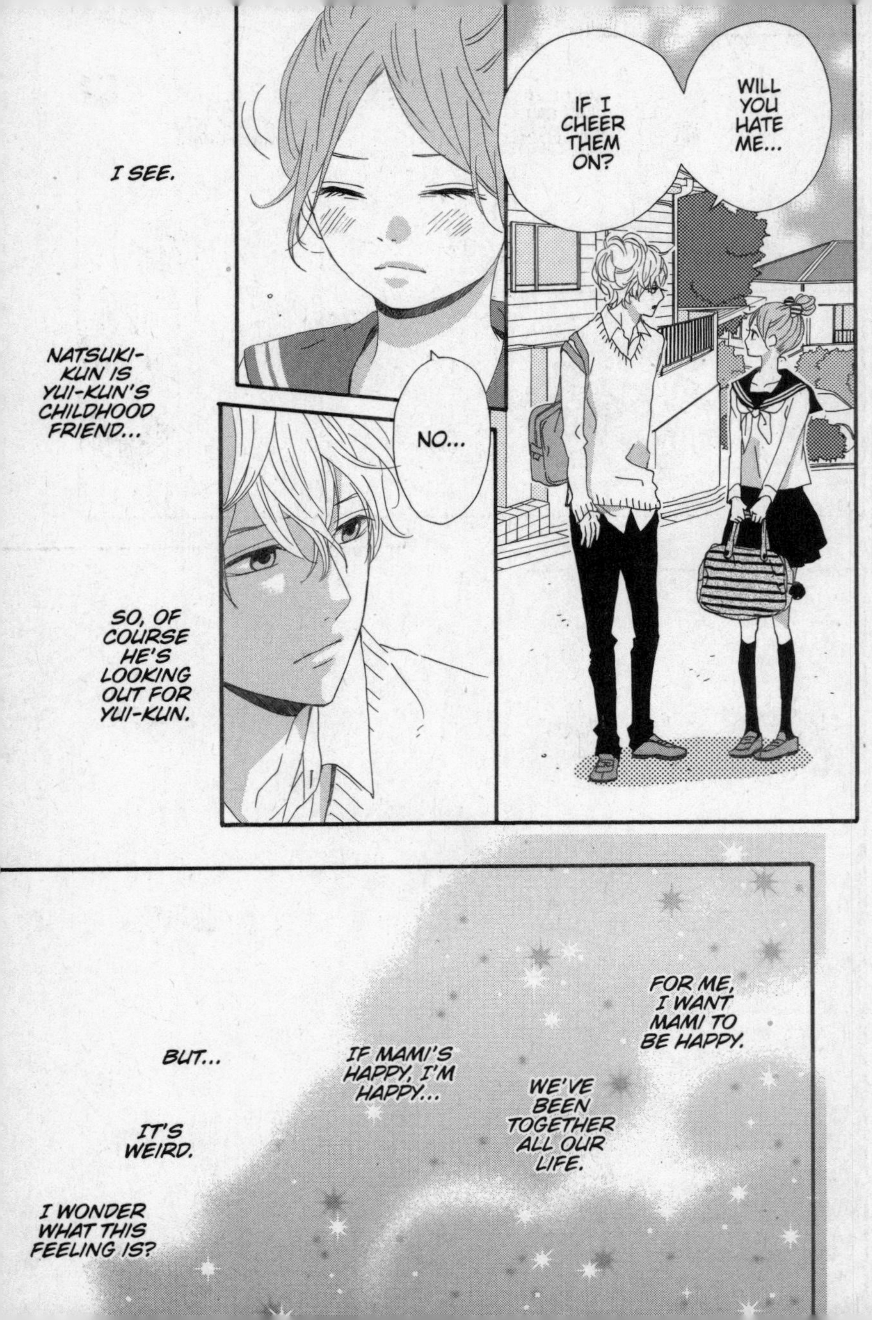
WILL YOU HATE ME...
IF I CHEER THEM ON?
NO...
I SEE.
NATSUKI-KUN IS YUI-KUN'S CHILDHOOD FRIEND...
SO, OF COURSE HE'S LOOKING OUT FOR YUI-KUN.
FOR ME, I WANT MAMI TO BE HAPPY.
WE'VE BEEN TOGETHER ALL OUR LIFE.
IF MAMI'S HAPPY, I'M HAPPY...
BUT...
IT'S WEIRD.
I WONDER WHAT THIS FEELING IS?

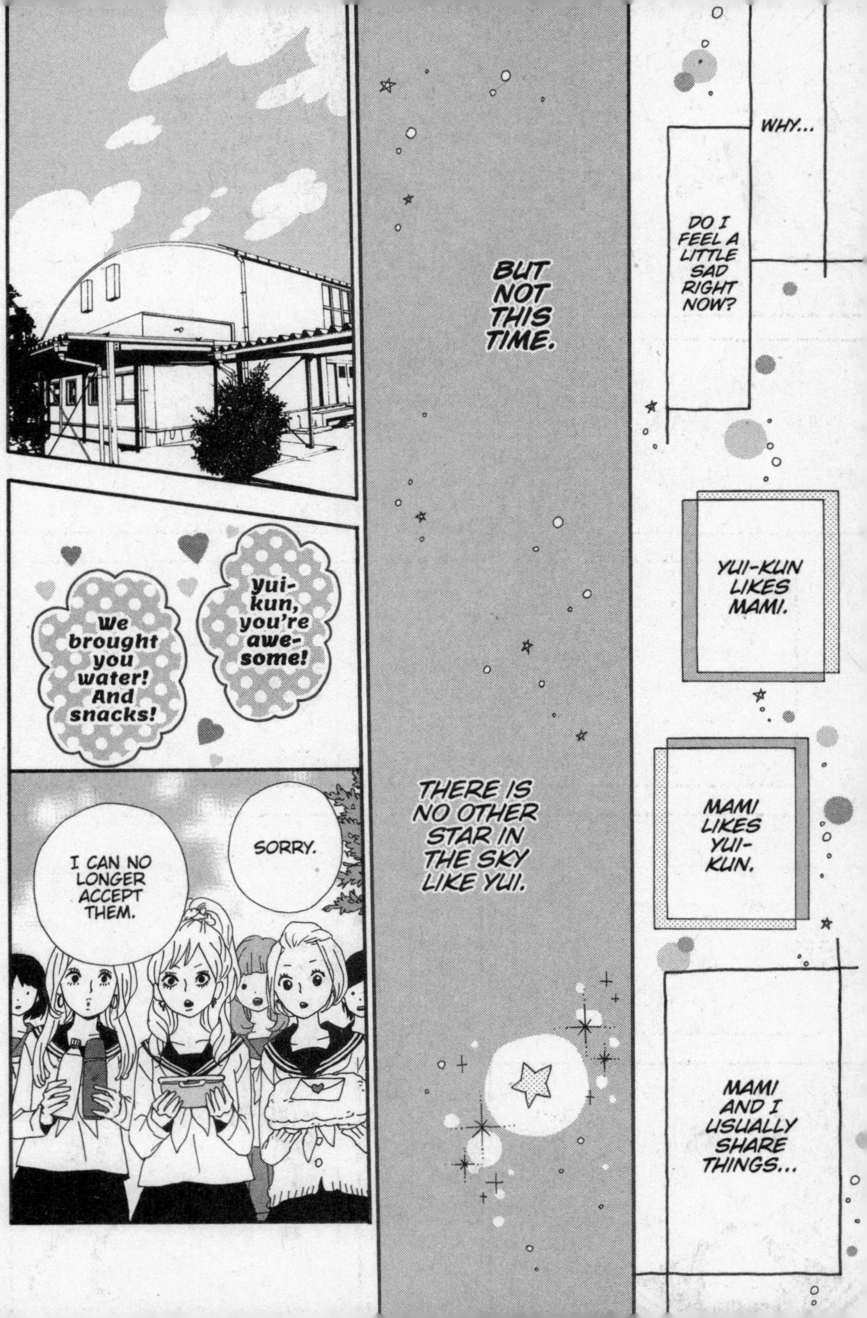
WHY...
DO I FEEL A LITTLE SAD RIGHT NOW?
YUI-KUN LIKES MAMI.
MAMI LIKES YUI-KUN.
MAMI AND I USUALLY SHARE THINGS...
BUT NOT THIS TIME.
THERE IS NO OTHER STAR IN THE SKY LIKE YUI.
Yui-kun, you're awesome!
We brought you water! And snacks!
SORRY.
I CAN NO LONGER ACCEPT THEM.

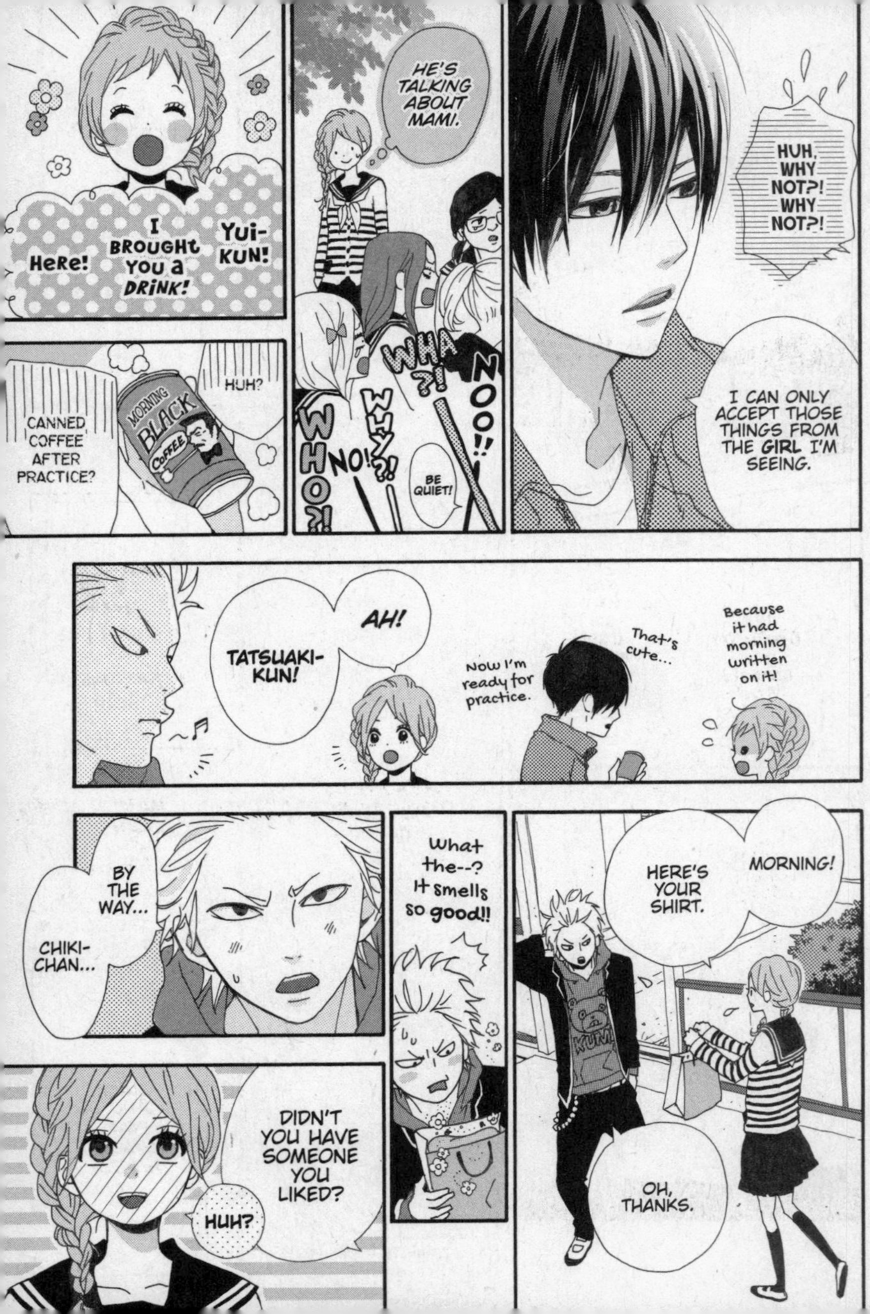
HUH, WHY NOT?! WHY NOT?!
I CAN ONLY ACCEPT THOSE THINGS FROM THE GIRL I'M SEEING.
HE'S TALKING ABOUT MAMI.
WHA?!
NOOO!!
WHY?!
WHO?!
NO!
BE QUIET!
Yui-KUN!
I BROUGHT YOU a DRINK!
Here!
HUH?
MORNING BLACK COFFEE
CANNED COFFEE AFTER PRACTICE?
Because it had morning written on it!
That's cute...
Now I'm ready for practice.
AH!
TATSUAKI-KUN!
MORNING!
HERE'S YOUR SHIRT.
OH, THANKS.
What the--? It smells so good!!
BY THE WAY...
CHIKI-CHAN...
DIDN'T YOU HAVE SOMEONE YOU LIKED?
HUH?

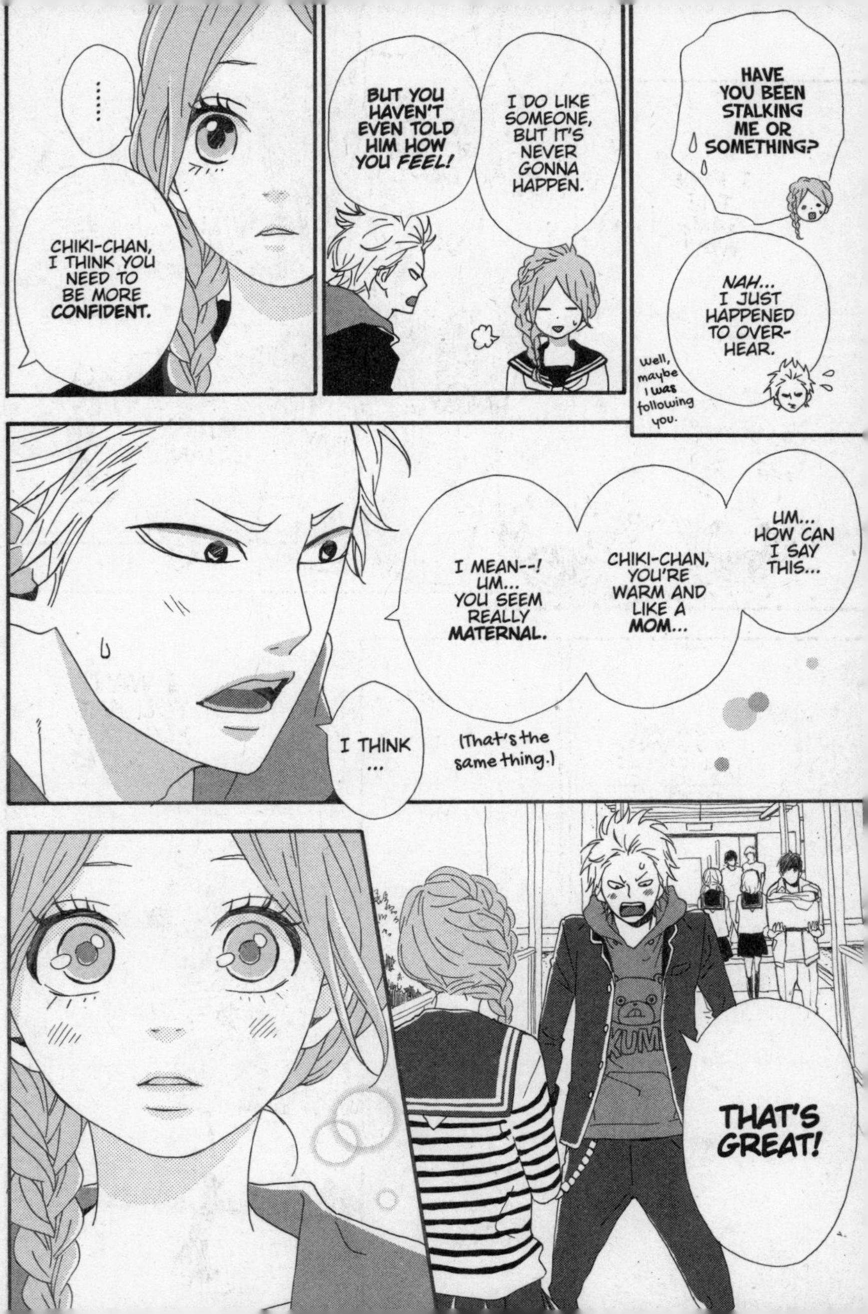
HAVE YOU BEEN STALKING ME OR SOMETHING?
NAH... I JUST HAPPENED TO OVER-HEAR.
Well, maybe I was following you.
I DO LIKE SOMEONE, BUT IT'S NEVER GONNA HAPPEN.
BUT YOU HAVEN'T EVEN TOLD HIM HOW YOU FEEL!
......
CHIKI-CHAN, I THINK YOU NEED TO BE MORE CONFIDENT.
UM... HOW CAN I SAY THIS...
CHIKI-CHAN, YOU'RE WARM AND LIKE A MOM...
I MEAN--! UM... YOU SEEM REALLY MATERNAL.
(That's the same thing.)
I THINK ...
THAT'S GREAT!

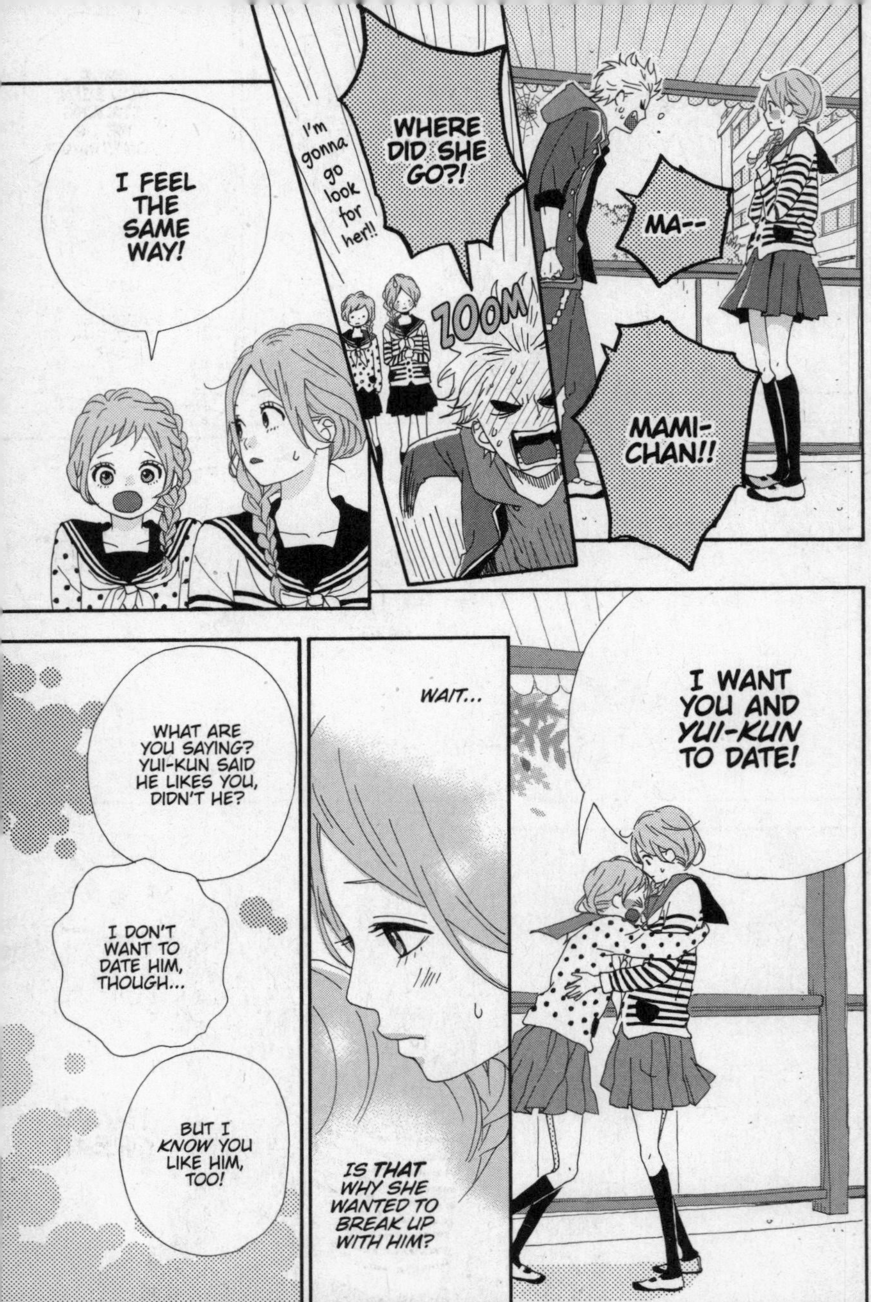
MA--
MAMI-CHAN!!
WHERE DID SHE GO?!
I'm gonna go look for her!!
ZOOM
I FEEL THE SAME WAY!
I WANT YOU AND YUI-KUN TO DATE!
WAIT...
IS THAT WHY SHE WANTED TO BREAK UP WITH HIM?
WHAT ARE YOU SAYING? YUI-KUN SAID HE LIKES YOU, DIDN'T HE?
I DON'T WANT TO DATE HIM, THOUGH...
BUT I KNOW YOU LIKE HIM, TOO!

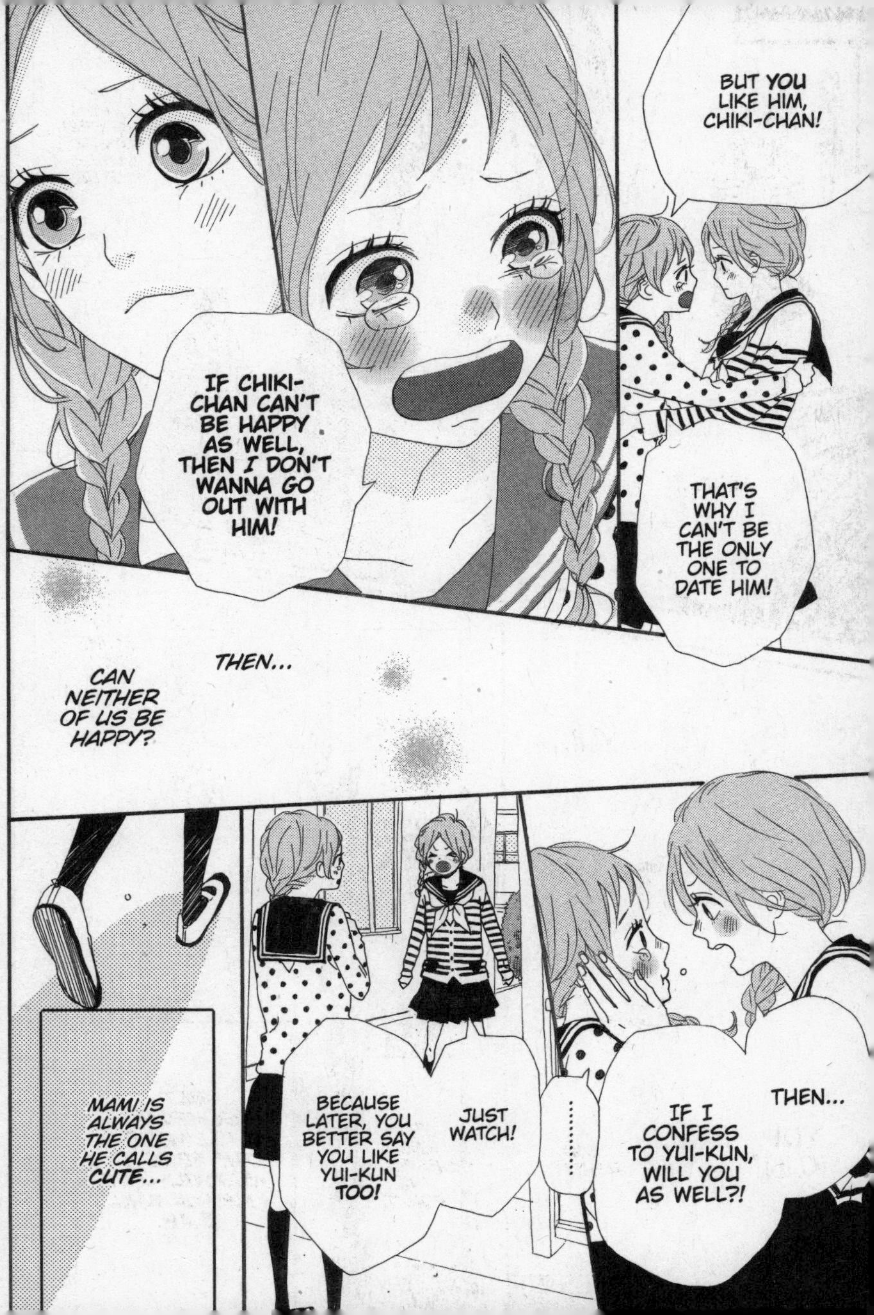
BUT YOU LIKE HIM, CHIKI-CHAN!
THAT'S WHY I CAN'T BE THE ONLY ONE TO DATE HIM!
IF CHIKI-CHAN CAN'T BE HAPPY AS WELL, THEN I DON'T WANNA GO OUT WITH HIM!
THEN...
CAN NEITHER OF US BE HAPPY?
THEN...
IF I CONFESS TO YUI-KUN, WILL YOU AS WELL?!
......
JUST WATCH!
BECAUSE LATER, YOU BETTER SAY YOU LIKE YUI-KUN TOO!
MAMI IS ALWAYS THE ONE HE CALLS CUTE...

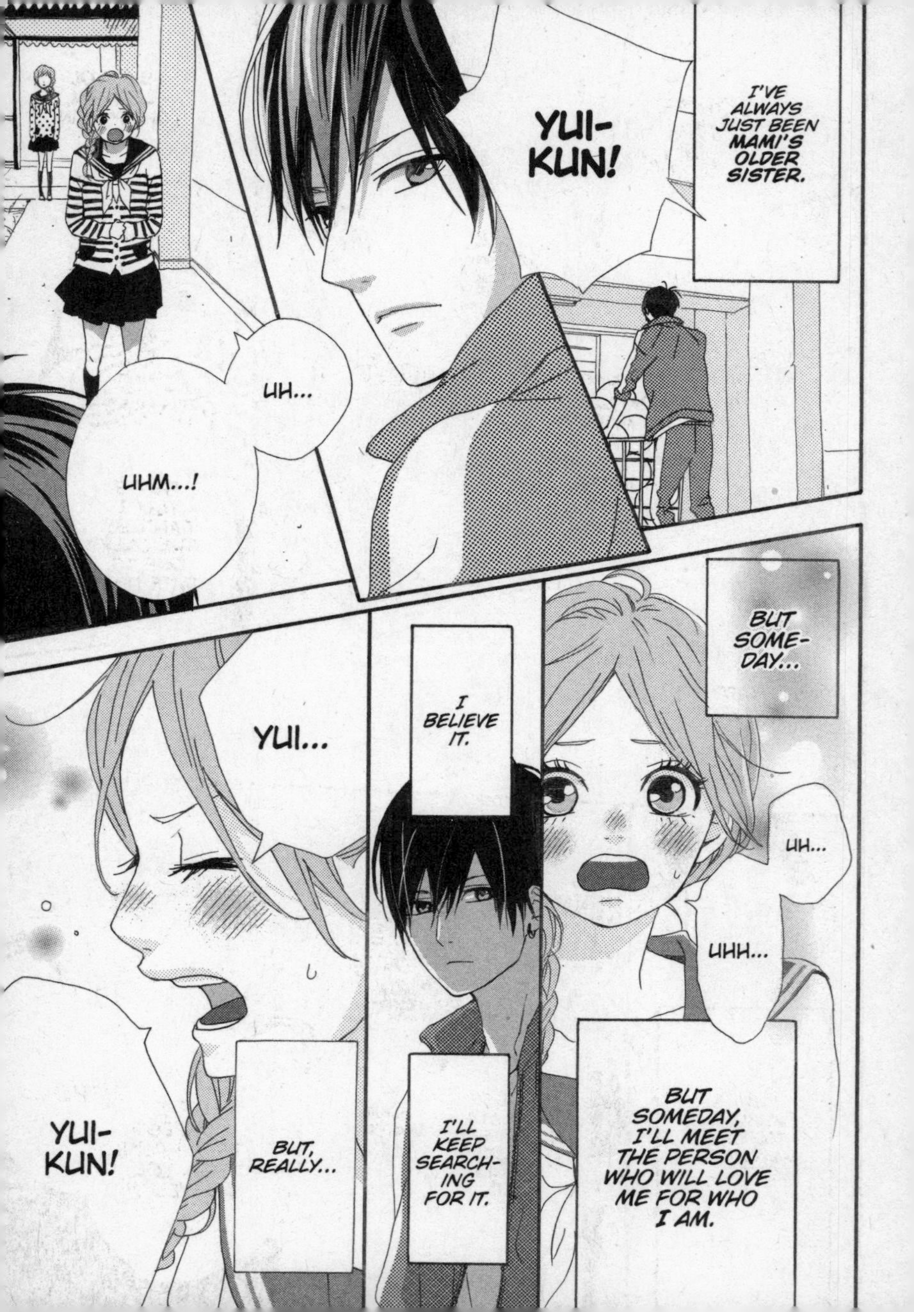
I'VE ALWAYS JUST BEEN MAMI'S OLDER SISTER.
YUI-KUN!
UH...
UHM...!
BUT SOMEDAY...
UH...
UHH...
BUT SOMEDAY, I'LL MEET THE PERSON WHO WILL LOVE ME FOR WHO I AM.
I BELIEVE IT.
I'LL KEEP SEARCHING FOR IT.
YUI...
BUT, REALLY...
YUI-KUN!

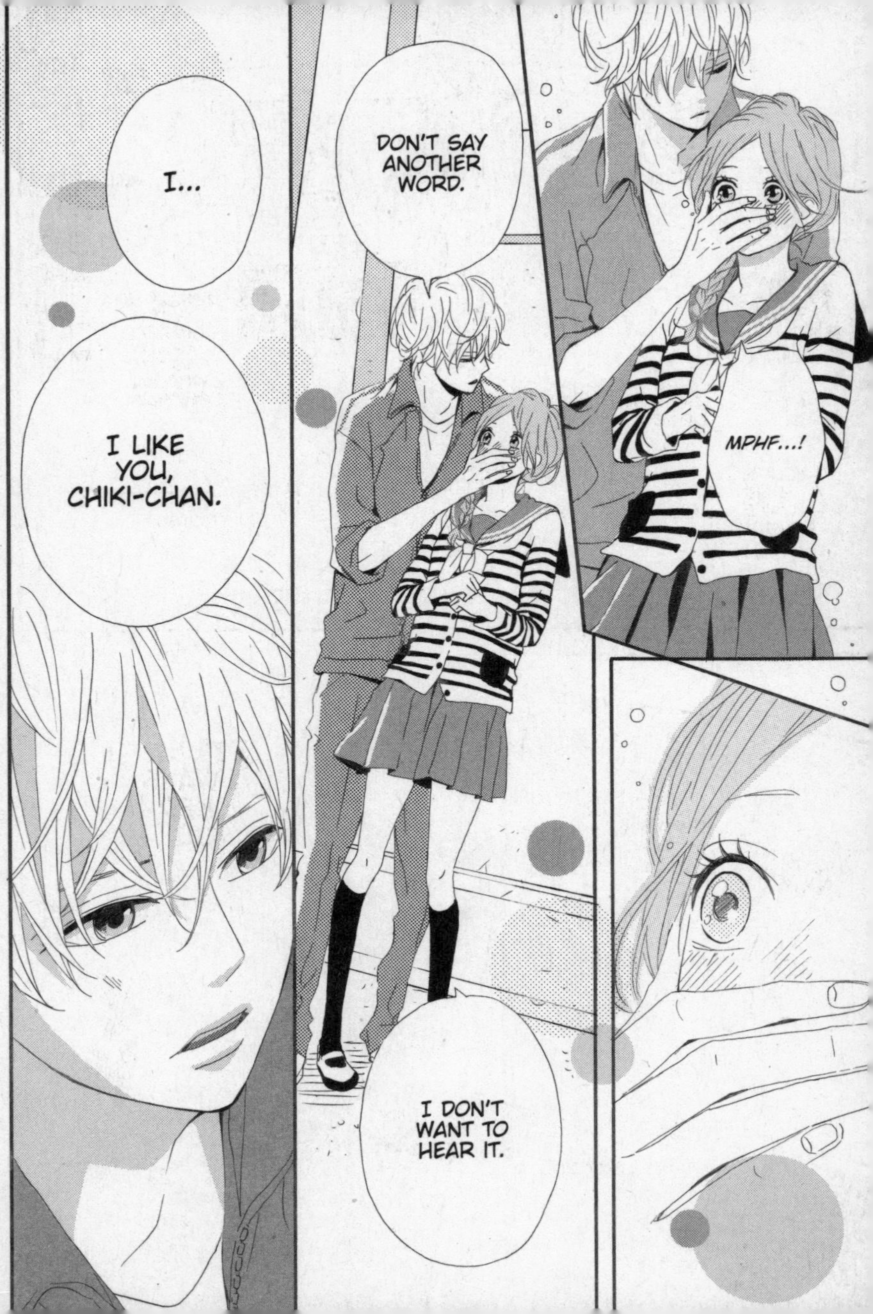
MPHF...!
DON'T SAY ANOTHER WORD.
I DON'T WANT TO HEAR IT.
I...
I LIKE YOU, CHIKI-CHAN.

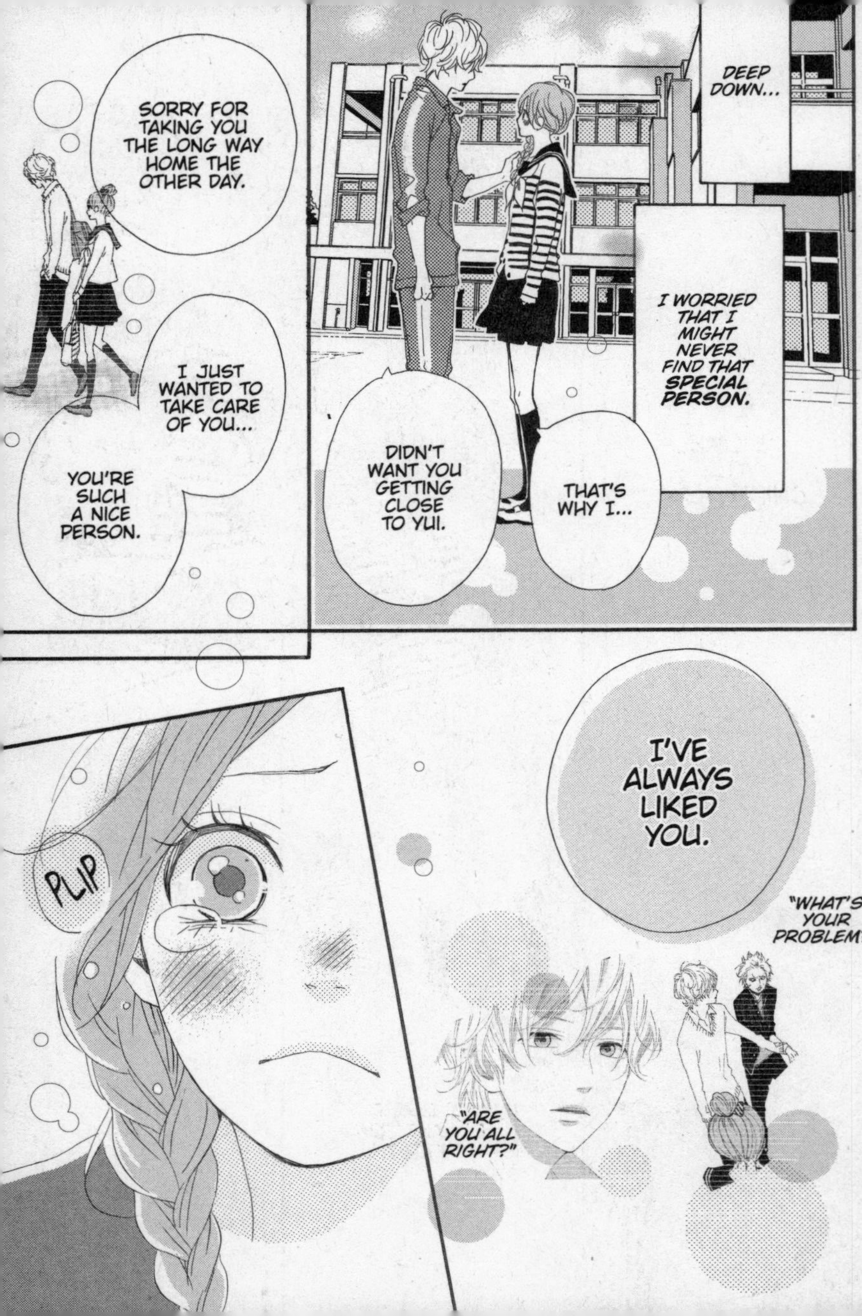
DEEP DOWN...
I WORRIED THAT I MIGHT NEVER FIND THAT SPECIAL PERSON.
THAT'S WHY I...
DIDN'T WANT YOU GETTING CLOSE TO YUI.
SORRY FOR TAKING YOU THE LONG WAY HOME THE OTHER DAY.
I JUST WANTED TO TAKE CARE OF YOU...
YOU'RE SUCH A NICE PERSON.
I'VE ALWAYS LIKED YOU.
"WHAT'S YOUR PROBLEM?"
"ARE YOU ALL RIGHT?"
PLIP

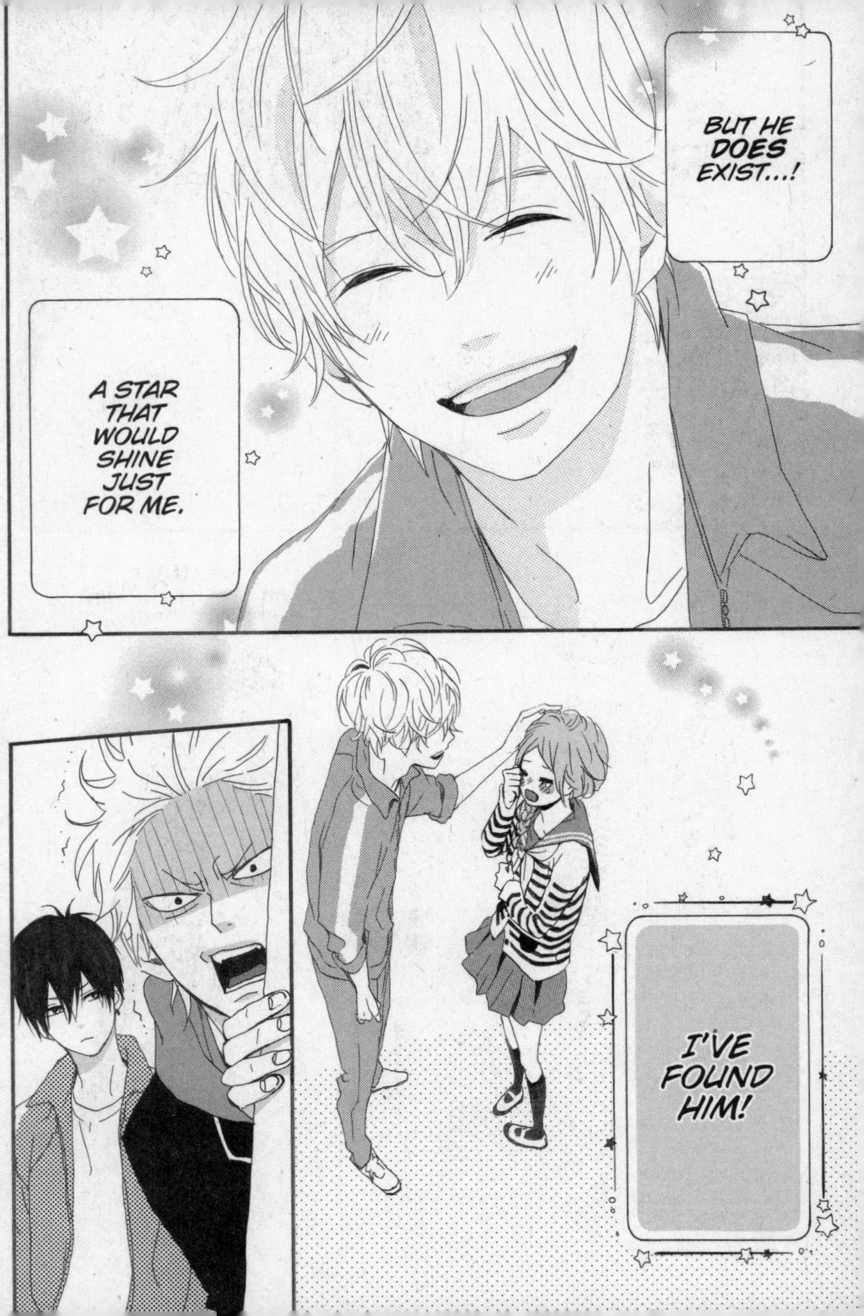
BUT HE DOES EXIST...!
A STAR THAT WOULD SHINE JUST FOR ME.
I'VE FOUND HIM!

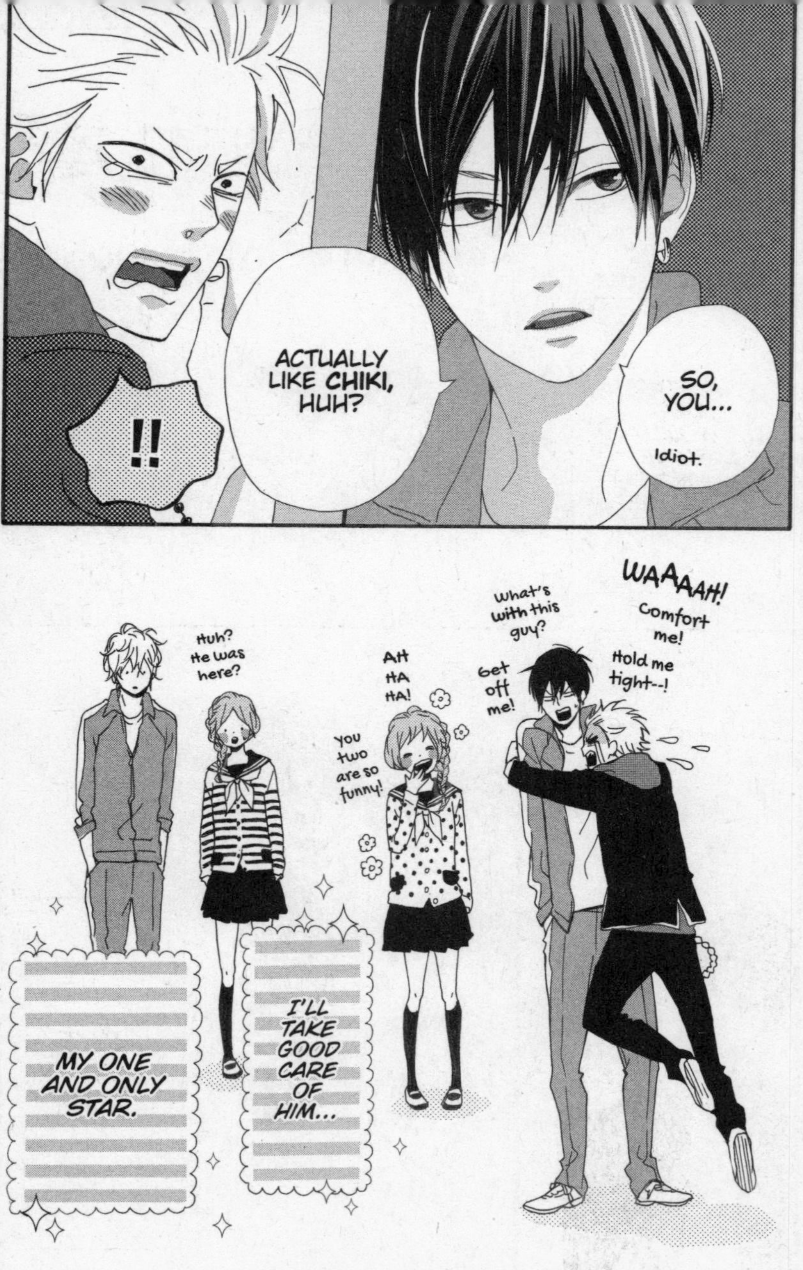
SO, YOU...
Idiot.
ACTUALLY LIKE CHIKI, HUH?
!!
WAAAAH!
Comfort me!
Hold me tight--!
What's with this guy?
Get off me!
AH HA HA!
You two are so funny!
Huh? He was here?
I'LL TAKE GOOD CARE OF HIM...
MY ONE AND ONLY STAR.

HARUIRO ASTRONAUT

A very loose... Character Introduction!

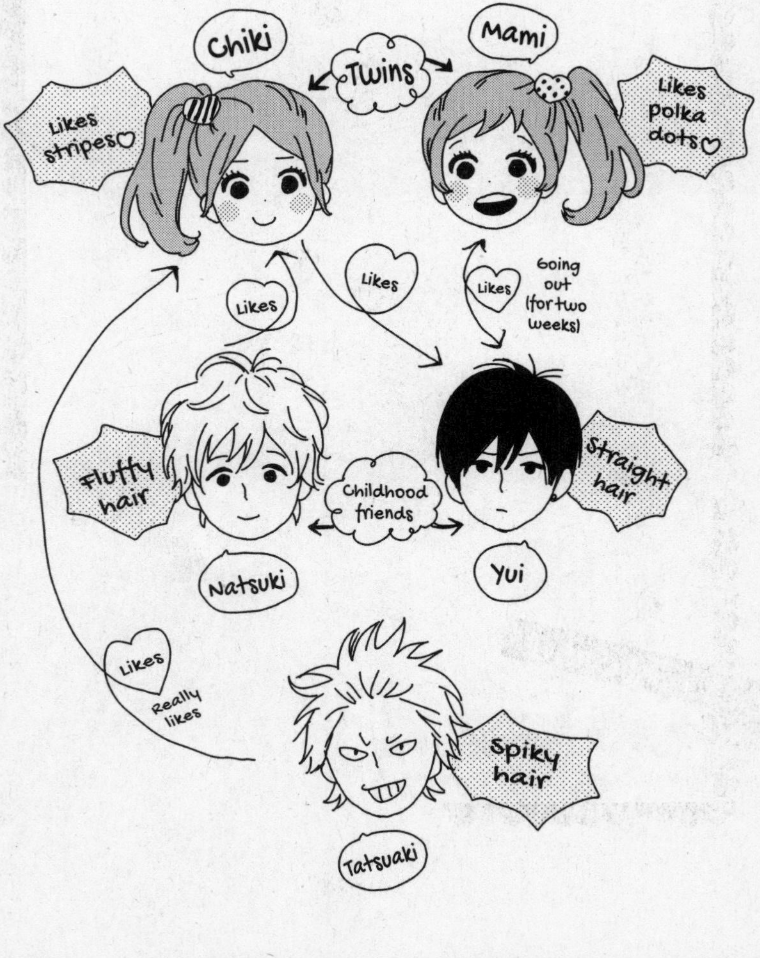
Chiki
Mami
Twins
Likes stripes♡
Likes polka dots♡
Likes
Likes
Likes
Going out (for two weeks)
Fluffy hair
Straight hair
Childhood friends
Natsuki
Yui
Likes
Really likes
Spiky hair
Tatsuaki

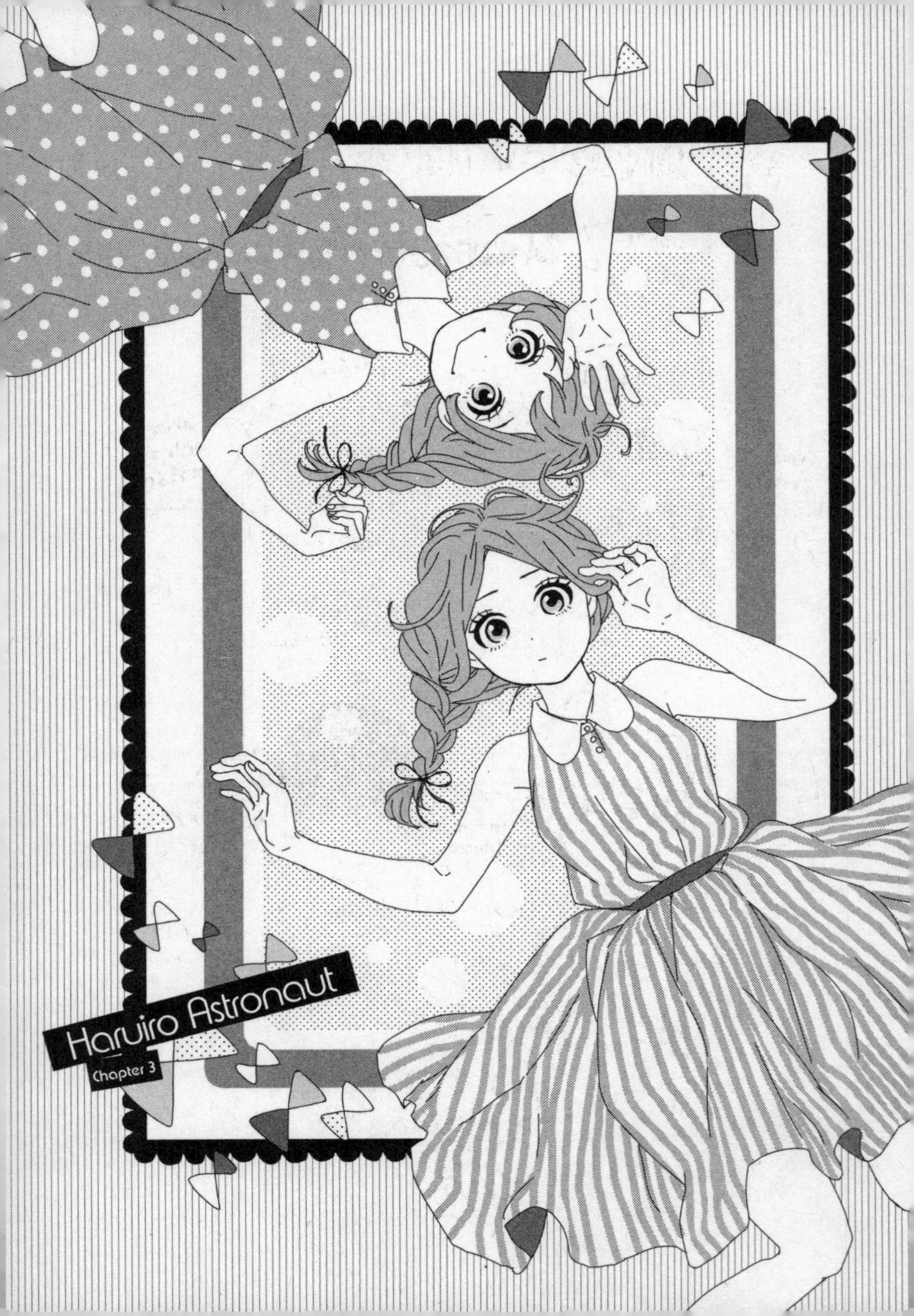
Haruiro Astronaut
Chapter 3

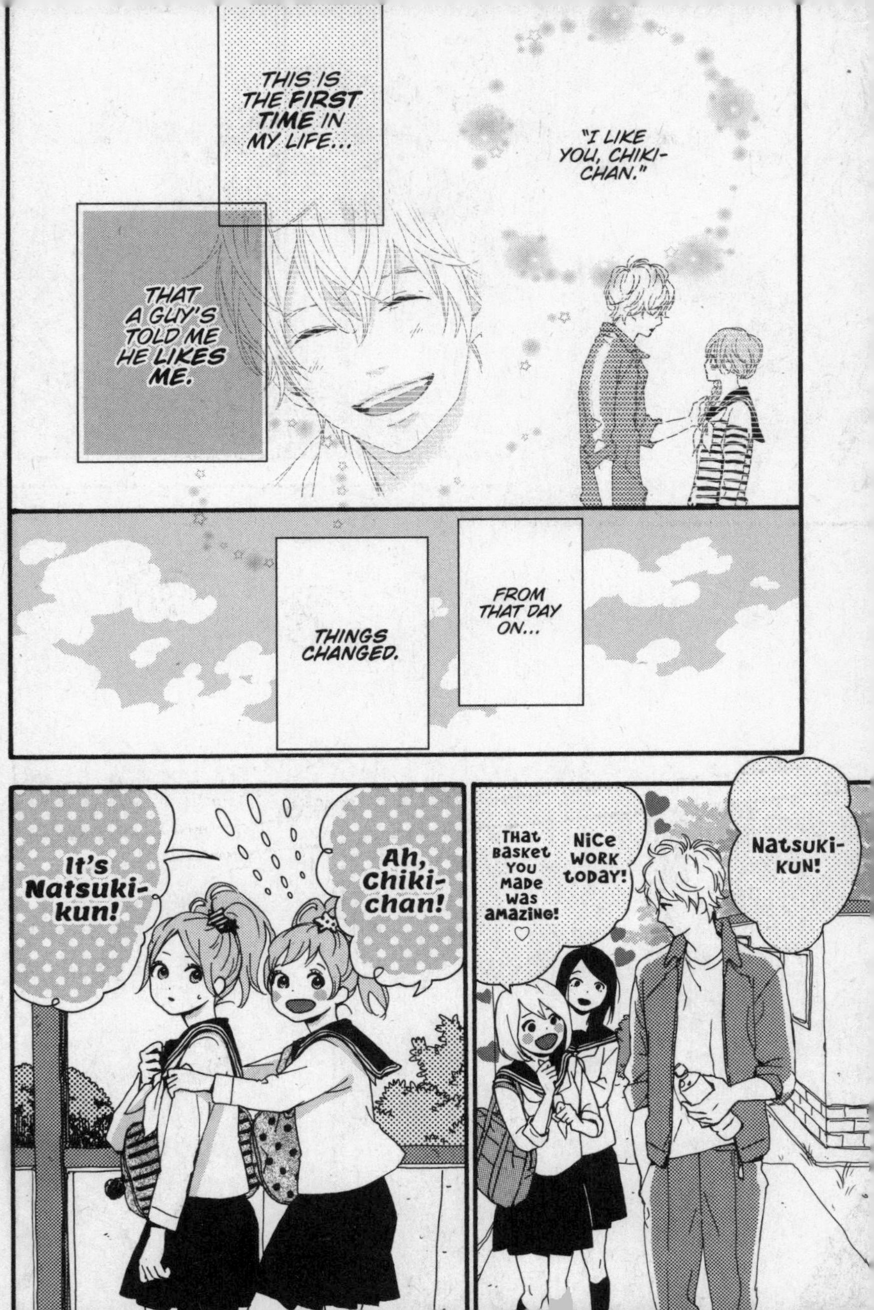
"I LIKE YOU, CHIKI-CHAN."
THIS IS THE FIRST TIME IN MY LIFE...
THAT A GUY'S TOLD ME HE LIKES ME.
FROM THAT DAY ON...
THINGS CHANGED.
Natsuki-kun!
Nice work today!
That basket you made was amazing! ♡
Ah, Chiki-chan!
It's Natsuki-kun!

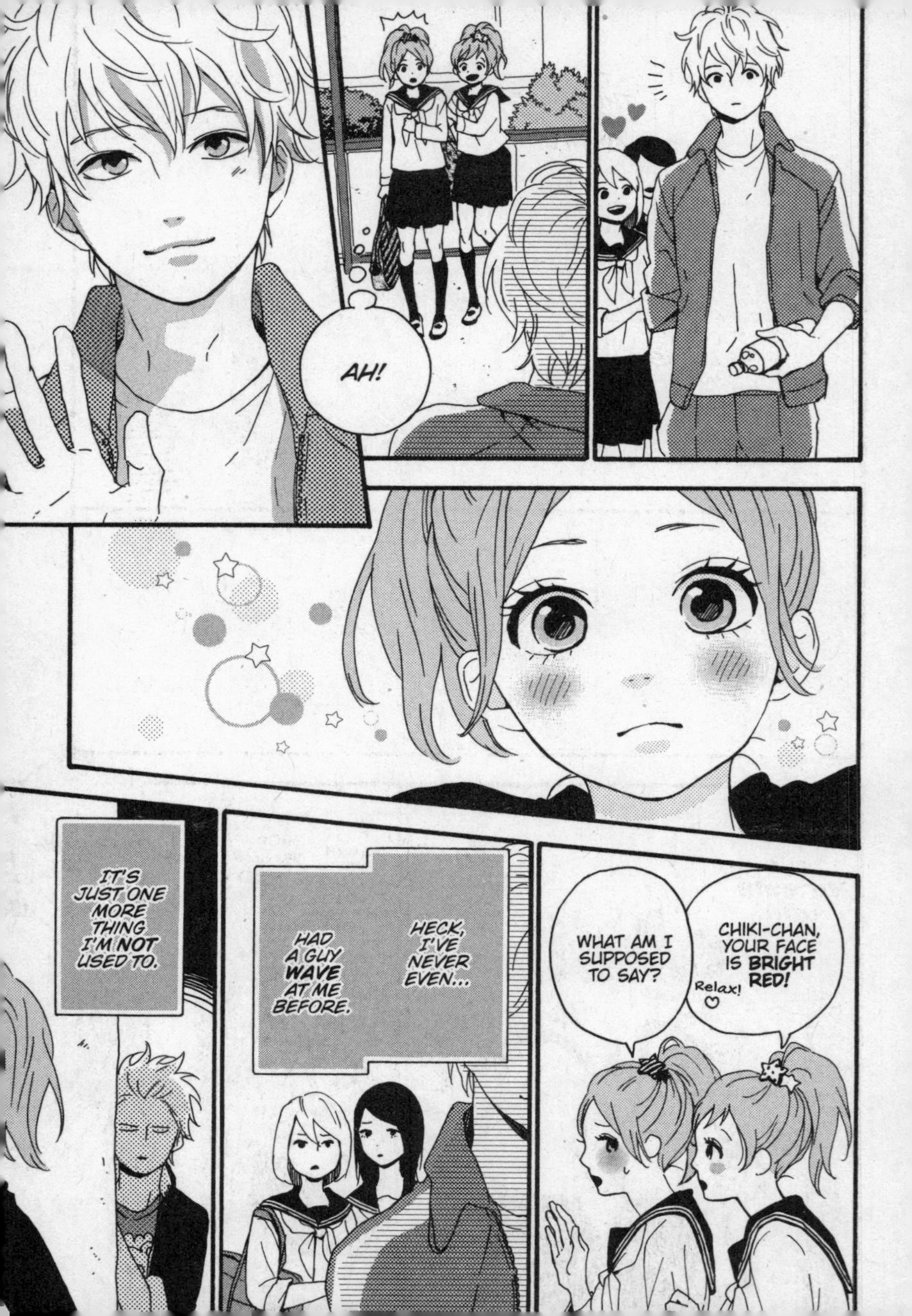
AH!
CHIKI-CHAN, YOUR FACE IS BRIGHT RED!
Relax! ♡
WHAT AM I SUPPOSED TO SAY?
HECK, I'VE NEVER EVEN...
HAD A GUY WAVE AT ME BEFORE.
IT'S JUST ONE MORE THING I'M NOT USED TO.

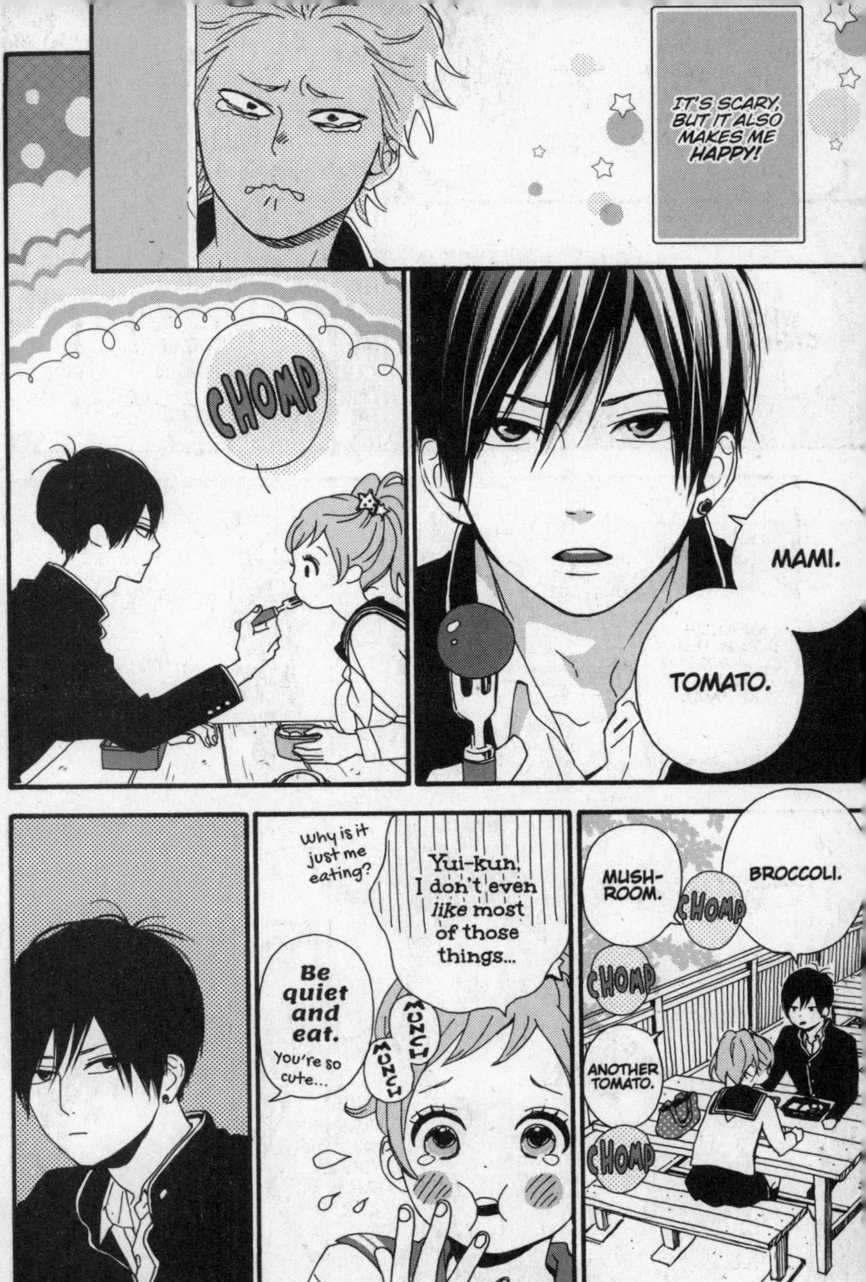
IT'S SCARY, BUT IT ALSO MAKES ME HAPPY!
MAMI.
TOMATO.
CHOMP
BROCCOLI.
MUSH-ROOM.
CHOMP
CHOMP
ANOTHER TOMATO.
CHOMP
Yui-kun, I don't even *like* most of those things...
why is it just me eating?
Be quiet and eat.
You're so cute...
MUNCH
MUNCH

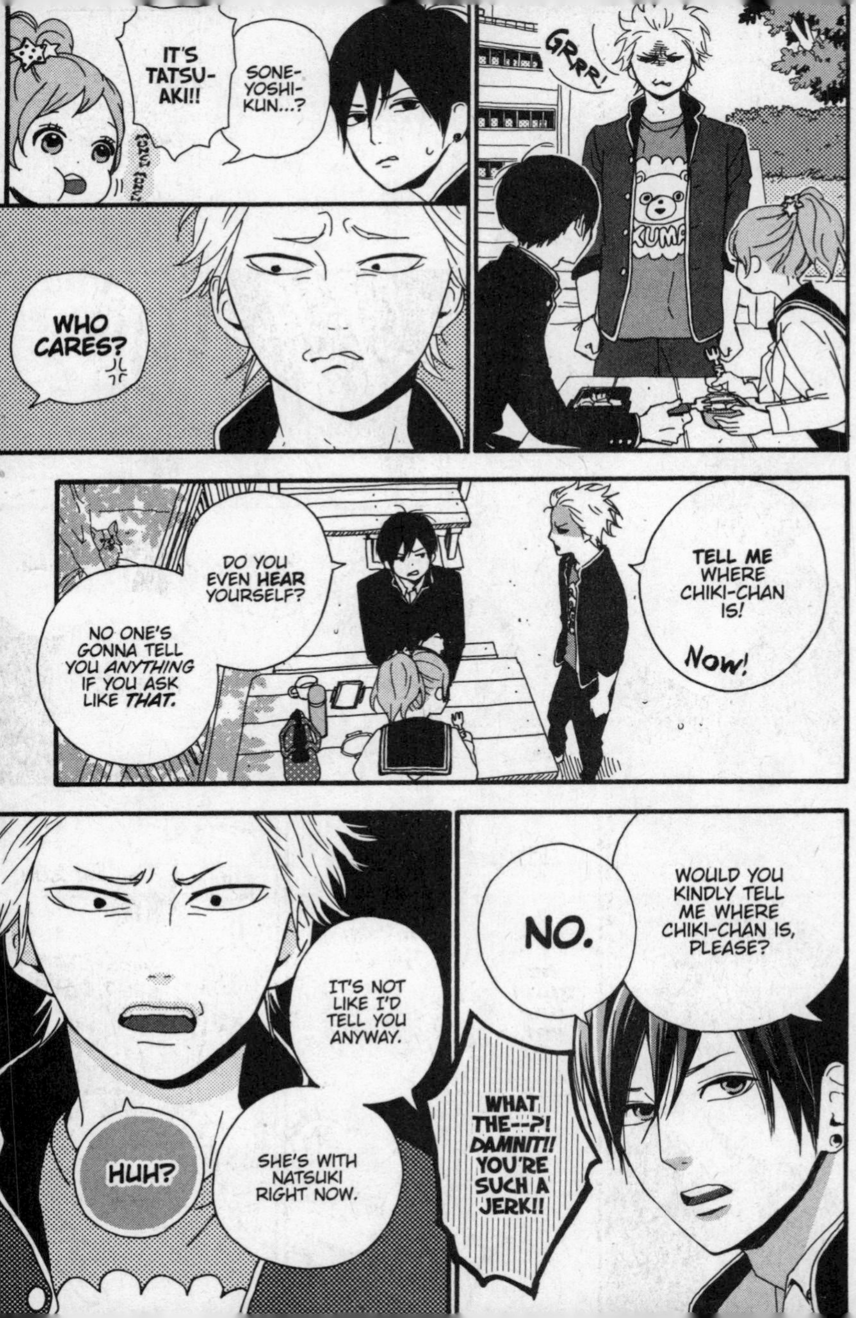
GRRR!
SONE-YOSHI-KUN...?
IT'S TATSU-AKI!!
MUNCH MUNCH
WHO CARES?
TELL ME WHERE CHIKI-CHAN IS!
NOW!
DO YOU EVEN HEAR YOURSELF?
NO ONE'S GONNA TELL YOU ANYTHING IF YOU ASK LIKE THAT.
WOULD YOU KINDLY TELL ME WHERE CHIKI-CHAN IS, PLEASE?
NO.
WHAT THE--?! DAMNIT!! YOU'RE SUCH A JERK!!
IT'S NOT LIKE I'D TELL YOU ANYWAY.
SHE'S WITH NATSUKI RIGHT NOW.
HUH?

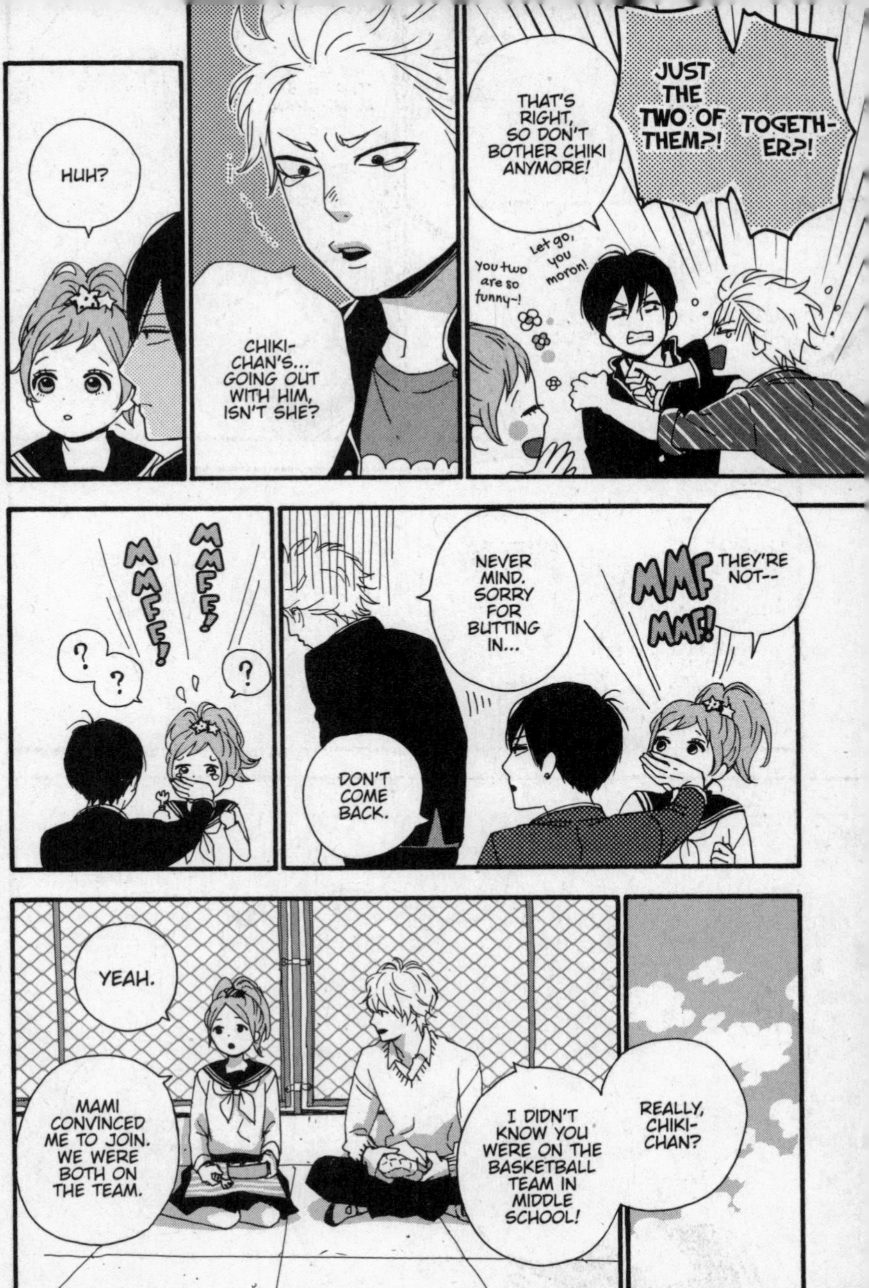
TOGETH-ER?!
JUST THE TWO OF THEM?!
THAT'S RIGHT, SO DON'T BOTHER CHIKI ANYMORE!
Let go, you moron!
You two are so funny~!
CHIKI-CHAN'S... GOING OUT WITH HIM, ISN'T SHE?
HUH?
THEY'RE NOT--
MMF MMF!
NEVER MIND. SORRY FOR BUTTING IN...
DON'T COME BACK.
MMFF!
MMFF!
?
? ?
REALLY, CHIKI-CHAN?
I DIDN'T KNOW YOU WERE ON THE BASKETBALL TEAM IN MIDDLE SCHOOL!
YEAH.
MAMI CONVINCED ME TO JOIN. WE WERE BOTH ON THE TEAM.

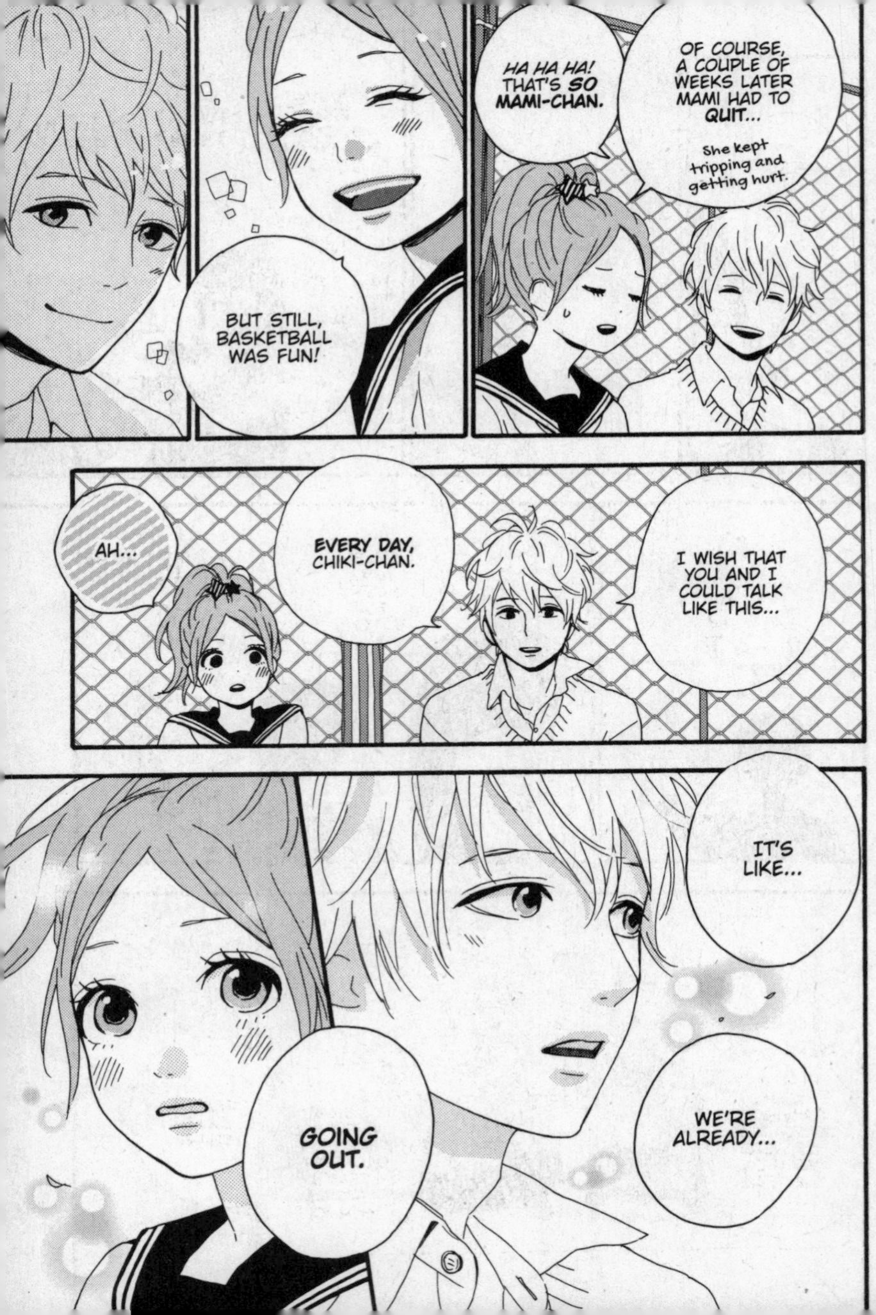
OF COURSE, A COUPLE OF WEEKS LATER MAMI HAD TO QUIT...
She kept tripping and getting hurt.
HA HA HA! THAT'S SO MAMI-CHAN.
BUT STILL, BASKETBALL WAS FUN!
I WISH THAT YOU AND I COULD TALK LIKE THIS...
EVERY DAY, CHIKI-CHAN.
AH...
IT'S LIKE...
WE'RE ALREADY...
GOING OUT.

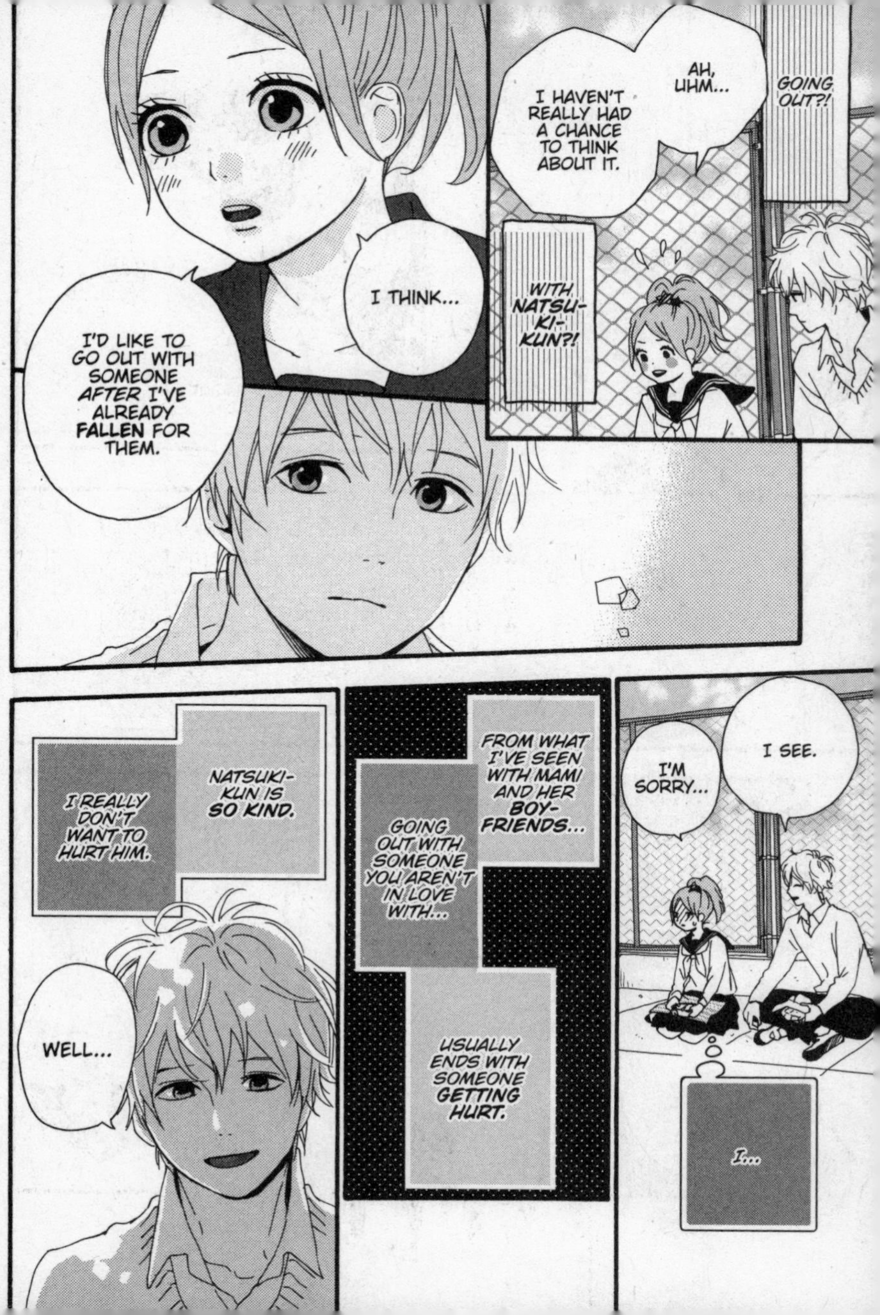
GOING OUT?!
AH, UHM...
I HAVEN'T REALLY HAD A CHANCE TO THINK ABOUT IT.
WITH NATSUKI-KUN?!
I THINK...
I'D LIKE TO GO OUT WITH SOMEONE AFTER I'VE ALREADY FALLEN FOR THEM.
I SEE.
I'M SORRY...
I...
FROM WHAT I'VE SEEN WITH MAMI AND HER BOY-FRIENDS...
GOING OUT WITH SOMEONE YOU AREN'T IN LOVE WITH...
USUALLY ENDS WITH SOMEONE GETTING HURT.
NATSUKI-KUN IS SO KIND.
I REALLY DON'T WANT TO HURT HIM.
WELL...

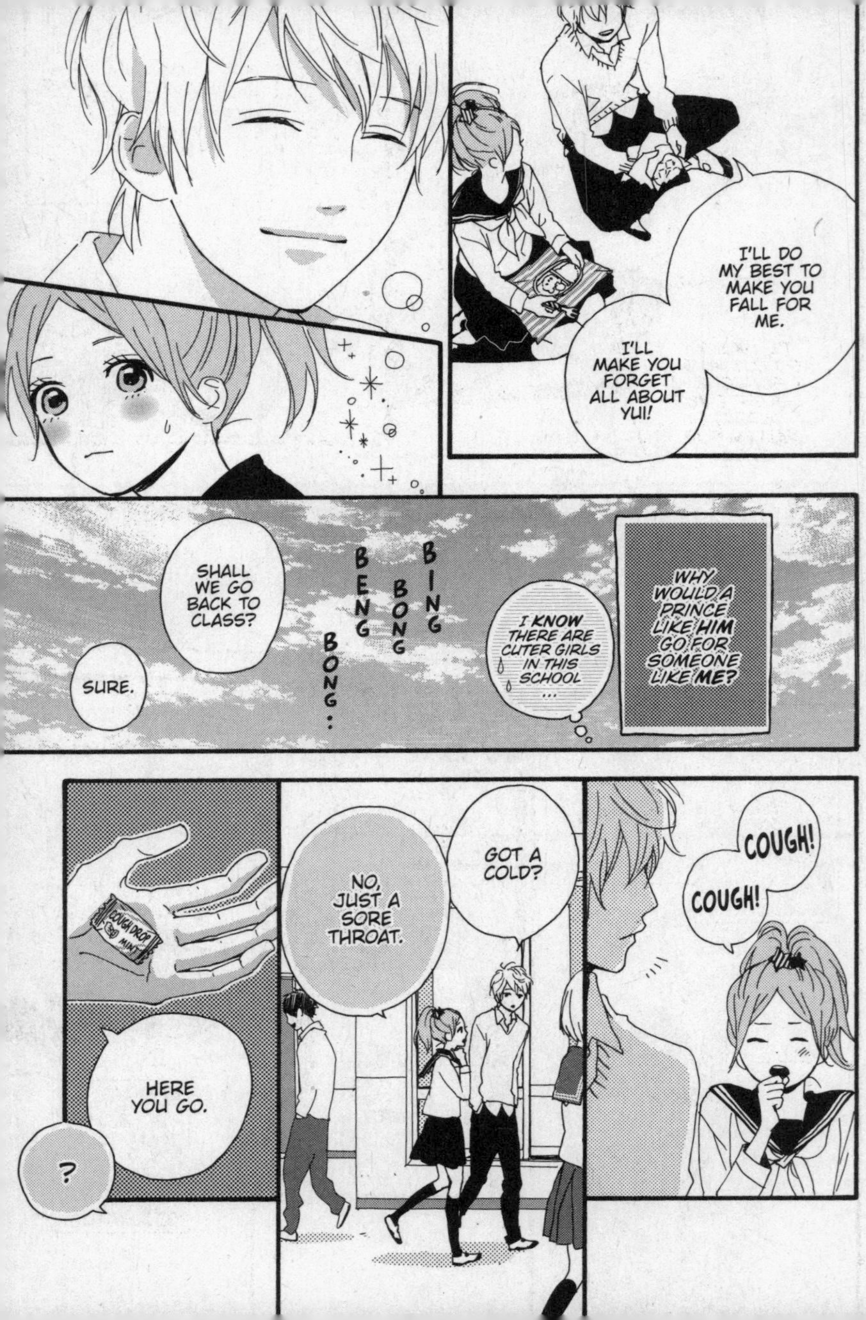
I'LL DO MY BEST TO MAKE YOU FALL FOR ME.
I'LL MAKE YOU FORGET ALL ABOUT YUI!
WHY WOULD A PRINCE LIKE HIM GO FOR SOMEONE LIKE ME?
I KNOW THERE ARE CUTER GIRLS IN THIS SCHOOL...
BING
BONG
BENG
BONG...
SHALL WE GO BACK TO CLASS?
SURE.
COUGH!
COUGH!
GOT A COLD?
NO, JUST A SORE THROAT.
COUGH DROP MINT
HERE YOU GO.
?

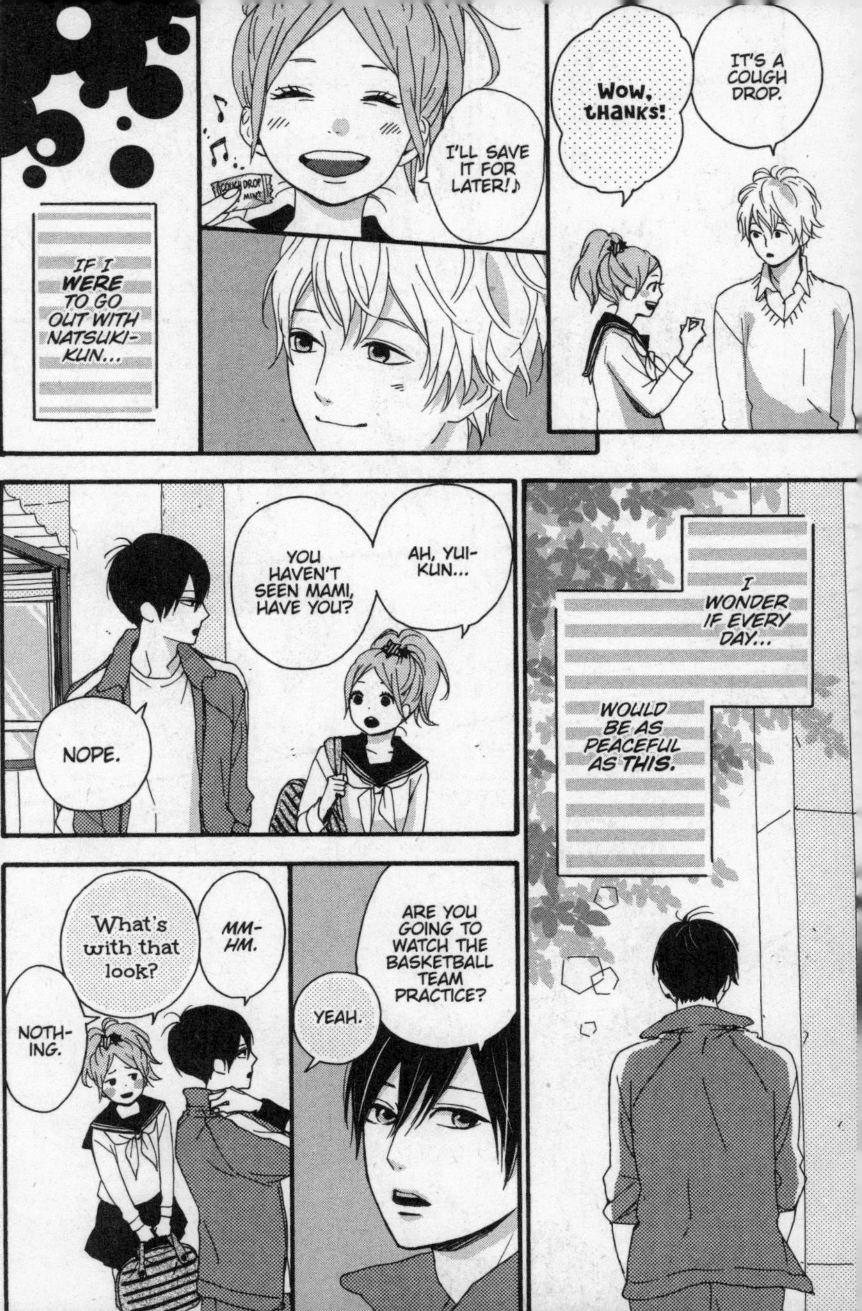
IT'S A COUGH DROP.
Wow, thanks!
I'LL SAVE IT FOR LATER!♪
IF I WERE TO GO OUT WITH NATSUKI-KUN...
I WONDER IF EVERY DAY...
WOULD BE AS PEACEFUL AS THIS.
AH, YUI-KUN...
YOU HAVEN'T SEEN MAMI, HAVE YOU?
NOPE.
ARE YOU GOING TO WATCH THE BASKETBALL TEAM PRACTICE?
YEAH.
MM-HM.
What's with that look?
NOTH-ING.

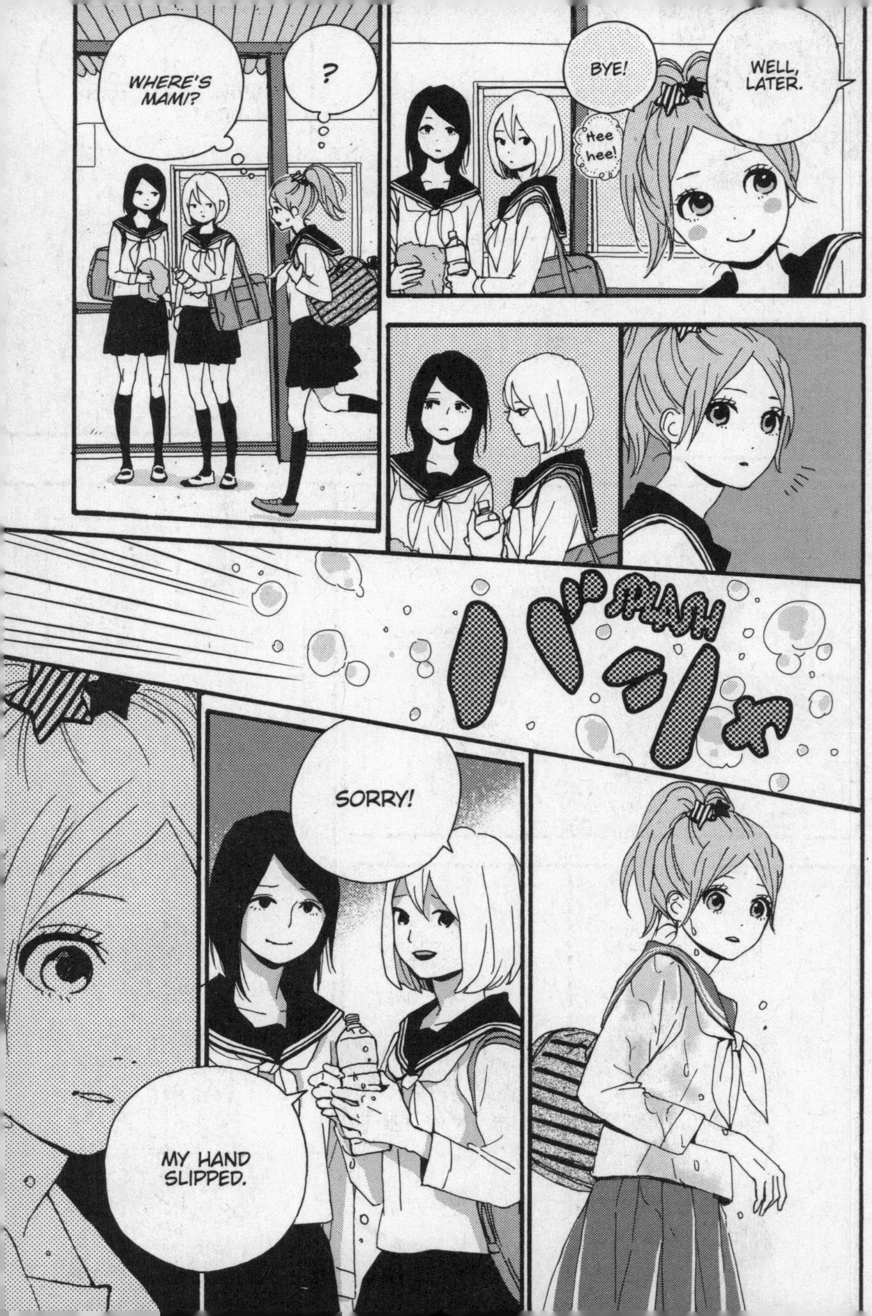
WELL, LATER.
BYE!
Hee hee!
WHERE'S MAMI?
?
SPLASH
SORRY!
MY HAND SLIPPED.

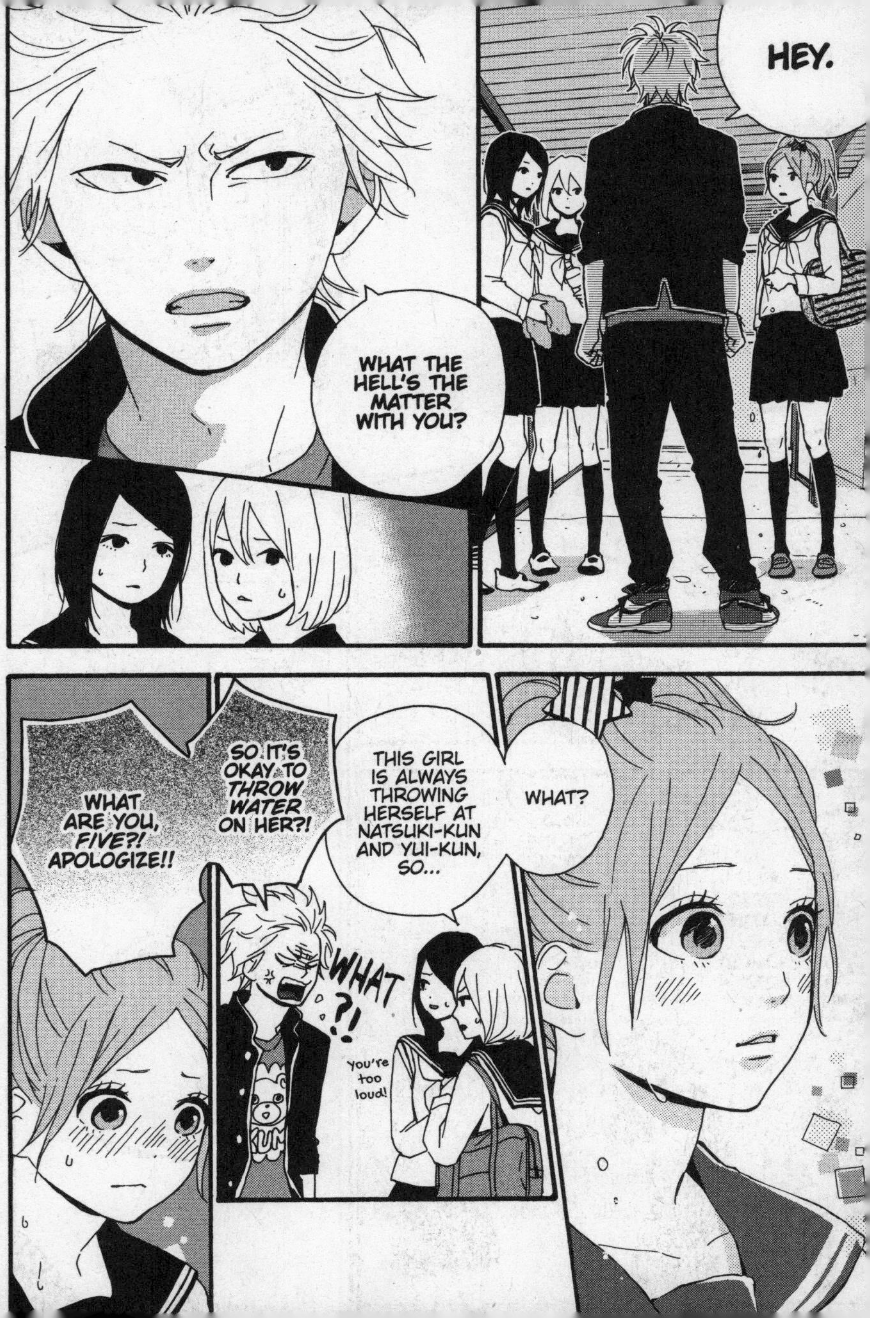
HEY.
WHAT THE HELL'S THE MATTER WITH YOU?
WHAT?
THIS GIRL IS ALWAYS THROWING HERSELF AT NATSUKI-KUN AND YUI-KUN, SO...
WHAT ?!
You're too loud!
SO IT'S OKAY TO *THROW* WATER ON HER?!
WHAT ARE YOU, *FIVE?!* APOLOGIZE!!

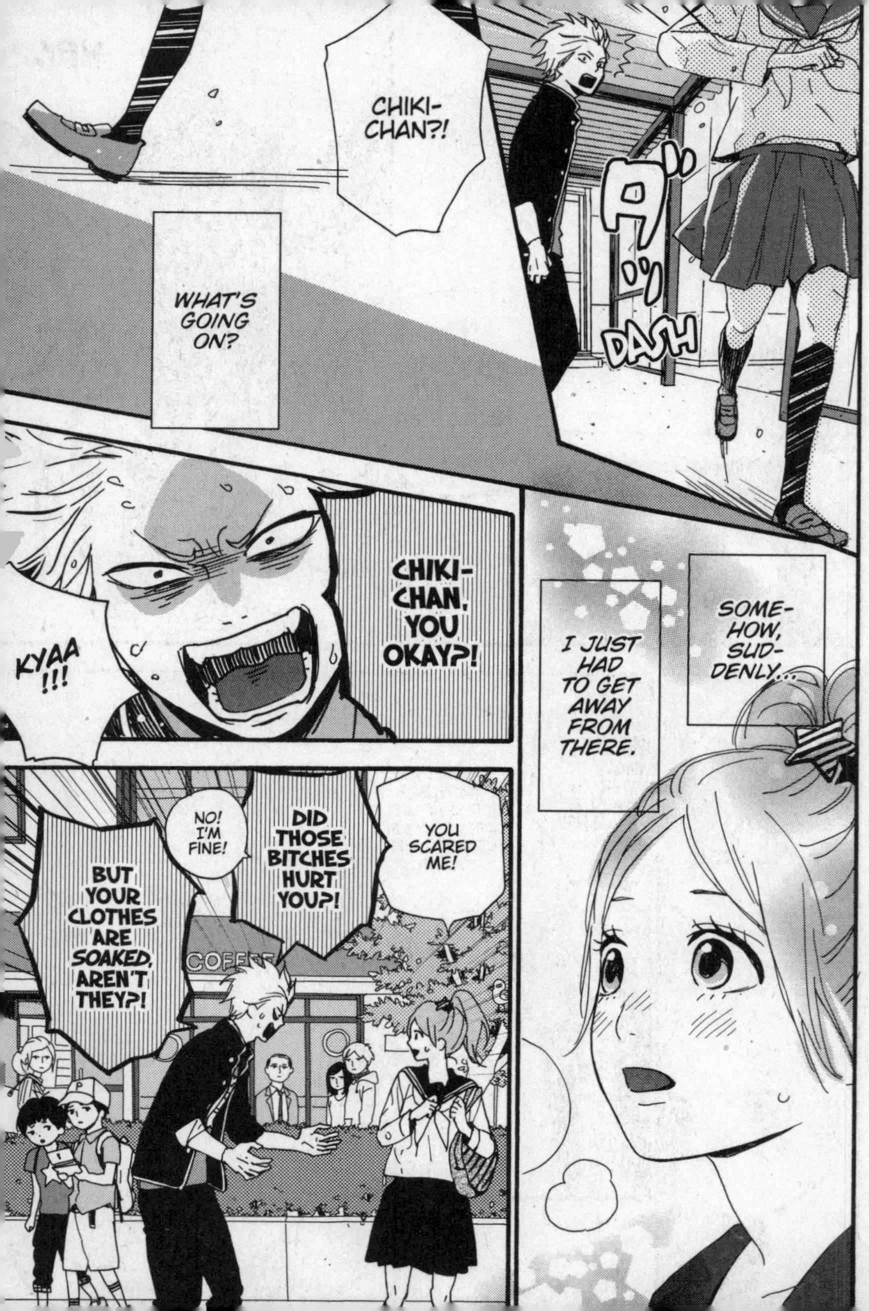

CHIKI-CHAN?!
ダッ
DASH
WHAT'S GOING ON?
SOMEHOW, SUDDENLY...
I JUST HAD TO GET AWAY FROM THERE.
CHIKI-CHAN, YOU OKAY?!
KYAA!!!
YOU SCARED ME!
DID THOSE BITCHES HURT YOU?!
NO! I'M FINE!
BUT YOUR CLOTHES ARE SOAKED, AREN'T THEY?!

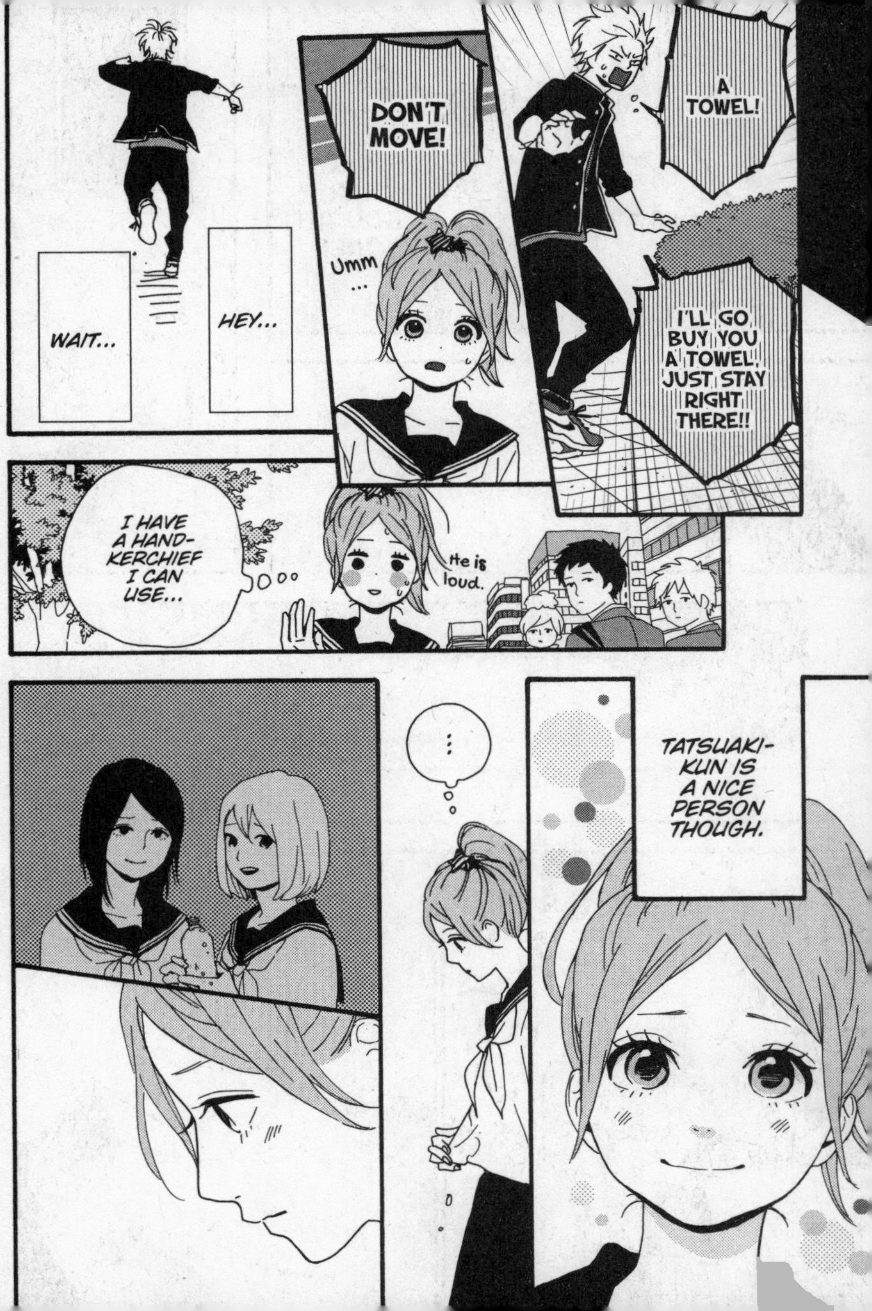
A TOWEL!
I'LL GO BUY YOU A TOWEL, JUST STAY RIGHT THERE!!
DON'T MOVE!
Umm...
HEY...
WAIT...
He is loud.
I HAVE A HAND-KERCHIEF I CAN USE...
TATSUAKI-KUN IS A NICE PERSON THOUGH.
...

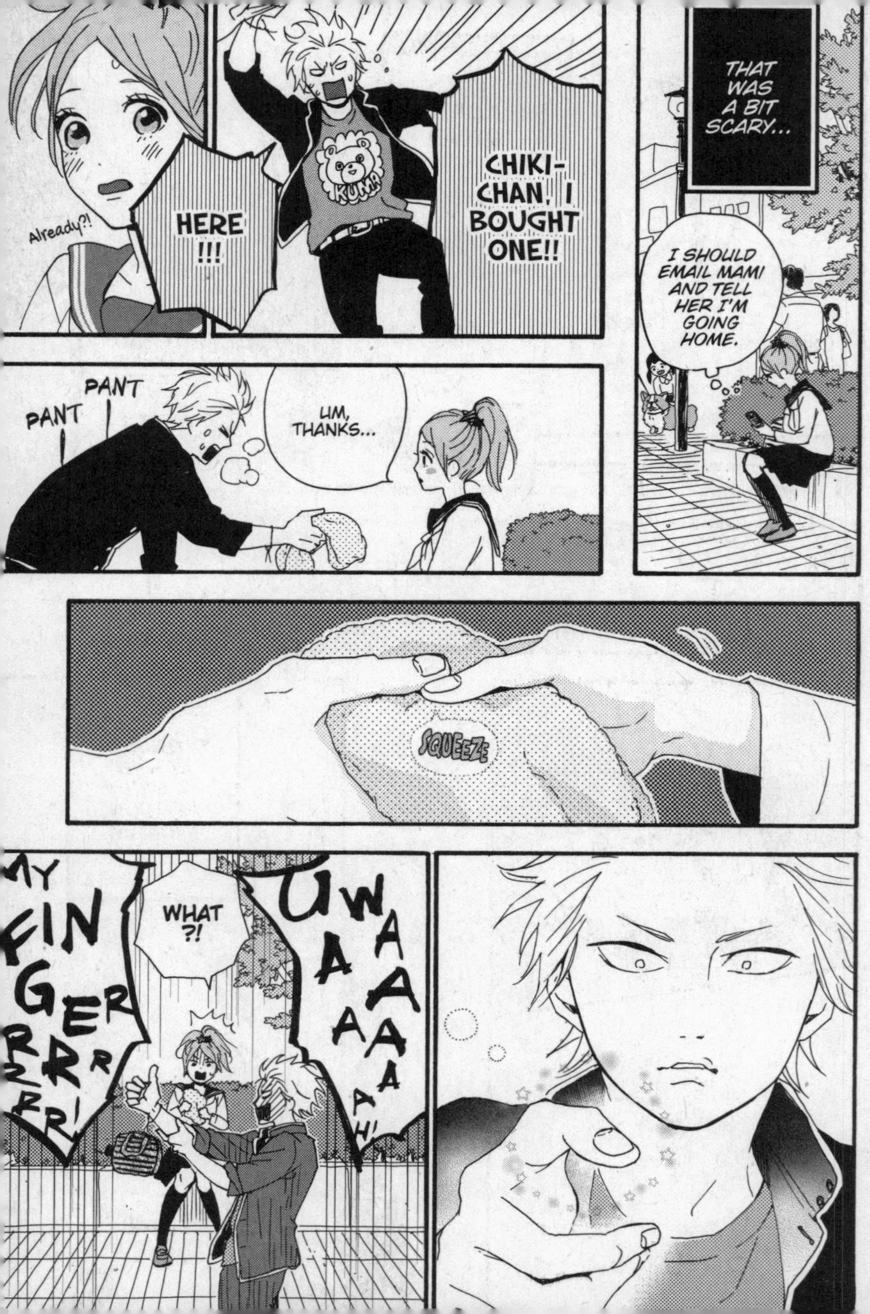
THAT WAS A BIT SCARY...
I SHOULD EMAIL MAMI AND TELL HER I'M GOING HOME.
CHIKI-CHAN, I BOUGHT ONE!!
HERE!!!
Already?!
UM, THANKS...
PANT
PANT
SQUEEZE
UWAAAAAAAAH!
WHAT?!
MY FINGERRRRRRR!

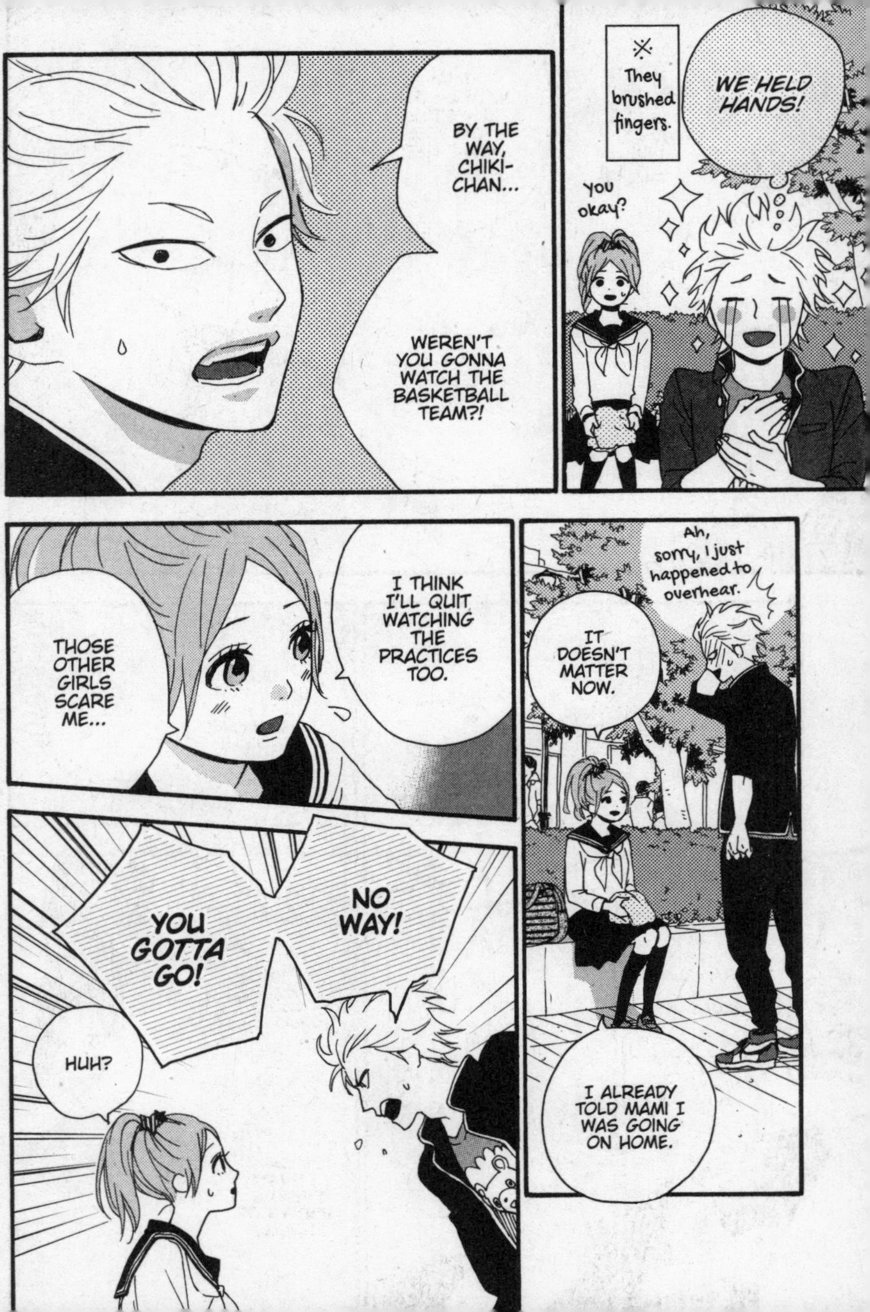
WE HELD HANDS!
※ They brushed fingers.
You okay?
BY THE WAY, CHIKI-CHAN...
WEREN'T YOU GONNA WATCH THE BASKETBALL TEAM?!
Ah, sorry, I just happened to overhear.
IT DOESN'T MATTER NOW.
I ALREADY TOLD MAMI I WAS GOING ON HOME.
I THINK I'LL QUIT WATCHING THE PRACTICES TOO.
THOSE OTHER GIRLS SCARE ME...
NO WAY!
YOU GOTTA GO!
HUH?

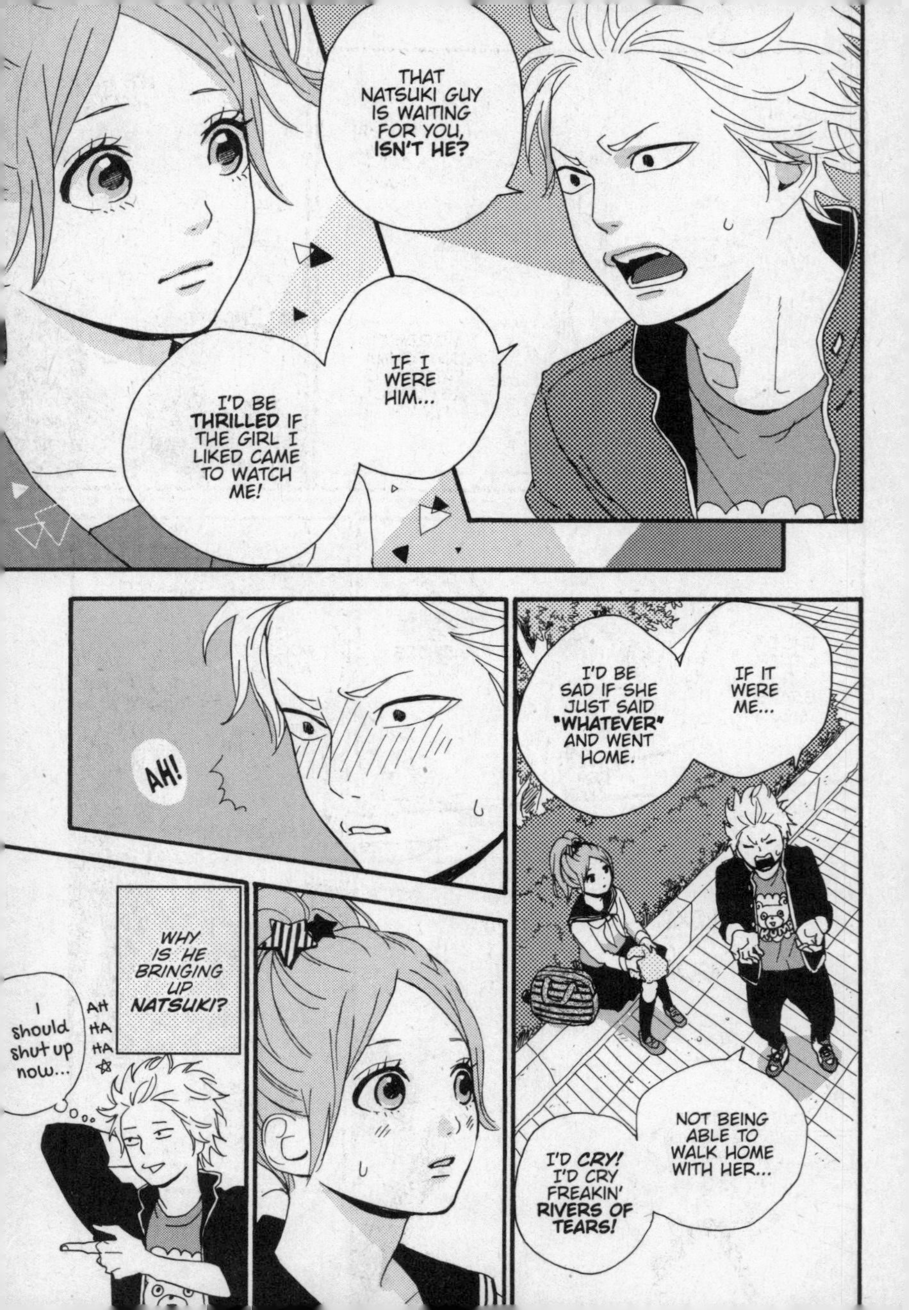
THAT NATSUKI GUY IS WAITING FOR YOU, ISN'T HE?
IF I WERE HIM...
I'D BE THRILLED IF THE GIRL I LIKED CAME TO WATCH ME!
IF IT WERE ME...
I'D BE SAD IF SHE JUST SAID "WHATEVER" AND WENT HOME.
NOT BEING ABLE TO WALK HOME WITH HER...
I'D CRY! I'D CRY FREAKIN' RIVERS OF TEARS!
AH!
WHY IS HE BRINGING UP NATSUKI?
AH HA HA ☆
I should shut up now...

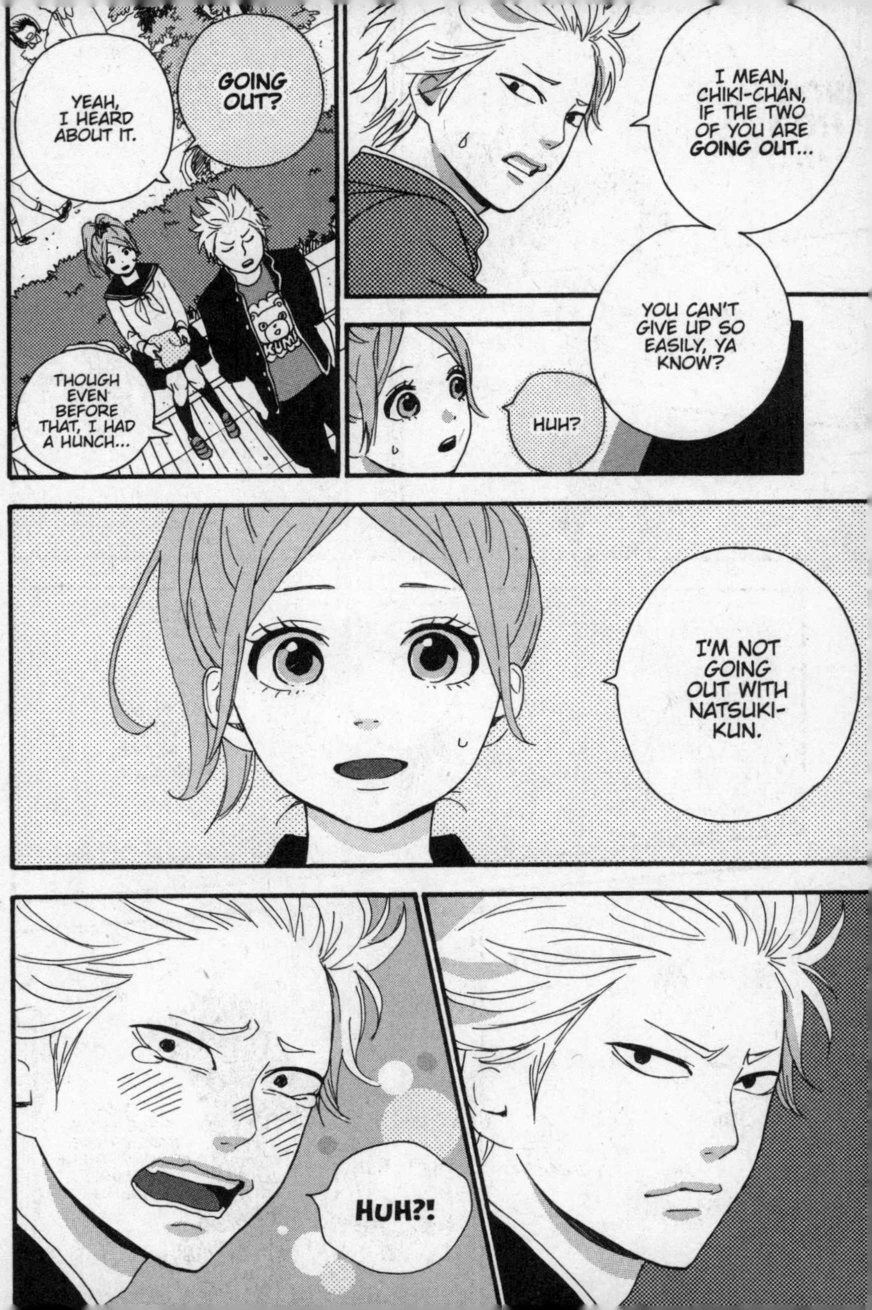
I MEAN, CHIKI-CHAN, IF THE TWO OF YOU ARE GOING OUT...
YOU CAN'T GIVE UP SO EASILY, YA KNOW?
HUH?
GOING OUT?
YEAH, I HEARD ABOUT IT.
THOUGH EVEN BEFORE THAT, I HAD A HUNCH...
I'M NOT GOING OUT WITH NATSUKI-KUN.
HUH?!

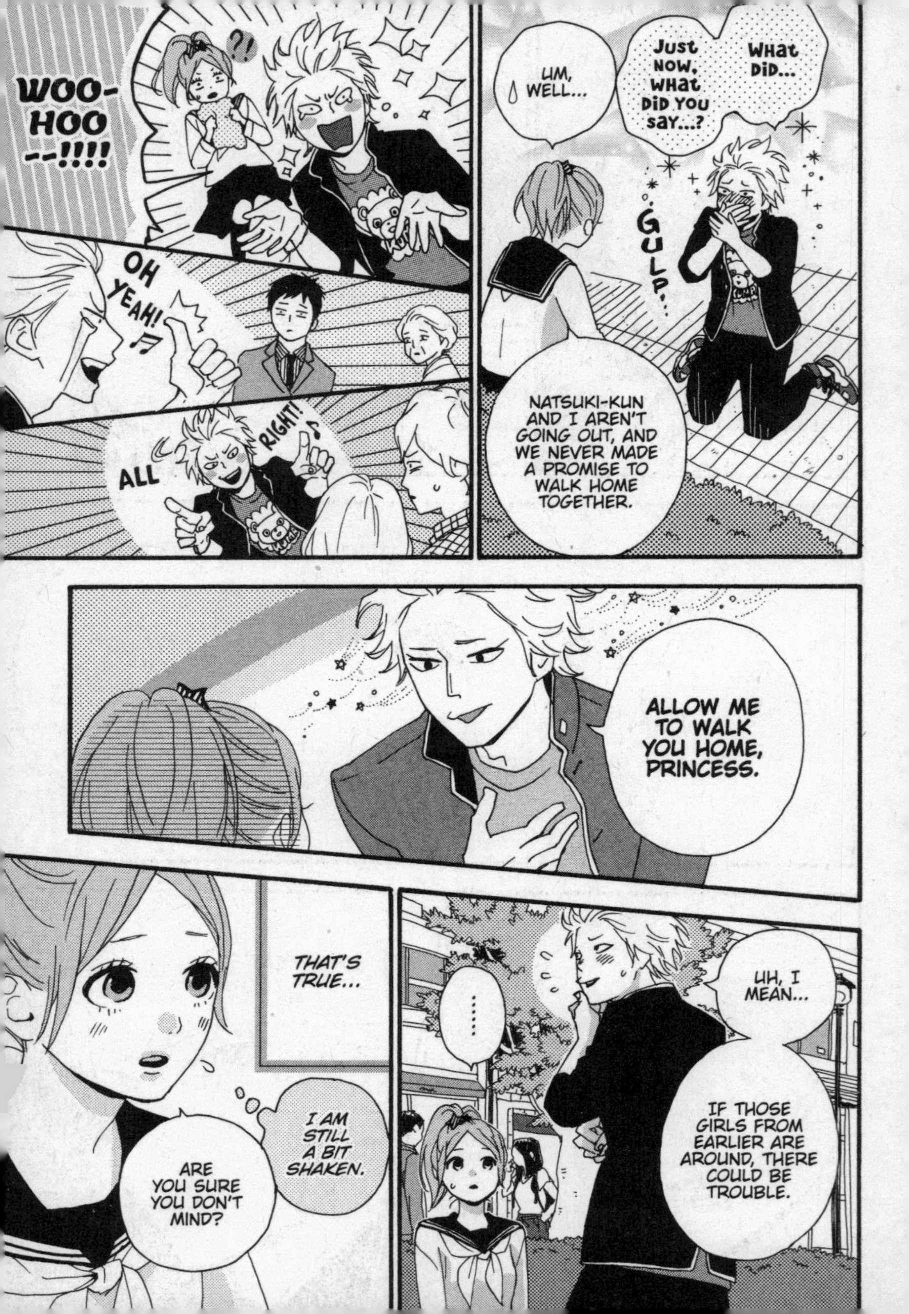
What did...
Just now, what did you say...?
Um, well...
GULP...
Natsuki-kun and I aren't going out, and we never made a promise to walk home together.
WOO-HOO--!!!!
OH YEAH!
ALL RIGHT!
Allow me to walk you home, princess.
Uh, I mean...
If those girls from earlier are around, there could be trouble.
......
That's true...
I am still a bit shaken.
Are you sure you don't mind?

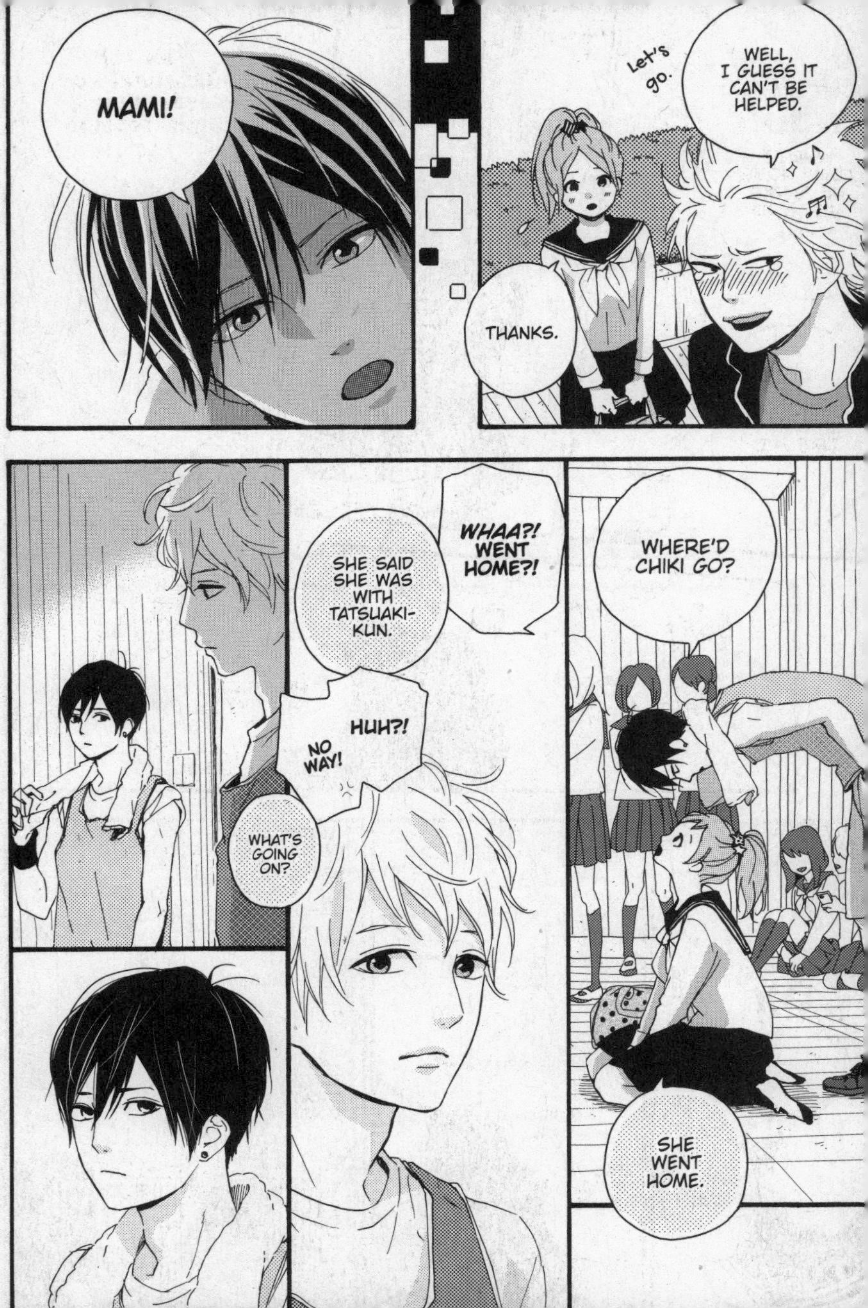
WELL, I GUESS IT CAN'T BE HELPED.
Let's go.
THANKS.
MAMI!
WHERE'D CHIKI GO?
SHE WENT HOME.
WHAA?! WENT HOME?!
SHE SAID SHE WAS WITH TATSUAKI-KUN.
HUH?!
NO WAY!
WHAT'S GOING ON?

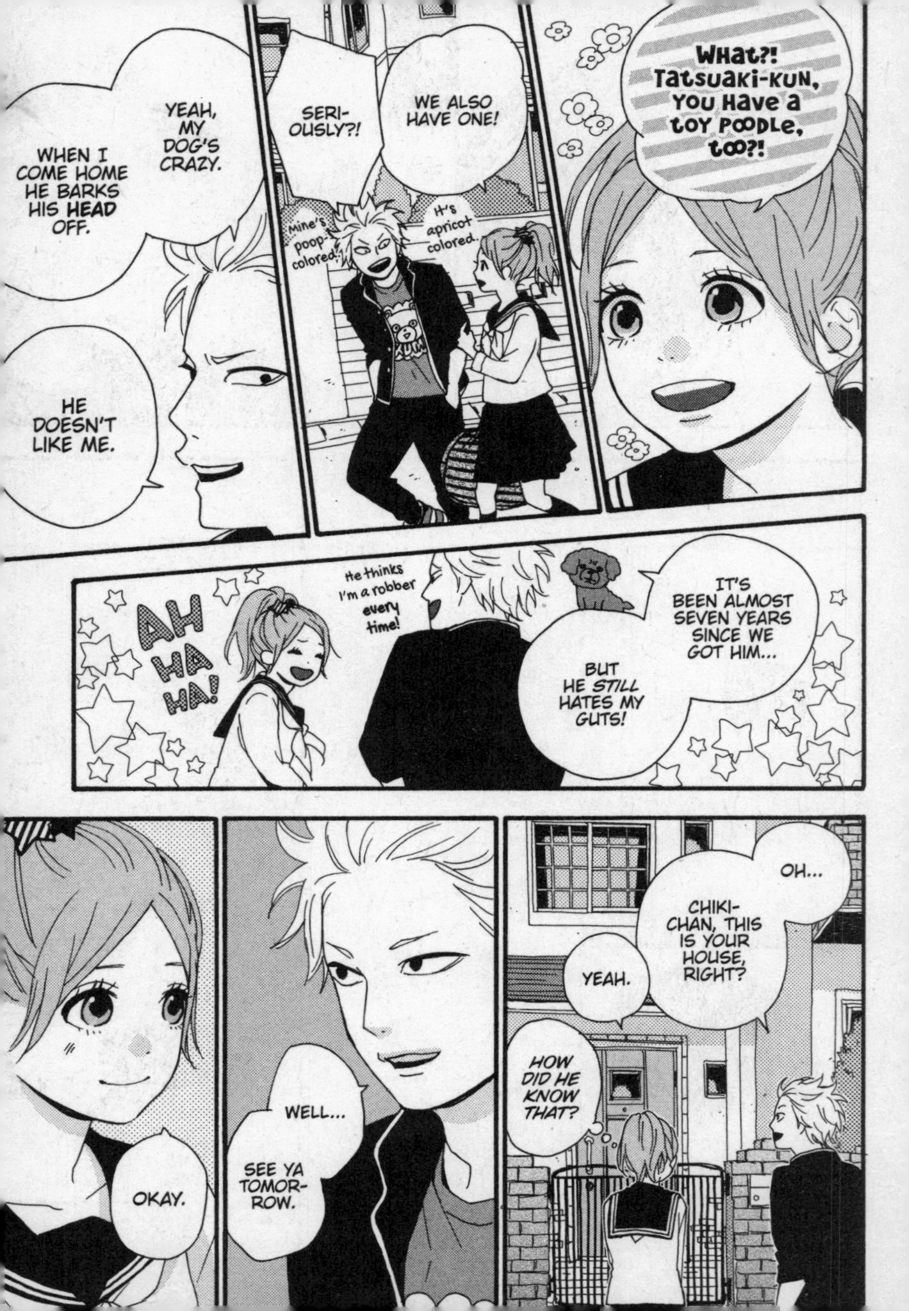
WHAT?! Tatsuaki-kun, you have a toy poodle, too?!
WE ALSO HAVE ONE!
SERI-OUSLY?!
It's apricot colored...
Mine's poop-colored.
YEAH, MY DOG'S CRAZY.
WHEN I COME HOME HE BARKS HIS HEAD OFF.
HE DOESN'T LIKE ME.
IT'S BEEN ALMOST SEVEN YEARS SINCE WE GOT HIM...
BUT HE STILL HATES MY GUTS!
He thinks I'm a robber every time!
AH HA HA!
OH...
CHIKI-CHAN, THIS IS YOUR HOUSE, RIGHT?
YEAH.
HOW DID HE KNOW THAT?
WELL...
SEE YA TOMOR-ROW.
OKAY.

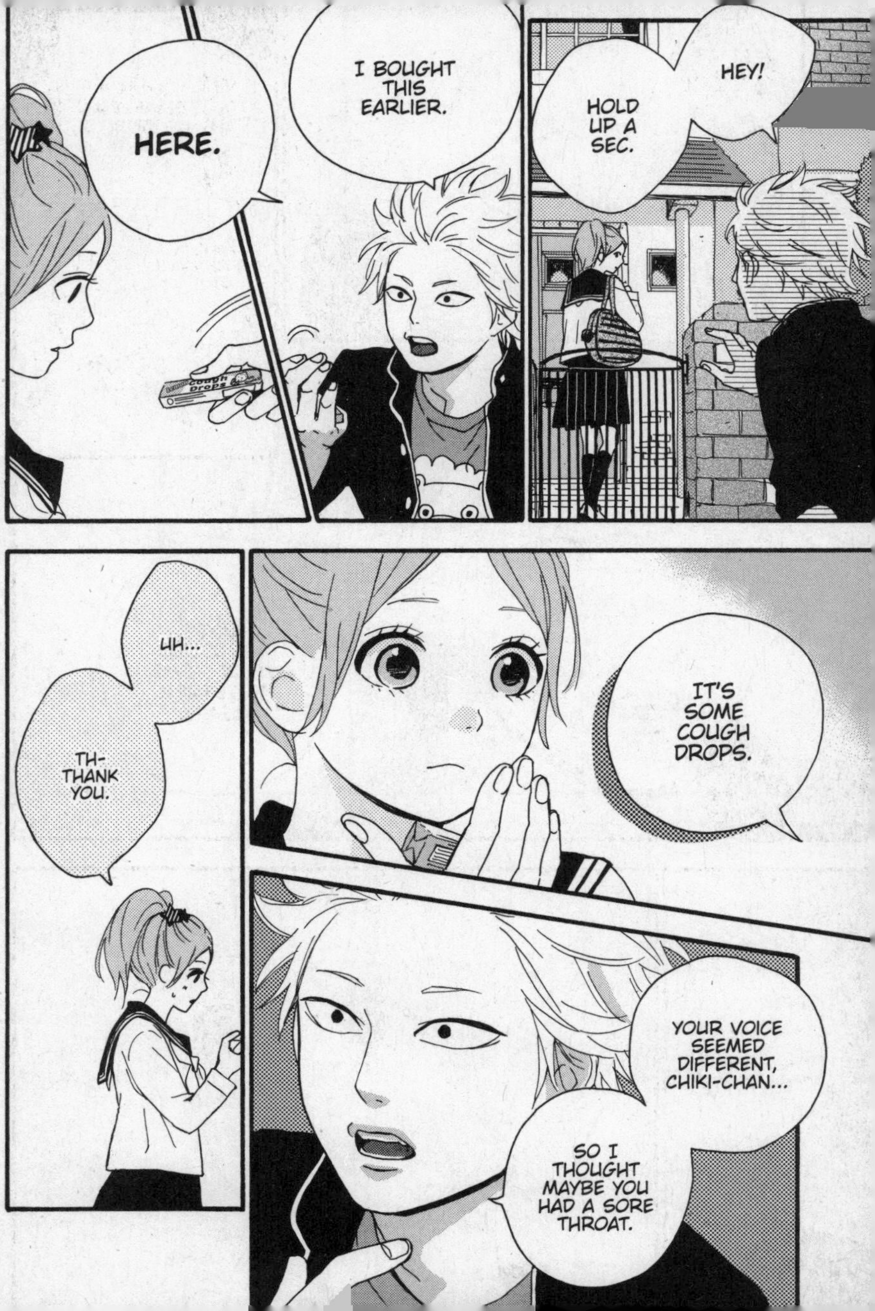
HEY!
HOLD UP A SEC.
I BOUGHT THIS EARLIER.
HERE.
Cough Drops
IT'S SOME COUGH DROPS.
YOUR VOICE SEEMED DIFFERENT, CHIKI-CHAN...
SO I THOUGHT MAYBE YOU HAD A SORE THROAT.
UH...
TH- THANK YOU.

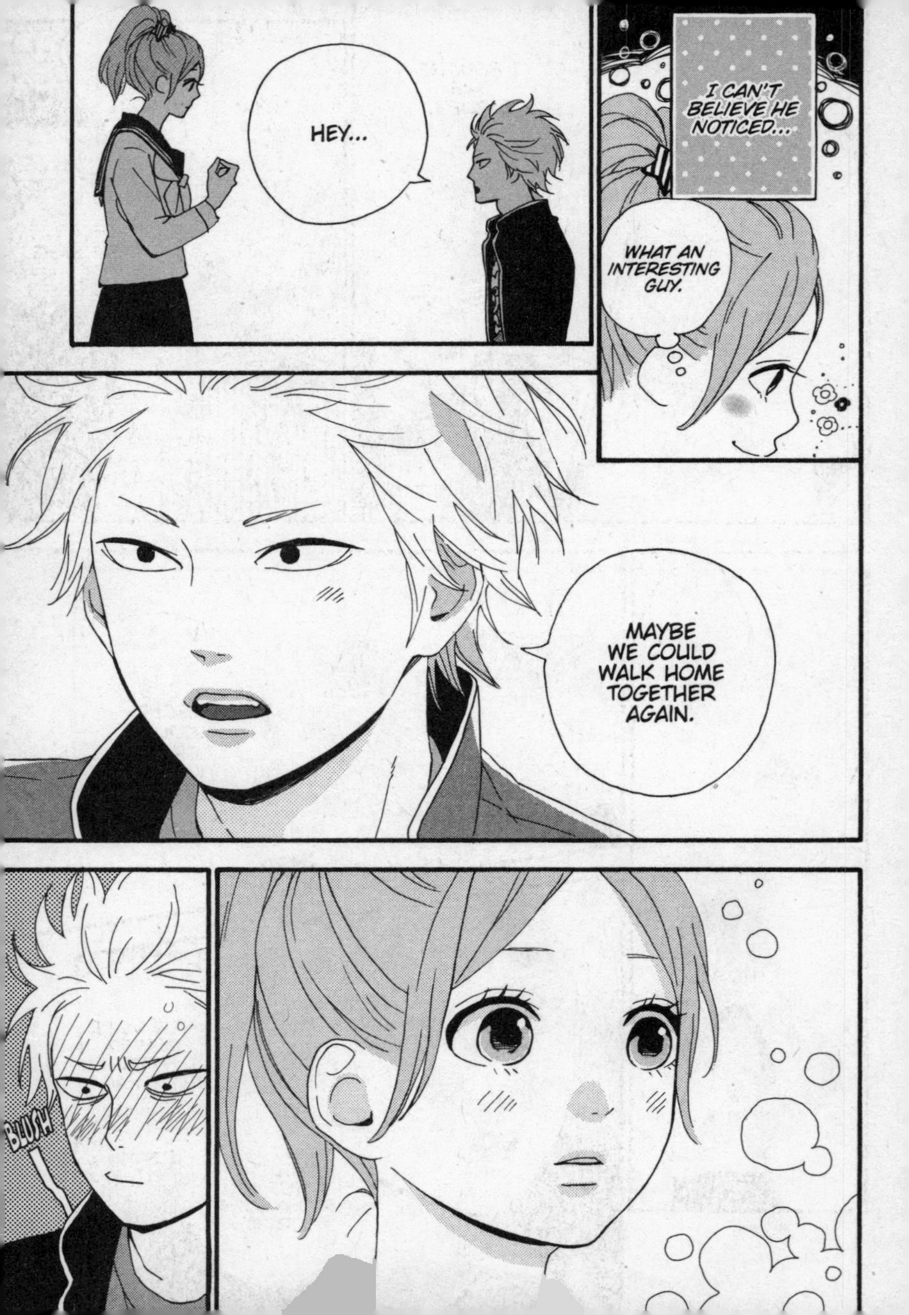
I CAN'T BELIEVE HE NOTICED...
WHAT AN INTERESTING GUY.
HEY...
MAYBE WE COULD WALK HOME TOGETHER AGAIN.
BLUSH

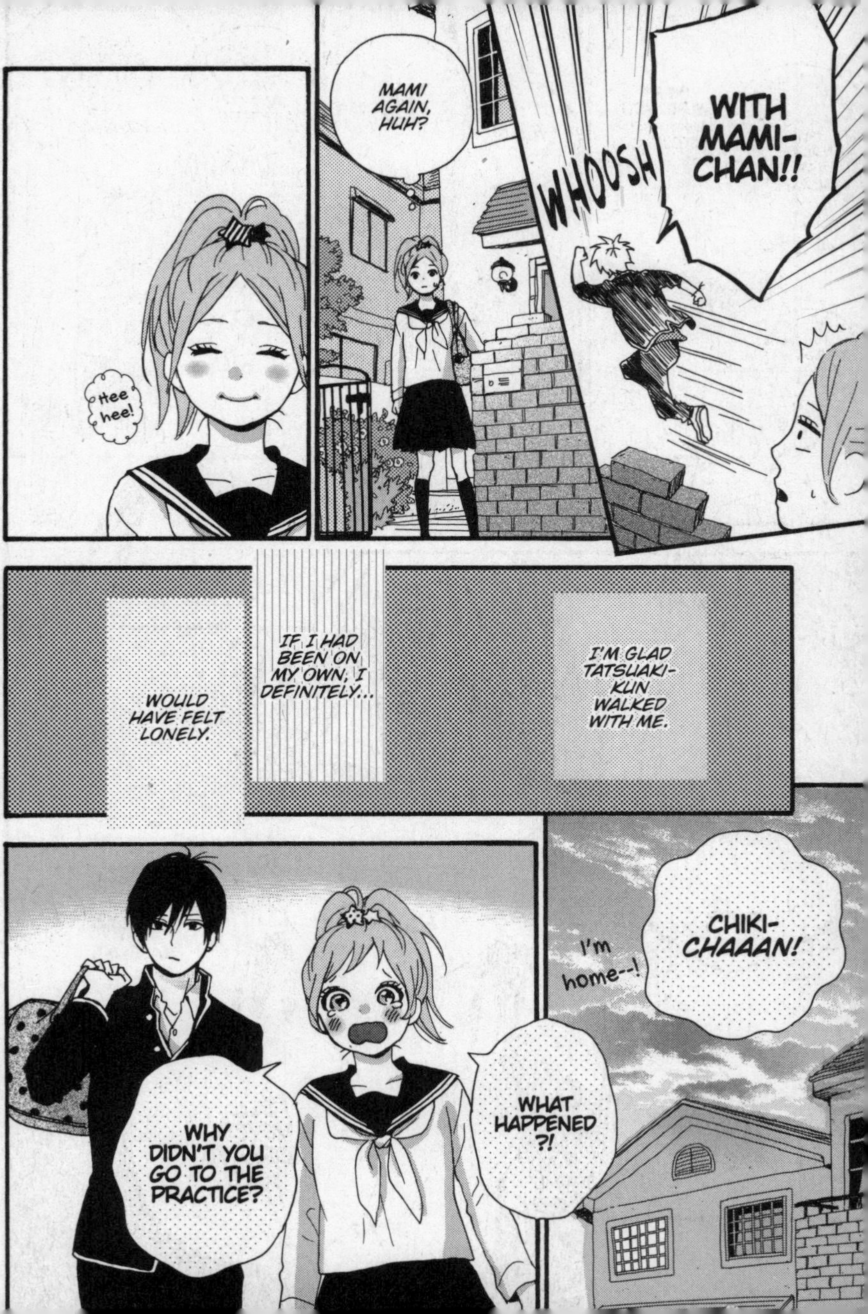
WITH MAMI-CHAN!!
WHOOSH
MAMI AGAIN, HUH?
Hee hee!
I'M GLAD TATSUAKI-KUN WALKED WITH ME.
IF I HAD BEEN ON MY OWN, I DEFINITELY...
WOULD HAVE FELT LONELY.
I'm home--!
CHIKI-CHAAAN!
WHAT HAPPENED ?!
WHY DIDN'T YOU GO TO THE PRACTICE?

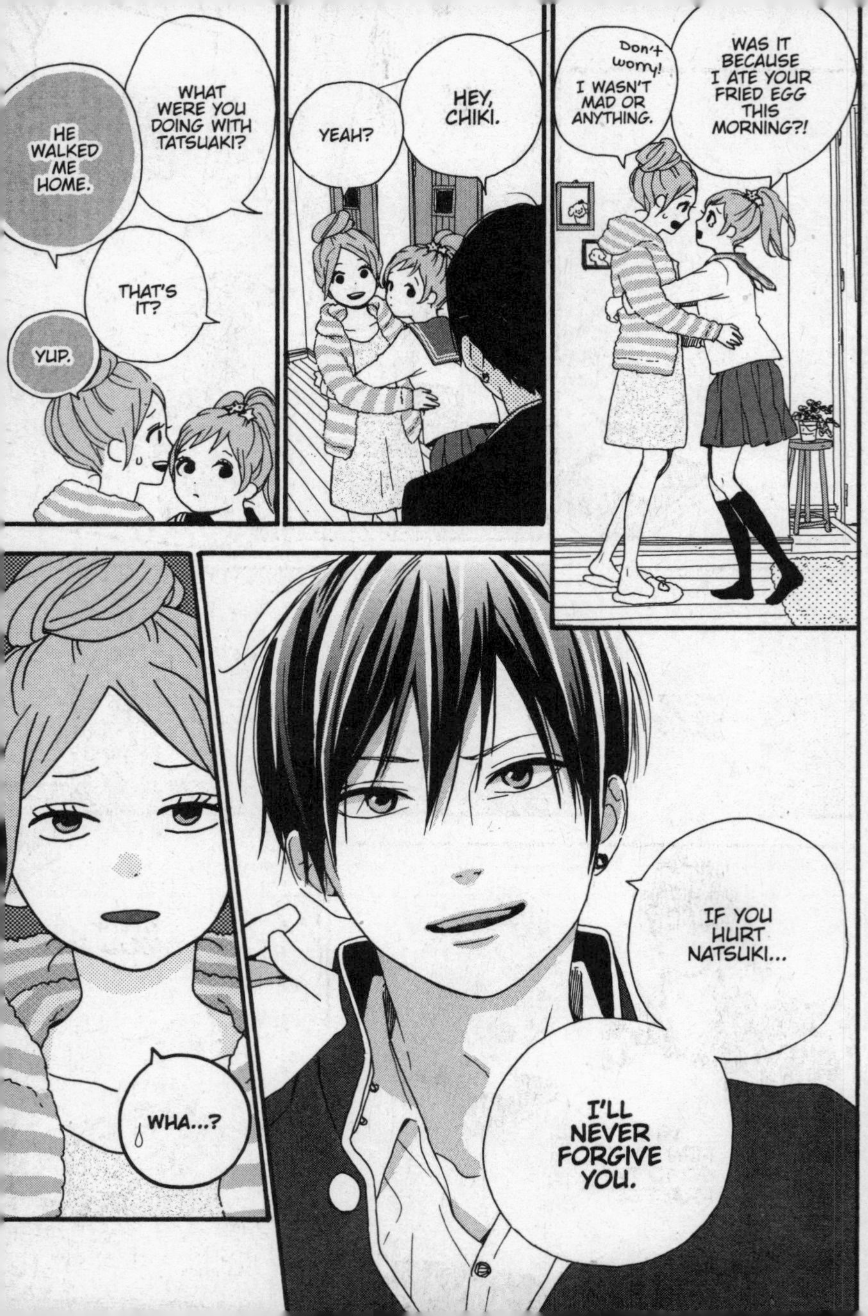
WAS IT BECAUSE I ATE YOUR FRIED EGG THIS MORNING?!
Don't worry! I WASN'T MAD OR ANYTHING.
HEY, CHIKI.
YEAH?
WHAT WERE YOU DOING WITH TATSUAKI?
HE WALKED ME HOME.
THAT'S IT?
YUP.
IF YOU HURT NATSUKI...
I'LL NEVER FORGIVE YOU.
WHA...?

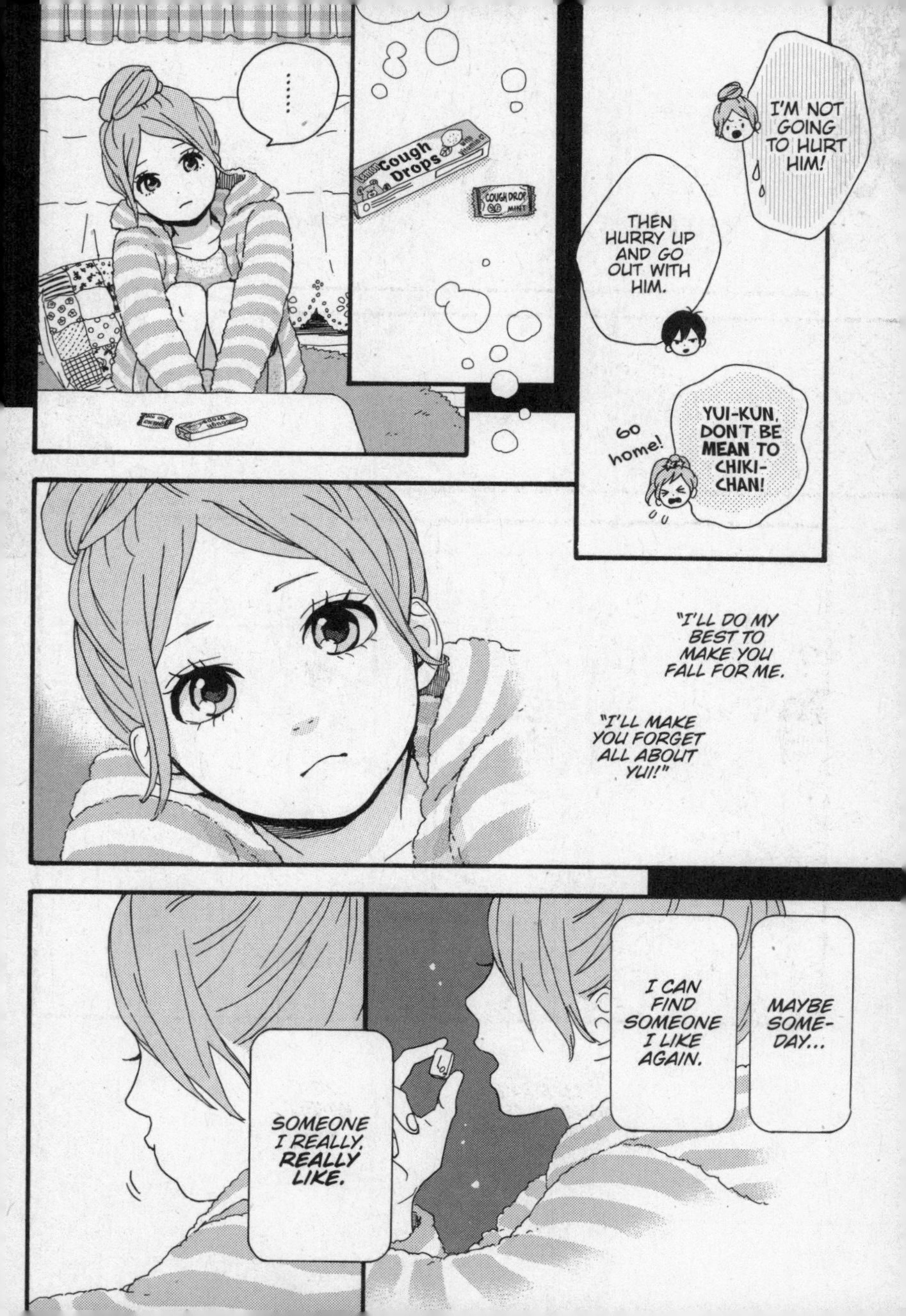
I'M NOT GOING TO HURT HIM!
THEN HURRY UP AND GO OUT WITH HIM.
YUI-KUN, DON'T BE MEAN TO CHIKI-CHAN!
Go home!
Cough Drops
COUGH DROP MINT
......
"I'LL DO MY BEST TO MAKE YOU FALL FOR ME.
"I'LL MAKE YOU FORGET ALL ABOUT YUI!"
MAYBE SOME-DAY...
I CAN FIND SOMEONE I LIKE AGAIN.
SOMEONE I REALLY, REALLY LIKE.

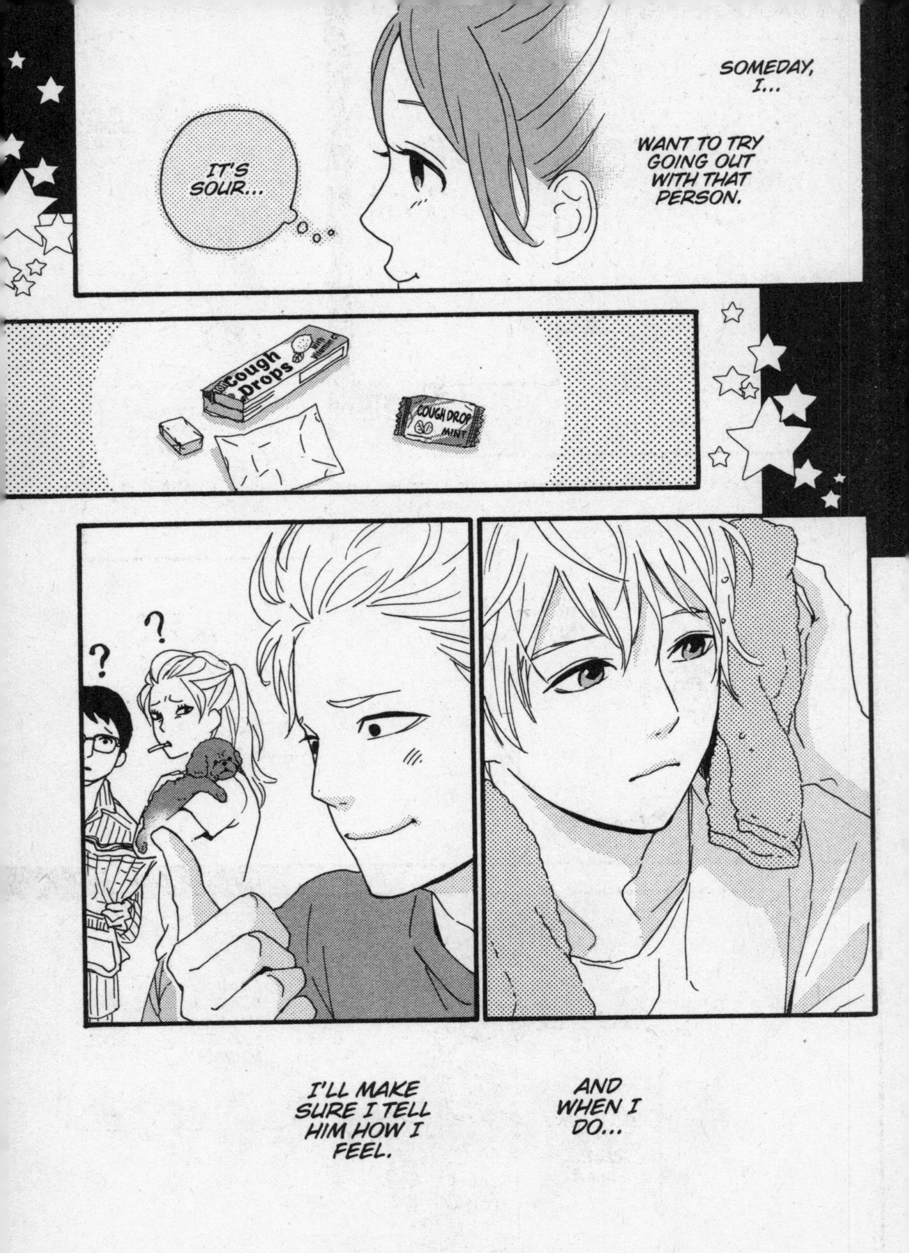
SOMEDAY, I...
WANT TO TRY GOING OUT WITH THAT PERSON.
IT'S SOUR...
Cough Drops
COUGH DROP MINT
?
?
AND WHEN I DO...
I'LL MAKE SURE I TELL HIM HOW I FEEL.

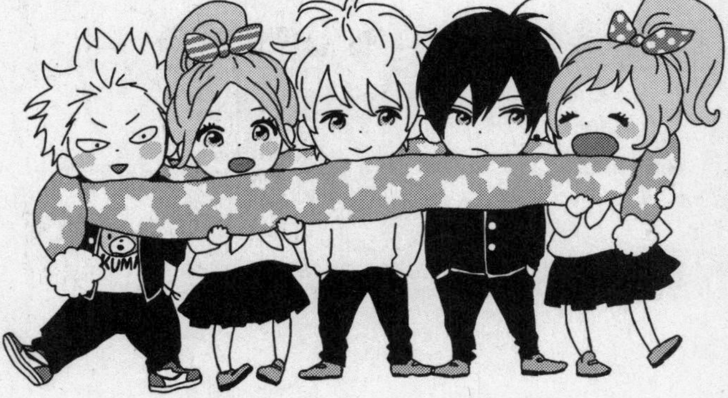
KUMA

HARUIRO ASTRONAUT

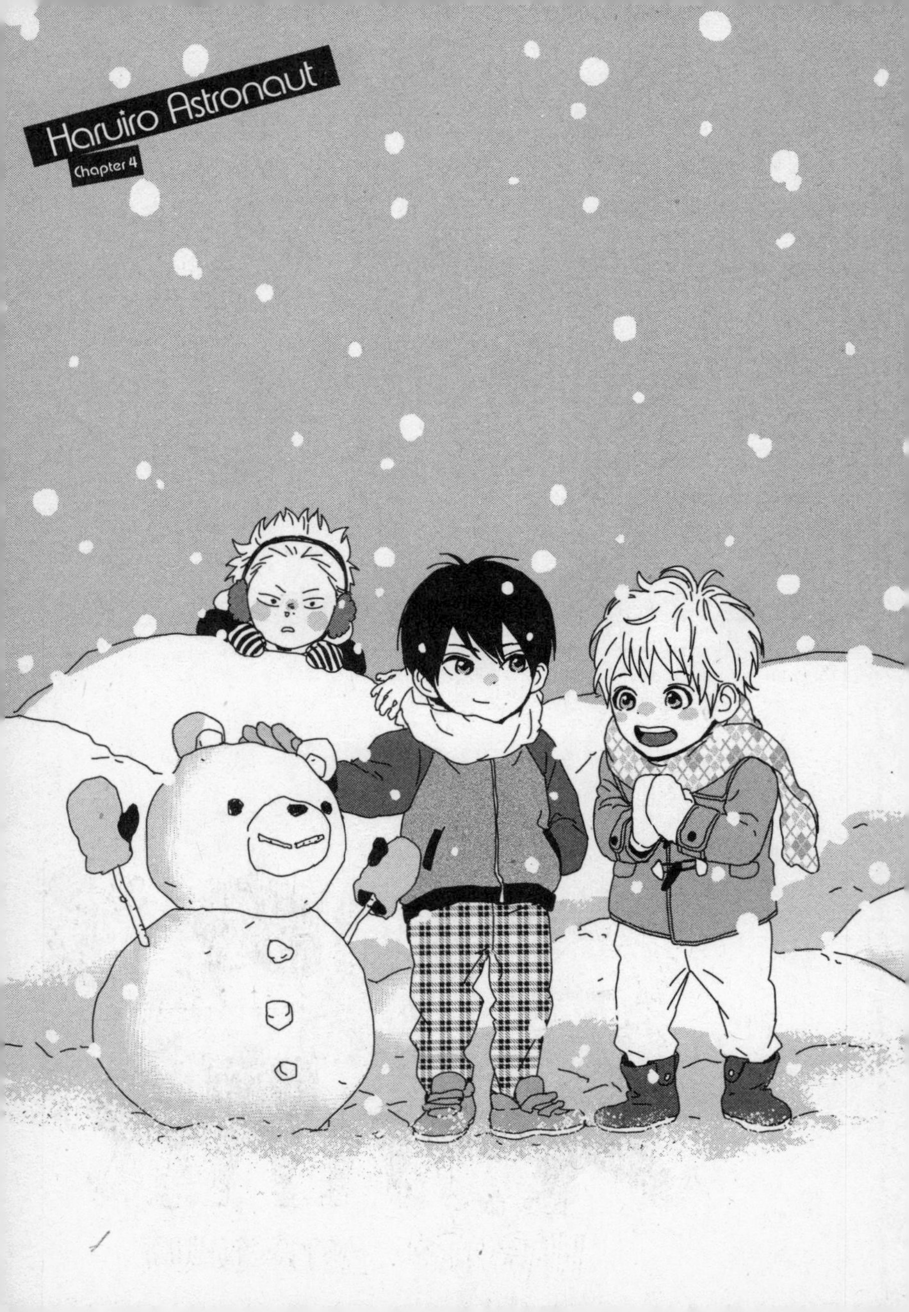
Haruiro Astronaut
Chapter 4

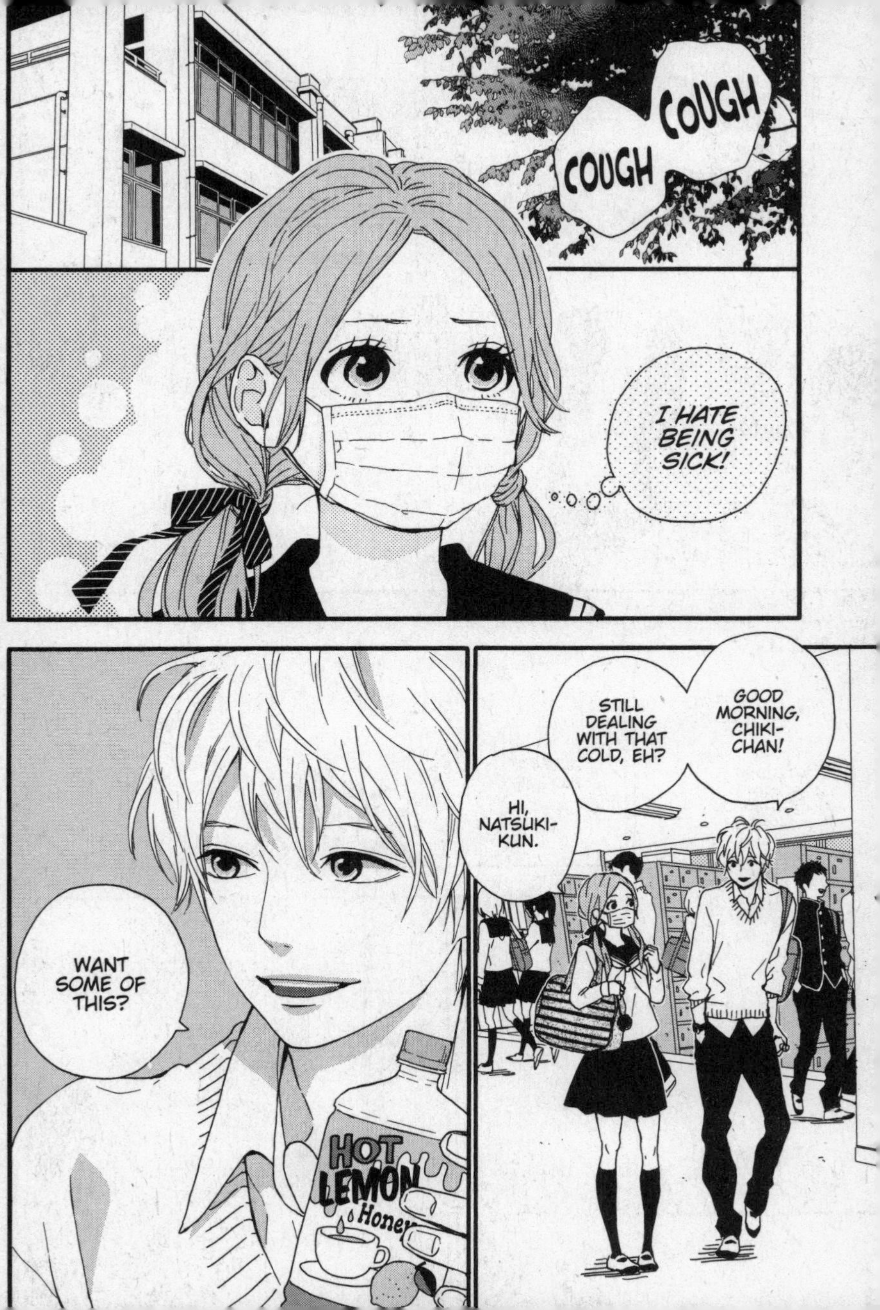
COUGH
COUGH
I HATE BEING SICK!
GOOD MORNING, CHIKI-CHAN!
STILL DEALING WITH THAT COLD, EH?
HI, NATSUKI-KUN.
WANT SOME OF THIS?
HOT LEMON
Honey

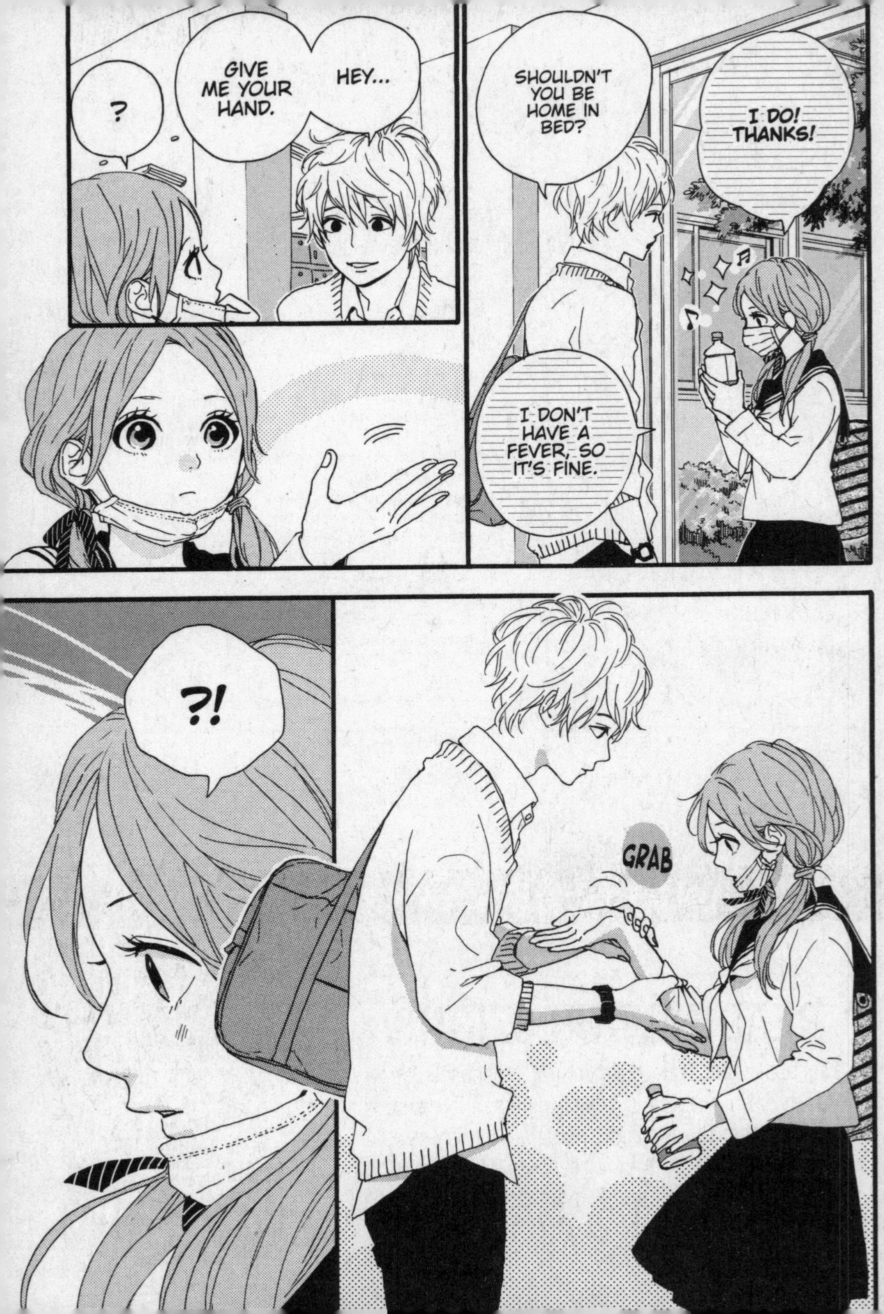
I DO! THANKS!
SHOULDN'T YOU BE HOME IN BED?
I DON'T HAVE A FEVER, SO IT'S FINE.
HEY...
GIVE ME YOUR HAND.
?
GRAB
?!

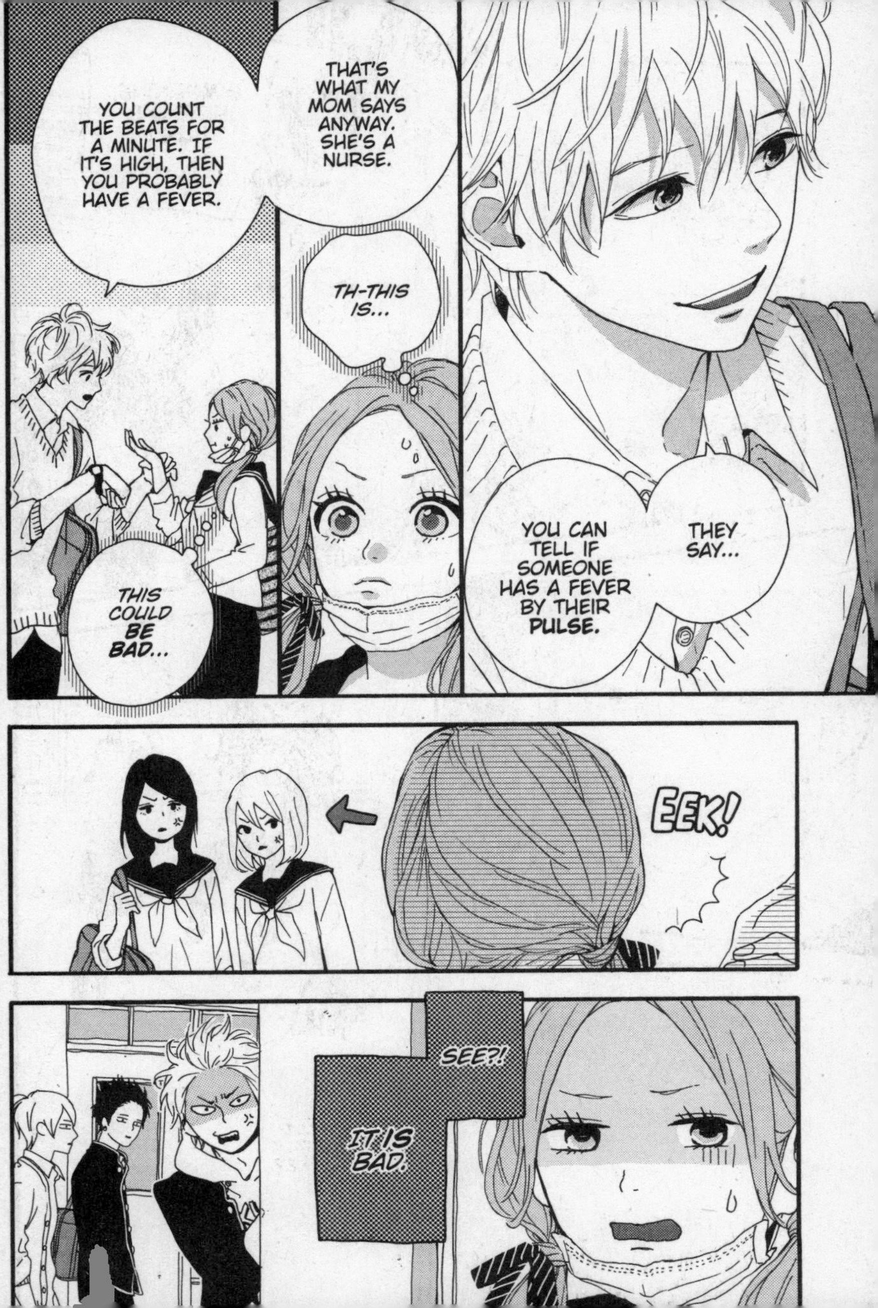
THEY SAY...
YOU CAN TELL IF SOMEONE HAS A FEVER BY THEIR PULSE.
YOU COUNT THE BEATS FOR A MINUTE. IF IT'S HIGH, THEN YOU PROBABLY HAVE A FEVER.
THAT'S WHAT MY MOM SAYS ANYWAY. SHE'S A NURSE.
TH-THIS IS...
THIS COULD BE BAD...
EEK!
SEE?!
IT IS BAD.

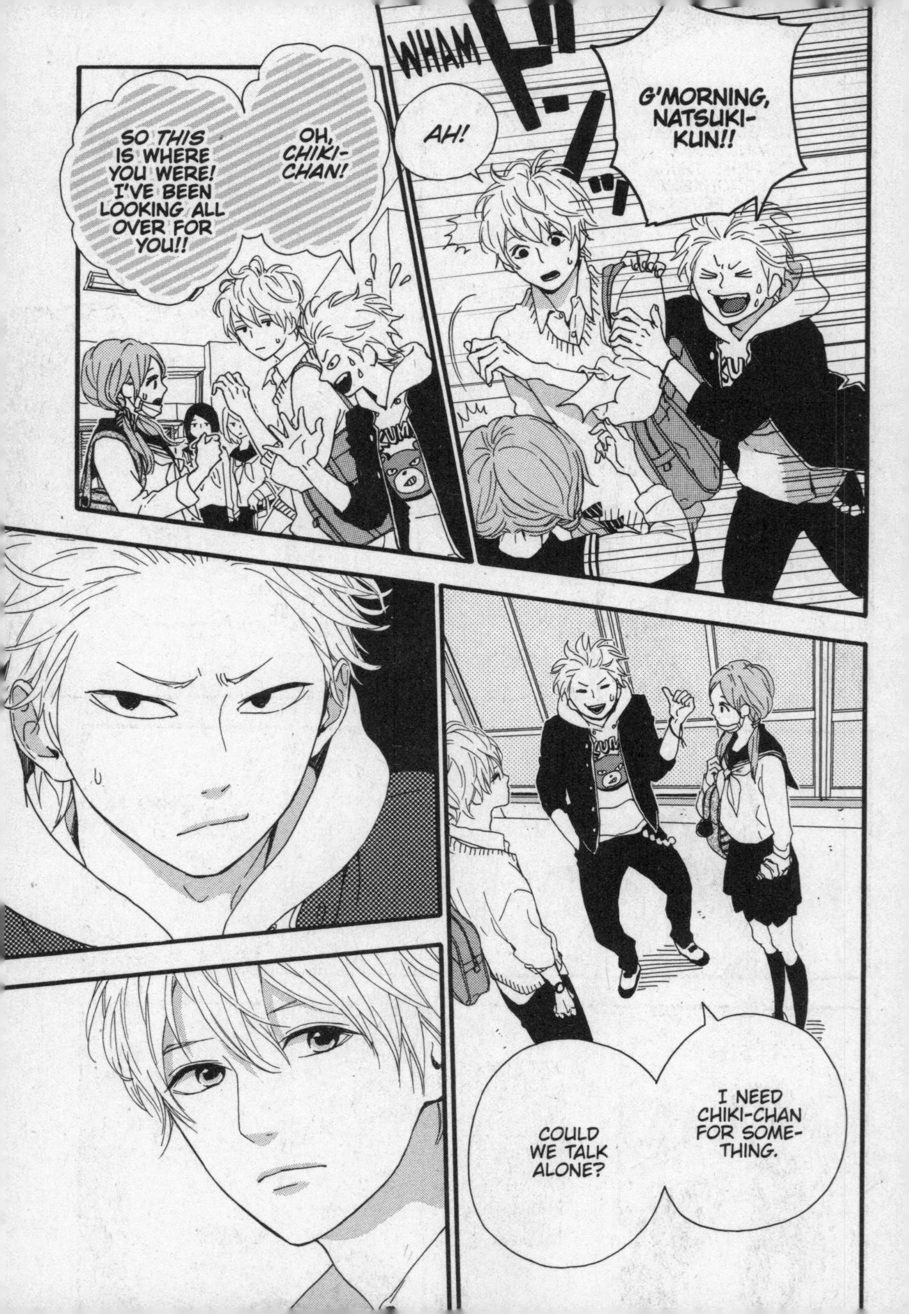
WHAM
G'MORNING, NATSUKI-KUN!!
AH!
OH, CHIKI-CHAN!
SO THIS IS WHERE YOU WERE! I'VE BEEN LOOKING ALL OVER FOR YOU!!
I NEED CHIKI-CHAN FOR SOME-THING.
COULD WE TALK ALONE?

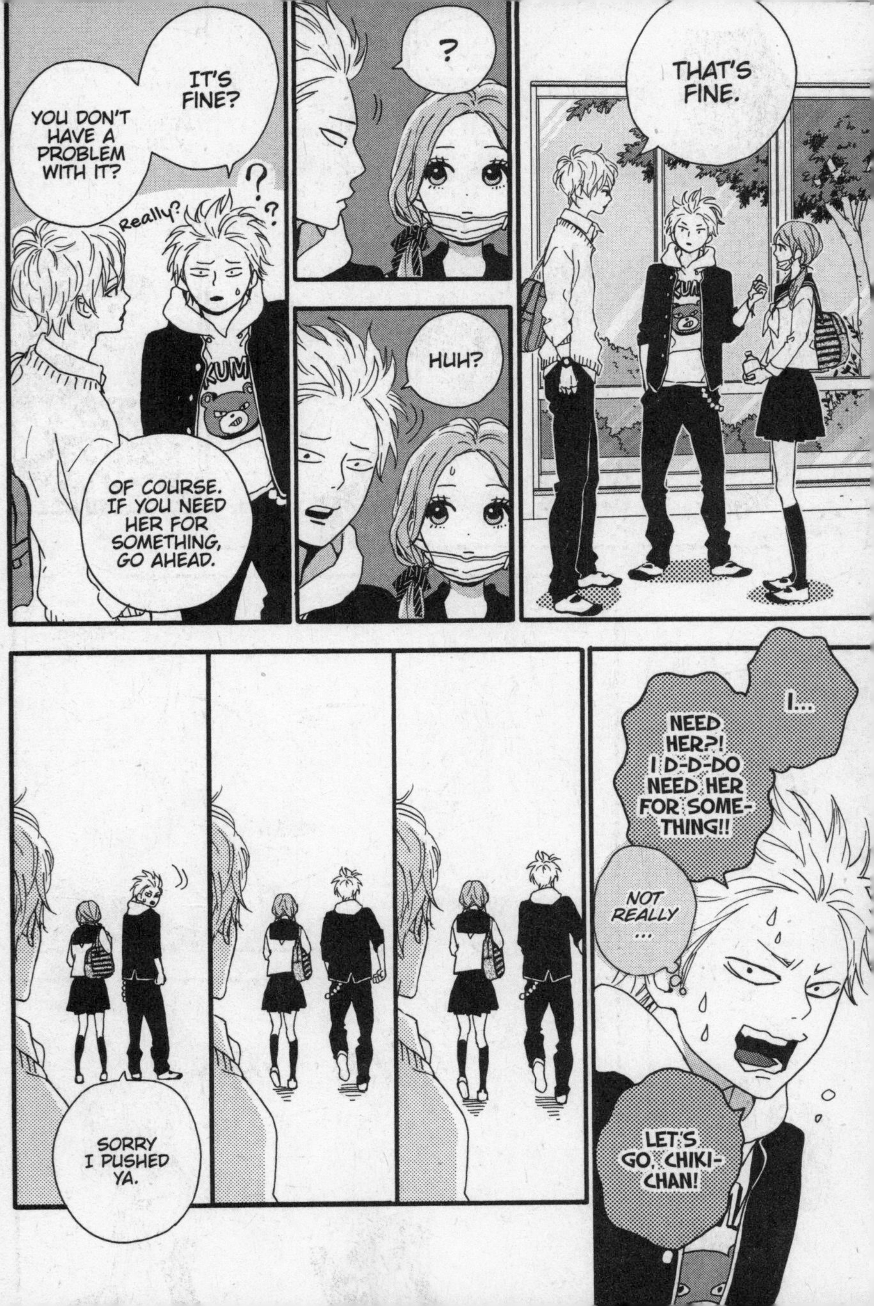
THAT'S FINE.
?
HUH?
IT'S FINE?
YOU DON'T HAVE A PROBLEM WITH IT?
Really?
? ?
OF COURSE. IF YOU NEED HER FOR SOMETHING, GO AHEAD.
I...
NEED HER?! I D-D-DO NEED HER FOR SOME-THING!!
NOT REALLY ...
LET'S GO, CHIKI-CHAN!
SORRY I PUSHED YA.

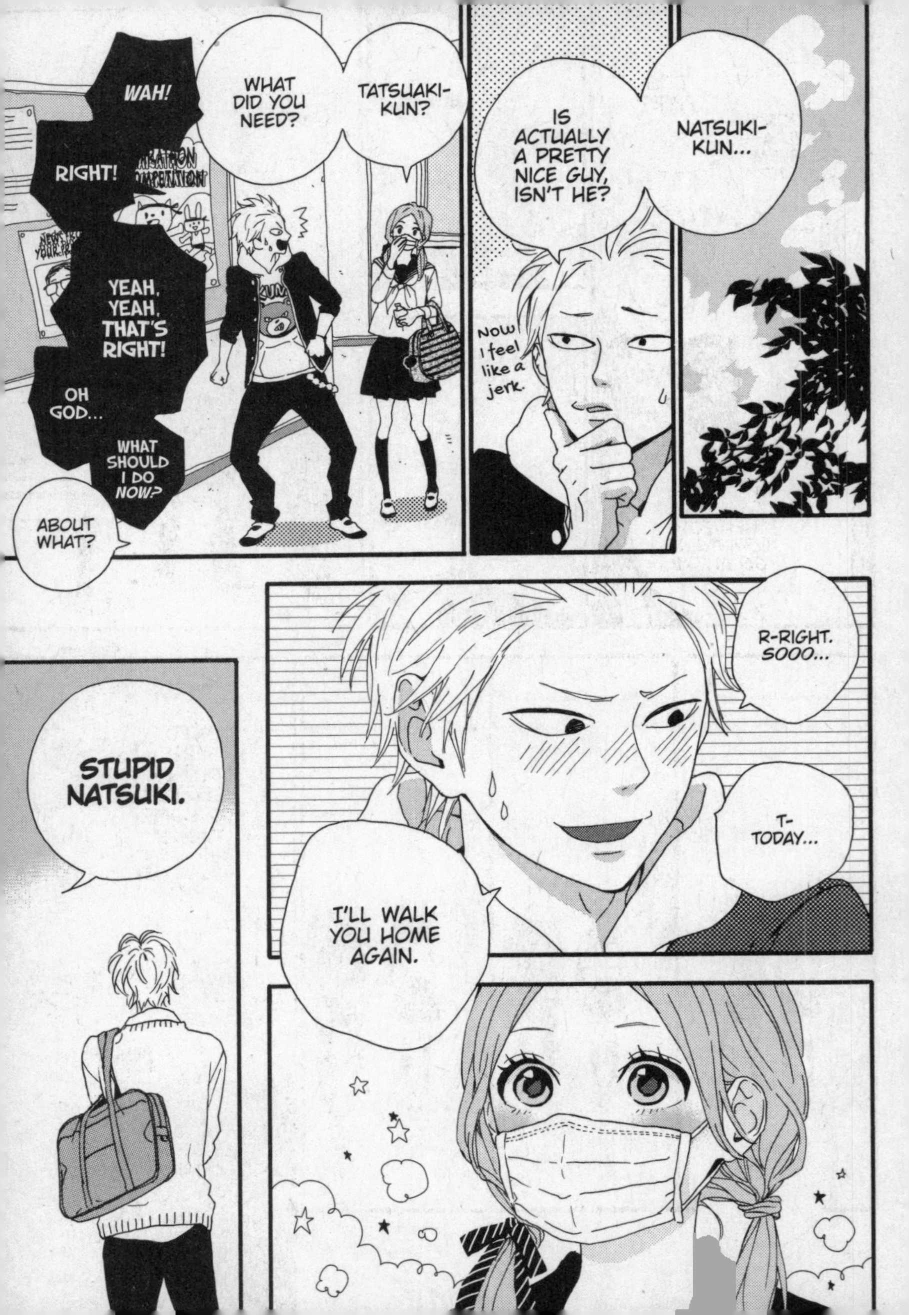
NATSUKI-KUN...
IS ACTUALLY A PRETTY NICE GUY, ISN'T HE?
Now I feel like a jerk.
TATSUAKI-KUN?
WHAT DID YOU NEED?
WAH!
RIGHT!
YEAH, YEAH, THAT'S RIGHT!
OH GOD...
WHAT SHOULD I DO NOW?
ABOUT WHAT?
R-RIGHT. SOOO...
T-TODAY...
I'LL WALK YOU HOME AGAIN.
STUPID NATSUKI.

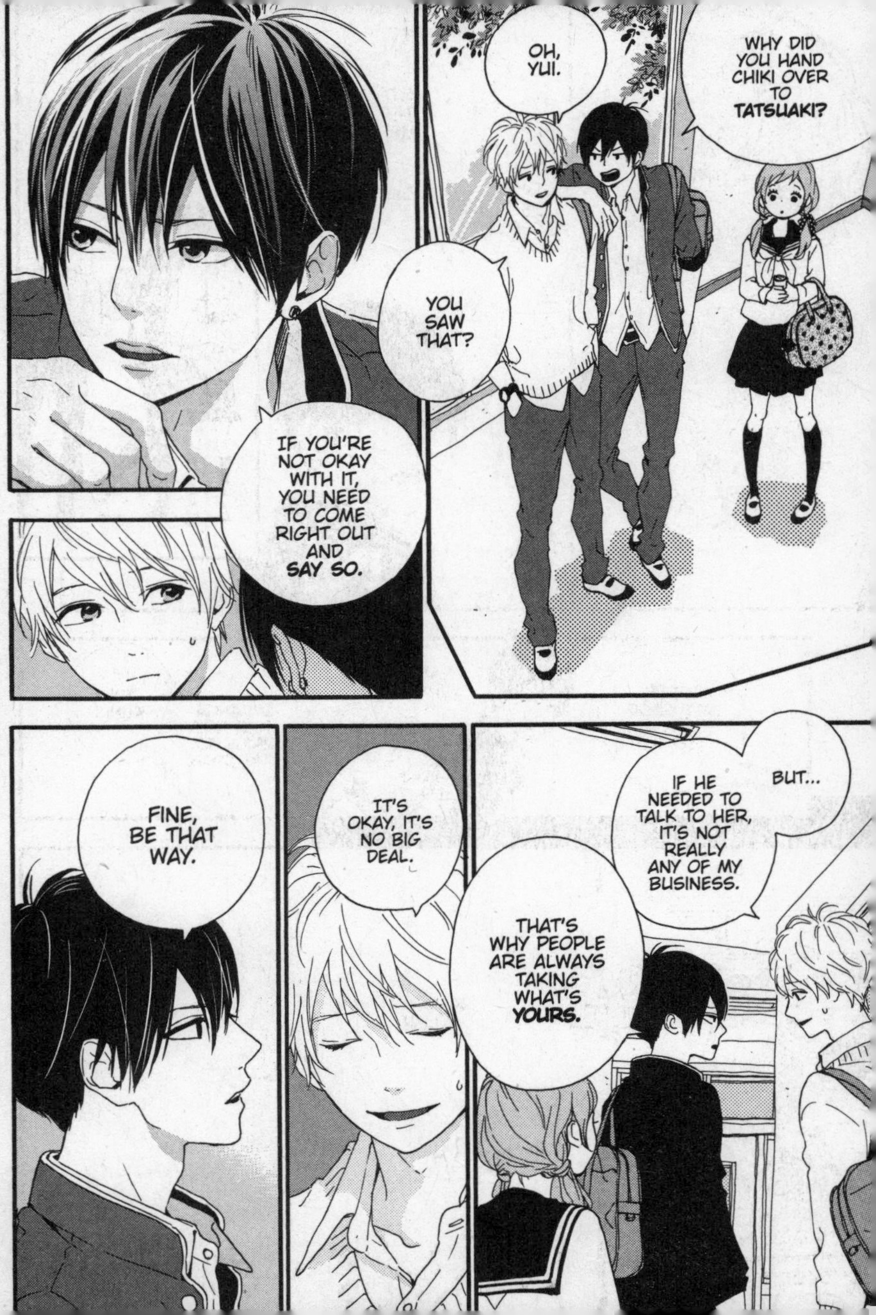
WHY DID YOU HAND CHIKI OVER TO TATSUAKI?
OH, YUI.
YOU SAW THAT?
IF YOU'RE NOT OKAY WITH IT, YOU NEED TO COME RIGHT OUT AND SAY SO.
BUT...
IF HE NEEDED TO TALK TO HER, IT'S NOT REALLY ANY OF MY BUSINESS.
THAT'S WHY PEOPLE ARE ALWAYS TAKING WHAT'S YOURS.
IT'S OKAY, IT'S NO BIG DEAL.
FINE, BE THAT WAY.

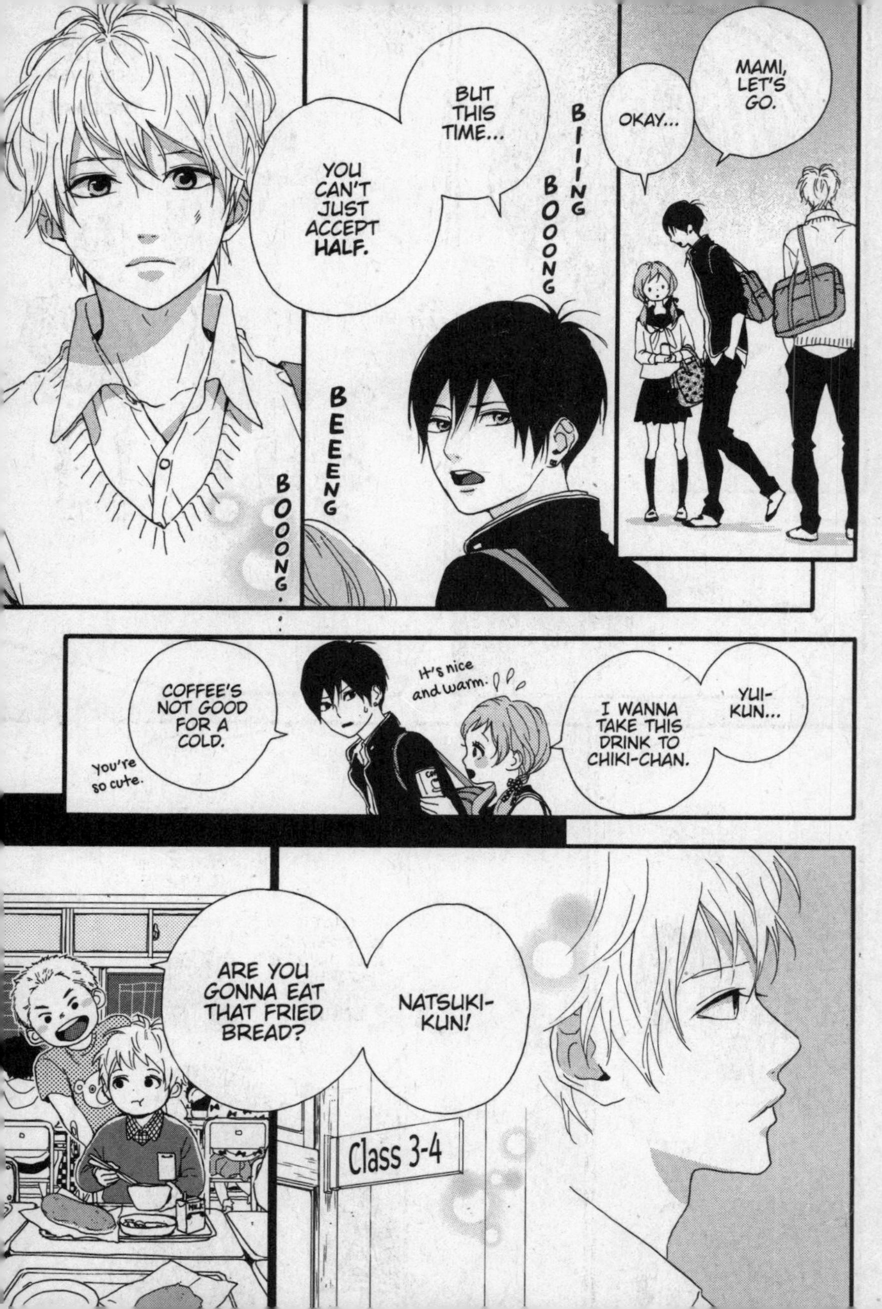
MAMI, LET'S GO.
OKAY...
BUT THIS TIME...
YOU CAN'T JUST ACCEPT HALF.
BIIING
BOOONG
BEEEENG
BOOONG...
YUI-KUN...
I WANNA TAKE THIS DRINK TO CHIKI-CHAN.
It's nice and warm.
COFFEE'S NOT GOOD FOR A COLD.
You're so cute.
NATSUKI-KUN!
ARE YOU GONNA EAT THAT FRIED BREAD?
Class 3-4

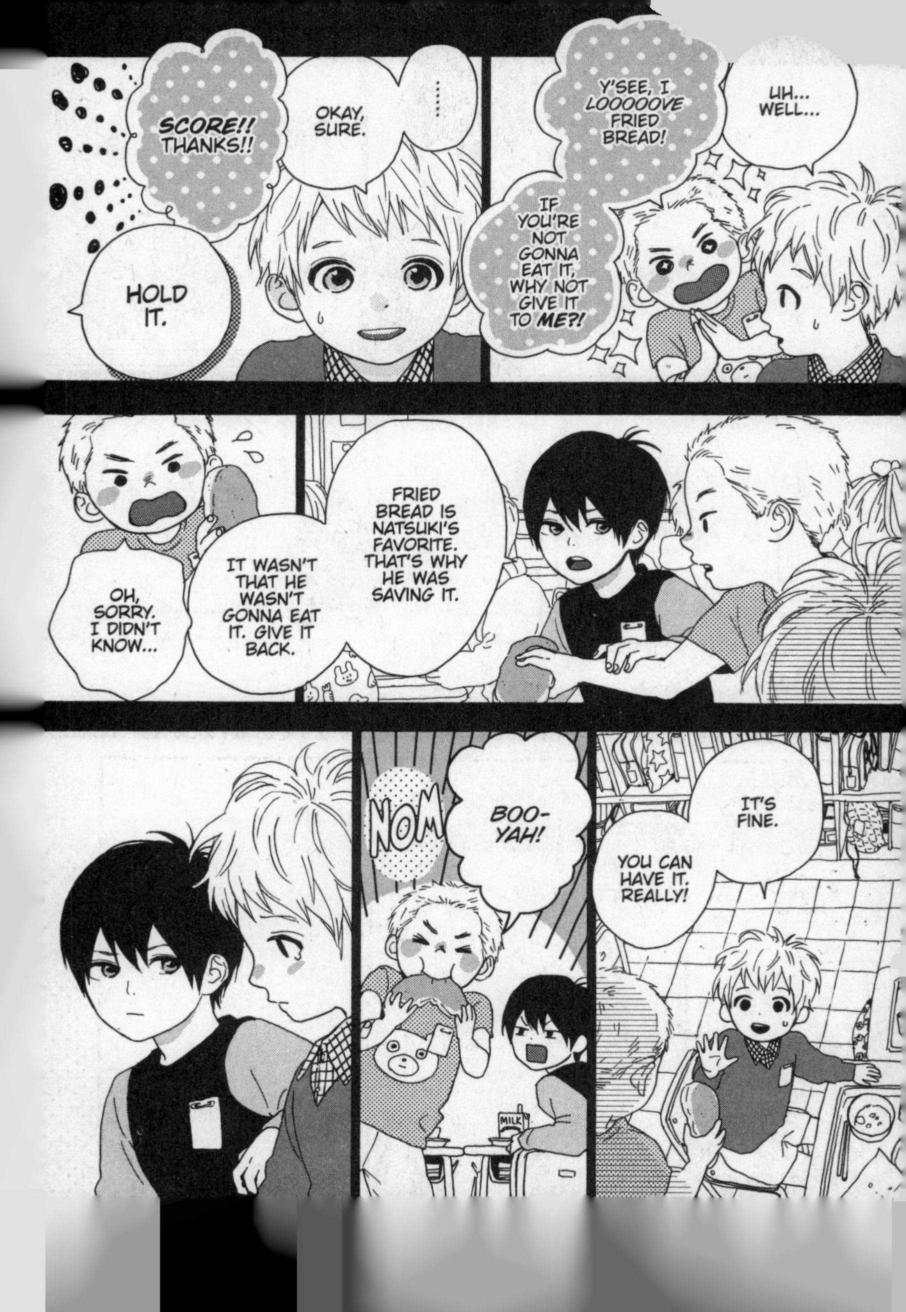
UH... WELL...
Y'SEE, I LOOOOOVE FRIED BREAD!
IF YOU'RE NOT GONNA EAT IT, WHY NOT GIVE IT TO ME?!
......
OKAY, SURE.
SCORE!! THANKS!!
HOLD IT.
FRIED BREAD IS NATSUKI'S FAVORITE. THAT'S WHY HE WAS SAVING IT.
IT WASN'T THAT HE WASN'T GONNA EAT IT. GIVE IT BACK.
OH, SORRY. I DIDN'T KNOW...
IT'S FINE.
YOU CAN HAVE IT. REALLY!
BOO-YAH!
NOM
MILK

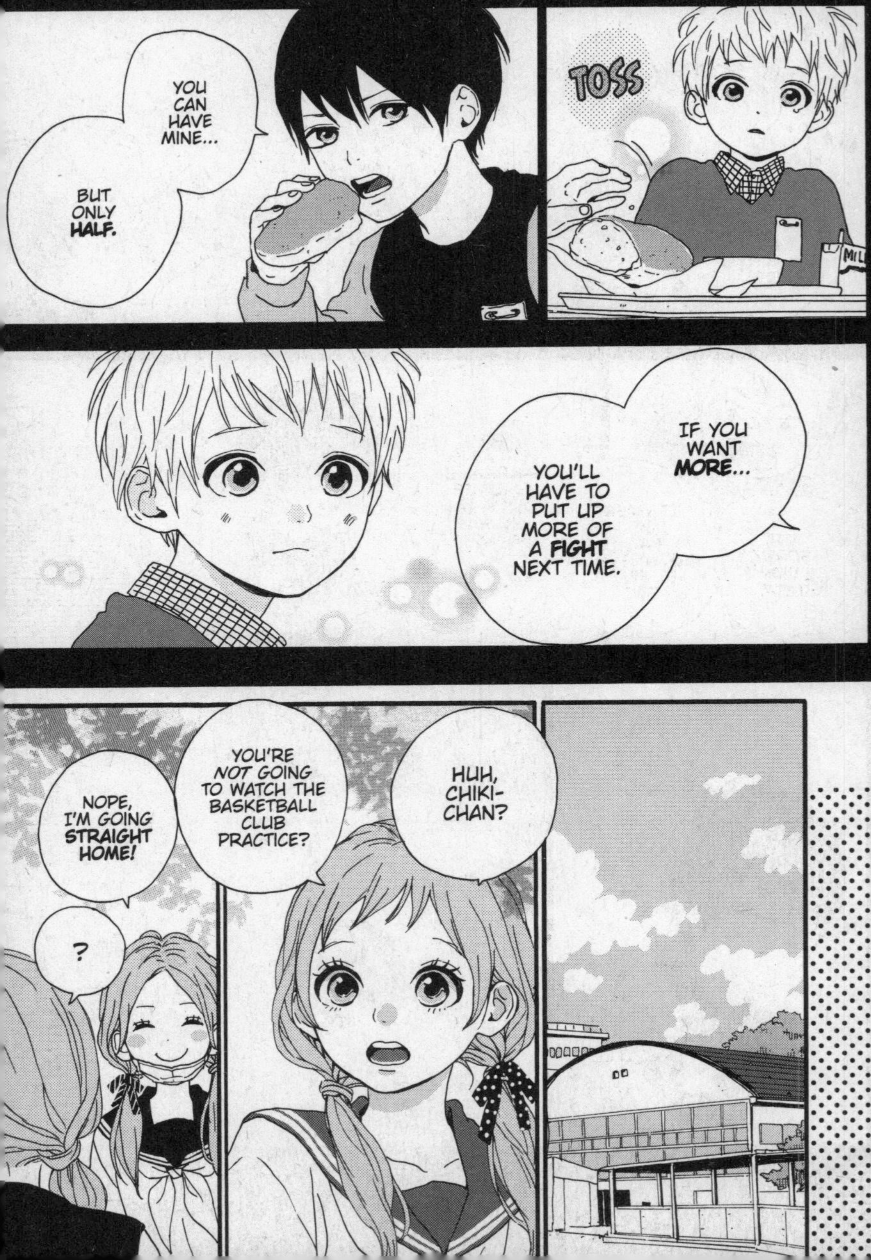
TOSS
YOU CAN HAVE MINE...
BUT ONLY HALF.
IF YOU WANT MORE...
YOU'LL HAVE TO PUT UP MORE OF A FIGHT NEXT TIME.
HUH, CHIKI-CHAN?
YOU'RE NOT GOING TO WATCH THE BASKETBALL CLUB PRACTICE?
NOPE, I'M GOING STRAIGHT HOME!
?

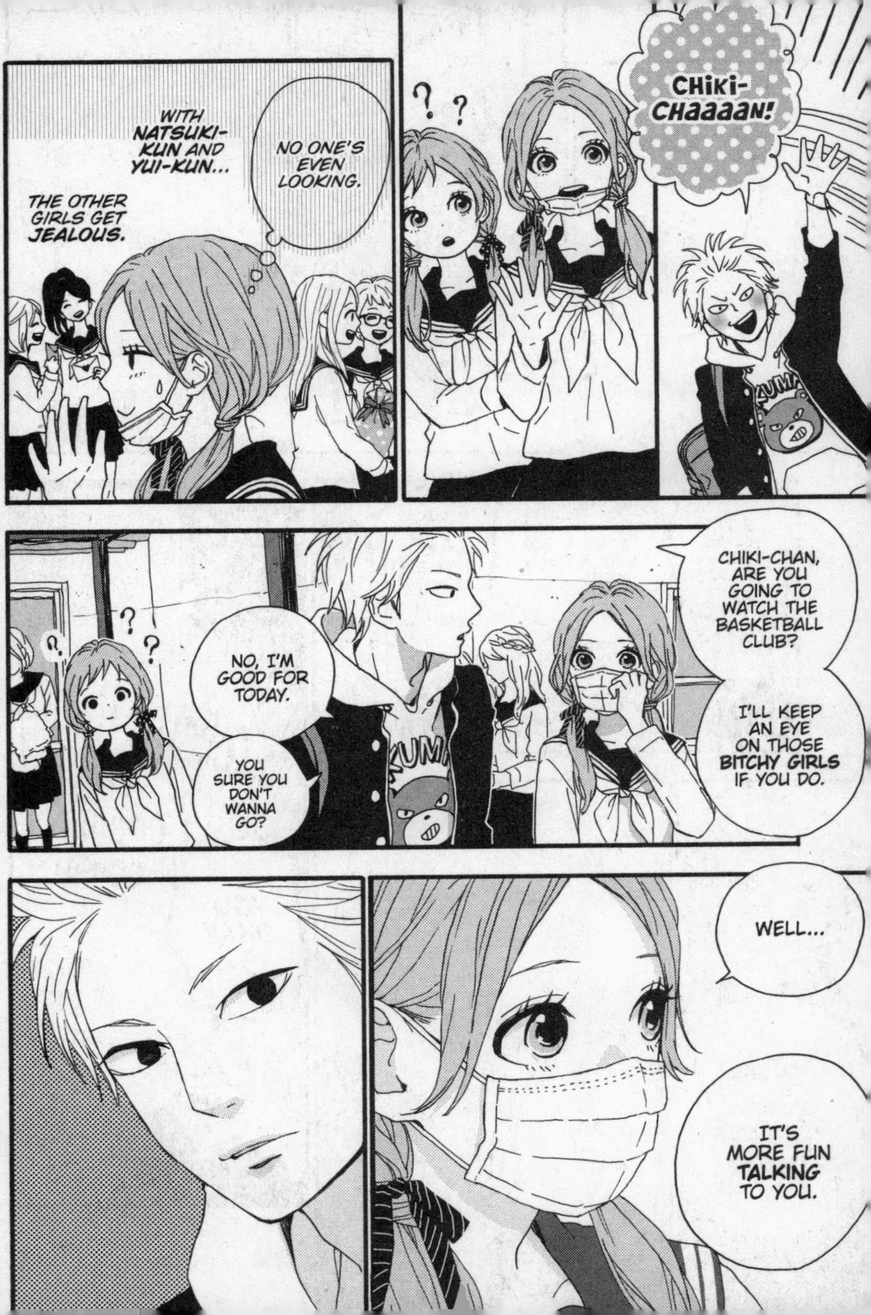
CHIKI-CHAaaaAN!
NO ONE'S EVEN LOOKING.
WITH NATSUKI-KUN AND YUI-KUN...
THE OTHER GIRLS GET JEALOUS.
CHIKI-CHAN, ARE YOU GOING TO WATCH THE BASKETBALL CLUB?
I'LL KEEP AN EYE ON THOSE BITCHY GIRLS IF YOU DO.
NO, I'M GOOD FOR TODAY.
YOU SURE YOU DON'T WANNA GO?
WELL...
IT'S MORE FUN TALKING TO YOU.

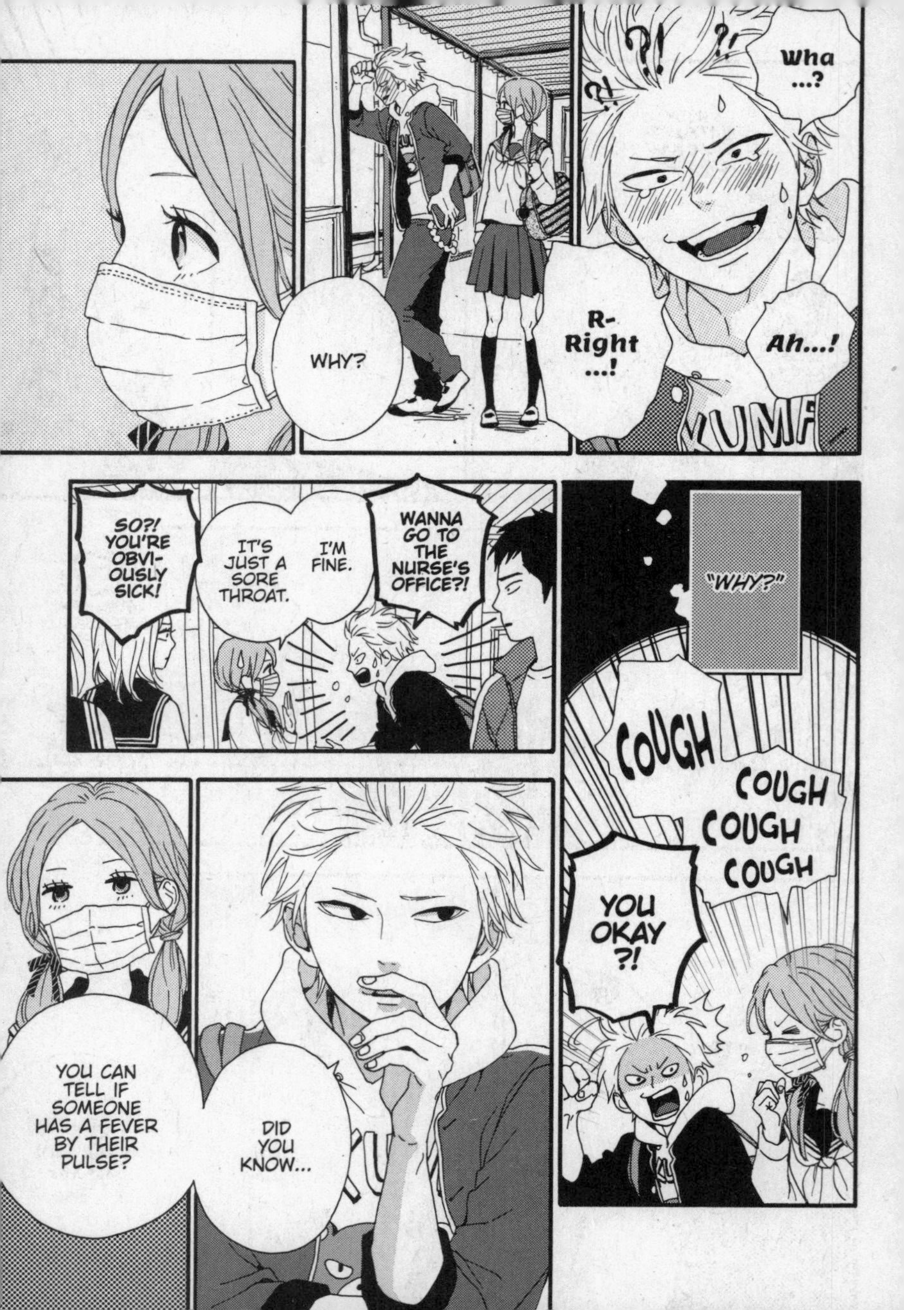
?!
?!
?!
Wha ...?
Ah...!
R-Right ...!
WHY?
"WHY?"
COUGH
COUGH
COUGH
COUGH
YOU OKAY ?!
WANNA GO TO THE NURSE'S OFFICE?!
I'M FINE.
IT'S JUST A SORE THROAT.
SO?! YOU'RE OBVI-OUSLY SICK!
DID YOU KNOW...
YOU CAN TELL IF SOMEONE HAS A FEVER BY THEIR PULSE?

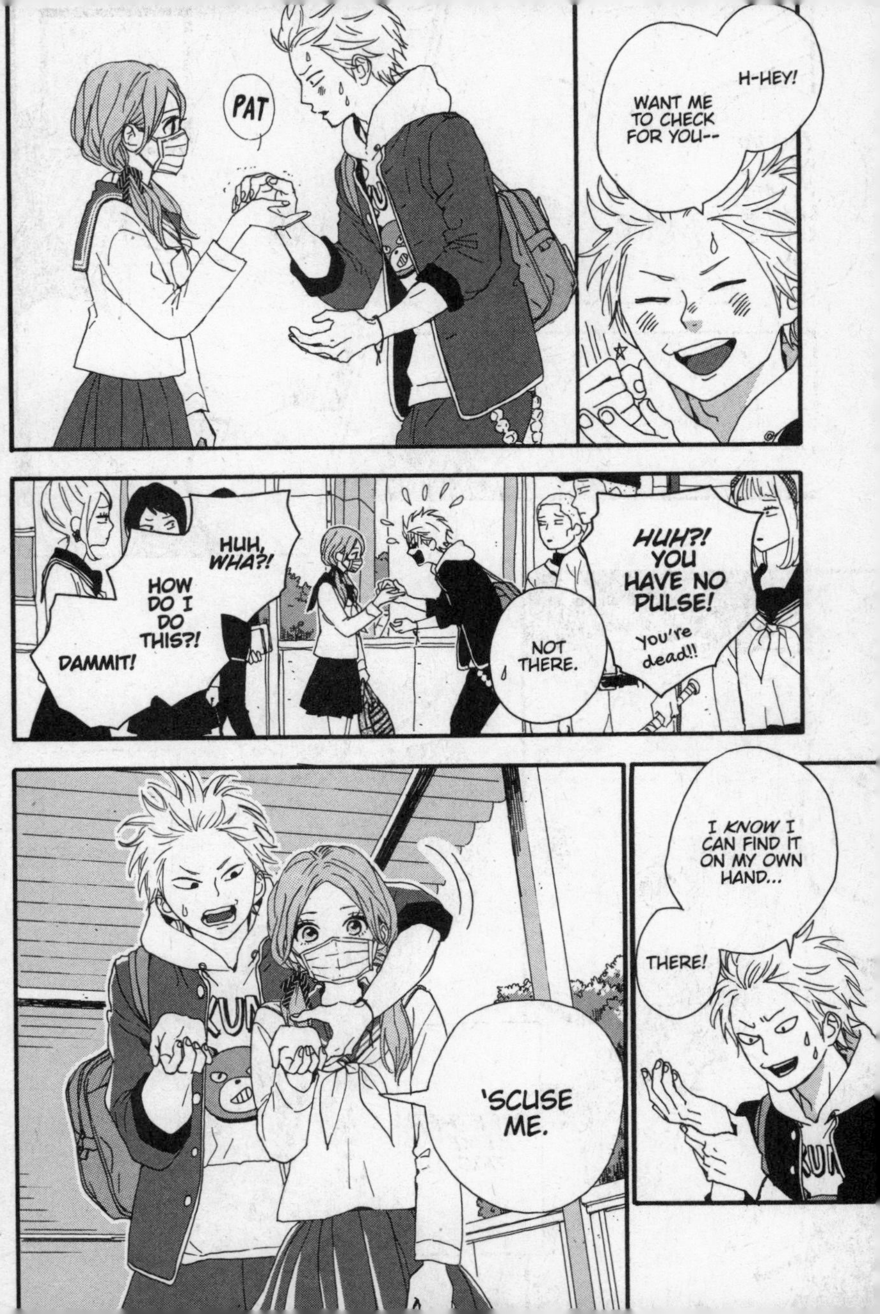
H-HEY!
WANT ME TO CHECK FOR YOU--
PAT
HUH?! YOU HAVE NO PULSE!
You're dead!!
NOT THERE.
HUH, WHA?!
HOW DO I DO THIS?!
DAMMIT!
I *KNOW* I CAN FIND IT ON MY OWN HAND...
THERE!
'SCUSE ME.

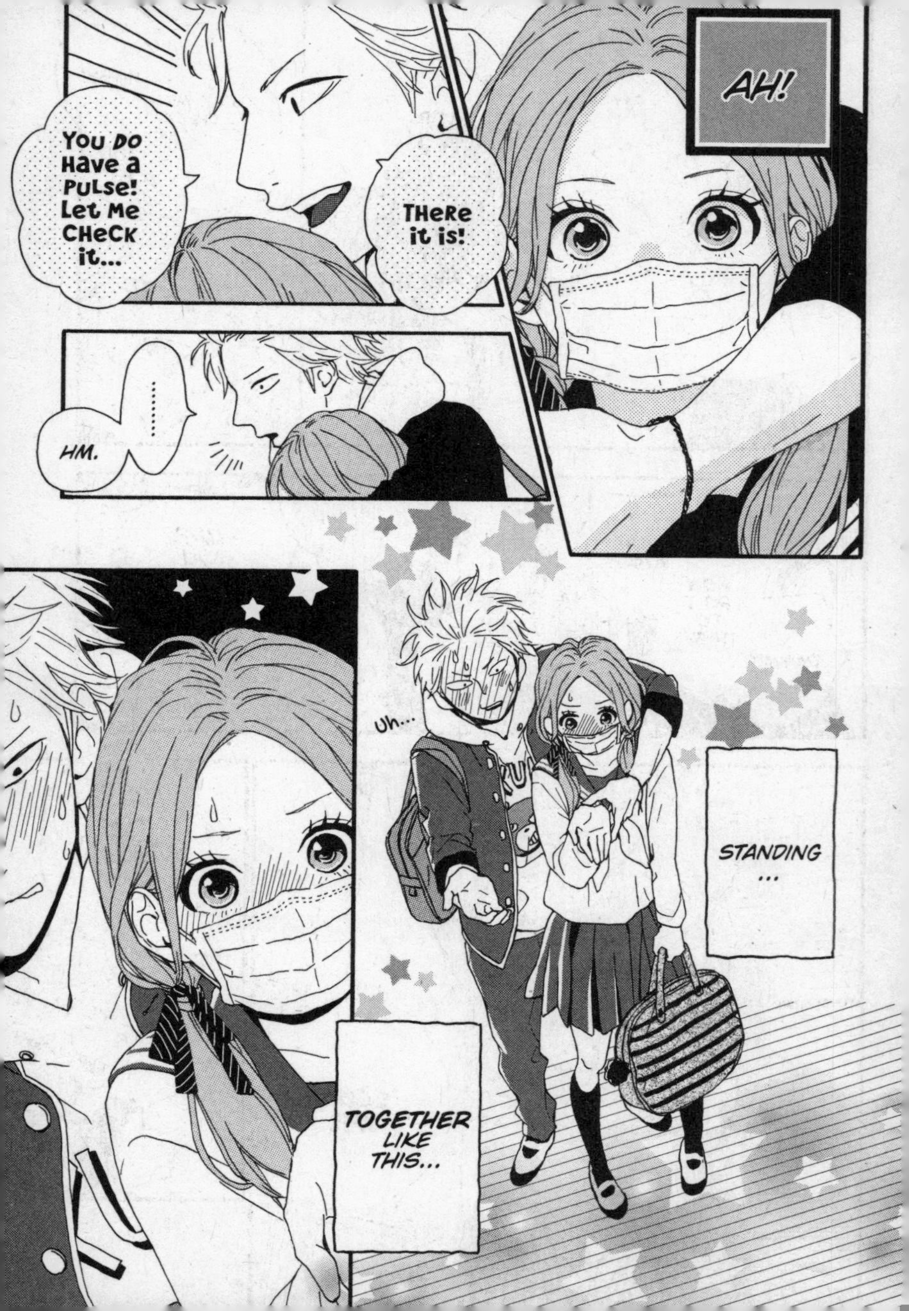
AH!
There it is!
You DO Have a Pulse! Let Me Check it...
......
HM.
STANDING ...
Uh...
TOGETHER LIKE THIS...

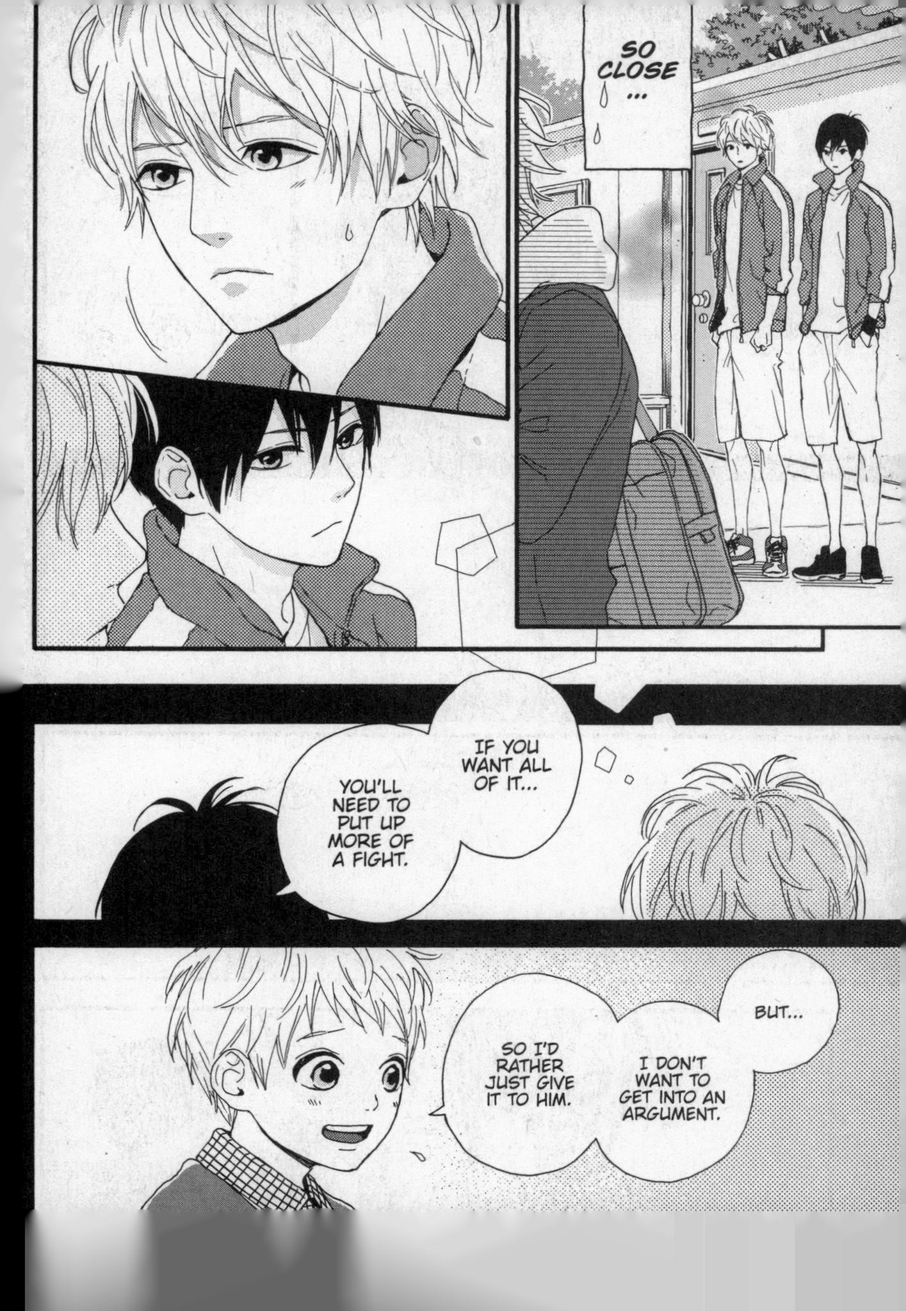
SO CLOSE ...
IF YOU WANT ALL OF IT...
YOU'LL NEED TO PUT UP MORE OF A FIGHT.
BUT...
I DON'T WANT TO GET INTO AN ARGUMENT.
SO I'D RATHER JUST GIVE IT TO HIM.

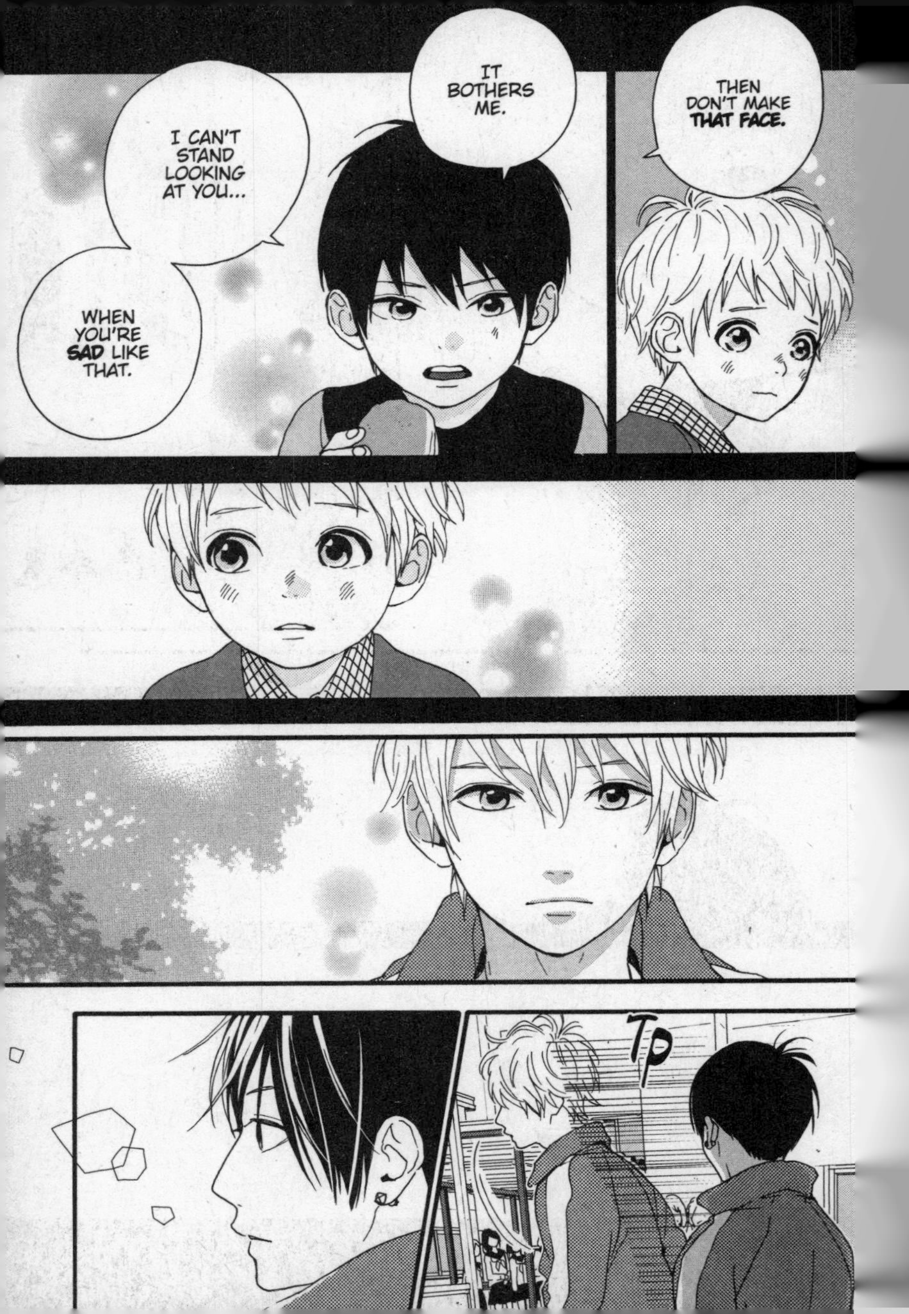

THEN DON'T MAKE THAT FACE.
IT BOTHERS ME.
I CAN'T STAND LOOKING AT YOU...
WHEN YOU'RE SAD LIKE THAT.
TP

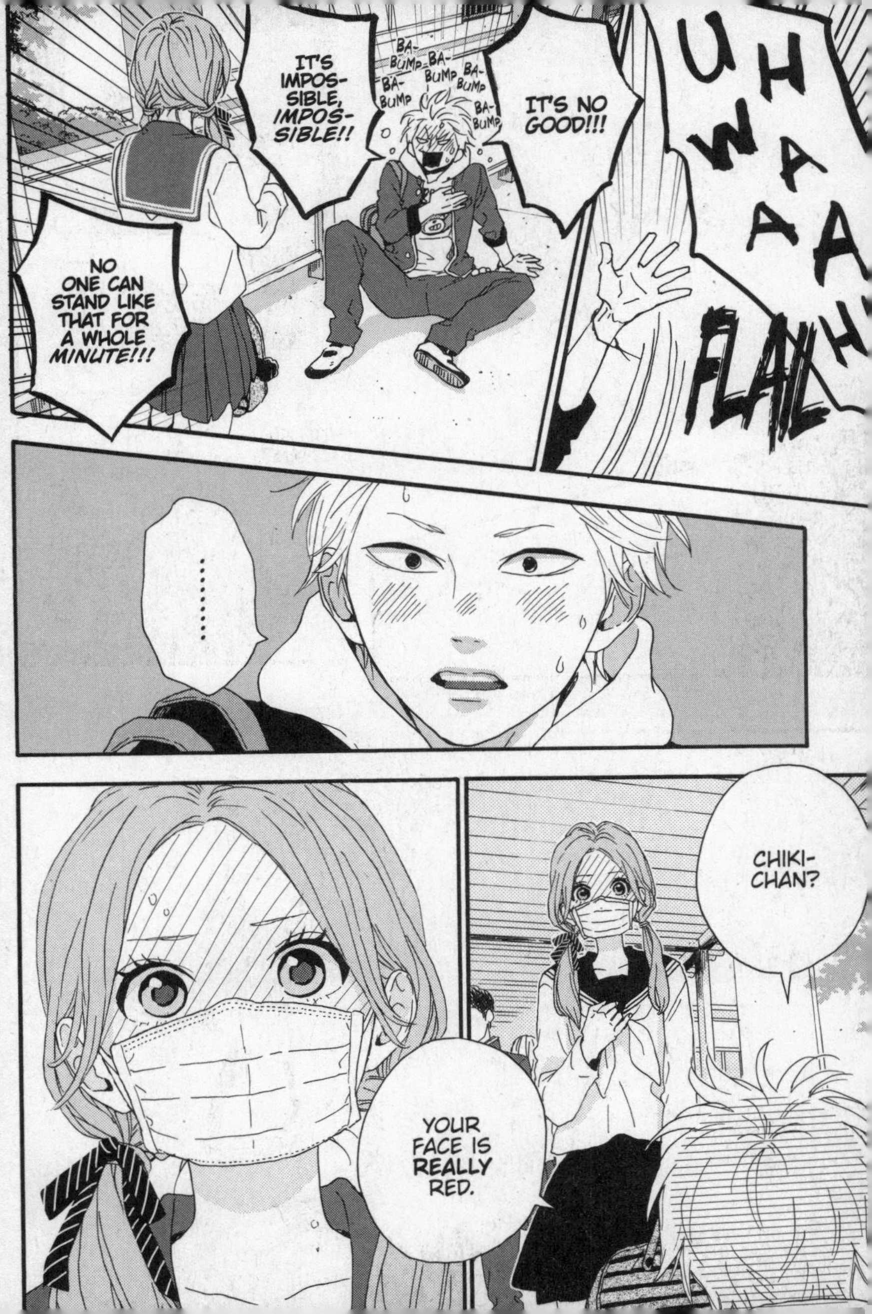
UHWAAAH
FLAIL
IT'S NO GOOD!!!
BA-BUMP BA-BUMP BA-BUMP BA-BUMP BA-BUMP
IT'S IMPOSSIBLE, IMPOSSIBLE!!
NO ONE CAN STAND LIKE THAT FOR A WHOLE MINUTE!!!
......
CHIKI-CHAN?
YOUR FACE IS REALLY RED.

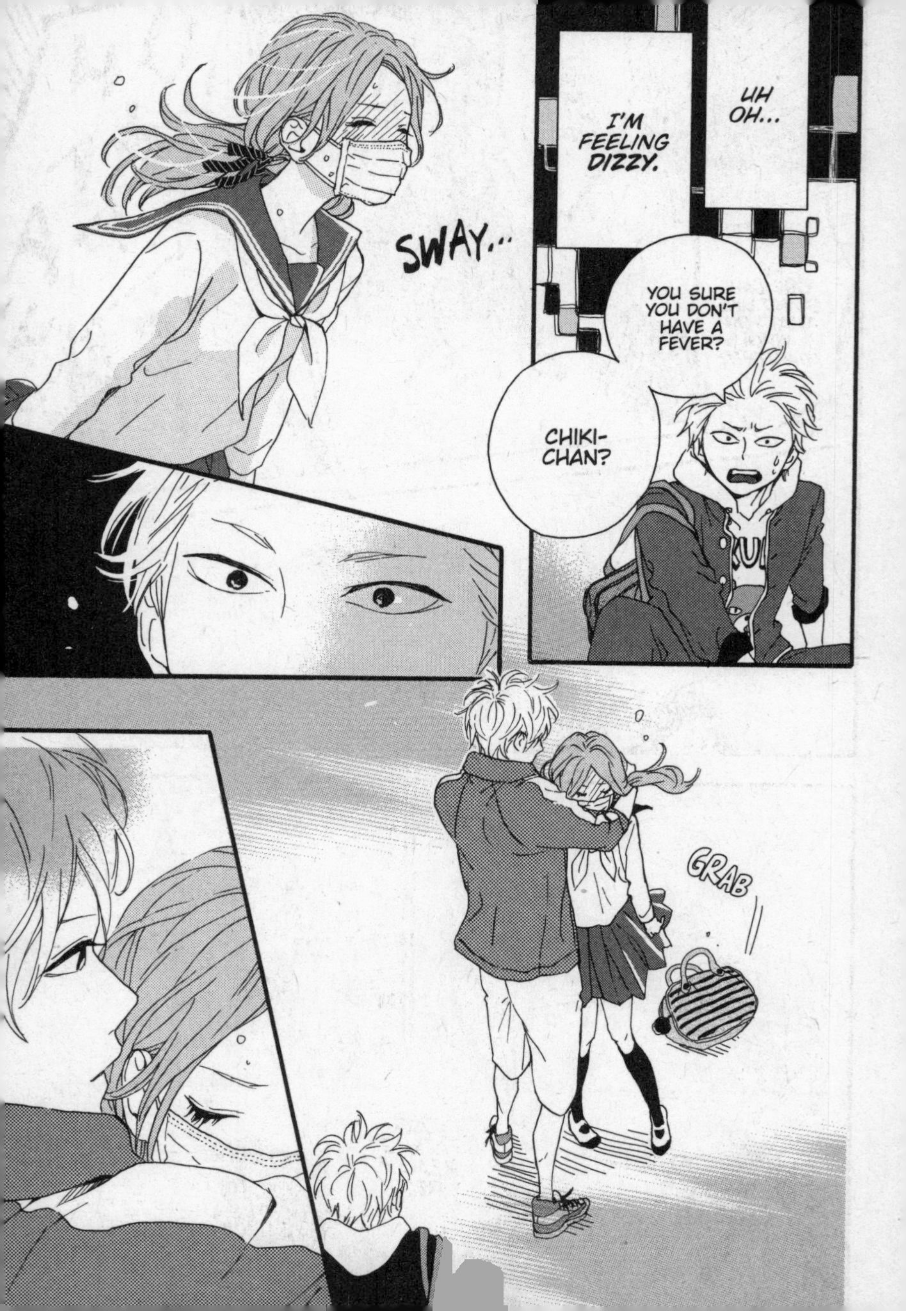
UH OH...
I'M FEELING DIZZY.
YOU SURE YOU DON'T HAVE A FEVER?
CHIKI-CHAN?
SWAY...
GRAB

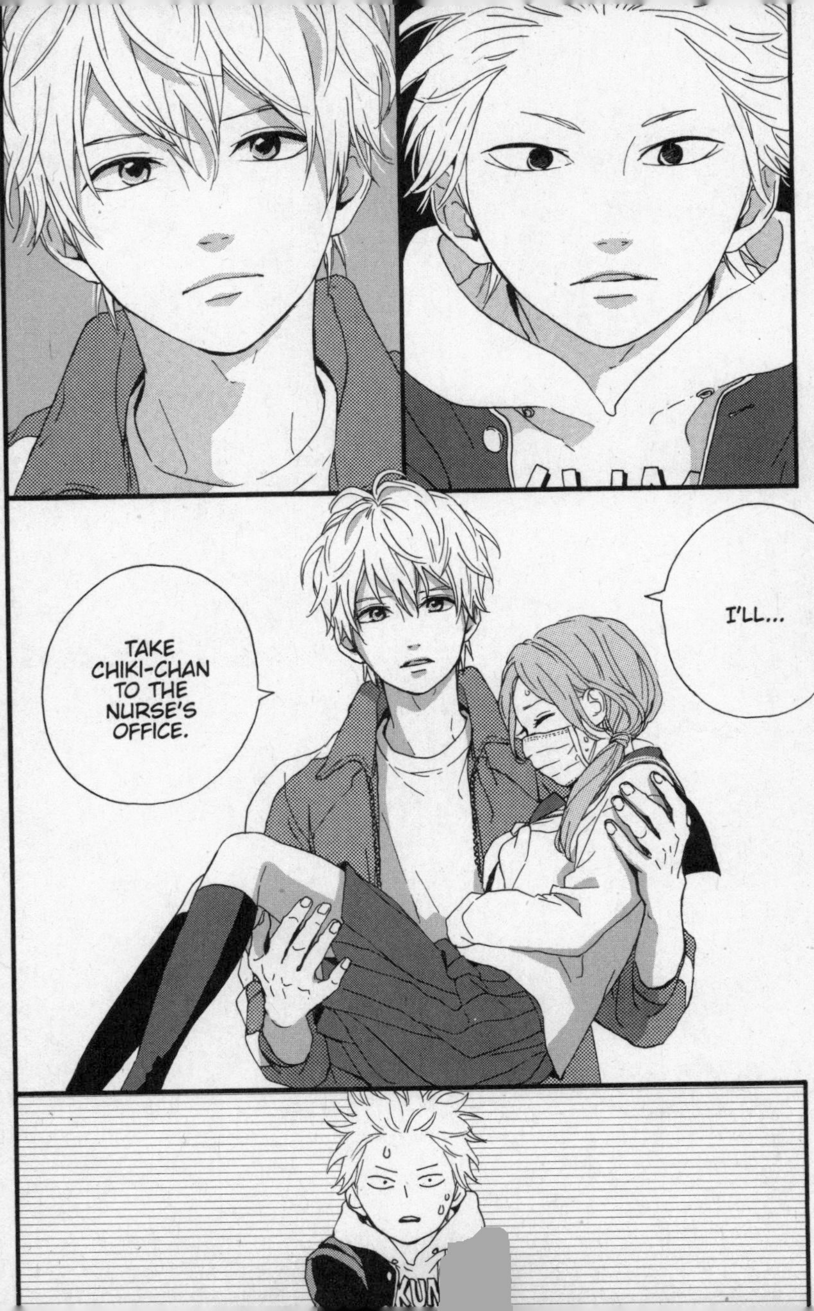
I'LL...
TAKE CHIKI-CHAN TO THE NURSE'S OFFICE.

Haruiro
Astronaut

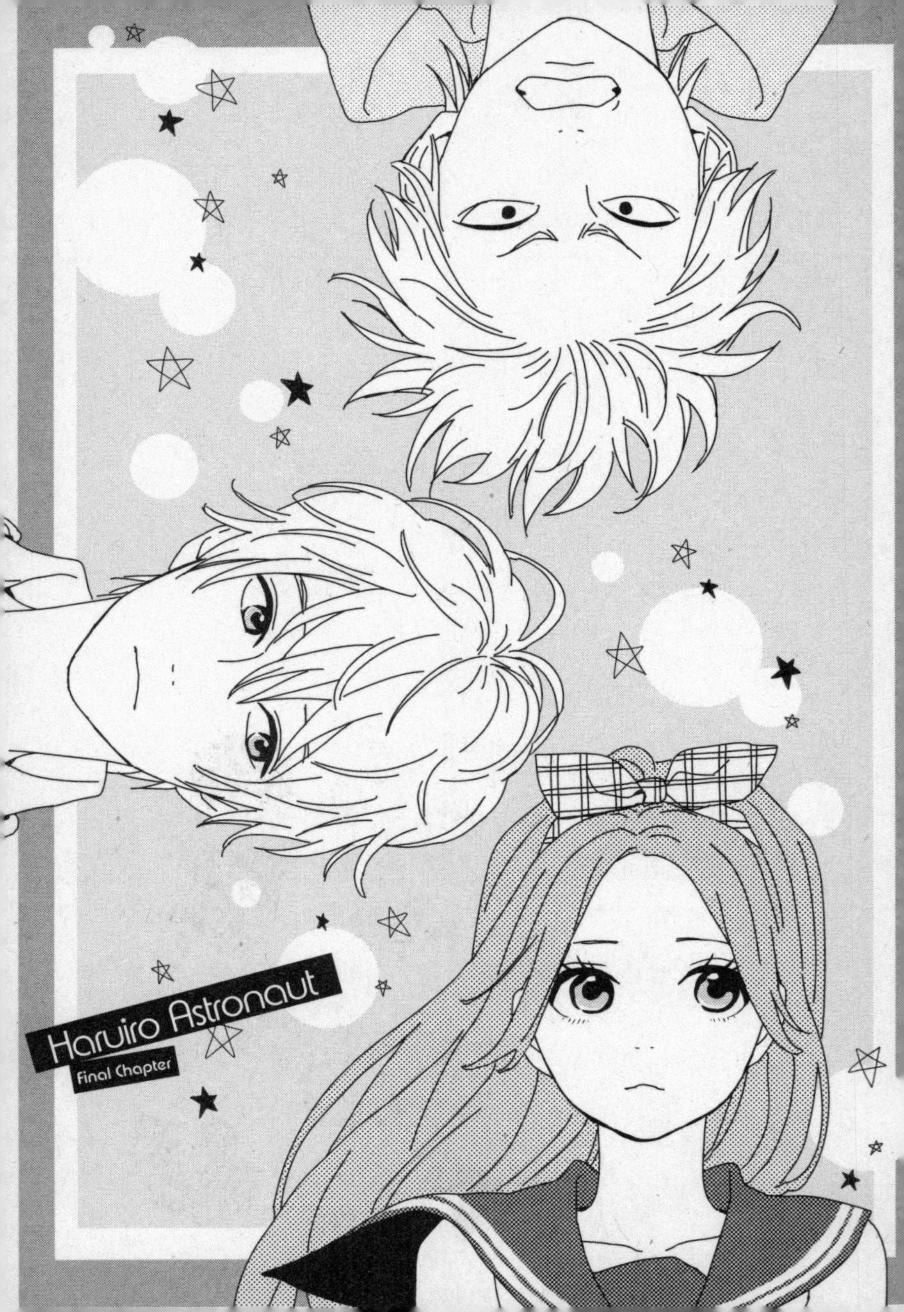
Haruiro Astronaut
Final Chapter

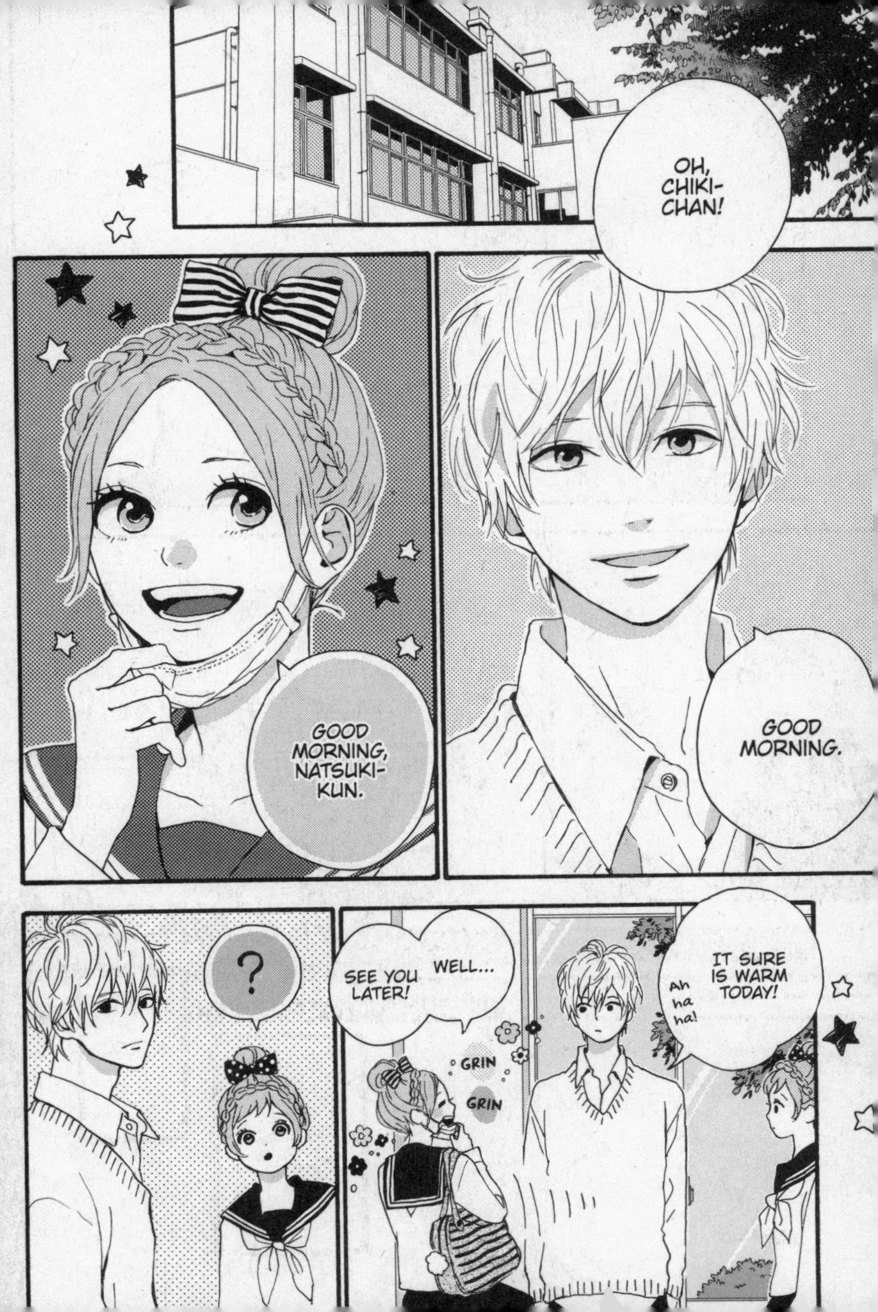
OH, CHIKI-CHAN!
GOOD MORNING.
GOOD MORNING, NATSUKI-KUN.
IT SURE IS WARM TODAY!
Ah ha ha!
WELL...
SEE YOU LATER!
GRIN
GRIN
?

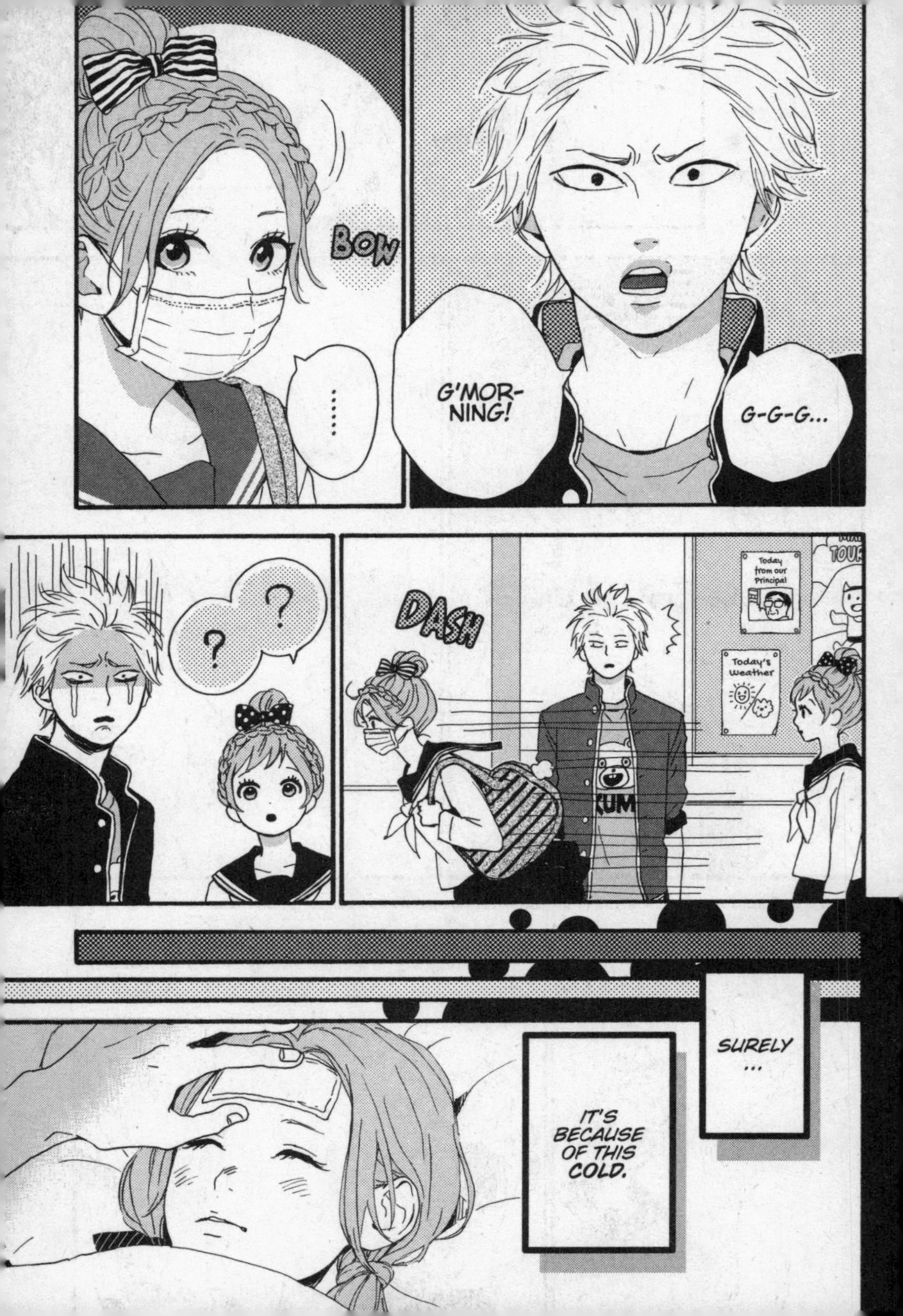
G-G-G...
G'MORNING!
BOW
......
Today from our Principal
Today's Weather
DASH
KUM
?
?
SURELY ...
IT'S BECAUSE OF THIS COLD.

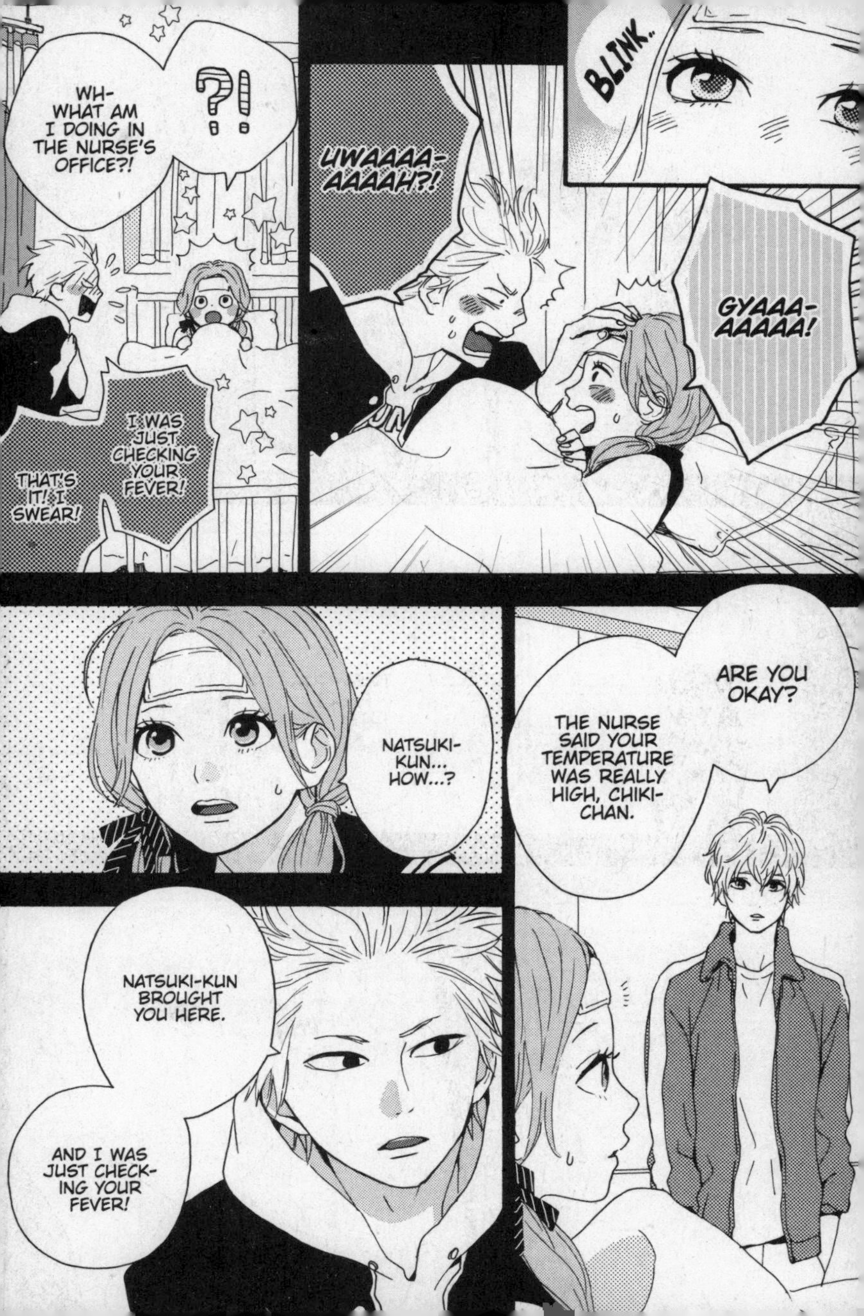
BLINK..
GYAAA-AAAAA!
UWAAAA-AAAAH?!
?!
WH-WHAT AM I DOING IN THE NURSE'S OFFICE?!
I WAS JUST CHECKING YOUR FEVER!
THAT'S IT! I SWEAR!
ARE YOU OKAY?
THE NURSE SAID YOUR TEMPERATURE WAS REALLY HIGH, CHIKI-CHAN.
NATSUKI-KUN... HOW...?
NATSUKI-KUN BROUGHT YOU HERE.
AND I WAS JUST CHECKING YOUR FEVER!

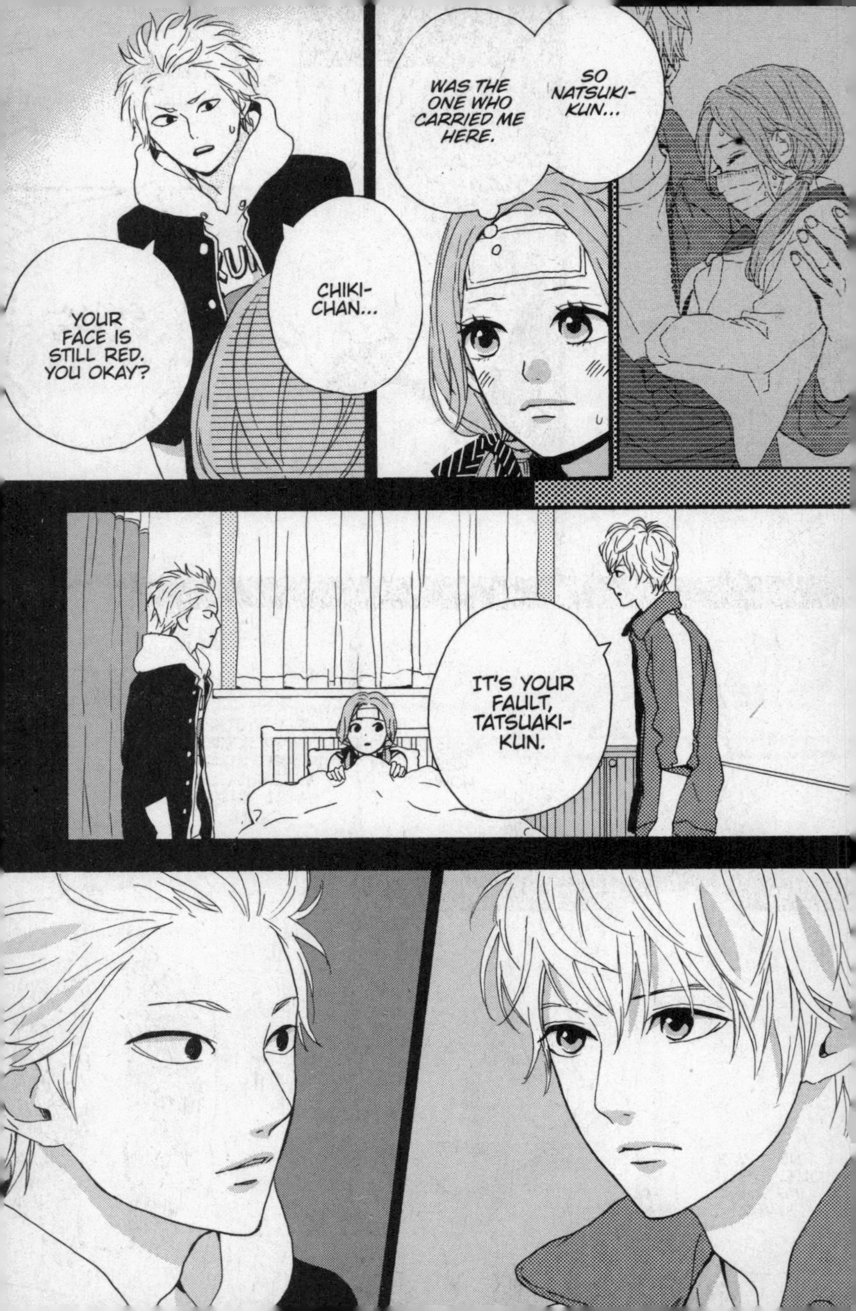
SO NATSUKI-KUN...
WAS THE ONE WHO CARRIED ME HERE.
CHIKI-CHAN...
YOUR FACE IS STILL RED. YOU OKAY?
IT'S YOUR FAULT, TATSUAKI-KUN.

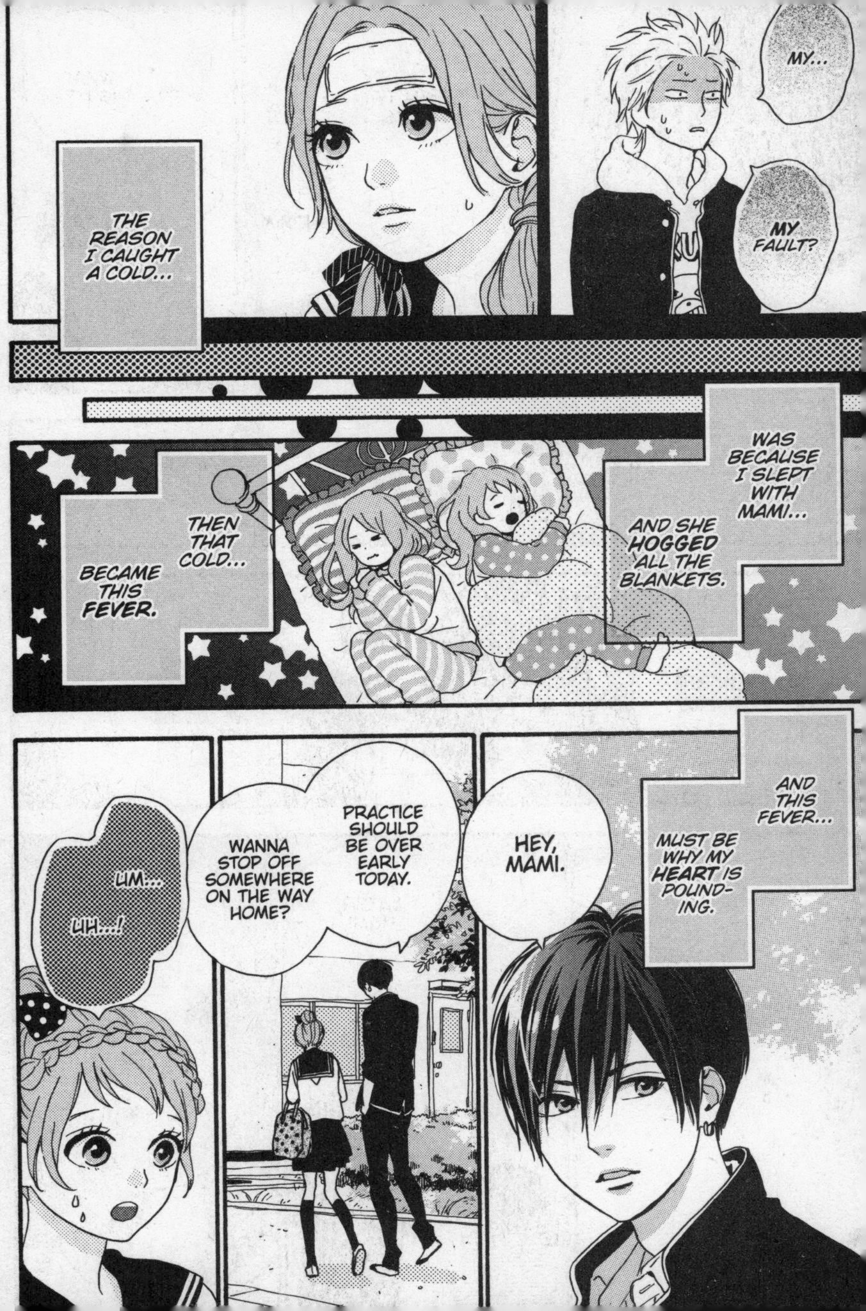
MY...
MY FAULT?
THE REASON I CAUGHT A COLD...
WAS BECAUSE I SLEPT WITH MAMI...
AND SHE HOGGED ALL THE BLANKETS.
THEN THAT COLD...
BECAME THIS FEVER.
AND THIS FEVER...
MUST BE WHY MY HEART IS POUNDING.
HEY, MAMI.
PRACTICE SHOULD BE OVER EARLY TODAY.
WANNA STOP OFF SOMEWHERE ON THE WAY HOME?
UM...
UH...!

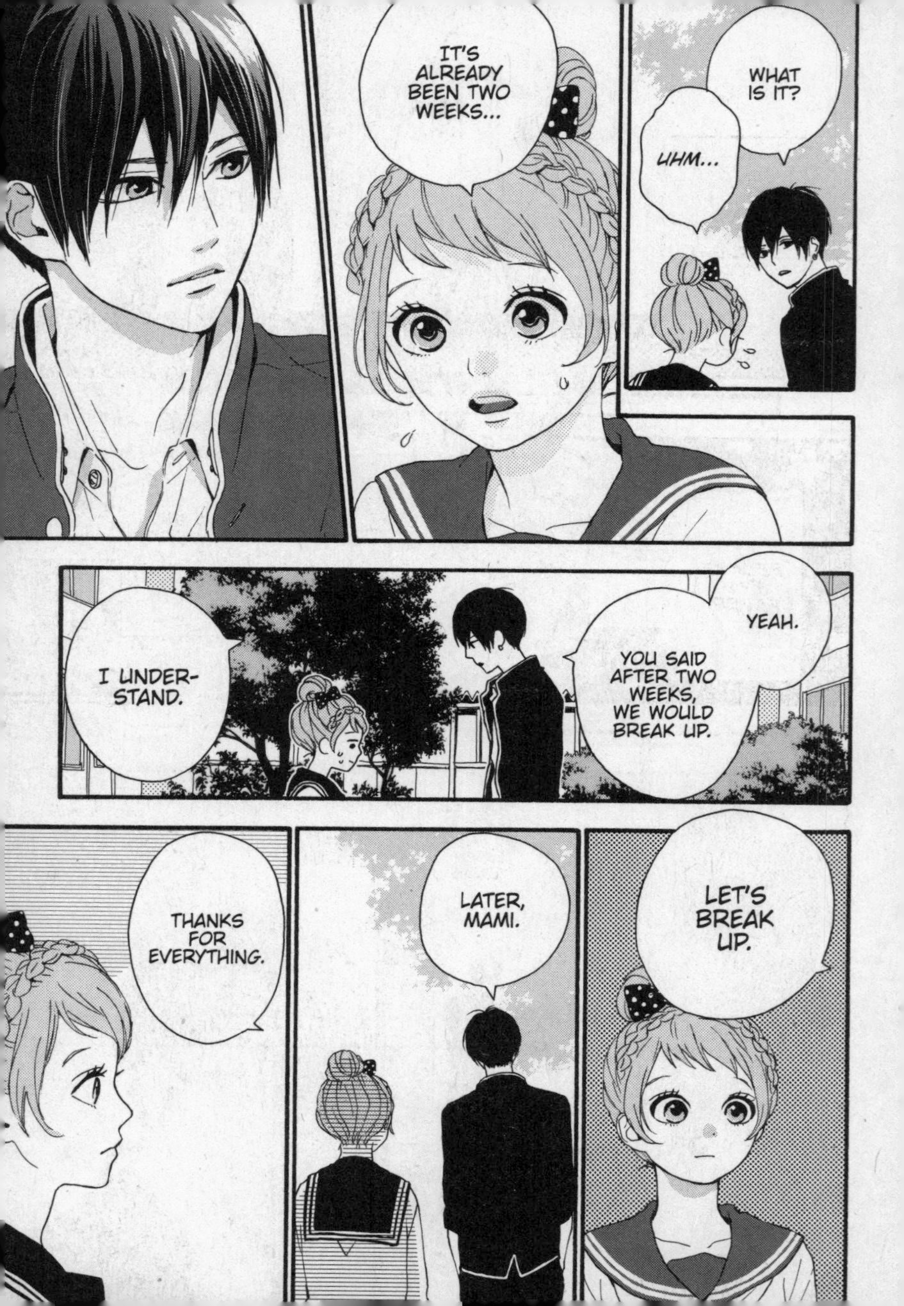
WHAT IS IT?
UHM...
IT'S ALREADY BEEN TWO WEEKS...
YEAH.
YOU SAID AFTER TWO WEEKS, WE WOULD BREAK UP.
I UNDER-STAND.
LET'S BREAK UP.
LATER, MAMI.
THANKS FOR EVERYTHING.

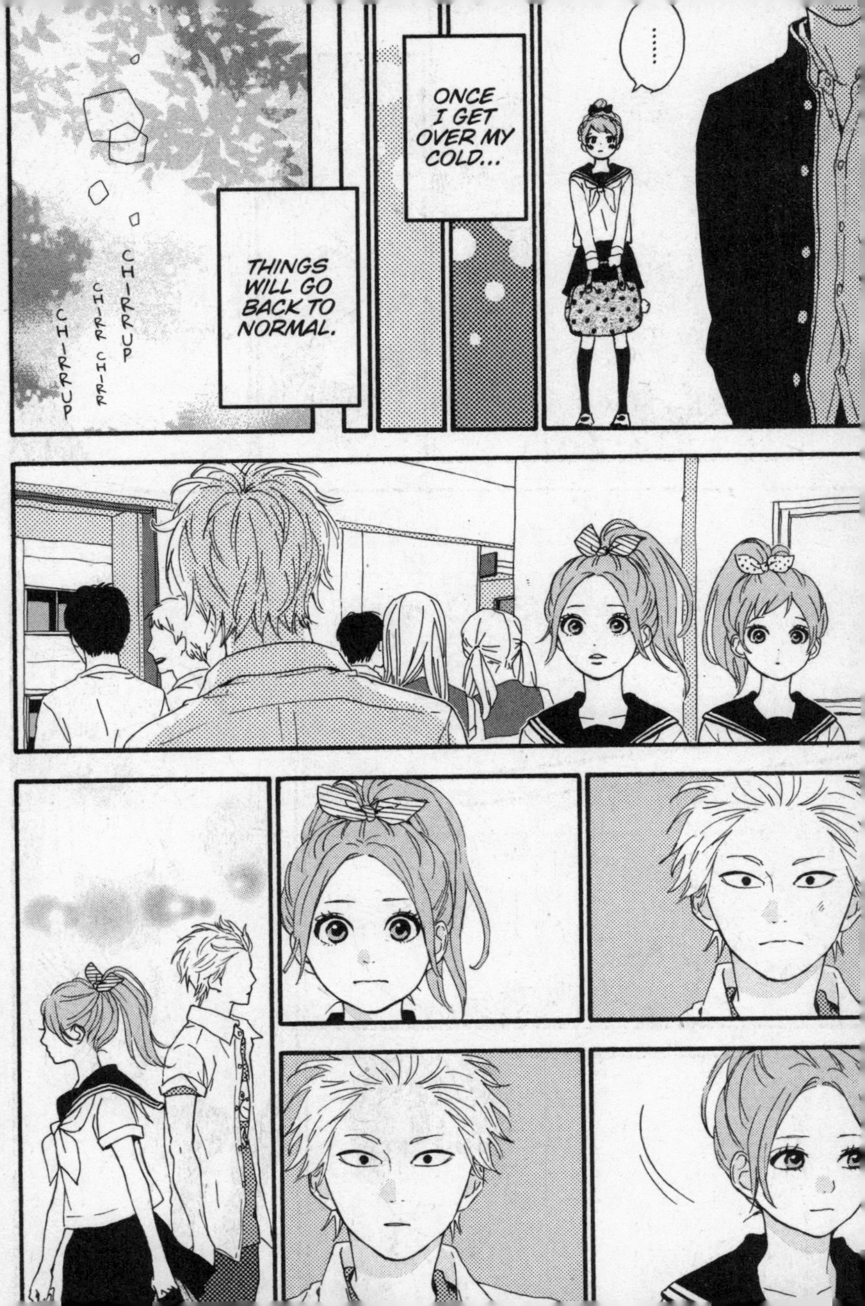
……
ONCE I GET OVER MY COLD…
THINGS WILL GO BACK TO NORMAL.
CHIRRUP
CHIRR CHIRR
CHIRRUP

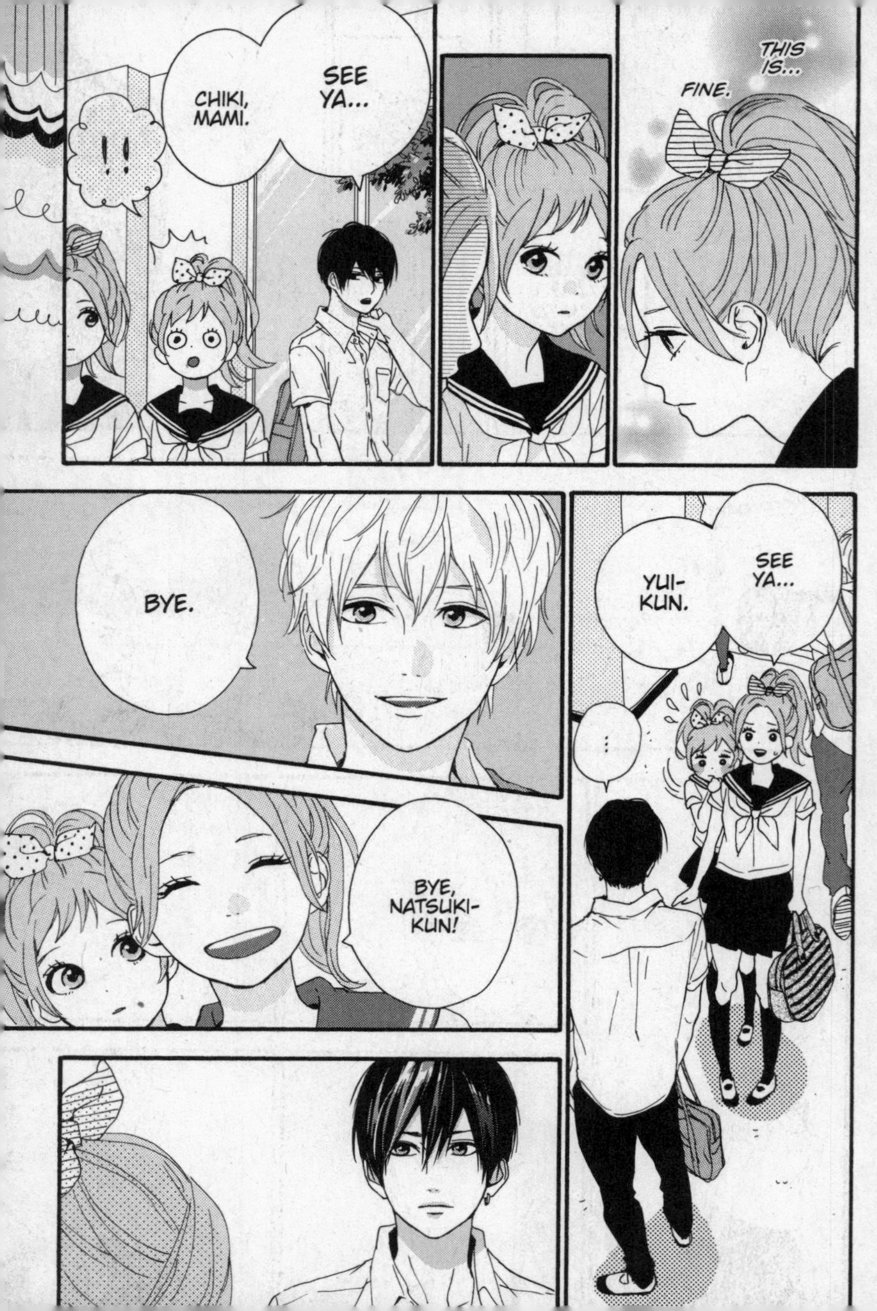
THIS IS...
FINE.
SEE YA...
CHIKI, MAMI.
!!
SEE YA...
YUI-KUN.
...
BYE.
BYE, NATSUKI-KUN!

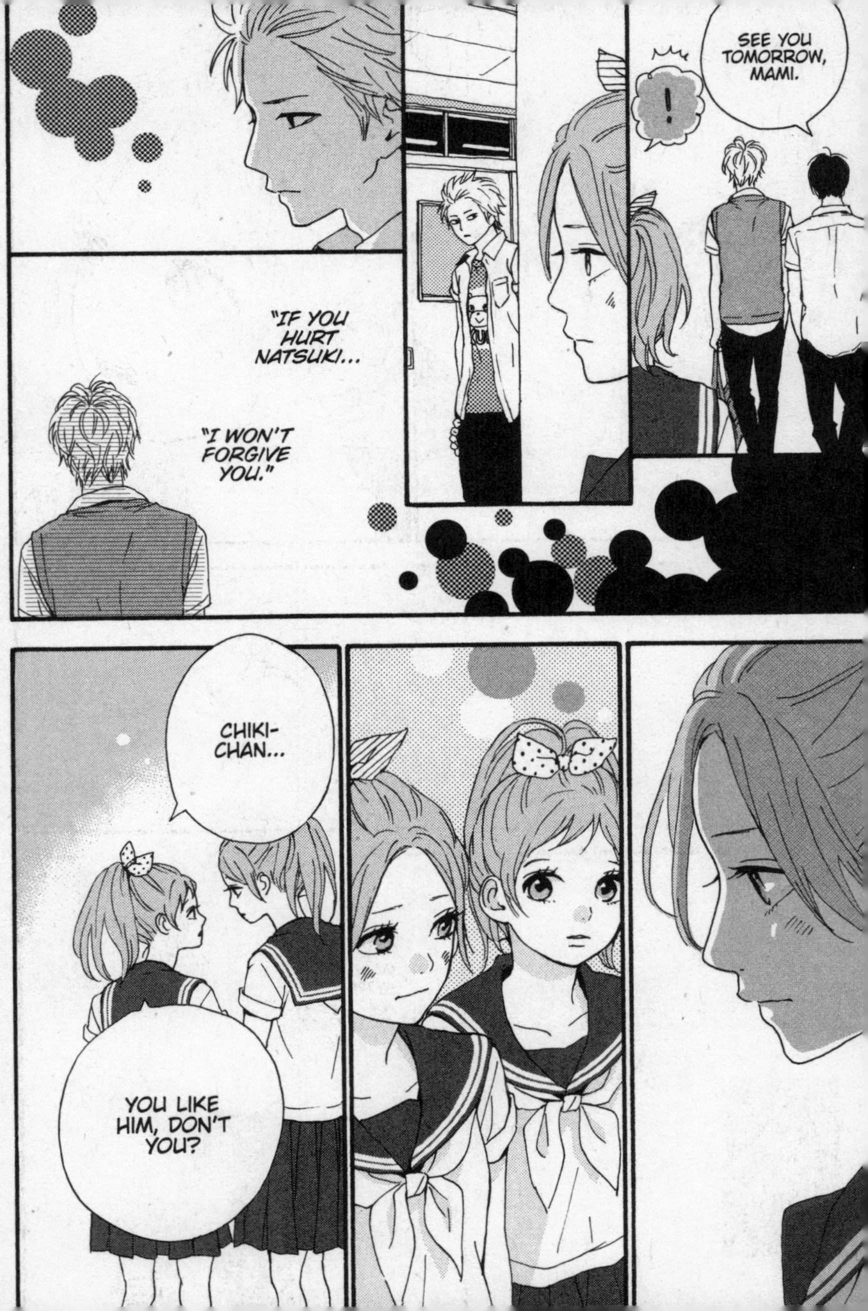
SEE YOU TOMORROW, MAMI.
!
"IF YOU HURT NATSUKI...
"I WON'T FORGIVE YOU."
CHIKI-CHAN...
YOU LIKE HIM, DON'T YOU?

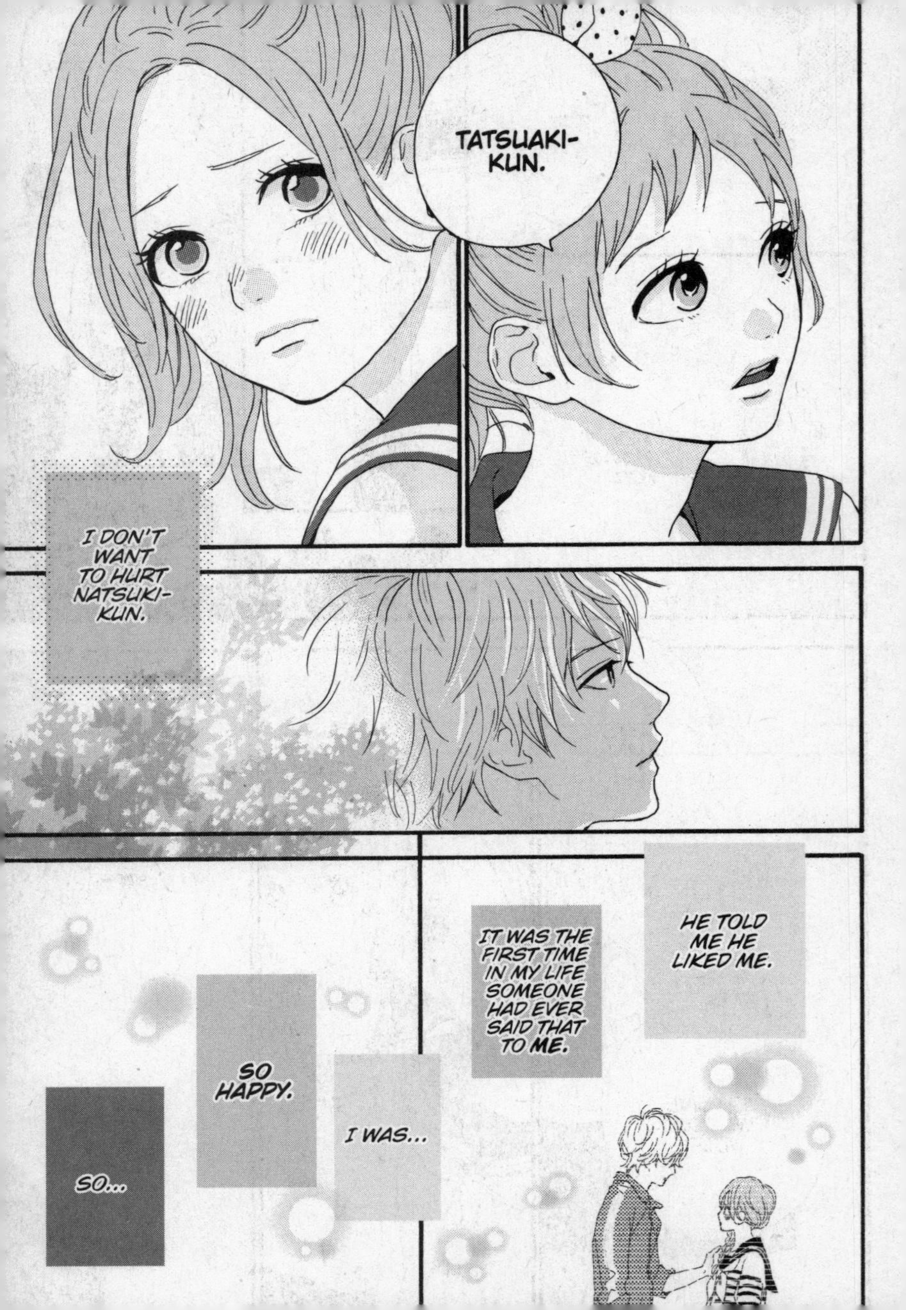
TATSUAKI-KUN.
I DON'T WANT TO HURT NATSUKI-KUN.
HE TOLD ME HE LIKED ME.
IT WAS THE FIRST TIME IN MY LIFE SOMEONE HAD EVER SAID THAT TO ME.
I WAS...
SO HAPPY.
SO...

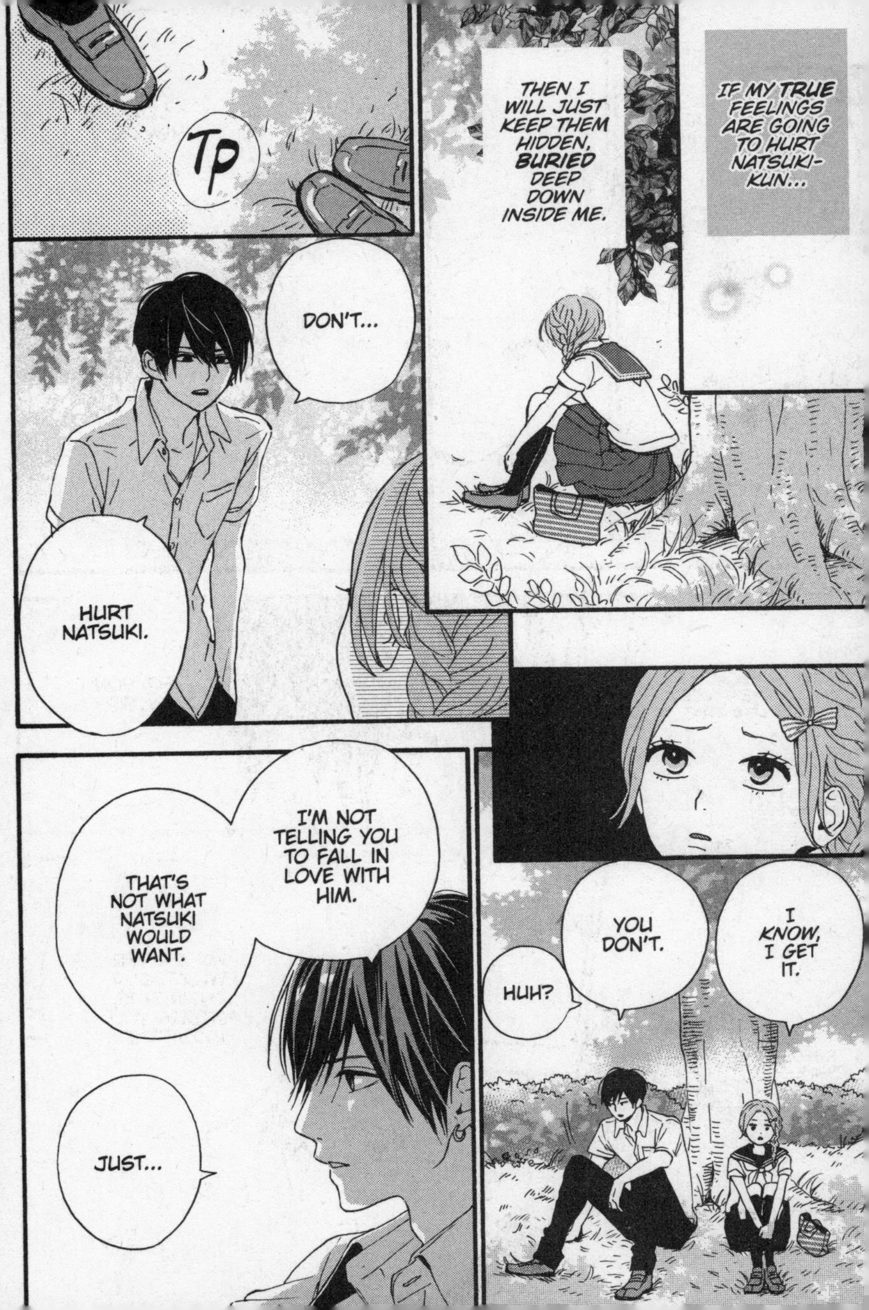
IF MY TRUE FEELINGS ARE GOING TO HURT NATSUKI-KUN...
THEN I WILL JUST KEEP THEM HIDDEN, BURIED DEEP DOWN INSIDE ME.
Tp
DON'T...
HURT NATSUKI.
I KNOW, I GET IT.
YOU DON'T.
HUH?
I'M NOT TELLING YOU TO FALL IN LOVE WITH HIM.
THAT'S NOT WHAT NATSUKI WOULD WANT.
JUST...

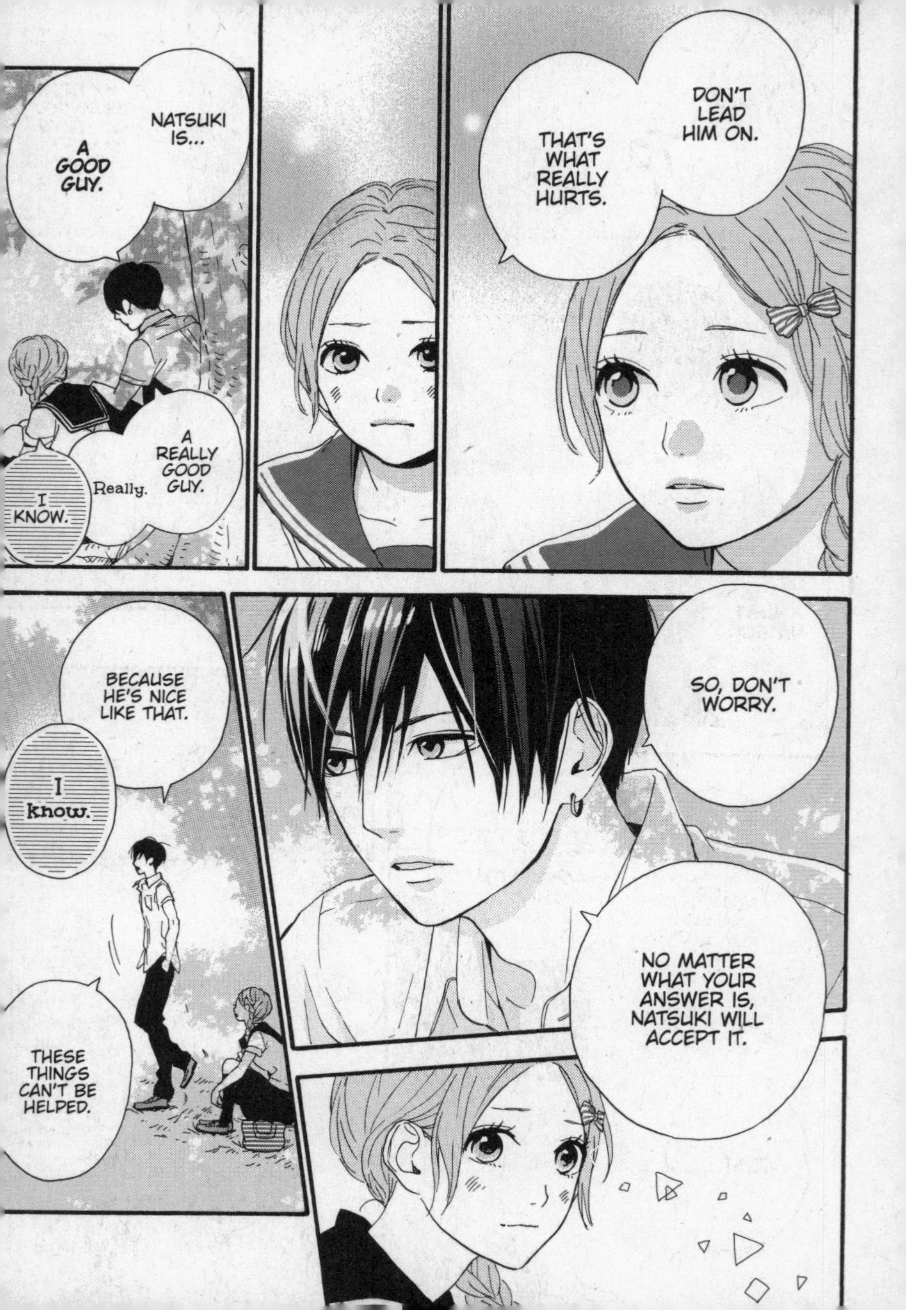

DON'T LEAD HIM ON.
THAT'S WHAT REALLY HURTS.
NATSUKI IS...
A GOOD GUY.
A REALLY GOOD GUY.
Really.
I KNOW.
SO, DON'T WORRY.
NO MATTER WHAT YOUR ANSWER IS, NATSUKI WILL ACCEPT IT.
BECAUSE HE'S NICE LIKE THAT.
I know.
THESE THINGS CAN'T BE HELPED.

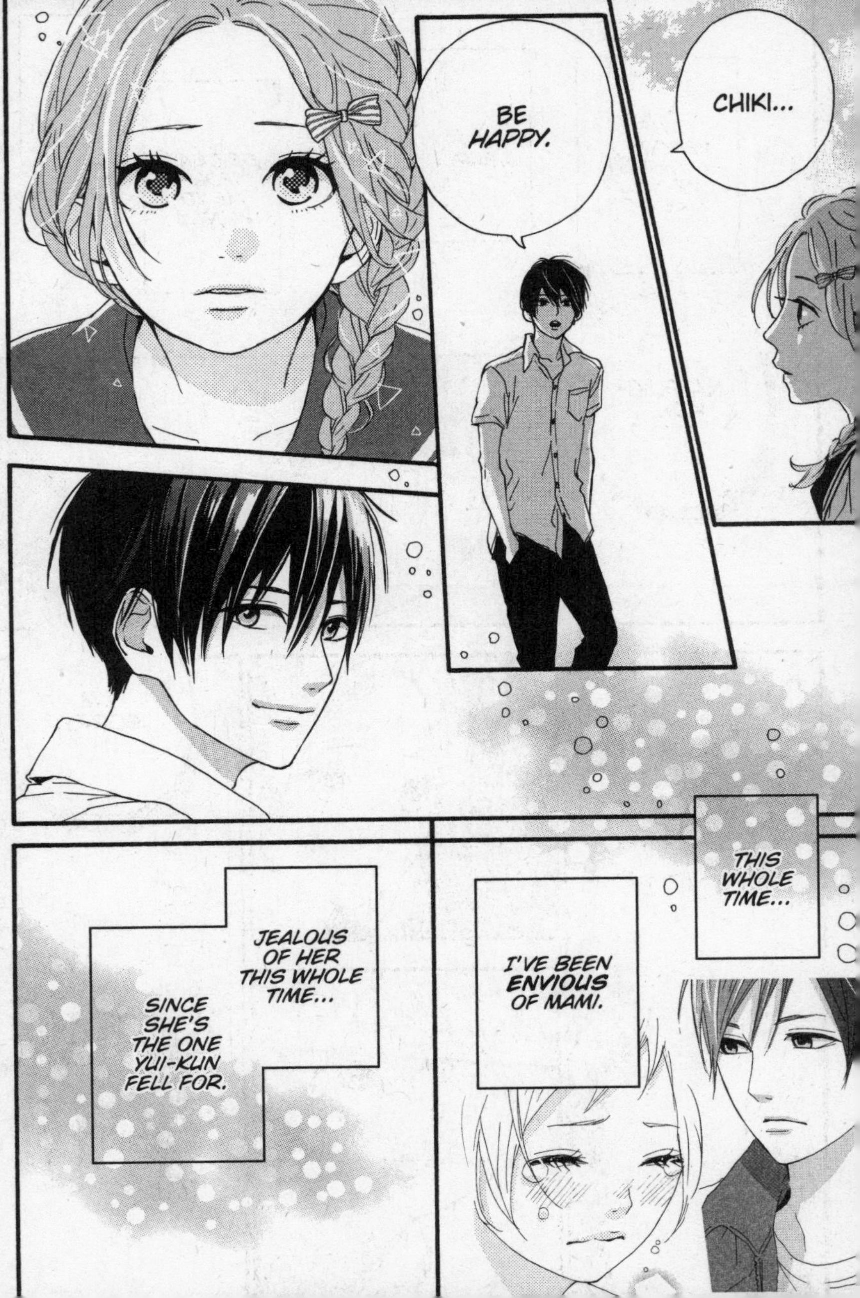
CHIKI...
BE HAPPY.
THIS WHOLE TIME...
I'VE BEEN ENVIOUS OF MAMI.
JEALOUS OF HER THIS WHOLE TIME...
SINCE SHE'S THE ONE YUI-KUN FELL FOR.

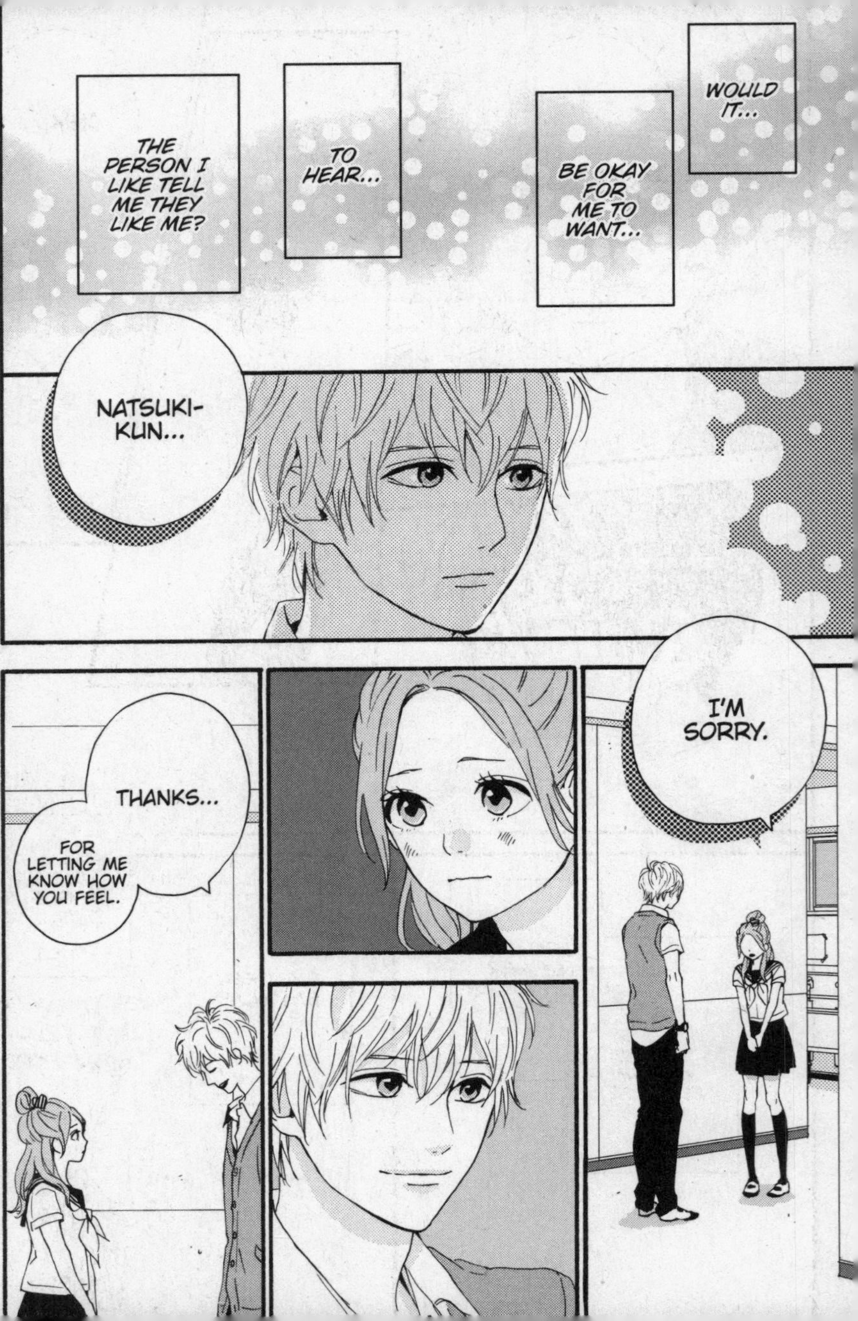
WOULD IT...
BE OKAY FOR ME TO WANT...
TO HEAR...
THE PERSON I LIKE TELL ME THEY LIKE ME?
NATSUKI-KUN...
I'M SORRY.
THANKS...
FOR LETTING ME KNOW HOW YOU FEEL.

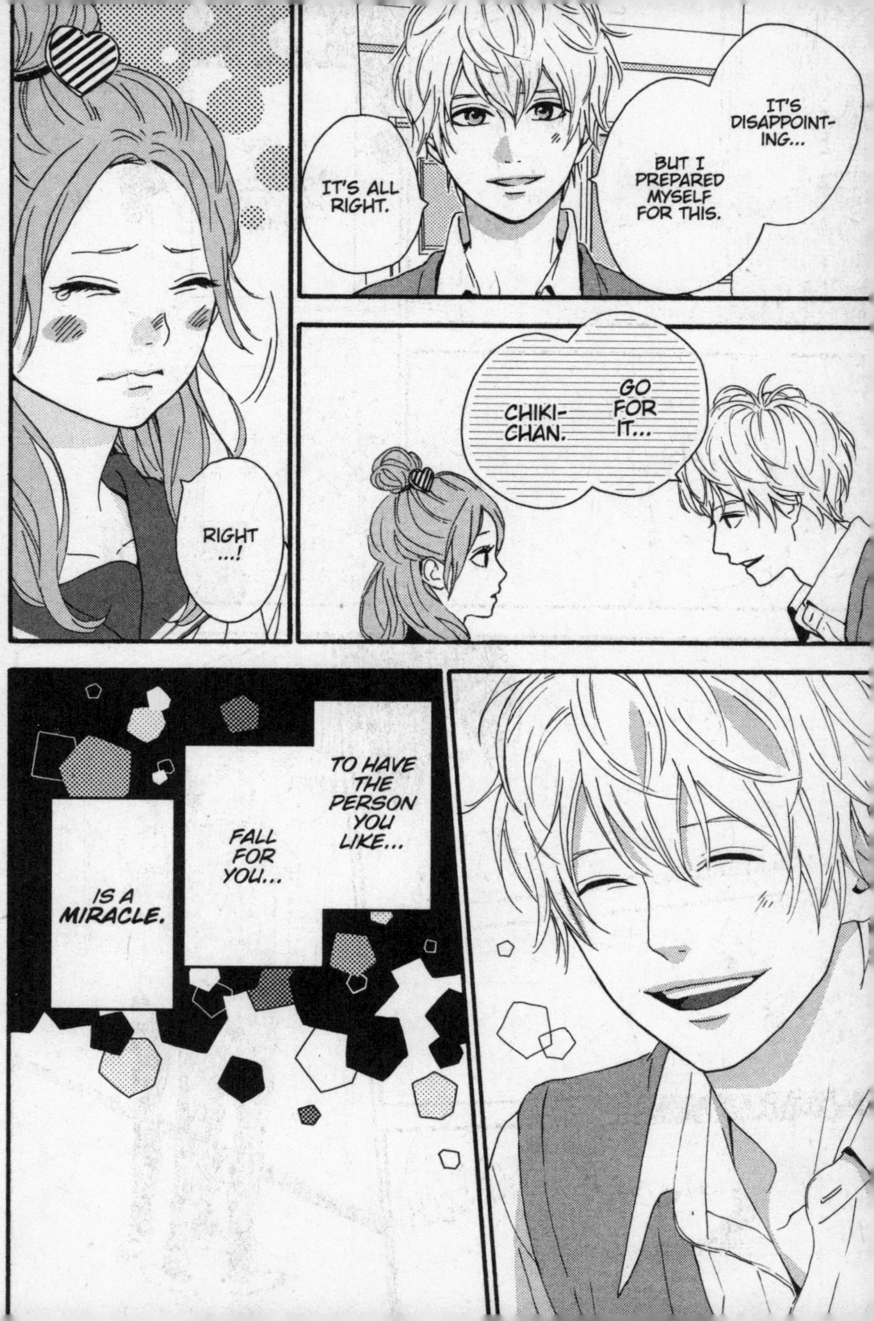
IT'S DISAPPOINTING...
BUT I PREPARED MYSELF FOR THIS.
IT'S ALL RIGHT.
GO FOR IT... CHIKI-CHAN.
RIGHT ...!
TO HAVE THE PERSON YOU LIKE...
FALL FOR YOU...
IS A MIRACLE.

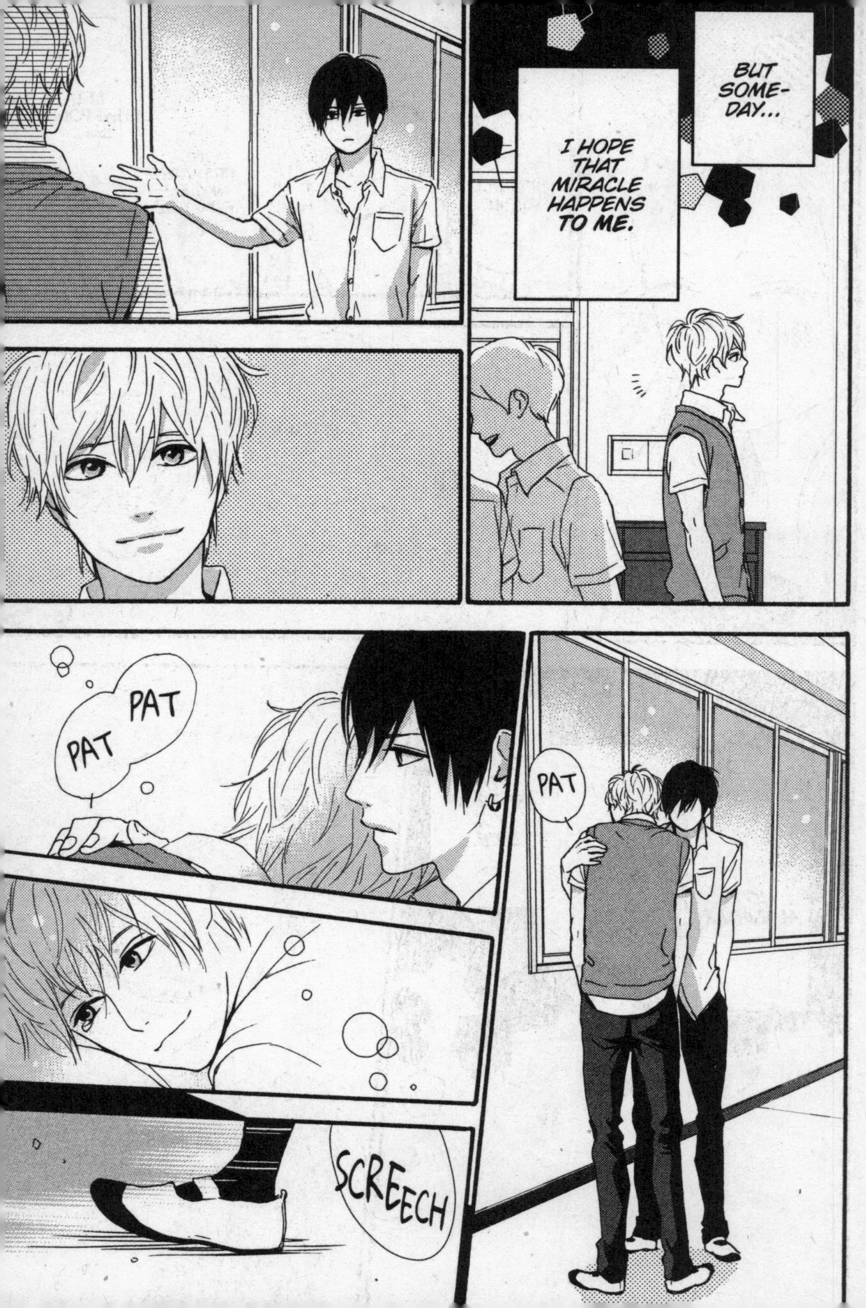
BUT SOME-DAY...
I HOPE THAT MIRACLE HAPPENS TO ME.
PAT
PAT PAT
SCREECH

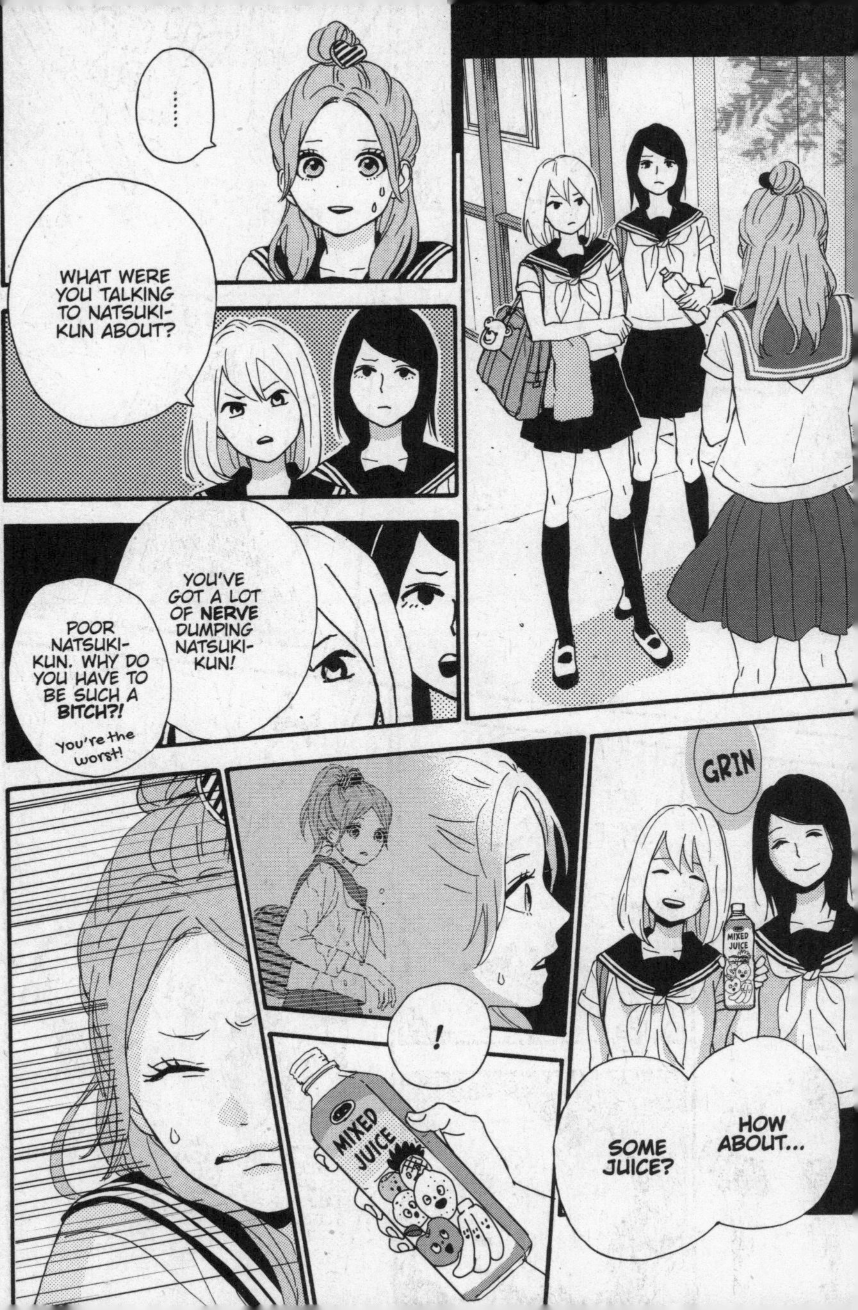
......
WHAT WERE YOU TALKING TO NATSUKI-KUN ABOUT?
YOU'VE GOT A LOT OF NERVE DUMPING NATSUKI-KUN!
POOR NATSUKI-KUN. WHY DO YOU HAVE TO BE SUCH A BITCH?!
You're the worst!
GRIN
MIXED JUICE
HOW ABOUT...
SOME JUICE?
!
MIXED JUICE

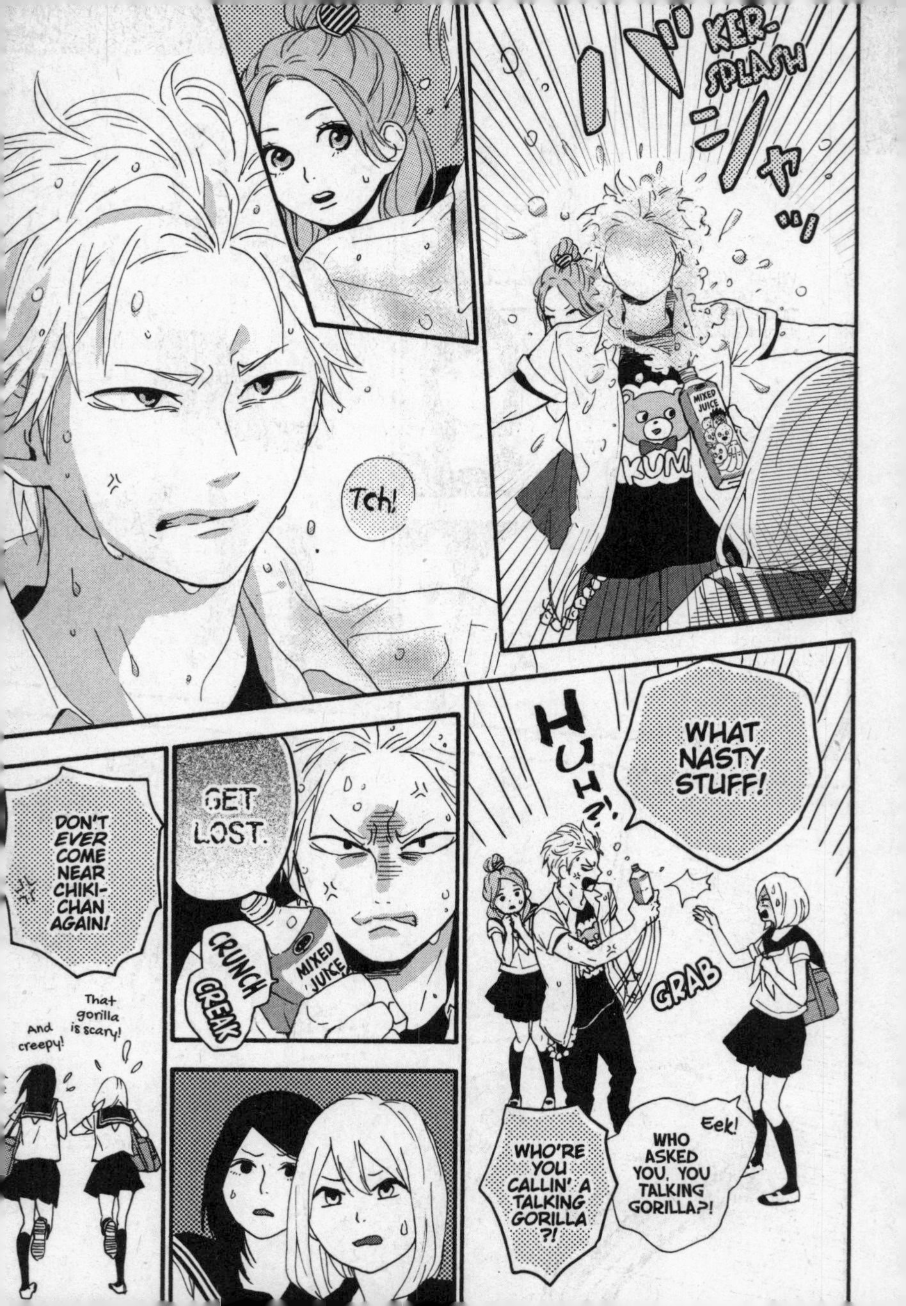
KER-SPLASH
MIXED JUICE
Tch!
HUH?!
WHAT NASTY STUFF!
GRAB
Eek!
WHO ASKED YOU, YOU TALKING GORILLA?!
WHO'RE YOU CALLIN' A TALKING GORILLA?!
GET LOST.
CRUNCH
CREAK
MIXED JUICE
DON'T EVER COME NEAR CHIKI-CHAN AGAIN!
That gorilla is scary!
And creepy!

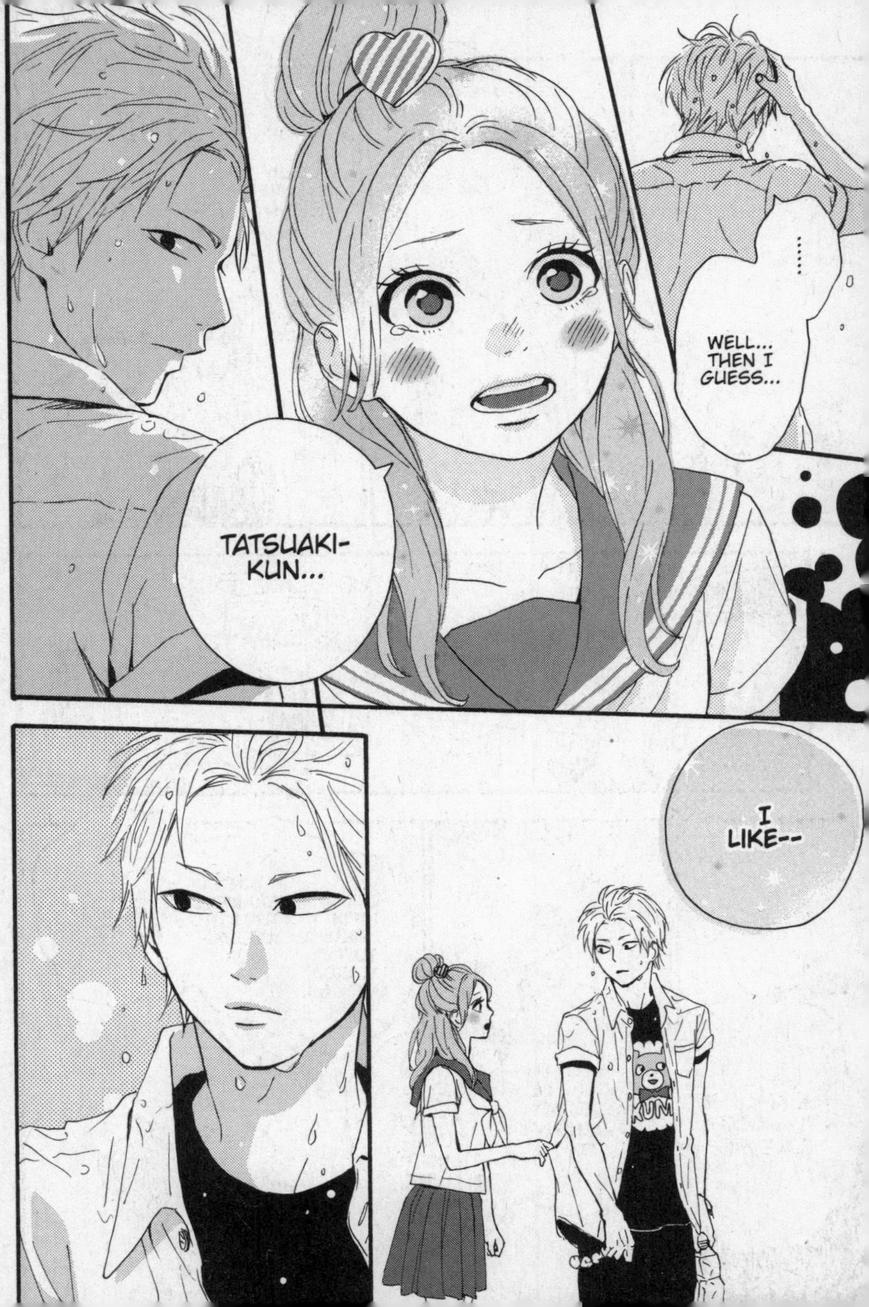
......
WELL... THEN I GUESS...
TATSUAKI-KUN...
I LIKE--

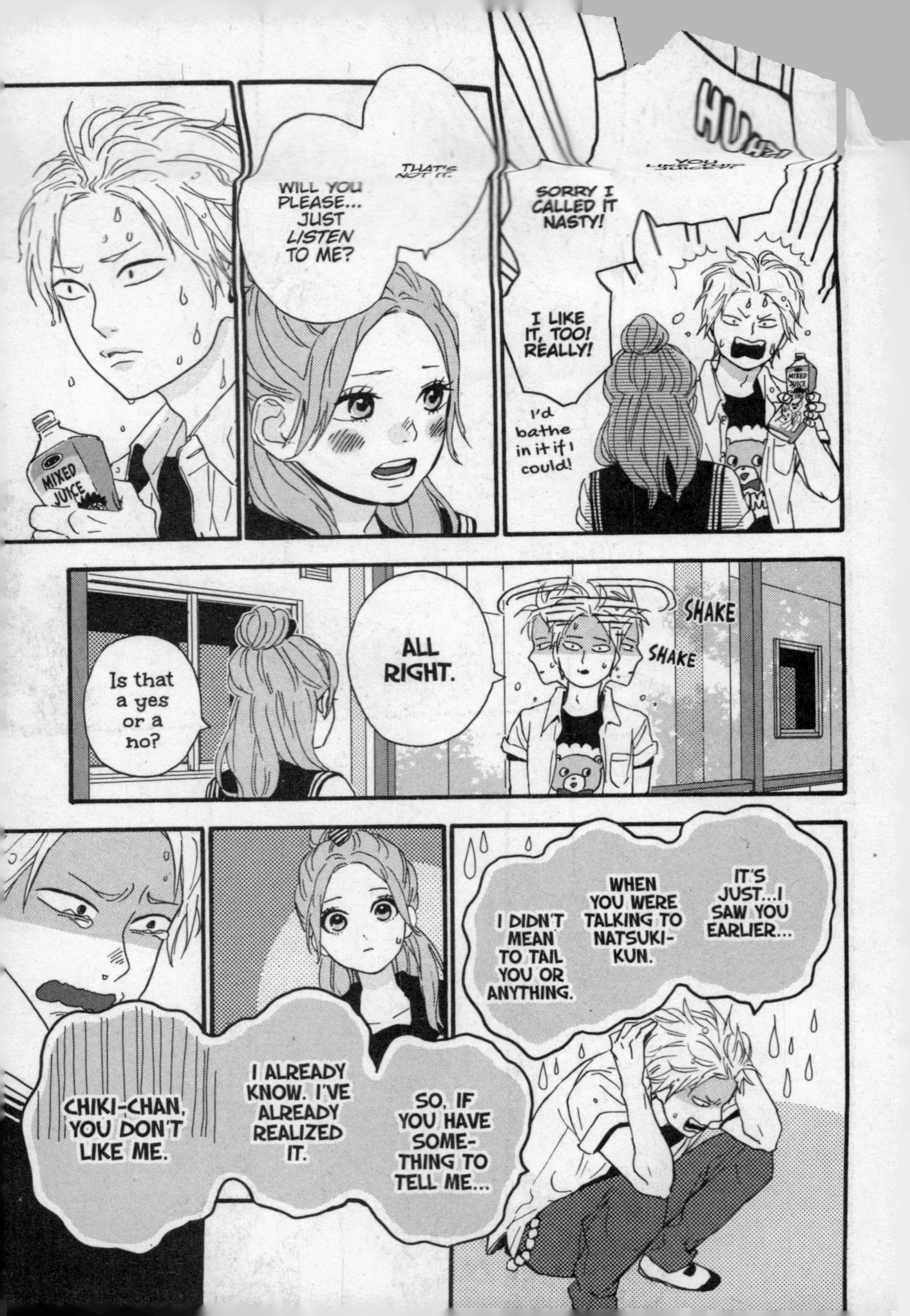
HUH?!
SORRY I CALLED IT NASTY!
I LIKE IT, TOO! REALLY!
I'd bathe in it if I could!
THAT'S NOT IT.
WILL YOU PLEASE... JUST LISTEN TO ME?
SHAKE
SHAKE
ALL RIGHT.
Is that a yes or a no?
IT'S JUST...I SAW YOU EARLIER...
WHEN YOU WERE TALKING TO NATSUKI-KUN.
I DIDN'T MEAN TO TAIL YOU OR ANYTHING.
SO, IF YOU HAVE SOME-THING TO TELL ME...
I ALREADY KNOW. I'VE ALREADY REALIZED IT.
CHIKI-CHAN, YOU DON'T LIKE ME.

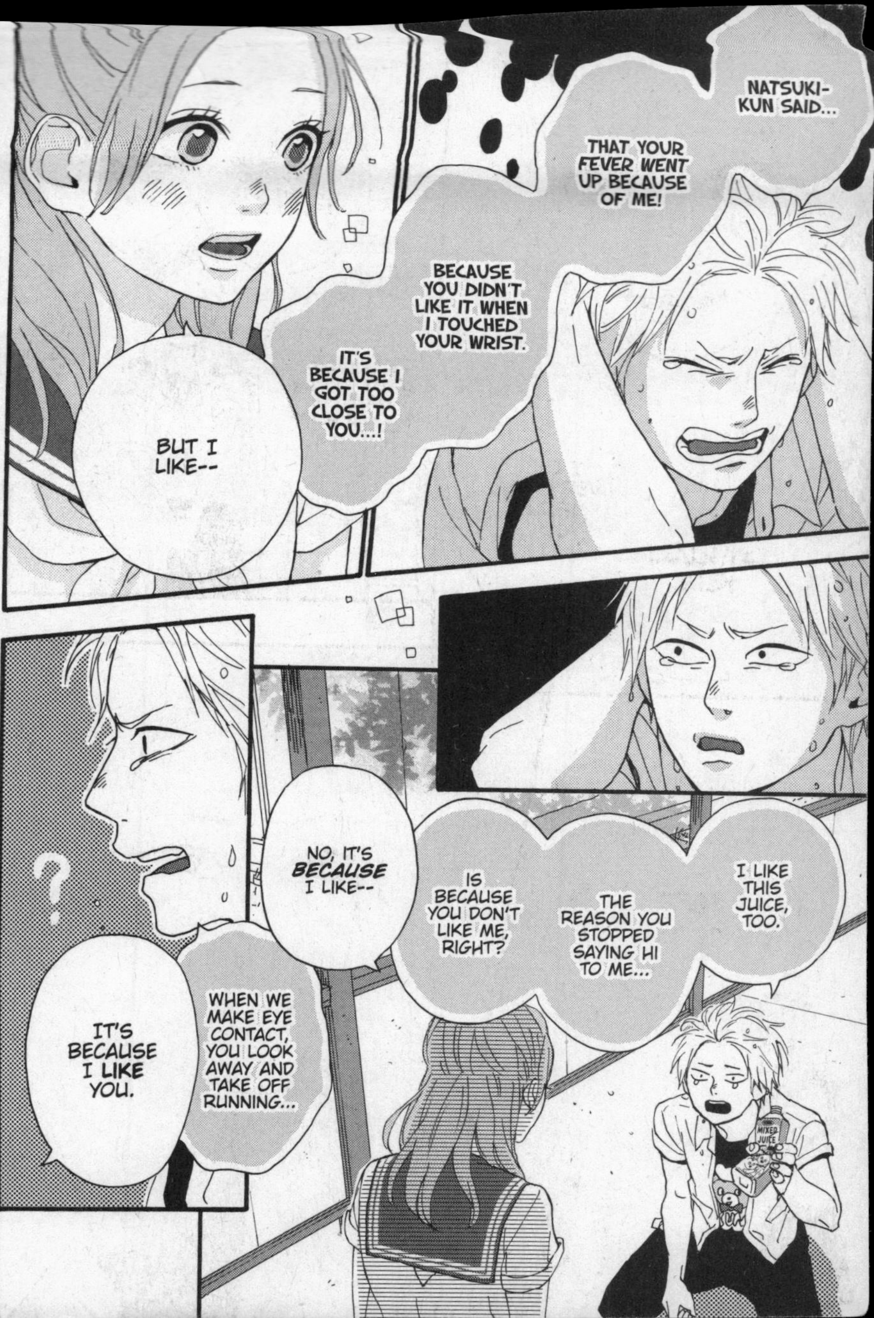
NATSUKI-KUN SAID...
THAT YOUR FEVER WENT UP BECAUSE OF ME!
BECAUSE YOU DIDN'T LIKE IT WHEN I TOUCHED YOUR WRIST.
IT'S BECAUSE I GOT TOO CLOSE TO YOU...!
BUT I LIKE--
I LIKE THIS JUICE, TOO.
THE REASON YOU STOPPED SAYING HI TO ME...
IS BECAUSE YOU DON'T LIKE ME, RIGHT?
WHEN WE MAKE EYE CONTACT, YOU LOOK AWAY AND TAKE OFF RUNNING...
MIXED JUICE
NO, IT'S *BECAUSE* I LIKE--
?
IT'S BECAUSE I **LIKE** YOU.

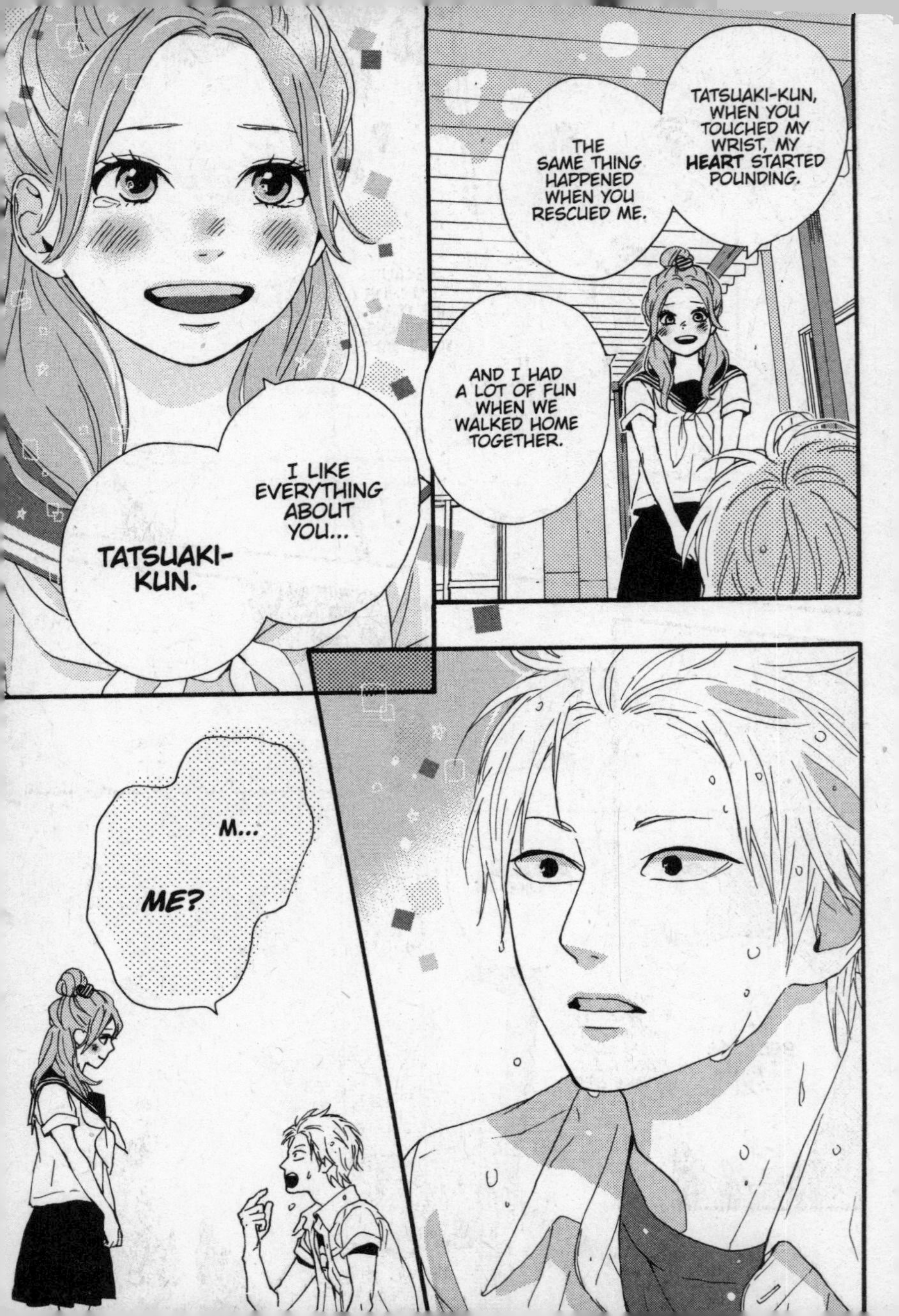
TATSUAKI-KUN, WHEN YOU TOUCHED MY WRIST, MY HEART STARTED POUNDING.
THE SAME THING HAPPENED WHEN YOU RESCUED ME.
AND I HAD A LOT OF FUN WHEN WE WALKED HOME TOGETHER.
I LIKE EVERYTHING ABOUT YOU...
TATSUAKI-KUN.
M...
ME?

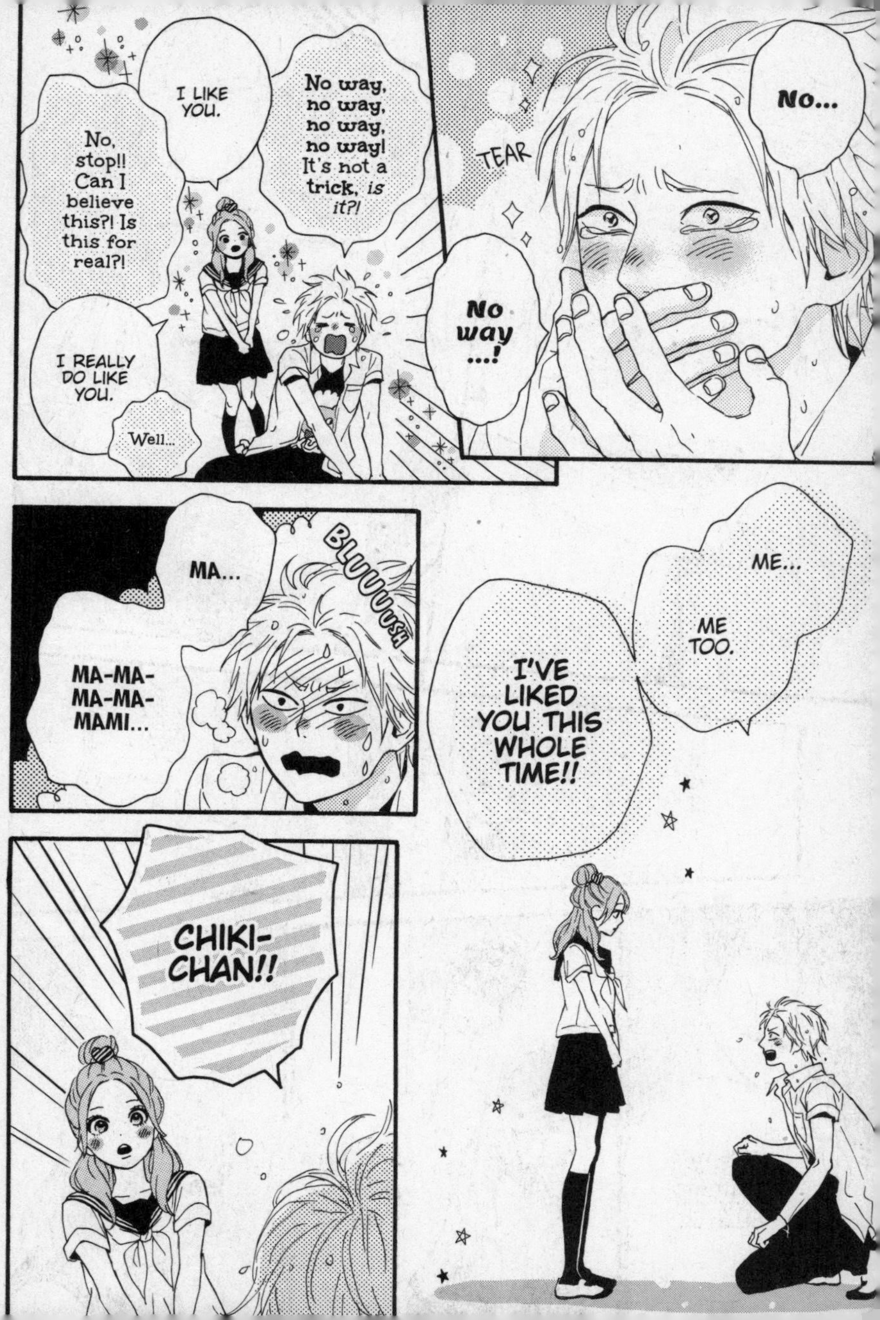
No...
TEAR
No way ...!
No way, no way, no way, no way! It's not a trick, *is it*?!
I LIKE YOU.
No, stop!! Can I believe this?! Is this for real?!
I REALLY DO LIKE YOU.
Well...
ME...
ME TOO.
I'VE LIKED YOU THIS WHOLE TIME!!
MA...
BLUUUUSH
MA-MA-MA-MA-MAMI...
CHIKI-CHAN!!

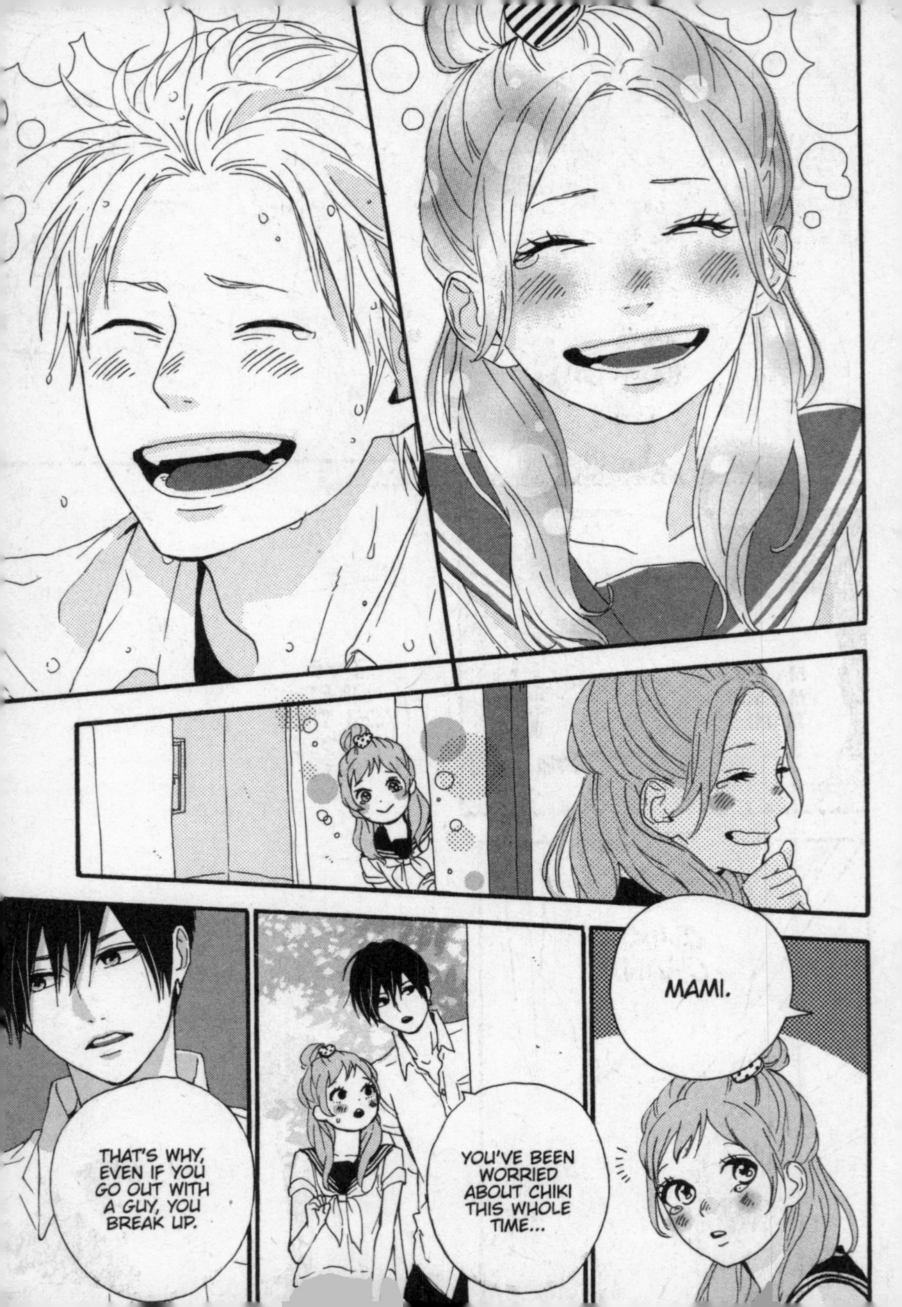
MAMI.
YOU'VE BEEN WORRIED ABOUT CHIKI THIS WHOLE TIME...
THAT'S WHY, EVEN IF YOU GO OUT WITH A GUY, YOU BREAK UP.

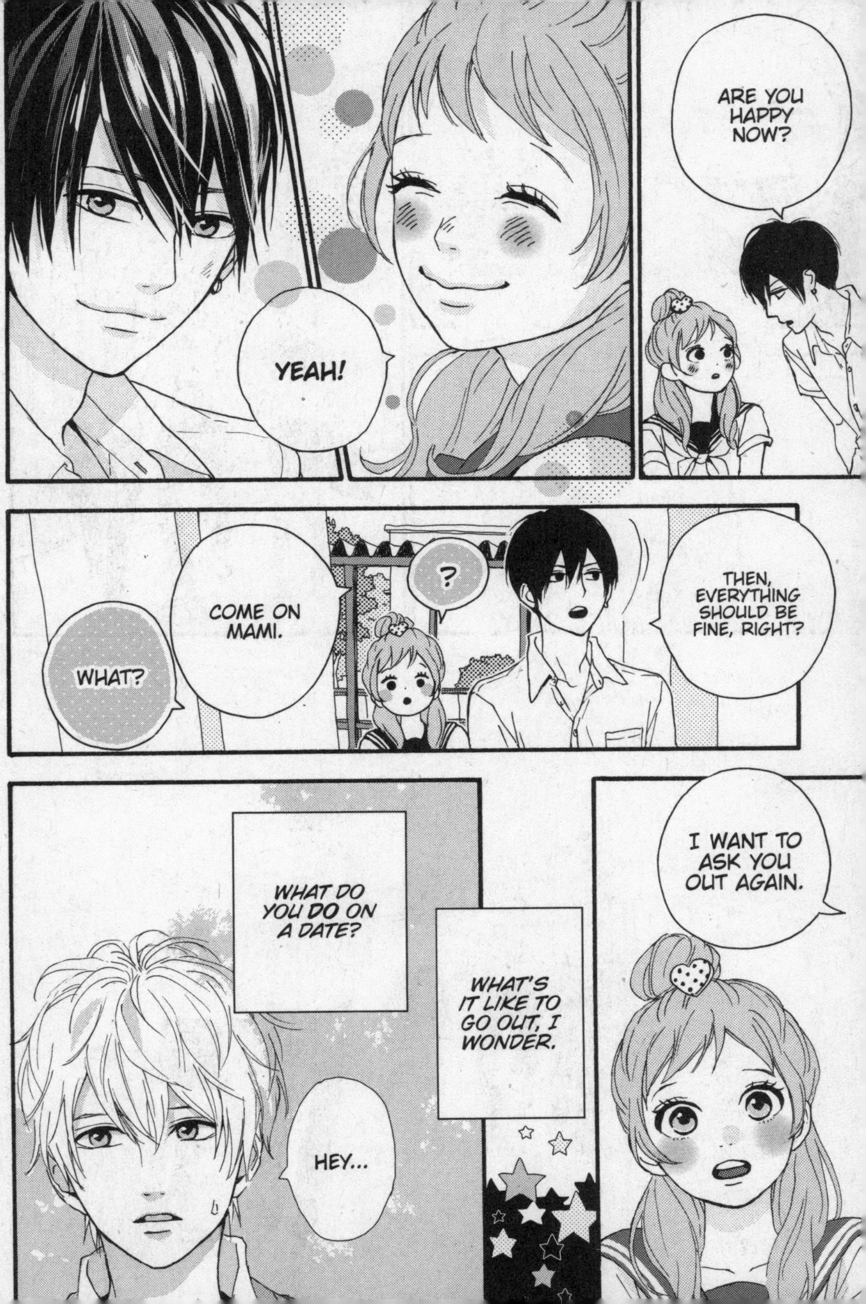
ARE YOU HAPPY NOW?
YEAH!
THEN, EVERYTHING SHOULD BE FINE, RIGHT?
?
COME ON MAMI.
WHAT?
I WANT TO ASK YOU OUT AGAIN.
WHAT DO YOU DO ON A DATE?
WHAT'S IT LIKE TO GO OUT, I WONDER.
HEY...

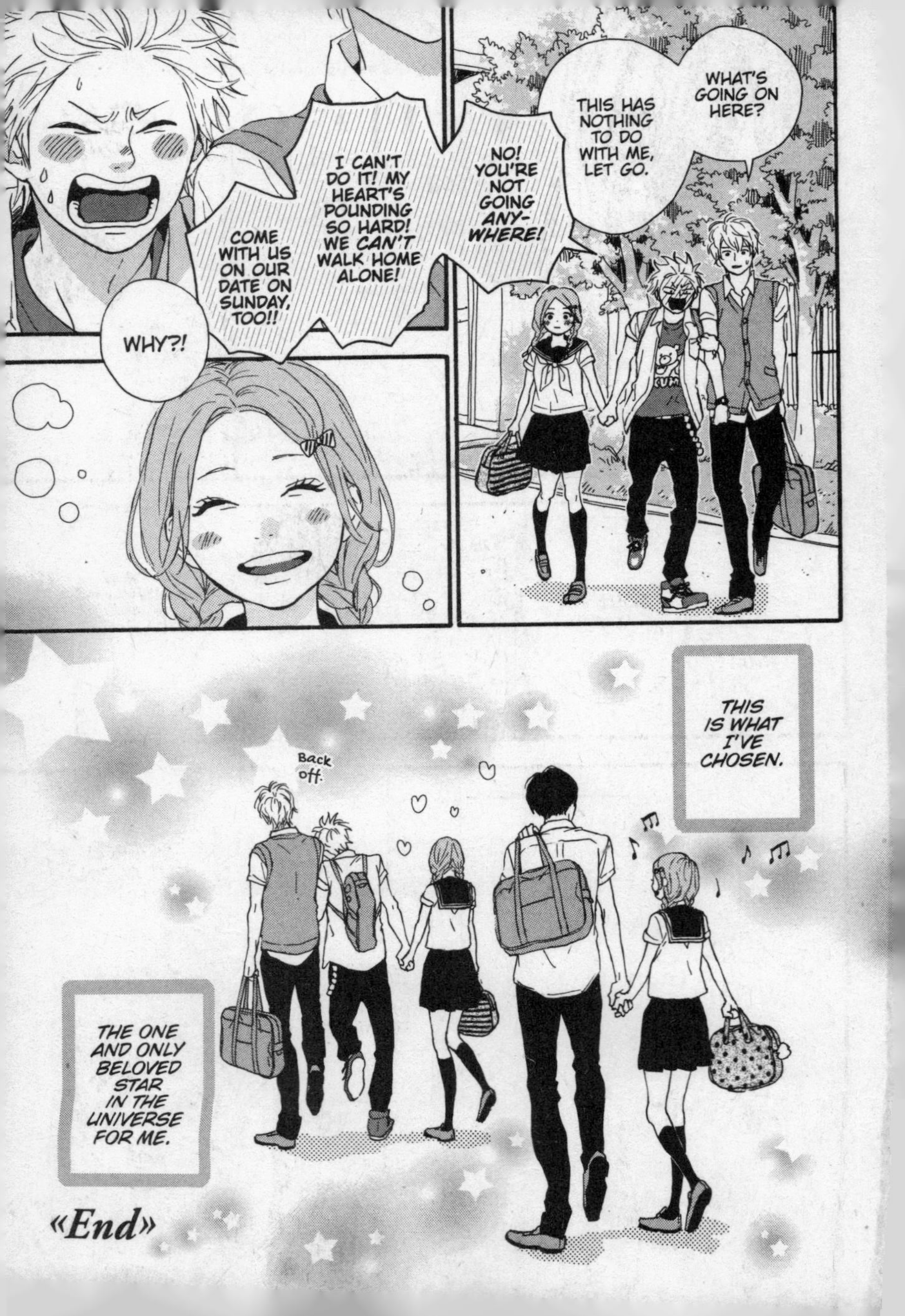
WHAT'S GOING ON HERE?
THIS HAS NOTHING TO DO WITH ME, LET GO.
NO! YOU'RE NOT GOING ANY-WHERE!
I CAN'T DO IT! MY HEART'S POUNDING SO HARD! WE CAN'T WALK HOME ALONE!
COME WITH US ON OUR DATE ON SUNDAY, TOO!!
WHY?!
THIS IS WHAT I'VE CHOSEN.
Back off.
THE ONE AND ONLY BELOVED STAR IN THE UNIVERSE FOR ME.
«End»

SEVEN SEAS ENTERTAINMENT PRESENTS

orange

THE COMPLETE COLLECTION 2

story and art by Ichigo Takano

TRANSLATION
Amber Tamosaitis

ADAPTATION
Shannon Fay

LETTERING AND LAYOUT
Lys Blakeslee

COVER DESIGN
Nicky Lim

PROOFREADER
Shanti Whitesides

PRODUCTION MANAGER
Lissa Pattillo

EDITOR IN CHIEF
Adam Arnold

PUBLISHER
Jason DeAngelis

ORANGE: THE COMPLETE COLLECTION 2 (VOLUMES 4-5)

First published in Japan in 2013 by Futabasha Publishers Ltd., Tokyo.
English version published by Seven Seas Entertainment, LLC.
Under license from Futabasha Publishers Ltd.

ISBN: 978-1-626922-71-6

Printed in Canada

First Printing: May 2016

10 9 8 7 6 5 4 3 2 1

FOLLOW US ONLINE: ***www.gomanga.com***

READING DIRECTIONS

This book reads from ***right to left***, Japanese style. If this is your first time reading manga, you start reading from the top right panel on each page and take it from there. If you get lost, just follow the numbered diagram here. It may seem backwards at first, but you'll get the hang of it! Have fun!!

1
2
3
4
5
6
7
8
9

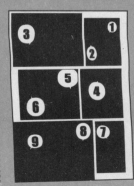